THE FREAK
FROM
BATTLE CREEK

A Novel

AJ Hartman

PAGE PUBLISHING
Conneaut Lake, PA

First originally published by Page Publishing 2022

ISBN 978-1-6624-5093-8 (pbk)
ISBN 978-1-6624-5094-5 (digital)

Printed in the United States of America

This is for Mom and Dad.

FOREWORD

Before you read any further, I want to emphasize that this is a work of fiction.

F.I.C.T.I.O.N.

By definition, that means that this work is made up from whole cloth, not a closely researched, inspired-by-real-events, as-close-to-the-real-action-as-you-can-get type of thriller. I've known two Secret Service agents in my life; both of them were in the anticounterfeiting division and never drew their weapons except for practice and cleaning. They also never gave me any idea about how they actually caught counterfeiters, or how counterfeiters actually plied their trade, and even if they had, I wouldn't put it in a book, because that would be stupid; and while I'm a lot of things—impulsive, occasionally crude, silly over the power of puns, and enamored of writing that sounds like real conversation—stupidity is not one of my problems.

In short, if you were looking for the real inside dope about the Secret Service, you've come to the wrong place. This is a procedural, but it's definitely a work of fiction, hence the lack of actual Secret Service procedures. I did draw on some guys I knew who were professional bodyguards, and I also relied heavily on the TV series *The West Wing*, because I know that Aaron Sorkin and his brethren tried to be true to the spirit of the Secret Service in their portrayals of agents and procedures.

Otherwise, I made it all up.

The military part is less fictional and more based on what I know from several really good sources. I had a great friend who was a Navy SEAL, who enlightened me on several levels about how special operators work, and my dad was in the Army, and I've had several other informants in the Army, Navy, Air Force, Coast Guard, and especially the United States Marine Corps, which is still the best military service in the history of the modern world.

So the military stuff is more accurate (perhaps) than the Secret Service stuff, but I still didn't give away any secrets I may or may not know, again, because to do so would be stupid, and we've already gone over that. You will notice that I did not name my friend in the SEALs, or any of his comrades he may or may not have introduced me to, or any of my other informants. (Sorry, but that's classified. Read the rest of the book and you'll get the joke.)

Before we go any further, a word or thirteen about the United States Marine Corps.

Last night, while you and I were snoring our asses off, or drinking beer, or watching porn on the internet, or whatever other silly shit we were doing, the men and wymyn of the United States Marine Corps (along with the rest of our armed forces, who I do not wish to in any way denigrate) were guarding us as we slept. From Mogadishu to San Diego, from the far reaches of the Indian Ocean to Savannah, Georgia, these men and womyn were defending the interests of our country in ways large and small, and most of them were putting their own asses on the line to do it. I'm a peace-mongering liberal who hates war and wants everybody to drink a Pepsi and get along, but I am fully aware that I get to be a fat, chickenshit old man who fights wars with words instead of having to put my lard-ass self on the firing line because these real-life heroes are doing it for me.

The United States Marine Corps isn't perfect, and it may seem anachronistic to some of you, but to me the men and wymyn of the oldest military service in the United States are those brave warriors who take care of us scared peasants; they're the castle walls that keep the dragons out, they're our finest example of sacrificing oneself for the greater good, and they deserve our utmost respect and undying gratitude for what they do every day. I hope that we can agree that most of us would shit ourselves if we had to do what the average Marine does every day as part of their duty and at least respect that they do their duty (and often above and beyond that) better than anyone else in the world.

I deliberately made my main character a United States Marine because of the motto of the United States Marine Corps, *semper fidelis* ("always faithful"), which is how I wanted the Freak to think and act. I think she does that, and she is definitely a tribute to all the Marines I've ever known. Semper fi, you tough motherfuckers, and thank you for your service.

Also, there is no such thing as a "former" Marine. There are dead Marines, retired Marines, imprisoned Marines, drunk Marines, wounded Marines, honorably discharged Marines (on temporarily detached duty), reserve Marines, still-serving Marines, and all other kinds of Marines, but there is nothing truer than this on the green earth: once a Marine, *always* a Marine.

Sorry for shouting, but I really wanted you to get it.

I'd also like to share a few words about the U.S. Secret Service.

Lately, the only thing we've heard about the Secret Service makes them seem like fools and buffoons who can't seem to do their jobs right. Nothing could be further from the truth—I'm afraid you've been bamboozled by media bullshit.

How do I know this is true? First and foremost, President Obama is alive and well, and there have been zero attempts on his life (that we know of). You see, the Secret Service keeps all its successes a secret—imagine that—and the only things we hear about are their very rare failures, because the Secret Service can't—and more importantly, won't—defend itself.

Even when congresspersons go on TV and thunder about how inept and inefficient the Secret Service is (neither of these things are true), the Service still can't/won't defend themselves, for two reasons.

First, the United States Secret Service does not comment on security procedures, ever, and for good reason. The brave men and wymyn of the Secret Service, like those in our armed forces, put their lives on the line every day when they go to work. It's their job to jump in front of the bullets that might rain down on their principals (protectees). For this reason, they can't tell that thundering congressman that the guy who jumped the fence and got in the White House only got to do that because the Secret Service doesn't instantly go to guns in those situations and shoot that asshole dead, since they might hit some innocent bystander. Look at the tape of the guy going in the door at the White House. There's a Secret Service officer there, but he can't shoot the guy, so he has to try to physically stop him without shooting. The Secret Service also doesn't get to patrol the perimeter of the White House with trained dogs like they should—it looks bad—which, again, severely limits their operational effectiveness.

The Secret Service as a whole is also severely understaffed, as well as underpaid for what they do. I mean, really, we can pay a congressperson $179,000 a year to sit on his or her fat ass, blat at the press, and get absolutely nothing done, but we can't pay Secret Service agents more than $70,000 a year (most of them start around $35,000) to jump in front of bullets? When you look at it that way, it's amazing we get anyone who wants to be a Secret Service agent, but we do, because, like the United States Marine Corps, Secret Service agents are incredibly faithful and 99.95 percent effective at what they do—you just don't get to hear about it because when they're successful, they *never* talk about it.

If you don't believe me about the underpaid or understaffed aspect, please look up Secret Service pay (it's public information) and look at how many people the Pope goes around with and get back to me.

The second reason the Secret Service can't defend itself against the thundering congressman (or the public) is that Congress (and, indirectly, you) have control of their budget. You don't get to tell your boss that he's full of shit, because she'll fire your ass and hire somebody else, so when he (or she) rains a raft of shit down on your head, you shut up, especially if you're the United States Secret Service, because you don't comment on procedure, ever, even if it means that some asshat who couldn't protect a doughnut gets to unfairly smack you around like a piñata.

When that congressperson thunders away on TV about the ineptitude of the United States Secret Service, what she's (or he's) doing is akin to beating up Helen Keller while she's tied to a stake. To paraphrase what my grandma used to say when she saw someone being treated unfairly, it's like Congress (and the press) is "knocking the Secret Service down and kicking them for falling."

It would really be nice if we all could get off the backs of the brave men and wymyn of the United States Secret Service, especially since none of us know the whole story (this is especially true of Congress, who, we all know, couldn't find their asses with both hands and directions).

If nothing else, please remember that the agents of the protective division of the United States Secret Service train to jump in front of bullets, or jump on a grenade, or grab the bomb and run away from their principals, and as much as all of us would like to believe we'd do the same thing, those of us who are honest with ourselves know we'd just roll up into the fetal position, stick our thumbs in our mouth, and call for our mommies in those situations.

So please shut the fuck up about the ineptitude of the United States Secret Service, will ya?

I should also say a word or five about the language in this book.

If you don't want to hear those words that George Carlin called the "seven words you can't say on television" (*shit, piss, fuck, cunt, cocksucker, motherfucker,* and *tits*) and a whole host of others, then you shouldn't read this book. I recently read a military thriller—a really good, well-researched, and well-written book, too, that had a great plot and story line and was consistently interesting—that rang false because there wasn't a single curse word in the whole thing, not even from the Russian characters.

The author had a Command Master Chief Petty Officer in the United States Navy give a speech that sounded like it was delivered by an English major during an Oberlin College debate class. While such a creature may exist, I've never met one, and I for damn sure don't believe that a CMCPO would exhort his sailors without at least one *fuck* in there, since most senior noncommissioned officers can Use *fuck* as every part of speech, often in the same sentence. Cursing in the military is ubiquitous and the norm rather than the exception, and any book that purports to portray military personnel who sound like Shakespearean actors at a small religious college is at best disingenuous, and at worst full of shit.

I'm sorry if this offends your tender sensibilities, but a vast majority of regular folk curse in their daily speech, and if you don't believe me, well, try being a schoolteacher (we don't get to curse, we just get to listen to the kids do it) or a bus driver or a police officer or any other profession that takes you out of your little comfort cocoon. The cursing in this book is not done to shock but rather to approximate normal speech as much as possible. The fact that the main character of this book is a Marine and a Secret Service agent foreordains that there would be cursing, and so there is. My fucking bad.

In writing the book, I've also encountered resistance to my hero being a heroine, mainly from misogynistic Neanderthals who've tried to tell me that no womyn in the world could ever beat them up, martial arts and throwback Neanderthal strength notwithstanding.

Fuck them.

I learned *aikido* from a 90-pound East Asian womyn who often beat me up without breaking a sweat while brushing her teeth, reading her grandchildren a bedtime story and weaving a rug. I fought a 5'5", 175-pound womyn during a *kendo* tournament who was so strong she lifted me off the floor using a stick in my left armpit—and I weighed a svelte 275 pounds. I've seen many womyn who were incredibly strong, including the USA's Ramona Pagel, who made the Olympic team for the shot put four different times (1984, 1988, 1992, and 1996) and was so strong the earth shook when she walked—and she was 6', 185 pounds (I'm guessing, but there was no way she weighed more than that the first time I saw her in 1981).

There are also many anecdotal stories about wymyn throughout history who had unusual strength without being behemoths, and the connection to the Basque Neanderthal gene is out there, although I haven't seen anything that I would call concrete evidence yet. There is no reason to believe there are not such throwback individuals among us, especially since recent events have proven that wymyn can, in fact, make their way through the U.S. Army's Ranger School (an arduous and elite special operations school that requires great strength and endurance). There is also no reason to doubt that this trend will continue. Boo-rah, First Lieutenant Shaye Haver and Captain Kristen Griest—Rangers lead the way!

I also need to explain the spelling of *wymyn* or *womyn*. The "y" sound is perfectly acceptable for the pronunciation of the words traditionally spelled *woman* or *women*, and it eliminates the need to be sexist—I'm a man who has always hated that wymyn have been forced to accept "man" or "men" within the description of their gender. This spelling change is my little contribution toward the equality of treatment that wymyn deserve.

You also need to know about the eating establishments in this novel. Every single one of them is real, and every single one of them has its charms. I have personally eaten at all but a very few of these places, and I do not mention any hot dog places that I have not eaten at. The hot dogs of Chicago are my favorites, and yes, I love Portillo's and Superdawg, which should be declared national monuments. The hot dog list is somewhat incomplete, since it doesn't include Mad Dogz (thanks Marco and Diane) up in Comstock Park, Michigan, home of 100 percent beef hot dogs named the Hound (chili, coleslaw, mustard, and onion), the Chi-Chi (chili, cheese, onion, tomato, sour cream, Fritos), and my personal favorite, the Goofy (chili, peanut butter [crunchy or creamy], pickles, crushed Fritos), or Johnny Dogs up in Munising, Michigan, just down the street from the Pictured Rocks cruises and home to the Reuben Dog, Philly Dog, and Bob Marley Dog (all just what you'd expect—jerk chicken on a hot dog is simply fabulous! Who knew? Thanks, John!), or lots of other fun joints. But I had to limit it somehow, so I kept it to Chicago. By the way, sorry for calling Doug of Hot Doug's a pussy—everyone knows you put your heart and soul into the place, but we miss you, man.

Why did I put the restaurants in here? Because the Freak is a foodie—only she likes real food, not vapors, froths, ramps, edamame, organic vegan tofu, or any other highfalutin' insult to diners everywhere that masquerades as food. I wanted her to be the All-American girl, and having a family hot dog list seemed to be a good way to do it.

The fact that I got to plug some of my favorite hot dog places was an act of pure serendipity.

So there you have it, the user's guide to this fictional work of fiction that is wholly fictitious. Anybody who thinks they recognize themselves or some permutation of their name, or someone they know, is delusional, drunk, or over- (and/or) undermedicated. Most all the names are made up, and the people are just characters in a fictional and wholly fictitious novel. I didn't write about you, unless it was accidentally, or wholly coincidentally, or from some deep, dark place in my slightly warped brain, and even then, it isn't about you, because—say it with me—this is fictional, even the names.

Except for one name.

That name is Thomas J. (for Justice) Vernon.

Tom was a friend of mine who built houses for a living, built a great family, and made the world a better place just by being himself. He was the best man I ever knew, an honest, open, simple person who wouldn't lie, cheat, or steal for any reason. The fact that he has passed makes life not as fun, as solid, or as wonderful as it once was, but in my family, we believe that as long as you remember someone, they aren't truly gone. I can't think of any better way to remember my friend and make sure he's not gone than to use his name in this novel, especially since the character in the novel parallels Tom's attitude and personality so well. I hope his friends and family who read this will recognize their father/uncle/cousin/brother/son/grandpa/friend even without the name, because I put all of Tom Vernon I could into the character.

I want to thank his wife, Deb Vernon, for her gracious permission to use Tom's name in the book. I hope Tom still sounds like himself when you read this.

Read on, gentle reader. Serious fiction awaits you (and if you buy that, well, I've got this property in Florida I'd like you to look at).

Remember, this is *fiction*.

AJ Hartman,
from the Highgate House
17 December 2021

PROLOGUE

I decided to let them hit me just three more times. I figured that an even twenty shots to the head and torso were enough, and they were at seventeen, so three more was my limit.

Unless they used an implement.

For some reason, being hit by their fists didn't bother me, but the thought of being whacked with an implement did. Maybe it was because of my childhood, when my brothers whaled on me with sticks as we played at "sword fighting" (which I was still convinced was brotherspeak for "Let's beat the shit out of our younger sister and get away with it"), or maybe it was because I really, truly didn't like bullies who whipped up on people weaker than them by using implements of destruction. But probably it was just because I was inherently afraid of penises and/or their symbolic representations (as my good friend Fiona the Freudian psychologist always told me).

Or maybe I was just tired of getting smacked around by three strong motherfuckers.

Especially since they were trying to force information out of me that (a) I was never going to supply and (b) was certainly obsolete, since my supervisor would have changed it the moment she knew that I was taken, and (c) the objects they wanted the information for were out of their reach, locked up in the White House behind a Secret Service screen that could be augmented by a Marine regiment in about five minutes (literally).

Or maybe I was just tired of being knocked around by three strong motherfuckers.

In any case, either three more shots with their fists or one shot with an implement and that was it. I was a stubborn, bullheaded, obtuse bitch with serious anger issues and an iron will, but enough was enough. These clowns were good—clearly well trained and in great physical shape—but they weren't SEALs and had never seen me in action and were in for a big surprise after just three more punches or one whack with an implement.

Which was why I was totally unprepared when one of them took out a big Ka-Bar combat knife and sliced my blouse up both sides. He tore the remnants of the blouse off, pulled my bra away from my body and sliced it between the cups, and then threw the whole mess behind him on the floor, leaving my considerable breasts exposed.

It must be said (so I'll say it before anybody else does) that I am not a good-looking womyn, but my boobs are spectacular in their shape, size, and effect on men. Every guy who has ever seen them (even in a business suit) is so awestruck that they pause for a moment in silent reverence for the God of Tits, who blessed me with my totally outrageous ta-tas.

Not these guys. They never really looked at them at all, which was when I realized that either (a) I was in the presence of three totally gay guys who couldn't care less about tits (highly unlikely, since these motherfuckers looked and acted mucho hetero) or (b) these were serious professionals bent on truly harming me.

I was betting on the latter, especially when the shortest one pulled a circuit board, battery, and some alligator clips on the end of wires out of a backpack. I realized at that point that it wasn't the information that they wanted—I was going to be a message for POTUS. After they had systematically tortured me, they were going to leave my body somewhere it would be readily discovered, and subsequently reported to POTUS, who would undoubtedly get the message that his daughters were next.

All this flashed through my mind right before the one with the knife yanked my hips away from the chair and slit my pants right down the middle (he cut through my Hermès belt, too, which really pissed me off). One of the other goons stepped up, and the two of them yanked my pants down around my ankles, which were still duct-taped to the chair legs. Knife Goon sliced through the bunched legs and threw the remnants of my pants into the same pile as my bra and blouse.

I wasn't really bothered about being completely naked in front of the three gomers, until gomer #3 lifted the front of the chair up and set a wide pan down, leaving my feet immersed in water when he gently let the chair back down. I knew what that meant—the next thing out of the backpack would be a probe of some kind that they were going to shove in my vagina or up my ass (if I got to choose, I'd have picked vagina, because at least it was used to being probed by my vibrator) right before they used more volts to fry me again.

The three gomers stepped away from me, and the one with the scar said, "Not very modern, are we?" They all glanced at my crotch and almost smiled, I assume because they had never seen a real Burning Bush before (which was what my one college boyfriend had always called my pubes). Having flaming-red hair is not a bad thing, unless you have pubic hair that grows like the Brazilian rain forest and covers most of your belly up to your *pipik* (your navel, for the non-Hebrews among us)—then it's a bitch. And no, I never considered having a Brazilian done, since I was sure that even Cedars-Sinai couldn't have stopped the bleeding from that waxing, and no, I wasn't going to shave it either—you know how bad it is when you have to stand absolutely still and your pubes itch? No? Believe me, it's as bad as having poison ivy in your crotch. And yes, I do know what that feels like.

Besides, my current sex toy liked the Burning Bush (I guess it was inevitable that the nickname would stick) just the way it was, so yeah, I had a mass of curly hairs just sticking up down there. The three gomers did pause just a bit to gaze at the Burning Bush, which was when I decided that having alligator clamps attached to my nipples and a probe shoved up my ass so some gomers could half-electrocute me for information that they clearly didn't give a rat's ass about just wasn't in the cards.

Like I said, the gomers had never seen me in action—clearly, they weren't part of the first team, all of whom would have been briefed on my abilities—which was why they were totally unprepared when I shrugged my shoulders and flexed my arms, yanking them up and out, which ripped the chair apart. I fell on my butt and rolled up to my feet before the well-trained gomers could react.

I hit the first one with a knife hand to the solar plexus, caught the second one with a hammer fist to the nose, and drove a reverse heel kick into the third one's left knee. I spun and aimed my front elbow at the first gomer's face, but he put his hands up to block, which was OK with me, since it was a feint. My trailing elbow came around in a short vicious arc and broke four of his ribs, dropping him from the fight. The second gomer was semi-recovered, so I kneed him in the balls and spun an elbow into the mastoid process behind his ear, breaking his jaw in at least three places and also removing him from the fight.

Gomer #3 had recovered enough to pull his Ka-Bar out again, which meant that I was going to get cut. Despite what you see all the time in movies, even the best martial artists (of which I was one—black belts in three different styles) cannot casually disarm someone with a knife. The rule was simple: if they get within 10 feet of you with the knife, you're going to get cut. No exceptions. Even Bruce Lee or Chuck Norris would have to be just stone lucky to not get cut—and even with luck, they'd probably still be bloodied up. Since this gomer was about six feet from me, I was going to get cut.

So I charged him, hoping he wouldn't hit anything vital until I could subdue him. He stepped back just a tad and then came in low with the knife, aiming right for the Burning Bush (my analytical mind reminded me that this was so I couldn't kick his hand up without taking the thrust somewhere in my body), so I planted my left foot and spun sideways into a desperate wheel kick, which was when my bra intervened.

That's right, my bra.

I know, I know, it's a cliché, right? The heroine is saved by some miraculous occurrence that is totally unbelievable, but this time it was just simple physics. Take 210 pounds of mass and move it along a vector with 850 foot-pounds of thrust at a rate of real quick and the point of the thrusting instrument will arrive at its destination in a certain time with a certain amount of force, provided that the thrust remains constant. This was what should have happened to me, except for the fact that another physical principle—that would be friction—was temporarily suspended at the anchor point of the thrust, changing both the thrusting force and vector of the strike.

The gomer stepped on my 100% silk bra with the foot he was pushing off with. Hand sewn by a little old Chinese American lady in my neighborhood in D.C., the silk bra did just what it was supposed to do: it slid smoothly across the floor, just like it slid over my boobs when I was wearing my shoulder rig, which was just about all the time. When your boobs are perfectly round perky 38Ds, you need custom bras, because nothing off the rack is ever going to fit right.

So when the gomer slipped on my bra, his aim was spoiled, and he didn't have nearly enough force to drive the Ka-Bar through my midriff (or my cooter, for that matter) and gut me.

He did, however, still cut me. The knife slid along my side from my hip up to my armpit, but I just clamped his hand and forearm between my arm and side and hip-tossed him to the floor. Not letting go of his arm, I reversed and spun his shoulder out of socket, broke his arm at the wrist and elbow with a judo hold, and kicked him in the trapezius, right where his neck met his shoulder. The gomer's head snapped down and back, then struck the wall at an unnatural angle, breaking his neck. I said a silent thanks to Mrs. Chen for her craftsmanship on the bra—and her insistence that silk was the only proper fabric for a bra—as I stood up from killing the third gomer.

I could feel the wound on my side burning where the knife had cut me as I ripped the tape and chair arm off my left wrist. I then carefully unwound the tape from my right wrist and used it to hold the edges of the wound in my side together. Fortunately, the knife had been razor-sharp—further evidence that these gomers were pros—and the wound hadn't yet started to really bleed. I slapped the tape flat over every part of the wound I could see, because I knew when I started to move it would open up. I also carefully unwound the tape from my ankles and used it as cross supports over the wound.

When I was finally tape- and chair-free, I stepped over to the first gomer, the one who had broken ribs and problems breathing from a solar plexus that was certainly bruised all to hell. I knelt down next to him and put my index finger right on the middle one of his broken ribs. He looked like he was thinking of trying to attack me, so I hitched up and put my knee right on his throat. The gomer had a face full of the Burning Bush and 167 rock-solid pounds poised to crush his hyoid bone and slowly suffocate him—and he was a pro who knew that I would do it, too. All the fight went out of his eyes, so I said, "Say, can we talk? I'm just bursting with questions after being assaulted, battered, and forced to defend myself against three big, healthy men—the exercise really gets your mind right, y'know?"

He sort of nodded, so I said, "All I want to know is this: Where is your boss?"

His eyes got big, and he slowly moved his head side to side. I suspected that he was more scared of his boss than he was of me, so I said, "Look, he's a scary guy, but I'm right here, right now, and if you don't tell me, I'm gonna have to really, really hurt you." To emphasize my point, I gently pushed down on his broken rib with my finger. To his credit, the gomer only grunted, so I stiffened my finger into an attack position and really dug in on the rib.

He screamed like a third grader and passed out, which was what I expected to happen. I went over and secured the still-unconscious gomer #2 with leftover duct tape. Gomer #3 was dead as a doornail, so I didn't duct-tape him up. I did put gomer #1's feet and hands together with duct tape so that when he woke up, I wouldn't have to wrestle with him at all.

He woke up in short order, at which point I again put my finger in an attack position and set it on the rib. I said, "OK, I'm only going to ask you one more time: Where is Tom Miller?"

His eyes lit up when I said Tom's name, so I said, "Look, I know what's going on, and I know who's leading the effort, so tell me where Tom is and nobody else has to get hurt. I know that you were just following orders, and I know why Tom wants to do this, but if I can't find him, I can't help him. Anybody else is just gonna shoot him on sight, so why not tell me where he is? I'll tell him it was gomer #3—the dead one over there—that told me. He'll never know it was you."

They tell me that I have a sincere and trustworthy face, which really means I can con anybody, but in this case, I meant what I said, and the gomer must have seen that. He blew out a breath and said, "We were supposed to meet him at the National Portrait Gallery, just inside the northwest entrance."

"By the Stuart painting of George Washington."

"Yeah. In fact, that bench was the wave-off spot. If we were compromised, or didn't finish the job, one of us was supposed to leave a copy of today's *Post* on the bench, folded open to the second sports page."

I stood up and said, "Thanks, man. I'll call an ambulance for you and gomer #2 as soon as I've seen Tom. Otherwise, it could be quite a while before somebody finds you." I stood up and had turned to leave the room when I realized that I had a problem.

No fucking clothes.

I was good at what I did—there was no better Secret Service agent alive—but I couldn't go after a bad guy who wanted to harm the president of the United States while completely nude. First of all, they'd never let me in the National Gallery, even if I told them I was just a model who was going to a nude sitting. Second, I was pretty sure that Tom Miller would notice a completely nude me trying to stalk him, and third, I didn't know where the fuck I was, and I didn't have any fucking money for a cab or a fucking car, although I was pretty sure the gomers had some kind of transport—it's hard to take an unconscious Secret Service agent on a bus or the metro.

There was no question everybody would get a load of the Burning Bush, which would stop traffic just long enough for the cops to arrest my ass and throw me in jail, thus defeating the mission of getting the bad guy.

In other words, I was fucked.

Unless…

I went back to the injured gomer and said, "Dude, I need to borrow your clothes."

"Why'n't you take his clothes?" the gomer said, inclining his head toward his dead buddy. "He ain't gonna need 'em no more." I couldn't argue with that logic, especially since the dead gomer was shorter than the other two. I stripped the clothes off his body—outerwear only, since I wasn't wearing anybody else's drawers (the only thing more gross than that would be using someone else's toothbrush—eeeyyeuuu!)—and put them on.

The shirt hung like a tent, and the pants were way too big everywhere, but they were clothes, so I just tightened the belt up, rolled up the shirtsleeves, and cut off the pants cuffs with the Ka-Bar. By then the wound scored into my side was burning and trying to leak, but it turned out that the duct tape was just as good as stitches, although nowhere near as good as whiskey for the pain.

I nodded at the conscious gomer and headed out the door.

It opened on a small warehouse, which was nearly empty except for a few boxes near what I guessed was the outside door. I went over and almost just passed by the boxes, but something about the markings made me stop to look at them. I opened one and suddenly knew where Tom Miller and his merry band of rogue SEALs were, and how they were going to get at the first daughters…and I was pretty sure that it was going to work too.

Shitpisshelldamnfuck!

CHAPTER 1

In the Beginning There Was the Freak

Ugliest. Baby. Ever.

There was no getting around it. I've seen the pictures of me, which are bad enough, but it's the pictures of all the people looking at me that really tell the story.

There's one of my Uncle Mort and Aunt Adele—two nicer people you will never find—looking at me in my mother's arms. Uncle Mort looks like he was having his annual prostate exam, while Aunt Adele appears to be sucking on several lemons flavored with goat turds. My mother has a sickly smile on her face that would scare an ogre, and my dad is trying to cover my face with my little baby blanket as he looks anywhere but at me.

All five of my brothers have baby pictures where people are beaming at them; they were so cute then you can almost hear the billing and cooing coming from the pictures.

There isn't a single picture of me that looks like that. No, I got lemons and goat turds, with the smell of rotting sheep carcasses thrown in.

Yes, I was an ugly, ugly baby, but I would improve in looks, right? All girls are cute when they're five, right?

Wrong again.

I'm 34 years old and still waiting to get cute, or even "handsome," the euphemism that people use when you're not pretty but still cut some kind of figure.

I have a feeling that I'll be waiting until hell freezes over, because I'm never going to be good-looking, unless you count my overly muscular jock body, which most guys don't, especially once they find out that they will never be stronger than me.

I am just an ugly freak—that's all there is to it. Oh, and fuck that sympathy I hear trying to come out of your mouth. I don't need sympathy, unless it helps me get laid—in that case, sympathy away. Otherwise, just fuck off.

Did I also mention that I grew up with five brothers who taught me to be just like them? No?

In any case, there I was, the world's ugliest baby in a family of beautiful people, but with redeeming sweetness and character aplenty...except for a few *minor* flaws.

When I was six months old, I entered my screaming phase, where I screamed at anything that touched me, went by me, or was, in any way, possibly going to be within 50 miles of me. My parents tried everything—car rides, walking the floor with me, covering my mouth with a pillow (not really, you outraged superparents—I think they used an afghan instead), but nothing worked. I screamed. And screamed. And screamed. And not just any old scream either. My dad always said it was a cross between James Brown, a Mongol war cry, and an F-15 fighter jet on takeoff, with a hint of Metallica on top.

Luckily for my parents, the phase was fairly short—it only lasted until I was four, four and a half tops.

Of course, my screaming phase did overlap with what my mom called my samurai phase.

When I was one and a half, I decided that I would stab, chop, or slash anything that I didn't like, which turned out to be everything except my eldest brother, Aaron (who, for some reason, I thought walked on water—he was my own personal shibboleth). Everything (and everybody) else got perforated, mangled, and/or carved up.

I stabbed the dog with a crayon. Good old Cyclops didn't even bite me, but he did forever shy away from crayons and anyone who came up on his blindside.

I nailed my cousin Irving to the wall with four colored pencils. Fortunately, the surgery was a success and he has gone on to a successful career in the dry-cleaning business, although he still won't come to family reunions when I'm there.

I tried to nail my brother Morris with a salad fork, missed, fell out of my high chair, and stabbed him through the foot, keeping him immobilized until Dad could get a pry bar and release him from the hardwood floor. Mo still prizes the 34 stitches in his foot, despite the limp.

The worst was when my mom went to get the phone while frosting a cake. She left the frosting spatula on the table, which was when I appropriated it as my "sword." I managed to hold off an entire regiment of people for nearly four hours—I crammed myself into a corner of the pantry and just kept slashing and stabbing, wounding at least 17 (a real number) until Mr. Hooper from next door brought over his cast fishing net and tossed it over me.

I still say that if that spatula had been sharp, I would've cut my way free and run off to Bora-Bora, but instead I got walloped by Dad, who didn't really believe in corporal punishment but didn't know what else to do with his "little sweetie" (his pet name for me until this incident). My brothers started calling me the Serial Maimer.

Nobody else knew what to do with me either. My brothers thought I was a terrorist, my mom doted on her boys, and my dad could only take so much. I'm still amazed that my parents let me live through that stage, and the stages that came after, but for reasons as yet unknown, they did.

Going to school for the other Glickstien children was a thing of joy forever. My brother Aaron, who would become a 6'5" All-State shooting guard before going to Northwestern on a basketball scholarship, was a superb student who made the dean's list every semester, even at med school. My next eldest brother, Marvin, who won the state cross-country championship three years straight before going off to Stanford, was even smarter than Aaron, making Phi Beta Kappa and getting a Rhodes scholarship. My brother Morris, who won the state math championship as an eighth grader, and every year after that until he went to Cal Tech, was a super-nerd genius who NASA hired to figure out how to make ships go at light speed (not really—light speed is impossible, but if anyone could figure it out, it would be Mo). My brother David (pronounced "Dah-veed") was a 3.95 student while winning All-State honors in football three years straight before surprising everyone and going off to Cornell to become a vet (he gave up a shot at the NFL to go to "doggy school"). My brother Gabriel was voted president of the student body his senior year before he took his perfectly sculpted All-State swimmer's body off to the University of Texas and then Yale Law, where he edited the law review. Everyone loved Gabe, who people usually said was "the sweetest boy ever." All my sibs were good at school and loved the experience.

Then there was me.

School sounded like a good idea, right up until I got there. Then it was hell on earth.

I got in trouble the first day of kindergarten, right off the bat. In fact, several people mentioned that I had set a new record at my school for "fastest in trouble."

My crime? I wouldn't tell Mrs. Swilley, the old bat that taught kindergarten like she was in charge of Stalag 17, my "real name." It went like this:

Old Bat: Is Glinda here?
Me: No, but Glinka is.
Old Bat: Excuse me?
Me: My name is Glinka Glickstien, not Glinda.
Old Bat: I'm sorry, dear, but Glinka is not a real name.
Me: Yeah, it is, Mrs. Swill.
Old Bat: I'm sorry, dear, but my name is Mrs. Swilley.
Me: Swilley isn't a real name…
Old Bat: Of course it is—
Me, *interrupting*: But Swill is. Just ask a pig.
Old Bat, *shrieking*: GO TO THE OFFICE!

My mother the lawyer came to school when they called her. I was sitting outside the office when she arrived, trying to figure out how to ditch school and get to my grandma's house, where I knew there was a nice retired lady who wanted nothing more than to give me cookies and knishes. My mom walked up to me and said, "On the first day? Really? This is what you decided to do to me? I have to endure 12 more years of this? Oy vey!"

Mrs. Swill came stomping out of the office with her hair on fire and said, "Mrs. Glickstien, your daughter refuses to answer to her correct name! Doesn't she know her name?"

My mom turned to me with *her* hair on fire and said, "Are you *kidding* me? You've known your name since you were *one*!" I smiled sweetly (I thought it was sweet, but with the way I looked, it probably wasn't) and said, "But, Mother, I tried to tell Mrs. Swill my name, but she said it wasn't real."

"What name did she give you?" my mom said, her exasperation with my antics clearly showing.

"I called her name, Glinda, but she tried to tell me her name was Glinka," the Old Bat said.

Mom raised her hand to smack me but stopped and looked at the Old Bat, puzzled. "But her name *is* Glinka."

"Nonsense! That clearly isn't a real name," the Old Bat said.

Her smugness was the wrong approach to use on my mom, who drew herself up into court-room pose and said, "Well, Swill isn't the greatest name I've ever heard either, but if you say it's your name, I'll believe you."

"Actually, it's Swilley, but that is entirely different from a name like Glinka," the Old Bat said.

My mom's eyes flashed, and she went into full hissy-fit lawyer mode. "Oh, really? Are you calling my husband and me incompetent because of the way we named our daughter, Mrs. Swill?"

It went downhill from there.

The rest of kindergarten was a nightmare—my teacher didn't like me (actually, she didn't like my mom, but I was the one who bore the brunt of her wrath). The Old Bat called me Glinda and I ignored her, while I called her Mrs. Swill and she punished me. I almost never went out for recess—I was perpetually busy writing lines (Usually "I will not ignore my teacher"), but when I did go out, I got in more trouble.

The Great Playground Fuckup started with a simple game of tag. I was declared "it" one day and promptly ran down one of my classmates in approximately a nanosecond. Unfortunately, I ran down Logan Brunner, the best athlete in kindergarten anywhere. His mom and dad had both been college athletes and owned their own sporting goods store, while my mumsy and pops had been geek-o-nerds that became an attorney and a CPA. Nobody could catch Logan Brunner, who everyone believed would be a professional athlete someday, but I caught him effortlessly.

What happened next became the stuff of playground legend. Logan thought he would just re-tag me, so he waited for me to move the requisite five steps away and then came after me, a cruel smile on his face. The smile soon vanished when he came up with air on his first tag attempt. He bellowed with prepubescent rage and gave chase again.

I kept him missing for at least ten minutes, effortlessly dashing away from him. He became so frustrated he changed the rules of tag, deputizing four of his pals to be co-its. All five of the boys rushed me, certain of victory, and all five fell down without touching me. I ran out into the wide-open space of the back playground to give myself room to maneuver, but also to taunt the already-weary Logan Brunner.

Five minutes later, three things happened simultaneously: (a) the bell rang for us to return to class, (b) I dodged so effectively away from my pursuers that three of them ran smack-dab into one another and knocked themselves out, and (c) Logan Brunner puked his guts out all over the spectators, causing several of the more delicate flowers to sympathy-puke.

I ran back to the door to go inside, none the worse for wear and grinning. I got back to the classroom and went to my seat, but none of my classmates showed up. The Old Bat was snoozing in her chair, so I sat perfectly silent for 10 minutes before she snorted herself awake and looked around the room. Her eyes swept right to me, then widened as she took in the empty room. Before she could say anything, our principal, Mr. Colley, a kindly man who would later be one of my best teachers in high school, came in. He looked at me, then beckoned the Old Bat out into the hall. I could see them but couldn't hear what they were saying, although it wasn't hard to guess what the subject was.

After a moment, the Old Bat put her face in her hands and rocked gently back and forth for a bit. She looked up at me through the window and was turning to stomp into the room when several of my classmates finally showed up, led by Elise Truby and Lauren Marker. They were the official officious twits of kindergarten, a role that they would play throughout our school years. Both little martinets bustled into the room, and Elise said, "Well, I hope you're happy! Poor Logan has vomited three times and has heatstroke. Jamie, Patrick, and Cooper were all knocked out and had to ride in a ambulance. Several others have vomited—"

"Puked their guts out," Lauren said.

"Yes, puked their guts out—and it's all your fault!" Elise finished.

She and my other classmates glared their outrage at me, but I just sat there without any expression at all. I knew I would be blamed for the Great Playground Fuckup, but I also knew that my babbling on wouldn't change that, so I chose to keep my dignity and await my punishment.

Mrs. Swill stomped in, grabbed me by the arm, and dragged me down to the office. I didn't resist, just let her bundle me along, although I was pretty sure that I could have stopped her. Call it a premonition, but there was just something inside me saying, "Shake her hand off—you can do it!" but I resisted, figuring I was already in enough trouble.

When we got to the office, I was glad I had, because my mom, dad, Uncle Mort, and *zayde* (Grandpa Abraham) were all in there with Mr. Colley, Logan Brunner's parents, and some guy I didn't know. They were all looking at me, and not with kindness and understanding either. My five-year-old brain realized that this was serious, but I still had an ace in the hole (I thought).

Before anyone else could speak, my *zayde* said, "I always said that God had to've given you some special gift to make up for…well, you know, but seriously, Gigi?" (This was his nickname for me: G + G = Gigi.) "Three out cold and mass vomiting? What kind of superpower is that?" He didn't smile, but at that moment, I knew I had at least one ally in the room, because I could tell that he was teasing me, and teasing Mr. Colley too.

That gentleman cleared his throat and said, "Well, we're all here today because young Miss Glickstien seems to have caused a ruckus on the playground."

My Uncle Mort, my mom's older brother, who had been a trial lawyer for as long as anyone could remember, said, "Your Honor, it is hardly credible that this little lady could have caused all the mayhem she allegedly caused without the participation of others."

Mr. Colley smiled and said, "Mr. Blumenthal, I'm not a judge, just a principal, but I would like to ask Miss Glickstien her side of the story before we proceed to summary judgment." My side all gave a little laugh, but the Brunners and their goon (he was almost as ugly as I was) didn't even move. Mr. Colley turned to me and said, "You're on, little lady."

So I told them the whole story, and when I got to the part about Logan deputizing his pals, my mom, my *zayde*, and Uncle Mort—lawyers all—said some variation of "That's against the rules of tag!" Mr. Colley held his hands up and said, "Please, I stipulate that Mr. Brunner's action was unfair and against the rules of tag." Once again, my side laughed, but the Brunners were still not amused, nor was their goon, who was taking copious notes.

I finally finished my side of the story, and Mr. Colley said, "Well, that jibes perfectly with the story I got from numerous witnesses, including three teachers and Mrs. Butler, the playground supervisor." I knew that development was a good one, because "Iron Butt" Butler was the most scrupulously honest person in the whole school. My brother Aaron said she would rather rip her tongue out than tell a lie (although how he knew that, I never knew), so having her tell the same story had to be in my favor. I was feeling pretty good until Mrs. Brunner, a bottle blonde with so much hair spray in her hair it looked like Niagara Falls in January, said the magic L-word.

Then all hell broke loose, kind of what I imagined Armageddon would look like, only with lawyers.

My mom, Uncle Mort, and *zayde* all started screaming and yelling like wounded whales. My mom threatened to get a restraining order against the Brunners, my Uncle Mort was yelling about a devastating countersuit, "Because Glinka might like owning a sports store," and my *zayde* was promising the Brunners would experience "a scorched earth attack on their character and a long, hellish road to trial and beyond."

The Brunners were yelling, too, mostly inarticulate athletic barking, but their goon (who I guessed was a lawyer too) was screaming about "assault, assault with intent, mental distress, and physical intimidation." This went on for a while, until Mr. Colley just bellowed, "All right, everybody shut up! Now!

And they all did too. Mr. Colley was pretty laid-back, but when he wanted to, he was like a rottweiler on a UPS guy.

Everybody stopped yelling and looked at him. He cleared his throat and said, "Miss Glickstien, did you hit Mr. Brunner?"

"No, sir," I said.

"Did you tease him at all?"

"No, sir. I tagged him It and he chased me, trying to make me It."

"Did he chase anybody else to make them It?"

"No, sir. Just me."

Mr. Colley nodded thoughtfully, then said, "Well, it sounds to me like an innocent-enough occurrence. Children at play, no teasing, no fault to either child, just tag on the playground." When all the adults drew breath to speak, Mr. Colley said, "And we are *not* making a federal or any other kind of case out of this, are we?" He looked hard at all the assembled legal powers, who all nodded meekly and said, "No, Your Honor."

"Good," my principal said.

My Uncle Mort couldn't help himself. He said, "Your Honor, can we at least stipulate that the boy keep away from my niece? Sort of a schoolyard restraining order?"

The Brunners' pit bull made a rumbling sound in his chest that might have been an objection, but Mr. Colley just cut through all the crap. "Indeed, counsel. I am ordering the two parties to stay apart on the playground for the next four weeks, at which time I will reconvene them for a re-evaluation hearing and determine if the order needs to stay in place. Are we agreed?"

The Brunners nodded, my side nodded, and Mr. Colley said, "Miss Glickstien, you stay away from Mr. Brunner on the playground until I tell you differently, OK?"

"Yes, sir," I said.

"Now, everybody go where they belong. I have a bunch of pukefest parents and kids to see."

And that would have been it, except for one or 13 things. It seemed that word got around that I needed my folks to defend me, so I became a target for every Morgan, Jessica, and Samantha who needed to make their bones in the pile of shit hierarchy that was school. I was constantly bullied by the entire school, at every opportunity. Some of the teachers tried to get between me and the bullies, but that just made it worse, because now I was not only a mama's girl but was also a brown-nosing teacher's pet.

School had become my own personal hell.

I tried to fight going, but my parents wouldn't have any of it; they just stood there like Scylla and Charybdis (look it up—it's not my fault your education is lacking), obdurate and immovable.

My brothers did their best to explain why I had to go to school, and they encouraged me in every way possible, but school held nothing except pain and tears for me, until I adopted a unique defense against the abuse.

I ran. From everybody and everything. I ran down the halls to the bathroom. I ran to lunch, ran to the bus after school, and ran around the playground as fast as I could (while leaving everyone else in school in the dust). I ran right through kindergarten, first grade, and second grade without making a single friend or feeling in any way connected to school except for my intimate association with ostracism. Forrest Gump had nothing on me.

And just a note before we move on: all of you snivelers out there who are feeling pity for the poor little ugly girl who was horribly bullied by an entire school, just cut that shit out right now. I would like to point out that I had five brothers who doted on me, and parents who were fiercely loving, that I lived in a great house in a wonderful neighborhood, that I ate well and often, and that I had a best friend, Marcia Warren, who lived right across the street (in the Battle Creek school district, as it happened) and who thought I was the best person ever. So stop that fucking pity machine, because I don't need or want it. Yeah, school sucked, but overall, my life was fucking awesome.

Besides, my challenges at school would all change one day during third grade, because of a telephone book and some two-by-fours.

CHAPTER 2

Little Red-Haired Freak

So third grade started up right where second grade left off: me trying to scam my way out of going to school, being picked on, running, running, running away from everyone and everybody—pretty much the sucky experience I had come to expect from school, only I was older.

So was my teacher. I thought Old Bat Swill was old, but Mrs. Tracy was the ancient mariner, apparently sentenced to teach for life by the teaching gods because of some unfortunate mouth breather she had flunked in the past (or maybe she had killed an albatross, although the mouth breather was a better possibility). Whatever motivated her to keep going also made her kind without being wimpy, demanding without being a jerk, and determined to reach every kid in her class, even the Running Girl. My previous experiences with the ogres they called teachers at Little Beavers Elementary—Old Bat Swill, Bad-Breath Sewer in first grade (her name was Seward, but well, I just couldn't resist dropping the *d*), and Ms. Wallpaper in second grade (completely invisible after the first day of school, just like the wallpaper in Grandma's House)—made me feel like I'd been taught by the Weird Sisters from *Macbeth*. All my teachers had been bad, but Mrs. Tracy wasn't half-bad.

School was still sucky, though.

Until *that* day. Ever since it happened, that's the way I think of it: *that* day.

We had another stupid assembly that was supposed to inspire us to be good citizens and toe the line and straighten up and fly right and get our priorities in order and all that other shit that they try to dump on you in school, but this one was somewhat different, because it was also illegal as hell.

The group that Swill (who was now principal, since Mr. Colley had taken the math job at the high school) brought in was a Christian group called He Is Our Strength, and believe me, they were prepared to preach to us, although they cloaked it in a carnival atmosphere, loud pop music, and demonstrations of physical strength. They also completely disregarded the separation of church and state, as well as the rights of the 37 Jewish students, 23 Muslim students, and the four atheists who attended the school, but that would come back to bite them in the ass, so I'll shut up about it.

So there we were, all prisoners of this propaganda carnival in the gymnasium, watching men and wymyn rip phone books in half, break boards with their hands, and generally make asses of themselves in front of a bunch of little kids. I sat there by myself, as far away as I could get from any of the other stooges in the gym, mostly bored stiff, until the audience participation portion of the show.

They started asking volunteers to come up and try what they were doing, and the usual cast of characters (all the popular kids, connected kids, pretty kids—you know, all the spoiled-rotten brats who thought their defecation was not odiferous) got up there and couldn't do it, at which point the preachment about "not just using your muscles to be successful" (you need Jay-sus!) really kicked in.

As they preached, they set out little balsa wood "boards" and let some of the elite break them with their hands (a really strong baby mouse could have broken those slats). Those twits were also a sexist bunch of Holy Rollers, because up to that point they hadn't let a single girl try anything. Finally, one of the wymyn in the group noticed me sitting all alone and said, "Would you like to try? You, the red-haired girl with the WTF T-shirt?"

I got up and dashed to the front of the gym, because I figured if I broke boards, at least I wouldn't be bored. When I got to the front, Lucas Brunner said, "Look out! She'll prob'ly just grab something and run, lady!" That got a general laugh. Old Bat Swill and Mrs. Sewer certainly were entertained, but the lady just looked at me and said, "Sure you want to try?" I nodded, but I looked at the real two-by-fours they had been breaking and then looked at the little piece of balsa. She looked in my eyes and said, "OK, but these are real boards. They're hard, are tough to break, and could hurt your hand."

I nodded and pointed at the two-by-four, at which the whole gym erupted in laughter. "She thinks she can break a real board!" Lucas Brunner said. "What a stooge! All that running has made all her brains leak out—now she's stupid *and* a wuss!" There was general agreement with him, but the lady just set a two-by-four up on the stand and said, "Anytime you're ready, sweetie."

Not to ruin the moment, but I just want to say that I hate people who don't know me calling me sweetie, or honey, or any other kind of treacly endearment. Come to think of it, I hate anybody calling me sweetie or honey—to a kid that's just "I don't give enough of a shit to know your name" talk. Anyway, onward.

I looked at that two-by-four and focused every bit of the hostility I felt toward school on it. I rested my hand on top of it and felt its solidness, a wooden rock for me to break my hand on, which was my intention all along—I figured that it would be a good way to get out of school for a while.

Just then, Logan Brunner said, "Aw, look, she's goin' to chicken out!"

I raised my hand in a tight fist and drove it down, smashing cleanly through the two-by-four and leaving it broken perfectly in half.

The silence that followed was, as they say, deafening. I turned and lifted a telephone book off a table and casually ripped it in half with no apparent effort. I dropped the pieces on top of the broken two-by-four, said "Thank you" to the now-stunned Holy Roller lady, and ran back to my corner.

The gym erupted in a cacophony of unrelated conversations. Everyone just started babbling at once, all about something different. Finally, the lead proselytizer guy, whose name tag said "Peter," was overwhelmed by the Holy Roller spirit and said into his microphone, "Behold the power of Christ! The red-haired child is a modern Samson, filled with the power of Christ! Praise the Lord!"

I didn't even hesitate. I put my hand up, and Peter said, "Quiet! She wishes to speak!"

The gym fell silent, and everybody turned to look at me. I stared at Peter and all the other well-meaning Holy Rollers, and all my schoolmates, and said, "Samson was Jewish, asshole! Jesus didn't have shit to do with his strength!" (Did I mention my five older brothers who taught me things? Cursing was a particular favorite.) and then ran out of the gym and back to my classroom.

Mrs. Tracy admonished me about my language, but not my sentiments.

From *that* day forward, my classmates stopped picking on me. And I stopped running.

School still sucked, though.

Anyway, Mrs. Tracy made me understand that I wasn't weird, just different (a good thing), and that all people had different strengths. After I read a book called *Freak the Mighty* by some guy named Philbrick (hey, I don't make this shit up—his whole name was Rodman Philbrick, and his book, which should be required reading for all teachers, bullies, and well, *everybody*, is still on my shelf), I asked my not-so-sucky teacher if I could make a poster for the wall. She looked at me and said, "Knock yourself out, Miss Glickstein."

So I drew an eagle flying, and a fish swimming, and an elephant lifting a giant stone, and a jaguar in a palm tree (at least they vaguely resembled those things, sort of). Then I wrote, "Birds fly, fish swim, elephants lift heavy loads, and jaguars hunt through the jungle," under the pictures. I showed it to Mrs. Tracy, and she smiled at me as if I had just finished the *Mona Lisa* and said, "Glinka, that is perfectly expressed."

She ran my little homily through the laminator and then hung it on her wall, where it hung until she died during my senior year of college. The not-so-sucky Mrs. Tracy left the picture to me in her will, along with a letter that is too personal to share here but which let me know how proud she was of me.

Truth be told, Rhea Tracy saved my life, both academically and personally. I never would have survived the next year, fourth grade, without her kind, gentle guidance, because old Swill had me assigned to Bad Breath Sewer's class. Through the entire year of what I came to call the Grand Guignol Tour (look it up—it's not my fault your parents weren't reading freaks), I just thought of sweet, not-sucky-at-all old Mrs. Tracy and carried on. Old Lady Sewer's attempts to crush my spirit and academic excellence went awry, leaving behind a very determined human being who was bent on succeeding at all costs, despite her teachers, if necessary.

That year wasn't any fun, but knowing that Mrs. Tracy was rooting for me made it bearable. It was also bearable because a few of my classmates felt sorry for me (it was the second time in three years that I never got to go out for recess—try it sometime and see how much fun that is) and because my family got into the act of making fun of Old Lady Sewer.

> My dad at breakfast: What's that smell?
> My mom at same breakfast: Glinka's teacher just walked by with her dog.
> My dad: Good thing the dog has just had a bath, or we would've retched.

It was silly, but it kept me going.

Fourth grade finally ended, summer passed in a blur, and school went back into session. I was prepared for more torture, but instead my life was changed forever.

That was the year I met the Great Pumpkin.

CHAPTER 3

It's the Great Pumpkin, Freak

Five-five, 225.

Blazing-orange (not red) hair.

Teeth like Secretariat's.

Thick, horn-rimmed glasses.

Voice like a foghorn.

A laugh that would scare Dracula.

Best. Teacher. Ever.

That was Miss Joslyn, a.k.a. the Great Pumpkin.

She came into class like Hurricane Katrina, a refrigerator with a bowling ball for a head (my apologies to Jim Croce, but that's the best description I could come up with) that began talking about learning when she woke up in the morning and stopped when she fell asleep at night. Miss Joslyn was a whirlwind of activity without ever moving from her desk, a one-womyn wrecking crew that stalked ignorance and killed it dead using knowledge, compassion, and the sheer force of her personality.

I fell in love with her on the first day, when she stood up in class and said, "How many people here think they're stupid?" Lots of hands went up, including mine. The Great Pumpkin looked at all the hands, and then she put her hand up with all the rest of the dummies (me included) and said, "Everybody is stupid about something—including me."

There was an audible gasp from the entire class, because we had never heard a teacher confess ignorance about anything. They were gods, and we were the dummies—weren't all teachers like the Pope, infallible and all knowing? (Hey, I'm Jewish, but I still know about the Pope—I have two degrees from liberal arts colleges.)

She read our minds. From her plain round face came the words that set all of us free (or at least gave us a chance in the cruel world). "Nobody's perfect, including me. I expect to learn as much from you as you do from me. For that to happen, we have to work hard, behave ourselves, trust one another enough to ask questions, and respect one another enough to listen to the answers to the questions we ask. We also have to remember the most important thing of all." She paused, looking for all the world like a real live Michelin womyn in an orange fright wig, or a pregnant hippo, as she waited for us to get it.

Almost without thought, my hand crept up into the pregnant pause, trembling a bit because I, the Running Girl, was about to do something that I had never done in class before: ask a question.

The Great Pumpkin looked at me and said, "Yes, Glinka?"

I wondered how Miss Joslyn knew my name, but I just said, "Uh, Miss Joslyn, what's, uh, the most important thing of all?"

She smiled and said, "Thank you for being brave and asking, Glinka. What do you think is the most important thing to remember?"

I said, "Well, we all need to get better at stuff?" (Hey, fuck you, it was fifth grade—I never said I was a Rhodes scholar or anything.)

The Great Pumpkin smiled and said, "Improvement is a worthy goal, but is it the most important thing to remember?"

Socrates had reared his ugly head, because there ensued a wide-ranging discussion of the most important thing to remember about our education, guided by the Great Pumpkin, that finally concluded when Amos Yoder, one of our Amish students, raised his hand and said, "Uh, Miz Joslyn, isn't everybody good at somethin'?"

The Great Pumpkin smiled like a jack-o'-lantern from a Tim Burton movie and sang (yes, sang), "At lassssttt, my dream has come alonggggg…"

Her voice was perfect, like a nightingale outside a bedroom window.

She looked at all of us and said, "Now you know what my gift is, what I'm best at. Amos is right, everyone is good at something, and our job is to find out what each of us is best at and nurture that talent, which in turn will enhance all the other skills you'll need going forward."

I will spare you the Socratic discussion of the words *nurture* and *enhance*, but the point is that no one fell asleep, virtually everyone participated, and best of all, no one felt threatened or bullied the entire time. It turned out that education could be conducted without beating the students (both literally and figuratively), and that the Great Pumpkin was dedicated to the idea of helping everyone find their "gift," as she called it. When she asked us to write an essay on what we thought we were already good at, we didn't know she was employing a diagnostic test, nor would we have cared. All we knew was that our teacher was interested in us and that she thought we were already good in some way.

It was like pouring water on the desert, especially for me. The Great Pumpkin made it impossible not to flourish, simply by believing in all of us, even Dave Spoelstra, who still couldn't really read, even in fifth grade, a problem that embarrassed us all (especially Dave), until the Great Pumpkin explained to us the difference between ignorance (fixable) and stupidity (ain't no fixin' stoopid), at which point Dave said, "Hey, I ain't stoopid, I'm just ignorant!" We all laughed, even the Great Pumpkin. And then the whole class helped Dave catch up in reading.

We were so blessed in that fifth-grade classroom. There was nothing the Great Pumpkin wouldn't do to further your education. She spoke in funny accents, made fun of herself, taught us to sing answers instead of just speaking them (as it turns out, that helps with long-term memory), and generally made learning a pleasure.

However, her greatest gift came to us care of a silly Halloween TV special about a cartoon character named Charlie Brown. Charlie Brown was the creation of the great Charles Schulz. He had a dog named Snoopy, a nemesis named Lucy, and lots of other characters in his comic strip, but his best friend was a kid named Linus van Pelt. Linus walked around with a security blanket, sucked his thumb, and was quite a country philosopher, but most of all, Linus believed in the Great Pumpkin, the rough Halloween equivalent of Santa Claus.

The Great Pumpkin knew that we'd all seen the hokey TV special, so on the day of Halloween, she came to school with a special surprise.

It was a Great Pumpkin suit.

I mean, she actually looked like a pumpkin. We were all waiting to go into school on that morning when we heard a funny whooshing sound, followed by the voice of Linus from the TV special saying, "It's the Great Pumpkin, Charlie Brown!"

Into the driveway rolled an orange Cadillac convertible driven by a guy dressed all in orange, and sitting on the back of the car was the Great Pumpkin.

Miss Joslyn.

Her suit was perfectly round. Her face stuck out near the top of the pumpkin, painted green like a pumpkin stem, and trailing some pumpkin vine leaves. Her arms and legs were encased in heavy orange fabric, and she'd painted her heavy old horn-rimmed glasses orange too. She really looked just like a pumpkin.

The Great Pumpkin alit from her chariot, led the rest of us into school, and proceeded to just teach the hell out of Charlie Brown, Linus, and the whole *Peanuts* gang. We examined religious beliefs around the world, where Halloween (and Christmas, and Easter) came from, why the Day of the Dead in Mexico and Halloween are different—we had one of those whirlwind learning days where the bell rings at the end of the day and you go "Awww, can't we stay a little longer?"

Miss Joslyn, still in the costume, which she had worn all day (we wondered how she went to the bathroom), took us out to the bus and said, "Well, gang, I'll see you tomorrow. Be careful if you are trick-or-treating." She was being kind, because Amos Yoder (Amish), Shelly Bonde (Jehovah's Witness), and Gerald Doane (born-again Christian) would not be getting any candy. "And remember, there is a spelling test tomorrow."

"Yes, O Great Pumpkin," we all said, just like we'd practiced during last recess. Miss Joslyn smiled and nodded, her round face just beaming like a huge green sun with horn-rims.

From that day forward, whenever someone in class raised their hand to ask a question, they would say, "Your leave to speak, O Great Pumpkin!" and she would say, "Do thou speak, O Gentle Sprout!" Our respect for her just soared, especially because she continued to teach like a crazed badger.

My own respect for her grew to the size of Montana when she handed me a book about Babe Didrikson Zaharias with the admonition that Babe and I seemed to share some characteristics. I devoured the book—it turned out that Babe was persecuted because she, too, could beat boys at sports. (Who knew? I came from an accountant and a lawyer, both of whom put together weren't as athletic as a beach ball.) And suddenly I realized that the Great Pumpkin was giving me a hint at what I might be best at.

I played Little League that year—baseball, not softball—and made All-Stars while hitting about .840. No kidding—I was so fast that if the ball bounced more than three times getting to a fielder, I was safe. It also turned out that I could hit the ball out of any Little League park anywhere—sixteen of my twenty home runs were out of the park. I was also a tremendous catcher who routinely threw out any runner trying to advance or steal.

It was all because of the Great Pumpkin and her philosophy that "everyone is good at something." For me, sports were a way to not be a freak but rather a "normal" person.

The Great Pumpkin also made me into a superior student, and made all of us in her class better, because of her self-effacing, humor-filled, learning-is-a-need-like-air-and-water approach to class. She taught us to question everything, to never stop in the pursuit of the whole story, and to suck the very marrow out of our academic life. If that sounds like the plot of the movie *Dead Poets Society*, I would like to point out that I had Miss Joslyn's class five years before that movie came out, and she was even more peculiar and demanding than Robin Williams's Mr. Keating.

The day fifth grade was over, every kid in the Great Pumpkin's room cried like we were three-year-olds. Dave Spoelstra could finally read, Emily Goodacre didn't wet herself every time a teacher called on her in class, and Rodney Harvey could talk without stuttering. There weren't any of us who couldn't write a three-page report on anything. And me? Well, I didn't run from anything anymore. I was studying karate and contemplating middle school sports and totally unconcerned because I was "different," all because the Great Pumpkin treated all of us like the special people we were.

She talked to each of us at our desks for a moment just before the last bell of the year rang, drying tears and offering the last advice we'd ever get from her. When she came to my desk, I couldn't even talk, until she handed me a sheaf of papers and said, "Glinka, you need to read these over the summer. Maybe they will explain some things about who you are. I hope that you'll come and see me before next year starts. I will be glad to discuss the reports with you."

I hugged her and said, "O Great Pumpkin, I will never forget you!"

"All hail the Great Pumpkin!" Dave Spoelstra said.

"Hail Great Pumpkin!" we all cried through our tears.

The bell rang, and the Great Pumpkin said, "Gentle Sprouts, *dis*missed! Go forth and conquer!"

And we left her there, her tears running down her fat Great Pumpkin cheeks as we struggled out of our seats and went to our buses. For the only time during the whole year, she did not walk us out but instead stood in her classroom and waved, wearing, of course, her orange Great Pumpkin pantsuit, her flaming-orange hair catching the afternoon light like an ancient beacon of knowledge.

I waved until I couldn't see her anymore, and then I cried all the way home. An eighth grader named Dirk (who the hell names their kid Dirk? That's a porno name, right?) Steensma tried to make fun of me for crying, so I punched him in the nose and knocked him back into his seat, and everyone else shut up and left me alone.

When I got home, I ran to my room and looked at my class picture in its little paper frame, hungry to see the Great Pumpkin again, despite having just left her.

I still look at that picture every single day, although now it's in a real frame, under glass, and protected. It is the only thing that I own that I'd run back in and save from a fire, a memory from a time when I was a freak and the Great Pumpkin came out of *Peanuts* to save me.

It also reminds me that everything has a cost associated with it because there ain't no such thing as a free lunch (TANSTAAFL)—everything in this life has to be paid for in one way or another, a lesson that we are loath to learn but always end up learning the hard way.

As I would find out early on in my young life.

CHAPTER 4

Freak Motivation

By now (if you've read this far) you are definitely wondering, "Dudette, what the fuck is all this whiny school history shit? Where's the damned action-adventure story that began in the prologue? Why am I still reading this shit about someone called the Great Pumpkin?"

Well, let me tell ya, gentle readers (I would've said *assholes*, but I was afraid you might be put off), knowing about my early years at school will definitely make it easier to understand my actions later on, so hold your horses and keep reading—or quit if you want, although you will miss some good shit later on.

So in the summer before sixth grade, I found out, thanks to Miss Joslyn, that not only was I not a freak but also that there are records of people through history who were just like me (well, in some respects—I'm not sure that Richard the Lionheart had a Burning Bush, although I guess it was possible).

I read about Kate Williams Roberts, Athleta Van Huffelen, Luise Krökel, Laverie Valee, Ramona Pagel, Maria Loorberg, Marie Ford, Anette Busch, Josephine Blatt, Kate Brumbach, Jillian Camarena, Michelle Carter, Anita Joslyn—and those were just the wymyn like me, superstrong freaks who did various athletic things and were not only successful but also admired for their strength. It turned out that the world beyond Battle Creek, Michigan, celebrated people with special talents instead of torturing them (at least some of the time).

Anita Joslyn?

I snatched up the packet of papers and found several articles about my teacher, Miss Anita Joslyn (whose first name I had never known).

From the *Daily Mining Gazette* in Houghton, Michigan, I found this one:

Local Girl Sets Records: Throws Ball Over 200 Feet,
Runs "Incredible Time" in 70-Meter Dash
May 27, 1979
by Kevin Pentikkonen
The Daily Mining Gazette

It isn't often that Muriel Llewellyn is surprised by something one of her students does. After 44 years in education, the Houghton Middle School principal thought she had seen it all, until sixth grader Anita Joslyn, the daughter of Brian and Lisa Joslyn, participated in the softball throw during the sixth-grade Field Day competition.

"Gunnar Hattula was probably the best athlete here at Field Day that I remember, but after watching Anita today, well, I can't say that anymore," the veteran educator said with a broad smile.

Anita Joslyn, an 11-year-old sixth grader, threw the softball an astounding 259 feet—a new record for boys and girls—and, according to girls' varsity track coach Shannon Gustafsson, ran an "incredible time" of 8.9 seconds in the 70-meter dash, also a new record for boys and girls. Joslyn also leapt 13 feet, 1 inch in the standing broad jump, just 2 1/2 inches off Hattula's record.

"I've never seen anything like it," a clearly startled Coach Gustafsson said. "If she makes any improvement at all, she'll be a great high school athlete."

Making this all the more remarkable is that Anita Joslyn is only 4', 3" tall. She has not grown taller since she was in fourth grade, but according to the new record holder, she has "gained considerable weight" since then. "I shop in the boys' husky section and then my mom alters my clothes," Joslyn said, enjoying a laugh with her friends after the competition.

Joslyn has made the honor roll every year in school and says that she wants to be a teacher when she graduates. She also plans on playing sports when she gets to high school, but she isn't sure which ones.

From the looks of it, she could play just about anything and be good. Coach Gustafsson agrees. "You can't teach that kind of strength and speed," she said, shaking her head in wonder.

I found several other articles about the Great Pumpkin. "Teen Shatters Junior High Shot Put Mark, Also Runs 12-Second 100-Meter Dash" was from her eighth-grade year, "Gremlin Athlete Anita Joslyn Breaks Division IV Shot Put Record at State Meet, Scores in Discus and 100 Meters" was from her sophomore year, "Joslyn Breaks State All-Class Shot Put and Discus Record" was from her senior year, and finally, "Gremlin Anita Joslyn Signs Track Scholarship Offer from Michigan State, Will Compete in Field Events." There were more articles about her college career—she medaled at the NCAAs nine times for Michigan State while competing in the shot, discus, and hammer throw, winning the hammer her senior year.

She also made the U.S. National Team and competed at the Olympics, placing fifth in the hammer throw.

My teacher was a freak just like me, so much so that we even looked (sort of) alike. I determined right then that I, too, would be a track-and-field athlete, just like the Great Pumpkin. I didn't know much about track yet, but my brother Marvin was a track star, so I went to him to get some pointers.

Me: I wanna be great at track. What have I got to do?
Marvin: Run fast and turn left.
Me: That's it?
Marvin: Remember to put shoes on.
Me: I mean, how do I train for it?

Marvin: Well, running is always a good idea.
Me: No shit, Sherlock.
Marvin: You're welcome.

Actually, after that conversation, Marvin hooked me up with his buddy Eric McNamara, who threw the shot and discus, and Eric helped me train. Marvin also helped me, especially with my running form, and then the rest of my athletic brothers (all of them except Morris, who was a math nerd and thought that exercise was something stupid people did for entertainment when they couldn't solve third-order regressions in their head for fun) began to help me run, especially after I beat my brother David (who would become a three-time All-State defensive back in football) in a 40-meter dash.

I ran my ass off that summer, threw the shot and discus, and lifted weights, although for me it appeared that it didn't matter whether I lifted or not—I was just flat strong, with or without weight training. Eric McNamara challenged me to a deadlift contest at the end of the summer, and I beat him, a fifteen-year-old high school sophomore who was 6'2", 200, by 40 pounds.

I couldn't wait to impress the Great Pumpkin that fall when school resumed. And yes, I drove my family crazy telling them that, but they never let me know how much, because I had finally become a real person, thanks to the influence of a fellow round, dumpy strength freak named Anita Joslyn, a.k.a. the Great Pumpkin.

So the first day of school, I ran from the middle school, where the bus dropped me off, to the upper el, where the Great Pumpkin was waiting for her students. I could see her, wearing a bright-green dress and standing near the area where parents dropped off their kids. I bellowed, "O mighty Great Pumpkin!" at the top of my considerable lungs, and she turned toward me. Her face lit up, and she said, "Welcome back, Gentle Sprout!" She waved, and I noticed for the first time that her considerable arms didn't jiggle a bit but rather moved like a python would.

I wasn't more than 50 feet from her when a dark-red Cadillac peeled around the corner into the drive and ran right over her.

One second the Great Pumpkin was waving at me, and the next she was gone, pinned under a 3000-pound behemoth.

I ran so fast I swear the air around me moved out of the way.

The door of the Cadillac fell open, and some guy stumbled out of it. He looked around and tried to stagger away, while his front tire was sitting there on the Great Pumpkin's chest. Her left hand was moving, and she was trying to talk, but it was impossible with the car crushing her.

I was screaming, "MOVE THE CAR! MOVE THE FUCKING CAR!" as loud as I could—people literally half a mile away heard me—but the guy kept staggering away, and no one else was moving yet. I got to the car and did the first thing I thought of—I grabbed the bumper and lifted the car off the Great Pumpkin.

And no, I'm not kidding.

I held the car in the air and bellowed to Mr. Fullriede, one of our custodians, who'd run out of the building, "Pull her out, Mr. Fullriede, PULL HER OUT!" He grabbed her arm and pulled her out from under the Cadillac. Once Mr. Fullriede pulled the Great Pumpkin clear, I let the car down and fell to my knees beside her crushed body, hoping to hear her say something, anything. But I could tell it was no use.

The Great Pumpkin was dead.

Her eyes were wide open and staring, but there was absolutely no movement in her body. My hero was gone, and I knew who was responsible. I reached out and closed her eyes, then stood up to my full 5'3" and looked for the staggering guy.

He was about 70 yards away, wobbling his way away from the school. I looked at Mr. Fullriede and said, "Call 911." He nodded at me, and I turned and sped down the drive to the road.

I hit the staggering guy right in the middle of the back, going as fast as I could. He went down like he'd been hit by a train. He was a big guy, 6'3", 250 or so, but I'd driven the wind out of him, so he didn't get right up. When he did, I hit him with a right just above the belt buckle, burying my fist as far as it would go into his considerable gut. He bent over, and I kicked him square in the balls. He fell to his knees, and I grabbed his hair, pulled his head back, balled up my left fist, and hit him a hammer blow right between the eyes.

He fell over like a deer hit by a .50-caliber rifle. I grabbed the back of his suit coat and shirt and dragged him right back down the road to the school. At one point, a cop car came screaming up and a nice policeman got out and tried to stop me from dragging the guy, but I hit him with an elbow in the balls and he stopped talking to me.

When I got back to the school drive, there was a crowd of people there, all standing around the Great Pumpkin, whose body was now on a gurney and covered with a sheet. I reached for the sheet, and one of the EMTs started to tell me to stop, but I glared at him and he backed off. I didn't notice it at that time, but everybody backed off.

I pulled the sheet back and contemplated the still, quiet face of the dead Great Pumpkin. I still had the big guy's clothes clenched in my fist, and when he began to stir and mumble, I jerked him up so that he was face-to-face with the Great Pumpkin. He recoiled and said, "Get it away from me."

I stared into his face and said, "Her name is Anita Joslyn, not *it*, and you're looking at her, you son of a bitch, so that you can see what you did!" I grabbed his chin and forced his head around so that he had to look at her. He closed his eyes, and I slapped him three times, my open hand cracking across his face like a bullwhip.

"Don't close your eyes, you *look*, asshole! Look at her! You murdered her, so LOOK!" I said.

And he did look. And said nothing. Finally, his face fell and he began to cry. I only let him blubber for about 30 seconds before I slapped him again and said, "She was the best person I ever knew, you motherfucker, and you murdered her! I hope you rot and burn in hell."

And then I hit him with three left hands and dropped his unconscious body on the ground, and dropped my body down next to the gurney that held the Great Pumpkin. I put my arms around her neck and held her, literally growling at anyone who came near us.

After a while, my brother Aaron was there, kneeling next to me. "Glinka, you've got to let her go," he said quietly, tears coursing down his cheeks. The cop I'd elbowed in the balls knelt on the other side of the gurney and said, "Miss Glickstien, I promise that we'll take good care of her, but the EMTs need to leave now." He also had tears on his face—getting hit in the balls can't feel good, but these seemed to me to be compassionate tears—so I nodded and let her go.

I carefully placed the sheet back over the Great Pumpkin's face and stepped away so the body could go in the ambulance.

"Sorry about the shot to the balls, Officer," I said to the cop.

He nodded and said, "I understand, miss, and I'll recover. And so will you. I'm sorry for your loss."

"No, I don't think I will recover, sir, but thank you for your kindness." I turned to where the staggering guy was lying in the drive and said, "You need to arrest that worthless piece of shit, or I'm going to drop the car on him."

The cop nodded, went over to the guy, and sniffed and said, "Smell that?"

A second cop came over and said, "Yep. Smells like gin to me."

I didn't know what gin smelled like—I'd never seen anyone in my family drink anything but Manischewitz—but his staggering finally made sense.

A drunk driver had killed the Great Pumpkin.

I stepped toward him, but at that very moment, my dad's old Subaru came roaring up and slammed to a stop. My dad jumped out and sprinted up to me, wrapping me in his arms and crying. He and Aaron and I held one another until my mom and *zayde* came roaring up in my mom's old Subaru and screeched to a halt. Then it was a five-way Glickstien-Blumenthal hug. I let go after a while, weeping my eyes out and wailing like a banshee.

I finally burned myself out and we turned to go. The elbow-in-the-balls policeman wanted my parents to bring me down to the police department when I was ready, and my parents said they'd get back to him.

We were walking toward my dad's car when the drunk driver said, "I'm gonna sue that bitch— she assaulted me!" His voice was wavering and rusty, but the words came out clear as a bell. My seventy-year-old peacenik *zayde* stepped over to him and spoke.

> *Zayde*: Walter Necker?
> Drunk Driver: Yeah. Say, you're Abe Blumenthal, right?
> *Zayde*: Yes, Your Honor, I am Abraham Blumenthal, and that girl is my granddaughter.
> Drunk Driver: I'm gonna sue that little bitch. Punched me and tore my clothes.
> *Zayde*: Sue this, you drunk bastard. (*Right hand to the face.*)
> Drunk Driver: Urgh. (*Head sprongs off car door and he falls to the pavement unconscious.*)

We went home, and later, I gave my statement. The incident was highly publicized, because it turned out that the drunk driver was the Honorable Judge Walter Necker, a criminal court judge for Calhoun County.

It turned out that he had been arrested twice before for driving while impaired.

It turned out that Judge Necker was driving on a suspended license.

It turned out that he didn't have insurance on his car.

It turned out that those in the court system stick together.

It turned out that no prosecutor in Calhoun County would file charges for vehicular manslaughter against Judge Necker, for fear of having to face his wrath in court later.

It turned out that the charges against Judge Necker were the very minimum they could be—driving while impaired and driving on a suspended license—and that his punishment was to have his license suspended for two more years, and a fine of $4,000.

It turned out that he didn't even have to give up being a judge, because his crimes were only misdemeanors.

It turned out that Judge Walter Necker didn't serve a day in jail or have to be inconvenienced in any way by his murder of the Great Pumpkin.

I went to every bit of the truncated court proceedings and listened to every sickening courtroom maneuver by Judge Necker's slimy defense attorney. My semiretired *zayde* sat next to me, just as angry as I was, but handling it better. And I almost made it all the way through all the posturing and obfuscations, right up to the point where a county cop lied.

Then I exploded.

Some asshole county sheriff sergeant testified that it was possible that the Great Pumpkin caused the accident by standing in the drive or that it was the school's fault for where they placed the drop-off zone, thus absolving the drunk guy of any responsibility.

Hurricane Glinka then came ashore, a Cat 5 of indignation, horror, and righteous anger. Like Carol Kane in the classic movie *The Princess Bride*, I called out the judge, the defense attorney, and the asshole sergeant, leaping to my feet and pointing at the jackass on the stand.

"LIAR!" I bellowed. "LIIII-ARRR!"

The sound was so loud, and my tone so commanding, that the presiding judge didn't even call for order. Into the shocked silence that ensued, I said, "Your Honor, that man is lying to protect a murderer. Miss Joslyn was at least 20 feet from the drive, the drive has been there with the same drop-off zone for 50 years, the defendant was drunk when he drove over her, going 30 miles an hour in a clearly posted 20-mile-per-hour school zone, and most importantly, the defendant never hit his brakes until *after* he had run over Miss Joslyn. Judge Necker is a *murderer* and deserves to go to prison!"

I got it all out, and then the judge came to his senses, pounded the gavel for order, and said, "You are out of order and have no standing in this court, young lady. Sit down and be quiet, or I will have you removed from court."

I looked at the judge and said, "Yeah? You and what army, you braying jackass?"

Hurricane Glinka had really come ashore.

The gallery began laughing, the judge was pounding his gavel and calling for deputies to take me out of court, the defense attorney was yelling that nothing I said was admissible, the lying sergeant was pointing at me and calling me a stupid little kid, and Judge Walter Necker was bellowing his innocence for the world to hear.

I just stood there, my eyes red-hot laser beams boring into the lying sergeant, and then the judge. Once I looked at them, they both stopped yelling and seemed to shrink away from me. The defense attorney and the drunk judge couldn't really see me, but I was glaring the death beam at them too.

Finally, two court deputies got to me to take me out. One of them reached for my arm, but I said, "If you touch me, you'll regret it," and he and his partner backed away. Apparently, word had gotten around about what I was capable of, because the deputy said, "Miss, will you please come with us?"

I nodded and said, "Yes, Officer, I've had my daily ration of shit for the day and need to come up for air."

He smiled at me (by then I was a seventh grader—that's how long it took to even get the drunk judge to court), and I was verbally very precocious (that means I could cuss like a drunken sailor), so the deputy nodded and turned to lead me out of the courtroom. His partner stepped up behind me, and my *zayde* followed us out of the court.

Once we were outside, the deputy in front turned and said, "You're free to go, miss, and I would, before Judge Schmucker decides to hold you in contempt. He can be cantankerous." Then he winked at me and my *zayde*, who said, "Thanks, Deputy. I'm aware that old Schmuck is a dipshit."

We all laughed, even the deputies, and then my *zayde* and I left. We were silent until we got in the car, and then I said, "Why?" knowing that he would understand what I meant.

My *zayde*, a.k.a. Abraham Blumenthal, Esq., attorney-at-law for over 45 years, looked at me with his "OK, here goes nothing" expression, and the following conversation ensued.

> *Zayde*: There are those in this world who think that you need to go along to get along—in other words, sometimes you have to sacrifice your principles in order to proceed with your profession.
>
> Me: What bullshit! What about honor, truth, and justice?
>
> *Zayde*: Many in the legal profession do not hold those things as important as proving their point, or winning cases.
>
> Me: You and Mom don't feel that way, do you?
>
> *Zayde*: Definitely not. We feel—your father feels this way too—that our principles define us.
>
> Me: So that Judge Schmuck is just helping out a pal so that he doesn't make an enemy? He's compromising his principles to get along?
>
> *Zayde*: So it would seem.
>
> Me: So he's taking the easy way out?
>
> *Zayde*: Yes.
>
> Me: That asshole! But you and Mom have never done that, right?
>
> *Zayde*: No, which is why we are the rarest of the *rarae avis*.
>
> Me: The rarest of rare birds? What is that?
>
> *Zayde*: Poor Jewish lawyers with Harvard degrees.

After my *zayde* dropped me off at home, I went to the kitchen and got a whole bunch of stuff, went to the storage closet and got toilet paper, and then went to my room and shut the door. I stayed there for three days, behind the sign that said: PRIVATE INTROSPECTION IN PROGRESS. PLEASE STAY OUT. (This means you, Mom and Dad).

They did, leaving me alone with my thoughts and packaged food.

On the third day, I emerged for supper—I could smell the corned beef for Reuben sand-wiches—and sat down with the rest of my family. None of my brothers said anything, and my parents acted as if I had been acting normally, but finally my brother Marvin said, "So what did you find out from the introspection, Gigi?"

"I'm going into law enforcement to make sure that what happened to the Great Pumpkin never happens again if I'm there." My mom looked like she'd eaten a maggoty piece of sour fruit, but my dad said, "Then aim high, Gigi—FBI, U.S. Marshals, something like that. None of this piddly county sheriff or city cop, even if it is a big city. Aim high." My father was a CPA, but he was also a master at motivation, because he never pushed an issue, he just laid it out there and let you draw your own conclusions (which usually ended up being what he wanted you to do, anyway).

"Yeah," my brother Gabriel said, "aim high. You're too good for some cheap job. And besides, if you're a U.S. Marshal, you'll get to beat up federal judges instead of county ones." We all laughed at that one, even Mom.

So that was why you had to read about the whiny school shit, because some of those experiences drove me to be the womyn that I am today.

It was also why, 20 years after the death of the Great Pumpkin, I became a Secret Service agent, with plans to use my time in the Service to then transfer into the U.S. Marshals.

Think of me as the female equivalent of Don Quixote, tilting away at the windmills of injustice.

And my plan almost worked.

Almost.

CHAPTER 5

The Freak of Battle Creek

So school went on without the Great Pumpkin, but I never forgot her.

After my adventure throwing around a 250-pound grown man, lifting a 3,000-pound car, and running so fast I could've beaten Usain Bolt in the 100 meters, my parents and my *zayde* took me to our family doctor for "tests," a euphemism for "Find out why our daughter is a freak, will ya?" After exhaustive testing, blood work, x-rays, MRIs, and every other acronym in the known universe, we all sat down in Dr. Watson's office (not making that up—his name was Dr. John Watson, OD. He'd been an Army doctor who took a bullet through the shoulder in Afghanistan and married a womyn named Mary Holmes, too; life is so crazy that you don't even have to make shit up, don't cha know?) and got the results.

> My Dad: So what's the diagnosis, Doc?
>
> Dr. Watson: A perfectly normal twelve-year-old girl.
>
> My Mom: But why is she so strong?
>
> Dr. Watson: Damned if I know. She got bit by a radioactive spider?
>
> My *Zayde*: But she can run like a deer! How does she do it?
>
> Dr. Watson: Damned if I know. Lightning struck a shelf of chemicals in the lab and bathed her in them?
>
> My Dad: But little girls aren't supposed to be like this! What the hell made her that way?
>
> Dr. Watson: Damned if I know. Does she have an abnormally heavy hammer she plays with?
>
> My Mom: But she's our little girl! Why is she so…abnormal?
>
> Dr. Watson: Damned if I know. Her workups are so normal it's hard to believe that she's a Jedi Knight.

Needless to say, my parents weren't satisfied with those answers, so they drove me over to Western Michigan University in Kalamazoo for more tests. Some PhD named Zabik ran a raft of new tests on me and discovered just one weird thing.

I had some proteins in my body that were only found in the Basque Country in the Pyrenees Mountains, a place where neither of my parents, or their parents, or anybody we ever knew, had ever been. Nobody knew why I had unusual blood chemistry, although this Zabik guy had a theory that I was a throwback to Neanderthal times, with the strength and speed of early protohumans (you try dodging saber-toothed tigers without those kind of assets—can you say extinction?).

In any case, my parents decided that if we didn't talk about my "condition" (the code word they used instead of calling me a fucking weirdo), it wouldn't be an issue.

It almost worked, but my seventh- and eighth-grade years led me to more organized sports, and I kept up with my martial arts training, especially in tae kwon do, where Master Paul, the American-looking but Asian-thinking sensei, quickly whipped me into a black belt. I also worked with Mistress Julia on becoming a black belt in *kendo*, the art of Japanese stick fighting (really sword fighting), but she was an even tougher teacher than Master Paul, so that took longer. I later became a black belt in classical *karate*, *aikido*, and judo.

I tried and discarded swimming, soccer, golf, and tennis—all great sports, but not for me—and got into basketball, track, and volleyball. I was forced to quit volleyball after our eighth match of my eighth-grade year, when I broke bones on three Battle Creek Lakeview players and knocked the floor referee unconscious after spiking the ball crosscourt and missing the floor (but striking his head).

After a lot of hysterical screaming from everyone involved, it was agreed that I was too dangerous for volleyball (those Lakeview girls were just snooty, pansy-ass, overprivileged bitches—if you can't take a few broken bones, you shouldn't play pansy-ass volleyball) and that, in the interest of safety, I should just retire (at age 13½).

Basketball was OK, but it didn't really excite me. I'd just steal the ball from the other team's guards, race down the floor (I would occasionally dribble as I did this), and then either make or miss a layup, whereupon the process would start over. By the time my freshman year rolled around, it was clear that basketball was also not the sport for me, so track remained my sole sport at that time.

Track and field was where everyone got their first look at the future Freak.

I broke the school record in the 100 meters the first time I ran it—in 12.2 seconds.

I mean, I broke the *high school* record, not the middle school record.

In seventh grade.

I also long-jumped 17 feet even (also a school record), high-jumped 5'6" (ditto), and threw the eight-pound middle school girls' shot 51'3" (which might have been a world record for middle school).

I also broke the school records in the 200 meters and 400 meters and pole-vaulted 9'6" without any training at all.

Everyone started calling me the Freak of Harper Creek.

But track and field was in the spring, and I had nothing to do in the fall, until I got a letter from the Great Pumpkin's parents on her birthday, August 5. They had written to me every year since she died, telling me stories about "our Anita" and trying to help me get over her loss. It certainly helped, but this letter would set me on the arc that became my life and would lead me back to righting a wrong that needed righting. It was the letter that led to me becoming the womyn that I know the Great Pumpkin would've wanted me to be.

Dear Glinka,

Brian and I are so glad that you are entering high school, and we hope that it is the same positive experience for you as it was for our Anita. She loved sports but always felt cheated that she never got to compete against the boys, because most girls were no competition for her. Her brothers all played football, but the school wouldn't let our

Anita play simply because they were afraid she would get hurt. Brian and I always told her it was because the coaches were worried that she would hurt someone else. They said the same thing about wrestling…

I read the rest of the nice letter but kept coming back to the part about what her school wouldn't let the Great Pumpkin do. I decided that in tribute to her, I'd do what she had never been able to do, prove myself against boys.

I didn't tell anybody about what I was going to do, except my All-State-football-playing brother, David. When I first told him what I wanted to do, he looked at me like I had fucking Alzheimer's, and then tried to talk me out of it.

> Me: I'm gonna play football and wrestle.
> David: Have you contracted fucking Alzheimer's?
> Me: Nope. They wouldn't let the Great Pumpkin play, so I'm going to play in her honor.
> David: You're a freak, but you'll get your ass kicked against boys. Urgh!
> Me, *holding his 200-pound body off the ground over my head by gripping his crotch and neck*: Wanna bet?
> David: Urgh. Nerk. Ponk megh dawp!
> Me, *after setting him down*: Say what?
> David: Tell them you want to play guard and linebacker.
> Me: Is that what you really said?
> David: Yerp.

So the first day of football practice, I reported like everybody else. I had my hair cut short because if I left it long, no helmet in the world would hold it (or protect my head). I wore shorts and a T-shirt, plus the best sports bra in existence, because I didn't want anything flopping around when I ran (yeah, I had breasts by then, and they would have flopped). I also wore a pair of cleats that I'd been breaking in for most of the summer. I had been training like crazy and was in the best shape of my life.

I also brought my *zayde* along, in case I was challenged by the coaches.

I stood in the freshman line, waiting to get a helmet, completely unaware of anybody looking at me. (It turned out they weren't looking on purpose—David told everyone that he would personally pound anyone who looked at me as other than a teammate. Sometimes big brothers are good things to have.)

When I finally got to the head of the line, the freshman coach said, "Name?"

"Glinka Glickstien."

"Related to David Glickstien?"

"His sister."

"Oh. Know your head size?"

"Seven and five-eighths."

"Here's your helmet. Try it on."

I did, and I said, "It fits perfectly."

The coach whacked me across the face and said, "Yep, it fits. Go over there to be weighed and measured."

I never did need my *zayde*.

I got weighed (152 pounds) and measured (5'5½") and then went off to physical testing: 40-yard dash, pull-ups, standing broad jump, cone drill, push-ups in one minute.

Which was probably why I never needed my *zayde*. In fact, the coaches sent him home right after I ran a 4.92-second 40-yard dash. I was pissed I ran that slowly, but the coaches were very excited.

Then I ran a 4.8 flat and beat the starting fullback on the varsity, and they went apeshit, a condition that continued as I did 34 overhand pull-ups without a rest, did 12'5" in the standing jump, and blew away the rest of the PT without really breaking a sweat.

The head varsity coach, Marv Horn, who had over 200 victories in his career and three trips to the state finals (no winners then), walked over to PT and watched for about two minutes. Coach Horn was a crusty old guy who was known for not taking any shit from anybody and always playing the best players, regardless of their age or connections. He finally engaged me in conversation after watching me do 152 push-ups without stopping.

> Coach Horn: Can you do more?
> Me: Yes, sir.
> CH: How many?
> Me: My record is 224.
> CH: Feel like knocking people down?
> Me: Yes, sir.
> CH: Good. Until we're in pads, you go with the JV.
> Me: Yes, sir.
> CH: Just one more thing.
> Me: Sir?
> CH: Your period give you cramps?
> Me: If it does, I'll play through it, sir.
> CH: Good answer.

Football opened up my world. Coach Horn and all the other coaches didn't care if I was female—all they cared about was whether or not I could do the job. They wouldn't let the guys harass me in any way about my gender, and quite frankly, once my teammates saw how I was going to help them, they treated me like one of the guys, which meant I got teased for all sorts of stuff—that's the way of good teams—but I never once got sexually harassed by anyone on my own team.

I loved it. The sheer physicality of football was just joyous for me. I finally got to let all my talents out without having to worry about hurting someone (remember volleyball?), and I got equal treatment from the guys. It was like heaven.

And then we put our pads on.

After literally 20 minutes of practice in pads, everybody on the JV team was terrified of me. I'd also hurt three people.

We started practice with a demonstration of how to tackle properly, led by my All-State brother. "Head up, back straight over the knees, put your shoulder right on the ball, drive with the hips, wrap up—see what you hit!" the coaches reiterated as David whacked three guys right to the ground using perfect technique.

We split into our teams for a simple drill called Oklahoma, which for my teammates soon became the see-how-fast-I-can-avoid-going-with-the-girl drill.

The premise of the drill was deceptively simple: one defensive player faced one offensive player, with a ballcarrier behind the offensive man. The action was bounded by two orange cones to denote the hole the ballcarrier was supposed to run through. The objective was for the defensive player to get past the offensive player and tackle the ballcarrier, with the offensive player trying to block the defender and prevent her (him) from actually tackling the runner. The coaches would signal the snap count to the offensive player and the runner from behind the defender, then call the cadence out to start the drill.

I found myself in the front of the defensive line (players formed two lines and rotated from ballcarrier to offense, from offense to defense, and from defense to ballcarrier). Opposite me was Jarius Walker, a 6'3", 255-pound sophomore who would probably be on the varsity after the first week of pads. Behind him was Stan Ball, one of the starting JV running backs.

I stood with my feet shoulder width apart, my right foot slightly back, and my weight square over my knees, which were out over my toes. My shoulder pads were canted forward, and I was in a state of perfect calm. I didn't feel any fear, trepidation, or any other emotion except one.

Idiot joy.

At last, I'd be able to show what I could do, without any restrictions. David told me that anything went in the Oklahoma drill, and I was as ready for anything goes as anyone in history.

One of the coaches said, "HIT!" and three things happened so fast most people watching almost missed it.

Jarius Walker put his head down and exploded out of his stance, much like a rodeo bull coming out of the chute (my apologies to The Fabulous Thunderbirds).

I jumped completely over Jarius, just like Cúchulainn doing the "hero's salmon leap" (look it up).

I hit Stan Ball like a sledgehammer hitting the Berlin Wall (with perfect form, I might add), separating him from the ball.

I scooped up the ball and ran 40 yards to the end zone of the practice field as fast as I could, then turned and trotted back.

There was dead silence over our part of the field, until Jarius growled, "Again!"

That meant he wanted another try at me, which I expected.

Stan Ball wasn't getting up anytime soon—he seemed to be experiencing navigational difficulties (concussion). So our coach put some other schmo back there and we went again.

This time Jarius didn't put his head down, but it didn't help.

I hit him square in the chest with both hands, stood him straight up, popped my hips forward, and launched him five yards downrange. The running back successfully evaded the flying Jarius, but he was unsuccessful evading me. I hit him like a peregrine falcon striking a poor duck; his helmet and one shoe flew off, the ball went bouncing away, and his shoulder pad straps broke, leaving his pads sideways and over his head.

I just scooped up the ball and ran 40 yards to paydirt again, then trotted back. As innocently as I could, I said, "Anybody else want to go with me?"

Thirty-seven other ballplayers all shrank away from me, slowly shaking their heads. My coaches looked frozen, until Clyde Rafferty, the head JV coach, said, "Holy whackin', Batman! Jarius, she opened a giant can of whup-ass on you!"

Everybody started laughing, even Jarius, who whacked me on the butt and said, "Damn, Freak, you gonna kick some serious ass when we get on the big field. You're a player!"

It felt like I'd finally found my place in the sun, because there is really no other feeling like the approval and acceptance of your teammates. Sex is better, I guess the birth of a child is supposed to be better, and pure, sweet love is probably better, but at that moment in time, all I knew was there were 37 guys who had my back.

And the Freak of Harper Creek was born.

By the next day, no one at football called me anything but Freak. By the end of the week, my parents even started slipping and calling me Freak on occasion. Only my *zayde* never called me Freak, but then he was a freak in his own right—who graduates from law school at 17?—so I guess he thought that I was trying to take his title away.

Also, by the end of the week, Jarius Walker and I went up to the varsity, where I became an instant starter at defensive tackle in our 4–3 defense. I was the second freshman to ever start on the varsity for Coach Horn, and I was determined to not let him down (every time I looked at him, I thought of the Great Pumpkin).

And I didn't.

I made All-Conference three straight years, and first-team All-State my junior and senior years (the only girl in the history of Michigan to do that). I caused more fumbles than any player in Harper Creek history, returned more fumbles for touchdowns than any player in state history, and blocked 32 kicks (still a state record). I also scared the shit out of every other team we ever played, so much so that I was often triple-teamed, which meant that my teammates got to go apeshit on the other team.

I did a bunch of other individual stuff, but the best thing of all was that by being so disruptive, I was able to help my team win big. We went to the state semifinals all four years and made the state finals the last three.

We won twice in the finals, the first and second state championships for the Fighting Beavers of Battle Creek's Harper Creek in football. Our only loss was my junior year, when a guy from perennial power Birmingham Brother Rice (a private Catholic school that recruited like crazy in the Detroit area and elsewhere) kicked an impossible 58-yard field goal with literally no time left on the clock to beat us 15–14. I still say that they didn't get it off in time and that I was held by three different guys (I was—watch the tape!), but it really was a hell of a kick.

We won my senior year 35–0, beating another private school, Orchard Lake St. Mary's. I had two touchdowns—one on an interception return, and one when I smothered a punt in the end zone. After the game, the Orchard Lake head coach told me I was one hell of a football player, and my own coach gave me the game ball for being the best player in the final game—still the best award I've ever won.

I was also hooked on wrestling, qualifying for the state finals four straight years and medaling all four years. I went undefeated as a junior and senior, wrestling at the very unladylike weight of 171 pounds. It was odd, but by my sophomore year, I was 5'7", 167 pounds, and nothing I did seemed to change that. I starved for wrestling that year, trying to make 160 pounds, but my weight never went below 164. I ate like a pig one year to try to bulk up for track, but my weight never went over 169. It was weird, but my wrestling coach didn't care—I was always quick and strong enough to wrestle up a weight, and I almost always won (177–9 for my career, but who's counting?).

Of course, track and field was still my best sport. It was the only one I could count on going to college for, because I was never going to be big enough for football, and no college wrestling coach would offer a scholarship to a womyn, no matter how good she was.

Of course, I had about 250 (really, no hyperbole) offers for college track and field. It really didn't surprise anyone; by my senior year, people were calling me the Freak from Battle Creek. I'd outgrown Harper Creek and become a citywide celebrity.

I ran the one hundred meters in 11.94 seconds; long-jumped 21 feet, 3 inches; threw the shot 54 feet, 9 inches (just off Michelle Carter's national record for high school girls); and broke the national record for discus when I threw 206 feet, 1 inch, at the state finals (sorry, Shelbi Vaughn). By myself I scored 40 points at state my senior year, winning all four of my events, and since we had three of the best distance wymyn in the state, plus two pole-vaulters, and a Latvian exchange student who could hurdle like Gail Devers, we won state going away.

I was voted the best athlete in Battle Creek, man or womyn, and I was a track All-American for everybody who picked such things. Longtime residents of Battle Creek said I was a better athlete than James Sheehan, the Harper Creek quarterback who won the Heisman Trophy at Michigan and was playing in the pros for the Bears. When the city newspaper conducted a poll for Athlete of the Decade, I beat Sheehan out for the honor, but it was clear who was going to have the longest legs as an athlete—my career would be over after college.

Speaking of colleges, they all clamored at me about attending, and I had those 250 full-ride scholarships offers, but there was no doubt about where I was going to school.

Go Green! Go White!

Michigan State University in East Lansing was my destination, right from the first day of my sixth-grade year in school. The fact that they offered me a full scholarship package based on track and field and academics was just frosting on the cake. (Did I mention that I got a 35 on the ACT and graduated with a 3.97 GPA? No? Well, I did.)

The best part was, on the day that I signed my national letter of intent for MSU, the Great Pumpkin's parents were there. My mom and dad surprised me by getting Mr. and Mrs. Joslyn to drive down from Houghton (eight and a half hours) for the ceremony.

I nearly fainted, because Mr. Joslyn looked just like the Great Pumpkin, except older and male. When he smiled at me, I swear I could see Miss Joslyn, and her mom's voice was so Great Pumpkinish that I felt like I was back in fifth grade.

They were the nicest people, and insisted that I call them Brian and Lisa. I did, but it was hard, because to me they were the Great Pumpkin—the largest authority figure in my life after my parents—and I had always called her miss or the Great Pumpkin. But we got along so well that it got easier, and by the time they left, I promised to keep in touch with Lisa and Brian (a promise I kept). They told me that they were proud of me and that "our Anita" would have approved of the way I lived my life.

I cried then, blubbering like a four-year-old whose favorite doll is lost, or a sixth grader who lost her favorite teacher ever.

Then I went off to MSU, where my life got even better, if that were possible. The only really bad thing that happened to me was my friend Tim Miller being murdered during my sophomore year. He and his twin brother, Tom, lived right across the street from us, and they both played football and wrestled, so we became friends. The twins were three years in front of me in school, but Tim and Tom were very cool about not noticing the age difference and often took me to the movies when they went (I couldn't drive yet).

Tim was apparently the victim of an enraged father, brother, or jealous ex-boyfriend. He was found in his car at a notorious parking spot just outside the Battle Creek city limits in Pennfield Township, strangled to death. It was apparent he had been sexually active that night, and the police speculated that someone was upset about it and murdered him after his girlfriend left—there were tire tracks leaving the scene.

The police also speculated that he left marks on his attacker—Tim was 6', 190 pounds of muscle from football and wrestling—but no one was ever found to match the DNA found at the scene. In fact, there wasn't much evidence except that DNA, and the police, both Battle Creek and Michigan State Police, never did solve the case.

That was about the only bad thing that happened to me in my young life, except the death of the Great Pumpkin, so I had it pretty good overall.

Going to Michigan State would make my life even better, because it was there that I met Leland David Thomas, the professor who would change my life just like the Great Pumpkin had, as well as get my first boyfriend, the Square Peg.

Going to State opened my eyes to the world and taught me that everything in this life has a cost associated with it, because, as L.D. Thomas pointed out to me many times, "there ain't no such thing as a free lunch" (TANSTAAFL).

It's just that sometimes the price is a life—yours or someone else's.

CHAPTER 6

Press On, State

So off I went to Michigan State University in East Lansing, Michigan. Everybody knows about State because of Sparty, football, and basketball (Coach Izzo is the best), but what most people forget is that it's a world-class university with a tremendous academic culture. The best program at State is probably the veterinary medicine department, but it is followed closely by a horde of others, including the law enforcement academy, which was what I enrolled in during my first semester. I figured that if I wanted to be a cop, that was a logical place to be, and no one back at good old Harper Creek High School tried to talk me out of it.

Even though I was going to be in law enforcement, MSU still required everybody to get a well-rounded education, so at 7:45 a.m. on my first day of classes, I ran to Berkey Hall for Econ 201: Introduction to Microeconomics. I thought it was odd that class was at 8:00 a.m.—most classes at State didn't start until 9 or so—but I figured that it was just another freshman lecture class run by a TA with a trace of farm boy in him or her.

Boy, was I wrong.

I got to the lecture hall assigned for my class and found a large group of large people sitting in the seats. Many of them were so large they almost looked like circus animals, including one specimen who I was sure was actually a dethawed mastodon.

And those were just the wymyn (at least they appeared female—several had breasts larger than my head).

The men were larger, far larger. One wee lad looked to be seven feet tall and three hundred pounds (remember, I played football and had seen large people before), and there were several who had to be missing from the Budweiser Clydesdales (they were almost certainly offensive linemen for the football team).

There were several other specimens who weren't as bulky but were far taller than my 5'7"—basketball players, men and wymyn. I recognized a couple of them from their time on national TV, especially Dre Morris, the MSU point guard, and Kelvin Richardson, MSU's 6'9" small (yeah, right!) forward, who had carried the Spartans to the Final Four the year before. No one looked very awake at 7:55 a.m.—that is, until all the lights went down and a medium-size balding individual wearing big black-framed glasses and a really sharp three-piece suit and clutching a sheaf of papers strode to the lectern.

There was absolute silence in the hall as the guy clipped a microphone to the lapel of his suit and said, "Turn off all your infernal devices, *now*." The bleeps and blips continued for a short time, and then it was deadly silent again. My part in the parade was very short, since I didn't have my cell phone with me. (I've got to be honest—cell phones never really caught on with me. I have one now but still just use it as a phone. Yes, I'm aware that I'm a freak and a dinosaur.)

The guy looked up at us and said, "You all know why you're here, and you know what will happen if I don't get your best effort, so I don't see any need to fuck around with some silly rules, including attendance. If you don't show up, I will know, which means that Coach Dantonio will know, and Coach Izzo will know, and all the other coaches will know, and"—he grinned evilly, looking like a demented gnome about to get even with a king by cursing him with crotch rot—"you will *run*. Until you vomit. At 5:00 a.m. in the rec center. And I will watch." Here he grinned again, clearly not in the least displeased by the prospect of us vomiting. "And I will sell tickets. And keep all the profits."

Then he laughed a great belly laugh, all by himself, because the rest of us were still silent.

I didn't know what to think, but I did have a question. I raised my hand—I wasn't even sure he could see us in the dark of the lecture hall—and he instantly said, "Glickstien, what the hell do you want?"

I didn't stop to be amazed that he knew my name, even in the dark, because in comedy (and life), timing is everything, so I just said, "How much?"

The guy looked right at me and said, "How much what?" A lively conversation ensued.

> Me: How much for the tickets you're hoping to sell, Dr. Thomas?
> L.D. Thomas: Are you sick, Glickstien?
> Me: No, Dr. Thomas.
> LDT: Because I am not a doctor, Glickstien. I have a PhD in economics.
> Me: Doesn't that mean you're a doctor, Doctor?
> LDT: No, it means I have a PhD, a doctorate, but not an MD, which is what the term *doctor* commonly means in our culture.
> Me: Sorry, Doc—er, Professor Thomas.
> LDT: Better, Glickstien. Now, how much what?
> Me: How much will you sell the tickets for when we have to run?
> LDT: Be precise when asking such a question, Glickstien. Per ticket, per person, per event?
> Me: Per person, per event.
> LDT: The cost will be $5 per spectator, per event.
> Me: I'll give you $10 each time I'm absent to not tell Coach Whitmer.

Professor Leland David Thomas just bellowed with laughter. We all followed suit, because it was obvious that we had done something right. When we finally all stopped laughing, he took out a pipe, stuck some tobacco in it, lit the pipe right under a big sign that said "No Smoking," and when the smoke showed the pipe was well stoked, took it out of his mouth and pointed it at me.

"Glickstien is on the right track, but as you know, she would have to pay me $10 per spectator in order for me not to tell Coach Whitmer, who, by the way, is among the lowest-paid coaches at this university." He took several puffs on the pipe and then pointed it at Kelvin Richardson and said, "Richardson, could you pay me just $10 per spectator in order to not tell Coach Izzo that you were absent for class?"

Kelvin said, "No, Professor."

"Why not? I'd give Glickstien that deal—why not be fair and give you the same deal?"

"It wouldn't be fair, sir," Kelvin said.

"No? Why not? Sounds fair to me," Thomas said.

"It sounds fair to me too," said one of the offensive linemen. Several other students chimed in, agreeing with the prof and the lineman.

Thomas just stood there with his pipe, patiently smoking and watching the conversation. When there was a pause, he pointed the pipe at Kelvin or me (I was sitting right in front of Kel, so it was impossible to tell who was getting the point) and said, "You two don't agree that it's fair, Richardson getting the same deal as Glickstien? Ten bucks per spectator to not mention your absence to your coach?"

"No," we said at once.

Kel tapped me and said, "Ladies first," so I said, "Professor Thomas, there are several reasons why a deal like that wouldn't be fair or equitable."

"Do tell, Glickstien."

"First, as a tenured professor at State, you make reasonably good money, so $10 per spectator wouldn't be much of an incentive for you not to report me. Second, my coach doesn't care about the money she could make from something like this, because she's not interested in making money off me, she just wants to protect an investment she's already made—she's trying to protect her sunk costs. Third, just giving you $10 to not tell about my absence will eventually mean a loss for you."

"How so?"

"Eventually, the spectators will stop coming when no one has to run—you won't be reporting me, right?—so I will stop paying per spectator and just give you the $10, which would certainly be less than you could get from paying spectators."

"All good points, Glickstien, but you didn't explain why it would be unfair for me to offer the same deal to Richardson," Thomas said, his eyes glinting mischievously.

Kel said, "Sir, you need to take into account a couple of other factors. If you have to kick back some of the profits from your selling tickets, you'd need to charge me more, because my total worth to the university and my team is more, and I have a much larger potential for future earnings." Everybody laughed, because he was a potential first-round NBA draft pick. And Kel said to me, "No offense, Freak."

"None taken," I said, impressed that the most famous athlete on campus already knew my nickname.

"You also have to take in relative wealth, or at least *potential* wealth, in this situation. When I'm done at State—barring injury, of course—I'm going to be a wealthy man, while Freak is not going to be wealthy, at least at first. She could eventually make as much as an NBA lottery pick, but not at first, so you should charge me more, because of my potential wealth," Kel said.

Thomas positively beamed at us, a benevolent tyrant who suddenly discovered that the rocks he bought to build his castle were filled with gold ore. He relit his pipe and said, "Do you know why I like having athletes in my classes?"

It was a non sequitur, and nobody switched gears that fast. He waited for a bit, hoping someone else would say it, and finally I put my hand up and said, "Because most people think we're dumb jocks, but in reality, we're no such thing?"

"Spot on, Glickstien. All that talk about dumb jocks is a canard bruited about by the weak and jealous, because no Big Ten offensive lineman can be stupid. Anybody who understands the game knows that offensive linemen have to be able to think and adjust on the fly within already-set boundaries, because if they don't, our quarterback will get killed, right?"

Even the non-football athletes nodded at that one.

"The same thing can be said for every other sport—you can't play basketball, run the 400 meters, throw the hammer, hit a tennis ball, kick a soccer ball, or do anything else in sports without understanding basic physics, geometry, algebra, history, and 10 other disciplines. You have to be better time managers than other students, and you also have an overarching code of conduct that governs all your actions, and at Michigan State University, you'd better believe that is true. Our coaches are fair, but they are also tough and committed to doing the right thing—all of them, without exception."

Thomas paused, puffed on the pipe, and said, "I've never met a stupid athlete. It may surprise you, but I requested this group for my class, because I see a vast untapped potential in all of you. In here we're in my arena—I'm way better than all of you at this game. But I'm going to see to it that all of you come as close to me as you can, because that's what coaches do, isn't it?"

We all nodded, so Thomas pointed the pipe at one of our wymyn's soccer players and said, "So, Teegarden, what was Glickstien talking about when she mentioned something called incentives?"

There ensued a Socratic lesson that kept everyone on their toes. Thomas had apparently already memorized all our names and could match them to our faces. He effortlessly kept the discussion going through judicious questions and prompts, always teaching but never quite lecturing. It was so good that when class was over, no one believed it. There were audible expressions of disbelief and disappointment as the class got up to head for their next class.

Leland David Thomas looked at us and said, "Go Green!"

"Go White!" we thundered back.

"See you on Friday," Thomas said. "Glickstien and Richardson, stick around a minute, please."

Everyone else left as Kelvin and I went down the stairs to the stage. Up close, Thomas was even shorter than me, about 5'6", but his eyes were the most intense I had ever seen, filled with an intelligence that reminded me of my brother Morris the Math Genius.

He looked up at Kel, and then down at me, and said, "You guys are both mis-majored. I need to talk to you about it, so I've scheduled time for you during office hours tomorrow. Be there at 7:00 a.m., would you, please?"

"Yes, sir," Kel and I said simultaneously.

"You owe me a Pepsi," I said to Kel.

"Agreed," he said. "The Union at seven tonight OK with you?"

"Absolutely," I said.

Just like that, I was drinking Pepsi with the most popular athlete on campus, almost like it was a date.

"I don't run a damned dating website, so why don't you guys go to your next class?" Thomas said. "And seven means seven, not seven oh-five."

"Yes, Professor," we said at the same time.

"Two Pepsis," Kel said.

Who was I to argue with him? (Did I mention he was absolutely gorgeous, and tall, and well-built? No? Well, he was. Imagine a 6'9" Taye Diggs, only better built. Yeah. Like that.) Girls whose nickname is Freak don't get to talk to guys like Kelvin Richardson, much less go on Pepsi dates with them, so I was pretty fired up.

"Glickstien, quit mooning and get your ass to biology. Richardson, quit drooling and haul ass for American Lit. Changing majors won't do any good if you dipshits flunk out first semester," Thomas said.

And so we ran to our next classes, already under the far-reaching aegis of Leland David Thomas and not realizing that the man really could make dreams come true.

We also forgot to remember to be careful what we wished for, but at that time, it seemed like heaven.

CHAPTER 7

A Freak Finds Love (Sort Of)

OK, so for the first time in my life, I was in love, head over heels for a guy so far out of my league that I would've had an easier time trying to date Prince William (after he was married *and* had had a kid).

Wymyn who looked like me, and acted like me, and could run like me, and could lift like me, and one thousand other things like me, *never* get to go anywhere with the biggest of the BMOC, especially not when the womyn is from the back of Bumfuck, Egypt (a.k.a. Battle Creek, Michigan), and the BMOC in question is from the Big Apple, that is, New York City, and especially not when said BMOC is destined for the NBA.

And that leaves out the fact that he was Black and most definitely Baptist (thanks for the article about Kelvin, *Sports Illustrated*!), and I was so white that fresh snow looked dirty in comparison—and I was most definitely Jewish.

Plus, I was a virgin, and I was pretty sure that Kelvin Richardson, All-American and future NBA gazillionaire, was not doing without in the "getting laid" department.

He could have slept with all the cheerleaders, most of the female faculty, and the homecoming queen by then, with really any side entertainments he wanted—several campus legends spoke of females hurling their panties at him during breaks in the games (in the stories, most of the panties had phone numbers written on them), or at open practices (which might have been what led Coach Izzo to close most practices—he wasn't a man who liked distractions).

And yes, before you roll your eyes and sneer, this was a young man who was on the Sexiest Man Alive lists for many national publications. He modeled for *GQ*, posed nude for ESPN's *The Body Issue*, and was given a cameo in a Scarlett Johansson film. (He was the guy making love to her roommate at college. I and every other womyn in Michigan ruined our DVRs running that scene frame by frame.)

In short, Kelvin Richardson might have been the best-looking man on the planet not named Clooney, Cooper, Damon, or Pitt, and it was close with all those guys.

He was better built than Michelangelo's *David*, too (and almost as tall).

That didn't even take into consideration his best feature, his huge…brain.

The guy got a 35 on the ACT and made the dean's list with a 4.0 over three semesters (he graduated early from high school and started at State when he was just seventeen years old). I could go on, but Kelvin Richardson was accepted at all the Ivy League schools (he almost went to Harvard, of all places, to play basketball—glad Coach Izzo beat out Coach Amaker) and was a real-life near-genius (his IQ was only 156, so he wasn't able to join MENSA).

I adored his brain as much as I lusted after his bod, probably more, because I understood even then that the body faded but the mind didn't have to.

And I had a Pepsi date with him.

Before we go any further, let me just help you wipe that stunned look of amazement off your faces, all of you who had just assumed something while reading.

I am a straight womyn who still lusts after luscious male bods and brains. (Well, sort of. I've got a boyfriend, but that doesn't stop me from lusting after someone like, say, the Detroit Tigers' pitcher Anibal Sánchez—what a cutie).

So no, I'm not a lesbian—not that there would be anything wrong with that or any other sexual orientation. It's just that I like guys. Sorry for the shocker, but I thought that we should clear that up.

So by the time my classes were over that day, I'd died a thousand times thinking about everything that could go wrong, or him calling it off, or getting blown off without any explanation, or getting sick and puking all over him, or just blurting out "I love you" at some point in the evening. My nerves were so shot I decided to go to the weight room and work out, because I needed to clear my head and the iron was always my friend in that regard.

I got to the weight room and began by doing bench presses and bounding over boxes. I did power cleans and jump ropes, dead lifts, Roman chair sit-ups and finished with squats and push-ups.

It wasn't until my second set of squats that I realized people in the gym were staring at me. Several large individuals, including two from my econ class that morning, were just watching me as I approached the safety rack for my second set. I stared back at them until Greg Bullard, an O-lineman and one of my classmates, said, "Uh, howzit goin', Glickstien?"

"Great, Bullard. What the fuck are you guys staring at? You never seen a womyn work out before?"

"Uh, well…not like you been doin'," Bullard said.

"You know that's 315 on the bar, right?" another guy said.

I shrugged and said, "Yeah, this is only my second set of five-by-eight." That means five sets of eight repetitions each. "So it's a little light. I'm just going for a good workout, not a huge one."

All the football players just kept staring at me, until Bullard said, "Well, do ya need a spotter?"

I looked at the safety rack, a piece of machinery designed to allow solo lifters to work out without fear of injury, then thought, *WTF? Can't hurt to make new friends,* and said, "Sure. It always helps to have someone critique your form."

They all came over to the rack to help. I got under the bar, set myself, and lifted it clear of the rack. Bullard was behind me and put his hands on the bar in order to make sure it didn't roll forward and break my neck. I went into the full squat position—my thighs were below 90 degrees—then stood up and did it seven more times. I moved forward, and Bullard guided me into the rack, helping me set the bar down.

"How'd they look?" I said.

"Perfect," Bullard and several other guys said. "Your form is flawless, Glickstien," Bullard added.

"My friends call me Freak," I said.

"OK, Freak," Bullard said. "What weight are you gonna do next?"

"I'm gonna jump to 375, the 425, then 465, but I gotta do my push-ups first," I said.

"Can we follow your workout?" one of the other guys said.

"Sure. I'm doing a light push-up routine—eight regular, eight wide, eight diamond, eight inverted, and eight pull-throughs. Follow along."

So we all went through my workout. Bullard and I worked on one rack, and everybody else took up stations around US. When we were all done, everybody kind of just stood around, until Bullard said, "Freak, that's the damndest workout I've ever seen. My ass is gonna hurt for a week."

I deadpanned it and said, "Well, I tried to take it easy on you, Bull. You oughta see my Wednesday workout." Everybody cracked up laughing, because all the guys recognized a pissing contest opener when they heard one, and it was obvious from the workout that even if I didn't have a penis, I could piss with the best of them.

Finally, Bullard said, "Freak, we lift Monday, Wednesday, Friday at 6:00 a.m. right here. You're welcome if you wanna come. We'll try to put you with the youngsters so nobody gets hurt." There was more laughter from the guys, and all at once I had a nice, solid group of new friends.

And a date with the biggest BOMC. Shit. Time to run.

So I did, showering in record time and fixing my hair (yeah, right!), then heading for the Union, fearful but hopeful.

My BMOC was waiting outside.

My heart felt like it was going to jump out of my chest like a coho jumping out of Lake Michigan. I was sweating like a cow. (Don't say pig. Pigs don't sweat—I didn't go to the best agricultural college in the world for nothing.) And I had to pee, but I was pleased to note that my stomach was not trying to crawl up my esophagus, my bra was adjusted correctly, and all my sphincters appeared to be holding up well.

Kelvin saw me and said, "Hey, Glickstien. You know that we're going to have some serious fun together, right? That econ class is going to be a real blast! Can you believe how lucky we are to be in there?"

I stared at arguably the best college basketball player in America and said, "You are the squarest jock I've ever met—we have a Pepsi date, and all you want to talk about is econ? What the fuck are you, the square peg that everybody tries to cram through the proverbial round hole?" The conversation that followed set the tone for the rest of our relationship.

> KR: What do you mean? (*Laughing.*)
> Me: Y'know, all ballers got to be sayin' some shit all th' time, 'cause they live fo' de game. (*In a really bad caricature of basketball dialect.*)
> KR: The fuck you all talkin' 'bout, homey? (*Ditto my caricature of basketball dialect.*)
> Me: 'Zxactly, bee-atch. Gots to be ballin' or I be dyin' and shit.
> KR: Wow, talking like this is really tiring. Can we just speak plainly?
> Me: You got it, Square Peg.

Long story short, we went in the Union, he bought the first Pepsis and I bought the second, and we spent three hours discussing economics and how to get the most out of a degree from Michigan State University.

We also discussed our families (he had five younger sisters, plus a brother who died young, and both his parents were attorneys), our high school experiences (his good, mine OK), our heroes (mine the Great Pumpkin, his Tim Duncan of the Spurs—he tried to say his dad, but I made him go outside the family), our tastes in music (me folk and classic rock, his classical and reggae), and how we intended to function after our sports careers were over (me law enforcement, him college professorship).

I was even more in love with this guy after all that conversation, especially because he never once wavered in looking at me as we talked. He didn't answer his phone, look around the Union, or notice all those people who were trying to get his attention—I was his sole focus.

As the end of the conversation neared (we had to be at Thomas's office at 7:00 a.m.), I said, "I'm sorry I'm not prettier. It must be hard for you to look at someone who looks like me for this long."

Then I fell more in love because Kelvin Richardson, near-perfect human being, said, "What the hell are you talking about, Glickstien? I've never met a more beautiful girl than you. And I will destroy anyone who quarrels with that opinion." His deep-brown eyes bored into mine, and I felt myself sliding closer to him (metaphorically, of course—we were drinking Pepsis with a table between us).

I couldn't talk at that point, so Kel stepped in and said, "In fact, that's what I'm going to call you, Beautiful Girl, if you don't mind the *girl* part?"

"And I'm going to call you Square Peg, if you don't mind the terrible implied pun in the *peg* part," I said.

"Deal," Kel said, taking my large hand in his huge one. (Did I mention that my hands were freakishly large? No? Well, they still are—I wear a size 13½ ring.) And he said, "To our new friendship, Beautiful Girl."

"You are going to catch so much shit for this, Square Peg. Giant NBA freaks don't hang with ugly Jewish girls from BFE," I said.

"Well, fuck 'em if they can't take a joke, or my choice in friends," he said, throwing back his head and roaring with laughter. I joined in, braying like a donkey. We eventually got asked to leave the Union (politely—the Square Peg was still the BMOC).

So we left, and he walked me back to my dorm at Kauffman Hall. When we got into the lobby, Kel took my hand again, bent over with a courtly bow, and kissed it. He looked at me and said, "Thank you for a lovely Pepsi date, Beautiful Girl. Until we meet again, I will remain your faithful servant."

My panties were soaked, but I managed to not fling myself on him and rip his clothes off. Instead, I said, "I accept your service, Sir Square Peg, and look forward with anticipation to our next encounter."

He nodded and said, "Au revoir, Lady Beautiful."

When he left the lobby and went out the doors, I literally fell to the floor, my mind and body stunned from exposure to so much beauty, grace, and intelligence for so long. Several people came over to me to see if I needed help, but I just pointed out the door and repeatedly said, "New friend. Kelvin Richardson. Likes me. Faithful servant. Whooee."

Not my finest repartee, but then how often does a freak like me get swept off her feet?

Turns out that would be the first and only time, so fuck everybody if they can't take a little incoherent love rambling.

I did have to change my panties and shower when I got up to my dorm room, because it turned out that freak love smells. Who knew? (I sure as hell didn't.)

I had no way of knowing the next day would change my life forever and would have nothing to do with love.

But that first day with Square Peg made me feel like I was normal for the first time since I'd been in the Great Pumpkin's classroom.

Unfortunately, I was still a freak, possessed of the luck of a freak (think Quasimodo and Esmeralda, find love, die in prison—look it up).

When I think of that day, I can still feel my panties squishing as I walked up to my dorm room. It was delicious!

CHAPTER 8

Your Fucking Highness

So the next morning, Square Peg and I showed up at Thomas's office at 6:55 a.m. (My *zayde* always said, "If you're not early, you're late," and so did Peg's *zayde*. One more reason to love this guy. Yay!). Both of us were still giddy from the night before (OK, so I was projecting for the Square Peg, but I was still over the moon, although my panties were dry).

I smiled and said, "Square Peg."

He smiled back and said, "Beautiful Girl."

Thomas opened his door and said, "Yuck! Make me puke, will ya? I had a rough department meeting yesterday at Leo's." It was the local bar where the faculty hung out—at least the cool ones. "Could ya spare me the lovey-dovey and get your asses in here?" We went in his office, and Thomas said, "I'll be brief. You both have fucked-up majors, and we need to get them switched, like, now, so you don't further fuck up your college careers, which in turn will fuck up your post college careers."

I put my hand up and said, "Uh, Professor Thomas, since I want to go into law enforcement, shouldn't law enforcement be my major?"

He shook his head and looked at me like I'd just jumped naked into a baptismal font during a christening. "Sure, Glickstien, if you want to be a local Barney fucking Fife and stop people who fucking jaywalk. Is that what you want? One bullet, big fucking ugly equipment belt, a fat fucking ass from eating doughnuts and surveilling teenage fucks who are out after fucking curfew tipping fucking cows?" (Just a note about cow-tipping, a favorite Midwestern entertainment for bored youths: Some cows sleep standing up, so the trick is to sneak up on one and then tip it over, although you can do it with cows that are sleeping on the ground too. Hey, it's better than drugs, alcohol, and/or illicit sex in the back of the Buick.)

I gaped at him, because I'd never heard a teacher who used the word *fuck* so much, but Square Peg put his hand up and said, "Professor Thomas, do you realize that you just used the word *fuck* as at least four different parts of speech?"

"Fuck yeah, Basketball Fucker," Thomas deadpanned.

We all cracked up.

Finally, I said, "Professor Thomas, I'd like to know what you think my fucking major should be," at which point we all cracked up again, until Thomas said, "Look, I'm the fucking king of this shit, just like the Square Peg is the fucking king of basketball and you are the fucking queen of track and field. I know my shit in this arena, but most of the people who come through the hallowed halls of Michigan fucking State won't listen. You two want to maximize your potential, and I'm damn well not going to let you fuck that up."

"Your Highness," I said, standing and curtsying, "I would love to maximize my potential. O Oracle of Majors, I doth beseech you to enlighten your poor servant."

"*Poor fucking servant* would have been better," Square Peg said.

"I beg your pardon, Your Highness. Your poor fucking servant begs your counsel," I said.

"Don't you mean Your Fucking Highness?" Thomas said.

We all cracked up again but finally calmed down enough to be semi-serious.

"Look, Glickstien, you obviously want to be a big-dog law enforcement officer, I'd guess FBI or U.S. Marshals. So why aim low with your major? The fact is, most of the people who get into those organizations have degrees in accounting, finance, or the law, with a few history majors with JDs thrown in. Your best route to a big-time law enforcement organization is to get a degree in something like forensic accounting, go into the military for four years, and then apply to one of the training academies. You'd never see the FBI with a degree in law enforcement. It isn't a bad major, it's just bad if you want to hit your target."

It made sense to me. After all, I didn't know jack shit about this stuff, while His Fucking Highness had a black belt in it. My mom, dad, and *zayde* always said, "The smartest people know what they *don't* know," meaning, "Don't try to be an expert at shit you know nothing about and listen to people who do."

"Your Fucking Highness, what about me?" the Square Peg said.

"Richardson, you're in prelaw, which, because of your background, is kind of like being a moose at a wolf convention. I've heard about your parents' work. You'd just be trying to measure up to them, which isn't going to fucking happen, since you actually want to help people. Just because your parents are asshole attorneys doesn't mean you have to fucking be one too. No offense intended to your parents."

"None taken. But how did you know that?" Square Peg said.

"Because I can fucking read. I looked over the transcripts and applications of everybody in the fucking econ for jocks class," Your Fucking Highness said. (Yeah, that was what Square Peg and I called Leland David Thomas for the rest of our time at State. He called us Freak and Square Peg. It was a very comradely thing to do; plus, it was just fucking funny every time we said Your Fucking Highness.)

"OK, leaving aside the fact that is just a freaky weird thing to do, what should my fucking major be?" Peg said.

"Well, I think it should be finance, so you know how to manage your money after you get the humongous bucks from the NBA," I said.

"Oh, my fucking stars, the Freak hits the target first shot!" YFH said.

"Really?" I said.

"Nah, but fucking close." We all cracked up at that too, but YFH said, "She's in the right ballpark, Peg. We all know that you're going to be a sporting man, barring injury, but even if you do get hurt, do you really want to go through all that goddamned torture that is the fucking law? No, you want to help people, so why not get a management degree and really help people manage their money? You've got the chops for it. You could've gone to fucking Harvard. What the fuck *were* you thinking? And there are only about 100 ways to take a management degree. Get a concentration in finance if you want, or better yet, get a concentration in public policy or urban management and help poor people manage their money and finances."

Square Peg started to nod, and YFH said, "Who's a kid in the inner city going to listen to, a white-bread fucking Harvard man or a fucking NBA star from good old MSU? You could change a whole generation's spending habits and start a revolution among Black youth, Peg. Hell, they might even name a fucking high school after you."

I looked at the love of my life's face and knew that he was hooked. In about 10 minutes, Your Fucking Highness had talked more sense to him than all the high school counselors in the world could have. (In all fairness, it isn't the fault of school counselors that they suck at, well, counseling. They have about 45 different jobs to do, there are never enough of them, and they always get dumped on whenever there is school drama, which is always. Very few people have as much to do as school counselors, and fewer still can actually do the job at all.)

"I'm in," Square Peg said. "I'm going to do it, even if I don't start a revolution."

"Excuse me, Your Fucking Highness, but what should my minor be?" I said.

"History," YFH and Square Peg said.

"You owe me a fucking Pepsi, Peg," YFH said.

"Your Fucking Highness, you owe *me* a Pepsi," Square Peg said.

"Why don't we meet at the fucking Union at eight?" I said.

"It's a date," YFH said. "Now, fucking blow! I got a class to teach in about 17 minutes, and your asses better be in a seat. No running off to play fucking kissy-face or some shit."

"Kissy-face?" Peg and I said together.

"Fuck off," YFH said. "I'm an old fuck."

"True that," Peg said. "And you, Square Peg, owe *me* a Pepsi," I said.

"Well, I don't mind paying off on the fucking debt," Peg said, smiling at me and making my panties damp again.

"Oh, for fuck's sake! Get out now and take the fucking Romeo and Juliet shit the fuck with you," YFH said as he slammed his door on our asses.

And we went.

As we walked to class, Square Peg took my hand in his and said, "Beautiful Girl, can we just hold hands as we walk to class?"

"I would really like that, Square Peg," I said.

I just hoped that I could keep from squishing as we walked across campus.

No such luck.

Class was once again so awesome that no one wanted to leave when it was over, but we did, because there were other classes to take and other shit to do, but Square Peg promised to meet me for dinner, and he did, and then we went off and had another grand bull session (and about 12 gallons of Pepsi, which we both loved—yaayyyy!), and then it was time to walk home.

We held hands as we walked to my dorm room. When we got there, I just blurted out, "Jessica'satherboyfriend'stonightallnightyawannacomein?" Just like that—all one word. Was I cool or what? After I blurted, I thought, *Ah, shit! He's gonna think I'm a slut and that I just want him for his body and fame! Why couldn't I have actually dated in high school? I don't even know if I'm doing this right. Shouldn't I be playing hard to get? Am I a slut?*

Peg saved me from any further strain on my fevered brain by leaning down close to me and saying, "Beautiful Girl, I want nothing more than to stay with you all night, but I care about you too much to do it. I know that we've only been friends for two days, but I feel like I've found what I've been missing all my life, and I don't want to mess it up, so can we just go really slowly for now?" His eyes were hypnotic and clearly full of love.

I forgot all about being a slut—true sluts, male and female alike, just fuck for diversion, not for love. I wanted to make love to this man forever, but I also didn't want to rush it, because a fire with too much tinder burns out too fast (thanks to Mom, Dad, and *zayde*, who all gave multiple lectures on the subject of love—embarrassing, but ultimately very useful), so I nodded and said, "Roger that, Square Peg."

He smiled even deeper and, still close to my face, said, "Besides, I'm a virgin, and sex scares the fuck out of me."

That did it. I leapt up onto his neck, wrapped my legs around his torso, and put my head on his shoulder. I was crying tears of joy and hugged him so hard I was afraid I'd hurt him, but he just hugged me back—hey, the guy was 6'9", 245, and built like the proverbial brick shithouse. (Although it always bothered me. Why were well-built people built like shithouses? Wouldn't it make more sense if they were built like the Empire State Building, or Frank Lloyd Wright Houses, or Buckingham Palace? Why shithouses? After all, a shithouse doesn't need to be that well-built, because all you do is go there and shit and/or piss? Another old aphorism that really doesn't make sense.)

"I'm so glad you said that I could just tear your clothes off," I said, "but I won't, because sex scares the fuck out of me too."

So we held each other like that a while before the inevitable happened—gravity got a grip on my 167 rock-solid pounds, and I started to ooze down Peg like a banana slug making a run on a slippery leaf. I finally let go and stood in front of him, still hugging him close, just with my head pressed to his navel instead of his neck.

"How strong are you, really, Beautiful Girl?" Peg said.

I bent down, grabbed him around the thighs, and stood up, holding him completely off the floor. He started laughing, so I spun him in midair, put my hands in the small of his back and between his shoulders, and military-pressed him over my head. He really laughed at that and said, "I'm the only guy on campus whose girlfriend can bench-press him."

"Except for whoever Karen Kamakawiwo'ole is dating," I said. Karen was a Hawaiian womyn who was on the track team (actually, she was on the field part of the track team, because at 6'4", 300 plus (definitely plus), Karen didn't have much connection with the track), who despite her immense size had such a beautiful smile and such easy grace that guys were always making passes at her—until they met her brother Ezra, who was a water buffalo-size defensive lineman on the football team that thought his "little" (Ezra didn't get descriptive adjectives) sister needed protecting. The prospect of getting stomped by Ezra cut down on Karen's dating life, but she still managed to sneak off with a couple of different guys now and then. One of them was Dre Morris, the MSU point guard and Square Peg's friend, which was why Peg laughed so hard at my little joke that I had to drop him on myself, which was why Dre Morris, who was also one of Peg's roomies, found us entangled in a heap outside my door.

"Well, got-damn, cain't y'all open a got-damn do-ah?" Dre said. He was from New Orleans (which he pronounced Nuh Awlins) and could make English sound like a foreign language. "A'int nuh raisin tuh be-ah foolin' 'rahound in no hallway, no."

Peg and I just laughed harder, because we knew that Dre had been visiting Karen, who lived just down the hall from me. Even if we hadn't known where Karen lived, we'd have known that something was up, because Dre was weaving around like he was drunk, and it was well-known that he didn't drink at all.

Peg said, "Dre, you OK? Need some help getting home?"

Dre nodded and said, "Dat id wayuh too much wo-man for po-ah ol' me, you. She-ah dun wore-ed me ah-out." (Just a word about Dre Morris: If it sounds like he was a moron, it's because there is no accurate way to record his New Orleans accent, short of resurrecting the great dialectician Samuel Langhorne Clemens and having him write it. Dre was as smart as the next guy, but when he got tired or excited, the New Orleans came out and required translation, which was what I tried to do here.)

So my boyfriend ("Squish, squish" went the panties) gently helped me disentangle from him and stood up to help his friend. I rose on my toes and kissed him chastely on the cheek, and he kissed my cheek as well. "Until anon, Beautiful Girl," Peg said.

"Forsooth aye, my Square Peg," I said.

"Y'all are too weir-ahd fuh me, you," Dre said.

"Why, yes, we are," Peg said. "It's a match made in heaven, the Freak and the Square Peg, forever together in poem and song." He gave me such a charming, goofy look of joy that I almost forgot how scared I was of having sex, but in the end, he staggered off with his exhausted friend. I was so wet with desire I just oozed under my door like a ragged old dishrag.

Who needs sex? I thought as I lay down on my bed.

Thank all that is holy for hands, or I'd never have fallen asleep that night.

CHAPTER 9

Freak's Three-Year Dream

And so it came to pass that, thanks to judicious and excellent counseling from Your Fucking Highness, the Square Peg and I changed our majors, and my three-year dream began.

I loved forensic accounting but decided to make accounting my minor because history at MSU was a blast, especially once I convinced my pals Karen Kamakawiwo'ole and Greg Bullard to join me in the Magical History Tour. We were the scourge of the history department—large, loud, and ferociously smart, wringing everything we could out of the experience.

Square Peg became a star both on and off the court. He was so good at management, public policy, and finance (Peg didn't do anything halfway—one of the reasons I loved him so much was his full-speed-ahead-and-go-all-the-way attitude) that he actually considered quitting basketball, until I bitch-slapped him all up and down at a 6:00 a.m. lifting session in front of the entire O- and D-lines. I still remember it: "Are you a *nitwit*, you dumbass? People would kill for your talent, you *mucking foron*! Quit *basketball*? Over. My. Dead. Body!"

The football players yelled at him too, and then Your Fucking Highness showed up (I'd called him) and added his considerable talents to the mix.

Then Coach Izzo showed up, and it got really interesting.

Square Peg continued with basketball, where his happiness with his change of major made itself most evident.

He led the team to a national championship during his sophomore year, won the Wooden Award as the best college basketball player in the country as a junior when we repeated, and was the leading rebounder and shot blocker in the nation his senior year as MSU three-peated, becoming the first team since Indiana in 1976 to go undefeated in a season. Peg had 25 points, 21 rebounds, 10 blocked shots, and 11 assists in the championship game as he had the first quadruple-double in NCAA finals history. The fact that it came over That Other School in Ann Arbor just made it all the sweeter.

The only problem for Peg came from the press, the NBA, and the agents, all of whom said he was "wasting his talent" by staying in college. It finally came to a head before his senior year, when a national publication (I won't mention any names, but think swimsuits) had three of its senior basketball writers offer their advice to Square Peg about turning pro, and predictably, all three said it was a mistake to turn down the big bucks from the pro game.

One of them said that Peg "owed it to the public and the NBA fans to make himself available for the draft."

Another said that it was "obvious that Richardson [was] afraid to test himself against the highest level of talent for fear of failure."

The third writer said that Peg was "stupidly foolish for clinging to an antiquated dream" about finishing college and that he should "grow up and face the real world."

After consulting with Coach Izzo, Your Fucking Highness, his parents, and me, Peg had the Sports Information Office at MSU schedule a press conference. He invited anyone who was interested to attend, including the three national publication writers and the Washington Wizards, who had the first pick in the soon-to-come NBA draft.

The press conference was in the Wharton Center at MSU, and it was a real-goat rope. Everybody thought that Peg was going to announce his entry in the draft, and there was enough press there to gag a maggot (another aphorism that only makes sense when you really think about it but makes perfect sense once you do), including the three national publication writers.

There was also a shitload of celebrities there. Michael Jordan (part owner of the Wizards), LeBron James (part owner of the Cleveland Cavaliers), Tom Cruise (who wanted to play Peg in a biopic—not kidding—but who is such an asshole), several celebrity agents (no names, but think huge assholes), a bunch of actresses, both major and minor, who wanted to snuggle up with the hunky Peg, a famous self-help guru (think not a doctor but plays one on syndicated TV), and Oprah, who wanted to share her experience as a "successful Black womyn" with Peg.

Peg came out and sat down in front of the goat rope. He was flanked by Coach Izzo, Your Fucking Highness, and his parents. He was calm and composed, staring up at the crowd through the bright TV lights and snapping flashbulbs. He looked offstage, where Dre, Karen, Bullard, and I, along with a bunch more of our crowd, were watching. I nodded and gave him the thumbs-up, and he smiled and turned back to the press.

"I have decided today to make my position vis-à-vis the NBA draft perfectly clear. I am not declaring for the draft, now or ever. I came to Michigan State as a student athlete—please note that *student* comes first in that phrase—and I intend to accomplish the goals I set for myself before I arrived. Those goals are, in this order: one, graduate from Michigan State University; two, wring the most out of my education here in accomplishing goal number 1; and three, play basketball for MSU to the utmost of my ability. At no time did I set a goal of becoming an NBA player. That will happen or it will not, but that was never my goal."

He paused, looked up at the three national publication writers, and said, "Furthermore, my goals are not foolish, antiquated, or out of touch. I am not acting from fear, nor do I owe anyone anything in relation to my athletic career. I owe my parents respect, I owe Coach Izzo for his relentless pursuit of perfection in my game, I owe my professors here my full attention and effort, I owe my teammates my best effort and my loyalty, I owe my girlfriend faithfulness, and I owe God for all that I have, but I *do not* owe the NBA and the public *anything*.

"Since when did it become old-fashioned or antiquated to want to complete a college degree? If I play in the NBA—that's *if*—my career cannot reasonably last more than fifteen years. Since I will be 22 years old when I graduate from Michigan State, my putative NBA career would be over by the time I was 37 years old. If I live the average for an American male, that would mean I would have 44 years of life *after* basketball was over. If I have a degree from MSU, those years could be very productive, perhaps even transformative. If I do not take my degree, I will be forced to rely on past glory and accomplishments, which is neither satisfying nor productive.

"I also wish to make it clear that there is no amount of money in the world that can persuade me to change my mind. A degree from MSU is worth more than gold, and certainly worth more than a career in the NBA.

"I would also like to point out to all those who are giving me advice, or who wish to give me advice, that I do not need any such thing from you. I have on my right the best basketball coach in the world to advise me on sports, on my left is the best faculty adviser in the world to help me with academics, and on both left and right are the best parents ever, to help me with everything else. I have the best girlfriend in the world, the best teammates, and the best friends, none of whom want to use me for any purpose, unlike all of you who are in attendance here today."

Peg looked at me again, his smile as broad as the Pacific Ocean, and said, "So today I invite all of you in attendance to depart and leave me in peace. I will be taking my degree at, and playing basketball in, the green-and-white of Michigan State University next year, and I will always be my own man, with my own goals.

"Also, for those of you out there who believe that you can work on me, or somehow persuade me to change my mind, I have today obtained a personal protection order from the courts of Clinton and Ingham Counties, which prevents any sports agent, representative of any NBA team, or any other person who might be employed by same to come within 500 feet of my person and my dorm room. I have asked the president of MSU to enforce such an order through the campus police, and he has agreed. This order also applies to journalists that are not pre-approved by the university. All press requests will go through the MSU Sports Information Office and will be routinely declined. Any questions?"

The goat rope exploded, but Peg just pointed at the sports reporter for the campus newspaper, a good guy named Rob Quinter. Robbie said, "Mr. Richardson, what do you mean *if* you play professional basketball? Are you considering not playing in the NBA?"

Peg smiled that slow, wicked smile that I loved to see and said, "Mr. Quinter, no one can know what the future holds, but there are several opportunities before me that appear worthwhile, including the NBA, law school, graduate school, and several intriguing job prospects. You will notice that the NBA is simply one opportunity, and not necessarily the most preferred by me."

The cacophony that filled the Wharton Center surpassed that of a flight of F/A-18s taking off from the USS *Nimitz*, but Peg ignored it all and again pointed at Quinter, who said, "Two follow-ups, Mr. Richardson: Does this mean that your passion for basketball has diminished? And could you give us a scenario where you might not play in the NBA?"

Peg smiled again, a deep smile of satisfaction that led me to believe that he and Robbie Quinter had set all this up beforehand (they did; Peg said that he and Quinter agreed over a Pepsi that there were certain questions that needed asked and answered and that the student newspaper was the logical source for those Q&As). He nodded at the reporter and said, "Excellent questions, Mr. Quinter. First, my passion for basketball has not at all diminished from when I entered Michigan State. If anything, it is deeper, as is my appreciation for the game itself and especially for the opportunity to play for the Spartan program. Our coaches are outstanding, and if I did not already have an excellent father, I would consider Coach Izzo an outstanding substitute. Playing here has made me better in every way as a player. I still don't know how I ever got a rebound in high school with my footwork." Lots of laughter at that, since Coach Izzo was well-known for his hounding of his players about footwork and positioning when rebounding. "And it has also made me a better man. I still love basketball, now more than ever, but I will not let basketball become my raison d'être. Remember, I play basketball, but basketball doesn't get to play me.

"As for a scenario where I might not play in the NBA, well...that one is easy. If I am offered a Rhodes scholarship, I will not be playing in the NBA for at least two years, because I will be at Oxford or the London School of Economics. The same scenario will obtain if I am offered a position by the administration in Washington, or the UN." Peg pointed at Quinter and said, "Another follow-up?"

Despite audible protests from the mainline reporters, Robbie Quinter said, "Is it possible that you might never play professional basketball?"

Peg said, "Yes." The place exploded again, and then he leaned into the microphone and said, "Thank you all for coming. No more questions." A howl went up from the rest of the press, but Peg just said, "Go Green!" into the mike.

"Go White!" the MSU faithful in the crowd bellowed back, drowning out the press and all the toadies who wanted a piece of Square Peg.

He came off the stage and hugged me, then shook hands with everybody else and said, "That should hold them for a while, don't you think?"

"Fuckin' A," we all said.

"Everybody owes everybody a Pepsi," Greg Bullard said.

"To the fucking Union!" Your Fucking Highness said.

"Roger that!" we all yelled. "More Pepsis!"

So we all kind of wandered away to the Union. As we walked along, we—well, Square Peg—got extended applause from the students we saw. Everybody seemed to know that he was staying, and several people complimented him on his loyalty to State. It was one of the most inspirational things I'd ever seen.

People started yelling, "Go Green!" at us, and we yelled back, "Go White!" It was a shitpot of fun walking across campus on a sunny day with a bunch of good people who were all enjoying themselves, and also the epitome of what a college experience should be.

I found myself walking with Peg's mom and dad, who both smiled at me. His mom, a brilliant lawyer named Corinne, said, "He's staying because of you, Glinka. He loves you beyond all belief, and his father and I are thrilled. Thank you for being there for our boy." I hugged her and Peg's dad, Harvey, and we all laughed and cried with joy and yelled, "Go Green!" at the top of our lungs until we got to the Union, where there were about ten thousand green-and-white-clad maniacs waiting for us.

We sang the State fight song and then did a few minutes of "Go Green! Go White!" before we all turned to go into the Union for owed Pepsis. As Peg, Karen, Bullard, and I went up the steps, there was a very dapper figure barring our way.

It was a very famous sports agent (no names, but think superasshole who drove a car worth more than Moldova), well-known for driving impossible bargains with NBA teams for giant contracts that he took 17 percent of right off the top. His hair was slicked back, and he was wearing a $10,000 Armani suit, a huge gold Rolex, and a pinky ring with a diamond the size of an egg yolk.

He was also wearing an MSU tie and shit-eating grin that was supposed to impress all of us with how cool he was.

Before he could speak, Coach Izzo said, "Hey, [superasshole sports agent's name], can you hear? There's a restraining order against you."

The guy said, "Now, Tom, let's be reasonable. I just want a minute of Kelvin's time so we can talk numbe—"

Which was as far as he got, because four MSU campus policemen surrounded him. One clapped a large hand on a wrist bearing a Rolex, bent the wrist behind his back, and said, "You were warned—the restraining order is in effect. The East Lansing police are waiting to arrest you at the main gate, sir. Let's go." They frog-marched him away to thunderous cheers, and we went in the Union and drank Pepsis until they kicked us out.

After that, pretty much everybody left Square Peg alone, except those people he wanted around.

My MSU experience was just a fucking dream.

I hung out with Peg pretty much all the time, and we had a few really good friends that we hung out with, too. Classes were swell (who knew I'd like chasing down historical triangulations so much?), and I had amazing success athletically.

My freshman year, I wrestled, finishing third in the Big Ten Championships and sixth in the NCAAs. In track, I broke the school records for long jump, shot put, discus, and the hammer throw and placed in long jump, discus, and hammer at the NCAAs. I kept lifting weights with the football team and got up to my most muscular weight, 167 pounds.

In my sophomore year, I again finished third in the Big Ten Championships and was fourth in the NCAAs. I won three of my four events at the NCAAs, helping MSU to a team runner-up finish. I also broke the NCAA record in the hammer throw when I flung one 244 feet, 7 inches (sorry, Jenny Dahlgren), and went 22 feet, 8 inches in the long jump, second on the all-time NCAA list.

My junior year, I won the Big Ten Championship in wrestling at 165 pounds and was runner-up in the NCAAs.

Track and field was crazy that year. Karen Kamakawiwo'ole started throwing consistently in the 55- to 58-foot range in the shot, our pole-vaulter hit 14 feet every meet (that's really high), and Denita Williams ran sub-twenty-three seconds in the two hundred (that's world-class fast). We also had some great distance people and a crazy javelin thrower from Finland named Ulla Virkkonnen, who almost set the NCAA record in our first meet. I was on fire, too. I broke the NCAA record for the long jump at 23 feet, 11 inches, threw the discus 206 feet, put the shot 54 feet, 7 inches, and broke the world (yeah, the whole world—who knew a kid from East Bumfuck, Michigan, could do that?) record in the hammer with a heave of 261 feet, 8 inches (sorry, Bette Heidler of Germany).

Our team broke the record for points in the final meet, we won the NCAAs, the first time ever for MSU, and I was named the outstanding athlete, also a first for MSU. All in all, it was a fucking glorious year for the Freak Show and MSU sports.

Plus, I had the coolest, hippest, best-looking, kindest, sweetest, smartest, and most fun boyfriend any womyn could ever have.

I still think that my junior year of college might have been the best year of my life up to that point, even though Peg and I still weren't having sex (by mutual agreement). We'd seen each other nude. (Did I mention that he was, uh, well-endowed too? No? Think as big as a…well, you get the picture. After all, this isn't *50 Shades of Green and White* or something, it's a thriller. I promise it's a thriller! Hold your horses!) And we'd even slept nude together, but no sex beyond some petting and kissing (which he was mucho good at too).

Of course, all good things must come to an end, just like my junior year.

First, Square Peg was selected as a Rhodes scholar. He came running into the Union screaming like his shorts were on fire. I'd seen him this excited before, but it was the look in his eyes that really caught me off. He was cranked up on high, but he was also scared—maybe his mom and I were the only ones who could have seen it, but it was there.

Fear.

Square Peg was *never* fearful, of anything. He guarded a 7' monster when we played That Other School in Ann Arbor and never displayed a second of fear. He routinely went into the bad places in Detroit to do service work and never flinched. We went hiking in the Porcupine Mountains in the UP one spring and he faced down a bear while buck naked.

OK, I'll explain that. We were lying out on a nice blanket (sans clothes, of course) in the spring sunshine on the three feet of snow still lying on the ground in the Porcupines when I noticed a black bear on the other side of the clearing from us. I mentioned it to Peg (OK, so I was gibbering in fear as I kept hitting him with my elbow and saying, "Buh-buh-buh-buh-buh"), and he said, without a trace of nervousness in his voice, "Beautiful Girl, just put your snowshoes on and we'll back out of here." He was so calm I just did what he told me, and we escaped the bear without any loss of life or limb, although our dignity was in a shambles. You ever tried to back through dense pine forest on snowshoes while nude? It would have made a great YouTube video, believe me, especially when that pine bough went up my ass.

Anyway, even then, the Square Peg didn't show any fear at all.

So when he finally came down from telling all of us about the Rhodes scholarship, I quietly said, "Square Peg, what are you afraid of?"

A tear slipped down his incredibly handsome face, and he whispered, "I don't want to leave you, Beautiful Girl. I can take everything else, but not having you there when I'm in London is going to be a killer. I thought about turning it down, but I knew that you'd kick my ass—"

"You mean I'd kick your fucking ass, you fucking moron," I said, smiling at him.

"Exactly—you and the rest of the world," he said, smiling back.

"Peg, this is what you've wanted since forever, right? You showed me your journal from your eighth-grade year that proved it. The Rhodes scholarship is your shibboleth, your holy grail, right?"

"I seek the Holy Grail," he said solemnly.

"And what is the wind speed velocity of a sparrow?" I said.

"A laden or unladen sparrow?" Peg said.

We both laughed. (If you don't get the reference, I feel sorry for you. Our whole crowd could do *Monty Python and the Holy Grail ad nauseam.* Never seen it? Rent the DVD, pop some popcorn, and be prepared to pee your pants—one of the funniest fucking movies in history.)

And then he kissed me on the lips, deeply and passionately, in front of all the people there screaming.

I looked at him and said, "Well, we'll always have Toledo," and we were laughing again, head over heels in love and not caring at all about our impending separation at that moment, just reveling in each other.

I stayed with him as he called Coach Izzo, who was appreciative of the accomplishment and very supportive of Peg's decision to accept the Rhodes and forego the NBA for a while. I stayed with him when he told his parents, his mom squealing with delight and his dad bellowing like a bull. I stayed with him when he called Robbie Quinter to set up the questions for the press conference the next day to announce to the world that he was skipping the big bucks to get an MBA at the London School of Economics. I stayed with him as he drank Pepsis with our crowd until he was all wound down, and we walked back to our dorm room (we shared a suite with K2 and Bull—boy, could that single bathroom get crowded!).

And I stayed with him as we made sweet love for the first time, all night long. It was a transcendent experience and made me feel like a real womyn for the first time (and that's all I'm going to say about that, you pervs).

Unfortunately, it turned out to be the last time I felt like a womyn for a long time, because our first time making love was also our last time.

Ever.

CHAPTER 10

The Freak Stands Alone

We woke up the next morning about 11, said tender words to each other (you don't get a view of everything, ya voyeuristic fuckers), showered, and prepared for the coming goat-rope press conference.

Peg put on a cool suit and tie, I put on pants and a cool blouse (thighs like mine do not bode well for dresses; hence, I have yet to put one on as an adult), and we walked slowly across campus to the field house. On the way, Square Peg told me what his nefarious plan was concerning the future, and I laughed my ass off. We laughed together and held hands just like always, but we both knew that this was the beginning of the end of our idyll at MSU. London is a long way from East Lansing, Michigan, and Skype isn't the same as having someone to hold when you're having a shitty day.

As we approached the field House Bull and K2 flagged us down.

"Peg, we got a small problem at Jenison—can you hold here for a minute?" Bull said.

"Let me guess—the press coverage looks like we just discovered space aliens in Cleveland," Peg said.

"Or Lady Gaga is singing nude at the Vatican," K2 said.

"Or Prince George just reinstated summary execution for anyone who doesn't give him ice cream when he wants it," I said.

"Or a bunch of assholes in the press think they own ya, Peg, just because you're a public figure," Bull said.

"Hey," we all said at once.

"We all owe each other Pepsis," Peg said.

"And what I meant was, the Stones just announced they've all went back to being 29 and they're going to do the Sticky Fingers tour again," Bull said.

"Now you're talkin', *ku'uipo*," K2 said. It was like a mountain calling a mastodon sweetheart, but watching them look at each other made it really sweet; they were definitely deep in love, and K2 meant it when she called Bull sweetheart in Hawaiian.

Bull's cell beeped, and he said, "Yeah? Ready. We're around the back, but we want to walk right in the front. Come get us, OK? The assholes are swarming like army ants on a pig with a broken leg."

Within a minute, the entire MSU offensive and defensive lines marched around the corner and surrounded Peg and me. K2 and Bull got into the phalanx, and Bull said, "Forward, march, Spartans! On to glory!"

The football players sliced through the press like a sharp *katana* through a rotten watermelon. We marched through the doors to Jenison Field House at 2:55 p.m. and reached the table at center court three minutes later. Peg sat down between Coach Izzo and Your Fucking Highness, who both looked at Square Peg like he was their son. Both men whispered something to him, but he never told a soul what they said, including me. Square Peg could keep a secret—that was for sure. He could also command a room like John F. Kennedy—poised, prepared, and imperturbable.

At exactly 3:00 p.m., Square Peg cleared his throat into the microphone and all conversation in the field house just died, like the president of the United States had entered the room or the Pope had called for prayer. The love of my life looked stolidly out at the mass of humanity before him and made them wait for it. All the talking heads were speculating that Square Peg was going to announce that he wouldn't play for the Memphis Grizzlies, who had the first pick in the NBA draft. The three nationally known reporters from that swimsuit magazine all confidently predicted that Peg was going to announce the teams he would play for, and all three seemed to agree that he would only play for the Lakers, the Spurs, the Warriors, or the Cavaliers, or perhaps the Knicks or the Nets, since those teams would take him "home" to the New York area.

At exactly 3:02 p.m., Peg said, "I have been offered a Rhodes scholarship to attend Oxford and the London School of Economics, which has been a lifelong goal for me. I have also been told that I will be the first pick of the Memphis Grizzlies in the upcoming NBA draft, which would lead me to the fulfillment of another lifelong dream. I also have been given the opportunity to go to Africa and work for Matt Damon and Gary White's Water.org for a year, which is another attractive challenge. I could also attend Harvard Law School.

"I have consulted with all my advisors, consulted with my friends, consulted with my parents, and most importantly, consulted with my girlfriend, who is the most sensible, grounded person that I have ever met, and I have decided that there is only one course of action that makes sense to me." Peg clicked a button on his cell, and the smiling face of Matt Damon appeared on the scoreboard screen.

"I'm really excited about you coming to work for us, Kelvin. Gary and I applaud your commitment to the largest problem on the planet and look forward to meeting you in person for the first time tomorrow. Are we still meeting in Chicago?"

"Yes, sir," Peg said.

"Hey, call me Matt," Damon said.

"See you tomorrow, Matt. Are we still going to Superdawg?"

"Yeah. I'm coming straight from the airport, so order me one ahead, will ya?"

"Absolutely," Peg said.

"You've got a lot to be proud of there at MSU, but this guy is really someone to be proud of," Matt Damon said. "Go, Spartans!"

Peg looked out at the still-stunned crowd and said, "I have deferred my Rhodes scholarship for a year so I can work for Water.org and will spend two years in London and Oxford after my time in Africa, which means that my NBA career is at least three years away, if ever I do play basketball in the future."

Jenison Field House exploded with a cacophony of sound not found in nature. I suppose that Krakatoa going off might have sounded like that, or all the Super Bowl crowds ever screaming inside the Seattle Seahawks stadium, or perhaps one hundred thousand second graders screaming for their mommies; but other than that, I could not imagine more noise, unless Godzilla was destroying Tokyo while every teenage girl who ever screamed at/for the Beatles did their thing.

The sporting press went crazier than a passel of shithouse rats.

Some of them were foaming at the mouth, some were talking so fast only an occasional word was intelligible, and one of the experts from that swimsuit magazine actually passed out while vehemently denouncing Square Peg's decision.

After literally ten minutes of caterwauling, the crowd began to wind down, so Peg put his hand up to calm the waters, at which point one of the other reporters from that swimsuit magazine stood up and yelled, "You ungrateful asshole! You owe it to the public to play in the NBA! This is just some kind of contract stunt!"

The football players who had escorted us in were all ranged around Peg's table in a semicircle, just out of sight of the cameras. Like a diesel engine slowly warming up, they all began laughing, as did K2 and I and everyone else who knew Square Peg, because (a) nobody on the planet cared less about money than Kelvin David Richardson, and (b) he never pulled stunts. Practical jokes on his friends—those were fair game, as were return practical jokes—but stunts required a sense of ego that Peg just didn't possess.

Eventually, the laughter slowed, although the football players continued to snort and giggle (yeah, it sounded like a herd of elephants giggling). Peg looked at the reporter and said, "Sir, I assure you that this is no stunt. I am going to fulfill my dreams outside basketball first, and only after I have kept my commitments will I entertain thoughts of the NBA. I also want to assure you that if—*if*—I do play in the NBA, it will not be for the money. I could simply go to Harvard Law, edit the law review, and graduate first in my class, and I would earn more money than any NBA career would ever bring me, with far less wear and tear on my body."

Peg looked the now-embarrassed sportswriter in the eye and said, "I also want to make it clear that I do not owe *anyone* any part of myself, except those I have already made commitments to. I have explained this once already. And I certainly do not owe any nebulous body known as 'the public.' I am my own man and will make my own choices about my life, which, I might add, have been endorsed by all those in my life I love and respect."

Then he said, "I will now take questions." He pointed at Robbie Quinter and said, "Mr. Quinter?"

The rest of the press groaned, because it was obvious that the presser wasn't going to go their way.

And they were right. Robbie asked 17 questions, not including follow-ups, and when he was done, Peg said, "Thank you for coming, ladies and gentlemen. And go Green!"

"Go White!" the crowd responded, just like a pack of trained gerbils (if you've been to MSU or are a fan of one of its teams, it is virtually impossible to not respond to this—it's a requirement to attend State).

The screaming hordes left, and the football team went after them, just in case any stragglers tried to turn back and horn in on Peg's time. I was hoping that somebody would, because it was always fun to watch the O-line and D-line rhinos go off on the field. I could only imagine how much better it would be if they went off on a sportswriter (luckily, the hospital was very close by).

Peg and I looked at each other with huge smiles on our faces. He'd asked me what to do over a week ago, and I'd told him to do what was in his heart, even though I knew that meant that he would leave me.

Yeah, that's trite, but before you go getting all "C'mon, this isn't an action story, it's a fuckin' soap opera" on me, understand that I knew with 100% certainty that Square Peg was going to fly away if I gave him permission, just like I knew that he was going to stay if I asked him to. It may sound trite, mundane, banal, and all the other words you can think of, but we were just that close. I couldn't resist him if he asked me for anything, any more than he could have resisted me.

I also knew that I had to cut the ties we had cleanly, or I would hurt Peg, hold him back, and possibly completely fuck up the best friendship I'd ever had. Whatever else happened, I didn't want to lose that friendship. If that sounds trite, well, go fuck yourself, the horse you rode in on, and the family dog. Sometimes the absolute, rock-bottom, bedrock truth is just that banal.

My friendship with Square Peg was more important than my own happiness, which is the absolute definition of true love.

Put that old chestnut in your pipe and smoke it, dear reader.

In any case, Coach Izzo looked at Peg and said, "You really are the Square Peg in the round hole, aren't cha?" He laughed that great Coach Izzo laugh and said, "Peg, anything you ever need, you let me know. I mean it. Whatever you need, you got it."

Uh-oh. Coach Izzo had just fallen into part two of Peg's nefarious two-part plan.

Peg's smile got even broader. He said, "Well, Coach, now that you mentioned it, there is something that I need from you." He outlined what he intended to do at the end of his three-year hiatus from basketball, and the part Coach Izzo had to play in it, which caused Coach Izzo to have a cow.

Your Fucking Highness, K2, and the Bull all busted a gut, both at the look on Coach Izzo's face and the audacity of Peg's plan. The Bull picked Peg up in a gigantic bear hug and said, "You are the coolest, smartest, most badass motherfucker since Michael Jordan, Square Peg! You're gonna conquer the fuckin' universe, and I'm gonna get to say I knew you when. Me and K2 are gonna name our firstborn after you, Captain Clang." (It was another nickname for Peg, used exclusively by the O-line at MSU. They all said that Peg's "balls clanged when he walked," which one of the linemen had transposed into Captain Clang.)

Your Fucking Highness said, "But can you make it work? What about the draft?"

Coach Izzo said, "Hell yeah, it can work! First, nobody's gonna draft him, this year or any other. He's officially a headcase, and also a dilettante, as far as the NBA is concerned. Second, he'll be completely off the radar, because he won't be playing in Europe or anywhere else the NBA recognizes as useful. Third, in three years, there'll be some other new hotshot, maybe not as good as Square Peg was, but still the new and improved superstar-in-waiting. This plan is so crazy it could work—talk about Captain Clang! You got the stones, Peg, and with your brains you probably intend to bring this scenario to its logical conclusion, right?"

Peg's smile got even broader, and he nodded, pleased that Coach Izzo got what he was going to do. I'd liked the idea as soon as I heard it, and I knew Your Fucking Highness would like it too. The whole thing was a real masterpiece—too bad the world would have to wait three or four years for it to come to fruition.

As it turned out, I couldn't be a part of phase three of the plan, because I was busy being shot at when it started, but that wasn't the worst part of that day. It turned out that I only had to wait one more day for my separation from Square Peg, not the two weeks I'd been promised.

Like the man said, shit happens.

How's that for trite? (And truth?)

So after the press conference, we really couldn't get any peace, despite the best efforts of the Bull and the Spartan football team. The phones rang off the hook, people kept trying to approach us, and our dorm room became ground zero for the press, despite the fact that MSU had them all ejected time and again.

We also figured out that it was a bad idea to watch TV or listen to the radio. It wasn't just because Peg got raked over the coals—the media even started calling me Yoko Ono, among other things that are still painful to me. One reporter claimed that I had control over Peg due to my "rampant raw sexuality" and that I was going with him to Africa "in order to keep him in line with sex." I laughed my ass off at that one—we'd had sex *once*, there, dude—but it still hurt.

Peg noticed and tried to apologize for hurting me, but I said, "Listen, it's the asshole media that's causing this problem, not you, so shut the fuck up, ya pissant."

Peg said, "But I—urk!" I snatched him off the floor and squeezed his lower belly as hard as I could—think of an anaconda squeezing an unsuspecting pig. It quickly became apparent that for all his athletic prowess, Square Peg was no match for his girlfriend, because he began to turn blue almost immediately. (Yes, he's Black, but he still turned blue, a very dark blue, but blue nonetheless. I still wish I could've taken a picture of that, but it took both arms to do the squeezing, which left no hands to take the pic—hey, I'm incredibly strong, but there's no big red "*S*" painted on my chest.)

Peg managed to weakly tap me on the shoulder, so I set him down and let him breathe again. After regaining control of his limbs and faculties (anoxia's a bitch), Peg said, "I won't apologize again because I want to live. But I hope this will fade away with time. I love you very much and want you to have the best life possible, with or without me. Nobody deserves to be harassed for something that they didn't do."

"OK, that I agree with, but I'm a big girl and I can take care of myself. You have to focus on you for once and stop with the noble shit. Just be selfish and take care of Kelvin David Richardson, OK? Remember, not even death can stop true love."

Everybody with us laughed; it was a line from our favorite movie (*The Princess Bride*—watch it and be prepared to laugh like a hyena) that we always used when it seemed that life was changing around us in a way that might not be pleasant.

This particular moment quickly became that kind of change to the *nth* degree. I could tell that Square Peg had something else to tell me, but before he could say anything, the Bull said, "Peg, the diversion is ready and the getaway car is waiting."

"What fucking diversion?" I said coolly (OK, so I was fucking freaking out, but nobody was going to know that from the way I looked, except Peg, and he was clearly fucking freaking out too).

Peg's face fell, but he went on like a man and said, "Beautiful Girl, I'm going to Chicago tonight. Matt Damon has a suite reserved for me at the Intercontinental on Michigan Avenue. Dave Kline is driving me in and sticking around until Matt and I are done meeting, just in case I need him."

Dave Kline was one of the assistant sports information guys for MSU—basically a press secretary—who helped all athletes with any outside communications and just about anything else they needed. Dave was one of those guys you couldn't help but like—helpful, determined to protect "his" athletes, a great writer, and absolutely fearless with the press. Dave had worked with the basketball program for a long time and was one of our favorite MSU staffers. He'd grown up in Chicago but now bled Spartan Green and White, so he was the perfect guy to take Peg to meet Matt Damon.

I stared at the love of my life and said, "OK, that's a great idea. What the hell is the diversion?"

Peg smiled and said, "Mr. Bullard, what has our contestant won?" in a game show host voice.

"Well, Monty, she's won brand-new couches for the athletes' lounges at the training complex!" the Bull said in his best TV announcer voice.

"You're going to cause a riot and burn the couches from the lounges," I said. "My god, Holmes, it's the perfect solution!" I said in my Dr. Watson voice. (My English accent was atrocious, but I used it anyway, because I was convinced it would get better with time. I also thought that I'd grow out of my short round phase—hope springs eternal.)

Peg and his fellow conspirators all smiled and laughed, pleased to have pleased me. The couches in question were the ugliest, most uncomfortable things in history. Some rich alumni had donated them, so they couldn't be touched, but if a riot occurred and they burned, well, there wasn't much that could be done about that. We'd need new couches for sure, and maybe we could actually have input on them.

I can't explain why I hated those couches so much, although the fact that they were covered in blue-and-gold checkered fabric and had been made in Ann Arbor might have had something to do with it.

I realized that the diversion could only be made better in one way, so I said, "Peg, the Bull, K2, and I need to go get ourselves arrested, or at least on the late news. If the press sees us there, they'll think that you're around, which means that you and Dave can escape without being seen."

The love of my life nodded and said, "Still the smartest person in the room, Beautiful Girl. How did I get so lucky?"

"Who could have resisted this?" I pointed at my overly muscular round body, topped by my butt-ugly face and weird red hair, as everybody laughed. Peg hugged me and kissed me passionately, stepped back, and said, "See you guys in two days. Have fun burning down the world to fight the Man."

I didn't cry, even when he looked over his shoulder and said, "Not even death can stop true love."

"As you wish," I said. Then he was gone to Chicago to meet Matt Damon, just like a 6'10", 255-pound (he'd grown a bit since his sophomore year) elf from *The Lord of the Rings* sailing away to Valinor across the sea. The Bull, K2, and I went off to distract the media, in the process almost getting arrested while helping over three thousand other students burn some ugly-ass couches and show the Man (whoever that was) that we weren't going to be pushed around, or whatever shit excuse we made up for the protest.

All in all, it was great fun, except for one minor detail: Square Peg never came back from Chicago.

It would be six long years before I saw the love of my life face-to-face again.

Shit.

CHAPTER 11

The Lonely Year

It sounds like I'm just being a whiny bitch, but even though I had a ton of friends left at State without Square Peg, I felt like I was all alone. I dragged my ass around for two weeks, spewing darkness and gloom wherever I went, until one morning at weightlifting, when the Bull said, "Freak, we think you oughta play football this year. We need a punt returner and a gunner for punts and kickoffs, and you're the fastest athlete in school, plus you're pound for pound the strongest person we've ever seen, so we think you oughta stop being a depressed dipshit and get off your ass and play football."

The giant O-lineman looked at me with what I can only describe as tenderness, and I got all choked up, and then the Bull said, "We all miss him, Freak, and we know that it's worse for you, but you need to snap out of it, or the rest of us are gonna have ta go off on your ass. Being a bag of shit that slopes around under a black cloud ain't you, Freak."

He was right.

So I went to talk to Coach Dantonio, who expressed concerns about my size and gender, until we went out to the practice facility and I outran Willie Treece, Melvin Arnold, and Donta Knight, the three returning members of the defensive backfield, in the 40-yard dash, at which point my size became less of an issue.

He was still concerned about my gender, until the O- and D-lines vouched for my "balls" and my weightlifting ability, and my ability to just be one of the guys. Coach Dantonio still looked wary, right up until I crushed Mark Brown and Cordell Wilkerson, the wide receivers who were the fastest men on the team, by almost four yards in the 40, at which point I became a Michigan State football Spartan.

Playing college football lifted my funk almost immediately. There was so much to learn that I never thought I'd get it all; plus, it was as much physical training as track, and almost as much as wrestling, and I had a full class schedule, so I really didn't have time to miss anyone more than two, 300 times a week (which was far less than the seven or 800 a minute I was originally missing Peg).

Plus, I got to take out all my physical and mental frustrations on the field, which really helped to take the edge off.

I started off as a gunner on the punt team and kickoffs. For the football deficient, that's the guy that tries to run down the field as fast as they can and break up the return or make the tackle of the guy carrying the ball. It sounds easy, but the other team generally throws the kitchen sink at you to impede your progress down the field.

In other words, the opposition tries to knock you on your ass so you can't get their guy with the ball.

The first punt we did in practice was a jogging-down and doing-your-job exercise—it was without pads and strictly no contact, at half speed. We did that several times, and the two guys who were trying to impede me just went through the motions. The last punt, the special teams coach said, "OK, no contact, but let's go full speed."

So I did.

I evaded the two nitwits trying to stop me and flew down the field at full hyperspeed. The guy catching the ball never had a chance to get it since I caught it out of the air. He began jumping up and down, talking about interference, but as several of our teammates pointed out, I hadn't done anything illegal—when the ball was in the air, it was up for grabs.

Coach Dantonio was so intrigued he asked us to run it again. This time I ran down and stood next to the guy catching the ball until he caught it, then wrapped my arms around him in a play "tackle."

The third time we ran it again, I ran down behind the guy catching the ball, let him catch it, and then snatched the ball out of his hands.

Everybody was cracking up and razzing the guys catching punts, and several people pointed out that it would be different in pads, but I saw Coach Dantonio watching me, and I could see him thinking that maybe pads wouldn't be so different.

Much the same thing happened on the kickoff team, except about every third kickoff, I caught it out of the air and ran it in for a touchdown.

We did our little dance without pads for the rest of the week. I worked out with the defensive backs and the punt and kickoff teams until the Saturday-morning practice, when we tried our first punt block. Again, for the football deficient (I'm not making fun of you guys; I'm just trying to explain), the punt block is where you try to break through the other team's front line and block their punter's attempt to kick the ball downfield.

I blocked eleven in a row before the special teams coach assigned me three personal blockers.

Then I blocked five more in a row.

I was on the punt receive team, too, especially when we were going for the block.

So on the following Monday, we put pads on. All the guys were laughing because they were sure that the girl would find out about the realities of college football now, since they were all big, strong, and mean, and I was just a teeny, tiny wittle girl (that's my attempt to Use baby talk).

Wrong again, asshole sexist pigs.

I learned that no matter what level of football you play speed kills, especially when it's combined with extraordinary strength.

We went through all our footwork for the secondary, and we did form tackling drills, and then we did a "fight off" drill, where we fought off a blocker and tackled a back in the open field. I was third in line and had to go with Cordell Wilkerson, who was 6'4", 225 pounds of very fast, very strong wide receiver, a guy who was destined to play in the NFL (thirteen years with the Vikings and Cardinals after he left State).

The coach barked "Hit," and we did our little dance, which resulted in three separate outcomes:

1. I knocked Cordell Wilkerson ass over tea cart.
2. I smoked the guy with the ball, a 6'2", 215-pound tailback named Jamaal Curtis (two-time All-Big Ten selection).

3. Everybody stopped treating me like a wittle girl and started treating me like a football player.

The whole team had a good laugh on Cordell and Jamaal, including themselves, but when Cordell jogged by me back to the end of the line and said, "Nice hit, Freak, won't happen again," he patted me on the butt, which is the ultimate gesture of acceptance for any football player.

And that was the only thing that was weird about the whole situation. Everybody associated with the Michigan State football program just accepted me as a football player and forgot that I was a womyn.

It was wonderful.

I was a part of the team and was rewarded or punished just like everybody else. There was no sexist conduct, no jokes about my genitalia, and no one said anything about my tits, which I found remarkable (they were my only really feminine feature and definitely stood out).

It got even better once the games started. I had worked my way up to be our "dime" defensive back—I came in when we used six defensive backs and usually took a smaller slot receiver man-to-man. It really worked, mainly because the rest of our DBs were so good, and all the dime position required was flat-out speed.

So I went into our first game against UCLA at home with me playing sometimes, and we were kicking off, so I went out to my gunner position, third player in from the left sideline. The ball got kicked and nobody even touched me as I flew down the field and blew up the poor UCLA kick returner at the nine-yard line.

My teammates were appropriately appreciative, and just two plays later, we went to our "dime" pass defense because UCLA had a third and 11 from our eight-yard line, and they had an excellent QB (quarterback, like Tom Brady, the guy who passes the ball), who liked to take chances and throw the ball all over the field.

I went with my slot guy, and when the ball was snapped, he dropped back two yards and broke for the sideline. It was a play called a screen. Two of his guys were going to block me while he caught a pass and tried to run for a first down. I recognized it immediately—our DB coach drilled us on their screen package during the week—and broke forward to get my guy.

Nobody touched me again as I dashed forward, and the QB didn't really look, since two of our defensive linemen were draped all over him, so he just threw the ball and I caught it and ran right in the end zone for a touchdown.

I got swamped by giant men jumping up and down like little boys, and I got a pat on the butt from Coach Dantonio, which really made my day.

We went on to absolutely cream UCLA, who was ranked 11th in the country at that time, by a score of 56–7. I had seven tackles, the interception for a touchdown, and blocked two punts and a field goal. I also caused three fumbles (when you make the other team drop the ball against their will), which we recovered, and knocked the UCLA kickoff guy unconscious when I smoked him with a perfectly legal hit (I never did hit anyone with my helmet—I was afraid of damaging my own brain, and besides, shoulder pads allow you to really smoke a guy without much chance you'll get hurt, which is one of the points of football) on our last kickoff.

After the game, a reporter tried to get Coach Dantonio to make a comment about my gender being a factor in guys taking it easy on me, which provoked the following response.

> Reporter: Coach, why do you think UCLA took it so easy on Glickstien?
>
> Coach Dantonio: Say what?
>
> R: Don't you think that Glickstien had a good game because UCLA took it easy on her due to her gender?
>
> CD: Freak had a great game because she's a great football player, and our game plan put her in a position to excel. She executed the game plan extremely well today.
>
> R: But don't you think that UCLA simply didn't take her seriously because she's a girl?
>
> CD: Did you actually watch the game? They put three guys on her on their third punt, and she still made the tackle, after she put the three guys on the ground.
>
> R: But isn't it hard for a male collegiate athlete to take Glickstien seriously because of her size and gender?
>
> CD: Well, I hope that's the case going forward, because if teams actually did that, well, we're going to win a lot more games.
>
> R: But she's too small, she's not as strong as the guys—she can't be, right?—and well, she's a girl. Girls can't complete with male collegiate athletes in football, right?
>
> CD, *pausing in thought for a few seconds*: Well, I'd say anyone who actually watched today's game would have to dispute that statement. Clearly, Freak's our best special team player, regardless of the fact that she's a womyn. I mean, did that *look* like a girl to you, or just a football player?
>
> R: C'mon, Coach—isn't this just a publicity stunt? You don't actually think that a girl can physically compete at this level against the big boys, do you?
>
> CD: If Freak's a publicity stunt, I'd like ten more just like her. I'd also say that any athlete that can squat five hundred pounds and runs a sub-4.3 forty can compete against major college competition.
>
> R: Say what? No way can Glickstien physically do those things!
>
> CD: Did you actually watch today's game?

After that, Coach Dantonio refused to answer gender questions about me, and after our second game, they all ceased, anyway, because we pounded the dogshit out of #3 Oklahoma State in their own stadium. I had five tackles, knocked down three passes, and blocked two punts, which my teammates obligingly picked up and ran in for touchdowns. I also caught a kickoff on one hop and ran it in for a touchdown.

Our offense was also a machine, scoring touchdowns on five straight drives as we dismantled the Cowboys 68–10.

Oklahoma State's coach said after the game that he didn't care if I was a girl, a womyn, or an android, because I was for sure "the most disruptive special teams player he'd ever seen"—and the guy had coached 10 years in the NFL and 20-plus years in college.

Our season went pretty well after that.

We won every one of our regular-season games, but our three favorite wins were against Wisconsin, That Other School from Ann Arbor, who was ranked #2 at the time, and that team from the Hairless Nut State (a *buckeye* is a hairless nut), who was ranked #1 at the time.

Against Wisconsin, I got picked up by three very large Badgers and hurled out of bounds on a punt (that's illegal, and the penalty flags were already flying), after which the three dudes just jumped on me like starving dogs on a pork chop. They were trying to grab me any way they could, and one of them kept saying, "Gonna rip your tits off, ya cunt!" like it was his Zen mantra.

Unfortunately for the Badgers, they'd hurled me out of bounds right in front of our O-line. These dudes averaged 6'6", 325 pounds, none of it fat, and they thought I was their little sister, so they reacted badly when the three Badgers attempted to rip my tits off.

Looking back on the replay, there was a small knot of red-and-white jerseys trying to pummel me, then there was a surge of giants wearing green, then there were three red-and-white dudes pinwheeling through the air as my big brothers hurled the screaming Badgers back out onto the field, and then there was an enormous roar from the crowd as my big brothers raised me on their shoulders so everyone could see I was OK.

After the dust settled from the brouhaha, the Badgers had been assessed 45 yards in penalties and were backed up to their own goal line. After three unsuccessful running plays, the Badgers tried to punt, but a screaming meemie in green wearing number 44 broke through, blocked it, and one of her teammates fell on the ball in the end zone for a touchdown.

We onside-kicked (we kicked it short in an attempt to recover the ball for our side) on the ensuing kickoff, and I caught it on a hop and ran past the startled Badgers for another touchdown.

And I caused a fumble on the next kickoff, which we recovered. Our offense took it in on the very next play as we scored our third touchdown in twenty-six seconds, all of them caused by me.

And that was just the first quarter.

They showed the sequence on Sports Center over and over, and then they showed the third-quarter highlight when two Badgers tried to block me on a punt return and I burst through them to drop the returner. When I got up, one of the guys took a swing at me and I dodged, whereupon he connected with his other teammate, who was also trying to hit me. They knocked each other down with haymakers to the jaw as I just jogged past them to the sideline.

My teammates all started laughing, which soon degenerated into the crowd laughing. It was so funny that the Wisconsin fans laughed, and even Coach Dantonio smiled and laughed, which was a major accomplishment.

They played that one on Sports Center over and over, and oh yeah, we won the game 65–0, against a team that had the leading rusher in the NCAA that year.

So when we went to La Casa Grande in Ann Arbor, both teams were undefeated. We were ranked #3, and That Other School in Ann Arbor was ranked #2, and the game was a classic, at least until the piss yellow-and-navy weasels kicked off.

Coach Dantonio had kept it under wraps, but he had a surprise for the team from our west, because I was out there with the kick-receive team for the first time, standing on the right wing of the formation. They kicked the ball to Eric Truckey, our kick returner, and he ran to his right. I immediately broke to my left, and when we passed each other, he handed me the ball on a classic kickoff reverse.

Then I turned on the jets and blew toward the left sideline, right past the piss yellow-and-navy bench. It was just me and one of the piss yellow-and-navy players on the sideline, so I put it in Freak gear and ran past him like he was a concrete weasel, 90 yards to the end zone, untouched, for our first touchdown, just 12 seconds into the game.

You ever heard 116,319 screaming fans (no shit, look up the attendance for the game—La Casa Grande will hold an absolute shitload of fans wearing piss yellow and navy) go from screaming for blood to dead silence in 12 seconds? I have, and it's awesome. It was so quiet we could hear Coach Dantonio say to our special teams coach, "Well, that went about as well as could be expected," which made us all laugh, because for Coach Dantonio that was the highest declaration of respect.

It went downhill for That Other School from Ann Arbor after that, because we did the Wisconsin-onside-kick trick again, and I did exactly the same thing, running it in from 48 yards out for a touchdown, and then we ran a fake on our extra point, so after 22 seconds of actual elapsed game time, we were ahead 15–0, and that piss yellow and navy team had yet to touch the ball.

It was 43–0 at halftime, and when That Other School from Ann Arbor tried a swing pass to start the third quarter and I intercepted it for a touchdown, it was 50–0 and a huge part of the 116,319 fans were streaming to the exits. Our offense scored one more touchdown, and we won 57–3 to become the #2 ranked team in the country, headed into our confrontation with the #1 Hairless Nuts the next week.

The coach from That Other School in Ann Arbor, a usually volatile and entertaining individual, really didn't know what to say about the game. He verbally meandered around for a while before he finally said, "Well, 44 just kicked our ass, and then she blocked that punt in the second quarter, and she caused that fumble after that, and well, that 44 is the best fucking special teamer in America, and she kicked our sorry asses eight ways to Sunday."

They played that one on a Sports Center loop, too (with a beep, of course).

So the biggest game of the year arrived, and we had to go to the horseshoe in the land of the Hairless Nuts to try and win the latest game of the century.

Five Hairless Nuts lost fumbles, three blocked kicks, and two punt returns for touchdowns later, we were in the Big Ten Championship game with a 51–0 win. I caused four of the fumbles, blocked two of the kicks, and returned one of the punts for touchdown, as well as had five tackles and the block that sprang the second punt return TD. I was also responsible for making the Hairless Nut punter shank one for a minus-two-yard net (his punt essentially went backward) when I faked like I was going to come at him (he might have flinched as he started to swing his leg) and had my first QB sack (tackling the QB for a loss on a pass play) when I blitzed from my dime corner spot in the slot and creamed the Hairless Nut QB.

We went to the Big Ten Championship game against the Minnesota Gold Gophers, who we crushed like we were the real Spartans against real gophers, and then made it to the national championship against Alabama, where we lost 18–17 on a 65-yard field goal with no time left.

I still say that they didn't get the kick off before the clock expired, a contention confirmed by ESPN and others, but it was a hell of a kick and maybe the best college football game ever. The two teams had literally the same amount of offensive yards, and although we kept them out of the end zone, they still won (all their points came via long field goals).

We almost won when I blocked a punt in the middle of the fourth quarter, but I got called for being offside (again, replay proved I was not), so I blocked the re-kick and the refs called one of my teammates offside (he also was not).

That's not sour grapes; it's just the facts. You can look it up.

In any case, once the season was over, I was named to the All-Big Ten first team as a special teams player and was also named to every All-American team for the same thing. Seven of my teammates were also honored with various awards, including four who were first-team All-Americans.

At our football banquet, Coach Dantonio said I was the catalyst for our season and that I was the best special teams player he'd ever coached anywhere, which was a great honor, and my teammates voted me Most Inspirational and Best Rookie, which was even more of an honor, and when I got called up for my football letter, I got a standing ovation.

I still missed my Square Peg, but football sure helped me stay sane.

Wrestling season was also very successful for me and our team. We lost to Penn State in the Big Ten and NCAA championships, but we beat everyone else to finish runners-up in both. I also finished runner-up, losing to a whirling dervish from Penn State named Randy Bucher-Pastrick in the finals on criteria. We were tied 1-1 after regulation and overtime, but the Penn State guy had three more seconds of riding time (keeping me on the mat, ya pervs) in overtime, which meant that he won on criteria. Yeah, it's cheesy, but them's the rules.

For the record, I was the first four-time All-American in MSU wrestling history and finished fifth, third, third, and second, which isn't bad for womyn wrestling against men at 165 pounds. I was also voted Most Valuable Wrestler by my teammates.

Come to think of it, that's not fucking bad for anybody, period.

So by then, it was the spring of my senior year, with track and field starting, and my decision on what to do after my graduation was looming like Mt. Kilimanjaro over the Serengeti. I talked to everybody about it, especially my *zayde*, my parents, my brothers, Square Peg, Your Fucking Highness, the Bull, and K2. Everybody agreed on one thing: I should do what moved me the most, not kowtow to some conventional premise about what wymyn should do, or fall into the trap of money.

Your Fucking Highness and my brother Eggy said essentially the same thing. "With a double major in accounting and history, you'll always be able to get a job and make money, Freak."

"Do what you want to while you're young, because your options start being limited as you age," Your Fucking Highness said.

"With those academic qualifications and your unique background, they'll be lining up to give you money, Freak, so do what pleases you. I could make more money, but I like Cal Tech, so I stay there to be happy. It's worth it," Eggy said.

Everybody was right, so I made my decision and then kept it to myself until track was over.

There wasn't any runner-up finish in track and field that year. My best female friend, Karen Kamakawiwo'ole, the giant K2, set a new NCAA record and won the shot put; our crazy Finnish javelin thrower, Ulla Virkkonen, set a new NCAA record and won her event; and our really crazy pole-vaulter, Katie Karsen, also won.

We got runner-up finishes from Suzette Roy in the long jump, Greta Hoogstratten in the high jump, and Felicia Rankin-White in the triple jump, and Mandy Royer was third in the high jump.

I had the best meet of my life. I broke the world record in the hammer throw, again, at 271 feet, 1 inch (sorry, Anita Włodarczyk of Poland), and set the NCAA record for the discus (sorry, Seilala Sua of UCLA) and won both events. I was also part of the record-setting four-by-one-hundred-meter relay team that won, and finished runner-up to K2 in the shot.

We'd already won the meet after just the field events, so when our two hurdlers scored in the high and low hurdles, our four-hundred-meter runner ran third, our steeplechaser was third, and Denita Williams set a new NCAA record in winning the two hundred meters, we were just gilding the lily. We topped it off with a win in the four-by-four-hundred-meter relay that was also a new NCAA record, after which we were pretty much declared the best NCAA wymyn's track team ever.

I got a tremendous amount of attention for the new world record in the hammer, and I gave all the credit to playing football, wrestling, and my excellent coaches at MSU, which were all true, and then baldly lied about trying out for the Olympic team, which I had no intention of doing, because I'd decided on a different path for myself.

I loved track and field, but I'd been doing it by then for 10 years, and I was really done with it. The camaraderie was great, I'd always had excellent coaches, and the competition was fun, but I just didn't see it being competitive enough for me going forward. It sounds really trite, but this is the truth: I needed a real challenge, one that would stretch my capabilities mentally and physically and let me try to actually achieve something that was in line with my considerable gifts. So far, all we've really focused on are my physical gifts, but I was a 3.95 student at Michigan State University with a double major and double minor. I did accounting, history, economics, and international relations, got one B in an advanced statistics class, fit all the credits in four years, all while lettering nine times in intercollegiate sports.

I wasn't just an athlete; I was an actual student athlete, with some emphasis on the *student* part. After I graduated from State, I wasn't going to be a washed-up crank talking about the old (implied better) days, because I was equipped to go out in the world and be successful.

But I wanted more.

I didn't have to make any announcements about anything until the U.S. Olympic Committee (USOC) called to tell me that I was one of the athletes that they intended to put on the cover of the newest bulletin about the next Summer Olympic Games.

Ah, fuck.

It was time to shit or get off the pot, so I shit, all over my sport, my family, and my school.

I declined to be on the bulletin, and I told the executive director of the USOC the reason, although I asked her to keep it quiet for a week. She was shocked and (dare I say) dismayed, but she agreed to keep it to herself.

I didn't really believe her, so I asked Dave Kline, our assistant sports information guy who'd helped Square Peg out, to set up a press conference for me in two days. I called my Mumsy, Pops, and *zayde* and asked them to gather those of my brothers that could get there, called Peg, and told him what I was doing, asked the Bull and K2 to provide security, got Your Fucking Highness and the MSU track coaches (Zelda Sipes, my throwing coach, and Frances "Frankie" Rupp, the head wymyn's track coach) to come, and then called one more person, my mystery guest, to attend the presser.

The day came, and the media showed up, along with several people from the USOC, USA Track and Field, the International Olympic Committee (IOC), and a ton of students.

So I talked about my track-and-field career, emphasized my love of the sport and the gratitude I felt for all the people who'd helped me along the way, and then dropped the shit-bomb by announcing that even though I was the world record holder in the hammer, I wouldn't be trying out for the Olympic team, for that event or any other.

Shit flew everywhere.

I got called unpatriotic, ungrateful, un-American, and a rotten bitch, among other things. I took it all until a USOC official called me a fucking cunt, at which point I slammed my hand down on the table in front of me and (accidentally on purpose) broke it in half.

In the sudden silence that followed, I pointed at my mystery guest, who stomped up and stood ramrod straight next to me, which really got everybody's attention.

"Despite the abuse you've just rained down on me, I am still firm in my decision. Backed up by my family, my professors, and my coaches, I have decided to enlist in the United States Marine Corps in order to serve my country and challenge myself in ways that I cannot yet understand," I said. I turned to my mystery guest standing next to me and said, "Gunnery Sergeant Karl, can you explain what I'm about to go through?"

Marine Gunnery Sergeant Steven A. Karl, my Marine recruiter, looked like he was 10 feet tall standing next to me in his dress greens. He nodded at me and said, "Of course, Ms. Glickstien." He gave a very succinct synopsis of what I'd be going through at Marine basic training at Parris Island, South Carolina.

He also caused quite a stir when he said, "And if the reee-cruit manages to pass through basic training, she will then be sent off to Marine Officer Candidate School, where she will be trained to lead U.S. Marines in battle. If she should pass through that school, then she will attend several other schools in order to ensure that she is fully trained and equipped to lead Marines in battle."

There was silence in the hall, and then Dave Kline said, "Any questions?"

There were several, mostly for me. I answered all of them honestly and fully, and then there was one for the Gunnery Sergeant.

The reporter from the *Chicago Tribune* said, "Do you really think that there's a chance that a world-class athlete like Glinka Glickstien won't make it through basic training?"

"Yes," Gunnery Sergeant Karl said.

"How good a chance?" the reporter asked.

"Better than 50 percent," the Gunnery Sergeant said.

There was silence, and the reporter for the *Detroit Free Press* said, "Even someone like the Freak from Battle Creek?"

"Yes," Gunnery Sergeant Karl said. "Marine basic training is the hardest initial training exercise in the world, bar none. Ms. Glickstien will receive no special treatment, no special rations, no special rest periods, no special training, but she will receive the most rigorous physical and mental training she's ever seen. Marine basic training will make her athletic career and her previous training seem like a Sunday picnic with her mommy and daddy.

"If, and I emphasize that word *if*, she survives Marine basic training, she will have become one of the world's elite combat personnel, but first, she has to survive the hardest test ever devised by humans. We will wash her out if she can't keep up, and yes, she will have to *prove* that she can keep up, elite athlete or not," Gunnery Sergeant Karl said.

"And that's what you're choosing over Team USA?" one of the USOC officials said.

"The United States Marines *are* Team USA," I said. "I chose the Marines because they're the best, and I want to see if I can hack it with the best. Plus, I want to serve my country like it's served me and my family."

"And her family completely supports her," my brother Doc said.

"Bet your ass," my *zayde* said.

"And we're so proud of her for choosing her own path," Mumsy said. "We raised her to be independent, and it looks like we were successful, eh?"

Everybody laughed, but the wymyn's Olympic track coach said, "But the world record? An Olympic gold medal? These don't mean anything?"

"Of course they do, but that's the easy choice," I said.

"Whattaya mean the *easy* choice?" the coach said.

"At the risk of being arrogant, if I train full-time for the hammer, I'll go out and win the gold medal, and probably set another world record, but what does that mean? I've already done it twice, I'll do it again, and I'll get covered in glory for my athletic career. But so what? How does that make the world a better place?

"On the other hand, becoming a U.S. Marine is the hard choice, but if I'm successful, I'll be doing something that really matters, because in the end the hammer throw or sports in general don't matter a bit compared to stopping the enemies of the United States, now, do they?"

"Booyah," Gunnery Sergeant Karl said.

And nobody could really argue with the truth.

So off everybody went to talk about the crazy Freak who turned down athletic glory so she could go in the Marines. I got some hate mail, some people on campus gave me shit, and five rednecks decided that they were going to "teach me a lesson 'bout messin' with 'Merica," as they told the cops from their hospital beds, but other than that, I wasn't too badly abused.

Everybody important to me was just grand, especially K2, who told anybody who'd listen how proud she was of me and how I was going to change the world for wymyn forever by being Marine Recon, or commandant of the Marine Corps, or the chairwoman of the Joint Chiefs of Staff. Believe me, when a 6'4", 300-pound Hawaiian womyn talks to you, you listen, so word went around that I was really a patriot, and pretty soon people were saying, "Semper fi, Freak," and "Booyah, Marine!" as they passed me on campus.

At graduation, all three speakers mentioned me as being a good example of "what it means to be a Spartan," and I got a standing ovation after the dean announced me as Glinka "Freak" Glickstien, queen of the Spartans.

It was one of the greatest days in my life, but it was soon over. I had to say goodbye to all my pals, which really hurt, and then I had to say goodbye to the Bull and the rest of the O-line, and then I had a tearful goodbye with K2, who was like my sister from another mother. I urged her to go for the Olympic gold (she came close—silver in shot put) and told her that I'd keep in contact when I could. She told me that she was going to marry the Bull after their careers were over (he was probably going to be drafted by an NFL team) and that she was naming her first child after me (she did, too—poor kid).

Finally, I went around and said goodbye to all my really excellent profs, finishing with Your Fucking Highness.

He looked me up and down and held out his hand to shake, but I said, "Oh, fuck that, Your Fucking Highness, that just won't fucking do," and pulled him into a hug. After a bit, we'd both stopped crying enough to talk, and Leland David Thomas said, "It's doubly hard, without fucking Square Peg around to shoot the fucking shit, isn't it?"

"Bet your fucking ass," I said, and finally we laughed. Truth be told, I'd tried to keep Peg out of my thoughts and mind but hadn't really been all that successful. Hearing Your Fucking Highness say his name and express what I was feeling actually made it easier, I think because I realized that I wasn't the only one who missed him.

It was still fucking lonely without him.

At last, it was time to leave East Lansing and Michigan State University. As I got on US-127 South for the last time and headed for I-69 to I-94 and home to Battle Creek, I thought about all the joy I'd experienced in college, and the very little heartbreak, and I finally realized what a lucky person I was, in every way possible. I also realized that life would never again be as carefree as it had been while drinking Pepsis in the Union and bullshitting with my friends, but it suddenly struck me that I was OK with that, because State had been ephemeral, like a long-term dream that simulated real life. Eventually, you have to wake up and get on with real life, like it or not, or your life will lack purpose and focus, and drifting along is only fun as long as the current goes the way you want it to.

So I drove home, got a huge surprise when the city of Battle Creek threw a parade in my honor and drove me around on top of a fire truck, and good old Harper Creek High inducted me into their Hall of Fame, and I was recognized as the best athlete ever for the Fighting Beavers (laugh all you want about our mascot—OK, it deserves the laughter—but it's still a top-notch school with above-average sports teams). Since we'd had two Olympians and an All-Pro NFL quarterback who also happened to be a Heisman Trophy winner, it was a pretty big deal.

Finally, all the hoopla was over and it was time for me to report to Marine Corps basic training at Parris Island, South Carolina. I kissed everybody goodbye and got on my plane, all the while figuring that since I was a world-class athlete and a college graduate, I was ready for anything that the Marine Corps threw at me.

Wrong again, dumbass.

CHAPTER 12

Semper Fi, Freak

The Marine Corps and I fit like a hand in a custom glove, even though they threw me (and everybody else) some serious curveballs during basic.

I reported for boot camp at Parris Island, South Carolina, with extremely short hair and a very positive attitude, which did not change when I got off the bus and found several well-muscled, leather-lunged female Marines screaming their heads off about what losers we were.

I will spare you the language (all those DIs were English majors—they could use the word *fuck* as every part of the English language, most times in the same sentence), but it was the absolutely no-nonsense, take-no-prisoners, don't-fuck-with-me attitude that I liked. These were very serious wymyn, with very serious jobs, and they did not disappoint when it came to esprit de corps, either.

I knew a little bit about what to expect, learned from a very unexpected source: my *zayde*. Before I left for boot camp, he took me aside and said, "You need to make sure that you don't look at the DIs, talk back, or ever hold up any exercise. If they tell you to run naked down the street, do it, and for God's sake, make your bed properly."

"Is it really that bad?" I asked.

"Worse," he said. "They are going to try to warp your mind into their idea of a good Marine, and you are not going to let them. You are going to be a good Marine, but not at the expense of yourself."

I looked at him, my earnest old grandpa, and suddenly realized that he was trying to tell me something that I never would have guessed.

"You're a former Marine," I said.

"Wrong. I *am* a Marine. There is no such thing as a former Marine," my *zayde* said. "Once a Marine, always a Marine, Mac." He smiled at me and ruffled my short hair like I was a little girl, but I could see the pride in his eyes, and the fierceness that I had seen in court when he still defended people against what he called "the awesome power of the state." Apparently, there was a lot more to my *zayde* than met the eye—just as there was to me. We shared a quiet moment, each of us contemplating how much we were alike, until he said, "And don't forget that you're going to get your ass kicked eight ways to Sunday. The Corps does not like those who stick out until it's time to stick out, and that time is *not* basic training. Your DI is going to hate you, right up until she loves you at graduation, so get it into your head right now—it's all a con. Be who you are, excel at all their little games, accept the punishment for being the best, graduate, and the corps will give you your choice of programs afterward."

"What do you think I ought to ask for after graduation?" I said, already accepting his advice about my Marine Corps career.

"First, they're going to ask you about OCS, Officer Candidate School. You want to go because you want the rank for later, but remember that it's sergeants who run the corps, especially Gunnery Sergeants, Top Sergeants, and the occasional Sergeant Major. Never forget that. And once you're an officer, always rely on your sergeants—they know where the bodies are buried and how to get things done. And don't call any sergeants *sir*. All sergeants will tell you that they work for a living, and they mean it. They will also kick your ass for calling them *sir*, so avoid that.

"Once you're done with OCS, you want to train for the law enforcement part of your career, so you want to be part of the shore patrol, what the Navy calls the Military Police component of the corps. That part of your career should take about three years, and then you want to apply for cross-deck training in the JAG, the Judge Advocate General's office."

"Not NCIS?" I asked, teasing him about his favorite TV show.

"No, that might be after the Corps, but you want to get real legal experience, in case you decide to go to law school. After eight years of the SP and JAG offices, then you can make up your mind," my *zayde* said. "I still think that you'd make a great legal advocate, but I know that it won't ever satisfy your need for physicality, so maybe after you're old that'll happen." He looked sad, but my *zayde* also looked proud of me for knowing who I was.

I stood up and said, in my best Marine recruit's voice, "*Sir*, I'm going to tear the corps up, and I'm going to try to live up to your standards and expectations, *sir*!"

Zayde smiled at me and said, "Don't call me *sir*, recruit. I work for a living!"

We laughed like crazy, and three days later, I left for Marine Corps Recruit Depot Parris Island, South Carolina.

I was off the bus about 30 seconds when I met Gunnery Sergeant Angela Thornton. Up close and personal.

I was milling around with the rest of the recruits when this person I never saw bellowed in my ear, "JESUS H. CHRIST! IT'S A GOT-DAMNED GINGER! I HATE GINGERS!"

I didn't drop my bag or piss my pants, but it was close. I flicked my eyes over at the insignia and name tag and said, "Gunnery Sergeant Thornton, this recruit will shave her head if it will alleviate your displeasure!" I didn't look at her, but I did straighten up to attention, as best as I could.

Then there was a real shitstorm.

"DID I *ASK* YOU TO SPEAK, REEE-CRUIT? DID I *ASK* YOU TO 'ALLEVIATE MY DISPLEASURE'? DID I? ANSWER ME, REEE-CRUIT!"

I knew that I was fucked either way, so I decided to just brazen it out. "No, Gunnery Sergeant! This recruit was out of line!" *Zayde* had told me not to apologize, to just admit my error and let the DI go on, so I did.

She definitely went on. "YOU ARE SURE AS SHIT OUT OF LINE, REEE-CRUIT! SEE THOSE FEET OVER THERE ON THE PAVEMENT? THAT IS THE LINE. NOW GET YOUR ASS OVER THERE AND DO NOT ADDRESS ME AGAIN UNTIL I ASK YOU TO DO SO!"

I hauled ass over to the line, stood on the feet, and looked straight ahead. I still didn't know what Gunnery Sergeant Thornton looked like—she'd hadn't been in my sight line, and I wasn't going to try to sneak a look—but her voice was huge, deep, resonant, and with a carrying power I'd never heard before.

I came to think of it as the voice of God, Marine Corps Division.

After we got sorted out and in a semblance of a line, a Sergeant Major named Gunnett stepped in front of us and said, "Reee-cruits, this is Marine Corps Recruit Depot Parris Island, home to 100 percent of female Marine Corps recruits. You are about to undergo thirteen weeks of training in order to qualify as a member of the greatest military corps on earth. Most organizations that recruit you try not to scare you off, but here in the Marine Corps, we believe in honor, duty, and truth, so I will not lie to you: this will be thirteen weeks of hell. We will train you within an inch of your life, physically, mentally, and morally, and if you do not meet *every* requirement, you will be told to leave and you will *not* become a U.S. Marine, which means you will *not* receive the highest honor that can be bestowed upon you. The Marine Corps motto is 'Semper fidelis,' which means 'always faithful,' and you better believe that we are that, and more! You will be divided into training platoons by your drill instructors. Follow instructions to the letter and *never* believe that 'your way' is the best way to do things, because for you there is the right way, the wrong way, and the Marine Corps way!"

She paused for effect and said, "Drill instructors, form your platoons! Welcome to hell, ladies!"

We got shoved into order by the DIs and sent off to do all the business of becoming Marines. I didn't need a haircut—mine was already regulation—but I still needed to do all the other shit, which consisted of being hurried from one place to another so that we could wait. Then we were "inspected, detected, and injected" (my thanks to Arlo Guthrie—you remember Alice?) and hauled off to our squad bay, where we learned to make up our rack and lots of other interesting stuff, like how to brush our teeth.

We went for the initial strength test, a real joke for me. (Flexed-arm hang for twelve seconds, forty-four crunches in two minutes, one-and-a-half-mile run in fifteen minutes? Was this supposed to be a test or a warm-up?) Until our senior DI, Gunnery Sergeant Angela Thornton, began screaming at me for dogging it, which was when it got real serious.

> Gunnery Sergeant Thornton: REEE-CRUIT, DID YOU MAX YOUR IST? OR WAS THAT JUST A JOKE FOR YOU?" (*I never did figure out how Gunnery Sergeant Thornton could read my mind, but she could.*)
> Me: Ma'am, this recruit passed all the requirements, ma'am!
> GST: DID I ASK YOU ABOUT THE MOTHER-LOVING REQUIREMENTS, REEE-CRUIT? DID YOU MAX THE INITIAL STRENGTH TEST?
> Me: Ma'am, this recruit did not max the IST, ma'am!
> GST: WHY THE HELL NOT, REEE-CRUIT? WERE YOU TRYING TO BE SELF-EFFACING, OR ARE YOU JUST A WEASEL WAITING TO LET YOUR TEAMMATES DOWN BY FUCKING UP AT A CRUCIAL MOMENT?
> Me: Ma'am, this recruit did not wish to discomfit her fellow recruits or appear to be grandstanding, ma'am!
> GST: DID YOU UNDERSTAND THAT THE IST WAS DESIGNED TO SEE WHAT YOU COULD ACTUALLY DO, REEE-CRUIT? BECAUSE THAT SOUNDS LIKE A FUCKING WEASEL TALKING!

Me: Ma'am, this recruit was ignorant of the purpose of the IST, ma'am! This recruit requests permission to take the IST again, ma'am!

GST: WHAT A NOVEL FUCKING IDEA, REEE-CRUIT! LET'S *ALL* DO IT AGAIN!

Me, *in my head*: Oh, shit.

After our repeat of the initial strength test, it wasn't only Gunnery Sergeant Thornton who didn't like gingers—everybody in Training Platoon 4004 didn't like them either, especially one from Battle Creek, Michigan.

Oh, yeah, I did 107 crunches in two minutes, did forty-four pull-ups (it was underhand grip, so it was easier), and ran one and a half miles in 8:27 (a 2:45 pace per half-mile).

Which still did not please Gunnery Sergeant Thornton. She expressed her displeasure at the volume of a squadron of F/A-18s taking off from the deck of the USS *Nimitz*, which, combined with her physical stature, left me almost intimidated.

Gunnery Sergeant Thornton was 6'2" or 6'3", around 200 very solid pounds, with shoulders like a really good linebacker, and the biggest hands that I had ever seen on a womyn. She also had very thick wrists, which experience had taught me meant serious physical strength. The Gunnery Sergeant was Black with strong features, especially a nose that looked like an ax blade rising from the center of her face (the nose showed evidence of being broken a time or three, as did the gold front tooth she sported). Her hair was very short, a real Marine Corps haircut, and she had dark-brown eyes that missed absolutely nothing. Her demeanor was forbidding, with a serious can of whup-ass roiling just below the surface.

I thought that she was the best example of a professional person that I'd ever seen. She reminded me of my mom and my *zayde* when they were going to court: organized, well-prepared, serious as cancer, and ready to do battle with anyone who crossed their path.

She also reminded me of Square Peg before a game.

I was enthralled by this person who would abuse me for thirteen weeks, pushing me beyond my physical, emotional, and mental limits. Maybe it was Stockholm syndrome, maybe it was infatuation, but probably it was just that she reminded me of the Great Pumpkin, only ten years later. I tried not to stare, watching her out of the corner of my eye, but once we fell out into formation, well, it was another shitstorm.

Gunnery Sergeant Thornton: Ginger, what the hell are you looking at? Have you been eyeballing me?

Me: Gunnery Sergeant, this recruit has been admiring your professionalism, ma'am!

GST: REEE-CRUIT, WHAT THE FUCK DO YOU KNOW ABOUT PROFESSIONALISM?

Me: Gunnery Sergeant, my family are all professionals, so when I see it in others, I admire it, Gunnery Sergeant!

GST: ARE THEY PROFESSIONAL *SOLDIERS*, GINGER?

Me: No, Gunnery Sergeant, they are lawyers and doctors! (*OK, I knew that was wrong as soon as I said it, but there it was.*)

GST: ARE YOU SAYING WHAT PROFESSIONAL SOLDIERS DO IS THE SAME AS WHAT SISSY-ASSED LAWYERS AND MOTHER-LOVING DOCTORS DO, REEE-CRUIT?

Me: Uh, no, Gunnery Sergeant, but, uh, well—

GST: DROP AND GIVE ME TWENTY, REEE-CRUIT!

I got used to that rather quickly, since Gunnery Sergeant Thornton said it at least ten times a day, sometimes more if I was particularly fucking up, and everything that I did was fucking up, even if it was right, because as far as the Gunnery Sergeant was concerned, I could do no right.

Marching, making my rack, polishing my boots, policing the parade ground, it was "Ginger, drop and give me twenty!"—that was the only thing I heard. Notice that I said *was* the only thing I heard, not *seemed like* the only thing I heard—all my platoon mates and even the other DIs noticed that the Gunnery Sergeant was really dogging me. It was like I was the proverbial redheaded stepchild (pun intended), and she was the wicked stepmother. The only person in history who had it harder was Cinderella—and she at least got to go to the ball with a handsome prince.

I got to go to the obstacle course.

But weird things happen when you're a freak, especially when you are built for speed and strength beyond what is natural or normal for someone of your gender and size. (Who am I trying to kid? I was stronger than 99 percent of the guys at boot camp.) So the obstacle course was where the course of my boot camp changed.

We got there (by running), got the walking tour of the layout (it was huge and really tough, especially the climbing parts), and then were told that we'd be running through it in pairs (for practice, not an official time).

I was sent off with Natalie Marchand, the least physically capable womyn in our platoon. Nat was my height and round like me, but her only real muscle was between her ears—she was probably as smart as my brothers (except Eggy/Mo, since nobody was that smart). She was terrified, especially about the wall and the wire crawl, where you got to crawl under barbed wire while they fired rounds over your head (probably blanks, but this was the Marine Corps, so who really knew?). I told her not to worry, and then we were shoved off.

"Go as fast as you can and don't worry about me," Nat said. "This is practice. Just go practice." She pushed me ahead, so I ran as fast as I could.

Which turned out to be mucho fast. There wasn't one obstacle that even slowed me down. I saw observers clicking watches and shaking their heads, and I started to get a fairly large ego boost, right up until I heard Gunnery Sergeant Thornton begin yelling at Nat. I was crawling under the second round of wire when I heard, "COME ON, REEE-CRUIT, GET YOUR ROUND ASS UP AND OVER THAT WALL! IF YOU CRY, YOU'RE GOING HOME, BUBBLE BUTT! GET UP THAT WALL!"

I was still a dumbass about the corps, but I knew one thing for certain: Marines do not leave other Marines behind, even during a practice run through the obstacle course. I crawled a wide circle under the wire, cleared it, and jumped up to run the course in reverse.

It felt like my feet didn't even touch the ground.

There were observers trying to turn me around, but I ignored them and just ran like the devil was chasing me. I got back to the wall, vaulted up, and looked down at Natalie Marchand trying to climb the rope. She was shaking so bad I could feel it at the top of the wall, so I said, "Nat, did you take your antiseizure medicine this morning? Need a shot of tequila to calm yourself? Thinking about that hunky Marine that serves the soup in the mess?"

She looked up at me and said, "I think it's the three pots of coffee I drank at breakfast," and I knew we were going to be OK. I smiled and said, "Grab the rope and hang on, Nat. Wrap your legs around it." She did what I asked, and I hauled her up the wall hand over hand. When she got to the top, there was dead silence—even the DIs were silent. Nat shook my hand and tried to thank me, but I said, "Later, Marine. Let's run!"

And we did. I really didn't have to help her with anything the rest of the way, although I did keep my hand on her butt when we crawled under the wire so that she didn't get her ass shot off. We got to the end of the course, and the rest our platoon cheered. Nat and I hugged and did a little dance. Jessie Coleman, another of our platoon mates, said, "G, my brother won the Oklahoma state powerlifting championships, and he could'nta done that! And the way you ran! Lord Almighty, that was the damndest thing I've ever seen!"

Our celebration was short-lived. "ATTENTION ON DECK!" a very familiar voice said.

We all snapped to attention and stood like statues. Gunnery Sergeant Thornton came right up to me and said, "FIRST, YOU LEFT YOUR FELLOW MARINE BEHIND, AND THEN YOU DISOBEYED DIRECT ORDERS FROM SUPERIOR OFFICERS TO RECOVER HER, REEE-CRUIT! YOU ARE HEADED TO THE BRIG FOR THAT LITTLE STUNT, AND THEN YOU ARE OUT OF THE MARINE CORPS! DO YOU READ ME, GINGER?"

I started to say something but bit it back just in time. I came really close to picking the Gunnery Sergeant up and throwing her about a mile down into the shooting range, but I bit that back, too, and stood there at attention, seething with rage and impotent to do anything about it. The Gunnery Sergeant didn't know it, but she was very close to going to sick bay that day.

But it seemed she did see it, because she said, "YOU GOT SOMETHING TO SAY, GINGER? IF YOU GOT SOMETHING TO SAY, JUST SAY IT, YOU PANSY-ASS, CHICKENSHIT REEE-CRUIT!"

She was right in front of me in her Smokey Bear DI hat, huge, menacing, and just as fired up as me, but that didn't deter me. If I really was leaving the Marine Corps, then I wasn't going quietly.

"GUNNERY SERGEANT, THIS REEE-CRUIT REQUESTS PERMISSION TO SPEAK FREELY!" I said.

"Go right ahead, Ginger," Gunnery Sergeant Thornton said. "It isn't going to matter in about sixty days, anyway. You're gone, reee-cruit."

I looked her right in the eye, absolutely not done in Marine Corps basic training, and said, "GUNNERY SERGEANT, THIS REEE-CRUIT DOES NOT CARE IF NATIONAL COMMAND AUTHORITY HIMSELF ORDERS HER TO STOP—SHE WILL NOT LEAVE ANOTHER MARINE BEHIND! DUTY REQUIRES SACRIFICING ONESELF FOR THE GOOD OF THE CORPS, AND MARINES DO NOT LEAVE EACH OTHER BEHIND, GUNNERY SERGEANT!"

"BOOYAH!" the platoon said.

Gunnery Sergeant Thornton got in my face, so close-up that I could smell her toothpaste. Her dark-brown eyes bored into mine, but there was no hatred or anger in those eyes. There was a fierce glee and respect, but no anger.

It all became perfectly clear: the whole thing was a test, just like those the Great Pumpkin, Coach Horn, Coach Garvey, and Your Fucking Highness had put me through. Gunnery Sergeant Thornton was looking for greatness, and real Marines, and toughness, and all those things that really great coaches look for in their athletes. The whole time, she had been testing me, trying to see if I was real or a fucking poser.

She looked in my eyes and said in a near-whisper, "Good answer, Glickstien. No Marine leaves another behind, especially one as smart as Marchand." She didn't smile, but her face wasn't contorted in anger either. "NOW, DROP AND GIVE ME TWENTY, GINGER! WHAT THE HELL DID YOU LEAVE YOUR PLATOON MATE BEHIND FOR IN THE FIRST PLACE?"

I did my twenty, and she said, "NOW GIVE ME TWENTY FOR DISOBEYING ORDERS!" so I did twenty more, and she said, "NOW GIVE ME TWENTY FOR EYEBALLING ME!" so I did twenty more, and she said, "NOW GIVE ME TWENTY FOR NOT LETTING MARCHAND PULL HERSELF UP THE WALL!" so I did twenty more, and she said, "NOW GIVE ME TWENTY FOR HOLDING UP THE REST OF THE PLATOON!" and I did twenty more perfect push-ups, for one hundred total. Gunnery Sergeant Thornton cracked a cold and evil smile and said, "NOW, GET ON YOUR FEET AND LEAD THE WHOLE PLATOON THROUGH THE OBSTACLE COURSE AGAIN, REEE-CRUIT!"

I think that she thought I was going to be completely gassed, but I routinely did a thousand push-ups a day, so one hundred weren't going to gas me at all. I jumped up, ran over to the rest of the platoon, said, "Follow me and Marchand!" and raced off. Nat ran with me as we led the platoon through the course. When we got to the wall, I ran up the rope to the top, then belayed the line while Marchand walked up. (Yeah, I may have helped her a bit—what's the use of being abnormally strong if you don't use it?) As she was coming up, I said, "Pinder, Angle, Kalas, you guys get up first! Then Hainrihar, Mitchell, Bugliesi, Seal, de Boer, and Turnage! We need to get two teams going so we can all get up now!"

Once Marchand hit the top, I said, "Nat, get Pinder, Angle, and Kalas down so we can help everybody down. Once there are eight down, you take off, then have Pinder and Angle follow you with eight each. You know who needs to go where—go from slowest to fastest. Kalas stays with me until we've guided everybody down, then we'll haul ass to catch up. Remind everybody at the wire to keep their asses down so nobody gets hung up or gets a bullet in the ass."

Nat looked at me and said, "Roger that, G!" She grinned and then jumped down, saying "Pinder, Angle, Kalas, on me! First eight down, form a pathfinder squad on me!" She relayed my orders as we proceeded to smoothly get everybody over the wall. Our platoon formed up into squads and followed Marchand's squad, but because we were in the right echelons, we all arrived at the last under-the-wire crawl at exactly the right time.

I had raced ahead of my squad to exhort my fellow recruits to crawl properly, right until Kayla Shanley fell off one of the obstacles and broke her leg. Shonda Kalas yelled, "G, Shanley is down! She can't move!"

I ran back, took one look at Shanley's crooked leg, and said, "Kalas, take the rest of the squad through the wire, asses down! I'm bringing Shanley. Get going!" The rest of the squad ran for the wire and began crawling through, but Kalas waited for me. I scooped Shanley up and said, "Kayla, this is going to hurt" and tore off for the wire. When I got there, I sent Kalas through, dropped on the ground, grabbed Shanley by the collar of her BDUs, and crawled through the wire while dragging her along. We got to the end of the wire, and Kalas dragged Shanley out, then we both took an arm and hoisted her up. I said, "Kayla, this is really going to hurt," and we lifted her up and ran for the finish line.

When we got there, the platoon was waiting. So was Gunnery Sergeant Thornton, Sergeant Major Gunnett, and a Colonel we didn't know. I saw them and said, "CORPSMAN, WE NEED A CORPSMAN HERE!"

They were waiting right behind the DIs and took Shanley from us. They laid her on a stretcher, and she said, "Semper fi, Marines!" even though she looked like death warmed over. We all "semper-fied" her until Gunnery Sergeant Thornton said, "ATTENTION ON DECK! FORM PLATOON! GLICKSTIEN, FRONT AND CENTER!"

We stood at attention as the DIs and the Colonel looked at us with serious faces. Finally, the Colonel, a tall, good-looking womyn in desert BDUs with "Benavidez" on her name tape, said, "Reee-cruit Glickstien, I have a couple of questions." The conversation that followed was a bit bizarre, since Colonels in the Marine Corps do not usually address lowly recruits. (You may have noticed that I always write it "reee-cruit" instead of "recruit," but that's the way everybody in the Marines says it, even general officers. I still don't know why, but even Gunnery Sergeant Thornton, who was from the north side of Chicago, said it that way. Welcome to the idiosyncrasies of the Corps.)

Colonel Benavidez: Why did you drag that reee-cruit under the wire?

Me: MA'AM, NO MARINE LEAVES ANOTHER MARINE BEHIND, MA'AM!

Col. B: Weren't you aware that you could simply call for a corpsman and leave her, due to the unsafe nature of your action?

Me: MA'AM, THIS RECRUIT WAS IGNORANT OF THAT COURSE OF ACTION, MA'AM!

Col. B: You weren't informed of this before you ran the obstacle course?

Me, *realizing that if I said no I'd be throwing Gunnery Sergeant Thornton under the bus*: MA'AM, THIS RECRUIT REGRETS THAT SHE HAS A FAULTY MEMORY CONCERNING THIS ACTION, MA'AM! (*Hey, it wasn't a lie—I was trying hard to remember it a different way than not being told.*)

Col. B: So you forgot that you could leave a clearly injured reee-cruit behind without penalty and jeopardized yourself and the rest of the platoon—the whole op, really—so that you could grandstand some hero shit? Is that accurate, reee-cruit?

Me, *knowing that I was probably fucking up royally*: MA'AM, THIS RECRUIT REGRETS
TO INFORM YOU THAT YOUR CONTENTION IS INACCURATE, MA'AM!
Col. B: Are you really contradicting me, reee-cruit?
Me, *plainly, absolutely fucking up*: MA'AM, YES, MA'AM!
Col. B: Reee-cruit, why is it that you were not jeopardizing the platoon and your mission?
Me, *thinking my Marine career was now clearly in the rearview mirror, so what the fuck*:
MA'AM, THIS RECRUIT REQUESTS PERMISSION TO DEMONSTRATE
THE INACCURACY OF YOUR STATEMENT, MA'AM!
Col. B: This ought to be good. Very well, proceed with your demonstration.

So I turned to Gunnery Sergeant Thornton and said, "Gunnery Sergeant, may I have your permission to involve you in this demonstration?" She looked totally nonplussed, perhaps because I had just taken responsibility for something she hadn't done. She looked at me and nodded, so I stepped over and said, "Keep your legs perfectly straight up and down and knees locked, Gunnery Sergeant."

Before she could protest or ask a question, I bent down and grabbed her legs above the knee and lifted her to the level of my chest. I threw her into the air and caught her feet at my shoulder level. "Keep your legs locked and stand on my hands, Gunnery Sergeant," I said. When her feet were set, I lifted her over my head so that she was standing on my hands. I locked my right arm in place and gripped the bottom of her feet, then removed my left arm from the lift.

Looking the Colonel right in the eye, I did a squat with Gunnery Sergeant Thornton over my head and standing on my right hand.

In fact, I did 10 full squats, and while I did, I said, "MA'AM, THIS RECRUIT BELIEVES THAT AS LONG AS SHE WAS NOT HIT BY ENEMY FIRE, SHE COULD HAVE PULLED RECRUIT SHANLEY ACROSS THE DMZ IN SOUTH KOREA, MA'AM!" (What the fuck, right? I was already giving a bird Colonel shit—in for a penny, in for a pound.)

There was dead silence until Colonel Benavidez said, "Please put the Gunnery Sergeant down." I stopped at the bottom of my squat and lowered Gunnery Sergeant Thornton to the ground. She stepped off my hand, and I stood back up at attention, wondering how I was going to explain my getting kicked out of the Marine Corps before I got in when Colonel Benavidez said, "I stand corrected, Marine. It's clear that you were simply following the Marine Corps way by not leaving your platoon behind. Well done." She turned to Sergeant Major Gunnett and Gunnery Sergeant Thornton and said, "Carry on, Sergeant Major, Gunnery Sergeant. And call me when you get to pugil sticks with this platoon."

The Colonel walked away, and the Freak of 4004 Platoon, Hotel Company, Third Recruit Training Battalion, was born. Word of my show-off feat of strength spread like a viral video of Kim Kardashian naked, apparently even into the male command that ran side by side with our training. I became the *de facto* leader of my training platoon and company, and the most popular recruit at Parris Island. Everybody talked about what I did, but it apparently made Gunnery Sergeant Thornton crazy, because I caught more hell than ever.

She ran me over hill and dale (and parking lot and golf course and beach and anything else available), made me do so many push-ups that I thought I was learning to be a professional push-up artist, and stood me at attention so often that I could do it while asleep with my eyes open.

She also had me do a fun thing called "dig a cube." It went like this.

My squad was responsible for policing the parade ground one day, and we scoured that puppy until even the dirt was clean. We stood at ease until Gunnery Sergeant Thornton came out to inspect our work, standing at attention until she gave us the OK to go to evening chow. It was cheeseburger night—my favorite—and we were all looking forward to it because we figured we might also have chili (everybody likes chili cheeseburgers, right?). Everything was going well, until the gunnery sergeant unwrapped a stick of gum and threw the wrapper on the ground over her shoulder.

Uh-oh, no way is this going to end well, I thought.

Right again, Freak.

The Gunnery Sergeant walked over in front of US and pretended to notice the gum wrapper. She pointed at it and said, "GINGER, WHAT THE HELL IS THAT ON MY PARADE GROUND?"

"Gunnery Sergeant, it is a gum wrapper, ma'am," I said.

She jumped right in my face and said, "WHAT THE HELL IS A MOTHER-LOVING GUM WRAPPER DOING ON MY PARADE GROUND, REEE-CRUIT? WEREN'T YOUR ORDERS TO POLICE THE PARADE GROUND?"

At this point, I was fucked either way. If I affirmed my orders, she'd be on me for disobeying orders, and if I pointed out that she had dropped the wrapper, she'd be all over me for lying (since, by definition, DIs were God in Marine Corps basic training, and thus perfect). This was your classic "fucked if I do, fucked if I don't" scenario. I decided to take responsibility and get it over with.

"Gunnery Sergeant, this recruit regrets doing an inadequate job of policing the parade ground. As squad leader, this recruit accepts responsibility for not completing the mission, ma'am."

Gunnery Sergeant Thornton cracked a thin evil smile and said, "Very well, reee-cruit. I want you to go get your trenching tool from your squad bay, on the double." I ran off to get the trenching tool, a multipurpose piece of equipment that was really a short-handled shovel.

When I got back, the squad was standing at ease, while Gunnery Sergeant Thornton was actually sitting in an office chair set in the shade from the barracks. She nodded benignly, and my stomach fell; this was not an easy womyn, and she was almost smiling at me. I felt like an antelope being eyed by the head lioness of a very large pride of lions.

"Ree-cruit, I want you to dig a perfect three-foot cube and bury that gum wrapper in it. It must be precisely three feet on each side, or you will have to dig it again. Am I understood?" Again, she almost smiled at me, causing all my sphincters to contract.

"Gunnery Sergeant, yes, Gunnery Sergeant!" I said.

"Good. The rest of the squad and I will supervise the activity. Begin." She lounged back in the chair, and the rest of my squad stood there, unable to help or look away.

So I dug a three-foot cube in the hot South Carolina sun. With a short-handled shovel. In packed earth that had been trod on by thousands of Marines. The ground's resemblance to concrete was purely coincidental.

Gunnery Sergeant Thornton lolled in her chair, had ice tea brought out for herself and my squad, and generally had a high old time while I dug my ass off like a crazed prairie dog trying to escape a hawk. I still wasn't sure how I was going to measure this cube, but the Gunnery Sergeant had a yardstick brought out to me when it looked like I was close to done. She didn't say anything, but I figured that if it wasn't perfect, she'd bitch me to death, or make me re-dig the whole thing, so I spent some time squaring up the cube and making it, well, perfect. After three hours of digging, I finally stood beside the hole and dropped the gum wrapper in.

Gunnery Sergeant Thornton got off her chair, measured the cube, and nodded at me. "Well done, reee-cruit. This is a perfect cube. Now, cover up that trash so we can get some chow." By then it was almost 9:00 p.m., and chow call was long over, but I figured the Gunnery Sergeant could pretty much walk on water while she was our DI, so food wasn't going to be a problem. I also wished for some of that iced tea, because I was completely parched, but when she didn't offer, I figured it was Sahara time for me, so I started shoveling the dirt back in the cube. My entire body protested. ("HEY, ASSHOLE, NEED SOME REST HERE! WATER, ANYONE? WHERE'S THE HOT TUB / ICE BATH?") But the Gunnery Sergeant sat back down on her chair and passively watched the sky, so I kept shoveling.

I put the last trenching tool load of dirt in the hole, whacked the dirt down flat and stood at attention, ready for water, chow, and a nice shower.

I was so thirsty that I'd probably have drunk cat piss at that point, and eaten the cat.

Gunnery Sergeant Thornton got up and ambled over to me. She looked at where the hole had been, looked around the completely clean parade ground, took the chewing gum out of her mouth, and said, "Reee-cruit, where is my gum wrapper?"

Oh, shitfuckpisshelldamnmotherfucker. I was pretty sure from her calm demeanor and innocent-sounding question that a shitstorm was about to hit. After all, Marine Corps DIs are not known for their calmness and innocence. No matter what I said was going to be wrong.

Roger that, reee-cruit.

"Gunnery Sergeant, this recruit buried it at the bottom of the cube dug for that purpose, ma'am!"

"WELL, I WANT IT BACK, REEE-CRUIT!"

I turned back to begin digging, but my squad mates beat me to it. They all started scraping out the dirt with their hands while they took turns on the trenching tool. Within twenty minutes, we had the dirt out of the hole and were sifting through it for the gum wrapper. Marie Hainrihar found it and gave it to me. I put it in my pocket, and we filled the hole in. When the dirt was all back in place, we all stood at attention.

I held out the gum wrapper on my palm and said, "GUNNERY SERGEANT, THIS RECRUIT HAS THE WRAPPER YOU REQUESTED, GUNNERY SERGEANT!"

Gunnery Sergeant Thornton took the wrapper, stuck the gum in it, and put the wrapper in her pocket. She looked over the squad and said, "Well done, reee-cruits! Now, haul ass over to the chow hall and draw sandwiches, then double-time it back to your squad bay, shower, and hit your racks. We got a little 15K hike in the morning, so you'd better get all the rest you can. Disss-missed!"

We ran for the chow hall and ate the sandwiches on the run back to the squad bay. I was still eating one when I showered; I drank about three quarts of water and still didn't piss until the next day at noon. We fell into our racks at about 1:35 a.m., and the reveille bugle sounded at zero dark thirty (0530, or 5:30 a.m.) when we all went for a 7.5-kilometer hike with full packs, then turned around and hiked 7.5 kilometers back, after doing PT (physical training, consisting of various torture activities) for an hour.

I drank several large bottles of water, pissed just once, and still felt like I needed an IV transfusion of fluids—but none was offered, so I decided to march my way through it.

And I did. So did all of my platoon. After all, we were trying to be awarded the greatest title in the world: US Marine.

Nobody said it was going to be easy.

Especially with Dracuzilla de Sade as our DI.

Boorah!

CHAPTER 13

M9 Freak

So basic training went on, and Gunnery Sergeant Dracuzilla de Sade (our new nickname sounded so much better than just Thornton) didn't let up on Platoon 4004, or on me. In fact, she got even tougher.

It all ran together, and it's mostly boring to talk about ("Leffttt, leffttt, leffttt-riiight-leffttt" gets pretty old in a fat-ass hurry), but there were three things that stood out: guns, self-defense training, and applied self-defense training. Coupled with the discipline, mental toughness, and sustained level of effort demanded by Gunnery Sergeant Dracuzilla de Sade, these experiences made me who and what I am today.

It is not bragging at all to say that they also made me a basic training legend in the United States Marine Corps.

So guns first. We went to the range and became acquainted with the M16A2 rifle, the standard training weapon of the Marine Corps. (In battle, we were much more likely to carry an M16A4, but that was for real Marines, not reee-cruits. It was rumored that real Marines had better toilet paper, too, but that was just scuttlebutt.) We were instructed by several people, including First Sergeant Gene Glenn, who could shoot the wings off a gnat at two hundred, three hundred, and five hundred meters and then park a round up the gnat's asshole before it hit the ground (direct quote from the First Sergeant: "You don't quibble with a man like that over a little hyperbole unless you want .223-caliber piercings where they don't belong").

The First Sergeant was the biggest badass we'd met thus far (he was really a gifted shot, and anybody with two Silver Stars, a Navy Cross, and two Purple Hearts was, by definition, a badass), until we were introduced to Master Gunnery Sergeant Jan Berkey during our training with the M9 Beretta, the standard Marine Corps sidearm.

The M9 is considered a defensive weapon by the Corps, for a very good reason: if the enemy gets close enough, you can use it like a hammer and hit them on the head with it and run your ass off while calling for artillery or helicopter gunship support. Seriously, it isn't very accurate outside five meters, but it makes up for it by lacking any stopping power.

The grips suck, too, especially if your hands get sweaty (think about where we've been fighting lately and assess the possibility that your hands will get sweaty—134 percent chance, right?).

In any case, Master Gunnery Sergeant Berkey was the reigning Marine Corps champion with the M9, and she'd also won the Interservice Pistol Championship, the NRA National Pistol Championship, and the World Pistol Championship in a single year. If there was a Super Bowl of pistols, she'd be Mean Joe Greene of the 1970s Pittsburgh Steelers.

Master Gunnery Sergeant Berkey had also served two tours in Afghanistan and one in Iraq, as well as being the only womyn to ever serve as an instructor at the Navy SEAL school.

Legend had it that she could shoot different birds out of the air at the same time with M9s in each hand or shoot the mites off a gnat's ass.

This was one bad motherfucking Marine.

She looked it, too. Six feet tall, broader shoulders than Gunnery Sergeant Dracuzilla de Sade, no neck (her traps came right up to her ears, which is theoretically impossible for a womyn), and a big round butt that looked like you could break bricks on it. She was slab-armed and had long, almost-delicate hands. Her face looked like a big pumpkin, round and ridged here and there, and her hair was a crazy shade of orange that couldn't be called red.

I fell in love right there because she looked like a larger version of the Great Pumpkin.

I had done all right with the M16 (all right, false modesty alert; I was the best in my company, and one of the best in the battalion), but I decided that I wanted to be more like Master Gunnery Sergeant Berkey, so I paid special attention to her pistol instructions.

After giving us the whole rundown, she made sure that we had our earmuffs on and then stepped up to the five-meter firing line and said, "This is what it's supposed to look like." The Master Gunnery Sergeant's M9 came up, and she loosed a fusillade of bullets downrange at the unsuspecting target. When the gun's slide clicked open on an empty clip, she pushed the button that brought the target back.

We all gaped in awe at the single hole in the center of the target—it was only slightly wider than an actual 9-mm round—because the Master Gunnery Sergeant had hit the same hole every time.

Suitably cowed by her perfection, we stepped back to our own lines to begin firing. When my turn came, I decided to shoot as fast as I could and see how I compared to the Master Gunnery Sergeant, so I settled myself in the proper shooting stance and loosed off an entire magazine, just hoping to hit the target every time.

I shredded the bull's-eye into a ragged hole, with no holes outside the center.

Both Gunnery Sergeant Dracuzilla de Sade and Master Gunnery Sergeant Jan Berkey seemed to just appear at my shooting station. They both silently inspected the target and simultaneously turned their blazing eyes on me.

"REEE-CRUIT, WHERE THE HELL DID YOU LEARN TO SHOOT?" Gunnery Sergeant Dracuzilla de Sade asked.

"Gunnery Sergeant, I learned to shoot in the United States Marine Corps, ma'am!" I said.

"BULLLLL-SHIT, REEE-CRUIT! I MEAN, WHEN DID YOU LEARN TO SHOOT?" the Gunnery Sergeant said.

"Gunnery Sergeant, I learned to shoot approximately 20 minutes ago here at the Marine Corps firing range, Gunnery Sergeant!" I said.

"QUIT DICKING ME AROUND, REEE-CRUIT! WHEN WAS THE LAST TIME YOU SHOT ANY TYPE OF FIREARM BEFORE TODAY?" Gunnery Sergeant Dracuzilla de Sade asked.

"Gunnery Sergeant, this recruit has never discharged any firearm before today, Gunnery Sergeant!" I said.

"Really?" Master Gunnery Sergeant Jan Berkey said, her voice as soft as rain on spring flowers. She looked me directly in the eye, and I said, "Master Gunnery Sergeant, that is affirmative. I learned to shoot from you, Master Gunnery Sergeant Berkey, right here at the PI range, ma'am!"

She took my M9, dropped the clip, slid a full one in the butt of the pistol, and handed it back to me. She ran a target down to the ten-meter line and said, "Do it again."

I racked a round in the chamber, took position, and loosed all eight shots within five seconds. Master Sergeant Berkey just looked down at the target and said, "Well, fuck a duck, reee-cruit, you appear to be Roy Hobbs. Everybody else carry on. Roy, Gunnery Sergeant Thornton, will you please come with me?"

We all walked down the back of the firing line until we came to the last three firing stands, which were empty. Master Gunnery Sergeant Berkey set up two targets and ran them down to the ten-meter line. She handed me an M9 and told me to clear it (make sure it was empty, so I didn't shoot off a tit—mine or somebody else's). Once the weapon was cleared, she handed me a full clip (all fifteen this time) and said, "Once you're loaded, shoot at each target alternately until the clip is empty, beginning with the right-hand target. Shoot as fast as you can but be deliberate enough to put each round on target. We clear?"

"Yes, Master Gunnery Sergeant Berkey!" I said.

She smiled and nodded as she dropped her earmuffs over her ears.

I racked a round into the chamber, took my stance, and commenced shooting. Within ten seconds, I emptied the pistol. When it racked open, I dropped the clip, made sure the weapon was safe (y'know, didn't have any rounds hung up so I didn't shoot myself in the ass), set the weapon down on the shooting bench, and stepped back.

All bull's-eyes again.

Both the Gunnery Sergeants looked at me with totally blank faces, which is about as close as a Marine Gunnery Sergeant who is a DI at basic training gets to jumping up and down and yelling, "Yippee-ky-yaaaa! I just won the lottery, you poor motherfuckers!"

The Master Gunnery Sergeant ran a target down twenty meters (about 65.5 feet) and said, "Do it again."

I fired off fifteen rounds and hit fourteen dead nuts in the center, with one a bit high and to the right. Master Gunnery Sergeant Berkey pointed to the off-center hit and said, "Your first shot." She looked at me, and I realized it was a question. "Master Gunnery Sergeant, it was my first shot. I corrected for the distance, Master Gunnery Sergeant."

She looked at me, this absolutely perfect example of the US Marine Corps, and said, "When we're alone and shooting, let's cut out all the basic bullshit, shall we, Marine? Address me with respect and I'll forget that you're a reee-cruit, OK?"

You could have knocked me over with a feather. The most recognizable Marine alive had just called me a Marine. It was one of those "Earth to Glinka, come in, Glinka" moments, because I was flying high. It was the Great Pumpkin all over again.

So I nodded and said, "Yes, Master Gunnery Sergeant Berkey?"

She nodded back and said something to Gunnery Sergeant Dracuzilla de Sade, who nodded back and stepped over to the firing station next to mine. She unholstered her own M9 and prepared to shoot. Master Gunnery Sergeant Berkey handed me a fresh clip and said, "Now we're going to see how you change distance. I'm putting a target at ten meters and one at twenty meters, and I want you to alternate shooting at them. Which one should you shoot first?"

"The near one, Master Gunnery Sergeant Berkey."

"Why? And before you answer, call me Gunny. Your way takes too long." She didn't smile, but I still realized she was joking with me—again, not typical behavior for a Marine Corps DI or basic instructor. So I smiled and said, "The closer the enemy is, the more of a threat they are, Gunny."

"Good, Marine. Prepare to fire." I picked up my pistol and took my stance. Right before the Master Gunnery Sergeant said, "Commence," Gunnery Sergeant Dracuzilla de Sade started firing, ideally to unnerve me and throw my aim off.

It didn't work.

I emptied the clip and had all bull's-eyes again. When the gun locked open, I took my earmuffs off and looked at Master Gunnery Sergeant Berkey. She looked back at me and said, "Question, Marine?"

"Gunny, that second target isn't at twenty meters—it's at least at thirty-five meters, probably forty. Was that a trick, like with Gunnery Sergeant Thornton trying to distract me?"

She did laugh then, a sound I never expected to hear at Marine Corps boot camp, unless it was derisive in nature. It was like looking at the statue of President Lincoln at the Memorial in Washington and having it say, "Four score and seven years ago, our forefathers brought forth on this continent..."

"Glickstien, you are going to be one handful of Marine," Master Gunnery Sergeant Berkey said. She nodded at Gunnery Sergeant Dracuzilla de Sade, who walked over and took something from her, then walked behind my left shoulder. The Master Gunnery Sergeant moved behind my right shoulder and stuck a full clip out in front of me. She said, "Just one last little fun test, Marine. Gunnery Sergeant Thornton and I are going to toss some things in the air, and we want you to try to hit one. Don't worry if you're unsuccessful. Just try for now. OK? Am I clear?"

"Crystal, Gunny. Try to hit what you and Gunnery Sergeant Thornton throw in the air."

"Exactly," she said. And they threw eight glass balls in the air.

I whipped the M9 up and fired eight times.

No glass balls hit the ground.

"Motthherr-fucckkerr," Gunnery Sergeant Dracuzilla de Sade said softly, wonder evident in her tone.

"We are gonna kick the Army's ass next year," Master Gunnery Sergeant Berkey said. "We got us a got-damned secret weapon named Glickstien."

Life was good.

I dropped the clip from the M9, ejected the round still in the chamber, and bent to police my brass (that's service-speak for "Pick up the empty shell casings").

"Belay that, Marine. I'll pick up the brass," Master Gunnery Sergeant Berkey said.

I turned to her and asked, "Gunny? Master Gunnery Sergeant, that's my job."

One of the best pistol shots in the world looked at me and said, "It'll be my pleasure to pick up the brass, Marine. I've got to think for a bit, and picking up brass always gets me to a Zen place.

You and Gunnery Sergeant Thornton have got to hustle to chow and catch up with your platoon. You run along and I'll see you next time." The Master Gunnery Sergeant then stuck her hand out for me to shake.

I about fainted, pissed my pants, and came all at the same time. I wasn't yet a Marine, but I knew that this was *never* done; no one of the rank and status of Master Gunnery Sergeant Berkey *ever* shook the hand of a lowly reee-cruit (I still can't stop doing it).

I shot a quick glance at Gunnery Sergeant Dracuzilla de Sade, and she gave me the briefest of nods, so I put my hand out and shook with the Master Gunnery Sergeant, which was about the greatest honor I'd had up to that point. Her grip was strong and firm, but not overpowering, and she looked me right in the eye when she shook. I saw then what it meant to be a Marine—there was honor, duty, and sacrifice in those eyes, as well as the strength to be a female Marine in an essentially male world. She reminded me even more of the Great Pumpkin then, and I resolved that this would be my role model for my Marine career.

We stopped shaking, and Gunnery Sergeant Dracuzilla de Sade and I double-timed it for chow. We were almost there when she stopped and whipped around to face me. She brought her face down as close as she could to mine—her Smokey Bear hat hit me square in the bridge of the nose—and said, "Reee-cruit, this doesn't change a damned thing about my approach to you or your training. If you think that this is going to give you some special treatment, you are sadly mistaken. I'm still going to scramble your eggs every which way to make you into a Marine, which you are *not* yet. Am I clear, reee-cruit?"

"GUNNERY SERGEANT, YOU ARE AS CLEAR AS CRYSTAL, GUNNERY SERGEANT!" I said in my best almost-Marine voice.

She wasn't fucking kidding either. If anything, basic got harder for me because of my ability with the pistol. No one cut me any slack of any kind except Master Gunnery Sergeant Berkey, and that was only when we were shooting (more on that later).

As for Gunnery Sergeant Dracuzilla de Sade, well, she really "scrambled my eggs" when it came to the self-defense training.

She brought in the men.

CHAPTER 14

Self-Defense Freak

Gunnery Sergeant Dracuzilla de Sade let me stew for a while, but then came the day when we began self-defense training.

My meat had arrived, and I was ravenous.

I was already primed by my prior training to be good at this phase, and I did not disappoint.

When we started, there were female trainers, but Gunnery Sergeant Dracuzilla de Sade was the primary trainer, and she was very, very good. We went through the basics and then started to really train with each other.

I put everybody in my platoon away like they were 90-year-olds who'd drunk a bottle of Jack Daniel's. The Gunnery Sergeant then expanded my horizons to include the entire company, with exactly the same results. She finally brought in all the toughest reee-cruits in the entire training command, including those in platoons about to graduate, but there was simply no one who could stand up to me. I'm not trying to brag, but it was like a really good rocket football player going against an NFL All-Pro, except the NFLer might have mercy.

I didn't.

I didn't intentionally hurt anyone (although some people got hurt), and I wasn't cruel, but I wasn't letting anyone beat me either. It really wasn't fair—I had extensive martial arts training and was also the strongest female in the training command, so it really wasn't a surprise that I dominated in self-defense.

The real fun started when I knocked everybody I faced off the platform with the pugil sticks. Nobody lasted more than four seconds with me (sorry, this sounds like braggadocio, but as my *zayde* always said, it ain't braggin' if it happened), so Gunnery Sergeant Dracuzilla de Sade decided to bring in the big gun.

She got on the fighting platform with me.

It looked like a mismatch from the start—big, strong, fully trained, and experienced Marine DI with a smaller, weaker, untrained, and inexperienced reee-cruit. And so it was.

Gunnery Sergeant Thornton never had a chance.

The instant the DI who was running the pugil sticks said "Fight!" I lunged forward in a straight thrust (in kendo this is called *tsuki*) and rammed my stick into Dracuzilla's crotch, spun the stick up to strike from low to high through her hip to her neck (a kendo move called *kiri-agi*), and then spun in a full circle, catching the Gunnery Sergeant just under her armpit and knocking her ass over tea cart and off the platform before the proctor could tell me to stop.

Start to finish, the "fight" took about four seconds.

I want to make it clear: This wasn't a Hollywood *An Officer and a Gentleman* moment. It wasn't that we were evenly matched, and my greater passion/integrity/fierceness made me win. The Gunnery

Sergeant had as much chance against me as a tethered goat against a full-grown Bengal tiger. I was dispassionate about the whole affair because I was trained to do this; in this particular case, I was the instructor, because of my training and the gifts given to me by my weird, throwback genes.

But Gunnery Sergeant Dracuzilla de Sade was a U.S. Marine and no quitter, so she staggered up, got back on the fighting platform, and said, "C'mon, reee-cruit, you hit like a girl! Let's really get after it, sissy-pants!"

She was trying to goad me into doing something stupid, so I made it look like I was. I let the pugil stick droop to my right and charged her like I was seriously pissed off.

She did exactly what I expected. Her pugil stick swung down in a short arc toward my left shoulder, and she tried to use her height and weight advantage to knock me down. It was a good strategy, as far as it went, but it was based on faulty assumptions and backfired completely. I dropped the head of my pugil stick all the way to the mat. This turned it completely horizontal and blocked her strike and also positioned me perfectly for *mayoko giri*, a horizontal cut designed to cut completely through the opponent from side to side.

I struck like a mongoose fighting a cobra. I felt the breath gush from the Gunnery Sergeant as I compressed her lungs with the strike, but in kendo one cut flows to another, so without stopping, I spun the stick up and struck her directly on the right ear, once again knocking her tits over ass and off the platform. This time she did a slow-motion cartwheel and landed bonelessly on the ground. It sounded like 200 pounds of potatoes in a sack dropped from a barn loft.

In the silence that followed, I jumped off the platform, threw down the pugil stick, ran to the Gunnery Sergeant, and yanked her protective helmet off. She wasn't unconscious, but it was close. Her eyes were unfocused and sort of crossed, and she looked up at me and said, "Aunt Alice, I really love Jimmy. I wouldn't let him get to second base if I didn't, but everyone laughs at me because he's so short. Why does whiskey taste so good if it's bad for you? Aunt Alice, is it true you can orgasm from intercourse, or is that a myth? How could we elect Monkey-Ears Bush president a second time? Can we go get lunch at Superdawg?"

The Gunnery Sergeant obviously thought that she was back in Chicago (home of Superdawg) and that she was talking to some wise old relative named Aunt Alice. She also had a problem with her timeline—old "Monkey-Ears" hadn't been president for some time (the world still sighs with relief). The real surprise was Gunnery Sergeant Dracuzilla de Sade's voice—it was so soft, mellifluous and girlish that it sounded like a character in a Disney movie. The platoon crowded around until the other DI told us to clear out for the corpsmen, but by then the Gunnery Sergeant was back to herself. She tried to sit up, but I pressed her to the ground and said, "Gunnery Sergeant, please let the corpsmen check you out first. Your head is going to hurt when you sit up, Gunnery Sergeant. Please stay down."

She looked at me and said, "Kee-riist, Glickstien, you are a freak. I've never had anybody, man or womyn, hit me that hard. You looked like you barely swung, and you knocked 209 pounds of Marine tits up and out. What the fuck was that?"

I said, "Gunnery Sergeant, that was years of training and some genetic freakishness."

Just then the corpsman arrived and shouldered me out of the way. I stood up, and our second DI, Staff Sergeant Patricia Rafferty, said, "PLATOON, FORM UP! BACK TO THE SQUAD BAY ON

THE DOUBLE!" so there was no time to say anything else. We took off when the Gunnery Sergeant was sitting up, but she caught my eye for just a minute and gave me a slight nod. I nodded back, but what I noticed was that she didn't look at all discouraged. In fact, she looked like she was deep in thought, at a time when her brains should have been scrambled.

Shithouse mouse, I thought. *She's already planning to get me. What the fuck did I just get myself into?*

The next day the men arrived.

We went out for morning PT, and there was Gunnery Sergeant Dracuzilla de Sade and Staff Sergeant Rafferty, but there were also two male Marines there. One was about 6'1", 185 (very muscular), and blond (had nice blue eyes too), while the other one was about 5'8", 225, and hugely muscular in that real-life-athlete way—he looked like the muscles were earned through doing something, not just pushing iron in some gym. He was dark-haired with funny ears and had a swarthy complexion—his name was Vigg. The blonde guy's name was Clark. Both were plain old sergeants, and neither looked like they were happy to be there.

We did our PT, went for chow, went on a little (eight-kilometer) hike with packs, and came back for more hand-to-hand combat training. We stretched, did some practice routines, and then turned to sparring with a partner.

Vigg was my partner.

I was fairly sure that this was not SOP (standard operating procedure), but it did explain Gunnery Sergeant Dracuzilla de Sade's shit-eating grin when we paired up for judo throws. We were supposed to walk through with no resistance first, and then we'd go half-speed before we met in one-minute matches where the throwing was live. Staff Sergeant Rafferty demonstrated technique for the 3,157th time (can ya tell we'd been doing this a while?), and then we went into the no-resistance phase. It went OK. Vigg just let me throw him, then threw me with the ease and economy that told me he'd done this before. In fact, from the way that he finished the throw, it was apparent that his muscles came from wrestling. And it was then that I placed him.

He was Walter Vigg, the reigning Marine Corps wrestling champion at 97 kilograms (214 pounds).

Shithouse mouse.

We went through the throw about 25 more times, easily throwing with no resistance, and then the staff sergeant said, "Move to half-speed!"

I took one look at Vigg's face and knew that there wasn't going to be any half-speed, so when he told me to throw first, I acted like I was an empty-headed Valley Girl and let him stop my throw and reverse me to the ground. I groaned for effect, like he'd really hurt me, and then attacked him at about 1/100th speed so he could throw me savagely to the ground. I wanted him to relax and think that my prowess had been overrated—he'd never seen me in action, after all, and there is a huge difference between someone telling you about an elephant charging and actually seeing it, so I just kept dogging it in the half-speed session.

I let him feel like he'd thoroughly discouraged me with his manly prowess. My groans and grunts were all fairly soft and small, but an experienced opponent would expect that. And I never broke into outright crying.

Gunnery Sergeant Dracuzilla de Sade said, "One-minute matches. First six pairs, Baldridge and McKenzie, Davis and Gelman, Pumphrey and Gonzales, Short and Vasquez, Sanderson and Phillips, Glickstien and Vigg." She was looking right at me when she said it, that evil little smile on her face and a glint of satisfaction in her eyes.

Too fucking bad, Dracuzilla.

Vigg and I faced each other, and Staff Sergeant Rafferty said, "ATTACK!" Vigg leapt at me like an anaconda: enormous, filled with destructive energy, and with overwhelming speed.

I'd already determined that it wasn't his fault that I had to fight a man, so I didn't hurt him permanently, but I did catch him in an *aikido* hold, throw him head over balls, and then completely immobilize him; one of my feet was pressed against his head, while the other was pressed into his hip, with his right arm rotated 135 degrees away from his body. If he tried to move, either his neck would break, his arm would dislocate at the shoulder, or his ribs would push through his chest cavity.

The sergeant really knew his stuff, because he said, "Good one, Glickstien. I tap out." I let him go, sprang to my feet, and offered him my hand. He took it, pulled himself up, and said, "You were dogging it during half-speed, right? Sucked me in like a newbie?"

"Yes," I said, staring straight into his eyes.

"Probably used my inherent sexism against me too, didn't ya?"

"Yes," I said.

He looked right back and said, "Not this time."

I smiled and said, "No, Sergeant, not this time."

We went at it like wild dogs fighting over a T-bone steak.

Vigg was too good for me to just overwhelm him, but I more than held my own. After the first surprise attack, we had seven one-minute "matches," about one Olympic wrestling match, and I "won" five to his two, including one spectacular throw-rethrow-rethrow series (think of it like a porno film where the actors start with the womyn on top, bouncing up and down, and roll around until the man is on top, and then roll one more time so the womyn is on the top again).

It was tremendous fun, and also very satisfying, in a finding-one's-limits sort of way, because I knew that if I could hold my own with Vigg, I could go hand to hand with anybody.

When Gunnery Sergeant Dracuzilla de Sade said, "TIME! CEASE EXERCISE!" Sergeant Vigg and I stopped attacking each other and shook hands. I said, "Sir, this recruit would like to thank you for the hand-to-hand experience, sir!"

Vigg laughed and said, "Fuck you, Marine. Don't call me *sir*. I work for a living!"

The entire platoon laughed. Marine noncommissioned officers, especially sergeants of every stripe, will not tolerate being called sir, because they claim that officers don't actually "work for a living." (No, they don't really believe this of Marine officers; officers are, after all, still Marines.) For Vigg to say that to me was the highest form of compliment.

As I was laughing and slapping Vigg's back, I noticed that we had an audience. I didn't really register who it was, but I recognized the gold star of a general officer, so I said, "AH-TEN, HUT! OFFICER ON DECK!"

Everyone snapped to attention, looking straight ahead, when the voice of Brigadier General Terrance McAllen said, "As you were, Marines. Sergeant Vigg, front and center!" Vigg stepped out in front, turned precisely ninety degrees, marched to the center of our formation, then turned precisely ninety degrees again to face the general, who ran the Parris Island Training Command. He braced to attention and said, "SIR! SERGEANT WALTER O. VIGG REPORTING AS ORDERED! SIR!"

Brigadier General Terry McAllen was a Marine's Marine. He was 5'11", 180 pounds, square-shouldered, and trim, with a face the color of Marine Corps coffee, and no need to prove he was a badass. His decorations spoke for him before he ever opened his mouth: Force Recon, Silver Star, Bronze Star, Navy Cross (twice), service in every war zone the U.S. had fought in over the last twenty years, including three tours of the Sandbox and twice in Helmand Province, and expert badges in every form of weapon the Marine Corps utilized. However, it was the pale-blue ribbon with the five white stars that got the most attention and had even senior officers stiffening to attention and saluting, because Brigadier General Terry McAllen won the Congressional Medal of Honor during his last tour of the Sandbox.

Everyone in the corps knew the story. Hell, probably half the world knew the story, since an NBC cameraman had filmed it all.

Major McAllen was on routine patrol while escorting an NBC News crew who was embedded with his company. He was the company S-2 (intelligence officer), who was tasked with showing the world where the Marines had already dug the enemy out. As their three Humvees eased down a road that led to a forward operating base, they were struck by an IED. The 12 Marines and two newsmen were all wounded, many of them severely. This would have been the end of the story in most cases, but this time the al-Qaeda fighters were ready at the ambush site, and they attacked the Humvees. Despite having his left foot literally blown off by the IED, then major McAllen had been the least injured of any of the Marines. With only two other Marines capable of returning enemy fire, Major McAllen had defended his wounded comrades from about 100 al-Qaeda who were armed with everything up to and including RPGs (rocket-propelled grenades).

He tied a tourniquet around his left leg in two places and ground dirt into his stub to stop the bleeding, then gathered his wounded behind one of the overturned Humvees that was armored on the bottom. He placed his two other effectives in the best firing positions he could, then dashed out to retrieve one of the journalists—the cameraman—and one of his Marines, who were exposed to enemy fire.

Major McAllen then took up all the arms and ammunition he could find and dashed into a flanking position, attacking the Taliban with an M4 assault rifle in each hand. He lured the al-Qaeda fighters in, then threw every grenade at his disposal, and attacked the remaining enemy on his left flank. Faced with a crazed Marine who made John Wayne seem like a huge pussy, the al-Qaeda fighters on that side made a strategic withdrawal (they ran like hell). Major McAllen then dashed across in front of his ruined Humvees and attacked the right flank of the al-Qaeda position with small-arms fire. During the entire engagement, the enemy were shooting only at him, because Major McAllen had ordered his two remaining effectives not to fire unless the enemies were within 10 meters and he was down, thus keeping the wounded out of harm's way as much as possible. He also kept up a call for reinforcements during this time. The tapes didn't lie. Major McAllen never raised his voice or lost his cool; he simply kept repeating his coordinates and the need for "more Marines."

When the Marines from up the road arrived with APCs (armored personnel carriers) and two AH-64 Apache attack helicopters, they found Major McAllen coolly knocking down al-Qaeda fighters with his M9 Beretta—his M4s were out of ammo. Still bleeding from multiple wounds (one severed foot, three bullet wounds, lots of nice shrapnel), Major McAllen directed the reinforcements into position before dashing back to check on his men and the journalists.

On the stump of a leg.

With bleeding holes everywhere.

As luck would have it, the wounded NBC camera womyn had kept the camera running the whole time, while her correspondent (who was also wounded) kept up a running commentary. (Can we all agree that those war correspondents and their camera people are crazy, brave, insane motherfuckers? 'Cause they are.) The people at NBC headquarters had been showing the patrol live at midday, so they interrupted regular programming and kept the battle streaming live, which was why, when the fighting was over, they got the definitive quote about Major McAllen from another Marine.

A lieutenant who was part of the reinforcements ran to the Humvee with the wounded to tell Major McAllen that medical relief was on the way. When the Marine lieutenant saw the major's stump, he turned green and instantly blew chunks, then straightened up to near-attention and, without spitting or rinsing his mouth or doing anything else, said, "Goddamn, Major, you are the toughest motherfucking Marine son of a bitch I've ever met, sir!"

It went out live all over the world, then went viral as everyone went crazy over this Marine who beat the shit out of al-Qaeda with his foot blown off.

And that wasn't even the best part of the story.

Brigadier General Terrance McAllen was also one of the few Marines who fought his way back into the Marines.

After they cut his leg off near the knee, and after his extensive rehab, and after being fitted for a new "bionic" prosthesis, and after promotion to Lieutenant Colonel, and after awarding him the Medal of Honor ("African American President Pins Medal of Honor on African American Marine" was huge news—yeah, Brigadier General McAllen was *that* Marine), and after all the hubbub surrounding his career died down, the powers that be tried to muster Terrance McAllen out of the Marine Corps.

He declined.

The corps insisted; he was officially "permanently disabled" from the loss of his limb. But Lieutenant Colonel McAllen said that "he preferred to stay on active duty, since the Marine Corps was his career, not some stepping stone to something else." The Marine Corps was still dithering when the senior (and I do mean *senior*) senator from Arizona, which just happened to be Lieutenant Colonel McAllen's home state, stood up in the well of the Senate and proposed a bill that would allow service personnel who were classified as "disabled" to remain on active duty if they were certified by a service physician to be physically able to perform their duties (whatever party you're from, you have to admire that old bird from Arizona—talk about one tough motherfucker). Since the senator from Arizona was technically "disabled" (which was bullshit—even Vietcong torture couldn't stop that squid), the bill carried a lot of weight and was clearly going to sail through Congress.

The corps immediately returned Lieutenant Colonel McAllen to active duty, where he had since distinguished himself enough to be promoted twice more. Brigadier general was probably as high as he would go—people in Washington and the Marine Corps had long memories, and many still believed that the brigadier general had broken some code by squealing to his senator, but there was still no denying that this was a Marine's Marine, and a Man with a capital *M*.

So Sergeant Vigg stood very straight as the brigadier general said, "Sergeant, are you going to tell me that you were going full speed against this reee-cruit?" (Even generals from Arizona do it.)

"Sir, I went all-out against reee-cruit Glickstien. She's the real deal, sir," the sergeant said.

"You didn't let up because she is female? Not fully exert yourself because of her gender?" the brigadier general said.

"No, sir. I went at her like I would if it were you, sir," the sergeant said.

The brigadier general nodded and said, "REEE-CRUIT GLICKSTIEN, FRONT AND CENTER!"

I tried to imitate the sergeant when I went to stand before arguably the best man in the entire Marine Corps, but the truth was that I was about pissing my pants. I managed to not embarrass myself (I still wish I had a Depends™ on) as I stood at rigid attention, eyes straight ahead.

Brigadier General McAllen said, "Reee-cruit, do you think that you could take me in open, hand-to-hand combat?" His voice was soft, but I knew that he was deadly serious and was looking for just the right answer. I also knew that Marines needed to be decisive, so I said, "Sir, this reee-cruit has always been taught not to judge a book by its cover, sir! The only way to answer that question would be to face you in combat, sir!"

"You wouldn't defer to my rank or my salad bar or my age?" Brigadier General McAllen said. "You wouldn't let up on a crippled old man?"

"Sir, no, sir! I would put you away just like anyone else, sir!" I said.

"Why is that, reee-cruit? Don't you have any compassion? What about my disability?" he said.

"Sir, Marines in battle do not have compassion, sir! Marines in battle fight until the enemy is subdued, or they are ordered to withdraw, or they die," I said.

"So you wouldn't even let up on your poor old *crippled* division commander?" he said.

I decided to go for broke. Wasn't it Chesty Puller who said, "No guts, no glory," because that was what Marines did? So I said, "Sir, if this reee-cruit met you in battle, she would respectfully put you away by tearing your prosthesis off and shoving it up your ass, sir!"

Brigadier General Terrance X. McAllen stood even straighter than before. I couldn't see his face, but I had the feeling that I might have perhaps, maybe, possibly, almost certainly overstepped a boundary line.

I was sure of it when the brigadier general stomped right up into my face and said, "What did you say, reee-cruit?" His eyes were ablaze and boring right into mine, but I no longer felt afraid, because while this general was a great man, he wasn't any better than anybody else when it came right down to it.

I steeled my resolve and said, "Sir, Marines are built to fight and respond to any challenge, so this reee-cruit would kick your ass eight ways to Sunday if she could and would shove your prosthesis right up your ass, sir!"

Brigadier General McAllen smiled and said, "Exactly right, Marine. Marines are built to fight, and you responded to this challenge right well. Boo-rah!"

"BOO-RAH!" the rest of the platoon said.

"Gunnery Sergeant Thornton," the brigadier general said.

"SIR!" Dracuzilla de Sade said.

"You have my permission to allow Reee-cruit Glickstien to train with male Marines in all physical combat exercises and to run the obstacle course with male Marines, unless, of course, she objects to this order." He shot me a don't-fuck-with-me-Marine look that all Marine officers had, so I said, "Sir! This reee-cruit is grateful for the opportunity to train harder, sir!"

"Good. Don't let me, or the corps, down, Reee-cruit Glickstien. Continue to train at the highest level and make yourself into the ass-kicking Marine I know you can be," the brigadier general said, his voice firm and serious.

I won't lie—my heart swelled up, and I was almost overcome with pride and ego. This was *the* ass-kicker in my little Marine Corps world, and he thought *I* could become an ass-kicker? Fortunately, my nearly swollen head came back to regular size as I remembered that Marines take pride in the performance of the Corps, not themselves, because no Marine wins a battle or completes an operation without other Marines—it's called *esprit de corps*, not *esprit de moi*.

So I swallowed my pride and said, "AYE, SIR! BOOO-RAHH!"

"Roger that, reee-cruit. Gunnery Sergeant Thornton, keep me in the loop when Glickstien and Sergeant Clark go at it with pugil sticks. That I would like to see," the brigadier general said.

"Aye, sir!" Dracuzilla de Sade said.

And so the next week Brigadier General McAllen was there when I turned Sergeant Clark into a practice dummy. To make a long story short, I hit him so many times that observers lost count. And he hit me zero. I busted his nuts, broke four fingers, damaged his thigh muscles, and knocked him around so that he was looking out the earhole of his headgear. I also knocked him down five times and off the platform three times. Poor Sergeant Clark suffered the final indignity when I knocked him completely unconscious and he had to be carried off on a stretcher. No one laughed, but there were some smiles, including from Brigadier General McAllen.

I felt bad about knocking him out, but Sergeant Clark was all man, and all Marine, so he wouldn't quit—and he wouldn't ask for a quarter either, so I did what I was supposed to do and put him away.

At that time, it felt good. I had no idea that it would come back to bite me, and one of my platoon mates, in the ass.

Literally.

CHAPTER 15

The Battle of the Shower Room

So basic training went on, and I continued to excel. I about shot my hands off, defeated all challengers in the physical realm, and continued to learn how to be a real Marine. The climax of my training came after I outshot everybody they sent against me on the combat pistol range, including Master Gunnery Sergeant Jan Berkey. We both shot the same score, but I beat her by .8 seconds on time. We shook hands after that and agreed that we were going to kick Army's ass at the Interservice Championships the next year (we did). I also kept working out with men (and routinely kicking their asses).

When we ran through the obstacle course the last time, Platoon 4004 set a new wymyn's record for time. I ran through the obstacle course and set an individual record for Parris Island (men and womyn), as well as having the best record ever for the "crucible," the combined mental and physical training necessary to being a Marine. (Think of all the exercises Marines do, then think Super Bowl, and you'll still not quite get it. The "crucible" is the toughest challenge in any of the services, except for Navy SEAL training—those motherfuckers can do shit no ordinary human can aspire to or tolerate.)

With a week left of basic until graduation, we were out on a final training run when Gunnery Sergeant Dracuzilla de Sade took offense at my running (she claimed that I was dogging it, which I was). When we got back to the parade ground, she kept me and one of my classmates, Noelani Esparza, for more PT (Esparza had laughed at me when the Gunnery Sergeant announced that I needed "some extra incentive to run hard").

So Noelani and I did extra PT while the rest of Platoon 4004 showered and went to chow. After forty-five minutes, Gunnery Sergeant Dracuzilla de Sade said, "ALL RIGHT, REEE-CRUITS, HIT THE HEAD AND GET YOUR ASSES OVER TO CHOW ON THE DOUBLE!"

Esparza and I ran back into the squad bay and then hauled ass over to the showers, where we disrobed and turned on the hot water. It was embarrassing showering with Noelani Esparza, because she had the most beautiful female body ever seen by humans. In fact, she was the most beautiful person that I'd ever seen, male or female. Her mother was Hawaiian, her dad was Mexican (he was what used to be called a mestizo, the product of Native Americans and Spanish ancestors), and their gene combination created Noelani (whose name meant "beautiful girl from heaven" in Hawaiian), and her phenomena body!: without blemish, perfectly curved, and with smooth, golden-colored skin that accentuated all her, ah, natural assets.

She made me feel like a leprosy victim who'd been hit by the whole damned ugly tree.

Hell, she made Kaley Cuoco look like a decomposing warthog who'd been mauled by a tiger and run over by the ugly truck.

This chick was smoking hot.

I was giving her shit about her perfection when she got a weird look on her face and said, "What the fuck?"

I said, "Hey, I'm not hitting on you, Noe, me heterosexual, you heterosexual, right?"

And a male voice said, "Me heterosexual too. And I'm all for fucking."

I whipped around to find seven male Marines in the wymyn's head. They were all grinning, apparently because they thought that they were funny, although my first thought was that Gunnery Sergeant Thornton was going to make them regret being born. My second thought was that they were going to be court-martialed and sent to Fort Leavenworth.

My third thought was that they were going to rape and possibly murder us.

I didn't get what their motive was until one grinning ape said, "You won't be making us look bad after this, Freak. We're gonna make it so that you can't walk for a while, much less run, although it may end up being fun for you. Be the first time an ugly girl like you got any, right?" (Hey, I wasn't pretty then, and I'm still not, but calling people ugly, especially a Marine, is always a bad idea.)

Esparza said, "You guys get out of here and we'll just forget about it, OK?" She was clearly scared (I wasn't scared yet, probably because I was pissed off at being called ugly), and her proposition was exactly the wrong thing to say, because it emboldened the motherfuckers.

They all kind of chuckled, and one said, "Oh, you're not going to forget this anytime soon, Esparza. We're going to give you and the Freak something to remember for a long time, if you make it. We got five guys outside who are going to want sloppy seconds—if there's any left after we get done with you."

I looked right at him and said, "My boyfriend is an NBA player, asshole. I wouldn't feel your thimble dick even if you could get it up." I figured being defiant was the only way to go, because I was pretty sure that they were going to fuck Esparza and me until we were either unconscious or dead. In my suddenly afraid brain, I decided that if I was going down to a bunch of redneck dickhead motherfucking asshole rapists, I was going down like a Marine.

I looked at the biggest one of the rapists and said, "Hey, Needle-dick, did you guys blow each other first to get your courage up? Or do you need to blow each other to just get it up?" I wanted them distracted so that I could get between them and Esparza. I thought maybe if they concentrated on me, she could get away and bring help, while the impotent dipshit cocksucking rapist sons of bitches took turns with me.

The biggest one's face got red, but he said, "You talking to me, cunt?"

I couldn't tell if he was going for a De Niro impression or not, but I could tell I was pissing him off, so I said, "Yeah, I'm talking to you, Needle-dick the Bug Fucker. Why'n't you and the rest of your asshole buddies go fuck a goat or a sheep? Aren't wymyn just a bit out of your league?"

He turned nearly purple, and the rest of them turned some shade of red, except for a guy with corporal's stripes, who kept his cool and said, "No more bullshit, Freak. Your ass is gonna be the size of a 155 [a large field artillery tube] by the time we get done fucking you, you overachieving cunt!" They split into two groups; two guys went toward Esparza, while the other five spread out in a semicircle around me.

When I saw them break up, I knew they wouldn't be surprised by me, so I went for broke while I got ready to fight for my and Esparza's lives. I smiled and said, "Not with your teeny-tiny dicks,

Corporal. All of you put together can't be more than five millimeters. Hell, I've seen mice with bigger cocks than yours, you limp-dicked, pig-fucking, shitfaced pussy!"

They charged me, including the even-tempered corporal, all of them deranged with too much testosterone and hatred. In a move typical of the long-range planning skills of men, they didn't really have anything planned beyond holding me down spread-eagled while they took turns raping me. Esparza was a bonus, and they would probably do the same to her after they got through with me. It kind of reminded me of the rape scene from that DeMille book *The General's Daughter*, except that was in the field under the cover of darkness and was supposed to be fiction. But our situation was looking pretty damned real to Esparza and me right about then.

The two guys rushed Esparza, and she tried to defend herself, but one of the guys hammered her in the gut with a big right hand and she ended up in the absolute worst position—head down, with her hands on the floor and her butt still up in the air. It looked like a naked downward dog, which meant that the puncher could move in and grab her hair and throat while the other guy moved behind her and began to drop his pants. He had a great big egg-sucking smile on his face as he dropped his pants to reveal an erect penis.

I bellowed, "MULE KICK, MARINE!" at Esparza and attacked the big Marine nearest me.

He thought that he was ready, but my adrenaline was flowing, and I reached him so fast he couldn't get his hands up. I hit him with double knife hands on the left side of his neck and then kneed him in the gut. He bent over, the breath completely knocked out of him and with his left arm useless. There was an enormous scream from near Esparza—a mule kick to the balls and throbbing penis were going to hurt like a 143-mile-per-hour fastball to the crotch and probably cause an orchiectomy and broken dick (that guy was sincerely unfucked, probably forever). So I spin-kicked the rapist I disabled in front of the other three on the left and turned my attention to the Marine who was grabbing me—he got a good grip on my left tit just as I felt a searing pain in my ass cheek.

I pinned the hand and arm locked on my tit into an over-under grip and twisted my body away from the pain in my ass (literally). When the Marine who had a grip on my tit was behind me, he did what anyone would do: he pushed into me. And I used his momentum to flip him right into the shower room wall.

He let go of my tit, and everything else, as he hit the wall like a 200-pound turkey hitting a truck window. I flicked a glance over at Esparza, who was holding her own with the lone Marine still trying to rape her, and spun toward the three rapists that I had spilled on the floor. They were all struggling to their feet, but one of them was holding a bloody combat dagger that he had used to stab me in the ass.

"COME ON, PINDICKS! GET IT UP ENOUGH TO AT LEAST RAPE ONE OF US, YOU LOUSY PIECES OF SHIT! I'VE WIPED TOUGHER TURDS OFF THE BOTTOM OF MY SHOES, YOU GODDAMNED COWARDS!" I bellowed, hoping to throw them again, because I knew that I'd have a hard time in a three-on-one fight even without a knife.

Three things happened simultaneously.

Esparza turned on the shower right in front of my three remaining rapists just before her rapist grabbed her from behind.

There was a huge shout from outside the head, followed by high-pitched screaming.

I launched myself at the feet of my three remaining rapists.

I hit them like a bowling ball, and they flew across the suddenly wet, slippery floor. I slid to my feet and hit Esparza's rapist on both ears with my open palms. It must've felt like a lightning bolt as his eardrums burst. He went "EEK!" like a giant mouse and passed out just as First Sergeant Gene Glenn, Gunnery Sergeant Angela Thornton, and three Shore Patrol guys burst into the shower.

Sergeant Glenn took the billy club in his hand and clocked one of the rapists, Gunnery Sergeant Thornton smacked a second one in the face and then punched him in the heart, and the three Shore Patrol guys fell on the remaining rapist with ASP expandable batons, relieving him of the knife and consciousness at the same time.

First Sergeant Glenn bellowed, "THESE ARE MY MARINES, YOU WORTHLESS MOTHERFUCKERS!" and began to kick the one he'd downed. Gunnery Sergeant Thornton (no more Dracuzilla de Sade for her) pulled a handheld radio from her belt and said, "I need more Shore Patrol over at the Hotel Company squad bay, in the head." She looked at us and said, "Are you guys OK? Did anybody get at you?" She meant, "Did anybody rape you?" but couldn't bring herself to use the term.

I looked at Esparza, and she shook her head, her lips trembling and her eyes wild. I wrapped my arms around her, and we both cried for a while, not out of fear, just letting the adrenaline rush bleed off. I give the Shore Patrol and First Sergeant Glenn credit; they simply kicked and shoved the rapists into a rough pile near the door of the head and never once gave two naked females the eye. In fact, I think if we hadn't been there, none of those guys would have made it out alive; the SPs were especially rough, yanking three of the rapists upright and handcuffing them even though they were unconscious. One of the handcuffed and unconscious rapists let out a moan, and the tallest SP whacked him on the shoulder with his ASP hard enough for us to hear the man's collarbone snapping.

"Oops," the SP said.

"Son of a bitch was trying to escape," a second SP said.

"Better make sure his handcuffs are still on tight," the third SP said, so the one who whacked him lifted the rapist up by his cuffs, shook him like a mongoose shakes a cobra, and then let him fall back to the floor without even attempting to stop his fall.

One of the conscious rapists said, "First Sergeant Glenn, these wymyn enticed us in here and then cried rape." The first sergeant whipped around and broke his jaw with the billy club, then kicked him three or seven times in the belly. The other conscious rapist looked at First Sergeant Glenn, who grinned like a demented orangutan and said, "Got anything to say?"

The guy wasn't very smart. He opened his mouth, and Gunnery Sergeant Thornton casually kicked his mouth shut as she stepped out of the shower room. The rapist fell over, and two of his teeth fell out as the Gunnery Sergeant came back with two blankets. After we were wrapped in them Gunnery Sergeant Thornton led us back into the squad bay.

We sat together on a bunk and she stripped two more blankets off the nearest racks and wrapped them around us. It was tender and caring and made Esparza and me feel safe. The Gunnery Sergeant stood up and said again, "Did any of them manage to successfully attack you?"

"No, Gunnery Sergeant," we said simultaneously.

"One of them stabbed Freak in the butt with a knife," Esparza said.

I wanted to slap her—it burned a bit by then, but I didn't want any more fussing—but Gunnery Sergeant Thornton immediately said into her radio, "I need a corpsman in the Hotel Company squad bay on the double! Where are the SP escorts?"

Her radio squawked back with something unintelligible, but she seemed satisfied. The Gunnery Sergeant looked at me and said, "Glickstien, do you feel dizzy? Hot? Disoriented?"

"I'm not in shock, Gunnery Sergeant, just pissed off at those assholes. One of them almost got his tiny dick into Esparza, but she mule-kicked his balls into orbit around Pluto. He won't be thinking about fucking anything any time soon."

We all laughed, and then a Shore Patrol Captain and six SPs with M16s at port arms showed up. He said, "Gunnery Sergeant, I relieve you. Squad, disperse into guard positions." The SPs got into a circle around us, with the M16s facing out. The Captain drew his M9 and stood barring the door. He looked over his shoulder and said, "Don't worry, Marines. You're safe. If anybody we don't like the look of tries to come in this squad bay, we'll shoot their asses dead."

He nodded at us and then looked back out the door.

Gunnery Sergeant Thornton said, "I'm going to leave for a bit, but I won't be far away. Glickstien, tell the corpsmen about your punctured ass. Esparza, make sure she does it."

I said, "Gunnery Sergeant, yes, Gunnery Sergeant."

Esparza nodded and said, "Yes, Gunnery Sergeant!"

Then the strangest thing happened. Gunnery Sergeant Thornton drew herself to attention and gave us a perfect Marine Corps salute. Without hesitation, we stood at attention and returned the salute (Pavlov was grinning right then—no Marine could ever not return a salute), and the Gunnery Sergeant said, "Semper fi, Marines! Seven to two, and you still outfought the bastards! Booyah!"

"Booyah!" we said. Then Esparza and I sat down and cried some more as the adrenaline slowly bled off. The corpsmen arrived—a man and a womyn—and attended to my stabbed ass. The blade hadn't hit anything important (like my hamstring or my anus), but it had gone deep into my buttock, so the corpsmen ran peroxide down the hole and gave me an antibiotic injection to help prevent infection. They gave me five stitches so I wouldn't bleed too much more but also informed me that I was going to see a doctor later who would probably remove the stitches to check for infection.

They also checked us for shock, but we appeared remarkably normal, considering we had just evaded a gang-raping by twelve angry (so-called) men. Turned out there were five guys guarding the door to the shower room, but they were all in the hospital due to First Sergeant Glenn, Gunnery Sergeant Thornton, and the three SPs smacking the living shit out of them with implements of destruction when the would-be rapists—ahem—"resisted arrest and defied a direct order."

After a 243-year wait (actually about 45 minutes), the SPs got a radio call and we got marched (gently) over to the infirmary, where two doctors checked us over and inspected my stabbed ass. Both docs said I was lucky but didn't appear to have any problem with the wound in my butt. Both docs also signed affidavits that we were not raped but that we had been assaulted. I finally remembered to tell them about my left tit, which was the only part of me that really hurt.

A corpswomyn gently peeled open the blanket and robe that were wrapped around me so they could see my injured tit.

The corpswomyn and both docs gasped when they saw the mess the rapist had made out of my tit. It looked like Salvador Dalí had taken a big load of acid, drank a quart of tequila, and then tried to paint using black and blue paint, leaving behind a design from an acid- and tequila-induced nightmare.

I didn't realize it at that time, but the rapist had a pretty solid grip on the left side of my rack. His fingernails had cut me, leaving streaks of semidried blood all down my tit, but it was the five giant blue-black streaks that looked like a messy giant's fingerprints that really made my tit spectacular. Each one had a black bull's-eye center, with blue-turning-to-black streaks radiating out from it toward the other five. The tit itself was so swollen that my nipple looked like it was engorged, even though it was not. The nipple also looked like someone had used sandpaper on it. When the air hit it, I winced because it hurt so badly.

The corpswomyn took pictures of the damage before she treated my poor tit. By the time she was done, it looked like I had a (very large) rotting eggplant on my chest. The docs decided to get the swelling down by applying ice, which hurt so bad I decided that the rapists needed to have their testicles removed with dull, rusty scissors and a plastic knife.

I was avowing as how this was the thing to do to those rotten, no-good, limp-dicked, misogynistic, pussy-assed motherfuckers when Colonel Benavidez came through the door with two JAG officers. Once again, Esparza and I leapt to our feet (old Pavlov had nothing on the training of Gunnery Sergeant Thornton) to stand at attention and salute. I still had ice bags swathed around my injured left tit, and it was still freezing my nipple off, and I still wanted to injure those fucking rapists beyond all repair, but a reee-cruit always saluted superior officers, and a Marine Colonel, Navy Captain, and Air Force Major were all superior to me, so all hail Pavlov, trainer of dogs and Marines.

Colonel Benavidez said, "At ease, Marines. These are JAG investigators Captain Henry Walton and Major Erin Aalberg. They are here to take your statements about the incident and to provide you with counsel should they feel you need it."

I was looking at her, and Colonel Benavidez saw the question in my eye. She said, "Reee-cruit Glickstien, do you have a question?"

"Ma'am, yes, ma'am! This recruit would like to know why she and Reee-cruit Esparza might need counsel, ma'am. They attacked us and we defended ourselves. Doesn't the UCMJ allow for self-defense, ma'am?"

The Navy Captain answered, "Of course it does, Reee-cruit Glickstien." (Even in the Navy? Was there a course for this dialect?) "The problem is that right now it's a 'she said, he said' situation, and those Marines are claiming they were lured to the head by reee-cruit Esparza, and then the two of you set upon them." Captain Walton took off his John Lennon glasses, polished them, and said, "It's all a load of horseshit, but you may need to defend yourselves, and here we are."

I looked at Colonel Benavidez again, and she made a "Be my guest" gesture, so I said, "Ma'am, this reee-cruit would like to know if this is an attempt to keep this incident quiet, for the good of the Corps."

Without appearing to move, Colonel Benavidez got right in my face. She said, "Glickstien, the best thing for the Corps is to get this right out there and send those rapist bastards to Fort Leavenworth. Don't you dare do anything but tell the truth, Glickstien, because I want all of them to get buttfucked by the hardcases in Leavenworth before we drum their pitiful carcasses out of *my* Marine Corps. Are we clear?" Her brown eyes blazed with the righteous fire of the true warrior, the one who believes in the old code of chivalry, where the strong protect the weak and knights do not stoop to rape.

I stood to attention and said, "Roger that, ma'am! Telling nothing but the truth, aye!"

"We both concur with that, by the way," the Air Force Major said. Esparza and I both glanced at the male, Captain Walton, who caught it and said, "Hey, I'll help with cutting off the stupid fuckers' dicks if I can. Just because I'm male doesn't mean I endorse rape, although it might be more effective to nail their nuts to boards."

It was smooth sailing after that.

All the rapists were convicted and sent to Leavenworth, after their injuries healed, of course.

Esparza and I went back to Platoon 4004, but the story of the Battle of the Shower Room preceded us, because when we got back to our barracks, there was a sign over the door that said, "Watch your balls! Freak and Mule on duty!"

We went through the hatch, and Natalie Marchand said, "Attention on deck! War fighters on the floor!" Everybody came to attention, and Marchand said, "Freak and Mule can kick an elephant's balls up between his shoulder blades!" and the rest of our platoon said, "BOOYAH! FREAK AND MULE RULE!"

Needless to say, it was a nice homecoming, right up until Gunnery Sergeant Angela Thornton said, "Can the shit, reee-cruits! We've got close-order drill to do, and the Freak and Esparza are so far behind after their goldbricking that we'll never catch up. Prepare to hit the parade ground in full gear in five minutes for a little practice session so we're not the laughingstock of this training command!"

Ahh, welcome back to Marine Corps normality, reee-cruit.

CHAPTER 16

Chow Line Wisdom

So Platoon 4004 returned to work on close-order drill on the parade ground. After about eleven seconds, Gunnery Sergeant Thornton (I told ya, after what she did in our defense the night before, we weren't going to make any more smart-ass remarks) said, "Platoon, halt! Glickstien, why the hell are you and Esparza so damned clumsy? How the hell are we supposed to work on close-order drill when you two act like you've never had a rifle in your hands? Drop and give me twenty, you two."

Ah, more normality.

Esparza and I were doing the push-ups when a truck pulled up and Sergeant Major Gunnett got out of the cab. She motioned Gunnery Sergeant Thornton over and said, "Gunny, have your reee-cruits stack those M16s and draw new weapons."

Gunnery Sergeant Thornton gave her an odd look and said, "Roger that, Sergeant Major! Sergeant Rafferty, get the platoon in line behind the truck and return weapons." We turned in the M16s and got brand-new M4 assault rifles. When that was done and we were formed back up, the two corporals who handed out the rifles began walking down our rows distributing ammunition clips, which wasn't unusual, but...

These held live rounds.

Each reee-cruit got six clips after they put one in their rifle, and our squad leaders all got hand-held radios.

This was unusual. In fact, it was never done until the last week of basic, and then only for those standing an outside access post like the main gate.

Adding to the confusion of the platoon were the orders we were given by Sergeant Major Gunnett. After all, only three of us—me, Esparza, and Gunnery Sergeant Thornton—knew what had occurred last night. The rest of the platoon (excepting Sergeant Rafferty, who the Gunnery Sergeant had surely told) were mostly in the dark except for scuttlebutt, which is notoriously unreliable (the Marines who hit the beach at Tarawa heard scuttlebutt that they were going to Tahiti—scuttlebutt was just a bit off on that one).

When all of us held fully loaded M4s, the Sergeant Major said, "Attention to orders! By order of the commanding general, ROE for Training Platoon 4004 is hereby 'weapons-free' should the platoon or any individual member of the platoon feel threatened by any internal or external forces while on field operations. The principal drill instructor and her subordinates are ordered to take any defensive action necessary to defend the platoon or any individual within the platoon from any form of attack by forces internal or external. The principal DI shall post one-in-four watches consisting of a full squad and one drill instructor while bivouacked in the field, and four womyn on one-in-four watches while in the squad bay or other base housing. ROE for all these actions is 'weapons-free.'

This should not be considered a drill. By order of Brigadier General Terrance X. McAllen, commanding Marine Corps Recruit Training Depot, Parris Island, South Carolina."

The platoon stood at attention, completely mystified by the orders, until Gunnery Sergeant Thornton said, "PLATOON DISMISSED FROM ATTENTION. EVERYBODY GATHER ON ME!"

We crowded around her and Sergeant Rafferty. The Gunnery Sergeant said, "Take a knee, reee-cruits." We all knelt down, and she proceeded to tell the story of the Battle of the Shower Room in a perfectly normal tone of voice. Her demeanor was calm, cool, and collected, like any sergeant who was also a professional soldier in the U.S. Marine Corps would be, even when she said, "There is no doubt in anyone's mind that Esparza and Glickstien would have been gang-raped had they not exhibited the highest level of composure and exercised their battle skills to the best of their ability. That they did this while nude and without any weapons except their training, Glickstien's freakish abilities, and their considerable intellect is remarkable."

It was then that Esparza and I lost it. We began crying our eyes out as our bodies shook with the release of the fear and embarrassment that we had suffered, although when you think about it, there was no reason for us to be embarrassed, since all we did was get attacked by a bunch of dumb-fuck, needle-dick, bug-fucking assholes.

After the catharsis was over, we all looked back up at Gunnery Sergeant Thornton standing there at parade rest in her perfectly turned-out uniform. Her face looked like it was carved out of a block of granite into an implacable mask, but her dark eyes were filled with a fury that I had never seen in another human being before. Her face was stone, but her eyes said, "Do not fuck with me or mine, motherfucker, or I *will* kill you."

The entire platoon could feel it as she said, "Those orders we just received were endorsed by the commandant of the Marine Corps, reee-cruits. Let me clarify what they mean: We *will* use any and all means at our disposal to defend ourselves should any other men get any ideas about payback. We *will* post guards, we *will* travel everywhere in squads, and we *will* be fully armed at all times, even in the head. We *will* be prepared for any eventuality and will permit no further harassment of our platoon or any other female on this post that we are in proximity to. If we are forced to defend ourselves, we *will* shoot to kill. Are these orders clear?"

"BOOO-RAHH!" we said.

Gunnery Sergeant Thornton said, "Just one more thing, reee-cruits. We will not rely on any other Marines, male or female, to support us. *We* will take care of *ourselves*. Is that clear?"

"Aye, aye, Gunnery Sergeant!" we said.

"GOOD. ON YOUR FEET, PLATOON! PREPARE FOR CLOSE ORDER DRILL," she said. We got up and did close-order drill for twenty minutes, until the Gunnery Sergeant said, "GLICKSTIEN, HOW'S YOUR ASS?"

"GUNNERY SERGEANT, IT'S SORE, BUT I CAN MANAGE!" I said.

"WELL, HELL, IF GLICKSTIEN'S ASS ISN'T THAT SORE, LET'S GO FOR A LITTLE HIKE!" the Gunnery Sergeant said.

It was music to our ears.

We got back after a short five kilometers and did more close-order drill. When it was time for chow, we all double-timed over to the chow hall, with our M4s slung over our shoulders. When we hit the chow hall door, there was quite a commotion, until Gunnery Sergeant Thornton said, "First squad, secure tables!" The eight recruits in our first squad got us four tables, and the Gunnery Sergeant stalked over to stand at their head. She drew her M9 Beretta and kept it at her side while the rest of us got in the chow line.

You could have heard a pin drop as we got chow; it was shit on a shingle (chipped beef and gravy) day, which, contrary to what it sounds like, wasn't half-bad. And there was fresh ice cream. I got my tray and turned toward the tables just as a gaggle of male reee-cruits came up for more ice cream (we didn't get it every day, but when we did, everybody ate like pigs, because even Marine Corps cooks can't screw up ice cream).

The male recruits quickly kind of enveloped me, and then things happened very quickly.

I had my M9 in my hand without realizing it, pointed at the nearest male reee-cruit.

The rest of my platoon had their M9s out and deployed.

Gunnery Sergeant Thornton was rushing across the chow hall like a mama bear headed for her cub.

The male reee-cruits all put their hands in the air, and one of them said, "We surrender! We surrender!"

Huh?

I looked at the one I was aiming at, and he said, "Permission to speak freely, Marine," like I was a DI or an officer or something, and it felt right, so I said, "Permission granted, reee-cruit."

He nodded and said, "Miss, my squad and I wanted to apologize for those assholes who tried to assault you, and we wanted to tell you that you made us proud to be Marines."

"Whaaat?" I said.

"Miss, everybody's heard about the Battle of the Shower Room, how two naked and unarmed Marines outnumbered two-to-one not only held out against their attackers but also took the fight to them. Everybody knows who won that battle, and...well, we just wanted to say semper fi, miss." He and all his squad snapped to attention and slowly saluted. Behind them the entire chow hall rose to attention and saluted.

I snapped to attention and returned the salute, holding it at the top like an officer would.

"GLICKSTIEN AND ESPARZA CLANK WHEN THEY WALK!" the squad nearest us said.

"BOOO-YAAH!" the entire chow hall said.

The tension ran out of the room as we all sat down to eat amid the wave of good feelings.

But nobody put down their M4s, and Gunnery Sergeant Angela Thornton didn't holster her M9.

When Platoon 4004 was done eating, we all hustled back to the squad bay and cycled through the latrine and shower room—under guard, of course—and then attended a short lecture on the care and maintenance of an M4 rifle as compared to an M16 (they were remarkably similar). We headed for our racks, and Gunnery Sergeant Thornton ordered 1st Squad to stand the first watch with Sergeant Rafferty.

"Third Squad, you have the next watch with me at 0100," Gunnery Sergeant Thornton said. Esparza and I looked at each other; we were in third squad. Gunnery Sergeant Thornton stared at us, challenging us to say anything, but we were Marines, so we shut our mouths and went right to sleep, because four hours of rack time went right quickly when you were going to be on guard at 0100.

So we slept, and then we exchanged places with 1st Squad and took up overwatch duty. At 0130, I heard a strange sound. It was barely audible—shuffle, clink, shuffle-clink, shuffle-shuffle-shuffle, clink-clink, shuffle—and I almost felt it instead of heard it. Apparently, it was audible to Gunnery Sergeant Thornton, who appeared at my side without a sound. "What the fuck is that sound, reee-cruit?" she said in the softest tone of voice that I'd ever heard from her.

"Don't know, Gunnery Sergeant," I whispered back.

She listened a moment more, then thumbed her radio and said, "Rafferty, get the rest of the platoon up and armed. Deploy them in Delta One, just like we talked about. Kill the main breaker and turn on all the lights. When I tell you, turn on the main breaker and then hustle over to reinforce 1st Squad." There was double click from the radio as Sergeant Rafferty acknowledged the order, and a second later, all the lights behind us went dark.

The Gunnery Sergeant glided down the 3rd Squad line, giving instructions, ending up right next to me. Her M9 Beretta was in her hand, and I noticed for the first time that she had four grenades on her web belt.

She put her head right next to my ear and said, "Glickstien, I'm going to challenge whoever thinks they're creeping us, then Rafferty is going to flood the area with light. Keep your eyes closed until I tell you to, then train your rifle downrange and prepare to fire. But don't shoot until I give the order." I turned my head and said, "Acknowledged, Gunnery Sergeant. Should I aim for their crotches or just shoot 'em dead?"

She smiled like a tiger about to drop on a wild pig and said, "Hit those motherfuckers dead center, Freak—heavy emphasis on the *dead*." I nodded back and looked downrange; the sound was louder, but still not at all loud. If we hadn't been in hypervigilant mode, we might have missed it.

Suddenly, a group of something—people?—was there at the edge of our vision, coming from the PT area, toward our squad bay. They weren't really creeping along, although they weren't exactly just out for a walk either—they avoided all the lights in the compound.

After they were five meters in the clear of the gate that led to the PT area, Gunnery Sergeant Thornton said, "HALT! WHO GOES THERE?"

It sounded like a bad war movie, but it got worse. The shadow people froze and then seemed to melt into the background. Gunnery Sergeant Thornton wasn't having any of that, so she said, "HALT! IDENTIFY YOURSELVES IMMEDIATELY, OR MY MARINES WILL OPEN FIRE!"

One shadow wriggled forward and said, "We are 1st Squad, 3rd Platoon Force Recon of the 2nd Marines." The voice was even-toned and very familiar, but the Gunnery Sergeant wasn't taking any chances.

"WHAT'S THE PASSWORD?" she asked.

"Athena," the shadow leader said.

"ADVANCE AND BE RECOGNIZED!" Gunnery Sergeant Thornton said.

The shadow people wriggled forward. When they were all within our parade ground, Gunnery Sergeant Thornton double-clicked her radio and said, "Steady, Marines!" All the lights on our parade ground came on, and we waited a three-count to open our eyes. The advancing men were temporarily blinded, and when their vision cleared, they were facing 34 Marines armed with live rounds and ready to shoot.

It was Brigadier General McAllen and eight easily recognizable Force Recon Marines—they all had their jump wings pinned to their blouses right over their left chests. The brigadier general said, "Permission to advance under cover of darkness, Gunny."

The Gunnery Sergeant said, "Permission granted, sir. Rafferty, douse those lights." Within seconds, there were just the ordinary lights around the squad bay. The Force Recon detachment came on until they were at our perimeter, and the brigadier general said, 'I'll bet that Glickstien heard my goddamned leg coming at her, eh? That's how you were ready, right?'"

"Yes, sir," Gunnery Sergeant Thornton said. "That and some small-unit leadership and Marine Corps planning for what the enemy could do, not what he might do, sir." Every Marine Corps noncom and officer—hell, every Marine—had that drilled into their heads. Always plan for what the enemy could do, not what he might, and always overplan your response, just in case.

The brigadier general and his squad all laughed along with the two DIs, but none of Platoon 4004 laughed or moved from our positions or dropped our guard at all. Our M4s were unwavering on the nine targets in front of us; we were ready and willing to defend ourselves if necessary.

Brigadier General Mad Dog McAllen said, "Your Marines are well trained and disciplined, Gunnery Sergeant. Your people have been through enough to last a week in the last 24 hours and deserve to rest. I formally request permission to take over the guard detail for your platoon."

Gunnery Sergeant Thornton said, "Sir, I will need to communicate with my squad leaders first." She didn't wait for his response, motioning for me, Esparza, Natalie Marchand, and Sergeant Rafferty to talk. She looked at US and said, "Whaddya think?"

"No fucking way!" Sergeant Rafferty said. "We don't need some *men* guarding us. We can do it—we're just as good a Marines as they are, the sons of bitches!"

I said, "Concur with Sergeant Rafferty, ma'am. I'm good to go for as long as it takes."

"Concur," Esparza and Marchand said.

"Roger that," Gunnery Sergeant Thornton said. She turned back to the brigadier general and said, "Sir, we decline your offer of assistance. My Marines would rather guard themselves, sir."

"I could order you to accept our assistance, Gunnery Sergeant," the brigadier general said.

"Yes, sir. And we would accept that order, but my Marines and I would rather not," Gunnery Sergeant Thornton said.

The brigadier general was clearly in a catch-22 situation—he could order us to accept, but then he'd just be another man big-footing a situation because we were wymyn; if he declined, word would get around that a bunch of wymyn had basically faced him down, thus weakening his authority. This wasn't really fun for him, although it was more fun than facing a bunch of guys trying to gang-rape you.

One of the Force Recon guys muttered something from behind the brigadier general, and he turned and said, "Good idea. Permission granted to step forward." The shadow came forward and resolved into a lean but muscular Master Gunnery Sergeant. He was about 5'10", 170, with a handsome face and combat badges from all corners of the globe. He stood at parade rest and said, "Gunnery Sergeant Thornton, I am Master Gunnery Sergeant Joshua O. Chamberlain, 3rd Battalion, Force Recon, 2nd Marines. I give you my word that we are not doing this because you are wymyn or because we regard you as weaker but rather that we admire your courage and adherence to Marine traditions of honor, courage, and fighting spirit. We are asking to relieve you because we want you to know that Marines can depend on one another, even if we are men. We also want you to know that those goddamned pussy, shit-for-brains goat-fuckers who assaulted members of your platoon do not represent the rest of the Corps."

He stood at attention and said, "From one Gunnery Sergeant to another, I request permission to guard your platoon while you sleep, Gunnery Sergeant. I would accept reciprocal treatment should my squad need it. Will you accept our assistance?"

What the hell could we say to that? This man had put himself out there, not because we were wymyn, but because we were *Marines*. I put the safety on my rifle and signaled everyone else to do so. Gunnery Sergeant Thornton heard us and said, "Master Gunnery Sergeant, we accept your offer of assistance and will render any assistance you need when requested. Thank you and your squad. We can all use the rest, although it should be noted that those pansy-assed, shit-eating, limp-dicked goat-fuckers *tried* to assault two of my Marines, they were *not* successful!"

Everybody laughed, and Master Gunnery Sergeant Chamberlain said, "Duly noted, Gunnery Sergeant! Nobody fucks with Platoon 4004!" We all laughed again, and then Gunnery Sergeant Thornton said, "Platoon, secure from guard detail and prepare to rack out."

We were heading for the squad bay when I noticed that the brigadier general was in battle dress and fully armed. He was putting on a helmet with night vision glasses attached, too. I looked at Gunnery Sergeant Thornton and raised my eyebrows. She arched a brow at me, and I looked out at the brigadier general. She got it instantly and said, "Sir, who is commanding the squad tonight?" as if she were inquiring about the chain of command, not as curious as a four-year-old at Christmas (weird analogy for a Jew, I know, but I had a lot of goy friends when I was a kid).

Brigadier General Mad Dog McAllen said, "I am, Gunnery Sergeant. Master Gunnery Sergeant Chamberlain will be my second-in-command." He said the words quietly, but his tone was in the mode of "You got a fucking problem with that?"

Gunnery Sergeant Angela Thornton was no dummy, so she fell back on the time-honored Marine tradition of questioning a superior office with a very bland "Sir?"

The brigadier general laughed and said, "Gunnery Sergeant, I was Force Recon before they took my leg. The Master Gunnery Sergeant and I worked together then. And I am still field qualified to command Marines." He looked through the darkness and said, quietly but emphatically, "Plus, these here wymyn are my Marines, too, Gunnery Sergeant. I didn't swear an oath to protect some of my Marines, I swore an oath to protect *all* of them, and that's what I'm going to do."

Gunnery Sergeant Thornton stiffened to attention and said, "PLATOON 4004, ATTENTION ON DECK!" WE STIFFENED UP, AND SHE SAID, "PRESENT ARMMMS!" We all saluted, and the brigadier general returned it with grace and panache. The Gunnery Sergeant said, "Very good, sir," and we went to bed.

And slept like babies until oh-dark-thirty.

That'll happen when you know that the finest soldiers in the world, led by a genuine hero, have your backs.

Platoon 4004 became Marines that night, and I finally figured out what "Semper Fidelis" really meant.

You do not fuck with U.S. Marines, or they will, without fail, fuck you up.

It also meant that you could sleep like a baby, because your brothers and sisters always had your back.

CHAPTER 17

The Freak Meets the War God

The rest of boot camp went by without incident. We got to the end, and it was surprisingly emotional. Even though she'd beaten the living shit out of us, nobody wanted to leave Gunnery Sergeant Thornton. When it came time for us to part, we all cried, until she said, "Cut the shit, Marines! You sorry pieces of shit aren't reee-cruits anymore, you're goddamn US Marines! So act like it! Cry when somebody dies, not when you get new orders."

We all managed to shape up and march through graduation. We were presented, accepted as Marines, and finally freed to be with whoever had come around to watch the proceedings. My whole family was there, so I was pretty cranked up. Esparza's family was there, as was Marchand's, but after the ceremony, we were all going our own ways, at least for a while. We all had orders to San Diego for AIT (Advanced Infantry Training), so we'd be in the same place, but 'Dago was a big place, and we knew our chances of seeing one another were really slim once we were there.

Everybody in the platoon hugged and mugged for pictures, and then it was time to go. I shook hands with my two best friends and said, "Well, at least we'll always have Parris Island," which got a way bigger laugh than it should've, and Esparza said, "See you in San Diego," and Marchand and I said, "Roger that." And they were gone.

I turned to find my family and almost shit a brick. Gunnery Sergeant Thornton was right behind me. I started to stiffen up for a salute, but Gunnery Sergeant Thornton said, "Stow that, Marine. I work for a living, and so do you. I just have one thing left to tell you." Her eyes were glowing with a brown fire that seemed to bore right through me as she leaned down until her face was precisely four inches from mine. She didn't whisper but said in her softest in-the-field-and-keeping-quiet-so-the-enemy-doesn't-hear-us voice, "Glickstien, you have a special gift for this line of work. If you fuck it up, I'm going to knock your ass into next week. When you get where you're going, just remember that I'm the toughest bitch who ever lived and you make me look like a goddamned fairy princess. You get your ass through the next phase of your training and then do some real good, for the Corps and for our gender. Don't forget that you're going someplace that no one else from the sisterhood has ever gone. All of us are depending on you, Glickstien, so don't fuck this up."

I was confused, so I said, "Gunnery Sergeant, I am just going to 'Dago for AIT. I assure you that I won't fuck it up, ma'am."

Gunnery Sergeant Angela Thornton did something that I never expected.

She smiled.

A genuine, I'm-so-happy-I-could-just-do-a-cartwheel smile, transitioning to a proverbial cat-that-ate-the-canary smile. She patted me on the cheek and said, "Change is the only constant in this world, Freak."

"Aye, Gunnery Sergeant," I said, really confused.

She saluted me, did a perfect about-face, and took her cryptic ass off at a parade march, right for the squad bays, where new recruits waited. I stared after her, convinced that she knew something that I didn't, but not what it was.

Turned out I was 100 % right, but I didn't remember that until after I had a party with my family, took 30 days' leave to go back and recruit in Battle Creek, and then reported for transport to San Diego.

By which time it was too fucking late to do anything about it.

Story of my life.

So the family and I went to a great restaurant over in Hilton Head that my *zayde* knew about and had a great, crazy time. We actually had too good a time and were asked to leave the restaurant (over a dozen Jews shouting "Mazel tov!" every five minutes was apparently not desirable conduct in the South), but my dad, of all people (he who would not say shit if he had a mouthful), said, "Hey, goddammit! My daughter is a U.S. Marine, and if we want to be loud, we will be! She's about to go off and defend the country so you can stick this snooty place up your ass!"

We all laughed because it was so out of character. Our dad just wasn't combative—that was Mom and *zayde*—so his outburst caught all as hilarious. The maître d' didn't know what to say, especially after *zayde* stood up and said, "I, too, am a Marine, and I was given to believe that this establishment was both friendly and welcoming to U.S. service personnel. Was I misinformed, sir? Is the ambience simply a charade or a facade, designed to appear hospitable while, in all actuality, being hostile?" (OK, so *zayde* was half in the bag after a couple of mint juleps that were mostly bourbon. When he got drunk, his diction and vocabulary became more grandiose as his logic deteriorated.)

Despite the eloquent protests, it looked like we were still leaving when a tall, ramrod-straight man with iron-gray hair cut in a Marine Corps high-and-tight marched up out of nowhere and said, "What the Sam Hill is this racket in my restaurant?" He sounded like Gunnery Sergeant Thornton, so I unconsciously stiffened to attention as he stared at the maître d', who tried to explain. After some sputtering about our obstreperousness, the tall man waved his hand and said, "Stop, Maurice."

He rounded on me and barked, "What's the sitrep, Marine?"

"Sir, I just graduated from Basic at Parris Island, and my family is helping me celebrate, sir," I said.

He said, "Is there any need for your family to sound like the circus came to town, Marine?"

"Uh, sir, we may have gotten a bit loud, but—"

He cut me off with a wave of his hand and said, "Marine, they can hear your ass over in Beaufort."

"Yes, sir," I said. "We'll be going now, sir."

He scowled at me and said, "Who the hell said anything about leaving, Marine?"

"Sir?" I said.

"I want them to hear your ass in Charleston, Marine. Is that understood?" I stood there like a dipshit, until his face broke into a smile. Then we all started laughing, and the man introduced himself.

"I'm John Thornton, USMC, retired," he said.

My eyes lit up, and I said, "Sir, are you related to—"

"She's my daughter," he said.

My *zayde* said, "Mr. Thornton, what rank were you in the corps?"

John Thornton straightened up and said, "Major General John Wainwright Thornton, USMC, retired. You?"

"Major Abraham Blumenthal, JAG Corps, USMC, retired," *Zayde* said.

"Let me buy you a drink, Major," General Thornton said.

So Gunnery Sergeant Thornton's father bought us all drinks, regaled us with stories of the Gunnery Sergeant's Marine Corps service, and reminisced with my *zayde* about the "old Corps." We partied like it was 1999, until my brother Aaron threw up in a potted plant, at which point we decided to close the show.

As we were leaving, Major General Thornton (USMC, retired) stopped me and said, "Marine, my daughter tells me that you are the best reee-cruit she's ever had. Don't fuck up this chance you've got. Angie would kill to go where you're going. Don't try to be historic. Just be the best damned Marine who ever lived, OK? I'd like to think that there are others out there who want the opportunity, and after my talk with your grandpa, I'd like to see them get it. The Corps needs to grow and adapt, or it will fall behind." He looked at me with a mixture of command and admiration, but I looked back with confusion.

"Sir? Where exactly am I going?"

His look changed to humorous, and he shook his head. "Same old Corps," he said, laughing. "They didn't tell you, did they? Well, I'd pay money to see this unfold, but...well, you enjoy your AIT, Marine."

I wanted to press him about it, but we were trying to pay and he wouldn't let us, so there was a check battle (Major General Thornton, USMC, retired, won), my *zayde* needed my support (I was the only one that didn't drink anything—only Pepsi for this teetotaling Freak), and about 37 other things were happening, but on the way home, I pondered what the cryptic Gunnery Sergeant and her equally cryptic Major General (USMC, retired) dad were talking about.

I thought I found out what they meant when I got shipped to Officer Candidate School instead of AIT, but unfortunately, I didn't really find out what my cryptic DI and her cryptic dad meant until after my leave following my graduation from OCS, when I reported to Detroit International Airport to catch a plane for the fleet base in San Diego and my advanced training. I got to the American Airlines desk and presented my travel voucher, and a nice lady said, "Oh, Lieutenant Glickstein, I'm afraid that you aren't flying to San Diego. We have a ticket for you to the Tampa-St. Pete Airport."

Uh-oh.

Shithouse mouse. There was only one reason for a Marine with special skills to fly to Tampa-MacDill Air Force Base, home to SOCOM—the US Special Operations Command.

It was the last thing that I expected, because the people who operate out of there are real freaks; it was (and is) the place where special people are trained to do special things that we don't talk about.

SOCOM was that place where you went to get trained to win medals that you could never display, or to disappear for months at a time, or be sent home in a Ziploc bag to be buried without explanation. It was either heaven or hell, depending on your perspective.

It was a bit of both, as it turned out. But more on that later.

So I got checked in to my flight, boarded the plane, and flew to Tampa-St. Pete. I wasn't 10 feet out on the concourse when two large MP sergeants wearing Air Force Special Operations Command badges approached me. The Asian one's name tape said "Fong," while the White guy's name was "Branch." Sergeant Fong said, "Glickstein." I nodded, and Sergeant Branch said, "Come with us, Marine." I nodded, and off we went, Fong, then me, then Branch.

We got outside, and there was a Humvee with SOCOM insignia waiting, with two more Air Force SOC guys in it. The driver was Sergeant Ibrahim, the passenger Sergeant Coles. We got in the back, with me in the middle, and drove off like the Humvee was stolen. Nobody said a word, so I looked at the four guys, automatically looking for telltale signs that might clue me in to their strengths and weaknesses.

There weren't any.

I mean none. The four sergeants all swayed with the movements of the Humvee but otherwise were completely still. Even Sergeant Ibrahim, the driver, never really moved as we hurtled along like we were in a war zone.

Except for their eyes. Their heads never moved, but their eyes constantly flickered across the scenes in front of us, taking everything in and cataloging it as friend or foe. (I found out about this later. One of them literally said, "I classify everything as friend or foe, every time." I thought he was kidding, but I found out that he wasn't—can't talk about that, though. It's still classified.)

After a really short, fast trip, we roared up to the main gate at SOCOM. Sergeant Ibrahim flashed his creds at the Army guy guarding the gate, and three other soldiers looked in our windows and asked for our military IDs. After we were all thoroughly inspected, and the Humvee checked top and bottom, we passed through the gate and roared up to a building with a sign that said, "Administration."

We all got out, and Sergeant Ibrahim headed up the walk to the door. The other three sergeants walked behind me to the door but peeled off when I went inside. I kept up with Sergeant Ibrahim as he strode down the halls, finally ending up in front of a door that had three big gold stars and "JSOC OPS, Gen. Buckner, Commanding" on it.

Sergeant Ibrahim opened the door and let me in, then stayed in the hall and closed the door.

I was alone in the office of a big-time general, I was wearing BDUs instead of dress uniform, and I was without a fucking clue as to what was going on. I didn't have any orders for this duty and I really, truly needed to pee.

Story of my life, right? But instead of freaking out, I just thought of the Great Pumpkin and her gentle advice to keep everything in perspective. I figured that there must be some good explanation for this, so I went up to the desk where a Navy lieutenant (j.g.) was typing on a computer. He was a good-looking guy, so when he held up a finger in a "Wait a minute" gesture, I used the delay to scope him out. He was wearing all the appropriate stuff on his salad bar and had a Surface Warfare badge, as well as a JSOC badge. He was kind of "coffee with lots of cream" colored, had pretty brown eyes, a large straight nose, and he was named Beaumont.

He was a real attractive guy, not like Square Peg, but still good enough to tickle a girl's fancy (or other body parts). I was trying to work up a fantasy when he looked up and said, "Glickstien, right?"

I revised my estimate of his attractiveness upward and said, "Yes." He smiled, and I almost wet my pants (he was climbing ever upward on the attractiveness meter), but Beaumont said, "The XO wants to see you ASAP. Through the door on the left." He pointed and started to turn back to his computer, but I said, "Sir? Any idea what this is about?"

Lieutenant (j.g.) Beaumont smiled again and said, "Marine, we never discuss JSOC business with outside personnel, and I personally don't ever discuss the business of my principals with anyone except them."

His tone was kindness personified, and I understood his logic perfectly, so I nodded my thanks and went over and knocked on the left-hand door. A voice said, "Enter," so I went in.

And I was staring into the face of Brigadier General Terrance McAllen.

It made sense now.

He knew what I could do physically and knew how tough I was, so General McAllen had requested me for SOCOM. But why? There must've been hundreds of Marines just as qualified and many more, well, male, for the job, so why me?

He smiled and said, "All will be made clear, Lieutenant, as soon as you prove that you are ready for this to some of the other brass. Shall we?"

I looked at him and said, "Sir, I still don't get this. It's outside SOP, sir."

Mad Dog laughed and said, "Well, that's totally irrelevant to this exercise so I'm going to follow my orders, if you don't mind."

"Uh, yes, sir," I said. *What the fuck is going on?* was what I thought.

He opened the door to his office and headed out the door. The lovely Lieutenant Beaumont said, "Sir?" and General McAllen said, "Ops training room, son." We went out of the office suite and headed to an elevator. General McAllen bypassed the elevator for some steps, and three stories later, we went down a short corridor to what proved to be a first-class gym, complete with workout mats, several types of weapons and weights that were so beautiful they almost made me cry.

There were several brass standing at the head of the gym, but no one that I knew, plus the four guys I'd ridden in with. The sergeants were all standing in the middle of the mats when we walked in, but General McAllen said, "Defend yourself, Marine," and the four guys became a raging group of attack dogs.

Fong and Ibrahim attacked me frontally, while Branch and Coles moved to flank me. Following SOP in this situation, I attacked Branch, who was moving to flank me on the left; behind him was the bulk of the gym, with lots of room for maneuvering.

He made a typical big-man mistake when fighting someone shorter—he crouched down to my level. I went to full speed and hit him with a flurry of lightning-knife hands. The last four hit him in the low throat, high throat, nose, and right behind his right ear—all neatly provided for me by his crouch. He went down, and I escaped to the open area and immediately attacked Fong from behind instead of running. He was slow to react and took several kicks to the legs before I hit him with three hammer hands in the small of his back. When he leaned back from the impacts, I spun and hit him with an elbow right on the mastoid process behind his left ear. Fong fell like he'd been shot, and I evaded Ibrahim and Coles just long enough to let them get a good look at their buddies lying like big shit heaps on the floor, and then I attacked Coles, who didn't look back fast enough. I was inside his guard before he realized it, caught his uniform at the shoulder and hip opposite each other, and threw him in a judo toss. Before he was really on the floor, I kneed him in the jaw and broke his nose with a perfect knuckle strike. (And yes, I struck down, not up, so get off my ass about possibly killing him. I wasn't even really trying to maim him. Well, maybe I was trying to maim him a little bit, but hey, it was four to one, so STFU.)

I popped up and moved laterally away from Ibrahim, who was totally relaxed and "open on all eight sides" (a kendo term that means ready for any attack). He was smiling a confident little smile, so I cut hard to my right, ran up the wall, and descended on him like a Valkyrie attacking a frost giant. (Hey, look it up. It's not my fault that you had a deficient education.)

Ibrahim was totally unprepared for my attack. On my descent, I realized that this was a trap, so I altered my trajectory, collapsed into a ball, and rolled right past, just missing his massive two-handed hammer-blow, which probably would have killed me.

I stayed on the mat and did a low spin kick, taking him off his feet. I lunged onto his back, circled his throat with my left arm, locked my right arm into my left, and choked him unconscious in eight seconds. I jumped to my feet and went over to where Branch was trying to get to his feet.

"Stay down, Branch. You got some real damage there, Hoss," I said.

"Fuck you, bitch," he said through clenched teeth. "I'm an Army Ranger. I'll fuckin' stay down when I'm dead." He got to his feet, and I kicked him straight in the balls, whereupon he took his macho self back to the mat for some alone time with both his bruised cookies and bruised ego. "Then you're out of uniform, shithead, because that blouse says Air Force," I said, but he didn't answer back (he was too busy communing with the Great Testicle God, who was warning him about playing with little girls).

I surveyed the human piles and saw that Coles also was trying to rise. I went over and said, "Got-damn, Coles! We're on the same side. Stay down or I'll put your ass in sick bay for a month, Green Beret or not." Coles looked up at me and said, "Ya put some tit into that last shot, Glickstein. I can't feel anything from my jaw down on the right side. It's like I'm paralyzed or some shit."

"Don't worry, Coles, it's just nerve shock. You'll be better in about an hour, but that tomato you call a nose is gonna hurt like a motherfucker. Make sure they give you the good drugs before they set it, you know what I mean?"

He tried to smile and weakly raised his hand. We fist-bumped, and Coles fell back. I turned around and said, "General McAllen, these men need immediate medical attention. I request you summon several corpsmen, especially for Sergeant Branch. He's in a real world of hurt and could have a problem with his testicles, sir. I nailed him dead nuts on, sir."

The brass all laughed at that, but General McAllen was looking at my face and did not laugh. He said, "Right away, Marine. Anything else?"

"Permission to speak freely, sir?" I said.

"Permission granted," the general said.

"Sir, the next time you try a stunt like that, I'm going to put everybody else in the room in the hospital, even if it means my court-martial, sir. I understand your motivation, sir, but that was low and completely despicable. Those men were not briefed, and even if they had been, it was still a dirty trick. Remember that I'm a womyn of my word, sir."

General McAllen made to speak, but he was interrupted by a four-star admiral who stepped out of the brass clusterfuck and said, "That was done on my orders, Marine." He was a trim-looking guy wearing a Navy dress uniform, and he was clearly upset by my little speech, because his face was red and he had that condescending I'm-your-superior-officer-so-can-the-shit look on his face, but I was the product of my training, so I said, "Sir, I don't give a flying fuck if God herself gave those orders—they were a dereliction of duty, and the demo was utterly absurd."

"Excuse me, *Lieutenant*," the four-star said in his best intimidation-through-rank voice. "When I want your opinion, I'll—"

I interrupted him and said, "Yes, sir, you'll rip off my head and shit down my neck. I've heard it before, sir, but the orders were just plain stupid. When the chairman of the Joint Chiefs calls you tomorrow and says, "I need your four best men for a classified mission of the highest importance," these four guys will be unavailable, because they'll still be in sick bay. And those are very good men who've seen the elephant, sir. They've been deep in the shit and come out the other side, and now you embarrass them and cause them to doubt their training, all to satisfy some residual macho impulse or to prove that you somehow earned those four stars, sir? With all due respect, Admiral, that is counter to Marine small-unit leadership doctrine, and worse, it's shortsighted and shows a lack of strategic thinking. If I'd done something like that in Basic my DI would've made me do 1000 push-ups and run a damned marathon, sir. Poor decision-making is poor decision-making, sir, regardless of the braid or insignia on the shoulder boards, *sir*." (I used my speak-truth-to-command voice, figuring that at least I'd get points in the brig for my *chutzpah*.)

The four-star looked at me and said, "I *am* the C-JCS, Marine, and I'm curious about your response to orders from your superior officers."

Oh, fuck a duck.

I'd just read the riot act to Admiral David Nelson Hardy, the chairman of the Joint Chiefs of Staff and the highest-ranking officer in the United States military.

So I stood as straight as possible and fell back on my training. I saluted him and said, "Sir, I am at your disposal to satisfy your curiosity, sir!" just like I was back in Basic and he was Gunnery Sergeant Thornton. I stared straight ahead and thought about my brief career in the Corps, because nobody gets to talk to C-JCS like that except the president, God, or his wife.

Admiral David Nelson Hardy had a booming laugh. It echoed off the walls of the gym as he walked right up to me and said, "Stand easy, Glickstien." I relaxed but didn't look at him, because only fools and drunks looked the C-JCS in the eyes (and no, I wasn't a fool, just a stubborn asshole bitch who knew she was right). Admiral David Nelson Hardy stuck his hand out and said, "Terry told me about you, but I didn't believe it, and yes, you are right about the demonstration. I'm old now, and I guess I was trying to make myself feel good, vicariously reliving my youth, although I certainly wasn't ever that good. In fact, I've only seen one person who was as good as you in my career." His eyes slid to the right, looking at a two-star in a Marine uniform.

I looked at the two-star and immediately stiffened back to attention, because I knew who this guy was, even if we had never met.

It was Rodney Alvarez.

A mustang officer—a mustang starts out in the enlisted ranks and then becomes an offi-cer—Alvarez was a Recon Marine, a Marine sniper extraordinaire, won the Medal of Honor in Afghanistan, and should have won it again for valor in an unnamed action where he put down twenty-five Russians before they knew he was even there and then exfiltrated right through an entire division (they gave him the Navy Cross instead). He was also the greatest living special operator in the entire U.S. military and the youngest commandant of the Marine Corps in history.

I was in the presence of a fucking legend in the flesh, so much so that everyone called him The War God.

I had goose bumps as big as the Himalayas.

I was also totally fucked sideways, because Rodney Alvarez was not going to react well to my little tirade. This guy was the definition of the squared-away Marine, even more than General McAllen, and discipline meant more to these warriors than my gentle sensibilities. I hadn't demonstrated this when I chewed out the Chairman of the Joint Chiefs of Staff. In fact, I'd been insubordinate; I was right about the four guys and the exercise, but I was still downright insubordinate.

Oh, fuck a duck.

General Alvarez got right to my ear, stopped, and said, "Can I play too?" Suddenly, he was right in my face, just like a DI would be. His brown eyes drilled into me like a .50-caliber slug boring into an elephant's heart as he said, "Whaddya think, Marine? Ya think that you can take me?"

I hesitated for a nanosecond, calculating his age, fitness, and training against mine. Before I could answer, he smiled and said, "Admiral, I believe that Glickstien and I are going to have a go-'round, sir, if that meets with your approval." He glided over to the rack of *kendo* sticks, grabbed two, and tossed me one.

"Let's see watchoo got, leetle girl," he said, trying to intimidate me with his Hispanic act, as well as calling me *little* to demean me and get inside my head, but he'd picked the wrong girl for that. After all, I'd grown up dealing with my brothers and parents and *zayde* my whole life, so psychological warfare was like mother's milk to me.

I was still scared shitless, though.

It wasn't David and Goliath; it was an ant (me) vs. a giant (The War God).

Then I thought, *Fuck it, go down fighting, Marine,* said a prayer to the sword-saint Musashi, and attacked The War God like a ginger tornado.

He was incredibly fast and fluid as water over smooth stones, and his footwork was like watching Leonardo paint, but what really made General Alvarez a tough opponent was that he clearly didn't care whether he lived or died. Everything he did was predicated on the fact that he would have to be killed, because he wasn't going to lose.

It reminded me of an old *Star Trek: Deep Space Nine* episode where Worf was being held prisoner by the Dominion and was forced to fight in a ring against Jem'Hadar soldiers. After he had beaten a bunch of them, he was forced to fight the top Jem'Hadar soldier, and he lost, but old Worf wouldn't quit. Finally, the Jem'Hadar turned to the camp commander and said, "I yield. I cannot defeat this Klingon. I can only kill him."

That was The War God in a nutshell.

We fought for twenty unrelenting minutes (you try it sometime; just make sure that you have your Life Alert bracelet charged up), wooden blades whirling and chopping as we sought each other's weaknesses. We hacked at each other, parried, lunged, dodged, issued strokes from every conceivable angle, and still neither of us had touched the other.

Then it was over.

I let him think that I was more tired than I was, deliberately slipped, just a bit (I was after a tiger, and tigers sniff out traps, so it had to be subtle) and then went on the offensive, making like a demented Weedwhacker from a Stephen King story. When I repeated the teeny, tiny mistake from before the attack, The War God pounced, issuing from above with a killing stroke so swift it defied belief, and so powerful it would have broken my bones.

Except it hit the floor. As the stroke was made, I was whirling in a semicircle, dancing out from under the killing blow and issuing a counterstroke to catch General Alvarez right at the waist. I held my stroke, gently laying the wood on his waist, but he knew what that meant, and so did I.

With real steel, I would have separated him into two neat parts.

We stood like that for what seemed like an hour but was probably only a second, engulfed by the silence of sheer surprise emanating from the spectators. The silence was broken by clapping as the brass applauded our effort, and The War God said, "You're now a member of Task Force Bravo, Operation Sphinx, Marine. Prepare to work your ass off for three months' training." He stuck out his hand, and we shook. He looked me in the eye and said, "I talked to Master Gunnery Sergeant Berkey the other day, and she told me a story about a Marine named Roy Hobbs. I almost didn't believe her, but then I got a call from Sergeant Major Gunnett, who told me about a Marine who kicked the living shit out of seven male motherfuckers who were trying to rape her and another female in the shower room, and then my old pal Terry McAllen tells me a story about the best Marine reee-cruit he's ever seen, and well… I decided I needed to meet this *wunderkind.*"

I was impressed that he used the word *wunderkind*—not a lot of call for the word itself, and I was pretty sure that General Alvarez hadn't used it much in his youth in East LA. So I opened my mouth for some smart-ass comment when he stepped even closer and said, "So what's the deal, Loot? You a bull dyke who wants to impress the ladies, or are you really a guy who had reassignment surgery so your body would be more compatible with your inner womyn?"

I went cold, so angry that I could have cut glass with the look I gave him. He stared right back at me, so I said, "Sir, permission to speak free—"

"Fuck you, Glickstien! I don't give a damn about the fucking protocols of rank here. It's just us special operators here, so what's your fucking deal, you raggedy cunt?"

I was beyond myself now, just a wisp of pure anger floating in the air, looking for someone to strike, but also so clear in my mind that I let it all go.

"Fuck you, the horse you rode in on, and the family dog, Alvarez. My sexuality isn't the question here. The question is, how do all of you special operators salve your wounded egos because you got your ass kicked by a *girl*, isn't it? Like I said, fuck you. I'm a got-damned U.S. Marine, tacohead, and I don't need any approbation or approval from some got-damned REMF greaser, gold stars or not, to prove it. You want me to piss standing up? Fine, I'll just piss down my leg, which will remind me of all the chickenshit men who've tried to use my gender against me to keep me down. You're supposed to be this legendary operator, beaner, but all you are is another sexist-pig motherfucker who thinks that his rank entitles him to lord it over the little ladies. You think what we just did was bad? You come at me without sticks and you'll find out, but you'll need to tell me one thing first."

"And what's that, you kike faggot?" Alvarez said.

I looked straight into his eyes and said, "Just tell me where you want your piece-of-shit body shipped, you wetback, guacamole-for-brains asshole."

We glared at each other for a bit, until General Alvarez said, "You weren't kidding, XO. She's really not afraid of anything, is she?"

"Not that I've found, sir," General McAllen said.

"Seems like a perfect special operator to me, Mars," Admiral Hardy said.

"Mars?" I said.

"Roman god of war," Alvarez said. "You're going to find out why in about forty-eight hours, G2."

"I'd prefer Freak, sir," I said.

"Freak it is, then," General Alvarez said. "Although G2 wasn't a bad handle."

"Because I'm short?" I said.

"Yeah, and remember, good things come in small packages," The War God said.

"Like C4, .50 caliber, and tactical nukes," I said.

"She's gonna fit into the unit like a well-worn shoe," General Alvarez said to Admiral Hardy.

"Sir, if I may ask an impertinent question. What are Task Force Bravo and Operation Sphinx?"

"Classified," everybody in the room said at once.

"You'll know when you need to know," Admiral Hardy said.

"And not one minute before," The War God said.

"And don't ask again outside a secure room," General McAllen said.

"Yes, sirs," I said.

"Oh, just so you know, Freak, my family are fourteenth-generation *Californios*, so the terms *beaner*, *greaser*, and *wetback* don't apply, although I suppose that guacamole for brains does," The War God said, a smile creasing his face. "Don't forget *asshole*, sir," General McAllen said with a straight face.

"Roger that," Admiral Hardy said. Everybody laughed and Alvarez said, "Concur, Chief," which set off another round of laughter.

"And I will be breaking the arms of the next person to call me *cunt* or *kike*, although *faggot* never did bother me," I said, smiling like butter wouldn't melt in my mouth.

"Roger that, Freak," The War God said.

"Sir," I said, but he cut me off. "We're special operators, Freak. We don't go in much for rank or protocol. Just talk, OK?"

"Roger that. So when do I start training, Mars?" I said.

"It started when you got off the plane and ID'd those sergeants as not Air Force personnel but still followed orders, even though it must have been driving you crazy," General Alvarez said.

"True tests are never obvious," I said.

"Old Frank Herbert's Bene Gesserit was some smart biatches," General Alvarez said. (Hey, look it up. It's not my fault that you didn't read classic science fiction.)

"Concur, Mars. When do we go see our operators in sick bay?" I said.

"Who says we have anybody in sick bay?" Alvarez said. I looked at him and didn't say a word. Finally, he nodded and said, "Terry told me that you were smart, but I didn't believe him. How'd you figure those are our guys?"

"You wanted a true test of my abilities, so you'd care enough to send the first team. Also, Ibrahim, Coles, and Fong are all faster than shit through a goose. Plus, they were all using standard special ops tactics and maneuvers. Branch is slow—injured in the Sandbox, I'd say, and not fully recovered—but he told me he's a Ranger, and we all know that there aren't any pussies in the Rangers. I'd say that Coles was probably a Recon Marine, and Ibrahim and Fong are probably SEALs. That trap Ibrahim laid on me was pretty sophisticated, and he thought of it in about nineteen nanoseconds…and that screams SEAL."

"Can I just promote her now?" Mars said to Admiral Hardy.

"Can I keep her as my S-2?" a guy I found out was General Buckner said.

"If I don't decide to keep her as my personal aide and bodyguard, it'll be up to you, Mars," the C-JCS said.

"Too good of an operator, sir," Mars said with a smile. "She's mine. Can you imagine caging a tiger in a Pentagon office and having to face it every day to get to your office?"

"When you put it that way…" the C-JCS said.

"And you haven't even seen her shoot yet, sir," General McAllen said. "Imagine that the tiger has 9-mil projectile teeth that never miss when she spits at you."

The chairman of the Joint Chiefs of Staff laughed and said, "All yours, Mars. I think that she'll fit right in with your merry band of warriors. Another sword in the scabbard, eh?"

All the top brass laughed at some inside joke and left the room. I was alone with Generals McAllen, Buckner, and Alvarez. They all smiled at one another, and General Buckner said, "Freak, I hereby assign you to General Alvarez until further notice. You are not to discuss this appointment with anyone except authorized personnel within the program. Are we clear?"

"Yes, sir. No sharing about my assignment with anyone."

"Good. XO, any last words of wisdom for the lieutenant?"

"Yes, sir, just one. Remember where you came from, Marine. Semper fi, Freak," General McAllen said.

"Boo-rah, sir," I said. General Buckner and General McAllen both shook my hand and left, leaving just me and Mars.

"Time to head down the rabbit hole, Alice," Mars said.

"Ooh, is it a tea party?" I said.

"Just like, except we're gonna be drinking blood 'stead of tea," Mars said.

"Will there be finger sandwiches too?" I said. "Like *real* finger sandwiches?"

"Oh, the warriors are gonna love you," Mars said.

And they did love me, and I loved them back.

And no, it wasn't that kind of love at all, you perverts (c'mon, you know you were all thinking it).

It was better.

CHAPTER 18

The Freak Goes Down the Rabbit Hole

You may have already guessed this, but in case you haven't, let me be explicit.

None of those names from the previous chapter are real, except the brass, because those guys are public figures. By now everybody knows who Rodney Alvarez was, and thinks that they know what he did. And yes, I was a part of that still-classified operation, which is why you won't find anything about it here.

I served with lots of great men, none of whom were named Ibrahim, Coles, Fong, or Branch; those are all pseudonyms, as are Task Force Bravo and Operation Sphinx. Special operators are secretive by their nature, and also by necessity. Unit safety requires anonymity, so don't expect any straight dope about what I did for special operations.

I will say this about my spec ops career.

We never killed anyone who didn't deserve to die.

We didn't kill anyone who wasn't a direct threat to the USA.

We never killed out of hate, only necessity.

We never tortured anyone.

We never left any of ours behind, except in one very special situation.

We never undertook any operation without direct orders from NCA (National Command Authority, a.k.a. the president).

We probably saved the world at least three times.

You probably won't believe me on this one, especially those of you of the liberal persuasion, but we never enjoyed killing anyone, even some of the evilest motherfuckers to ever walk the earth.

We did what we did because it was necessary for the survival of our country and, in at least three cases, probably our species.

We did what we did because we were the best trained, best equipped, and best suited for doing it.

Almost all of what we did will never be known to the public, but if it was, most of you would approve. (Again, sorry hard left-wingers, but it's true. If it's any consolation, trickle-down economics still don't work, but the hard right-wingers still cling to that delusion.)

I would absolutely do everything that we did again, except one thing, and that is just a matter of tactics (it should have been done with a nuclear weapon, preferably a cruise missile).

I served with people named T-Bone, Scalper (tickets, not heads—jeez, ya cretins!), Spoony, Zapper, Kreskin, Tweedle-dee and Tweedle-dum, Snortz, Gummy, Hot Pants, Lemonjello (pronounced Leh-mon gell-o), PDQ, Shorty, Gunga Din, Beef, Barf, Snerd, Bucky, Big Johnson (yep, ya pervs got that one right), Roo, Froggy, Mad Dog, Brisket, Funkalicious, Bonzai Bob, Big Kahuna, Big Bird, Matador, Muggsy, Snake, Paavo, Oscar the Grouch, Furburger (don't ask), Sinbad, Forks,

Geezer, Double Axel, Mouse, Fish, Tiny, Tink (for Tinkerbelle, but only one person dared call him that), Monet, Mitb (hey, if Hoda Kotb can do it, why not a special operator?), Dinger, Popeye, Shaka, Zulu, Farmboy, Dracula, Adonis, Xeno, Whisper, Bad Doobie, Kid Galahad, Titless, Porky, Swabby, Wanker, Twanger, Iago, Gordo, Badass, and Boris Badass, which is all you're ever going to get to know about the guys I served with as special operators, except for a few guys you'll meet later.

I will say this: they were the best brothers a girl could ever have, and I would still do anything for them.

As for all the work we did…well, not to be too cliché, but it's all still classified, so fuck off and die.

And that's all I'm gonna say about that. (My thanks to Tom Hanks.)

CHAPTER 19

The Freak Comes through the Looking Glass

So after eight years I can't and won't talk about, I decided to become a civilian again. It wasn't because I was tired of Spec Ops so much as I couldn't stand losing people I loved anymore, so I decided to leave the Marine Corps for a different kind of life.

I became a Secret Service agent instead.

I know, I know, out of the frying pan and into the fire, but working for the Secret Service meant that I got to guard and not kill people (often). It especially meant that I could continue in an organization that I admired, that offered me a sense of belonging, and that treated me with dignity.

And before we go any further, don't let all the recent negative press fool you—the Secret Service is as competent an agency as can be found in the U.S. government, or anywhere in the world, for that matter. All the public ever hears about are the fuckups, which are always sensationalized by the media. The Secret Service is treated by the world kind of like teachers are: all you ever hear about is the hot teacher that slept with one of her students, not the 1.9 million teachers who worked their asses off so your rotten little urchins could get an education. Like the CIA (those fucks), the Secret Service never advertises its successes, so all that ever gets out are the negative actions of a few idiots. Anybody who doesn't understand that the Secret Service, America's teachers, and the CIA (those fucks) are filled with highly trained, extremely competent people who flawlessly execute their job 99.99 percent of the time is either stupid or a Tea Party fanatic from East Bumfuck, Idaho.

Don't believe me? Try attacking the president some time, or counterfeiting 100 dollar bills, or shoving something into the hands of the first daughters.

Just tell me where you want the body shipped first.

In any case, I left SOCOM as a Marine Corps Major, applied for a job with the FBI, Secret Service, U.S. Marshals Service, and every other three-letter agency. (Except NSA and the CIA—no way I'd ever work for those fucks again! Sorry, still classified.)

I figured that I'd have quite a wait, since government has two speeds, glacial and full stop, but the Secret Service called first, only two days after I'd finished the application. The only way that happens is if someone bigfoots your app up the line. I wondered who my rabbi was in this case.

I found out when I went in for my first interview and the three-person panel was made up of a womyn named Marchand; a guy named Kalas, who looked just like General Terry McAllen (except this guy was White); and Charlie Hassenger, then Secretary of the Treasury and soon to be the president's Chief of Staff. Hassenger and I had gone to high school together at Harper Creek, but I hadn't seen him in years.

Mystery of the rabbi explained. I had at least three, including one really big gun. Even though the Secret Service is currently under the domain of Homeland Security, it had been the property of the Treasury Department for over 100 years. SecTreas still pulled a lot of water with regard to the

Secret Service. It probably didn't hurt that I'd given Hassenger a blow job after the junior prom, but I doubt if that was the primary consideration after 20-plus years.

The Marchand lady turned out to be Natalie's aunt Sarah; Kalas was Delvin P. Kalas, USMC, retired (as a Major General, he and General McAllen were at the Naval Academy together and remained close), and you've already met Charlie Hassenger.

My interview was short, to the point, and completely unnecessary, since the first thing that Hassenger said was, "Major Glickstien, you've got the job if you want it," but we went through the form anyway.

When it was over, we all shook hands, and Hassenger said, "Your second interview is tomorrow at 9:00 a.m., at the Hays-Adams Hotel. Don't be late, Freak." He smiled at me and then was gone, again leaving me to wonder what the fuck was going on. It hit me as I was leaving the building.

The Republican presidential candidate wanted to meet me.

Remember, I knew this guy. He was seven years in front of me at good old Harper Creek High, and I had beaten him out for the Athlete of the Century in Battle Creek, so we had a small history.

And his wife hated me, which I figured might be a plus. FLOTUS (work it out—remember that she was the first lady) and I stopped getting along when my brother Aaron beat her out for valedictorian during high school, but the hatred started when I beat up her three brothers for picking on Suzy Glanders (yeah, I know, anybody named Glanders is getting picked on in school) for being "stupid." Since Suzy wasn't stupid—she was a Down syndrome girl—I objected to the characterization and threw down with the three much-larger-than-me brothers of the future FLOTUS (it really isn't that hard if you think about it).

I proceeded to royally thrash the three lunkheads in full view of several people who could have stopped it but didn't really want to, since the brothers of the future FLOTUS (see, I knew you could do it—got it now, dontcha?) were (a) total silver spoon pricks who thought that their status as the kids of a Kellogg's board member (Battle Creek is the Cereal City for a reason) made it perfectly OK to lord it over anybody they wanted, even special kids who couldn't defend themselves, and (b) even the teachers didn't like the three lunkheads, all of whom fancied themselves athletes, gentlemen, and massively intelligent scholars. Since that usually translated into lame questions, grade grubbing, and outright insubordination, the eleven teachers who saw me open a can of whup-ass on the three lunkheads waited until they were all whacked silly and then lied like rugs and said that the lunkheads had attacked me without provocation.

The three lunkheads got three days off school, and I got a new friend in Suzy Glanders, who turned out to be just about the best person I ever met. I also got an anonymous gift from the entire teaching staff—a get-out-of-class-anytime permanent pass—for putting the lunkhead brothers of the future FLOTUS (Okay, remember that she was the first lady of the United States. Did you go to school at Pennfield? [Note: local BC school that was thought to contain many unintelligent people]. Bellevue? [Note: Ditto previous note.] Keep working on it.) down for being overbearing jackass twerps. The teaching staff also conspired against the future FLOTUS (if you haven't got it, I'm not telling you) to make sure my brother was valedictorian. (Did I mention that she was a grade-A, class-one, ball-busting bitch? No? Well, she was all that and a bag of chips. Seriously, look in the dictionary under *megabitch*—you'll find her high school graduation picture.) They did it by giving her three A-minuses, which just barely dropped her GPA below Aaron's 4.0.

She blamed me for the A-minuses, and she was right, but that didn't stop me from letting her have it when she tried to confront me about it with her posse of bitchy girls.

> Future FLOTUS: So you're the *girl* (*finger quotes*) that beat up my poor brothers.
> Me: I pee just like you, so yeah, I'm that girl. And since you're all financially wealthy, you
> must be referring to your brothers' state of mind, which I agree with.
> FF: Huh?
> Me: Being poor indicates an inferior state of mind, which I agree your brothers possess.
> FF: Huh?
> Me: It's another way to say they're puerile and intellectually unpromising.
> FF: Huh?
> Me: It means they're stupid, dipshit.

It actually went downhill from there.

All this went through my head as I thought about meeting with James Patrick Liam Sheehan, University of Michigan grad (boo, hiss, finger cross against evil! Go Green! Go White!), Heisman Trophy winner, former governor and congressman and current junior senator from the great state of Michigan, and the presumptive Republican nominee for president.

I hated the idea of this guy, even though I kind of liked him personally. He was literally an altar boy for St. Philip Catholic Church. He was tall, built like a brick shithouse (Midwestern for "Look at that killer body!"), smart (1590 on the old SAT, 35 on the ACT, summa cum laude from U of M), witty, genuine (well, as much as any politician can be), patriotic, and a slam-dunk public speaker.

This guy was the real deal, despite the fact that he was an asshole Republican governor that cut funds for roads, schools, and law enforcement so that he could get his wealthy donors a tax break or 11.

So the next morning, I met Senator James Sheehan for breakfast. It went better than I thought it would.

> Senator: Freak, howarya?
> Me: Good, Golden Boy. You?
> Senator: Can't complain.
> Me: Well, that's good. Nobody'd listen, anyway.
> Senator: Except for *Face the Nation*, the *Free Press*, and the RNC.
> Me: OK, you win the pissing contest.

We all laughed at that, just like old friends, even though we really weren't. And then the senator said, "So how are your parents and your grandpa? I should get that guy to be AG when I'm president—he could outargue anybody else we could ever get, right?" He looked at me with that "sincere" look that politicians use, even though he didn't have to, since my *zayde* really could have outargued anyone. His use of a politician's trick made it doubly satisfying to say, "Senator, my *zayde* died last year."

This time the look and tone were both really sincere. The governor's eyes welled up just a bit, and he said, "Glinka, I'm sorry. I didn't know. What happened?"

I looked him straight in the eye and said, "A teenage driver was on his cell phone when he hit a pothole and veered off course. He hit my *zayde* head-on and busted him up. It took the EMTs over forty minutes to get there to help, and by that time my *zayde* had bled out."

The silence was deafening. Two years before, as governor of Michigan, the senator had signed a budget bill that cut public services (including the number of EMTs) in the state, failed to fully fund desperately needed road repairs, and had vetoed a bill that banned talking on your cell phone while driving, claiming that it violated the rights of "ordinary Americans."

The fact that I was lying about it all was irrelevant; it was just fun to stick a pin in this master of the universe (MOTU).

Can you tell I didn't give a flying fuck about getting the job?

After what seemed like an hour, the senator said, "And you blame me, right?"

"No," I said, "I blame that asshole who was on his phone and not controlling his car. But I did want to remind you that actions have consequences, senator, many of them of the unforeseen variety."

"So you and I are good?" he said.

"Yeah, but I wouldn't go anywhere near my mom and dad, or Aaron, or David. They'll still kick your Irish ass, senator or not," I said.

"Agreed. I truly am sorry about Mr. Blumenthal. I liked and respected him," the senator said. "He was one of those guys that made Battle Creek such a good place to grow up." His eyes were really watering now, and a small tear ran down his cheek. It was the most genuine moment that I'd ever seen from any politician and touched me deep in my heart.

"Well, he was 87 years old, and he'd lived a good life, so at least he didn't suffer along in need of relief," I said. As governor Sheehan had also vetoed the legislature's attempt at an Oregon-style law allowing assisted suicide. I had to take the shots when I could, because if this guy became president while I was with the Secret Service, I wouldn't be able to, and besides, he deserved it, the arrogant prick.

As if he had read my mind, Governor Sheehan said, "I deserved that one too." He laughed, and I laughed, and then I said, "And what about the bit—er, putative first lady? She and I really don't hit it off."

He laughed and said, "Oh, fuck her! I get to help those I want to help, and I don't need her input. I looked at your service jacket—a lot of redaction there—and I've known you a long time. You want the job?"

"Yes, Governor, I really want to be a Secret Service agent," I said.

He looked at me and said, "Well, that asshole Charlie! He didn't tell you?"

"Tell me what?" I asked.

"That I intend to have you on the presidential protective detail once I'm elected president."

You could have knocked my fat white ass over with a feather.

James Sheehan laughed and said, "I'm going to win the election next year, Freak. I've got the money, my organizations are in place across the country, and the electoral math looks good. I can't compete in New York or Pennsylvania, but I'm already polling ahead in California, Virginia, Ohio, Florida, and Michigan. And the Democrats are going to tear themselves apart over the current administration's policies, which I have nothing to do with. My state is going great, and I'm going to be the tallest, best-looking person at all the debates. And you know that I can do that."

It was true; he led our debate team to the state championship three straight times and could probably outtalk P. T. Barnum, and he was smarter than hell.

I nodded, and Sheehan said, "So I'm thinking ahead. I talked to Charlie, and he thinks that you'll have to spend at least two years on the counterfeiting side, which means that you'll be ready to transition to the protective detail during my transition, right? What could be better than having the president of the United States as a rabbi? Do they actually call it that, a rabbi?"

"Nah, that's an old term from cop shows past," I said. "We call it having someone bigfoot your career, you know, to stomp the opposition to your moving up with a big foot." I paused and looked him straight in the eye.

He said, "What? You've got a question or two?" The semator smiled and sat back in his chair with that smug asshole look that MOTUs (remember? Masters of the Universe) get when they know that we lesser mortals are going to do their bidding. So I gave him a ration of shit, because I knew that I was going to do whatever I had to in order to get the protective detail.

"Why me? Why tell me now?" I asked.

"My daughters are 12 and ten right now, and they need someone to guard them when I'm president. Who better than you?" he said.

I stood up and responded, "Fuck you, Golden Boy. I hate kids, and only a psychotic masochist would take on two teenagers, especially ones who have been pampered and catered to all their lives."

His face fell, and his jaw literally dropped. The future president made an inarticulate sound and then stared at me. I don't think that he'd been talked to like that in a very long time, so I stuck the needle in a little further, just to see if I could get away with it. (And before you get all concerned because I was ruining my future or souring my relationship with a powerful person who could directly affect my career, please remember that I was a Marine and special ops veteran; powerful people didn't impress me unless they had been there and done that, and all this guy had faced were 300-pound men intent on harming him, but with *rules* and *restrictions*. Go into combat against people whose only job is to kill you and come out the other side and I'll be impressed. Otherwise, just shut the fuck up.)

"And I got your wife knocked down to salutatorian, mainly because she's a prize bitch," I said.

He jumped to his feet, and his eyes got red. Go figure. He really did love that skinny twat, even with her 100% bitch personality. And I said, "Oh, don't get your panties all in a bunch. It isn't like you were Athlete of the Century in Battle Creek. You got beat out by a *girrrlll*." I dragged it out just like a playground insult, enjoying the sudden rage on his face. And then he got it.

"You're busting my balls, right? There's no way you'd say that to anyone else or even remotely give up a chance to be on the protective detail, not after being a special ops warrior. You just want to give me shit, Fighting Beaver to Fighting Beaver, right?" he said.

"Yeah, I'd pretty much guard that asshole Dick Cheney if it meant getting on the detail," I said. "Although in that case, I might be a step slow when it came to a gun." We both laughed, and he shook my hand.

"I still would like to know why you'd want me to guard your daughters, Golden Boy," I said.

"Well, your nickname sort of says it all. You're the Freak from Battle Creek, but beyond that, I've never seen a more physically or emotionally capable individual in my life, and I played 12 years in the NFL. I can't imagine anyone getting close to my girls with you around, and even though she still doesn't like you, Laura feels the same way. And yes, I asked her before this meeting," he said.

"So you want me to guard your bratty teenagers just because I'm a physical freak? That's not the greatest endorsement I've ever heard," I said.

James Sheehan took my hand back, looked down at me from his 6'5" vantage point, and said, "I trust you. Your physical attributes are a plus, but I read as much of your file as I could and it confirmed what I already knew: you are a good person, from a good family, and you are worthy of any trust that I can invest in you."

It was the sincerest thing I've ever heard from a politician. Not only did he mean it, but my acceptance also seemed to lift a weight off his back. His eyes looked almost relieved, as if he'd been carrying something around. I wondered about it at that time, but then his chief of staff said, "Sir? We've got to get to the committee meeting?" and the spell was broken.

I said, "Sir, I'd be honored to guard your daughters." We shook hands, and the next day, I was told to report to the Department of Homeland Security for training as a Secret Service agent.

I should have thought harder about why me, but I'd been dazzled by the bullshit, which would come back to bite me in the ass.

Like, literally bite me in the ass.

Again.

CHAPTER 20

Chicago Freak

Let me get one thing straight: I. Love. Chicago.

My first posting after training was to the Windy City, and I was ecstatic. I'd loved the city since I was a kid, and my *zayde* took me to the Art Institute of Chicago. We went in the front door, right between the lions, saw world-class art, then walked over to Portillo's on Ontario Avenue and had the best hot dogs I'd ever eaten—and I was hooked, forever.

You can find world-class entertainment in Chicago, from the Chicago Symphony Orchestra to some of the best blues clubs anywhere (Buddy Guy's Legends on Wabash leaps to mind), two Major League Baseball teams, an Original Six hockey team (Boo! Hiss! Go Red Wings! Sorry, Michigan girl—gotta hate the Blackhawks), an iconic NBA franchise, and one of the true originals in the NFL (da Bears) playing in a stadium that has the echoes of the origins of professional sports in America, not to mention the world's greatest art museum, the Art Institute of Chicago.

That list doesn't include the Field Museum of Natural History (the best natural history museum outside the Smithsonian), the Shedd Aquarium, the Museum of Science and Industry, the Adler Planetarium, two high-rise observatories at the Sears Tower (yeah, it's the Willis Tower, but fuck them, everybody still calls it the Sears Tower), and the John Hancock building (where you can see across Lake Michigan), the Cultural Center, and a hundred other museums and arty places. And don't forget Navy Pier.

You can walk down the Magnificent Mile and find literally anything that you want to buy, from Coach purses to the best popcorn ever popped, ending up at the Water Tower Place mall, a collection of stores that will satisfy any shopping need.

There's always a parade in Chicago, and parades need food. If you ever want to see the perfect orgy of food, you need to get to the Taste of Chicago (usually the second week in July) and try to eat the world, because this is the largest picnic you'll ever see. Whatever you want is available, reasonably cheap, and just plain *good*.

One year my family and I tried to see how much we could eat. Did I mention that my brother Morris and I once ate fifty hot dogs each on a bet? No? Well, we did it for the American Cancer Society fundraiser in Battle Creek. Our math teacher, Mr. Colley, bet us that we couldn't eat 25 hot dogs in four hours and said he would pay us $5 a dog if we got to 25. So we went for 50 and got it. For the record, I actually ate 53, and Mo ate 51, but we rounded down for the sake of our teacher, who was not rich but gladly offered up the $500 after the contest.

We found that we were considerable eaters, especially when it came to hot dogs. We ate every hot dog we came across and decided that for our family it came down to about five places.

Before we go any further, please note that Chicago also has pizza, barbecue, steaks, Italian, Chinese, Mexican, Armenian, Russian, Polish, and literally any other kind of food you want, and most of it is world-class. It has to be in order to compete, but this isn't a food book, so I'm not going to write about that.

But I will rank hot dog places according to the Glickstien family.

And before you get all wanked out about me leaving your favorite place off the list, well, fuck you—this is my family's list, not your family's. Write your own damn book if you want to complain.

And before we get any further, we are talking about Chicago-style hot dogs. That means a steamed poppy seed roll, bright-green relish, tomatoes, onions, yellow mustard, a spear of dill pickle, sport peppers, and celery salt, along with an all-natural-casing Vienna Beef hot dog (or its equivalent). No whole wheat buns, no low-fat or skinless dogs, no fancy mustard, steamed or boiled dogs, and absolutely, positively no fucking ketchup.

My family decided, after several samplings both at the Taste of Chicago and the restaurants themselves, that our list would be as follows:

1. Superdawg (6363 North Milwaukee, Chicago). The classic place, a drive-in with dogs-in-a-box and with Superfries. Their dogs are a custom-made recipe and have a great snap and flavor. Don't ask for ketchup.
2. Portillo's (100 West Ontario, Chicago). Excellent dogs and also great Italian beef and Maxwell Street sausages. You will need a cake shake. Trust me. Don't ask the nice singing lady at the counter for ketchup or she'll throw something at you.
3. Gene and Jude's (2720 River Road, River Grove, out by O'Hare Airport). They pile the fries right on the dog, and it works—the dog is just superb. Don't even think about ketchup.
4. Phil's Last Stand (2258 West Chicago Avenue, Chicago). Okay, this dog is char-grilled, but it is so tasty that it doesn't matter. Get the hand-cut, twice-fried fries, too. Ketchup for the fries upon request, but don't push it!
5. Wolfy's Hot Dogs (2734 West Peterson Avenue, Chicago). Great-tasting dog, superhot sport peppers, and Green River soda on the beverage menu. Also, the best celery salt on the planet. I doubt if they ever heard of ketchup.

We'd have put Hot Doug's on here, but Doug Sohn closed the damned place, leaving all of us craving one more hot dog creation and the duck-fat fries. They had a great classic Chicago dog, real snap in the casing, as well as the most inventive other types of dogs ever seen.

But to hell with them. They're closed, so they can't be on the Glickstien family list, the pussies. (OK, so Doug was *always* there, and he may have been just a teeny bit tired. Sorry for calling you a pussy, Doug, but we miss you.)

Feel free to argue with the list all you want, but please remember, this is like asking 10 economists for an opinion on the future and getting back 37 opinions. Nobody is really wrong; they just have different preferences.

In any case, I was posted to Chicago for my first counterfeiting assignment, and I was over the moon. I took a tiny apartment in Wrigleyville on the north side, right near the Wishbone Restaurant on North Lincoln Avenue, learned about all the Metra and El stops needed to get where I needed to go, and reported for work on a bright Monday morning in February.

Did I mention that I liked cold weather? No? Well, I love cold weather, because I hate bugs, and because when the temperature rises above 70 degrees I start to sweat, and because I don't want to have to expose my round body to ridicule—sweats and a T-shirt for me, with a nice sweatshirt over the top.

Anyway, it was 27 below with the windchill (no shit, it got colder that day) when I reported to the Secret Service office at 525 West Van Buren. I was less than two miles from the Art Institute, the CSO, and a host of other great places, and I was working for one of the best organizations in the world.

Life was good.

I went up to the office and met my boss, Agent-in-Charge Jerry Clune, a bluff, hearty Irishman who was a 22-year veteran of the Service. He was just an inch or two taller than me, thick without being fat, and the second-best pistol shot in the Chicago office (as soon as I entered the building—sorry if you think that is arrogant, but it ain't bragging if you can prove it). He took me to my desk and introduced me to my immediate superior, Narita Singh, who ran the counterfeiting investigations in Chicago.

Ms. Singh was an incredibly beautiful Sikh womyn who looked to be about 50 years old. She was whip-thin but had good muscle definition and moved like a ballet dancer. She looked me over and said, "Whattya no 'bowt funnee monee, rook?" (which I later found out meant "What do you know about funny money, rookie?") in the purest New Jersey ("N' Joisie," as she called it) accent I'd ever heard. It was so incongruous that I started laughing and couldn't stop. Jerry and Narita laughed, as did the rest of the office, which made life feel even better. It's great to work at a place where people laugh, because it sure lightens the workload.

When we were all done cackling, Narita said, "Okay, Glickstien, what do I call you?"

"Everybody calls me Freak," I said.

"Say what? Why the hell would they call you that?" Narita said.

I turned to a guy who was sitting in a nice chair at the desk next to mine and said, "Can I use your chair for a minute?"

He smiled and said, "Sure. Anything for a rookie." He started to get up, and I said, "Just sit still." Before he could respond, I dropped into a squat, put my hands under the chair and lifted it off the ground to chest level, positioned it so that the back of the chair was to me, and then pressed the guy and the chair over my head. I turned back to Narita and said, "This is just one of the reasons they call me Freak." I wasn't straining at all, and my voice didn't quaver a bit.

There was dead silence until Jerry Clune said, "Well, fuck me blind, I've never seen anything like that!"

"Holy shit!" Narita said. "Calvin weighs 210, plus 20 pounds of chair. Holy shit!"

"I'm telling you now that I'm not working out with this womyn," Chair Boy said.

"My, what a pussy you are, Bumble!" another agent said.

"Better a live pussy than a dead hero," Chair Boy said.

"I'm also a black belt in aikido, tae kwon do, karate and kendo," I said.

"Well, fuck me, I'm a pussy too," the guy who ribbed Chair Boy said. He came over and stuck out his hand and said, "I'm Stanley Rzepzynski. Call me Gunny, Freak." He was a bald White guy, 6"2", 200, and very fit, with a bit of a challenge in his eyes.

I steadied the chair with my left arm and stuck my right hand out. Rzepzynski and I shook hands during a chorus of "Holy shits!" "Motherfuckers!" "Are you fucking kidding mes?" and "Jesus Christs!" Rzepzynski gave me a nod and let go of my hand, I put Chair Boy down, and everybody took a few minutes to marvel at my freakishness.

I was introduced around. Chair Boy was Calvin "Everybody Calls Me Bumble" Beemond. There were two other female agents, Emily "Ed" Devlin and Siobhan "Mac" McKee, and four more guys: Garrett "Weasel" Wei, Bill "Joe" Cocker, Quentin "House" Bowe and Nolan "The Greek" Laskarides. There were four other agents in the office, all out on investigations. After introductions and some more frivolity, we all decided to actually do some work. I was partnered with Bumble for the day, and he showed me the ropes, got my passwords set up, and took me around.

Right after lunch, Narita had a briefing about current investigations and the potential for other investigations. She also pointed me out again and said, "Freak isn't just another pretty face—she's coming from Special Ops Command and also worked a case or two for NCIS, right?"

"Classified," I said.

Everyone laughed, and Narita said, "Good one, Freak. Whadja do for NCIS?"

I stared back at her without the slightest smile on my face and said, "Senior Agent Singh, that's classified."

Her stare hardened, and she said, "Really?"

"Yes, ma'am," I said, my own stare as hard as diamond.

"Oh," she said. "I thought you were bullshitting us."

"No, ma'am," I said in my best drop-this-now-please voice.

"Shit, Freak is the real deal," Stan "Gunny" Rzepzynski said. "Carry on, Squid."

"Fuck you, Gunnery Sergeant. I'm a fucking Marine," I said.

"Boo-rah!" Rzepzynski, Laskarides, and Bowe said.

"Concur," I said.

"Not this military shit again!" Emily "Ed" Devlin said. "We all appreciate the spirit of camaraderie, but we could do without the macho chip on your shoulders. We Smith girls are delicate."

"Military my ass," I said. "We're Marines, not some chickenshit wing-wipers or dumbass ground-pounders in the Green Machine. Hell, we're not squids, we're Marines."

"No, you most certainly are not Marines. You are now Secret Service agents," Ed said, her mouth set in a prim, disapproving curve.

"That is correct," Siobhan (pronounced "she-vawn" for those of you who are not Gaelic) "Mac" McKee said. "And we Bryn Mawr girls do not approve of such appalling language. We are professional people in a professional setting, are we not?"

"Oh, fuck you, Mac," a new voice said. It came from a really, seriously good-looking Hispanic guy in a very snappy suit who was came through the door of the briefing room. "You remember that case at the Wrigley building? You cussed that security guy out so bad that even House got embarrassed, and we all know that he can use *fuck* as every part of speech."

"It's true, Mac. I turned fuckin' red that time!" Quentin "House" Bowe said. Bowe was 6'6", 280, and so black his skin shone.

"And remember that time when we went to San Antonio and that waiter dumped that tray of drinks on you?" Garrett "Weasel" Wei said. "Holy fuck, fuck! You let fly with that Gaelic shit, and the waiter nearly fried, like, literally."

"Oh, go fuck yourselves, the horse you rode in on, and the family dog," Mac said. She looked at the four Marines and said, "You asswipe, knuckle-draggin' gobshites can be any fookin' thing ya want to be, ya silly shits."

"That's our girl," Bill "Joe" Cocker said. "She even got one of those Gaelic swear words in there! What the fuck is a *gobshite*, anyway?"

"Look in the mirror," everybody said at once. "And you're buying the Pepsis, Joe," Mac said.

"It's a good thing that you can sing, Joe, or we'd have to get rid of your stupid ass," the good-looking Hispanic man, whose name was Emiliano "El Gato" Zaragoza, said.

Everybody laughed, and Bumble said, "Old Joe went to Harvard and finished first in his class, and then finished first at Stanford Law. He's about the smartest guy in the whole unit, and that includes the hackers down at Cyber Crimes."

Joe and I looked at each other for a second, and then we both said, "Wait a minute…"

"You owe me a Pepsi, Joe," I said.

He said, "Done. You're Roady's little sister, aren't ya?"

"I am," I said. "Marvin never talked about anybody at Stanford except Pill and JC. That's you, right?"

"It is. Roady was the best goddamn trial lawyer I ever saw. He won our moot court cases, and I got all the credit. Did he get that clerking job with the Michigan Supreme Court? Justice McCormick?"

"Nah, he called some pal and went to work for Justice Sotomayor. He's with some big Manhattan firm right now, making a shitload of money. He says that he wants to be a federal judge someday, or AG," I said.

"Boys and girls, if the Freak is half as smart as her brother, you all are going to have to catch up, 'cause you are all as dumb as a box of rocks compared to her," Joe said.

"Well, could we fucking prove it sometime today by getting some work done?" Narita Singh said. "We'll let old home week ride until 5:01?" (It actually came out like "Wull, cud we proive et sumti'm tuhday b' gittin' sum woik don?" It was like she was doing a stage act that required a Jersey accent. I admit, I snorted every time she talked the "foist munt'" or "t'ree I woiked dere.")

So Bumble introduced me to our caseload, which seemed pretty pared down compared to special ops. It was also fairly tame. Bumble told me that there hadn't been any shooting in the three years he'd been in Chicago.

"We chase paper and paper pushers. We ID the paper, and then we arrest the pushers. It isn't exciting, and we spend a shitload of time on the computer, but it is useful work and satisfying when we catch the assholes who keep counterfeiting our currency." I shot him a look, and Bumble said, "Ask anybody. It sounds trite and all patriotic, but counterfeiting really hurts the average American by decreasing their purchasing power and making their wages effectively shrink. Every time we make an arrest, I think of my old gramps and grandma sitting in their house in Dothan, Alabama, and how much more their Social Security is worth when we put those counterfeiting cocksuckers in jail."

I looked at this tall handsome Black man and saw the kind of patriotism that I identified with—quiet, understated, and so real it was almost tangible. This wasn't a "'Mericuh right or wrong" patriot but a thoughtful man who decided to prove his love of country by doing the right thing and actually living up to the American ideals. I knew then that this was going to be a good posting, because it was clear that everybody in this office was on the same page.

So we discussed some cases, Bumble gave me advice about procedures, and I got started actually reading case files. I'd read about forty when I opened one up and found something that caught my eye, primarily because it said "Kalamazoo, Michigan" on the subject line.

It turned out that somebody was passing bad paper in Kalamazoo until about three months ago, when it just stopped. There wasn't enough evidence to really fire up on something that had gone cold, just a few bad 10s and 20s and some bank reports, but I read the whole thing anyway.

It hit me about halfway through that the places mentioned where the bad paper was passed had something in common.

I turned to Bumble and said, "Are you familiar with this case? Bad paper in Kalamazoo, Michigan?"

"Yeah. We had some unemployed guy who got fired from a local brewery and set up shop in a warehouse printing bad 50s and 100s and trying to get his friends to pass 'em at his former employer's retail outlet…what the fuck was the name'a that place? Bill's? No, no, it was Bell's Brewery. They make that tasty Oberon shit. It's a seasonal brew. Took about 30 seconds to catch the guy," he said.

"Nah, not that one. The dribble of bad paper at Kalamazoo restaurants? Just stopped about three months ago? We took a couple of reports, but it stopped before we really investigated. We got a report from the sheriff of Kalamazoo County 'bout it?" I said.

"No, I didn't look at that one. I don't remember anyone talking about it either," Bumble said. He stood up and said, "Any of you motherfuckers ever heard of a case in Kalamazoo, Michigan, where the paper just stopped comin' 'bout three months ago? Some shitkicker county sheriff sent us a report?"

"Was that the case with the brewery that makes that tasty Oberon brew?" Gunny Rzepzynski said.

"That is some goooood shit, bro," Nolan "The Greek" Laskarides said. "We drank about two cases of that shit at Gato's wedding, din't we?"

"Yeah, we did, but that ain't the case Bumble's talkin' about," Weasel said. "You mean the one where it looked like someone was passing paper at restaurants but then just abruptly stopped, right?"

"That's it," I said. "There's something hinky about it."

"Is that the case where we got a report from Sheriff Richard Fuller of Kalamazoo County? He had a deputy look at it and found something that might be a case for US. It was bad 10s and 20s?" Joe said.

"Fucking photographic memory," Mac said. "Asshole," she added to general laughter.

"Guilty of having an eidetic memory, but is that the case?" Joe said.

"Yeah, it is," I said.

"Well, what the fuck is hinky about it? We don't want to have to slap the shit out of you to find out, Freak," Gunny said.

"Concur," several voices chimed in.

"Just spit it out, Freak. It's the way we operate," Mac said.

"OK. Well, all these restaurants are hot dog stands," I said. "It seems weird that every restaurant that had bad paper passed is a hot dog stand."

"That is weird. I wonder what time the paper was passed," Steven "Jewey" Silverberg said. He was 6'8" and about as hairy as Chewbacca from the *Star Wars* films, hence the easy nickname. Jewey had gone to Penn, graduated from the Wharton School, and was approximately as smart as everybody in the town of Nutley, New Jersey, put together.

"What does the time have to do with it?" Ed asked. Then she tapped her head and said, "Got it. We need to find out."

"Got what?" the Greek asked. "Why is the time important at all?"

"And it's weird that they were all hot dog stands, but that doesn't make it a case," El Gato said.

"I'll bet all those bills were passed between 11:30 and 12:30, probably for a dog and a drink," I said. "That's how I would do it."

Bumble said, "Sure, they're trying to catch really busy places at their peak and bum-rush the bills. Nobody stops to check bills when there's a line at lunchtime."

"OK, this sounds like a scam, but why stop?" El Gato asked.

"County sheriff was sharp, and the targets were too few," Mac said.

"A test run, don't you think?" Jewey said.

"Well done, young Padawan," Joe said. "Of course it was a test run. Freak, would I be right in assuming that those hot dog stands are all close enough to one another to walk to?"

"More or less," I said. "They can't be more than three miles from one another."

"And they're all near some kind of commerce so that a vendor wouldn't be surprised to see the same customer regularly?" Bumble said.

"They'd kind of expect it. Most of these are just lunch places, all within walking distance of lots of offices. Most of them probably take call-in orders, too, which makes it easier for the paper pusher," I said.

"East to west, or west to east?" Ed said.

"With Michigan, it's more likely to be north to south. Some of these aren't open during winter, right?" the Greek said.

"That I don't know, but I think that we should find out," I said.

"Let's do it this way," Joe said. He was obviously the planner of the group, so everybody listened to him. "We'll open an active case file instead of shitcanning it, then we'll use four pairs and check the four vectors. We've got other cases. Gato, you and Sparky"—he was referring to Agent Carly Cronenwell, whom I hadn't had the chance to meet yet—"still got that thing with the 50s at Macy's, right?"

"When she gets her perky ass back from the dentist," Gato said.

"And, Greek, you and B are testifying in federal court Wednesday and Thursday?" Joe said.

"At least," the Greek said. "Could be Friday, too. They're going to grill us on the takedown and the chain of custody. My bad."

He looked forlorn, so I asked, "What happened?"

The Greek couldn't even get his mouth open before Bumble said, "The suspect claims that he was tortured by old Mr. Laskarides."

"And he was," Mac said.

"It wasn't intentional," the Greek said.

"Still, chemical warfare and torture," El Gato said.

"It wasn't even that bad," the Greek said.

"Bull-sheeeee-it!" House said. "You likely fumigated the whole warehouse with that burner!"

"I could smell it *outside* the warehouse," Ed said.

"Confirm that," Gunny said. "There were rats running out, wearin' gas masks!"

"Fuck you all very much," the Greek said.

"You, uh, you passed gas near the subject?" I asked.

"Nooooo!" they all chorused.

"The Greek farted right in the subject's face from a range of about three inches," Bumble said.

"Might have been two. He was pretty much right up the old anal canal when the Greek let go," Joe said.

"Sounded like a 12-car pileup bein' shredded by a Transformer," said Weasel. "I was in the car, and I heard it."

"People in Joliet heard it," Gunny said. "Didn't we get a call from U of C asking about a seismic occurrence?"

"It was pretty violent," the Greek said.

"OK, what the fuck happened?" I asked.

"It was fairly straightforward. There were four subjects, we caught 'em by surprise, and everything was copacetic, and then two of the gomers decided to bug out. They were goin' to outrun us, jump in their car, and take off into the sunset, but I ran track at Illinois, and B was a four-sport varsity star at Nebraska, so we ran 'em down," the Greek said.

"And it must be said that the Greek made a picture-perfect tackle and took the first guy down in about five steps," Ed said.

"And Bumble did the same with his guy," Joe said.

"Except my guy fell on the Greek's ass," Bumble said.

"And I had Indian for lunch," the Greek said.

"And when his gut hit the floor, the mighty wind was released," Gunny said.

"Right in the second subject's face," Weasel said.

"Who promptly puked," Bumble said.

"Well, it did smell like the sewers after St. Patrick's Day," Joe said.

"And porta potties after the Taste of Chicago, you know, when the guys forgot 'em in the hot sun for two days," Weasel said.

"Hell, it smelled worse than Fallujah, and I didn't think that was possible," Gunny said.

"It smelled so bad it made Waziristan smell like a bed of roses," House said.

151

"It was the worst motherfucking smell I've ever smelled in my life, and I grew up on a hog farm in Iowa," Mac said.

"It was so bad that some Chicago copper called HQ and their NBC team showed up in full gear," Ed said. We all just about died laughing at that one. The NBC Team, the unit tasked with investigating and containing nuclear, biological, and chemical attacks on the city, really did show up, thanks to gentle urging from Gunny and Joe and an eager young Chicago patrolman who was convinced that the counterfeiters had rigged poison gas to the stacks of fake currency as a deterrent to theft.

"So you guys have some 'splainin' to do in court," I said.

"Yeah," the Greek said.

"So here're the teams," Joe said. "I'll take Ed and head east, Gunny will take Mac and head south, Weasel will take House and head west, and Jewey will take Freak and head north."

"What the fuck? What is it, Hebrews United Month?" Jewey said. "Seems kind of religionist to me."

"Oh, blow me, Jewey," Joe said. Everyone laughed again, and Joe said, "One computer nerd, one bulldog per team. It doesn't have anything to do with your Hebrewness, ya big mook. Besides, I can't put Freak with Weasel—"

"Because we inscrutable Orientals hate those big-nosed Jews, always trying to take our jobs at high-tech firms and orchestras," Weasel said.

"And I can't put her with Ed—"

"Because she's too cute and I might make a pass at her. We lesbians can't resist new meat," Ed said.

"And I can't put her with Gunny—"

"Because I just got divorced again and, given my past record, I'm bound to be attracted to a fellow Marine who's built like a brick shithouse," Gunny said.

"And we all know that office romances are *verboten*!" they all chorused amid general laughter. "As long as we got it straight that it isn't going to be Hebrew Central or Jews on Parade just because Freak and I share a religious heritage," Jewey said in his deep, Darth Vaderish voice.

"Nah," Joe said. "We all know what Guru would say about that," Joe said.

"Quit yer bitchin' and get the jawb dunn!" the team said.

There was a lot more laughter, and then we got to work.

It seemed like we'd only been working a minute when Ed sang out, "Gotttt onnnne!" We all looked up, and she said, "Tony Packo's, Toledo, Ohio. A month before the Kalamazoo stuff, four 20s and three 10s passed in an eight-day period, then nothing."

"That's like Portillo's in Chicago," I said. "Always busy, tourist attraction, tons of regulars."

"It fits the profile, but keep looking," Joe said.

There was some clacking of computer keys, and then Joe said, "Got another one: the Coney Hut Drive-In in Jonesville, Michigan. Three 20s and a 10, two weeks after Tony Packo's and two weeks before Kalamazoo."

"I've been there. They make their own root beer and have really good Chicago dogs. And home-made Coney sauce," I said.

"Help an Irish girl from Iowa out. What the fuck is Coney sauce?" Mac said.

"It's chili without beans," Weasel said.

"The fuck it is!" Ed, Gunny, and I said at once.

"You both owe me a Pepsi," I said.

"And it is chili without beans," Weasel said.

"Greek!" Gunny said.

"Yo, Gunnery Sergeant," the Greek said, poking his head out of the office, where he and Bumble were working.

"Is Coney sauce chili without beans?" Gunny said.

"Bite your tongue!" the Greek said. "It's a complex meat-based sauce with herbs and spices, plus onions and garlic. You simmer it for a day or two and then put it over top-quality hot dogs on a good bun, with a stripe of mustard."

"Best you've ever had?" I asked.

"My aunt Mary Kokanakis's, out in Boone, Iowa. She grated fresh nutmeg and cinnamon into it and added some shredded kosher dill pickle. She also used a lamb/hamburger mix that gave the sauce great flavor but less grease. Whoever told you it's chili without beans is one dumb motherfucker."

We all pointed at Weasel and the Greek said, "Figures. Damn chinkese don't know dick from good *American* food."

"Big talk coming from a guy whose last name means 'we eat dogs' in Greek," Weasel said.

"Nothing wrong with a good roast dog once in a while," the Greek said.

"I like 'em stewed," Weasel said.

"Can't argue with that either," the Greek said. He went back in the office, and Ed said, "Got another one. Allen's Root Beer Junction in Coldwater, Michigan. Four 20s and two 10s, four days after the Jonesville pass." (A note on the name of this hot dog stand: I've used the old name of the place, which used to be one of the best Chicago hot dog stands outside Chicago. My family ate there at least twice every year from the time I was four years old. They had carhops, fresh-brewed root beer, and the best onion rings and deep-fried mushrooms you've ever eaten. And their dogs were on par with Superdawg. Unfortunately, the place was sold to some people not named Allen, and it has become just awful. I'm not going to bash the new owners, but they wouldn't know a good Chicago dog if it bit them in the ass. If you are using this as a tour guide, avoid this place—your digestive tract will thank you.)

Ed looked thoughtful for a minute, hit some computer keys, and then a big map of northern Ohio and southern Michigan popped up. She keyed in the places where we'd found bad paper being passed, and little red circles popped up on the map.

They were virtually a straight line from Toledo to Coldwater, right down US-12.

I said, "I'll bet if you look you'll find something in Sturgis, Michigan, probably at Coney Island Pizza, or maybe at Bill's Hotdog Factory in Battle Creek," I said.

"Four 20s at Coney Island in Sturgis, four 20s and three 10s at Bill's, three days before it started in Kalamazoo," Ed said.

"Look at the map," Mac said. "They left Sturgis and went up M-66 to Battle Creek, then took I-94 to Kalamazoo."

"I'll bet that they took King's Highway, M-96, from Bill's to Kalamazoo," I said. "It goes right in the back door to downtown, gives them access to all the stands there."

"OK, we all concur that we've established a pattern. What's their cover? They aren't spending enough to live, unless they're spending all funny money," Gunny said.

"Can't be. We'd notice it right away. They must be using this as their test run under the cover of doing something else," Jewey said.

"Could be roadies for a band," House said.

"Some of those places are too small for that. Jonesville is just a burg, and Sturgis isn't much bigger. Besides, roadies wouldn't be in the lunch rush—they'd still be hungover," I said.

"Could be county fair carnies," Mac said. "We used to get 'em in Iowa."

"But then they'd eat at the fair," Gunny said.

"And those places aren't in the right place for the county fair. The one closest to Sturgis is way north in Centreville, the St. Joseph County seat," I said.

Joe said, "Look at this," and keyed in more data to the map. A series of blue, green, yellow, pink, and purple circles appeared on the map, radiating out in all directions from Toledo in more or less straight lines, and all terminating in some fairly good-size towns within driving distance of Toledo.

Including the red line, which proceeded to Kalamazoo.

"What would a group of four or five guys be doing to make lines like this?" Ed asked.

"Itinerant workers of some kind, but what? It can't be agricultural. It's the wrong time of year, and the pattern is wrong," Jewey said.

"Got it!" Joe said. He looked at Jewey and said, "Young Padawan, what type of labor is done in the open, while traveling during good summer and fall weather?"

"Cement and—"

"Roofing," Mac, Ed, and I said.

"Pepsis on me," Mac said.

"Of course," Jewey said. "And not gypsy roofers, either."

"Explain," Joe said.

"They must be part of a company, or at least an organized subcontractor," Jewey said. "Those lines indicate a succession of planned jobs, one after another. If you look at the timelines, I bet you'll find they went all the way out and worked their way home, or vice versa."

"We need to look at the time interval too," Ed said. "If each job is three or four days apart, that would confirm it's a company. Gypsies wouldn't be able to be that organized."

Weasel clacked some computer keys, and numbers began appearing on the map. Every line radiating out from Toledo had either a three or three next to it, except one that was a seven. The line to Kalamazoo went in twelve- to fuourteen-day intervals, except from Sturgis to Battle Creek, which was two days, and Battle Creek to Kalamazoo, which was three days.

"That seven is either a commercial job or a weather delay," Mac said.

"Concur," Jewey and Joe said. "I'll bet that these are small businesses being serviced," Jewey added.

"One-day prep, one-day roofing, one-day getaway?" House said. We all looked at him, and he said, "I did some roofin' during summers in college. It was hard work, kept me in shape, and pretty good money too. I seem to remember that was the deal: we'd scrape the roof clean, put the tar paper up, shingle like hell for a day, and then finish up by noon the next day. We'd eat lunch at places like we're talkin' about, then haul ass for the next job and get set up to scrape."

"And why did you eat at places like hot dog stands?" Joe said.

"Because roofing is a damned dirty business. We always sweated like motherfuckers and smelled like we'd been in the sandbox for a month or two with no water. No way we'd go into a restaurant lookin' like poster boys for the Great Depression and smellin' like a dead goat's ass," House said.

"We got a case," Joe said. He picked up his phone, hit speed dial, and said, "Guru, can you get the boss and come down here? We got something you need to look at."

"Ending with a preposition?" everybody but me said.

"It's the common touch. It makes Guru think that I'm just one of the guys, not the smartest motherfucker this side of U of C," Joe said. "And yes, I'm buying the Pepsis."

"Yeah, and I'm a fuckin' ballerina," House said, his 280 pounds resting comfortably in a custom Herman Miller chair. (And don't get your panties in a bunch about government employees wasting your taxpayer dollars. Quentin "House" Bowe played ten seasons for the Chargers and Rams in the NFL and had invested very wisely. He used his own money for the chair, because government issue wasn't going to cut it.)

"And I'm a personal-grooming model," Jewey said, hair sticking out everywhere.

"And I play tight end for the Bears," Ed said. She was 5'6", maybe 130 pounds soaking wet, and clearly not a professional athlete.

"I don't give a fuck, as long as I don't have to go to East Bumfuck, Michigan, looking for funny paper," Weasel said. "I can't take those little burgs without a Starbucks and Wi-Fi. I start hearin' the theme from *Deliverance* once I get past Hegewisch on the South Shore."

"Damned city boy," Mac said. "Where do you think those sausages that you love at Mary's come from? A Pez dispenser?"

"I don't give a shit where they come from, as long as she has 'em and I don't have to travel to the damned country to get 'em," Weasel said. "I like to eat pig, not raise 'em or give a flying fuck about their lives."

"Aren't you from L.A., Weasel? Isn't it, like, obligatory to care about the poor, lesser creatures of the firmament?" Ed said.

"I'm from East L.A., sister, not Holly-fuckin'-weird. We East Angelinos were all too goddamn busy trying to dodge bullets and make a semi-honest living to get involved with causes," Weasel said.

"I get that, Weasel," Gunny said. "Tell 'em the truth about it."

Weasel Wei was this tall, really skinny Asian guy who was almost a stereotype but who just missed it, mainly because he didn't wear thick glasses, have his hair in a bowl cut, or play a musical instrument. He also sounded more like a Valley girl than he did an Asian just off the boat, probably because his family came to L.A. in 1905. He was as smart as anybody I ever met when it came to computers, could get into the minds of criminals without trying, and was truly gifted at poker.

He looked at all of us and said, "OK, I'll tell you guys about my brother and sister, but if you decide it's a joke, I'll erase your lives from cyberspace." Nobody said anything; when a guy has a BSci degree in programming from Cal Tech, and a master's degree in computer systems from MIT, having your life erased from the net is a very serious threat. So Weasel said, "When I was 21, my brother and sister were gunned down in our family's fruit stand. There were some people who objected to some other people, and they decided to throw down right at the entrance to our store. Amanda and Robert were doing what my whole family did, taking their turn in order to pay for their college, so that eventually we could sell the store and all become rich computer nerds."

We all looked at him, completely speechless, and he said, "So strange as it may seem, I don't want to leave the city. I know what to expect from it, know how it moves, and know its internal structure, and if I go to East Bumfuck, Anywhere, I'm too far from the bad guys. That's why I joined the Secret Service, to catch bad guys and put their asses in jail, especially those gangbangers who use funny paper to finance their dumbass turf wars, or pissing contests, or whatever the fuck they do. So if it's OK with you, I'd rather stay in the city, where the real bad guys are, while you guys go to Outer Bumfuckolia, looking for some stinky-ass roofers who are passing bad paper."

Weasel looked at Joe and Guru, and Guru said, "Message received and understood, Agent Wei. We'll keep your ass close to the computer for support and let the rest of these hunyocks go round up these paper pushers." She turned to Joe and added, "The boss'll be right here, but give me the broad outlines."

So Joe sketched out the stuff we had so far, and Guru said, "Damned good catch, Freak. How'd we get all the reports on the funny paper in Kalamazoo and all those other one-horse towns?"

"We don't know yet," Joe said. "In Kalamazoo it appears to be a sharp sheriff's deputy or the sheriff himself. The rest of the stuff came up from bank reports, bills that didn't pass the Test and were tracked back by the banks." All the other agents nodded, but I was still new, so I said, "What do you mean, the Test?"

So Joe explained it to me, and I said, "Oh, you mean [the technical name for the test]," and they all nodded again.

And before you get your knickers in a knot (or panties in a bunch, or balls in an uproar, or whatever cute colloquialism you use), no, I'm not going to describe the Test to you. There are all kinds of public knowledge about how to detect counterfeit bills, but there are some that aren't public, and the Test is the best one. If you expect me to expose Secret Service procedures, you can kiss my wide muscular White ass—you've got a better chance of Colonel Sanders revealing the secret blend of herbs and spices in Kentucky Fried Chicken (and he's been dead for decades).

The agent in charge showed up, and we presented our evidence all over again. After he heard what we had, Jerry Clune said, "OK, we definitely got a case here. Guru, whaddya say we send Sparky and El Gato down to Toledo and let them track the money back to Kalamazoo after that court stuff they got? We'll send Freak, Mac, Gunny, Ed, House, and Joe on to Kalamazoo to run with it there. Joe, you'll be the team leader and organize the liaison with local law enforcement. We'll keep Jewey and Weasel here for computer support and coordination. You guys will also handle all the logistics for both trips so the field guys don't have to waste time fuckin' around, gettin' cars and rooms and shit."

Guru nodded and said, "And if we find a trail somewhere else, we can detach two agents from Kalamazoo to chase it down."

"Concur," Clune said. "Any questions or comments, guys?"

"What's the fastest way to get to Kalamazoo?" Joe said, looking at me.

"Fuckin' wagon train," Weasel said.

"Sled dogs," Gunny said.

"Pulling a toboggan, right?" Ed said.

"You're all full of shit," Mac said. "Ya gotta get a birch-bark canoe and paddle your ass across Gitcheegumee."

"Is that an STD?" House said.

"Don't you gobshites read?" Mac said. "Gitcheegumee is Lake Michigan. You know, 'By the shores of Gitcheegumee, by the shining big sea water'?"

"There's a goddamn international airport in Kalamazoo," I said. "Pfizer's there, Stryker Medical, Kellogg's is over in Battle Creek. It's not like going to East Steerfuck, Oklahoma, or Nome, Alaska."

"What the fuck is a Gitcheegumee again?" Gunny said.

"It's from *The Song of Hiawatha* by Henry Wadsworth Longfellow," Guru said. "It's a reference to the Native American name for Lake Michigan. Jay-sus, even I know that and I went to Rutgers."

We all laughed, and then Jerry Clune said, "Go home and pack your bags, kids, because you're goin' to Kalamazoo to check out hot dog stands and funny paper."

That was when it became apparent to me that despite the kidding and easy attitude of the office, these people were real professionals. By the time we all were packed and assembled at O'Hare, Jewey and Weasel had us all set up with tickets, itineraries, cars, and hotel reservations, Joe had our Kalamazoo assignments all drawn up, and Guru had numbers and contacts for local law enforcement.

I also had permission from Jerry Clune to buzz over and see my folks in Battle Creek, as long as it didn't interfere with the work.

And that, dear readers, is where the real shit hit the fan, even though I didn't know it at that time.

CHAPTER 21

Freak and Team in the 'Zoo

We landed at Kalamazoo / Battle Creek International Airport at 7:45 p.m., and the ribbing started at 7:46 p.m.

"Is that cow shit I smell?" Gunny said.

"Look, it's an Amish limousine," Ed said, pointing at a snack cart on the concourse.

"Are the lights still on? It's after nine here in the country," Joe said.

"Will there be anybody to get our horses out of the stable?" Mac said.

"Should a brother be worried 'bout the po-leece in dis here burg?" House said.

"Fuck you and the horse you rode in on, ya hunyocks," I said. "There're two colleges in this town, not to mention twenty-four-hour restaurants and a nice nightlife."

"Is there movin' pitchers, too?" Ed said.

"Keep fuckin' around and we'll miss last call at Bell's Eccentric Café," I said. "You know, where they brew that Oberon shit you guys like to drink?"

We got our three rental cars and hit the road in record time after that. It turns out that Oberon shit's one superb motivator for those of the beer drinking persuasion.

After a great meal at Bell's (and several brewskis for those partaking—everyone but me), we staggered to our cars and rumbled three blocks down the street to our hotel, the Radisson Plaza at the Kalamazoo Center (really swanky digs for the 'Zoo; thanks, Weasel)—checked in and had our briefing meeting for the following morning.

Joe pulled us all into his room and said, "OK, here we go. Gunny, you and Ed are going to meet with the manager of the Fifth Third Bank, a guy named Jonas Birgy. That's where a majority of the funny paper was caught. It's also where most of our target businesses bank. All you have to do is walk out the door and turn left. The bank is just east of here. We need to know what alerted them. It can't have been just the Test."

He looked at Mac and me and said, "Mac, you and Freak are going over to meet with the manager of the Educational Community Credit Union, a womyn named Sarah Shelhammer. Two of our target businesses bank there, and the credit union is the only one to get a funny 50. Mac, you know the drill, and, Freak, observe everything you can. Especially look at the funny paper and try to tell what tipped them off.

"House and I are meeting with the local sheriff and chief of police at the chief's office, also located conveniently close," Joe said. "You guys at the banks'll probably be done before we are, so let's plan on meeting back here before we head out and hit the restaurants, OK? Any questions?"

"What the fuck kind of name is Fifth Third Bank?" Gunny asked.

"Mergers be makin' banks' names for shizz," House said.

"What's with the ghetto accent, House? Didn't you go to Boston College by way of Beacon Hill?" Mac asked. House's dad was an investment banker, his mom a pediatrician, and both of his siblings were college professors. He'd grown up in the exclusive Beacon Hill neighborhood of Boston, so the accent was kind of funny.

"I thought that it might impress the locals. You know, handsome, tough Black guy fed on the prowl for the perps," House said.

"Where you gonna find the handsome guy to play you?" Gunny said.

"You need a tough guy too. I saw you cry when we went to the movie where that tree-man died saving his friends," Ed said.

"What the fuck is a *perp*?" Mac said. "Sounds like something that grows on your ass. I had a perp, but I got rid of it with an antibiotic."

"What the fuck was the name of that movie?" Joe asked. "Isn't that the one where the aliens kidnap the kid? With a sexy green chick?"

"Yeah, the green chick was Zoe Saldana. She's scrumptious," Ed said.

"Tree dude's name was Groot, the movie was *Guardians of the Galaxy*, and he died saving his friends, but a shoot survived," House said. "And I wasn't the only one crying." He looked at the rest of us, and I said, "Well, I wasn't there, but I cried too."

"And she's the toughest one of us," House said. "She's a Recon and Special Ops Marine, and everybody knows they're tougher than a junkyard dog. So fuck off and die about my crying when a brave tree died, motherfuckers." We all laughed, and Joe said, "Off to beddy-bye. We're starting early and working late if we need to, so let's not dick around."

We all nodded, and Gunny said, "What's the rule on this, Freak?"

"Eat, drink, piss, shit, and sleep when you can, Gunnery Sergeant, because you never know when it will happen again," I said.

"Booyah!" everybody else said. And off we went to sleep.

Weasel got us four rooms. House was too big to share even a king-size bed, and Ed didn't like to make us straights nervous by sleeping in the same room, so Mac and I roomed up, as did Joe and Gunny. Everybody had their lights out within five minutes, so the next morning came easy.

Mac and I got out of the hotel and headed for the Educational Community Credit Union, which turned out to be on the far western reaches of Kalamazoo, off M-43 on Ninth Street. We pulled into the parking lot, and Mac said, "What's the difference between a bank and a credit union?"

"About seven letters or one word," I said.

"Wow, fuckin' hilarious, Freak," she said. "Really, what's the difference?"

"Your education at Smith was sadly lacking," I said. "A bank is for-profit and owned by shareholders, who expect a return on their money. Banks are part of the Federal Reserve System and have certain reserve requirements. Credit unions are nonprofit and are owned by the shareholders, who expect to be able to borrow freely from the credit union as long as they're a member. Credit unions also aren't subject to the same rules as banks. Their only purpose is to service their members."

"So there isn't much difference, except for the profit thing?" Mac said.

"Yeah, but most economists will tell you that banks are riskier because they fuck around with your money in ways that credit unions can't," I said.

"Derivatives and shit," she said.

"Right. Heavy on the shit," I said. We laughed and went in the nice-looking ECCU building (that was what they called it, ECCU, which was right there on the building in big green letters) and showed our creds to the nice lady at the welcome desk. The badges got her attention, like they always did, and in a jiffy we met the credit union manager.

She was a big womyn, not fat, just tall and broad shouldered, with an attractive face, a big straight nose, and deep-brown eyes. Her hair was long and well kept, and her business suit was tailored for her *zaftig* (pleasantly round and curvy) figure. She stuck out her hand and said, "I'm Sarah Shelhammer. Let's go to my office and talk."

We got to her modest office, and she said, "I'd offer you something, but it's been my experience that you want to get right to business."

"It's too early for a Bell's Oberon," Mac said.

"You probably don't have a cold Pepsi in the place," I said.

"Besides, we did come about the funny money," Mac said. Poor Ms. Shelhammer looked a bit nonplussed, so Mac said, "We really would like to see the counterfeit currency and talk to whoever found it."

Ms. Shelhammer picked up her phone, punched a button, and said, "Greg, can you bring the counterfeits and come down here? Thanks."

About three seconds later, a tall thin guy with a frown on his face came through the door and said, "Hello, agents. Hello, Sarah. I've got the stuff right here." We shook hands as we introduced ourselves, and the guy, whose name was Greg Klett, said, "I'm the former head teller at ECCU. I'm in wealth management now, but I still go out and help the new head teller when needed. I found the counterfeit currency."

"How?" Mac said. "We assume that something tipped you off and then you applied the Test to confirm your suspicion."

"That was exactly it. We got in several large deposits late on Friday afternoon, and as I was counting one, I felt a funny 50," Mr. Klett said.

"You felt it?" I asked.

"Yes, it was too soft. Like it had been run through the washer," he said.

"How did you know it hadn't?" Mac said.

"It was a part of a corporate account, Dogs with Style—it's downtown, near the State Theater—and I know the owner. Her husband is a teacher, and there is no way that she had a 50 in her pocket and forgot about it when she did her laundry. I was suspicious, so I set the 50 aside and counted all the rest of the deposit. I found three 20s and four 10s that also felt too soft, and they all failed the Test. No other bills in the deposit did," Mr. Klett responded.

"And who found the second batch of funny paper?" Mac said.

"I found it the same day that I found the Dogs with Style counterfeits," Mr. Klett said. "It was in another deposit from someone I knew, Mansour Mohammed. He has a hot dog cart downtown on weekdays."

"An Arab?" Mac asked. One of the ways that some terror groups funded themselves was through funny money. It isn't fair, but Secret Service agents perk up when they hear Arabic names near funny paper.

"Again, I know this man," Mr. Klett said. "He and I went to school together. He converted to Islam when he married his wife, Malika Mansour. He's also worked at the highest levels for the U.S. government. He was a physicist at the Jet Propulsion Lab in Pasadena, California, for twenty years."

"His security clearance is probably higher than mine," Mac said.

"Concur," I said.

Mac knew that my work with Spec Ops left me with a clearance higher than hers, so she surreptitiously gave me the finger and said, "If this guy was a physicist, why's he got a hot dog cart in Kalamazoo?"

"Dr. Mohammed is a member of the faculty at Western Michigan University. He has a hot dog cart to protest the low wages the faculty gets paid," Ms. Shelhammer said. We both looked at her, and she said, "Kalamazoo is a fairly small town. Everybody who goes downtown knows Dr. Mohammed. Lots of people buy hot dogs from him because they think he's right about the professors at Western."

"His name before he converted was Lonnie Waldron," Mr. Klett said. "I've known him all my life. No way is he a counterfeiter or in cahoots with counterfeiters."

"Cahoots?" Mac and I asked.

"You owe me a Pepsi," I said.

"Concur," Mac said.

She looked at Mr. Klett and said, "Cahoots? You mean conspiring with other criminals to commit a fraud against the American people?"

"I don't know how you talk," Mr. Klett said. "I was just trying to put you at ease." His face was red, and he appeared to be trying to squirm himself into his shoes.

Mac and I laughed, and she said, "Mr. Klett, we appreciate your efforts to put us at ease, but we are investigating a serious crime, not looking to be put at ease. Also, you don't know how we operate, but if Agent Glickstien or I uttered the word *cahoots* around our colleagues in this investigation, we'd never hear the end of it. We're Secret Service agents, sir, and we use humor to let off steam and keep ourselves grounded during serious investigations. We're sorry if we appear to be making fun of you. We are not. We are simply trying to keep ourselves sane. Is there anything else you can tell us about this incident? Please don't leave anything out."

So the former head teller told us his long convoluted story, we took notes, and just before he wound up, Klett said, "Oh, I happened to see Dr. Mohammed, and I told him about the counterfeit bills that I found in his deposit. I asked him if he'd had any suspicious characters around, and he told me that the only nonregulars he'd had that week were a bunch of roofers—they were working on one of the downtown buildings."

Both Mac and I sat right up. I said, "Do you know how to contact Dr. Mohammed? Or where he'll set up his cart today?"

"I have his cell number, and since today is Tuesday, he'll be set up outside the medical school buildings downtown," Mr. Klett said.

"We need his number and all the currency, separated by the deposit it came in," Mac said. She took the currency and sealed it in separate evidence bags, signed the chain of custody line, and said, "If we could get a complete written statement from you in the next two days, Mr. Klett, and from you, Ms. Shelhammer, we'll send an agent around to collect them and have them notarized."

"Of course," the manager said. "What else can the ECCU do to help you?"

"Keep this guy involved with any commercial deposits and notify us immediately if you get any more funny paper," Mac said. She handed Ms. Shelhammer her card, with the main office's number circled.

"And we could use directions to the med school," I said. She gave us the directions, we all shook hands and said our goodbyes.

Mac and I went out and got the car, and she said, in a perfectly natural Irish accent, "A trained physicist notices a bunch of roofers at his hot dog stand? Jay-sus, Mary, and Joseph, me granda was right—'tis better to be lucky than good."

"Concur. He's a trained observer. Wanna bet that he can at least give some accurate physical descriptions?" I said.

"No bet. Now, where the fuck is Stadium Drive?" she asked.

"Follow me. I know the way," I said, imitating the Denholm Elliott character from the *Raiders of the Lost Ark* films.

"Wasn't that motherfucker notoriously lost?" Mac said.

"Yep," I said.

And so were we. We found Stadium Drive right away, but once we got back to downtown Kalamazoo, we were confronted with a confusing array of one-way streets, a bizarre area that was a pedestrian mall, and construction of every stripe. We finally stopped at a downtown hole-in-the-wall restaurant named Taco Bob's for directions. Mac and I walked in the door, took one look at the place, and both said, "Bingo."

"You owe me a Pepsi," Mac said, "and we need to talk to the owner, or manager, of this establishment."

"Wanna bet they came in here at least once?" I asked.

"No bet again. This is exactly the kind of place they'd come after a hard day's work on the roof, especially since they could also get a couple of beers," Mac said.

So we flashed our badges and got to talk to the owner. Taco Bob was a pleasant-looking guy with a mustache, a bluff, a hearty smile, and a willingness to help. We asked him about the funny paper first, figuring we'd see if he could get us to the roofers without any suggestions on our part.

Jackpot.

Taco Bob said, "We did have some 10s and 20s that came through here that we thought were weird."

"Define weird," Mac said.

"Well, they were all soft and unwrinkled, like when you forget bills in your jeans and they go through the washer and dryer," Taco Bob said.

"Do you remember when this happened?" I asked.

Taco Bob looked thoughtful and finally said, "I think it was during my regular bartender's vacation." He yelled up the ramp from the bar and said, "Hey, Alicia! Come down here a minute, willya?"

A pretty, dark-haired young womyn with three diamond studs in her lip came down the ramp and said, "Yo, boss man." We showed her our badges and introduced ourselves, and Taco Bob said, "Do you remember when you were bartending this spring?"

"Sure," she said immediately. "It was every other night the last week of May and the first week of June. Jason went on vacay, and Mike and I took turns."

"Did you get any of those weird, soft bills while you were doing that?" Taco Bob said.

"Sure," she said. "That one Friday night, I got three soft 10s. It was the night those roofers were celebrating getting their jobs here done. One of 'em said they were going to do a job in New Buffalo and asked if I knew any place to get a burger and beer there, so I told 'em about my sister, who works at the Stray Dog. They were so happy they all tipped me a five or 10—40 bucks for the five of them."

"Were either of the fives soft?" Mac asked.

"No. The tens were, and one of the roofers made a crack about washing money at an unfamiliar laundromat," she said.

"Do you remember what the wisecrack was? What he said exactly?" I said.

"It was something like 'We're bad money launderers,' or 'We aren't very good at laundering money,' some smartass thing like that," she said.

Mac asked, "Why would you—"

Alicia interrupted. "He was cute. He had a cute butt, and he kept smiling at me. I sorta thought maybe he'd ask me out, but they never came back after that night."

Mac and I looked at each other, and Taco Bob said, "I don't have any more of those bills, but you should go talk to Dr. Mohammed. He's got a hot dog cart over by the med school today. I remember these guys talking about eating at his cart. They were complaining about not being able to get a beer with their dogs. Dr. Mohammed doesn't hold with alcohol. He's a Muslim."

"We'll certainly go over and talk to him, but right now, we'd like Alicia to give us some descriptions of the guys, if she would," Mac said.

The waitress/bartender looked at Taco Bob, who said, "Sure, but if it gets busy, I may need her."

"What time's the rush?" I asked.

"Eleven forty-five," they both said. "You owe us a Pepsi," I said.

"You do that in Chicago too?" Taco Bob asked.

"I'm originally from Battle Creek," I said.

We had some old-home-week jawing, and then we got descriptions from Alicia. We gave them both cards and thanked them for their cooperation. We also got directions to the med school and were pleasantly surprised that we could walk there (good fuckin' thing—navigating Kalamazoo takes two Siris and a Tom-Tom), but Secret Service agents never set off on foot. (It's rule number 8: never leave your ride if you can help it. And no, we're not imitating Gibbs' Rules from NCIS; the Secret Service has its own rules, thank you very much.) So we drove the two short blocks to the med school.

It didn't take long to spot the hot dog stand. There were five cop cars parked near it, and Dr. Mohammed turned out to be a Black guy who was bigger than House. He was wearing a very colorful dashiki, stood 6'7" in his bare feet (yeah, they were bare; his sandals were so big they could be mistaken for *Perry*-class frigates in the U.S. Navy), and was as wide as a barn door (remember, I played football at Michigan State, and my boyfriend there was a 6'10" All-American basketball player—I still know real size when I see it).

We pulled into a no-parking zone right in front of the cop cars, and before we could turn around, a cop came up to us and said, "No parking there, ladies. You'll have to move your car before I—"

I opened my creds and showed him the classy Secret Service badge, then flipped them sideways so that he could see my picture. His nametag said "Roush," and he had three stripes on his arm, so I said, "Sergeant Roush, I'm Agent Glinka Glickstien of the Secret Service. This is my partner, Agent Siobhan McKee. We need to talk to Dr. Mohammed about a case. Shouldn't take long, and we don't want to park in BFE, if that's all right with you."

"Not a problem, ma'am," Roush said.

"Thanks, Sergeant, and if you ma'am me again I'm going to kick your ass. It's Agent Glickstien, or Freak. My mom's a ma'am, not me," I said.

"Sorry, ma—uh, Agent Glickstien. It's an old habit from the Marine Corps—if you don't know someone's rank or status, you—"

"Salute 'em and ma'am or sir 'em. Better safe than sorry," I said.

"You in the Corps, ma—Agent Glickstien?" he said.

"Force Recon and Special Ops, out of MacDill," I said.

He stiffened up and looked like he was going to salute, so I said, "Sergeant Roush, I don't outrank you. I'm out of the Corps. I'm an entry-level agent for the Secret Service, nothing more. Just act normal and let me do my job, OK?"

Roush looked at me and said, "Wait a minute, you're the Freak. You won the President's Cup and led the Corps to wins over the other services for, like, five straight years. You're a legend, ma— Agent Glickstien."

"Jay-sus, Mary, and Joseph, he looks like he's about to genuflect. She ain't the Pope, boyo, she's just a damned Secret Service agent," Mac said, teasing the sergeant.

Roush looked very serious and said, "Oh no, ma'am. The Freak never missed a pistol shot in the President's Cup—not one in seven straight years. That's not possible, ma'am, but the Freak did it. She's a legend with the M9, ma'am. I heard other stories, too, about her physical capabilities, they might just be stories, but the shooting stuff is on record. It's an honor to meet you, Agent Glickstien." He stuck out his hand, so I shook it, but I also said, "Enough of this legend shit, Sergeant Roush. We need to interview Dr. Mohammed in connection with a counterfeiting investigation. Since it's about to be rush hour, maybe we could get to it?"

By then several other cops had come up to us, and many of them had heard Roush's celebration of me, so one of them said, "We're qualifying tomorrow morning if you want to show us your pistol expertise, Agent Glickstien." He said it like he didn't believe a word, so I decided that I'd take up the challenge.

"When and where?" I asked. The cop, whose name badge read "Wilkinson," said, "Seven a.m., at the county jail range. It's at the sheriff's department."

"I'll be there," I said.

Mac said, "Jay-sus, why'n't ya just pull your dicks out and measure them here?" Everybody laughed, and then Mac said, "And Roush, how old are you? Thirty-five?"

"I'm 34, ma'a—"

"Then stop that ma'am shit for me too, ya hunyock! I'm thirty-eight, so you don't get to ma'am me either. And no, I won't kick your ass, I'll just run you over with the rental car and blame it on a car thief, ya gobshite." Her Irish was back, even though she was kidding.

"What's a *gobshite*?" Roush said.

"Look in the mirror," we all said. Everybody laughed again, until Mac said, "Just so we're clear, I'm Mac, she's Freak, and we're gonna interview the giant hot dog man over there, if you'll let us."

"No problem, Mac. And get the chili cheese dog," Roush said.

"I'd get the Chicago dog," Wilkinson said. "Dr. Mohammed's originally from Chicago, and he's still got some connections. His dogs are 100 percent beef, kosher, and from an old family recipe."

"The dogs are so good that you could eat 'em cold and not be disappointed," a third cop, named Phillips, said.

"But the dogs are halal, not kosher," Roush said. "Dr. Mohammed's a Muslim."

"They mean the same thing," I said.

"You sure?" Wilkinson asked.

"Trust her, she's Jewish," Mac said. "Besides, it turns out Freak is something of a hot dog expert."

"Well, she's gonna love Dr. Mohammed, then. Get the New York with kraut and Gulden's mustard—best dog in history!" Phillips said.

"Message received and understood," Mac said. "Now get the fuck outta the way and let us work." She went over to the by-now-bemused hot dog vendor and said, "Dr. Mohammed, I presume?"

The giant Black physicist laughed and said, "Right you are, Stanley. Credentials, if you please, agents." We showed him our creds, and he said, "How can a humble purveyor of hot dogs help the Secret Service?"

"You worked for the JPL for 20 years, and you expect us to believe you're a humble purveyor of hot dogs? Sorry, Dr. Mohammed, but I'm guessing that your doctorate was from Cal Tech or MIT, and none of the places you get a physics PhD are humble," I said.

"OK, you got me, Agent Glickstien. I went to Iowa, then Princeton, then Cal Tech—and you're right, none of them are humble. I'm going to guess on my own and say that this is about the fake bills Greg Klett found in my deposit," Dr. Mohammed said.

"Right through the uprights on the first try, Doctor," Mac said.

"I think it was the roofers," Dr. Mohammed said.

I was impressed, but Mac didn't bat an eye, she just said, "What roofers?"

"There were these five roofers who showed up for three days that week. They were very jovial, asked about my background, told me that they were headed for Chicago, then hit me up for places to go for hot dogs when they were in the city," Dr. Mohammed said.

"So what? How does it make them the culprits on our little funny money scheme?" Mac said.

"First of all, it isn't some little scheme," Dr. Mohammed said.

"How'd'ya figure that?" Mac said. "We're just here to ask questions about a couple of funny 20s."

"Sure you are, but Greg told me he found around 120 dollars in fake bills in my deposit, and my friend Ray over at Ray-Rays on Miller Road told me he had several bills that were hinky, and Taco Bob told me the same thing, and I will bet that Nagle's Top Dog over on Burdick Street and the Root Beer Stand had the same thing. You're in pursuit of a counterfeiting ring, not some little funny money scheme," Dr. Mohammed said.

"Obviously PhD doesn't mean 'piled higher and deeper' in your case," Mac said.

"No," Dr. Mohammed said. "I'm not just smart, I'm also a keen observer of everything," he added. "Did anyone tell you what I did at JPL?"

"No, just that you were a physicist," Mac said.

"Actually, I have two fuds, one in astrophysics and one in applied mathematics," Dr. Mohammed said.

"Wow, a double-doc," I said. "You sound like my brother Eggy—he got a fud from Cal Tech in astrophysics and one from Georgia Tech in finite math."

The double-doc hot dog vendor looked at me and said, "Hey, wait a minute. Is your brother Dr. Morris Glickstien at Cal Tech?"

"The same egghead," I said.

"Wow! That guy makes me feel stupid, and I'm impressed that you've refrained from speaking until now. Morris would've cut me off long ago—no room for nonsense in his world, is there?" Dr. Mohammed said.

"Nope. He's always been like that, and if I'd known that you were on his level, I'd have taken over the questioning. Mac was trying to see if you might be connected to the counterfeiting by being obtuse," I said.

"How do you know he's not connected? It's still possible that all his palaver is a smoke screen," Mac said.

"Nah," I said. "If Dr. Mohammed was involved we wouldn't be here."

"How the fuck you know that?" Mac said.

"Because if he travels in the same circles as Eggy, he's too smart to get caught," I said.

"Thank you for the compliment, Agent Glickstien, but nobody travels in Morris's circles, although you're right. If I decided to counterfeit, you'd never catch me, or you'd catch someone working for me who was laundering the money," Dr. Mohammed said.

"What did you do at JPL?" Mac asked.

"I was in charge of observing near-earth objects and computing their orbits in order to determine if they were going to collide with earth," he said.

"Shit, you're right, Freak. No way this guy had anything to do with it. He's probably smarter than Jewey and Weasel put together, and they're smarter than the rest of the unit put together," Mac said.

"Concur," I said. "So why was it the roofers?"

"They were too nice—no way five redneck roofers should be that nice to a big, black egghead wearing a dashiki. Their truck had Bush/Cheney and Romney/Ryan stickers on it, and clearly I'm not of that persuasion. They should have hated me on sight, not sought me out for three straight days. Plus, I think that they were trying to distract me so I wouldn't notice the bills," he said.

"Man's got a point," Mac said.

"Yeah, especially since it worked. You didn't notice anything hinky, did you?" I said.

"Sure didn't," he said. He looked sincerely distressed and said, "It worked perfectly. I was thinking about how nice these guys were compared to most guys with Southern accents, and I never noticed anything remotely amiss. It was only afterward that I started to think about it, and by then it was too late. They were gone."

"Southern accents?" Mac and I said at once. "You owe me a Pepsi," I said.

"Deal. What about these accents?" Mac said.

"They were from Georgia or South Carolina," Dr. Mohammed said.

"You a linguist too, Double Doc?" Mac said.

"No, just a smart motherfucker," he said. "And my mom was from Savannah, so I know that accent."

"Clean up yore room, boyah! Wash those dissshes! Mo' that yar-ed!" Mac said. We both looked at her, amazed at her sudden, near-perfect Georgia accent, and she said, "My grandfather on my mom's side was from Hinesville, right there at Fort Stewart."

"I've been to Fort Stewart," I said.

"Me, too," Double-Doc said. Neither of us bothered to explain why, and Mac smartly didn't ask.

"So they had that kind of accent?" Mac said.

"Yeah, but remember that South Carolina is right across the Savannah River—and all those crackers talk like that."

"Understood," Mac said. "Now let's see if we can get a description of the guys."

It turned out that Double-Doc was an absolute wizard at noticing details. His regulars were starting to show up, so he dished dogs and talked to us at the same time.

One of the guys had distinctive hair, black with a white streak over the left temple. "He told me that he got it when his brother dropped a crowbar on him while they were roofing in Tuscaloosa," Double-Doc said. "He told me the same thing while he was hitting on me," one of the regulars said. She was a pretty girl named Lily Hedges who was trying to become a medical doctor. "He also told me that he'd played baseball at the University of South Carolina but that he'd flunked out because of calculus. He seemed smart, looked nice, but smelled bad and had bad teeth," she said.

"He tell you his name?" Mac asked.

"Elvis," Lily Hedges and Double-Doc said at the same time. "You owe me a Pepsi, Doc," Hedges said. He nodded and handed her a Pepsi. She opened it and said, "I thought he was full of shit, but he showed me a Georgia license, and the first name was Elvis."

"What about the last name?" I said.

"Linemann," she said. "Like a football player, but with an extra *n*."

"Hey, the tall one with the birthmark must have been his brother," said another regular, a guy named Patrick Cirino. "We started talking about fishing, and he mentioned he'd been on the Bass Pro Shops Tour, you know, the one with Kevin VanDam? He told me he was Roy Linemann. I recognized his name. He really was the guy—I looked him up on the internet and confirmed it."

We didn't blow it; both Mac and I knew we had solid leads, but we just continued to listen and write everything down. By the time lunch rush was over, we had four names and five good physical descriptions, courtesy of Double-Doc Mohammed and his regular lunch crowd.

We knew that two of the roofers were brothers, Elvis and Roy Linemann; that one of the roofers was a very muscular man with green eyes, named Carl Horne; and that one of the roofers had dull-red hair and was named Chip or Chipper, and that the only one without any name attached was about 6'2", 200, and was missing the ring finger on his right hand.

"We shook hands, and he told me thanks for the great dogs," Double-Doc said. "He didn't talk much at all. He was the strong, silent type, and he may have stuttered or had a lisp."

"How do you know that?" Mac said.

"I'm a former stutterer. The best way to cover it up is just not to speak, and I got the feeling that he had practiced his little speech. He's also the only one that didn't join in the banter. They all had the peculiar habit of calling each other Bob. Elvis called all of them Bob at one time or another, but the strong, silent one didn't. Bob is hard to say for a stutterer. That *B* sound can just cause you to break down and fry," Double-Doc said.

We thanked him and his regulars for their help, promised to contact them later in the day or tomorrow for help with an ident-a-kit drawing, and turned to leave.

"Hey, Mac, Freak, aren't you guys forgetting something?" Double-Doc said.

"I'll take two chili dogs and two Chicagos without sport peppers," I said. "And two Pepsis."

"And I'll have a New York with kraut and a Chicago dog," Mac said. "Two Pepsis for me too."

We got our dogs, overrode Double-Doc's offer for free stuff, paid with a tip, and headed back to the car. The local cops were all gone, except Sergeant Roush. He looked at us eating our dogs and said, "Well, at least ya ate well here in the 'Zoo. Can we local yokels help you with anything?" He was eyeing Mac eating her New York with kraut dog, trying for casual but clearly interested in more than just the case. In fact, he was nearly salivating watching Mac eat, but I didn't think that it was the New York with kraut dog he was imagining her eating.

She cut him off with a full mouth of dog and some panache. "Probably, but that is above my pay grade, Sergeant. My AIC and your chief are meeting with the sheriff and will have to work out the details. I just go where the AIC points me. We appreciate the offer, though." She was classy; she didn't insult his manhood or just tell him to fuck off, but she made it perfectly clear that he'd probably seen the last of her.

Roush took it like a man too. He said, "Roger that, Agent McKee. I had to offer, y'know?"

She smiled and said, "No harm in the offer, Sergeant. Thanks." We all shook hands, and Mac and I jumped in the rental and headed back for the hotel to meet with the team. We looked at each other and laughed, and Mac said, "OK, for the record, he was good-looking and charming and friendly, but I really was raised Catholic, so I have a thing about that type of come-on. Those nuns were real she-bitch brides of Christ when I was a kid, and it stuck. I'm not against a hookup, but that was just too casual."

"Can I have him, then?" I said, fake-panting and fanning myself.

"Fuck you and the horse you rode in on, Freak," Mac said. Her laughter was like a middle-C bell, filling the car with a joyous sound.

"We do have a serious lead," I said.

"Yes, indeedy-doo," Mac said. "Wanna bet we blow the boys out of the water?"

"Welll," I said, "it's possible that they have leads too. If the people at their bank were as forthcoming as ours were, then they must have gone to see the other subjects, right? Isn't that SOP for cases like this?"

"Yeah, but I'm betting that nobody else was like Taco Bob or Double-Doc and his regulars. These are top-shelf wits. I'm not saying anything against the rest of the team, but didn't we get lucky finding Taco Bob? And having Double-Doc's regulars come by just as we were there? Better to be lucky than good, Grandma always says."

"Concur," I said. "My *zayde* always says the same thing. Doesn't mean we can't lord it over them when we get there, right?"

"Bet your ass we're gonna lord it over them. We got the best shit with a half-rookie team, which means they gotta kowtow to us," Mac said. The look on her face showed she was relishing the thought of whacking everybody else with our information. A sly look came over her face, and she said, "Freak, ya wanna have some fun? I've got an idea about this…"

She outlined a plan for practical joking that was simple and yet quite funny. After she was done, we looked at each other and began giggling, until we finally found our way back to the Radisson (fucking one-way streets in Kalamazoo).

We gave the car to the valet, and I held out my fist to her. "Wymyn against the machine," I said.

"Roger that, Freak," Mac said. "We're gonna freak those fuckers right out, and it's gonna be great. Too bad Guru's not here—she'd shit a brick."

"Damned skippy," I said. "Let's go amaze our friends!"

Mac nodded, and we went up to our rooms not knowing that we were about to blow the lid off what would become the case of the century.

Beware the law of unintended consequences. It's a mean bitch that doesn't care who gets pissed. Or dead.

CHAPTER 22

Follow the Breadcrumbs Home, Freak

We got up to the room and found out that the other agents had taken over a small conference room downstairs, so we went back down and found them in a nicely appointed room with three computer screens and a big conference phone station.

"Mac and Freak arriving," I said when we came in the door.

"Great," Joe said. He laid a few bars of "You Are So Beautiful" (the guy actually sounded like the real Joe Cocker) on us and then said, "House figured out what they're doing."

"Really? Do tell," Mac said. She sat down and idly began messing with one of the laptops.

"They're bleaching ones," House said. "It's the only way that the paper is so perfect. Joe and I looked at it under a microscope, and it's the real deal. It also explains why nobody really noticed the fakes. We went to Nagel's Top Dog and the Root Beer Stand and they hadn't noticed a thing, but they definitely had someone passing funny money."

"Wow, that's something," Mac said. She was still fiddling with the laptop, seemingly just pushing a button here or there.

The guys and Ed were really fired up, and they kept talking a mile a minute, not noticing that Mac and I weren't joining in the enthusiasm.

"And we can track the paper once we get it on a mass spec [mass spectrometer]. It gives you the unique chemical signature of anything that you put in it. It would reveal the place and time the bills were printed and where they were first distributed," Ed said.

"Then we can backtrack and find out where they went after distribution…"

"But we'll have to check the ink, too, before we can…"

"If they were stupid and just collected them from the same area, we can get on their trail right away…"

"Of course, we'll have to have a bigger unit, probably a task force…"

"Got to get Captain Cork and Guru involved ASAP…"

"I mean, it could be they're also turning over fives, but it isn't as likely…"

"And plates aren't really a problem if you can find a gold- or silversmith…"

"Yeah, they might be able to use a 3D printer to set the plates, but that's plastic, not metal, so how long could they use one set?"

The whole time the maelstrom was swirling around us Mac and I kept nodding, "Uh-huhing," "Yepping," "Isn't that somethinging"—you know, making all those sounds and gestures that you use when your grandma or coworkers or casual acquaintances get on a roll that you don't give a flying fuck about, but you don't want to be rude by just cutting them off. My mom used to call it pseudo-convo, or synthetic conversation. My *zayde* called it small talk skills.

The Marine Corps called it bullshitting, and like most times, I tended to agree with the Corps.

After five minutes of conversation flying all over the conference room, Joe finally noticed that Mac and I were just not that excited about their discovery. He said, "Freak, you don't seem too enthused about this break. What the fuck is going on?"

"Oh, I'm enthused," I said with about as much enthusiasm as you'd have for a root canal.

"Mac, are you watching porn or what? We've got a real break in the case," Joe said.

"Un-huh. That's really somethin'," Mac said. The printer in the corner of the room began to hum and spit out some pages. She looked up from the laptop and said, "Did I miss something? Freak?"

"Uh, Joe and the guys have a real hot lead on how the counterfeiters are making the funny money?" I said, acting like it was a real puzzle why everyone was so excited.

"Oh, that," Mac said. "I thought it was something important."

"Fuck you," House said. "It won't take very long to backtrack this shit and get on their trail for real."

"That's nice," Mac and I said.

"You owe me a Pepsi, Freak," she said.

"Concur," I said.

"What the fuck is wrong with you guys? We're going to break the case in short order," Ed said.

"We almost can't miss. These guys will be sitting ducks right quick," Gunny said.

"We've got a direct line to the entire ring, once we get on the ground where they're picking up their paper," Joe said.

"That's nice," Mac and I said in unison.

"We owe each other a Pepsi," I said.

"Concur," Mac said.

"What the fuck?" Ed said.

"Did you guys drink lunch?" House said.

"Or sniff too much funny money ink?" Gunny said.

"And what the hell is with the 'that's nice' routine?" Joe said.

Mac went over and picked the sheets off the printer. The rest of the team watched her, clearly frustrated but not saying anything. She looked at the top sheet, nodded slightly, and said, "Freak, will you please explain "that's nice" to the rest of the gang?"

"Of course, my liege," I said. "One time there were five old ladies enjoying a lunch on the veranda in Savannah, Georgia. The first old lady said to the rest, 'See this diamond ring? It's five carats and worth $50,000. My husband gave it to me for our anniversary.' The rest of the old ladies 'Oohed' and 'Ahhed' over it, except one, who just said, 'That's nice.'

"A second little old lady said, 'Well, see that new Mercedes in the driveway? It's an S-Class and worth $100,000. My husband gave it to me when our first grandchild was born.' The rest of the old ladies 'Oohed' and 'Ahhed' over it, except one, who just said, 'That's nice.'

"A third old lady said, 'Of course y'all've seen my house. It has twenty rooms, five bathrooms, and four maids. It's worth a million dollars. My husband gave it to me just because he loves me.' The rest of the old ladies 'Oohed' and 'Ahhed' over it, except one, who just said, 'That's nice.'

"Finally, one of the little old ladies said, 'Bernice, why do y'all just keep saying 'That's nice'?"

"Bernice said, 'Well, my mama always said that a lady shouldn't swear, so when I wanted to say 'Fuck you,' I should just say 'That's nice.'"

To their credit, everyone laughed, but Joe said, "Why 'Fuck you'? I mean 'that's nice?' What'd we do?"

"Oh, it's not what you did, Joe," Mac said.

"Y'all are just fine," I said.

"Why are y'all telling us, 'Fuck you'?" Ed said.

"Oh, we just solved the case," Mac said.

"That's nice," the other four said at once. They sorted out who owed who a Pepsi, and then Gunny said, "No fuckin' way, Mac. We'd need names and phone numbers, or driver's licenses, or social security numbers."

"Freak, can we run our checklist?" Mac said.

I jumped to attention and said, "Ma'am, yes, ma'am."

She stood up and said, "Names?"

"Check," I said as she turned over the first sheet of paper from the printer.

"Phone numbers?" Mac said.

"Check," I said as she turned over the second sheet.

"Social security numbers?" Mac said.

"Check," I said as she turned over the third sheet.

"Pictures of the three with criminal records?" Mac said.

"Check," I said as she fanned three more pages out on the conference table.

"Holy shit!" Ed said.

"Motherrrfuckerrr," House said.

"Fuck me blind and call me a whore," Gunny said.

"Sweet Mother Hubbard," Joe said. "Ya solved the whole goddamned thing in one swell foop!"

"OK, dish, you assholes," Ed said. We recounted our steps, including the tip on where the paper pushers were headed.

"So they must be in Chicago right now," Joe said.

"That's what we figured. It was probably their target all along," Mac said.

"Sure it was," Gunny said. "Hell, they could pass funny paper in Portillo's at rush hour and there wouldn't be any way to tell. The people at the cash registers aren't trained to detect it, and they're in a hurry because they're trying to be as fast as possible for the customers."

"And cash flows through there like shit through a goose," Ed said.

"Guaranteed that no one at the Ontario Street restaurant counts the cash by hand—they just load it into a counter and band it," House said.

"So no one would even notice at the store, or the bank, not until the cash goes back in circulation. And remember, this funny money makes the grade except for the Test," Joe said.

Just then, the phone rang. Mac hit the speaker and said, "Fat Helen's Soup Kitchen. Fat Helen ain't here. This is Shee-vawn speakin'. How kin ah hep' you?"

Jewey said, "Cut the shit, Mac. We've got lots more on the guys you touted. I'm sending a secure email to your phone with the info, but I can tell you that we have positively identified them all."

"Go, Jewey," Mac said.

"First, all these guys work for an outfit called Wilson Roofing, headquartered in Toledo, Ohio. Weasel is working on the company. All we know right now is that it's owned by somebody named Tommie Wilson. I've got thumbnails on the five guys.

"Elvis Linemann, 35, married, with three kids; hometown Savannah, Georgia; one conviction for check kiting; served 60 days in county lockup. Played baseball for two years at the University of South Carolina before he flunked out of school.

"Roy Linemann, 34, brother of Elvis, married, with two kids; same hometown; no convictions or arrests; former professional fisherman; has a graphic art design degree from the University of South Carolina.

"Carl Horne, 36, married to the Linemanns' sister Carol, with two kids; one conviction for fraud; one conviction for receiving stolen goods; served 60 days in the county lockup on the receiving charge; served a year and a half on the fraud charge; it was a credit card scam.

"Charles 'Chip' Fowler, 35, maternal cousin of the Linemanns, married to Horne's sister Lena—her real name—with one kid; one arrest for credit card fraud in the same beef as Horne; served 90 days in the county lockup; a hothead, mouthed off to the judge, or he'd've just had 60 days. Also attended the University of South Carolina, left voluntarily before graduation.

"Mark Roberson, 34, half-brother of Fowler, divorced from a Linemann cousin, no children, raised by his grandmother when his parents died in a small plane crash, no arrests or convictions, has a business degree from South Carolina State University, where he played varsity football. He's apparently the foreman of the traveling crew from Wilson Roofing."

"Great job, Jewey. We're gonna follow up here tomorrow and then come home. We think that these guys are already in town," Joe said.

"Guru said the same thing. Weasel and I concur and think that all the stuff before Chi was a test run," Jewey said.

"We came to the same conclusion," Joe said. "Keep us posted via email and really dig in on the roofing company. It's hard to believe that these clowns came up with this scam on their own. Might be this Wilson guy is the mastermind."

"Roger that. We'll be all over them. The Greek and Bumble are done in court, and Captain Cork has assigned them on our end. Let us know if you need any additional support. See you when you get back," Jewey said.

We all fist-bumped, and Gunny said, "Damn good job, Mac, Freak, especially since you're half-rookie. Way to catch on to the witnesses the way you did. It was a stroke of genius."

"Nah, just good luck and good timing," Mac said.

"Hell, if we hadn't gotten lost, we'd never have been in the right place at the right time," I said.

"Still awesome work, both of you," Ed said.

"Concur," Joe said. "Let's get our paperwork done and we'll catch some supper. Freak, where the hell should we eat in the 'Zoo?"

"Whaddya want to eat?" I asked.

"Prime rib," House said.

"That sounds like a winner to me. I'll bet that there are some cows just waiting to give it up out here in East Bumfuck, Michigan," Gunny said.

"Well, it ain't Omaha or Kansas City, but it does seem that we might get some good cow out here, like farm-to-table shit," Ed said.

I looked at Joe and said, "Well, there is a really great old restaurant just east of here in Marshall that has the best prime rib on this side of the state, and well…" I just trailed off, so Joe said, "Yeah. And what else, Freak?"

"If we went there, I'd be able to see my family," I said. "We used to eat there all the time. My mom and my *zayde* were kind of regulars because they went there with clients all the time."

"Hey, now we gotta go," Joe said.

"Concur," the rest of the group said.

"Just one question, Freak. Do they have beer?" Gunny asked.

"And wine, and mixed drinks, and the best creamy garlic salad dressing you've ever had," I said.

"Sold, but I ain't drivin' home," Gunny said.

"Roger that," House said.

"I definitely deserve a drink or five," Mac said.

"Freak and I will drive home," Joe said, "as long as nobody gets slobbering toasted."

"It's a deal," I said.

I called my mom, and she said they'd meet us, so we went over our notes, wrote up our contact reports, and got ourselves organized for the next day. Once we were all done, we loaded up our cars and rolled down I-94 to Marshall. We parked in the lot across the street and went into Win Schuler's restaurant.

Schuler's is a grand old place that's been there for over 100 years. It has an old-world feel when you walk in, all dark wood and subtle lighting and some of the best food in Michigan. Their prime rib is about as good as it gets, and they do everything the right way, from service to appetizers (get the fried oysters from the pub) to main dishes, especially beef. The people at Schuler's are friendly, dignified, and interested in you having the best experience possible.

We had a blast.

After we met my family—Mom, Dad, *zayde*, Dog-Boy (my brother David, a veterinarian) and his wife (Phyllis), and Shyster (my brother Gabriel, an attorney in the family firm) and his wife (Ivara)—we settled in for scintillating conversation, food that wouldn't quit, and general good fellowship.

"These oysters are fabulous," Ed said. "And this remoulade they use for dipping sauce is yummy. I'd almost drink it if this wine weren't so tasty."

"I'm going to get another salad so that I can drink some of this dressing. Creamy garlic is the shizz!" House said.

"Just tell 'em to bring you another pitcher and use it on your prime rib," Shyster said. "It's better than the horseradish sauce."

We had quite an argument about that, and then my mom said, "Ladies, let's go to the restroom." We all stood up, the men all stood up, and we trooped off to the restroom. We went in, and my mom and I volunteered to wait since there weren't enough stalls.

That was when it happened.

And my life changed forever, even though I didn't know it at that time.

"Poor Mrs. Miller just got out of the hospital again," Mom said.

"Still can't get over Tim?" I said.

"Well, she claims she heard him talking to her about getting the person who killed him," she said.

"Who was it this time?" I said.

"She claims he told her it was pre-fall Lucifer, the right hand of God," my mom said.

"Oh, shit. That poor womyn, I'm surprised she's even lucid anymore," I said.

"That's the weird thing. I talked to her the day before she went in, and there was no sign of anything wrong. We had a great talk, she promised to bring me some greens from her garden, and then boom, right back in the loony bin," my mom said.

"Sounds like PTSD," I said. "I've seen some of that and had to help people deal with it."

"Well, she did mention getting your number and talking to you about what happened, now that you're an investigator for the Secret Service," my mom said.

"What? I don't investigate murders. I investigate funny paper. How'm I going to help?" I said.

"She specifically told me that you were the perfect person to look into it," Mom said. Just then, two stalls opened up and we went in to do our business. When we got back to the table, Ed said, "Who's Mrs. Miller? And what's driving her crazy?"

"And why does she want to talk to you?" Mac said.

So we told the sad story of Karen Miller and her twins.

"We lived right across from the Millers when I was a kid," I said. "The week before she was due with twins, Mrs. Miller and her husband, John, were hit by a drunk driver who crossed the center line and smashed their car. She lived, and the twins were delivered alive and healthy by Caesarian section, but Mr. Miller was really mangled and died during surgery.

"All that happened a week after my birthday. The twins are three years older than me. We grew up together, and Mrs. Miller recovered from her husband dying, although she never remarried or even dated that I know of." I looked at my mom, but it was my dad who said, 'She was married to the job of mom. And she did an excellent job of raising those boys.'

"And she worked her ass off at Kellogg," my *zayde* said. "She became a shift supervisor and was being groomed for higher management when, well…" His voice trailed off as we all contemplated the hell Mrs. Miller went through on her twins' 17th birthday.

"When the twins turned 17, there was a big party at the Millers' House. Mrs. Miller threw a shindig with food and live music, and everybody from Harper Creek showed up. The boys were popular athletes and literally Eagle Scouts, and they were just plain fun to be around. So was Mrs. Miller back then, so the party was crammed.

"About 9 that night, the party had been in full swing for two hours and didn't show any signs of letting up, but nobody could find Tim. He was the younger twin. Everybody thought that he was with someone else, and lots of people saw his brother Tom and assumed it was Tim. Anyway, when the party started winding down Mrs. Miller got concerned because she still couldn't find Tim. It became clear that no one had seen him for over five hours, so Mrs. Miller sent out search parties to try to find him. I went with his brother, Tom, to look." I stopped for a minute to collect myself, remembering that awful day.

"So I told Tom that no one had seen Kristy O'Dowd, Tim's girlfriend, either, so we decided to cruise the local make-out spots in case he was on a booty call. We went by two, and there was no one there, but there was a car we didn't recognize in the third one, so we decided to sneak up on whoever it was. I think we were going to scare Tim and Kristy, if it was them.

"Unfortunately, we found Tim, all alone and very dead. His head was twisted at an odd angle, he had bruises on his throat, and he was nude," I said. I smiled a wry smile and said, "Not very appetizing conversation right before prime rib, right? Anyway, having her son murdered—the county ME determined that it had been death by strangulation or asphyxiation related to some weird sexual practice—drove Mrs. Miller over the edge. She was in the hospital for at least two years, and she has never been right again."

"Jay-sus, Mary, and Joseph, the poor womyn," Mac said. Everyone made some sound of sympathy, and then the food came, and we talked about better days while we ate the best prime rib in West Michigan.

After the meal was over and everybody had had their aperitifs in hand, Joe said, "So whose car was Tim Miller found in?"

"And what about his girlfriend, Kristy O'Dowd? Where was she when Tim died?" Ed said.

"And strangulation—wasn't this guy a hotshot athlete? Strangling him would be tough unless somebody slipped him a roofie. Were there any signs of resistance?" House said.

"I also wonder about DNA. It was a while ago, and they may be able to get something now they couldn't before," Gunny said.

"Was there any sign of sexual activity? A nude body usually signals something going on, especially if the ME thought there may have been a sexual game going on," Mac said.

"Wow, did you pick the right group to be affiliated with?" my brother Shyster said. "These people are like white on rice—they're just like you, Freak."

I really felt like a million bucks at that moment. I knew that Shyster was trying to tease me, but it felt like one of the best compliments of my life, like when my CO in special ops complimented me (and that's all I'm gonna say about that—it's still classified). Not only were the people I worked with real professionals, but they were also real people who just plain gave a shit. They were my unit, and my people, and I was supremely glad to have been picked to serve with them.

That people would die because of their professionalism never even crossed my mind at that point.

So we spent more time at Schuler's, drinking good drinks, eating great desserts (hummingbird cake, raspberries and cream bread pudding, and classic crème brûlée, all of which make you fat just from smell alone), and discussing the case of poor Mrs. Miller. After we'd chewed it over for at least an hour, Joe said, "Freak, there's just too much mystery here. We need more info to go on, or we're not going to be able to help poor Mrs. Miller. I need some help here, guys." He looked at the other four agents, and House immediately said, "When my uncle Poot was murdered, my grandma 'bout went out of her mind until a sergeant named Belson came 'round from the Boston PD and told her how it happened. She said all she needed were some answers, and her disposition improved once that happened. Sounds like Mrs. Miller needs some answers to keep on goin'. I say we get some for her."

"I was an MP for a time, and I don't mind acting like one again so we can get Mrs. Miller some answers," Gunny said.

"If it were my son, I'd want to at least know that somebody at least gave a shit, and I'd want all the info I could get," Ed said. "Of course, it goes without saying that I'd want to catch and kill whoever did it."

"Concur," we all said. "I owe all of you a Pepsi," my dad said.

"Freak and I worked well together today. I'd be pleased to be her partner again tomorrow and help Mrs. Miller at least get some hope by digging up all the info we can," Mac said.

"I knew I could rely on you weirdos to have a heart," Joe said. "I'm going to detach Mac and Freak to Battle Creek to investigate the funny money at Bill's near the airport, and they're probably also going to have to liaise with the Battle Creek PD, maybe for some time. The rest of us are going to do our follow-up in Kalamazoo, then book it for Battle Creek to help with the investigation at Bill's. Since we'll probably need at least half a day, we'll have to get Weasel to change our flight to late Thursday night from the Kalamazoo/Battle Creek International Airport."

We all nodded and winked, and my mom said, "Why don't you check out of your hotel tomorrow and plan on coming to our house and staying? We've got plenty of room, and if we don't, Shyster and Dog-Boy (my brothers Gabriel and David) have spare rooms. In fact, why don't Freak and Mac stay there tonight? It'll give them an earlier start."

"That is a generous offer and brilliant planning, Mrs. Glickstien. We accept," Joe said.

So Mac and I went off in one car to the House of Glickstien Motor Court Motel while the rest of the team went back to the 'Zoo. Mac and I agreed to get started at 7:00 a.m. I was going to take her to breakfast at Speed's Coffee Shop (another Battle Creek institution—their coffee was so strong it could be eaten from your hand if you didn't mind the burns), and then off to the Battle Creek PD. I was bound to know someone there, although I wasn't sure who was left.

We got to the House of Glickstien Motor Court Motel, and everybody went off to bed, except my dad, who came to my room door and said, "Freak, you know your mom and I are damned proud of you, right?" I nodded, and he said, "Never more than tonight, girlie. This is a *mitzvah* (an act of charity without regard for reward) to end all *mitzvahs*. Your friends are very Jewish for goys, and we are incredibly proud of the fact they respect you so much. It lets us know that you're on the right path."

I didn't cry, but I did well up a bit. My dad was always worried about me but seldom expressed it. What he really meant was, "We love you," and I was really touched. He kissed me on the forehead, and I hugged him tight.

When I lay down on my old bed from high school, all I felt was loved, respected, and cherished. I did not feel the turn my life had taken, which, just like Alice, would lead me down the rabbit hole into a world I didn't even know existed.

I also didn't know that I was going to change world history because of our *mitzvah* for Mrs. Miller, but if I had, it wouldn't have stopped me. Right is right, regardless of the consequences, or at least I thought so at that time (OK, I still think so, despite what happened).

I just wish people hadn't died for my hubris.

CHAPTER 23

St. Freak and the Mitzvahs

So the next morning, I called the Kalamazoo Public Safety Office and left a message telling Officer Wilkinson that I still wanted to shoot against him but that he'd have to call me to set up a time because duty called.

Mac and I said goodbye to the family and headed for Speed's to eat breakfast, but the family just followed us, so we all ate too much, had coffee that would peel paint (don't get me wrong—the coffee at Speed's was and is excellent, but it's got about 37 times the normal caffeine punch, and they serve it Marine Corps hot, which means just below the temperature of molten lava), and then Mac and I headed for the Battle Creek PD (and if you watched the short-lived eponymous TV show, it's nothing like that, and no, none of the cops look like Dean Winter or Josh Duhamel).

We went in, showed our creds, and were sent back to the bullpen, where we got really lucky right off the bat.

The lone detective in the bullpen had shiny blond hair and really broad shoulders. He stood up, and I said, "Denver, Denver!" in my football voice. Without turning around, he said, "Okie, over, Okie," in a deep bass voice. Mac looked at me, and I said, "Sorry, but that gorgeous hunk of man over there is one Bengt Olafsson, former tackle for the Harper Creek Fighting Beavers and all-around good guy."

Bengt turned around and said, "Freak, ya need tah poot a few pownds on, eh?" in a classic Minnesota accent (and fuck you, Minnesotans, ya do have an accent dere, dontchaknow?). He was exactly 6'8" in his bare feet, still weighed 275, and had the ugliest broken nose I'd ever seen—it was like a sweet potato in the middle of his face, but bent slightly to the left. He was also a sharp guy who could've probably been prime minister of his native Norway if he hadn't stayed in Battle Creek when his cereal executive dad was transferred (he stayed because of American football, which he loved, although he would have been All-State in *futbol*—the guy kicked several field goals for us that were over 50 yards, including a 59-yarder that was good by about fifteen yards).

He was also one of my best friends from high school—one of the only guys that never tried to take advantage of my ugliness to get into my pants or get his hands on my boobs. (A sidenote: I don't know why guys, especially high school guys, assume that ugly girls will just give it up for the attention. I was perfectly happy not being pawed by a bunch of hunyocks, and I never needed the attention. I had a family, after all, from whom I got plenty of attention. We ugly girls may not be pretty, but we do have standards, and it would be nice if you moronic thumb-suckers that call yourselves men would get the picture. Ugly girls are people too, and that "Ugly girls are easy" stereotype is about as true as "All Jews are rich" or "All football players are dumb." And you are annoying all of us unattractive types when you do it.)

I ran over and jumped on Bengt (I know, I know, not Secret Service standard behavior, but fuck you, I'd known the guy for 25 years) and gave him a monster hug. He hugged me back and said, "So what can I do for the Secret Service, eh? Yer lookin' for funny money and you t'ink a Battle Creek detective knows aboot it? Mebbe out t' Bill's by t' airport?"

I was prepared to lie like a very old Persian rug, but there was no way I was going to lie to Bengt, so I introduced Mac and told him the truth. He listened to the whole spiel and just nodded. When I was done, he got up without a word and went through the back door of the office. In less than three minutes, he was back with a file box in either hand. He set the file boxes on a clear table at the back of the bullpen and said, "C'mon back. Ya can work here."

We came back, and Bengt said, "Let's talk aboot da case first, eh? I'll tell you what I know, and ya can tell me what ya know, and mebbe we can make some sense of it all."

We nodded, and he said, "Well, here's the top-sheet rundown: Tim Miller was a 17-year-old junior at Harper Creek High School, played football, wrestled, and ran track, was on the honor roll every trimester, and was well-liked by teachers and schoolmates. He was in prime physical condition, had no distinguishing marks or tattoos, and had sex either while or just before he was killed. Forensics found three used condoms in a plastic bag in the car, all of them consistent with his blood type. The samples have been preserved but not tested for DNA. You'll understand why in a minute.

"Cause of death was definitely strangulation—his hyoid bone and larynx were both crushed. The ME estimated that it must have been done by a man with oversize hands, as well as great physical strength, because manual choking is hard to do on a man as physically fit as Tim Miller.

"Besides the bruising on the neck, the ME also found bruises on his buttocks, maybe from being kicked or slapped really hard. There was also a small bruise on the back right quarter of his head. It looked like he'd hit his head on something fairly recently.

"The weirdest thing was that he had no defensive wounds at all, nothing under his fingernails and no sign of a struggle. Other than the bruises, he was pristine. Another weird thing: he had no body hair except on his head and eyebrows—his entire body was shaved." (It should be noted that during the entire case rundown, Bengt's English was perfectly clear and unaccented. Weird, eh?)

"Say what?" Mac said.

"He and Tom did it during wrestling season. They believed it helped them make weight and that it made them slippery, hard to hold down. This was only a week after state, so he probably hadn't let the hair grow again," I said.

"Ya, dat's da same t'ing we t'ought," Bengt said.

Mac added, "Detective, you haven't said a word about motive. Why would somebody do this to a kid?"

Bengt looked very pensive, then opened one of the boxes and pulled out some pictures. He looked at them, selected two, then said, "Well, at t' time da detectives t'ought it was a crime of passion, but da boy's girlfriend was 5'7", 125, so dat d'int fly. Den dey t'ought it was a random t'eft t'ing, since we never recovered his wallet or his watch, and it was a good watch dat his gramps gave him for winning state wrestling as a sophomore, but dat wouldn't fly because dere was $250 in 10s and 20s in one of his shoes in t' front of t' car." He stopped and looked at us, and I said, "OK, obviously you've looked at this case. What do you think?"

Bengt Olafsson's face had always been an open book, and now was no exception. He looked down at the table, his face got red, and he seemed to shrink a bit. "I t'ink a man of God did it in anger and den felt remorse." He looked up at me, and suddenly it hit me: Kristy O'Dowd's uncle was a 6'6", 290-pound-plus priest named Pat O'Dowd, Bishop Padraig O'Dowd, the head of the Kalamazoo-Battle Creek diocese and the principal/superintendent of the Battle Creek Area Catholic schools. Bishop O'Dowd was one of the most respected people in all of Battle Creek. He was on every board, at every function, and could have easily been elected king of Battle Creek if that were possible. I knew the man personally; he'd been in our home, because he and my *zayde* were friends, and he'd even written a letter of recommendation for me when I went to Michigan State.

No wonder the case never went anywhere and Mrs. Miller was going crazy; accusing Bishop O'Dowd of murder would be like accusing the Michigan Wolverines of colluding with the Ohio State Buckeyes to throw their annual border war football game.

Bengt and I shared a look, and Mac said, "What?" so I explained who Bishop O'Dowd was and why the detectives 20 years ago might have been less than eager to pursue the case. Mac thought about it for a minute and said, "OK, so the scenario is like this: Tim and Kristy slip away for some fun time, they go at it for a while and her uncle just happens upon them either during or right after the fact, at which point he gets Kristy out of the car and loses it on Tim. His rage is off the charts and his size advantage is so great that he strangles Tim without meaning to. He's probably just trying to shake him up. Once he realizes that Tim is dead, he bundles Kristy out of there, swears her to secrecy, and goes to confession but never once unburdens his soul, because he's got to keep the secret that he's a murderer."

"Ya," Bengt said very softly. "It all fits t'gedder real good, and t' bishop had no alibi for dat night. I checked as best I could, and he was simply nowhere to be found."

"Ahh, shit!" Mac said. "Even with no statute of limitations, we can't go accusing a Catholic bishop of something like this. We've gotta talk to Kristy and run down the bishop's whereabouts without alerting him. If he really did it, we've got to have the case done up eight ways to Sunday, because otherwise we'll all be chasing reindeer turds in North Bumfuck, Alaska," Gunny said.

"You're gonna have a hard life if you're wrong," I said. "Ya, I'll be headed back to Norway wit'out my wife and kids if it isn't true, and dey'll probably convert to Catholicism, because dey already love t' bishop." It turned out that Bengt's eldest daughter played volleyball for the St. Philip Tigers; she was a starter on the team from the school where the bishop was superintendent and principal.

"De only good thing about dis is yer timin'. Da bishop's in Detroit for four more days while t' Pope's dere. We could make inquiries wit'out attractin' too much immediate attention," Bengt said.

"First of all, Mac and I will do all the digging. You're sitting this one out, Big Bengt. No way are we going to let any of this blow back on you. Mac and I can take the heat, especially once we let it slip that you were less than helpful," I said. My old friend's faced was less red, and he was clearly relieved to not be stuck in the middle of what promised to be a fair-size shitstorm.

"One thing still bothers me, though," Mac said. "What about the rental car? How did Tim Miller end up dead in it instead of his own car?"

"He didn't have his own car," I said. "Tom had a car. Tim had a motorcycle. Their mom couldn't afford a car for both of them, so the twins decided to split the difference. Tom had a tired old Subaru wagon with 275,000 miles on it, while Tim had an old Honda 350 that probably had 100,000 miles on it."

"OK, but where did the car come from?" Mac asked.

Bengt said, "Dat's why I first considered t' bishop, since t' car was part of a courtesy fleet rented by t' Catholic Charities o' Battle Creek/Kalamazoo. The diocese was havin' dere annual charity auction, and dere were lots o' local celebrities in town who din't have wheels. T' bishop signed for t' cars, altho' dere was no way t' tell who was drivin' 'em."

"Oh, shitalicious," Mac said.

I said, "We have to do this fast. Let me call some people and see if we can get a line on Kristy, then we'll go talk to Mrs. Rhinebolt."

"She died last year, but I already got Kristy's address in my notebook," Bengt said.

"She *died*?" I asked.

"Who the hell was Mrs. Rhinebolt, and why the hell are you screaming?" Mac said.

"Ellen Rhinebolt was the editor of the *Battle Creek Enquirer* for about 350 years, and she knew everything about everybody in the Battle Creek area. She was like a human resource library, only nicer and easier to access," I said. "How old was she, Bengt?"

"One hunnert an' seven," he said.

"No shit?" Mac said.

"No shit. She was sharp as a tack till t'day she died," Bengt said.

"So what the hell happened to her?" I asked.

"She got attacked by t'ree pit bulls while she was taking her daily walk. Some city guys saw t' attack and ran over w'it shovels, but one of t' dogs had opened an artery, an' she bled out before t' paramedics could get her t' Leila Post," Bengt said as a tear ran down his face, but the look on his face wasn't quite sad, so I said, "What happened to the dog owner?"

"*Owners*. Dey was two brudders who was tied up wit' some meth dealers," Bengt said. "Unfortunately, dere house burned down wit' dem in it, so dere wasn't a trial, and a crowd o' people seem ta have kilt da dogs, al'do it was pointed out dat it was t' guys who were responsible, not t' dogs."

I looked at my old friend and knew that the fire had been no accident, but I couldn't figure out why he looked, well, triumphant about the whole thing. He looked at me and said, "Ya, well, dese two guys were out on bail an' some folks objected to dat, and dere was an attempt at a public lynching, but o' course, dat was stopped by Battle Creek's finest, so dese guys kinda t'umbed dere noses at everyone, including da cops and, well…everybody loved Mrs. Rhinebolt…so, uh, y'know, dat internet is somethin' else. Somehow dese guys's address was posted on a website, and t' dogs got loose from t' kennel somehow, and well, t' fire department got a call to help out t' Bellevue department way out near Olivet, and jeeze, dere doors were jammed and dey had boarded up all t' windows from inside, so…" He didn't smile, but Bengt Olafsson wasn't at all distressed by what had happened, a point that was proven when he said, "It was a real tragedy for all o' Battle Creek."

"What the fuck kind of asshole judge would give a couple of dumbfuck drug dealers who'd clearly committed at least manslaughter bail?" Mac said.

Bengt looked at me with that flat cop gaze, the "I'm not sure you want to hear this, but I'll tell you if I have to" look, and I suddenly knew who it was. Before Bengt could say anything, I said, "It was His Honor Walter Necker, wasn't it?"

"Ya," Bengt said. My face must have flushed red, and my special ops look must have jumped up, because both Mac and Bengt took a step away from me. Mac said, "Easy, Freak. Stand down from that mission in your head, whatever it is, and let's concentrate on this mitzvah for Mrs. Miller. One mission at a time, right?" She was being reasonable, but as all my memories of the Great Pumpkin came flooding back, I wasn't in a reasonable mood, so I turned for the door to go visit Judge Necker's chambers, which were just a few yards away from the PD. As a federal officer, I'd be able to carry my twin 10-mils into the courtroom, but I was thinking more about ripping him limb from limb (and yes, I could have done it; hell, I'm old now, and I could still do it).

Bengt stepped over to the only door out of the bullpen and said, "I know I can't stop ya, Freak, but I'll slow ya down just enough ta let t' judge escape. Remember dat I have kids, OK?" He settled in front of the door in a relaxed pose, his huge hands ready to defend himself. I felt Mac slide to my right, into a position where she could jump me from my blind spot if she had to.

I looked at Bengt's hands in front of his chest, and a sudden thought hit me. I stopped moving, thought hard for a minute, and said, "Bengt, did the ME have an estimate on how big someone's hands had to be to strangle Tim Miller?"

"What?" he said, clearly startled by my change of direction.

"What the fuck does that have to do with some asshole judge?" Mac said.

"Nothing. Fuck Necker, the horse he rode in on, and the family dog. It has to do with who killed Tim Miller," I said.

Bengt looked thoughtful, went over to the desk with the files, and removed a folder, looked at it a minute, and then handed it to me without a word, his finger showing me which line to read. I looked at it, then handed it to Mac. She read the line and whistled, then looked at me. Bengt said, "Defining characteristic, eh? I'm a big guy, and my hands aren't near big enough t'wrap completely around a 19-and-a-half-inch neck."

I looked at Bengt and said, "You've got the biggest hands I've ever seen on a person. They're bigger than my college boyfriend's, and he's an NBA star. Whaddya know about the bishop's hands?"

"Not a t'ing, but I can get someone who does," Bengt said. He pulled out his cell phone, hit a speed dial number, waited a second, and said, "Ya, Dad, it's Bengt. How big are Bishop O'Dowd's hands?"

There was a big booming voice out of the phone that clearly said, "Oh, jeeze, not even a report on da grandkids, eh? Just some outta-da-blue question about some Cat'lick? I hain't seen him in 'bout two weeks. He's gone ta Washington or some such. He ain't been at da pinochle game."

Bengt said, "Ah, jeeze, we're comin' out tomorrow w'it da kids, but dis is really important, Dad. Are his hands bigger den yers?"

"Well, fer sure dey are! He's got da biggest hand I've ever shook, even bigger den yers!" his dad roared from the phone. Bengt thanked him for his time, told him they'd definitely be out, and hung up.

"Strike two on the bishop," Mac said.

I looked at my old friend and said, "OK, now we have to talk to Kristy. Where can we find her, Bengt?"

The huge detective handed me a piece of notepaper with two phone numbers and two addresses.

"Top one is da work address and number, the bottom one is da home info, dontchaknow?" he said. "I still t'ink I should be goin' along. It in't right dat youse should be doin' all da legwork."

I smiled at the big man still trying to protect people; he was a hell of a pass blocker in high school, and then at Kalamazoo College, but now it was me who had to protect him. If this all went tits up, it was going to be on the U.S. Secret Service, not Detective Bengt Olafsson of the Battle Creek Police Department.

After all, I didn't have any kids to take care of, and I didn't have to live in Battle Creek if the result of the mitzvah was a shitstorm of gigantic proportions.

So we said our goodbyes to Bengt, thanked him for his help, and headed to Kristy's place of business, a restaurant named the Canal Street Café, which was just outside Battle Creek in the tiny town of Augusta.

We cruised down M-96 and got to Augusta about eleven thirty. Bengt had assured us that Kristy would be working; she was a teacher at Harper Creek Middle School, and the summer waitress gig was strictly so she could actually survive. (Not to be all political, but Michigan teachers are paid like shit. Big surprise, right? They are teachers, after all, not anybody important [cue sarcastic music], and most teachers that I know work summer jobs to supplement their incomes, which seem to keep shrinking.)

There were only two cars in the parking lot when we pulled in, so we called Joe for a sitrep in the 'Zoo before we went in. He told us that they had wrapped everything up and were going to catch lunch and then head for Battle Creek. I gave him directions for the Canal Street Café and said we'd wait until they got there so we could all go in at once and scare the shit out of Kristy O'Dowd without saying a word. Two Secret Service agents are bad, but six federal agents are like a pride of lions—armed and definitely dangerous.

Mac looked at the restaurant and said, "What kind of country shitkicker place is this, Freak? Burnt steak, weak coffee, fries from a bag?"

"No fucking idea, Mac. It used to be called the Barking Frog. It was kind of a blood-and-guts sorta biker bar. I haven't been here since I kicked the shit out of four creepy hunyocks over them grabbing a girlfriend's tits," I said.

"Do tell," she said, so I told her the story about how I and Beth Vernon stopped for a drink when I was home on my 30-day leave before my first deployment.

"Beth was my best female friend in school. She was a big old girl who had a laugh like a braying ass's and an ass like a goddess's," I said.

"Whaddya mean an ass like a goddess's?" she said.

"She was about 6'3" and proportional, and her ass was perfectly heart-shaped. She was in high demand just about everywhere we went, and this was no exception. Some greasy-haired, too-much-meth, mentally impaired stoners tried hitting on us, but we told 'em to get lost, so they waited until we left to ask us again. Three of them backed Beth against the dumpster there and began giving her a free mammogram, while one of them tried to keep me busy with my own country shitkicker chest exam. Like most guys, they misapprehended the real threat. I put my guy down and proceeded to break several bones on the other three. Beth kicked two of 'em in the nuts, and then some real tough guys came out of the bar, found out what was happening, heard me when I said I was a Marine, and proceeded to really stomp the shit out of them," I said, a smile on my face as I remembered the scene. Beth really got a kick out of it (sorry, bad pun, but accurate description) once we got the guys off her boobs, and I enjoyed watching the bikers whale on the meth-heads. Guys who try to rape get what they deserve (and you know I know what I'm talking about with that).

"Anyway, it sure doesn't look like that now," I said. "And we're not here for the food. We're here for Mrs. Miller."

"Doesn't lessen the good deed if they got a decent cheeseburger, does it? Is there some Jewish rule that says you have to suffer when you help people?" Mac said.

"Nah, but there is a rule that says you can't enjoy the cheeseburger until you get the bad guy," I said.

"Really?" Mac said. "Jewey never told us that one. All he ever talked about was disappointing his mother by not being a doctor and not dating *shiksa* girls."

"It's all part of the Jewish guilt police rules," I said. "And it's not *shiksa girls*. A *shiksa* is a girl, specifically a Gentile girl who's attracted a Jewish man, although a lot of Jews don't use it as a disparaging term anymore."

"Learn somethin' new every day," Mac said.

"Good. Now, let's get out of this car and find out what Kristy knows about the night Tim Miller was murdered," I said as the car with our fellow agents pulled in right next to us.

The Kalamazoo contingent got out, and I said, "We need to catch this chick unawares before the restaurant becomes busy. We'll debrief both sides later, OK?"

They all nodded, and Joe said, "What's the play?"

"We go in like the feds, all big, scary, and mostly silent, and then Mac and I pick her apart about the night in question. Throw in anything that you think is appropriate, but mostly stand there and glower," I said.

"Ah, yesss, the old 'scare the shit out of her so she blurts something out' approach," Ed said.

"I like it," Mac said. "Simple, direct, and very effective, especially because we have a secret weapon."

"Dat we do," House said in a fake ghetto accent. We all laughed but abruptly stopped when we hit the door. A middle-aged blond womyn said, "Six?" but I cut her off and held my badge right in front of her eyes as I said, "Agent Glinka Glickstien of the U.S. Secret Service. We're looking for Kristy O'Dowd. Is she on the premises?" The womyn flicked a glance back at the kitchen and said, "Uh, may I—"

I cut her off again. "Agent Bowe, Agent McKee, secure the back entrance of this establishment. Agent Cocker, Agent Rzepzynski, check the bathrooms, then return and guard this entrance. Agent Devlin, with me. We're going in the kitchen through the front door." We were all moving within five seconds, but before we could carry out any of the tasks, the kitchen door opened and a stunning young womyn with blond hair and very blue eyes came through the door and said, "I'm Kristy O'Dowd, Agent Glickstien." She looked straight at me, and I saw the recognition in her eyes.

"You're…you're *her*! You're the Freak from Battle Creek," she said.

"I am, Miss O'Dowd, although that has no bearing on why I'm here. We have a case that touches peripherally on a case you were involved with, and we have some questions for you. Can we step around the bar to the front of the room and talk?"

The blond hostess, who turned out to be one of the owners of the café, said, "Of course. I'll take your table for now, Kristy." I nodded at her, and we went around the bar. I had Kristy sit on one side of the table, while Mac and I sat on the other. Joe and House went and stood behind Kristy's chair, while Gunny and Ed stood behind Mac and me. Their eyes were like laser beams trying to bore into her brain, never leaving her face. It was the perfect intimidation setup, and Mac and I were about to make it better.

Mac smiled at Kristy and said, "Miss O'Dowd, you are not under arrest, nor do we consider you a suspect in any crime. If you would like to have a lawyer present, you can certainly do so, but I assure you it won't be necessary." Her tone was gentle, and she was looking at Kristy as if she were her favorite niece.

She smiled back at Mac and said, "I… I don't think that I need a lawyer, but I don't know how I can help the Secret Service. I like the president."

You'd be surprised how many people tell us that; most people think that we all guard the president and that everything that the Service does has to do with that. Our smiles weren't evident, but they were all there on the inside. Mac said, "I'm sure that you do, Miss O'Dowd, and we appreciate that, but we just have two or three questions."

She smiled again and said, "Well, I can answer two or thr—"

I went over the table until my face was right in front of hers and said, "What the fuck happened the night that Tim Miller was murdered, you twit?"

Kristy O'Dowd was so surprised by my demeanor, invasion of her space, and malevolent tone that she didn't even think; she just blurted out, "I was fucking his brother Tom! Tim and I broke up that morning, and I was pissed, so I tried to get back at him by fucking his brother! I never saw Tim!"

We all believed her; there was no way she came up with that story in the millisecond she had before her brain engaged after my snap question. Add to that the fact that she couldn't have known what the question was and there was no doubt: Kristy O'Dowd was telling the truth, which meant that Tim Miller hadn't had sex with her.

So who did he have sex with? And could it still be that the Bishop had something to do with it?

"Kristy, where did you and Tom have sex?" I asked.

"My house," she said. "My parents were at the graduation party. It was easy to slip home, have sex, and then sneak back."

"Did anybody see you?" Mac said.

"No. We went down the hedgerow and then in through my window off the patio. I'd left it open so we could," she said.

"Did you tell anybody about it afterward?" I said, even though I already knew the answer.

"No," she said, quietly crying. "I… I… I couldn't tell anyone, because the next day we found out that Tim had been murdered! I… I'm still guilty about it. If I hadn't done that, maybe Tim would still be alive."

I didn't see the logic in that statement, but it did lead me to my next question. "So why did you and Tim break up, Kristy?" I said.

"He was afraid that I would get pregnant. We were having sex a couple times a week, and we were both Catholic, so we weren't using any birth control. And he said he just couldn't do it anymore. I wanted to stay together and just not have sex, but Tim said he couldn't keep his hands off me, and he knew I liked having sex with him, so we decided to just take some time off and consider the problem. That's what Tim said, 'Let's take some time off and consider the problem,'" she said.

"And you went along with it?" Gunny asked.

"Yes," she said. "I loved him, but I was scared too."

"How was the sex with Tim?" Ed said, her voice as soft as a silk scarf.

Kristy's face turned red, but she said, "It was dreamy. He was a very considerate lover—gentle, kind, and always concerned about my satisfaction. He… Tim was the best lover I've ever had, even better than his brother, who was pretty good too."

"Do you know where your uncle was the night Tim was murdered?" I asked.

She looked confused at the sudden change in the direction of the question. "My uncle Pat? He was at the party. He was shooting baskets with some guys, then he was playing cards with Mr. Koszlowski and his friends. I don't…he was at the party when Tom and I got back," she said.

"You're sure he was at the party when you got back?" Gunny asked, his voice also soft and gentle.

"Yes. I saw him shake Tom's hand in the kitchen. Uncle Pat was getting beers for the guys, and Tom was getting a Pepsi. I remember because Uncle Pat had all four beers in one hand—he has ginormous hands—and Tom had just started drinking a little pop after wrestling was over. They were laughing about something, and Uncle Pat said, "You're one of the ones I trust, Thomas, because you were baptized by a saint." And they laughed again, because Uncle Pat had baptized Tim and Tom when he was just a parish priest," Kristy said.

"When did your uncle leave the party, Kristy?" I inquired.

"He took me and my mom home. My dad wanted to stay and play some more cards, so we all went home in his Cadillac, even though it was just three blocks. 'Can't be too careful with my girls,' he said."

"Do you know where he went after he dropped you off?" Gunny said.

"No, I don't th—wait a minute. He did say that he was going to see a sick parishioner, someone who lived out of town, south off M-66," she said.

"Did he mention any names? Anything at all about the parishioner?" I said.

"No names. All he said was the person had just finished chemotherapy and had to stay home for a while so they didn't get sick," Kristy said.

"What time did he drop you off at home?" Gunny said.

"Exactly midnight. He made a joke about turning into a pumpkin when the clock struck 12," Kristy said. "It was one of his regular jokes." I nodded. I'd heard the bishop make that very joke with my own ears. I also nodded because it meant that the bishop wasn't off the hook; the ME had put Tim Miller's death between midnight and 2:00 a.m., which meant the "sick parishioner" might have been a cover story so the bishop could strangle the young man who had defiled his niece.

I could see that Mac was on the same page, so we asked Kristy a few more questions, then tried to fold up our tent.

"Thank you, Kristy, and sorry about scaring you earlier," I said. "We only have one day in Battle Creek to investigate this, so there isn't much time for subtlety."

"Oh, that's OK. I'm just glad that somebody is looking at it. The sheriff did all the work last time, and no one even asked me any questions," she said.

"What?" we all said at once. "You all owe each other a Pepsi," Kristy said.

"Miss O'Dowd, Kristy, did you mean that no law enforcement officer asked you any questions at all about your relationship with Tim Miller?" Joe said.

"Well, yeah," she said. "The sheriff asked my mom where I was all night, she told him the Miller's party, and he never talked to me. He didn't talk to Tom either. We both thought it was weird at that time."

"Just to clarify, the sheriff never talked to you or the victim's twin brother," Joe said.

"Right. We never heard from them at all," Kristy said.

"And the Battle Creek Police never talked to you either," I said.

"No," she said. "We heard that BCPD wasn't involved in the investigation because it was outside their jurisdiction. Since Tim was found outside the city limits, he was killed in the county, not the city."

"And you don't know of anyone talking to your uncle about it either," House said.

Kristy O'Dowd wasn't just a pretty face; she started to say something when it hit her. It was like the proverbial light bulb going on over her head. Her face flushed red, but she sat up straighter and said, "You think that my uncle Pat killed Tim. Because we were having sex." Her tone was flat, but her eyes flashed with anger.

"We don't think anything yet. We're just doing what we do, asking questions and trying to see if we can find any answers. We don't have any preconceived notions. We're just asking questions," Joe said, but Kristy wasn't buying it.

"Bullshit. All this has been about Uncle Pat, but I can tell you that you've got it wrong," Kristy said.

"Do tell," House said from over her shoulder. She turned in the chair, looked him right in the eye, and said, "Uncle Pat knew the first time that Tim and I had sex, and he knew that I liked having sex with Tim, and he knew that we didn't stop having sex after the first time."

"How?" House said. "The man's a priest. He ain't a mind reader."

Kristy said, "No, he's a *bishop*, and he's also an active priest in Battle Creek." She stopped, challenging House to say something. The giant agent smiled and said, "Got it, Miz O'Dowd. Uncle Pat is a bishop, but he also hears *confessions*, don't he? Including yours, I'll bet."

Kristy nodded and said, "And Tim's. We both confessed it to him."

"And if he's anything like my cousin Mel the Preacher, he tried to counsel you out of it, might even've told you to break with Catholic doctrine and use protection," House said gently.

Her face was enough to tell us that House was right. It didn't let the bishop off the hook completely, but it did damage the sudden rage theory.

House put his hand on Kristy's shoulder and said, "Ain't nothin' wrong with lovin' someone so much you want to make them happy, and there ain't nothin' wrong with enjoyin' it, but ya'll can't carry 'round this burden 'bout Tim's death. Some asshole cooled him, not you, and ya'll couldn't've stopped it nohow. Ya'll need to confess it one last time and then lay it down, little sister, 'cause it'll just eat you up otherwise."

Kristy stood up and hugged him for a while. House patted her head, and she said, "Thank you, Agent Bowe. I will do that." She shook all our hands, and we nodded at her as she went back to work.

"What the fuck was with the down-home accent and diction there, Big Man?" Ed said.

"Sho' 'nuff were a pow'rful lesson," Gunny said.

"Isn't 'little sister' a line from *True Grit*? Isn't that what John Wayne called Kim Darby?" Mac said.

"Ah thought that ya'll wuz gonna break into a hymn there, big brother," Joe said.

"Fuck each and every one of you," House said in his perfect Bostonian accent. "Everything I said was true, but if I said it like this, it would never have the power of down-home country wisdom. Sometimes you have to meet people's preconceived notions about you in order to get them to open up, or at least get them to listen to what you're saying. It's a tactic that works, and fuck you all again for not appreciating my efforts to help the young lady."

We all were so busy laughing that we didn't understand that we'd just made a huge break in the case. In fact, if we hadn't been so busy amusing ourselves, someone in that group of excellent thinkers would have realized that House's analysis was dead-on and that we weren't looking at the case from the right perspective, but once we all stopped laughing at House, the first thing we thought of was confirming that the bishop hadn't killed Tim Miller.

Joe said, "We've got to run down the bishop's whereabouts after midnight, and we've got to find out how he was acting before and after the murder."

"We'll need hospital records for two weeks before the murder, and we need to interview his card-playing chums," Mac said.

"We also need to eat lunch first, and we are in a restaurant," Gunny said. We agreed that food was needed, so we called the hostess over and asked for menus. Kristy came over and waited on us, and we had an outstanding meal. It turned out the co-owner's daughter was a first-class chef and the Canal Street Café was a first-class place to chow down.

We finished our meal with desserts. The place had some retired guy working for them, and the lemon cheesecake was superb. The hostess tried to give us the meals for free, but we pointed out that it was probably illegal, and besides, we were on expense account (the owner was paying for our meal either way; the least we could do was generate some cash flow).

Before we hit the road, I took Kristy aside and said, "Why are you still here, working in a restaurant? You could go anywhere and do anything. You're beautiful and smart. So why the Canal Street Café? It's a great place, and I'm sure that teaching is great, but why Battle Creek?"

She looked at me and said, "My first child was born just about nine months after Tim's murder. His full name is Timothy Miller O'Dowd, and he needs to be near his grandparents. Especially his Grandma Miller. She'd go really crazy if I tried to take him away, and I can't have that on my conscience too." There were tears in Kristy's eyes as she spoke, and I finally got the full depth of her guilt.

"Ahhhh, shit," I said. "Tom's?"

She shook her head and said, "No, Tim's. That's why I slept with Tom, so I'd have a fallback position if I couldn't get Tim back. I figured that the DNA would match—identical twins, right? And back then I was a scared kid trying to sort out her future. I also hadn't told Tim, and once he broke up with me, I just couldn't tell him. Even as fucked up as I was, I realized that would just be trapping him, and that was no good, so I slept with his brother before I knew about his condition, thinking it would be an out for me. Luckily, I told Tom the truth, and he told me about his condition, and then I went to college, met my boyfriend Jerry, and had another kid. And BC remained my home. I've been lucky."

"What condition?" I asked.

"Oh, Tom's sterile," Kristy said. "He had the mumps when he was a kid. The MMR vaccine didn't work on him for some reason. Weird, huh? It worked perfectly on his twin brother but left Tom sterile. He's a great uncle, by the way. He loves Timmy like a son and would do anything for us. Every time he's home on leave, he comes over with something for Timmy, or me, or Jerry—he loves Jerry too—and of course, he writes us letters from all over the world."

I looked at her and asked, "What's Tom do now?"

"Oh, you didn't know? He's still in the service. Tom's a Navy SEAL now," Kristy said.

"Really? I'd heard he was in the Navy, but a SEAL? Didn't know that," I said.

"Yeah. He's probably going to retire soon," Kristy said. "He told Timmy last time that one more tour ought to do it. I think he's tired of the constant deployments and he wants to come home to be with his mom, and us, too. He told me that we're just taking vengeance on people who have nothing to do with our security now, not really defending the country."

If only I had been paying attention, or if Gunny hadn't said, "Bus is leaving, Freak, let's hit it," or if I'd been able to spend five more minutes with Kristy, the shitstorm that became the case of the century would never have happened. But if wishes were fishes, we'd all cast nets. (There's some country wisdom for ya. The Great Pumpkin Used to say that, and I'm still not sure what it means.)

Sometimes I'm too stupid for words. This was one of those times.

Fuck!

We went back to BC by two cars. Joe rode with Gunny and me. We were headed for the Calhoun County Sheriff's Office, while the other three went to Leila Post Memorial Hospital to take a look at their records for the two weeks before Tim Miller's murder.

Gunny was driving and Joe was in the back seat as we turned onto M-96 and headed for the sheriff's office on East Michigan Avenue. I didn't know the current sheriff, a guy named Frank Giltner, and since Michigan County sheriffs are elected, he might not even have been sheriff at the time of the murder. But I was betting that my mom and *zayde* knew all about that. As I raised the phone to call them, Joe said, "You know why the sheriff's office handled the investigation, right?"

"Cover-up," Gunny and I said.

"I'll buy those Pepsis," Joe said. "It had to be a cover-up. I'll bet the B.C. chief of police was and is tight with the bishop. Also, the city police would have had to talk to both Kristy and Tom Miller, and that would've led to a whole can of worms nobody wanted to open up."

"Brent Dolbee has been the police chief in B.C. since before time. He and the bishop are really tight, and Dolbee is a professional policeman, so he would have put all this together in about 10 seconds. Once he or his guys questioned Kristy, it would have been open season on the bishop, because back then there were crime reporters for both the B.C. and Kazoo papers, and the TV stations would have had a field day. The sheriff's office would've had a far lower profile and wouldn't have stirred up as much fuss, even if they found anything out," I said.

"So we need to see the current sheriff and find out what the fuck went on back then, but we need to do it so that nobody figures out what the fuck is going on," Gunny said. "Sounds like a job for you, Joe."

Joe nodded and said, "You guys are the strong, silent types this time, unless there's some insider shit I don't know about, Freak, then step in and keep me from making an ass of myself, OK?"

"Can I let it go on just for a tick or two? It would really entertain the troops," I said as Gunny laughed like a hyena. We all laughed, and Joe said, "I know. It's always funny to see a self-assured asshole like me get his comeuppance, but if we're going to get this mitzvah done today…"

"We need to cut the shit and just get it done," I said, letting some faux sadness creep into my voice.

"Roger that," Joe said.

But it turned out that we didn't need a stealth approach, because when we got to the sheriff's office, there was a big old classic black Cadillac Eldorado parked in the first visitor's space. There was a priest leaning over the front fender with a polishing rag, but when we pulled in, he looked up, saw me in the passenger seat, and strolled around the car. He opened my door, and when I got out, he said, "Oh, you heathen Jew, you are in soooo much trouble with His Grace. You're gonna get it now!"

Gunny was moving to intercept him, and Joe had his hand on his weapon before I could stop them. I put up a hand to each of them and said, "Stop! This is Father Edward G. Robinson. He and I have known each other all our lives. He's kidding, because even though the bishop isn't going to be very pleased, he'll at least be polite, unlike this mannerless street urchin."

"Ya heathen Jew, please notice that I'm wearing the collar and soutane of a Catholic priest now. The street urchin in me is long gone," Father Ed said.

"Or superbly repressed in that Jesuit computer you call a mind," I said.

"Fair point," Father Ed conceded. "I have indeed become a master of repressing my baser instincts, all praise be to God."

"Otherwise, you'd be in Jackson State Prison, or dead," I said.

"Truer words have never been spoken, Lady Freak," he said, finally opening his arms and hugging me. Eddie and I had been on the wrestling and track teams together before he went off to Georgetown and got an education and religion; no one in Battle Creek could believe that a wild-assed hoodlum and street urchin like Eddie Robinson had graduated from Georgetown, or become a Catholic priest, but he did. Eddie's parents were crack users who basically abandoned him when he was ten. He lived in various places, including Hacienda Glickstien for a while, but until Georgetown, Fast Eddie didn't like to stay in any one place for too long; anyone who watched him run track or cross-country or wrestle could see that right away. In wrestling he was unstoppable; he just kept attacking his opponents from everywhere on the mat. We used to say that once Fast Eddie had a foot out the door of the locker room, he was a threat to shoot a double-leg takedown. And we weren't far off. In the state finals his senior year, Fast Eddie took down a previously undefeated wrestler five times *in the first period* and went on to pin the guy in the second period.

He was just like that at Georgetown, where he was salutatorian of his undergrad class, then finished first in his class at Georgetown Law. He also got a PhD in economics from American University, which he used to help make the Battle Creek diocese one of the most efficiently run and best-funded Catholic institutions in the state. Rumor had it that several cardinals had approached Fast Eddie about Vatican appointments, but he'd always refused.

Bottom line, Father Edward G. Robinson was one sharp motherfucker, and in this case our friendship would mean exactly zero. He was here to let me—us—know that the bishop was not going to be fucked around with, or in any way legally discomfited, without being well represented. His presence was a gauntlet thrown down by Bishop Padraig O'Dowd, but I wasn't afraid of Fast Eddie, and I was pretty sure that Joe and the rest of the gang wouldn't be either.

"Father Edward G. Robinson? What the fuck—excuse me, Father—kind of name is that? Whatarya, a damned gangster priest from a 1950s movie?" Gunny said.

"Yeah, I'm not buying that moniker either, Father. I'll need a copy of your birth certificate and sworn witnesses before I'll believe you aren't a Jamaal Jameson, or Ray Stark, or a Latavious Percivalnanian," Joe said.

"C'mon, Father, show us your tommy gun," Gunny said.

"As long as you have a class IV or V license for it," Joe said.

"Otherwise, we'll arrest your ass—excuse me, Father—just like any other dirtbag," Gunny said.

"Fuck you, hard cases," Fast Eddie said. "Where'd ya get these dipshits, Lady Freak? Central casting? You sent out a call for a big, dumb Polack and a pugnacious Mick and this is all they had left?"

The tension broke and we all laughed until we snorted, when Joe said, "Excuse me, Father? C'mon, Polack? You can do better than that."

"Forgive me, Father, for I have sinned. It has been 21 years since my last confession," Gunny said.

"I believe that, Agent Rzepzynski. You must be Agent Cocker," Fast Eddie said to Joe. He shook both their hands and said, "None of the O'Dowds are dummies, and Kristy's as smart as me. She also has an eidetic memory. And she's not shy about calling her uncle Pat, especially when a bunch of tough motherfuckers scare the shit out of her."

"We didn't have a choice, Fast Eddie. We're outta here tomorrow, so we had to work fast. Kristy was the only option we had," I said.

"His Grace and I kinda figured that was it, which was why we came straight here from the airport. We just got back from D.C. when Kristy called, and His Grace wanted to talk to you straight away, even though he's old, tired, and not involved with any shenanigans whatsoever," Fast Eddie said, his look and tone telling me not to fuck around.

"Father, not that we don't trust a man of God, but we'll need to determine that for ourselves," Joe said.

"Of course," Fast Eddie said, "but don't fuck His Grace around, or try any tricks, or step over the very thin line that you're walking on, because if you do, I'm going to fuck you so far up that you'll wish for death."

"Understood," we all said at once.

AJ HARTMAN

"We'll buy each other a Pepsi," Fast Eddie said. "Let's go see His Grace."

We went in, and the deputy at reception sent us right back to the sheriff's office.

When we came in, the sheriff stood up and said, "I'm Frank Giltner. This is my undersheriff, Marv McMillan, and this is—"

"Bishop Padraig Liam O'Dowd. And I already know the lady," the bishop said in his best giving-the-homily voice. I'd forgotten how big he was—at least 6'6", 300—with very little jiggling as he stood in front of us. His hair was a bit more gray, and he had some more wrinkles, but it was hard to tell that the bishop was over 70 years old. He held out his gigantic hand, and I shook it. Gunny and Joe both said, "Your Grace," and kissed his big ring with the amethyst, observing Catholic doctrine even while on the job (by the way, in case you're wondering, Jews don't kiss rings, or anything else for that matter; we're kinda stiff-necked in that respect).

We all sat down around the sheriff's conference table, and the bishop said, "Agent Glickstien, I want to say categorically that I did not have anything to do with the death of Timothy Miller. I'm not required to even respond to any questions about this." He paused and looked at Fast Eddie, who nodded. "But I would just like to clear the air before you ask the questions I'm sure you have."

I looked him right in the eye with my special ops look and said, "Thank you, Bishop O'Dowd. Why did you get the sheriff to investigate the death instead of the Battle Creek Police Department?"

"Who says he did?" Fast Eddie said.

The bishop held up his hand and said, "Father Robinson, let's stipulate that Agent Glickstien is as smart as we think we are and dispense with the fencing, shall we? I don't see this conversation being recorded—these agents don't even have notebooks out—so let's just proceed down the path Agent Glickstien lays out for us."

Fast Eddie nodded, but he didn't look chastened and his attention never wavered.

"I did it because Chief Dolbee and I are known associates and have a close personal relationship. He is also a very fine professional police officer who would have had to ask too many inconvenient questions, many of which would have been about my 17-year-old niece's sex life, which I was loath to have in the newspapers and on television, so I asked him to determine that the crime was committed in the county's jurisdiction, which it technically was, so that the sheriff would do the investigating."

"Exactly why was the sheriff so preferable to Chief Dolbee?" Joe said. His tone said, "OK, Bishop, I kissed your ring, now let's get down to business."

"Because the previous sheriff—Todd Phillips, his name was—was a complete idiot who couldn't find his ass with both hands and directions," the bishop said. "By the time it became clear that he and his department couldn't handle the investigation and brought in the state police, it was too late: the evidence was old, the trail was cold, and certain areas of inquiry had been sanitized."

"What do you mean 'sanitized'?" Gunny said.

"My niece was pregnant. She made it known that the baby was Tim's, and Mrs. Miller declined to push the state police to look further into her son's murder. In fact, she bought the theory that Tim had fallen down in the car and hit his head and that he had strangled himself over the seat back," the bishop said.

Gunny and I'd seen that alternate theory in the case file, but the ME's findings pretty much rendered it a moot point. There had been hands on his neck, and those hands choked the life out of him. Although the ME had gone out on a limb and said that the head shot might have rendered him unconscious, no serious investigator would have believed the theory, but if the mother of the victim pushed it, well, it apparently flew well enough for the former sheriff to sell, and the state police hadn't picked up anything else.

But Mrs. Miller went quietly crazy about a week after the investigation was officially closed, which made all of us think that not only did she not believe her own theory but also that she knew it wasn't true. The problem was, Mrs. Miller wouldn't—couldn't?—talk to anyone about Tim's murder without going even crazier, which meant that there was really no place to go with any further investigation, unless Mrs. Miller, a devout Catholic, knew that the bishop had done it and that was what drove her crazy.

So I asked the obvious question (hey, I was the only non-Catholic in the room, and Joe and Gunny were thinking the same thing, but openly accusing a bishop of the Church isn't something you could just take back—thank God for Jews). "Isn't that rather convenient for you, Bishop? It doesn't take a genius to figure out that Tim Miller was fucking your niece and you were an obvious suspect. Doesn't the fact that you just admitted that you manipulated the investigation further implicate you in the crime?" I had deliberately come right over the top and used *fucking* instead of something gentler because I wanted to shock the man and gauge his reaction.

Everybody else stiffened up a bit at the tone and language, but I give Bishop O'Dowd full credit. He looked right into my green eyes with his green eyes and said, "Thank God for Jews, especially Jews who are the product of lawyers and the U.S. Marine Corps. You get right down to the nitty-gritty right away, don't you?" His tone was soft and gentle, his mannerisms one of a man who was in complete control of the situation.

Wrong move.

Before anyone could stop me, I exploded out of my chair and grabbed the front of his soutane and jerked him out of his chair so that his head was six inches from mine. "Cut the shit, you fat-assed, mackerel-snapping clown! Did you strangle Tim Miller in the back of a goddamned Catholic courtesy car?" Everyone was so shocked nobody moved, so I lifted the bishop off the floor and shook him until his teeth rattled. "C'mon, you oleaginous piece of wafer-huffing, wine-guzzling papist shit! Did you murder Tim Miller?"

Gunny and Joe were grabbing me and Fast Eddie was yelling and the sheriff and undersheriff were moving on me when the bishop said, "No! I did not kill Tim Miller! I loved him like a son!"

I was the only one looking at his face, but it was enough for me. The bishop was hiding something, the look on his face a mixture of anger, frustration, and deep sorrow, but it wasn't murder. I gently set him back in his chair and said, "You guys get your hands off me or somebody's gonna go to emergency."

Something in my tone made everybody realize that I wasn't fucking around, and they all backed off. I looked at the bishop and said, "Please forgive me, sir, but Tim was my friend, his mom was always good to me, and I was tired of your little game. What are you hiding, sir?"

The sheriff spoke before the bishop. "I was a lowly patrol deputy when Tim Miller was murdered, and so was Marv, and we both knew right away that we had to get the investigation in our shop. Marv and I are cousins—our moms are sisters—and we had already talked about it when it came up. Marv's married to Todd Phillips's sister Meg, so he pushed his sister, she pushed her brother, and…well, we got what we wanted."

"Why in the hell would you do that?" Joe said. "That makes you an accessory after the fact if the bishop did it. It's also obstruction of justice."

"We did it for our family," the undersheriff said.

"Yeah," the sheriff said, "we were trying to protect our family."

"I know for a fact that the bishop isn't your family—he's got a brother and a sister, and neither of you are related to them," I said.

"That's true," the sheriff said.

"Well, what the fuck—excuse me, Your Grace—were you doin', then?" Gunny said.

And then it hit me: I think I just knew what the hell was going on, like a sudden flash of juice from an Ouija board just injected itself into my brain.

"You're both Cullens. Your moms are two of the four Cullen sisters," I said.

The sheriff and undersheriff both nodded, and Joe said, "Who the fuck are the Cullen sisters? And why the fuck—excuse me, Your Grace—do we care?"

So I told him about the Cullen sisters, four valedictorians from Battle Creek Central High School who were in fact a singing group at one time, that all went to the University of Michigan on scholarship and changed their worlds. One became a doctor who helped pioneer heart stents, one became the president of U of M and changed the way the university did business with the world, one became a research scientist who went to work for the Upjohn Company (which was later bought by Pfizer) and helped develop Viagra (she had eight kids, which apparently meant that her husband was part of the clinical trials), and the fourth, Colleen Cullen Flaherty, became world-famous as the Secretary of the Treasury, and later the U.S. ambassador to Ireland.

When her U.S. senator husband died, Colleen Cullen Flaherty had just finished five very successful years as the Secretary of the Treasury. She left government service to mourn but was appointed U.S. ambassador to Ireland by the next president. She turned out to be one hell of a diplomat and held the post for seven years, after which she negotiated a truce between North and South Sudan that earned her the Nobel Peace Prize. She surprised the world after the ceremony for the Peace Prize when she thanked everyone for all the opportunities she'd enjoyed and retired to her ancestral home… Battle Creek, Michigan.

Colleen Cullen Flaherty became the grand dame of charitable causes and the talk shows, but she continued to live in a modest house out off M-66 South, and she'd died of cancer about ten years after Tim Miller's murder, after successfully beating the first round of cancer the same year as the murder. I remembered the local news stories about her battle with cancer and how the bishop and the rest of the parish had been praying for her. It was a big deal because she was probably the most famous person from Battle Creek after the Kellogg brothers and Tony the Tiger ("They're greeaaate!").

And I knew why she was important to our story.

I looked at the bishop and said, "Sir, are you sure you want everyone here to hear what I'm about to say?"

Bishop O'Dowd said, "The Cullen boys already know, and Fast Eddie is my confessor, so he already knows. I would appreciate it if you and your companions would promise to keep this between us, if you would. Not for me." It seemed he was mistaking the look on my face for anger. "But for the memory and legacy of a truly great lady."

"I can speak for my colleagues in this instance. They don't call us the Secret Service for nothing, sir," I said. "We just want to get to the truth about Tim Miller's murder and alleviate Mrs. Miller's suffering." Both Gunny and Joe got up and went over to kiss the bishop's ring again. He looked touched at the gesture and put his hands on their heads in a genuine act of benediction. He looked up at me and said, "In that case, ask your question, Agent Glickstien."

"Sir, where were you from midnight to 4:00 a.m. on the night Tim Miller was murdered?" I said, my voice formal and as stiff as the Pope's collar.

"I was in the bed of Colleen Cullen Flaherty, the former ambassador to Ireland," the bishop said, his voice filled with the gravity of the admission. The silence in the room rivaled that of Tut's tomb before Howard Carter ripped it open in 1922, but unlike the Boy Pharaoh's gold, this secret was going to remain buried.

"We got there the next morning at six to tell our aunt, and His Grace was still there. They didn't try to hide the fact that they were lovers from the family. My mom'd already told me," the sheriff said. "That was why we had to get the sheriff to take over the investigation, to protect our aunt and His Grace."

"We knew that Phillips would fuck it up—sorry, Your Grace—because we knew that he'd never ask any real questions," the undersheriff said.

"Todd Phillips is still as dumb as a post," Fast Eddie said. "He was the perfect stooge."

"And I also knew that Sheriff Phillips would fuck it up. The man once asked me if Catholics kept kosher like the Jews, and he later asked me if Catholics believed in Jesus," the bishop said.

"Well, that ignorant motherfucker," Gunny said.

We all laughed, and I said, "Was his dad Mr. Phillips the science teacher at Harper Creek?"

"Yeah," Fast Eddie said.

"Ohmigod! You mean that Calhoun County elected Booger Phillips sheriff?" I asked. There was more general laughter, and Joe said, "We don't need to hear that story, Freak."

"Nobody does—it is truly gross!" the bishop said, his tone so mournful that we all laughed again. After the laughter subsided, I said, "Sir, I want your blessing to tell Mrs. Miller a white lie in order to give her some hope and closure."

"I'm a man of the cloth, Agent Glickstien. I can't condone lying," the bishop said with a straight face. We all laughed again, and he said, "What's the white lie?"

I told him what I planned to tell Mrs. Miller, and everybody nodded their approval. The bishop stood up, raised his right hand, made the sign of the cross, and said, "In nomine Patris, et Filii et Spiritus Sancti, te absolve."

"Thank you, sir," I said. "Sorry about the explosion earlier, but I'm not a big fan of unctuousness. It's probably a result of being Jewish."

"'Tis true, we mackerel-snappers are often unctuous assholes," the bishop said in a very Irish accent.

"His Grace means that we're obtuse motherfuckers," Fast Eddie said.

"A far better way to put it, Father Robinson," the bishop said. We were all laughing and snorting until the bishop said, "I'd like to explain myself a bit, if I might, Agent Glickstien, about the ambassador and why her memory needs to be respected."

I wanted to tell him that wasn't necessary, but I was curious, so I just nodded, and he said, "It was because of Gaelic that we met, and because of French that we became involved, and because of Russian that we realized what we felt was true love, not just an infatuation."

"Sir?" I said, completely mystified of what he was talking about. Everyone else also looked confused, so at least I wasn't doing a Lone-Ranger-on-meth routine.

"The ambassador and I met at a luncheon for visiting dignitaries from the Old Sod, a trade delegation that came to see Kellogg's in action and perhaps secure some jobs back in Ireland," the bishop said. "Several local dignitaries were invited to make them feel comfortable, and the ambassador and I both spoke very fluent Gaelic, so we addressed the head trade commissioner in the old tongue and sparked quite a conversation. One thing led to another, and Mr. O'Rourke basically agreed to the terms Kellogg wanted right there at the meet and greet. He told the Kellogg CEO that the ambassador and I being able to speak Gaelic made the delegation feel like they were negotiating with another Irish company, so we got invited to the dinner celebrating the trade deal and were seated together.

"During the meal, the ambassador turned to me and said, 'Well done, my friend. We appear to have been the team that decided the issue.' I said, 'Il n'a pas de quoi,' French for 'It was nothing,' a common way to de-emphasize one's role and maintain the illusion of modesty. She smiled at me with a twinkle in those brown eyes and said, 'Faux, mon bon évêque.'—'Untrue, my good bishop'—in perfect Parisian French. So we began a conversation in French that led to me complimenting her dress, hair, and shoes and her explaining how she had always liked men who could speak fluently in tongues other than their native one, and we both realized we'd gone a bit too far, because almost everything in French sounds like 'I love you,' so we parted and I determined that I would not be around her again, because I was sorely tested by her charm, erudition, and intelligence, not to mention her physical presence, which was mesmerizing.

"In any case, I resisted, but in this case resistance was futile. And yes, I felt like Jean-Luc Picard dealing with the Borg in that *Star Trek: Next Generation* television show. We kept getting thrown together, and finally I said, 'This situation is intolerable,' in Russian, and she said, 'Da.' And we had a Russian conversation where she said that we were like Romeo and Juliet. I declared that we were like Zhivago and Lara. We realized that we could not deny the power of our biology." The bishop paused, his eyes leaking a few sad tears.

"And it was easy to keep secret, because you and the ambassador were always being invited to all sorts of public events, and it was only natural that you'd collaborate on things like the school and the Catholic literacy effort and…just about everything else in B.C., because you two were the biggest fish in this pond," I said.

"Exactly," the bishop said. "She'd always come to the church, but I rarely celebrated Mass—that was what Fast Eddie here was for. But once we began having our affair, I did more in that respect too. She decided to take a seat on the school governing board. Of course, no one objected, because who could resist having a genuine, famous person on their board, especially one who was so smart? And we needed to meet about that…" His voice trailed off, and Joe said, "So there was no hint of scandal, because you hid in plain sight. You didn't need to sneak around, just carry on with business as usual."

"I see that you've associated yourself with intelligent people, Agent Glickstien. That was exactly what happened. Our physical relationship was glorious, but entirely clandestine. No one suspected an old bishop and old ambassador of having a sexual relationship, much less one that was consummated at two o'clock in the afternoon after a lunch meeting about the Catholic Charities Casino Night," the bishop said.

"The two of you loved each other more than the church," Gunny said. "That's true love, Your Grace."

"Yes, my son, it was. In fact, it is, because as the great William Goldman said in his book *The Princess Bride*, not even death can stop true love. I love her still, more even than I love Christ, and I would gladly confess my sin and cover myself in ignominious condemnation, but I will not do anything to tarnish her legacy or my memories of her," the bishop said.

"And you won't have to, sir. All we wanted was to disqualify you as a suspect in Tim Miller's murder, and I am positive that my colleagues and I are in agreement that we have done so," I said. Gunny and Joe nodded, as did the sheriff, the undersheriff, and Fast Eddie.

We all stood up, and the bishop put out his enormous hand and shook mine. He laughed and said, "By the way, Agent Glickstien, it is good to see that some things never change."

"Sir?" I said.

"You were aware that you picked me off the floor with no visible effort, right?" he said.

"Oh, that," I said. "It's true, Bishop Pat, I've still got the chops, just like you taught me at the powerlifting club."

He smiled and said, "Tell your family hello for me, and tell that old curmudgeon that he better make the pinochle game on Wednesday. I've got to take some of his Jewish lawyer war chest to pay for more communion wine."

"I will do that, Bishop Pat. Take care of Fast Eddie, and thank you for your honesty," I said.

He nodded and said, "It was the least I could do, considering what you're doing. As for Father Robinson…well, I think it will eventually be the other way around." He let everybody have a smooch of the ring and left the room. Fast Eddie shook our hands, gave me a hug, and said, "Find out who did it, Lady Freak, and I'll help you kick their ass into the deepest, darkest prison we can find."

"Roger that," I said. "You take care of him, Fast Eddie."

"Depend on it," Father Edward G. Robinson said. He nodded to everyone else and left.

The sheriff said, "I'll let you know if we find anything else. Marv and I are going to do a cold-case investigation on this and two other unsolved murders. If you find anything out or need my help, let me know, OK?" We exchanged cards, and then we went outside to stand by the car.

Before anybody could say anything, Joe's phone rang. He answered and said, "Yeah, Mac. Un-huh. Four names? OK, let's meet back at Freak's house and we'll talk. No, definitely not on an open line. Roger that." He hung up, we got in the rental car, and we took off.

I'd driven about a block when Joe said, "Mackerel-snapping clown? Oleaginous piece of wafer-huffing, wine-guzzling papist shit? Are these normal terms of endearment for a sitting Catholic bishop?" We all laughed, and Gunny said, "And you picking the bishop up by his lapels—did you guys practice that or what?"

"Nah, I really picked him up," I said.

Both agents got quiet, and then Gunny said, "Just how strong are you, Freak?"

"Got a quarter?" I said. Joe handed me one from the back seat, and I held it in my right hand between my thumb and forefinger. I looked at Gunny and pinched my fingers together, bending the quarter into a perfect half-moon. Both guys gawped at me, their eyes wide and their mouths open. I tossed Joe back his quarter and drove on. The car was very quiet until we were turning into my parents' driveway.

"So the nickname means 'freak of nature,' not 'freaky,'" Joe said.

"As in 'freakishly strong,'" Gunny said.

"And fast too," I said.

Joe asked, "How fas—"

I reached across and snatched Gunny's creds out of his jacket pocket while taking Joe's glasses off his face before either of them could move.

"Pretty fuckin' fast," I said as I handed their stuff back.

"I would guess that someday that might come in handy on this job," Gunny said.

"Probably already has, since you came from special ops," Joe said.

"Classified," I said, deadpanning it so they would laugh, which we all did.

We got out of the car, and Gunny said, "I hope to see you use those gifts on a perp someday. It would make my old heart swell up with Marine pride."

We all laughed again, mainly because we didn't know that my fellow agents would get to see me in action.

It's all fun and games until somebody gets dead.

CHAPTER 24

St. Freak and the Mitzvahs

We went into Casa Glickstien and found Mac, Ed, and House already there. Mac said, "We've got the name of three potential wits for the bishop, but we think we know which one it was." She smiled at us to let us know that she was smarter than we were, which was probably true (except for Joe—that was one smart motherfucker) in most cases, but not this one.

We all smiled back, and Joe said, "Do tell," so Mac said, "We think that it was Colleen Cullen Flaherty, former SecTreas and U.S. ambassador to Ireland. She and the bishop were on a lot of boards and committees together, and one of the nurses remembered him coming to visit her when she was having a chemo treatment."

"Wow, good work, you guys," I said, not being condescending but impressed with their logic.

"So what did the wit say? Did you confirm it with her?" Joe said, trying for maximum "Gotcha!" effect.

"We couldn't. The ambassador died a while back," Mac said. "But we're contacting her family to see if they might be of any help," Ed said.

"What a great idea," Joe said.

"An excellent idea," Gunny said. "Why didn't we think of that?"

The other three got the picture, and House said, "Why'n't you assholes just tell us, instead of dickin' us around like we're Feebs?" *Feebs* was the Secret Service nickname for the FBI, sometimes also known as Feeble Buttfucking Idiots—there was, and is, such a thing as interservice rivalry, which wasn't, and isn't, such a good idea operationally but which still exists because people are people and bureaucracies live for funding, which makes them competitive, which leads to… Feebs, etc.

So we told the story of the bishop's confession to our suitably impressed colleagues, and Joe said, "All you guys did was give us confirmation of what we found out—the bishop didn't do it."

"Well, fuckin'-A, he didn't do it," House said, "but that still leaves us with the 64-million-dollar question."

"Yeah, like who the fuck did kill Tim Miller?" Ed said.

"We don't know, and we can't find out in this time frame, but Freak has an idea about how to help Mrs. Miller get closure, maybe alleviate some of her guilt," Joe said. So I told them about my idea, the bishop's granting of absolution for any lies that might be told, and our tactics in carrying out this mitzvah. Everybody agreed that it was a good plan and that they'd help with the mitzvah. In fact, the team surprised me.

"I'm going to look into this further on my own time," Ed said. "I feel like there is some little thing that could help us figure it out if we just had the time."

"It does sort of just stick there in your frontal lobe, doesn't it?" House said. "I actually fell asleep last night dreaming about the mechanics of actually strangling someone without them resisting."

Mac said, "I've decided to look at the possibility that he was messing around with someone more sophisticated who asked him to play a game, and that it went too far."

The other guys all chimed in, and we discussed it until my mom and *zayde* got home. They had been in the Kalamazoo County courthouse on a case all day, so we got a treat—they brought home pizza from this place called Erbelli's that my dad found one day when he was consulting on some CPA stuff with a colleague in the 'Zoo. Dad brought home a bunch of beer—Pabst Blue Ribbon, pizza eatin' beer, as he called it—and we ate a ton of great pizza. The Disco Q (Cajun crust with smoked grilled chicken and blue cheese sauce), Meat Monster Mania (heart attack on a crust, but damned yummy), and Smooth Ace (homemade Alfredo sauce, marinated chicken breast, pepperoni, fresh-sliced mushrooms, spicy capicola, applewood smoked bacon, feta cheese crumbles, ranch, and hot sauce drizzled on top) pies were all devoured forthwith. We had to stop Gunny from eating the cardboard that the Smooth Ace was on—he was convinced that some of the sauce had soaked in and that it shouldn't go to waste.

After all the pizza was gone and we all brushed our teeth and gargled away the PBR smell, my mom called Mrs. Miller and asked if I could come over with my "team." Mrs. Miller said yes, so we all got tarted up and walked over to her house.

I knocked, and Mrs. Miller opened the door right away. I hadn't seen her in four or five years, and I was shocked. She looked like the portrait of Dorian Gray, only older. Her hair was thinning out so that she was nearly bald, her eyes were what people used to call rheumy—bloodshot, crusty, and almost like they had a semitransparent cover over them—and the hand she put out for me to shake had no more substance than a few pipe cleaners held together with thread. Altogether, she looked as if she had been aboard the *Titanic*, sunk with it, and then starved for two hundred years.

And she was younger than my mom by two years.

I introduced "my" team (we all agreed it would sell better if I was in charge, since Mrs. Miller knew me), we all showed her our creds and shook her fragile bird-hand, and then we all sat down. She looked at me and said, "I… I still miss him, every day. He was the one who was going to stay, while Tom went off and saw the world. They were twins, but very different in that respect. Tim loved Battle Creek and Kalamazoo and Marshall—the farthest he liked to go was Lansing, or Grand Rapids, sometimes up to Traverse City or Petosky. He loved the small-time, as he called it, while Tom loved the bright lights and big city. They always used to kid each other about it." She looked at us with eyes bright with pain, even after all these years, and it was so real, so visceral, that every one of us had to stifle a reaction.

It got worse.

Mrs. Miller put her hands to her face and shrieked, "I'm all alone now! I'm all alone! Tom is somewhere I don't know where, and Tim is dead! HE'S DEAD! HE WAS MURDERED! AND NO ONE CARES! AND I CAN'T EVEN GO TO CHURCH AND ASK GOD ABOUT IT! I'M ALL ALONE!" Mrs. Miller just sobbed her eyes out, and so did we, the toughest men and wymyn the Secret Service had to offer.

When she finally wound down, House went over to her, got down on one knee, and gently touched her hair. She tilted her grief-ruined face to look up at him, her eyes set in a 1000-yard stare. The giant man said, "Ma'am, I care. So does the rest of our team. We can't know what you are going through, and we didn't know Tim, except for Glinka, but we care. I believe that Dr. King was right, ma'am, that injustice anywhere is a threat to justice everywhere, and this injustice offends my sense of honor. I pledge you my solemn word that I will not rest until we find out who killed your son. I'll have to do my job for the Secret Service and catch counterfeiters and such, but I am making this my part-time, after-hours job. I promise you on the heads of my twin sons, someone is going to pay for the murder of Timothy Miller, so help me God."

Mrs. Miller touched House's cheek with her withered, fragile hand and said, "Why, thank you, Agent Bowe. That's all I ask, that someone try to find out who did this and bring them to justice. Even if he's not caught, just the effort would bring me comfort." House took her hand and held it, and she squeezed his hand and leaned over and kissed him on the cheek.

I said, "Mrs. Miller, we know why you think you can't go to church."

She looked at me, startled and very wary, and she said, "I... I... I...uh, I...can't...uh, I can't even go to confession because uh...uh...uh..." She trailed off, clearly about to have an episode of some sort, and I said, "Ma'am, we have conclusively proven from two different sources that Bishop O'Dowd had nothing to do with Tim's murder. He was in another place that was nowhere near where it happened. He'd been there long before the murder occurred, and he left long after. Bishop O'Dowd is innocent, ma'am."

Tears ran down her face and Mrs. Miller began rocking back and forth. She kept saying, "Thank God, thank God," over and over. House hugged her as she rocked, until finally she said, "You're sure?"

Gunny said, "Ma'am, do you remember Bengt Olafsson, who played football with Tim?" She nodded, and Gunny said, "Ma'am, he worked with us to confirm one source that proved the bishop couldn't have done this. Detective Olafsson is satisfied with the bishop's innocence, and we also have another source."

Ed began explaining how the other team had confirmed the bishop's alibi, and I had an idea. I stepped into Mrs. Miller's hall, whipped out my phone, and bumped Fast Eddie on his cell. He answered on the first ring and said, "Freak, whattya need?"

I said, "Bring the bishop over to Mrs. Miller's right now. Tell him to bring his mumbo-jumbo stuff, for confession."

"Well, I'm not gonna call it that, but we're just leavin' the school, so we'll be right there," Fast Eddie said.

I love working with smart people—he knew what was up and didn't even waste the breath for a question.

"See ya in five," I said.

"Roger that," he said, then hung up.

I went back into the living room, where Mrs. Miller was grilling everyone about the bishop not being guilty. My team was treating her like a queen, answering every question with grace and aplomb, allowing her to regain some of her own dignity.

She looked at me and said, "Freak, does this mean that I'll be able to go back to church now?"

"Better," I said. "It means that you're going to be able to go to church tonight." Mrs. Miller's quizzical look was matched by my team's confusion—this wasn't a part of the plan—and then the doorbell rang. Everyone except Mrs. Miller got it. I said, "May I let them in, ma'am?" She nodded, still a bit mystified, until Bishop Padraig Liam O'Dowd filled the doorway to her living room.

He went right to her, knelt, bowed his head, and said, "I did not come sooner, Marion, because I did not think that my presence would be a comfort to you. I shamefully took the easy path and avoided you, in order to not be faced with your wrath. I comforted myself when the Lord commands me to comfort my flock. I've been a bad priest, and a bad friend. I hope that you can forgive me."

Marion Miller put her hand on his head in a gesture of benediction and said, "Te absolve, Padraig. I, too, need to beg forgiveness, for doubting you and believing evil of you, when in fact you were completely innocent."

"Not completely innocent, but I did not harm Timothy and would have rather that I died in his stead," the bishop said, his plain words and quiet tone proof of his sincerity.

"Perhaps we should forgive each other and move forward with the Lord," Mrs. Miller said.

"I would like that," the bishop said.

"Forgive me, Father, for I have not been to confession for over 12 years," Mrs. Miller said. She looked better already, but I knew that she would feel even better if she had a private session with the bishop, so I stood up and said, "Mrs. Miller, my team and I have to go, but we will keep you updated on our investigation. If you ever need to contact one of us, my mother has all our numbers, and the number of our office in Chicago. Please don't hesitate to call at any time."

She gave us all hugs, kissed everyone on the cheek, and was profuse in her thanks. We left her in the hands of the bishop, who was laying out all his regalia for confession, and filed out of the house. Fast Eddie was on the porch, and I said, "I owe ya one, Father."

"Nah, it doesn't work that way, Freak, not when it comes to matters of faith. Let's just say that the big guy upstairs wanted this to happen. It's all part of the plan, y'know?"

"Roger that, my brother," I said as we exchanged fist bumps.

My crew and I walked back to my parents' house. When we got on the porch, House said, "I'm gonna find the motherfucker that did this, and I'm going to rip his arms off and beat him to death with 'em."

"More fun to stick a red-hot piece of wire up his urethra and then clamp it to a power source and watch him fry slowly," Ed said.

"Prison," Joe said. "Raped nightly by the baddest dudes we can find. I'll pay 'em."

"We find a biker bar filled with Harley riders, preferably gangbangers, we throw him into their bikes so that they all fall over, then we watch the bikers stomp him into a grease puddle," Mac said.

"Piranhas, a big vat full. We cut off one of his toes and just lower him into the knees, then to the hips, then to the waist. Make sure they can get at his balls. And then we leave his ass there, dropping one inch every minute until it's over," Gunny said.

"And then we crush his bones to powder and send that shit up to the space station so they can scatter his ashes in the cold pit of space," Ed said.

"But not before I rip his arms off and beat his bloody dead corpse with them," House said.

They weren't kidding either.

Each member of the team decided then and there that it was a matter of honor that we find the murderer of Tim Miller and that we separately and individually pursue his killer until we caught him.

Joe wrote up our charter, and we all signed it, making the Find That Motherfucker Association official. We sealed the deal by drinking more PBRs and eating more pizza, this time from Pizza Sam's in B.C., which we decided wasn't quite as good as Erbelli's but was still very consumable (get the Al's Choice, Big Daddy Supreme, or York Fantastic; they're good munchie material).

In the middle of our celebration of the mitzvah, I got a call from Sergeant Roush of the Kalamazoo Public Safety Department, asking if we could shoot the following day, and since our flight home wasn't until eleven thirty, I said we'd be there at 7:00 a.m., armed and ready to defend the honor of the Secret Service.

When the revelry was winding down, Joe said, "We are gonna find this asshole and put him away, right? We weren't just bullshitting on the porch. You guys are going to keep looking even if our unit is split up, right?"

"Bet your ass," we all said at once, sounding like a sleuth of growling bears. "We owe each other Pepsis for a month," Gunny said. We all agreed that sounded fair, and Mac said, "We need to divvy up responsibilities and then shift our focus once in a while. You know, to keep ourselves fresh and get as many eyes on as much information as we can." We agreed that was a good idea, so we spent an hour drawing up an organizational chart and getting organized.

By then it was 11:30, and we were scheduled to shoot at 7:00 a.m., which meant up and out at six, so we all trooped off to bed. I was sleeping downstairs on the couch, so I went over and flopped. My mom came in to turn off the lights, saw me, and said, "That may be the best thing you've ever done, Glinka. We're all very proud of you for the mitzvah for Karen."

"Thanks, Mom," I said. "We really didn't do very much, just looked into a couple of things."

"Nonsense! You gave her church back, you gave her hope. Essentially, you gave Karen her life back, which is a mitzvah if I've ever seen one," my mom said.

"Who saves one life saves the world," I said with a smile.

"Exactly," my mom said. "Now there's only one more thing to do."

"What's that?" I said.

"Catch that motherfucker and put his ass in jail," my mom said. We both laughed, she kissed me good night, and I slept the sleep of the righteous.

I would not have been able to sleep so righteously if I had known how deep and wide the circles of blood and heartache from one simple mitzvah for a crazy old lady in Battle Creek, Michigan, would ripple outward.

But that was much, much later, after lots more water under the bridge.

CHAPTER 25

Freak Show on the Range

So we all got up early, had coffee and doughnuts from Sweetwater's Doughnut Mill, the best doughnut house in Michigan (and maybe the world—their Boston crème doughnuts are the food of the gods), said goodbye to my family, and left for the Kalamazoo County Sheriff's shooting range.

We were met by a gaggle of deputies led by a lieutenant who wasn't wearing a name badge and didn't give us his name, but Sergeant Roush was there, and Wilkinson with his mustache, and Officer Phillips, so we felt welcome, especially after Wilkinson said, "The sheriff told us if we didn't beat you, we'd have to patrol in Parchment for a month, so one of us has to take you, Agent Glickstien." All the deputies groaned; apparently, Parchment was someplace you didn't want to be, and Gunny said, "Hell, none of you children can even shoot with me, so I don't know how you're going to beat the best fucking pistol shot in the history of the Marines." There was more groaning and good-natured bantering, and then we went into the range.

It was well kept up, had 12 shooting booths, and had great depth; it probably went back 550 feet, which meant that this range might be used for long guns. I looked at Sergeant Roush, and he said, "We've got five inches of steel plate reinforcing the back wall. It's sandwiched between two layers of block. We can shoot a Barrett Light .50 in here if we're careful, and yes, we have competition shoots with .308s and such."

"This is an impressive range for a county sheriff's department," Gunny said.

"Sheriff Fuller expects a lot of us, but he also gets a lot for us," Wilkinson said.

"Good sheriff?" Mac asked.

There was general agreement that Sheriff Richard C. Fuller III was a good man and good sheriff.

"He has to get elected, but he isn't some political asshole," Officer Phillips said.

"He's a professional lawman," Wilkinson said, "and he acts like it."

"We get a lot of training that other deputies might not," Sergeant Roush said. "It really helps in serving the public."

"He doesn't expect us to do anything that he's not done or prepared to do," the no-name lieutenant said.

"Fucker is a little short for a sheriff, though," Wilkinson said, drawing general laughter. After it stopped, Gunny said, "Head-to-head, winners advance?"

"Sounds good," said the nameless lieutenant. Everybody got earmuffs and looked at the numbers inside. We decided to shoot number one earmuffs versus number two earmuffs, etc., until all the Secret Service agents had been engaged. We all wanted to watch, so all the matches would be just two shooters at once in side-by-side booths.

"Bull's-eyes the tiebreaker?" Gunny said.

"Sounds good," said the no-name lieutenant.

"I've got number one," said Ed.

"I'm number two," said Officer Phillips.

They stepped to the line, pulled their weapons, checked their actions, and then Ed picked up her SIG Sauer P228, Phillips picked up his Glock 22, and the lieutenant said, "Shoot." Both of them loosed all their rounds in about six seconds and then set down their empty weapons. Phillips was a bit slower than Ed, but not slow.

The targets came back from the 25-foot line, and it was clear that Ed had won. Phillips had one round that hit high on the outer ring—his second, I'd bet, didn't anticipate the recoil very well—and had a good grouping just outside the 10-ring, but all of Ed's rounds were inside the nine and 10 rings, and she had two near bull's-eyes. "Got me," Phillips said. Everyone agreed that Ed would move on as Gunny (number three) and the nameless lieutenant (number four) moved into their booths. The targets were sent downrange, they went through the ritual, and then they shot.

Both men loosed all their rounds in under five seconds, but as soon as the guns racked open, the lieutenant said, "I fuckin' hate Parchment!" Everybody laughed as the targets came back from downrange, and sure enough, the lieutenant had a round in the seven-ring, while all of Gunny's were in the 10-ring, except for two bull's-eyes and one just into the nine-ring.

There rest of the shooting was fairly even. A good-looking deputy named Pastrick beat Mac clean, and Sergeant Roush beat Joe two bull's-eyes to one, while House squeaked by a deputy named Heaton three bull's-eyes with one dead center to three bull's-eyes but none dead center.

Finally, it was down to Wilkinson (number 11) and me (number 12). He looked at me and said, "Got a C-note, Agent Glickstien?"

"Got five of 'em," I said.

Sergeant Roush said, "Easy, Wilk. She's the—"

But Wilkinson said, "Yeah, I know, Sarge, but I'm tired of talkin'. I want to see her do it with a bit of pressure. Maybe five Cs of pressure."

"We good at 500, then?" I asked.

"Bet your ass," Wilkinson said.

I was straddling the line between the two booths so that I could see both targets. I smoothly pulled my Smith & Wesson 1076s from their shoulder holsters—smooth is fast—and loosed all 10 rounds from both guns in under three seconds.

"Whatthefuckwasthat?" Wilkinson said.

"Holy fuck!" Gunny said.

"Wait'll ya see the targets," I said. They came droning up from 25 feet, and there was a silence so profound outer space seemed noisier. Finally, Wilkinson pulled his wallet out of his pants, got down on a knee in front of me, and held it over his head. I took the wallet—it was as silent as Tut's tomb before Howard Carter opened it—took out five $100 bills, closed it, and gave it back. Wilkinson got up and bowed, backing away from me while continuing to bow.

Gunny finally broke the silence. "BOO-RAHHH!" he bellowed. "Holy fucking A! It's the Freak from Battle Creek!" He grabbed me around the waist and picked me up, swinging me in a circle. The rest of my team rushed us and started pummeling me, and jumping up and down, and screaming inarticulately, until House started chanting, "Freak! Freak! Freak!" at which point the whole team began chanting, until everybody in the room started chanting, "Freak!" After about five hours (OK, it was about a minute, but it felt so good I'm sticking to the hours theory) the chanting stopped, and the no-name lieutenant said, "I've been shooting since I was five years old—42 years—and I've never seen anything like it. That's not just incredible, it's impossible. If I hadn't seen it, I wouldn't believe it! Sergeant Roush, you ever seen anything like it?"

"No, sir," Roush said. "I heard stories in the corps, but it was usually just scuttlebutt, rumors, and so I kinda discounted it. Shouldn'ta done that, ma'am," he said, turning to address me.

"Roush, ya dumb fucking jarhead, I told ya that I'm not an officer anymore, I'm just an agent," I said, laughing with everybody else.

"Sorry, ma'am, but anybody who shoots like that will always be an officer to me. Sorry, ma'am, but that's the way I was trained." Roush drew to attention and said, "Ah-TENN-hut! There's an officer on deck!"

His voice was so perfectly pitched, and his intent was so pure that anybody who'd ever been in the service came to attention. Roush said, "PREE-ZENT… ARMSZ!" and everybody saluted. I let them hold it a second, drew to attention, and returned the salute.

It may have been the greatest moment of my life to that point.

After three counts, I said, "ORDER…armsz!" and everybody dropped their salutes and began talking at once. Wilkinson looked at me and said, "What are you shooting out of those monsters, Freak?"

"I'm loaded with Cor-Bon 165-grain jacketed hollow points," I said.

"That a big enough load? It seems like you oughta be shootin' 180 grain through a 1076—they are 1076s, right?" Wilkinson asked.

"Yeah, they're modified 1076s, old FBI issue. I had rubber Hogue grips put on. Had to have them modified because of the decocking lever on the side, and I had all the springs upgraded so there wouldn't be any ejection problems, although I won't shoot the FBI Lite rounds through them, anyway," I said.

"Aren't they a bitch to control because of the recoil?" Phillips asked.

"I've kinda found that to be myth," I said. "I use the Cor-Bon JHPs because they're only about 540 feet per second at the muzzle, but they still deliver 1,250 feet per second on target. That's enough to stop anything short of an elephant or water buffalo. It'll rip anything human to shreds at ranges up to 150 feet. Since the average range to a hostile is about 12 feet, I figured these Cor-Bons will work nicely. I have shot Buffalo Bore 180-grain JHPs through 'em, and they do kick a bit more—muzzle velocity's about 750 fps—but they also deliver about 100 more feet per second on target."

"In case you need to stop an APC or Apache helicopter," Gunny said.

"Which is why I shoot the Cor-Bon 165 JHPs. If I can't put enough hurt on the target with those, I'm not going to stop it with the 180s, no matter how fast they streak out of the barrel," I said.

"With that kind of accuracy, you could probably use .22 shorts and stop most targets," Wilkinson said. Everybody had a good laugh at that one, and then the good-looking deputy named Pastrick said, "Ma'am, could you give us one more demonstration? I'd like to see how you group at fifty feet."

"Send a target down," I said. I put my spare mags in the 1076s, reloaded the first mags, and prepared to shoot. I put the loaded weapons down on the counters and said, "Before you put your muffs on, I want to remember that anything outside 25 to 30 feet is a crapshoot with a pistol, especially under combat conditions. The only way you can be effective is to know your weapon's tendencies, and your own shooting tendencies, and you have to practice perfectly. And then do it again under stress conditions. The Marine Corps training proves that this works, but only if you put the rounds through your weapon and correct for your own tendencies. Keep everything you shoot at, analyze your groupings, and especially your misses, then work to correct everything as a whole. When you pull your weapon, it should be as natural as taking a breath, regardless of the situation."

I looked at Phillips and said, "Your miss against Ed. It was your second round, wasn't it?"

He nodded and said, "I still have trouble with the second round because of recoil. I can't seem to anticipate it, and my hand is always surprised."

"Try firing rounds one and two at the same time. Double-tap one and two into the body, then steady on three and put it through the target's head. Remember, I can give you all the advice in the world, but if you don't put the rounds through your weapon, it won't make any difference."

Everybody nodded, some of the deputies were writing in their little notebooks, and I said to Pastrick, "We all set?" He nodded, so I put my muffs on, smoothly palmed one 1076 into my right hand, steadied in my modified Weaver stance, realized the target was at about 75 feet instead of 50, adjusted my aim, and loosed all 10 rounds in just over two seconds. The 1076 clacked open, and I whipped off my muffs and said, "Fuck you, Pastrick. Putting the target at 75 feet isn't going to fool me, but it does kind of piss me off, so if you want to play, put a target as far away as you can."

His handsome, chocolate-colored face immediately flushed, so I knew that I was right. He hit the switch, and the 75-foot target came back the same as the 25-foot targets.

Every round dead center.

The center bull's-eyes on all three targets didn't exist, and there were no marks outside it either. It sounds really amazing, and I suppose it was, but remember (and I'm not being melodramatic here), I fought in some really hairy places where a miss on a target literally meant death for me, and for everyone else with me (sorry, still classified).

Besides, I'd shot better than this under far worse conditions.

No one made a sound as the target motored down to the 150-foot line. I decided to really show off this time, so I smoothly palmed a 1076 into my left hand, settled in my Weaver stance, and loosed all ten rounds in just over three seconds. I'd gone a bit slower than usual because I wanted the target to be perfect, and as the last round left the barrel, I was sure it would be. Pastrick hit the button, and the target came back.

It got about 10 feet from the shooting area, and House, Gunny, and Ed started laughing. By the time it came to a stop, everybody else was laughing. Pastrick stepped over to me, got on one knee, and offered me his wallet, just like Wilkinson had. I opened it, took out the three $100 bills I found there, and handed it back. He stood and bowed while backing away from me.

"What the hell kind of shooting is that?" a new voice asked.

It belonged to Sheriff Rick Fuller, who was as advertised, just a bit short but dressed like a lawman and definitely acting like one. The no-name lieutenant said, "Sheriff, this is Agent Glinka Glickstien of the U.S. Secret Service, and she's the best pistol shot you've ever seen." He pointed at the shredded 25-foot targets, and the shredded 75-foot target, and then at the 150-foot target. The sheriff looked at me and said, "I'll bite. What's it stand for?"

I pointed at the perfect F outlined on the target and said, "Freak, sir, they call me Freak, so I thought I'd leave the deputies with a gentle reminder that they all got their asses kicked by a girl."

Sheriff Fuller roared with laughter, as did everybody else, and then they all told him the story of the other three targets, and then we all had a good time telling stories, and then it was time to go, because my team and I had to catch a plane.

We shook hands all around—the sheriff and his deputies were all pretty cool—and Wilkinson said, "Freak, would you mind signing these targets? We'd like to put 'em up as a reminder that we need to keep improving, and that we got our asses kicked by a girl."

We all laughed one more time, I signed the targets, and we left for the Kalamazoo/Battle Creek airport and Chicago, where we were going to catch some roofers who were counterfeiting the currency of the good old USA.

As we were waiting to board the plane, Mac said, "So is it just great teaching and a shitload of practice, or is some of it talent?"

"I have 20/5 vision in both eyes, my reaction times are the fastest anyone has ever seen, and I can hold a 100-pound weight straight out from my shoulder at a 90-degree angle from my body without straining, so some of it's raw physical ability. The first time I shot in the Corps, I really couldn't miss. It was like I instinctively knew what to do, as if I'd been shooting all my life. After Master Gunnery Sergeant Berkey got done with me…well, I've got enormous physical gifts, and I was trained by the best pistol shooter I've ever seen…so…" I didn't know what else to say, because it sounded like I was bragging, so I stopped.

House looked at me and said, "It ain't braggin' if you can do it, Freak. You don't need to be ashamed to be the best."

"It's an honor to be a fellow Marine, and to watch you shoot," Gunny said, his tone indicating that he wasn't kidding.

"It's also good to know that if we go to guns, you're going first," Mac said. "That way, I won't have to shoot anyone, because once you get done, the bad guys will all be dead."

"Dead as a doornail," Joe said.

"Because they've been nailed by the Freak from Battle Creek," Ed said.

"Booyah!" House said.

As we got on the plane for Chicago, I looked at my team and felt like I was going to burst with joy. It was like being back in special ops—the camaraderie, the professionalism, the black humor—except this time we were more likely to die from a thousand paper cuts than from being shot up by a shitload of bad guys. Or so I thought.

It's funny how you can underestimate some shit, especially when it comes to the future well-being of you and yours.

I'd forgotten the old Yiddish proverb "*Mann traoch, Gott lauch.*" "Man plans, God laughs."

Shit, I could've just listened to Public Enemy and remembered it, but I wasn't listening to rap that century, so I fluffed it.

The result was murder.

Literally.

CHAPTER 26

Trigger Finger Takedown

So we got back to the office and had a sit-down meeting with Captain Cork, Guru, and the rest of the team. Joe briefed everybody on what we'd found out, Weasel put up the pictures and vitals of the roofers, and we discussed our plan of action.

"Are we sure they're here?" Captain Cork said.

"If they aren't, they will be soon. This is where they need to be in order to make a big score," Joe said.

"Or St. Louis, or Memphis, or Indianapolis, or any other major city," Carly "Sparky" Cronenwell said. "I don't see why it just has to be Chi." We'd just met. She was at the dentist my first day, and we missed meeting. But I already liked her. She was tough, no-nonsense, and willing to just be one of the guys. And she was also a great flatfoot agent, according to Gunny. "That chick can pound the pavement, and she ain't afraid to just keep goin'. Sometimes the Guru has to literally send two of us out and drag her back to the office, because she ain't ever heard of working hours—she thinks every hour's a working hour. She'd make a great Marine if she hadn't been a wing-wiper." (He meant that she'd been in the Air Force).

"How do we think that will be done?" Guru said. "They can't just keep spending it and keeping the change—that's just not big enough."

"I think they're going to keep spending it, but that the big score will come from cashier's checks," Jewey said.

"Oh, you clever young Padawan," Joe said. "I didn't think of that at all, but I'll bet that it works like a charm."

"Of course it will," Captain Cork said. "These guys work with their hands at small jobs. They could pull it off, especially if they stay in their work clothes."

"Especially if they also do driveway sealing or say that they do," Sparky said.

"OK, you assholes, what the hell are you talking about? I'm just a simple boy from the *barrio*, and I don't get all this fucking stuff," Emiliano "El Gato" Zaragoza said.

"I forgot that you're a boy from East L.A., where the freeways are also the parking lots," Joe said.

"And where all the roofs are made out of Spanish tile, so's no real men have to get their hands dirty with shingles and tar," the Greek said.

"Yeah, yeah, and tile doesn't burn in the wildfires, and it's better for the environment. Make all the fuckin' Cali jokes you want, but I'm still confused about this big score," El Gato said. I was glad he said it, because truth to tell, I wasn't really sure what they meant either. I'm smart, but not a fucking genius, like some of my teammates were. Also, my favorite jobs involved the chase and capture of nefarious individuals. (Yes, I used *nefarious*—it's a great word and perfectly describes all the dirtbag, pond-scum assholes I'd spent my special ops years on. No, I'm not saying anything more about that—classified.) I preferred to leave the heavy thinking to those best suited for it, while I concentrated on the physical side, which was my best side.

Captain Cork said, "Look, it makes perfect sense. These guys will come in with cash and some small legitimate checks to several banks. Their cover story is that they are working for a big company out of Toledo. Wasn't Toledo where we found the trail?"

Joe nodded, and Captain Cork said, "So they develop a relationship with the tellers—they apologize for smelling bad, or being dirty, or whatever. They open a checking or savings account in the company's name and deposit the cash, say, 5K or so, then over the course of the summer and fall, they keep making small deposits at all their banks, all under 9K, so they escape the notice of any computers or sharp-eyed federal boys and girls. Business is good, so their accounts grow pretty big pretty quickly, but they probably got lotsa deposits in lotsa banks, so they keep all their accounts under a mil. Of course, all this business is conducted under the company name, so these guys got no real access to the money."

"Who cares? How would they even open the accounts, and why would they if they couldn't get at the money?" El Gato said.

"First, they give the bank a letter from the company authorizing them to open the accounts but not withdraw any money without express permission of some higher-up in the company, probably the treasurer or CFO. Then the company sends a letter to the bank allowing the two trustees to access the money, but only so they can send it back to the parent company by cashier's check," Jewey said.

"And before you ask, Gato, this way they inspire trust with the bank. These guys can't be scammers or bunco artists, because they have a legit company behind them, and oh yeah, they can't get at the money anyway, because they're trustees for the company, not actual account holders," Captain Cork said.

"So there must be some mastermind somewhere, probably in Toledo," Mac said.

"They could be anywhere, but yeah, this operation is too sophisticated for some roofers from Savannah, or wherever the fuck they're from," Guru said. "The company they work for is the washing machine for all the funny money."

"And they claim almost all the cash transactions and pay taxes on it, because that keeps the IRS off their ass, and who gives a flying fuck? Because it's all funny money, anyway," Joe said.

"We should also look at coin-operated laundries, vending machines, and casinos," Weasel said.

"Yeah, we should," Captain Cork said. "It makes sense that they have a supplier of dollar bills under their control, or at least that they have access to a shitload of small bills."

"OK, all this sounds plausible, but wouldn't a group of large deposits under a company name show up somewhere? The IRS or the fed or even the Service?" Bumble said.

"Ah, there's the rub! But these guys are smart, or whoever's runnin' the show is, because they've got their deposits under a whole bunch of dummy company names, so nobody ever links them together. They probably send two guys into each bank, to sign the deposit cards and give ID, but they can use lots of combinations and cover tremendous ground because they don't have to do any legitimate work at the start," Captain Cork said.

"What if somebody got a look at their work trucks and the name didn't match the account?" Mac asked.

"I'll bet that they have about two hundred of those magnetic signs for their trucks, and I'll bet that they have work shirts made up the same way. That way, they can be from multiple companies in the same banks, if they use different pairs of guys," Joe said.

"Concur," Jewey said. "They probably keep a log about who goes where and with what company name so there aren't any fuckups, and I'll bet they drain the deposits when they get to 250K or so."

"Why?" the Greek said. "Wouldn't it just be easier to load up, pull up stakes, and hit the road to somewhere else?"

"Sure, except remember the amount of time and effort they spent getting set up. These guys don't want to go through that rigmarole any more than they have to. They're looking for the big score, and Chi Town is the place to get it, just because of the sheer size of the metro area. They could do some jobs out in the 'burbs, start using suburban banks or credit unions, and voilà, they've got unlimited places to cash in the funny money," Captain Cork said.

"And they'll be good at the jobs they do take on. I'll bet that they're licensed in Ohio, and probably bonded too," Weasel said.

"Yeah, they kinda have ta be," Ed said. "Everybody would notice if they were rip-off artists, and that's the last thing they want. They can't have any form of law enforcement looking at them, because they've got to send the money somewhere, and that would leave a pretty easy trail to follow."

"So these are legitimate guys who do at least average work and send most of their cash "home," wherever that might be," Sparky said. "So we gotta go out and pound the pavement, take their pictures to banks, and try to match them up with accounts."

"Nah," Jewey, Weasel, Joe, Guru, and Captain Cork all said at once. We all laughed, and Captain Cork said, "I've got the Pepsis, but, Weasel, why'nt you explain why that's a bad idea?"

"We need to catch 'em completely by surprise, all of 'em at once. We can't let anybody get to a computer or a bank, because they could drain the accounts before we even came close to catching up with them, and then all the cash is in the Caymans, or Lichtenstien, or Switzerland, and semi-legitimate," Weasel said. "We're way better off trying to take them away from the banks, and we don't show anybody their picture until we absolutely have to."

"Because one of them might have cozied up to a teller or 10," Ed said.

"Remember the chick in Kalamazoo who said that she would've gone out with the cute one, Elvis Linemann?" Mac said. "If they wanted to, these guys could get an in with most of the banks just by hitting on the tellers. They have lots of cash available and could buy all manner of gifts or treat them to expensive dinners or whatever. If that's the case and we show one of the wymyn they've befriended their picture…"

"Poof! They're gone with the wind," Bumble said.

"Or at least the cash is," Jewey said.

"Exactly," Weasel said.

"We can get after them by looking at recent applications for Illinois business licenses, by checking every roofing company in and around Toledo and by looking for anything in their personal accounts, probably without a warrant," Guru said. "This feels like economic terrorism to me."

"I think that Weasel, Joe, Ed, and I can find their scam using the magic boxes, but we need a way to physically find them once we do. They're probably staying in some no-tell motel in the 'burbs and paying cash," Jewey said.

"I'll bet they got themselves an Airbnb place, someplace to park the truck outta sight and be able to store the cash too," House said.

"Concur—that much funny money would take up considerable space, and they'll need to load it without being seen," Bumble said.

"And Airbnb people have no problem taking cash. It keeps Uncle Sugar from getting his cut and maximizes profits," El Gato said.

"OK, so we're going to designate the four wizards to work on the magic boxes and ferret out these assholes and their parent company, but how the hell are we going to get a physical location for these birds?" Captain Cork asked. "We can't just put surveillance on random banks."

"Oh, that's easy," the Greek said.

"Do tell, O mighty Oracle of Delphi," Gunny said.

"Hot dogs," the Greek said.

"Have you lost your motherfuckin' mind?" El Gato said.

"Nope," the Greek said. "These guys already proved that they like using hot dog stands to pass funny money, but what if they did it because they like hot dogs, especially Chicago dogs? Where would people go for hot dogs, especially during the day on their lunch hour? Or at night when they want a beer?"

"It depends on where they're at, but most likely a Portillo's, or maybe SuperDawg, if they're out that way, or even the little stands at the Field Museum," I said. "Those places are crazy busy and wouldn't notice if they were being passed bad paper at lunch hour or the dinner rush, for that matter."

"So we put three-person teams around the city at hot dog places, but we pay special attention to Portillo's, because if they're in the city, sooner or later they're going to go there for a dog and a beer at lunch," the Greek said.

We all looked at one another and realized that the Greek was right. Despite being a huge town in every way, Chicago was also kind of small in some ways, and Portillo's was an institution. These guys had a pattern that they'd stuck to across the Midwest, and there was absolutely no reason for them to change now, so we could surveil just a few places and perhaps get lucky while our computer geniuses worked their magic boxes. Once the wizards came up with company names, we'd have other avenues to get at them, but until then it was just good old police work.

We all liked that, because it meant we were doing something, even if it wasn't immediately productive. It also meant that we got to hang out in hot dog joints, which would naturally lead to eating hot dogs, which, at least for me, was better than a cash bonus. I was pretty sure that it didn't bother the Greek, El Gato, Gunny, House, or Bumble either. Even Captain Cork looked kinda geeked at the prospect of going to Portillo's, which also had the best Italian beef in the city, and cake shakes—they put a slice of chocolate cake into the ice cream and milk and mixed it all up, and yes, they taste as good as they sound. Wipe that drool off your chin.

So Captain Cork and Guru split us up into teams, and we decided on tactics if we found the roofers. We all agreed that it would be better to track them to their humble abode and then arrest them while they still had the funny money in their possession, so we had three-person teams with one "inside" operator and two outside "trailers."

I was going undercover at the Portillo's on Ontario as a cashier, with Bumble and El Gato as my trailers. Sparky was going undercover at the Portillo's in Skokie, with House and the Greek as her trailers. Mac was going to work at the Forest Lake Portillo's with Gunny and a guy from Financial Crimes named Tom Greenman as her trailers. Guru was going to be our mobile floater. She'd wait at a spot in the center of the triangle our three posts formed and be ready to go where needed. We were going to give it a week and then branch out to other suburban locations if the wizards didn't come up with anything.

As much as he wanted to go into the field, Captain Cork decided to stay in the office and coordinate everything. He also kicked the results of our preliminary investigation upstairs and had the local FBI Hostage Rescue Team (HRT, the federal equivalent of a SWAT team) ready in case we found the roofers and decided we needed to shock and awe them into submission. It struck us all as funny at first, but then we remembered our training.

> Gunny: Like we need some Feebs to rescue us from five roofers. What are they going to do, shoot us with their nail guns?
>
> Mac: And with with the Freak on our side, are they going to outshoot her with their pneumatic staplers?
>
> House: Besides, they won't even know we're coming. Are they going to use their magical construction powers to prepare an ambush?
>
> Bumble: I'm scared. They might attack us with hammers. I hate hammers.
>
> Weasel: Roy Linemann has a class V federal firearms license. He legally owns a Browning automatic rifle, two .45-caliber Thompson submachine guns, a full-auto AK-47, and an M60 light machine gun.
>
> Me: Gotta plan for what the enemy could do, not what they will do.
>
> Gunny: Roger that, Freak. Get those HRT Feebs ready with their sniper rifles and shit.
>
> Mac: Tell those great Americans to bring some damned grenades, too, just in case.
>
> Bumble: Do they have a tank?

So we went out to our stations while the wizards worked on their magic boxes. I got "trained" at Portillo's by a really nice womyn named Pattie Brundage, who told me that I'd love working at Portillo's—and yes, there was free food at the end of my shift.

Unfortunately, I never got the chance to take advantage of it.

The first day I was working, it was a madhouse from 11:00 a.m. onward. People came into Portillo's in a steady stream, and we kept the cash registers humming like Indy 500 cars. Most of the people were really nice, and some of them were downright hilarious, and suddenly there was Elvis Linemann right in front of me, third in my line. I glanced at the rest of the line, and there was Carl Horne and Chip Fowler standing together. I finished the order at the counter, and they all moved up in line. I looked over the other line, and there was Roy Linemann with a streak of white in his hair, and Mark Roberson right behind him. As I was looking, Fowler said something to Roberson, who waved at him with a hand that only had four fingers.

I went back to concentrating on orders, and when Elvis Linemann got to the counter, I said, "Welcome to Portillo's. What size would you like on your drink?"

He smiled—definitely bad teeth—and said, "A large Coke, please, darlin'. I'd also like tw Chicago dogs." He had a definite Southern accent, and he was kind of cute, but all I really wanted to do was ask him one more question.

I put on my best airhead voice and said, "Oh, are you from New Orleans? I *love* your accent."

Linemann smiled and said, "Sorry, darlin', I'm just from little old Savannah."

"In Georgia?" I asked in full airhead mode.

"The very one," he said.

"Oooh, I've always wanted to go to Savannah," I said, pouring it on.

"Well, ya'll tell me when you get off work and I'll come by and getcha and we'll talk about it," he said.

"I'll get off at eight thirty," I said.

"And what do I call you, darlin'?" Linemann said.

"Shevaun," I said. "It's Irish."

"And beautiful," he said, handing me a $20 bill.

I said, "Ah, $11.37 out of $20.00. Your change is $8.73. And I'll see you at eight thirty."

He winked and said, "Count on it, darlin'."

I could hear my trailers in my earpiece. "Roger that. The targets are in the store right now," Bumble was saying to Captain Cork. "Freak, I've got them coming out of line to stand in the waiting area," El Gato said. "Nod if that's true."

I nodded at the next people in line and said, "Welcome to Portillo's. What size would you like on your drink?"

There was a lot more tactical chatter; the other teams were coming in to the Ontario Street location, and the HRT team was going on standby, just in case the roofers somehow got rambunctious before we were ready for them. I just kept ringing people's orders up as if I'd been doing it forever, while Gato and Bumble took their beers over to a table near where the roofers were sitting and began talking about how the Cubs really had a chance this year, what with all the young talent and the deep pitching staff.

I looked up from my register and saw Guru slip into the back of my line. She was talking on her phone about getting a babysitter for her five kids, which I was sure meant she was arranging more surveillance teams for our group of merry roofers. When she got to the end of the line, she went to the other cashier so that I wouldn't have to wait on her. She didn't even look at me, just paid for her order and went to stand in the waiting area. She ordered her food and three beers and went over to sit at a table a couple of rows behind the roofers.

She was joined about a minute later by Mac and Gunny, who sat down and began talking as Guru shared the beers. The roofers kept eating and talking, and eventually, Fowler and Horne went over and got five beers. The roofers drank them down and got another round as Gato and Bumble got up and left. The place was really full of people, but the Greek and Sparky had been just standing around, looking to sit down, so they pounced on the empty table and sent Buzz Greenman to get their food. We had the roofers covered every which way, so I relaxed and just did my job.

It was hard work, but it really was fun. I bantered with the customers and the people I was working with until it was my break time. I left my register just as the roofers were getting up to leave, so I sort of wandered that way, acting as if I didn't see them.

Elvis Linemann touched my arm, and I looked up with an airhead, deer-in-the-headlights expression. My face softened, and I said, "Oh! It's you, Mr. Savannah! I thought that you left!"

He smiled at me and said, "Say, She-vaun, do you happen to have a friend? My brother Roy there, he's a famous bass fisherman, might want to ride along with us, and I thought…if it wasn't askin' too much…"

If I didn't know that he was a) married and b) a counterfeiting scumbag I'd have almost been charmed, even though he had terrible breath and the worst teeth this side of a British soccer fan. I did my airhead smile and said, "My friend Becky was coming to pick me up, but she likes to party so I'm like, sure she won't mind. She likes older men, too."

"We'll be here then, ready to party," Elvis Linemann said.

"Oooh, goody. Maybe we can go to the Billy Goat Tavern and get some beers," I said.

"Depend on it, darlin'," he said. The roofers headed out the door, followed by Gunny and Mac, who were going to hail a cab—it was actually a Chicago PD undercover, driven by a cop named Gregerski who knew Captain Cork. Bumble and Gato were already in two other undercover cars, and I was pretty sure that I'd heard Captain Cork say something on the tac channel about a helicopter.

I waited until I was sure the roofers were gone and went over to Guru's table. "Can I get you anything else, ma'am?" I said in my best Portillo's voice.

"How about two more fucking surveillance cars and a valet delivery?" she said, a smile creasing her face. She spoke into her mike, telling Captain Cork that we were about to become part of the tail detail. He came back and said, "Wait one. We're having a brainstorm here at the Nest." There was a very short pause and he said, "Guru, Freak needs to stay put until I get there. We are also recalling Mac to Portillo's. Everybody else goes out on surveillance of the subjects, but Freak and Mac stay put."

"Acknowledged, Captain Cork. Freak and Mac maintain position, the rest of the team on surveillance of the subjects. Guru, The Greek, Sparky and Gunny joining the surveillance net. We are on comms at 125.9." She looked at me and said, "Well done, Freak. You're gonna be part of your first take-down tonight." She slapped my palm and left with the other agents. They would split into teams at the door and go to two other nondescript vehicles in order to join the team already trailing the roofers. With five vehicles and a helicopter it would be impossible for the roofers to know they were being tailed, and virtually impossible for the detail to lose them.

We had them in our sights, and now we just needed to take them down.

Mac got back about 10 minutes after Guru and the rest of the gang left, and Captain Cork arrived about 10 minutes after that with a man and womyn in tow. They turned out to be the FBI HRT commander, Erlacher, and his deputy, Goméz. They were both of a piece: about 5'10", maybe 175, brown-eyed, muscular, fit, intense, and very professional.

We went upstairs to the balcony room above the main floor of Portillo's in order to plan for the return of the two roofers. Captain Cork said, "First off, great job, Freak. Having Elvis ask you for a date is going to make this part a piece of cake. We'd like you to get the guys to stay inside for just a bit—tell them that you guys get free beers because you work here, and that you need to wind down after a long shift. Drink your beer normally and you'll give us enough time for the HRT guys to get set up, right?" He looked at Erlacher, who said, "Affirmative, sir. We're going to clear the immediate exit area and saturate it with our guys in plain clothes—should take us about five minutes."

Captain Cork said, "And Agent Goméz has a little present for you." The HRT deputy commander handed us each a device that looked like a TV remote, except for the prongs sticking out the end. She smiled and said, "These are the latest iteration of a taser—they'll incapacitate an elephant if any two of the three prongs are making contact. They're especially effective if you jam 'em in an armpit, neck or groin."

"Five bucks says that I get mine in the groin first," I said to Mac.

"Fuck you, Freak, I'm gonna jam mine up old Roy's ass before I pull the trigger," Mac said.

"I wouldn't if I were you—he might like it," Goméz said. We all got a good laugh before she demonstrated the taser, which turned out to be easier to operate than the revolving door at Portillo's.

When we were ready Captain Cork said, "This has to be perfectly casual and natural, because we don't want them close to you if they're suspicious. Don't look for backup—it'll be there, but you can't be looking around—because these guys could get hinky, OK?"

"Can we prime their pumps a bit—dress a bit provocatively, show some tit and leg?" Mac said.

"I don't see why not," Captain Cork said. He looked at Erlacher, who said, "Sure. It'll keep their minds in the gutter and off being taken down. Plus if they're ogling your tits they'll have a harder time reaching for a weapon—especially if they're ogling yours, Agent Glickstien."

I stared at him and the tough HRT guy kind of quailed away from me a bit. "No offense," he said. I laughed and said, "Don't worry, Commander, I'm with ya on that. I've found that letting men look at my tits also helps keep them from examining my face too closely, which might also be a plus in the takedown."

"No shit, Sherlock," Mac said. "If I had tits like yours George Clooney would've married me instead of the lawyer chick."

"If I had tits like yours I'd've been Miss California and probably Miss America," Goméz said. "Instead I joined the FBI and got stuck in an elite unit where I always have to wear a damned Kevlar vest."

"Can you even get a vest over those things?" Mac said.

"Yeah, if I wear a men's large," I said. "Otherwise I get nipple chafe."

"That's the worst," Goméz said.

"It is a bitch—and it would be worse for you, Freak, because you can't really go without a bra."

"Well, I *can*, but it isn't advisable," I said.

"Causes traffic accidents, don't it," Goméz said.

"And divorces," I said.

Captain Cork looked up at the speaker in Portillo's ceiling and said, "I want it to be known that neither I nor Agent Erlacher initiated the Great Tit Debate. We at no time harassed anyone, nor did we discuss the feminine attributes of any of the female agents present." He looked like he was testifying at a Congressional hearing, which made us all laugh again.

"So "Becky" and I are going to be off duty and dressed casually—with maybe a pinch of slut thrown in—and we're gonna get these schmucks to drink a beer with us so that HRT can get set up. Once we exit after our beer can I suggest to them that we go to the Billy Goat for some more drinks? That way we can use "goat" as the trigger word for the takedown," I said.

"You already said something about that to the target, right?" Captain Cork said.

"I did—and I can pump him up about it, too, while we're having our beer," I said.

"Isn't my apartment right around the Billy Goat?" Mac said. "My two-bedroom apartment with two king sized beds?"

"Perfect," Captain Cork said. "And keep up the airhead act—these guys are from the South, which means they probably don't think much of wymyn anyway."

"Wow, what an insensitive stereotype, sir," Mac said.

"Am I wrong?" he said. We all laughed again and agreed that he was probably right on the button. We set up the rest of the plan and Mac and I went back to work. We weren't sure if the brothers would show up early, so it had to look good.

Captain Cork talked to the manager, who agreed that we'd get off "early," around 8:00 p.m., so that we could change and get ready for our date. He was the only one at Portillo's who was in on the scam, because we wanted this to be natural and easy for the brothers.

Eight o'clock came, and we changed into our street clothes. I left the top four buttons of my shirt undone and had Mac's bra on; it was about eleven sizes too small, but it gave me a great push-up effect that I was sure would get Elvis's attention. Mac went commando and pulled her blouse up, tying it up just below her breasts. It looked good, and her muscular torso also drew attention. I was wearing jeans that were molded to my hips, and Mac had on spandex pants that made her ass look like a work of art. I thought of John Singer Sargent's *Nude Egyptian Girl* in the Chicago Institute of Art.

We were ready.

Mac and I heard all our backup check in on our wireless earbuds. We were also wearing body mikes so the backup crew could hear everything, but obviously, we couldn't talk back without alerting the bad guys, and we were feeling pretty good about it all when the counterfeiters walked in.

Fuck a goddamned duck.

They brought Mark Roberson with them.

Two tasers, three bad guys.

Fuck a goddamned duck.

I looked at Mac and said, "Becky, did you remember to pick up your check?" She slapped herself on the forehead and said, "Oh, shit. I *knew* I forgot somethin'. Be right back." Mac headed back into the manager's office as I greeted the counterfeiters.

"Hey darlin'," Elvis said. "We scare off your friend?" All three of them smiled and I realized that these weren't really bad guys, they were just lazy guys who had a fool-proof plan to defraud the U.S. government and taxpayers. Hell, they weren't all that different from Congress when you got down to it.

Except that people who feel trapped often turn into someone they're not, sort of like Bruce Banner and the Hulk (ummmm, Mark Ruffalo… Chris Hemsworth… Chris Evans… Anthony Mackie…love the Avengers…concentrate, you dipshit), which meant that we needed a change in plan.

So I said, "No, she just forgot her check. Becky's kind of an airhead." They all smiled and Roberson said, "She'll get along fine with Roy then—he once cast after bass during a fishin' tournament and forgot to put bait on his line." He had a soft, hesitant voice that was still somehow commanding. It was obvious from the way that the other two reacted to him that Roberson was the alpha dog, which meant that we had to be doubly careful of him during the takedown.

Before I could answer Captain Cork's voice filled my ear. "Herd the Linemanns away from Roberson—tell him to get a cab—and we'll rush him once the other two are down. The Feebs think that Roberson is the brains of the outfit, which makes him the most dangerous. You're still covered, but we want separation in case the HRT guys have to go to guns. Acknowledge by making a joke about Mac."

"Well, Becky forgot her underwear and did the splits during a basketball game," I said. "Her mom was so mad at her that she tried to make Becky become a nun." We all laughed just as Mac walked up. She rolled her eyes and said, "You told them the cheerleader story, din't ya? And my ma wantin' me to be a nun?" We all laughed some more and she said, "Well, let's get a beer and decide what we wanna do, and I'll tell ya some more about my cheerleading days."

"Ya gotta tell 'em the story about that time Mr. Fenstermacher came into the locker room when he thought we were all gone," I said. "Uh, oh, sounds like some guy got an eyeful," Roy said.

"Ya got no idea," Mac said.

We went over and all got beers, then sat at a table for ten minutes while Mac regaled us with a story about dancing naked on the bench in the locker room when the principal came in with some basketball officials. Everybody was laughing and drinking a beer when Captain Cork said, "The street is secure. Remember, send Roberson to the corner to get a cab before you fry the other two."

So we all got up and went through the revolving door. The cross street was empty, but Ontario still had traffic, so I said, "You guys park around here somewhere?"

Elvis said, "We come in a cab—we felt like it made us real city dwellers." We all laughed again and I said, "Well, we need another one if we're goin' downtown. Mark, will you step out to Ontario and flag one down?" He was the closest to Ontario, so it was perfectly normal that he'd be the one to do it. Roy Linemann was already making moves on Mac and Elvis was right next to me, so we were in the chips.

Mac fumbled her cell phone and dropped it on the sidewalk. She went to a knee to pick it up and said, "So are we gonna go to the Billy Goat?" At the word "goat" she came up with her taser, stuck it right in Roy Linemann's crotch and pulled the trigger. I whipped my taser out and stuck it in Elvis Linemann's neck and fried him. He made a noise like a demented pig and flopped straight backward onto the ground. Roy Linemann didn't make any noise at all, he just collapsed right on top of Mac, squashing her into the sidewalk.

That's when Mark Roberson reached behind him and pulled a gun out. He immediately aimed it at Mac, who was trying to get out from under Roy. Roberson had a serious look on his face and murder in his eyes. His face flushed red with anger and he was clearly going to shoot someone, probably Mac, who went still when she saw the gun pointed at her.

It was a good gun, a .38 Smith & Wesson Chief's Special, aimed at Mac from about eight feet away. It would be hard to miss her at that range, especially since Roberson was in a solid shooting stance and really locked on the target.

I was about 10 feet from Mac, about 18 feet from Roberson, and I instantly looked at my shooting backdrop, sort of clear, except for the McDonald's across the street and the parking lot full of people getting in their cars, and I realized that I was going to have to do some fancy shooting. I already had my 1076 in my hand, and I said, "Mark, you're surrounded and about to die. The FBI has an HRT squad here, and their snipers are trained on you."

"Bullshit," he said. "They ain't gonna shoot with me out here among the civilians. And I ain't gonna be captured so's I can go to prison, not if I got me an FBI agent under my gun." He smiled an evil smile, and I realized that it was time for my Annie Oakley act, so I shot his trigger finger off before he could shoot Mac.

My bullet chopped his finger off and smashed against the trigger guard, flattening itself on the gun's frame and not ricocheting at all, just like I planned it. The impact knocked the gun out of his hand, spun Roberson around and knocked him to his knees. Before he could get up Gunny and House sprinted from across the street and knocked him down flat. They cuffed him as the rest of my squad cuffed the two still twitching Linemann boys. Captain Cork came out of the McDonald's and sprinted across the street, straight for Mac.

"You all right?" he said, helping her to her feet.

"The fuck ya think, Boss? That damned redneck about made me puke, then the redneck with the gun about made me shit my pants, then Freak *did* make me shit my pants."

She got up, came over and hugged me tight. We just stood there a second or two, until Captain Cork gently took my pistol from my hand—SOP for a Secret Service agent involved shooting—and Mac said, "You shot his fuckin' finger off? Seriously? That's like Wild West legend shit. I..." Mac shuddered and then wobbled a bit—shock's a bitch—and then she said, "I just don't believe it. Nobody can shoot like that. Nobody!"

"I didn't have a choice. The background was full of civilians, and I didn't want him to shoot you, or the Feeb snipers to kill him, so I went for the shot, knowing that I could kill two birds with one stone," I said.

"Well, I owe ya a Pepsi for that one," Mac said as she hugged me one more time. "Now I need to go change my panties, 'cause I'm pretty sure I at least pissed myself." An ambulance rolled up and we put her in it so they could treat her for shock. Ed came out of Portillo's with a chair and made me sit in it, which was good, since I was pretty sure I was going to do a face plant in the sidewalk after all of the adrenalin that'd been pumped into my system.

My squad crowded around me and Joe said, "I dub thee Queen Freak, for never hath I seen such a thing in all my born years."

"Hell, I fought in two wars and I never saw anything like that—all those stories about you that ran through the Corps weren't just scuttlebutt, were they?" Gunny said.

"Classified," I said, which got everybody laughing. We all sat there and watched while the three counterfeiters were hauled off, two in cop cars and one in an ambulance. House looked at me and said, "Your heart rate even go up a scoche?"

"Well…uh…not really," I said.

"You are truly the Freak from Battle Creek," he said, shaking my hand and pulling me into a hug. Erlacher, the HRT commander, walked over and said, "Glickstien, if you ever need another job just let me know. I'll shitcan my snipers and doorbusters and just let you corner suspects and shoot their trigger fingers off. It'll sure as hell save time and money." He shook my hand and said, "No shit, that's the best shooting I've ever seen. There's nobody at the Bureau who can even come close to that."

I thanked him, shook a few more hands and said, "Captain Cork, we got two more bad guys out there—we gonna go pick 'em up?"

"We are, but you are not," he said. Before I could protest he said, "Freak, you know the procedure—agent involved shootings require debriefing as soon as possible. There are people waiting for you back at the House—they're waiting for Mac, too, so you guys are going back while we tool out to the Holiday Inn where the other two paper pushers are and arrest their fraudulent asses. We're taking HRT with us, so you can relax your trigger finger for a while, OK?"

Gunny said, "Rest easy, Freak, we're not taking any chances with these guys. They're goin' down for the count without even knowin' what hit 'em." The rest of the squad was nodding and making noises of agreement, so I just nodded back and said, "OK, boss. Mac and I are going to RTB. Do we get a driver, or should I just carry her ass on my back?"

"We already got you a driver, so just get in the car and do what the de-briefers tell you, OK?" Captain Cork said. He gave me a hug, squeezed Mac, and we piled into a Service car driven by an agent neither of us knew and sped off to the office, where we were met by Jewey and Weasel, along with an entire detail of de-briefers led by Francis Wong, the Agent in Charge of the entire Chicago office.

We were immediately separated and taken to interview rooms. My de-briefers were thoroughly professional, noncommittal and mercifully brief (sorry about the pun). When we were done both Mac and I were sent back to our squad room, where Weasel said, "We got the other two without incident—they're under arrest and the rest of the guys are headed back. The only one who got hurt was the bad guy whose finger you blew off, Freak."

I was so relieved that I just flopped down in a chair and blew out a big breath. Mac came over, sat down and put her arms around me. "Thank you for saving my life," she said quietly. "Sorry it came down to that," I said. "Well, I'll never feel unsafe around you. No one who saw that shooting ever will again," she said. "You're like Annie Oakley with the balls of Elliot Ness. As long as you have a gun in your hand it'll always be us over the bad guys, with the bad guys scoring zero."

I really wish that she hadn't said that, because as my *zayde* said, "Man plans, God laughs."

We should have heard the laughter then, but hubris trumps good sense in most cases, and this was one of those cases.

CHAPTER 27

Pyrrhic Victory

So all five of the counterfeiters were in custody, and the next day Francis "Charlie Chan" Wong, the AIC of our office, called the squad together and said, "First of all, well done. I've already determined that the shoot was righteous—the tape clearly shows Roberson aiming at Agent McKee when Agent Glickstien fires, and that is supported by all of the witnesses, including the FBI's HRT team. Both of their snipers were about two pounds of trigger pressure away from killing the subject, so we're good to go there. I want to explore what we do next. Jerry?" He looked at Captain Cork, who said, "Our computer guys have some info on that. Agent Wei?"

Weasel said, "We don't think that the flow of funny money comes from the roofing company in Toledo. They don't really have any place to store the stuff, and they don't have the intellectual capability to do it, either. We've gathered a ton of information on the owner of the company, Tommie Wilson, and the first thing that everybody said about him is that he's as dumb as a box of rocks. His chief bookkeeper, a guy named Chris Williams, is also mentioned as a member of the moron team, and we already know that the guys we caught aren't going to win any intelligence contests, which means that we're still looking for the brains of the outfit. We may have a lead on that." He looked at Jewey, who said, "So I called my cousin Mort, who works at a brokerage house in Philly, and asked him to sniff around for a company that might be washing the cash. He's tied into the NASDAQ, AMEX, and NYSE computers and he hears things about the financial world." He stopped and looked at all of us, his face lit with a sly grin.

"C'mon ya big Hebrew, what the fuck didya find?" Sparky said.

"Always with the melodrama," Joe said. "Geniuses always have to prove their brilliance by making we mere mortals wait."

"I'm about to bust some big Jew's head. We Mexicans are excitable and sometimes have a problem with our tempers," Gato said, using a Speedy Gonzales "Mexican" accent.

"OK, OK—I was just trying to heighten suspense, but if everybody's going to get their panties in a bunch," Jewey said. He punched a button on the conference table and a company logo popped up on the video screen in the squad room. It said "Italia's Quality Seafood," followed by "World's Largest and Finest Fresh Seafood Selection." There was a lobster underneath the words, with "Excellence in Wholesaling Since 1909" and "Luigi Tromboli II, Proprietor," followed by an address, "207 South Street, NYC." It was all done in bright red using a fancy font. Altogether it looked pretty cheesy, especially since none of us had ever heard of this "world's finest" company.

"A seafood wholesaler since 1909 that I never heard of? In the Big Apple? I spent my yout' woikin' in da Fulton Fish Market, and I nevah hoid o' dese goombahs. It ain't possible," The Greek said in a massive fail attempt at a New York accent. "Besides, that address is for the Fulton Stall Market. All of the fish guys moved to the new state of the art facility in the Bronx—it's on Food Center Drive, if I remember right."

"And I grew up ri't next tah two guys who woiked at Joe Monani's Fish Company—the old man started the company in like 1935," Guru said. "I never hoid ah dese goombahs, eider, so I t'ink I'll call Tony Manacci, my old comrade in arms who still woiks dere." She went over to her office and made a call.

"So why this company?" Captain Cork said.

"Mort says that they were around for a while, then they about faded out—apparently the latest CEO is a truly profound numbnuts. He's called 'Little Luigi,' to distinguish him from his father, 'Big Luigi,' who at least kept a few guys employed and did some business with the big boys. Apparently, when Big Luigi died, the company nearly went bankrupt. Little Luigi flunked out of at least three community colleges and never quite got the hang of the business. Then one day, voilà, they began to turn a profit. The problem is, when Weasel did a quick dig on them, they didn't appear to be doing enough business to justify their profits."

Guru came out of her office and said, "They're a front for the cash. Tony Manacci says that Big Luigi ran about eighteen trucks that carried fish for some of the bigger fish at the Fulton Street Market. He wasn't too bright but he was honest, so he made a decent living. When he died Little Luigi took over and proceeded to run the business into the ground. He cut wages for his drivers, upped his rates, and alienated just about everyone at the old market. When the market moved to the new venue, he refused to carry product there without what he called 'a piece of the action'—he wanted a percentage of the business's profits that he carried fish to. Tony says that not only is Little Luigi stupid, he makes up for it by being venal and dishonest. No way does this guy have enough business to justify his balance sheet."

"So they aren't a publicly traded company, then?" Joe asked.

"Nah, they're not big enough," Weasel said. "But they did borrow over three million dollars from the Chase Manhattan Bank against their property and assets, including the fine fish company at 207 South Street. Oddly enough, their loan was approved by someone named Darcy Fowler, who just happens to be…"

"Related to Chip Fowler, one of the roofing counterfeiters," Ed said.

"Right down the middle, first time," Weasel said, raising his arms in the "it's good!" signal from football. "She's his sister. She went to William and Mary, graduated with a degree in finance and has been a loan officer for Chase since 2010. Her record seems to be solid without being spectacular—she specializes in smaller businesses that are looking to get bigger in order to go public."

"Doesn't Chase have backups for this kind of thing? Don't they have to investigate the assets, assess the property, things like that? Remember, I'm a copper, not a finance geek," Sparky said.

"Yep, of course they do. It appears that the inspection of the property was done by a guy named Tim Servent, who just happens to be married to a womyn named Melissa Goren, whose sister is a womyn named Teresa Horne," Weasel said.

"She's married to Carl Horne," Bumble said.

"Give the man a cee-gar," Weasel said.

"In other words, this is a huge criminal conspiracy that involves not only counterfeiting, but also a fraud perpetrated against the largest commercial bank in the world," Captain Cork said.

"A-yuh," Jewey said.

"Shithouse mouse, this fucker is turning into a giant-sized case," Captain Cork said. "We need to get Financial Crimes involved, and also get the Director up to speed. How sure are we of this info?"

"Ten of 10—I got all of this off public records, plus I called a guy I know at Chase who says that this Darcy Fowler is sharp, but that she doesn't really exert herself like she could. She doesn't cut corners or fuck off, she just does the job and goes home, like she doesn't really need the money," Weasel said.

"And we all know that isn't normal for people in this type of position—it's *all* about the cash, because that's how you get up the ladder," Joe said.

"So all of these mutts got together and started this conspiracy to counterfeit, but what's the three million dollars for?" Gunny said. "Why take the risk?"

"They needed startup cash for their tools, their space and their stock," Ed said. "The paper they're passing is perfect, except for the Test—we already know that they must have a method that works since very few of these bills have been detected, even by people who handle money every day."

"They have a method to bleach ones and turn them into 10s and 20s," El Gato said.

"Sí," Jewey said. "It's the only thing that fits. They probably went to strip clubs, casinos, laundromats, even arcades, in order to change bills into ones so they could print up a bunch of funny money. It's simple, essentially foolproof and mostly idiot proof, too."

"And once they get going it's a self-perpetuating system, too," I said. "Once they start spending a few of the funny money bills they'll always have a way to procure more ones for the printing process, because of the change they get."

"I'm convinced that we need to pursue this, and fast," Charlie Chan said. "If these guys were feeding money to the roofing company in Toledo, they probably have some sort of timetable to follow, especially if the company in Toledo is feeding money back to the fish company to be washed."

"Concur," Captain Cork said. "But Boss, we need to keep this as quiet as possible, because these people are likely to have literally tons of cash at their disposal, funny money so good that it passes everything but the Test. They could send it out of the country on a ship and use some of it to just disappear and we'd never find them again."

"There's another problem with not keeping it quiet," Jewey said. He poked another button and put a different picture up on the screen. It was a bottle blonde in her forties who looked like she'd had a complete plastic surgery makeover, from huge fake boobs to a face that looked like it hadn't moved since the Carter Administration, and a short fat guy in his late sixties with a terrible comb-over and a doughy face that hid behind a cheesy mustache—he looked like a fat Super Mario brother. They were both decked out in beautiful clothes, and the lady was wearing about 75 pounds of diamonds, emeralds, and rubies in her earrings, necklace, brooches, and rings.

Shithouse mouse, indeed.

Everybody knew what the rocks meant; these people had portable wealth that they could legally take out of the country any time they wanted to, cash notwithstanding. Diamonds and other precious gems are the most portable, most easily exchanged currency in the world. They are relatively small, lightweight, easy to hide, and desirable from Auckland to Timbuktu, and everywhere in between. In many places in the world, they serve as *de facto* currency, and on the black market they are considered preferable to cash. After all, you can't counterfeit diamonds.

"This is Mrs. Leona Tromboli, Little Luigi's fifth wife, and the Super Mario look-alike is Little Luigi himself, at a fundraiser for the Republican candidate for governor of New York. She is wearing at least $2.5 million in stones, because a reporter asked about it and she said that was why her husband had hired bodyguards for the evening. Little Luigi also pointed out that he was personal friends with a designer from Friedman and Son Jewelers, a well-respected jeweler on Forty-Seventh Street in the diamond district, and also that he played golf with old Isadore Silverman, who happens to be the CEO of one of the biggest diamond importers in the country. They have an extensive showroom on Fifth Avenue," Jewey said.

"Ahh, shit," Joe and I said at once. "You owe me a Pepsi, Joe." He nodded, and Captain Cork said, "Ahh, shit, what?"

"If Little Luigi is in tight with diamond dealers in New York City, he has access to international networks and markets that allow him to ship stuff anywhere, as well as cash in stones virtually anywhere in the world. He can buy, sell, trade with impunity, and he won't have to do it at a discount," I said. "Instead of going through the black market at 40 cents on the dollar, he can simply sell his stones to someone in the network, probably for a profit, because Friedman and Son and Izzy Silverman don't deal in junk. These are first-class dealers in precious stones who enjoy worldwide reputations. Nobody in the business would even question you if these guys gave you *bona fides*."

"She's right," Joe said. "I'll bet you that Izzy Silverman has contacts in Antwerp, Tel Aviv, Johannesburg and Amsterdam that would buy up anything that you offered them just because he said to. If Little Luigi is in with him that means he has access to the Diamond Bourse on the Pelikaanstraat—the richest and largest gem market in the world. He could dump every diamond he's ever bought and it wouldn't even be a gnat bite on an elephant's ass."

"It's instant cash," Sparky said.

"Absolutely," Joe said. "That's why we need to get on this ASAP and keep it close to the vest. We can't afford to spook anybody in the funny money chain, because they'll all bolt with a suitcase full of untraceable loot."

"Concur," said Charlie Chan. "I'm going to the Director about this, but I think that we should be the point unit—we can keep it in-house in Chicago and only liaise with other offices when we need to. I also think that we need to interrogate the roofers and get intel on the Toledo operation so we can roll it up. Jerry, I'd like you to lead the interrogations."

"Boss, I'm gonna defer that to Agents Beemond, Silverberg and Glickstien," Captain Cork said.

"Why?" Charlie Chan said.

"Bumble used to work for the New York City Homicide Bureau, where he was considered the best interrogator in a unit filled with great interrogators. Jewey has a PhD in clinical psychology from UCLA and was a Psy Ops operator for the U.S. Army, and Freak—well, she is a former Spec Ops operator for the Marine Corps. She knows how to get intel out of subjects right quick, sir," Captain Cork said. "I'll supervise, but these guys are our best bet to get maximum information in the shortest period of time."

"OK, Jerry. Get going right now," Wong said.

So Bumble, Jewey and I went down to the Cook County jail, where four of the counterfeiters were currently housed in isolation. Carl Horne was still in the jail wing of Cook County General while his thumb healed. We decided on the way there that we were going to concentrate on Roy Linemann, because he appeared to be the weak intellectual link, as well as a vain man who had been semi-famous once. That type of person almost always has to boast to someone about his accomplishments. We worked out a complicated plan of attack that involved camaraderie building, a sneak attack from me, since he was psychologically vulnerable to a strong womyn and browbeating good-cop, bad-cop from Bumble and I if the first approaches didn't work.

It turned out to be all bullshit.

We got Roy into an interview room and he said, "I waive my right to an attorney. Whattya wanna know?"

"Uh, what?" Bumble said.

"Get me the form to sign—I want to waive my right to an attorney so that I can answer your questions," Roy said. So we got all the forms for his signature, made sure that the video camera and audio recorder were running and proceeded to interrogate him.

"Who's the boss of the outfit? Tommie Wilson?" Bumble asked.

Roy snorted and laughed and said, "Tommie? Tommie's not smart enough to pour piss out of a boot with directions printed on the heel. That motherfucker's the biggest stooge in history."

"He's listed as the CEO of Wilson Roofing, and that appears to be where the funny money is coming from," I said.

"Ya'll need to investigate further, because the only people dumber than Tommie Wilson are high school principals and Congress," Roy said. "Tommie just does what Darcy tells him to do—she fucks him once in a while to make sure he does what he's supposed to, but truth be told Tommie's a little bit afraid of her. Truth be told, we all are."

"Do you mean Darcy Fowler, the loan officer at Chase Bank in Manhattan?" Jewey said.

"Yeah, she's the mastermind of this whole thing," Roy said. "She's also one mean bitch—Chip gave her some shit one time and she beat the hell out of him. She knows some karate shit and he didn't have a chance. Whacked his nose outta shape and busted up his knee."

"Darcy Fowler is the mastermind of the counterfeiting ring?" Bumble said.

"Oh, yeah. She thought it up, got aholt of all of us and laid it out at a family wedding," Roy said. He smiled and said, "It sure has been a sweet gig—nobody even got a whiff of it until ya'll."

"How much funny money do you think that you've put into circulation?" Bumble said.

"At least $3 million, maybe $4 million," Roy said. "We been doin' it for a while, and we ain't the only crew."

"How many more crews?" Jewey said.

"Least three, but there could be one roamin' the wilds of California," Roy said. "Ol' Darcy's got a brother that lives in Long Beach, and they was tight when they was little. He owns a landscaping company, so he could do what we been doin' without any trouble."

"And how much counterfeit currency do you think is left to distribute?" I said.

Roy Linemann laughed until he about puked. He finally got himself under control and said, "Well, I'd say about a warehouse full. I don't know how much it is in dollars, but Darcy said she had a warehouse full of bills, includin' some test 50s. She also told me and Mark that it'd take 'bout 20 years to use it all up at the rate we was goin,' which meant that we'd be able to keep it up until most of us was ready to retire."

None of us showed a thing on our faces, but I was betting that comment was setting off a shit-storm outside the room. Roy said, "Ya'll are tryin' to keep a straight face, but I'll bet ya'll's assholes just slammed shut, because that is a shit-ton of cash. I'm tellin' ya, ol' Darcy is a fuckin' genius and ya ain't never gonna catch her. She's just too smart for ya'll." He looked so smug I wanted to smack his ass across the room, but I was saved from having to restrain myself when Jewey gave a soft laugh, rose from his seat to his full 6'8" and said, "Mr. Linemann, with what you just told me, and what you didn't tell me, I can put Ms. Fowler away for the rest of her life. But that isn't important, because she's not the mastermind of the scam."

"Yer wrong, big boy, ol' Darcy's the one that put us out there in the first place. She's the one done thought this up and made it happen," Roy said.

"Nah," Jewey said. "If she was the one who started it all she'd have never told a dumbshit like you about it, because she'd know eventually you or your dumbshit accomplices would get caught and sing like a canary, and she'd sure have found a bigger, better way to change the funny money than using dumbshit roofers washing cash in the thousands." Jewey just looked down on Roy, pity in his eyes, and then he said, "Don't feel bad about her lying to you, Roy. She's just doing what she has to do to protect the operation. I'm sure that Ol' Darcy's boss gave her the idea in order to insulate the real top dogs in case you got caught."

Roy looked all impassive and totally composed, but a look crossed his face. It was quick, but it was there, and we all noticed. I was going to prod him some more, but Bumble and Jewey both got even more still, so I stifled my impulse and did my best gargoyle routine. It worked.

"Ya'll better talk to Mark," Roy said. "He's married to my sister Enid, and he's a pretty smart feller. He thinks like ya'll, even tho' I ain't never seen no evidence that ol' Darcy ain't the head honcho. Mark said all along she was playin' us for fools, but the money was so good we just didn't worry 'bout it."

We all got up, reconfirmed that Roy had been advised against talking to us without an attorney, thanked him for his honesty and went out to talk to the rest of the team.

"We gotta take 'em all at once," Captain Cork said. "A dollar to a doughnut hole says this Fowler womyn has an escape plan, probably triggered by some signal we don't know, and another dollar to a doughnut hole says it's preceded by sending a whole lot of washed cash out of the country to some place like Lichtenstein, or another one of those goddamned countries with Byzantine banking laws, the fuckers." Captain Cork really didn't like banking secrecy laws, or the countries that promulgated them.

"Concur," Joe said. "We've gotta talk to Roberson, then we've gotta quietly arrest Wilson and the Toledo crew. In fact, we oughta take them the same time we take Fowler, so that there's no way to alert anyone else in the chain."

"Concur," Weasel said from his computer, "especially since I've been able to determine that the washed cash probably amounts to $35 million or so, and that's just in Chase accounts controlled by Fowler's computer. Remember, those are just the ones that I can see now—anything under another name is still hidden. If we tip her off in any way she's almost certain to have the money set to drain into other accounts overseas—the Caymans, Lichtenstein, even Switzerland—and even if we find it we won't be able to recover it."

"OK, so let's get set up to take everybody at once," Captain Cork said.

"Don't forget, we gotta take Little Luigi, preferably at his warehouse," Joe said.

"Yeah, we need to take his ass, too, because if there really is a warehouse full of cash, like Roy said, it's gonna be Little Luigi who has it," Guru said. "He's the only one who really has access to a warehouse, and let's face it, the fish business would be a perfect cover for it."

"Concur," Captain Cork said. He put his chin in his hand and thought for a minute, then said, "OK, tell me what you think of this. We let Jewey and Weasel keep digging on this end, and they coordinate the simultaneous operations, while Guru and I take the rest of the squad to New York to arrest Fowler and Little Luigi. We'll detail agents from the Detroit office to get the Toledo roofing company, but I want to take the real movers and shakers on our own."

"New York'll be pissed—you know they don't like other people on their turf," Guru said.

"Fuck 'em, the fucking glory-hounds," Captain Cork said. "We did all the work so that they can get all the glory? Not on my watch. We'll take some of their agents as backup, but we're going to make the arrests, period."

So that's how we came to be outside a warehouse on Fulton Street in New York City. Guru and Ed were at the Chase central bank with eight agents from the New York office to arrest Darcy Fowler. Bumble, El Gato, Sparky, Joe, Gunny, House, The Greek, Mac, and I were led by Captain Cork and backed up by two New York office agents whose names I didn't get, and, oh yeah, we had the NYPD's SWAT team on standby just in case.

According to our intel Little Luigi and his wife were in the warehouse with two of their fish company employees, and there were three trucks backed up to their loading docks, which meant that there were also three truck drivers in the warehouse, but those guys didn't really concern anybody. We were focused on Little Luigi, because after looking at his financials Jewey and Weasel were convinced that he was the mastermind—he had over $50 million stashed all over the NYC area in all sorts of accounts. The warehouse was in his name and he also owned a fleet of fish trucks, in addition to the property at the Fulton Street Stall Market.

Little Luigi was also friends with several bigwigs in and around the NYC area, including the newest mayor, who had received over $50,000 in campaign contributions from Little Luigi and his employees. We all knew where that money had come from—this warehouse in the Bronx—and so we figured there'd be a shitstorm when we actually completed the bust.

It didn't take that long.

We went in the building and immediately saw Little Luigi and his wife Leona, along with their two employees. We went in and Captain Cork walked right up to Little Luigi with the arrest warrant in his hand. Mac and Gunny were just behind and on either side of him, and the rest of us were spreading out across the warehouse when my phone rang. I looked at the caller ID and saw it was Weasel, so I dropped back near the front wall and answered it.

"Weasel, wha-" was all I got out before Weasel said, "Freak, watch Leona Tromboli! She's the granddaughter of Salvatore Bonnarino!"

"What?"

"Leona Tromboli is the granddaughter of Sally Bones, the head of the Bonnarino crime family! Jewey and I think that she's the mastermind of the funny money scam!" Weasel said, nearly screaming in panic.

I must have realized what was about to happen, because I dropped the phone and whipped one of my 1076s out, just as Captain Cork said, "Luigi Tromboli, I'm Agent in Charge Gerald T. Clune of the U.S. Secret Service, and I have a warrant for your arrest on federal counterfeiting charges."

It was a shitstorm of epic proportions.

Leona Tromboli stepped away from her husband as he reached under his coat for the butt of a pistol. Captain Cork rushed in and grabbed him in a bearhug so he couldn't draw the weapon and several things happened at once.

Leona pulled a very small weapon from her impressive décolletage and shot Mac in the back of the head from about three feet away, then ducked down behind a three-stack of loaded pallets.

The two employees ran into the alleyways between the pallets and immediately disappeared.

Several other shots rang out—two shotgun blasts lifted Gunny off his feet and knocked him backward. Three rifles opened up—my mind immediately classified them as AR-15s or M16s—and El Gato, Bumble, Sparky and the two New York guys took hits and went down. Three more shotgun blasts rang out and The Greek and House were down. Joe was trying for cover up under the pallets as the shotguns and rifles all targeted him.

It had all taken literally one second.

In the next second came a volley to finish people off. I saw Captain Cork trying to take Little Luigi to the floor when a rifle round hit him in the back. He let go and slid down and another round hit Little Luigi right in the face and blew the back of his head off. Other shots echoed through the warehouse, but most of them appeared to miss.

Nobody aimed at me. Later the forensic techs would determine that I was in the only blind spot in the warehouse, but at the time all it meant was that all those motherfuckers shooting were going to die.

I identified targets as I pulled my second 1076 and went off like the battleship *Iowa* delivering a broadside.

I drilled a guy with a shotgun trying to get at Joe through the right eye, nailed a rifle guy with a double-tap to the chest and took down two more shotgunners with head shots. The two employees who had run popped up with handguns and blazed away. I double tapped both in the chest and finished them with head shots. I ran right up and over Joe's head and onto the leading pallets, firing the rest of my rounds where I thought that the remaining rifles were, then dropped down and filled the 1076s with fresh clips.

The rifle on the right let fly on full auto—M16, I thought—so I spun left and looked up at the corner of the warehouse. There was another rifle there, about 150 feet away, so I barreled him up and shot three times—two in the chest and one in the head.

That left the one rifle shooter on my right, and I didn't waste any time. I just stood up, locked on him, and let fly ten shots.

I hit with every shot. He looked like a bloody bowl of shredded wheat as he slid toward the floor.

All the shooting had taken less than 15 seconds.

229

I yelled for Joe and he said, "Freak, keep your head down! I still have a shotgun loose in front of me!"

"Count 'em for me, Joe!" I said.

"Three shotguns and three rifles, plus the two handguns!" he said.

I stood up and yelled, "COME OUT AND PLAY, YA MOTHERFUCKER! I'LL SHOOT YOUR NUTS OFF!" When nothing happened, I said, "Joe, call in the SWAT guys to make sure we're secure, then call for busses—we got wounded!"

"Already on it!"

I walked back to where I'd seen Leona slither, my 1076s at the ready and prepared to shoot anything that was not us. As I neared Leona's hiding spot I heard her talking on the phone, which kicked my rage factor up by about 1,000 percent. I flew around the corner of the pallet she was behind and heard her say, "Grandpa, I think they're going to try and pin this one me. I—"

I tore the phone from her hand, knocked her down, stepped on her neck and screamed, "SALLY BONES YOU WORTHLESS PIECE OF SHIT COCKSUCKING ASSHOLE, I'M COMIN' FOR YOU NEXT! GO TO MASS YOU SLIMEBALL BUTTFUCKING GUINEA, BECAUSE YOU'RE GONNA BE MEETING ST. PETER SOON!"

I dropped the phone and kicked it over to the wall, reached down and hauled Leona to her feet and said, without any emotion at all, "Leona Tromboli, you are under arrest for counterfeiting, conspiracy to commit fraud and the murder of Secret Service agent Siobhan McKee. You have the right to remain silent. Anything you say can and will be used against you in a court of law. You have the right to an attorney. If you cannot afford an attorney, one will be provided at no expense to you. Do you understand these rights as I've read them to you?"

She looked at me with eyes that reminded me of a snake trying to mesmerize a bird and said, "I didn't murder anyone, and I have no idea about any counterfeiting." She smiled—it didn't reach her eyes—and looked at me with all the condescension and privilege she could muster.

I looked at the tiny derringer she'd shot Mac with. She looked down at it and said, "That's not mine—I saw the red-haired womyn drop it. I think that she was trying to plant it on m—urrggh!"

I jerked her right off the floor by her dress front and started shaking her. "DO YOU UNDERSTAND YOUR RIGHTS AS I READ THEM TO YOU?" I kept saying over and over. I became aware of the SWAT guys and Joe trying to stop me, but it wasn't until I saw the fear on her face and she pissed herself that I set her down—but I didn't let go of the front of her dress.

Joe said, "Leona Tromboli, you are under arrest for counterfeiting, conspiracy to commit fraud and the murder of Secret Service agent Siobhan McKee. You have the right to remain silent. Anything you say can and will be Used against you in a court of law. You have the right to an attorney. If you cannot afford an attorney, one will be provided at no expense to you. Do you understand these rights as I've read them to you?"

She started to try and speak and Joe said, in a very soft voice, "Be careful, Leona. I can't stop her from shaking you until your organs fly out of your body. Be wise, OK?"

Leona Tromboli looked at me and then said, "I-I-I...uhhh, er—I understand my rights and I'm invo-invo-invoking my r-r-r-right to an at-at-at-attorney." I let go of her dress as the SWAT guys handcuffed her and turned to survey the carnage.

There was no doubt that Mac was dead. There was a pool of blood under her red hair, and her eyes had that flat lifeless stare that I'd seen too many times before. Leona's derringer looked to be a tiny, one-shot job, which meant that it was a .22 or .25 caliber, which meant that the slug would still be inside Mac's head. She looked peaceful, probably because it looked like Leona had hit her in the medulla oblongata, which meant she was literally dead before she hit the ground.

Gunny was also obviously dead. His vest probably stopped most of the shotgun pellets from the first two shots, but a third blast had caught him right in the face. It was ugly to look at, but probably also nearly instantaneous. I did smile though—even though he was going down for the count and caught completely off-guard Gunny had drawn his service weapon and was trying to orient toward the enemy…a Marine to the end.

Sparky was dead, and The Greek was going to join her. Both had been hit in the head with rifle rounds, and The Greek had two more through his vest. He was breathing, but just barely, and the EMTs were ignoring him, which meant that their triage was over and they were trying to help everybody who had a chance. The two New York agents were also dead, both hit in the head with rifle fire.

House was trying to get to his feet, so I went over and said, "Stay down, big man. We got it under control." He was hit high in the chest with shotgun pellets, and had a through-and-through in the calf of his right leg. He looked up at me and said, "Motherfuckers ambushed us, Freak. Somebody fuckin' squealed, goddamnit! Motherfucker's gonna pay for this shit!" I squeezed his hand and said, "All but one of them are dead, House, and the other one is gonna ride the needle for it."

He smiled and said, "Mac?" I shook my head and he started to cry, so I left him and went over to El Gato. He was hit in the torso by rifle fire and had an ugly wound to his thigh. He was muttering as the EMTs got a line into his arm for blood expanders, finally saying clearly, "Got to get over to The Greek—he got hit more'n me…" I took his hand and squeezed it, and he squeezed back, but then passed out.

I turned to see Captain Cork looking at me. There wasn't a medic there yet, so I went over and said, "Don't get up, Captain. Help's on the way."

His sad Irish eyes bore into me and he said, "Couldn't get up if I wanted to—can't feel my legs. I really fucked this one up—no chance I'll ever be AIC of the Chicago office, and Assistant Director is just a distant memory."

I realized that even through the pain he was joking, so I said, "Yeah, you're probably right. Guru's just been waiting for you for slip up, and here you go handing her the perfect opportunity to slide past you. What a fuckup you are—pretty typical for an Irishman, though, ain't it?"

We both laughed a little bit and Captain Cork said, "How many?"

"Three of ours, plus the two New York guys, all of theirs except Leona. Joe and I weren't hit," I said.

"Who besides Mac?"

"Gunny and Sparky, probably The Greek. Everybody else looks like they should make it," I said. He squeezed my hand and then the EMTs pushed me out of the way to work on him. I stood up and saw Joe motioning to me from the door. I went over and we went outside into the sun.

We both smelled of cordite as we stood there in the pandemonium that surrounded the warehouse. Joe held out his hands and I took my 1076s out of their shoulder holsters, de-cocked them and handed them over. Joe said, "I've got to take possession of these as the senior agent left, but we both know that's just temporary—there has never been a more righteous shoot." He dropped the pistols in his jacket pockets and then gave me a big hug. We both broke down and cried for our lost teammates. When we finished Joe said, "Who tipped them off?"

"They had some kind of signal that was automatically tripped—maybe when we got the roofers, but probably the Fowler womyn sent something, maybe by phone. We didn't leak, Joe, it was just one of those things that no one could predict. Besides, Weasel got me just before all hell broke loose—Leona Tromboli is the granddaughter of Salvatore Bonnarino."

"Holy fuck-fuck—she's Sally Bones's granddaughter? Is this an OC thing, or is Leona just using her training to be a player?" Joe said.

"I'd say that she's just trying to keep up the family business, because no flags went up with OC when we enquired about the other mutts," I said. "Also, you notice that the riflemen iced Little Luigi right away? That means that Leona was the mastermind, and Little Luigi was the weak link. The guys ambushing us had orders to take him out because he was the stooge, which makes Leona the real bad guy."

"Concur. We got the three truck drivers in custody—they were all trying to get out during the shooting—let's go talk to them. Maybe they know something about the setup here," Joe said.

"OK, but don't forget we need to find the funny money—it's gotta be in this warehouse somewhere," I said.

Joe nodded and we went over to where the SWAT guys were holding the truck drivers. They all looked scared as hell—their eyes were wild and they were all shaking—which let Joe and I know right away they weren't part of the ambush team. These guys looked like scared truck drivers who weren't used to gunplay, much less actually shooting people.

Two of the truckers were Black men who told us it was their first run to this warehouse, or for Italia's Best Seafood Company. They were both supposed to go to the commercial train terminal at Grand Central Station. Their trucks were already loaded with ticketed loads to Toledo, Ohio and Phoenix, Arizona.

Bingo. The loads were going out for distribution through the roofing and landscape companies that were already washing the funny money.

But it was the third trucker, a Hispanic man, who was the real prize.

He looked at Joe and I and said, "My name is Arturo Orrieta. I am a U.S. citizen, but I originally came from Nicaragua, where I was a CPA. I am going to school nights at City College so that I can take the CPA exam here in America—I am only driving this truck until I can pass the exam and go to work for a big New York firm. I know this will happen, because I was a very good accountant in Managua working for an international exporting firm before I came to New York. My wife and I decided to move because we wanted our children to have the best education in the world, and therefore the best chance at success in later life."

Joe and I looked at him with our best basilisk stares, our eyes boring into his but our mouths as silent as the tomb, waiting with what psychologists call 'silent expectation,' letting the patient (or witness) offer more than they otherwise might.

Mr. Orrieta did not disappoint.

"This is my fifth trip to this warehouse, and something is very wrong here." He looked at us, but we didn't speak, so he said, "These people, especially the lady boss, are doing something illegal from this warehouse."

"How do you know that?" Joe asked, using his "arctic blast" Secret Service voice.

"Two reasons," Mr. Orrieta said. "First, my loads are too heavy. I am supposedly picking up fresh fish, but my loads weigh like frozen fish with lead in their bellies. Second, all of my loads are being sent to Managua, where I used to live and work. We have no need of fresh fish from New York in Managua—the city is right on Lake Managua, where fish teem, and also close to Lake Nicaragua and the Pacific Ocean, where Nicaraguan fisherman catch all the fish that the city can use. I have also noticed that many loads are returned from Managua to this company, although not all of them come to this warehouse."

Double bingo.

Joe said, "Mr. Orrieta, what do you suppose is going on here?"

The trucker slash CPA smiled and said, "I believe this company is what you call a laundry—they are washing cash from some illegal source, probably drugs, in order to legitimize it and make it so the owners can freely spend without suspicion falling on them."

Fuck bingo, we hit the lottery. Joe looked at me and nodded, and I said, "Thank you, sir. We are going to need to ask you some more questions, so could you please sit tight here? We'll be sending some people over for you." Mr. Orrieta nodded and sat back, a small, quiet man who had just helped solve a huge crime. The other truck drivers looked at each other, and finally one said, "I might be able to tell you some things about the guy who owns the company—Mr. Tromboli? My brother works for him over at the stall market."

The second guy said, "And my cousin works for Legal Seafood—you know the big restaurant in Paramus, at the mall north of Manhattan? They tried to deal with these guys, but there was some fuckup—uh, they couldn't get it together in order to supply the restaurant?"

Joe said, "You guys stay put and we'll send some Secret Service agents over. Until then don't talk to each other and don't try to leave, OK?" They all nodded and we went back to where the medics were treating our friends.

Mac's body was covered up, and so was Sparky's, but The Greek was still breathing, although it was visibly slower and the breath was rattling in his chest. Someone had covered him up to his neck with a sheet, so Joe went over, fussed with the sheet and said, "Greek, we got some gyros and twelve bottles of Stroh's. Soon's you sit up we're gonna have a party because Freak killed all of the bad guys except the ringleader, and she shook that evil bitch until she pissed herself. So you got a lot to look forward to, ya Peloponnesian son of a bitch."

The Greek opened his eyes and said in a clear, bantering tone, "Drink one for me, willya?" and he died. Joe and I both put our heads down for a moment, then we stood up to check out the rest of the team.

Most of them were gone, except for the bodies, and Bumble, who was actually sitting up while two EMTs were trying to get him to lay down. Joe and I went over and Bumble said, "Tell these guys to let me up—my vest got the shotgun pellets and the rifle shot's a through-and-through on my bicep.

I'm not in shock, and we need to talk, like now." Joe motioned to the EMTs, who backed off but didn't leave.

"What is it, Bumble?" Joe said.

The big man spoke in a very soft voice so only we could hear him. "There was one more guy—he ran back to the rear of the building and tried to get into the back wall. There's gotta be a door back there into where they keep the money. He fumbled around, couldn't get in and then pulled out a cell as he went for the rear exit. Somebody here has a key on them for the door, and we need to get it, now, before anybody else gets here."

"It's Leona. I'll bet that it's in her purse," I said. I stood up to go over and get the purse and Bumble said, "Stop, Freak. Our warrant only covers the warehouse, it doesn't cover her purse. If the keys are inside, they're not in plain sight, which means you got no right to them."

I stopped, because he was right. Having our search tossed because I was an aggressive asshole wouldn't help us any, and we needed to make this airtight if we were going to put everybody involved away for life. I thought of way to do it and started toward the purse again when Joe said, also in a very soft voice, "And there must be cameras somewhere in this warehouse, which means that if you kick the purse and it comes open that's the same thing as just opening it." He'd read my mind.

"But if a delirious agent who was trying to walk out of the ambush under his own power because he was a macho sumbitch fell on the purse and it came open then that would be another matter altogether," Bumble said.

Joe and I didn't say another word, we just went over to the EMTs and engaged them in conversation. "Our pal is really macho and he wants to try and walk out under his own power," Joe said.

"He's in shock—if he tries to stand up, he's probably gonna crash and burn," one of the EMTs said.

"We know that, but he's a Marine—you know how those semper fi motherfuckers are—and he needs to at least try," I said.

The second EMT said, "Well, he can try but he's just gonna fall over." At that very second Bumble said, "Oh, fuck me" as he crashed down to the floor after trying to stand.

"You mean like that?" Joe said.

"Looked like a big tree hitting the floor," I said.

"Hey Bumble, you get a 9.5 from the Jewish judge," Joe said.

"Fuck you, you raspy-voiced lounge singer. At least I made an effort, unlike all those other slacking sumbitches who just let these guys carry 'em out," Bumble said, just in case there was sound to go with the video. The EMTs hustled over to him and proceeded to get him on a gurney for transport. Bumble didn't argue, he just got this beatific smile on his face and started humming "Bye-Bye Blackbird" under his breath.

Joe and I both went over and took his hand for a moment. He squeezed and said, "Find the shit, guys. For the squad." We nodded and the EMTs hauled him off.

We turned and looked around like we were waiting for more Secret Service to show up—we were, actually, because the Agent in Charge of the New York office was on his way up, and with our AIC out of commission he would certainly be here ASAP—but what we were really looking for were Leona's keys.

And there they were, just sitting there in plain sight next to her open purse. Joe bent down, picked up the keys and said, "I wonder where all the funny money is, Freak?"

I said, "I don't know, Joe, but it's possible that there is a secret part of the warehouse that requires a key. Maybe the boss lady had it on her key ring?"

Joe said, "What a great thought, Freak. Let's see—Mercedes keyless entry fob, Chubb House key, small padlock key and—well I'll be! What have we here?" Joe held up a long key, almost like an old-fashioned door key, but with wards on the top and bottom.

I said, "Joe, the logical place for that key to fit would be on the back wall, there. Why don't we look for a hole that fits the key?" We sauntered back to the back wall and immediately saw the door and the keyhole. The door was about 10 feet wide and 12 feet high so that forklifts would fit through, and it had one of those big recessed rings that you had to pull up and yank on to open the latch. There was a big white sign with red lettering over the door that said, "KEEP DOOR CLOSED EXCEPT WHEN LOADING OUT. COLD STORAGE ROOM. NEVER PROP DOOR OPEN. AUTHARIZED PERSONEL ONLY."

"Not only are they counterfeiters and murderers, but those motherfuckers also can't spell," I said. Joe laughed and said, "That's how we catch 'em, Freak—the stupid assholes always fuck up somehow, and the smart guys move in."

We looked carefully at the door before we opened it, wary of any booby traps, but it was evident from the wear on the door that it was regularly used, so Joe turned the key in the lock and we yanked on the ring and the door came open. Cold air rushed out as we stepped through the plastic streamers that helped keep the cold air in when the door was open. We got inside the room, and we both just stopped.

"Motherfucking-A," Joe said. I was speechless, just staring at a mountain of cash that rose forty feet in the air. There was a pit dug down twenty feet in the cold room, and inside the pit was a stack of cash, baled and stacked on skids like hay in a barn. The stack was about 40 feet on a side, and it rose 20 feet above the pit, which meant that we were looking at a perfect 40 cubic feet of cash.

It didn't take long for the wonder to wear off, though. I noticed a big red button that said "SCRAM" next to the door. It was hooked to a timer that had five minutes programmed in, and the timer had wires that ran all over the warehouse. Some of them ran into the stack and some of them ran to tanks that were spaced along the sides of the pit. All of the tanks had several pipes leading into the pit, where they ended in a fan shaped attachment.

"Shithouse mouse!" I said. "They've got the cash booby-trapped! Don't touch anything, Joe!"

He had been moving closer to the cube of cash, but stopped and said, "It could be they have pressure plates somewhere to set it off, but I did want a look at the stuff on the outside of the cube. I think it's some kind of plastic explosive, but I'm sure the tanks are full of either kerosene or high-pressure natural gas."

"Ah, fuck! They got it wired for an FAE," I said.

"Of course. They know they can't burn all the cash—it doesn't burn that well, and the inside stacks wouldn't even be burned by a fire that burned for a day, but they could just vaporize everything within two miles—that'd cover their tracks, wouldn't it?" Joe said.

"Yeah, an FAE would leave nothing but a crater. Only a nuke would do more damage, and that would just be the radiation," I said.

FAEs—fuel-air explosives—are a fairly simple concept. You take pressurized gas and put it in a container that you can quickly vent, put the container in an enclosed space, vent it and then set off a priming charge, commonly called a squib. When the squib ignites the gas there is an explosion that under certain circumstances can imitate a nuclear detonation. (For a better, more technical explanation read Tom Clancy's *The Hunt for Red October*—he has it cold.) The tanks we were looking at would discharge their pressurized contents in two or three seconds, filling the airtight cold room with rapidly expanding gas, and then the squibs would ignite. The resulting explosion would be big enough to wipe out the entire warehouse, all the funny money and most everything else for at least a couple of thousand yards. Outside the immediate blast zone there would still be massive damage, but at least most of the earthworms would survive.

I said, "We need to leave and get the bomb squad, and now we know that Sally Bones is involved."

"Concur on both counts, Joe said. "Let's get the fuck outta here, nice and easy."

So we exited, much more gingerly than we entered. Joe immediately said, "Stop talking on your cell phones NOW! There is a booby-trapped room back here, and it's just possible it can be set off remotely by cell phone!"

Everybody dropped their cell phones, and most of them moved towards an exit.

"Good idea," Joe said. "Let's exit and see if we can get the bomb squad in to disarm this bitch." We all streamed out of the building, but as I was leaving, I saw Mac, Sparky, Gunny and The Greek still lying on the warehouse floor. I went over and got Sparky and laid her on top of Mac, put both of them on top of The Greek and stacked them all on top of Gunny. I silently asked them to forgive me for the indignity of piling them on top of one another, then stooped and picked up the four bodies in my arms and walked out of the warehouse through the open overhead door.

When I got to the loading dock everybody outside just stopped talking and stared at me. I walked down the ramp with my friends' bodies in my arms and went to the first open ambulance that I saw. An EMT there rolled a gurney out and popped it up. Three NYC firefighters came over and gently put Sparky's body on the gurney. Another gurney appeared and they repeated the process with Mac. When the third gurney appeared I gently laid The Greek on it, and did the same for Gunny. Two EMTs rolled each gurney to an ambulance. As they moved across the tarmac somebody said, "Ah-ten-HUT!" Everybody there came to attention and the same voice said, "Present, ARMS!" We all saluted, and the four ambulances slowly rolled away toward the road out, their lights going as they carried the fallen members of my squad away.

The ambulances had just cleared the parking lot when about 4000 cars came screaming toward us down the road. Guru and Ed jumped out of the first one and came running toward us. "Who?" Guru said. "Who?"

She and Ed skidded to a stop, and Joe said, "Mac, Sparky, Gunny, and the Greek are dead on our side, and everybody except Freak and I are wounded. Captain Cork is paralyzed below the waist, and El Gato is really bad—he's got at least four holes in him. Everybody else looks as if they'll make it." He stopped, and I said, "We found the funny money, but it's booby-trapped. We'll have to wait for the bomb squad." Ed and Guru didn't cry, but their faces were crumpled like old cigarette packs thrown in the gutter. "Freak shot all the bad guys except Leona Tromboli—she's the mastermind of the scam. She's also the granddaughter of Salvatore Bonnarino," Joe said. "Oh yeah, Freak literally shook the piss out of her."

Guru said, "How'd they get the drop on you?"

"It was an ambush. They were definitely waiting for us," I said.

"That *bitch*!" Ed said. "I'm gonna rip off her tits and stick 'em up her pussy! Then I'm gonna rip off her head and shit down her neck! I *knew* that computer key meant something!"

"Darcy Fowler saw us coming and hit a single key on her computer," Guru said. "She just smiled at us when we arrested her and said she wanted an attorney. We both thought it was odd behavior, but now it seems like she had a prearranged signal built into her computer—hit one key and it sounds the alarm."

"It probably also triggered a massive cascade failure in her computer," Joe said. "Good luck finding that information."

"She'll be fucked there—Jewey and the guys from Financial Crimes captured her computer early this morning and copied all of the information to our secure server," Guru said.

Then THE MAN arrived. His armored SUV rolled up and several young agents prostrated themselves so that his feet wouldn't touch the dirty pavement. He walked across their backs and then descended to the red carpet that had been rolled out for him (in case you didn't get it that's a joke—but it seemed that way at the time). He strode up to us as if we were supposed to genuflect and kiss his ring, but fuck it, I'm Jewish, so all I did was say, "Whattya want, Mac?"

He looked at me and said, "I want to be addressed properly, Agent Glickstien." His stare was supposed to intimidate me, but I don't play that game, so I said, "Well, people in hell want ice water, but they ain't gonna get it. Who the hell are you?"

He straightened up and said, "I'm Edward Otis Whitney, the Agent in Charge of the New York Secret Service office, and I don't appreciate your cavalier attitude, Agent Glickstien."

"I could give a shit Eddie—I don't appreciate watching four of my friends get killed, but that's what I had to do, and what I have to live with for the rest of my life. So if you'll forgive me I'm not going to genuflect, kiss your ass, or give a flying fuck what you do and don't like, yer worshipfulness."

Oops. Not supposed to talk to the brass that way, especially a guy who was the heir of the Otis elevator fortune and the great-grandson of the New York Whitneys (think museum) and was probably going to be the director of the Secret Service someday soon.

Hurricane Freak to weather control—there's a shitstorm of epic proportions coming to a warehouse parking lot near you.

Soon.

Like now.

CHAPTER 28

Shitstorm Fallout

Edward Otis Whitney, scion of wealth, privilege and power looked at me and said, "I understand, Agent Glickstien. You blame yourself for this incredible snafu and need to lash out—and I happen to be the best target right now. In situations like these—"

"Which you've never been in, which means you know nothing about it, which means that you should just shut up now, Eddie, because you're about to really piss me off, which would be really bad for you. Oh, and fuck you! I don't blame myself or any other agents for the 'situation,' I blame the goddamned criminals who undertook this scam. And it wasn't a snafu, it was an ambush that we couldn't have anticipated or stopped. So just go talk to the cameras and look good for your promotion while we mourn our dead, OK?"

Edward Otis Whitney was surrounded by other agents, and one of them started to leap to his defense when something really extraordinary happened.

"Stop, Agent Flynn. She's right," Edward Otis Whitney said. He nodded at me and turned to the squad with him. He ordered them to get the bomb squad in to disarm the booby-trap, told everybody to stay off the radio and cell phones until it was all clear, then walked up and through the overhead door to look at the scene, despite that fact that some of New York's Finest tried to tell him there was a big-assed fucking bomb in the building.

You could have knocked us all over with a feather.

At that point I really didn't give a flying fuck about some hot dog's sensibilities, AIC or not, and I really didn't care about getting fired, because I did blame myself—but I was never going to tell Edward Otis Whitney that. So when he walked away, we all looked at each other in absolute amazement, because very junior Secret Service agents did not talk to very senior Secret Service agents—especially Agents in Charge of their own offices—and not get killed, fired, or at least sent to East Bumfuck, North Dakota, which was the same thing as getting killed or fired, just without the dirt nap.

"I was going to get the AED to restart your heart after the big dog killed you dead, but apparently he didn't want any red meat today," Joe said.

"I was gonna give you my alpaca sweater, 'cause those winters in North Dakota are a real bitch unless you're properly equipped," Ed said.

"I'm gonna get your ass a Dale Carnegie course, Freak, 'cause you do not know how to win friends and influence people at all," Guru said. We all laughed at that, just because we needed some relief, and because Guru was right. I needed to lighten up and apologize when old Three Names came back out, or in all likelihood I was going on to private contractor work.

So when Edward Otis Whitney walked out the door and headed right for us, I had my little apology all prepared (thanks to Joe, Ed and Guru, who all gave me advice on it)…but I never got to use it.

"Who's got her gun?" he said.

"I do, sir—it's guns," Joe said.

"Give 'em back, right now," Edward Otis Whitney said.

"Pardon me, sir, but protocol is for an investigation into the shoot before an agent is released back to duty," Joe said.

"I just investigated—if that shoot wasn't righteous then Bob's yer uncle," Edward Otis Whitney said. Joe handed me my 1076s and I put new clips in, jacked rounds into the chamber, de-cocked the pistols and put them back into their shoulder holsters. Edward Otis Whitney watched me take care of my weapons and said, "Why didn't any other agents get any shots off, Agent Glickstien?"

"They were all taken down by the first volley except Agent Cocker. For what it's worth, Agent Rzepzynski had his weapon out and oriented toward the bad guys despite two shotgun blasts to the chest," I said. I said it in a deliberately dismissive tone, because I still didn't like or trust Old Three Names, mainly because I knew where he was going next.

He rounded on Joe and said, "You weren't hit, Agent Cocker, but you still failed to discharge your weapon. Why?" He was back to being a supercilious, condescending prick MOTU (master of the universe, for those of you who were trying to figure it out).

Joe said, "Sir, I went for cover and was pinned down by automatic rifle fire. I had no angle on any of the shooters and would have had to expose myself in a cross-fire in order to get to a position to do so. Also, I was covering the backside of the warehouse in support of Agent Glickstien, who was actively engaging the shooters." Despite just being called an incompetent agent by Old Three Names, Joe was remarkably calm.

"But you could have gone to the corner of the pallets up front and got an angle on at least one of the shooters. Why didn't you, Agent Cocker?" Edward Otis Whitney said, his face almost distorting into a nasty sneer. This was agent-speak for calling Joe a coward, hidden behind that massive wealth, privilege and power.

Joe said, "Sir, I didn't have time to do that. It was imperative that I maintain my position so that the shooters were aimed at me."

"Why? Why not at least pop up and take a look around before dropping back down? What kept you from doing that, Agent Cocker?" Old Three Names said in a tone that pleased his acolytes, who were obviously enjoying what they thought was Joe squirming.

"Because that's TV shit, Eddie," I said. "The guys with the rifles were trained on Joe's position, which meant that I had clear shots on them. He was the goat in the trap, and I was the shooter. If he'd popped his head up as soon as his hair cleared the pallet in front of him the shooters would've launched a three round burst and he'd have been splattered—they'd've blown his head off."

"But why were you the shooter instead of the senior agent who was unhit?" Edward Otis Whitney said.

"Because I'm the best pistol shot in the world, bar none, and Agent Cocker isn't. Even if he'd gone to the corner, he couldn't have made the shot on the rifle shooter in the corner. Sorry Joe, but you know you couldn't have hit him," I said.

"Agent Glickstien is correct, AIC Whitney. The shooter was over one hundred feet from me with an M16. It would have taken dumb luck for me to've hit him, and even then I'd probably've been hit," Joe said. "I also couldn't've fired after the first two seconds, because Agent Glickstien went over the top in front of me and engaged all the other targets."

"Why weren't you hit when you went over the top if the shooters were already aiming at that point? Shouldn't you have been 'splattered,' as you so colorfully put it?" Edward Otis Whitney said.

"No, because the shooters were looking for someone to pop up, not transit the area from the top down, and especially not to fire off multiple rounds and then be gone. The reason I got the shooter on the left was because he immediately reacted to my transit by firing an entire magazine on full auto at Agent Cocker's position, not mine. When I heard his M16 click empty I stood up and took the shot, which induced two shotgunners to get bold and try to attack Agent Cocker's position. They also got dead because of their boldness, as did the two shooters with handguns," I said, my insolence clearly a big 'fuck you' to the head of the New York office.

Edward Otis Whitney said, "Your arrogance surprises me, Agent Glickstien. After all, there are three agents dead and three others wounded and you are standing here proclaiming yourself the 'greatest pistol shot in the world, bar none'? If that were the case wouldn't everybody be alive and unhurt?"

I was instantly cold as ice with a fiery rage that would consume worlds. I had just been called incompetent, arrogant and a braggart, and I was not going to tolerate it. I slowed my breathing, looked at Joe and smiled. He reached in his pocket, took out a quarter and showed it to me, then wound up like a baseball player, ran three steps toward the empty part of the parking lot and heaved the quarter up and out into the clear New York air.

I smoothly drew the 1076 under my right armpit, cockedaimedfired and watched as the shiny quarter blew apart from the impact of the 165-grain Cor-Bon jacketed hollow point. I de-cocked the 1076 and stored it back in its holster. I turned to the group around Edward Otis Whitney. They were all gaping like dead fish. I said, "Fuck you, Eddie. I'm done playing. If we had any warning about the connection to organized crime, or if the Fowler womyn hadn't sent an emergency signal, nobody would be dead, except any bad guy who tried to take us down. Because I respect your rank, I'll let you calling Joe an incompetent coward and me an incompetent braggart go this time, but if you ever talk to me like that again, I'm goin' to federal prison and you're goin' to the morgue. You grok me, Eddie?" I hadn't raised my voice, but everybody who heard me moved back a step, except Joe, who prepared to tackle me if I came completely unglued.

Edward Otis Whitney slowly nodded, then said, "I apologize for it all, Agent Glickstien. I... well, sometimes I play a role and forget where I came from and how much I don't know. Agent Cocker, I totally understand the situation now, and I apologize for questioning your courage or tactical handling off the situation."

"Just doing your job, sir, but she killed five of them in less than two seconds, and two more in the five seconds after that. I've never seen anything like it, sir, not even in a video game," Joe said.

"You shot a quarter out of the air," one of Edward Otis Whitney's guys said. "You shot it out of the air."

"And that's my nondominant hand," I said. "I don't say shit that I can't back up, Eddie."

He nodded and said, "OK, the tactical situation was such that we only had one agent engage, but our second agent safeguarded her so she could shoot. We need to move forward with the investigation, specifically with the connection between this scam and OC, and especially between the counterfeiters and Salvatore Bonnarino."

"Sir, I believe that our computer geeks in Chicago have already made a connection," Guru said, looking up from a text on her secure phone. "Can I put this on speaker?" Old Three Names nodded and Guru said, "Jewey, Weasel, you have us and the entire New York office, including AIC Whitney."

Jewey identified himself and said, "Agent Singh, Agent in Charge Whitney, we have conclusive proof that the counterfeiting scheme operating out of Italia's Quality Seafood is definitely connected to organized crime, and specifically to Salvatore Bonnarino. We have multiple points of contact, and Mr. Bonnarino is definitely profiting from the scheme."

"Agent Silverberg, how confident are you in your evidence?" Edward Otis Whitney said.

"Sir, we've conferenced in the FBI's Organized Crime unit to back us up," Jewey said.

"Ed, this is Assistant Director Antonio Escalante—we met at the anti-terrorist thing last year?" a voice said.

"Yes, sir, I remember. Your son plays *futbol* for Columbia," Edward Otis Whitney said.

"I'm glad you remember. The information developed by Agents Silverberg and Wei is 100% accurate as far as the Bureau is concerned. Our guys are saying that we have the key to Bonnarino's whole operation, once we start sorting it out. I was just going to start the process for warrants when you called," Escalante said.

"Is it possible that we can get in on the arrest? My people have worked really hard on this and I'd like to let them have the satisfaction of actually being there when we arrest him," Edward Otis Whitney said.

Esperanza laughed and said, "Ed, I was going to have them draw up warrants for you—although I wouldn't mind having some Bureau observers there when it happens."

"Approved," said a third voice. "Ed, this is Director Hessler. Agent Wei contacted the home office, and I wanted in on the conference call. We're going to go in full force and arrest everybody, including the family dog. The FBI is going to loan us an HRT, and NYPD is sending their SWAT guys with us. I want you to arrest Sally Bones's ass in full view of the press I'll be calling right after you tell me you're in position." By all accounts, Siri Hessler was no one to trifle with. She was about five feet nothing but had the personality of a grizzly bear and the intelligence of Stephen Hawking. Our nickname for her was "Nails," as in "tough as nails." It was readily apparent why she was the Secret Service director. We were going to get the credit, and the good publicity that went with it, as well as taking one of the few remaining OC figures left in New York City off the streets, which would probably amount to greater funding in the near future. Hey, nobody likes the politics, but get real: the only way to take care of the troops was to have access to a bigger budget, and Director Hessler wasn't shy about bellying up to the trough, which was why she was director, and I shot bad guys. (You've already seen my political "prowess.")

"Should we wait for the warrants, Director?" Edward Otis Whitney said.

"No, Ed. Go arrest that son of a bitch and drag his ass down to the Tombs. Make sure he gets a nice runaround so that he doesn't just walk out an hour later," Director Hessler said.

"I may have to move him to the Staten Island holding facility if I can't guarantee his safety at the Tombs," Edward Otis Whitney said with an absolutely straight face.

"That's unfortunate, but Mr. Bonnarino is a top suspect in the death of three agents, and also the apparent mastermind of a huge counterfeiting scheme that defrauds the American public. Ordinary citizens deserve their day in court on this. You do what you have to in order to make that happen," Director Hessler said.

"Understood, Director. I will confirm with you when Mr. Bonnarino is in custody. Whitney out."

Guru shut the phone down and looked at Edward Otis Whitney, who said, "Agent Singh, I would appreciate it if you and your remaining agents would accompany me to arrest Mr. Salvatore Bonnarino for murder and counterfeiting, assuming that suits you."

Guru said, "Sir, we would be pleased to do so. Shall we wear vests, sir?"

"Bet your ass," Edward Otis Whitney said. "We're going to pretend that Sally Bones is a wounded Cape Buffalo about to charge us." He turned to one of his aides and said, "Where is he?"

"At lunch, sir. The FBI has him at L'Artusi, sir, on the West Side," the aide said.

"So let's go to 228 West Tenth Avenue and see our friend Mr. Bonnarino. He may be a criminal, but he's got good taste. L'Artusi is a very fine dining establishment," Edward Otis Whitney said. "I'll bet he's taken a table downstairs, where it's noisier, makes it harder for the FBI to eavesdrop on his conversations." Everybody laughed, because the idea that somehow any decent intelligence agency couldn't bug your conversations because of ambient noise was, well, laughable. The idea of privacy had gone out the window after 9/11, and with recent technological developments…well, I could tell you, but I'd have to kill you (not kidding—classified).

We all went to get in cars, and Edward Otis Whitney said, "Chicago unit, please ride with me," so we all got into his Suburban and sped off. Old Three Names waited until we were on the surface roads before he said, "You know that I'm looking to be the next director of the protective detail, right?"

I didn't know it, but apparently, everybody else did, because they all nodded. Guru said, "You and Andy Tolbert. He's got the edge because of his experience. He was chief of the VP's detail, plus he worked security with the U.S. Marshals."

Edward Otis Whitney laughed and said, "Well, the Chicago office doesn't hold back, does it? You're right, Agent Singh, but you're wrong. Andy is going to be the next assistant secretary for Homeland Security, and I'm going to move up to the protective division chair after Jerilynn Nelson retires. There's no hurry, but I just wanted you to know that you all have places in the protective detail if you want them. I like people who get the job done and speak the truth, although sometimes I act like an asshole because of the constant role-playing I'm forced to do in this job." He looked at all of us, and Guru said, "Thank you, sir, but I'm a counterfeiter catcher for life. I only qualify with the pistol because I have to, and I'm too old to want to cowboy up and play games."

"Sorry, sir, but I'm with Agent Singh. I like the intellectual contest with counterfeiters, and I like the pursuit of funny money pushers. I'm also an old dog, and I don't want to learn any new tricks, but I do appreciate the offer," Joe said.

Ed said, "AIC Whitney, I may take you up on your offer, on one condition."

"What's that?"

"I want to work with her," Ed said, nodding in my direction.

"What about it, Agent Glickstien? Think that you could work for me?"

I smiled sweetly and said, "Well, Eddie, if you can avoid being a pompous asshole with serious shithead tendencies." The car was really still for a nanosecond, and then Edward Otis Whitney bellowed with laughter. We all laughed, even his driver, and when we were done, the future director of the protective detail said, "I grok you, Agent Glickstien, loud and clear."

"Good. We just need to make some things crystal clear, like I shoot, you plan. You make strategy, but you don't ever try to tell me about tactics, because let's face it, Eddie, you're not the next big thing in field operatives, and I'm never going to be briefing the president of the United States. I'm too ugly for the one, and you're too much of an Ivy League twit for the other."

"A perfectly accurate sketch of my character and our differing abilities, Agent Glickstien," Edward Otis Whitney said.

"Sir, you've gotta quit calling her that," Ed said. "She's the Freak, without any doubt at all. Even Agent in Charge Wong calls her that, sir."

"Francis Wong will be moving up too—he's the perfect assistant director for me because he does have so much field experience. Is it the shooting? Is that why they call you Freak?" Edward Otis Whitney said.

"Gimme a quarter," I said. Seeing the look of alarm on his face—the driver about jerked the car off the road, too—I said, "C'mon, ya maroons! I'm not gonna fire off a pistol in an armored car. Just give me the quarter."

The driver pulled a quarter out of his pocket and handed it back to me. I put it between my thumb and forefinger and squeezed it in half, then put it in my other hand and squeezed it in half again. I handed the folded-up coin back to the driver and said, "Thanks, man."

Edward Otis Whitney said, "Dalton, could you do that?" to his driver, a muscular guy whose name was Dalton DeBoer. Agent DeBoer shook his head and said, "Sir, that ain't human. My uncle Dale was the strongest guy I ever saw, and he couldn't've done that. She's a freak, begging your pardon, Freak."

"No offense taken, Agent DeBoer. It's just the truth. I can also outrun anybody in the Service, unless Usain Bolt has joined up," I said.

"You'll make the perfect protective agent," Edward Otis Whitney said. "I don't give a damn if you call me Eddie, or Asshole, or Numbnuts—you've got to come work for me when I go up."

"Deal, if I get to arrest Sally Bones," I said.

"Just remember that he has to really resist before you get to tear his arms off," Joe said.

"And you can't beat up his gorillas just because you don't like their cologne," Ed said.

"And absolutely no shooting him unless he actually pulls a gun, and then you should shoot him in the nuts," Guru said.

"Which one, right or left?" I said.

"Oh, definitely the left," they all said at once, laughing along with DeBoer and Edward Otis Whitney.

"You guys owe me a Pepsi," I said. "Now, let's go arrest the bad guy."

We got to the restaurant and got out of the car on the sidewalk. There was a SWAT van on the corner, and the FBI's HRT guys were also waiting. Edward Otis Whitney had them deploy outside the restaurant, with some of the HRT team inside the vestibule of L'Artusi in case they were needed.

We went right in, with Edward Otis Whitney leading 24 Secret Service agents. The SWAT guys came right behind us, wearing all black and carrying their M4 rifles at the ready. We stopped at the host's stand, and Edward Otis Whitney asked about Sally Bones. The host responded by pointing in the right direction, and we streamed into the dining area with pistols drawn. The diners all reacted by shying away from us, or gasping, or generally looking concerned, but we didn't stop for them—we headed for the only table where there wasn't any reaction to our presence.

We walked up to the table. There were eight goombahs around it, and I walked right up to Sally Bones himself, a tall lean man with a big Roman nose and thick black hair. He looked up at me with his jet-black lizard's eyes, then contemptuously said, "They send an ugly cunt to arrest me? I don't think I feel like getting arrested by anybody today, especially an ugly, fat FBI cunt with shitty hair."

I smiled and said, "Well, you're in luck, Mr. Bonnarino, because I'm a fat, ugly, bad-haired Secret Service cunt. Please stand up, sir."

He smiled a lazy crocodile smile and said, "And if I don't?"

I snatched him out of the chair so fast it looked like a magician's trick. One minute he was slouched back in his plush chair, and the next he was on his feet, with one hand behind his back.

"No problem," I said. "I like helping the elderly. Salvatore Bonnarino, you are under arrest for the murder of Secret Service agents Siobhan McKee, Carly Cronenwett, Nolan Laskarides, and Stanley Rzepzynski, for counterfeiting, for conspiracy to commit fraud, and for racketeering under the Racketeer Influenced and Corrupt Organizations Act. You have the right to remain silent. Anything you say can and will be used against you in court. You have the right to an attorney. If you cannot afford an attorney, one will be provided at no expense to you. Do you understand these rights as I have read them to you?"

I had the cuffs on (too tight) and had spun him around to face me and the gang of agents. I had my hands on his forearms as they snaked around his back, so when he reared back to spit on me, I just lifted him off the ground. His spittle went over my head and hit Edward Otis Whitney right in the face. I looked back at Sally Bones and I said, "Mr. Bonnarino, we will be adding assaulting a federal officer to your charges, but I must ask you again if you understand your rights as I've read them to you, sir." I was still holding him off the ground, and I could see the surprise in his eyes at the power in my hands and arms. He finally nodded and I said, "Sir, if you could verbally confirm that you understand your rights it would be helpful."

"I understand my rights," Sally Bones said, trying to kill me with an evil look. He said to one of his henchmen, "Call Corsetti and tell him to meet me at the Tombs. I don't want to be in that dump any longer than I need to be. Call my wife and tell her that we will still be going to the opera tonight." Sally Bones had stones, I'll give him that, but his stare wasn't working on me, which baffled him.

We were waiting for Edward Otis Whitney to wipe off his face—Ed told me later that the smile never left his face, that he just reached into his pocket, pulled out a hankie, wiped off and dropped the silk square on the floor—when I felt other eyes on me. I looked around the table and saw a compact, neatly groomed and dressed man with hair parted down the middle and an old-fashioned haircut looking at me, his face set in a gentle smile. 'Shooter,' I said in my head. He nodded at me and said, "You're the broad told Mr. Bonnarino that you was comin' for him next."

"Yeah," I said.

"You used some un-ladylike and discourteous language," he said.

"Yeah," I said.

"You shouldn'ta oughta done that," he said.

"Yeah?" I said.

"I'll be seeing you, maybe we can talk about it," he said.

"I'd say you should fuhgeddaboutit, but that's probably too central casting," I said.

"Say what?" he said.

"It ain't gonna happen," I said.

"Yeah?" he said. "Why's that?"

"You and I meet there's probably gonna be very little talking," I said.

"Ooh, you talkin' 'bout a date?" he said, his little smile a bit wider.

"No," I said, "an ending. For you."

His eyes narrowed and the smile disappeared. He said, "Paul Monteverdi, Agent Foulmouth. I'll be seein' ya." He was supposed to be menacing, but it was so New York, so La Cosa Nostra, that I couldn't restrain myself. "Not if I see you first, Mr. Green Mountain. Enjoy the rest of your lunch."

He nodded at me, but the look was clear: he and I were going to have a go at it if we ever met. I couldn't wait, because I was thinking of my dead friends, but I also realized that it was prudent to alert everybody to the threat at the first opportunity, because I was good, not immortal, and Paul Monteverdi looked like he knew something about shooting people.

We went out of the restaurant and there were lots of TV trucks outside, with reporters and cameramen waiting. We stuffed Sally Bones in a Suburban and Edward Otis Whitney gave instructions to Agent DeBoer, who jumped in the vehicle and sped off with two other SUVs taking up positions fore and aft of the vehicle with Sally Bones in it. The AIC turned back to the waiting reporters and motioned us to come and stand around him.

The impromptu press conference started with a question from the bottle blonde reporter from WNYW, Fox 5.

"Agent in Charge Whitney, why has the FBI come in force to L'Artusi restaurant today?"

"Shelly, the U.S. Secret Service has today arrested Salvatore Bonnarino on a variety of charges, including capital murder and counterfeiting. We were able to connect Mr. Bonnarino to a massive counterfeiting ring, and when the Secret Service went to arrest Mr. Bonnarino's associates they opened fire, killing six Secret Service agents and wounding several others."

"Agent in Charge Whitney, how did you discover the counterfeiting and its connection to organized crime?" the red-haired reporter from CBS 2 said.

"Through the diligence of our Chicago office," Edward Otis Whitney said, looking as if he'd been born in front of the cameras.

"Could you elaborate on that?" the young, good-looking, gay reporter from ABC 7 said.

"Only to the extent that this operation originated in Chicago, and that our agents, led by their section AIC Gerald Clune, came to New York to effect the arrest of Mr. Bonnarino's associates, with assistance from the Ney York office. AIC Clune was wounded, as were several of his fellow agents, when the Bonnarino thugs ambushed them. I can also confirm that six agents are dead, but will not be releasing their names until their families have been notified."

A slick dude with a hipster's sideburns and three-toned sunglasses said, "Eric Fortner, *New York Post*. How did the Bonnarino shooters get the drop on a team of Secret Service agents? That sounds like they weren't fully prepared to take down an OC operation." His sneer hung in the air like week old garbage, right up until Old Three Names unloaded a batch of industrial strength Febreeze.

"That would be an absolute mischaracterization of what actually happened. Our team moved in on what was thought to be the ringleader of the counterfeiting operation, a small-time operator named Luigi Tromboli, just as other agents developed the intelligence that the operation was actually tied to the Bonnarino crime family. An associate of Mr. Tromboli was also arrested at this time, but managed to send an emergency signal to the Bonnarino thugs who were in cahoots with Mr. Tromboli. This is the only reason that the Secret Service team was ambushed—bad timing for us, and good timing for the bad guys." His tone left no doubt about it—we had done good, but had been victimized by bad luck.

The *Post* reporter tried one more time. "But why did Tromboli's associate have time to send any signal? Doesn't that mean that the agents arresting him were slow, or that they were incompetent?" Once again the shit was flying in our direction, splashing all over our reputation and effort.

Edward Otis Whitney looked at the reporter with a smile and said, "Mr. Fortner, how far away from me are you?"

"About…maybe 10, 12 feet?" the reporter said.

"Would you do me a favor and come toward me as fast as you can? If we could just clear a path for Mr. Fortner, please?" Old Three Names said. Everybody moved out of the way and Edward Otis Whitney said, "Just rush me as fast as you can, Mr. Fortner, and try to touch my arm. Ready? Please proceed."

The reporter was game—stupid, but a trier—and he rushed Old Three Names at top speed. The New York AIC calmly took his phone out, hit one button and put the phone back before the reporter could touch him. The *Post* guy stopped before he touched Old Three Names, his face red with exertion and embarrassment.

Edward Otis Whitney smiled even broader and said, "Mr. Fortner, I just alerted my wife that I would be home late this evening, and that she would have to pick our son up from wrestling practice, and that I would like her to cancel our opera tickets—all with the push of one button. You see, in today's world it is almost impossible to sneak up on anyone and achieve tactical surprise before they can at least hit a button on their phone or computer to trigger a pre-arranged signal.

"It is also impossible to believe that one of the largest counterfeiting operations in United States history would fail to take these elementary precautions, or that they would fail to have several tripwires safeguarding their operation. I think that we should focus on the fact that we penetrated an organized crime operation, took down the counterfeiters—and by the way, Secret Service agents killed all but one of the ambushers, despite their use of shotguns and automatic weapons against Service pistols—and helped to safeguard the currency in the hands of ordinary citizens, rather than trying to assign blame for what went wrong. This was a first-class operation that was an unqualified success, despite the tragic loss of six of our agents."

Take that, you "gotcha" REMFs.

The on-air reporter for WNBC, 4 New York, said, "AIC Whitney, how much counterfeit money was seized?"

"Preliminary estimates are that we seized $900 million in counterfeit 10s, 20s and 50s," Old Three Names said, acting as nonchalant as if he were quoting Keats.

There was an audible gasp from the reporters, and all of them started shouting at once. Edward Otis Whitney finally pointed at the 4 New York guy, who said, "Uh, do you mean this operation today seized almost a billion dollars?"

"Why, yes, I believe I do," Old Three Names said.

Things got considerably friendlier for the Secret Service after that.

The press conference ended and one of Edward Otis Whitney's aides came up with a phone for him. He listened for a moment and his patrician face opened up in a great big smile. He said, "Understood, Director. We will do so immediately. Thank you." He hung up and said, "Agent Singh, how would you and your team like to assist in arresting all of Sally Bones's associates still in the restaurant?"

"We will assist you in any way we can, sir," Guru said. "Of course we are honored that you would want us to assist." She was being formal because of the reporters still in the area, but you could see the glee on her face.

Old Three Names looked at me and said, "We have confirmation that all of the individuals in the restaurant were involved with the counterfeiting scam. Monteverde was in charge of security and ordered the men to the warehouse for protection. The womyn taken into custody, Darcy Fowler, is singing like the proverbial canary. She has laid out the entire operation in what she believes is an immunity deal, and an FBI wiretap recording confirms her story."

"'What she believes is an immunity deal'?" Joe said. Edward Otis Whitney laughed and said, "While she was waiting to be interrogated Ms. Fowler asked to talk to the "person in charge." She was being watched by two NYPD detectives, so the senior one entered the interrogation room and Ms. Fowler made an offer of cooperation in exchange for immunity from prosecution. The lead detective realized what was happening and brought a NYC prosecutor into the room. Ms. Fowler repeated her offer and the prosecutor accepted. The paperwork was all done, Ms. Fowler was appointed an attorney—a public defender who apparently was unaware of the details of the case, and who advised her to take the immunity—and she is still providing details of the entire operation."

"But that's just immunity for the state crimes—this is a federal case and governed by federal counterfeiting statutes," Ed said.

"Unfortunately no federal prosecutors or agents were present at the time—so no deal was struck with federal authorities," Old Three Names said, with a smile on his face that would have lit up Times Square.

"And she waived her rights with an attorney present? Oh. My. God." Joe said. "It's all legal—she's confessing to life in prison for counterfeiting, accessory to murder, assault with intent on federal officers… Oh. My. God."

We all looked at each other and burst out laughing at the stupidity of even "smart" criminals. Finally Ed said, "The Greek would've loved this—it would have appealed to his Greek sense of irony."

"And Gunny would've loved it because all the shitbags are going to do really hard time, preferably at Marion Maximum Security," Joe said, referring to one of the toughest federal prisons in the U.S., located at Marion, Illinois.

"And Sparky would've loved it because some silly douchebag thought she could outsmart the Chicago Outfit," Guru said. "She would've said we had better Jews and Asians than the greaseballs."

We all laughed again, and Old Three Names said, "Let's go get those shitheads before they're done with their cannoli." The NYPD SWAT guys followed us in again, and we went back to the same table where all the goombahs were. They were all on their phones and didn't stop talking when we approached. I walked right up to Monteverde and said, "Time to say goodbye, Paulie. You got an appointment." He smirked at me, so I reached out and took the phone from him, said, "He'll call you back" and tossed the phone to Ed, who shut it off.

Monteverde surged to his feet, his hand darting under his coat for the pistol at his hip. I hit him with a knife strike to the solar plexus that took his breath away, right before I used a hammer hand to break his right collarbone. He dropped back in the chair like he'd been shot, completely out of breath and in incredible pain (broken collarbones are a bitch—can't lift your arm and the nerves up there just go crazy—it makes you sick to your stomach, it hurts so bad. I know from personal experience—can't tell you why—classified).

I stepped behind him, pulled out my second set of cuffs, yanked his good arm behind him and said, "Paul Monteverde, you are under arrest for counterfeiting, conspiracy to commit murder, accessory to murder, violation of the federal RICO statute, and anything else that pertains to the counterfeiting scheme run by Salvatore Bonnarino and others. You have the right to remain silent. Anything you say can and will be used against you in court. You have the right to an attorney. If you cannot afford an attorney, one will be provided to you at no cost. Do you understand these rights as I have read them to you?"

Monteverde was a tough goombah. He gritted his teeth against the pain and said, "I unnerstan' my rights. I wan' my lawyer."

I smiled at him and said, "No problem sir." Then I jerked his right arm behind his back and locked the cuffs, at which point Mr. Monteverde fainted as the broken bones from his collarbone slid across each other.

"Oh, dear," I said, "Mr. Monteverde appears to have fainted. Perhaps we should call an ambulance for him." I let go of his wrists and he rolled straight down until his face was resting on the table. He had a soft landing, because a bowl of spumoni was right there to catch him. I made sure his airway was clear and said, "Who's next on the resisting arrest parade?"

Everybody stood up and put their hands behind their backs without even being asked.

We arrested their goombah asses, read them their rights and sent them off to the Tombs for processing. An ambulance took Paul Monteverde to Bellevue Hospital so he could spend some quality time in their locked ward. We watched them all go and Old Three Names said, "Oh, my. I knew I was forgetting something."

He turned to his aide and said, "Samuel, where did we send Sally Bones?"

"We sent him to the Tombs, sir, but the shift commander there said he couldn't guarantee Mr. Bonnarino's safety, so he was transported to the Staten Island holding facility."

"And has he arrived yet?"

"Yes, sir, but it appears as if Staten Island is full, so he will be moved to the holding facility in Hoboken, New Jersey, which has a brand-new wing that is as yet unoccupied by other prisoners," the aide said with a straight face.

"Since this is a federal crime, I believe he should be in a federal facility," Old Three Names said.

"Well, we could take him to the federal detention center in Buffalo," the aide said. "They have ICE detention there, but also some high-level individual cells for high value targets."

"I believe that we must consider Mr. Bonnarino a high value target, especially with his OC connections. For all we know he may be in this venture with other underworld figures, who may wish to harm him in case he tries to rat them out, don't you think?" Edward Otis Whitney said.

"Absolutely, sir," the aide said.

"I concur completely, sir," Guru said.

"Better safe than sorry," Joe said. "La Cosa Nostra has a long reach. We might want to check him in under an assumed name, just in case."

"And we might want to hit him with a FISA warrant, in case he's tied to world-wide terrorism," Ed said. "If he's sent money to the Caymans, or Luxemburg, or Lichtenstein he could be tied to al-Qaeda, or ISIL."

"Only too true," I said. "We may have theoretically fought those guys in a couple of places—we wouldn't want to let a known OC criminal send aid and comfort to the enemy. I concur with Joe—better safe than sorry."

"Well, that is settled then," Old Three Names said. "Once he gets to Hoboken, we should notify his lawyer that he's there, and then we should send him on to Buffalo under a FISA warrant, just for his own personal safety."

"Shall we drive him there, sir?" the aide said.

"Of course, Samuel. Let's see if the Hoboken police will loan us one of their paddy wagons, and we'll send an FBI and Secret Service agent along with him. In a separate car, of course—I think Mr. Bonnarino can ride by himself in the back, don't you?" Old Three Names said.

"Oh, yes sir," the aide said. "I would be glad to volunteer to ride along with Mr. Bonnarino and make sure he is properly housed."

"Good, and thank you, Samuel. Please make all that happen, would you? We are going to the hospital and see about the wounded Chicago agents. Call me if I need to smooth the way for Mr. Bonnarino," Edward Otis Whitney said.

Old Three Names got into his waiting SUV and we all piled into the back, and off we went to the hospital to check up on our guys. No one said a word until we got to the hospital, when Edward Otis Whitney said, "You guys have performed magnificently, and as soon as we do all of our debriefing and get the loose ends tied up you'll be going home, but I want to reiterate my job offer when I go up. No need to answer now, but be ready for a call, OK? And I won't hold it against you if you decline the offer, except you, Freak. I have a job in mind for you, and let's face it, you're much more suited for the protective division than the counterfeiting unit."

"Well, she can bench press a horse," Ed said.

"And punch out a polar bear," Guru said.

"And shoot the balls off a gnat at 100 feet," Joe said.

"Actually, shoot either ball off a gnat at 100 feet," I said. The tension of the moment broke as we all laughed. We got out and Old Three Names shook all of our hands, and we went in to find out about our guys.

And the tears flowed again.

CHAPTER 29

The Freak Squad Meets a President

We got up to the ward where our guys were supposed to be and approached a nursing station. Edward Otis Whitney flashed his ID and asked what rooms our agents were in. He bent down and the nurse said something in a tone only he could hear. Old Three Names got pale, but he stood up and said, "Thank you. Room 530?" The nurse nodded and we all followed him down the hall. When we got to the room there were two New York agents outside the door. Old Three Names nodded to them and said, "Go get some coffee and come back in 15, OK?" The agents nodded and left, and he turned to us and said, "This won't be easy to hear, but Agent Bowe has died. He had an embolism from a compound fracture in his femur and died before anything could be done. I'm sorry."

Tears sprang into my eyes and ran down my cheeks without volition. Joe, Ed, and Guru were also silently crying. We all stood there like dumb cows contemplating the slaughterhouse, and I said, "You sent Bonnarino to Buffalo to keep him away from us."

"Correct," Old Three Names said. "I didn't know this had occurred, but I feared that if there were complications and something like this happened Mr. Bonnarino would have difficulty arriving at his appointment with the federal justice system intact. I though perhaps you would rip off an arm and jam it up his ass, or perhaps write your name on his torso with a clip from your pistol."

"We're professionals, and we would never do that," Guru said.

"That is very true, but you are people, too, and people can only take so much. I was right to do what I did, and I'd do it again," Edward Otis Whitney said. He looked at each of us and said, "Despite being a pompous ass and political whore I take care of my people, and you are my people, even if you worked in South Bumfuck, Arkansas. This way all you can do is support your friends, because the bad guy is beyond your reach. It will also give you a chance to harden your resolve before you testify against that son of a bitch at his trial."

No one could argue with his logic. I know that I would have gladly beaten Sally Bones into a semi-functional bag of meat jelly, and that was before House died. After a long pause spent in contemplating telling House's wife and children about his death, we all nodded, and Old Three Names said, "Agent Beemond is in this room. His injuries are severe, but he is going to survive barring further complications. Agent Zaragoza and AIC Clune are still in surgery—and neither of them is out of the woods. I am going to try and find out details while you visit with Agent Beemond, and then I'm going back to my office and meet with the Director and Assistant Director. You will have a car waiting and will follow as you see fit. You are under no time pressure, but the debriefing will begin as soon as possible after you are done here. I will be back to see you before I leave." He turned and went back to the nurses' station, and we went in to see Bumble.

He was semi-awake when we came in—you could almost see the pain meds coursing through his veins—but perked up when we came in. After hugs and kisses on the cheek Bumble said, "What's the score?" When nobody answered he said, "I saw Mac and Gunny get it, so I know they're gone."

"Sparky got hit by two rifle rounds, one in the heart and one in the head. The Greek took multiple hits and hung on like a piece of gum on your shoe, but he didn't make it, either. House died here at the hospital—threw a clot from a compound fracture and died before the docs could do anything," Joe said, holding Bumble's hand.

"Ancient Chinese gentleman," Bumble said.

"Say what?" Guru said.

"You know—ancient Chinese gentleman," Bumble said.

"Oh, yeah—House used to say that when he was trying not to swear around his kids," Ed said. I must have looked perplexed because Bumble said, "Ancient Chinese gentleman's name was Ah Phuc, Freak."

I couldn't help it—I laughed and said, "Sorry, but I just got an echo of House saying that in my head." We all laughed a bit, and Bumble said, "Captain Cork? El Gato?"

"Both in surgery—no word yet," Joe said.

"We got shot to shit," Bumble said. "How many of the bad guys did we get?"

"All of them but one," I said. "They all expired due to extreme exsanguinations, mainly because they were completely perforated by ten-millimeter holes, the shitheads." Bumble looked at my face and said, "How many did you get, Freak?"

"All of 'em," I said, "but too damned late." The tears ran down my face, again without my permission or volition. I felt like my heart was going to burst in my chest, just like I did when we lost guys in Specs Ops. (I'd tell you about it, but…say it with me…it's classified.)

Bumble held up his good hand (one shot had gone through his upper left arm, which was strapped to his side so he wouldn't start bleeding again) and said, "Bullll-shit! There was no way to anticipate what happened, and if you hadn't shot those motherfuckers we'd all be dead, because they would have just waited until we were down and finished us off. Then they would have waited for Guru and Ed to show up and shot them, too. So stop that weepy shit right now. You saved my ass, and everybody else's, too—it ain't your fault those motherfuckers had rifles and shotguns and could shoot. Blame the right people—those motherfucking asshole counterfeiting fucktards…not you, Freak."

"Man's got a point," Guru said.

"A good one, Freak. We all feel like shit, but we can't shoulder this one," Ed said.

"Besides, our guys all knew the risks. Gunny and The Greek both fought in wars, Sparky was a cop before she joined the Service and Mac was a tough broad who shot three guys during a bank robbery when she was off duty," Joe said. "No virgins or naïve rookies in the bunch—just tough professionals who got ambushed, and the rest of us who were saved by their superhero friend. Nobody can fault you, or anybody else involved, Freak. As usual Bumble is right—you got to let it go so we can put those motherfuckers in jail forever."

I realized they were right, and vowed to myself to honor the memory of my fallen comrades by being the best agent I could be and putting all of those really responsible for their deaths behind bars for a very long time. It sounds trite, but I really did that in my head, mainly because I didn't want the agents who were left to razz me until the end of time about being a maudlin pussy (which they would have gladly done).

Just then there was a knock on the door and Edward Otis Whitney came in. He said, "Agent Beemond, we haven't been properly introduced. I'm AIC Whitney of the New York office, and I am glad to tell you that Agent Zaragoza is out of surgery and the prognosis is good. He had a collapsed lung and some damage to the hepatic artery, but the doctors caught both problems in time. AIC Clune is still in surgery."

We all thanked him, and Bumble said, "Sir, I want you to know that Agent Glickstien saved our lives. She drew her weapons and was firing less than a second after the bad guys opened up. It was extraordinary, sir, and she deserves some recognition."

"And I assure you that she will get it, right after we debrief. I'm leaving now, but the rest of you stay as long as you like. Agent Beemond, I may send agents to debrief you here if you are up to it. If not just say so and we'll wait. Until everyone is back up to speed there will be Secret Service agents on your door, just in case some random 'bad guy' gets any ideas," he said and left.

We all sat around and shot the shit for a while, but our people were still dead, and inevitably we all felt the need for action. We waited until Bumble fell asleep (morphine trumps adrenalin every time) and went to see El Gato in recovery.

He was out like a light, but looked surprisingly good considering how badly he'd been hurt. While we were staring into the ICU a doc came up and said, "You the Secret Service people?"

"Yeah," Guru said. "What's up with our dude that was in surgery?" Her voice was flat and cautious at the same time, because we all knew where Captain Cork was hit. There weren't any Secret Service agents that were paralyzed.

The doc looked at her and said, "He's alive, but we aren't sure that he's ever going to walk again. The bullet ricocheted around in his spinal column and broke at least three bones. That's the bad news. The good news is that the spinal cord is intact, but it took serious trauma. We took three fragments out of the spinal column that were impinging on the cord, but it'll be at least three days before the swelling goes down and we know anything. Until then we've got him in a medically induced coma so that he can't move around and hurt himself."

"Give us a ballpark on his recovery," Joe said. The doc looked at him like Joe'd asked him to grow tits and be Miley Cyrus, so Joe said, "C'mon, Doc. I've worked with the guy for 11 years—nobody's gonna hold you to any guess you make."

The doc swallowed hard and said, "I'd say he has a 60/40 chance of regaining some function, but there is no way to even ballpark a full recovery chance. In fact, chances of a full recovery right now are zero, because when he went under there was no movement or feeling in the lower extremities."

"Can he at least use his arms?" I said.

"Yes. His heart function and upper extremities are not in jeopardy—he's suffered no trauma that caused any problem above the waist," the doc said.

"Can we see him?" Ed said.

"Nothing to see," the doc said. "Right now he's just a lump of clay that's sleeping so deeply he can't even remember what consciousness is."

"Don't people in comas still hear things?" I said.

"Well, yes, but we don't know how much they actually understand or retain," the doc said.

"But giving him some comforting words could help, right?" Guru said.

"Theoretically," the doc said.

"OK, then I wanna see him," I said. I looked at my fellow agents and said, "I'm going to give him a brief rundown of what's happened, including a scorecard. It might give him some encouragement." I smiled my most evil smile, and my pals responded in kind.

We went to the ICU and I went through the rigmarole (and yes, I know why it's necessary and I mean no denigration of ICU procedures) required to get in and a nice nurse led me into the area where Captain Cork lay bundled up like a dozen Roman senators in their formal togas. I went up close to his ear and said, "Captain Cork, I just wanted to let you know that I made like Cuchulainn the Hound of Ulster (look it up, dear reader—and remember that it isn't my fault that your education is lacking) and blew all of those motherfuckers who ambushed us to the furthest reaches of hell. The womyn is alive, but bound for federal prison, and we got the asshat dirtbag asshole shithead buttfucking sonofabitch who started the whole thing. Everybody's taken care of, and you are going to get better. Do what they tell you, and we'll get your wife here by tomorrow. Rest easy, Captain, and Erin go Bragh." I patted his hand and left, stopping when I got to El Gato and giving him the same message, only adjusted for his national heritage (I said El Cid instead of Cuchulainn and tossed in some *chinga tu madre* for good measure).

When I got out of the ICU Guru was saying "Just get over there and get her to the airport. The Director is sending a Service plane for her and Gato's wife. And make sure that it's you and Jewey telling House's wife and kids, OK? Yeah, her parents live in Vegas—no, they live there, she was from Vegas—and The Greek's sons and daughter live in Providence. They're all covered, but you gotta get to House's wife and kids, then pick up Maureen and get her to Midway, to the private aviation terminal. OK. Keep me posted, Weasel. Don't you and Jewey lose it. OK." She hung up and said "They're both crying like first graders, but they'll get the job done. Now we gotta go debrief so that we're here when Maureen gets here."

We went downtown to the New York office and did the debrief dance. By the time we were done I felt as if I'd been washed over Niagara Falls and then tumble dried. My head hurt, my feet stank and I definitely didn't love Jesus when it was all over (thanks to Jimmy Buffett for that phraseology—it fit perfectly in this circumstance). I finally got done after five hours of debriefing, went to our hotel and fell into a deep sleep for five hours.

I woke up to a gentle shaking of the bed and found Ed jostling the mattress with her foot. I sat up—still in my clothes—and said, "What time is it?"

"Five a.m. Maureen Clune and Selma Bowe are coming in on the Service plane—Guru wants us all to meet them."

"Roger that. I'm gonna step in the shower and change. Five minutes."

"You got 10. Old Three Names is sending us a convoy with sirens so we can get to the airport without so much trouble," Ed said.

I performed my ablutions and went to catch my ride. It was silent all the way to the airport, all of us lost in our thoughts, until Joe said, "We gotta be solemn, but we also gotta be positive for Maureen, so let's try for dignified distress, OK?"

"What? Ya tryin' ta be Martin Scorsese now, Joe? What the fuck is 'dignified distress' anyway?" Guru said.

"Aw, fuck, I don't know," Joe said.

"Ah Phuc? Skinny guy, ancient Chinese gentleman in the La Choy commercials?" I said.

"I think I knew that guy—did he used to do shirts over on Kedzie Avenue?" Ed said.

We all laughed, and Guru said, "Just be us, OK? Maureen has a bullshit detector that won't quit, and you know that Selma must have one, too, if she stayed married to House for 26 years."

So it was a subdued, but not funereal group of agents who met the two ladies from Chicago. Maureen Clune was short, stout, and clearly torn up about her husband. Her eyes were red from crying, and she was trembling when she hugged all of us. Her makeup was askew in that way that told you she was just mailing it in, and she couldn't really bring herself to speak.

Selma Bowe was just as torn up, but the first thing she said was, "I hope you all put those motherfuckers that killed my Q deep down in the cold-ass ground." She was a short round womyn who looked like a church lady that sat in the Amen pew, but her manner was pure South Side of Chicago.

"Mrs. Bowe, I put eight of them down, and the rest are going to Marion Federal Penitentiary for the rest of their lives," I said.

"Good. I intend to attend every day of their trials and make sure they see what I lost. My Q was worth a 100 of any chickenshit counterfeiters that ever lived, and I want to see them squirm when they realize their assholes are about to be the size of the Grand Canyon," Selma Bowe said. She smiled a grim smile and we all joined her, even Maureen Clune. Selma turned to Maureen and said, "Don't you worry, Mo, Jerry is one of the toughest white men I've ever seen. His Irish ass is too happy to pass on. We'll sit down here and pray about it after I see my Q, OK?"

Maureen Clune nodded and said, "Could I go with you? I liked Quentin very much, and Jerry said he was one of the most honest men he'd ever met. I'd like to pay my respects."

A tear ran down Selma Bowe's cheek and she said, "Of course you can come with me. We'll stick together—and thank you for thinking of an old widow womyn in her time of need." They set off for the morgue with Guru, while Ed, Joe and I waited for word on Captain Cork.

Joe said, "Freak, you're gonna have to watch your ass with Monteverdi. That motherfucker is a killer."

"Concur," Ed said. "He wasn't kidding about shooting you."

"I agree, and I will watch my ass. The only good thing about it is I think the moron wants to do it himself, and that asshat is too fucking ugly to sneak up on me." We laughed again and I finally lost it. The tears ran down my face and I slumped down in one of the plastic chairs outside the ICU, just spent all the way down in my soul. It wasn't the first time I'd lost people in battle (still classified), but this was very much more personal, and also more senseless. It was just paper they died for, not some noble cause, and I was having a hard time making sense of it. I cried and cried, inconsolable for the loss of the good men and womyn who were killed over man's love of filthy lucre, which every holy book and common sense said was the root of all evil.

I stopped when several men in suits and earpieces swept into the room, their eyes searching everywhere and seeing everything at once. It was clear that they were somebody's protective detail—Secret Service for sure—and the lead guy confirmed it when he said, "Agents, I'm Karl Stephens, the head of the president's protective detail. I'd like to ask you to surrender your weapons, just for a short time while the president looks in on AIC Gerald Clune. It's SOP that we're the only ones who are armed while in public with the president." He smiled to take the sting out of it, and both Ed and Joe reached for their weapons.

I did not.

I looked at Stephens and said, "Fuck you, the horse you rode in on, and the family dog. If you want my weapons, come and get them, asshole."

Stephens acted like I'd just shit my pants in church. He and the rest of the detail recoiled and then surged forward like I was trying to gun the president down. I just looked at them with a stare I'd perfected in other places in the world (sorry, still classified) and they all stopped.

"It's a reasonable request, Agent…," Stephens said, not sure who I was.

"Glinka Rose Glickstien, U.S. Secret Service," I said, my voice as cold as space. I held up my creds and said, "Let's see yours, fuckface. I don't know you, and this could all be an elaborate scheme to get at my AIC. Get 'em out, you lame shits."

Creds came out and we all looked at them, and Stephens said, "What bug crawled up your ass, Glickstien? This is SOP for any presidential visit. You don't need to be such a pissant about it. Now give me your weapon and let's get this over with."

I looked at Stephens and stepped toward him. I give him credit—he was brave and didn't back up, even though everybody else did. I got within six inches of his face and said, "Agent Stephens, my creds look just like yours, and I swore the same oath you did. Your SOP is idiotic and insulting, and you should know that seven of ours went in the ground today. Those of us who are left were threatened by the perpetrators of a vicious ambush that caused those deaths. If you think that I'm going to give up my weapons at any time just because the president of the United States is coming to visit you are out of your motherfucking mind, and I definitely won't give them up on today of all days. If you think that you can make me you are sadly mistaken. So either bring His Worshipfulness in or don't, but you are NEVER going to get your hands on my weapons, you supercilious asshat." My voice would have cut steel, even though I didn't raise it at all.

Stephens looked in my eyes and saw the truth, but his face was saved when the president, who apparently had heard my whole little soliloquy, said, "I agree with her reasoning, Karl. Nobody has to give up anything today—I think that Agents Laskarides, McKee, Cronenwell, Bowe and Rzepzynski gave up enough for all of us."

I hadn't voted for the Republican son of a bitch, but I would have right then.

I looked at him and said, "Thank you, Mr. President. My colleagues and I appreciate it."

"Where'd you learn to swear like that, Agent Glickstien?" the president said.

"Sorry, sir, but that's classified," I said.

He laughed and said, "Well, I'm the president, so I'm probably cleared."

I looked right back at him without a smile and said, "Sorry, sir, but you're not cleared for this, and the rest of the room most definitely is not. I can tell you that my vocabulary was significantly improved during my time at Parris Island, South Carolina, during basic training for the U.S. Marine Corps, sir," I said.

"Are you always like this, Agent Glickstien?" the president said.

"Sir, yes sir. Every day of my life since I was born," I said. The president looked at me and smiled. He shook all of our hands and then said, "I am very sorry for your loss. I did not know any of these agents, but I know my Secret Service agents, and they are the best men and wymyn in government. Given Agent Glickstien's reaction to being asked to give up her pistol I'm going to assume that the people we lost today are the same as my agents—top-notch professionals who went above and beyond the call of duty."

We all noticed the incorrect present-tense grammar—like most people, it was taking the president some time to accept that our guys were dead—but the sincerity in his voice moved all of us. Joe said, "Mr. President, you have no idea. These were the best people I knew, funny, smart, capable, and completely devoted to their duty, and they loved being in the Secret Service. I was at the Shedd Aquarium once with Agent Bowe and his kids, and some guy in front of us was joking about not smearing the ink on a 50 that he had just printed that morning. Agent Bowe very gently tapped the man on the shoulder and held up his badge, identified himself as a Secret Service agent, and asked to see the bill. He inspected it, determined that it was authentic, and handed it back, then apologized to the guy about the shakedown. The guy wasn't mad, but he said, "I was just kidding around. I'd hate to be that suspicious of people." And House—Agent Bowe—just looked at him with his best Secret Service stare and said, "You don't have to be suspicious, sir. That's why you pay the U.S. Secret Service. I'll guard the currency and American way of life by being suspicious for you." Those were the kind of people we lost today, Mr. President."

Even the president's protective detail had a lump in their throat, and Ed, Joe, and I all had tears streaming down our faces. The president took a hanky out of his pocket and wiped his eyes, while the rest of us used Kleenex to clean up.

Agent Stephens said, "Sorry I asked you to give up your weapon, Agent Glickstien. It really is SOP, you know."

"Understood, and sorry about the tirade, but it's been a tense day, and I snapped. We haven't had the training like you guys, but we'd all take a bullet for him, and so would the guys we lost," I said.

"Gunny would've tried to catch it in his teeth," Ed said.

"The Greek would've thrown up a gyro with extra peppers, then ate the gyro, bullet and all," Joe said.

"Mac would've just shot the motherfucker before he got the shot off," I said. "Sorry about the technical terminology, Mr. President."

"I didn't know Mac, but I like her idea best. And there are a lot of motherfuckers who'd be glad to take the shot," the president said. We all laughed—the guy was really sincere and trying to put us all at ease. The laughter stopped when Selma Bowe and Maureen Clune walked in the door.

Their eyes about popped out of their head when Joe said, "Mrs. Clune, Mrs. Bowe, this is the President of the United States, come to pay his respects." The president shook their hands and said,

"Mrs. Clune, Mrs. Bowe, I am truly sorry for your loss." Maureen Clune's eyes welled up and she said, "So Jerry is gone, then?"

I grabbed her arm so she wouldn't fall over and said, "Mrs. Clune, we haven't heard yet. The president doesn't know all of the players like we do. He was just being polite, as well as insensitive and ignorant." I glared at the president and he hung his head like a fourth grader being berated by the principal.

We were all saved from further embarrassment by the doc, who walked in and said, "Mrs. Clune? Your husband is out of danger and stable, and he is moving ALL of his extremities." The doc had a great big smile on his face and we all found ourselves smiling. Mrs. Clune just reached out and hugged him, and as the doc hugged her back, he said, "I think he's going to be OK after some rehab, but no guarantees that he'll be 100%. If he's as tough minded as he is in his body we've got no problems."

Maureen Clune smiled and said, "Well, he's an Irishman from County Cork, so I think that we can assume he's at least a wee bit stubborn, can we not?" We all laughed the laughter that relieved people use, and then those of us who knew him laughed even harder, because Captain Cork wasn't going to quit anytime soon, at anything, and especially not at being an AIC.

The president finally said, "Mrs. Clune, I know that you will want to see your husband first, but if I might look in on him after you are done I would appreciate it." Maureen looked apprehensive, but the president said, "Just me, Mrs. Clune—no photographers or anyone else, not even my chief of detail. I just want him to know that I and the American people are grateful for his sacrifice and dedication."

My estimation of him as president went up about 100%.

Mrs. Clune nodded her approval and went off with the doc to see her husband. Selma Bowe waited until they cleared the door and said, "Mr. President, pardon me for being forward, but I hope you see to it that the people who perpetrated this crime go to federal prison for the rest of their lives."

"I would think that they will probably get the death penalty, given that they murdered seven federal agents and tried to defraud the American public for over $900 million," the president said. He had run on trying to restore the death penalty when he was governor of West Virginia, and even though he was unsuccessful remained a staunch death penalty supporter. He had signed several pieces of national legislation that mandated the federal death penalty for certain crimes.

Selma Bowe drew herself up to her full height and said, "Oh, nossir, Mr. President, we can't let them off that easy. My Quentin didn't hold with the death penalty for any crime, because it let the criminal off too easy. He also thought that the death penalty was un-Christian, because only God gets to judge. He always said, "Throw 'em in prison for life and let God sort 'em out"—and he meant it, Mr. President."

Joe said, "That's true, Mr. President. House didn't think that the state should take retribution on criminals, because that lowered our standing in the eyes of God and the world. If he were here House wouldn't go for the DP, sir."

"How do you feel about it? The death penalty?" the president said to us.

"Totally opposed, Mr. President," Joe said.

"For the reasons already stated, and because it is a barbaric, bloodthirsty practice that reminds me of the Colosseum in Rome, I'm also totally opposed, Mr. President," Ed said.

Everybody looked at me, and I said, "I understand the impulse to go all Old Testament and get an eye for an eye, but that's just a vindictive retribution tactic that implicitly condones further violence, Mr. President. If it actually stopped people from murdering each other it might be justified, but since it doesn't justice requires that we incarcerate the individuals who murder so that they can actually pay for their crimes for life. I don't mind paying taxes for that, especially if it means they go to Marion, or Super Max."

"I might've expected a different answer from federal law enforcement officials," the president said.

"Hey, I'm the product of liberal Jewish parents in Battle Creek, Michigan—we were the first state to ban the DP, in 1846, no less. I've always hated the idea of the state sanctioning its own kind of murder," I said.

"And yet you killed people when you were in the Marine Corps," the president said.

"Completely different story, sir," Ed, Joe, Selma, and I all said at once. "I'm buying the Pepsis," Selma said.

"Why is it different?" the president said.

"Sir, those were armed enemy combatants who paid their money and took their chances. It's true that if they were going against me and the rest of my guys it was tantamount to murder, because none of those assholes were going to ever beat us, but they were armed and they did have a chance. Strapping someone to a gurney and shooting poison in their veins is murder, whether the state sanctions it or not," I said.

"And it's too easy, Mr. President," Selma said. "They get to just shuffle off this mortal coil, and yes, most of 'em are going to Hell, but they get relief, sir—no more worries for the dead. I want them to suffer the hell that my children and I will suffer the rest of our lives without my Quentin, not let them off by killing them."

"And that doesn't even cover the fact that we may be killing the wrong people," Ed said. "If the state murders even one innocent person how is that justice?"

"When you put it that way it seems as if the death penalty is never appropriate," the president said.

"Exactly," we all said. "I'll buy the Pepsis for that one," Maureen Clune said as she came through the door of the patient's lounge. "Captain Cork would want me to, although since he's going to live I'll probably let him pay." We all laughed again and the president said, "Thank you all again for your service, and I'm sorry for your losses, especially you, Mrs. Bowe. Thank you for the frank talk, too. I don't get much of that anymore. Karl, I'm going to walk down the hall and see AIC Clune. Please don't let anyone else in, OK?" He raised his hand to us and left. We all looked at each other and finally Selma Bowe said, "Did the president of the United States just ask us about the death penalty and actually listen to our answers?"

"He seems like a normal guy," Ed said. "I always thought that he was an arrogant prick with a serious ego problem."

"He's shy," Karl Stephens said from the door.

"Oh, come on Stephens," Joe said. "He ran for president twice and kicked everybody's ass who ran against him—and he's shy? How'd he pull that off in the last debate? Seventy million people watched it."

"He's really shy, but when he goes out in public, he pretends it's just him and the moderator, or one of us," Stephens said. "When he was debating Olsen the last time, he stared at me the whole time, like he and I were having a discussion. That arrogance you see is actually an introvert trying hard not to embarrass himself."

"Well, I was surprised that he actually listened," I said. "I doubt if he'll change his mind, but the way he acted like everything we said was important impressed me, and I'm not easily impressed."

"And he didn't act shy with all of us," Guru said. She looked at Stephens and said, "What the hell is the president doing here anyway?"

"First, it wasn't an act. He really cares about what the Praetorians say. He calls the Service the Praetorians because he thinks if the Roman emperors had listened to their elite bodyguards more Rome wouldn't have fell—he thinks we know more about the 'ordinary' citizens than he does, so yeah, he was really listening and inputting the data you gave him. And yes, he is seriously smart, in addition to being the nicest president I've ever served.

"And that's why he was here to see AIC Clune. He'll also want to go down and visit the other agents in ICU, which is why most of my guys are down there right now trying to sanitize the floor. We were in NYC so he could address the UN, and when we got done the AG told him about the dead agents, so here we are." Stephens looked at me and said, "I know that you haven't taken the training, but I could really use four more agents to protect POTUS. Know anybody who might be able to do that?" It was a very subtle apology, as well as an invitation to a new job tryout. It also wasn't the kind of thing that you could say no to, so we all nodded and away we went to guard the president of the United States while he visited with our wounded comrades.

It was pretty boring, and obviously totally unnecessary, right up to the point where the guy came around the blind corner with a gun in his hand.

We were escorting POTUS (do we really have to go through this again? A really smart fifth grader gets the acronym) to his waiting limousine. Joe and I had point and were just strolling along when a guy popped out from a blind corridor and pointed something down the hall at POTUS (you should have it by now—and I'm not telling you, so look it up).

Joe bellowed "GUN!" and everybody went for their pistols, but the guy was too close to me for that. I figured that he'd have to hit me in the body before he could hit the president, and I also figured that by now POTUS was buried under a swarm of Secret Service agents, so I hammered the guy with a special-teams tackle from my Michigan State days.

I wrapped my arms around his body, pinning his gun arm straight up in the air, and drove right through him with my legs. We slammed into the wall with enough force to break through the drywall. I twisted him away from the president, grabbed his gun hand and slammed him to the floor using a really cool judo throw. I yanked up on his arm, dislocating the shoulder and breaking his wrist, yanked the now empty hand down to the small of his back, cuffed him and pulled my 1076s, scanning for further threats while kneeling over the guy.

It all took less than two seconds.

Joe and Ed told me later it looked like the scene from *The Avengers* movie where the Hulk slams Loki all over the place, but all I remember was that after it was over my mind identified the gun as a camera—still possibly a threat, but not a gun.

I would've apologized to the guy, but he was out cold. Apparently the *New York Post* didn't make its reporters pass a physical fitness test, or they weren't used to facing an energized Secret Service agent, because the guy was never conscious when I saw him, the pussy.

Apparently he had a source in the hospital that told him the president was there, and also told him how to get an unauthorized picture of POTUS (I'm assuming that you got it by now) on his mission of mercy, so they concocted this plan where they could surprise the president of the United States, which is always a bad idea, kids, especially if I'm on point.

It could have been worse. If the guy had been even five feet from me instead of inside my personal space he'd be dead from three 165-grain Cor-Bon jacketed hollow points. Instead, he got physical therapy and a great story to tell, although his source in the hospital got fired and nearly prosecuted (POTUS persuaded the hospital administrator not to prosecute, once again proving that he was a fair guy).

I got a commendation from the president, and from Karl Stephens, who said, "Goddamndest thing I've ever seen! It was like you were on hyper-drive or something! I've never seen anyone move like that—you had the guy down and out before anyone else even cleared leather! You are a freak!"

"Exactly," Ed, Joe and Guru said. "I'll get the Pepsis this time, guys," I said.

The best reward I got was the whole next day off so I could sleep, because by the time POTUS (got it?) sped off in his armored limousine my ass was dragging—all of us were. Guru made us promise to go to our rooms and sleep—she'd already cleared it with Director Hessler, although the day after that would be more de-briefing and certifying statements and other administrative bullshit.

I almost got the sleep, too.

Almost.

261

CHAPTER 30

Freak and the Polygon Peg

So there I was, deep asleep in a post-adrenaline-rush coma when my phone started ringing Mozart's *Eine Kleine Nachtmusik*.

Square Peg's ringtone.

He and I had talked over the years, but it had been almost a year since we'd said anything to each other. I was busy, he was really busy with basketball (second for MVP behind LeBron James, ninth consecutive All-NBA and All-NBA defensive team honors, led the Pistons to the league finals for the fourth straight year) and his charitable foundation (educating kids everywhere, especially in economically downtrodden areas), plus it was kind of awkward, because I still loved him and wouldn't date anyone else, while he appeared to be the only celibate NBA star since A. C. Green.

It didn't stop me from taking his call.

"Peg, what the hell? It's only 6:30. Everything all right?" I said, trying to be civil even though I wanted about 350 more hours of sleep to counterbalance the 800 gallons of adrenaline I'd mainlined yesterday.

There was silence on his end before he said, "You know that I love you, Beautiful Girl, right?"

"Well, yeah," I said. "You know the feeling is mutual, Square Peg, right?"

He sounded kind of like a little kid when he said, "Yeah, yeah I do, and I just wanted to say that I'm sorry I sucked you into that."

I was instantly indignant and said, "Fuck you, Peg—nobody sucked me into anything. You're the most honest person I know, you're the kindest person I know, you're the most moral person I know—what's not to love? I would've loved you if you hadn't loved me back, that's how much I love you, so fuck right off with the 'sucked me in' shit. What the hell's wrong with you?"

Once again there was an uncharacteristic silence, but when he spoke it was the old Peg. "What was that thing that your *zayde* always said about making a decision?"

"He says that if you have two choices to make, a hard one and an easy one, the hard one is probably the right thing to do," I said. "What choice do you have to make, Peg? Are you going to retire from the NBA? Disavow your race? Run for president?"

He laughed then, warming the cockles of my heart (I'm not sure what it actually means, but my *bubbe* used to say it about my *zayde's* voice before she died, and it's appropriate for how he makes me feel), and I smiled, thinking about younger days.

Peg said, "I'm going to make a monumental announcement today, Freak, and I needed to tell you first." He waited for me to ask the question, but when I didn't, he said, "It won't affect the way that I feel about you, Glinka." Square Peg never used my given name except when he was deadly serious, so I got the picture: this was a life-changing announcement. Maybe a part of me already knew what he was going to say, but at the time I just kept thinking that he was leaving the Pistons, or basketball, or that he was an alien from the planet Ozonus.

OK, so somewhere in my subconscious I already knew. That didn't lessen my conscious shock when he said, "I'm going to tell the world that I'm gay, Beautiful Girl. I've wanted to for years, but now I've found someone to share my life with and I don't want to hide anymore."

At first—just for an instant—I felt deeply hurt, but my second reaction was 'Oh, so that's why we only had sex once?' My third reaction was 'Fucking-A, how did he keep this a secret for this long? Square Peg is the man—nobody could keep this a secret.' My fourth reaction was intense pride that Peg would trust me with his secret before he announced it—the best person that I knew thought I was worthy of his ultimate trust.

"So who's the guy?" I said, acting as casual as if he'd said he was going to announce he was a tall Black man.

"Typical Freak," he said, laughing again. "Does anything ever surprise you?" So I told him about the photographer from yesterday, and the shootout, which felt good to dump on someone else, especially since it was someone that I knew I could trust.

There was some thoughtful silence and then Peg said, "Are you OK, Beautiful Girl? Do you need me to postpone my announcement and come out there? I could catch a flight from Detroit and be there in less than four hours." Typical Peg—always worried about his peeps before himself.

"I'm all right, Peg. Just tell me who the guy is," I said, although I really wanted to tell him to come so I could feel comforted by his massive presence.

"It's Amos Gutierrez," Peg said.

"Well, that makes perfect sense," I said. Amos Gutierrez was the sixth man for the Phoenix Suns and had been the NBA Man of the Year last year for his work with the Make-a-Wish Foundation. He'd donated money, expertise, and his very recognizable face for a national fundraising campaign that solicited funds for sick kids to make their dreams come true. Amos Gutierrez had personally bought a wheelchair van for one little boy who just wanted to see the Suns play one time before he died from leukemia—and then he personally drove it to U.S. Airways Arena (now Talking Stick Resorts Arena), brought the kid into the locker room, and made room for him on the Suns bench. He also scored a career-high 44 points, had 23 rebounds, and 11 assists that night, then drove the kid to a local ice cream parlor for a big-time party, which he also paid for.

When the boy died later that year, Amos Gutierrez gave the best eulogy anyone ever heard, crying at the end of it about the loss of his friend. He also petitioned the league to change his number from 43 to 8, for the number of years his young friend had lived. He still wore the number and kept a picture of the kid in his locker.

The Phoenix locals called Amos Gutierrez El Gigante Compasivo, "the compassionate giant," which seemed appropriate for a 6'9", 250-pound forward who also adopted dogs from the local shelter—he had at least 17 at his modest hacienda just outside Phoenix. He was universally loved in Phoenix and was respected league-wide for his integrity and professionalism.

He and Peg would fit together like James Bond and a bespoke suit from Savile Row.

"What about the dogs?" I said.

"I loved the dogs—he has 12, but only two actually live in the house. The rest have their own house out back, with a play yard, their own pool, and kennels that are nicer than some of the houses I used to live near in Harlem. I don't think that the dogs will be a problem," he said, something unspoken in his voice.

"Your mom and dad know?" I said.

More silence on the line, then a sigh, then "They're my next call," he said. "I'm scared to death that they'll be disappointed, especially dad, mainly because I'm the last male in my line—having all sisters means that there are already plenty of grandkids—but there's no one else to carry on the family name since my brother Franklin died. I know there are other Richardsons in the world, but there won't be any more of my branch."

"Well, I'll bet ya a grand that your mom already knows," I said. "And your dad doesn't give a shit—he just wants you to be happy, Peg, and you know it. The guy couldn't be more laid back if he were Jimmy Buffett after a pound of Jamaican ganja. Not to be making a really bad stereotypical pun, but aren't you just being a bit of a limp-wristed, sissified, pansy-ass?"

Square Peg roared with laughter and said, "That's why I love you, Beautiful Girl. You know just how to get me going and soothe me at the same time. That's why I called you first."

I was very flattered, but the need to sleep was really coming on, powered by the 700 gallons of adrenaline still working its way out of my system, so I said, "OK, Peg, what time's the announcement?"

"Three o'clock today—we're at home against the Suns, so Amos and I thought that this was the best time. We're going to do it together, then go out on the court and try to bash each other's brains out," he said, laughing again. "Sounds like love, right?" We both laughed and I said, "Call me after and we'll talk. Right now I gotta sleep. And call your parents, ya chickenshit, or I'll tell the world that you wear ladies' undies and like disco."

"Ahhh, shit, ya can't tell 'em about the disco, Beautiful Girl," he said in mock desperation.

We both laughed again, and I said, "I'll be watching, Peg. Call me after." We hung up, and I went back to sleep after I set my alarm for 2:55 p.m.

It went off. I got up and peed and turned on ESPN. There were Square Peg and Amos Gutierrez sitting side by side in front of a few cameras and looking remarkably relaxed. When it was straight up three o'clock Peg said, "Thank you all for coming. I have asked my friend Amos Gutierrez to sit in on this announcement, as it concerns him as well."

The rude sports reporter for WJBK—the Fox affiliate in Detroit—said, "So are you going to be raising money for Big Brothers and Sisters, too, KR?" Peg hated that people called him by his initials, and he also didn't like stupid people who weren't prepared, so he waited a moment and said, "I should have called Amos my fiancé, since we have decided to get married. Of course we will be working on all sorts of projects together once we are married, but our primary concern will always be the Make-a-Wish Foundation."

There was a stunned silence and then all hell broke loose. The WDIV sports reporter started yelling "Get me the network! Get me the network! Call Lester Holt if you have to!" Can anybody say 'Let's climb the ladder on the back of a sex scandal'?

264

The Fox reporter kept yelling, "When did you turn gay? When did you turn gay? When did you turn gay?" It sounded like a question from *Dumb and Dumber, To*—and it connoted the same level of intellectual development.

The local ABC reporter from WXYZ yelled, "Was it seeing all of the naked players on your team that turned you gay? Was it all those big, studly bodies? Was it?" Uh-oh, sounds like somebody needs to read up on their Freud (my thanks to Dr. Freud for his lifelong pursuit of the human psyche. Penis envy is bullshit, Siggy, but latent homosexual tendencies…well, the ABC dude's questions were pretty good anecdotal proof).

The WWJ reporter, a pretty blonde womyn who was rumored to be in line for a promotion to CBS headquarters, kept her cool, but still said, "Is your condition due to taking those ballet lessons as a child? Or because you played the clarinet in the band?" Oops, Boopsie, there goes the network job. Nobody who asks a question that stupid should be on network news—I was pretty sure that Scott Pelley wasn't quaking in his boots.

Through all of the crazed frothing at the mouth Peg and Amos just sat there with serious expressions, waiting for the stupidity storm to calm itself. When there was a brief pause while the reporters sort of composed themselves a reporter raised her hand to ask a question, and Peg said, "Ms. Ifill?"

It was Gwen Ifill of the PBS NewsHour, in town for a fundraiser for Detroit Public Television, WTVS, and one of the most respected reporters on television. She calmly said, "Mr. Richardson, Mr. Gutierrez, did the Supreme Court's decision in *Obergefell, et. al* influence your decision to announce your marriage?"

Peg and Amos laughed and Peg said, "The decision that gay marriage is legal certainly didn't make my decision, but it made it easier for me." He looked at Amos, who said, "I was tired of hiding in the closet—it's not easy for a guy my size to get in there"—the reporters couldn't help themselves, so they laughed at the joke—"and once I met Kelvin socially and had a chance to talk to him I realized that I needed to step up like a man and tell the world who I really was. *Obergefell* just made it easier for me, too, but I'd already made up my mind to out myself."

"Where did you meet?" Gwen Ifill asked.

"Working at a basketball camp," Peg said. More laughter from the reporters, and Peg and Amos laughed along.

"Was the attraction immediate?" Gwen Ifill said.

"After we beat each other's brains out playing one on one for the campers we started talking about classic literature, reggae music and non-profits and I was really attracted to him," Peg said.

"It took me a while, not because I didn't want to think of myself as gay, but because I didn't believe that a man as good-looking, smart and accomplished as Kelvin would be attracted to me—guys from East L.A. never get what they want, or so I thought at the time," Amos said.

"How do your parents feel about this announcement?" Gwen Ifill asked.

"Mine are ecstatic—Kel makes more than me and has better endorsements," Amos said. There was silence until Gwen Ifill laughed, and then the rest of the realized he was joking, so they laughed, too, and Amos said, "My family is very pleased—they were hoping that I would find someone to love."

"So they already knew you were gay?" Gwen Ifill said.

"Yeah—I told them years ago that I was gay. My father just put his arms around me and said, "You are my son, and I don't care who you love, as long as you respect your mother and I." My whole family was pretty much the same way," Amos said.

"My parents were both incredible—they cried tears of joy, and my dad asked me if Amos was a good man that would treat me right and respect our vows. I assured Dad that he would, and my mom and sisters immediately started the wedding planning," Peg said. I believed it—his sisters would do anything for him, and they all loved doing shit like that. Peg and Amos were going to have to deal with a plethora of advice and ideas—they'd be better off just turning it over and saying "OK, sure" every chance they got—it'd be just like *Say Yes to the Dress*, only with giant men in tuxedos who didn't give a shit about the details.

"Are either of you afraid about the reaction of your teammates?" Gwen Ifill asked.

"My guys in Phoenix are cool with it—they've known since 2013," Amos said. "We haven't had any problems since I came out to them, and they've all kept it private, so I think we're cool."

"I was worried about some of mine, especially Priest Bailey," Peg said. The locals laughed nervously, because they knew that Daniel "Priest" Bailey, the shooting guard for the Pistons, was going to be a Catholic priest when he quit playing in the NBA, and wasn't afraid to tell people about the Lord and his plans for the priesthood.

"And what was his reaction?" Gwen Ifill said.

"He told me that Pope Francis said it wasn't his place to judge gays, and that if the Pope wasn't going to judge, it wasn't up to a potential priest to judge. He also said the same thing to the team. He quoted Matthew 7:1, "Judge not lest you in your turn be judged also," to them, and nobody except Luther said a thing," Peg said.

"You mean Luther Wilson, your center on the Pistons? What did he say?" the reporter for WDIV said.

Peg's face got red—yeah, Black people blush, too, and I could tell he was embarrassed, but all he said was, "Well, Luther asked me if I was going to keep scoring, rebounding and playing defense and I said yes, and he said that as far he was concerned that I could—ah, er, uh—well, sleep with anybody I wanted, as long as we finally beat LeBron and then Durant to win a ring. I assured him that I would continue to work to that end and he said, uhh—'cool' and gave me a hug."

"Just like that?" the WXYZ reporter said.

"There may have been a few more words in there, but that's the gist of his comments," Peg said, still blushing but smiling. All of the locals laughed, because they knew about Luther and his vocabulary. The year before he'd gotten a technical foul against Cleveland in the conference finals for saying "Hey fuckhead, your fucking eyes are fucked up, you fucker" after the ref had called him for goaltending that clearly wasn't. Peg told me that Luther could use the F-word as all the parts of speech, and that he could use it tonally as both a word of derision and approbation, and I believed him, because I'd heard Gunnery Sergeant Thornton do the same thing. The fact that Luther was a 7'2", 290-pound White boy that had played college ball at Southern Methodist University just made it all the funnier.

"Where are you going to get married? Where will you live?" Gwen Ifill said.

"We are going to get married here in Michigan, primarily because it's about midway between my family in New York City and Amos's family in LA," Peg said.

"We're probably going to live here in Detroit, because we both want to be part of the revitalization of the city," Amos said. "I've got my teaching degree from UCLA, and Kel would make a great college prof, so when we retire, we may go into teaching, or maybe even open our own school. But that's a while away, because neither of us needs to retire anytime soon."

"How will you handle the competition when the two teams play once you're married?" the blonde from WWJ said. Maybe she still had a shot at headquarters—that wasn't the dumbest question I'd ever heard.

"We don't think much will change. I'm still going to go out and try to beat everybody we play, and that includes Amos and the Suns. If he tries to shoot over me, I'm going to reject it, just like I would with anybody else," Peg said.

"Dream on," Amos said. Everybody laughed, and he said, "Seriously, I love Kelvin, but I don't like anyone once the jersey is on. We'll be like lawyers on the opposite sides of cases. We'll go as hard as we can until the buzzer sounds, then go rest up for the next game."

"Will you stay together when the Suns are in Detroit, or when the Pistons are in Phoenix?" the WWJ reporter asked. OK, so my first impression of her was off a tad. That was another pretty shrewd question.

"No," they both said at once. "You owe me a Pepsi, Kelvin," Amos said. "So I do," Peg said. He looked at WWJ blondie and said, "That would be unprofessional, and besides, that would make our teammates uncomfortable. During the season it's 'us' versus 'them,' and Amos is one of 'them.' I wouldn't want my brothers on the team to feel as if my loyalties were divided."

"What if there's a fight between the two teams and one of your brothers tries to hit Amos?" the WWJ blondie said.

"Then I'll do the same thing that I've done since grade school—I'll go over and sit on the bench until the fight is over," Peg said. "I don't fight, regardless of the situation. I play a game called basketball; I don't box or wrestle or play hockey or do MMA. Amos can defend himself, and my teammates already know how I feel."

Everyone nodded and then the questions began to degenerate in their meaningfulness, so I shut off the TV and hustled up a sandwich. I'd just finished when the phone rang and Peg said, "How'd we do, Beautiful Girl?"

"Not bad for a couple of basketball nerds," I said. "You guys also have better comedic timing than I expected—maybe you ought to think about touring when basketball kicks you out."

"Amos is a lot like you—he has a great sense of humor, he isn't afraid to take a chance and he's really smart."

"And he loves you," I said.

"Yeah," Peg said, and I could tell he was about to launch into another apology, so I said, "It shows—you can see it on his face. Watching the two of you made me feel privileged to be a human being. Two massive sports stars—and massive men—proving that love is blind and that all the haters are full of shit when they try to stigmatize LGBTQi people. Do you two have any idea how many people you helped today? Or how much it meant to that basketball player in East Bumfuck,

Tennessee, who finally gets to say he's gay and still play the game he loves? What're the haters going to say to him? You're a fag, and fags don't play basketball? All he's got to do now is say, "You wanna say that to Kelvin Richardson, or Amos Gutierrez?" and a lot of the pressure is gone. I'm so damned proud just to know you, Square Peg, much less to have been your girlfriend at State. You did good."

It took me a moment to realize that he was crying. Finally he said, in the tiniest voice I'd ever heard him use, "I was afraid that you'd be bitter, or hostile. Most people don't like being told they're in love with someone who likes the opposite gender."

"Listen to me, you dumbass—you and I are bonded for life, no matter who we sleep with, who we marry, or where we go. Whenever you need me I'll be there, because I'm your best friend ever, and you are the same for me. Whatever comes between us will never come between us, because like Wesley said, not even death can stop true love." (We both loved the movie *The Princess Bride*, and especially that line. Thanks, William Goldman, for writing a great book and screenplay. It's *inconceivable* that the world would be better without it.) I paused, and when I heard Peg weeping again I said, "Whether or not you get it, I love you for you, ya schmuck, not for your body. I'm never going away until God comes and gets me, so stop worrying. What are ya, a lily-livered pansy-ass?"

He laughed then and we had a great conversation about the announcement and Amos, and what their lives would be like after today. As we were talking my phone beeped that I had a call coming in. I saw it was Guru, so I said, "Peg, I've gotta go—it's my boss. We're all going to the hospital to see our AIC who's recovering. Call me later and we'll talk some more, OK?"

"Got it, Beautiful Girl. I can't tell you how much better I feel because I'm not hiding out any more—it really wore me down over the years. I can't imagine the kind of pressure someone would have felt when we were even in college, much less when we were in high school. It could really warp your personality," he said.

"Well, thank God yours was already warped," I said. We laughed our way off the phone and I suited up to go see Captain Cork and the other wounded members of my unit.

Another piece of the puzzle had fallen into place, but because of the turmoil in my professional life I didn't have a snowball's chance in hell of realizing it right then.

It's too bad life's such a bitch, but my lack of focus would cost several people their lives.

CHAPTER 31

The Freak Squad Reconfigures

So we all went off to the hospital to see Captain Cork. When we got there Edward Otis Whitney was just leaving, so we met with him for a minute outside the room. The New York AIC looked like he was going to pose for a GQ spread, and he also looked like the cat that had just swallowed a canary.

"What is it, Eddie, and don't say we gotta go out and arrest some more bad guys," I said.

"No, you've all done more than enough the last two days—you've all gone above the call of duty," he said. "No. I just met with AIC Clune, and he tells me that the president gave him assurances that you all would be moving up a pay grade, and that AIC Clune would be able to go back to his old job and reconstitute his own squad. I also am told by AIC Clune that there will be commendations for all personnel, including myself." He smiled a private smile and I said, "Give it up, Eddie—your poker face is for shit. I've seen third graders who could keep a secret better."

"It won't be a secret for long. I'm being promoted to Director of the Protective Division at the start of next year. Director Hessler has also authorized me to take any of you on as agents. I'll be asking you again soon to consider life on the other side of the Service, but for now enjoy your promotions and your time together as a counterfeiting unit in Chicago. Working with you has been a pleasure, and I look forward to doing it again." He shook all of our hands and took his leave, preceded and followed by his own security detail.

We all looked at each other as we went in to see Captain Cork. He was propped up in bed, and Maureen and Selma Bowe were with him. When we came in his eyes lit up and he said, "Well done! Got all of the shitheads in one bag and dropped 'em in the river of justice." We all laughed and Joe said, "Captain, people'd know you were Irish just by the poetry of your blarney." We all laughed again and Selma Bowe said, "My Q would have loved the fact that you all were honoring his memory by getting all of those assholes. I see why he liked all of you."

We all shed a few tears then, but Selma said, "Don't worry, House died doing what he loved and was born to do, and his children all know just who their daddy was. Ain't nothin' to be worryin' about now, just everybody gettin' healthy and back to work catching bad guys." There didn't seem to be any better way to put it, so we all cheered up a bit and shot the shit until Captain Cork said, "Ladies, my team and I need to talk business for a while. Could you go and find us some Pepsi?"

Maureen said, "Fuck you, Jerry, you got legs, get your own damned Pepsi. Selma and I are going to get a real drink." Maureen laughed along with the rest of us and gave Captain Cork a kiss on the head. She and Selma left, talking about whiskey and tequila and gin.

We all swung back to our fearless leader, who said, "Yeah, my legs are coming back. That's why I'm awake and not in some damned coma—the swelling's gone down and it looks like I'm going to be fine." He looked at me and said, "We all owe you, especially me. I was helpless and they woulda put several more in me if you hadn't done your Annie Oakley imitation."

"Annie Oakley couldn't shoot like me," I said. "Besides, I've only got two other friends, and both of 'em live far away from Chicago, so I needed to shoot well in order to keep my social life active in Chi." I was very uncomfortable with the compliment, mainly because we had four people lying in the morgue and three more in intensive care, which didn't seem like such good shooting to me.

Captain Cork read my mind and said, "Bullshit, Freak. You don't get to flip away a compliment that also happens to be the truth—and stop with the self-effacement, willya? It gets on our nerves. Without you being a superhuman everybody in the detail would be dead, probably even Ed and Guru, because they would have come to find us after they arrested the Fowler womyn, and the bad guys would have murdered them, too." Guru and Ed both nodded, and Guru said, "Dose iceholes wudda gotten away wit' it, too, 'cause der wudnta bin no boddies, Fweak."

"Concur," Ed said. "We would've walked in there and been blown away by the same ambush—and so would some more of the New York office boys."

"And I would most definitely be dead, because the only thing that saved me was the greatest display of pistol shooting in the history of the world. I don't know how or why you can do it, but that was the beyond the pale of possibility. It was the greatest display of marksmanship I've ever seen—you used a notoriously difficult to control handgun with massive rounds, and every bullet hit its intended target. It will go down as the single greatest shooting exhibition in history, and yes, it saved our asses, so take the compliment," Joe said.

"Second greatest exhibition," I said.

"What?" they all said.

"You all owe me a Pepsi, and it's the second greatest exhibition," I said.

"Well, I'd tell you to give it up, but it's probably classified," Ed said.

"Another Freak story we don't get to hear," Joe said.

"This tough bitch told the president that she couldn't tell him about stuff because it was above his classification," Guru said. Everyone laughed their asses off at the thought of me telling the president that it was classified, until I said, "Ah, fuck it! So my unit was posted to Anbar Province, and we had to stop this group of—uh, foreign fighters—who were going to hit our guys from the rear, and they hit us with a wave of RPGs…" And I told them the story of the Russian Incursion, which was sure as shit classified, complete with everything except the name of the OpFor—they could figure out that it was the Russians without any help from me. After all, these were the brightest people that I ever worked with, before or since.

There was dead silence after I finished and then Joe said "How many?

"Thirty-eight confirmed kills with my pistol. I don't know how many bad guys went up with the tank rounds and ammo dump, but I did get three T-72s and a T-80," I said.

"Holy shit," Ed said.

"Holy fucking shit," Guru said.

"Holy motherfucking-A shit," Captain Cork said. They all started bowing and saying "We're not worthy, we're not worthy" and then we all laughed like hyenas who just found an abandoned wildebeest carcass, until a nurse came in and said we were disturbing the other patients. We quieted down and Captain Cork talked about who to get to fill up the squad back in Chicago. Guru tossed in some ideas, as did Joe and Ed, but I didn't know enough agents to say anything, so I did what my *zayde* always told me to do when one is ignorant: educate yourself by shutting up and listening.

After 40 minutes of chewing the fat, we'd pretty much decided on who would be joining us, and we already knew that all transfers would be approved ($900 million in bad paper brings you some privileges), but we didn't know who was going to say yes, so everybody turned to me.

"Got anybody you want to recommend?" Captain Cork said.

"Well, the only agent that I think would fit like a glove has a few, uh, detractions," I said.

"Such as?" Ed said.

"Well, he's as gay as a bright spring day, he's just over five feet tall and he's directly related to the Marquis de Sade, a distinction that he takes very seriously," I said.

"Uh-oh. I think I know where this is headed," Ed said. "Well, I don't," Guru said. "Who the fuck cares who he's related to?"

"He really likes to dress in all leather, he carries a leather whip in his briefcase and he has a group of fellow de Sade followers who call themselves The Merry Flagellators," I said. "He's their Chief Tormenter."

"It could be worse," Joe said. "They could call themselves The Merry Fellators, which might be more than even the Service could take."

"Or he could carry a giant dildo with a suction cup for easy shower use," Guru said. We all looked at her and she said, "What? I was single for a long time and I read a lot of literature about self-help."

"In what—Penthouse?" Ed said.

"I always got it for the articles," Guru said.

"Jaysus, Mary and Joseph! Will ye lasses stop with such talk? I'm a sick old man, and besides, I still haven't heard why we want such a creature in our squad," Captain Cork said.

"He's as smart as Jewey and Weasel, and he can disappear when he's undercover," I said.

"Tell us more," Joe said.

"He looks like he's about 12 years old when he shaves off his goatee, he can speak in any accent you've ever heard, because he's a polyglot—he speaks 11 or 13 languages—and he can squeeze into the smallest spaces you've ever seen. He can literally hide in plain sight," I said. "He was also valedictorian of his class at MIT and got his doctorate from Stanford in Renaissance literature after taking master's degrees in accounting from Vanderbilt and civil engineering from Georgia Tech."

"He does sound like Weasel and Jewey," Ed said.

"And he has a fifth-dan black belt in Shotokan karate," I said. "He sometimes calls himself Mamba because he's as deadly as the snake, although he also calls himself the Gay Blade because he's better-looking than Ryan Gosling."

"How big is this guy?" Guru said.

"He's 5'2½", and he's really sensitive about that half-inch. He weighs 135 pounds, but don't let that fool you—he's stronger than a Bulgarian weight lifter and more agile than a Chinese gymnast," I said.

"Male or female gymnast?" Joe said.

"Definitely female—he's the only person I've ever met who's close to me in the strength department," I said.

"There are just two more questions to be answered about this Renaissance Man," Captain Cork said. "What's his name?"

I smiled and said, "This is his name—no shit, and yes, it's his real name." I paused for dramatic effect and said, "Almont Phillipe Gilbert de Coucy; his title is Comte de Condé, but most of the time he just runs it all together."

"WTF—a real French aristocrat? And this guy is a Secret Service agent?" Ed said.

"Graduated in my class—he was working for the State Department before he came to the Service," I said.

"That still leaves the last question unanswered," Captain Cork said. He gave me his most solemn look and said, "Does. He. Have. A. Sense. Of. Humor?"

"You'll laugh your ass off," I said. "In medieval times Monsieur le Comte would've been a court jester who kept the world in stitches—he actually made several of my classmates piss themselves because they couldn't stop laughing. He'd be a real pain in the *tuchas* if he wasn't so funny—and so smart. He'll love chasing funny money, and we'll have the best surveillance guy that has ever lived."

So Almont Phillipe Gilbert de Coucy, Comte de Condé, got added to our list of possibles for refilling the squad. Maureen Clune came back and kicked us out of the Captail's room, saying he needed his rest. We all went off to see our other wounded comrades.

Bumble and El Gato were both out of ICU, but not out of the woods yet. Gato's nurse told us that he'd be out of action for at least six months, but that he'd be fully functional when he came back. Bumble's prognosis was less optimistic. His doc told us that the big man's leg injury could leave him permanently disabled, at least as far as being a Secret Service agent was concerned, but his overall outlook was good—it didn't look like he was going to die.

Gato said, "We need to get Carmen Stokes from the Memphis office to fill up the squad. She's a tough broad and smart as hell."

"Already on the list," Joe said.

"Good," Gato said. He looked at me and said, "Thanks for killing all of those asshole motherfuckers, Freak. I owe ya one."

"Nah. I just did my job—and you'd've done the same for me," I said. We shot the shit some more, but El Gato got tired quickly, so we went off to visit Bumble, but he was asleep and the nurses said he needed the sleep more than he needed to see us, which made perfect sense, so we all went back to the hotel and prepared for our departure.

The New York office had all of our depositions, but we'd still be needed for the trials of Darcy Fowler and Leona Tromboli, assuming there weren't any plea bargains, and we'd have to testify at the trial of the Toledo Five, although we had word they were all going to plead guilty because Tommie Wilson wasn't smart enough to shut the fuck up and had already basically convicted everybody. That meant that we could go home and start putting the squad back together, but Captain Cork wanted us to interview Darcy Fowler and Leona Tromboli before we left, so Ed, Joe and I would stay one or two more days and do the interview while Guru went home and started to pull transfers together and get us back up to speed in Chicago.

It always amazed me how fast people got over trauma and got back to work when they had a job to do. Captain Cork pointed out that counterfeiting hadn't stopped just because we'd been ambushed, and he also pointed out that we were the people best equipped to catch those funny money bad guys—"And I have $900 million to prove it," he'd said.

He was right. We'd done all we could on this case and we'd cracked it in short order, and we needed to do the same thing to the next ring, and the next, and the next, regardless of our personal feelings or losses. If we didn't the counterfeiters would win, which was unacceptable to everybody.

So the next day we went back to work. Our interview with Darcy Fowler began at 9:00 a.m. and ended just 10 minutes later, but it was fairly productive.

She came into the interview room at the federal courthouse downtown like she was a princess. Since she was their star witness against Leona Tromboli the City of New York had been putting her up in a good hotel, so her hair was nice and neat, her eyes were clear and she was in very good spirits. We were the first federal officials she'd spoken to since her arrest, so we were very careful to read Ms. Fowler her rights and make sure that she understood them.

She and her PD exchanged a look and Ms. Fowler said, "I understand my rights and I waive them, because I already have a deal for immunity with the New York DA's office. What is it that you'd like to know, detectives?" She was a pretty blonde womyn who looked like a runner—she was slim and well-built, but had that gaunt look around the face of someone who spent lots of time with sneakers on her feet. She smiled at us and relaxed in her chair, as did her PD, who was looking at her like he might be willing to take out his fee in trade if he were a lawyer in private practice.

"Agents, actually," Joe said. "We're with the U.S. Secret Service, and they call us agents, not detectives."

"I'm sorry, agents," Fowler said. "How can I help the Secret Service?"

"We'd like to know your connection to Luigi and Leona Tromboli," Joe said.

"Lee and I are in the same running club—FleetFeet of Islip?—and we have homes near each other there," she said.

"And who decided to start the counterfeiting ring?" Ed said.

"We were discussing it one night after dinner at the Russian Tea Room—we'd just come from the theater—and we were all joking about printing our own money in order to afford such things in the future. One thing led to another and Lee mentioned her grandfather's connections, and I mentioned my cousins as a distribution network, especially with my position at Chase, and Little Luigi mentioned that there was an area at the warehouse that might be perfect to store some cash, and, well, the joking became more serious. Three days later Lee told me that her grandfather had a way to get blank Treasury quality paper, and I discovered the printing process that would let us print bills, and Mr. Monteverdi got us in touch with a printer…and the rest is history." Darcy Fowler smiled as if she had the world by the balls, but what she'd just done was put herself in prison forever, or at least until the two mob guys she'd also put in there had her ass killed for squealing on them.

"So Salvatore Bonnarino and Paul Monteverdi were in on the ground floor of the enterprise?" I said.

"Oh, yes. We couldn't have done it without them," Darcy Fowler said.

"And you set up the washing network through Chase?" Joe said.

"Of course. I went to the College of Charleston and got my accounting degree, but I minored in finance and information systems—it was easy to do, especially since my boyfriend worked in the financial transfers department. Our cash was just a little trickle in the giant flood of money that moves around the world every day," she said, still smiling like a lioness that just ate a zebra.

"His name?" Ed said.

"Reggie Carlini. He's the head of the transfer section at Chase," she said. One more poor schmuck for the welcome to prison team, served up by Lady Oblivious.

"And did you also set up the security measures for the enterprise? Specifically, did you set up the transmission that alerted the warehouse shooters to deploy in order to ambush the law enforcement officials trying to arrest Leona and Luigi Tromboli?" Ed said.

Darcy Fowler looked at her court appointed attorney, who smiled and said, "It's a normal question, Darcy. They need to establish who did what to whom so they can convict the higher ups. You can answer the question." She smiled back at him and said, "Yes, I did."

"And was this done on your own initiative, or did someone ask you to do it?" I said, as nonchalantly as if I were reading my grocery list to my dog.

"Mr. Bonnarino brought up the idea, just in case of emergencies, and Mr. Monteverdi supplied the guys for the shooting, but we all worked out the details together," she said.

"When you say worked out, do you mean that you had a meeting about it, or did the information get shared some other way?" Joe said.

"Oh, we had several meetings about the details of the operation," Darcy Fowler said. "Mostly we met at L'Artusi, Mr. Bonnarino's favorite restaurant. That's where we finally decided to set the safety precautions, just in case someone got on to us somehow. We never thought that it would happen, though, because we set the operation up in segments, with cutouts between each segment. Only Mr. Bonnarino, Leona and myself knew all the details."

We all looked at Bonnie Holderman, the Assistant U.S. Attorney we'd brought into the interview with us, and Joe said, "Enough?"

Holderman, a big old girl with shoulders like a linebacker and a brain the size of Johannes Kepler's (what a shitty education you had if you don't know that name—look it up) said, "Oh, more than enough. I would like to know about the money transfers, though."

"So where did the money go after you got it at Chase?" Ed said.

"Oh, I already gave all that information to the first detectives that interviewed me," Darcy Fowler said.

"We'd like it if you'd give it to us again, just for the Secret Service records," I said, so sincerely appreciative that butter wouldn't melt in my mouth. (Did I mention that I was a great liar who routinely beat lie-detector tests? No? Well, let's just say that I could have sold ice cubes to Inuits, or conned more people than Dick Cheney.)

"OK. I sent most of it to numbered accounts in the Caymans, and then Reggie and I went there on vacation and flew back with suitcases full of clean money. Some of it went to the accounts of our distributors, and some of it went straight to Mr. Bonnarino's accounts in Luxemburg. I also had several slush funds at Chase that only I could access. Oh, yeah—I also set up brokerage accounts for Lee and I through the Chase traders at the NYSE. Mine's worth almost $50 million, can you believe

THE FREAK FROM BATTLE CREEK

it?" Darcy Fowler said, her face lit up like a little girl at Christmas. "I'm rich!" she said, laughing as if she was just going to be able to waltz out and spend the money.

Even her PD looked at her strangely when she said that, and Bonnie Holderman said, "If you're rich why do you have a public defender? Why didn't you retain your own counsel?"

"Why, that's my retirement account. If I spend any of it there are severe tax penalties, so I've sequestered that money from my budget. Plus, Mr. Bonnarino said if I had a public defender it would be easier to appeal, since they don't do the best job all the time. Sorry, Stan—no offense."

"None taken," her PD said, his face as red as the proverbial beet. It got redder the next minute, because Bonnie Holderman said, "Cuff her" to Ed and I, then said, "Darcy JoAnn Fowler, you are under arrest for the murders of Secret Service agents Siobhan McKee, Nolan Laskarides, Stanley Rzepzynski, Carly Cronenwett, Quentin Bowe, Mark Lemon and Lucien Tavares. You are also under arrest for conspiracy to commit murder, conspiracy to commit fraud, fraud, interstate transportation of stolen goods, conspiracy to violate the Currency Act of 1998, money laundering, violation of the RICO statute and securities fraud. You are entitled to remain silent. Anything you say or do can be held against you in a court of law. You are entitled to an attorney. If you cannot afford an attorney one will be provided for you at no expense. Do you understand these rights as I have read them to you?"

Darcy Fowler and her attorney sat in their chairs with bemused smiles on their faces while Bonnie Holderman spoke. When she was done Darcy Fowler said, "Oh, I understand my rights, but do you understand that I have a deal for immunity? I've already been arrested on those charges, but they're going to be dismissed in exchange for my testimony against everybody else. Show 'em, Stan."

Her PD pulled some papers out of his briefcase and slid them across the table to Bonnie. She looked carefully at them, then slid them back to the PD and said, "Yeah, so?"

Her attorney said, "So you can't arrest my client for anything she says here today, or that she's said in the past. She. Has. Immunity."

Bonnie Holderman smiled like a lioness that just took down a fat antelope, and we smiled like the rest of the pride who knew they got to share. Darcy Fowler and her PD stopped smiling, and Fowler said, "Stop smiling like that—you're creeping me out."

"Imagine what life in prison is gonna be like," Bonnie Holderman said. "Clap the iron on her, ladies." Ed cuffed Fowler and took one arm. I took the other as we prepared to lead her out of the room.

"What part of immunity do you not get?" Fowler said.

"Oh, I get it," Bonnie said. "There's just one teensy little problem with that agreement."

"It's airtight, the PD said. "There's nothing wrong with it."

"True," Bonnie said.

"Then what the fuck?" Fowler said.

"That immunity agreement is with the District Attorney for New York County," Bonnie said.

"So what? Immunity is immunity," the PD said. "Fuckin'-A," Darcy Fowler said.

We all smiled again and Bonnie said, "Sorry, kids, but you have immunity from *state* charges." She held up her badge case and said, "My ID is signed by the Attorney General of the United States, and their IDs are signed by the president of the United States. You have as much immunity from *federal* charges as I do from syphilis, which is to say NONE. I'm arresting you for the people of the United States of America, and I could give a fuck what kind of deal you got from Cyrus R. Vance, Jr., although I do like that man's suits and ties."

"He is a snappy dresser," Joe said.

"But he can't hand out federal immunity for anything," Ed said.

"Noooo, homey can't do that," I said.

"Homey?" Bonnie said. "The guy is whiter than the Tea Party."

"He's whiter than the *original* Tea Party," Ed said.

"He's whiter than a yeti in a Himalayan blizzard," Joe said.

"Now that *is* white," Bonnie said, her flawless coffee-with-creamer skin shining under the bright Federal Center lights.

Darcy Fowler exploded with rage, trying to wrench herself out of our grasp (good luck with that) and spewing curse words like a drunken Marine. "Goddamnyoubitchcuntmotherfuckingasshole cocksuckingfederalrugmunchingqueerfuckshitasstwatfourflushingshiteatingdonkeyfuckers—I'VE GOT FUCKING IMMUNITY!"

"Wrong again," Bonnie Holderman said. "Take her down to the lockup and get her processed into the federal system, and make sure she's under guard at all times—old Sally Bones ain't gonna be happy when he hears that she rolled over on him."

"I'VE GOT IMMUNITY!" Darcy Fowler said again, her voice cracking.

"Not so much, and certainly not from federal charges," Bonnie said.

"How you think old Mr. Green Mountain is gonna feel about being rolled over on?" I said.

"I'd say mighty, mighty pissed," Ed said.

"I'll get this stuff thrown out! This is entrapment!" the PD said, his face even redder than the proverbial beet.

"How?" Bonnie said. "Did you ever meet with any federal officials? Consult with me or my boss, the U.S. Attorney for the Southern District of New York? Talk to the Attorney General or one of her representatives? Did you ever ask me for a guarantee of immunity? Did I ever offer one? No? Then I'd say you're shit out of luck, counselor—your client is free from *state* prosecution, but certainly not from any *federal* charges."

"Oh, fuck a duck," the PD said. He turned to Darcy Fowler, who had stopped ranting and was trying to intimidate us with her Chase bank death stare, and said, "Don't worry, Darcy, I'll get bail set at a reasonable level and we'll have you out in no time."

We all hooted with laughter, and Bonnie Holderman said, "Dream on, Junior. Your client helped kill seven federal agents, and she has money stashed in the Cayman Islands, which makes her a flight risk, and oh, yeah—she helped kill seven federal agents."

"She still has a right to ask for bail," the PD said.

"Which she'll get when pigs fly out my ass smoking little cigars," Bonnie Holderman said.

"I think I can convince a judge that this whole exercise is unconstitutional," the PD said.

"Well, I think you're barking up a dead goat's ass, but give it your best shot, bub," Bonnie said.

"Oh, I'm gonna have to steal that one from ya, Bonnie," Joe said.

"Be my guest," Bonnie said.

"You think this is funny?" Darcy Fowler said. "You think my going to jail is funny? You think ruining my life is funny?"

I was prepared to rip her limb from limb, but Joe said, in a voice as clear and cold as a northern Michigan stream, "No, Ms. Fowler, we're only laughing because we don't want to cry anymore. We're laughing because your actions caused the deaths of seven people we loved and cared about, seven people who only wanted to do the right thing and stop criminals who hurt every American by counterfeiting the currency and lowering its value. These were good people who weren't criminals but the finest kind of citizens of the United States, because they cared more about their country than themselves. So please pardon us for laughing over your plight, because we know what you are, Ms. Fowler—you're nothing but a common criminal, who we are sworn to find and put in jail. While we were going to put you there on the evidence we already had, you just made it easier for us to make it stick. We thank you for that, and please pardon our laughter, but it's just the sounds of our sorrow, our mourning dirge for our fallen comrades who you helped murder."

Darcy Fowler and her attorney stared at Joe for what seemed like a year before he said, "Get that pile of offal outta my sight before I puke." Ed and I took her out the door and into the custody of two New York agents, who took her down to Central Booking in the federal courthouse.

Ed and I went back in the room and Joe said, "Please tell me that that bitch isn't getting bail."

"Not until I get married to George Clooney, win the Nobel Prize for chemistry and am named the sexiest womyn alive by *People* magazine," Bonnie said.

"So definitely no, then," Ed said.

"Arrgh, go fuck yourself," Bonnie growled as we all laughed. For the record, the bail hearing took less than 10 minutes, whereupon Ms. Fowler was remanded to federal custody until her trial was over. Every time the PD tried something Bonnie Holderman intoned *'seven dead federal agents'*, until the judge said, "OK, I got it. Remand without bail and the accused will surrender her passport." Bonnie Holderman was as fierce as a momma bear in defense of her cubs when it came to defending the law, and putting away those who broke it.

We also interviewed the Toledo Five, who confirmed all of our suppositions about how they distributed the funny money. They also expressed their admiration for the fact that none of them got shot in the takedown except Mark Roberson, who said, "That was my own fault—I shoulda never taken aim at someone I didn't intend to shoot anyway."

"So you weren't going to shoot Agent McKee, even though you threatened to do so?" Joe said.

"Nope. I thought that ya'll would let me jump in a cab and I could escape before you could get organized. I only had birdshot loads in the gun, so if I'd hit her anywhere in the body I wouldn'ta killed her anyway," he said.

"So your intent was to escape and evade, not commit grievous bodily harm or murder," I said.

"Oh, no, ma'am, I wasn't goin' to murder no one. Hell, if I'da knowed I was up against Annie Oakley I woulda just put the gun down and run back inta the restaurant fer 'nother beer before I went to jail," Roberson said, a smile of apology on his face.

"For the record, Mr. Roberson, I shoot better than Annie Oakley. I also had no desire to shoot your finger off, either," I said.

"Oh, don't you apologize fer that, ma'am—ya coulda blew me away and been right ta do it. It was all mah mistake, and all mah fault. Cain't nobody with somethin' besides shit and wet cardboard for brains hold no grudge over that. 'Sides, that's still the best shootin' ah ever did see, and ahm just grateful ah got ta see it first hand, as it were," Roberson said.

"Or first finger," I said. We all laughed, even the federal prosecutor.

After our interviews all of the Toledo Five said they were going to plead guilty, not only because they all felt guilty about our dead agents, but also because they believed it was the right thing to do. "Man's got to own up to his actions if he wants to still be a man," Elvis Linemann said. "Wanna dance ya got ta pay the piper," Carl Horne said. "A fuck up's a fuck up, and ev'rybody's got ta pay for their fuckups," Chip Fowler said. "Ain't right to shirk your responsibilities," Roy Linemann said, "'specially if it's yer own damn fault yer in hot water."

We found that commendable, and all of us testified that we believed Mark Roberson was not going to kill Siobhan McKee, but rather was threatening an assault because he was out of his depth. He was convicted of intent to assault a federal agent, not the charge of assault with intent to commit great bodily harm, which shortened his sentence considerably.

In the end, justice was done for all concerned. Salvatore Bonnarino and his henchmen all got life sentences, with Bonnarino and Paul Monteverdi getting seven consecutive life sentences, plus two hundred years for their roles in the murders and counterfeiting. Leona Tromboli also received seven consecutive life sentences, plus 100 years for her role in the crimes. Darcy Fowler got a seven consecutive life sentences plus 50 years for her role and was the only one who was not convicted of state charges, because of her immunity deal. (BFD, right? Consecutive life terms meant they all had to serve each term one after the other, which meant that none of these schmucks was ever coming out of federal prison.)

Of course, the federal prosecutors put on full cases, but the deciding evidence in every case was the lovely (digitally recorded in living color) testimony of Darcy Fowler, who the judge took pity on and sent to the Big Sandy United State's Penitentiary in Kentucky, where she might have a chance to not be knocked off by Sally Bones's OC connections. No one swore revenge on her, but it wasn't hard to interpret the looks all the big-time defendants gave her taped testimony when it was shown in court.

In any case, in a relatively short period all the bad guys were headed for lockups while their appeals processed, and we were all back in Chicago to catch counterfeiters and other ne'er-do-wells. Our case of the century became a matter of history and legend, and it was back to the humdrum of everyday, small-time crooks who were trying to cheat the system.

Until some more defecation hit the air conditioner, from a place we never expected.

CHAPTER 32
The Freak Squad 2.0

When we got back to Chicago Guru had already brought on some replacements for the squad. We kept the guy from Financial Crimes, Tim "Buzz" Greenhoe, because he was useful at lots of stuff and looked like the character "Buzz Lightyear" from the *Toy Story* movies.

We got a former U.S. Olympic volleyball player from the Memphis office, Carmen "Coach" Stokes, who was a real physical specimen (6'3", 200 pounds of solid muscle), tougher than shoe leather, and smart as hell. Her nickname came from the fact that she coached for years before deciding that she'd had enough of kids at any level and wanted to put bad guys in jail (yeah, that's an unintended commentary on education right there—sorry for the editorializing, but it's just the truth).

We also got Susan "Betty Crocker" Fleming, who was a graduate of the Culinary Institute of America in Chicago and a former chef that went into the Secret Service after her former partner bankrupted their restaurant by defrauding the taxman and others. She was a very tall (6'2"), very thin (118 pounds) womyn who looked like she might be a human spider, but she ate like a crazed bull mastiff, cooked like a wizard, and possessed an excellent sense of humor. She was also smart as a whip.

We couldn't get a couple of guys everybody wanted, so we went to the alternates and picked up LaDavious Bell, a collegiate wrestler who graduated from Oklahoma State and then tried out for the national team. He was short, compact, muscular but lithe, and very, very quiet. He also had a degree in forensic accounting and could type faster than any human being I ever saw, often while doing research at the same time.

That left one more spot on the squad.

God help us all, we filled it with Almont Phillipe Gilbert de Coucy, Comte de Condé, a.k.a. "Mamba."

Guru started our first briefing with an update on our wounded. All of the guys were looking good, especially Bumble, whose leg wound had healed quite nicely thanks to great surgeons and post-surgical nurses. El Gato was going to have some physical therapy, and Captain Cork was going to have to use a wheelchair for a while, but they were all doing better than could be expected.

Just as she started to get to memorial service information for our murdered colleagues our new French nobleman breezed in. He was wearing a black Armani suit that looked like it cost more than the whole budget for the Chicago office, as well as custom made Ferragamo loafers that cost enough to feed most of New Mexico for a month. His tie and pocket square were matching lavender silk (I couldn't see them, but I knew that his socks and underwear would match, too), and his Rolex Oyster Perpetual had been a gift from his mother when he got his PhD—as was the large amethyst bracelet he wore on the other wrist. His royal signet ring was a large ruby carved in the family crest and set in platinum.

He was also wearing a Phi Beta Kappa key that he earned at MIT.

Oh, yeah, his hair—also a beautiful lavender—was combed up and over his head in a semi-pompadour.

Did I mention that Mamba knew how to make an entrance?

Before he could speak Jewey said, "Monsieur le Comte, just how fucking rich are you?"

"More than the Queen of England, less than Christina Onassis," Weasel said.

"That's not the Queen of England?" Joe said, pointing at Mamba. I looked at him and he said, "Hey, their hair is the same color."

"And who does your hair? The same person who does My Little Pony's?" Ed said.

"That's what he reminded me of—My Little Pony," said Coach.

"I thought it was Prince at first, until I realized that Prince is taller," Buzz said.

"And Prince's purple is darker, and more velvety than that Armani *schmatta* he's wearing," Jewey said.

"Golllleeee, Ah ain't never seen nobody all gussied up like that," LaDavious Bell said. Everybody looked at him and Joe said, "I heard him first—naming rights on the newbie."

"Concur," all of us old timers said.

"I dub thee Gomer Pyle," Joe said. "Welcome to the best squad in the Secret Service." He shook LaDavioUS's hand and we all laughed, because LaDavious Bell, All-American wrestler from Oklahoma State University, sounded just like the old Jim Nabors character from the TV show *Gomer Pyle, USMC*.

"Oh. My. God." Almont Phillipe Gilbert de Coucy, Comte de Condé said. "This is a squad full of vicious *savages* who apply *nicknames* to the poor *unfortunates* who happen to be stuck in *Chicago*. How am I *ever* going to be able to actually *work* in such a *poisonous* environment?" He was lisping like he was Nathan Lane in *The Birdcage*, as well as doing his prissy San Francisco queen act.

"We already decided to call you 'Mamba'," Ed said.

"Well, in that case let's catch some fuckin' bad guys," Monsieur le Comte said. Everybody laughed, and Guru said, "We got us a live one! Captain Cork's going to love this guy."

"What's not to love?" Mamba said, looking at his immaculately manicured fingers. There was more laughter and everybody shook hands, except me. I just hugged my old Academy friend and said, "Yer Worshipfulness, I'm honored by your presence."

He hugged me back and said, "Lady Freak, I see you still shop at Goodwill during the clearance sales." We shared a private laugh and then Guru said, "As I was saying before I was so rudely interrupted—"

"Sorry, Lady Boss Whose Name I've Forgotten, but I brought a small present for the squad, a gesture of respect and thanks for taking me in," Mamba said. He opened the door to the conference room and said, "Bring in the gift!" Both doors opened and a host of caterers came in with enough food to feed the crowd at a Bears game. There were five kinds of eggs; five kinds of omelets; corned beef and pastrami hash; fried potatoes, latkes (kind of like potato pancakes, for the *goyim* among us); corned beef, pastrami and brisket sandwiches; platters filled with lox, capers, tomato, onion, cucumber, olives and bagels; tomatoes stuffed with tuna, chicken and egg salad; matzo ball soup; three kinds of mac-n-cheese; fresh fruit of all kinds; chopped salads; three kinds of cake; and my personal favorite—tubs of sodas that included Green River from Chicago, Dr. Brown's sodas from

NYC and Vernor's Ginger Ale from Detroit. All the caterers were wearing "11 City Diner" on their aprons. This joint was at Eleventh and Wabash in the South Loop near our office and was famous as an homage to a neighborhood New York City diner. Given the high-quality food (they smoked their own meats in-house and had Brooklyn egg creams at their sofa fountain) and great atmosphere at the restaurant it was no wonder Mamba had decided to fete the office from there.

We all just sat there with our mouths open as the caterers set up, until Mamba took a soda, held it up and said, "In memory of absent friends and friends new-found—a toast to the company!"

We all held up our sodas and Weasel said, "To Gunny, Mac, Sparky, House and The Greek. They would have loved this."

"Hear, hear," we all said.

"And they would've wanted us to chow down," Joe said.

"Fuckin'-A right," Jewey said.

And we did chow down, like we hadn't eaten in a month.

As we stuffed ourselves Guru told us about the memorial services. House and Gunny were here in Chicago, Mac in Springfield, Missouri and The Greek in Monterrey Bay, California. She also told us that we were going to be put on paid leave to attend them all, and that the Service was picking up the tab for our room and travel. We all expressed our gratitude by scarfing down more food while telling tales about our lost comrades, until finally we couldn't eat any more.

I polished off one last latke—I love potatoes in any form, as my lack of figure can attest to—and drained the last of a Green River soda (I can't describe it if you've never had it—it's sort of like Seven-Up meets a limeade…but not). The room was full of burps, groans and people discretely unzipping and unbuttoning, all as we looked at the huge pile of food that remained. Mamba said, "Take it away, boys," and the caterers moved in to clear the debris away.

"Where's it going?" Joe said.

"I know a great shelter that always needs food," Ed said. "Don't just throw it away."

"C'mon, Mamba, put some of it in the fridges here so we can eat it all week," Weasel said. He was trying to save money for a racing edition Corvette that was 100% original, so he scrimped on everything from clothes to food. The feast was a windfall for a guy who often only ate twice a day (you think I'm kidding, but don't think that Secret Service agents get paid a luxurious salary—you pay us, and you don't do it very well, and no, I'm not bitching about it, I'm just pointing out the facts).

"What do you take me for, a *Philistine?*" Mamba said. "I've already arranged to have the leftovers transported to the Salvation Army kitchen at the LaVillita Corps Community Center on Twenty-Fourth Street—I know the couple who helps run it for the community. As for you—well, I *suppose* I can tell you the rest of the surprise." We all looked at him with laser focus, and he said, "Oh stop *staring*—it's so *gauche.* Every day that we're here I'm going to have lunch catered, so we can break bread together and get better acquainted."

"Three cheers for Monsieur Mamba, le Comte de Condé!" Jewey said. We cheered, shook hands again and then got back to work. We all had our assignments and we dug right back in. I liked keeping busy because it kept me from thinking about not saving my four comrades, which I still blamed myself for, even though I knew it wasn't rational or reasonable.

The work day got over and Mamba said, "I'm going for drinks at a dive over on Adams if anybody wants to come along."

Joe, Ed, Jewey, Coach and I all raised our hands, but Guru said, "I can't—I promised my kids we'd go for pizza. Next time, OK?" Mamba nodded and said, "Your children should always take precedence over anything else, especially some old queen scrounging for companions to carry him home after he blacks out," and after the laughter subsided Betty Crocker, Gomer Pyle, Weasel and Buzz all offered some version of "Thanks, but I can't afford it even though I'd like to," which is when Mamba said, "Oh, I *invited* you, so that means that I'll be *buying*," at which point everybody agreed a drink might be a great idea. We left the office and went out to stand on the sidewalk. We were all talking about who was driving when we realized we didn't know where we were going.

"Where is this place?" Joe asked.

"Oh, it's just a dive I know up on Adams," Mamba said. "You can all ride with me—I've already hired a car." At that moment a huge stretch limo pulled up and a giant black chauffeur got out. The guy looked like he could play tackle for the Bears, or wrestle an elephant, or maybe hold the car up with one hand while he changed a tire with the other. The giant nodded as he walked over to the rear door and said, "I am sorry for my late arrival, Monsieur le Comte, but this Chicago traffic is simply brutal. Drivers here show no courtesy it all, and turning on some of these streets involves making multiple turns. Paris is almost easier to drive in." He heaved a huge sigh that sounded as if he was carrying the weight of the world on his shoulders—and they looked like they might hold it, too.

His accent made him an Australian, but he didn't look aboriginal, at least to someone whose knowledge of Australia was learned from books.

Mamba said, "No worries, mate—we're just on the tarmac from a long, hot day of catching counterfeiters and need a beer. Remember the place we talked about this morning?"

"Oh yes, sir," the black Australian giant said. "It won't take but a minute or seven to get there, sir." He smiled and you could see what he looked like when he was a kid—if a kid could be 6'7", 275. Mamba said, "Excuse my *execrable* manners. Peeps, this is my friend James Campbell, who also happens to be my major domo, chauffeur, and masseur, as well as my bodyguard when I go out on the town. James, these are the people in my new unit." He introduced all of us using our real names, then told James all of our nicknames.

James smiled and said, "It is my pleasure to meet you, sirs and ladies. Please make yourselves comfortable while I maneuver this beast to our destination." We all piled in the limo and James whisked us away from the curb and into the dreadful Chicago traffic (he wasn't kidding about that—try it sometime).

"A giant black Australian chauffeur," I said. "Really? That's even a little bit over the top even for you, Mamba."

"Oh, James is far more than just an employee. He's my boon companion, my friend, and the best man I know. I owe him my life, and so I employ him at an exorbitant wage and enjoy his company, while he supports his family with honest and interesting work."

"Owe him your life?" Ed said. "Is that just melodrama, or is it real?"

"No, when we were children, I was playing by the banks of the Seine in Paris and fell in. The river was mighty, and I was a very small boy. Even though I was a great swimmer, I couldn't make headway for a bank, and sooner or later, I would have gone under. James was standing on the Pont Neuf when I was swept by its pylons, and he didn't even hesitate. He jumped off the old bridge, swam me down, put me on his back, and carried me to shore. He pulled me out and whacked me gently on the back so I'd spit up the gallons of dirty river water I'd swallowed, then carried me to the nearest hospital for inspection. He called my parents to tell them where I was, only after he explained to the doctor in flawless French what had happened. He refused all treatment for himself until I was declared fit. We were both 11 years old. It turns out that James and I share the same birthday, as well as similar tastes in nearly everything else. We became best friends, and I nearly died again when his parents took him back to Australia when we were 13."

"So how did you reconnect?" Betty Crocker said.

"Well, James wasn't hard to find, especially after 2016," Mamba said.

"Wait a minute—he's *that* James Campbell?" Coach said.

"Ah, knew ah'd herd his name b'fore," Gomer Pyle said. "Never thought Ah'd meet him, though."

The light dawned on all of us at the same time. I looked up at James and said, "It's not a come-down to be driving some silly French git around after winning an Olympic gold medal?"

"Oh, no, Miss Freak. I love the travel, Monsieur le Comte pays extremely well and he is an excellent traveling companion. Plus, he gives me the winter off so that I can pursue my career, so what's to feel bad about? No, every day is a joy at this job, which really doesn't feel like a job. How many people get to spend every day with their best friend *and* get paid? I couldn't ask for better," he said with a broad, happy smile.

"Gold medal at what?" Ed said. "I'm not up on the Olympics—I have season tickets for the Sox and missed all the excitement at the Olympics."

"James Campbell led Australia to the rugby-sevens gold medal in Rio de Janeiro," Coach said. "It was the first time that rugby had been at the Olympics since 1924, and it was also a first for Australia—they were the last team to qualify and they beat Japan, Russia, Great Britain, South Africa and especially New Zealand."

"It wuz also the first tahm th' Aussies beat New Zealand—th' behst team in th' wurld," Gomer Pyle said.

"Steady on, there, lad—we beat their sevens, *not* the All-Blacks," James said with a big smile. "We've got to climb that mountain next, if it's even possible."

"All-Blacks? Is rugby primarily a white sport? Who the hell names their team the All-Blacks? That's just racist," Ed said.

James laughed, as did the rest of us in the know and Mamba said, "Ed, the national team of New Zealand are called that because they wear all black uniforms, not because they're racist, or the sport is racist. The two best players on the New Zealand team are black—Maoris—and even South Africa has black players."

"Oh," Ed said. We all laughed again and James said, "Don't worry, Miss Ed, you are still partly right. There were many of my countrymen who were not glad it was me who led the squad to victory. I still get hate mail, and I don't even play ruggers anymore."

"You said you were working on your career—what are you doing instead of rugby?" Betty Crocker said.

"I play rucker for the Geelong Cats in the Australian Football League," James said.

"What the fuck is a rucker?" Jewey said.

"It sounds like a dirty sex move," Betty Crocker said. We all stared at her and Betty said, "Hey, a single girl has lots of time to read. You wouldn't believe some of the shit out there."

"A rucker contests all the bounced balls, like a jump ball in basketball, and also plays the mid-field region. I'm too big for a traditional rucker—'far too heavy' according to most AFL analysts—but I didn't lose a ruck last year, so the Cats fans leave me alone about it. I also scored more goals than anyone in the AFL, and more behinds, because I can kick the ball home from the fifty-meter line, and I can mark it with anybody, thanks to my rugger experience and my height. The fact that I'm native-born but not aboriginal is a huge topic of conversation, but everybody in Geelong loves me, so it's all good, mate," James said.

"I only understood about 50% of that, but I'm intrigued," Coach said. "I'd love to have you teach me the finer points, when you have time."

Mamba and I looked at each other and laughed. Everybody else caught on and started laughing, but all Coach said is, "Hey, motherfuckers, I'm 6'3" and built like a moose—you know how hard it is to find, smart, good-looking, and athletic men my size?"

"Not to worry, Miss Coach, I would be honored to explain 'footie' to you. We can even work out, if you like, because I have to stay in shape even if I'm just a chauffeur for now," James said, a twinkle in his eye that promised all kinds of fun for Coach.

"Score!" Ed said.

"Why can't I find somebody like James? Is it because I look like the world's largest pipe cleaner?" Betty Crocker said.

"Don't feel bad, Betty—try finding a gay man who likes someone that looks like a child," Mamba said. "Most guys feel like child molesters if they're attracted to me—and remember that they're already fighting that stereotype."

"Even though most child molesters are straight," I said.

"Life's a bitch, and then you die," Coach said.

"Or you marry one, and you wish you'd die," Jewey said.

"Or you go to work for the federal government so you can pay for dying," Joe said.

"You're such a cheery bunch! Thank all the gods that there's alcohol at the end of the trail," Mamba said.

"Too true, mate," James said. "We're here, Monsieur le Comte."

We looked out the window and Ed said, "Wow! We're at 17 West Adams!"

"The Berghoff!" we all said together. If you don't know, The Berghoff is an institution: it's the "oldest restaurant in Chicago," founded by Herman Joseph Berghoff, an immigrant from Dortmund, Germany. Herman and his brothers started a brewery in Ft. Wayne, Indiana and brought their beer to Chicago for the Columbian Exposition (World's Fair) in 1893…and never left. When Prohibition hit The Berghoff couldn't rely on just beer sales, so Herman opened a full-service restaurant, and also began selling Bergo soft drinks, which The Berghoff still sells. The food there is good German fare (their wiener schnitzel is outstanding) and other solid restaurant fare, but it is the *bier* (German for 'beer'—it seems appropriate to call it that, in honor of Herman and his bros) that's the real attraction. The very professional waiters (it takes years to get a job waiting tables—you have to serve an 'apprenticeship' of hosting, bussing tables and filling water glasses and carrying food) and dark paneling, old, soft leather and comfortable chairs are just a bonus that make The Berghoff one of those places where the world seems just a little bit removed from reality, where you can sit and drink *bier* and dream of better days.

Captain Cork says The Berghoff is an adult version of Disney World, only with better service, better food, and the best *bier* in Chicago—and no annoying children or waiting in line.

It may be the perfect place to enjoy the company of friends while having adult beverages of exceptional quality.

"The forecast for tonight is beer, with increasing drunkenness toward closing time," Weasel said in a perfect imitation of George Carlin's 'Hippy-Dippy weatherman' skit.

"Oh, liter steins of original lager how I love thee!" Jewey said, singing like he was in church.

"There will be satisfied funk druckers tonight!" Ed said, deliberately flipping the first letters of 'drunk fuckers' to make US all laugh, which we all did.

"I could really use a dark *bier*," Joe said, "in honor of Gunnery Sergeant Stanley F. Rzepzynski, who once drank 12 one-liter steins in one sitting, God bless his leather-necked soul."

"Twelve liters in one sitting?" Betty Crocker said.

"Of dark beer?" Gomer Pyle said. "Hoe-lllleeee sheeee-it."

"Still a world record for world-class dark *bier*," Joe said.

"How's about we quit talking about it and get the fuck out of this limo?" I said.

"Concur," said everyone else. "And you all owe me a *bier*," I said.

We piled out of the limo and into the lobby, where we were met by Harold Biesbacker, the head waiter at The Berghoff. He greeted us and said, "Monsieur le Comte, we have a table in the back room near the window for you. If you would follow me?"

We all trouped off like baby ducks following their mama until we arrived at a beautiful table for twelve, where Harold deposited us and apologized for not being our server. Mamba said, "We understand completely, *Herr* Biesbacker. There is an order to things, as all intelligent people know, so we will suffer along without the best headwaiter in Chicago, and indeed perhaps the world. If you could just let our waiter know that the check is to be deposited in my hand only? I would consider it a personal favor."

The head waiter stood at attention and clicked his heels together (I really couldn't make this stuff up—go to The Berghoff and see what happens) and said, "But of course, Monsieur le Comte." He departed in a flourish of starched shirt, tuxedo pants and perfectly placed towel over his arm and a very brisk, neatly dressed, and mustachioed waiter bustled in with his own towel over his arm. "I am your waiter, Mario," he said. "Welcome to the Berghoff. What is your desire?"

We all called out our orders and he diligently did not write them down, but when he returned just a few seconds later (I told you—time seems to distort at The Berghoff) he put everybody's *bier* or soda in exactly the right place without being told again who ordered what.

Joe stood up when everybody had their drinks and said, "To Gunny!" We all rose and said, "To Gunny!" and took a drink. I'm not much of a beer drinker—I rarely drink alcohol at all, and prefer good whiskey (that's Gaelic for 'single malt Scotch') when I do, but I have to admit that the Original

Lager at The Berghoff can make your day a whole lot better, even if you just married Chris Pine and won the lottery.

Weasel stood up and said, "To The Greek, who taught me how to say 'gyro' and how to eat *saganaki* the right way. Opa!" We all stood and said "Opa!" as more *bier* disappeared from our glasses. I must say that Gomer and James, who had changed out of the chauffeur's outfit into jeans and a Geelong Cats jersey before joining us, were drinking Bergo black cherry soda. It didn't stop them from being festive, but it did mean that we had two designated drivers, plus two people who could help us get into our respective domiciles if it got too drunk out.

After that Ed rose to toast House, and I rose to toast Mac, and Jewey rose to toast Sparky, and everyone's glasses were near empty, so we toasted Captain Cork, El Gato and Bumble. There was a collective decision that the *bier* and soda were too fine to waste, so we ordered food before we got a second round. Once again Mario assiduously did not record our orders, and once again he placed the food perfectly. It was uncanny, and I said so to him.

"Miss, every waiter at The Berghoff is required to keep orders in their head, because it facilitates service and ordering. When one has to pause to write things down it slows the process and irritates those dining, as does an incompetent waiter who does not know where to place food and drinks. We strive for the perfect drinking or dining experience here at The Berghoff, hence I will never write down an order, nor will I err in placing food or drink."

"That's incredibly professional, and also nice of you," I said. "I understand precision and the quest for perfection when trying to please someone else, so I really appreciate your efforts. I would say thus far that you've achieved your goal, Mario."

"I must admit that my efforts are not entirely selfless, miss," Mario said with a twinkle in his eye.

"Oh? Then what motivates you, good sir?" I said.

"My friend Harold will not live forever, Miss," Mario said, a winsome smile on his face.

"Ahhhh, I get it," I said. "You want to move up one more rung when *Herr* Biesbacker retires."

"It is my grandest aspiration, and would be the crowning achievement of my life—to be the head waiter at The Berghoff. What more could a man of my station and abilities wish to have?"

"It is good to know where one fits in the world, isn't it Mario?" I said.

"Yes, miss, especially since most people mask their dreams and desires with just doing their duty. Being the best waiter at the best restaurant in Chicago isn't just my dream, it's my fondest aspiration, because it would mean that I've maximized my potential. Too many people reach past their potential and try to fit someone else's model of what they should be or do. This pursuit of the head-waiter's position—which I cannot hope to hold unless Harold has died—is exactly what I should do. I am content with the pursuit, even if I should never attain my desire, because I am serving the purpose for which I was intended."

He moved me, so I stood up and shook his hand and said, "Well said, Mario. *In bocca al lupo.*"

"*Grazie, signora. Crepi il lupo,*" he said, shaking my hand back and kissing me on both cheeks (sorry about the Italian—a friend of mine in Spec Ops was Italian, and he always said this when we were about to go work—it literally means "In the mouth of the wolf" and it is the equivalent of saying "Break a leg" to an actor about to go on stage. The traditional reply means "May the wolf die!"—also appropriate for people about to undertake a grave task—and stop holding your breath, because I'm not going to tell you about any missions—still classified).

We ate the excellent food and were preparing to order a second round when Weasel said, "I know that it's bad manners, but where the hell does your money come from, Mamba?"

Monsieur le Comte said, "My family was rich on both sides. My mother was a du Pont, and my father really did inherit all the family lands in France. He also started and managed the largest hedge fund in Europe and owned eleven vineyards in the Bordeaux region before he became the finance minister of France, and then the French ambassador to the United States. I was born here in the United States during his second term as ambassador, and when he went back to France to be in the government again, my mother and I stayed in Delaware at one of her ancestral estates, commuting to see my father when he wasn't coming to see us. When I was nineteen years old, she flew back to France to see my father and died in a car accident just outside Charles De Gaulle—my father had a heart attack and died when he was told, and I was suddenly a very rich orphan."

Weasel said, "I'm sorry for your loss, but just *how* rich did that leave you?"

"Out of bounds," we all said, giving Weasel the raspberry at the same time. Mamba waved his hands and said, "Oh, I don't mind telling you that I could buy Bulgaria." We laughed, but then Weasel said, "C'mon, I've never met a truly rich person before, and I may never again. How much?"

"In all but seven countries in the world, I would be the richest person in the country," Mamba said. He said it matter-of-factly and without a trace of condescension or superiority. Everybody was silent for a moment, until Gomer said, "Whoo-eee, that's a real shitpot of money!"

"It is," Mamba said, "and I would gladly give up every penny to have my parents back for just one more day. In fact, I would burn it all up and jump in the fire if it meant I could spend an hour with *ma mère et père*."

You could hear the pain in his voice, and the truth…and we all paused for a moment, unsure of what to say or do. Mamba looked at all of us frozen in place and said, "That's why we need to drink more *bier*, and have chocolate cake, and enjoy ourselves, because if I can't bring them back I can at least make them proud of my generosity, and the way I don't let money affect me, by showing the world the greatness of their spirits shining through me. They were the most generous of parents and people, and I intend to honor their memories by being the same way. It may seem flippant at times, and it is certainly irreverent, but that is because I am the man they raised me to be." He gave a very Gallic shrug of his shoulders and said, "I'm like Gimli the Dwarf in Tolkien's *Lord of the Rings*. Freak, do you remember what Galadriel said to him at the parting feast before the Fellowship of the Ring left Lothlórien?"

I nodded and said, "*I do not foretell, for all foretelling is now vain: on the one hand lies darkness, and on the other hope. But if hope should not fail, then I say to you Gimli son of Glóin, that your hands shall flow with gold, yet over you gold shall have no dominion.*" (Thank you, J. R. R.)

"And so it is with me, my friends, for money means less to me than an old piece of chewing gum, unless I can spend it to bring joy or effect change. It's one of the reasons that I decided to join the Secret Service, because it's dedicated to protecting people's hard-earned money. I can't stand the thought of people who have worked their asses off to make a buck losing any part of it because some motherfucker decided to defraud them, not when I never worked at all for my billions. I know, I know—it sounds corny and trite, and just a little bit melodramatic, but it's the truth. I guess I'm just a damned idealistic fool, but that's my story and I'm sticking to it," Mamba said. He looked up and said, "OK, let me have it—it's open season on the sentimental old Mamba."

We were all smiling, but not in preparation to chide him for being an idealist. A tear ran down Weasel's face, and he said, "Mamba, did you ever pick the best squad you could be in. What you said—that's exactly why I joined up. My folks came from Hunnan province in the PRC and worked their asses off so my sisters and I could go to college—my dad worked three jobs, my mom two, and they wouldn't let us work because they thought our job was school. I won't let anyone rip those stubborn old Chinamen off, either, because the only reason there is a me is them."

"My dad and brothers are incredibly well off—I could also have gone into the family business and been rich, but I chose to serve instead. My grandpa fought with Patton on the way to relieve Bastogne and always told me that I owed the country something for the way it treated Jews. I listened to him, looked at my family working like dogs and decided that I would make sure the fruits of their labor were protected and pay back the Silverberg debt," Jewey said, tears rolling down his cheeks.

"My brother was murdered when I was sixteen. He walked in on a robbery at our local grocery store and tried to stop it, and they shot him dead. I made up my mind then that I was going to be in the law enforcement sector, because I couldn't stand the idea of someone else going through what I went through. I also decided that thieves were the scum of the earth and needed to be caught, so I dedicated my life to that pursuit. There are no bigger thieves than counterfeiters, so here I am, just a dumb old idealistic schmuck who thinks that we can actually affect the lives of everyday people by stopping funny money," Joe said.

"Are we all just all idealistic idiots?" Mamba said.

"Yeah," I said. "Welcome aboard the USS *Idealistic Idiot*, Captain Jerry Clune, Commanding, Commander Narita Singh, XO."

"If Captain Cork were here he'd be crying his eyes out," Ed said.

"El Gato would be making an excuse for all the water pouring from his eyes—you know that Hispanic men don't cry," Weasel said.

"Yeah, right—remember when we took him to see *Finding Nemo*? Fucker cried like a third-grader," Ed said.

"Just face it, Mamba—we're all like you. Why else would we do this job? It sure isn't like we get paid an exorbitant salary, or get rave reviews from our adoring public, or are respected for our integrity. We all have our little place inside that motivates us and keeps us from becoming cynical about the job. We all joined up because we want to make a difference—and we do, every day and in every way. I admire you for your desire to give back, but don't think that you're alone, because you're not. We're all in this together," I said.

"Thank you all for that—I do feel ever so much better," Mamba said. He smiled and said, "Now let it rain *bier* and soda! The gay guy is paying!" We all laughed and sent Mario for our second round. He came back bearing the nectar of the gods, but also brought us another person.

"Bruce!" Mamba said. "Everybody, this is Bruce Keller, the manager of The Berghoff. Our families knew each other, and Bruce and I have been friends for a very long time."

"Monsieur le Comte, please pardon me for intruding on your party and taking advantage of our friendship, but I have a small problem at the front desk."

"What is it?" Mamba said.

Bruce Keller pulled a $100 bill out of a leather folder and handed it to Mamba, who held it up to the light and rubbed the bill. Keller said, "I have six Asian men at the front desk who are all trying to pay their tabs with $100 bills. This is not unusual—we get 100s all the time—but this bill felt funny to the cashier, so she sent for me and gave them our standard spiel about getting manager approval for such a large bill. I took the bill back to the office and came straight here."

Joe said, "Jewey, Ed, look at the bill. Give me one, too, Mr. Keller."

The experienced agents looked at the bills, rubbing them in their fingers and holding them up to the lights. Jewey took the bill Ed gave him, rubbed it up and looked at Joe and Ed, who both said, "Run the Test for confirmation."

Jewey ran the Test. It came back positive. "Funny money," he said flatly.

"Confirm that the money is counterfeit," Joe said. He looked at us, then at Bruce Keller.

"Asian guys, you said? Any idea where in Asia they're from, Mr. Keller?"

"One of my staff believed they were speaking Korean, but he said it could also be a dialect of Mandarin," the manager said.

"A thousand says they're Korean—North Korean," Weasel said. Mamba said, "I'd take that action, except that I read a disturbing memo last week. Could they be government sponsored counterfeiters?" The Service had long known that the North Koreans were prolific counterfeiters, especially of $50 and $100 bills, which meant that these guys could certainly be government agents.

"I guess we'll find out when we brace them," Joe said. He was the senior agent present, so he laid out a plan to keep everything cool while still asking the Korean guys about their fake bills. When he was done Jewey said, "Joe, you are one devious motherfucker. Are you sure you aren't Jewish?"

"You did that all in three minutes?" Mamba said. "I'm usually the one who gets there first, but I bow to your superior mental processes on this one."

"Clever, simple and easily done with the personnel available. I think the brass better watch out—you've got a touch of Machiavelli in you, Joe. It might be time for you to move up the chain," Coach said.

"It's just like a Spec Ops plan—deceptive, simple and has a high probability of success," I said.

"Ah'd say it has a one hunnert percent chance of success," Gomer said.

"No plan survives first contact with the enemy, especially with our serious lack of intel," I said. "Everybody needs to be completely focused and not get overconfident. Everybody do your jobs perfectly and we *might* be successful." I looked at Gomer with my hard Spec Ops laser beam look and he said, "Sorry, Ma'am. It won't happen again."

I said, "You bet your ass it won't happen again if you 'ma'am' me one more time, because I'm gonna kick your ass myself, Gomer. I'm Freak, or Agent Freak. I. Am. Not. A. Ma'am. *Are we clear?*" My Marine DI voice was still in good shape, because he straightened up and said, "Crystal clear, Agent Freak."

"Good. Now let's go kick some Korean ass," I said. As we were moving to our assigned positions Betty Crocker said, "How will we know if they're government agents?"

"Their reaction when we brace them with the counterfeit claim should tell us all we need to know," Joe said.

As usual Joe was right.

Unfortunately it told us more than we wanted to know.

And cost us.

Again.

CHAPTER 33

Never Eat Spicy Korean Food with German Beer

We looked out at the Korean men around the cashier's station and Joe said, "Everybody get really ready—those Asians don't look like boy scouts." In fact, they looked a lot like the Spec Ops boys I used to play with: not too tall or short, muscular but very fluid in their movements and hyperaware of their surroundings. We could only see five, but Mr. Keller assured us there was a sixth one out there. Everybody in our group was in position when Joe got a blurt on his cell phone that the other group was ready. "Go," he said to Betty and I.

We walked out across the lobby hand in hand like a married couple, talking about walking the dog when we got home. We exited the lobby to the little enclosed niche that opened out onto Adams Street. We didn't look when we left, but Weasel and Jewey were in the café on our left, with Ed and Gomer on our right toward the bathrooms. Once we cleared the door Betty and I immediately turned around and crept back up the stairs, ready to close the door off when Joe gave us the signal.

We saw him come out with Mr. Keller and walk up to the desk. Jewey and Weasel were probably finishing up their alert calls to our office and the Chicago PD, and if I knew Weasel he'd already looped the FBI in, because any kind of investigation into foreign agents would have to involve them anyway. In a case like this the more people at the party the better.

We crept the door open and Joe said, "...and as the owner's representative I wanted to personally apologize for any inconvenience. We've had a rash of counterfeit bills lately, and so our corporate board implemented this new policy. In fact, we want to take 10% off your bills, and offer you free drinks the next time you come to The Berghoff as an apology for the delay."

The lead Korean said, "Oh, we completely understand, Mr. Cocker. We're not inconvenienced at all, but we'd still like to take you up on your offer, because the beer here at The Berghoff is excellent. We'd be glad to come back and drink more, especially if you're buying." His English was flawless—sounded like he was from Michigan, or Indiana, or Ohio—and he used it colloquially. His face had a genial look on it, and he laughed when he was done talking, as did his companions. If we hadn't seen the counterfeit bills we might have bought it, but his coal-black eyes didn't laugh, and his four companions kept looking around as if they could smell the trap.

These were not boy scouts—I was betting that they were trained operatives.

Joe said, "Excellent sir, and thank you for the compliment on the beer. We'll just take care of your bills and Mr. Keller will get you the gift certificate for your free beer. Thank you again for your patronage."

Just as Joe stuck out his hand to shake with the lead Korean Mamba and Coach entered the lobby. Coach was almost dragging Mamba, who was wearing a T-shirt and jeans and bitching his head off like only a teenager could. If I hadn't known who they were I wouldn't have looked twice at them—it looked like just another typical American teenage brat and his mom.

"I don't wanna go to gramma's, mom. She smells and she always pinches my cheek and I hate her cats and she's stupid and…"

"I don't give a shit, junior. If I havta go you havta go, so quit acting like a crybaby," Coach said.

They continued to natter at each other until they were directly behind the two Koreans who were behind the lead guy. As soon as Mamba was behind his guy he struck just like the snake that was his namesake. He had the guy down before the Korean even had a chance to twitch. Coach had her guy down and Joe was wheeling his guy to the floor. Betty and I burst in the door while Ed and Gomer sprinted in to take down the fourth and fifth guys. Jewey and Weasel were right behind Betty and I as our strategic reserve. It looked like a textbook takedown when all hell broke loose.

Mamba's Korean did some kid of explosive escape maneuver and was out and on his feet. Coach's guy tried the same move, but she caught him and piled-drived his head into the hardwood floor. It hit with an explosive crack and he went limp. Joe's guy twisted loose and jumped up into a martial arts stance, bouncing on the balls of his feet and looking confident. Mamba's guy saw how little he was and actually smiled as he prepared to duke it out.

The fourth guy was also preparing to fight. Before I could get to him Gomer charged in, trying for a double leg takedown. Unfortunately the Korean launched a taekwondo roundhouse kick just as Gomer changed levels, and a kick which would have struck him in the ribs (and probably broke them—the Korean was definitely a pro) caught him full in the throat.

Unlike the movies and TV, kicks directly in the throat are not recoverable. Gomer went down like he was shot, his face immediately starting to turn blue. The Korean gave an exultant yell which was cut off by Ed saying, "Fuck this shit!" and pulling her pistol. The remaining Koreans were suddenly surrounded with pistols, and because they were pros they began giving up.

Two put their hands in the air, while the third guy looked at Coach, who was still exposed in front of him. Before he could decide to jump on her Jewey advanced from the rear and said, "Coach, back away to your right." Jewey looked down from his full 6'8" and said, "Mr. North Korean, if you twitch, I'm going to shoot you so many times that your corpse will be in pieces. Do you understand me, Mr. North Korean? I'm going to blow you away if you move. Put your hands up if you understand me."

The guy put his hands up. So did the fifth guy. I couldn't blame them.

Joe said, "Weasel, Ed, Coach, handcuff those wankers. Betty, Mamba, get some first aid on Gomer."

Just then the head guy bellowed something in Korean and the sixth Korean, who must have been hiding in the café, ran right through the plate glass window next to the door and escaped on to Adams Street.

"Freak, Mamba—get him!" Joe barked. We holstered our pistols and ran out the same broken window. I looked east and saw the Korean hauling ass down Adams. Less than two blocks away Michigan Avenue—the busiest pedestrian sidewalk in all of Chicago—beckoned to him. If the Korean got there and turned either way we'd lose him, because that was the fabled Miracle Mile of Chicago—the place where all the shops, museums and high rises were. There was also an El station, the Van Buren Metra station and Millennium Park, where finding a random Asian would be like looking for a Yankee fan in the right field bleachers at Yankee Stadium.

If he got there we were fucked.

I just exploded down the sidewalk, running as fast as I'd ever run. I gained on the Korean immediately, but I probably would have still missed him if a womyn looking at her cell phone hadn't ran right into him and knocked him almost down. He also made a tactical error and looked back to see where I was, which made him slow down just enough. I screamed "HALT! U.S. SECRET SERVICE!" just before I caught him. Some people don't like this idea—they think that it tips off the subject and gives them a bearing on your pursuit—but I took my tactic from nature, where tigers roar just before leaping on their prey. Zoologists have proven that the prey freezes up for a split second, which in these types of situations makes all the difference.

The Korean froze for just that split second I needed—and I tackled him to the sidewalk right at the corner of Michigan and Adams.

I'll give him credit—he was well trained and very muscular. I felt like I'd tackled a bag of snakes, because he twisted away from my grasp and popped up ready to fight (it was just like tackling that Wisconsin tailback who rushed for 2000 yards—take a brick wall, add some pythons and a gazelle and you've got a vague approximation what it felt like).

He smiled at me and said, "No guns, eh cowgirl? Too many people—you might hit an innocent bystander, and then you'd be crucified, even if you got me." He laughed, but I just dropped my jacket and unhooked my shoulder holsters. Mamba was standing at my shoulder and I handed him the stuff, never taking my eyes off the Korean. I said, "Mamba, if he gets by me shoot him. I don't care about collateral damage—that's an order. Comprenez vous?"

"Oui, mon capitaine," he said.

The Korean's eyes got even more flat and implacable, but he put a good face on it and said, "After I put you down the little man is going down, and then I'm just going to melt away into Koreatown. You'll never catch me, cowgirl."

I smiled—one of my Spec Ops pals told me I looked like the mythical basilisk before a fight (looking at one froze your blood and turned you to stone)—and I put all of that power into my stare. The Korean didn't turn to stone, but he stopped smiling and immediately attacked me, scything his legs into the air in a taekwondo combination kick that was supposed to knock me back and bounce my head off the sidewalk

A security video showed the fight perfectly well afterwards. The Korean launched his attack and I blurred into motion, moving inside the kicks and blocking the second one with my right arm. The block spun him a quarter-turn away from me and I hit him with three hammer hands—kidney, neck, and head—further spinning him away from me. He was hurt, but he was also a trained professional. The Korean tried to continue the turn and attack me coming out of the spin, but I was inside his turning radius. His hand flew futilely past my head and I planted my left knee right in his balls while hammering a punch into the pit of his stomach.

He puked then, a graceful arching stream of beautiful golden German lager that fell all over the people who were watching the fight. I didn't give him time to recover or attack me again. I hit him fourteen times—all in the body—before he fell to the pavement. Also, unlike the movies or TV, taking that kind of punishment from someone who knew how to punch and could bench-press a Fiat (the small one, OK?) was unrecoverable.

The Battle of the Miracle Mile (as it became known) was over.

I stepped over, cuffed the Korean and pulled his semi-conscious self into a sitting position. I took out my creds, held them in his face and said, "I'm Agent Glinka Glickstien of the U.S. Secret Service and you are under arrest, sir. You have the right to remain silent. Anything you say can and will be used against you in court. You have the right to an attorney. If you cannot afford an attorney one will be provided to you at no expense. Do you understand these rights as I've read them to you?"

The Korean puked again, blowing chunks all over the now-empty sidewalk. Chicago pedestrians are smart—it only takes one drenching with puke for them to get the message. The spectators all started to applaud, and somebody said, "Do not FUCK with the Secret Service!" and everybody laughed. I didn't laugh or even nod, because I was sure I'd left a dead man behind me—no way Gomer survived that kick to the throat.

Just then Jewey and Coach pushed their way through the crowd with their credentials out. Jewey said, "All secure, Freak?" I nodded and said, "Gomer?"

"It was the damnedest thing I've ever seen—tell you about it when we clear the scene," Jewey said. "I don't know if he'll be right, but he's still breathing—he's headed to Stroger for treatment." The John H. Stroger Hospital of Cook County was the closest Level I trauma center to The Berghoff.

I nodded and then whole carloads of Chicago PD, FBI and Secret Service cars rolled up and chaos swallowed us up. We went through all of the bullshit that a crime scene entailed, talked to hordes of detectives, agents and supervisors, filled Guru in on what happened—she was in the second wave—then explained the same thing to Charlie Chan, who shook my hand and said, "Good work, Freak. I just talked to Joe—none of these guys have diplomatic immunity. It appears that they are an espionage ring, although they all have a cover as South Korean businessmen who have legitimate green cards."

"Weasel went online, eh?" I said.

"And he called Buzz at home, and he came back to the office right away—let's get back to The Berghoff so we can coordinate with the rest of your squad." We were so close that we didn't ride—we just walked down Adams and showed the Chicago PD guys our creds. We went into the lobby and found the rest of our team except Betty and Gomer. There was a blood stain on the carpet in the middle of the room, but it wasn't enough for someone to have bled out—and we hadn't seen anyone bleeding when we left. There was also the strong smell of booze in the air.

I looked at Jewey and he said, "Betty did a tracheotomy on Gomer using a steak knife and a ball point pen."

"What the fuck?" Mamba and I said at once. "You owe me a Pepsi, Freak," Mamba said. "Agreed, but what the fuck?" I said.

"Betty realized that Gomer was asphyxiating, so she got Keller to bring her a sharp steak knife. She got down on the floor, had Coach hold his head still and had me sit on his legs, then poured some bourbon over his throat and started muttering to herself. She sounded like a mage praying over a dead body, but it turns out that it was dialogue from a *M*A*S*H* episode."

"What the fuck?" Mamba and I said. "I owe you," Mamba said, "but what the fuck?"

"There was a *M*A*S*H* episode where Hawkeye had to walk Father Mulcahey through a tracheotomy and Betty remembered it. She talked her way through the dialogue and did a perfect trach—she even put a ball point pen in the air hole and taped it up. Gomer started breathing again, and when the EMTs got here they couldn't believe it. She used 90-proof Knob Creek bourbon to sterilize everything, which is why it smells like a distillery in here. Since she performed surgery in their lobby to save a man's life The Berghoff has decided to give her beer for life."

"They gave her what?" Mamba and I said. "We'll each buy a case of Pepsis," I said.

"I'm sure she'll share," Jewey said.

"She better, or I'll sic the Freak on her," Mamba said. The rest of the squad wanted to know, so I told the story of the Battle of Michigan Avenue again. They all listened intently, especially Charlie Chan. At the end of the story he said, "So this was definitely someone who trained—an operative, not just a guy who studied taekwondo?"

"Definitely," I said. "He was very good and would have probably beaten anyone else in the squad up and gotten away."

Charlie Chan looked at Mamba, who said, "She's right, sir. I'm very well trained and can handle myself quite well in most situations, but a good big man beats a good little man every time—and this guy was big and very, very good. He just ran into a stronger, better opponent, and it didn't hurt that she was a womyn."

"He's right sir—the guy was definitely arrogant and overconfident. He came at me hard, but probably not at 100 percent. Not that that would have mattered," I said.

"You should have seen her—she hit him eighteen times, and he never laid a finger on her. It looked like a tackle for the Bears against an eight-year-old Pop Warner football player. Her hands moved so fast you almost couldn't see them, and her knee's impact on his testicles was most impressive. He puked a fountain of beer," Mamba said.

"Hopefully we'll get a video of it," Ed said. (We did—the security tape was a hot commodity for quite a while in our office, and later in the protective detail offices.)

"I always like a good beat down of the bad guy, especially when he pukes," Charlie Chan said, surprising everybody. We all must have looked it, because he said, "Hey, being an AIC doesn't mean you're some kind of superhero—I'm just a guy who enjoys a good ass-kicking like everybody else, especially when one of mine is the kicker and not the kickee." We all laughed then—it felt good to dump some of the adrenalin out of our systems—and then we went back to work.

Charlie Chan had us literally walk him through what happened. We went back through The Berghoff and did it all over again. Mr. Keller, the manager, explained how the whole thing started. We talked to the cashier who first suspected the bill was counterfeit, and outlined what we had done to confirm the suspicion. Our waiter Mario confirmed that no one had more than one glass of beer—he showed Charlie Chan the bill to prove it—so that no one could say anyone was impaired at the time of the operation. We explained again to Charlie Chan, the FBI AIC and the Deputy Chief of the Chicago PD why we didn't wait and follow the guys, or confirm they were foreign agents, or consider calling for help before we began.

Nobody raised the slightest question that we had done the right thing, especially after I relayed the comment the Michigan Avenue guy made about melting away in Koreatown. Charlie Chan said, "Even if you had followed them, once they hit Koreatown the only agent who could have kept up the surveillance is Agent Wei, and he's Chinese, not Korean. There is a difference, and everybody in

Koreatown knows it. He'd've stood out like a guy with a neon sign saying 'I'M NOT KOREAN'—and of course we'd've lost the guys completely. Your reasoning was sound and your execution was masterful, except for their physical abilities, which you overcame without any discharge of a firearm and hopefully no losses on our side. Barring any further developments I'm calling this a good op."

The FBI guy and the deputy chief concurred, and in fact complimented Joe for coming up with the plan so quickly. They gabbled on a bit, until Joe said, "Sir, we need to figure out a way to keep this as close as possible, so that we can try to backtrack the source of the funny money for the North Korean cell."

Charlie Chan looked at his watch and said, "In about two minutes that won't be a problem, Joe."

Less than a minute later several guys came into the room like they owned it, and one held his creds over his head and said, "I'm Assistant Director of Homeland Security Nathan Jones, and this operation is officially classified as a matter of national security. We are classifying this as an attempt at domestic terrorism—it appears that these men were attempting to set up a bombing of the Willis Tower (he meant the Sears Tower—fuck those Willis people). Anyone who knows anything about this case is hereby enjoined from discussing it unless in the presence of two or more Homeland Security officers with Top Secret clearance. Everyone is enjoined from further discussion of the case with anyone until they are fully debriefed. Am I clear?"

We all mumbled some version of affirmation, and then everybody was bundled out of The Berghoff and to the Homeland Security offices. We were piled in with Homeland Security agents so we couldn't talk about it, but Joe and Mamba were in my car, and I really wanted to talk to them about my theory of why the case was going this way. As we rode in Joe said to one of the Homeland guys, "Does Uzbekistan have an embassy here in Chicago?" The guy said "How the fuck'm I s'posed to know?" but another one said, "They have a trade mission, but not an embassy." Joe smiled at me, and at Mamba, and we both smiled back, because we realized what Homeland was going to do with the incident. I started smiling then, because I was pretty sure what they wanted me to say, and I was pretty sure that I was going to say it.

When my turn with debriefing came it was with AD Nathan Jones and two other guys who didn't introduce themselves. AD Jones asked me if I needed anything and I asked for a Pepsi, which one of the no-name guys immediately brought to me. I took a healthy swig and Jones said, "So Agent Glickstien, any idea where the guy you fought was from?"

"Uzbekistan, or maybe Kyrgyzstan," I said. "He was vaguely Asian, but the language I heard from him didn't sound like Japanese or Mandarin. It was more guttural and not at all sing-songy like true East Asian dialects."

Jones looked at me and smiled. He made a notation on a pad in front of him and said, "Other witnesses said they thought he might be Korean or Pakistani. What is your assessment of that?"

"Well, he could be Mongolian, I suppose, but there is no way he was a Pakistani—I've spent time there and know the people pretty well, plus I'd recognize the language. I also don't think he was Korean—he wasn't really Asian enough," I said.

"What were you doing in Pakistan?" Jones said.

"Stuff," I said.

"What specific kind of stuff?" Jones said.

"Sorry, sir—I can't tell you that," I said.

"Why not?" he said.

"Classified," I said.

"I've got a security clearance," he said. "I'm an assistant director of Homeland Security."

"Sorry, sir, but your clearance doesn't include this," I said.

He told me what level he was cleared to, and I told him what level the information was classified at, and he looked at me and said, "No shit?"

"No shit, sir—I might be able to tell the president, but I'd want it cleared first," I said.

One of the no-name guys laughed and I looked at him. He shrank away from me and I said, "I'm not kidding—and I know these two schmucks aren't cleared."

"Fair enough, Agent Glickstien. So back to the guys you saw—you think they were Uzbeks? Or Kyrgyzstanis?" Jones said.

"Or Mongolian, sir, but my money is still on Uzbekis. They were trained in martial arts, but I didn't see any evidence that they were employing taekwondo, which I would expect a Korean to use. Their style was too rough and tumble for Koreans, sir," I said, keeping myself serious so I didn't start laughing.

"Well, Agent Glickstien, several of your fellow agents concur with your assessment, although one agent thinks that they were Indonesians using *muay Thai*, or some bastard form of it. Possible?" Jones said.

"I hadn't thought of that, but it is possible, sir. I suppose it could also have been a bastard form of *krav maga* (a martial art form the Israelis teach their armed forces and spec ops troops), but these guys were more near Asians than south Asians. I'm sure they weren't Indonesians, sir," I said.

Jones nodded and said, "Thank you for your cooperation, Agent Glickstien. It's very fortunate that one of your team overheard these men discussing their plot to attack a Chicago landmark and alerted Agent Cocker to the threat. We're grateful for all that the Secret Service did, but this is our case now and we will be pursuing it. Your squad is officially off the case. Are we clear on what that means?"

"Oh, absolutely Assistant Director. Homeland Security is taking the lead on this one—if you want us you'll let us know, right?" I said.

"Exactly," AD Jones said. We shook hands and I was shown out to a waiting car. Joe, Coach and Ed were already there, along with two Homeland guys, so we took right off for our offices. By then it was coming up on three a.m. and we were all tired, so nobody said anything. We got to the office and Charlie Chan was waiting.

"Everybody get some sleep and report to the office at 10:00 a.m.," he said. "Staff meeting tomorrow to set our priorities going forward. Don't talk to each other, either—we'll have a nice, long talk tomorrow, OK?" Everybody nodded and plodded off to their cars, but I'd come in by train and there was no way I was going to try to fight my way back to Wrigleyville, so I just went up to the office and crashed on the couch in the lunch room. I always left a change of clothes at the office, and I'd just shower in the wymyn's locker room, if I woke up on time. I was so tired that I didn't even think of Gomer and his throat, or the Uzbeki Koreans who were about to become Muslim terrorists.

And I didn't realize that another clue to the crime of the century had revealed itself.

It would've saved a lot of bloodshed if I had.

CHAPTER 34

Surreptitious Freak

The next morning the news was all good. Gomer was out of danger, Betty had a new career in medicine thanks to Hawkeye Pierce and the story had broken about a gang of Uzbeki terrorists who were planning to bomb the Sears Tower (I don't care who owns it—Sears built that motherfucker so it's the Sears Tower) but were stopped by a joint Secret Service/Homeland Security task force. Most information about the plot was classified, but it appeared that the Uzbeks were ISIS sympathizers who were caught scouting their target before they could assemble a bomb. Five pictures of the suspected terrorists were shown on all the major and minor networks and people were convinced that we had dodged another Muslim bomb.

There were predictable reactions to the news, but not one word was said about any Koreans, and at The Berghoff the staff was supporting the story by telling everyone that *Herr* Biesbacker and Mr. Keller had overheard the Uzbekis plotting in broken English and alerted the Secret Service friend of Mr. Keller, Monsieur le Comte de Condé.

We were all refreshed by the sleep, but especially by the news about Gomer. When Betty came into the office we all stood and cheered, and then started bowing and saying "We're not worthy! We're not worthy!" She blushed and couldn't talk, but joined us when I said, "Three cheers for Hawkeye Pierce!" We all started chanting "Hawkeye! Hawkeye!" until Charlie Chan stepped in the door and said, "Staff meeting downstairs. Follow me."

We trooped downstairs and found a Service car waiting—Guru was in the back already, with two agents I didn't know in the front, and Mamba's limo was waiting with himself in the back and James behind the wheel. Wong said, "Get in and follow me to the staff meeting."

We jumped in and Mamba said, "Anybody know what the hell is going on? Where are we going for a staff meeting—and why? Don't we have perfectly good staff rooms at the office? Oh, yeah, we do have perfectly good staff rooms at the office because we ate a sumptuous meal in one just yesterday. WTF?"

We were in heavy traffic, headed north on the Kennedy Expressway, which meant we could be going anywhere, so that was no help, but Joe finally said, "I think that we need to have an off-site meeting because we're going to be playing a game with this case."

"What kind of game?" Ed said. "Homeland basically told us to fuck off, and so we're fucking off."

"Well, they didn't exactly tell us to fuck off," I said. "Jones told us that *officially* they were in charge of the case. But this morning he also told the world that these guys were terrorists from Uzbekistan, and we all know that isn't true."

"Ah," several people said at once. Mamba didn't say anything, just opened the cooler in the limo and started handing out Pepsis. As there were gasps of carbonated satisfaction all around Weasel said,

"So when I denied those guys were Korean and suggested they might be from Indonesia I was saying exactly what Jones wanted me to."

"Yeah, you were," Joe said. "I told him they were probably Uzbeks, which made me kind of feel like shit."

"Why? Who gives a fuck? They're Koreans," Ed said.

"Did you sleep last night?" Joe said.

"No, I had to fight with Della when I got home—she was sure I was out cattin' around, and she kept at me until I had to leave for work. When she sees what really happened she'll feel like shit, but that won't bring my sleep back. Just pretend that I'm brain dead today and explain everything slowly and using small words." Della was Ed's wife; she was notoriously jealous, but she was also a real knockout who loved Ed fiercely. I was amazed that she ever gave Ed crap about staying out late—when your spouse is a Secret Service agent they're probably not going to be keeping regular hours (duh!)—but Ed said she was just acting out from watching her mom cheat on her dad.

In any case, Joe said, "Anybody else feed Jones the Uzbeks?"

Jewey, Coach, Mamba and I put our hands up. "And did anybody suggest that these were Asian Muslims, not Middle Eastern Muslims?" Joe said.

Jewey, Weasel, Mamba and Coach put their hands up. "So I felt like shit because we kind of threw an innocent country under the bus. Now the Uzbeks'll have to try and prove that they didn't know anything about it, which will lead to turmoil and more terrorism possibilities."

"But why are we doing this at all?" Ed said.

"I think that Jones wants to turn us loose on the North Koreans while he points everyone else at Uzbekistan, so we can roll up the whole North Korean counterfeiting ring before they even know we're on to them," Weasel said.

Mamba drew out another ice-cold Pepsi and said, "For you, sir, in honor of your intellectual prowess."

Joe put his finger next to his nose and said, "Spot on, laddie" in a perfect Scottish accent. "We're going to a meeting with Jones or his boss, and they're going to tell us that while they have the lead we have the important job of interdicting as much North Korean counterfeiting as we can before they stop the Uzbek investigation. Homeland is going to run the false flag op while we do all the real work."

"If you think about it, that's really the optimal working conditions—we get to act like cowboys while they have to act all formal and do things by the book. If we're really lucky they'll use their typical Homeland big-foot tactics and we'll be able to lay in the weeds and knock off the North Koreans," Jewey said.

"Interdicting?" Betty said, raising a cynical eyebrow to Joe.

"To halt or interrupt a flow of supplies, in this case funny money," Mamba said.

"Fuck you, Mamba, I went to Smith, so I know what it means—I just wondered if we had to start talking good or what," Betty said. We all laughed and Joe said, "Sorry, I was just trying to talk like an assistant director of Homeland Security. In fact, I'm gonna bet that's an exact quote."

"No bet. I've heard enough bureaucrat-speak to know that you're almost certainly right," I said. "Although I think old Jones is just putting it on for the bosses—that guy's got lots of good, old-fashioned copper in him."

"I got that feeling, too. He was giving off cop vibes when we talked," Mamba said.

"Or he was giving off romantic vibes," Ed said. "The guy's as gay as a *Birdcage* dance review. Maybe he likes you."

"And I just thought he had a *gun* in his pocket," Mamba said. Once again we all laughed, because Mamba was a master of tones and accents—he did stereotypical 'gay' speech and actions better than most drag queens, which made it all the more hysterical, since he actually was gay. Think gay Marx Brothers and you'll almost get it.

The laughter subsided as we left the Kennedy for Bryn Mawr Avenue and then kept straight on until we were on Avondale. When we turned right onto Nagle Avenue Joe, Jewey, Weasel, Ed, and I all said, "We're going to Superdawg®!"

There were Pepsis all around and general cheering, because Superdawg® is another one of those Chicago institutions. It's a drive-in restaurant with a tiny inside dining room that you have no trouble finding once you're on Milwaukee Avenue, or Devon, or Nagle, because when you approach that tri-corner you can see the 12-foot-high "Tarzan and Jane" hot dog figures with neon eyes that still blink just like they did in 1948, when Maurie and Flaurie Berman opened the place. The place is distinctive looking, but that's not the best part.

The Superdawg™ is. As they will tell you if you ask, this isn't a wiener, or a frankfurter, or a red-hot, it's a Superdawg™. Maurie and Flaurie came up with a unique proprietary blend of spices and other ingredients, added them to a pure ground beef and came up with the best hot dog—

Superdawg™!—I've ever eaten (we've already established that I'm a hot dog expert, right?).

The fact that they peel and hand-cut their French fries and cook them fresh every day is just gilding the lily.

Ahead of us Charlie Chan's car pulled into the Superdawg® lot and parked by a speaker. The limo wouldn't fit in the lot, so we all got out and went up to order at the window while James drove around the block. Charlie Chan stuck his head out the car window and said, "Get it to go" and pointed across Devon Avenue at the nature preserve.

We ordered enough food to feed everybody at a Taylor Swift concert and piled back into the car with our boxes of Superdawgs™ and Superfries™ (they pack the dogs and fries in neat little boxes with the Tarzan and Jane figures on them) and cartons of chocolate malts. The smell was like heaven met a deep fryer and had a baby. We were all slavering like Pavlov's dogs when we got out of the limo in the public area with the picnic tables at the nature preserve (the "Clayton F. Smith Woods Preserve" was on a big sign by the entrance) and found Assistant Director of Homeland Security Nathan Jones and a man and a womyn waiting for us. They also had Superdawg® boxes on their table—Jones was munching on Superfries™ as we walked up.

The other two people got up and turned around and I nearly dropped my precious bag of Superdawgs™—the womyn was my old boss in Spec Ops, Lieutenant General Natalya Muzghov-Franklin. She was a tough broad with a very Russian face—long straight nose, chin like a work boot, big white teeth, blonde hair that was almost white, and wide-set cornflower blue eyes that were topped with bushy blonde eyebrows. Her body was all gristle, sinew and corded muscles, even though she was nearing sixty years old. General Natalya Muzghov-Franklin wasn't pretty, but she was striking—and she was utterly implacable when it came to destroying the enemies of the United States.

In Spec Ops we called her SWWFYU—pronounced "swiff-yu"—an acronym for "She Who Will Fuck You Up."

I'd never had a better boss.

She looked all of us over and then did a slow swivel of her head back to look directly at me. Her rock-hard face split in a wide, wicked smile and it was apparent that General Muzghov-Franklin could have any man she wanted, because when she smiled like that the Pope would have been tempted.

Without any conscious thought I put my Superdawg® bag down, straightened to attention and snapped my hand up in a perfect salute. I couldn't have stopped myself if my *zayde*'s life depended on it. SWWFYU also stood at attention, saluted and said, "At ease, Major Freak. We're all just friends here, meeting at the park to discuss the Cubs, and Bears and a huge major international counterfeiting ring." She dropped her salute and I said, "Aye, ma'am! Standing at ease, ma'am!"

She came over and hugged me. "It's good to see you, Freak. I hear you gave these guys an idea about shooting in your alternate universe—still like a video game for you?"

"Affirmative, ma'am. My skills might even be better," I said.

"Impossible—they were already perfect," SWWFYU said. She turned to her companions and said, "Meet the best special operator I've ever seen. She'll definitely do for this op, and if she vouches for the rest of the team I'm satisfied."

Nathan Jones said, "OK, but we need to eat first, because if I don't get a Superdawg™ down in the next 10 seconds my gut is going to fall out through my asshole."

Nobody could argue with that, so we all sat down and ate like we were going on a survival hike in the Gobi Desert without food.

When the burping commenced and the air began to fill with the smell of dill pickles, green relish and onions Nathan Jones said, "Most of you have probably figured this out, but Homeland Security wants you to interdict as much North Korean counterfeiting as you can before we stop the Uzbek investigation. Homeland Security is going to run the false flag op while you do all the real work."

We all looked at Joe, and then we burst out laughing. I said, "We're not worthy" and bowed to Joe, and the rest of my squad mates followed suit. Guru and Charlie Chan also laughed, and were joined by Nathan Jones, who said, "Picked my pocket, eh Agent Cocker?"

"Word for word," I said. "If I didn't know better I'd say that you fed it to him, but Joe is just that good."

"Since we're already on the same page about what we want to do, I need to tell you that your director has already signed off on this," Jones said. He looked at Charlie Chan, who said, "Director Hessler has temporarily detached us from all other duties in order to concentrate on this case. We are also getting eight computer geeks to assist—they'll be coming from the Financial Crimes section in San Francisco, arriving tomorrow."

"Wow, they're sending the first string," Jewey said. "Those guys are on the front line of cyber crime attacks on the currency, especially from Asia, and probably are experts on the North Koreans already."

"And they are super-smart, super-up-to-date hackers too," Weasel said. "I can code with anybody, but those geeks are playing a game I'm not familiar with."

"Nice theft, Weasel," I said.

"Thank you—it's always nice to work a sports quote into the operational briefings—it promotes teamwork, don't ya think?" Weasel said.

"What the fuck are you dipshits talking about?" Ed said, her sleep deprivation asserting itself.

"Bobby Jones is one of the immortals of golf—he practically invented the game here in the United States and was the founder of the Masters. He watched Jack Nicklaus win the 1965 US Open and said, 'Nicklaus played a game I am not familiar,'—imagine Michael Jordan watching Kevin Durant play and saying that. Or Ted Williams watching Miguel Cabrera—it's the ultimate quote of respect," the other guy with Jones and SWWFYU said.

"Meet Mr. Brown of the CIA," Jones said.

"Oh fuck that code name shit. These are real warriors—they deserve more respect than that, dontcha think?" the guy said. "I'm Jack Grimké, formerly the station chief in Seoul and now head of the Asia desk at Langley. I've been assigned to assist you in any way possible because I'm well versed on the nefarious DPRK, or the Marx Brothers of International Terrorism, as I like to call 'em," the CIA guy said.

"And this is Lieutenant General Natalya Muzghov-Franklin, commanding officer of the Combined Special Operations Unit of the United States military," I said, "my former commanding officer and a legendary special operations soldier in her own right."

"Except I'm old now and don't go into the field," Muzghov-Franklin said. "I do still have the privilege to command the best Spec Ops unit in the history of the world, and we've recently had our own run-in with the Marx Brothers that involved us killing a bunch of them and capturing a small block of cash in the form of $100 bills that proved to be fakes, which is why I'm here."

"You mean you captured a block of counterfeit $100s, ma'am," Betty said.

"What's the difference?" Muzghov-Franklin said.

"A fake is like one of those million dollar bills that you use as a prop—there is no intent to deceive and they are not what we would call structurally correct—they're obvious fakes," Betty said. "If there is intent to deceive—if the bills try to look right and have the proper insignia, lettering and other features found on real currency—then they are counterfeit. I will assume from your tone and emphasis that these $100 bills looked like the real thing at first glance, but turned out not to be," Betty said.

"Hence they are counterfeit, not fake," the general said.

"Four-oh, ma'am," Betty said.

"Army?" the general said. "Four-oh" is a military term—*4.0*—the highest score one can get on Fit Reps (Fitness Reports—the basis for advancement in military rank) and promotion boards, etc., so her guess was a good one.

Betty smiled and said, "I hesitate to tell you this, but my grandfather was Augustus R. Fleming, USN."

Admiral Augustus R. "Gus" Fleming was a legendary sailor who rose from the enlisted ranks to become the Chief of Naval Operations, and later the Superintendent of the United States Naval Academy, where he turned out quality naval officers for over 20 years. He was also one of the fathers of the new stealth navy, having championed that technology as the future of the surface Navy since it became available for aircraft.

But the real reason everyone knew Gus Fleming in the military world was because he was the guy who went to Congress as the CNO and bitched them out about how poorly our sailors, soldiers and Marines were paid (and treated) if they were not at the general officer level. He especially stood up for the enlisted ranks, who he said were "criminally underpaid and overworked."

When one particularly obese Congressman challenged his contention Admiral Gus Fleming said, "Sir, it doesn't look like you've missed many meals during your time in Congress, but many of our enlisted personnel who have families and live off post do. Maybe you should try trading salary and perqs with them sometime, instead of going to cocktail fundraisers so you can get re-elected."

Which is not the thing to say to a member of the Ways and Means Committee, especially when the guy is the chairman of the Armed Services sub-committee.

Fortunately Admiral Gus Fleming wasn't just an old salt who liked to bitch. After the obese Congressman got his licks in verbally Gus Fleming got his in, both factually and viscerally. In front of lots of reporters and TV cameras the CNO brought in 25 sailors and Marines who told stories of grinding poverty, lack of food for their children and the poorest housing imaginable. The fact that they did this in full dress uniform (even the seven who had empty sleeves or legs in their uniforms due to service-related amputations) gave their testimony almost as much impact as the 29 spouses of sailors and Marines who had died in combat that told their stories of life in service while waiting for loved ones that never came home.

When one young widower talked about taking care of his five kids while working full time and waiting for his wife to come home from a non-combat position in Afghanistan, only to return one day to find a Marine sergeant and captain waiting to tell him she'd been killed…well, even the fat congressman had tears over that one.

And surprisingly something got done: *60 Minutes* did an investigation and so did the *New York Times*. An intrepid Fox News reporter went along with a group of military wives who pooled their resources every month and fed their kids collectively in order to save money, and the president of the United States actually got involved, suggesting legislation that tied military pay to the rate of pay earned by Congress. (Okay, so you can stop screaming now. I tried every other word I could think of in that sentence, and *earned* is the only one that worked. I agree with you about Congress—sorry, men and wymyn of the legislative branch, but it's really not work when you [a] have a staff that does 99.9 percent of the actual work and [b] no one notices when you're doing nothing, especially when you're doing nothing most of the time—and yeah, *earned* was still the only word that worked. Sorry.)

So Gus Fleming got the job done and enlisted pay was raised above the poverty level, but there was a price to be paid for his cavalier and condescending attitude toward Congress. They forced him out as CNO, and tried to force him to retire.

But four-star admirals don't go easy, especially when they feel like they've been fucked over for telling the truth, so Gus Fleming cleverly got the Pentagon to put him out to pasture as the commandant at the Naval Academy, where he educated young naval officers until his death at age 70… after 52 years in the United States Navy.

General Muzghov-Franklin straightened to attention when Betty mentioned her grandpa's name, as did all of the rest of us who had served, because Gus Fleming was not only a *mensch* (Yiddish for "one tough motherfucker"), he was also the epitome of the fighting sailor/soldier/Marine/air force personnel that were only rarely found in any armed services around the world. He'd seen the elephant, stood up straight in the face of overwhelming opposition and also stood for the men and wymyn under his command at great personal risk…and he came out the other side unbowed and unbeaten to do one of the most important jobs in the Navy.

I thought SWWFYU was going to salute, but all she did was nod at Betty and say, "That was one hell of a sailor, Agent Fleming. He was someone I'd go to war with."

Betty returned the nod and said, "You know that he was born a warrior, right?"

"What d'you mean?" SWWFYU said.

"Grandpa was born on Thursday, 26 March, 1934. He was born on the day named after the Norse god of war, in the month named for the Roman god of war and under the astrological sign named for the Greek god of war. He always said he was a warrior born, not made," Betty said.

SWWFYU nodded again and said, "So he was. Everyone still in the service owes him, and I'm not just talking about the pay thing." She stuck out her hand and Betty shook it, and then SWWFYU turned to look at me and said, "Now it makes perfect sense, Freak. You were born that way."

Betty looked at me and said, "Really? You were born in March?"

"26 March, 1977," I said. "It seems that I was born under the same star as your grandpa." Betty put her arms around me and gave me the best hug I'd ever had from anyone (remember that before he discovered that he was gay my boyfriend in college was a huge basketball player—and gay or not, Square Peg knew how to hug).

"Not to break up a touching moment, but can we do this after we catch the motherfucking North Korean assholes who are counterfeiting our currency and trying to undermine the world economy?" Jack Grimké said.

Typical CIA asshole—the joke in Spec Ops was that CIA operatives had good skills but no heart; it wasn't because of a lack of respect that my unit always called them "Tin Men," but rather because their studied dispassion always made them seem arrogant and uncaring, without any results to back their conduct up. Spec Ops operators always knew that we had a direct and indirect impact on the world—our actions had consequences in the real world—but the CIA men and wymyn we dealt with always acted like they were conducting a lab experiment for a new hard-on drug; the results would be interesting no matter what happened, but it didn't really concern them if guys took the new pill and got a hard-on for 12 days.

I started to say something harsh, but then something hit me. I looked at the rest of the squad and they were all thinking hard, too, so I said nothing. I rolled the thought around in my mind and finally said, "General, where did you come into possession of the counterfeit currency?"

"And who did you catch with it?" Joe said.

"And how was it packaged?" Weasel said.

"It was overseas—Manila, or Taipei, or maybe Kuala Lumpur," Mamba said.

"And you were tracking it, because it was connected to a splinter group of terrorists who were trying to overthrow the government," Buzz said, pointing at Grimké.

"Not Muslims...it must have been that group in Manila last month, the one that had a U.S. serviceman who fed them intel because his cousin was the leader of the group," Coach said.

"Wait a minute—there must have been multiple U.S. personnel involved, because it was a very hot story one day, and then gone the next. It was as if the story dug a hole and pulled the hole in after itself," Joe said. "Since it wasn't in Russia, it must have been us who did that." He looked at SWWFYU and Grimké, who just sat there like statues.

"Of course," I said, "it was an elite unit that did it—so they sent you to get them, ma'am."

"Army Rangers," Betty said. "SEALs wouldn't do it, and if it was the unified Spec Ops command they wouldn't have sent General Muzghov-Franklin's troops, so it had to be Army Rangers."

"Could have been Marine Spec Ops," Weasel said.

"No way," several of us said at once. "Besides, Marine Spec Ops are under her command anyway—they'd have sent somebody else," I said.

"And you were the bird-dog, because you have somebody in the splinter group," Mamba said, pointing at Grimké.

"And you want to advise us so that we don't blow your asset," Joe said.

"And so CIA can get some of the credit when we do bust these gomers," Jewey said.

Grimké and SWWFYU both laughed, and the CIA guy said, "OK, OK, we give—you got us. I didn't realize that your unit was full of geniuses."

"Actually, the plural of genius is 'genii'," Mamba said.

"Really?" Grimké said.

"Nah, I'm just fuckin' with ya," Mamba said. We all laughed again, and SWWFYU said, "To answer all of your questions: we found it packaged in a small bale, like it had been taken from a larger bale—there were grooves in the plastic that looked like they may have been made by packing straps."

"Was it thick, heavy polyethylene, or was it lighter, like the plastic on magazines?" Weasel said.

"It was definitely lighter—one of my guys thought it might be shrink wrap because the bale was very tight," SWWFYU said.

"And exactly who were the guys you found with it, ma'am?" Jewey said.

"Eight members of First Platoon, Company B, Third Battalion, 75th Ranger Regiment," SWWFYU said. "They were part of an anti-terrorist training group that was deployed in a joint exercise with the Philippine Army. The story about the intel going from one soldier to his cousin was a cover—these guys were all Caucasian and were simply washing cash. At first we thought it was drug money, but then Agent Grimké showed up and we changed our minds."

"Why? Ah, I get it—you were already tracking the money because of where it was showing up after it left the PI," I said.

"Give the womyn a cookie," the CIA agent said. "We started noticing loads of cash—literal, physical cash, not wire transfers—being spent by North Korean agents who were trying to acquire miniaturizing technology so they can make little nukes and deploy them against us, but it was funny, because usually these guys are really slick, and the guys spending the cash were just too clumsy. They actually offered one of these bales to one of my guys at a scientific conference in Beijing—he was there to observe the Chinese nuclear scientists and ended up getting approached by DPRK agents. He sort of confronted them by playing the 'I'm a patriot' card and they couldn't back water fast enough—they claimed it was all a misunderstanding and that they were South Korean, but my guy has tons of experience with the DPRK and I trust his judgment—these were North Koreans."

"But why come to us? Surely CIA has its own assets in place to follow the supply of counterfeits—and the Secret Service really doesn't do international cases," Guru said.

"They came to us because we are somehow already connected to the money," Joe said.

"It really is the only thing that makes any sense," Mamba said. "Your unit is somehow connected to the cash, probably from an old case."

"Not very old," Weasel said. "I think that this bale of funny money is from our mountain of cash at Little Luigi's."

"That bitch!" Jewey said.

"That fucking bitch!" Joe said.

"That motherfucking bitch!" Guru said.

"Damn that cunt to eternal burning hell!" I said.

We all started talking at once, until Joe shushed us. He looked at the three outsiders and said, "Let me guess—the money looked and felt right, except that it was a little soft, like it had been in a dryer, and when you subjected it to scrutiny it passed, except for the Test."

Nathan Jones said, "Absolutely correct. We have several former Secret Service personnel in Homeland, and they all said the money was legit…until they did the Test, and it wasn't right."

"The paper was perfect and the ink was right on?" Guru said

"And this bale of funny money was a million dollars, right?" Jewey said. "Didn't have a bill out of place?"

"Absolutely true," SWWFYU said.

"Oh, that smarmy shitbitchmotherfuckingassholecunt!" Weasel said.

"Who's the bitch?" Grimké said.

"Darcy Fowler!" we all said.

"More Pepsis for everybody," Mamba said. "Who the fuck is Darcy Fowler?" the CIA guy said.

Guru explained, and SWWFYU said, "Holy shit—this is an international conspiracy to undermine the dollar with counterfeit money. The North Koreans are committing an act of war."

"No wonder those assholes were so clumsy—they've got a mountain of cash and they're all hands on deck to wash it right into the U.S. economy where it can do the most damage. They're using terrorists to wash it, too, and probably to carry the funny money to places where they can buy drugs and weapons and all sorts of other stuff to keep the global turmoil going," Grimké said.

We all nodded, and Jewey said, "If they get enough counterfeit in circulation it'll be a fucking disaster—a tsunami of funny money that undermines faith in the dollar as the world's reserve currency, and once that happens…"

"Fuckin' ka-boom goes the U.S. economy," Coach said.

"And that sucking sound you hear it the rest of the world's economies going down the shitter," Betty said.

"Oh holy fuck-fuck," I said. "We've been letting Fowler have access to her attorney, she's talked to dozens of prosecutors, there've been sworn statements using court reporters—didn't her attorney have three paralegals interview her in order to file the writ to suppress her confession?"

Joe went pale and said, "Oh, no. We've got to get surveillance on all those people, and we need to tap their phones and computers, and we need to check everybody's bank accounts for sudden deposits of any size—and we need to do it yesterday."

"We can't do that—we'd need a thousand warrants," Charlie Chan said.

Nathan Jones got it right away. "Luckily I don't need any such thing—I'll get 'em later," he said. We all pulled out our cell phones and called the office, asking for the Financial Crimes unit.

Jack Grimké said, "Why do I always feel like the slow one around here? What the fuck is going on?"

SWWFYU said, "I believe all of these smart people know something we don't. I'm guessing that they are going to be hungry when they all stop talking on their phones, so let's go get some more food, shall we? All will be revealed when we return."

They went across the street and came back with more boxes of Superdawgs™, which we promptly devoured like a pack of starving wolves. When we were down to the chocolate malts Weasel said, "General, when did you seize the bale of counterfeit 100s?"

"8 June 2018," she said.

"At what time of day?" Weasel said.

"2330 hours," she said.

"So you got the funny money at 11:30 p.m. on the same day that we arrested Darcy Fowler at 1:00 p.m.," Joe said.

"She's got another distribution warehouse that's independent of the one in the Big Apple," Jewey said.

"Of course—she signaled the warehouse in NYC, but is letting the other one go forward, probably because she's still convinced that her lawyer is going to get her off," Guru said.

"And I'll bet that she's using that weaselly fuckhead to send messages to her henchmen about continuing to distribute—she knows that we're not set up on any other funny money because we've never said a peep about it," Ed said.

"General, where are you keeping the Rangers that you caught with the counterfeits?" I said.

"The three who survived are in a place I'm not going to talk about, but I can get access to them if I need to," SWWFYU said.

"You need to," Charlie Chan said. "We're going to give them the old flim-flam if we have to, unless we can find some other leverage."

I thought about it and said, "What do people in the south do more than any other region of the country?"

"Fuck their cousins," Coach said.

"Drive pickup trucks and fuck their sisters," Weasel said.

"Eat barbeque and fuck their hogs," Ed said.

"Hogs are synonymous with cousins in this case, aren't they?" Betty said.

"They live in trailers, shoot guns at road signs, drink cheap beer, make meth *and* fuck their relatives," Mamba said.

"Nice generalization of who they fuck—covers a lot more bases," Coach said.

I laughed along with everybody else, but Joe and Jewey looked at me and Jewey said, "The original question was what do Southerners do more than any other region of the country, right?"

"Correct," I said.

"They join the service," Joe said. "The armed forces get more recruits from the South because it's a tradition there."

"And our original distributors of funny money were from the south," Jewey said.

"And Darcy Fowler is related to those clowns, and also from the south," I said. "She went to William and Mary."

"General, we need the service records of all the Rangers involved," Charlie Chan said. He turned to Guru and said, "We also need to get a list of all of Fowler's regular clients at Chase, especially those that are from or work extensively in Asia."

"Stereotyping the poor Asians?" Weasel said in mock outrage. "Couldn't this have been pulled off by a bunch of round-eyes?"

"Probably," Jack Grimké said. "But my mole in the terrorist gang tells me that the money men have all been Asian wymyn out of Hong Kong. The mole knows for a fact that they aren't hookers or drug mules—they appear to know exactly what is going on as far as the money is concerned."

"How does he know that?" Betty said.

Grimké smiled and said, "Sorry, but that's a bridge too far."

Betty bowed and said, "My apologies, good sir—that was a dumbass question. Of course you can't reveal anything about your agent, even though we'll probably identify him during our investigation."

"Wanna bet a thousand dollars you don't even get a whiff?" Grimké said.

"I'll take that action," every person on the squad said at once. Pepsis were passed around and Grimké said, "OK, I'll take all the action, but if I lose, I'm paying in $100 bills."

We laughed our asses off all the way back to the office.

And one more clue to the crime of the century was right before us, although it would take us far too long to realize it.

CHAPTER 35

Boob Job

So we all went back to the office and went to work. We got the records of the Rangers involved and found a link to Darcy Fowler right away.

Sergeant First Class Durwood Moody was married to Marilyn Gilroy, whose brother Jimbo Gilroy was married to Samantha Chouinard, whose brother Gaetan Chouinard was married to Marcy Horne, whose brother was Carl Horne of the Toledo Five. It got weirder, because the Chouinards, who were Cajuns from Iberia Parish near New Orleans, were the first cousins of both Durwood Moody and the Hornes, while Marilyn Gilroy was a first cousin of the Chouinards and Darcy Fowler. It was a convoluted course to the truth, and vaguely incestuous, but it all fit together.

Our two crimes were interconnected.

"I'll bet that bitch set the international connection up at a family reunion, too," Jewey said.

"If they had time—it sounds like family reunions were an excuse for a fuck-fest," Betty said.

"Maybe they just had orgies and used 'family reunion' as a euphemism," Ed said.

"*Eeeeyyyuuuuuu!*" Mamba said, "That is just *dis-gusting*. Straight folks are just *pigs*."

"Depravity is an ugly thing," I said. "But we have established a connection between Fowler and the Rangers, which means we only need to find the connection between the Koreans and Fowler to establish that it was the same counterfeiting ring in both cases."

That piece of information filling in the gap in our case came when Weasel said, "Guess what the Koreans we caught were doing in business?"

"How the fuck're we supposed to know that? We don't even know who the fuckers are," Coach said.

"Well, one of them is named Park Mun-Hee," Weasel said.

"Give it up, motherfucker," Joe said.

"I was looking at databases and found out that some people who do business with the state of Illinois have to be fingerprinted—like anyone who works in a prison," Weasel said.

"Park Mun-Hee is a prison guard?" Joe said.

"No, but his business deals with prisons, and sometimes in the early days he delivered there, which meant he had to be bonded—and fingerprinted," Weasel said.

"They deal in vending machines," Mamba said.

"Give the man a cheroot," Weasel said. "Park Mun-Hee is the CEO of Red Star Vending, Inc., which deals in all types of vending machines, from condoms to packaged food. From their yearly statement it looks like Red Star has a virtual monopoly on soda vending machines in the Midwest—they operate over 500,000 Pepsi and Coke machines in Illinois, Wisconsin, Minnesota, Indiana, Michigan, Ohio, Iowa and Missouri."

"Those double-dipping motherfuckers," Jewey said. "A half a million machines? Now we know where the majority of their dollar bills come from."

"They're making a profit while *really* making a profit," Buzz said.

"Sounds like they're running dog capitalists to me," Betty said.

"And I'll bet that they invest most of the profits here in the good old New York Stock Exchange, then send the washed money home to good old North Korea," I said.

"That is *definitely* running dog capitalism," Mamba said.

"Check for known business associates," Joe said.

"Already on it. Well, lookee here," Weasel said. "Red Star works closely with Wanchu Associates, an LLC that runs the Asian Angels Gentleman's Clubs across the Midwest. Asian Angels is run by Sung Yong Hoon, who has also been fingerprinted because he's bonded. Both companies work with Ginger Flower Catering, which is run by Choi Shin Ook, also bonded when he worked for Red Star before opening Ginger Flower."

"Also places where lots of ones change hands," Guru said. "These guys are good, and I'll bet that they've been here a long time—did they go to college here?"

"Yeah—right here, in fact. All three of these guys went to the University of Illinois—Chicago in the business college. They were part of a five-person group that enrolled under a scholarship exchange program with the Asian studies departments of UIC and the University of Seoul," Jewey said. "The other two guys in their group were Lee Kyung-Sook and Jeong Ho-Sung."

"Fuckin'-A, bingo-bongo-boingo! Got you motherfuckers!" Weasel said. He hit some keys and we all got information cross-decked to our computers. Within seconds there were smiles all around.

Guru picked up a phone and said, "CC, you'd better come down here right now." The AIC was in our bullpen within 30 seconds and found a bunch of agents grinning like the Cheshire Cat from *Alice in Wonderland*. Charlie Chan raised an eyebrow and Joe said, "CC, we are about to cook some Korean goose. Go Weasel."

Weasel said, "We've established the connection on both ends, and they both come back to Darcy Fowler. She's got a shirttail relation that was in the Ranger squad that was supplying the funny money for guns in the PI, and she's deeply connected to the Koreans who are supplying the ones to be bleached and counterfeited." He looked at Jewey, who said, "We've got three Koreans in custody who are all in heavily cash businesses that get lots of ones, but it's the two who aren't in custody that establish the connection at this end."

Two photographs of Asian guys came up on our plasma screen. One was Lee Kyung-Sook, the other was Jeong Ho-Sung. Lee's pic was from the American Bar Association, but Jeong's was from an ID card from Chase Bank, Chicago branch.

"Oh Holy Mother of God, please tell me that Jeong works with Fowler," Charlie Chan said.

"He is the senior supervisor of the mail room," Weasel said. "Fowler supervises all non-electronic outgoing and incoming correspondence."

"Hail Mary! We just won the lottery! She's his FUCKIN' BOSS!" Charlie Chan said. Werner Oland would have been so disappointed—Francis Wong just destroyed the stereotype of the inscrutable Asian. We all started screaming like we really had won the lottery, and then Weasel said, "Oh, yeah, Lee Kyung-Sook is the corporate counsel for all three of the companies owned by our incarcerated Koreans. He deals directly with their financial services representative at Chase…"

"Darcy Fowler!" we all said.

"Bet your ass," Weasel said. "That bitch is gonna get fried."

"Hope she likes Cuban food, 'cause her ass is headed to Gitmo!" Coach said.

"I can't wait to see the look on her supercilious face when we drop this in her lap," Ed said.

"You know, this is basically giving aid and comfort to the enemy. If we can get two direct witnesses to her criminal activities we might be able to prove treason, which means we could shoot that cunt," Guru said.

Joe laughed and said, "And to think that this all started because of some hot dog stands." There was more laughter and hilarity, but when we calmed down Charlie Chan said, "OK, now we do everything by the book. We get the computer wizards from financial crimes and we nail down dates, times, transactions and all that other stuff, plus we get Nathan Jones on the horn and tell him what we're doing, and we need to get set up on the two Koreans we don't have in custody, and we need to talk to the FBI and CIA about our Koreans—do we think these guys are deep-cover sleepers?"

"It's a virtual certainty that these guys are North Korean agents," Joe said. "This whole operation has been years in the planning and execution—I'd bet that the Koreans we have in custody are handlers who came in to check up on our boys and see that they're still on mission and not going native."

"Concur," I said. "This is something that their military dreamt up and executed, probably so they could fuck us with the counterfeits. The weapons they're buying with the funny money is just gravy."

"We don't want to spook the two Koreans that we don't have, either," Betty said. She looked thoughtful and said, "We need to insert someone at Chase to catch them red-handed—if this Lee Kyung-Sook is any kind of agent he's gonna wanna get in one last lick against the imperialist running dog Americans."

"I vote for Coach," Buzz said. "I could do it, but if Lee is used to working with a womyn why not keep it the same for him so that he doesn't get his guard up? Especially when we have someone as qualified as Coach to play the part?"

We all looked at Coach, who said, "Ah, fuck. Yeah, I majored in finance at Nebraska. I could con the son of a bitch, at least until we can tell if he'll incriminate himself."

"We've got enough to arrest him right now, but catching him in the act would really be the icing on the cake," Joe said.

"I'll call Edward Otis Whitney in the New York office and get him to set it up," Charlie Chan said. "Coach, Ed, Weasel, and Jewey, you guys get ready to go to New York. Joe, Freak, Betty and Mamba, you are going to interview our pet Koreans and see if we can get anything out of them now that we have some names. I already called Jones at Homeland—they've been keeping the Koreans in isolation at Marion. He'll have them at the Cook County jail this afternoon at five so you can try to talk to them. Guru, Buzz and I are going to coordinate here—oh, and Captain Cork is coming back tomorrow. Maureen called and said if I didn't let him come back she was going to have to take out a hit on me. Apparently the good Captain is a wee bit of a handful when he's not keeping busy."

AJ HARTMAN

We all laughed, relieved that our fearless leader was OK after being shot up, and more so because he was a great tactician when it came to preparing court cases against counterfeiters. We were still giggling about him driving Maureen crazy at home when Joe said, "Hey, we should get Jack Soo in on this. We'll need a translator in case they stick to the 'we-no-speakee-English' routine—he speaks Korean, Japanese and Mandarin, right?—plus he's a pretty sharp interrogator."

"Who the fuck is Jack Soo?" I said. "Hey wait a minute—wasn't that the actor who was on *Barney Miller*?"

"Jack Soo—his real name was Goro Suzuki—was Detective Nick Yemana on the show with Hal Linden, Abe Vigoda, Max Gail, Ron Glass and a bunch of other guys. Our guy is actually Alec Hwang, but he is a dead ringer for Jack Soo, so he got the name and it kinda stuck," Guru said.

"He's affected the mannerisms of the character, too—he's got the driest sense of humor in history," Joe said.

"Tell him I said he can leave everything else for right now and go with you, and let's get our poop in a group on this. We don't want to give these shitheads any wiggle room on this one," Charlie Chan said. We chorused our agreement and all got busy breaking the biggest counterfeiting ring in history.

At 4:30 Joe, Mamba, Betty and a guy who looked exactly like Jack Soo came up to my desk. I was introduced to him, and "Jack Soo" said, "Oh, I just made coffee? You want some?" We all got a good laugh—it was a running gag from *Barney Miller*, where Detective Nick Yemana made the worst coffee ever—and then we went off to interview our Koreans.

"There's a good chance they still won't talk, even with all the info you have about them now," Jack Soo said.

"They're probably afraid we're going to burn them at the stake, or drop a nuke on their families," I said.

"Ah, I see you've met North Koreans before," Jack Soo said.

"Hypothetically," I said.

"What the fuck you talking about, Freak?" Jack Soo said, his voice and mannerisms a dead ringer for the real Jack Soo.

"It's classified," I said.

"Oh," he said. He looked at the other guys and they all nodded. He shrugged his shoulders and said, "If you don't wanna talk you don't wanna talk." Once again we could have been on the set of *Barney Miller*.

"How many episodes did you watch?" I said.

"Every one he was on, and every one after that. It was my favorite show, because the only other shows with Asians were *Bonanza*—good old cardboard cutout Hop-Sing—and *Kung Fu*, where a round eye played an Asian. Fucking David Carradine was about as Asian as the pet dragon in *Mulan*. I still worship Jack Soo—he's my hero."

"I'm so glad for you, but are the North Koreans seriously that paranoid?" Betty said. "How could they after being here for years?"

"They were all brainwashed as kids. From the moment they can listen little North Koreans are told the USA is going to invade their country, that Americans hate them, that all of the apparent

312

wealth and good things in the USA are just props to hide the evilness of the people—you really can't believe the level of paranoia and fear that they have instilled in them," Jack Soo said.

"But all of the things that they see—don't they believe any of the news or magazines, or anything on the internet?" Betty said.

Jack Soo, Joe and I laughed. "They're like mushrooms—they're kept in the dark and fed horseshit," I said. "If you access the internet in North Korea they execute you. *National Geographic* is banned—it's the death penalty for having a copy. Smart phones? International news? An old encyclopedia? All death penalty crimes in North Korean."

"She's right. Anything that isn't about the Dear Leader—the title of Kim Jong Un, the current dictator—is considered capitalist propaganda and carries the death penalty. North Korea is the most repressive country in the world, maybe in the history of the world, and these guys are going to be very, very tough to break, because they're probably also DPRK Army officers, which means that they have been brainwashed again. They believe that the Dear Leader can see and feel disloyalty, and anything that isn't in line with his thinking is disloyal," Jack Soo said.

"Those poor bastards live on around 500 calories a day, while the elite eat like pigs and enjoy all sorts of modern comforts. North Korea is living proof that if you control the information you control the population," Joe said.

"They have one TV station, one radio station and no—zero, zilch, nada—access to the internet," Mamba said. "There is only one truly acceptable newspaper in the whole country—Rodong Sinmun, the paper of the ruling class. The rest are all just window dressing to prove they have freedom of the press."

"Which is the joke of the half-century," Jack Soo said, "since the government has to approve and accredit all reporters before they can write a word. If you write the wrong words after that—bang, you're dead. No trial, no appeal, no proof necessary—you color outside the party lines and you're dead."

"So how do we get these guys to talk?" Betty said.

"Strippers?" Jack Soo said.

"Fine whiskey?" I said.

"Vulcan mind-meld?" Mamba said.

"Appeal to their better angels?" Joe said.

"After we get them drunk, bring in some blonde strippers and mind-meld with 'em," Jack Soo said. We laughed again, but Betty was persistent. "Seriously, what do we hope to get out of them?"

"I don't think we'll get jack shit, but Charlie Chan wants us to try, so I'm going to trick them into using English, and when that doesn't work—and it won't, if these guys are who we think they are—I'll translate while you genius interrogators pummel it out of them," Jack Soo said.

"We could get something out of them if we surprise them with their names and details of the counterfeiting ring," Betty said.

"I could be elected Queen of England, but it's highly unlikely," Mamba said.

"Would you settle for Queen of the May?" Jack Soo said.

"If it's the best I can do—is there a height requirement?" Mamba said.

"No, you just have to be able to be a queen," Jack Soo said.

"Well, then I'm *highly* qualified," Mamba said.

As we were laughing when Joe's phone rang. He listened, then said, "Going on speaker."

"Lee Kyung-Sook and Jeong Ho-Sung are both on vacation in San Francisco. They booked a wine-tasting tour and are apparently in the Napa Valley. The FBI is scrambling teams to follow them around, but I'll bet I already know what is going on," Jewey said.

"They're getting drunk on high quality grape juice after paying with counterfeit money, the assholes," I said.

"It might help if I told you that they are flying out through Long Beach," Jewey said.

"Oh, ho," Joe said.

"I gotta give credit where it's due—they're clever assholes," I said.

"But isn't Long Beach way south of San Fran?" Betty said. "Who the fuck was their travel agent—that's crazy when they could fly direct from Cali to Chi."

"Except that the Port of Long Beach is the busiest port in the U.S., and one of the busiest in the world," Mamba said.

"Ahhh," Betty and Jack Soo said. "You owe me a Pepsi, Jack," Betty said.

"Would coffee be OK? I just made a fresh pot," Jack Soo said.

He was totally in character.

We thanked Jewey and laughed our way to the parking lot at the Cook County jail. Located on North California Avenue about three blocks south of Belmont Avenue on Chicago's northwest side and just off the Kennedy Expressway, the jail was bigger than most towns in South Dakota (and North Dakota, for that matter) and typically housed too many inmates. It was a great place to interrogate people, because it was so busy that no one would notice some random Koreans and Secret Service personnel, plus it had more interview rooms than the Palmer House Hotel had rooms (believe me when I tell you that the rooms at the Palmer House were much nicer even after a drunk rock band had trashed them).

We went in and showed our creds to a fat sergeant behind five inches of bulletproof glass and got passed right through. There was a giant Chicago cop waiting for us—he was so big that he blotted out the fluorescent lights. He was also hiding Nathan Jones and two other people behind him. One was clearly an FBI guy—short hair, JCPenney suit and a serious look on his face. The other was the best-looking womyn I'd ever seen. She was about 5'10", curvy and caramel colored, with deep-brown eyes and a nice Michelle Obama hairdo. She was also very well dressed in what looked like a Vera Wang dress and Jimmy Choo shoes and had a figure that could only be called voluptuous (the same way that Kate Upton is voluptuous, only just a tad thinner—and no, I'm not dissing Kate Upton—she is absolutely gorgeous just the way she is).

This womyn made me look like a contestant in a pig-judging contest—and I was the pig.

Jones said, "Hey, kids. This is FBI Special Agent Don Mort, and my Intel chief, Assistant Director Marla Ahumada." He turned to the giant Chicago cop, who stuck his hand out and said, "I'm Lieutenant June Walton from the Intelligence Division of the Chicago PD." His voice was the kind of bass that registered on the Richter scale. It would have made Barry White jealous and was so melodious that it almost seemed as if he were singing.

It also got the attention of the two wymyn and gay man present, as we all quivered to sexual attention. We shook his hand and Mamba said, "Lieutenant, you are an exquisite giant. Has anyone ever told you that you look like a Black copy of Michelangelo's *David*?"

"Oh, sure. My wife of 37 years tells me that all the time," Lieutenant Walton said with a straight face.

We all backed down from being on sexual point, and Walton said, "'Course, she also tells me that my ass is as big as Wyoming and that my rotund self is gonna die from heart failure if I don't lay off the Superdawgs™, so I guess she's jist tryin' to keep my morale up after all the bitchin'."

Even Nathan Jones laughed. Finally Lieutenant Walton said, "I'm disappointed in you-all—don't nobody wanna make a joke about my name?"

The Secret Service detachment all looked at each other and said, "John-Boy" at exactly the same time. "I'll buy the Pepsis," Mamba said. "And you can stop with the dumb city cop *schtick*, John-Boy," I said. "You were the left tackle that led the Illini to the Top 10 back in the '80s—and you were an academic All-American. Then you made the Texans and got hurt, right?"

June Walton smiled and said, "Yeah, that was me. I would like to know how you remember all that. I was pretty obscure."

"She remembers all of that sports trivia because she's a *freak*," Mamba said. "She knows all the batting averages of the 1984 Detroit Tigers, too."

"All of that is great, but shouldn't we be interviewing the Koreans by now?" Marla Ahumada spoke for the first time and her perfect image was shattered.

She had a little, screechy voice with just enough petulance in it to make it sound like fingernails on a chalk board. It was what my mom called a "my defecation is not odiferous" voice, and what Square Peg and I always called a "bitch on wheels" voice.

We all immediately disliked her as much as we all liked Lieutenant June Walton.

"Oh, I just got it," Betty said, as if Marla Ahumada hadn't spoken. "You thought that we were going to make fun of your first name."

"It does have some feminine *overtones*—June Cleaver comes to mind—but in reality June is a *male* name," Mamba said.

"Do tell," Lieutenant Walton said, perfectly aware that the two Homeland personnel were getting antsy, but perfectly willing to tweak them a bit.

"The name 'June' means 'young' in Latin and is one of the oldest surnames in the world," Mamba said.

"Didn't the name originate in France? I seem to remember that it was recorded in the Domesday Book around 1299 CE," Joe said. "Wasn't it Richard le Jeune?"

"Give the man a cheroot," Mamba said. "It's an old English name that originated in the medieval French. Before it got to America it was almost exclusively male, but here it became a unisex name, at least as a given name. There is still a Lord June in Britain, although that particular line is dying out. So no, Lieutenant Young Walton, we do not want to make fun of your name, although we won't be using it in any case."

"Because you're John-Boy from now on," Jack Soo said, still in character.

"Then you must be Jack Soo, or should I say Detective Nick Yemana?" John-Boy said.

"Got any coffee?" Jack said. We all laughed, except the now flawed (but still easy to look at) AD Ahumada. She harrumphed a sigh and John-Boy said, "Oh, don't get your knickers in a knot, girl. Those Koreans aren't going anywhere and we can grill 'em for as long as your FISA warrant holds out. Hell, we can even get 'em sent to Guantanamo Bay and we can grill 'em there. Which don't sound like such a bad idea, since I ain't never been to Cuba in June." He turned to us and said, "How 'bout you?"

We all got it, and responded with a chorus of Sinatra's "How About You?" which was rather incongruous since we were in the Cook County jail about to interview North Korean secret agents, but it really pissed Miss Bitchy Voice off, so we hit it again just to make sure she got the point.

When we were done Nathan Jones said, "Nice number. Can we get our asses in gear and see if these guys will talk?"

"Of course," Joe said. "Let us at 'em."

So we went into the bowels of the jail and found Homeland agents standing outside the doors of three separate interview rooms filled with Koreans. As per procedure, multiple agents had to be in each room in order to interview, so we decided to hit each guy with three teams, with each team getting 30 minutes or so before we debriefed each other and then went at them again.

Joe, Jack Soo and I took the room with Park Mun-He, Betty, Mamba and Nathan Jones took Sung Yong Hoon, and John-Boy and Miss Bitchy Voice took Choi Shin Ook. We were pretty sure they weren't going to talk, but we needed to interview them anyway, before we tried the two whose names we didn't know tomorrow. Better safe than sorry, right?

As soon as we got in the door to interview Park Mun Hee Jack Soo let fly with a stream of Korean. Park Mun-Hee didn't even blink; he just sat there looking straight ahead. Jack Soo paused, looked at the impassive Park and let fly with another stream of Korean invective. Still no reaction, so Jack began to talk in a low, soft voice directly into Park's ear. After a few seconds Park's eyes began to move around the room, but he still wouldn't speak. After the low, soft attempt Jack Soo said, "I give up. Got any ideas?"

Joe said, "I don't know. How do you say 'talk or don't talk, motherfucker, we still got ya for counterfeiting' in Korean?"

Jack Soo translated for Park Mun-Hee, which was ridiculous since we knew that he'd graduated from UIC, but it had to be done. No reaction at all.

I looked at him and said, "Look, Mr. Mun-Hee, we know all about your spying for that fat little piglet Kim Jong Un, and we know that you were helping distribute counterfeit currency in the U.S. You're going to prison, so why not at least confirm your name is Mun-Hee Park?" I deliberately screwed up his name and insulted his Dear Leader, and it almost had the desired effect. Park looked at me and then looked away, then slowly slid his eyes back for another look, but he wasn't looking at my eyes.

He appraised my tits like a true connoisseur, and then just went back to his stony straight ahead imitation of the Sphinx. It was something, but it didn't pan out. Our 30 minutes with him came and went and we were on to Sung Yong Hoon.

It was much the same, but this time Sung began looking at my tits before I spoke. Hmmmm.

Let me reiterate: I am not good-looking in any known universe, but I do have outstanding tits. It didn't hurt that I was wearing a real bra instead of the industrial strength sports bra I usually wore. It meant that my tits were very perky in their 100% silk "C" cups, and it gave me the start of an idea, which I let ferment in my head for a minute.

We wore out Sung, but he wasn't any more forthcoming than Park, so we moved on to Choi Shin Ook. We were about five minutes in when I excused myself and went into the observation room to look at Park being interviewed by Betty, Mamba and Nathan Jones. As soon as Betty spoke Park's eyes slid over to check out her tits. Mamba had bigger tits than Betty Crocker; Park just glanced over and immediately dismissed her.

Gotcha, motherfucker!

Or rather, I was going to get Sung Yong Hoon.

When we all came out to debrief I didn't even let anyone else open their mouth. "I want to shuffle our teams. I want AD Ahumada and Jack Soo with me, and I want to take on Sung Yoon Hoon first."

"Why?" everyone else said. Nathan Jones said, "You got something cooking, Freak?"

"Sir, what do Asian men like better than good scotch, gambling and Kobe beef put together?"

"Round-eye boobs, the bigger the better," Jack Soo said.

"What?" AD Ahumada said. "That's a ridiculous stereotype."

Jack Soo leered at her ample figure and said, "No, uh, it's actually the truth, pretty lady" in his perfect Detective Nick Yemana voice.

"Explain," Nathan Jones said.

"Look, a majority of Asian wymyn have funny little tits, and most Asian guys, especially Japanese and Korean men, have serious mommy issues. Nothing says 'mommy' like a pair of nice round, full tits attached to some beautiful non-Asian womyn. I'm not saying every single Asian guy ever born likes tits better'n anything else, but it's a fair guess that at least one of these guys does," Jack Soo said.

"Speaking from personal experience, Agent Hwang?" Nathan Jones said.

"I married a blonde California round-eye with perfect breasts and a PhD in psychology from Cal Berkeley," Jack Soo said. "Draw your own conclusions." After we all got done laughing—except Miss Bitchy Voice, who clearly wasn't amused—Nathan Jones said, "So what's your idea, Freak?"

I told them about my observations and what I planned to do. Joe said, "Clever yet simple—and you picked the right target. I didn't know what he was looking at, but Sung definitely reacted to you. I thought it was because you screwed up his name and insulted the Dear Leader, but you had a better sightline."

"He was definitely looking at my tits," I said. "All we need to do now is get AD Ahumada and me into costume and we'll be good to go."

"What do you mean 'get into costume'?" Miss Bitchy Voice said.

"We're going to go commando in front of Sung, push all of his buttons and get him to start talking—once we get him going it's possible that he will be so intoxicated by the sheer volume of our cleavage that he'll let something slip," I said.

"You may want to let something slip to help him along," John-Boy said.

"How many people can fit into that observation booth?" Joe said. "I'm sure you'll need experienced interrogators to make sure that it's being done properly."

"I'm thinkin' you, me and Jones can get in there OK, but I'm not sure about anybody else," John-Boy said.

"I'm absolutely not participating in any such charade," Miss Bitchy Voice said. "It's disgusting and outside protocols, and I won't be a part of it."

Nathan Jones looked at her like she'd just said she was going to take a shit on the White House lawn during a presidential press conference. He shook his head and said, "There is nothing disgusting about using whatever means necessary short of torture to get information out of a foreign national that is trying to cause an economic meltdown of our economy. I won't order you to do this, but I strongly urge you to think about it before refusing." In bureaucratic speech that translated into "Are you fucking crazy? You're committing career suicide."

Miss Bitchy Voice said, "It is disgusting—it's like being a prostitute. I won't be pimped out for any reason, and I'm going to take this up with the Secretary when I get back to D.C." Her face was set like Mount Rushmore, and you could see her quivering in anger.

"No one's asking you to do anything lewd or lascivious, AD Ahumada. No one is pimping you out or asking you to be a prostitute. All we need you to do is use your natural gifts to influence someone we desperately need to talk," Jones said. He was cool under pressure—she'd just told him that she was going over his head to his boss on a sexual misconduct charge—but Miss Bitchy Voice was adamant.

"No, I won't do it," she said, pouting like a little girl who didn't get a pony for her birthday.

"AD Ahumada, this is deadly serious business," John-Boy said. "We all understand your objections, but it would seem that the needs of the country outweigh your tender sensibilities. Believe me, I know pimping and prostitution—and this isn't it."

"You're not in my chain of command, and I don't care what you know about pimping and prostitution. I'm not going to parade naked in front of anyone, much less someone we can't even confirm is a foreign agent," Miss Bitchy Voice said, her voice arching in a triumphant tone. She thought that she was not only going to win the argument, but also come out of it smelling like a rose. Maybe she even thought that she would get promoted for sticking to her principles and/or being the victim of sexual harassment.

"No one is asking you to parade naked," Nathan Jones said.

"All we want is for you to take off one undergarment and sit there. Freak will do the actual interrogating," Joe said.

"I don't care what some ugly freak does with herself, but I won't be a part of such blatant sexual exploitation," Miss Bitchy Voice said, the triumphant tone still in her screechy voice.

"Absolutely no one here is asking you to be sexually exploited," John-Boy said. "I see sexual exploitation every day and you have no idea what you're talking about. Your outrage doesn't really work in a city where wymyn are beaten, raped and tortured for sexual pleasure, and then asked to do it again the next day because it's their *job*."

"This is definitely outside the purview of my job, and your argument doesn't hold water—no one is asking you to take off any of your clothes," Miss Bitchy Voice said.

"Of course not," John-Boy said, "but if the detail were busting down the door of drug dealers known to be armed and dangerous who do you think would be in front?" She looked at the giant cop, but Miss Bitchy Voice wasn't going down that easily.

"It's an entirely different situation," she said.

"How? You got gifts, but so do I. It just happens that mine is always being the biggest and strongest person in the room. For the first ten years of my career in this department I was called "Door-Buster"—they always said it just like you'd say "Ghost Busters"—but I was always the first one through the door. My superiors made a joke of it by saying that it would take a cannon to hurt me anyway, but what they meant was "so we get the nigger killed? So what—niggers are disposable." Did I mention that my other gift was an IQ of 178? Do you think I didn't know exactly what they meant, or what a sawed-off shotgun would do to me?"

"Would you have done it nude?" Miss Bitchy Voice said, clearly enjoying the repartee.

"Yeah, because it was my duty to do it, and because I knew we had a better chance to stop the bad guys. That's all anyone is asking you to do, and quite frankly your sense of propriety and pious indignity rank far below stopping a world-wide economic meltdown on my list of priorities," John-Boy said.

"But it's my body and I refuse to take part in any strip show, regardless of how it is couched." Miss Bitchy Voice said.

"Oh, fuck it," Betty said. "I'll do it. My tits are really small, but my nipples are huge, so all we have to do is turn the air conditioning down so it's cold and Sung won't be able to stop looking, especially if Freak's tits are bouncing around, too." Nobody laughed, because it was clear that Betty meant it. In fact, everybody made some gesture of appreciation to her for her commitment and willingness to getting the job done.

"Oh, so you'll prostitute yourself?" Miss Bitchy Voice said, her voice rising in triumph again. "Well, I won't, not to satisfy some old-boy club notions or to take part in some cockamamie plan hatched by a freak."

"OK," Nathan Jones said. "You've made your position perfectly clear, Marla. You object to participating in an operation to further our intelligence concerning a significant threat to the country, and you object to the plan itself. I will note it in my after-action report to the Secretary. I am sorry if you were offended, but you will notice that I am not ordering you to do so."

"But you did ask, and that is just as repulsive and disgusting as actually making me take part," Miss Bitchy Voice said. "Let's make it clear: you were in favor of me prostituting myself as part of some idiotic plan hatched by a deranged Secret Service agent and based on some glances by subjects under interrogation. And I refused to debase myself in this plan and you brought more pressure to bear to *make* me do it. That is the very definition of sexual harassment."

Jones started to speak but I'd had enough, so I cut him off. "You are needed for a joint operation between the Secret Service, Homeland Security and the Chicago Police Department to stop the havoc that would be wreaked on the world economy if these perpetrators continue to spew counterfeit currency into the money supply and you are refusing because you feel sexually harassed. We get it. But you're going to do it anyway."

Miss Bitchy Voice smiled and said, "No, actually I'm not. And you're not in my chain of command." Before she was done speaking I was right in her personal space. I didn't touch her, but it must have made her about pee her pants—one second I was 10 feet away, lounging against a wall, and in the blink of an eye I was right next to her, almost standing on her Jimmy Choos.

"Bad guys working for these men shot Nolan Laskarides three times at close range, then shot him in the head with an automatic rifle. Carly Crowell took a shot through the heart and through the head. Stanley Rzepzynski was hit at least five times, twice with shotgun blasts to the head after he was down. Siobhan McKee was shot from close range in the back of the head. Quentin Bowe was hit five times and died from a pulmonary embolism as a result of his wounds. Two New York guys were also murdered. Several other agents were wounded. I don't care about your sensibilities. You are going to do this," I said, my tone of voice completely calm and relaxed.

"I will not. I'm sorry about your agents, but that doesn't mean that I have to prostitute myself," Miss Bitchy voice said. "Principles only mean something if you stand up for them when you're tested."

I looked up at her and said, "You don't get it, do you?"

"Oh, I understand perfectly," she said. "You're an ugly girl who sees a chance to get ahead by exploiting the size of your chest and ingratiating yourself with those above you because that's the only way for you to get noticed. You may be willing to 'do whatever it takes' to get information, but I'm not willing to pros—"

I cut her off by gently putting my finger to her lips. "Shhhh. We all got it—you won't prostitute yourself. But this isn't about me. Right now Johnny Smith is out in East Bumfuck, Iowa on his tractor, getting the ground ready for his corn crop. Johnny's a good guy—he and his wife Susie have raised three good kids, they go to church every week, Johnny serves on the local school board for no pay and they've saved their whole lives so that one day they can retire, although neither of them can imagine not working the farm.

"Then one day Johnny and Susie are watching the noon news when Scott Pelley breaks in to say that the dollar is tanking so bad that trading of it on the New York Stock Exchange has been suspended. The Chinese, the Germans, the Indonesians, even the Canadians are dumping dollars because of a story in the *Wall Street Journal* that says there's billions of dollars in counterfeit currency in circulation, which means the dollar can't be trusted as the world's reserve currency anymore.

"Overnight Johnny and Susie are bankrupt, because the value of their investments dropped a thousand percent, and all of their reserves are in dollars, which are now worthless. The result is a world-wide depression that makes 2008 seem like an all-expenses-paid vacation to Disney World, but Susie and Johnny don't have to worry about it, because they decide not to suffer anymore. That's why you're going to do this, because your oath was to defend this country for Johnny and Susie, because they can't do it themselves," I said, taking my finger from her lips.

Miss Bitchy Voice said, "Despite your cute little simile I still refuse."

I smiled—everybody else in the room involuntarily moved away from us—and I said, "Well, first of all it was a homily, but there's another reason you're going to do it."

"Oh, really?" Miss Bitchy Voice said. She arched her eyebrow and smiled condescendingly. "What's that? Are you going to somehow force me into prostituting myself?"

"No, you supercilious cunt, I'm going to drag you into the nearest wymyn's restroom and yank your La Perla bra off myself. Then I'm going to superglue your lips together, staple your hands in the pockets of that Vera Wang knockoff and strap you to a wheelie chair so that I can get you in the room and jiggle your tits around whenever I want. After we get the information we need I'll probably get fired, arrested and almost certainly have to go to prison, but Johnny and Susie will be safe, and so will the rest of the world, because my unit will run the bad guys' asses down and my pals in Spec Ops and the CIA will stop the pipeline overseas. You'll still have your dignity intact, but that superglue is a bitch to get off your lips—oh, yeah, and I'ma kick yo' ass when I'm done, too."

Miss Bitchy Voice was so shocked she didn't even blink when I reached in her pocket and pulled out the nifty little digital recorder she'd been using to make sure everyone knew who the good guys were in this battle for moral supremacy. Like most career REMFs (surely you've figured this one out by now) she had forgotten to plan for what the enemy would do, not what they could do. In her world there were no physical threats because it was not only bad form, but also detrimental to your career advancement. The problem was, when she was faced with someone who wasn't playing the get-ahead game Miss Bitchy Voice didn't know what to do.

I showed the recorder to everybody and then crushed it in my hand. I took it over to a waste basket and let the pieces trickle into the can, watching Miss Bitchy Voice gape at me. I went back over and stood close to her again and John-Boy said, "You best be gettin' out of that bra like right now, missy, or the Freak is gonna take you apart."

"And I'm going to help her," Betty said.

"Me, too," Joe said.

"I'm absolutely in," Mamba said.

"I'll hold her head still," Jack Soo said.

"And I know I have five or nine very healthy matrons here at the jail that would *love* to help," John-Boy said.

"And I'll help her kick your ass afterward," Nathan Jones said. "Come to think of it, I'm going to kick your ass downstairs either way, so get that damned bra off and let's stop these motherfuckers right now."

I knew there was a good cop inside him.

Miss Bitchy Voice, Betty and I went into the wymyn's bathroom and took our bras off. I looked at Betty and she said, "Solidarity, my sister. And backup, in case her highness decides to bolt."

Betty didn't have any tits, but her nipples were enormous. Miss Bitchy Voice had ordinary nipples, but her tits were so perfect that they took my breath away—and I'm as hetero as hetero can be.

She saw me looking and said, "They've been this way since I was a senior in high school, and believe me that everybody noticed. I've lost three boyfriends because their fathers hit on me, and I'm sure I wasn't promoted the last time because I wouldn't let someone above me in the food chain get a look, or cop a feel. I've tried my whole career to minimize my physical attributes and succeed on my merit alone, but thanks to you I'll probably be demoted, and I'm prostituting myself to boot. You have no idea how hard my life has been, looking like this."

I believed her—beautiful wymyn have problems the rest of us can't even conceive of—but I was really tired of her whining, so I said, "I got it, MBV, you've had a tough row to hoe because you're gorgeous, but can we skip the 'curse of beauty' lecture this time and get this counterfeiting asshole to slip up and tell us something that might help stop their operation? I'll give ya that being as beautiful as you must present problems that an ugly girl like me can't understand, but right now I don't care. I want to get these guys because they're a threat to our country, and because they helped kill my friends. You and I can discuss this at length after we're done, but right now it's time to STFUAGTJD, OK?"

"And lay off the 'prostituting myself' routine, willya?" Betty said. "Nobody's sticking his cock up your ass, or beating you while fucking you like a pig, or jamming his dick down your throat until you puke. You're not giving blow jobs in an alley, or freezing your ass off on a street corner in Minneapolis in January, or being gang banged by a fraternity, or chained to a bed while guys come through for hours on end and fuck you until you bleed to death, so shut the hell up about prostituting yourself and be a real federal agent."

Miss Bitchy Voice said, "What the hell do you mean, Glickstien? What is MBV? STFUAGTJD?"

"Miss Bitchy Voice, and shut the fuck up and get the job done," I said.

"I—I—don't have a bitchy voice," she said, her tone belying the words.

"You do, but I could live with that if you'd just help me crack this guy. Usually men use our tits as weapons against us, but this time we can turn the tables and hoist this guy from the yardarm by just suggesting that he might get to *look* at our tits. That isn't prostituting yourself—that's using every available legal resource at our disposal to crack the case. What's wrong with that?" I said.

"Nothing," Betty said. "And for your information, I've been terrorized my whole life for *not* having any tits, so it would be nice to see a bad guy get broken because of a perfect rack. You dig, MBV?"

Miss Bitchy Voice nodded. "What do you want me to do?" she said without her usual whine.

"Just follow my lead, OK? I've got an idea to get him going—just act like an intel officer instead of a Yale Law grad forced to be a public defender in night court and we should be good," I said.

Miss Bitchy Voice looked utterly stricken; her face fell and she looked like she was about to cry.

"Let me guess—you're a Yale grad," I said.

"Yale Law—I made Law Review," she said, her voice so soft you could hardly hear it.

"Excellent," I said. "Now we know why you're such a superior bitch. Pretend that Betty and I went to Columbia and we should be fine."

Betty and I smiled at her and Miss Bitchy Voice thawed just a bit. She nodded at me and said, "I act like a superior bitch because I *am* superior to most people. I didn't make Law Review because of my pretty face."

"Acknowledged, MBV," I said. "Now let's go kick some bad guy ass."

We came out of the bathroom and found Mamba and Jack Soo waiting for us. "I think that Mamba should go in with you," Jack Soo said.

"Why? We need a Korean speaker," I said.

Mamba rattled off a spate of gobbledygook and Jack Soo said, "Yeah, it also doesn't hurt that you're a gay man, but you know what the primary reason is." Mamba hit him with some more gobbledygook and Jack Soo said, "Yeah, your Korean is just perfect, and even your accent works." Mamba hit him again and Jack Soo said, "Yeah, we want to surprise that eater of bats. And yes, that's a great expression that I've never heard in Korean before."

We all laughed and Mamba said, "Bottom line, Sung Yong Hoon won't suspect that I'm fluent in Korean, and that means he won't expect me to be able to decipher anything that he says—it's a tactical advantage for us, Freak."

"Concur," I said. We got to the door of the interview room and I said, "Showtime. Let's ham it up and see if we can break a North Korean field agent."

Mamba went in, MBV followed and I came in last, firmly shutting the door but not locking it. Deliberately screwing up his name I said, "Mr. Yong Hoon, we really need some answers concerning your involvement in the counterfeiting scam at The Berghoff." I put my hands up behind my head and stretched as far as I could, bending over backwards in case he didn't get a big enough eyeful.

I couldn't see his eyes from my position, but Mamba gave me a discreet thumbs up signal that he was interested. As I relaxed from my stretch MBV moved in close to Sung and laid her perfect tits on his forearm that was sitting on the table. The North Korean agent reacted as if he'd been poked with a live wire. His eyes bugged out and he twitched—it was a tiny flinch, but it was there. He also had some sweat pop out on his hairline, and his breathing became a bit more labored.

"I just want to know if your name is really Sung Yong Hoon, because I think that is the perfect name for a businessman who runs gentleman's clubs." Her voice was a gentle coo that caressed his ears as much as her previous voice had grated on ours. When Sung didn't say anything she said, "I've always wanted to work in a gentleman's club—I think I'd be good, don't you, Mr. Sung?" Her voice sounded like a sweet honey candy wrapped in milk chocolate tasted.

And Sung was hungry. He gulped for air like he was just coming up from a coal mine cave-in and the sweat poured off him, along with that acrid odor that signified physical desire. I didn't want to break her rhythm, but I wanted him to be as susceptible as possible to her sudden charm, so I bent over the table and said, "Mr. Hoon, all we need to know is that you weren't aware of the fact that your $100 bill at The Berghoff was counterfeit and our bosses will let us stop bothering you." My tits were on full display, bulging out of my blouse so far that I was afraid that they'd pop right out of there in all their nipply glory. Sung's eyes got so wide I was afraid that they were going to pop right out of their sockets, and then MBV moved in for the kill.

"I might be able to make $100 tips if I worked in one of your clubs, don't you think, Mr. Sung?" she said, purring in his ear while her breasts slowly dragged across his upper arm and shoulder. She didn't stop there, but continued to drag those puppies across his neck and shoulders to end up on the other side.

Sung looked like he was about to come right there, muttering in Korean as he tried (and mostly failed) to maintain his composure. Mamba immediately said something back in Korean and Sung twisted to look at him. "Really?" he said in English. Mamba nodded and said, "It was the greatest day of my life." The North Korean agent said something else in Korean and Mamba said, "No, I didn't pay. If she likes you she'll show you for free, although she of course charges to touch them."

Sung looked back at MBV with drool practically running down his chin and said in English, "Is that—would you really—I would pay to be able to…" His voice trailed off as MBV stood up straight and said, "Well…if you would just confirm that your name is Sung Yong Hoon, I might be able to give you a little peek." She put her hands on either lapel of her blouse like she was about to part the silk sea and let him get a good look at her perfect tits.

Sung nodded and said in English, "I am Sung Yong Hoon, owner of the Asian Angels chain of gentlemen's clubs."

Gotcha, motherfucker.

The iron rule of interrogation says that once you get them talking they are going to keep talking, especially if the subject thinks they're somehow insulated or safe. Sung Yong Hoon thought that we were just interested in a single $100 dollar bill, not an international counterfeiting conspiracy. Besides, admitting that he was a business owner automatically gave him rights, right?

And it might also give him a look at Miss Bitchy Voice's perfect tits.

MBV moved her blouse apart just a tad so he could see her cleavage and leaned over like I had so he could see right down her blouse. Sung's eyes were turning like pinwheels when MBV said, "If only we had some privacy I could show you so much more," MBV cooed, her chest starting to heave just a bit as she laid it on thick for the North Korean.

"We—we, uh, er,…we could go to one of my clubs here in Chicago. They all have private rooms for uh, er…dancing," Sung said.

"Ooh, I love to dance," MBV purred.

"Me, too," I said. "Perhaps we could both dance for you, Mr. Hoon?" I put some of the coquette into my voice, but not nearly as much as MBV.

Fortunately, Sung Yong Hoon was already in la-la-land over the two sets of round-eye tits in front of him to care about that. He also had been in the U.S. too long, and liked it too much, because any training he had before he got to the land of the free and home of the brave had gone right out the window.

"I…would…love…to have…both of you…dance for me," he said, his voice skipping along with his heartbeat.

"But we can't," MBV pouted, "all because of that stupid old fake $100 bill."

"Oh, that is easily explained," Sung said. "I had several men in my club on Halsted Street from California who bought lavish drinks and food for their party and several of my dancers. They all paid in $100 bills, which my upscale clubs get quite often, but my careless manager did not examine the bills. It must have been that these men gave my club counterfeit bills, and that I foolishly trusted my manager when he gave me the club's receipts. I paid off a small gambling loss to my friends Mr. Park and Mr. Choi, and my investors Mr. Hwang and Mr. Bang. I bet against the mighty Bears, and they all took my action." His use of the slang was supposed to convince us that he was just another Asian-American working hard to assimilate, but nobody bought it.

I gave him another good look down my blouse, and MBV laid her perfect tits on his arm again, and Sung really came to attention.

"But these men at your club—surely you know something about them if they spent so much money," I said. "You are the boss, after all."

"Oh, I am the boss of my clubs. I own over 50 percent of the company stock, but am forced to rely on managers because of the success of the business—I have over 20 locations. Unfortunately, the only thing I know about these counterfeiters is that my worthless manager heard one of them speaking Japanese to one of our Japanese dancing girls. I questioned her after discovering the counterfeit bills, and she confirmed that they were Japanese businessmen from, uh, Long Beach, California." There was a slight hesitation in his recitation when he got to Long Beach, as if he could not think of anyplace else in Cali.

I looked at MBV and gave her an arched eyebrow, and she moved the conversation in a different direction. "You must make quite a lot of money if you have investors," she said. "I really love the feel of fur on my bare skin, but of course I cannot afford such things." Her voice was making me hot, and I couldn't imagine what it was doing to the guys behind the two-way mirror.

Mamba murmured something in Korean and Sung said, "That is so—I am a very rich man, thanks to my college education at the University of Illinois-Chicago and my excellent business sense, but often one needs cash to expand, so one takes on minority investors. I am the victim of my own success." He looked sideways at MBV's tits, which were still resting on his arm, and which she immediately thrust forward so her blouse gaped open virtually all the way. The tops of her nipples were showing when she said, "But surely the success of your clubs gave you enough cash to expand. Or are your managers stealing from you, the big boss."

Mesmerized by the perfect round globes before him Sung said, "They are my California investors. They help run my clubs in Long Beach, which are called Delights of the Orient Gentlemen's Clubs."

"Oh, so you are so successful that you have clubs in two places," MBV purred. "That means that you can afford furs, and perhaps jewels, if someone were to please you."

Sung murmured something in Korean while staring at MBV's tits, and Mamba, who looked like he was asleep, sat up in his chair and softly murmured back. Sung Yong Hoon said, "Of course I can afford it—don't we have a pile of cash in our warehouse in Long Beach?"

It was a fuckup of epic proportions. I immediately said, "But Mr. Sung, if you questioned your Japanese dancer about the $100 bills why were you using them at The Berghoff?"

"Park said they were so real not even the U.S. Secret Service could tell the difference," Sung said dreamily.

MBV and I both stood up and buttoned our blouses. "He was wrong," I said in my normal voice. "And you are in serious trouble, Sung Yong Hoon," MBV said in her normal, bitchy voice.

Sung's little wet dream paradise suddenly vanished as he realized that he had let too much slip. He then compounded the error and tried to backtrack.

"I have rights," he said. "I was not read my rights for this interrogation and therefore anything that I've said is inadmissible in court."

The door to the interrogation room slammed open and Nathan Jones came in. He looked at Sung and said, "Who said anything about court, Mr. Sung? We're going to charge you under the USA Patriot Act and the Espionage Act, neither of which require us to let you see the inside of a courtroom. You are a foreign national who doesn't have right one in the USA, and you can bet that we're going to grill you before we either PNG you, or try you in the FISA courts and lock your ass away forever."

Sung Yong Hoon got a funny look on his face and said, "I am a South Korean national who has a legitimate passport and a green card. I am a respectable business owner and known to many Chicago politicians. I believe that you have got the wrong man." He looked very self-satisfied, until Nathan Jones said, "Yeah? Bullshit, Mr. Sung. We've already contacted the KCIA and guess what they told us?

There are eleven Sung Yong Hoons in South Korea—and they are all accounted for. There is a Sung Yong Hoon who currently has a legitimate passport, but unfortunately he died at age two, along with his parents and three brothers when their house burned down. The number on your passport corresponds to his national insurance number, so quite frankly you're fucked, Mr. Sung—or whatever your name is."

We'd all heard of this scam, and we all knew that we had some agents who had obtained passports the same way, and we knew that Sung knew, so we all just held our breath for a second, hoping that Sung would break.

He looked at us, smiled a wistful, self-deprecating smile and said, "One supposes that in the age of computers keeping one's identity secret will become ever harder. I am tired of hiding out and being someone else. My real name is Moon Bon-Hwa, and I am an agent of the DPRK's Reconnaissance General Bureau. I was sent here directly by our Glorious Leader, Kim Jong-Un, to subvert the U.S. economy by taking in and distributing counterfeit currency, as well as spying on other U.S. activities." He stopped talking and looked at us like a kid who has just told his parents that he stole one of their beers—sure of punishment, but hopeful for mercy because of his honesty.

I looked at him and said, "Mr. Moon, if you ever want to see my breasts you're going to have to do better than that. Is there anything else that you want to tell us?"

"Yes," he said, "although it does not require any exposure on your part, Agent." He looked wistfully at my tits and said, "Who is in charge of this operation?"

"I am Nathan Jones, Assistant Director of U.S. Homeland Security. I'm the ranking officer in this group," Jones said.

"Ah, good. I am requesting political asylum in the United States in order to escape persecution in my homeland of the DPRK (that's the Democratic People's Republic of Korea, the technical name for North Korea). I am willing to outline several DPRK operations in exchange for asylum, especially if I may one day apply for citizenship in this great country," Sung/Moon said.

"Well, I can't adjudicate that, Mr. Moon, but I can grant you political asylum. We will need to debrief you somewhere else, somewhere safer, but I would like our agents to be able to question you some more before you leave, if that is acceptable to you," Jones said.

Moon smiled and said, "If we could make it the team that I am already familiar with that would be most gracious." He looked at MBV, Mamba and I with something akin to friendship, and I was moved. Moon had been duped by two sets of awesome tits, but he was no boob.

Nathan Jones said, "Done, Mr. Moon. I'll arrange for transport to a secure facility and for some food to be sent to the room. Do you have any preferences as to what you would like to eat?" The Assistant Director was not only a good cop, he was a smart cookie—being deferential to defectors or other people you've turned is always good business (sorry, can't tell you why I know that—still classified). Also, after this coup Nathan Jones could afford to be generous—he was definitely going up the ladder after busting a North Korean spy ring.

Moon said, "I would love to share a Leona's pizza with my interrogators."

"You really wanna eat all that cheese?" I said. "Is this a secret plot to kill us with gas warfare when your lactose intolerance kicks in?"

"No," Moon said, laughing at my stereotype joke (we'd already caught him with the old 'Asians love round-eye titties' one—why not give another one a try?). "No, unlike many of my countrymen I have no lactose intolerance—and I can hold my alcohol, too. I believe that this is because I have some non-Asian blood in my bloodline, perhaps because my ancestors were sailors who traveled across the ocean to many lands."

"So pepperoni, sausage, green peppers, onions, mushrooms, green olives and garlic on the pizza?" Mamba said.

"Double mushrooms," Miss Bitchy Voice said.

"Double sausage," I said.

"Double garlic and add black olives," Moon Bon-Hwa said.

"A man after my own heart," I said.

Who knew that Leona's pizza would put me one step closer to figuring out the crime of the century, or that it would take gallons more blood before it was all over?

Not me. I was still blissfully oblivious to the giant shitstorm hurricane that was going to engulf my whole world.

CHAPTER 36

A North Korean Canary Sings the Star-Spangled Banner

So we got several pizzas from Leona's, opened Pepsis, and began our interrogation of Moon Bon-Hwa, a.k.a. Sung Yong Hoon. By then we had an assistant U.S. attorney with us, a U.S. Marshal, several FBI people (there was one hell of a fight about us interviewing Moon and not the FBI's Counter-Intelligence unit, but Nathan Jones won that round), a certified court reporter, and lots of other people behind the scenes who were recording everything that was said for later evaluation.

We all sat across from Moon with Pepsis in hand and pizza boxes all around. None of us were taking notes—there were lots of other people doing that. We kind of looked like a bunch of people picking our fantasy football league, rather than interrogators and a defector from a hostile foreign power.

"So who are those other guys we've got?" I said.

"The one you know as Park Mun-Hee is our leader. His real name is Kim Jung-Soo, and he controlled all of our efforts in the USA. He is a very hard-line supporter of the regime, and especially of Kim Jong-Un. Choi Shin Ook was another distributor, like me. He really is a gifted chef, but his real name is Rhee Gi-Guk. Shin Won-Shik joined us after we graduated from U of I and was our enforcer, although he was never needed, since we had no trouble paying our confederates with counterfeit currency and no one ever got out of line. Shin is the one that you defeated on the street, Agent Glickstien." Moon looked at me with wonder on his face and said, "You are truly gifted, because Shin—his real name is Lee Kang-Dae—is the most skilled martial artist in our service, and perhaps the entire DPRK. To my knowledge he had never been defeated before."

"He underestimated me because I was a girl. I thought that your worker's paradise was completely egalitarian—men and wymyn are equal there, right?" I said. Moon laughed and said, "Do not believe all that you read, Agent Glickstien. My culture is heavily biased toward men, and there is no such equality, nor has there ever been. We are male-centric and always will be."

"Why?" Mamba said. "Communist doctrine as set down by Marx and Engels requires equality in order to work."

"Please remember that our version of the worker's paradise is filtered through the writings and interpretations of Mao Zedong, and that worthy gentleman no more believed in the equality of the sexes than he believed in God," Moon said.

"In any case, Lee Kang-Dae won't be winning any martial arts contests any time soon—he won't be done with surgeries and rehab for a couple of years at least," I said coldly.

"Indeed. The other men you hold are Chung Kyung-Soon and Choi Suk-Chin. They are RGB agents sent to check on our operations and make sure that we are still politically reliable. When they are PNG'd back to the DPRK they will be shot for not stopping my defection, even though I had no

THE FREAK FROM BATTLE CREEK

such intention when they knew me. Our regime is very strict when it comes to such things, because it discourages any such behavior among the other people who have such chances," Moon said.

"Mr. Moon, is there anyone else we should know about in relation to the counterfeiting scheme?" MBV said, her voice well-modulated and respectful.

Moon looked at her and sighed. His eyes never left her beautiful face, but you could tell he wanted to look at her tits, which were still loose in her silk blouse. He smiled wistfully and said, "Yes, Agent Ahumada, there are others, especially Lee Kyung-Sook, whose real name is Kim Yong-Sun. He controlled the distribution of the counterfeit currency and is currently in Long Beach checking on our warehouse there. He has Jeong Ho-Sung, real name Song U-Woong, with him. Song is our distribution expert—he runs the mail room at Chase Bank and worked closely with our American confederate, Darcy Fowler, as did Kim."

"Did Fowler know who she was working with? Was she deliberately cooperating with North Korean agents, or was it just greed?" MBV said.

"Oh, she was just a very greedy womyn," Moon said. "We never tried to recruit her because she was so perfectly venal as she was—it was all about becoming rich for her. She had no idea that we were agents of a foreign power."

"So she helped you for the money, but how did she help? How much was she getting?" Mamba said.

"She got 10 percent of all the cash we washed into the system, plus she got $250,000 in counterfeit per quarter to do with as she saw fit. I do not know where it went, but I would bet on a brokerage account with a large New York firm, because Ms. Fowler understood how to grow cash," Moon said. "She and Kim arranged the movement of the cash through the system, and made sure that our contractors—like Luigi Tromboli and his father-in-law Salvatore Bonnarino—did not jeopardize the operation through greed or stupidity.

"Once the pipeline for the counterfeit currency was fully realized it went like clockwork, although very slowly. Kim and Rhee correctly realized that the stream had to be slow at first so as to not arouse suspicion, and they always preached caution to all of us and our domestic contractors," Moon said. "They were brilliant at this, and also very correct to do it the way that they did."

"How much counterfeit have you distributed so far?" I said.

Moon thought for a moment and said, "Perhaps as much as $2 billion, at face value. We have eleven warehouses in the United States, four in Hong Kong, and seven more in London. Kim knows the figure exactly, but I believe we have just over $300 billion in reserves, with more coming from our production facility in South Korea."

We all sat up a little straighter when he said that—South Korea? WTF?

Moon saw our faces change and said, "We surreptitiously own two novelty factories in the ROK—the kind of places that produce truly fake currency, as well as other things. It is the perfect cover for our operations, because we can ship anything we want anywhere and no one ever questions it. We can also print the counterfeit in plain sight and again, no one really notices. Most of the employees at our production facilities are South Korean workers who are just trying to make a good living—we pay somewhat better than most other factories, and we get away with it by requiring better quality from our workers. The plants make a profit without the counterfeit, so obviously it is working."

"Can you please describe the process in detail? I'm afraid that I don't have it straight in my mind," MBV said.

"It is simplicity itself," Moon said. "When we started we used a close copy of the paper used by the U.S. government to print it notes, but your Secret Service detected this too easily, and our agents kept getting caught. Then we discovered a process to remove the original denomination and replace it with a larger denomination, so we began to collect dollar bills here in the US and send them to the ROK, where we scrubbed them and made $1 bills into $20, $50, and $100 bills. We then simply reversed the shipping routes and began distribution operations."

"So the pipeline is a two-way one, going from the US to South Korea and then back again," Mamba said. "You collect here, process in the ROK, then distribute here. That's simple. But why take the chance on doing the work in South Korea? Why not just do it in the DPRK and make sure it stays a secret?"

"We used the factories in South Korea because they could get the laser and holographic printing that we needed in order to make our bills the most realistic counterfeits ever printed without attracting any attention. Plus, your counterintelligence agencies look for unusual activity in and around *North* Korea. Using a South Korean factory and shipping from the ROK also let us take advantage of the KORUS-FTA."

"You were smart, Mr. Moon," I said. "The Korean-US Free Trade Agreement meant that most, if not all of your shipping containers wouldn't be checked—and you exempted yourself for excise taxes and customs duties."

"Yes, we did," Moon said. "It seemed appropriate to use every advantage we could—it made us seem like more legitimate businessmen."

"Of course—maximize profits and cut all the legal corners that you can," Mamba said. "It's the American way."

"The Korean way as well," Moon said, laughing. "Business is business, regardless of where it is practiced.

"And you supplied all of the dollar bills to be scrubbed?" MBV said.

"Kim, Rhee and I all had businesses that supplied $1 bills in great quantity, and we had other operations that collected them as well. We also continued to mix in our own paper counterfeits, using them for very large payments like those to Darcy Fowler, or as profits from our businesses. We always inflated the size of our business profits, but not so grossly that they aroused suspicion. We also paid our taxes in full, but we always laughed when paying the government, since we were paying in counterfeit currency.

"All of us also spent large quantities of the counterfeit to buy all of the trappings of our stations—I once paid for a brand-new Mercedes-Benz 500 series with counterfeit cash, and Son U-Woong bought a building on Lakeshore Drive by cashing in his "life savings"—all counterfeit," Moon said.

"And because you all spoke perfect English and went to college in Chicago you were just a part of the American Dream—just another bunch of hard-working Asian immigrants who worked hard, played hard and paid your dues while getting ahead," I said.

"Yes," Moon said. "We were well trained and we always kept our heads down—until The Berghoff you never had a hint we were operating this way."

"No, we didn't," I said. "We thought that this was a domestic operation—it was well compartmentalized, except for the connection through Darcy Fowler."

Moon said something in Korean, shaking his head. Mamba said, "Once again man is betrayed by his penis? What do you mean, Mr. Moon? You were betrayed by your penis?"

Moon laughed and said, "No, Agent de Coucy, I had an entire stable of willing Korean, Chinese and Japanese girls to satisfy any of my hungers, and a beautiful blonde mistress as well. No, it was Song U-Woong and Kim Yong-Sun who were overcome by their desire for an American mistress. Both of them had relations with Ms. Fowler, each thinking that they were her exclusive lover. When she pushed Kim for more money he began to grow more reckless in his dispersal of the counterfeit—it was he who authorized her to let parts of her family enrich themselves while serving our purpose of distribution.

"It was Song who pushed for a more aggressive contract for Ms. Fowler, insisting that she needed to be compensated—in counterfeit, of course—for the chances she was taking while washing our cash into the system. By themselves these actions did no damage, but once you pulled at the other end of these threads it was only a matter of time before you discovered us," Moon said.

I wasn't supposed to ask the next question, especially since Moon Bon-Hwa was being so forthcoming, but I had to know the answer, so I threw protocol out the window and said, "Mr. Moon, why are you doing this? Why have you decided to defect after all this time?"

Mamba and Miss Bitchy Voice both looked like they'd just smelled Gary, Indiana on a bad day, but Moon laughed and said, "Agent Glickstien, I have come to love America with all of her faults, while I despise the Democratic People's Republic of Korea with all of her defects. It isn't that the people of North Korea are bad, but rather that the lies told by the elites, and especially the Kim family, are just too disgusting to follow any longer. I knew after I took my first political philosophy class at UIC that my country was based on a lie, and after watching America closely I can tell you that most people here can't find the DPRK on a map, much less have any desire to invade it."

Moon Bon-Hwa looked at our shocked expressions and said, "That's right—I'm a North Korean that has been seduced by the charms of the capitalist swine herd called the United States of America. I am also a very good businessman who would like to make an honest living and keep making money. Worst of all I love my golden-haired girlfriend, who I would like to make my wife."

"You've become an American," I said. "You got turned by the cheeseburger gun."

"I am not familiar with the term 'cheeseburger gun'," Moon said.

"There's no reason that you should be—one of my college profs thought that the way to overthrow the North Korean government and make the world a safer place was to put a McDonald's in the center of Pyongyang and serve free food for a year," I said. "He contended that after the North Korean people got to actually eat real American food they would revolt on their own to get more of it. His position was that American culture and its inherent prosperity would subvert the North Korean government far more efficiently than fighting a war, and also that it would save millions of lives. We all thought that he was crazy, but after hearing your story I'm not sure he wasn't right."

"I would say that your professor's 'cheeseburger gun' would be highly effective if it could be brought to fruition, especially if it were accompanied by cake shakes from Portillo's," Moon said. We all laughed at that, and Mamba said, "And perhaps some beer from The Berghoff?"

"And a steak from Chris's Ruth Steak House," MBV said.

"And ribs from the Montgomery Inn in Cincinnati, Ohio," Moon said. "If I did not love Chicago so much perhaps I would live in the Queen City. It is stately, beautiful and so All-American."

From there it was a walk in the park (that pun had to be made—sorry). Moon Bon-Hwa gave up all the information about the counterfeiters and their operations we could ever have wanted. He also told us he believed that Kim Jung-Soo, Lee Kang-Dae, Rhee Gi-Guk and the two RGB agents were not going to be turned. "Even after all the evidence to the contrary these are true believers, especially Kim, who is related to our Glorious Leader," Moon said. "However, Song U-Woong may feel as I do and may be susceptible to the charms of life in the West. I believe that he loves Ms. Darcy Fowler, and I know that he has come to love Italian food and money."

After we had interviewed him for over eight hours—well into the next day—Nathan Jones came in and said, "Sorry to break up the party, but everybody needs some sleep. Mr. Moon, we're going to send you off with the U.S. Marshals until tomorrow, when you will be debriefed by some other people. You probably already know the drill—you're going to be interviewed by several teams of people from multiple agencies until we are satisfied that we have all that we need, and then we will do it all again. I look forward to seeing you again, sir."

Moon, who was still shackled to the D-ring in the floor, stood up and shook Jones's hand. He shook all of our hands, lingering over Miss Bitchy Voice's while trying to stare down her blouse, and then John-Boy came in to unshackle him, followed by four U.S. Marshals. Before they could march him out Moon said, "Ah! I forgot the most important part! There is a signal that must be sent every seven days or the pipeline will stop sending the counterfeit by established routes and the two factories in South Korea will burn down. It was last sent four days ago, so it must be sent the morning of the third day—now the second day?—from today, on the thirteenth of the month."

"What is the signal and how do we send it?" Jones said.

"You must put an advertisement on-line with Craig's List—it is always an advertisement for some service or other," Moon said.

"What service?" Jones said.

"Unfortunately I do not know—it was always Kim or Lee who sent the signal. The rest of us would be informed only in the case of those two dying or being captured. I am sorry I do not know this, but it was done this way for operational security."

Jones nodded and looked at Mamba, MBV and I. "I believe him," I said.

"Me, too," Mamba said.

"I also believe Mr. Moon," MBV said. "He is an honorable man and has no reason to lie now." Moon smiled at her and gave a small bow, and she smiled back.

"OK, that means we need to move our timetable up," Jones said. He turned to the marshals and said, "Let's get Mr. Moon to Dirksen—set him up in one of the holding rooms downstairs so we can start talking to him at 7:00 a.m. We'll take the other four there after we're all set up on Mr. Moon tomorrow—let's just keep them here tonight."

The marshals nodded and escorted Moon out the door and to the Everett McKinley Dirksen Federal Building down on Dearborn Street in the Loop. Jones said, "Everybody else get some rest—we've got a briefing at 6:00 a.m. before we go at these guys again. You guys all done good today." He looked at Marla Ahumada and she said, "I was out of line earlier, and I apologize. I understand if you want to pull me from this detail, Assistant Director."

Jones said, "Anybody know what the fuck Ahumada is talking about? Why'n hell would I pull my intel chief from the biggest intelligence coup of our lives? What'd ya do, fart when you were interviewing Moon? He's from North-fucking-Korea—I guarantee he's smelled worse."

The look on Miss Bitchy Voice's face was worth all of the shit we went through to get her to take off her bra. If it had been a cartoon her jaw would've literally hit the floor and her eyes would've bugged all the way out of her head.

Mamba started laughing, and pretty soon we were all laughing like hyenas. It had been a long, tension filled day, and we were all walking on clouds, because we were about to break the biggest case the Secret Service and Homeland Security had ever had, so it felt good to just spew. Even Miss Bitchy Voice started laughing when she realized that Jones was letting her off the hook. After it all calmed down Mamba said, "My car is waiting—anybody need a ride?"

We all did, even John-Boy.

Once we were in the car I got Betty and MBV in a huddle and said, "I have an idea." I told them what I thought that we should do and Betty said, "Oh, that's just excellent, Freak. Count me in."

Miss Bitchy Voice looked at me and said, "Well, I suppose it's only fair. Shall we do it tonight, or wait until tomorrow morning?" She smiled and it was amazing how beautiful she still was, even at 2:00 a.m. after eight hours of interrogating someone.

"Tonight," I said, which is how we wound up at the Dirksen Federal Building at 2:35 a.m. We got through the security and went down to the holding room where they were getting Moon settled. I went up to the head marshal, a guy named Steve Atwater (not the great Denver Bronco strong safety, but a guy who was built like a pro football player) and said, "Steve, we've got just a couple more questions for Mr. Moon. We're not going in the room—we're gonna ask our questions through the mirror. Can you guys step away for just a minute?"

"Sure, Freak," he said. The marshals stepped out into the corridor and we went into the observation room. I hit the switch that un-blanked the two-way mirror and tripped the speaker button.

"Mr. Moon?" I said. He turned around and said, "Yes, hello."

We all yanked up our blouses at the same time and flashed him with three sets of All-American tits. "Welcome to America, Mr. Moon," we all said.

"America really is the land of opportunity," he said. We all laughed our asses off, even Miss Bitchy Voice, who looked like she really enjoyed the exhibitionism (I think we all did).

Why did we do it, you ask? Hey, this guy was the reason we were going to roll up an operation that could have hurt the whole world…and after all, a little encouragement never hurt anyone, and clearly he was motivated by tits.

It wasn't like we prostituted ourselves, and it felt like the perfect end to a nearly perfect day.

Too bad the blood would flow the next day.

CHAPTER 37

Operation "Yuck Fou, North Korea"

The 6:00 a.m. briefing was truly an interesting meeting, even though the Chicago contingent only had three hours of sleep. There was the Director of the FBI, the Secretary of Homeland Security, the Secretary of the Treasury, the president's National Security Adviser, the Deputy Director of Operations for the CIA, the Attorney General, the chief of staff for the Senate Intelligence Committee, the chairwoman of the House Intelligence Committee, the Vice-Chairwoman of the Joint Chiefs of Staff, the Director of the Secret Service and Lieutenant General Natalya Muzghov-Franklin, among others.

Ever heard the old story about too many chiefs and not enough Indians?

Or does the term cluster-fuck ring a bell?

We spent time we didn't have on introductions, the pissing contest for positioning at the table, and outright big-footing using titles and precedence to establish the pecking order. It was a disgusting display of stupid bureaucratic wrangling at its very lowest. We low-life, scum-sucking line animals just sat there against the wall like we were at the kid's table for Thanksgiving while our "superiors" did their idiotic dance of dunces. Everyone except SWWFYU had already made one bid for supremacy, and they were going on their second round when Nathan Jones came up to me and said, "Freak, I've got an idea. Come with me."

I raised an eyebrow and he said, "Not here—outside." We went out into the hall and he said, "OK, I'm all for productive discussions"—that's bureaucrat speech for 'bloviating without result due to a need to get credit for something you may or may not have anything to do with'—"but we need to get our plan together now, because the clock is ticking. Here's what I want to do." He told me, and I said, "I'm definitely in, Mr. Assistant Director. Want me to use my cell phone?"

"He did give you his direct number," Jones said. "It would be very effective, especially if you were to dial it in there, and I was to put it on speaker."

"Your boss is going to have your ass for this, Mr. Soon-to-be-former Assistant Director," I said. "I hear that Thule Air Force Base is nice for about three days in August." I was referring to the U.S. Air Force Base in Greenland, where it was rumored that those in the U.S. government who displeased their superiors were sent to contemplate the end of their career advancement.

"Ah, fuck him if he can't take a joke. All I care about is getting our shit together so we can take all of these counterfeiting, espionage-making motherfuckers down for the count. I want 'em all in Super Max or dead ASAP, because this could be a goddamned disaster of epic proportions for the world that my three kids, wife and parents live in. I don't give a fuck about credit, my job or any other consideration, as long as we coordinate everything and take these assholes out forever. I also want to give Kim Jong Un and his pals a big shit sandwich to eat, because maybe they'll step out of line and we can finally nuke the sons of bitches."

"Wow, tell me how you really feel, Jones," I said. "Usually it's me doing that kind of ranting."

"You've been out in the weeds fighting this kind of thing for real. Tell me you like all of this fucking around," he said.

"Nah, I'm just impressed that you can express yourself like that. Usually guys at your level are a bit more—uh, circumspect about their opinions," I said.

"I'm a cop at heart—I started with the Wayne County Sherriff's office in Detroit, went to the Michigan State Police and then Homeland," Jones said. "I'm just tired of fucking around when I know how to get this job done."

"Not to go all Dr. Phil on ya, but let's dooo it," I said.

"Fuckin'-A," he said. We went back in to the room and the Secretary of the Treasury, a good guy but a born bloviator, was saying "…and the Department of the Treasury was formed right after the Defense Department—they called it the Department of War then—so my position takes precedence over the Justice Department, or Homeland Security, so I should be the head of this committee…"

I tuned him out and hit a speed dial button on my phone. The voice I expected answered after two rings, and I used my Marine Corps voice to say, "Sir, it's Agent Glinka Glickstien. Fine, thank you sir, but we're having a problem getting organized with so much firepower at the table. No, sir, we are still trying to establish who will lead the effort. Yes, sir, we've been meeting for 45 minutes now. No, sir, nothing of substance. Yes, sir, it definitely is—yes, sir, by the 13th. You want to be on speaker? Right away, sir." Everybody was looking at me like I had been transported from the starship *Enterprise* into a meeting of the Romulan Senate (sorry if you don't get the reference, but anybody who doesn't get *Star Trek* doesn't make any sense to me), but I just pointed at Nathan Jones, who punched the button on the speaker and said, "Sir, you have the working group."

"Well, it sounds like the non-working group to me," the President of the United States said. "Why the hell are we not planning how to take down the entire North Korean counterfeiting operation instead of wrangling over who's getting the credit?"

The Attorney General said, "Mr. President, this line may not be secure. We need to—"

"Oh fuck that, Paul," the president said. "I don't give a flying fuck whether this line is secure or not. I want you to get organized and set up on this before noon, and I want to be briefed at 1:00 p.m. today. I realize that the debriefing of our new friend will take some time, but we only have until the 13th of this month—and that's less than two days away, right?"

"Yes, Mr. President, but how did you know that, sir?" the Secretary of Homeland Security said.

"Assistant Director of Homeland Security Nathan Jones filled me in on the details early this morning," the president said. The Secretary of Homeland Security looked at Jones with her phasers on full vaporize, but Jones just looked right back, his dark brown eyes returning fire with quantum torpedoes (another *Star Trek* reference—see previous reference for how I feel about you not getting the reference).

"And before you try and fry him with your famous 'you jumped the chain of command' look, Angela, *I* called him," the president said. "I also previously gave Agent Glickstien my private number and told her to call me if she ever needed my help. I assume she got tired of the listening to all the palaver and called to see if I could cut through the bullshit."

"Mr. President, I believe that we were just about to name a chairman based on the establishment of cabinet departments," the Secretary of the Treasury said. He and the president had been friends since college and he probably thought that gave him the inside track.

Wrong.

"I understand that reasoning Sherm, but it was the Secret Service that got on to this first. With the help of Spec Ops and the CIA they made the connections, arrested the first group of counterfeiters, and took down most of the key parts of the domestic network. It seems logical to have them at the front of this. Director Hessler, are you there?"

Nails said, "Yes, sir, I'm here."

"Good. I'm naming you chairwoman of the working group on this operation—what are we calling it?"

"Operation Striking Eagle, sir," Director Hessler said.

"Well, I don't like that at all—too melodramatic," the president said. "Agent Glickstien, what would your group like to call it?"

"Permission to speak freely, sir?" I said.

"Carry on, Marine."

"Sir, we'd like to call it Operation Yuck Fou," I said.

"Why?" the president said.

"Sir, because Operation 'Fuck You, North Korea' doesn't really cut it for public consumption," I said.

The president laughed and so did everybody else, and then he said, "Well, I like *that*. Chairwoman Hessler, I'm authorizing you to take over Operation Yuck Fou, with Natalya Muzghov-Franklin as your deputy, and with DHS Assistant Director Nathan Jones as your second deputy. You are authorized to use whatever assets from whatever departments you need, and all of the other people at this meeting are to give you every bit of their considerable cooperation. You may use the working group as your advisory board or you may dismiss them and brief later. No one with a security classification lower than code-word clearance is authorized to be read in on this operation unless it is specifically necessary, and even then they must be cleared by the Secretary of Homeland Security. Any questions?"

It was as quiet as the tomb until Siri Hessler said, "No sir, we read you loud and clear."

"Good," the president said. "I don't give a flying fuck whose nose is out of joint, and I really don't care about who you think ought to get the credit—there will be plenty to go around. Now get your asses in gear and bust all of these shitheads. Oh, Agent Glickstien? Assistant Director Jones?"

"Sir," we both said.

"Good decision on making the phone call. It's very refreshing to have line animals who take the initiative," the president said.

"Just doing my duty, sir," Jones said.

"Concur, sir," I said.

"I wish more people got what that means," the president said. "Now get to work." He hung up before we could answer.

Everything went as smooth as silk after that. Nails was an organizational dynamo who didn't really need anybody's help, although she kept most of the group around, because she could also play the political game with anyone, especially if it meant that her service would benefit.

She said, "First of all, would everyone who isn't cleared for code-word materials please leave the room?"

The chief of staff of the Senate Intelligence Committee squawked at that, but Nails went all 'Director Hessler' and said, "You heard the president, right?" She smiled at him like a saber-toothed tiger looking at a giant elk. She was only five feet tall and about 110 pounds, but 100 of it was brains and balls—she wasn't afraid of anybody or anything, and she especially wasn't afraid of any congressional staffer, regardless of who her boss was.

Almost everybody left the room, but I just sat there on my chair against the wall. Finally the Attorney General looked over and said, "We need to clear the room, Agent Glickstien. Nobody with lower than code word clearance needs to be in here." He wasn't being a dick, he was just trying to be helpful, so I just looked at him and said, "Thank you, Mr. Attorney General, but until instructed by my direct superior I need to stay. Thank you for giving me a heads-up, sir."

Everyone turned to look at me and the president's National Security Adviser, who delighted in being a dick, said, "Just because the president singled you out doesn't mean that you get to circumvent the rules. I wouldn't go getting an inflated opinion of my importance there, missy."

I hated being called missy, honey, sweetie, sugar, snookums or any other thing that was designed to put me in my place, and I especially hated it when it was some REMF doing it, but before I could reply SWWFYU said, "She's staying because her security is the highest in the room except for the DDO. It's actually higher than the two Secretaries." Her voice would have cut glass, and the look she gave the National Security Adviser would have stopped an elephant in its tracks.

"And don't call her 'missy' or anything else except Agent, or Agent Glickstien—she's a sworn Secret Service agent who also happens to have the Navy Cross, the Silver Star and four Purple Hearts," Nails said, her voice set on 'evisceration.'

"Ma'am, that's classified," I said.

"Thanks for the heads up, Freak," Nails said. She turned to the NSA and said, "Repeat that anywhere outside this room and I'll have your ass put in Leavenworth, Mr. National Security Adviser," in the same icy cold tone as before.

"She's cleared for intelligence that would get you shot, Glenn," Arthur Ishikawa, the DDO of the CIA said. He and I had worked together before, the shithead. I looked at him and nodded, and the NSA said, "Oh, you know each other?"

"Classified," we said, joined by SWWFYU and Nails. "I'm buying the Pepsis," Nails said. "Now let's get our shit together and get this done."

The discussion of how to take down everyone who needed to be taken down was vigorous, but very productive once everybody got that they all had a part to play. I sat in my chair and listened for the first 20 minutes, until Director Hessler said, "Freak, get your ass up here and sit at the table. We need your operational expertise."

I went up and sat at the grownups' table, right next to SWWFYU. It felt like old times (sorry, classified) and by 11:30 we were good to go.

Everybody left the room to contact all of the relevant parties, so that the pieces that needed to move could move into position. After everybody left it was just Nails, SWWFYU, Ishikawa and me in the conference room. We all looked at each other and the DDO said, "You need to get your team and bring them in now, Freak. You're gonna take down the Chicago unit of North Koreans, including Kim Yang-Sun and Song U-Woong—they're at O'Hare as we speak, being followed by FBI agents."

"I thought we were going to take Kim down in the Chase offices in New York," I said.

"Change of plans—Kim and Song are stopping here to rendezvous with the three Chicago based distributors and their watchdogs, probably to report on the warehouses in Long Beach," Nails said. "Mr. Moon's information on the sites was good—we sent agents to surveil them about an hour ago, including one agent who posed as a truck driver and confirmed that one of the warehouses has a room with separate locks and loading doors."

I nodded and called Joe, who came in the room a few seconds later with the rest of the team, including Captain Cork in his wheelchair. We all shook hands and SWWFYU said, "I've got to go make sure that my guys are all in position, but I'm sure we'll all have to debrief on this, so we'll see each other again. I just wanted to let you know that your work on this case has been exemplary, and that I'd take any of you at Spec Ops Command if you wanted to join up." She looked at me and snapped to attention and saluted me with the type of precision she was known for. "Permission to depart, OOD," she said.

I stood at attention and said, "Permission to depart is granted, ma'am! Commanding Officer, departing!" We laughed one more time, hugging each other, and she said, "Watch your ass, Freak."

"No can do, ma'am—my neck doesn't twist that far," I said. There was more laughter and SWWFYU left, still the epitome of the warrior that every military in the world can't do without.

We were briefed on our part in the takedown by Director Hessler and Ishikawa. Joe looked at him and raised an eyebrow, and the DDO said, "Don't get your knickers in a knot, Agent Cocker. I'm fully aware that the CIA can't operate in the US, but there is nothing that says we can't *plan* an operation in-country. All of my kids will be operating outside the borders, but we did get onto the two flying in today—it turns out that they actually flew to Macao for a day to meet with some nice Chinese fellows who were apparently members of Guojia Anquan Bu, a.k.a. Guoanbu. They're an arm of the Ministry for State Security and appear to be responsible for penetrating high tech industries. My agents in Macao heard rumors that perhaps the North Koreans had a way to grease the wheels a bit for the PRC—through investments that are covered as purchases by American companies."

The DDO let that sink in. Finally Mamba said, "Well, fuck us all blind. They think that they're going to use the funny money to buy the Chicago companies using American nominees, and then sell those to gain positions in tech companies."

"Where they'll have access to whatever they want in the tech sector—nobody says no to a director of the company who wants specifics about a new product, or anything else that they want to know," Jack Soo said.

"If they had enough directors they could also manipulate the company's stock price, which could in turn affect the entire tech market," Buzz Lightyear said.

"It's the ultimate insider trading, and it would give them a means to make a fortune before they crashed the company, after divesting themselves of dollars and going into say, gold," Joe said.

"Exactly," Ishikawa said. "That's why I'm here—we're going to have to eliminate some loose ends after we've arrested all of the people we can get our hands on, and we're going to have to watch others for years, just to make sure that they don't still have access to piles of cash we didn't find."

"Well, then, let's find them all so that we stop the whole thing at once," I said.

"Is that what you said before a Spec Ops raid?" the DDO said.

"No, we always said 'Kill 'em all and let God sort 'em out'," I said.

"Oooh, I like that one better," Betty said.

"We also said 'Fuck them, the horse they rode in on, and the family dog'," I said.

"How about 'Eat shit and die, you counterfeiting motherfuckers'?" Weasel said.

"Short, sweet, to the point—I think I like that one best," I said. "Way to go, Weasel—the unit has its slogan."

"Now all we gotta do is put these assholes outta business," Jewey said.

"Concur," everybody said. "I'm buyin' those Pepsis as soon as we strike those sons of bitches outta the funny money business," Guru said.

So two days later we were all in our assigned positions when Lee Kyung Sook, real name Kim Yung Sun, and Jeong Ho-Sung, real name Song U-Woong, strolled into the warehouse they leased on Western Avenue near Jarvis. They thought that there was a meeting because the warehouse had been sold to another investment group. Nails thought there was a chance that we could get them to offer us some funny money, either for a deal to buy the warehouse, or in order to cut us in on the exchanging process.

We knew that they did such things, because the previous owners of the warehouse were already in federal custody after our computer wizards discovered that their finances were being augmented by huge cash purchases—one guy bought a brand-new Porsche with actual cash (not a cashier's check), while another put a 20% down payment on a $5 million lake House using $20, $50, and $100 bills. This wasn't illegal, but it did cause our wizards to follow up, whereupon they found other evidence that sent our agents to talk to the warehouse owners, all of whom admitted they were getting massive under-the-table payments from their "Chinese" customers to basically never go to the warehouse, and to ignore any other irregularities they might encounter.

They all thought that it was simply an IRS problem for them, until we clued them in to the fact that this was a national security investigation involving the North Koreans, with the participants perhaps getting an all-expenses paid vacation to Guantanamo Bay. They were absolutely cooperative after that, and agreed that they didn't need lawyers, or to be seen in court until the Koreans were all rolled up.

So the entire unit was on hand, with Coach, Joe and Captain Cork playing the new owners of the warehouse, while the rest of us were scattered around. I was the secretary for the new owners, sitting just outside the warehouse office with my 1076s concealed in my voluminous jacket, just in case the two guys got froggy. John-Boy was hanging around with a Chicago PD SWAT team, and Miss Bitchy Voice was also somewhere around, monitoring our operations across the globe and waiting to let us know when everyone else was in custody.

SWWFYU had three Spec Ops teams deployed to take down the factories in South Korea and the two we'd found in the Philippines. Both were undercover as Homeland Security teams, because they had to cooperate with the local authorities, but they were armed with their full kit and they were taking the lead. God help the North Koreans who tried to resist in those places, because the Spec Ops team always shot first and asked questions later—and I knew they never missed (sorry, classified).

Her third team was deployed onboard a U.S. frigate in the Pacific Ocean. They were going to hit a ship that was carrying a whole shitload of counterfeit currency to the Port of Long Beach. The vessel was Liberian registered, but it was leased by the North Koreans through a shell company in Hong Kong. It was in international waters and the Spec Ops team was going to sink the ship, the funny money and any crew who resisted. The rest of the crew would be set adrift in lifeboats, where they would be promptly rescued by a different U.S. Navy frigate. The crew would tell a tale of Russian or Chechnyan hijackers who proclaimed to want the cargo in order to finance their guerilla war with the government.

It would all fly, because guys who are faced with hard men with guns rarely remember things the way they really were, since they were too busy being scared shitless.

The warehouses in Long Beach were all going to be hit by a combined Homeland Security/Secret Service task force. Word was the warehouses were stuffed with drugs—cocaine and heroin that had been run from East Asia by a nefarious drug cartel (pick one)—but the Secret Service would later announce that they had discovered a giant mountain of counterfeit currency.

Imagine that.

Our computer wizards were poised to freeze any and all accounts associated with the North Koreans, and we were prepared to lean on the Cayman Islands, Switzerland, Luxembourg, Lichtenstein, the Isle of Man and Jersey (all places where criminals try to hide their profits from nefarious enterprises like counterfeiting) in order to freeze assets there, too.

In the words of John-Boy, "We's 'bout to commence fuckin' up the North Korean counterfeiting operation and save the world economy."

So Kim and Song came in and I let them in to see the new "owners" and loosened my pistols in their holsters. We were all wired into the comms, so we were all listening when Captain Cork said, "We are meeting with you because we would like to continue the relationship with your companies that our predecessors enjoyed."

"We are still confused as to why this warehouse was sold to you. We were under the impression that the previous owners were perfectly happy with the terms of our contract, and that they owned several warehouses in the area," Kim Yung-Sun said. He was clearly being cautious, and it seemed he was confused about having people he was paying so handsomely (albeit in counterfeit currency) sell out from under him.

"Mr. Lee, we bought several warehouse companies here in Chicago," Coach said. "We already own several warehouse systems in Seattle, Long Beach and San Diego, and we were cash heavy, so we decided to move east into Houston, Minneapolis, Chicago, Boston and New York. My uncle—" she tipped her head toward Captain Cork "—is recovering from a bad fall and back injury, but his business acumen has not failed him. We got excellent deals on all our systems, but in order for them to keep being solid investments we need to keep our current customers happy, which is why we're having this meeting."

"We are not used to dealing with wymyn in our businesses, except as employees," Lee said. "Would we be dealing primarily with you or your uncle?"

"You'll be dealing primarily with me, Mr. Kyung," Joe said. "I will be running the central division of the company, including Minneapolis, Houston, and Chicago. I will be based here and will travel to the other two locations on occasion. I must emphasize, however, that Ms. Clune and her uncle are the primary owners of our company."

"I will be running the East Coast operations and my uncle will be returning to his home in Los Angeles," Coach said. "I understand if you do not want to deal with me, but I will have a say in all the decisions made for this system." Coach wasn't being pissy, she was just being firm, like a good businesswomyn would.

Lee and Song both chuckled collegially and Lee said, "Oh no, Ms. Clune, we did not mean any offense, or that we could not work with you. On the contrary, we were merely pointing out that we were not used to working with wymyn. My cousin Mr. Song works closely with many wymyn, and his direct supervisor is a womyn. In South Korea most of the capital is held by men, which means that most business deals are done between men. If your terms are favorable we will have no problem working with you."

There were smiles all around and Coach said, "Well, that is a relief. Your business is too good for us to just let you go, Mr. Lee. I assure you that we will offer competitive rates, and that we really have no desire to change our interaction with you from what it was previously."

"Is it possible that you could tell us who you already work with on the West Coast?" Song asked.

"My closest associate in Long Beach is the Carpenter Group," Captain Cork said. "Nash Carpenter and I are old friends—we went to high school and college together."

Lee and Song perked right up, because the Carpenter Group owned the warehouses they already used—and Nash Carpenter was a notorious figure who was reputedly tied to several criminal enterprises, but he had never been convicted of anything.

"And who might you be working with in the East Coast?" Mr. Lee said, his voice very polite, but his eyes lit up with an avaricious light.

"We already work with Luigi Tromboli and the Bonnarino Trucking Company in New York City," Coach said. "The warehouse systems we acquired were personally recommended by Mr. Salvatore Bonnarino."

Both North Koreans looked at each other and you could see the dollar signs whirling in their eyes. Lee said, "Will you excuse us for a moment? We need to confer with one of our colleagues."

"Of course," Captain Cork said.

The two guys came out of the office and Lee hit a button on his speed dial. That call went straight to voicemail, so he hit another button, and when that call was answered he immediately began saying something in Korean. The conversation went on for just over three minutes, and when he hung up Kim smiled and said something to Song in Korean. Both men smiled and they went back into the office.

I didn't know what Moon Bon-Hwa said to Kim, but it must have been good, because I could see from his face he was about to totally fuck himself up, although I'm sure he thought he was about to bring more glory to the DPRK and its Glorious Leader.

"We would like to confer privately with you if we might," Kim said.

"Of course," Captain Cork said. Coach closed the doors and Kim said, "We would like to offer each of you a bonus for giving us the most favorable terms for our next year of operation, to be paid in cash." This was the point where if we were honest we'd start screaming about kickbacks and the SEC, but instead Coach said, "We might be receptive to that, depending on what terms you actually want."

They should have been far more cautious, but these guys had no idea the Secret Service was on to them, plus they thought that they were slicker than James Bond, and they were true believers in the superiority of the North Korean culture. Add in personal arrogance, being too long undercover and accepting our *bona fides* at face value—they heard the right criminal names, which convinced them we were just more venal Americans—and they were about to undo years of work.

"We have certain, uh, delicate products that we would like to store in your warehouses. We would also use only our employees when moving these, ah, products. We would like your employees to stay away from our shipping containers, and we would like to ensure this by having a separate, locked area within your warehouses," Lee said.

"That would be possible, depending on how much we were paid," Captain Cork said.

"Oh, we would pay you the usual rate for the storage, and we would also pay to have the separate locked facility built in any warehouse that does not already have it, but we would like to not have any of the payments appear on your books in our names," Lee said. "If we could keep this private it would be worth $250,000 per quarter to us, to be divided between you as you see fit."

"So you want to pay us under the table to keep your name out of it and store your goods privately," Captain Cork said.

"Yes, if that would suit you," Lee said. "It might be helpful to your bottom line without involving your Internal Revenue Service, would it not?" Both the North Koreans were smiling now, sure that they had more Americans on their payroll.

At that moment, Miss Bitchy Face came over the comm and said, "Attention Task Force Yuck Fou, we have secured all foreign targets. We are moving on domestic targets now."

I picked up a nail file and hit my nails with it to tell the agents in the office that we needed to play these guys just a bit longer.

"We would have to know something about these 'delicate products'," Coach said. "If they are something that is detectable by say, drug dogs, then we would need to make different arrangements than currently exist in our warehouses."

"We could make our payments to you $500,000 per quarter if that would suit you better," Lee said. "Our other partners would like us to keep the shipments as private as possible, but I can assure you that nothing in them is detectable by dogs of any kind."

Captain Cork said, "Would you excuse us for a moment, gentlemen? If you could just step into the reception area for a few minutes I'd like to confer with my colleagues." The Koreans rose and were just getting to the door when Miss Bitchy Voice said, "Attention Task Force Yuck Foo—all domestic targets are going down now, now, now! Execute all takedowns now!"

The door opened just as I said into the intercom, "Mr. Forkyou please come to reception, Mr. Forkyou to reception."

The North Koreans walked out into the area in front of my desk and stood talking in Korean. Thirty seconds later the office door opened again and they looked up to see the three warehouse owners coming out. Their smiles grew wider right up to the point that I pulled one of my pistols and said, "U.S. SECRET SERVICE! YOU ARE UNDER ARREST—PUT YOUR HANDS ON YOUR HEAD!"

Both North Koreans started to turn and found themselves facing a plethora of pistols pointed at their heads. Every exit had SWAT guys pouring through them, and the three owners had pistols in their hands and pointed right at their Korean heads, too.

"Attention Task Force Yuck Fou, all domestic targets are down, I repeat, all domestic targets are down," Miss Bitchy Voice said in my ear.

Kim looked at me with snake's eyes and said, "I have a green card and am a citizen of South Korea, a U.S. ally. Why am I being subjected to this treatment?" Song didn't say anything, but his eyes were rolling around like a cat's at a Rottweiler convention.

"Save it, dipshit," I said as I advanced on him. "We've got Kim Jung-Soo, Moon Bon-Hwa and Rhee Gi-Guk in custody, and they've been singing like little North Korean canaries. You're going to be visiting Guantanamo Bay for a while, and then I expect you'll be going back to the DPRK, where I'm fairly sure that your Glorious Piglet isn't going to be too happy with you—we've just popped your whole counterfeiting ring like a soap bubble. Now get your hands on your head."

Song already had his hands on top of his head, but Kim Yong-Sun was moving a bit slower. His left hand brushed his lapel and I realized what he was doing, but eight feet of separation was too far even for me. Before I could stop him he swept his left hand to his mouth and popped something in. I knocked him ass over tea cart and tried to get his head in my hands, but he twisted away from me and defiantly swallowed, glaring at me as if he could kill me with a look.

I spun off the floor and bashed Song U-Woong's hand down as he was reaching for his mouth. A button hit the floor and rolled away as I took him to the floor and slapped the iron on him.

I stood up and looked at Kim. He had a thin trace of froth on his lips, and his eyes were still staring, but his body was going stiff. About 10 seconds later he stopped breathing and the light went out of his eyes. His body shuddered once and then was still.

"I never thought he was that much of a fanatic," I said. "We didn't think of poison, did we?"

"No," said Captain Cork, "but we also don't really care, because he was gonna die when he went back to North Korea anyway. He just took the easy way out while doing his duty, so maybe Kim Jong Un won't kill his family, too."

"Oh, all of our families will die when news of this breaks," Song said from the floor. "Our Glorious Leader does not suffer failures well, and he visits his displeasure on the families of those who fail and fail to return, even if it is his own family."

"Do you want to die, too?" I said. "Right now, by taking poison?"

"I do not wish to die at all. I am a patriot, but we were few against your many counterintelligence officers. I am not to blame for any of this, but that will not stop the Glorious Leader from executing me and all of my family," Song said. His despair was palpable and understandable—Kim Jong Un had executed his own favorite uncle because the man didn't get him an ICBM, and he'd killed his former girlfriend because she made fun of his shoes (or so the western news said—I heard she made fun of something else, and that perhaps the Glorious Leader wasn't so glorious in the sack). In any case, what Song was saying was almost certainly true—his life expectancy had certainly gone down in the last five minutes.

I looked hard at him and said, "Honorable Song, are you *sure* that you don't want to die right now by doing your duty and taking poison?" His eyes locked on mine as he got what I was saying. He looked at Captain Cork, who said, "It'd be a shame if you died right now from taking poison, Mr. Song. Why, we'd have to write up reports about how we let you get to the poison, and how you died with the Glorious Leader's name on your lips."

"That's right, a true patriot of the DPRK to the end," Joe said.

Song asked a question in Korean and Mamba answered him. Song thought for a moment and then said something else. He, Mamba and Jack Soo had a spirited conversation in Korean, and then Song said, "I wish to die from taking poison." I took the cuffs off him and tore a button off his shirt. He sat up, took the button from my hand, and swallowed it.

About 10 seconds later he shuddered and fell over, then shuddered again and lay still. His body began to stiffen just like Kim Yong-Sun's had, and soon he was completely still.

"Goddamn it, Freak! How'd you let that second shithead get to his poison?" Captain Cork said.

"Sorry, Boss, but I swore you said to let him go. Shit!" I said.

Joe calmly called on his comm to Miss Bitchy Voice and said, "Control, we need two busses here. Both suspects took poison before we could stop them. No hurry, but we should do it ASAP—we want to clear the scene."

"Acknowledged," she said. "Both targets down from self-inflicted poison. Ambulances are en route, ETA three minutes.

So we stood around for the four minutes it took the EMTs to get there and get set up. The first guys picked up Kim's body and covered Song's with a sheet. They left with Jewey, Weasel and Joe, who were going to ride with the body to the hospital in order to keep the chain of custody intact. Before he left Joe said, "Freak, you guys come with the other body and we'll all leave together. I nodded at him and stood next to Song's body with Mamba, Jack Soo, and Ed.

When the second ambulance got there Coach was wheeling Captain Cork out in his chair. As they passed by he said, "Too bad that second guy died. We really wanted to take one of these guys alive." Both EMTs looked at him, and Coach said, "Yeah, we could've really used a live one, Boss. Too bad the poor guy wanted to die a patriot and took that poison."

"Who would've ever thought they had poison in a button?" Captain Cork said.

The EMTs gave each other puzzled looks as they rolled their gurney over to Song's body. They pulled the sheet back and one of them went for his throat to check for a pulse, just like they always do. "He's dead from poison," I said in a quiet but firm command voice I learned in the Corps. The EMT looked at me and I slowly winked at her.

She got it. She acted like she was feeling for a pulse but never touched Song. She straightened up and said, "He's gone. Let's get him on the gurney before he lets go of anything, or gets close to rigor." Her partner helped her and they lifted Song onto the gurney and rolled him to their bus. We all got in the back and the EMT got in the front and we rolled away from the warehouse.

After a block I said, "What were you guys talking about with Song?"

"He was asking if we could get him into a program so the North Koreans wouldn't be able to find him," Mamba said.

"We told him we certainly could, and then he asked us about where we thought he should be relocated to," Jack Soo said.

"He was worried that he'd inconvenience our interrogators, since he knew they would want to talk to him about all sorts of stuff," Mamba said.

"Especially since he knew all of the bank accounts offshore and in the U.S., as well as the emergency routes for extracting cash and agents from the U.S.," Jack Soo said.

"I voted for the Virginia tidewater region," Mamba said.

"I told him to hold out for Cypress, California, or Carmel-by-the-Sea," Jack Soo said.

"I also told him that Asheville, North Carolina was nice," Mamba said.

"And Seattle-Tacoma is a really nice area," Jack Soo said.

"Too bad that motherfucker was such a patriot," Ed said. "He could've asked for asylum like Moon Bon-Hwa did."

"I wish to seek asylum in the United States," Song said from under the sheet.

"Now we're talkin'," I said. "Welcome back from the dead, Song U-Woong."

"Asylum is a wonderful antidote to poison," Jack Soo said and we all laughed, even Song. When we got to the hospital there were U.S. Marshals waiting for us at the morgue. They took charge of Song and gave him a change of clothes and sunglasses. They completed the disguise with a nice Panama hat and a paste-on mustache that looked real. We all shook hands with him and Song left looking nothing like a dead patriot, or a North Korean, for that matter. He looked like a guy who was headed to his pinochle game, or maybe the track.

I never saw him again, but I heard that he settled in Santa Barbara, California, married a nice Japanese lady and became a real fan of Santa Anita Racetrack. His best friend was a guy who used to be named Moon Bon-Hwa, who lived in Yorba Linda, California and was also a fan of Santa Anita. In addition to helping us crack everything we didn't already know about the counterfeiting ring, Song and Moon also convinced Kim Jung-Soo and Rhee Gi-Guk that they should "die from poison," and actually get to live a life. As far as I know they all did a fairy tale and lived happily ever after.

All the Secret Service did was seize $270 billion in assets and counterfeit cash, convert four North Korean agents to our side, stop the influx of funny money that could have destroyed the world's economy and tweaked the Glorious Leader's nose in view of the whole world. It cost us dearly, because even though we did all that The Greek, House, Gunny, Sparky, and Mac were still dead; but overall it was a pretty good op.

As a dryly funny BBC commentator said, the score was "U.S. Secret Service 270 billion, DPRK nil."

Or, as my friend Almont Phillipe Gilbert de Coucy, Comte de Condé put it, "Yeot-meogeo, Chosŏn Minjujuŭi Inmin Konghwaguk."

Fuck you, North Korea.

CHAPTER 38

Nothing Lasts Forever, Freak

Needless to say, that was the high point of my anti-counterfeiting career with the Secret Service. Our unit came back from our losses. Betty, Coach, Mamba and Buzz fit in like they'd always been a part of the group, while El Gato, Bumble and Gomer came back from rehab and Captain Cork literally got back on his feet. It wasn't the same, but it was still good.

We also testified at a shitload of trials putting away all of the bad guys—nobody that we arrested during any of the operations that busted the largest counterfeiting ring in the history of the world escaped the scales of justice (if it sounds like I'm bragging, well, I am—we lost five good agents so we could catch these shitheads, and it really was the largest funny money operation anyone had ever seen…it ain't braggin' if it really happened). There were the North Korean defections, lots of people, including the Toledo Five and Darcy Fowler, pled guilty and the two North Korean agents who were checking on their sleeper agents were PNG'd back to the DPRK, carrying with them the story of the brave North Korean agents who took poison rather than give up state secrets to the CIA.

That made all of the CIA/NSA/Homeland Security types happy, because it meant that they had more time to interview the intrepid defectors, and the defectors were happy because it meant that they didn't have to go home to the starvation diets of their homeland.

Of course, we continued to investigate and bust counterfeiters, but nothing compared to the Toledo Five/New York Massacree/North Korean Affair.

Oh, there was the case where Bumble and Mamba discovered a neat scam in Milwaukee. A group of grandmothers printed fake $10 bills during their "crochet circle," had bake sales and rummage sales where they bought everything at the sale that wasn't legitimately sold (they washed some of the 10s by using them for change), and then deposited the money in a fund operated by their church that sent pilgrims to the Holy Land. Because they were all retired the grandmas then rigged the selection criteria to make sure that some of them were picked to go on the trips—and nobody at the church resented it, because what jerk gets mad about a nice, old grandma getting a break?

They might have gotten away with it except for two things: Bumble happened to see a report from Israel that mentioned an influx of fake U.S. $10 bills, and one of the grandmas handed a stack of 10s to a cashier at her credit union that were in mint condition and gave off just the hint of fresh ink. The teller checked, the bills had consecutive serial numbers—so she called us. Mamba charmed his way into the crochet circle by playing the "gay best friend" card with one of the old ladies. He asked so many questions about what was going on that the old lady finally couldn't take it and spilled the beans.

They all got 20-year sentences, but several people (including two Secret Service agents) asked the judge for leniency, because they didn't really profit from the operation and besides, they were all at least 70 years old. The judge listened and they all got a year at a minimum-security prison, with 19 years' probation. They also had to forfeit their ill-gotten gains and crochet a large number of afghans for the church to sell in order to legitimately replace the lost Holy Land fund.

Everybody in our unit bought one, and Mamba bought all the leftover crocheted treasures to give to his connections at the LaVillita Corps Community Center so they could serve the less fortunate among us.

Everybody was happy about that result.

There was also the case where Ed, Betty, El Gato and Weasel caught a bunch of street punks trying to pass off counterfeit $50 bills. They used cupcakes, a singing act, four hookers and a homeless guy to set up a sting operation, which was hilarious after they cast Weasel as the homeless guy. He hammed it up so bad the punks were convinced that he was, in the immortal words of the (not so) brilliant leader of the criminal enterprise, "a fuckin' freakazoid piss-bum."

In his Emmy nominated role Weasel led the unit to over $1.1 million in funny money, which got the counterfeiters 20 years in federal prison and got Weasel kicked out of his girlfriend's apartment until he took several hundred showers, because his "disguise" included pouring his own piss all over himself, augmenting it with deer urine he bought at a sporting goods store, and taking a bath in his clothes, three bottles of Thunderbird, and ten gallons of milk, which saturated the clothes and eventually went rancid, creating a cloud of odorous vapor not found outside a dozen restaurant dumpsters left in the hot sun for three days.

Ed and Betty claimed he'd also shit his pants and failed to clean it up, but Weasel denied it. No one believed him.

And there was the famous case where Joe, Coach, Gomer, and I caught five guys from Wayzata, Minnesota, who were pumping out fake $100 bills in an old printing house and using it to fund their ersatz Asian barbeque restaurant chain in Minneapolis (they didn't have a single Asian person working there, and these guys were white-bread Lutherans, whose closest approach to Asia was when they watched Rick Steves in Bangkok on PBS, dontcha know). They were looking for some investors who they could then dump the restaurants on while cashing in on their stash of funny money.

We found out about them when a contractor complained to our Minneapolis field office that he'd gotten several fake $100 bills from one of three clients who paid him in cash. The Minneapolis office was short-handed and very involved in a Somalian warlord who was sending funny money to local Somalis, so they asked us to take a look at the disgruntled contractor's case. We confirmed that the bills were fake—they were perfect except for being printed on regular paper (not all cases are launched by criminal masterminds)—and then took a closer look at the three possibilities.

Gomer confirmed almost right away that the five ersatz Asian restaurant guys had cash flow that seemed to just appear in their restaurants, despite the fact that a rudimentary investigation revealed that the restaurants had as many customers as a New Orleans bar on Ash Wednesday (go to Mardi Gras and you'll understand—the party stops at 12:01 a.m. on Ash Wednesday and they ain't not kiddin', no they not, you).

We dug deeper and found out that all five guys had been drowning in debt until very recently, when their five restaurants around the city had been refurbished and their cash flow had increased dramatically. Joe found out they were looking for investors, so we all flew to Minneapolis to meet with them while posing as restauranteurs who were interested in something that they could franchise.

The five guys took us to one of their restaurants, wined and dined us and then pitched the deal. The food was terrible, but they were going to let us buy the chain at a discount if we used cash and let them report the sale to the Minnesota authorities while signing a non-disclosure agreement about the sale price. We said we'd have to let them know after we consulted with our "silent partners" which made them smile. We may have sort of implied that we were connected to the Chicago Mob. Hey, all's fair in love and anti-counterfeiting.

Two days later Coach called them to come to Chi and meet in one of "our" restaurants. We'd already decided we wanted to be as Asian as possible with our approach, and Gomer said he knew a great sushi restaurant down on Rush Street, so we took them there. The place was a hole in the wall (no, I'm not going to give you its name—can you say "lawsuit"?) and we'd already told the owner what we were doing, so he played along.

The sushi was excellent and we told them we wondered about their funding source to start the chain. Coach played our funding guru, with Joe as backup, but the questions they asked seemed to really spook the guys, and it looked like they were backing off a bit. We thought we'd lost them, but fortunately we had an experience that was a really good bonding agent and kept them off their guard.

It seems that the guy who delivered the high-quality tuna for the sushi didn't notice that the refrigeration unit on his truck had gone out until the next day, which meant that our tuna had been traveling around Chicago for six hours without direct refrigeration.

We had just stepped outside the restaurant when the vomiting festival began. Gomer erupted like a Mount Vesuvius of puke and I hurled right after him. Two of the guys from Wayzata also began worshipping the great god Urk, and then the rest of the group added their contributions to the gutters, sidewalks and at least two groups of diners at the outside tables of the restaurant next to the sushi place (I was really yakking by then, so I wasn't really clear on the number of tables involved, although I know there was some sympathy puking by the *al fresco* diners).

Then it got almost serious as our group of Porcelain Goddess acolytes all went down to their knees (we were just looking for a stable platform so we didn't fall down in the rivers of gastric distress running for the gutters) during the second round of the Revenge of the Sushi Surprise Tournament sponsored by Ralph's Markets (sorry about the pun, but it fits here way better than it doesn't).

Two of theirs and one of ours (Coach) went to the hospital, and all of us had our electrolytes replenished intravenously (God love those Chicago EMTs for pumping us full of good shit, or we might have died of explosive dehydration). While we were waiting at the hospital to see how our friends were Joe said, "After all this I can't blame you for not wanting to deal with us," but their number two guy (we could still hear number one loudly proclaiming his allegiance to the Porcelain Princess) thought maybe we just might be able to work something out, as long as we met in Minneapolis the next time. When everybody was all better we met again in one of their places (the food was still horrible and not Asian at all, but it was still better than the sushi place on Rush since we only had to taste it once) and they pitched another deal.

We'd already decided that we weren't going to press the issue of their financing, but their number one brought it up when he said, "How about we show you at our main office in Wayzata, say at 9:00 a.m.?" We agreed to meet them, although I'm fairly sure they didn't expect the other 25 guys we brought.

The next morning we arrived and determined that everyone was there, and the five guys told us how much they trusted us after "all we'd been through together" and that they could tell we were "stand up guys." They showed us into the warehouse area of their main office and showed us the nice mound of counterfeit $100 bills they had, at which point Joe, Coach, Gomer, and I all oohed and aahed about their ingenuity and skills, right up until the moment the rest of our unit busted into the warehouse, at which point we arrested their stunned Lutheran asses.

It seems they couldn't believe that Secret Service agents would poison themselves to make an arrest. One of them said, "But you were all puking and sick just like we were! You could've died! How could you do that?" which is when Gomer said, "Hey asshole, we jump in front of bullets for a living—do you really think that we're afraid of some *bad fish*?"

It was an immediate legend.

We called it the Worshipping the Porcelain Goddess Gambit.

There were lots of other cases, but we all knew it was too good to last. Captain Cork announced he was moving to D.C., to work in the Top Dick Squad (as we called it—it's actual name is the Criminal Investigative Division, and it oversees all Secret Service criminal investigations in the world), and that Guru would be moving up to his spot as AIC of the Counterfeiting Office in Chicago. Joe was moving up to be number two in Counterfeiting. Jewey and Weasel were moving down the hall to head up the Financial Crimes office—not really a big move, since they would continue to work hand in glove with Counterfeiting, but still moving away from the old unit.

We were all sad, but also happy for our friends, so we went to The Berghoff and partied harder than normal, which meant that when my phone went off at 5:00 a.m. I was not only not ready for it, I was damned mad at it for ringing. My consequent grab-and-chuck-it-against-the-wall maneuver was completely successful in killing the evil, ringing piece-of-shit technology, but unfortunately that was only my personal piece-of-shit technology. Whoever wanted me had been talking into it when I murdered my private phone, so they simply went to my Service phone, which was (a) too robust to get broken just by being chucked against a wall and (b) was too far away for me to reach in time to kill it before a message was left.

Shit.

I love working for the Secret Service—it really is a privilege—but I hated the stupid "on call twenty-four hours a day" rule, as well as the "you must call back if a message reaches you" rule, which definitely applied here.

Fucking shit.

So I hit the callback button on my government issued piece-of-shit technology and a nice lady said, "This is the main Secret Service switchboard. How may I direct your call?"

"I'm calling you back. I don't know what sadistic son of a bitch called me at 5:00 a.m., but if you find out let me know and I'll kill his or her overachieving ass," I said, and hung up. I fell back into bed after stuffing the government sleep-killer into my gun box and locking it.

I was out like a light and already dreaming when the gun box fell off the shelf from the cell phone vibrations.

"Goddamnedmotherfuckingshitcuntfuckhellbitch!" I said, clearly happy about the second interruption of my badly-needed-to-avoid-the-mother-of-all-hangovers sleep. I stuck my right thumb and left ring finger in the biometric locks of the gun box and pulled out the cell phone when the top of the box popped open.

It was the same goddamned number as last time.

They say that insanity is defined by doing the same exact thing every time and expecting a different result, so technically I shouldn't have been surprised by what happened when I hit re-dial again.

"This is the main Secret Service switchboard. How may I direct your call?" the same perky voice said again.

"We gotta stop meeting like this," I said. "Some asshole keeps calling me from this number. Unless you want me to come in and shoot the damned phone system to death you need to find out which asshole it is and get them to stop, or connect me to them so that I can get the asshole to stop."

"Uh, who is this?" the perky voice said.

I gave her my name and ID number and she said, "Oh, Agent Glickstien! Please hold for the Director."

I didn't really have time to say "WTF?" before another perky voice said "Good morning, Freak."

"Define good, asshole," I said, and hung up.

The phone rang about eight seconds later and I said, "We are not amused by the timing of this call, dipshit."

"Oh, is there someone there with you?" the perky voice said.

"No, it's just me and my head filled with a bowling league knocking down pins, Eddie," I said. "And what did they make you director of, the fucking Asshole Rise and Shine Club?"

"The Protective Division, actually," Edward Otis Whitney said. "You're my first call, and guess what I want?"

"A blowjob, but you're not gonna get it from me," I said.

"Well, that's a relief, because then we couldn't work together, and I already have your first protectee picked out," Old Three Names said. I paused and he said, "Don't hang up, because you know that you want to know who it is, Freak."

Damn his button-down ass, I did want to know. "OK, I'll bite—who the fuck do you want me to guard?" I tried to downplay it, but Old Three Names was too good at reading people.

"It is a unique and quite frankly dangerous job that will require a great amount of preparation and patience on your part," he said.

"You really wanna tease me when you know that I can shoot your balls off, or rip you limb from limb AND I have a hangover of epic proportions?" I said.

"Actually, that probably isn't my best tactic," he said. "Aleta Greenhoe Soper."

I looked at the phone and said, "Are you shittin' me, Eddie?"

"Most assuredly not. She wants a body agent who can keep up with her, and only seven people fit the criteria necessary, and she wants a womyn...so you're up, Freak."

Great. My first assignment for the Protection Detail would be safeguarding the most hated political candidate in recent memory, a womyn who won an Olympic silver medal in the steeplechase and ran on the gold medal four-by-four-hundred relay for the U.S. wymyn and hadn't slowed down yet in her run as the first openly lesbian candidate for president. And oh, yeah, she was married to a supermodel who had been on the cover of the *Sports Illustrated* Swimsuit Issue and had one of the most recognizable faces in the world—and who went everywhere with her wife.

Fuck me.

I seriously thought about trying to cross-deck to the U.S. Marshals Service like, yesterday, but then my competitive juices started flowing and I realized that I was probably the best candidate for the job, maybe in the world, because she may have won Olympic medals and be smarter than Neil deGrasse Tyson, but I could outshoot the U.S. Seventh Marine Division, played football at Michigan State and was still the wymyn's world record holder in the hammer throw.

Plus, I'd get to run the show when it came to security, so I'd show her arrogant ass who was boss right quick.

Theoretically.

"OK, I'm in for the protective detail, but I want to bring three people with me," I said.

"Agents Beemond, Devlin and Zaragoza have already agreed, if you were in," Edward Otis Whitney said. I realized then that Old Three Names was even smarter than I thought he was, because I wasn't going to move to the Puzzle Palace without some company, even if we were on different details. I really hated the thought of leaving Chicago, which had become a real home to me, but I could do it if I had friends who felt the same way.

"I thought I was your first call," I said.

"I lied. Get over it," Edward Otis Whitney said.

"When do we report?" I said.

"Next Monday," Old Three Names said. "Once you close up shop in Chicago you need to go to Marion before you report in DC."

"Why the hell am I going to Marion?" I said. The federal prison at Marion, Illinois, looked like Vlad the Impaler's castle and gave everybody the creeps, and I had no earthly reason to go there that I could think of.

"There is someone there that wants to talk to you, and I said yes on your behalf," he said.

"Talk about what?" I said.

"It's a surprise, but I will tell you that it surprised me, and I am not easily surprised," Edward Otis Whitney said. I believed him—I never met a more composed, decisive person than Old Three Names, and I served three presidents of the United States and a hundred other high-powered people.

I agreed to go to Marion and get my surprise, and then I got dressed and went to the office, where I found the unit already there. We looked like the Little Sisters of the Hangover Impaired, but everybody was functional. I walked in and said, "OK you assholes! You hung me out to dry with Old Three Names and now I gotta move to the Puzzle Palace and guard a renegade lesbian who thinks she can be president. Which one of you motherfuckers wants to die first?"

"Can't kill me, I'm already dead," Ed said, holding her head in her hands.

"If you kill me I won't have to listen to all of this incredibly noisy shit playing on the radio," Bumble said.

"The radio ain't on, Agent Bumble," Gomer said.

"Maybe not in *your* head," Bumble said.

"Why is there a big ol' worm 'bout ten feet long hallucinatin' purple cows in our squad room?" El Gato said, his voice cracking.

"And why is Steve Goodman singing live in here?" Betty Crocker said.

"I thought that old boy bought the farm," Weasel said.

"He *did*," Betty Crocker said, "which why him singing doesn't make any sense."

"Jesus Hubert *Christ*, the *ghost* of Steve Goodman is *singing* in our goddamned *squadroom*," Mamba said, defaulting to queen mode in his hangover distress.

"Will you guys shut the fuck up? I'm trying to keep my eyes from popping out of my head and it sounds like every Canadian goose in history is honking its way around the office," Captain Cork said.

"Don't shoot at 'em Captain—I think it's just the ghost of Steve Goodman," Guru said.

"Oh shit, somebody call *Ghostbusters*," Coach said.

We all started singing "Who ya gonna call? Ghostbusters!" through the haze of our hangovers, and then we started laughing, and then we started getting a little teary eyed, because the old gang was breaking up, so we all had a good cry.

When the crying stopped Guru announced that she was moving Joe up to Assistant Agent in Charge of the Counterfeiting squad, and that Buzz, Betty and Gomer were staying on. She announced that Charlie Chan was also going to the Puzzle Palace as an Assistant Director of the Protective Division, which made those of us who were also going there feel better.

We reminisced some more before Joe said, "There's one thing that we can't forget about, Freak, at least those of us who were there can't forget about it."

"Mrs. Miller," Jewey, Ed, Weasel, Bumble, and I said. "I'll buy those Pepsis if you'll tell me who Mrs. Miller is," Mamba said.

So we told all of the new squad members the story of Mrs. Miller, and when we were done Mamba said, "I would like to join your *tontine, mes amis*. It sounds like Mrs. Miller deserves some answers, and we are the people to give them to her, are we not?"

"Indeed we are," Joe said.

"I agree completely, but if any of us want to get out of here we need to clean up all of our outstanding shit," Captain Cork said.

And so we did.

I asked Coach and Mamba to come to Washington, too, and they agreed. Mamba was driving me down to Marion for my surprise and then we were leaving from Carbondale, the home of the Southern Illinois University Salukis, where we would catch a puddle-jumper to Louisville for the flight to Reagan International Airport in D.C.

I was ready when Mamba and James showed up at my former apartment at 5:00 a.m. James threw my two bags in the trunk of the limo and I climbed in to find Guru, Coach, Jewey, Weasel, Buzz. Betty and Gomer in the back with Mamba. It was a great surprise, and when I said so Mamba said, "Did you know it's less than two hours from Marion to St. Louis? Do you know how many great rib joints there are in St. Louis? Don't those left behind deserve an excursion in order to defray the sorrow of losing all of our comrades in arms? Aren't I a rich fucker who can afford to take some friends out to drown their sorrows in St. Louis ribs and coleslaw?"

We agreed with him, and I said, "Shit, let's go there first. I'm sure that my surprise will wait, and ribs sound pretty good." The limo was filled with laughter.

We shot the shit the rest of the way to the federal prison. Coach finally said, "You got any idea what the surprise is, Freak?"

"I can't think of anything that I need to be here for—I've racked my brain and it just doesn't compute," I said.

"Well, it must be something that matters, because Edward Otis Whitney is definitely not a frivolous person. He wouldn't send you off on a wild goose chase," Mamba said.

"Which is why this doesn't make any sense," I said.

"So it must be important," Weasel said. "It stands to reason that it has something to do with your reassignment to the Protective Division, but I can't figure out how."

"Maybe he wants you to meet with someone who knows about protection—is it possible that there's a protection maven at the penitentiary?" Buzz said. "Some guy with special insight into your new job?"

"Fuck if I know," I said. "I never heard of anybody at the place, I mean, no names leap out, and I've been around some of these commercial protection guys, and none of these people seem the type."

"Well, all mysteries will become clear soon," Mamba said. "We're here."

The hulking prison was there in front of us, and Mamba was right about the mystery being dispelled.

I've never been more shocked in my life.

CHAPTER 39

A Patriot Apologizes

The limo pulled up at one of the official gates and I got out. The limo took off—everybody wanted to pee and get coffee and none of those chickenshits wanted to stay at Castle Dracula any longer than they had to.

I didn't blame them. I was scared to go in, and I've been in some pretty bad places (no I'm not gonna tell you—say it with me…it's classified).

But I went in anyway, got processed as an official visitor, finally gave up my 1076s at a man-trap portal and then was ushered into the visitation room. Two guards stood at either end of the room, and two minutes after I got there two more came in with a prisoner.

Paul Monteverdi.

I stood up and thought '*WTF?*' as they brought him over to the table I was at. One of the guards said, "You want him hooked up?" while pointing at the steel D-ring set in the floor, and I said, "No, thank you. Mr. Monteverdi and I are old acquaintances. We'll be fine."

The guards nodded and then went over to stand on the two empty walls, so that there was a guard on every wall. I looked Monteverdi over and thought that he looked pretty good for a guy in prison, and the look on his face was…contrite? Apologetic? Almost friendly? It was unnerving to see a mobster looking at you like you were his granddaughter and not one of the people who sent him to prison for 25 years.

"Thanks for comin', Agent Glickstien. I can't shake your hand—we can't touch—but I would if I could," Monteverdi said. I sat down and said, "Yeah, why is that?"

"Because we treated you like shit when you was just doin' your job, which you was right to do, given the circumstances," he said.

"Come again?" I said, my astonishment clearly written on my ugly face.

"Mr. Bonnarino asked me to apologize to you, and I'm apologizin' for myself, too," Monteverdi said.

"Apologizing?" I said. I felt like I'd been transported to an alternate universe where I was a fairy princess whose very presence turned evildoers into Big Bird and Fozzie Bear.

Or maybe there was LSD in that coffee I drank on the way down.

"Say, you feelin' OK? You got a hearing problem or something"?" Monteverdi said.

"No, but I have to tell you—you could knock me over with a feather duster," I said. "I've never heard of a man like you—uh, no offense—apologizing for anything."

"Well, Mr. Bonnarino and me are bad men, sure, but we're also real men who love their country. Mr. Bonnarino and me both served in the Army, and all three of my sons been in the service. If we'd a known that this thing was run by some commies we'd a never been any part of it. Hell, I'd a dropped a dime on those Korean commie shits myself if stupid Leona'd told me they was supplying the product," he said.

"I, uh…where'd you serve, if I can ask?" I said.

"Mr. Bonnarino and I both served in the 'Nam, and two a my boys was in the first Gulf War. My third boy served in Afghanistan after 9/11 and won the Silver Star," Monteverdi said, clearly proud of his boys. "Did you serve?"

"United States Marines," I said. "I ended up a major."

"Yeah? An officer? Where'd ya serve?" he said.

I told him and his eyes got wide. "No shit?" he said.

"I shit thee not," I said.

"Jesus, you wasn't just window dressin' then," he said.

"No, I was a real Spec Ops operator," I said. I told him about a couple of my adventures in the field (and no, I didn't tell him anything that was classified) and he just shook his head and said, "And all you had was your pistol?" I nodded and he said, "Agent Glickstien, ya got some balls on ya, I'll say that." We both laughed at that one.

Monteverdi said, "Mr. Bonnarino wanted to apologize for his callin' ya an ugly cunt, too. He said to tell ya there ain't no excuse for that kind of behavior or language, and that if he saw ya again it wouldn't happen the same way."

"Please tell Mr. Bonnarino I'm sorry about my outburst toward him, too," I said. "I was in shock."

"Yeah, well that one is on me," he said. "I wanna apologize about that, too. My shooters was supposed to shoot Leona and Luigi so's they couldn't talk, not get in a damned firefight with the Secret Service. Leona bought 'em off with some a that cash, but that don't excuse my part in it. I'm sorry for the loss of your friends." He was so sincere that I almost reached out to take his hand before I realized that I couldn't.

I finally got it. "You're principled men," I said. "And you're not kidding at all about being patriots, even though you're members of an organized crime family."

"No, we ain't kidding about nothin', Agent Glickstien. Yeah, we're guineas who became made men at an early age, and yeah, we're a couple of vicious sons of bitches, if you'll excuse the language, but that don't mean we're piece of shit traitors, or that we don't have no principles. I mean, Mr. Bonnarino been married to his wife for forty-eight years, and he ain't never looked aside, and I woulda been married to my Florence for forty-seven years this year if she hadn't a got the cancer and died." He paused, and the heartsick look on his face said it all.

"I'm sorry for your loss," I said, meaning it more than anything because he suddenly reminded me of my *zayde* after my *bubbe* died.

"Thank you. I'm as tough as an old leather shoe but I loved that grand old broad, and I didn't never touch another womyn while we was married, and I ain't never gonna touch another one, out of respect for her stickin' by me even though she knew I was involved in some serious shit," Monteverdi said. "As for the patriotism thing—hey, Mr. Bonnarinno and I was in business to make a buck, but we wouldn't run no drugs, all of our girls was above age and willin' to work for good pay, we never, ah, eliminated no one who wasn't like us and we always paid our taxes, because the country needs to have good bridges and dams and shit or how are we gonna have a business?

"It's also a fact that Mr. Bonnarino and I are major contributors to the fireworks in the harbor on the Fourth of July, we both march with all the other vets in the Memorial Day parade and we're volunteers at the Long Island National Cemetery out there in Farmingdale," Monteverdi said.

"Doing what?" I asked.

"We help people find the graves of their loved ones, and we also help form the Honor Guard at U.S. Army burials. We've also paid for a few burials for old Army guys whose families got no way to pay for it," he said.

"Well, knock me down and kick me for fallin'," I said. "You guys probably wear red, white and blue underwear, too." We smiled at each other and Monteverdi said, "Maybe not, but every day Mr. Bonnarino and I put flags up at our houses, and we pay for every school in our neighborhood to get new flags when they need them. It's the least we can do for the country that took in our guinea grandparents when they couldn't even 'speaka da Eenglish' and gave them a chance to have a good life. Ain't nowhere else on earth where a buncha wop greengrocers can come so far up in the world that they got box seats at the Metropolitan Opera and own a theatre on Broadway—and got season tickets for the New York Yankees." Monteverdi looked at me with his deep-set, intense dark eyes and said, "I don't want ya ta think we're some kinda saints, Agent Glickstien, 'cause we ain't, but when Mr. Bonnarino and I say 'God bless America' we ain't kiddin' around, ya know?"

"I believe you. My family's story is much the same, except we're Jews who needed a place after Hitler got done trying to kill us all," I said.

"That asshole," Monteverdi said. "Excuse my French, but we shoulda sent a couple of Sicilians in to whack his ass right after he started all that shit in Europe, and we wouldn't a had to lose so many good people. You sorta know what I'm talkin' about when I say that Mr. Bonnarino and I love this country, am I right?"

"Very much so, and I appreciate it, Mr. Monteverdi," I said.

"And you know we're sincere when we say—again, please excuse my language—fuck those North Korean commie shitheads and the donkey they rode in on," he said.

I laughed and said, "Oh, I get that all right. Can I just say that my whole unit feels the same way, only we were not quite so delicate in our assessment of them?"

"Oh, so you added 'and the family dog' to it, right?" he said. We both laughed at that, and I was struck again by the complexity of human nature—I was in the middle of one of the most fearsome federal prisons in our country, sitting with a gangster patriot who had killed men, and whose men had almost killed me, having a pleasant but bizarre conversation about some people he wished he hadn't done business with.

Only in America.

I looked up and Monteverdi was again looking intently at me, his eyes sparkling but his face serious. He finally said, "Agent Glickstien, you remember how you felt the first time you saw me?"

"I won't ever forget it. I thought that you were one dangerous customer, and that I should be on my guard at all times around you," I said. I didn't say that I'd been just the teeniest bit afraid, but I had been.

"Good," he said. "So you was afraid, just a little bit, that I might be able to take you, right?"

"Well, yeah," I said. "Who wouldn't be just a little bit afraid of a big-time mobster?"

"Nah, that ain't what I'm talkin' about. I'm talking about that feelin' in the pit of your stomach that feels like you mighta got a bad clam in there, the one that makes ya think maybe you're gonna puke," he said.

"Oh, that," I said. "Yeah, I got that, too."

"Good, 'cause that's what guys like me call a 'healthy respect for the possible.' It means that your guard needs ta stay up even when ya think it don't need ta," he said. "You was surrounded by firepower and had the drop on us, and yet ya right away singled me out and homed in on the danger I represented—and ya was right to do so, because if I coulda figured a way to not get Mr. Bonnarino killed I woulda popped you right there. No offense, nothin' personal, but I'm not in the habit of lettin' Mr. Bonnarino get insulted and lettin' the person who did it get away with it, ya know?" He was smiling, but it was very apparent that Paul Monteverdi was completely serious, and also that he was trying to tell me something.

"I completely understand, Mr. Monteverdi, but why are you telling me this?" I said. "I'm also a killer, even though I'm a womyn, and I've met lots of bad guys, some of them worse than you, and, well, they're all gone and I'm still here, ya know?"

His smile got broader, and he said, "I know you're a killer—a tiger takes notice when another tiger comes into their part of the jungle, right?—but even tigers can get taken down, especially if they don't see the hunter comin'."

"OK, what the fuck're you talkin' about, Mr. Green Mountain?" I said.

He looked at me with what I could only assume was sympathy and said, "Stupid Leona told Mr. Bonnarino that she was approached by a gentleman who wanted some people whacked, government people who were getting too nosy about certain things. Being a stupid twit she decides, without talkin' to either of us, to have 'her' guys, who I thought were my guys, take the job. They paid her in cash up front, $2 million in a numbered account in the Caymans, which number I'm gonna give you before you leave, but that ain't the important part, if ya know what I mean." He looked at me, waiting to see if I got it.

I got it.

"The attack at the warehouse wasn't about the counterfeit—it was a hit on my squad," I said.

"Bingo," he said.

"But why? If it wasn't the counterfeiting operation, what was it?" I said.

"Yeah, it don't make no sense to Mr. Bonnarino and me, either, but according to stupid Leona the guy specifically wanted you, Agent Cocker, Agent Polack—I know that ain't his name, but these Polack names I just don't get—and Agent McKee to go down. The rest of your squad was supposed to go too, but the guy was very specific about the four of ya getting it first. Stupid Leona said he wasn't worried about the time frame for the rest of the squad, but the four of ya had to go right away," Monteverdi said.

"But why? Did he give her any reasons? And if it wasn't the counterfeiting ring, what the hell else could it be?" I said. There was a maddening tickle at the back of my mind, but it wasn't an itch I could scratch just yet.

"That stupid airhead twit didn't ask about no reasons, and the name he gave her was bogus, 'cause I had it checked out. The only thing that she said was she thought he was the FBI at first, like some Fed tryin' to set up a sting, except the FBI don't do that with murder for hire, and they don't go depositin' any money in the Caymans, either," Monteverdi said.

"And I guess they don't usually name Secret Service agents as the targets, either," I said.

Monteverdi made a gun with his left thumb and forefinger and shot me with it. He said, "In all my time with Mr. Bonnarino we ain't never took a contract on no government people of any kind except one city councilman who was cheating on his wife. That ain't a good idea in any case, but it especially ain't a good idea if your wife is a Sicilian from the Genovese family."

"So you never made war with the FBI?" I said, half kidding him.

He got the joke and laughed at me. "Mr. Bonnarino always said—correctly—that tryin' to fight the FBI was a losin' proposition, because they had more soldiers than we did, and they could stop our money whenever they wanted. Plus, it was easier to just buy them off. The government don't pay so good, even when you put your life on the line."

"Tell me about it," I said. We had another laugh at that one, until I said, "Any idea at all who this guy was?"

"I been lookin', because Leona the Airhead used Mr. Bonnarino's name to set up the hit and we don't want no part a that. So far I ain't found nothin', except one thing." He stopped and I looked at him, waiting for him to continue. He looked back at me and then glanced at the guards standing against the walls.

I got it. Monteverdi knew something, but he was afraid of being overheard, which meant it had something to do with someone or something important. I leaned closer to him and said, "I have excellent hearing" in my best sub-vocal mike voice. That's a really quiet tone with very little lip movement that Spec Ops operators use when talking into their very special throat mikes (and that's all I'm saying about that…it's classified).

He leaned closer to me and said, in the thinnest, quietest semi-whisper I'd ever heard, "One a my guys that seen him said the guy was carryin' a nice Glock 23 in a pancake holster next to a badge."

"Star or shield?" I said, asking about the badge.

"Gold shield," Monteverdi said, so quiet that I wasn't sure I wasn't just lip reading.

"Shit," I said. The FBI carries the Glock Model 22 or 23 in .40 caliber. They also carry gold shields.

"And that's how you make really good arancini. It's all in the rice—and don't shred the cheese. Ya gotta keep it in a cube so it just melts in the middle, not into the rice," Monteverdi said in his normal voice.

"Thanks for the recipe," I said. "I love Italian food."

"Tell me about it," he said. We laughed again and I said, "I really appreciate you telling me about this, Mr. Monteverdi. It's incredibly kind of you."

"Nah, it's about honor. Mr. Bonnarino's name was used to do somethin' he had no part of—and Leona the Birdbrain used my name to try and keep it quiet, which means we was both besmirched. Men in our positions can't let that happen—we owed you a debt, which we have now repaid. *Capsiche?*" he said.

"*Sí, grazie nonno,*" I said.

"Fuck you, Agent Glickstien, I ain't that old yet," Monteverdi said, laughing at my attempt to call him grandfather in Italian. "Pardon my French."

I laughed back and said, "If it's any consolation I don't think you are, either, but I thought that you'd feel patronized if I called you '*amico*'."

"Nah, but it wouldn't be the truth, either. I don't see no way a person like me can have a person like you for a friend, altho' that don't mean we can't be friendly," Monteverdi said. He looked so sad about it I said, "You mean two tigers can't share a nice juicy goat once in a while?"

We both laughed and Monteverdi said, "OK, OK, we can share a goat once in a while, but you ain't gonna make it a habit to come back to this piece a shit place ta see me on visitors day, are ya?"

I looked at the honorable semi-old gangster and said "Hey, *nonno,* if I wanna come to see you on visitor's day, I'll come to see you on visitor's day, OK? In all likelihood I'm gonna be too busy guarding a bunch of silly political candidates, but ya never know."

"I think I'd like ta see ya, and I know that Mr. Bonnarino still wants to apologize in person," he said.

"So why isn't he here now, instead of you?" I said.

"Oh, Mr. Bonnarino's in solitary for a while," Monteverdi said.

"Somebody threaten his life?" I said, thinking that a guy like Bonnarino must have some enemies in a place like this.

"Nah, as long as I'm around ain't nobody gonna do that," Monteverdi said, not bragging but meaning every word. "Some guy tried to cut Mr. Bonnarino in the cafeteria line, and that kind of disrespect can't go unchallenged, so Mr. Bonnarino beat the crap out of him with the lunch tray. Guy got fifty stitches and Mr. Bonnarino got solitary." He looked at me and said, "It would be a mistake to think that we're the only tigers in the world, *mia nipotina.*"

I stood up and said, "Thanks for the talk, Mr. Monteverdi. I appreciate the apology and accept it without reservation."

"Hey, it's an honor thing, plus Mr. Bonnarino and me like your moxie. Look out for hunters and remember that anything could be a trap," he said.

I was touched by his obvious concern and wanted to do something to acknowledge his honor, so I said, "I know we can't shake hands and I can't hug you, but there is something that I would like to do."

I stood at attention and saluted. "Major Glinka L. Glickstien, United States Marine Corps."

Montevedi snapped to attention and offered a crisp salute. "First Sergeant Paul G. Monteverdi, United States Army."

"Booyah, First Sergeant," I said.

"Back atcha," Monteverdi said.

"See ya around, First Sergeant," I said.

"Watch yourself, *mia nipotina,*" he said.

Two of the guards came and hooked him back up in the chains and took him out one of the doors, and the other two escorted me back out of the room. As we walked down the corridor one of the guards said, "What was that old con yapping about back there?" I didn't answer him, so the guard said, "Hey, I'm talking to you, Agent Hotshot. What was that wop talking about?"

I whipped around so fast that he almost ran into me. I pushed my way into his space until there was about a playing card width between us and said, "That's Agent Glickstien, and anything said between myself and Mr. Monteverdi is privileged information regarding an ongoing Secret Service investigation. If I ever hear that any of it went anywhere except in my ears I'm not going to invoke the U.S. Code and have you prosecuted, but I am going to come back here, drag you out in the yard and stomp your ass until there's nothing left but a grease spot and a steaming pile of shit. Are we clear?" I never raised my voice, but I was definitely in tiger mode, and it scared him.

He nodded, but I said, in a very gentle tone of voice, "Please verbally acknowledge that you understand."

"I, uh, I, yes, ma'am, I understand that your conversation is privileged, Agent Glickstien, ma'am, and I'm not to repeat any of it to anyone, ma'am," he said.

I turned to the other guard and said, "You got any questions?"

"No, ma'am. I understand perfectly," he said.

"Oh, just one other thing," I said. I looked at their name tags and said, "Roberts, Strouse, if anything happens to that old man or the old man that he hangs out with while they're here I'll come back and rip off your heads and shit down your necks. Are we clear?"

"Yes, ma'am," they said, truly scared by my completely dead tone of voice and the look on my face.

"Good. Now get me the fuck out of this godforsaken place on the double," I said.

They obliged me, and then I was out in the open air, the limo with my friends was waiting and it was time for me to enter the next phase of my life, guarding people's lives while my own might be on the line.

I just wished that I knew what the fuck was going on.

It would've solved the crime of the century before more people had to die.

CHAPTER 40

Every Asshole Who Runs for President Gets Protection (Good Thing it's the Law)

So I got in the limo and told all my pals what Paul Monteverdi had said. Their initial reaction was the same as mine: it didn't make any sense.

"We were all on this case, all the time," Weasel said. "And the Feebs didn't have anything to do with it—it was 100% Secret Service."

"And why would the Feebs try to hit our unit anyway?" Guru said. "They had to know that we'd be split up soon enough—the Service doesn't just leave people in place, especially when they have talent and get shit done. It seems stupid on their part."

"And if we're on somebody's shit list why did they let us run with what turned out to be the biggest case of anybody's career?" Mamba said. "After the hit didn't stop the unit they should have gone for a different approach, like divide and conquer."

"Exactly," Buzz said. "If they'd gotten us all spread out it would have been much easier to get rid of the important players, which obviously would have derailed anything else we were working on. It sounds like a stupid person panicked about something and just ordered the hit hoping it would work."

"I guess it did—we're gonna be all over hell's half acre," I said, "but we still need to keep our guard up, because the way Monteverdi acted there might still be someone out there with us in their sights, and it might be the FBI." I told them what he'd discovered during his investigation, and everybody agreed that it sounded like it was still serious.

"I'm especially bothered by the Glock 23 and shield business," Mamba said. "That really sounds like a typical FBI suit, but I still can't figure out what benefit there is to anyone in this."

"Yeah, *cui bono* also occurred to me," Coach said. "I can't figure out how anyone could benefit from your removal, even if it was about the North Korean Affair. Not to be an asshole, but the fact that you discovered the whole scheme was just dumbass luck."

"And let's face it, we weren't looking after we busted all of that New York funny money," Guru said.

"First of all, we like to refer to 'dumbass luck' as 'serendipity coupled with proper procedure'," Weasel said. "But yeah, if Mamba hadn't come on the unit we wouldn't've been at The Berghoff, and the manager wouldn't've known to seek us out with a counterfeit 100."

"So it was dumbass luck," Gomer said.

"Sure as shit," I said. We all laughed and Buzz said, "So does that mean that Mamba ordered the hit, since his rich ass got us in the second batch of trouble?" We all laughed again, but Weasel, Mamba and I stopped before everybody else, because a sudden thought hit all of us.

"Asians!" we all said at once. "I'll buy the Pepsis," Weasel said, "but why didn't whoever wanted us gone get the North Koreans to do it when we came after them? They could've hired any number of Asian gangs to assassinate us—some of the Vietnamese gangs'll kill you for $50—and the North Koreans coulda paid them in funny money and no one'd be the wiser."

"And it would've looked organic to the investigation, too—nobody would see anything even remotely odd about Asians killing you after you broke up their counterfeiting operation," Mamba said.

"And there'd be no chance to ever catch or interrogate any of the assassins, because they'd just leave the country," Coach said.

"Or disappear into Koreatown," I said.

"We aren't dealing with some great criminal mastermind, are we?" Mamba said.

"If it is the FBI, or some rogue FBI agent I'd think that would be patently obvious," Guru said. We all laughed again and then James said, "Freak, we're at the Carbondale Airport."

We got to the departures area—just a spot on the pavement outside the very small terminal that wasn't even guarded—and I got out. So did everybody else, and whirlwind hug time ensued. Even James got out and hugged me. I said my goodbyes and asked Guru to give Joe a call about the FBI thing, told everybody to be careful and went into the terminal. The limo pulled away, headed to St. Louis and ribs, and I went inside to catch my plane to Louisville, and from there to D. C.

My Delta flight was on time into Reagan National, where I was going to rent a car and a hotel until I could get a place to live close to the district, because I certainly couldn't afford to live in it. I headed out of the plane and onto the concourse to find a tall, blonde guy with a goofy smile and a sign that said "FREAK" on it waiting for me.

I didn't have to ask for ID, because I knew this guy.

"Attention on deck!" I said, using my command voice. He straightened up almost to attention before he caught himself and located me. The goofy grin got wider and he said, "Booyah, Freak!"

"Booyah, Badass," I said, his nickname when we were in Spec Ops. His real name was Tanner Goodenough, and he was one Marine Special Operations operator who lived up to his name. He was 6'3", 190 pounds of rawboned country muscle who came from the outrageously named town of Paw Paw, Michigan (he affectionately called it the 'Twin Cities'). Badass was also a very smart individual who got a law degree from San Diego State University during his spare time while serving at the Marine Corps Training Depot in San Diego.

Badass was tough, sincere, intelligent and as competent a person as I'd ever known. That he was in the Secret Service was welcome news to me, because it meant that I wouldn't have to be worried about my back, even if he wasn't on my detail. Goodenough had earned his nickname by being a true badass in the field—I'd never really seen anyone who was any tougher (except maybe me and two other guys…but that's classified. Sorry.)

We hugged each other and I said, "They got you being an errand boy?"

Badass's smile broadened and he said, "Nah—the CoD (Chief of Detail) thought it'd be nice if you saw a friendly face right off the bat, so she sent me."

I smiled and said, "Together again, Captain Badass?"

"Bet your ass, Major Freak," he said. We shared a good laugh, like two old comrades in arms should be able to. I hugged him again—think oak tree meets walrus (I was the walrus)—and I picked him up for a twirl through the air. It brought back good memories of bad times, but it mostly felt comforting to know that no matter what happened in the puzzle palace that is Washington, D.C., I was going to be in it with a true comrade who would die before he let anyone get near me. I could tell he felt the same way—who could blame us for being relieved to have someone we knew we could absolutely trust, especially in the Land of Liars, Thieves and Pedants?

"I need to get a hotel," I said.

"Nah, ya already got a place out in Anacostia, across from the Navy Yard," Badass said.

"Come on, I can't afford to live there. You know what I make," I said. He looked at me and smiled that goofy grin and said, "Seems that someone paid for you to have a nice apartment that you'll never be in. I got the keys—and the keys to your car, too."

"What the fuck?" I said…and then it hit me.

Mamba.

"Let me guess, it was a fellow agent who's a weird looking midget with a giant Australian chauffeur," I said.

"I thought that he was right spiffy, and his chauffeur was James Campbell, who's the rucker for the Geelong Cats, my favorite Australian Rules football team, so all in all I didn't mind meeting them," Badass said.

"Those assholes flew out here over a weekend and got me a place and a car, didn't they," I said.

"Not just you—your neighbors are Emily Devlin, Calvin Beemond and Tara Kywfterelian, who's also new to the detail, and me. Emiliano Zaragoza and his family have the first floor of the apartment building and the CoD will be moving into the top floor next week," Badass said.

"How the hell did he pull that off?" I said.

"Oh, he bought the whole building," Badass said. We both laughed as I pulled my bag off the luggage carousel. We went out to "my" car—a nice green 2013 Subaru Outback—and Badass said, "I'm drivin' today, just because we need to get there and you're definitely not used to this kind of drivin', but after today you're on your own. The good thing is that ya won't need the car for work, 'cause our building is about three blocks from the Metrorail Green Line station—ya can get anywhere for cheap and ya don't have to park. Damn Metro takes ya right to the office, too. Of course, some places ya got to drive, which is why you'll have this baby in our parking structure."

We got in and he sped off like a real Spec Ops veteran would—800 miles an hour and without regard for anybody else. By the time we got to the apartment building I'd decided that the Metro sounded pretty good, especially if Badass was driving. I wasn't really afraid of much, but D.C. traffic made Chicago look like everyone there drove those battery-powered kids toys—the people were crazy, the streets were designed like an archaic bumper-car layout and the speed limits appeared to be suggestions that no one paid any attention to.

You also had to be adept at sign language while driving like a bat out of hell, and God help you if you didn't start flying low the instant that the light turned green—there'd be a torrent of horns, verbal abuse and sometimes actual refuse flying in your direction (one guy threw a perfectly good chocolate malt out the window in an effort to get a car going—*before* the light turned green).

Traffic in Fallujah was safer, and no, I'm not kidding. Not everybody in Fallujah had a gun.

In any case, we arrived at our nice-looking building on Talbert Street SE and stowed the car, then went up to my second floor apartment. We weren't in it for two minutes when there was knock on the door and I let Ed in.

"Whattya think?" she said.

"Fuckin' Mamba's got a mommy complex—he's gotta make everybody happy," I said.

"Ain't altogether bad, havin' a rich friend who wants to be generous," Badass said.

"Concur," Ed and I said. "You guys owe me a Pepsi each," Badass said.

"Hell, I'm living in a rent-free apartment," Ed said. "I'll buy ya a case."

"Deal," he said. He looked at me and said, "We got a duty call tomorrow at 0700 sharp—the CoD's a good boss, but she is a big believer in 'on time means you're late'—think of Stinky Mel and you'll get the picture. We can catch the Metro, which means that we'll have to be on the 0613 train. I'll come collect you guys—I'm used to the routine."

That was Badass to a T—he automatically delegated jobs to those who were best suited for what was needed, and he wasn't condescending about it at all. It was a great strength in the field to have someone who could instantly analyze a situation, break it down and put the components of a response in exactly the right places to optimize your success. It was also comforting, because you knew that you weren't going to waste any time getting organized, or hurry up and wait (a real problem in the military).

I guess it made me feel at home, and like the transition from my old unit to my new one wasn't going to be all that difficult.

And I was mostly right.

I said, "Got it, Badass. We need to lay up so we can be ready to run free tomorrow."

"Roger that, Freak. You're gonna want all the rest you can get, especially since you're meeting our protectee—she's in D.C. for three days, testifying before the House Health and Human Services committee," Badass said.

"I know that you won't want to say anything out of school, but how is she?" I said. He looked at us as he was pondering what to say. Finally he said, "Well, ordinarily I'd tell ya to just gather your first impressions yourself, but you're gonna find out anyway, so..." He hesitated, which was very unusual for him—he didn't just talk all the time, but once he decided to talk he was usually very decisive. Ed and I looked at him with our heads cocked at an angle like we were baby birds looking to mama for a worm. He heaved a sigh and said, "Freak, you remember Colonel High?"

"Don't you mean 'Colonel Armand J. High, Commander of the First Ranger Brigade, United States Army'? I remember that asshole—he wanted you to repeat his full title every time. And nobody else got an opinion around that motherfucker because he was always right about everything. Remember how he tried to take command of our unit outside Peshawar, even though he had no idea what our mission was, or that Stinky Mel was in the field? That guy was a total douche bag with serious shithead tendencies...ahhh, shit!" I said. I looked at my old friend and he just nodded, and then we all said, "Ah, shit!"

"I'm still on the Pepsis," Ed said, "but I have a feeling I know why our protectee needed an almost all new detail." She looked at Badass and he said, "I'm usually the point guy—use the right tool for the job, right?—so I don't have to be right near her all the time, but I probably won't last too much longer, since (a) I'm a man, and (b) I'm just a stupid grunt and (c) did I mention that I'm a man, and therefore the right hand of the devil?"

"Uh, oh," Ed said. "Now I remember this chick—she wrote *Men are the Devil*, didn't she?"

"Yep," Badass said.

"And isn't her girlfriend that Sports Illustrated swimsuit chick who came out after she got the cover, and then wrote *Using Your Assets Against the Patriarchy*?" Ed said.

"She's her wife now, but yep," Badass said.

"And didn't she and her girlfr—wife—just march topless in New York in support of wymyn being able to go topless just like men?" Ed said.

"Yep," Badass said.

"And weren't they arrested in the process?" Ed said.

"Yep," Badass said.

"And I'll bet that her whole detail had to go to jail with her, because they couldn't not protect her," I said.

"Everybody but me and the CoD," Badass said.

"And she was pissed because it lessened the impact of her arrest," Ed said.

"Almost her exact words," Badass said.

"Oh fuck a goddamned duck," Ed said. "She's a goddamned militant feminist, meaning she's delusional by definition."

"Whattya mean?" Badass said.

"OK, she's a lesbian feminist who thinks that wymyn should overthrow the patriarchy and take their rightful place as the lead gender in our society. I'll bet she natters on about the patriarchy suppressing wymyn by using force and tradition against us, and I'll bet that she calls for wymyn to physically resist their oppressors by turning to their like-minded sisters for love, thus denying the patriarchy their chief weapon in the ongoing war between the sexes. She probably also thinks that wymyn should only do business with other wymyn, and that any man who tries to help a womyn is just oppressing her, either overtly or covertly," Ed said.

"Almost got her word for word," Badass said.

"Oh fuck a goddamned feminist duck," Ed said.

"She's a real piece of work," Badass said. "I should prob'ly let the CoD tell ya this, but we've already had a real attempt on her. We were in Atlanta two weeks ago and a guy came up with a knife. We were disarming him before he got really close, but she saw us doin' it, so she ripped her shirt open and said, 'Let the assassin strike! I am unarmed!' which really pissed us off, since it gave the guy incentive to resist and he cut two of the detail," Badass said. "That's why we have a new detail—nobody wants to work for her. In fact, the two agents who got cut just flat out quit. They claimed it was her fault they got cut in the first place, and I can't really dispute that."

"She's a bitch on wheels," I said. "She's also a thief."

"Say again your last?" Badass said.

"She didn't invent that dramatic phrasing. Senator Thomas Hart Benton said, 'Get out of the way and let the assassin fire! Let the scoundrel use his weapon! I have no arms!' when Senator Henry

S. Foote attacked him on the Senate floor during a slavery debate in the 1840s. She may want the world to think that she's an original, but it sounds like she's just another charlatan," I said.

"Believe me when I tell you that she is," Ed said. "I explored all of this before I joined the Service, and I realized that it's just a big load of crap. It isn't men oppressing wymyn, it's the strong oppressing the weak, and since our world no longer runs on plain old brute strength wymyn are getting on more of a level playing field. All of her blather is just keeping her lesbian ass in the spotlight—she's a female Donald Trump trying to leverage her way to relevance."

"Remember, though—the people of California elected her governor three times, and she actually did a pretty fair job, for a weasel politician," Badass said.

"Yeah, but that was three years ago. She probably wants to be president, but she can't run just on her own merits, so she needs to get into the debate with a splash so she can attract donors," I said. "What better way to do it than pissing lots of people off while attracting rich gays to support her?"

"Ya got a point," Badass said.

"But you can never forget—she's a narcissist twice over," Ed said.

"Whattya mean?" Badass said. "Remember that I'm just a dumb grunt tryin' to understand this intricate shit."

"Yeah, right—and I'm a fucking ballerina," I said. "Look, she's a big-time athlete, a big-time politician and a big-time LGBT advocate—she's got an ego as big as Montana and she thinks that the sun rises and sets out of her ass, and her ass alone, unless she also allows her girlfriend into the 'I'm better than you are' club she's created for herself. Either way, she's convinced that she alone is in possession of the wisdom of the universe, because everything she's done up to now she's been very successful at, and she's been praised like she's the second coming by every person she's ever been in contact with through academics, sports and politics. Her ego has been so warped by all the hero worship and praise and self-congratulation that she's sure that her defecation is not odiferous."

He laughed and said, "Freak, I'll be goddamned and go to hell—you just captured "Hippolyta" to a T—but I don't think you should share any of that with her or the Ice Goddess," Badass said, "or you might need a new gig, y'know? Ya can't forget that the Ice Goddess is her wife, not her girlfriend. Old Hippolyta is real sticky about that."

"Well, excuse me all to hell—her wife is almost certainly a bitch on wheels, too, am I right? As for getting fired…well, fuck that—I was lookin' for a job when I got this one," I said.

"By the way, who the hell was Hippolyta? She was real insistent on setting that as her Service code name," Badass said.

"She was the mythological queen of the Amazons who had a magical belt given to her by her father Ares, the Greek God of War, so that she could defeat any man in battle," I said.

"And the bitch on wheels once again shows her ignorance," Ed said.

"Whattya mean? I'm really not up on this mythology shit," Badass said. "My favorite pastimes are shootin' up the enemy, readin' John Sandford novels and building beds for the homeless. Mythology is just that for me—mythology, as in it-was-so-long-ago-I-can't-remember-that-shit."

"She wants a code name that celebrates a strong womyn, except the bottom line of that mythological story is that Herakles seduces Hippolyta and gets her to give him the girdle, but Hera intervenes by disguising herself as an Amazon and tells them that Herakles is going to kidnap their queen. The Amazons are royally pissed and charge Herakles's ship, so he kills Hippolyta and sails away with the girdle," Ed said. "Hippolyta was a prop for the guy in the story, and not a real tough cookie, either—just some broad a man seduced, used and then essentially murdered."

"I wouldn't tell her that story, either," Badass said.

"We're gonna have a real problem with this protectee, aren't we?" I said.

"Why? Just because she's everything you hate—supercilious, shallow, narrow, small-minded and arrogant—and because she's convinced that she's a match for an armed person comin' at her, and that we're superfluous Nazis, or that she thinks she invented physical training, or because she's convinced that her shit don't stink? Now why would that be a problem for the best Marine and Spec Ops operator, not to mention the toughest individual, I've ever seen? It's gonna be a walk in the park, Freak—she's gonna love you," Badass said, grinning like a hyena that just found a fresh wildebeest carcass without any lions eating it.

"Fuck you, asshole," I said, projecting all the humor I could into that phrase that Spec Ops troops used as a term of endearment (hey, it was just like Mandarin—all about tone and inflection).

We all laughed and Ed said, "She's what my grandpa used to call a charlatan—'all hat and no cattle'."

"Yep," Badass said. We all laughed some more, until Badass said, "OK, it's definitely rack time. We gotta catch the 0613 train, so be ready on the line at 0600. Dress is professional—the CoD also likes us to maintain the reputation of the Service by looking like we're the shit, so make sure you cover those sidearms with a nice jacket." He made a small face, like he'd just smelled a bad fart that was seeping under a door and I laughed, remembering how little my old partner in crime (I already told you, nothing we did was a crime, at least as far as Uncle Sugar was concerned—and besides, it's classified) liked playing dress-up for the brass.

"So is the CoD also a pain in the *tuchas*?" I said.

"Nope—she's a by the book boss, but she's fair and lets us operate within optimal parameters," Badass said.

"As good as Stinky Mel?" I said.

"A-yuh,' Badass said in imitation of a Down East accent. "Finest kind."

Ed arched an eyebrow at me and I said, "We're not gonna have any problems with the CoD, Ed me friend. She-ahs a keepah." We all laughed, and Ed said, "I don't get the joke, but I'll take your word for it, Freak."

We all went off to bed. I slept like I was dead, but woke up at 5:03, just like I did every other day of my life. Like the great Jack Reacher (if you haven't read Lee Child you're really missing the point of reading) I had an alarm clock in my head, only I couldn't set mine worth a damn. Every day at 10:45 p.m. it said, 'sleep,' and every day at 5:03 a.m. it said 'time to get up,' so I did…well, most of the time (there were some exceptions to the rule—sorry, but you know the drill…it's classified). In any case, I was on the line the next morning when Badass came out the door. A minute later Ed, El Gato and a womyn I didn't know came out, too, and Badass said, "Good. We'll pick de Vries up on the way—he lives across the river in the Navy Yard neighborhood—so let's go. Freak, this is Tara

Kywfterelian. She was in the Coast Guard and decided to cross-deck with the Service because she wanted more excitement and glamour in her life."

Kywfterelian was 5'9", 150, with a dark olive complexion that featured flawless skin, a long, straight Roman nose, full lips and a pair of intense black eyes—her irises were black, not like she'd been punched out. With her long, shiny black hair and well developed muscles that were clearly the result of long hours of some kind of training she was a striking womyn, if not altogether beautiful. Her handshake was firm but not crushing, but then she smiled, and striking became at least pretty, or semi-beautiful.

"Tara Kywfterelain," she said, her voice smoky and hot.

"Glinka Glickstien, but call me Freak," I said. Kywftererlain shot me a look and I said, "All will be made clear in time. They know why"—I gestured at the other agents as we walked down the street—"and so will you at some point. And no, before you ask, it not only doesn't bother me, I prefer it."

"OK. I never had a nickname, except when the Turkish girls at my school called me a dirty infidel," she said.

"Yeah, the Turks really don't like Armenians, do they? You guys are the Jews of south-central Europe," I said.

"Who says I'm Armenian?" she said, kind of bristling at my remark.

"Oh come on—Kywfterelian? If that's not Armenian then I'm a loyal member of the KKK," I said, making everyone else start laughing. "Besides, you act like it's a bad thing—the Armenians were the first nation in the world to adopt Christianity, which means you are People of the Book, which means we're cousins, since my people wrote most of the Book. The only people who think being an Armenian is a crime are the Turks, those genocidal assholes. We daughters of minorities who've survived genocide need to stick together, don't we?" I said.

"You're Jewish?" she said. "Well, duh—Glickstien is as Jewish as Kywfterelian is Armenian," I said.

"And I'm Germano-English, and El Gato is Hispanic, and Devlin is Black Irish and Beemond is Black American and all our names mean 'we're in deep shit' if we don't get to work on time," Badass said. "De Vries is Flemish, whatever the hell that is, and he's already a nasty shithead, so let's get our Metro cards and get on the train, shall we, fellow abusees?"

"Abusees?" El Gato said.

"Those who are abused by someone or in some situation that abuses them," Bumble said.

"Spot on, old boy, and a perfect description of being close to Hippolyta and the Ice Goddess every day," Badass said, his English accent a perfect imitation of Basil Rathbone as Sherlock Holmes. We all laughed our way onto the train and rode across to the Navy Yard stop, where a guy got on whose demeanor, outfit and physical makeup immediately screamed "I'm a soldier."

He was about 5'10", 180, with light hair cut in a Marine Corps high and tight, hard light blue eyes that saw everything while looking everywhere, square shoulders and big arms that got that way honestly, maybe by holding a SAW (the Corps' standard light machine gun; designated the M249 Squad Automatic Weapon, it was 16.5 pounds and could fire 750 rounds of 5.56 mm ammo a minute—and it was heavy enough that it made you grow muscles just looking at it). His posture was

Marine Corps straight and he was wearing the worst suit I've ever seen—it was a dark brown color that reminded me of dogshit and the cut was tight in all the wrong places, and loose in places you'd rather it was tight.

I knew this was de Vries, so using my command voice I said, "Marine, you need to get your kit squared away. That suit looks like dogshit, fits like dogshit and probably smells like dogshit. If that's your excuse for Class-A dress we've got more of a problem that just your awful fashion sense."

"Ma'am?" he said, unconsciously squaring to attention. "Are you deaf, Marine? Did I fucking stutter?" I said.

"No, ma'am!" he said.

"That suit is an abomination to the senses and has to go, Marine. We can't be seen in public with someone wearing that dogshit suit. Isn't this supposed to be a full dress uniform situation?" I said.

"Yes, ma'am!" he said smartly, his training evident in the way he was squirming under my bull-shit without moving.

"And how do we rectify this situation, Marine?" I said.

"Get a new suit, ma'am?" he said.

"Well, booyah and semper fi, Marine. You're not as dumb as that suit makes you look," I said. "I'm Glickstien, call me Freak."

He smiled at me and said, "Semper fi, Freak. I don't have no sisters, and this fashion shit kicks my ass. Mebbe ya can help me. Oh, yeah, I'm de Vries, call me Patsy." We shook hands and I said, "After work today we're taking you shopping, Patsy, because none of the rest of us can ever be seen near that suit in public again, or we'll die of embarrassment.

"After we finish puking our guts out," El Gato said.

I looked at Badass, who said, "I tried to tell him, but he wouldn't listen. Claimed that piece of doghsit made him look dapper, according to the nice lady who sold it to him."

"Man, she musta been a lesbian who hated men," Ed said, "'cause that suit makes you look like a blivet." Blivet is a military term: it means 10 pounds of shit stuffed in a 5-pound bag.

Everybody laughed, even de Vries, and El Gato said, "Patsy?"

De Vries said, "I love Monty Python, and in *The Holy Grail* King Arthur's page—you know the guy who runs along behind him clacking the coconuts together so it sounds like the king's riding a horse?—is named Patsy. A pal of mine and I did a scene from the movie for a talent show when we was graduating from basic at 'Diego and I got tagged—and it stuck." He had a small rueful smile on his face that made us all start laughing, until Badass said, "What he doesn't tell you is that the pal was his brother, who was killed in Kandahar in 2006, where Patsy won the Navy Cross by destroying several Taliban positions and capturing 26 enemy combatants by himself. He may have a nickname, but that's a real Marine you're talkin' to."

We all stared at him—his face turned red because he was embarrassed, ours turned red because we were embarrassed, too—and finally I said, "Only one thing to do, eh, Marine?" He nodded and I said, "Ah-ten, HUT!" We all stood to attention and saluted him, and Patsy snapped off a perfect salute in return.

We all relaxed, until Kywfterelian said, "But that suit still sucks, and we *are* getting you a new one, Patsy, come hell or high water." We all laughed again as the train lurched closer to the home office on H Street NW, right behind the White House and just up the street from the Capitol.

The train got more crowded as we went along, until we were at the Archives station, when it got just packed.

It was then that someone decided to grab my ass.

At first I thought that they were just shoved into me, but when they tried to put their hand down my pants I decided that this was a deliberate groping.

And then a hand came around my body to cup my left tit from underneath.

Definitely a planned attack.

The train was packed, but I was The Freak from Battle Creek, so I grabbed the wrist of the hand on my left tit with my right hand and squeezed until it let go. The hand then tried to gracefully withdraw, but the owner of the hand gripping it was monster pissed and about to lose her shit, so it couldn't get away. The hand trying to get into my pants did beat a hasty retreat, but I didn't care about that one, since I was sure it was attached to the same body as the other hand.

After securing the wrist I slowly turned until I'd forced my way 180 degrees around and found the owner of the wrist I was gripping so it couldn't get away. He was about 6', maybe 190 and spectacularly good-looking, like an underwear model for Gucci, or that guy from the fragrance ad for Dolce and Gabbana, the one wearing a swimsuit that was more of a suggestion than a real thing. He gave me a weak smile and said, "Sorry—purely unintentional" in a deep, manly voice he'd probably studied with a voice coach. His smile got weaker as I hardened my face into the look that many people had seen just before they met The Freak for the first (and often last) time. I squeezed his wrist at about half strength and his smile went away, replaced by a look of pain tinged with fear.

I yanked his hand up into the air and said, "Are you saying that you accidentally attached this tentacle to my left breast?" My voice was Marine Corps loud, like the one I used when getting Marchand through the Crucible.

He tried to chuckle and laugh it off. "It's a crowded train," he said. "I apologize if I accidentally bumped your, uh, anatomy."

I grabbed his other hand and yanked it up, too. "You mean that you accidentally latched on to my breast while trying to stick this hand down the back of my pants? Both incidents are unrelated and entirely accidental?" My voice was louder, and his face began to redden.

"Well, I never!" he said. "I did no such thing!" The people in my squad who knew me were trying to move toward us, but the crowd was too dense. Good.

"Try to sell that defecation somewhere else, pretty boy," I said. "You groped me fore and aft, it wasn't accidental and I demand satisfaction." My voice was so loud they could probably hear it in the next car, and now everybody around us was trying to edge away. Good.

"I, uh—what? Satisfaction? Whatever do you mean?" he said as sweat popped out on his forehead and he strained to get away from my grip. I increased strength and his face blanched as he lost all feeling in his hands. Good.

"I challenge you to a duel at sunrise, with swords," I said, still holding his hands up.

"I—I, uh, well… I'm not fighting a *duel*," he said.

Ed and Badass both bawked like chickens, while Patsy started whistling *The Yellow Rose of Texas*. Pretty boy got it, and his face turned a nice tomato color. He looked at me, putting on his hardass expression (I was sure he practiced that, too) and said, "It's the 21st century—we don't fight duels anymore."

"OK, then next time I'll get satisfaction another way," I said. I released his hands and he said, "How could someone like *you*"—meaning a squat, dumpy, ugly womyn—"ever get satisfaction from someone like *me*?" meaning a tall, successful, handsome man. His sneer was perfect, just like his face, and he was back to exuding that particular maleness that men use when they've been embarrassed, but think they see a way to recover. Good.

My right hand moved with the speed of a striking cobra as I grabbed him by the belt buckle and lifted him in the air, successfully squashing his balls and giving him the mother of all wedgies. I reached in my coat pocket and brought out my creds, flipping them open to my badge. I pulled him down on an angle so that they were right in front of his face and said, "By having you arrested for sexual assault, assaulting a federal officer and sexual harassment."

"I, uh, errr…uh, din't know…you…a federal o-o-o-o-off-uhhhhggg," he said, clearly having a tough time with his balls up in his throat and his pants yanked up into his butt.

"Well, now you do," I said. "And even if I wasn't a federal officer, I'm still a womyn who deserves to decide who touches her body and who doesn't. I'm gonna bet that this isn't the first time you've done this, so I'm just gonna say that if I ever hear of this happening again I'm going to drag you behind the train for eight or ten stops and then arrest whatever's left. *Capsice, paisan?*"

He tried to nod, but I wasn't going to let him off that easy, so I gently shook him and said, "What is it you're not gonna do anymore?"

"T-touch wymyn without their, unnggghhh, permission," he said. His balls had to hurt as much as his poor wounded pride, so I shook him a little bit more, just to make sure he got the point.

He did.

I lowered him to the floor and said, "Good, we understand one another. Now produce some ID, sir, so I can put a name to your face."

He pulled out a leather folder and handed it to me, looking at the floor and trying to play it cool while getting his pants out of the crack of his ass. I flipped open the folder and found out he was Jordan Winters, spokesman for the Assistant Secretary of the Treasury for Public Affairs.

I wrote down all of his information in my little notebook and gave him back the folder.

He finally looked at me and said, "I'm, uh, truly sorry if I offended you, Agent Glickstien. I really had no intent to harass you." He was trying for the sincere puppy-dog look, but I'm the wrong Marine to try that shit on, because I know that look is always bogus. He smiled his perfect smile and held out his hand to shake.

I looked at his hand, looked at his face, then looked back at his hand and said, "Unless you want me to rip that off and stick it up your ass you'd better pull back there, Jordy. You had every intent to intentionally touch a womyn without her permission, only you happened to pick the wrong womyn this time. If you ever try to touch me again for any reason I will guarantee you a visit in the hospital, followed by some time in a nice prison for attempted rape. Tell me you understand." My tone was as cold as an Antarctic seal's ass, and as serious as Mother Teresa about fighting poverty.

Winters looked at me and then slowly put his hand in his pocket. He nodded and said, "I understand."

Good call, asshole.

The speaker overhead said, "Gallery Place, Chinatown" and we all got off the train to walk to the office three blocks away. My fellow agents didn't say anything, until finally Kywfterelian said, "So you just hoisted that dude right off the floor like he was a piece of paper. What's up with that?"

Everybody laughed, especially the agents who'd seen me in action. Badass said, "We should just save it for the CoD, 'cause sure as shit she's gonna ask, too, but I can tell you I saw her lift the front end of a jeep out of the mud and put the tires on dry land—saw it with my own eyes, not heard about it. I can also tell you that there wasn't one guy in our Spec Ops command who would spar with her hand to hand except me."

"And you just did it because you're a masochist," I said. More laughter ensued, and I said "Remember Pepe le Pew?"

Badass said, "Shit, how could I forget? You picked that axle up and held it over your head, and when he said, 'Yeah, but you can't press it' you did 100 military presses and Pepe offered to marry you." We laughed, joined by our fellow agents who didn't know the story or the characters, but knew it was a great story and feat of strength.

"So you're like, what? Super strong? Do you lift weights?" Patsy said. He didn't look like a weakling—he'd clearly done some lifting in his day—so I knew he'd get it when I said, "I can dead-lift 575, bench 375 and squat 550—and I don't know if those are maxes, because I've never maxed. I also once lifted my brother's jeep a foot off the ground and I threw a javelin right through a solid oak barn door. I have what several doctors have assured me is a sort of throwback strength, like I'm a Neanderthal womyn. I'm also faster than shit through a goose, and my hand-eye coordination is off the charts—my eyes are both 20/5—which is better than most pro athletes. And no, I'm not bragging—I'm just a freak."

"She ain't lying about any of it, either," Badass said.

"How did it happen? Were you struck like lightning, or did you get bitten by a radioactive spider?" Kywfterelian said. We all laughed.

"Those weights are above all of the world records for your weight class, aren't they? Are you an alien, or mutant?" Patsy said, not only clearly perplexed but also impressed.

"Fuck no—I'm not an X-Man, and I didn't come from Alpha Centauri. I'm just the Freak from Battle Creek—for whatever reason I was born this way, although the docs at Stanford think I really am a throwback to Neanderthal times," I said. "And yeah, if I ever maxed out I'd probably have the world record for all three lifts, and total, too."

At that moment we were about a block from the office, and Kywfterelian said, "Let's race!" and tore off down the pavement. Patsy tore after her—and so did I. Ed and Badass just kept walking, because they'd already seen me in action.

I waited at the door for the other two racers and said, "What took ya so long?" with this big, drippy smile on my face, and both of them said, "Fuck you, Freak." We laughed until the other two arrived and Badass said, "I coulda told ya what was gonna happen. She can run backwards and beat most people, and God help ya if you're out for a run in full pack—she ain't never gonna lose a run under load."

"Veritas," I said. We went in the office laughing, and Badass took us straight to the boss's office, where we met Andria Rogers, a.k.a. CoD.

She was about 5'8" and kind of round, but not fat. She had short dark hair and hazel eyes that were as intense as a Marine officer's on patrol in Kabul. There was a jagged scar on her neck and she had a set of crooked teeth that were still really white. Her overall demeanor was much like I'd seen in general officers: competent, engaged, authoritative (but not authoritarian) and above all else just plain tough. It was clear that nobody had ever given Andria Rogers anything—everything she had she'd earned by working hard and being smarter than the average bear.

After introductions all around she said, "Call me CoD—it's easier and faster, plus it's less formal, which is going to be the rule for this unit. We aren't the Marine Corps, although we have some Marines with us—" She paused, and Badass, Patsy and I all said, "Booyah!"—"so we can afford to relax a bit. Yeah, I'm in charge, but the only difference between us is that I'm older and have more experience, whatever that is. I'm not a lord or a martinet, so it would be nice if we could all just use whatever names we're comfortable with, OK?"

She looked at Badass and he said, "Badass is best for me, although Freak is the biggest badass in the outfit."

"And I really am used to being called Freak—the only person who doesn't call me that is my *zayde*," I said.

"I'm Patsy," Alexander de Vries said. "Just think of Monty Python and clacking coconuts."

"I'm Ed," Emily Devlin said. "I like it better than Emily or Em because it sounds tougher."

"Even though you're a cream puff?" I said.

"Fuck you, asshole," she replied.

"See, that's what I'm talking about—camaraderie over rancor," CoD said. We all laughed and Tara Kywfterelian said, "You can call me Tara—I don't really have a nickname."

"What'd you do before this?" Ed said.

"I was in the Coast Guard," she said.

"Semper paratus," I said.

"God bless you," Patsy said.

"It's the motto of the Coast Guard, you asshole. It means 'always prepared,'" Kywfterelian said.

"What'd you do for the Coasties?" Ed said.

"Rescue swimmer," she said. We all put the jocularity aside for the moment and thought about how tough you had to be to jump out of a perfectly good helicopter into a sea that was trying to kill you—and then swim through it to rescue someone. Clearly Kywfterelian was as tough as a piece of fried liver, so she needed an appropriate nickname.

"Naming rights," Ed said.

"I got a good one if you think you need it," Badass said,

"Me, too," I said. "But I can tell from your face it's all but done."

"In honor of the Coast Guard motto, and in appreciation for your service swimming through seas that were incredibly rough and savage I am giving you the royal name of "Flipper," because no other creature better represents the qualities exhibited by Coast Guard rescue divers," Ed said.

Patsy and I started clapping the backs of our hands together and did our best impression of the 1960s dolphin who was the star of his own TV show. Kwyfterelian blushed and said, "My first nickname—Flipper sounds about right. I'm not sure how my mom will feel about it, though."

"Well, everybody who has to communicate with you is damned glad—Flipper is sure as hell easier to say that Kywfterelian," Badass said.

"Amen to that," CoD said. "It's also easier to put on a duty roster, and it might actually fit in the little space where you have to sign for secure comms."

"And it'll be a lot less embarrassing if we have to yell for ya across a crowded room," Patsy said. "I'd fuck Kywfterelian up for sure."

"He ain't kiddin'. You shoulda heard him trying to get Goodenough right. How long'd it take—two weeks?"

"Hell, almost three," Patsy said. "I still got problems with that one, but Badass I can handle."

"OK, since we've got all the important stuff done I want to let all of you know some serious shit. We got another threat this morning," CoD said. She hit a computer key and a note came up on her seventy-inch plasma. It was in Garamond, 12-point font, on plain paper, and it was explicit.

"Only an idiot or deluded fag would vote for you. All rug-munchers should die, and we're going to make you the first one, you filthy bitch. Make peace with whatever deity you and your so-called wife worship, you bull-dyke cunt, because you'll be meeting it soon." It was signed "The True Christian Knights."

"Office of Threat Assessment thinks it's credible?" Badass said.

"Yes," CoD said. "It's well written, is grammatically correct and seems sincere in its dislike for the candidate. Also, it seems that it was mailed from Cincinnati, which is where we'll be trooping off to right after the candidate gets done testifying before Congress. We've got an advance team out there, but obviously we have to be prepared before we go, since we're a new crew and it'll be our asses on the line at the three speeches she's giving there."

"I thought that it was two," Badass said.

"Well, the candidate accepted a speaking engagement at Morehead State University," CoD said.

"Ah, shit," Patsy, Badass and I all said at once. "I'll buy the Pepsis if I don't have to go on the trip," Badass said.

"Why? What's wrong with Morehead State?" Ed said.

"It's in motherfucking Kentucky," I said.

"Which state is not very fond of our gay brethren and sistren," Patsy said.

"You can say that again," CoD said.

"You can say that again," we all said, Greek chorus style. "Pepsis all around," CoD said, "but we've still got to protect her and her ubiquitous wife."

So we went through procedures and probabilities and a thousand other mundane details that were part and parcel of keeping someone safe even when they didn't necessarily want you to do so. I got all sorts of tips from Patsy, Badass and CoD, all of whom had closely guarded other people.

I was told just how close to stand, when and how to interpose myself between the protectee and a potentially hostile public, how to sneak away to the bathroom when the protectee was "under the umbrella" of some other security detail, or in a safe place that didn't require security…and we went over it *ad nauseum.*

Finally, after what seemed like days of tedium (but was really only two hours) CoD said, "Well, it's time to meet the candidate." She gave a heavy sigh and stood up like she was going to her own execution. "Is there something else we need to know, CoD?" I said.

She looked at all of us and said, "Just remember that every asshole who runs for president gets protection, and in some cases it's a good thing it's the law." She let that sink in before beckoning us to follow her. We went down the hall and turned left into a very large conference room where a gaggle of people were waiting.

We filed in and lined up behind CoD (just say it like 'cod'—you know, the fish?—and it works much better) in a single row from tallest (Badass) to shortest (Ed). While we waited for the candidate to finish talking on her phone I gave her the old eagle eye.

She was obviously an athlete: lithe body, developed muscles where I could see them, big knobby hands and large feet, that easy big-cat grace that most world class athletes have. She had brown eyes and close-cropped brown hair, with thick eyebrows and a very strong, almost cleft chin. Her face was high-cheeked and wide, with a tan that was uneven and probably from being outside instead of a tanning booth. Her lips were full and mobile as they flapped a mile a minute on the phone. Her voice had a pleasant alto tone but was harsh as she said, "I don't give a fuck how many goddamned protesters there are—I'm giving that speech. You can't run for president by being a chickenshit." She listened for a minute and then said, "Just set the fucking podium up and make sure there's a pitcher of water—and fuck the protesters. Yeah, I'll have some asshole protection-types with me." There was more squawking from her phone, but she cut it off and said, "Five, I guess, plus my guys. The last group couldn't take it—too much pressure for those Secret Service shitheads. You know—government types who all look good until the going gets a little tough and then they bail." More squawking, which she shut off by saying, "Yeah, yeah, I'm taking the threats seriously, which is why I'll have my own taser. Of course Josie'll have one, too. Right. Exactly. So just get the podium set up and tell all the sisters to stop worrying about the protesters. Yeah, see ya soon."

She hung up and then looked at CoD, who said, "Dr. Soper, this is your new protective detail. You already know Agent Goodenough, and these are Agents Tara Kywfterelian, Alexander de Vries, Glinka Glickstien and Emily Devlin. Agent Glickstien will be your new body agent, with Agent Kywfterelian as her backup. I have to go finish the details of your Cincinnati trip, so I'll leave you to get to know each other a bit. I'm just down the hall if you need me. Agents, when you're done please stop back at the office for a minute. Ma'am." CoD left and all of the people in the conference room started talking about a variety of topics, but no one even bothered to look at us, much less address us, so we stood there like the poor hick relations from the country while the city slicker cousins made nice with Grandma so they could get her fortune when she died.

Soper was talking a mile a minute about the sisterhood and the chance to break through in the south, especially if the speech at Morehead State was disrupted by the protesters. After just two minutes it was clear that she hoped the speech was disrupted, and that she planned to provoke the crowd by being deliberately inflammatory in her two previous speeches at the University of Cincinnati and Xavier University. I listened right up until she said, "And if we get lucky some red-neck will bring a weapon, hopefully a gun..." And then I lost it.

"Everybody except Dr. Soper clear the room—NOW!" I said in my Marine command voice. Gunnery Sergeant Thornton said the command voice was just like the Voice that was used by the Bene Gesserit in the *Dune* books to control people—and it needs to be as powerful as Pavlov's tuning fork, even on people who have no training (haven't read Frank Herbert's *Dune* series? Shame on you—it might be the best science fiction ever. Whattya been doing your whole life?). Clearly my command voice still worked since several people were already moving for the exit, but Hippolyta wasn't having any of it.

"Hold it! Agent Cluckstien, you don't get to give any orders, because while I'm here I'm the boss," she said, using what she thought was a hard tone. "Everybody stay put."

I looked at her with a real hard look and she visibly gulped and squirmed in her seat. I looked at the rest of the room and said, "Everyone. Else. Out. Now."

They all left.

The only other person who stayed was the supermodel who I recognized as Josephine Boroviak, Hippolyta's wife. She looked at me and raised an eyebrow, asking for permission to stay, and I gave her a slight nod and a look that said, 'But don't fuck with me, lady.' She gave me a nod back and sat up straighter.

I turned on Dr. Aleta Greenhoe Soper and said, "Dr. Soper, it's Glickstien, but let me make it a bit easier on you. You can call me Freak, like everyone else does. What you cannot ever do is disregard my instructions when it comes to security matters. When there is *any* security question, I. AM. THE. BOSS. PERIOD. Are we clear?"

"Uh, I don't like your tone, Duckfield. I think that you just shot yourself in the foot and lost a job. I'm going to have Super Agent Rogers kick your ass off my squad—nobody talks to me that way," Soper said.

"Fair enough," I said. "Let's go, guys." I opened the door and the rest of the detail started out the door.

"Hey, I just said I was getting Funkenstien booted, not the rest of you. The rest of you stay right here. I might be attacked by some pastry chef with a spatula." She chuckled, obviously trying to get her wife laughing, but Josie Boroviak was supernaturally good-looking, not stupid. She not only didn't laugh, she also got up and moved three chairs further away from Hippolyta, shaking her head at her partner's boorishness.

"They won't do it," I said, "because we're sworn to protect our principals, but we aren't slaves, or dumb automatons that you can just treat like dogshit. You don't want to listen to your protective detail? Fine. You want to act like a spoiled brat? Fine? You want to countermand my orders regarding security? Not only not fine, but hell no, Ms. Soper. You act like this is some kind of joke, but it's our asses on the line. No one is going to put themselves between you and a bullet if you refuse to listen to us and let us do our jobs so you can campaign without fear of being murdered. So you gonna listen? Or do you just want to prove you can get my ass reassigned? And by the way, both Agent Devlin and I have already been on the president's protective detail, so that's all you'll be able to do, get me reassigned. Decide now or we're outta here."

Hippolyta looked absolutely shocked. She started to open her mouth and Josie Boroviak said, "Hear her out, luv. She's an expert in her field, just like you are in yours and I am in mine. Do it for us, luv." Her accent was the female equivalent of Sean Connery—a deep, rich Scottish alto that was so sexy it could catch your panties on fire. I looked at Badass and Patsy and saw that it had the same effect on them, just in case Josie Boroviak was a switch-hitter.

Soper looked at her and you could see that Boroviak's voice had the same effect on her, because she curbed her anger and came back to me with a tight smile on her face but a fierce irritation in her eyes. She got her shit together and said, "OK, *Freak*, I'll hear you out, but remember that I don't like being told what to do, even by strong wymyn, and I'll *never* take orders from either of the *men*"—she sneered the word like she was saying '*stupid motherfuckers*'—in your squad, ever." She defied me to say anything about her conditions, but I was all done fucking around with this bitch.

"Wrong again, dumbass," I said. "If either of these men give you an order you'd better follow it like your life depended on it, because it does. Both Agent Goodenough and Agent de Vries are decorated combat veterans and skilled protective service agents—they've seen the elephant and lived to tell about it, so their word is law, just like anyone else's in the detail. It's not negotiable—we need instant obedience of we're going to do our jobs and keep you alive and unhurt. All your arrogance and intransigence does is ensure that your wife will be a widow. You really want that?"

You could see the war going on in her mind on her expressive face. She was used to being the smartest person in the room, and when her intelligence didn't get her what she wanted she just bullied people with verbal barrages that were driven by her giant ego. Finally love won out and she nodded while rolling her hand to say 'get on with it.'

"Before we go there's just one more thing," I said. "You call me anything but Agent Glickstien or Freak, or try to use me as the butt of a joke again, and you're going to the hospital. Nod if you understand me."

She stiffened and said, "If you think you're womyn enough, Agent Freak, let's dance."

I smiled and said, "No ma'am. That's a guarantee that you go to the hospital."

"Says you—but you're not willing to back it up? I can understand that, since I'm trained in *tae kwon do*, but I promise to just show you some stuff, not hurt you," Hippolyta said, her arrogance shining through her eyes and physical posture.

The rest of the detail was trying not to laugh—they all knew what I was capable of, and Badass and Ed had seen me in action. My smile got even wider, but Badass snorted, and Soper said, "You want to say something, Agent Goodenough?"

"Yes, ma'am. Your course of action would be very unwise and I recommend that you not undertake any sparring of any kind with the Freak. It's a very bad idea, ma'am," he said.

"Oh really? Why is that?" Hippolyta said.

"Because the Freak's at least a 5th degree black belt in four different martial arts, not including krav maga, which doesn't award belts, she's a combat veteran and she's the strongest person in this building by a factor of five. I've never met anyone who is her equal in self defense, and I was a

Marine Corps unarmed combat instructor for three full tours," he said, his voice totally devoid of any histrionics.

She frowned and looked hard at me again (I think that she was trying to intimidate me, but as you already know that shit don't fly with me), her forehead furrowing into deep ridges as she sought to control herself and respond. Waves of anger were pouring off her when I realized how to stop all of her bullshit.

"How about this, Dr. Soper: let's race each other so that I can prove why you shouldn't challenge me physically, and why you should let me do my job?" I said. She was so inordinately proud of her physical prowess that I knew I had her, and I wouldn't have to beat her ass into a pulp and go off to Leavenworth prison.

Her eyes lit up and she said, "How far?"

"You pick the distance, ma'am," I said.

She looked at my dumpy, sack of potatoes body and at her own lithe, streamlined Olympic body and said, "A thousand meters ought to be a good challenge for both of us, don't you think?" She was smiling like a shark before it eats a seal pup, but inside I was the one smiling, because she had no way of knowing that four days a week I ran 800 meter repeats at the high school track by my apartment, or that I worked out like a crazy person the other three days, too. Like most people Hippolyta had forgotten the 5th Rule— You are taking yourself too seriously—and the wisdom of the Tao Te Ching, where Lao Tzu said "There is no greater disaster than to underestimate the enemy (opponent)."

Too bad for her, the shithead. She was about to find out about the Freak from Battle Creek.

"Let's do it right now," she said. I nodded and we all went outside to look for a place to run. We walked out the door of the building and Badass said, "If we blocked off G Place NW"—the street right in front of us—"we could go down and back 3 times to get approximately 1000 meters."

"How do you know that?" Hippolyta said.

"The average city block in the District is one-tenth of a mile, or 528 feet. A thousand meters is approximately 3280 feet, which is six-tenths of a mile, which means we need six circuits to get to 1000 meters, give or take a few meters," Badass said.

"You just had that information in your head?" Hippolyta said, clearly not believing he was that smart.

"Well, I knew that a meter was approximately three point two feet, and the District block size is useful to know for motorcade detail, and I just did the conversions in my head. It's not like it was rocket science, ma'am, but you're welcome to check my math," Badass said. He was a former Marine and Spec Ops sniper, so he'd been doing those kind of conversions since sniper school (yeah, it's classified—I probably shouldn't've told ya he was a sniper, but what the hell—got to live dangerously once in a while).

Soper just shook her head and said, "Block off the street and I'll change my shoes." She took running shoes from a backpack and put them on while Patsy and Flipper went down to the east end of G Place NW. Badass and Ed walked down to the west end and got their creds out, holding them up while standing in the mouth of the street. Nobody even blew their horn—this was Washington, D.C., where streets were sometimes blocked off at a moment's notice—and I wandered over to stand near them.

Patsy waved to let Badass know that the street was secure at his end. Badass said, "If you went down and back three times and ended in the middle of the street at that No Parking sign it'd be almost exactly 1000 meters."

"Done," Soper said. Her entourage had wandered out with us, and they were laughing and yukking it up in preparation for watching their goddess destroy the uppity fat-ass with the funny red hair who dared to challenge the great and powerful candidate to a race. Didn't I know who she was, and that she was invincible? Several of them were even making fun of my shoes, pointing at them while pointing out that they weren't running shoes, but what they forgot was that we in the Secret Service ran *alongside* the limos our protectees rode in. My shoes were state of the art Rockports that had all sorts of special features for running, which these schmucks had no idea about. They thought that running over obstacles on relatively flat surfaces with people screaming at you from the stands was the equivalent of running for your life over 13,000-foot mountain passes with the Taliban (and others) trying to kill you with small arms and artillery fire.

They were about to find out how wrong they were.

Soper walked over to where I was standing and said, "You ready, Agent Glickstien?"

"Yep," I said.

"Somebody give us an 'on your mark, get set, go' call," Hippolyta said.

"On your mark, get set, GO!" one of the schmucks said.

I tore off like a tiger that'd just escaped from the National Zoo after it had been starved for a week was intent on eating my fat white ass. Soper took off at a more moderate pace, and I knew exactly what she was thinking: this idiot is going to die and come back to me, so I'll show her what an Olympic athlete can do.

I got to the end of the block, slapped Flipper's hand and tore back the other way. I passed Soper and she had a sly smile on her face, certain that I couldn't keep it up. I just kept hauling ass to the end of the street, slapped Ed's hand and roared the other way. When I passed Hippolyta this time she no longer had a smile on her face, and she was picking up the pace, but she still didn't look worried.

Until I went faster.

I slapped Flipper's hand to start my second trip down the street—I was just past 450 meters—and she hadn't reached the end of the street yet, so she was really surprised when she made her turn and I was only 25 meters from her. We passed each other and I could see she was really worried now—and that her stride was starting to falter just a bit.

I hit Ed's hand and just exploded down the street after Soper. I caught her before she made the turn for her second trip down the street, slapped Flipper's hand and then passed her again as I headed down the street for the last time. She just stared at me as I continued to run like I was being chased by a horde of starving cheetahs who wanted to gnaw my tits off. I hit Ed's hand for the last time and simply flew to the finish line, where Soper's schmucks were all standing with their mouths open. Herself was just coming down to finish her second circuit when I blew past the No Parking sign and began braking to a stop. I gathered myself and waited until Soper came back by me, falling in step with her as she plodded along to make the penultimate turn.

Neither of us said anything as we made the turn and then ran back down the street. We made the last turn and ran though the finish line. When we had both come to a complete stop I looked at Soper and said, "You and Ms. Boroviak back to the conference room, everybody else stays in the lobby."

Soper didn't speak, but she nodded at me and put her hands over her head to let more oxygen into her lungs. I went to the front door and said, "Badass, cover her with the detail until she can get in and on an elevator."

"Roger that, Freak," he said, a big, fat smile in his voice but not on his face. I could see Soper talking to Josie Boroviak, and I sure hoped that helped her disposition, but I was having a blast reading all of the shocked body language from everybody except my detail.

Take that, Queen of the Amazons.

CHAPTER 41

Laying Down the Law

I went up and sat in the conference room when CoD came in, looked around and said, "Ya killed her already? Rest of the detail disposing of the body?" She was so earnest and matter of fact that I wasn't sure she was kidding, until she winked at me. We both laughed and I said, "We had a small difference of opinion, but I don't think that will be a problem anymore. You should leave, though, in case I need to whack her later."

CoD brayed with laughter and shook her head as she walked out the door and back to her office. Less than five minutes later Soper arrived with Boroviak in tow, with the rest of my detail right behind. Badass walked over and handed me an ice cold can of Pepsi and said, "I had ya in 2:45, but it's probably a little short of a true 1000 meters."

"Thanks, Badass," I said. "I don't really train for the 1000, and all that turning slowed me down."

"Not too much. That time's about 16 seconds off the world record," he said.

"No shit? Maybe I oughta train for it—I could still make the Olympics," I said, smiling a little more than necessary.

"Nah," Ed said, "I don't think they take dumpy middle-aged broads in the Olympics."

"Especially since running isn't really your thing," Flipper said. "How far do you think that you could throw the hammer now?"

"Probably farther than I did before—my ass in much bigger, and of course I'm bigger around overall, so that would mean more momentum. Even if I couldn't throw it anymore I am still the world record holder, so fuck all those gigantic Eastern European wymyn and their mustaches."

"And you forgot that you can't guard a presidential candidate and have time to train," Patsy said. "Hard to stop a guy with a gun with a hammer, unless you've also got an AWACS system in your head."

"Shit," I said. "Goddamned job gets in the way of all my fun. I shoulda married a gazillionaire instead of being the best personal protection agent on the planet."

"And so modest, too," Badass said. "What a privilege it is to be in your presence, Yer Worshipfulness." The detail and Josie Boroviak laughed, but Aleta Greenhoe Soper just stared at me. Finally she said, "Where did you learn to run like that?"

"I didn't," I said. "It's a gift from the gods, just like my strength and intelligence, although I had some help with the intelligence."

"You've always been able to run that fast?" she said.

"Proportional to my body, yeah—I routinely beat the boys on the track team at 100 meters when I was in 8th grade," I said.

Suddenly a light went off in her head. "Wait a minute—are you *that* Glickstien? U.S. record holder in the discus?"

"And the hammer and the javelin, at least for a while. I still have the hammer record, but the other two've been broken," I said.

"You went into the service instead of trying out for the Olympics," she said.

"Yep," I said.

"Why? Why wouldn't you pursue your dream?" she said.

"I loved throwing stuff, and wrestling, and football, but they were recreation, not my dream," I said.

"But if you were that good—didn't you ever wonder how good you could have been if you made it your dream?" Soper said. "Didn't you ever want to be the best at something? To prove yourself?"

I looked at her for a few seconds and finally said, "I do, but I want it to mean something. Sports are fun, but they don't mean anything in the grand scheme of things. They're kind of like masturbation: it gets you off, but when it's over there isn't any deep feeling of satisfaction, and there is no connection to something grand like love, or even lust you satisfied…there's just an ephemeral satisfaction that just leaves you emptier than you were before you started. My dream is just too grand to fit into a picture like that—I want my dream to change the world, and some stupid athletic contests can't do that."

"So what is your dream?" Josie Boroviak said in her luscious voice.

I snorted and said, "Well, I hesitate to tell you, because it's really funny."

"Funny?" Boroviak said. "Whattya mean?"

"Ever been at a beauty contest?" I said.

"I was Miss Great Britain in the Miss World pageant," Josie said. "I would've won, too, except I'm pretty sure that Indonesian wench gave the head judge a hummer, which I was loathe to do, even though he asked." I liked her better already.

"So you already know what my dream is," I said.

Her face lit up as she got it, and she said, "Oh no, Agent Glickstien! Not that!" There was laughter in her eyes as she said it, and I decided I'd let her old lady live just because Josie was so nice.

"What? What's the dream?" Patsy said.

"Oh my god! I just got it!" Ed said. "You want world peace!" Everyone started laughing, even me, but after the laughter stopped Soper said, "Of course that can't be all of it, Agent Glickstien. What is your real dream?"

"I really want world peace," I said. "What's the point of building stuff up if some asshole just comes along and knocks it down? Why make beautiful art if somebody calls it decadent and burns it? Why make music that promotes happiness if someone else decides to pervert it and use it to promote hate? Without world peace nothing else matters, because it's just another piece of ephemera."

"You're an idealist? After the Army—," she started to say.

"Marines," Badass, Patsy and I all said. "You guys owe me a Pepsi," I said.

"OK, Marines and the Secret Service? How is that possible?" Soper said.

"It's the only way that I could do what I did, or what I do now. I am going to promote world peace until I die, in everything that I do or say. I'll always love sports, but they aren't as worthy a goal as stopping all of the killing and hatred around the globe. In fact, sports actively encourage such things at times, even in the name of peace," I said. "That's why I never went to the Olympics, or went pro in a sport…it's just too trivial for me."

"Well, I guess I see your point, although sports have pretty much been my life until now," Soper said.

"In any case, I was that Glickstien. Now I'm Agent Freak, and my task is to promote world peace by keeping you alive so you can run for president. We have many credible threats against you, so this is going to be a very active detail for as long as you continue running. As your body agent I'd like to go over some ground rules, OK?"

Soper and Josie nodded, so I said, "First of all, neither of you will be armed at any time when we are guarding you. You will not be carrying a taser or any other weapon."

Instantly the self-important, imperious and arrogant Aleta Greenhoe Soper was back. "Of course we will! We have a constitutional right to do so, and we both intend to exercise it. I'm not letting some nut-job harm me or Josie, and the best way to do that is to make sure I'm packing." She said it with great force and pride and was totally unprepared for the detail to burst out laughing.

Her face turned red and she said, "Did I say something *funny?*"

"First of all, ma'am, no one says 'packing'—that's a term from the 1930s. We all say 'carrying' when we're armed. Second, that was a nice speech, but it doesn't mean shit to me. The only right you have in this case is to live, and we're not going to jeopardize your chances of survival by letting you have a weapon so you can interfere with us doing our jobs," I said.

"You expect me to just sit there while someone attacks us and not respond?" Soper said.

"Oh, no, ma'am, I expect you to run, or that some of us will have swamped you and covered you with our bodies. I never want you to even consider standing and fighting," I said.

"I'm very good with my taser," she said. "I've been trained and I practice. I have very good hand eye coordination."

"Are you armed now?" I said. She nodded and I said, "OK, show me. I'm attacking you—yank your taser and let me have it."

"What if I accidentally pull the trigger and fry you?" she said, dead serious.

"I've got great insurance—no problem," I said.

She leapt to her feet and reached behind her back to yank the taser out and point it at me. She nearly shit herself when she found the barrel of my 1076 five feet from her head, so close that the barrel opening must have looked like the Lincoln Tunnel.

Sweat stood out on her forehead as she realized what could have happened. She looked in my eyes and saw a look she'd never seen before—the look that said "I can kill you, and I will if you fuck with me, lady."

I kept the weapon pointed at her head and said, "The average person's reaction time to danger is between 1.2 and 1.3 seconds. Average people really can't get into motion much faster than that, and they always hesitate—like you know you just did—before they train their weapon on the target. That's also assuming they get the target right. My reaction time is under two-tenths of a second and I never hesitate. You'll also notice that while drawing and training my weapon on you I closed your position to render your taser useless—I'm too close to you for the weapon to fry me—and also greatly increase the chance that I won't miss you if I did shoot. The fact is that everyone in this detail is faster and better trained that you or Ms. Boroviak. If you're armed all you can do is get in the way of your professional guards and guarantee that somebody gets hurt."

"What if you miss your target, Agent Glickstien? What then?" Soper said.

"You'll see a unicorn before that happens," Badass said.

"She never misses," Ed said. "Never."

"I heard the stories when I was going through basic training, ma'am, and I heard a Marine Gunnery Sergeant say that she'd never seen a deadlier pistol shot in her life, and that Gunnery Sergeant was damned good with the M9, ma'am," Patsy said.

"Must have been Gunny Thornton," I said. "She saw me when I took down every target at the President's Cup, including the target they tried to trick me with."

"Yes, ma'am," Patsy said. "She said you even beat Master Gunnery Sergeant Berkey head-to-head, and I saw Gunny Berkey knock down a target at 100 meters with an M9, and that ain't human. Freak never misses, ma'am, and neither will any of the rest of us."

I holstered my pistol and Soper put her taser away, and she said, in a very small voice, "How do I know that my wife and I will be safe, even with you there?" I got it then—she was putting on the tough bitch act so her wife wouldn't be scared. Soper thought that if she acted like she wasn't scared then Josie would be OK, which might have been true if Josie wasn't so smart. I decided another demonstration was in order.

I looked at Badass and said, "Show her your scars, Captain." His face got red, but he took off his coat, unbuttoned his shirt and took it and his undershirt off. I heard all of the sharp intakes of breath around the room, and Josie said, "Oh Jesus, Mary and Joseph."

"Holy fuck-fuck, Cap'n," Patsy said. "What the fuck kind of IED did you get hit with?"

"The enemy hit us with rockets, heavy machine gun fire and several of our local allies decided to change sides, so just when I took heavy shrapnel from an RPG a lovely Afghan freedom fighter hit my post with a Molotov cocktail," Badass said. His scars were a starburst pattern of purple triangles on his left belly, overlaid with burn scars that disappeared below his belt and crept up his chest and around his shoulder. They were incredibly ugly.

"Tell her what you did next," I said. Badass got redder, but I hitched a shoulder at him and said, "C'mon, Marine, tell her."

"I, uh, I picked up my M249 Squad Automatic Weapon and engaged the enemy I could see. I managed to locate one of their mortar firing positions and eliminated that threat, and then I found one of their MGs and knocked everybody out there, too. The enemy was trying to flank us, so I turned my position 90 degrees and engaged them until more of my unit came up to support me," Badass said.

"While you were on fire," I said.

"What?" several voices said.

"The Molotov cocktail caught Captain Goodenough on fire, but he refused to stop fighting," I said. "Tell her why."

By this time Soper and Josie were holding hands and looking like they might puke, but I give them credit, because neither one looked away.

Badass stood up at parade rest and said, "I didn't even think about being on fire, because the rest of my squad needed me to do my job or they would've been killed. I'm a Marine, and you better believe that the enemy better put two in my head, ma'am, and make sure that I'm dead, because as long as I'm breathing I'll kill any motherfucker that tries to come at someone I'm sworn to protect." He looked Soper right in the eye and said, "Sorry about the language, ma'am, but I swore an oath to protect and defend the Constitution, and the Constitution says you got a right to run for president without some assholes hurting you, and I intend to see that you get a full, fair chance at it."

Both wymyn had tears running down their cheeks, but Soper said, "It doesn't bother you that we're lesbians? That doesn't affect your calculus in a life or death situation?"

"Ma'am, I don't care what you do in your bedroom unless you're doin' it with me, and I care even less who you're doing it with. It ain't any of my business, and it ain't nobody else's business, either. My job is to guard you, and that's all I care about. If you want to sleep with an iguana you go right ahead, although I will tell you that anybody who isn't jealous of you isn't right in the head," Badass said.

"Why is that, Agent Goodenough?" Soper said.

"Ma'am, you chose a right good wife—beautiful, kind, talented and intelligent is a 4.0 combination, ma'am," Badass said. He looked at Josie Boroviak and said, "Sorry if I was too blunt, Ms. Boroviak, and no, I'm not trying to hit on you. I'm just tellin' the truth. No offense intended." We all laughed and Soper said, "No offense taken, Agent Goodenough."

"You are incredibly brave and gallant, Agent Goodenough," Josie said.

"I do have a question, Agent Goodenough," Soper said.

"Ask away, ma'am," Badass said.

"How did you get out of the situation you were in? How did you stop the enemy from killing or capturing you?" she said.

"That's classified," Badass and I said. "You owe me a Pepsi, Freak," Badass said. I nodded at him and said, "With pleasure, especially if you'll suit up again." He got dressed, but Soper was a persistent bitch, and she said, "Agent Goodenough, I know that the story is classified, but *hypothetically* what happened to save you?"

Badass looked at me, and I gave him a tiny nod. As he tied his tie he said, "Well, ma'am, hypothetically the Heavenly Host showed up and bailed our asses out."

"The Heavenly Host? I don't understand," Soper said.

"Ma'am, the Heavenly Host showed up, led by the Archangel Michael with his flaming sword, and killed the enemies of the righteous," Badass said.

By now everybody was looking at Badass like he'd lost his mind, and Josie Boroviak said, "Are you some kind of religious fanatic, Agent Goodenough?"

"No, ma'am, but that's exactly what happened," he said, a grim smile on his face as he remembered that day from the past when he almost died. "I was prepared to die right there, but out of nowhere Michael appeared and smote the enemy with his flaming sword, killing everyone he touched until there was no longer a discrete enemy, but rather a bunch of leaderless bandits who ran from us."

"Is this a device to keep the classified stuff classified, Agent Goodenough?" Soper said.

He smiled for real this time—a glorious sight, because Badass was one seriously good-looking dude, especially when he smiled—and said, "Ma'am, you've probably never seen a .50 caliber machine gun loaded with tracers go off, but when one goes off at night it looks like a flaming sword, and .50 cal kills anyone it touches. I always thought that Michael would be taller, but it turns out he's about five-feet-seven and the best gunner I've ever seen—he killed at least one hundred of the enemy that night, first with the Flaming Sword, and then with two Beretta M9 pistols. It looked like the Heavenly Host had come, because his three other angels knew what they were doing—they flanked the enemy and hit them with SAW fire, too. The enemy was brave, but Alexander the Great's troops would've broken under that kind of fire—and it didn't hurt that Michael was screaming "Hell awaits, motherfuckers!" at the top of her voice."

"And this 'Michael' and the 'Heavenly Host'—they were your comrades that you don't want to identify? Because the incident was classified?" Soper said.

"Ma'am, let's just say that when you're president there'll be lots of stuff in your security briefing that will surprise you, and this uh, incident, will be one of them," Badass said. Everybody looked at him with wonder in their eyes, but he looked at me and arched an eyebrow. Josie Boroviak noticed, and she looked at me with eyes that were asking a question, but she was smart enough to not to say anything.

But Soper was smart enough to read her wife, and she looked back at me and said, "It was you—you were Michael, weren't you."

Badass said, "Ma'am, that operation is *really* classified, and we can't confirm anything, but I will say that Freak has saved my life several times, and each time I was grateful, but there was one time that still stands out in my memory—it was really hot out, that time." He stared at her with his ice blue eyes wide, telling her that nothing else would be forthcoming.

She blinked first, lowering her eyes and then looking at me with a different face. "I understand," she said.

"You also need to understand that we're all like Agent Goodenough," I said. "It's time for a little biographical information and career synopsis. Agent Devlin, lead off, and don't be modest."

We all went through our bios. Ed told her about being a county sheriff, a state trooper and then joining the Secret Service. She paid particular attention to the time she faced down and killed three assholes when she was an off-duty state trooper in a bank they were trying to rob.

Patsy told her about his time in the Marines, and winning the Navy Cross, and the death of his brother. Flipper talked about fighting in the MMA, and then deciding to serve her country in the Coast Guard, where she jumped into 30-foot seas to rescue three kids who'd been stupid enough to take their power boat out in the San Juan Strait during a huge storm. I told her about the warehouse massacree, and about playing football at Michigan State, and about beating up Judge Walter Necker after he murdered The Great Pumpkin.

When we were done it was like the Tomb of the Unknown Soldier at Arlington National Cemetery…completely silent and solemn. Finally Aleta Greenhoe Soper said, "Sometimes you get so caught up in your own struggles that you forget everybody else in the world. You forget that other people have honor, that they also serve a higher purpose, and that they have faced incredible adversity and come through the other side as whole, normal people. I've tried so hard to express myself about the struggles of people like me I forgot you don't have to be like me, or even like me, to do your job and do it well." She looked at Josie Boroviak and said, "My wife knows that I can be a bloviating asshole on occasion, but she also knows that I'm willing to listen to people with a good point. Since I left the governor's office I haven't heard many of those, but I get your message, Agent Glickstien. We're in your hands and we'll do what you say, even though I may bitch about it sometimes."

"May?" I said.

"Sometimes?" Josie said.

We all laughed, and Soper reached out and hugged her wife, and finally I said, "I appreciate it, ma'am, but there is one other thing that I have to tell you that you won't like."

She held up her hand and said, "Before you give me more bad news I'd like to make a radical suggestion, if it doesn't violate some Secret Service protocol that means we'll be less safe." I thought I knew what she was going to say, so I said, "Whatever would that be, Ms. Greenhoe Soper?"

She laughed and said, "I guess I'm easier to read than I think I am. I want to dispense with all of this formality. I'm a candidate for president, not for sainthood. In reality I'm no different than any of you are, and I would feel much more comfortable if we could address each other comfortably, rather than the way we're doing it. Everybody I know calls me Soper, except for my wife, my mom and my uncle Nedrick, who all call me Aleta, but I don't want it to seem too familiar, so if you could just call me Soper, and leave the 'ma'am'-ing for when I'm president?"

I laughed and said, "Well, for the sake of brevity if we need to communicate under duress I'll do it, but only if you call me Freak."

"Done," she said. "What do I call the rest of you?"

Badass said, "My name in the detail is Badass, but I'm not sure the public is ready for that, so just call me Bad-A." She nodded and Ed said, "Ed works for me, Soper."

"I'm Patsy, Soper." Patsy said. "After the King's squire in *Monty Python and the Holy Grail?*" Josie said. "Yes—uh, er—" Patsy said, unclear on how to proceed.

"Everybody call me Josie, although if you want to remind me of my sainted grandmother Drusilla you can call me Josephine Julia Argyle Boroviak," she said, laughing at the ridiculousness of such a moniker. (Hey, fuck you PC types—when your name is Glinka Rose Glickstien you can make fun of other people's names—you try wearin' that shit for a while.)

"And I'm Flipper," Flipper said. "Trying to get anyone to pronounce Kywfterelian correctly is a real nightmare anyway."

Soper said something in what I later found out was Armenian, and Flipper (typing 'Kywfterelian' is almost as big a pain in the ass as saying it) responded. There was a spirited exchange in Armenian, after which Soper said, "Well, you can speak it anytime around me, although we are being rude and excluding everybody else."

Flipper said, "Soper did an internship with an international corn broker and spent time in Armenia—she learned the language in college. Can you believe it?"

"I also speak French, German, Italian, Kyrgyz, Russian, Gaelic, Spanish, Inuit, Lapp and some Portuguese, although I understand it more than I speak it," Soper said.

"So in addition to being beautiful, intelligent, well-educated, athletically gifted and a great public speaker you're also a polyglot?" I said.

"Well, yeah," Soper said. "I also play the piano, guitar and cello, and I'm learning the Irish harp."

"Fuck you, asshole," I said, using the language and phraseology of the Marines and Special Forces to convey my approval of her prowess, and hoping that she got it.

She did. She laughed and we all had a good time laughing with her.

"I am a pretentious bitch, aren't I?" she said.

"Bet your ass, Soper," Badass said, sparking more laughter. When we finally wound down I said, "Not to be a fun-sucker, but there is one more thing that we need to discuss."

"You'll be covering Aleta and not me," Josie said. She might have been the most beautiful womyn in the world (I'm not kidding—she was in the ether beyond what the term beautiful could convey and into otherworldly range), but Josephine Boroviak was also whip-smart. She knew what our mission was, and it didn't bother her, or at least she acted like it didn't.

"Of course they'll be covering you, J. If they're covering me they're covering you," Soper said.

She looked at me and I slowly shook my head. "Only so far as she is directly under your umbrella of coverage," I said. "Our first and only priority is you, and we also don't have a legal mandate to cover Josie."

"But we're together so much—surely you won't just abandon her to save me?" Soper said. She looked at five stone-faced Secret Service agents and realized that we would, indeed, abandon Josie to save her. A tear ran down her cheek as she looked at us for solace, so I said, "Let me make this perfectly clear, Soper. If we are faced with any kind of a choice in protecting one of you we'll choose you first, last and always—you're our *only* priority." She started to protest, but I put my hand up and said, "Let me finish, OK? We're not going to abandon Josie—most of the time protecting her means protecting you, but if push comes to shove we got you, and Josie's on her own. We can't divide our attention, or split up the detail, or in any way compromise your security, because we're tasked by our Director with *your* protection, and no one else's. I know the Bible says you two are one flesh, and that the law says you're a single legal entity, but our priority is the business half of the partnership—the candidate—and that is definitely you. We'll do everything we can to protect you both, but you deserve to know the reality of it—and so does Josie."

We all sat there as that sank in for Soper. At first she looked absolutely stricken, but then you could see why she was elected governor of the nation's largest state three times. She squared her shoulders, reached out and took her wife's hand and then said, "OK, Freak. I got it. I even understand, but try not to let either of us get hurt, OK? The three of us have a lot of life ahead, and I'd like to live to see some grandchildren."

Three?

Oh, fuck a duck.

"How far along are you, Josie?" I asked.

"Two months, two weeks and four days," she said. "We did in vitro using sperm from Aleta's brother, so the baby would have both Boroviak and Soper bloodlines. We found out last week that I was definitely pregnant."

"Well, that changes things just a bit," I said. "We need to consult with CoD, like now. Patsy, can you get her?"

About 30 seconds later CoD came into the room and said, "What's going on, Freak?" So I told her about Josie being pregnant, and the detail being too small, and maybe I could request some people that I was already comfortable with? CoD said, "Got somebody in mind?"

"I'd like Ed to be Josie's body agent, and then get Calvin Beemond and Emiliano Zaragoza to fortify the squad," I said.

"Done," CoD said. She turned to Soper and said, "Ma'am, we're all set on the Cincinnati trip, and I'm just confirming that we're taking the bus to Morehead State."

"Yeah, and from there we're going to Indianapolis, Ft. Wayne, Goshen and South Bend, Indiana," she said. "We're doing a west side swing into Michigan, and then heading out to Illinois and Iowa via Gary, Hammond and Chicago."

"All by bus, right?" CoD said.

"Yes," Soper said. Most of what we're doing is going to be by bus, although there is some flying later this month."

"My ass hurts already," Ed said.

"All our asses will be sore, but it's the only way that I can think of to be president," Soper said, laughing.

"No problem, Soper, as long as you don't ask me to eat any rubber chicken," Badass said. "That shit makes me have gastric distress."

"Just like MREs do," I said.

Everyone who'd ever eaten one shuddered at the thought of MREs—Meals Ready to Eat—that were meals in name only.

"And I am *not* kissing any babies," Patsy said. "They always puke on me."

"You dipshits got the wrong idea about what's gonna happen on the campaign trail—Soper's going to do all that glad-handing shit—we're gonna be watchin' her and Josie's ass," I said.

"Fine by me," Ed said, a twinkle in her eye.

"Ah, another member of the sisterhood," Josie said, a twinkle in *her* eye.

I put my hands on my hips, rolled my eyes and said, "Oh, fuck me. Two lesbians I can handle, but three lesbians are a committee, and that I cannot deal with without going crazy." We all got a good laugh out of that one (I know it seems that we're laughing all the time, but we really were—these were all smart people who got jokes quickly and enjoyed using humor to defuse the constant tension and pressure we were under. Besides, the detail really was kind of fun), and Soper said, "It's good to know that at least one member of the detail understand what it's like to be so *misunderstood*." She put the back of her hand to her forehead and did one of those silent film collapses on the chair, with an expression that looked like she was having a gas attack (I'm sure she thought it was a put-upon look, but I was reaching for the Tums).

"It's a good thing that Mamba isn't here, because then we'd have a whole coven of gay folks, and we all know where that train ends up," I said.

"Disney World?" Patsy said.

"A nail parlor?" Flipper said.

"Nah," Badass said, "that train ends up in the Swishy Town shopping mall."

We all laughed like hyenas, and I think that Soper peed her pants a little.

CoD had been on her phone, and she hung up and said, "Jesus! Soper ain't gonna be president if we kill her off from oxygen deprivation—at least let her catch a breath."

"Roger that, boss," I said.

"We got Beemond and Zaragoza, plus I'm bringing in two other agents so we can make sure we're not caught with our pants down," CoD said. "You're welcome."

"Thanks, CoD. Who are the other two agents?" I said.

"The Koenigsblett sisters," she said. "They were stuck in Legal because they have law degrees from the University of Michigan, but they played softball at Bowling Green State University, and I've heard they can shoot, so we can't waste 'em being junior prosecutors, or doing oversight, or whatever the fuck those dipshits in Legal do, so I convinced them to join the Protective Division."

"Hey…" Badass said. His face lit up and he said, "Are those the twins that played on the Service softball team last year? The blonde and blue twins?"

CoD had an evil smile on her face, and she said, "Why yes, yes they are. Is there a problem, Agent Goodenough?"

"Oh, no ma'am, boss. Excellent choice to augment the detail with—I'm in awe of your management skills. I'm sure they'll work out, ma'am," Badass said, really smarming it on.

"Yeah, cut the shit, Badass. Just make sure that you keep your mind on guarding the right bodies, big fella," CoD said. "Ya never know when you'll have a problem, and ya can't be caught off guard because your concentration wandered when an attractive set of hindquarters passed before your eyes."

We all got a laugh out of that one, and CoD said, "All kidding aside, just remember that the difference between life and death is just a couple of seconds one way or another. Ya wander off in your head for that second and one of ours dies; ya keep your concentration and the bad guys get a shit sandwich, right?"

No one ever dreamed that CoD was a seer, or that that future was hurtling toward us like the meteor that killed the dinosaurs.

But it was.

CHAPTER 42

Red Paint

The Koenigsblett sisters arrived—beautiful, vivacious, smart as hell and definitely physically capable of doing the job. They were a little over 5'8", around 155 pounds of lithe, curvy, fast twitch muscle and great hand-eye coordination, with blonde hair and blue eyes. Sarah was the more gregarious of the two, shaking hands with everybody and teasing Badass about his haircut (it wasn't a Marine Corps high and tight, but it was close), while Darah was a bit quieter and less ebullient, but no less engaged. She shook my hand and said, "Great job on the counterfeiting case, Agent Glickstien. Catching the Korean before he could disappear probably saved the rest of the case."

"Yeah, maybe, but it was really just good old-fashioned teamwork," I said.

"I saw that, too. It's one of the reasons that I'm happy to be here—I really miss being part of a team," Darah said.

"You're about to get over that. This is going to be a good one, especially since we've got the coolest boss in the world," I said. "She knows her shit and she's totally chill about it."

"We know her," Darah said in her calm, measured voice. "Her niece played ball with us at BGSU. She seems to be laid back, in a professional, watch-everything-like-a-hawk way." She smiled a quiet little smile, and I said, "A great physical package and a sense of humor, too? You'll fit right in with the rest of the weirdos."

"I just worry about Sarah—she has such a hard time making friends," Darah said. We both laughed as we watched Sarah regaling Patsy, Badass and Ed with a story that had them all laughing, too.

As we were standing there Bumble and El Gato came in to the conference room, and everybody had to get re-acquainted all over again. Once that was done CoD gave us our assignments for Cincinnati, including what the command structure would be.

"If anything renders me unable to function Badass is next in line for the big chair, with Freak, Patsy, Ed and Flipper in that order. We really need to stay on our toes—this southern Ohio slash Kentucky swing is really a pain in the ass, especially since we got a bag full of credible threats from that area *before* Soper scheduled the trip. We also need to be really careful in South Bend, because some of that Notre Dame crowd are Shiite Catholics (if you never heard that before you need to catch Jim Gaffigan, because CoD stole that line about "Shiite Catholics" from him), and they definitely don't appreciate Soper's point of view," CoD said.

"What a nice way to say that they hate her ass, boss. Have I complimented you on your management skills yet today?" Badass said.

"Fuck you, asshole," CoD said. We all laughed and then CoD looked at her watch. "The protectee finishes at the committee in 15—we're going straight from there to the bus," she said.

"Everybody clear on where you're supposed to be?" We all nodded and she said, "Good. Now get your asses into the cars and let's get over to Capitol Hill. We got a trip to take."

When Soper and Josie came out of the Capitol we were waiting. Ed, Patsy, Bumble and I got on the bus. CoD, Sarah Koenigsblett and El Gato went in the lead car, with Badass, Darah Koenigsblett and Flipper in the trail car.

We finally cleared the northern edge of the city and got on I-70 West until we merged onto I-68 West. The country was beautiful and we turned north on I-79 just outside Morgantown, West Virginia, crossed the southwest corner of Pennsylvania and then caught I-70 again and went due west all the way to Columbus, Ohio, where we merged onto I-71 South.

We stopped in Columbus at the original Max and Erma's restaurant on Third Street for supper. It was an easy place to protect Soper and Josie, since the stop was unannounced and we sat in the back right near an emergency exit. Before we got back on the bus I allowed as how it sure was nice riding a bus with a bathroom, a point that I emphasized to the car bound agents, who all cordially told me to go fuck myself. We didn't stop again until we got to Cincy, where the bus rolled off of the brand-new exit at Martin Luther King Drive East and arrived at the Kingsgate Marriott Conference Center right next to the University of Cincinnati.

Everybody piled out and we hustled Soper and Josie off to their suite—there were already donors lined up to have their five minutes with the candidate, and they all had to be vetted before they got up the elevator, so everybody had plenty to do. Badass and I were the least busy of anyone, since all we were doing at the moment was guarding the door of the suite while everybody else checked out the donor line.

I looked at Badass and said, "You surprised?"

"Yeah," he said. "I thought there was this concerted movement to protest everything that she does, everyplace she goes. Where are all the protesters?"

"Something is wrong here," I said. "There oughta be protesters ass-deep to a tall born-again pastor, but there isn't one guy with a "burn in hell" sign. That's not right."

The door to the suite opened and Josie said, "Aleta would like it if you came in for a minute." We both went in the suite, which was really clean, well appointed with every amenity and full of fresh flowers, which made it smell almost too good. Soper was on the phone, but hung up when we came in. She swept her arms around the room and said, "I just wondered how you liked your suite?"

Badass and I both got it at the same time. "Fuck you, asshole," I said. Soper and Josie laughed and Badass said, "That was well, done, Soper. Ya got another suite reserved somewhere else, and ya got some of your volunteers there in order to fool the protesters, dontcha."

She smiled and said, "It was CoD's idea—she called here and cancelled my reservation, then called back and made it in your names. She also called another hotel on the other side of campus and made a reservation for a block of rooms, which will be cancelled at midnight. She's done the same thing in Morehead, and probably for the rest of the trip. Josie used to the same thing when she was still modeling, and I imagine that we aren't exactly alone in doing this kind of thing."

She smiled again and said, "They'll find out sooner or later, but it's nice to have one peaceful night, isn't it?"

"Yeah, but it's about to get hectic again," I said. "How do you want to play the donors? And before you answer, remember that I'm not going to leave them alone with you unless they're close personal friends. Crazies come in all shapes and sizes, and lots of them are perfectly nice, reasonable folks until someone whose very existence they despise sends them over the edge. So how do you want to play the donors?"

She thought for a bit, looked at Josie and then said, "I don't want you to leave at all. Josie and I will be together, so they won't have any expectation of privacy anyway, and if they don't like you in the room then fuck 'em, I don't want their money."

"Glad to hear it. So Badass and Bumble will stand right outside the inner sanctum, with everybody else strategically spread out, except for Ed, Patsy and Darah Koenigsblett," I said.

"What will they be doing?" Josie said. Before we could answer she smacked her forehead and said, "Well, that was an embarrassingly stupid question. Of course they'll be sleeping—they've got the overnight shift."

"Bingo," I said. "We'll probably send everybody else to bed as soon as the last donor comes up, except CoD and I, who won't go to bed until you're secure in here," I said. "We've got nothing public until tomorrow night at the university."

"Actually, I'm going to address a small auditorium of students at Mount St. Joseph University tomorrow at 10 a.m., but it's unscheduled. One of my former professors at the University of Chicago retired to Cincinnati—his family is from here—and then decided to unretire at Mount St. Joseph, and I promised him some time with his kids," Soper said.

"CoD know this?" I said.

"I just got off the phone with Dr. Buckner," Soper said. "I hope that isn't a problem."

"Of course it's a problem, hon—your detail needs to do advance work wherever you go, regardless of the risk profile, which has to be pretty low for a liberal arts school, even if it is a Catholic university," Josie said. "You can't just throw stuff at them if you expect them to do their jobs properly."

"Actually, it's OK," I said. "We already did background on all the universities and colleges in Cincinnati, plus if your professor is the only one who knows we should be OK, although CoD is going to want to send somebody over first thing in the morning." I looked at Badass and he said, "I'm on it, Freak. I'll send Bumble and Flipper up right away." He nodded at Soper and Josie and said, "Ya owe me one, Soper—I'll for sure not get to sleep tonight. Oh woe is me." He tried for a pitiful look, and Soper said, "Fuck you, asshole" in the perfect put-down tone, and then she rubbed her index finger and thumb together.

Badass looked at her and said, "Yeah, yeah, I got it—you're playin' *My Heart Bleeds for You* on the world's smallest violin. Thanks for the sympathy, ya twerp."

We all laughed and Josie said, "Shall I have a case of Pepsi delivered to Mount St. Joseph? To help you stay awake?"

"Now there's a real lady—she actually cares about the poor line animals that do the work," Badass said. He smiled and left the suite. I had a thought and said, "Wait a minute—is your former prof Dr. Gary Buckner? Nobel Prize laureate? Studied the effects of human capital on economic systems? *A Treatise on Families as Economic Actors*? That Dr. Buckner?"

"You know him, too?" Soper said.

"Only by reputation and his writings—the guy knows his shit and changed economics and sociology, as well as opening up the discussion on rational choice theory as applied to economics and crime," I said. "He's a damned genius, with the ability to explain stuff in plain language and the research chops to back it up."

"Was your degree in economics, Freak?" Soper said.

"No, but I come from a high-powered Jewish clan that believed in education across the spectrum, even in the dismal science," I said. "Well, tomorrow you can ask him anything you want, as long as you remember that at age 90 he's still one of the five smartest people on earth," Soper said. "And be careful when you ask him stuff, because you're always going to get more than you asked for—and he's relentless in his teaching, so it will be a lesson." She smiled and I could see that she looked like when she was younger and presumably more carefree. She was still good-looking, but I'll bet that she'd been irresistible to both sexes 25 years ago when she was an undergrad. Before we could converse any more there was a knock on the suite door. Bumble leaned in and said, "Soper, there's a guy named Sean McCannell who wants to see you? He's also got a Lisa Silverman and Daoud Al-Hashem with him?"

"Please send them in—they can come in any time they want," Soper said. "You guys already know they're my campaign manager, finance director and foreign policy adviser, right?" I nodded and she said, "So even if I'm sleeping these three can see me right away, as long as they knock, OK?"

"Roger that, Soper," I said. "These guys have the equivalent of unlimited Oval Office access."

"Exactly—when I'm president it'll just be these three and Josie who have that kind of access," Soper said.

I took out my little notebook, stuck my tongue out and pretended to swipe my pen across it, while making a doofus face like I was an old-time reporter trying to spell a ballplayer's name right. "Lemme just write that down here, just in case you forget after the election—I hear that yer memory goes right quick once you become the Illustrious Potentate," I said, channeling my inner Ray Stevens (another hilarious dude who had a song called "The Shriner's Convention" that will just crack your ass up—find it on YouTube).

"Fuck you, asshole," Soper said, making Josie and I crack up.

"Up yours, too, lady," I said just as her campaign manager came in the door.

"Whoa, there, Agent! Maybe you need to watch your mouth around the governor?" he said, with some pugnacity. I looked at Sean McCannell for the first time and liked what I saw. He was 5'10", 160, with brown hair and eyes, a smooth, good-looking face and a very trim body that was encased in a really well tailored suit. Overall he was about an 8.5 on a scale of 10, with the possibility of moving up to a 9 if he was single.

I also liked the fact that he was being protective of Soper, probably because of all the abuse she'd had to endure already, and not just being an all-purpose asshat.

Before I could say anything Soper said, "It's OK, Sean, it's just insider banter. I'm learning that it's a Marine Corps and/or Special Forces thing. Believe me, Freak's one of the good guys."

"Uh, Freak?" McCannell said, clearly confused by Soper's attitude. I was betting that he was having a flashback about the last time he saw her with a Secret Service detail, which meant the poor guy probably thought that he was on acid.

I stuck out my hand and said, "Mr. McCannell, I'm Special Agent Glinka Glickstien. I'm the governor's new body agent, and third in command of the entire detail. The team and the governor have agreed that it makes communication easier if we are less formal in private, although we will be on a more formal basis when the public is present. I'm dreadfully sorry if I put you out with my language, sir." I was oozing sincerity, since I didn't know how much of a sense of humor this guy had.

"No she-e-e-'s not-t-t-t," Soper said in a sing-song voice. "She's just trying to tell you that we have a very informal manner of communication, which I've been bitching at you about since we started this thing, have I not?"

"Yes, you definitely have," McCannell said. "And I've been trying to tell you that it's un-presidential and allows people too much familiarity with you, which clouds your objectivity. You've got to remind people that you've already been a national leader, or Castro, McCaskill, Booker, Patrick and Klobuchar will look better at the leadership angle just because of their titles."

"Yeah, well, fuck 'em if they can't take a joke," Soper said. McCannell looked like he'd just swallowed a clan of badgers (OK, technically it's a 'cete' of badgers, but I like 'clan' better—besides, what the fuck is a cete?) and the other two campaign twerps about fainted. I give him credit, though—he kept his cool enough to say, "Uh, governor?"

"Look, I don't give a damn about the looking like a leader argument"—McCannell started to protest, but Soper held up her hand to stop him—"and no, I'm not saying you're wrong, I'm just saying that we disagree, and it's my name at the top of campaign posters, so from now on we're going with less formal, OK?" She looked hard at the campaign staffers, and finally McCannell said, "So you're just going to make your points until the money dries up and then hope you get picked for VP? Is that about it?"

"Fuck you, asshole," Soper said, getting just enough scorn and derision overlaid by genuine affection into her voice to let McCannell know that she was serious about changing policy, and that even though he was probably right she was changing tactics whether he liked it or not.

I was so proud of her—she was natural at the intricacies of 'fuck you, asshole' and she'd only been at it for three days.

I was also proud of McCannell. He bore up, got the tone of her voice and said, "OK, Soper. Less formal address it is—can I just call you 'Dipshit,' or how about 'Dumbass'? Just let me know. Now about the format at Cincinnati…" And they were off about what they were actually doing at the university the next day. About five minutes later the first wave of donors hit the door, walking past our guys at the door and into the inner sanctum. That kept on until midnight, when McCannell finally said, "Governor, you need to get some sleep—busy day tomorrow."

Soper thanked everybody who was still there, had a quick word with her campaign people and then said, "Freak, Josie and I would really like to get some sleep. Can you barricade the door on your way out?"

"Sure thing, Soper. Rest easy—we've got the place locked down, unless somebody tries to get at you with a Predator drone," I said.

"Jesus! Thanks for that image," Josie said.

"All kidding aside, that's not something that you should ever worry about," I said.

"Why not? Isn't it possible?" Josie said.

"Theoretically, but it's very unlikely. Commercial drones just aren't big enough to carry anything to get the job done, and if it's a military drone you'll never know what hit you," I said. "It's like fearing death—there's no good reason to be worried about dying, either."

"Doesn't everybody fear death?" Soper said.

"Sure, but I'm talking about worrying about it—there's nothing wrong with not wanting to die," I said, "but that's different than having a phobia, or obsession with it. I had a friend who was just paralyzed by his fear of death, until I told him what Epicurus said about it."

"The Greek philosopher? Didn't he subscribe to the absence of pain and the finding of pleasure as his foundational principles?" Josie said.

"In part, but this is what he said about fearing death: Why should I fear death? If I am, death is not. If death is, I am not. Why should I fear that which can only exist when I do not? If you think about it the guy was right, at least about that. Epicurus pointed out that it's illogical to fear death, which is why worrying about a missile strike from a drone is also illogical," I said.

Josie laughed and said, "A Secret Service agent who knows philosophy? Another result of your educated Jewish upbringing? Or are you a closet classicist?"

"Oh, I'm not in any closet," I said before I remembered who I was talking to. They both roared with laughter, and Soper said, "Well, I'm glad—we both kicked the motherfucking closet door down years ago."

I laughed too, and said, "Night Soper, night Josie. Sleep well—the U.S. Secret Service is guarding your crib tonight."

I shut the door and found Ed, CoD, Patsy and Darah all staring at me. "What can I say? I was a comedian in another life," I said.

"If you didn't already have a perfectly good nickname I'd call you 'Anne Sullivan'—I'd never heard her really laugh until today, and I've been on her detail for six weeks. You're a fucking miracle worker," CoD said.

"Nah, CoD, I'm just an honest womyn who won't put up with any shit, from a political superstar or the head of the New York Office, or anybody else," I said. "She just needed to know that we're 100% on her side, and our actions proved it to her. Smart people are easy to work with if you just identify what they need to trust you and supply it."

"And if you have big enough balls to tell them," Ed said, "which you do."

"Freak does clank when she walks—and that's a compliment, Freak, not a comment about your sexuality," Patsy said.

"Semper fi, Mac," I said, holding out my right fist for a bump.

"Semper fi, Mac," Patsy said, bumping me.

"OK, time for us to go beddy-bye. I'm first on the speed dial if needed, then Badass and Freak. I ain't kidding—if you don't like the way something sounds get us up and we'll come runnin'. Don't worry about pissin' me off—get me up if there's any reason at all to do so," CoD said.

"Roger that," they all said. "You owe me a Pepsi," Darah said. "Bullshit," Patsy said. "You're junior, so it should be your turn." We left them arguing, and turned in.

Just 17 or so minutes later (it was actually six hours) my alarm went off and it was time to go back at it again.

After the report of the overnight gang—no hassles of any kind—it was two non-stop hours of donors, favor seekers and other supplicants. One nice lady wanted subsidies for men age 55 to 60 who lost their jobs while the companies they worked for still made a profit; when Soper pointed out that there were already lots of programs to assist them the nice lady said, "But they don't give my husband enough to support our winter home in Boca Raton." Sheesh! I was glad that Soper was running, not me, because I'da popped that lady on the beezer for sure.

At 9:15 we entrained in town cars and headed for the nice little campus of Mount St. Joseph University, right off Neeb Road and hard by the banks of the mighty Ohio River (it's not hyperbole—that body of water is a motherfucking powerhouse in every way—what a great place for a campus). We detrained right in front of the Admin Building, where we were met by the president of the Mount (which is what everybody called the place), Sister Adele Maria Patrice, who just happened to also be the Mother-General of the Sisters of Charity of Cincinnati. She shook Soper's hand and said, "We are glad to have you here, Governor Soper, and are grateful that you consented to talk to our economics lecture with Dr. Buckner." She appeared to be sincere in her pleasure, which seemed a bit odd for the head of an order of Catholic nuns and the president of a Catholic university greeting an avowed lesbian.

Soper didn't say anything but the look she gave Sister Adele Maria Patrice must've said the same thing, because Sister Patrice, a 50-something womyn who was dressed in a sharp blue suit, said, "Oh, I don't think that you have a pair of horns and serve the devil, governor. We have LGBTQi students at the Mount, and I am sure that several of my sisters have that bent as well, but we agree with the Holy Father: you are a child of the Lord, and if He made you as you are, then who am I to quarrel with God? I personally don't think that your sexuality is any of my business, either, so don't sorry about your reception here. We are in the education business—we leave the judging to the Lord."

"I'm glad to hear that, Sister Patrice," Soper said. "Please call me Soper, or Aleta."

"Ah, you speak the truth, but are footloose," Sister Patrice said.

"You're a Greek scholar? Or an etymologist?" Soper said.

"No, just an old English teacher who loves words," Sister Patrice said.

"Not so old," Soper said.

"Well, Aleta, my mother always said 'It ain't just the years, it's the mileage,' and I think she was right," the sister said. Everyone laughed except the Secret Service personnel, because we don't laugh in public, even when it's a great line from a really classy nun.

We got to the lecture hall and it was just crammed—students were standing anywhere they weren't already sitting, and the maintenance guys were setting up chairs on the two balcony wings above the main floor. Just inside the doors Nobel Laureate Dr. Gary Buckner said, "Well, Soper, now you see the power of the god-forsaken social media culture. I told my class literally five minutes ago you were speaking this morning and they twitted it all over campus—and now we got a fucking goat-rope." He saw the university president and said, "Sorry, Sister Patrice. When you're not around I'm just a normal guy who swears like a sailor."

"And has a Nobel Prize, and who works for peanuts, and enriches our campus, and gives our students the best economics education in the entire Midwest. I don't care about your language, now or ever, Dr. Buckner. I'm honored to be in your presence, and I look forward to hearing your star pupil address our students today," Sister Patrice said. The ancient economist snorted and said,

"Thanks for the kind words, but if you think that Soper is my star pupil you're fucking crazy. She's a good egg and all, but when it comes to economics she's a loony-toon."

"Are we gonna argue about this again, Dr. B? I thought we agreed to disagree about macro-economics, especially about the role of government," Soper said.

"If people all made rational choices without having a government issued binky there wouldn't be any need for outside actors in the economy at all and we could practice true capitalism." Dr. Buckner said.

"And if everybody had the same access to goods and services—like a college education—then we wouldn't need any government binkies, because everyone who wanted to work could do so, and actually optimize their assets in a free and fair environment," Soper said.

"And if—" Dr. Buckner started to say, but Sister Patrice interrupted him by saying, "Pigs had wings they might fly out of my butt smoking little cigars, but it's highly unlikely, so could we please deal with the fact that we have a lecture hall full of students who are expecting to hear from a presidential candidate?"

Everybody laughed, except Soper's Secret Service detail, who had sudden coughing fits (OK, so we all laughed like crazed gerbils—that nun was one funny lady—but officially we coughed). After the laughter subsided Buckner said, "Well done, Sister Patrice. You managed to focus two economics PhDs on the same subject without resorting to violence or multiple appearances on a national TV show—now let's get the show on the road."

He walked up to the microphone at the podium and said, "Good morning! Now sit your asses down, turn off your infernal devices and shut the fuck up while we listen to Aleta Greenhoe Soper, PhD, the former Governor of California and current Democratic candidate for president." Buckner paused and scanned the crowd, and when it got so quiet you could've heard a mouse pissing in cotton he said, "Dr. Soper is doing us an enormous favor by conducting this forum, and she is also literally risking her life with this campaign, so I would be very displeased if someone surreptitiously recorded this time we have together. That displeasure would manifest itself in me making it my life's work to see that such a surreptitious recorder never found a job for the span of their life, or ever had a year without a visit from the IRS, where one of my students is the permanent Assistant Director. Do I make myself clear?" He spoke in an even-toned, deadly voice that reminded me of Vincent Price in a classic horror film, and when he was done several people shut off their phones, and several people nodded, and lots of people said, "You got it, Dr. B" or some variation thereof. I was impressed—the whole detail was, when we talked about it later—because this very old man clearly resonated with these college kids, who just as clearly respected him.

It's a matter of public record that no recordings of this campaign stop ever appeared in the media, or on YouTube, or anywhere else.

Buckner abdicated the podium and Soper stepped up. She scanned the crowd and said, "Good morning. I'd like to talk to you about the president's obligation to control and run the economy of the United States, after which I'd like to just talk about your questions for me. I'm not going to give you any stump speech, or try to fill your head with the usual bullshit you get from the rest of the candidates, who are all trying to not offend anyone so they can secure the nomination, and ultimately fill the Oval Office as president. I don't give a flying fig if I offend some of you—my very existence probably offends some of you—because if I can't really be honest with you then I'm wasting my time running around the country campaigning. I won't try to sell you a bill of goods and then renege on a bunch of campaign promises, because I'm only going to make you one promise: I will faithfully execute the Office of President of the United States, and will to the best of my ability, preserve, protect and defend the Constitution of the United States."

Soper looked at the expectant audience and let her words sink in. She said, "Some of you probably recognize that phrase—James Madison wrote it in 1787 at the Constitutional Convention, and it remains the oath we ask our presidents to swear or affirm upon taking office. It is also the only absolute obligation of the person who is elected to the office of President of the United States. Some of you are already going to protest—about being commander in chief, about the State of the Union address, about being able to make treaties—but the constitution doesn't say that the president has to *exercise* any of those powers except the state of the union, and she can do that by dropping Congress a note that says "Everything's OK" and she's fulfilled her constitutional obligation. No, all she has to do is faithfully exercise the office of president and preserve, protect, and defend the constitution—and that's the only thing that I promise you I will do to the best of my ability, which is considerable."

Soper looked at the now stunned crowd—no promises of a better life? Or more income? Or no new taxes? What the hell kind of campaign stop was this? She smiled and said, "I know—right now this isn't computing, because you're used to promises, and promises, and more promises of the sort most associated with Pollyanna. I told you up front, I'm not doing that campaign thing, but I am trying to be the next president of the United States. My reasons for that are simple: we always react to the crisis of the day, so we never get to anything substantive, we never plan for the long term, we never invest in our future, and we never try to tackle the really big problems, because they don't fit into a news cycle and therefore don't help us to get re-elected. We live in the richest and greatest country the world has ever seen, but we're paralyzed by the sheer volume of problems before us, kind of like a group of travelers facing the Himalayas without any maps of the passes. We're like the grizzly bear facing a pack of dogs…which one do we face first? How do we fix anything when it seems like we need to fix everything?"

She saw faces coming alive in front of her. I was focused on a guy about 15 feet up in the third row, just right of center. He had a zealot's eyes and nervous, fidgety hands that were hovering around the open flap of his backpack in a way I didn't like. I raised my hand and said into my wrist mike, "Badass, Darah, eyes on the guy with the red backpack in the third row, slightly center right, white tee shirt with 'Catholic Charities' and a cross printed on it. Report."

"On him," Badass said. "Can't see into the backpack yet."

"Has something red in there—I can just make out some color, but I don't see anything like a weapon," Darah said.

"Stay on him," I said, just as Soper said, "So what I'd really like to talk about is the president's role in the us economy. I'll bet that most of you have some thoughts about this, so I'll just give you mine and then let you ask me questions about it." She paused and the crowd leaned forward to hear her revelation.

And the nervy guy in the third row shoved his hand into his backpack, brought out some kind of projectile, cocked his arm and launched it at Soper.

Without any thought I hurled myself through the air in front of the projectile. I was standing on the stage 10 feet from Soper's right hand, so I had the perfect angle. As I traversed the short distance I identified the projectile as a red balloon, hurtling end-over-end and probably full of some liquid. I heard Badass bellowing "GUN! GUN! GUN!" as he charged up the stairs to tackle Soper, and I knew that Darah, Ed and Bumble already had her dogpiled on the ground and buried from any immediate harm.

Remember when you were a kid in high school and they had all those homecoming games? Well, even though I hated homecoming on general principle and even though the games were seriously, absolutely, undeniably lame, I was still good at two of them: the tug-o-war and the egg toss, where you and a partner tossed a (preferably cooked, usually raw) egg back and forth until it broke or you dropped it, all the while moving further and further apart. My special ed friend Karen Jorgenson and I were the absolute champs at it—we both had soft hands and could lob the egg back and forth in just the right arc so that it didn't break. We won all four years we were in high school, and it turned out those skills were valuable…and transferable.

I caught the balloon and immediately shot-put it right back at the attacker. I didn't see it hit him because I was busy doing a roll to get back to my feet, but when I popped back up he was drenched in fluorescent red paint—like the kind you find in dye-packs banks use in stolen money?—and he was right in front of me, just 10 feet away.

I launched myself at the attacker like a hungry cheetah attacking an antelope, while noting that El Gato and Sarah Konigsblett were rock steady behind the sights of their pistols as they aimed at him. My outstretched forearm hit the bright red student around the neck, and he went down like he'd been hit by a thunderbolt.

I recovered and flipped him over to slap on the cuffs. He was conscious but stunned, both physically and psychically. It was clear that he couldn't process that his perfect little plan to drench Soper in red paint—some kind of statement, but I didn't know about what yet—had gone from perfect to shit in the space of five seconds, but that's about what happened.

It might've been a full 10 seconds since he launched the balloon, but I didn't think so.

The asshole picked the wrong group to fuck around with, and he was really lucky not to be dead, because we're trained to shoot and ask questions later, but my freakish physical gifts meant that I'd taken him down before that could happen. It had all happened so fast that the students were just starting to scramble away from the guy when the paint splattered him, and most of them stopped when they saw me yank the guy to his feet, both of us dripping red paint.

One of the young wymyn said, "Hey, that's Craig Rickter, the anti-abortion guy who holds up signs at the Bengals games."

Another young womyn said, "You asshole! You coulda got us all shot!"

"And you don't even go to the Mount," another said. "What the fuck are you doin'?"

"What the fuck is wrong with you, you stupid asshole?" another young womyn said.

A big guy said, "Jesus! All we're doin' is tryin' to listen to somebody talk about bein' president. Why'd ya have to ruin it, ya shithead?"

I hauled the protestor (who was sort of recovering) out of the seats, signaling to the rest of the detail that we needed to get him out of there before we had a fucking riot, when Soper stood up and shook

CoD, Ed and Darah off her. She looked to where Bumble was getting off of Josie, saw that her wife was OK, and turned back to me. She came forward to the edge of the stage and said, "Freak, can you wait a minute?"

I stopped with the guy just below her feet, and she jumped down to look him in the eye. He tried to look back, but her eyes were ablaze with so much emotion that he quickly looked away. "Why?" was all she said.

He started to answer, and then stopped. She said, "Tell me why and I won't press any charges." He looked back at her, started to speak, and finally said, "You're a-a-a...baby killer. You love abortion!" His eyes were now whirling in his head, and he looked like a crazed killer, but Soper did the strangest thing.

She reached out and put her hand on his dripping fluorescent red shoulder and said, "Sir, you could not be more wrong." She pointed at Josie and said, "Do you see my wife up there? The beautiful womyn in the green shirt and jeans?" Her voice was soft and reasonable, and the guy's eyes lost some of their craziness. He nodded and Soper said, in a voice like a steel sword encased in the softest silk, "She's pregnant, sir, and I am ecstatic about the prospect of having a child, but if she told me today that she had decided to have an abortion I would respect her wishes, not because I love abortion, but because the only person who gets to make that decision is *her*, not me, not any other womyn here, and certainly not *you*, or any other man. I would argue against it until I was blue in the face, but in the end I would respect and defend her choice, just like I am going to respect and defend your right to the freedom of speech the Constitution gives you."

The guy's eyes had lost all of their craziness now, and he was staring at Soper like a man who just found 100 gallons of fresh water in the middle of the Sahara. "Wha-what?" he said.

"Wasn't your goal of splattering me with red paint to protest what you saw as my embracing abortion?" she said.

"Well...yeah," he said.

"Fair enough," Soper said. She stepped in and hugged him tight, smearing herself with red paint. She stepped back and said, "Take the cuffs off him, Freak. I'm not pressing charges against a citizen who is trying to exercise their 1st Amendment right to free speech." I wanted to dissuade her and started to protest, but then I caught the look in her eyes and said, "Roger that, Soper. No cuffs, no charges." I unhooked the guy and Soper stuck out her hand and said, "We even?"

The guy shook her hand and said, "Well...yeah."

"Good," she said, turning to the rest of the students who were by now gawking at her with their mouths open. "Anybody else need to throw anything, maybe a pack of Handi-Wipes, or a bucket of Mr. Clean and water?"

The students roared with laughter—hell, we all roared with laughter—and then the students started applauding, until finally there was a 15-minute standing ovation while Soper wiped some of the paint off.

I expected her campaign manager to be raring to whisk her away, but when I looked at Sean McCannell and pointed at my watch he just shook his head and mouthed "No problem" at me. Soper wiped off as well as she could, checked on Josie, who said she was OK, and then said, "Just one thing before we go on. If you want to say something personal or symbolic to me please just ask, because I'd hate to think what might happen to you if my Secret Service detail didn't exercise restraint. We OK with not getting them involved anymore?"

"The red-haired dude *is* a freak," someone said.

There was more laughter, but Soper said, "Well, first of all, that 'dude' is actually a womyn, Special Agent Glinka Glickstien, and she isn't a freak, she's *The* Freak, The Freak from Battle Creek. She's also a decorated Special Operations Command operator and a veteran of the Unites States Marine Corps, and the best pistol shot in the world. And what you just saw was normal speed for her—you really don't want to see her when she's trying to be truly fast."

Nobody laughed.

They all looked at me, and I nodded to Soper and went back to my position on her right, while Badass took up his position to the left and CoD went to stand right behind her. Soper acted like nothing had ever happened and went on to give a great talk about how to energize the economy without breaking the federal bank, and the students responded like I hadn't seen a group do since our econ class with Your Fucking Highness.

When the talk was over she asked for questions and answered every one, without exception. She patiently explained everything in language the kids could understand, and didn't duck any questions, and didn't leave until the last kid exited the auditorium almost three hours later. Even the red-paint guy, Rickter, stayed and asked questions, although we stationed Sarah Koenigsblett right behind him the whole time, just in case.

When the last kid left Dr. Buckner looked at her—still covered in red paint—and said, "I've never seen anything like it, and I've seen a lot of shit. I'm just sorry you don't have a chance to get the nomination, Aleta."

Soper smiled and said, "Thanks, Dr. B, but I've got to carry it out all the way, even though you're right—it's a lost cause."

Sister Patrice looked annoyed at their defeatist attitude. "Surely you must have at least an out-side chance? If you get your message out to a broader audience and continue to rally young people? I am also a worldly person and I was moved by your compassion, and your strength and—"

Soper, Josie, Buckner, McCannell, Lisa Silverman and Daoud Al-Hashem cut her off with ironic laughter. "Sorry, Sister, you're a good womyn and I'm sure you've been places, but in politics you're a naïf. Aleta is too far left to even be nominated."

"She just let a felon assault her and then let him go," Josie said. "She's too soft on crime."

"She's a vicious abortionist who wants to let doctors murder babies," McCannell said.

"She's a damned socialist who wants the rich to pay more taxes even though every penny they ever made was the result of their own labor," Silverman said. "She's probably a closet Jewish Red."

"And she's a sexual deviant who's probably into child molesting, or child pornography," Al-Hashem said.

"And that's just what her fellow Democrats will say about her," Josie said. "It will get worse if the Republicans get in the act."

"But…you're so rational, so composed, so on target about the issues of the day. You're a realistic person who's proposing realistic solutions to problems. Doesn't that count for anything?"

"No," they all said at once. Soper said, "I'll buy the Pepsis. Sister, conflict and fear and doom all drive the needle of politics—reason and actually solving problems is nowhere on the radar. Keep the enemy—the other party—down and promote outside fears so that the money flows. If we actually solved problems Congress could become a part-time body like it was supposed to be, and the president could retire to Sagamore House for the summer like a civilized diplomat should do. I'm afraid that's a practical impossibility, just like my getting the nomination."

"And you forgot that you're a bull-dyke queer whose very existence is perverted, and you're illegally married to another damned pervert, who you just announced is pregnant, which is an absolute abomination according to the Christian holy book," Buckner said.

"But I'm still going to carry it through, no matter what the obstacles, until I just can't afford to anymore," Soper said.

"But why?" Sister Patrice said. "Why not just throw in the towel and come at it from a different direction?"

"The little girl in Biloxi," McCannell said.

"What little girl in Biloxi?" Sister Patrice said.

"Sister, right now in Biloxi, or Atlanta, or Omaha, or Butte, or Nashville—just pick a place anywhere—there's a little girl or boy who thinks that they're dirty, or perverted, or bad, or immoral, or unworthy of love because they're LGBTQi. They think that they can't be president, or a parent, or even a "normal" member of society, whatever that is. They are so far buried in the bowels of society that every day is nothing more than a giant shit sandwich—and that's the only thing that little girl in Biloxi gets to eat, every day of her life. I'm going to keep going so that all of those kids know that no matter what kind of reception you get from the public, and no matter what kind of shit they throw up to keep you in your place, you don't have to take it. I'm going to keep running even if some nut-job kills me, because I'm not willing to sacrifice that little girl in Biloxi," Soper said. "I'm going to make sure that she knows it will get better."

I know I had a tear in my eye. So did the rest of my detail. Sister Patrice had tears running down her face, because she knew she'd just heard the most heart-felt reason for being president that she'd ever hear. The nun didn't say anything, but she walked over and wrapped Soper in a warm embrace. After a moment Sister Patrice said, "God bless you, child." She stepped back and made the sign of the cross, saying "In nomine Patris, et Filis, et Spiritu Sancti, go with God, Aleta Greenhoe Soper."

Soper inclined her head and said, "Et tu, soror mea." We all turned and went out the back to the staff parking plot. Soper said her goodbyes to Dr. Buckner; I never did get to talk to the old Nobel geezer. We got in our vehicles and whisked ourselves away. As we were leaving there were protestors setting up outside the gates to the Mount, but for once they were too late. Apparently Dr. Buckner's admonition about infernal devices had stuck, just long enough for us to escape without any incident.

We got back to the hotel and got Soper and Josie up to their suite, where they had time for a shower and a short nap, after which we got right back in the cars and headed for the University of Cincinnati, where Soper had a date with about 13,000 screamers at the Fifth Third arena on campus. CoD and Badass were already on there, and we had a battalion of help from the local PD and Ohio State Police. Also, Soper was going to be further away from the crowd, on a raised dais at the end of the arena with no one behind her, so we were in a very good position. There were also portable metal detectors and a horde of LGBTQi student organization members who were helping to have a good talk by their preferred candidate, so all in all I was only moderately worried.

The cars came and I went to collect Soper and Josie. They looked refreshed, and Soper didn't have any red paint anywhere I could see, but I couldn't help myself, so I said, "You want to stick with that blue *schmatta*? I thought maybe you'd go with a nice red pantsuit, maybe compliment it with some ruby jewelry and a pair of oxblood Jimmy Choos. I mean, you are a winter, right?"

"Oh, fuck you, Freak," Soper said. Her tone was perfect, and Josie and I got a good laugh. I said, "I'm not supposed to say this, but you wanted informal, so just let me say that I've never seen somebody do what you did today. I realize that you're probably not going to be president, but after watching you today I realize that's just politics. You've got the stones for it."

"Right back atcha—I always thought that I was the best athlete in the room, but when you're around I feel like a fifth grader. I've never seen anyone move that fast, ever, and I was in the Olympics," she said. "You're amazing, Freak."

"Thank you, Soper. It's a natural gift, although my training has certainly enhanced the gifts. I wasn't a Marine just because I was another pretty face," I said.

"You can say that again—how many people did you kill when you were in?" she said.

"Sorry, but that's classified," I said.

"It figures," she said. "I do want to ask you something. You said I have the stones to be president, but do I have the stones to be a Marine?" she said, about half teasing.

I drew myself to attention and said, "Ma'am, yes Ma'am! This Marine is certain that you would be an asset to the Corps in every way, ma'am!"

She looked touched at my sincerity. She and Josie shared a look, and then Soper said, "Thank you, Agent Glickstien. I'm going to accept that as the highest compliment I've ever gotten."

"You should, because I don't say it to just anybody," I said. We were almost to the arena, so I broke the mood by saying, "And try not to get hit with paint, or blood, or a flying Danish, willya? I gotta stand up there next to you and I've only got so many clothes—and I'm not married to a fashion model with access to an unlimited wardrobe." I smiled at them both and Josie said, "Thanks, Freak. We'll do our best to avoid being splattered."

We arrived at the back entrance to the arena—it was an old arena, so the back entrance was actually the alley and loading dock where they stored the garbage. We wound our way through the narrow corridors and got to the stage in time to meet the chancellor of the university, the president of the campus LGBTQi organization and the president of the student senate, as well as several faculty and university board members. Soper shook every hand, made small talk and would've kissed a baby if there was one available.

I stayed on her right hip, Badass stayed on her left hip and CoD led the way. The rest of us were already deployed out front, and Ed reported that she'd already seated Josie, and that the crowd appeared pretty calm, although there was a big section of boys in the left front rows on the floor that were a concern.

"They're too quiet," Ed said in my ear. "And they're staring at Josie, and it isn't lustful."

"Roger that," Bumble said. "Gato and I are gonna cruise 'em a few times and get the lay of the land."

"CoD, Seven has the stage secure across the front," Sarah Koenigsblett said.

"Five confirms secure stage," Darah Koenigsblett said. The twins didn't have names yet, so they were designated 'Five' and 'Seven' for tonight's extravaganza.

"Flipper confirms secure stage," Flipper said.

"Patsy confirms rear overwatch secure," Patsy said. He was at the back of the stage and was making sure that he could see as much of the crowd as possible. Bumble and Gato would circulate until Soper got to the podium, then take positions on either side of her at the foot of the aisles that led down the side of the arena. When she got to the stage Badass and I would flank her at about 10 feet, with CoD 10 feet directly behind her. Ohio state troopers and Cincinnati PD were tasked with positions all up and down the aisles, at the top and any place else CoD thought we needed them. I'd talked to some of the troopers, and they seemed like good law officers, even if they were younger than I thought they should be (I admit it, I was jealous of their youth. I know 34 isn't old, but it's older than 24, if you know what I mean—and if you don't know now, you soon will—time's a bitch).

Finally it was time, the chancellor introduced Soper and we went out onto the stage. She got to the podium and the group of boys to her left immediately began to boo. Several of them pulled out signs and unfurled them, and a group of girls right behind them started to chant "Im-MOR-al! Im-MOR-al! Im-MOR-al!"

Soper looked at them and smiled, which seemed to infuriate them and intensify their booing and chanting. Most of the signs were just crude putdowns of lesbians, like "Rugmunchers go home!" "It's Adam and Eve, NOT Susie and Alice!" (who the fuck were Susie and Alice? They couldn't do minimal research and find out it was Aleta and Josie?), "If you had a real man you wouldn't be a queer," and other such tripe, but the one that amused Soper was the one right in front, held up by an enormous fat boy who looked like an ambulatory bowl of green Jell-O (I hate to insult Jell-O like that, but it gives you the idea) with a complexion like the surface of the moon and enough jowls to make a hog feel envious.

It said, "Dikes suck!"

Soper looked up at the sound booth and pointed at the roof three times, telling the engineer to turn her mike up. She saw the state troopers moving to grab the signs from the protestors and said, "Officers, you can leave the signs alone. The students have a right to free speech, and I don't want to impinge on that." The engineer had the sound up really loud and her voice boomed across the arena like the voice of God.

A ragged group of cheers rang out for the freedom of speech, but the booing and chanting kept on, until Soper said, "Hey, big guy in green!" The kid was wearing a hideous lime-green shirt and fluorescent green pants with dark green stripes—it seemed to be our day for fluorescent colors. She pointed at him and the bowl of green Jell-O comically pointed at his chest and mouthed "Me?" She nodded and said, "I think the citizens of the Netherlands would disagree with you, young man."

The booing stopped, because the booers thought they were about to get their licks in—the candidate had just violated the rule of "Never engage with the rabble, because it will always turn out bad for you." The chanting also stopped, because the "Im-MOR-als" thought the same thing.

The bowl of green Jell-O said, "Sayuh whut?" sounding just like the complete idiot in a *Saturday Night Live* comedy sketch (think Bill Murray, although the younger set may want to think of Bill Hader).

"The people of the Netherlands may disagree with you," Soper said. "The Low Countries would all be flooded if it weren't for their dikes, and that was before global warming."

"Wuhl, they ain't no good Christians, then, if'n they lahk dikes," the bowl of green Jell-O said, smirking like he'd just scored a point.

"Oh, you mean *lesbians*," Soper said. "I thought you were referring to the earth and concrete dams that protect the people of Holland and Belgium from the Atlantic Ocean."

"Say-uh whut?" the bowl of green Jell-O said.

"Can I ask what your major is?" Soper said.

"Geography," the bowl of green Jell-O said. The crowd in the arena burst into laughter so loud I thought the roof would come off. The bowl of green Jell-O and the rest of his redneck pals and pal-ettes all started to laugh, until they realized that the rest of the crowd was laughing at *them*, not Soper. One of them decided to show the 'dike,' so he yelled out, "It ain't natural, what y'all do with each other! It's against the Bible!"

"So your objection to my campaign is that what my legally married wife and I do in our bedroom is against the Bible?" Soper said, her voice as reasonable as could be.

"Yuh, it shore is!" the bowl of green Jell-O said.

"Can I ask what you and your girlfriend do in the bedroom?" Soper said, so innocently that butter wouldn't melt in her mouth.

"HAAILL NO!!!" the bowl of green Jell-O bellowed, his jowly face flapping and beet red. "THAT AIN'T NONE A YORE BIDNESS!"

Soper said nothing. She simply stared at the bowl of green Jell-O and his cohort. Her face was set in neutral, but her eyes were lit up like a giant spotlight on a U.S. Navy aircraft carrier lighting up the whole flight deck (they got 'em, too—you stare into one of those and you might go blind). The crowd continued to yell and gesticulate, but Soper never wavered—she just zoomed in on the bowl of green Jell-O until he got it.

And he did. So did most of the rest of the crowd.

"It ain't the same thing," green Jell-O said.

"How is it not?" Soper said. "I have no more business in your bedroom than you do in mine. That would be like giving you fashion advice and making it the law. I might want to do it so that I can protect you from making a grievous error—like wearing two shades of green that really clash so much they make my head hurt to look at them—but that would be wrong, because what you wear is your business, not mine. It's no different than trying to legislate morality, or worse, who you can fall in love with."

A girl right behind the bowl of green Jell-O said, "But the Bible says it's wrong—it's against God's law. If y'all keep at it y'all are going to hell." The coed looked genuinely distressed, as did many of the other kids in her section.

"I understand and thank you for trying to keep me from doing that, but the Bible also says that God gives us free will to decided things for ourselves, and it says that we don't get to judge each other," Soper said. The crowd kind of roiled away from her, like she was about to burst into flame, and she said, "Matthew 7:1 says "Judge not, lest ye in your turn be judged also," does it not?"

"Well, ya-yuh," green Jell-O said, "but the Bible also says it's an abomination for a man to lay with a man. It's purty clare that homosexuality is a *sin*. God don't lahk *sin*, and neither do we."

"I'm not asking you to like sin, I'm asking you to respect my privacy, my perfectly legal love for my wife and the words of Jesus, who said that anybody who believes in Him shall have eternal life," Soper said. "You will note that the Lord said 'whosoever believeth in me,' not 'whosoever is straight and believeth in me' when He outlined the path to eternal life."

"But the Bible does say homosexuality is a sin," another coed said. "You can't deny it."

"I can and I do," Soper said. "And before you decide to tune me out, please remember that Jesus is the Redeemer, who washed away all that came before with His blood. He re-wrote all the old Jewish rules in the Bible and it says so plainly in John 3:16, and Jesus himself said so to Martha in John 11:25 and 26—"Jesus said unto her, I am the resurrection, and the life: he that believeth in me, though he were dead, yet shall he live: And whosoever liveth and believeth in me shall never die. Believest thou this?" And she did, and went to tell her sister Mary about it." She looked up and even the bowl of green Jell-O was nodding at her.

"The Lord didn't say anything about being straight, or gay, or color, or *anything else*. He said 'whosoever'—meaning *anyone*—and I take the Lord at his word. My wife and I are Presbyterians, and we believe fervently in the Lord Jesus Christ as our Savior, even if we don't bruit it about all the time—we both believe that our faith is also our business—but I will also tell you that if I'm elected president I will fight, and die if necessary, in order to protect your right to worship any way you want, or not worship, for that matter, because as president I will swear to protect, preserve and defend the Constitution…and freedom of religion is part of that defense. So is free speech." Soper looked out at the now mostly quiet crowd and said, "And that's all I'm asking you for—a chance to exercise my right to free speech. It may require us to agree to disagree"—she looked at the bowl of green Jell-O and gave him a nod, which he returned—"but at least then we could have a conversation of ideas, not just scream our opinions at each other. Can we agree to do that?"

The bowl of green Jell-O nodded, but he said, "It stahl sez it's abomination, whut y'all do, even though Ah guess it ain't really none o' mah bidness."

"Yes, sir, it certainly says that in Leviticus 17:22, but it also says in Leviticus 19:28 that "Ye shall not make any cuttings in your flesh for the dead, nor print any marks upon you: I am the Lord"—and yet I clearly see a tattoo on your forearm. I am also sure that those clothes you're wearing are of two different threads, that many of us have worked on the Sabbath and that no one here thinks that a rebellious child should be stoned to death, but that's exactly what Deuteronomy 21:18-21 says. Rather than go through the whole Bible, can't we just move on to the purpose of this gathering—to talk about the state of our nation, and what we can do about it?" Soper looked at the bowl of green Jell-O, and he nodded at her, so she said, "Good. Anybody who wants to scold or heckle me about my sexuality please come to the "Boo and Chastise Soper" mixer in the Student Union right after the speech, wouldya?"

There was some laughter, and then Soper outlined her credentials. She briefly described her undergrad degree at the University of Minnesota, masters at Penn, and PhD at the University of

Chicago. She told them about her Olympic medals. She spent more time talking about her three terms as governor of California, which led her to the things she really wanted to talk about.

Soper laid out all of her economic proposals one by one, connecting them into a seamless blueprint for raising economic prosperity for everybody. She was especially popular when she said that all college should be affordable, that the minimum wage should be $15 an hour and that pay for the same job should be exactly the same for both genders.

She also explained the virtuous cycle for economics and why it would work, which also drew large cheers…and then we were done. She thanked the audience and then the strangest thing of the night happened.

Soper got a standing ovation.

Even the bowl of green Jell-O and his henchmen stood up and cheered. The kids and other spectators weren't agreeing with her sexuality, they were acknowledging her courage and her message. I was impressed—twice in the same day she'd turned open hostility into at least grudging respect with logic, passion and honesty. It just proved how smart and committed she was, but it also made it clear that Soper would never be president. There was no way the big-money donors would ever get on board with her agenda—the reform of the tax code alone would disqualify her in their eyes—and without the money she couldn't keep spreading the word.

Fucking Supreme Court and *Citizens United*.

But it wasn't my job to be political, it was my job to guard her, so I forgot the politics and concentrated on getting her to the bus so we could head down the road to Morehead State University in Morehead, Kentucky, where I was sure that our job wouldn't get any easier.

We were heading out at night to stay away from traffic and because Soper had a big donor breakfast the next morning at nine, so rather than get up at the crack of dawn and try to fly down the highway we were going to take it easy and roll tonight.

We went out the back loading dock and there was the giant land cruiser, with Soper's picture and her slogan—"Making All Americans Prosperous is the Mission"—painted on the side. Ed, Badass, Bumble, Patsy, CoD and I would be riding in it, while the rest of the detail would be in the chase and trail cars.

I was surprised and somewhat dismayed to see the bowl of green Jell-O and some of his friends standing around the rope line near the bus. I moved over to Soper's left and right next to her side so that Badass, Bumble and I formed a solid wall between her and the guys, but she said, "I'm going over and talk to those guys for a minute." She veered left and I lifted my wrist mike and said, "Everybody up now. Soper's on the rope line and the green Jell-O gang is there. Within seconds there were 10 Secret Service agents around her, but Soper went right up to the bowl of green Jell-O and said, "What's your name, sir?"

Bowl of green Jell-O's mouth fell open, but he said, "Elvin Clyde Bliss, ma'am."

"Mr. Bliss, I'd like to talk to you some more, but I've got to get to Morehead State—you got time for a three-hour road trip on my bus?" Soper looked at him hesitate and she said, "I'm not looking for you to make an endorsement—you can call me a flaming asshole bull-dyke after we talk if you want—but I do want to talk with you about some things. Can you pick three other guys to come along, and four girls, including that one in the red shirt?"

Elvin Clyde Bliss looked at his friends, some of whom were nodding, and said, "Yes, ma'am. But why us? We don't even like you."

"That's exactly why," Soper said. "When you run for president everyone around you tries to tell you what you want to hear, and I want to hear everything, so I need someone to tell me what I *don't* want to hear—and that's your focus group."

"EC, I'll do it," a tall, skinny kid with curly hair said. "Me, too," said another kid. There were several more who expressed an interest, so Elvin Clyde Bliss said, "Well, it looks like we got enough guys—Steve, can you ask the wymyn?" The tall guy with curly hair nodded, took out his cell and fired off a text. Within a few seconds multiple phones were chirping, chiming and clanking, apparently with affirmative answers, because just a minute later Elvin Clyde Bliss said, "Ma'am, we'll go along, but one a the girls wants to know how we're gettin' home."

"I'll turn the bus around and take you right to your door. My wife and I are flying to Sa—"

I cut her off and said, "Sorry, Soper, but these guys don't need to know where you're going." I looked at the guys and said, "You men understand why I'm not going to let her tell you where she's going, right?" I knew we were making a flying trip to San Francisco for a fundraiser, but I didn't want the entire world to know it.

Bowl of green Jell-O—Elvin Clyde Bliss—only appeared stupid, because right away he said, "We don't want to know, because we're not the ones who sent the death threats. If we don't know we can't give anything away to whoever wants to hurt the governor. I mean, we don't want to hurt her, we want to *save* her. So we'd prefer it if you didn't tell us anything." (I've stopped trying to accurately depict Elvin Clyde's accent—sorry I'm not Mark Twain.)

"Good, 'cause we're not going to. I'd like it if you guys all turned your cell phones off, too, just as an added security measure," I said.

Elvin Clyde Bliss proved his worth to me then, because he just switched off his phone and handed it to me without another word. So did tall Steve, a short kid with blonde hair and a guy with no neck who had to be a wrestler or football player. "Y'all don't be tweetin' or textin' 'bout this until we get back on the bus and the governor is outta here, OK?" Elvin Clyde Bliss said. There were nods, and 'you bets' and 'Sure thing, ECs' from the crowd, and as far as I know they lived up to their end of the bargain.

I put Soper and Josie on the bus, the guys piled on and the girls came, turned over their cell phones and also got in. We buttoned it up and headed down I-75 south toward Lexington, where we would catch I-64 east to Morehead State.

There were reporters on the bus, but Soper only gave them about 10 minutes before she grabbed the kids from Cincinnati and took them back to her private quarters at the rear of the bus. I went with them and listened to their very interesting conversation all the way to Morehead (it turned out the U-C students were actually pretty fucking smart; they just sounded stupid when they were trying to stay true to their parent's religious beliefs), where we pulled into the Holiday Inn and Soper got them all rooms, so they could continue talking after she got done with the donors the next morning.

We all went to bed, got up the next morning and watched a procession of people parade through Soper's suite trying to buy influence, and watching her resist giving them any promises beyond defending the Constitution. She wouldn't commit to their pet interests, and most of them wouldn't pledge any monetary support without it. I'm not really a political animal, but it looked like she was just trying to see if her ideas would fly at all, not really looking for big money, which even I knew wouldn't sustain her campaign.

When the donors left she ordered lunch brought up to the suite and continued her conversation with the eight U-C students. I was amazed at her energy, as well as her easy way with the students and the enormity of her knowledge about all things economic, but I also found myself liking the womyn and agreeing with many of her ideas. It was her sheer intelligence on how the economy could function if properly incentivized that really won me over.

Her talk at Morehead State was scheduled for 7 p.m., so about 4:30 she shooed everybody out and went to take a nap. I took one too, as did the rest of the detail except Patsy, Sarah and Flipper, who'd all had a nap earlier so the rest of us could stand down.

I woke up five minutes before I needed to, rinsed my mouth out, brushed my teeth and gargled with Listerine (I like the green kind, although the blue kind was OK, too) and went up to the suite.

Flipper met me down the hall and said, "We got a small problem. Somebody got Josie's cell number and left her a nasty message while they were napping. She seems OK, but Soper is on the warpath." I nodded at Patsy and Sarah. "She's at Force Five," Patsy said. "Concur," Sarah said. "Looks kinda like Hurricane Sandy in there right now."

"Roger that—I'll go in and see if I can calm her ass down," I said. I knocked and then went in. Soper was on the phone, talking in a very loud voice to the FBI director (I guessed), since she said, "Mr. Holland, I want to make this very clear—the Secret Service is performing admirably and with great skill, but *you* are responsible for our communications being secure." Michael Holland, the FBI Director and rumored Republican vice-presidential candidate, must've said something, because Soper said, "I've already talked to the NSA Director, and she assures me that they are capable of doing security, but that you would have to relinquish your power in writing."

Holland must have replied that he wasn't going to do that, or something on that order, because Soper snapped, "Then do your fucking job and make sure we aren't harassed!"

She snapped her phone shut and said, "You heard?" I nodded as CoD entered the room and said, "Sitrep?"

I nodded at Soper, who said, "Some asshole got Josie's number and left her a filthy message while we were napping. I listened to it, too, but neither of us recognized the voice. It was disgusting." She shook her head and looked like she had a bad taste in her mouth.

"Can you play it on speaker for us?" CoD said. "You don't have to listen to it again, but we need to hear it."

I'm not going to replay the entire disgusting message left by some sick asshole with a tiny dick and mommy issues, but there were two parts that got our attention. In the first part the guy—unless they were using a really sophisticated voice synthesizer it was a guy—said, "And we're gonna make you watch while we cut your girlfriend's tits off and fuck her to death right in front of you. Then we're gonna cut her head off and send it to her parents in Aberdeen. We're also gonna send them the tape of us raping you to death with a red-hot poker up your ass—and we're gonna hack your pussy out and send that to your parents in Minneapolis, ya damned rug-muncher."

That was a fairly specific description of how these peckerheads intended to murder our protectee and her wife, which meant we had to take them seriously, but the second thing that caught our attention was even more alarming, because they guy said, "And we'll be waiting when you get off the plane at Gate 17 in the homo capital of the world, you dyke bitch queer."

That information was way too specific for a random guess. Somehow the guy—guys?—had specific information that was supposed to be very closely held. We had to be proactive about that, and we had to do some changing of arrivals, because no way were we going to assume that these guys were anything but serious.

But right now I needed to reason with Hurricane Soper, and the only way I knew to do that was to be brutally honest. I could feel Soper's eyes on me, burning through my jacket like the white-hot fire of a thousand suns. I turned to her and Josie and said, "Those motherfuckers have the worst problem with redundancy. I mean, 'dyke bitch queer'—isn't that redundant and a mixed message? I'm not gay, but I can certainly be a bitch, like I will be when we catch these guys and I fuck them up so bad that their mothers won't recognize them."

Soper just stood there and stared at me, but Josie smiled, and then started to laugh. CoD and I joined her and finally Soper's anger just dissolved, and she laughed, too. "I just get so damned mad at those cowards!" she said. "Threatening my wife? Isn't that supposed to be out of bounds?"

"Of course it is," CoD said. "When you love someone you think more about them than you do yourself, so it hurts worse. It'd be like somebody threatening my kids—I'd wanna rip off their balls and make 'em eat the shriveled little raisins, but all you can do is just move on from it, and know that there is very little chance they can succeed. Cowards love to brag about shit like this, but I'd like to see 'em take on 10 Secret Service agents and the horde of local cops we're going to be surrounded with."

"I agree with CoD. These chickenshits aren't going to try anything, even though it scares the hell out of you and pisses you off to the point you wanna nuke 'em," I said.

"I like the imagery of ripping their balls off," Soper said, smiling just a bit.

"Only one problem with that, sister," CoD said.

"What's that?" Soper said.

"Oh, I don't think that you could find these guy's balls with an electron microscope," CoD said. More laughter ensued, until CoD said, "I'm gonna go do some shit to change our itinerary—I'm not even telling you guys—and then we'll have to get going for the venue. You OK?" She looked at Soper and Josie, and Josie said, "Andria, we're just fine. You and the rest of the detail make us feel safe, even when someone manages to break through the electronic barrier and gives us pause. Thank you."

"Aw, shucks, ma'am, Ah'm jist doin' mah job," CoD said in a weird accent.

"Was that supposed to John Wayne?" I said.

"Yeah," CoD said. "Whaddya think?"

"Don't give up your day job," Soper and I said together. "I owe ya a Pepsi, Soper," I said.

"Good—my throat feels like the Atacama Desert," Soper said.

"I'm not surprised, yelling at the FBI Director like that. Poor thing probably hasn't recovered yet. He is very sensitive to criticism," CoD said.

"Well then I'll fire him when I'm president, because the FBI directorship shouldn't be held by someone who can't stand the heat in the kitchen," Soper said, smiling (but meaning it, I think).

"Just don't tell him I said so," CoD said. "He's also a vindictive son of a bitch."

"Our secret," Soper said. "We're OK, Andria. Go do your thing and then we'll go to the arena."

CoD nodded and left the suite. Soper looked at me and said, "Nice misdirection, Agent Glickstien—were you a magician before you came to the Service?"

"Nope, I was just the best special operator that SOCOM had ever seen, plus I had a few of the same experiences," I said.

We were interrupted by a waiter from the hotel restaurant with a tray full of Pepsis and big glasses of ice. We gladly poured them, stashed the leftovers in the suite fridge and sat down.

"You were going to tell us about some of your experiences," Soper said. So I told her and Josie about The Battle of the Shower Room, and the story of the Great Wisconsin Tit Rip-Off, and several other funny and interesting anecdotes about my life of being harassed for being different. I also told them about being a straight womyn who everybody assumed was gay because of what she did.

"But that's idiotic—it only takes about five minutes with you to see that you are completely heterosexual," Josie said. "I don't even sense any ambivalence in you, and I would if it were there."

"Yeah, I imagine being that beautiful does give you access to some lustful feelings in both men and wymyn, whether they're on the fence or not," I said.

"It does, although I've never understood why anyone would be on the fence. Sex is just a physical release, and who you release with would seem to depend on who you associate with—gender seems irrelevant. Bisexuality seems to me to be the only prudent course, since sex is just one small part of love. I can't imagine being without Aleta simply because we happen to be the same gender. Not being able to consummate our relationship physically might poison all of the other aspects of the relationship, and that seems silly," Josie said.

Soper nodded and said, "I've always been bisexual, simply because that seemed the most logical course when it came to sex. I've been attracted to men, and had physical relationships with them—and enjoyed it—but then I met Josie, and…well, uh—" She trailed off, her face reddening.

"She got bowled over by love and the power of our attraction," Josie said. "It was like the opposite poles of two incredibly powerful electromagnets—it was irresistible, although Aleta tried to deny it at first."

"You're kidding," I said. "I've never seen two people more in love than you two, if you'll excuse my forwardness. How could you deny that?"

"Well, look at her! How could somebody who looks like that be in love with a womyn who looks like me?" Soper said.

"Oh, fuck you, Soper," Josie and I said. "My Pepsis, Freak," Josie said.

"Done, and thanks for letting me in on your story. As for how she can be in love with you, Soper, what's not to love? Smart, funny, passionate, athletic, accomplished, good-looking—no, don't protest, because *nobody* is as good-looking as Josie—hello, *Sports Illustrated* cover model?—but you're still good-looking by any objective standard. Now if she'd fallen in love with somebody who looks like me you'd have an argument, but that's not the case," I said.

"You're very attractive, Freak," Josie said.

"Your athleticism alone would make you attractive," Soper said.

"Yeah, to Bulgarian shot-putters who are more chemistry experiments than people," I said. I held up my hands before they could protest and said, "You're damned right I'm attractive, but I'm talking about overt physical attractiveness, and we all know that I don't have that. I've got other gifts, but being physically beautiful isn't one of them. What I mean is this: I think that you could've looked like one of those Bulgarian shot-putters and Josie would've still been attracted to you. The fact that you're physically beautiful is just a bonus. The way she looks at you…it doesn't have a damn thing to do with the package, because Josie sees the real you, the one that few people will ever see. She loves the present inside, Soper, not the pretty package. And that…well, that is damned rare. Cherish it, willya?"

The both nodded at me and I nodded back just as there was a knock on the door. I moved over to flank the door and CoD came in looking at her watch. "We're about 15 minutes from departure, Soper, and Flipper just let me know that the venue is about full up. I've already sent most of the detail over there, because the local sheriff loaned us his SWAT team as our outriders."

Soper said, "Good. We'll be ready in 10." She and Josie went into the bedroom and CoD said, "Freak, I'm going to try and get you the Nobel Prize for Protective Services—she's like a different person. Whatever you did, it's working. If you could bottle that shit we'd be able to retire."

"But we wouldn't, CoD, because this is what we're good at," I said.

"Bet your ass," CoD said.

They came out and we left, got to the arena at Morehead State University and faced an almost identical situation as the one the night before. This time the protestors were more vocal and rowdier, right up until Elvin Clyde Bliss stood up at one of the microphones the university had set up to ask questions and said, "Y'all need to be quiet and let her talk."

We had no idea at the time that his well-meaning quelling of the crowd would lead to bloodshed and death, but it did.

CHAPTER 43

Collisions

The arena at Morehead State was a madhouse, filled with screamed profanity, hundreds of signs protesting both sides and passive cops who really weren't helping things any. We were all apprehensive because it appeared that this would be a much tougher crowd to try and corral if something happened, until Elvin Clyde Bishop stepped up to one of the microphones the university had set up for questions.

"Y'all need to be quiet and let her talk," he said.

The crowd seemed taken aback that someone speaking their language—"Kaintuckian"—would say such a thing. He looked out at the mass of hostility and said, "Ah'm frum Flo'rence, Kaintuckee, and Ah thought I'd hate her, too, but Ah don't. Don't rightly agree with everythin' she says, neither, but Ah still think she's got a raht to speak, so y'all be quiet now and listen. Y'all kin call her anythin' yuh want after she's done, y'hear?"

The crowd went still.

It was absolutely amazing.

Soper got up and said, "We're not supposed to be able to talk because we come from such different cultures. That's what this is—a clash of cultures, a collision between your born-again culture and my secular one, a collision between your adherence to the Bible and my adherence to the Constitution, a collision between your desire for a perfect world and my desire to protect the imperfect world we already have."

They were all listening now, because she sounded so reasonable. Soper looked around at all the shining your faces and said, "But we all inhabit the same world, and cultures can talk to each other, if they'll just do two things: acknowledge that the other side has a point, whether we agree with it or not, and actually listen when the other side talks. If we can do that what happens is that we begin to identify all of the things that we have in common, instead of just tending to our grievances with each other…"

When the event was over three hours later Soper got her third straight standing ovation. She stood under the lights after answering 50 questions and said, "Remember, not all collisions lead to wrecked cars, as long as we acknowledge the worth of all people and listen when people talk. In that case we may disagree, but at least we'll know why. Thank you, Morehead State University, and go Eagles!"

There was more cheering, and congratulations from the university chancellor and president, lots of student leaders who wanted to talk some more and all sorts of other hullaballoo, so it was 11:45 before we all got on the bus to get the hell out of there. We were going to the airport, where Soper, CoD, Badass, Bumble, Darah Koenigsblett and I were going to jump on a plane for San Francisco, where Soper was going to a fundraiser, while the bus was going back to Cincinnati to drop the U-C kids off before it looped back west so we could catch it in Louisville, and then head north for an Ohio-Indiana-Michigan swing.

It was happy on the bus, and Soper stood to publicly acknowledge Elvin Clyde Bliss for "his invaluable assistance with the crowd." She was going on, but just then my phone rang, so I stepped to the back of the bus and ducked in the "living quarters" to take the call.

"Glickstien," I said.

"It's your uncle Paulie," a voice said. "From the castle in Illinois."

"What the hell?" I said. "What are you doing calling at midnight, Uncle Paulie?"

Paul Monteverdi seemed to be stuttering as the cell signal fluttered, so what I heard was "…just got some info you need to…possibility that law enforcement could be in on…source says it's goin' to happen soon, but…don't know…somethin' about narrow streets…got to look out, 'cause these are serious… Mr. B said to warn you, 'cause of he don't know these…but he knows they're really bad guys…they got to some two-bit cop…gotta be careful…"

It was right then that I realized we were making one more turn through narrow, twisty streets in Morehead, Kentucky—and I didn't know why. I still had my phone in my hand, and I could hear Paul Monteverdi trying to tell me something as I stepped out of the back of the bus. I saw that Soper was standing in the aisle talking to Elvin Clyde Bliss, still wearing his green Jell-O clothes. She looked up, saw the look on my face and was asking me a question as I went forward to talk to the driver about our route to the airport when I saw a huge dark shape hurtle out between two buildings on our left.

It slammed into the side of the bus like the meteor that killed the dinosaurs, knocking everything and everybody ass over tea cart, and then everything went dark for a while.

CHAPTER 44

The Battle of Morehead

I wasn't out more than 10 seconds, because when I came to the giant cement truck that hit us was still trying to grind its way through the bus. I got up from the floor—my body seemed to be working—and looked out the side window. All the glass was smashed out, so I got a clear view of the driver of the truck as he jammed the truck into a lower gear and gunned the throttle.

My 1076 leapt into my hand and I shot him in the head. The truck immediately throttled back and stopped trying to gnaw its way through the side of the bus. I put my pistol away and bounded down the aisle looking for Soper.

I found her plastered into the two seats opposite where she'd been standing when we were hit. She'd slammed into the two people sitting there—I couldn't tell who they were—which had saved her life, because otherwise she'd've slammed into the metal skin of the bus, which clearly would've left her dead, since the person in the seat closest to the side of the bus was pretty much splattered all over it. Then I realized there were three people there, and that the splattered one was CoD. Andria must've seen the truck and wrapped her arms around Soper to cushion her before everybody in the bus was churned around like they were in a washing machine.

I noticed that lots of people were unconscious but alive, but then I heard something that chilled my blood.

It was another heavy engine revving up and coming closer.

Shit.

We were about to be under attack again. I didn't know where the chase cars were and I didn't see any other agents upright until Patsy's head popped up from the front of the bus. He looked OK, but when he said something it sounded like gibberish. "Repeat your last, Patsy!" I said.

"T'ere's a theckond twuck," he said.

"OK. Get the front door open and I'll bring Soper. We gotta get out of this goddamned bus coffin," I said.

"Wog'er dat," he said.

I didn't want to move her, but I couldn't leave Soper in the bus to get hit by another heavy truck. I gently picked her up and carried her in my arms to the door.

Which was stuck.

Patsy was trying everything to open it, but his left arm was just hanging there, and his left foot looked fucked up, but he was still throwing everything he had into the door. I laid Soper across the front seat, reached out and moved Patsy out of the way and kicked the door wide open. I stepped down out of the bus and ripped both doors right off their hinges, then went back up and got Soper. I looked at my brave friend and said, "Come, Patsy," which made him gurgle with laughter (ya gotta watch *Monty Python and the Holy Grail*) and spurt blood out of his mouth at the same time. He followed me out of the bus and we could hear the second truck coming closer. We moved away from the bus with Patsy in the lead, his pistol in his hand that still worked, and me carrying Soper.

I didn't know who was about, or where to even try to escape with my protectee when I heard the best sound I'd ever heard.

"FREAK! PATSY! CoD! Where the fuck are ya?" It was El Gato, coming down the street toward us. I bellowed "Gato! The front of the bus!" He came running with Bumble and Ed, and I began to breathe again. I said, "You guys get Patsy and Soper outta here—go to the nearest hospital and don't let anyone near Soper, not even any cops except our own or U.S. Marshals. Call home and tell 'em we were attacked. I'm gonna try to get some people out before the next truck gets here." We could hear it growling, but with the maze of streets and the low buildings reflecting the sound it was hard to tell exactly where the other truck was.

Gato, Ed and Bumble never even blinked. Bumble picked up Soper, Gato took the lead and Ed trailed. They went down the street as fast as they could, but Patsy didn't move.

"Get the fuck outta here, NOW!" I said.

"Thuck woo, Fweak," he said. "I'm a dod-damned U Eth Mawine! We don' weave any'n behin'!"

"Well, semper fucking fi," I said. "We gotta get people outta the bus in case we can't stop that truck. We aren't gonna get any more help, and I can outshoot you, so you're gonna have to start getting people moving, OK?"

Patsy said, "Woger dat, Fweak!" He headed for the bus just as a giant cement truck turned the corner about five blocks away.

"Hurry!" I said, turning to square up on the truck. I pulled up my 1076 and calmly put 9 rounds into the engine of the truck, which seemed to have no effect at all. I smoothly drew my other 1076 and prepared to park a magazine in the cab when Darah Koneigsblett appeared at my side with her pistol in her hand. She was bleeding from a major scalp wound and from her nose, but she smiled at me like the Buddha and said, "Shall we shoot, Freak?"

"Indeed," I said. "Fill the cab with lead, friend." We both let off full mags, and I smoothly refilled my 1076s with new mags and the truck was just two blocks from us when all hell broke loose.

Patsy and Badass opened up on my left, Darah let fly from my right and somebody opened up with a fully automatic weapon from the rear of the bus. I pulled up both pistols and let off all 18 rounds in just under two seconds. Every one of them hit, shredding the engine block of the cement truck, which promptly gave a gigantic "CLANK!" and stopped running. The truck wandered off the road, running into a store front about three-quarters of the way down the last block before it would've rammed the bus. The first truck was still running, but then the engine abruptly cut off and it was quiet.

I said, "Who the fuck was firing an automatic weapon? Sound off motherfucker, 'cause I've reloaded and I will shoot you." A voice came from the front of the bus. "I'm Curtis Jeffries, Deputy Sheriff of Rowan County, Kentucky. I don't know what the hell is going on, but I seem to be the only deputy that made it here, which seems pretty fucked up, since people been callin' 9-1-1 about the bus for at least 10 minutes. I'm comin' 'round the bus with my hands in the air, agent."

He came around the bus, a slender man who moved like a dancer and was wearing a Rowan County sheriff's uniform. He had a weapon on a sling that was riding muzzle down on his back, and both his hands were way up in the air. He was a good-looking man with a nice mustache, good hair and one eyebrow cocked in a quizzical look. When the eyebrow didn't de-cock I realized it must be a permanent feature. Jeffries saw me looking at it and said, "I fell out a hay loft when I was a kid and had a closed-head injury. My face kinda froze in this position, but it didn't affect anything else, unless you talk to my wife," he said. "Then it affected *everything*."

OK, so he was funny, too, but I had bigger problems to wrestle with, so I held up a finger and said, "Badass, you operational?"

The big man said, "I'm good to go, but Darah's got a concussion like you wouldn't believe, and her head is still bleeding. We need to get some docs here, because Patsy's even more fucked up than usual. His ankle's gonna need surgery and his arm is broken." I looked at him, hunched over but still standing and said, "You three sit your asses down and keep your weapons at the ready. I still don't know where Sarah and Flipper are, and according to Deputy Jeffries there is something about the response of local law enforcement that is fucked up, so let's defend ourselves until reinforcements we can count on arrive. I'm gonna assess the people on the bus, and Deputy Jeffries here is gonna give us some perimeter security, aren't you, Deputy?"

"Yes ma'am, and call me Curtis, or Curt. Who should I let through?" he said.

"U.S. Marshals or Secret Service personnel, but nobody else until I figure out what the fuck is going on," I said. "And call me Freak, OK?" He nodded and went to stand at the corner of the bus where he could see up the two streets that formed the crossroads we were at. I went to the bus doors and started in when we all heard car tires screeching to a halt.

"Got a car here with two ladies in it," Curtis said. "One's blonde and the other one looks like she's an Arab. Both of 'em look right pissed off, too." Before I could get around the bus I heard Sarah say, "U.S. Secret Service, asshole! Get your hands off that weapon or I'm gonna blow big ugly holes in your country shitkicker ass!"

Flipper said, "Agent Tara Kywfterelian, U.S. Secret Service! Drop the weapon or we will shoot you!"

"Sarah! Flipper! He's with us! Come to the front of the bus!" I said. Within seconds they were there, eager, excited and, best of all, uninjured. Sarah looked at Darah sitting propped up against the front tire of the bus and said, "Freak, this was part of a plan. We were deliberately turned so we couldn't follow you—I'll bet the bus is off track, too."

"We'll sort that out later," I said. "Right now you two and Deputy Jeffries are on perimeter security—we want either Secret Service agents or U.S. Marshals—no locals."

Badass said, "Flipper, help Freak." Before I could protest he said, "She's a rescue swimmer—you need her for triage and first aid. I can help with security while Patsy keeps Darah from bleeding to death and you guys eval and evac. No argument." He made perfect sense, so I nodded and went into the bus with Flipper behind me.

By now it'd been 20 minutes since we were attacked, and even the country shitkickers of the Morehead PD, or the Rowan County sheriff's department should've been able to get to the scene. There was the distinct smell of shit pouring down on our heads—this stunk so bad that I was sure we were all going to die. The sheriff and city PD had to be in cahoots with whoever planned this, because there was no other way for them to be able to hit us at exactly the right spot and exactly the right time. They also had a backup truck, which meant that there was a plan A, and plan B…"Oh fuck me blind!" I said. Flipper said, "Freak? What's going on?"

"If you carefully planned for an op and had a backup plan might you have another backup, just in case there was a need for plan C?" I said.

Flipper paled and said, "We need to set up a perimeter and get ready, because somebody else is coming."

"Bet your ass they are," I said. I bolted off the bus and said, "Everybody here at the front of the bus, now!" We all gathered and I said, "Curtis, what's the usual response time to get EMT personnel on scene here in Morehead?"

"I been worryin' about that, Freak. Our response times are really good—seven or eight minutes max, and we're goin' on 25 minutes, and I heard the 9-1-1 calls. Somethin' is up, and the sheriff is involved, else we'd have every EMT within 20 miles here already, plus a bunch of deputies and city cops."

"OK, whoever this is, they're going to hit us again, and soon. We need to get ourselves in position to stop them, even though we got Soper out of here. We need to safeguard these people, and we need to get to Soper, because three agents may not be enough to protect her against people who have three plans to hit her and have the cooperation of local law enforcement," I said.

"I got an idea about some reinforcements," Curtis said. He whipped out his cell phone and hit a speed-dial number. Somebody answered and the deputy said, "Lonnie, it's uncle Curtis. Is your squad around? Y'all got duty tomorrow? Good. Can you put them uniforms on and start your duty a bit early? Now. The corner of North Wilson and West Second. Y'all got any firearms? Well, bring everything you've got, and bring all your ammo, too. Good. Shake your ass, Lonnie, 'cause I really need ya here yesterday."

He looked up and said, "We'll have eight more soldiers in about five minutes—my nephew is the commander of the guard for the ROTC detail at MSU tomorrow. Them boys aren't very good at anything yet, but they're eager, they're armed and they're on our side for sure."

"We're gonna need 'em," Badass said. "Hear that?"

We did. It sounded like a swarm of angry bees, and it was headed our way.

"What the fuck is that?" Sarah said. It was getting closer, and we could hear what sounded like growling, or a group chanting, or a sloth of bears having a "let's eat some Secret Service agents" convention.

"There's only one thing that would make Sheriff DuPuis be derelict in his duty, and that's the Klan," Curtis said. "If I had to bet I'd say that was the Klan marching on our position."

Sarah laughed and said, "Oh come on. A bunch of guys in bed sheets? I think that's mostly legendary, isn't it?"

Curtis shook his head and said, "Y'all are from up north or you'd know—the Klan ain't legendary, and them bed sheets are holy robes to a Klansman, and they usually have a shotgun or rifle in 'em, too. This ain't no laughin' matter, agent. Our asses are in hot water, and it's about to be boilin'. Them Klansmen ain't fond of no federals, and they really hate lesbians and such. They'll kill us all if they get the chance, and the sheriff won't be able to find a single witness against 'em, if he even looks.

Sheriffs are elected here in Kentucky, and old DuPuis knows he can't win with the Klan against him." Curtis looked grim, but determined.

"Why aren't you out there instead of here?" I asked. He looked at me and said, "I ain't no Klansman—my family is Jewish, from the Jeffries family in Savannah, Georgia. Besides, I swore an oath to uphold the law, and the Klan ain't no part of that. I also don't like people tryin' to kill somebody in my town just because of who they love. That just ain't right, and I won't have any part of it."

"I'm glad to hear it," I said. "Now here's what we're gonna do to those bed-sheet bastards when they get here." I told them my plan, everybody agreed it was the best we could do, so we went ahead and executed it.

The ROTC boys arrived just as we were getting the last pieces into place. They were young, eager and armed, and we were about to face what sounded like 2000 angry and armed Ku Klux Klansmen, so I welcomed them in.

The first boy out of the first truck looked so much like Jeffries that I figured he must be the nephew, so I walked right up to him and said, "What's your rank, Mr. Jeffries?" He was startled, but his military discipline kicked in and he said, "Captain of Cadets, ma'am!" I smiled and said, "Captain, I'm Major Glinka L. Glickstien, formerly USMC and U.S. Special Operations Command, now the Secret Service agent tasked with defending this place. I need you and your men to follow my orders to the letter, and I need your assurance that you'll shoot to kill."

His eyes got round, not with fear but with surprise, but his voice was calm when he said, "Ma'am, my squad and I are at your disposal. I give you my word as an officer that we will follow whatever ROE you designate, ma'am."

"Four-oh, Captain," I said. I gave him his orders and set his men (I'm not calling men who were willing to go into combat boys, even if half of them didn't shave yet) into their firing positions. "Remember, ROE is weapons free, Captain. We need those Klukkers down and out, not down and still fighting," I said.

"Roger that, ma'am," Captain Lonnie Jefferies, USROTC said.

I turned to survey our defenses just as the lead part of the Klan turned down the street and headed for the bus. We'd blocked the side streets and the street behind us, but they could still probably get around our roadblocks, so I had Badass and one ROTC guy guarding our backs, with Patsy and Darah inside the bus keeping the people in there, most of whom were waking up and hurt, as calm as possible and watching the flanking streets, with Sarah and Flipper outside the bus. The rest of my troops were oriented toward the main body of the Klan, which was finding out that getting around a cement truck, a big SUV (it was a Yukon that belonged to Curtis) and three other vehicles (ROTC cadets are really enthusiastic to help, especially when you tell them that if their vehicles are damaged the U.S. Secret Service will buy them a brand spanking new vehicle of their choice) wasn't as easy as burning crosses on somebody's yard. We wanted them bottled up so that when they were fully engaged in the roadblock we could fire off a non-lethal volley, freeze them and then have a palaver to try and talk them out of dying. I had no hope that talking to them would help, but I had to try before we slaughtered them, which is exactly what I intended to do if they didn't stand down.

Sorry if that sounds bloodthirsty and over-the-top, but I was pretty sure that they wouldn't extend us any courtesies, and besides, they started it when they killed my Chief of Detail and tried to kill a womyn they didn't even know just because she was a lesbian running for president. I must admit that the fact that most of these bed sheeted idiots probably voted for President Shrub (Bush 43) gave me a mild rush.

Plus, I swore an oath to protect and serve, and I fucking meant it.

In reality, I wasn't going to lose any more people because of stupidity, and I hoped that the initial wave of dead Klukkers would persuade the rest of them to at least stop long enough to reconsider their motivation before they rushed into the little field of fire we had set up.

"Hold steady until they get to that building with the two lights over the sign. When they get there Curtis and I are gonna let the front rows have it. If they stop, or retreat, hold fire. If they don't stop, or they try to charge us we're all going to open up on them until they do. Am I clear?" I said.

"Yes, ma'am," everybody said. I felt as good as I could with 15 troops against 2000, limited ammo and no real backup plan, or route to retreat.

And then I heard the faintest whisper of something that made me excited and filled with dread at the same time. Others heard it, too, because I saw Curtis's head go up and quarter the sky. One of the ROTC guys started looking around, and from the back of the bus Badass said, "Freak! You hear that?"

"Yeah, but whose is it?" I said.

Suddenly there was a great rush of wind and two giant spotlights transfixed the leaders of the KKK column.

"Holy sweet Jesus!" Curtis Jeffries said.

A black helicopter with a shining white eagle on its forward fuselage and the name "Buck Rogers" in white script just below the eagle came over our heads and descended to hover 25 feet above the street between the KKK and the bus. It had stubby wings with big rocket pods on them, and an M230 30mm chain gun that immediately centered on the crowd of bed sheeted Klukkers.

A giant voice filled the air. "This is Lieutenant Colonel J. A. Rogers of the 101st Tactical Air Wing, United States Army, and by the order of the president of the United States you are ordered to disperse. If you continue your advance I will open fire on your position. You have two minutes to comply with this presidential order. This warning will not be repeated." The helicopter's hover was perfectly stable, and the gunner spun up the chain gun, which made a sound like the humming from a giant hornet's nest that's been disturbed.

"Holy motherfucking hell!" Badass yelled. The wind around us increased to gale force and I looked back over the bus to see four enormous CH-47 Chinook helicopters hovering just behind our position. Doors were open on both sides of the humongous dual-rotor aircraft, and men were rappelling out and down, the white eagle patches on their shoulders gleaming in the light of the spotlights that showed them the landing zone. The soldiers didn't wait to form up, they just began streaming toward the front of the bus. As they came up on our position two soldiers detached themselves from the rest. The taller one said, "Where is General Glickstien? I need General Glickstien!"

"I'm Glickstien," I said, bellowing to get over the sound of the helicopters.

"Ma'am," the shorter one said. "I'm Colonel Lucas Tomilo of the 3rd Battalion, 101st Airborne. This is Command Sergeant Major Luis Delgado. The president has ordered me to place Brigade

Combat Team Bastogne at your disposal until such time as Secret Service reinforcements can be brought in. What are your orders, Ma'am?"

I looked at the Colonel and said, "What the fuck? Sir, I'm only a Major who retired from SOCOM. I'm not a general."

Colonel Tomilo smiled and said, "Sorry, Ma'am, but this here order is signed by NCA himself, and it says you're a Marine three-star general, and that I'm under your command for the duration." I must have looked like a deer in the headlights, because he gave me a hard look and said, "Your orders, ma'am?" in a tone of voice that said "get your shit together, lady."

So I did.

"Colonel, secure the perimeter around this bus out to 500 meters, and deploy your anti-snipers as you see fit, just in case. I also have wounded and need medics ASAP. Oh, and get rid of all those assholes in the bed sheets at the end of the street."

"Roger that, Ma'am," Tomilo said. "Command Sergeant Major, you are over watch on the General until relieved." The CSM nodded and said, "Yes, sir." He drew his pistol and stood directly behind me, broad, menacing, capable and hyper-vigilant. You didn't attain Delgado's rank without being special.

The Colonel spoke into his throat mike and said, "XO, this is Sword-Actual. Set up perimeter at 500 meters and get anti-sniper teams deployed. Send medics this location now, and send three platoons down each side of the street to take a position 100 meters from the crowd. ROE Echo-8 are in effect."

I looked at the hovering attack helicopter—it was an AH-64D Apache, Longbow variation, the deadliest attack helicopter in the history the world (I'm not making that shit up—look up what its capabilities are and then tell me I'm wrong—those motherfuckers are scary)—and then looked at the crowd, which was milling around but not dispersing, and I had an idea. I said, "Colonel, can you get me on the command channel to that bird?"

"Yes Ma'am," he said. He pulled a headset with a mike on it out of one of his pockets and plugged it into a small battery pack from another pocket. He turned the frequency control to a specific freq and handed the headset and battery to me. I seated the headset, clipped the battery to my waistband and said, "Call sign, Colonel?"

"Buck Rogers, Ma'am," he said with a grin. I smiled back and said, "Buck Rogers, this is Sword-Command. Report."

"Command, Buck Rogers. There's about 15 seconds left on our timeline, and I'd rather not fire on a bunch of civilians, over," the pilot said.

"Buck Rogers, Command. How about you pull up and back 100 meters and torch the last two pickup trucks in the line? Say 10 seconds on the M230, over?" I said.

"Command, Buck Rogers. Roger your last. Firing in 20 seconds, over," the pilot said.

"Buck Rogers, Command. Execute pull up and back maneuver and fire in 20 seconds, over," I said.

"Command, Buck Rogers. Acknowledged."

The Apache lifted gently up and back and the crowd cheered and started to roil forward, until the Apache stopped and the co-pilot/gunner targeted the two ROTC pickups and triggered the 30 mm chain gun.

Then the Klan crowd ran like hell for anywhere but there.

The Apache looked like an alien spaceship when the chain gun pounded the two pickups into their constituent parts. Every other round was a tracer and it looked like the Finger of God was raining fire on the two hapless vehicles. One second they were there—discrete pickup trucks—and the next they were just small pieces of metal. There was surprisingly little shrapnel, and there wasn't any fireball, just a finger of flame that incinerated the trucks, leaving behind only after images on our retinas.

"Command, Buck Rogers. Mission accomplished. Requesting new mission parameters, over."

"Buck Rogers, Command. Well done. Ascend to a safe altitude and assume over watch for this area. Advise command on this channel of any vehicle or personnel movement toward this position. How fuel? Over," I said.

"Command, Buck Rogers. We are three-zero minutes from bingo fuel. Be advised that three more 64 Deltas are en route this position, two-zero minutes out. We will stay on mission until relieved. Buck Rogers will now assume over watch. Out."

I looked out at the 1st Brigade Combat Team of the 101st Airborne (Air Assault) Division—the "Screaming Eagles" of World War II fame, and the only air assault division in the world—and I said, "Command Sergeant Major Delgado, on what freq do I reach Colonel Tomilo?"

"One-two-five, Ma'am," he said.

I dialed my radio into 125 and said, "Sword-Actual, Command. Please report to my position at your earliest convenience."

He immediately radioed back and said, "Command, Sword-Actual. Acknowledged and on my way."

I called out to Lonnie Jeffries. "Captain, you and your men are relieved. Please gather your squad on my position for inspection."

"Right away, ma'am," he said. The ROTC men gathered around me and I said, "Stand easy until Colonel Tomilo gets here." About 30 seconds later the 1st BCT commander came up, followed by a team of 16 medics.

"My wounded are in the bus, but I have three here who need attention, too," I said to the lieutenant that was at the head of the medics. "I need them as stable as possible, and then I need 'em transported to a secure hospital."

Colonel Tomilo said, "General, we've got eight Blackhawks with our incoming Apaches. With your permission we'll lift the wounded to Fort Knox and secure them there, ma'am."

"Good plan, Colonel. I'm also going to need one of those Blackhawks to take me to the hospital where my protectee is," I said.

"Not a problem, ma'am," he said.

"Good. I also need to make sure that these ROTC men get home safely—their vehicles were destroyed by Buck Rogers," I said.

"Ma'am, pardon me for speaking up out of turn, but that was way cool! That pilot and gunner were really disciplined. I'm really glad that those guys are on our side," Lonnie Jeffries said.

"Believe me, Captain, you aren't alone in that sentiment," Colonel Tomilo said. "I might be able to get you a check ride in one, if you wanted." The Colonel was smiling, but he was clearly serious.

"Sir, I'd really like that—we all would," Captain Jeffries said.

"Good," Colonel Tomilo said. "You'll have time for that when you and your squad come to Fort Campbell to visit us for a week or two this summer. I'm also going to recommend to my Division commander that we grant you another patch for your uniform sleeves—kinda like this one." He pointed at the Screaming Eagle patch on his uniform, and Captain Lonnie Jeffries and his men all got super still, their eyes growing as round as the proverbial saucers. They all drew to attention, and it was obvious that they were about to salute when I said, "And Major, if you salute the Colonel or myself I'm going to personally kick your ass, unless the enemy snipers out there realize I'm a big time target and shoot me first. We don't salute until we know the battlefield is secure, right?"

He looked at me and said, "Uh, sorry, Ma'am. And I'm only a ROTC Captain ma'am."

"Not anymore," I said. "As a lieutenant general in the US Army I'm entitled to make battlefield promotions, so I hereby brevet you to Major until such time as this issue is resolved, effective immediately. I'm also going to recommend you to West Point, or any of the other service academies. Your unit was brave, committed and incredibly useful—and you were prepared to act as real soldiers if we hadn't had our asses bailed out by the best goddamned fighting unit in the world. I'd go to war with you anytime, Major Jeffries." I shook his hand and nodded at his men, who were all trying not to cry (I didn't blame them—if the 101st hadn't shown up when they did I would've probably pissed my pants—and I was 35 years old).

"I concur with the general, Major Jeffries. I imagine that as a West Point graduate my word may carry some weight in the matter," Colonel Tomilo said. "That goes for all of your men, too." The ROTC boys looked like they were about to jump out of their uniforms and run naked down the street with joy.

I turned to Command Sergeant Major Delgado and said, "Command Sergeant Major, would you please take a platoon and escort Major Jeffries and his men back to their dormitories or homes? You'll have to walk because we seem to have destroyed their trucks, but we'll send a Blackhawk to bring you back."

"Yes, ma'am, but if I might suggest that you keep the 'Hawks close for the wounded instead of sending one for us? We'll tag the bus site in our GPS and exfiltrate on foot unless absolutely necessary, ma'am."

I looked him, every inch a professional soldier, and I said, "Very well, Command Sergeant Major. Make haste, if you please."

"As you wish, ma'am," he said. Within 30 seconds CSM Delgado had a squad of men around him and was marching with the ROTC cadets toward their dorm. I turned to Tomilo and said, "Those are very brave future officers."

"Concur," Colonel Tomilo said. His smile let me know he was aware of what was coming next.

"I do have a few questions, Colonel," I said.

He smiled and said, "I'll bet you do, ma'am. Fire away."

"How are you operating here? The U.S. Army can't legally operate inside our borders unless there is an insurrection, which this was not. What gives?" I said.

"General, NCA loaned us to Kentucky as part of their National Guard training. Technically my unit is a part of the Kentucky National Guard right now. All the president did was nationalize a unit or two of the Kentucky National Guard to assist a presidential candidate, and that is legal," Colonel Tomilo said. His smile got bigger, because he knew what my next question was.

"OK, I'm gonna assume you know your law on that one, but how in the hell did you get here in time? Even if you were sitting in the barracks all loaded up for a nice 25K jog it's still going to take you longer to get here than it did. Those Chinooks are great birds, but they aren't supersonic jets—even if you were at Knox it'd take longer to enplane than it did for you to get here," I said.

"General, you're absolutely right, except we were already airborne," Colonel Tomilo said. "We had to swing east when we left the base for night maneuvers because Senator Sheehan was doing a campaign stop there and they wanted us out of any civilian approach flyways. We weren't more than 15 minutes from here when we got the orders."

We'd been saved by a guy I knew—Senator Sheehan was James Sheehan, who I'd beaten out for athlete of the decade back in Battle Creek. He was the Republican junior senator from Michigan and was running for his party's nomination for president. The fact that he was in the right place at the right time had saved our asses, even though he didn't know a thing about it.

"And how did that happen? How did the Chairman of the Joint Chiefs get you orders that fast?" I said. "Wouldn't something like that take at least a little time? And how the hell did he even know we were in trouble?" I said.

"General, we got the call directly from the president himself. Apparently he got a call from Agent Emily Devlin that said you were under attack, and the president called the governor of Kentucky, nationalized the Kentucky National Guard and then called me direct. My CO will be pissed because he got bypassed, but the president is the Commander-in-Chief, so I didn't question him. We changed course and hauled ass, led by our Apache escort. The president also sent authenticated orders to our secure fax aboard the Jolly Green Giant (a nickname for the Ch-47 Chinook helicopter), which I am supposed to give you now that we're secure." Tomilo handed me a sheaf of papers.

I looked at the top sheet, but I didn't get very far before Flipper leaned out the door of the bus and said, "Freak, you better come in here." There had been a fairly steady flow of wounded out of the bus, but something in her tone made me look away from the orders. Flipper had a grim look on her face, but she wasn't crying. I got on the bus and saw Sarah Koenigsblett standing by a seat with two medics. She wasn't crying, but she had a fearsome look on her face, like she was going to explode and tear someone a new ass. Badass was there, too—he appeared to be holding someone's hand that was in the seat—and when he felt my eyes on him he looked up and said, "We found Josie, Freak."

I'd forgotten all about Soper's wife. I ran down the aisle, but as soon as I got closer I saw that it was bad news. I looked down at Josephine Boroviak Soper's beautiful blue eyes staring out in death. Her body didn't look damaged, but one of the medics said, "General, she was sitting right where the truck hit. The force of the crash basically broke all of her ribs and jammed them through her body cavity like twelve swords. She was also squashed from the other side by this young man, who rebounded off the wall of the bus and crashed directly into her."

The medic pointed at Elvin Clyde Bliss, who was laying in the seat opposite Josie, his face mashed in and his neck clearly broken. One of his eyes had popped out of his head and was hanging by the optic nerve down on his cheek, and there was a piece of glass driven completely through the center of his chest that came out his back. He was dead three times over, and looked it, but Josie looked like she was just taking a nap with her eyes open.

I'd seen stuff like it in other parts of the world (sorry, still classified), usually from an IED attack where someone was thrown around in a vehicle. Poor Josie had been directly impacted and then indirectly impacted when she slammed into Elvin Clyde Bliss, kind of like a butterfly that had been slammed between the pages of an open book.

I was going to have to tell Soper.

Some days are just shit sandwiches, and you have to eat them just like they're the best brisket sandwich you've ever eaten.

This was one of those days.

I was also going to have to tell the parents of Elvin Clyde Bliss.

I would've sworn more, but there just didn't seem to be any words that fit. The kid had proven himself to be a thoughtful young man who was actually trying to learn something, not just some knee-jerk hater of everything that he didn't know. I never knew if he came to agree with Soper's sexuality, but he certainly listened to her about issues, and gave back solid, reasoned opinions that helped her understand the real people she was talking to about becoming president.

Now the kid who looked like a bowl of green Jell-O at the start of our association was just a big sack of dead meat, killed for no other reason than somebody decided they wanted to quell a voice they didn't agree with.

And another reasonable voice was silenced by violence.

Sometimes America sucks.

It's a good thing that the Founding Fathers of our supposedly free democracy didn't act that way, or most of them would have ended up in early graves. Thomas Jefferson and John Adams had quite the love-hate relationship, but they settled it by writing scathing letters to each other and various other correspondents, not shooting at each other, or by running over each other with a heavily laden wagon. Oddly enough, the two men died on the same day—July 4, 1826—exactly fifty years after signing the Declaration of Independence. Even more oddly, Adams' last words were "Thank God, Jefferson still lives"—he didn't know that Jefferson had died earlier in the day (look it up—sometimes truth is stranger than fiction).

All that ran through my mind in just a second or two, which is when I decided to find out who killed this kid, this good womyn and my friend Andria Rogers and kill those motherfuckers as dead as Benedict Arnold.

I looked at Josie again and said, "I'm going to carry her out, then I'm going to carry Elvin Clyde Bliss out, then I'm going to carry CoD out."

The medic—his name tape said "Zimont"—said, "General, beg pardon, but this is a crime scene. The FBI is going to want to photograph everything *in situ* before they give us permission to move the bodies." He looked apologetic, but I'd gone beyond being at all reasonable anymore, so I just looked at him and said, "Fuck the fucking fuckers of the fucked up FB-fucking-I. Does that clear up my position on your statement, lieutenant?"

"Yes, ma'am, it surely does," he said. "I'll get stretcher bearers."

"Not necessary," I said. I bent down, gathered Josie into my arms and carried her down the aisle and out of the bus. There were two corpsmen waiting with a field stretcher. I laid her gently down, walked back onto the bus and down the aisle and bent to pick up Elvin Clyde Bliss. The medic said, "General, the young man weighs a considerable amount, and the dead are notoriously hard to balance. Could I get a stretcher for you?"

I am told by those who were watching that I looked at the well-meaning medic like I was a tiger about to fall on a wild pig. Badass said my arms looked like they were giant anacondas inside my jacket, and apparently my green eyes went so dark they looked like chips of obsidian. I looked at the medic, bent down and grabbed the seat in front of the one Elvin Clyde Bliss was in and ripped it right out of the floor of the bus. I threw the seat on top of the two in front of it, picked up Elvin Clyde Bliss as gently as I had Josie and walked down the aisle and off the bus to place him on a stretcher as well.

I got back on the bus to find the medic, Flipper, Badass and Colonel Tomilo standing by CoD's body. The medic stood at attention, his eyes huge from fear—not many people on earth could do what I just did, and he knew it. The other three were also standing at attention, and I said, "Colonel, I'd like an honor guard for this womyn, if you please."

"Roger that, General." Tomilo called for a squad to come back to the bus, so when I got off carrying her body Andria Rogers had eight members of the First Brigade Combat Team, 101st Air Assault Division, United States Army, standing at attention. When my foot hit the ground Colonel Tomilo said, "Pre-SENT, arms!" and all of the soldiers within earshot snapped a salute that they held until CoD's body was carried away on a stretcher. I said, "Flipper, stay with her until she's in the morgue, then call me and someone will come and get you."

"Roger that, Freak," Flipper said as she followed the stretcher.

I turned to Colonel Tomilo and said, "Colonel, I need you to dial up a Blackhawk to transport the rest of my team to the hospital where they've got Soper. I would also like to take the squad that guarded CoD with us, with Command Sergeant Major Delgado, if he's back."

"Yes, General," he said. "I might also suggest that I send two of my Apache birds with you as escort."

"I'll take it, Colonel." I said. "Until you are relieved by me personally, or by a direct superior, I want you to keep the perimeter enforced and not let anyone in this area except Secret Service, U.S. Marshals or the FBI. Absolutely no locals will be allowed on this site until all federal agencies are satisfied that they have no more use for it."

"Roger that, General," he said. Our comms crackled and a voice said, "Sword-Actual, this is Sword-XO. Sir, I've got locals on the perimeter demanding we let them in. One of them says he's the sheriff of Rowan County, over."

I looked at Colonel Tomilo and said, "Find out where they are and then let's go see them."

"Sword-XO, this is Sword-Actual. State position, over," Colonel Tomilo said.

"Sword-Actual, Sword-XO. Sir, we're five hundred meters directly behind your position—right on the street. These guys are practically foaming at the mouth, sir."

Colonel Tomilo looked at me and I said, "Tell him we'll be right there."

"Sword-XO, Sword Actual. On my way—hold tight."

"Sword-Actual, Sword-XO. Roger that."

We went around the bus and I said, "Deputy Curtis Jeffries, where are you?" My voice was incredibly loud and clear, and Curtis came right up to me. I said, "Can you come with me to identify the sheriff? I'm not asking you to do anything that'll get you in trouble with your department, I just want to make sure it's really the sheriff."

"I'm already in trouble with the sheriff—apparently all deputies were instructed to stay away from here and ignore any calls for help. I didn't check my phone for messages when I heard the 911 calls, I just did my duty and came on the run," Jeffries said.

"Wasn't your phone on? Don't you have an alert tone?" I said.

"Not when I'm fishing," Jeffries said. "Besides, I told ya before, I swore an oath and I god-damned well meant it." Curtis Jeffries looked at me and smiled a Cheshire Cat smile and said, "Besides, I'm tired of this half-assed county and its half-assed sheriff's department. I was thinkin' of trying to get into the U.S. Marshals, and I'm thinkin' that a three-star general with Special Forces experience might be able to grease my way in, especially since I'm already qualified."

Both Colonel Tomilo and I laughed, and I said, "Well, Curtis, since I believe in TANSTAAFL, and since you already paid and are about to pay some more I'll see what I can do."

"Concur, general," Tomilo said. "There ain't no such thing as a free lunch, and Deputy Jeffries has already paid." We were almost at the barrier where I could see a bunch of guys waving their arms and acting like the bunch of country shitkickers they were. I turned to Lieutenant Zimont and said, "Lieutenant, I need an accurate casualty count."

"General, we have five KIA and twenty-eight wounded," he said. "Besides the three you carried out we lost one of the college girls, and the bus driver, who we think was trying to stop the crash by accelerating out of the way of the cement truck."

"How bad are the casualties?" I said.

"Seven of them are in critical condition with internal bleeding and in need of trauma surgery. The rest are serious but not life threatening—fractures, concussions and lacerations that we've mostly stitched up," Lieutenant Zimont said.

"Thank you, lieutenant. Keep me informed about the casualties, please, even if we're in the middle of the palaver with these individuals," I said.

"Roger that, general."

We got to the barrier and a Major with "Kolesaar" on his name tape said, "General, the big fat guy in the middle says he's the sheriff here, and he's demanding to get in to inspect the damage to his town." The Major saw the look in my eyes and said, "Ma'am, those are his words, not mine, ma'am."

"Very well, XO," I said. "Let's talk to the sheriff, shall we?" I looked at Curtis and he said, "Ma'am, that fat tub of lard is indeed Rowan County Sheriff Antoine DePuis, called Ant by his friends and lotsa other nasty names by everybody else. The big ugly guy next to him is Undersheriff

Colt Weaver. Both of them are about as smart as a bag of hammers, but they make up for it by being mean bullies who like to drink moonshine and shoot people's cats."

Let's see how they do with me," I said. "Colonel, let those two assholes through and prepare for trouble. Badass, Sarah, as soon as they're all the way through get your cuffs out, because we're going to arrest them for conspiracy in this goddamned goat rope."

"That's a bad idea, Freak," Badass said. "I concur with Badass, Freak," Sarah said.

"Why?" I said, my anger over the senseless deaths overpowering my good sense.

"Because we need to have an impeccable case against these assholes before we arrest them, or we run the risk of them concocting some bullshit excuse for a defense that even a federal judge might buy. If they are in cahoots with someone up the food chain they'll have a field day with the arrest— you know a judge is going to ask you for proof about why you arrested them, and we haven't got any yet," Sarah said. "We need to have them all sewn up before we put them in prison."

"What she said," Badass said. "Plus, being pissed off and making strategic decisions aren't always the best idea."

"What he said," Sarah Koenigsblett said. "Remember the Klingon proverb: Revenge is a dish best served cold."

"Concur," Badass said.

I got it, and they were right. I let the anger run through me, and then I said, "Colonel, let those two guys through, but no one else.

"Yes, ma'am," Colonel Tomilo said. He nodded at his XO and the Major pulled the two pieces of portable fence that had been barring entry to the street aside, letting the two county lawmen through, and then pulled them back closed. Neither of the arrogant pricks seemed to notice that their posse wasn't following them. Instead, the sheriff, who was a mouth-breathing, fat-necked, red-faced pustule of quasi-humanity said, "Ah don't know who you think you are, buddy boy, but Ah'm the sher'f hereabouts and Ah am in charge of this here crime scene."

He was glaring at Colonel Tomilo, because his tiny little sexist carbuncle of a mind couldn't conceive of the fact that someone besides a man might be in charge, so I walked right up into his face and said, "I'm Lieutenant General Glinka L. Glickstien, USMC, and I'm in charge of this crime scene until I'm relieved by someone in my chain of command, so why don't you and your pitiful excuse for lawmen fuck off and die, Sher'f?"

The fat, scummy bag of puke said, "What the fuck do y'all think you're talkin' a-bout? Y'all caint tell me what to do! I'm the sher'f of this county, and ya'll ain't got no jurisdiction here, whoever the fuck you are!" He looked at Colonel Tomilio, who said, "Sir, I'd advise you to listen to the general. She's also a Secret Service Special Agent and has arrest powers in this situation. Also, on a personal note, she's my commanding officer and if she tells me to just shoot you I will, as will the other members of the 101st Airborne (Air Assault) Division here present." Tomilo was almost smiling, but anyone with half a brain could see he wasn't fucking around.

But this was the sheriff of Rowan County, Kentucky, and apparently you didn't need even half a brain for the job, because Ant DePuis said, "Fuck you, soldier boy! This here is mah county, Ah'm the duly elected sher'f and Ah say that y'all can jist get the fuck out of here before Ah have y'all arrested." He turned his piggy eyes on me and said, "That includes y'all, ya uppity cunt."

Every soldier near me raised his weapon and turned it on Ant DePuis and his ugly undersheriff. Colonel Tomilo looked as if he was about to start spitting bullets out of his clenched jaws, but I couldn't help but laugh. It was the kind of grim laughter that got people's attention, especially when I said, "I've got five KIA, twenty-eight wounded, and I don't give a shit who or what you think you are, you pestilent bag of horseshit. If you don't shut the fuck up I'm not going to arrest you, I'm going to reach down your throat and yank your vocal cords out. Are we clear?" My voice was as cold as the void of space.

The sheriff was a stupid asshole bully, but his lizard brain must have recognized the danger he was in, because he looked around at all the weapons trained on him and the ugly undersheriff, started to say something and then just shut his mouth and nodded. I reached up and patted his cheek and said, "Good boy. You and your pile of useless peckerwood rednecks clear this area and remember that the Kentucky National Guard, led by the 101st Airborne Division, is in charge of this crime scene until further notice. Acknowledge that order."

Ant DePuis narrowed his piggy eyes and said, "Ya'll have got control of the crime scene, but Ah'm gonna call the guv'ner soon's as Ah'm at my radio an' find out fer how long."

"That's certainly your right, DePuis," I said. I turned to Colonel Tomilo and said, "Now get this gigantic piece of shit out of my sight before I decide to just shoot him, Colonel."

"Gladly, ma'am." As they got to the barrier the ugly undersheriff turned and said, "Y'all better hope the next time Ah see y'all there's plenty a soldiers around, or Ah'm gonna punch your tits off, gen'r'l or no."

All of my guys laughed like hyenas over a fresh zebra and I said, "Well, you're welcome to try, deputy, but I will need one thing before you give it a go."

"Whassat?" he said.

"The name of the funeral home where you want your body shipped. Now get the fuck out of my sight," I said.

I held out my hand and Major Kolesaar handed me the bullhorn he was holding. I stepped up to the barrier and said, "I'm Lieutenant General G. L. Glickstien of the Kentucky National Guard and I'm ordering you to disperse. If you do not disperse in five minutes I'm going to order my men to open fire on you as being in insurrection against the Unites States of America. This not a joke; disperse or face the consequences."

The crowd apparently took me seriously, because those chickenshits, many of whom probably just changed out of their bed sheets to come over to the party, were gone in less than a minute. They just melted away like lard on a hot grill, and the Battle of Morehead was over.

I turned to Colonel Tomilo and said, "I'll take that Blackhawk now. I'm taking my agents, plus my squad of Screaming Eagles. Once I get Soper squared away the lads will come back with the Blackhawk. You're in charge until the FBI, U.S. Marshals or Secret Service relieves you, Colonel." I stuck out my hand to shake and he said, "Ma'am, I'd be glad to serve under you any time. You'd have made a damned fine air assault commander."

I smiled at him and said, "Thank you for maintaining the charade of me as a general, Colonel. And thank your men for me—they are professional soldiers of the highest caliber. It has been a pleasure, sir." I stood at attention to salute, but he said, "Sorry, ma'am, but regs state that inferior officers salute superior officers first."

His right hand snapped up to the edge of his black beret and said, "Ah-TENN-HUTT! Pre-SENT, ARMS!" All of the Screaming Eagles snapped to attention and saluted. I returned the salutes with some panache and bellowed, "THE SCREAMING EAGLES HAVE BALLS OF STEEL!"

"HOO-AH!" the air assault troops said, and then returned to their duty stations.

I went down to the loading area for the Blackhawks and found Curtis Jeffries standing with Badass, Sarah, Darah and Patsy. I looked at Badass, Darah and Patsy and said, "You three need medical attention. Why aren't you with the medics? In fact, get your asses on one of these birds that are going to Knox with the other wounded and get yourselves treated."

"Sorry, Freak, but I'm just beat up. I'm standing watch over Soper with you until we can get another detail to relieve us," Badass said. "I had a doc look me over and she said I'm good to go."

"I've had a concussion, but it's mild and there isn't anything they can do to fix it, except I'm not supposed to get into any other car wrecks any time soon," Darah said. "And Badass made me get checked out—they're sure I don't have a fractured skull, or any other internal injuries, although my tits are going to be bruised for a few weeks."

"What?" I said. "What the hell happened to your tits?"

"I was knocked out of my seat into the aisle and I landed tits down—luckily they're resilient and bounced right back, although the medic said showering will probably hurt for a while."

"I can help you with that," Badass said. "I've got soft hands."

"Are you hitting on my sister, you big doofus?" Sarah said.

"Bad timing?" Badass said. "Too soon after a trauma?"

"Actually, it's about time," Darah said. "At least I know that you're OK, if you're thinking about your love life."

"An' 'm not dohing awa', ehther," Patsy said. "We nee' ethery 'ody we can geth, so 'm dohing w' you." I looked at Badass, who said, "He has a dislocated shoulder, three broken fingers on his left hand, torn ligaments in his left ankle and he will need at least fifty stitches in his tongue, but the doc says if he can stand it he's not going to do any further damage."

I looked at Patsy and he said, "Ah t'an 'thand it. 'M a U Eth Mawine, dod-dammit!"

"Roger that," I said. "Let's go find our protectee, team. Deputy Jeffries, I assume you're here just until the crime scene is taken over and you give your statement to whoever shows up first?"

"Yes, General, I am," Curtis said.

"Good, but from now on it's just Freak, OK?" I said. "You did good, and let me know if I can be of any help to you after this is over."

"Roger that, General," he said, smiling.

I said, "Come, Patsy" in my horrible English accent and picked the mangled agent up before he could protest. We all laughed our asses off as we got on the Blackhawk with the squad of Screaming Eagles, led by Command Sergeant Major Delgado.

Badass had the address of the hospital and he gave it to the pilot, who asked for permission to take off. I gave him the universal whirling finger signal and the bird left the ground, swung around and headed for the hospital, leaving death behind us, and sadness ahead of us.

I had no way of knowing that this death was the trigger for everything that came after it.

Including more death and sadness.

CHAPTER 45

Maternity Ward Wisdom

We landed on the helipad at Saint Joseph Mount Sterling Maternity Services in Mt. Sterling, Kentucky about fifteen minutes later, despite the arm-waving group of people who tried to wave us off. Command Sergeant Major Delgado and the squad from the 101st got off first and most of the arm-waving stopped, and then we got off and went straight toward the arm-wavers. I said, "Who's in charge here?"

"I'm in charge and you need to get that helicopter off my helipad! I've got triplets inbound, ETA less than two minutes and they're in trouble, so if you goons could move your part of the military-industrial complex I'd appreciate it! And if you assholes could call off your attack birds that are circling in our airspace and tell them to get the hell out of the flight path of my triplets I'd be forever grateful!"

The person talking was around four feet tall, very curvy (voluptuous is the word that comes to mind), with a huge topknot of white hair that made her look about six feet tall. She also had a beautiful mezzo-soprano voice and the most striking pink eyes I'd ever seen.

She was an albino dwarf.

I thought I had a concussion that was finally kicking in, but just then she said, "Did I fucking stutter? My triplets are on final approach and your fucking army shit is still in the way! Move your asses, shitheads!"

I recovered from my shock and ducked back into the Blackhawk. I told the pilot to stand off clear of the medivac bird and to send the Apaches back to Morehead. "After the medivac delivers I'll get it airborne and you can set down, Captain," I told the pilot.

"Roger that, General. I think I'd better lift now—that dwarf apparently doesn't like us sitting here." He pointed out the windscreen. I looked out to see the albino dwarf doc giving us both barrels of the All-American finger salute. When she saw me looking she gave us a right hand bird while pointing skyward with her left hand. I had to admire her grit—not many people would stand right under the turning rotors of an Army helicopter, but she clearly didn't care. I jumped out of the Blackhawk and the pilot immediately pulled a combat lift-off and clattered out of the way.

I walked over to the doc and said, "My apologies, doctor. I'm Agen-"

"Unless you're the second coming of Jesus fuck you, and even if you are the second coming I'm an atheist, so fuck you," she said. "I couldn't care less who you are unless you can deliver a baby. Can you deliver a baby, Army?" She took a breath to continue her rant and I said, "Yes, I can deliver a baby."

The clatter of a descending medivac helicopter was rising behind us as we walked away from the helipad. She looked up at me and said, "I'd love to hear about your obstetric skills, but I'm gonna be kinda busy for the next three or four hours. If you're still around I'll buy you a cup of coffee for being such a bitch."

"I'd love to tell you about it, but I won't be able to—it's classified," I said.

"Typical goddamned military-industrial complex shit. Delivering babies is classified? Bureaucracy much?" she said, snorting at the idiocy of the military bureaucracy (which I have to admit is pretty fucking stupid, until you need ammunition in a firefight and there's three or 17 times as much as you need—then you praise the paperwork in triplicate while reloading to save your ass...and yes, that's classified).

"Oh, fuck you, doc," I said, hoping she got the sarcasm slash admiration.

She was a smart doc, because she got it.

"Oh, amen to that, Army," she said, laughing. "Blame my mouth on my dad—he was career Navy."

"Well, I'm actually a Marine, so you can stow that Army shit," I said. The doc looked over at the troopers from the 101st and said, "Well, those Army guys seem to think you're someone important, so I think that this is a story I want to hear, but duty calls."

She pointed at the helo that was settling in the middle of the helipad and said, "Gotta run, Marine. Try not to get into too much trouble while I deliver my little bundles of joy."

"You got it, doc," I said into the rotor wash, but she was already running under the rotors to get at the expectant mother coming off the helo. I turned around and went to where Badass was standing in front of an open door with Command Sergeant Major Delgado and his squad. We went in the hospital and Badass said, "They're up on the fourth floor in an empty maternity suite. Soper is OK, but she has a severe concussion and her right radius and ulna are broken. She also has several lacerations that they thought were significant, but it looks like CoD shielded her from the brunt of it. She's awake, but anxious—she's concerned about Josie and CoD. So far we've been able to put her off because of the drugs, but she's going to be a handful in about half an hour...and she's asking for you now."

We all got on the elevator and I said "I'm going to tell her right away."

"Concur. She deserves to know—I'd want to know about my wife," Badass said. "Under it all she's a tough broad, although losing Josie will take some of the starch out of her. They really were perfect compliments for each other." He looked like he was going to cry, and I felt like I was going to cry, and Soper was definitely going to cry, so there really was no reason to wait.

We got off the elevator on the fourth floor and were met with two Secret Service agents flanking the doors with their weapons in their hands. I said, "Ed, El Gato, stand down. Command Sergeant Major Delgado, please sit on this elevator and don't let anyone down the hall to Ms. Soper's room unless they are Secret Service or U.S. Marshals, or I order you to."

"Yes, General. If I might speak freely, ma'am?" he said.

"Command Sergeant Major, you can talk to me like I'm just another numbnuts off the street if you want to—you've earned it," I said, nodding at his salad bar of decorations.

"Thank you, ma'am, but I wouldn't do that even if you were a numbnuts. You're a three star to me, so I will simply say that your approach to Ms. Soper's loss is the best, if she really loved her wife. She's going to thank you for it later, even if she curses you now."

"They teach you that in Sergeant Major school?" I said.

"Oh, yes, ma'am. I can also knit, bake a cake and do a cartwheel, although that may be a result of my service in four different wars," he said with a very small twitch of his face which I believe he thought was a smile. "But I do have two other questions."

I nodded and he said, "What about the FBI? They will be investigating this incident and they are going to want to talk to Ms. Soper—and you."

"Fuck 'em. They'll have to wait until I'm relieved or my boss gets here," I said.

"Something wrong with the FBI, ma'am? You don't seem to trust them," he said.

"Command Sergeant Major, do you read?"

"Yes, ma'am," he said.

"Me, too. I like thrillers and mysteries, especially well written ones where the heroes are real people who can get hurt but manage to get by even when they're down. There's this guy named James Lee Burke who writes about a detective from New Orleans called Dave Robicheaux?" I said.

"*In the Electric Mist with Confederate Dead*," he said.

"You read him too? So do you remember who Robicheaux's best friend is?" I said.

"Clete Purcell. Ah, I get it. Fart, Barf and Itch," the Command Sergeant Major said.

"What the fuck are you two talking about?" El Gato said.

"This guy in a book calls the FBI "Fart, Barf and Itch" because he says they can fuck up a wet dream," I said.

"And you don't trust them, either," the Command Sergeant Major said. "Is there a reason for your antipathy?"

"Great word, Command Sergeant Major. Let's just call it a bad feeling. Something isn't right about this, especially since they haven't found a single person who sent a death threat to Soper," I said.

Command Sergeant Major Delgado's eyes widened and he said, "Ma'am? They haven't found even one of the letter writers? Out of how many credible threats?"

"Over forty," I said. I watched him process and then arrive at the same conclusion that I had. He straightened and said, "Roger that, ma'am. No FBI unless you admit them. What about the nurses?"

I looked at El Gato and he said, "They're all good. There's this albino dwarf doctor who's been up to see Soper and she vouched for 'em. Bumble seems to think it's OK."

"So do I," Ed said. "Besides, it'd really be a suicide mission now—we got the 101st Airborne with us. Unless they bring a tank we should be OK, especially since Old Three Names is on his way with reinforcements."

"Your phone been burning up in your hand?" I said.

"Especially when Director Hessler got on there—she can swear as much as you do, if not as creatively," Ed said. "About melted the phone and my eardrum."

"Nurses are OK, Command Sergeant Major Delgado," I said. "I'm going down to see Soper. El Gato, Ed, catch a quick break. Everybody else, wait outside while I talk to Soper, and then we'll divvy up duties, OK?"

They nodded and I knocked, said, "It's Freak, Bumble," and went into Soper's room. My friend holstered his pistol and said, "She's in and out, Freak. They've tried to put her on drugs for the pain, but she objected because of her concussion. She's also asked for Josie about every 30 seconds." He looked at me, and I gently shook my head. Bumble's shoulders slumped, and he gave a snort, like he had something in his throat. The big man shook just a bit, then stood up straight and said, "It OK if I take a break, Freak? I assume we're all secure?"

"Barring a nuke or heavily laden cruise missile, I think that eight Secret Service agents and a squad of 101st Air Assault troopers led by a Command Sergeant Major can hold the fort. Go get food and rest up, because Badass, Patsy, the Koenigsbletts, and I are gonna flame out soon."

"Eight agents? What about CoD and Flipper?" Bumble said.

"Flipper is standing honor guard for CoD," I said, feeling lower than whale shit when I thought about Andria Rogers.

"What happened to her?" Bumble said.

"She wrapped me in her arms and shielded me from the force of the crash," Soper said, her voice sounding like she'd been smoking two packs of unfiltered Camels a day while guzzling Jack Daniels from the neck of a fifth. Her eyes were open and they were boring in on mine like twin blue laser beams trying to shoot down a space ship.

I looked right back, my green eyes blazing with tears and frustration, and I said, "Josie's dead, Soper. Her neck was broken and she died instantly. Elvin Clyde Bliss tried to protect her like CoD did for you, but he wasn't as successful, because they were closer to where the truck hit the bus." I figured that a little creative license with the truth right now was better than the absolute truth, which might send Soper further over the edge than she was headed. Strictly speaking they weren't lies, because nobody could tell what really happened, although I was fairly sure that the Army medic knew his shit well enough to have painted a pretty good picture of the accident.

I went over to Soper as Bumble opened the door to leave. He stopped, turned around and said, "Soper, I'm truly sorry for your loss. Miss Josie was a good womyn who never hurt a soul that I saw. When we find these bastards they better hope Freak can stop me, cause I'm gonna get some payback, if you don't mind."

"Thank you, Calvin, but no payback, OK? Josie hated violence, and she wouldn't want you—or them—to get hurt. Arrest them and throw them in jail, will ya?" Soper said.

"Roger that, Soper, but they may bump their heads when I put 'em in the car, y'know?" the big man said.

"Nobody could object to that," Soper said. Bumble nodded and hit the door, leaving us alone. Soper said, "She didn't suffer?" I put my hand on the bed and she took it. She was looking out the window, but she wasn't crying. We stood that way for a while and then she looked at me and said, "And Elvin Clyde Bliss? What about him?"

"He's also gone. Apparently he took most of it, because he was truly messed up, but the truck hit right where he and Josie were sitting. I'm going to notify his parents as soon as we get relieved, and I need to go back to D.C. to tell Andria's family. I didn't know if you wanted to tell Josie's parents, or if I should do that, too. If you'd been unconscious I would've done it, even if it made you mad, but having you conscious makes the decision easier, at least in that respect."

"I'll call my in-laws, but won't the media announce it as soon as they get it?" Soper said. "I need to call them right away, just in case."

"Rest easy," I said. "They're at Fort Knox at the military hospital, and the personnel there are under strict orders to continue EMCON. Emissions control," I said. "They don't have cell phones and even if they did a three-star general told them to keep their mouths the fuck shut, and they're members of the 101st Air Assault, so they'll follow orders."

"What general? I don't know any generals," Soper said, her voice grinding and almost cracking completely.

"Sure you do—me," I said.

"WTF?" she said, so I told her about the Battle of Morehead.

Soper was a real trooper, because she said, "You fired on civilian vehicles to stop the Klan?"

"Fuck the Klukkers," I said. "I had wounded, I was undermanned until the RCT was fully deployed and those boys deserved new trucks for putting themselves in harm's way. Plus, it was fun to see a bunch of bed-sheet wearing cowards running like a gaggle of schoolgirls caught in the rain."

"I want justice for her, so bad that it hurts worse than my injuries, but I cannot stop this campaign," Soper said. "Even though they killed my wife and baby."

I'd forgotten all about the baby. More shit to rain down on Soper's head.

Even with all that I guess I wasn't surprised about the campaign, because she'd shown her toughness and determination, but I was surprised she was thinking about it right now. Her wife and baby weren't dead four hours and that's the first thing she thought of? I tried to pull my hand away and she clutched it tighter than tight. I could have broken her hold, but when I looked at the tears rolling silently down her cheeks and I stopped trying to pull away.

She cried silently and hugely for 10 straight minutes.

Finally she said, "You need to understand, I promised Josie that if something happened to her I'd keep going. She made me swear on the life of my nieces and nephews, because she knew it was always possible that someone would get to her to try and stop me. If I don't press on now I'll never campaign again, not even for dogcatcher. I don't want to think about it—*I just want her back!*—but I can't stop. Even though they took all that I love… I CANNOT STOP! Do you understand?"

Soper's face was twisted into a gargoyle shape that left her unrecognizable as the beautiful, vibrant womyn that had transformed a hostile crowd into an attentive audience just four hours ago. Her grief had become a physical thing that was changing the topography of her face into a bitter mask of anger and resentment that she would never shed if something didn't happen to stop it.

So I broke the law like a motherfucker.

I said, "Raise your right hand and repeat after me." She looked at me, puzzled, but she saw that I was serious, so she raised her casted hand and I said, "I swear that I will, to the best of my ability, preserve, protect and defend the Constitution against all enemies, foreign or domestic. I give my promise as a United States Marine that I will die before I break this oath."

She repeated it, and I said, "Congratulations. You're now a fully sworn member of the U.S. Marine Corps, and as your superior officer I am informing you that you are bound by that oath to never divulge what I'm about to tell you. Are we clear?"

"Yes, but—"

"No buts, Lieutenant. I'm a three-star general, and I'm ordering you not to divulge this information, not even to the president of the United States, upon penalty of life in Leavenworth prison, or possibly death. Are you accepting my order?" I said, my face and voice telling her how serious I was.

"Yes, ma'am, I accept your order," she said.

"Good. There was a time that I was in Pakistan under attack. My unit was ripped to shreds by a Russian division, and I was carrying three guys who were hurt when the gomers engaged us with mortars and .50-cal fire. I didn't have a rifle, all I had was my M9 Beretta sidearm and my Browning Hi-Power backup gun, and I was taking direct fire on my position and we were all going to die, so I blew up the Russian hospital where the mortars and .50 cals were firing from. It made a fireball so big that I thought I'd torched off a nuke. It killed at least 900 Russians, and I don't regret it one little bit. Right before that I'd wanted to just stop and lie down and let 'em kill me, because I hadn't really slept in 60 hours, and I was ready to die, but one of my guys had kids at home, and he said, "Give it all you got, Freak, for my kids," so I got my guys up and dragged 'em back to our exfiltration point and we got the fuck outta there.

"If I'd laid down it woulda been all over, so I just refused to lay down until my guys were safe. So yeah, I do know what you mean. Just remember that when this is all over you need to cry, and then talk to somebody about it, because PTSD is a bitch you don't want anything to do with, Marine. You read me?" I said, looking at her eyes clear and her face unclench. Not all the lines went away, but the gargoyle face did, and that was enough for right now.

Soper looked at me and said, "I read you, ma'am. Permission to ask a question?"

"Granted, but be aware that I may not answer it," I said.

"Understood. Russians in Pakistan?" she said.

"Classified above your pay grade, lieutenant," I said.

"Yes, ma'am. You blew up a hospital?" she said.

"That one I can answer. It was actually an ammunition dump that those sons of bitches made up to look like a hospital. I'd already determined that was the case, so I wasn't shooting on a wing and a prayer. And the goddamned Russians I blew up were regular Red Army motherfuckers, so don't cry any tears for them, either. Fuckin' Putin, that asshole!" I said.

She looked quizzically at me again and I said "Enough stories. Remember your oath and never refer to this incident again—it's classified," I said with the hint of a smile.

Soper smiled to and said, "Thank you, general, for enlightening me. At least one person will understand what I'm going to do in the next few hours."

"Oh, I think lots of people will understand, Soper. The citizens love it when their leaders show they've got balls and guts, and I'd guess you're about to do that," I said.

"You bet your ass I am, general, but I am going to take your advice about PTSD," she said.

"Good. Now get some sleep so you look almost rested at the press conference," I said.

"What makes you think I'm having a press conference, Freak?" she said, almost laughing.

"Fuck you, Soper," I said. We both laughed a little bit and I said, "I gotta go check on my guys, but I'll be back. Sleep now."

"Yes, ma'am," she said.

"Actually, a good Marine would say 'Sleeping, aye!'" I said.

But she was already asleep.

So I went out and disposed my guys. I kept Patsy in the room with me so I could keep an eye on him—he was still declining medical attention—and I put Badass and Bumble right outside the door. Ed went forward with the 101st (after I gave her a hug and promised to bear her children if she wanted—making the call to the president had definitely saved Soper's life, and the rest of ours, too) so that she could report to me if necessary. Sarah, Darah and El Gato were in the hall between the 101st and the door to our room.

It should have been foolproof, but it wasn't designed for one particular type of assault.

An albino dwarf doctor with a God complex the size of Montana.

Hurricane Albino came ashore about two hours into our vigil and stormed past all the firepower by yelling "Fuck you, assholes! This is my hospital and I'll go wherever the fuck I want, you dumb-shits! Now get out of my way before I punch you all in the nuts or cunts, both of which could cause irreparable damage to your pitiful sex organs! MOVE!"

I opened the door to Soper's room and said, "Hey, we're tryin' to sleep in here! Injured patient needs rest! Doctor's orders! Could you herd of wildebeest keep it down? And somebody shut off that goddamned foghorn before I shoot it!" Everybody was laughing so hard that all of the tension seemed to just melt away.

Even Hurricane Albino was laughing, which I counted among the best things that I had ever done in my life.

She looked up at me with her pink eyes (yes, pink! They were incredibly arresting and attractive) and said, "Thanks for that, Agent. It's been very tense here for about five hours, most of it's my fault and I really do apologize, although you have to admit having armed soldiers descend on you from a giant military helicopter could put your teeth on edge and your sphincter in a knot, especially when you're about to deliver triplets that've had problems *in utero*. I'm Dr. Tully Whited." She reached her surprisingly large hand up to shake mine.

"Agent Glinka Glickstien, U.S. Secret Service. I'm also temporarily Lieutenant General G. L. Glickstien, United States Marine Corps, commanding the First Regimental Combat Team, 101st Air Assault Division. Everybody calls me Freak. And no way is your real name Whited," I said.

"Blame it on my dad. He emigrated from Poland to Lexington in 1959, and his name—Boris Bialyy—was a bit too Russian for the rednecks here in Kentucky, and explaining that it was Polish was just as bad, so he started telling people he was the great-grandson of an obscure Scottish lord—the Earl of Whited—thus changing his name to an English one without losing the meaning in Polish. Then I came along, and voilà, instant irony!"

She looked me up and down and said, "Freak? You escape from the circus or something?"

I laughed and said, "You could say that. I've got some unusual physical gifts."

"Tell me about it," Tully Whited said. We laughed some more before she said, "What kind of unusual physical gifts?"

"I have abnormal strength, speed, and hand-eye coordination," I said. "I'm stronger than 99 percent of the rest of the world, even the men, and I can outshoot anybody anywhere, and no, I'm not being arrogant or bragging—it ain't braggin' if you can do it," I said.

"How strong?" Whited said.

I opened the door to Soper's room and said, "Come in here. It'll be easier to show you." She came in, and Soper said, "Dr. Whited, I'm glad you came up. I... I... I need to talk. You heard that my..." She couldn't go on, and more tears ran down her face.

Whited and I took her hands, and Whited said, "Just cry it all out, Soper. You have a right to do that. We'll talk after Freak shows me her abnormal strength."

I looked at Soper, and she actually smiled through the tears. I stepped back from her side, said, "Lay perfectly still, Soper," put my arms under the hospital bed, and picked the whole arrangement off the floor, holding it at shoulder level like I was a forklift lifting a pallet of whiskey kegs. I turned 90 degrees so I could see Whited again and said, "Abnormal like this."

The doctor's face looked like Edvard Munch's *The Scream* (yeah, I know there are different versions—just pick one), but she quickly recovered her composure and went into doctor mode.

"Are your muscles trembling? Is holding the bed and patient up difficult? Are you in danger of dropping her?" Whited said.

"Negative to all, Doc," I said. "I couldn't hold her here all day, but it won't get heavy for another 15 or 20 minutes."

"And you've done stuff like this before," the doctor said.

"Lots of times," I said.

"OK, why don't you put her down," Whited said.

"OK." I put Soper and her bed in the exact position they'd been in before and looked back at Dr. Tully Whited. She was standing with her chin in her hand, looking at some far off place in her mind. After a while she said, "Have you been tested about this?"

"A long time ago, when I was still a kid. They didn't find anything abnormal," I said.

"So you weren't born a hermaphrodite? You don't currently have any testicles? Your genes are actually XX?" she said.

"No, no, and yes—I'm a real live womyn."

"And you have a normal sex drive?" she said.

"Define normal," I said. "If you mean do I want sex periodically, and do I sometimes act on those urges, the answer is yes. I'm not a hyper, or hypo, sexual person. Sex drive normal, aye."

"And you obviously don't do steroids, because that would be readily apparent. Are you hypertrophic? Are your muscles unusually large?" she said.

I took off my coat and flexed my bare arms (I like short sleeved blouses—easier to pull my pistols and shoot bad guys) in the classic 'muscle-man' pose. She poked my arm and said, "Not hypertrophic, and it can't be Marfan's Syndrome, because you'd be a lot taller, and your feet would be bigger." She looked at me again and said, "Well, you don't look it, but are you a Basque?"

"No—wait a sec. That's one thing the doctor from my testing asked about. He said I had some kind of protein that was only found in the Basque people, some remnant gene from the Neanderthals," I said.

"OMG!" she said. "You must have Le Sendoa's Syndrome!"

"Come again?" I said.

"There are only eleven documented cases of Le Sendoa's Syndrome across the world. It's a rare condition that's linked to proteins we think are throwbacks to Neanderthals, because all eleven cases have been in the Basque population of the Pyrenees. Eight men and three wymyn have exhibited extraordinary strength and/or speed without any other genetic problems or deformations. You would be the first case outside the Basque, if we could do tests to verify you really have the proteins," Whited said. Her eyes were lit up like a pink Christmas tree on Christmas Eve (hey, Jews have eyes—we never had a Christmas tree, but we were surrounded by gentiles back in Battle Creek), her hands were fluttering and her chest was almost heaving as she contemplated my "condition."

"Great, we might know what makes me a freak," I said. "I'll give you whatever you need, but first I gotta make sure that Soper is safe, get debriefed about the assassination attempt, give statements to the appropriate federal agencies, notify three families that their loved ones have passed and try to get some sleep and food, so can we forgo the clinical analysis for a bit?"

"Yeah, but I get dibs on writing the paper for the *New England Journal of Medicine*," Whited said, laughing. I had to admit I was being a whiny bitch, so I laughed, too. I looked over where Patsy had been sitting quietly in the corner and realized he was asleep, which with a concussion could be a bad thing, so I went over and shook him while Dr. Whited was checking Soper's vitals.

He woke right up and looked a question at me, but I said, "Easy, Patsy. Just wanted to make sure that you weren't stroking out on me. It's all quiet on the Kentucky front."

He looked bad, but he gave me a thumbs up, so I was just going to leave him alone when Hurricane Dr. Pink-Eyed Albino Dwarf Tully Whited bellowed, "What in the hell is going on?" She scared the shit out of Patsy and I, as well as Badass and Bumble, who both burst into the room with their hands on their pistols.

"Wha' th' fuh?" Patsy said.

"Are you having a stroke?" I said. Bumble and Badass looked at me and I said, "I don't know what her problem is. Ask her."

Before we could say anything else Dr. Tully Whited said, her tone quiet and even (which scared the shit out of US worse than the bellowing), "How long have you been like this, Agent?" She was looking right at Patsy, who looked right back and said, "Juth fo' a bih."

The pink-eyed hurricane looked at me and said, "You knew he was like this? Aren't you his commanding officer, or whatever term you Secret Service assholes have for it?"

"Not exactly, but even if I were I'd have to restrain him in order to get him to leave his post before he knows that our protectee is safe," I said.

Patsy looked at the Pink-Eyed Hurricane (she was pretty much given the nickname by consensus; we later shortened it to just Hurricane) and said, "Ah ca' tahk car' o' myselth."

"Oh, really?" Hurricane said as she advanced on him with her stethoscope and blood pressure cuff.

"Yeth! Ah'm a U Eth Mawine! We don' leaf anyone behin', or dethert our pothsss!" Patsy said. I thought the space between them was going to ignite from the heat in Hurricane's pink eyes, but she said, "OK, Marine, but I at least need to check your vitals, OK?" Her voice was gentle and her manner kind, and I caught an inkling of what made her such a great doc.

Patsy nodded and she did his vitals, then said, "Well, you're doing much better than I expected. I would like to give you a preventative antibiotic for the cuts and such, and also give you a shot for your immune system, just in case you were exposed to staphylococcus germs, OK? You can stay at your post until your relief comes, as long as you take these two shots. Fair enough?"

Patsy nodded and Hurricane went out in the hall, called for a nurse and said, "Jamie, bring me a prophylactic shot of Keflex, and five milligrams of Versed, willya?" She waited until the nurse came with the two shots, took them and said, "Thanks, Jamie, I can do it," and then walked over to Patsy. He took off his jacket, which was covered with so much *schmutz* that it looked like the cloth was alive, rolled up his sleeve and waited for his shots.

Hurricane looked up at him and said, "I'm 4'4½" tall," she said. "If you don't mind I'd like for you to sit down so I can reach your arm, OK big boy?"

Patsy said, "Thorry, Dock'er" and sat down on the chair. Hurricane swiftly swabbed his arm, shot him up with first one and then the other hypodermic, walked over and put the needles in a sharp's container, and went back and took Patsy's hand.

"Than Ah ast yoo a q'esshon?" he said.

"Sure," Hurricane said.

"Why are you tho thort?" Patsy said.

We all braced for the Hurricane, but she just said, "My parents both had double-recessive genes that were set for dwarfism, so when they mixed their DNA I got lucky and became a little person. I hate that term, by the way. My brother is 6'4" and as dumb as a box of rocks. My sister is 5'8" and she had three children by three different fathers before she was 21. I've got a PhD in clinical psychology and an MD in obstetrics, and I'm kind of a genius in my field, but they're "normal" and I'm a "little person." Does that make any sense?"

"Noooo," Patsy said. His eyes were starting to droop—Versed is a so-called 'twilight drug' that docs use to start the process in anesthesiology. He wasn't going to last much longer, but he said, "Ah ha' one mo' q'esshon, OK?"

"Sure, Marine, fire away," Hurricane said.

"Wha' arh yoor eyth pin'?" he said.

"Oh, I have a condition called oculocutaneous albinism. It's caused when the MC1R gene malfunctions and a person doesn't produce any melatonin at all. Luckily my brain case is as big as yours—or any other "normal" person's, so even being a short, white, pink-eyed monster I can be a productive member of society. Cool, huh?" Hurricane said, a small trace of bitterness creeping into her tone.

"Ah thin' yoo are beau'ifu'," Patsy said. "Ah will figh' anybod' who says diff'ren'," he said as his head nodded and he fell asleep. Hurricane said, "Get over here and use your freakish gifts to put him on the gurney, Freak. And if I didn't get the fact that he's a faithful man and you're both Marines I would rain a whole shitpot of abuse down on your head, and then I'd challenge you to a duel with swords, you stupid asshole."

I picked Patsy up and gently laid him on the gurney the nurse rolled into the room. I looked at Hurricane and her pink eyes were fierce on mine, but she was quite gentle when she said, "He could've had a skull fracture and died. There are a whole host of other problems he will probably have to live with because of his courage and determination, but you weren't hurt, and you're supposed to look after him. No, don't try to explain," she said, holding up a hand. "I get it—my dad is a Marine, and we have an obstetrician I work with who's a Marine. Duty, death before dishonor, I'm a goddamned U.S. Marine, all that other shit they fill your head with, it's all fun and games until somebody gets hurt, and then some doc somewhere has to try and put it all back together. That macho shit drives me crazy."

"It's not machismo, it's a real commitment to what we do. Patsy would be shamed for life if he came off the line for what he perceived as less than a life or death matter. He would also tell you that his life while guarding his protectee was worth less than hers, and that dying while ensuring her safety was not only proper, but necessary. Just because we don't think like you doesn't mean we're wrong or stupid or trying to impress people—we swore an oath, just like you did, and we don't mean ours any less than you did yours. In fact, your wimpy-assed Hippocratic Oath doesn't hold a candle to our oaths as Marines, or as Secret Service agents, because we're willing to die to prove we mean ours, and all you do is hedge your bets with "first do no harm." What the fuck kind of oath is that? And by the way, if you don't get that about Patsy and all the rest of us here, well, fuck you, the horse you rode in on, and the family dog, Dr. Hurricane," I said.

I was tired, and I wanted to cry and scream and tear my clothes for the loss of our people today, good people who didn't deserve to die, but I couldn't, because I swore to do a job and I by God was going to do it, come hell, high water or Hurricane.

Those pink eyes were sparking up as Hurricane prepared to hurl a reply at me, but we were interrupted by Soper, who said, "Doc, can I get some of that shit you gave Patsy? I hurt all over, my wife is dead and I'd like to just dream of better days for about a week. Whaddya say?"

Hurricane turned to Soper, her look softening as she went over to the bed and climbed on a stool that had been set there by the nurse who took Patsy away. Hurricane said, "Sorry, Soper. I forgot what I was here for. I just go crazy with all of this duty and honor shit. It's a hard way to live a life, and it can get people killed, y'know?"

"You mean like those people who killed my wife and baby, and tried to kill me and the rest of the people on the bus?" Soper said. "Without Freak and her comrades I'd be dead now, too, and so would a bunch of other innocent people. They do what they do because it's hard-wired in their DNA, just like being a doc is in yours, and running track is in mine. Just accept that people do what they do and get on with it." She took Hurricane's hand and said, "I'm not kidding about hurting, and wanting to sleep."

Hurricane said, "Will it be OK with you if I put you out when you might still be in danger?"

Soper laughed and said, "With the 101st Airborne, the Secret Service and the mighty Freak at my side? They only way I could feel safer is if Achilles and his Myrmidons were outside that door, and I'm not sure Achilles could take Freak. I need to sleep, Tully. Please."

Hurricane nodded and said, "One sec." She went over to the door and said, "Jaime, I need 3 milligrams Versed." The nurse brought her the stuff and Hurricane came over and put the needle in the port of Soper's IV. She said, "Nighty-night, Soper. I'll be here when you wake up."

"Me, too," I said.

"I'm counting on it," Soper said, and fell asleep.

"Can we call a truce?" I said.

"Fuck you, Freak—if you think that's fighting you've got a lot to learn about me," Hurricane said. "I just needed to vent—when I get worried about someone I get testy. When I get really pissed you'll know—my eyes literally get red and I have tears running down my cheeks. Oh, and I start punching anything within reach, so watch it." She cracked a grin to let me know that she was OK, and I said, "Hey, Patsy really seemed to like you. It could be the start of something beautiful."

"Nah, he's too nice. I like the bad boys—bikers, Force Recon assholes who think they're tough, reformed junkies, that type," she said. "Besides, I don't really have time for a love life—it's mostly hit and run."

"Tell me about it," I said. We both laughed, and she shook my hand and said, "I get the code, and believe me when I tell you that I live the same way, although the Hippocratic Oath really is kinda wimpy-assed compared to the Marines and Secret Service."

"Yeah, but getting to fix people up instead of fucking them up is way more rewarding," I said.

"Well, most days," Hurricane said. "Other days it would be nice to just light 'em up, especially when you're always answering questions like "how's the weather down there?" or "how do you drive a car?" Assholes."

I knew about people being so insensitive, so we had quite a talk about being different in a world that seemed to hunger for conformity. I kept asking for sitreps from my people, and everything was quiet, so we kept talking. Hurricane called downstairs to see how Patsy was doing; he had a concussion, torn ligaments in his ankle that would require surgery, a partially dislocated shoulder and a cut on his tongue that took sixty-two stitches (Hurricane thought that he probably bit himself), but it looked like he was going to recover, so we kept talking.

Hurricane had just told me about her first serious boyfriend's fear of making love to her because he was afraid that he might hurt her due to the size of his penis.

"And then I saw it and I couldn't help but laugh—he couldn't have hurt a mouse with that thing. He explained his worry again that he would hurt me with his eight-inch organ, and I said that if that was eight inches I was 6' tall, and then I thought of the joke about Needle-Dick the Bug Fucker, and I guess I laughed too much, or too loud, or I just offended his sense of dignity, and, well, he left in a huff and we never saw each other again," Hurricane said.

"Well, fuck him if he couldn't take a joke," I said.

"Actually, un-fuck him," Hurricane said.

It was right then that I heard the elevator bell ring down the hall. I put my 1076s in my hands and swept Hurricane behind me. Command Sergeant Major Delgado said, calmly and clearly, "This floor is restricted admittance, sir. Please produce ID before you try to clear the elevator."

A voice tried to tell him to calm down and Command Sergeant Major Delgado said in the same calm, clear voice, "I'll calm down after I put you in the ground if you don't produce ID *immediately*, sir."

In the movies this is the moment when the good guys all charged their weapons, but this was real life, so all I heard was Command Sergeant Major Delgado say "I've got the tall one in the overcoat." I could see the rest of the air assault troopers looking down the barrels of their M4 assault rifles, fingers on triggers and safeties off, preparing to let off the rounds from rifles that had been charged since we got on the helo from Morehead.

Luckily, whoever was trying to get off the elevator produced ID. Command Sergeant Major Delgado said, "Slide it over to me, sir." His voice was as calm as if he were ordering a cheeseburger, but I knew that his M9 Beretta never left its target. After ten seconds, he said, "One moment, sir."

My radio popped. "Command, CSM Delgado. His ID says he's Edward Otis Whitney, Director of the Protective Division. He's 6'1", 190, brown eyes, salt and pepper hair, wearing a $10,000 suit and excellent shoes, and he has that air of "my defecation is not odiferous" about him. He also has a scar under his chin and is wearing a Harvard ring on his right hand, and a large gold wedding ring on his left."

"CSM Delgado, Command. Sounds like our guy, but let's make sure. Send him down the hall—make him leave the coat in the elevator, and have him take his suit coat off, too—but keep everybody else on the elevator," I said.

"Command, CSM Delgado. Roger that, ma'am." He relayed the commands to whoever was at the elevator, and a few seconds later I heard someone's shoes tapping down the hall. I hadn't told them to, but Sarah, Darah and El Gato stopped and searched him. The shoes came down the hall until they were stopped by Badass saying, "That's far enough, sir."

The door opened and Bumble stuck his head in. "It's him. You want to come out or for him to come it?"

I put one pistol away and said, "Send him in." Bumble held the door open and Edward Otis Whitney came into the room. He looked odd without his suit coat, and his shoulder holster was empty, but otherwise it was Old Three Names. He opened his mouth to say something and I said, "Are you under duress, or are those our guys out there in the elevator?"

"They're ours. I also have another squad downstairs led by Assistant Director Francis Wong," he said. I felt like I was going to faint—I got light-headed and my vision blurred momentarily, and I must have swayed on my feet, because Hurricane was right there at my elbow holding me up. Old Three Names said, "You look like shit, Freak, but I'm damned proud of you anyway. Well done. You can stand down now." He put out his hand and I took it. We shook and I said, "This is Dr. Tully Whited, and I wouldn't make any sudden moves or she is liable to tear your head off and shit down your neck, sir. Don't let the tiny but exquisite package fool you—she's a killer. If she wasn't such a good doc I'd say you should hire her."

Edward Otis Whitney shook Hurricane's hand and said, "It's a pleasure, doctor. Thank you for taking such good care of our wounded, and our protectee. The country owes you a debt of gratitude."

"Yeah, thanks," Hurricane said. "Now that you're here I need to take care of the rest of the Secret Service detail, so I'm prescribing twelve hours of rest before any debriefing begins. No argument from you either, buster, or I'm gonna call your boss and tell him that you're interfering with a doctor trying to do her duty. We clear who's in charge here?"

"Perfectly," Old Three Names said. "I'm not a doctor, but I was going to suggest a twenty-four-hour waiting period before we began debriefing. Is that acceptable, or is twelve hours all that's needed?"

"Twenty-four is better, and Agent de Vries isn't going to be able to talk for at least three days, so his de-brief will have to be in writing," she said.

"Done," Edward Otis Whitney said. He turned to me and said, "If you'll call off the airborne I'll get you relieved." I stepped out into the hall and said, "Command Sergeant Major, these are the good guys. Let 'em off the elevator after you check all of their IDs."

"Roger that, General," he said.

"Still not taking any chances, are you Freak," Old Three Names said.

"No sense in stumbling right at the finish line," I said. He reached out and shook my hand again. "There was a reason we met. You're right where you need to be," he said. "The president and Director Hessler send their thanks, and we'll have to talk about moving you up the chain when you're ready."

"I'm not leaving Soper, sir, until she is done or we're pulled," I said.

"Understood, but the Director may have other ideas," Edward Otis Whitney said. "The president is asking for you full time."

"Well, fuck 'em both," I said. "There is nothing wrong with the president's detail, and if Director Hessler thinks that I'm coming off this assignment before it's over she's lost her mind. Soper is my team's protectee, and it's gonna stay that way, at least for me. I'm not sure about anybody else on the detail. That's non-negotiable for me, or I quit and guard her as a private citizen."

Old Three Names looked at me and smiled. "You just cost me $100, Freak. I bet that you'd accept reassignment, but Director Hessler said you'd say almost exactly what you did. Good people are worth a little extra, and I'm glad to pay that money."

We went out into the hall and walked down toward the elevator. Several agents had been cleared by the Command Sergeant Major and his men and were headed down the hall. The elevator dinged again and Charlie Chan came off first. He saw me and made to move down the hall, but two 101st troopers stopped him, and Command Sergeant Major Delgado held out his hand and said "ID, sir."

I laughed and said, "Stand you and your men down, Command Sergeant Major. I know this one by sight—he's as trustworthy as Colonel Tomilo."

"Yes, ma'am. Squad, stand down and resume guard positions," Command Sergeant Major Delgado said. He looked at me and said, "Should I dial up our bird, General?"

"Affirmative, Sar'nt-Major," I said. "And you can secure from this detail and stand easy. Thank you for your help." I shook his hand, and shook the hands of his troopers, and Command Sergeant Major Delgado said, "We're yours to command General. You don't need to thank us—you're our superior officer."

"I'm just Agent Glickstien now, Sar'nt-Major, although I'd be honored if you just called me Freak, like all of my friends do," I said.

"Ma'am, I would like to do that, but until we're out of your sight you're still Lieutenant General G. L. Glickstien, United States Marine Corps, TDY to command of First Regimental Combat Team Bastogne, 101st Air Assault Division, and we are going to by God treat you with the respect you deserve. Squad, Ah-tenn-HUT! Present arms!"

The troopers saluted me and Command Sergeant Major Delgado said, "The Old Lady clangs when she walks!"

"Hoo-AHH!" the troopers said.

I never got a better compliment in my whole life.

I returned their salute and said, "Command Sergeant Major Delgado, you and your squad can expect a citation from the president of the United States, and you have my personal gratitude. If you ever need anything you let me know and I'll do my best to help you. You are dismissed from this duty and should rejoin your unit forthwith."

"Yes, ma'am," he said. He looked behind me and I turned to find the rest of my detail right there. "We'd like to shake some hands, Freak," Ed said. "Well, fuck yeah—shake away," I said.

There were shakes, and hugs, and lots of attaboys and other palaver, and then it was time for the troopers to leave.

They got on the elevator and Command Sergeant Major Delgado put his hand out to stop the door from closing. "There is just one thing, General," he said.

"Anything you want, Sar'nt-Major," I said.

"I would like the chance to shoot against you, one time," he said, that competitive spark in his eye.

"I'd like that, Sar'nt-Major, but you should know that I never shoot without something on the line," I said.

"A case of fine Scotch?" he said.

"Make it Pepsis and hot dogs and you're on," I said.

"It can be arranged, ma'am," he said.

"Shall I call ahead so you can practice, Command Sergeant Major?" I said.

The troopers all laughed and he said, "Oh, no, ma'am. I have a key to the range at Campbell—and I shoot every day." He smiled at me, looking like the crocodile from Peter Pan.

"You're a freak," I said, smiling my own little crocodile smile.

"Takes one to know one, ma'am," he said, smiling as the elevator door closed.

I turned around, as weary as I'd ever been, and said, "Darah, Badass, downstairs to get checked out, then sleep. Everybody else on my detail, sleep. I'm going back to Soper's room to wait for her to wake up. Ed, you get an extra quarter out of petty cash for being the smartest agent in our detail and calling the right guy to get the job done. All around great job, everybody."

I got to Soper's door and Charlie Chan said, "We got it, Freak. Director Whitney said to go sleep and we'll get to it when you wake up."

I looked at him like he was speaking in Urdu and said, "Sorry, Charlie, but I promised Soper I'd be there when she woke up. Plus I've got phone calls to make, and a kid's parents to see. No rest for the wicked, I'm afraid." I smiled a weak-ass smile, shrugged and went to push past him when there was sharp pain in my butt. I whipped around to find Hurricane standing there with an empty syringe. She was smiling and she said, "Nice speech, Freak. Too bad you're so full of shit that your eyes have turned brown and your breath stinks."

"Goddamn it, Hurricane, I've got work to do. I can't just go off and sleep—what about that poor kid's parents? And I promised Soper I'd be there for her. You can't just go around shooting people in the ass with Versed, ya pink-eyed hooligan."

"Do I tell you how to shoot?" she said in a soft voice.

"No," I said, knowing where she was going.

"Then you should probably not tell me how to doctor, right?" she said. Nurse Jamie rolled a wheelchair up and Hurricane said, "Sit down before you fall down, Freak. Sleep deprivation is a bitch, because it's cumulative and hampers your ability to think and react—not what you'd want in a Secret Service protection agent, am I right?—plus you've got some PTSD thrown in, plus that Klonopin I gave you is going to take the edge off so fast it won't matter what you want to do—Morpheus is waiting just on the other side of your eyelids. We'll hold the fort here until you get some sleep, and then you can go back to saving the world, OK?"

"Fuck you, Hurricane," I said as I slid into the wheelchair. My eyelids were feeling pretty heavy, but I wasn't ready to give in yet. Hurricane stepped up to me and said, "You're a hero, Freak, and a real swell gal, but you still need sleep. Nobody's gonna hurt Soper, or think less of you because you sleep, so let go. Oh, and one more thing, you need to introduce me to that Badass man, the tall blonde one? He kinda flips my switches, if ya know what I mean. So get some sleep, 'cause I want that introduction." She spoke in a voice so soft I thought that I imagined it, but as I fell down a long hallway toward sleep she said "I'm gonna leave ya with this piece of maternity room wisdom: even fucking heroes need sleep, Freeeeeeeeeeeeeak."

'*Well, that sounds true,*' I thought, and then it was dark for a while.

CHAPTER 46

Conspiracy, Anyone?

I woke up in a room decorated with pink bunnies, blue ducks and dancing green hippos. At first I thought that I was having an acid flashback, but then I remembered that I never did acid, so I decided I was still in a maternity hospital in Mt. Sterling, Kentucky, where I was a prisoner of the crazed albino dwarf doctor named Tully Whited, a.k.a. the Pink Hurricane.

I was mUsing about how good I felt, considering—*'Wow! Sleep good! Ogg like sleep! Crazy tiny doctor right about sleep! Ogg happy to sleep more!'*—when I heard snoring and looked at the other bed in the room, where Ed was indeed sawing logs with great vigor. Someone on the other side of me cleared their throat, so I looked over there to find Edward Otis Whitney sitting quietly in a chair. He nodded at me and said, "Good afternoon. I'm thinking that you feel much better after twelve hours of sleep. You certainly look more human than you did yesterday, not that your look wasn't well-earned. You did a more than superb job the last two days—I am very proud to be your colleague."

"Odd, I didn't see you shooting there, Wild Ed," I said.

"It's true that I was not on the firing line, but I do have other responsibilities that make the firing line possible, you know," Old Three Names said.

"Sorry about that, Eddie. Don't let my cavalier attitude fool you—I do respect you and your position," I said.

Old Three Names said, "Oh, I know that, and I appreciate it, but don't tell the president or Director Hessler that—you currently can walk on water, cure leprosy and bring world peace at the end of your 10-millimeter handguns. I would say that you could ask to be promoted to Goddess of the World and they would at least consider it."

"But I can't raise the dead," I said. I felt terrible about Josie and Elvin Clyde Bliss, but I knew that was on the sons of bitches that hit us with a goddamned cement truck. Speaking of which…

I looked at him and said, "Can I get a Pepsi or five in here? And some food? Preferably big, fat roast beef or corned beef sandwiches loaded with mayonnaise and three or 12 bags of chips? I think I could eat a water buffalo with just my Ka-Bar and a fork."

"I already ordered sandwiches for you and Agent Devlin, who I see is now awake," he said. I looked over at Ed, and she was looking back at me, so I said, "Don't take this wrong, pal-o'-mine, but after we eat, I'm gonna hug you and give you a big wet, sloppy kiss. You saved our bacon back there, kid."

"Just made a phone call to a friend for a friend," she said, her brown eyes warm and sparkling. "I did what any agent would have done, given the same resources and situation."

"So you don't want a hug and a kiss?" I said, teasing her.

"I didn't say *that*," Ed said. "Never turn down a good hug and kiss—that's my motto." We both laughed. Ed was the least promiscuous person I knew. She was good-looking, sexy as hell, and really, seriously smart, but she didn't flaunt any of it, which just made her more attractive. I'd never seen her even remotely come on to anyone, because she took marriage very seriously, and apparently her wife was the jealous type (who wouldn't have been?).

We shared that look that only good friends can, and I said, "Did you get any calls after you called the president?"

"Yeah, a weird one," she said.

"Let me guess, it was my uncle from Illinois," I said.

"Oh, Mighty Karnak, you know and see all," she said (Johnny Carson was dead, but not exactly gone). "Your uncle tried to tell me that someone in the, uh, superstructure of a certain three-letter agency might have it in for you, and that they might be organizing a—ahem—*party*, in your honor."

Edward Otis Whitney cleared his throat and said, "Let's stop beating around the Bush, shall we? I also got a call from your uncle in Illinois, and he told me flatly that someone in the FBI was trying to set you up to be killed. His sources couldn't tell him who, but they did mention trying to get someone else to do the job who would not bring suspicion on this mysterious person."

"That's why it took you so long to get reinforcements here," I said.

"Correct. I only brought agents personally known to me, only those that I could implicitly trust with your safety and the safety of your protectee," Old Three Names said.

"Well, I was talking to my uncle when we got hit. Our transmission was breaking up, but I got enough to know that those sons of bitches were using Soper as a decoy so we'd focus our attention on her as the target and not me," I said. "That doesn't make any sense at all. What the fuck do I know that would get the FBI to assassinate me?"

"We don't know that is what happened, although it would seem that your uncle is better connected to that side of things," Edward Otis Whitney said. "I must ask, have either of you mentioned this to anyone else?"

"The call was breaking up when the truck slammed into us—my phone was knocked out of my hand and I really don't know where it is. I sure didn't tell anyone face-to-face."

"I was too busy calling the president and trying to figure out how to protect Soper with just three people—and where to get her medical attention. I haven't talked about it with anyone face-to-face, either," Ed said.

"Good. Please keep this between us—that way we can use this without alerting the guilty party. We can also keep the media from going down this road," Edward Otis Whitney said. "I have not even alerted Director Hessler. This is an internal matter that the three of us may have to deal with alone. In the meantime I have started our disinformation plan—the media thinks that this was entirely the Ku Klux Klan trying to get at Soper."

"Trying to assassinate Soper," I said.

"Well, yes, but we don't nee—"

Ed interrupted him. "No, sir, call it what it is, or was: an assassination attempt by a radical group inside the U.S. It's the best way to put the people who are after us off the scent, and it has the added benefit of being the truth. We won't even have to sell it—the media will go into a feeding frenzy and they'll sell it for us."

"Domestic terrorism," I said. "We can make it an orgy of coverage if we call it an assassination attempt and domestic terrorism. Both sides of the aisle in Congress will go crazy, every correspondent in the world will want to investigate the incident, and best of all it will totally fuck up the Klan."

"We'll get a three-fer, sir, killing all of our little birdies with one stone," Ed said.

Old Three Names sat there with his chin in his hand, but not for long. The guy could be a bit stiff and stuffy, but I give him credit—he knew a good idea when he heard one. He stood up and dialed a single digit on his cell. "I need three reporters for a pool report about the assassination attempt on Ms. Soper. Yes. We'll make at least two of the agents available, probably three. This afternoon?" He looked at us and we were nodding, so he said, "Definitely this afternoon—let's say 4:45 so that they can get it on the evening news. How about CBS, Reuters and PBS—make sure we get Gwen Ifill or Judy Woodruff, or Hari Sreenivasan, and that Mason gentleman from Reuters. It would also help if we could get David Martin or Bob Orr from CBS. Well, after talking to two agents who were there it is very clear that this was definitely an act of domestic terrorism. Because they saw the Klan coming toward them with weapons, and the Klan is domestic, no? OK, get on it now, and if you need me for emphasis do it. Yes, I do know Scott, and Gwen, too. Good. Thank you."

Edward Otis Whitney said, "It is a great idea for several reasons, and I'm going to claim it was your idea, because it plays right into the "we were blindsided by domestic terrorism" narrative, and it will emphasize that we are looking exclusively at the Klan. We can simply let them run as far as they want, and if someone should stumble on to something that doesn't jibe with our domestic terrorism narrative they will come to us first for comment, at which point we can express surprise and use their notes as cover for our own investigation."

"Good," I said. "We need to have Darah, Ed and Patsy at the interview. That way they can get a photogenic group on camera, and only Ed will know about what is really happening."

"Two things, Freak. First, it has to be you at the interview, not me, because whoever is after us, you seem to be the focus. Second, how are you going to get Patsy past the Pink Hurricane?" Ed said.

"Ah, shit," Old Three Names and I said at the same time. "I've got the Pepsis, Freak, but she's right—Dr. Whited is never going to go for it, even though I agree that we want the visual of the battered agent who wouldn't desert his post even in the face of domestic terrorism," Edward Otis Whitney said.

"You realize that that's what actually happened, right? Patsy wouldn't get any attention until the Pink Hurricane whacked him with a sedative," I said.

"Of course I recognize it. More importantly, so will Gwen Ifill or David Martin. Let them make the claim that he's a hero—which he is—because then the Service gets some good publicity without having to say a thing. In fact, I think that Agent Devlin is right. You led the defense of the candidate, assisted by your two injured comrades—didn't Agent Koenigsblett have a concussion and facial lacerations? Even better than that will be the image of two wymyn and one severely injured man leading the defense of the candidate against long odds. It will also piss the Klan off that they were turned away by a womyn, which means that they may do something stupid in response," Old Three Names said.

"Which will give somebody the chance to whack their stupid, bed-sheet wearin' asses," Ed said.

"Yeah, but does anybody really want to see this on national TV?" I said, pointing to my rather unlovely face (hey, blame my parents' genes for making me ugly—I know I do).

"Even better," Old Three Names said. "Everyone will know that you are a real field agent, not some pretty face we stood up so the Service could look good. No offense, Freak."

"None taken," I said, still not completely sold on the idea.

"Freak, Badass told me you put the first truck driver down and stopped that threat. Darah told me that you put three full mags into the second truck and stopped that threat. Patsy told me you took command of a regimental combat team of air assault troops and stopped the Klan from getting any closer to the bus than five hundred meters to stop that threat. I saw you take command of this situation and put a stop to any threat here.

"Who gives a flying fuck about how pretty you are? Was Eisenhower pretty? Chesty Puller? McAuliffe? Skinny Wainwright? Spruance? They were all ugly men, and who gave a shit? They were heroes because of what they did, not what they looked like, so fuck you if you don't get interviewed on TV just because you think you're ugly," Ed said, talking to me like I was her little sister.

I concluded that she was right, so I said, "Got it. Be on TV, ignore breaking camera lenses and looks of revulsion, provoke Klan and con unknown subject, aye!" We all laughed, which is when Soper came in the room. She was in remarkably good spirits, considering what had happened to her in the last forty-eight hours or so, and she heartily approved of Old Three Names' idea, especially because she wanted to participate.

At first he was reluctant to let her, but Soper pointed out that she was the aggrieved party, and that she wanted to help provoke the Klan while paying tribute to the Secret Service's dedication and effective service to their protectees. After some arguing about it Old Three Names gave in and accepted Soper as a participant in the interview.

She left, Old Three Names stepped out of the room, Ed and I got dressed and Edward Otis Whitney came back in with a load of food. Ed and I fell on it like ravenous vampires on unsuspecting virgins. As the food flew down our gullets he said, "We know that this is a conspiracy, because someone got to the local sheriff, and we're sure that either the same or a different unknown subject, perhaps from the FBI, arranged it, so we can mention a conspiracy, but it has to be something local."

"Don't worry about it, Eddie. I got ya covered on that one—it's gonna be the Klan, the Klan, the Ku Klux-fucking-Klan. Which gives me another idea—we need to bring one more person in for the interview to help support our local conspiracy theory," I said around a hunk of Italian beef and cheese sandwich.

"Curtis Jeffries," Edward Otis Whitney said. "I've already had him brought here so that his sheriff didn't have him lynched. He is persona non grata in Rowan County, even though they can't really think of a reason to fire him. I take it that he helped you?"

Ed and I clapped the backs of our hands together while barking and saying "Family seal of approval" (an old joke, but one that immediately signals one's approval of an action and also lightens a mood that may be too tense), and I told him all about the deputy and his nephew, the ROTC and how Curtis was the only deputy to arrive to help us. We also discussed his comments about the sheriff and the Klan, and also his desire to move into the federal law enforcement field.

"He's also a good guy with an automatic weapon," I said. "He hosed that second truck down like a pro, and I'm sure that he was prepared to shoot people from his hometown because it was the right thing to do. We could do worse than helping him become a U.S. Marshal."

451

"I concur. If he's qualified and can get through the interview process I will definitely support him," Old Three names said. "Now we need to discuss how we're going to treat this interview." We talked about it for 20 minutes or so before Hurricane whipped the door to our room open and said, "How are we feeling, Miss Glickstien?" in a prim and proper doctor voice.

"Fuck you, Hurricane," I said. "I got a great big lump on my butt from some quack whackin' me with a sedative and now I've gotta do an interview 'cause my boss is a lily-livered pansy-ass who can't deal with the press and who the hell put me in one of those hospital gowns anyway?"

"So you're just fine, is what you're saying," she said.

"I'm about as good as I could be. You were right about the need for sleep, by the way. Thanks for stabbing my tired ass with that nighty-night juice. Morpheus and I had quite a tango," I said. "How's Patsy?"

"Agent de Vries is doing fine—sixty-two stitches in his tongue, torn ligaments in his foot and his left shoulder was dislocated. Oh, yeah, he has a nasty concussion, but fortunately his head is really hard—I'm not kidding, the guy has an exceptionally hard head—and that kept him on the no skull fracture list. He should be good to go in two or three days," Hurricane said.

"He needs to be ready to go in about four hours," Edward Otis Whitney said.

"Yeah, nice one, Headquarters Guy," Hurricane said, like she thought Old Three Names was kidding.

"We've been introduced—I'm Edward Otis Whitney—and I'm not joking, Dr. Whited."

"Absolutely no fucking way will I release him for anything more strenuous than lifting a Pepsi to his lips," Hurricane said. "And that will *probably* be some time later—like two days later."

"He must be ready for an interview with three national media correspondents by five p.m. today," Old Three Names said.

"He can't travel, his tongue looks like Dr. Frankenstein's been working on it and he's had enough pain meds to choke a yak—what part of rest do you Secret Service assholes not get?" Hurricane said.

"This is a national security matter with life-or-death consequences," Old Three Names said. "I am concerned for Agent de Vries's health and well-being, but he must participate in the interview. I cannot emphasize how vital this is to the safety of our great nation." He looked at Hurricane with a patriotic glow suffusing his face, as his eyes encouraged her desire to be a good citizen to overmatch her decisions as a doctor.

"Fuck you, Eddie. You can take your patriotism and cheap manipulations and shove them up your fat, white ass. I'm a doctor, first, last and always, and my patients' welfare ranks so far ahead of patriotism that it isn't in the same country." Old Three Names tried to interrupt her, but Hurricane held up her hands to forestall him and said, "Don't get me wrong—I love this country and I realize how good I've got it, but *nothing* gets in the way of my patients' health—and I do mean *nothing*. Don't you have enough other people to sit down with whatever punks they send to get their puff interview?"

"The punks that are coming here are Gwen Ifill, Jeff Mason and David Martin, and they're not interested in a puff piece—they want to know the truth about the assassination attempt on Soper, from the point of view of the Secret Service," Old Three Names said.

Hurricane looked at us with suspicion written all over her face. She started to talk and then stopped, putting her chin in her hand. She looked down at the floor for just a few seconds and then it was like a gigantic spotlight went off over her head. She looked up and said, "OK, what the fuck is actually going on? Why do you need the visual of the battered Secret Service agent, especially so soon after the attempt on Soper's life? You guys and the FBI will be investigating this for months, maybe a year—but you've gotta have a seriously hurt guy ready for a media interview now? Why? It doesn't make any fucking sense, unless…there's something that I don't know, isn't there? What the fuck is it? Why do you need the visual of Patsy?"

"Why, whatever do you mean, Dr. Whited? We simply want to include our brave comrade in the interview so he can—"

"Cut the shit, Eddie! I've got an unmeasurable IQ and I've read so many thrillers they'd fill up the New York City library. This is clearly an attempt at disinformation, but against who? Why now? Why use a battered agent instead of the clear, concise briefing officers the media usually sees? Clearly you have to be authentic—those interviewers you just named are way too tenacious and too smart to fool with some press release—but why Patsy?" She turned her fiery pink eyes on me and said, "What the fuck, Freak? Can you explain it to me, or are you just Eddie's stooge on this one?"

I burst into laughter, and Ed joined me. Old Three Names and Hurricane just looked at us, and then at each other, but neither one spoke. I finally looked over to Edward Otis Whitney and said, "Hurricane's too smart to fool, Eddie. If we don't tell her she'll just keep digging, and who knows what she'll tell the press."

"Or worse, what she'll ask 'em," Ed said.

"Exactly. She has a need to know, and she wouldn't make a bad visual in the interview, either," I said.

"What do you mean?" Old Three Names said, clearly puzzled.

I looked at Hurricane and said, "Don't take any offense at any of this until I'm done, OK?" She nodded and I said, "OK, so what are all the ignorant prejudiced fucktards out there going to think of Dr. Tully Whited? They're going to think that she's an idiot, or incompetent, or at least not a threat, because "little people" have diminished capacity, right? They're not normal, and she certainly became a doctor because she had special privileges. No little person—and most people will call her a midget, even though that term is offensive—can be fully competent in today's world, because they're too short. Am I right?"

I looked at Hurricane and she said, "That's 100% right, Freak. I'm not a true dwarf—most people we consider dwarves are afflicted with achrondroplasia, a genetic condition that leads to a shortening of limbs and other characteristics. I'm just the victim of short grandmothers on both sides if my family—neither of them ever reached 4'4", and my mom is only 4'8. But Freak is totally right—my teachers in grade school always had me referred to special ed testing because I had to be mentally deficient, even when I pointed out in fourth grade that my brain case was exactly the same size as my classmates."

"So if we use Patsy we should use Hurricane, too, because it will encourage the opposition to believe that we don't have a clue. In fact, we can press our case more easily against the Klan if we use Hurricane, because they really won't like her," I said.

"Especially when I reveal that I'm a Soper voter out of sympathy for her sexuality," Hurricane said.

"A dwarf albino *lesbian* doctor? The Klan will be foaming at the mouth, and, well…" I said, stopping to look at Old Three Names. He nodded and said, "Go ahead, Freak, tell her it all."

So I told Hurricane the whole thing, and about our plan, and how we needed Patsy to flush out our opposition by convincing people that it was the vicious Klan who were the sole perpetrators of the crime.

"The Feebs can't have any idea that we even have a clue there is a conspiracy outside the Klan," I said. "Whoever is in there and wants me out of the way has to have some serious juice."

"Yeah, it's gotta be at least an assistant director, although a senior field agent could probably pull it off if they had your exact schedule of movements," she said.

"How do you figure assistant director? That means it's a senior FBI official, someone who I've met and probably worked with. I would be very careful bandying such scurrilous rumors around. You could sink the careers of several good men and wymyn," Old Three Names said, his face trending toward red.

"First of all, it's just us chickens in here, and second, I'd be just as surprised if it wasn't a senior FBI official," Hurricane said. "You need to yank your head out of your ass and smell the coffee, Eddie. It's the only way that the attack in Morehead could work—somebody with detailed knowledge of Soper's itinerary and timetable tipped the sheriff so that he could set up the ambush with the Klan as backup. It would've taken a day at least, maybe two."

We all sat there as the reality of her assessment sank in. Someone on what was supposed to be our team was working against us—and we didn't know who or why, just that it had to be true.

Fuck a goddamned duck.

Hurricane saw us accept the facts and said, "Not to be all Chicken Little on you here, but I know how I'd cover my tracks on this one."

"Elaborate," Old Three Names said.

"I wouldn't want you to figure out that somebody was passing out information they shouldn't be interested in or have access to, so I'd have somebody gathering up such information about all the campaigns and distributing them through my PIO apparatus to any local parties who might have an interest, say on a weekly basis. That way it'd become a routine thing, started long ago with nobody remembering who originated it. All you'd have to do is give the sheriff a little anonymous call and point out how easy it would be to really fuck up or end that godless lesbian bitch who's embarrassing the good old USA by running for president," Hurricane said.

"And you could probably pose as a Grand Pisser or whatever they call their higher ups in the Klan, thus giving your info more weight," I said. "And if you did pose as a fellow Klan member you might even be able to suggest how to do it so that you could keep the Klan out of it, unless the first attack didn't carry home, in which case the Klan could move in behind their hoods and beadsheets and finish the godless sinner bitch abomination, thus keeping the country safe for white heterosexual men."

"And you could've used a subordinate to actually suggest the information gathering in order to keep the Bureau abreast of any situations that might fall within their bailiwick. That would provide you with an extra layer of separation from the actual order," Ed said.

"You would simply be another tree in a forest of trees, despite your rank and influence. If you were a subordinate suggesting it to a superior they might even take the idea for themselves, leaving our conspirator entirely out of the loop, which means that we could never find him or her, at least that way," Edward Otis Whitney said, his face showing his frustration.

"It would still take at least a field supervisor, although I think that an assistant director still makes more sense, especially now," Hurricane said.

"Why?" Old Three Names said. "It could be a field agent."

"No, no it couldn't," I said. "It has to be somebody with some juice, because where are the Feebs? Why aren't we hip deep in cheap suits, mirror sunglasses and officious pricks? Why isn't some SAC trying to engage you in a pissing contest, Eddie, in order to prove who's in charge?"

"I'll bet that they're all at the scene in Morehead, trying to get through Colonel Tomilo to turn over the scene," Ed said.

Just then Old Three Names' phone went off. He answered it, said, "This is Edward Otis Whitney, Director of the Secret Service Protective Division. Yes, she is. I would be gla—" There was a distinct tone about the sounds that came from the phone and he said, "One moment, Colonel."

He handed me the phone and pulled out another one as he ducked out of the room. I said, "Hello, Colonel. Let me guess: the FBI is there and they want you to relinquish the scene to them— they're probably spouting national security concerns and trying to scare you."

He was silent for a second and then Colonel Tomilo said, "Yes, ma'am. There is a Special Agent in Charge named Daniel McNeill who insists that I release the scene to him and his men, or he will have me taken to Guantanamo Bay for violating the USA Patriot Act."

"Scared yet, Colonel?" I said.

"Not remotely, ma'am. I've seen tougher shithouse rats, even though this SAC is just as crazy as one. What would you like me to do, ma'am?" Colonel Tomilo said.

"Turn the scene over to him, Colonel, but I would like it if you and some of your men watched these agents operate and give me a verbal report on their actions and methods. Is that possible?" I said.

"Of course, ma'am. I'll put CSM Delgado on it and get back to you when we clear the scene. My command staff and I will have to be the last people out, of course. Should I call this number when we are ready to report?" Colonel Tomilo said.

"Yes, thank you, Colonel. And Colonel, thank you for your service and professionalism. My people and I are very grateful. You did good yesterday and today. We owe you one, sir," I said.

"No, ma'am, you most certainly do not. I had my orders and I followed 'em. The fact that I had a superior commanding officer just made it easier to get the job done. It was a pleasure to serve under your command, General Glickstien," Colonel Tomilo said.

"Boo-rah, Colonel," I said.

"You bet your ass, ma'am," he said.

I looked up and said, "The Feebs just got there, headed up by some guy named Daniel McNeill. They apparently tried to threaten my RCT, but Colonel Tomilo managed to contain his fear and keep the site clear. I told him to go ahead and release the scene, since I'm sure the team you had there is all done, Eddie." I looked at Old Three Names, who had just come back into the room.

He laughed and said, "Of course we've been there, although I'm sure most people didn't realize it. I am surprised that they sent McNeill—I don't know him, but he is an Assistant Director in the Personnel department."

"Well, he must be crazy, or stupid, or both if he tried to threaten the RCT—what'd he do, drive over from Ft. Knox with a division of tanks?" Hurricane said.

"No, they just sent somebody with rank so they can say they were taking this seriously, and no one will question it, because he's an assistant director. That will also explain their lack of speed getting there—he had to get clear of his commitments, and assemble a staff, and get briefed, et cetera. I'll bet that this was somehow arranged by our nemesis, too. It makes it less likely that they'll find anything incriminating," Ed said.

"Speaking of briefing, the U.S. Marshals and Inspector General's contingent are here to debrief you before the press arrives. This will only be preliminary—you know that there will be much more detailed questioning—but we need to do this so we can start the smokescreen as soon as possible. We want the focus on the Klan, especially since we have the two of the three correspondents we wanted for the interview," Old Three Names said.

"Who'd we not get?" I said.

"CBS is sending their political guy, John Dickerson," Old Three Names said.

"Well, that's OK—he's the host of Face the Nation, right? Good-looking blonde guy with a disarming smile and easy laugh? He'll do," Ed said.

"He seems intelligent and he asks solid questions, so he should help us. He's not known to be over the top, or given to flights of fancy, so he should set up the conspiracy theory for us without much effort on our part," Old Three Names said.

"God help you assholes if Patsy tears his stitches, because I'm gonna go off like Krakatoa once the TV jackasses leave," Hurricane said.

"I'll worry about that after the debriefing," I said.

And so we all went off and got debriefed. There were three U.S. Marshals, all of a type: lean, muscular and weathered. They all had brown hair and brown eyes, with what I could only call regular, normal faces. Their voices were all gruff, but not unnaturally so, and they asked all of the appropriate questions without being judgmental. They interviewed me for about an hour, and then I was debriefed by the IG's people, who were much the same as the Marshals. Finally I gave my official statement to the Secret Service investigators.

After three hours of talking to strangers I entered the hospital cafeteria, glad to be back among friends. My entire detail was there—Flipper had been relieved as an honor guard by two of Old Three Names' people—and it was good to see Curtis Jeffries again. We all had snacks (I only ate four Italian beef sandwiches and a bag of chips, so get off my ass about the snacks), drank some Pepsis and discussed the upcoming interview. It was a great time to decompress, and we got a head start on our camouflage when El Gato said, "It'll feel good to call the goddamned Klan out on national TV. Those sons of bitches deserve to get it up the ass after what they did to everybody on that bus, especially CoD, Josie, that kid from Cincy and Soper. We need people to know that these fucking chickenshit bedsheet bozos are murdering cowards, not heroes. Shit, my family was living in Durango, Colorado *before* there was a United States—and some motherfucker in a pointy hood is just trying to protect the American way of life? Fucking assholes—I say we just arrest all their asses and let them loose on the south side of Chicago."

We all agreed he had a perfectly valid point, and Bumble said, "What makes me mad as hell is that those Klan fuckers killed some of ours and we only got two of theirs—and we can't prosecute the rest of the fucktards unless we can prove conspiracy, which will be damned hard, since these fuckers seem to take the vow of silence pretty seriously. Unless we can prove that the sheriff organized the thing, and that some of the rest of these fuckers actually helped get the bus in position and us out of position we're only going to get the two we put in the ground.

"Don't get me wrong, I'm not like these bloodthirsty motherfuckers—I don't wanna put 'em all in the ground, I just want them to face justice, and go to prison for their crimes. I just want them in general pop at a federal facility, where they can meet some nice Mexicans, and some wrongfully convicted Blacks, and some Columbians, and especially some Russians and Ukrainians, and maybe some ill-tempered Asians, preferably from the Hong Kong triads, 'cause those boys know how to dispense their own brand of real justice, you dig? That's all I want for those haters, 'cause some things are worse than death…and those Klan fuckers deserve it."

"I can't get over the fact that they attacked somebody because of who she loves," Darah said. "I've read the Bible and I get Leviticus, but all of that Old Testament shit got wiped away by Jesus—he said "Love thy neighbor as thyself" and "Let he who is without sin cast the first stone," not kill anybody who doesn't agree with you. Conspiring to kill Soper because she's a lesbian is the equivalent of conspiring to kill your sister because she doesn't like ice cream."

"You don't like ice cream?" Flipper said to Sarah. "What the hell, girl? I'm not sure we can be friends." We all laughed and Sarah said, "It's true that I don't like ice cream, but I like apple pie, Chevrolet and the USA—and I agree with Darah, even though she's too nice to come right out and say it: these fuckers are crazy as shithouse rats. Jesus is about love, and peace, and turning the other cheek, not hating everything that you don't know or understand. The Lord certainly isn't about judging who someone else falls in love with, and then killing them because you disapprove. I agree with Bumble—the stupid shits need a little reality check in the Big House to think about it."

"I want naming rights on this one," Bumble said. We all nodded our assent and the big man said, "At the risk of being disrespectful and causing some tension here, Sarah Koenigsblett seems like a Sparky to me. I hasten to add that I mean no disrespect to a previous Sparky some of us knew, but she and Sarah would've been best buds if they'd ever met." He looked at El Gato, Ed and I, and Gato said, "I never thought of it, but now that you say it Bumble, I think you're right. She is like Sparky."

"I can see it, and I think that Sparky would be honored," I said.

"Concur," Ed said. "I knew Sparky for five years, and to tell you the truth she'd get a kick out of knowing that her spirit and nickname lived on."

"I hereby dub thee Sparky 2.0, and welcome you to the world as our sister," Bumble said. We all cheered a little bit, except Patsy, who was saving himself for the interview.

When the cheering stopped I said, "Naming rights on Darah Koenigsblett."

"Proceed," El Gato said. "I have been thinking of this and have an alternative if yours is not accepted."

"After the Battle of Morehead it occurred to me that Darah had depths that she kept to herself, an iron discipline under her college-girl exterior, and an unflappable streak that borders on supernatural. I would like to name her Buddha, in honor of her impression of Gautama Siddhartha," I said. "No offense to your religious beliefs."

"All is one, and one is all," Darah said. We all laughed and El Gato said, "Goddamnit, Freak! That was my name, too!"

"No shit?" I said. "Then Buddha is doubly blessed!" She put her hands together, bowed and said "Namasté" and we all laughed our asses off again, which is how Edward Otis Whitney found us when he came to take us to the interview.

Which worked so well that we weren't able to find out who in the FBI was after us until later.

Which meant that more innocent blood was spilled.

Shit.

CHAPTER 47

Freak Camouflage

So Patsy, Buddha, Curtis Jeffries, Soper and I went into a hospital conference room for our interview with Gwen Ifill, Jeff Mason and John Dickerson. I want to say right off that you couldn't ask for three nicer, smarter or more professional people. They had their cameras set up, explained that they would all be asking questions, thanked us for doing the interview, offered their condolences for our losses, told us to call them Gwen, Jeff and John and basically did everything they could to make us comfortable.

Gwen Ifill explained that each reporter had a list of questions to ask specific people, and that they were going to try and not pepper us with questions, but rather just listen to answers and edit the tape later. "And we won't be trying to make you look like fools with the editing—this will not be any kind of gotcha interview. We've agreed that you're the victims here, and that you're doing us a favor explaining exactly what happened. OK?" We all agreed and the interview got going.

They identified us for the audience, explained what was happening and then began the questioning. Dickerson asked Soper to describe the reason she had Secret Service protection, Mason asked Soper about the day leading up to the assassination attempt, and Ifill asked Soper about the Cincinnati students who came along to Morehead State. Ifill followed up by asking how she felt after the crowd at Morehead State lost its hostility, specifically, "was her message getting through?"

"Just like most places we go, Josie and I found that if people could meet us and actually see that we were just people in love, not hideous lesbians who wanted a new lesbian world order, and that we knew what we were talking about, especially concerning economics, well, more of them liked me than didn't."

A tear ran down Soper's face and she said, "I'm sorry, but talking about Josie still makes me cry. I still don't get that she's gone."

"Take your time," Ifill said. When Soper recovered the reporter said, "This question may seem a bit obvious, but how do you feel about the people who caused this accident?"

I didn't even wait for Soper to answer, I just butted in. "It wasn't an accident, it was an assassination attempt. Don't confuse a truck running a stop sign with what happened—there was a deliberate setup and plan for an end game."

Everyone looked at me and I said, "Sorry, Soper. I didn't mean to step on your answer."

She smiled at me and said, "Not to worry, Freak. You just gave me time to properly frame my answer." She turned to Ifill and said, "I hate their guts and I hope they all get leprosy, every last person who participated in the murders of my wife, Andria Rogers and Elvin Clyde Bliss."

"You don't want them to die?" Mason, the Reuters reporter said.

"Oh, I want them to die, I just want them to suffer first," Soper said.

"So you don't want them tried, convicted and given the death penalty?" Dickerson said.

"All of it except the death penalty. I didn't believe in the death penalty before three people I loved were murdered and I don't believe in it now," Soper said.

"But you just said that you wanted them to suffer and die. Wouldn't the death penalty fulfill that requirement?" Ifill said.

Soper looked at all of them and said, "If it would satisfy the parents of Elvin Clyde Bliss, of Josephine Boroviak, or the children and husband of Andria Rogers then perhaps it would be appropriate, because their suffering is going to go on forever. There are some wounds that time cannot heal, and having the state exact vengeance by humanely killing the people responsible will never fill that void." Mason started to ask a question, but Soper held up her hand and said, "I know what you're going to ask, so let me just say that while Aleta Greenhoe Soper, private citizen and wife, wants all of those sons of bitches dead by the most cruel method possible—leprosy, tertiary syphilis, being torn apart by wild dogs—Aleta Greenhoe Soper, governor, possible president and citizen of the greatest nation on earth, doesn't think that the state should be in the revenge murder business. Put them all in prison for life, so that Elvin Clyde Bliss's parents can send them postcards that they have to read every time he would've had a birthday? No problem. Putting them in prison for life so that all of Andria Rogers's children can send them videos of their weddings that the bastards have to watch? I'll pay for the videos. Put them in prison so that I can send them copies of Josie's *Sports Illustrated Swimsuit* shoot every year on our anniversary? I'll get it blown up to three feet by five feet, so that they can't miss her beauty and joyfulness…because I'm going to miss that the rest of my life. But despite my personal feelings about watching those cowardly twits die, I still don't condone murder by the state—it's just too easy to step over the line and start making death a punishment we casually dispense, and it's simply wrong. Only God gets to exact revenge."

"But most people, especially Republicans and the Christian Right, support the death penalty," Dickerson said.

"Then they need to read their Romans—it says right there in Romans 12:19, 'Dearly beloved, avenge not yourselves, but *rather* give place unto wrath: for it is written, Vengeance *is* mine; I will repay, saith the Lord.' They should also read their Proverbs, 20:22 and Matthew 7:12—'Therefore all things whatsoever ye would that men should do to you, do ye even so to them: for this is the law and the prophets.' Or doesn't the Golden Rule apply to Republicans and the Christian Right?" Soper said, her manner gentle as the hand of a mother stroking her sleeping child's face.

The reporters all looked astonished, and Ifill said, "Well, you certainly know your Bible. So regardless of the situation you are against the death penalty? Even though they killed your wife?"

Soper shook her head and said, "Gwen, I'm going to paraphrase from the TV show *The West Wing*: If we caught all the guys I'd want to kill 'em myself—and that's why it's a good thing that we don't let the victim's families and loved ones on juries. The death penalty is wrong because it's irrevocable, and barbaric, and about vengeance, and as I said before, only God gets that privilege. Even if I were president I wouldn't be God, just a womyn from California who wants the country to be better off and doesn't think that state-sanctioned murder will accomplish that. Not to be bitchy about it, but can we move on to something else, like these brave people and how the attack made them feel?" She gestured at the rest of us, clearly in need of a respite from the questioning.

All the reporters looked a bit sheepish, but they were pros and got it, so John Dickerson looked at me and said, "Agent Glickstien, we understand that you were the first person to recover after the first truck slammed into the bus in the assassination attempt. How did you recover from the shock so quickly, and what was the first thing that you thought about when you did recover?"

"Mr. Dickerson, I have no idea about how I got up so fast, and the first thing I thought was "Where the hell is Soper?" My only concern was for her safety."

"You're a former Marine—" Dickerson started to say, but Patsy interrupted him and said, "Nuh."

Dickerson looked a bit confused, but recovered and said, "Agent de Vries, did you have something to add?"

Patsy said, "Thee ithn't a *fawmer* Mawine, thee's a *Mawine*. On'th a Mawine, awways a Mawine. Thee's awtho th' bwavest perthon Ah've evah met." His face was red, but he wasn't embarrassed, just trying to talk around 62 stitches in his tongue.

"My apologies, Agent de Vries, Agent Glickstien. So do you think that your Marine training helped you recover so quickly?" Dickerson said.

"Certainly, sir. But there isn't any kind of training that can help you recover from that kind of crash quickly—I was lucky not to hit anything hard, as silly and trite as that sounds," I said.

Jeff Mason looked a bit sheepish again, but he said, "Agent Glickstien, preliminary reports are that you shot the driver of the first truck before you went to Ms. Soper's side. Is that true, and if so, why did you do that?"

"I identified the truck as the vehicle that had rammed us, saw that the driver was trying to either push through the bus, or overturn it, classified him as hostile and shot him once in the head so I could make sure there were no more injuries," I said.

"How could you tell he was hostile?" van Vlaminck said.

"I observed him downshift into a lower forward gear rather than reverse, and then try to accelerate right through the bus. Luckily he didn't back up first, or probably none of us would be here," I said.

"Did you try to warn the driver before you just shot him?" Dickerson said, annoying Ifill, who probably had a better question than the dumb one he asked.

"Sir, when our protectee is determined to be under attack our ROE—sorry, rules of engagement—is weapons free. Essentially anyone who is making what we determine to be a hostile gesture will be shot without warning. I wish it wasn't that way, but it is. I would've had to get out of the bus, run around the front and expose myself and my protectee to possible hostile fire in order to warn him," I said, not rubbing Dickerson's nose in it, but letting him see how ignorant his question was. He was a smart guy, because he said, "So at that point you went to Ms. Soper's side?"

"Yes. I determined that she was alive and was not gushing blood anywhere and then determined that we needed to get her off the bus in case of another attack," I said.

"And you were joined by Agent de Vries at this point?" Ifill said.

"Yes, ma'am. He saw me checking Ms. Soper and immediately moved to open the doors so we could egress the bus," I said.

"And you were already severely injured at this point?" Ifill asked Patsy.

"Yeth, ma'm," he said.

"So why did you keep going? Wasn't your left shoulder dislocated, and your left ankle ligaments torn? How did you fight through the pain to keep going?" Ifill said.

"Ah di'nt feel any pain," Patsy said. "Too mu'h adwenalin in mah sithtem."

"So you're saying you weren't in any pain, and you just did your duty by helping Agent Glickstien?" Mason said. "That's really quite remarkable, Agent de Vries."

"Than' yoo, thir. Ah jus' di' mah duty—Ah twhor to protet Soper, an' Ah men' it," Patsy said.

"Where did your strong sense of duty come from, Agent de Vries?" Dickerson said.

"Ah'm a U Eth Mawine," Patsy said.

"Are you saying that you will—" Dickerson started to say, but Patsy stood up, looked him right in the eye and said, "Ah will die bfwor Ah don' prote't the people Ah thwor to prote't. Death bfwor dithhonor."

All three reporters took a moment to let that sink in for the audience, and then they started to ask more questions of all of us. We answered truthfully and briefly, walking though our actions from the appearance of the second truck until we got to the appearance of the Klan, and shortly thereafter the arrival of the First RCT (Bastogne) of the 101st Air Assault Division.

Gwen Ifill said, "We've already heard a remarkable story, but here is where I get very confused. You've set up your perimeter defense because you can't move many of your wounded, using the remaining Secret Service agents, Deputy Jeffries and eight ROTC cadets, when the Ku Klux Klan allegedly comes around the corner and begins marching toward you."

"It wasn't allegedly, ma'am," Curtis Jeffries said. "I've lived in the South my whole life, and it was definitely the Klan marching toward us. It's hard to miss all a them pointy hats."

"OK, but according to some reports they stopped when a U.S. Blackhawk helicopter came and hovered in the road between them and your position? Is that right?" Ifill said.

I looked at Old Three Names, standing behind the interviewers where we could see him, and I waited, because this part was very important to our camouflage. Jeff Mason said, "We see that you are looking at Protective Division Director Edward Otis Whitney. Is there something that you don't want to tell us, Agent Glickstien?"

"No, sir, but Director Whitney is my boss, and in charge of our investigation, and the rule is, if you don't know what the investigation is releasing you keep your mouth shut. I've been in here, and I couldn't be a part of the investigation anyway, so I'm just checking with my boss so I don't screw anything up," I said.

Everybody in the room looked at him and Old Three Names hammed it up by putting his chin in his hand and striking the famous JFK pose from the Cuban Missile Crisis. After a pause that was just long enough he gave me a very brief nod, like "go ahead and tell them all of it."

So I did. "Sir, it wasn't a Blackhawk, it was an Apache AH-64 Longbow attack helicopter attached to the First Regimental Combat Team, Bastogne, of the 101st Air Assault Division."

"The Screaming Eagles?" Ifill said.

"Yes, ma'am. They really saved our bacon. Of course it didn't hurt when the rest of the First RCT showed up," I said. Everybody laughed, including the three newsies. Then we had to go through all of the rest of the story—thanks to the professionalism of the three reporters it was quick, efficient and comprehensive. Many of the questions helped fill in the narrative by being right on point, and then we finally got to the Big Enchilada.

Gwen Ifill asked the group, "So who do you think orchestrated this attack?"

"I' wath th' Klan," Patsy said, his voice flat and definitive.

"Do you think they acted alone?" Dickerson asked.

We all looked at Old Three Names, who gave us a short nod.

"Yes, I do," Buddha said.

"Why?" Mason asked. "Couldn't there have been a larger conspiracy?"

"I suppose so, but the Klan were the only ones who could have pinpointed the exact time of our departure from the arena and have the local knowledge to set up the diversions for our lead and trail cars, and set the trucks in just the right place. There was just too much local knowledge for it to have been some outside conspiracy," Buddha said.

"So you think that it was a conspiracy, but that it was the Ku Klux Klan that orchestrated it?" Ifill said to me.

"Ma'am, I'm with Agent Koenigsblett. If the Klan had co-opted the local sheriff—and that also seems likely, especially with the information that Deputy Jeffries is about to give you—then the Klan could easily have done this—and it seems like the kind of thing that they would do, although I don't know as much about them as some here present," I said, setting Curtis up for the kill shot.

"I'm not sure I understand. Deputy Jeffries, what does Agent Glickstien mean?" Dickerson said.

So Curtis told them about the sheriff's email and messages about not assisting us, about how the sheriff needed the Klan to get re-elected and how the Klan had been active in Rowan County forever, et cetera. He said, "Y'all don't need to look too much further than the Klan—they hate everybody, but a flaming liberal lesbian married to a purty white womyn, and who might could be president? Why, hell, they'd hate her if she weren't running for president. The very idea that she might someday sit in the Oval Office would make their blood boil, and everybody knows them boys ain't above killing black folk—they've been doing it since 1866 or so, every since the War of Northern Aggression." We'd argued about his phrasing on this—Old Three Names wanted him to say "lynching" instead of killing, but both Curtis and I thought that it'd be better if the reporters said the word, because then nobody could say we put it in their minds.

Thank God we won the argument, because after Curtis was done we got the gift we were all hoping for, all because Gwen Ifill, Jeff Mason and John Dickerson were very smart, very professional and very focused reporters. The feeding frenzy began with Dickerson, who said, "So you think that the Ku Klux Klan was coming to *lynch* Ms. Soper?"

Curtis Jeffries could've won an Academy Award, or at least an Emmy, on his performance. He looked confused, then he looked a little bit disgusted, and then he looked a bit wry as he shook his head and gave a grim smile. He looked right in John Dickerson's eyes and said, "You bet your ass I am, sir."

"And what do you think about that, Agent Glickstien?" Gwen Ifill asked me.

"When I saw all of those bedsheets I was pretty sure that we were going to die," I said.

"But did you think the Klan was going to lynch Ms. Soper?" Ifill said, thinking that she was pressing me into the answer she wanted.

I paused for effect, and said, "Again, I'm not entirely familiar with the Klan like Curtis—Deputy Jeffries—is, but I suppose in the back of my mind I considered the possibility. I've found out since the attack that they might've tried to hang me, too, since I'm Jewish and the Klan doesn't like Jews, either," I said.

"So the possibility of lynching did cross your mind?" Mason said.

"Well, like I said, it must have, but what really crossed my mind was that after I ran out of ammo for my weapons I was going to need Mjollnir so I could do a Thor versus the frost giants," I said.

"Excuse me?" Mason said.

"I was trying to decide how to engage the Klan in hand-to-hand combat and I was wishing for the magic hammer of the Norse god of thunder," I said.

"In other words, you were sure that the Klan was going to kill you," John Dickerson said.

"Sir, like I said—there were thousands of marchers bearing down on us with apparent bad intentions. My mom always said, "If it looks like a duck, quacks like a duck and walks like a duck it's probably a duck." The crowd was almost all dressed in Klan regalia, at least the part I could see. I could clearly see that some of them had weapons. I only had eight full magazines—eighty-two total shots—and our unit at that point only numbered 16, with far less than enough ammo to keep shooting until the entire Klan crowd was dead or fled—all I was thinking about was how to save our butts until some cavalry arrived," I said.

"Several reports have said that you personally ordered the Apache helicopter to fire on the crowd, and that it's a miracle that no one was hurt," Dickerson said.

I really threw them off then. I laughed like a crazed hyena that smells freshly killed zebra, and all of my colleagues joined in. Even Old Three Names chuckled, and one of the cameramen was also laughing. I noticed a tattoo on his forearm—a large red "1" inside an infantryman's badge, so I decided to include him in the discussion.

I pointed at the cameraman and said, "Sorry for laughing, Mr. Dickerson—I assure you that none of us are laughing at you—but even your cameraman knows that's kind of a silly statement."

"Why is that? Jeff?" Dickerson said, looking at the cameraman.

"Sir, if she had wanted that crowd dead, and she had a fully armed Apache Longbow at her disposal, well…none of the crowd would be alive today. We worked with those birds when I was in the First Infantry Division and people on the ground have as much chance against them as Yale would of beating Ohio State in football. She must have told them *not* to shoot at the people, or every funeral home in Kentucky would be full," the cameraman said.

The reporters looked at me and I said, "He's right, sir. I did in fact give the Apache pilot the command to fire, but I deliberately targeted the trucks at the rear of our barrier in order to scare the crap out of the crowd, not to kill anyone. The Apache has a thirty-millimeter chain gun that can chew through steel—and the crowd was trapped by our barrier and the narrow street behind them. I didn't have any intention of killing anyone I didn't need to, but I wasn't going to let them get at my wounded, either. It's like the French say, *pour encourager les autres*, but it's right out of Sun Tzu—basic tactics are terrify first, then hit the enemy in the mouth, because if you scare 'em enough you might not have to hit."

"But you would have fired on them?" Dickerson said.

"Yes, sir," I said without hesitation.

"And you wouldn't have hesitated, or waited to see if help arrived first?" Mason said.

I shook my head and said, "No, sir. In that situation my first priority is to my protectee, then to my wounded, and then to my men and wymyn. Since the crowd was surely going to harm my wounded and fellow agents I wouldn't have had any choice."

"And what if there had been collateral damage, or if the helicopter pilot had literally mowed down a thousand people?" Ifill said.

I acted like I was thinking about it, and then said, "Ma'am, all due respect and without any rancor, I would place the blame for such an occurrence on the people who joined up with the Klan for the express purpose of attacking and possibly killing, or, to use your word—*lynching*, my protectee. I would have grieved if there had been any innocents injured or killed, and I would have asked God for forgiveness for breaking the Sixth Commandment, but I still would have fired on them, because every action has a reaction, and we just got lucky that our reaction was defensive in nature and stopped the bloodshed before it escalated any further."

"And we can assume that you would have sent the troops into action against the crowd, again without compunction?" Dickerson said.

"Yes, sir, I would have ordered the First RCT into action against the Ku Klux Klan without hesitation. All actions have a consequence, sir, and I had wounded to protect."

"Would you have done anything differently?" Ifill asked Buddha.

"Ma'am, I completely concur with Freak. Her actions as a commander minimized the death toll and saved everyone involved," Buddha said.

Curtis Jeffries jumped in and said, "I couldn't believe it, tell you the truth. Old Freak never missed a beat. She took control of the unit, perfectly deployed it and had that Army colonel do exactly the right thing—I will bet you that several of those bedsheets had stains on 'em that won't never come out."

"It doesn't bother you that there may have been innocents killed?" Dickerson said.

"Thir," Patsy said, interrupting Dickerson.

"Yes, Agent de Vries?" the reporter said.

"Thorry to intewupt, but ith Fweak ha' stayd in th' Corps thee woul' be a general by now. Thee di' evewwyt'ing wight, thir. Thee thaved uth all an' din't kill a thingle innothent thivilian. Na' one, thir. Na' many people coul' hath done tha'." Patsy said. He nodded at me, and I looked back and nodded.

The reporters were silent for a moment, until Ifill said, "Point taken, Agent de Vries. I think that we each only have one more question. Jeff?"

The Reuters reporter said, "I just want to confirm: you all believe this was an attack by the Ku Klux Klan, and therefore an act of domestic terrorism?"

"Yeth, thos' wacist baswards," Patsy said.

"Yes, especially since Curtis told us about the sheriff's actions just before and during the attacks," Buddha said.

"I'm absolutely sure that it was, for the reasons I already said," Curtis said.

"I'm convinced it was the Klan because this is an Occam's Razor situation, you know?" I said.

"The simpler explanation is better?" Mason said.

"Well, when you have two competing theories that make exactly the same predictions, the simpler one is the better," I said. "We could all become conspiracy theorists and claim that the World Council wanted Soper dead, but the facts as we have them now all point to the Klan and the local sheriff. I can only believe the evidence I have before me, because anything else is speculation. That takes me back to the old "if it looks like a duck, and quacks like a duck…",", I said.

"It's a duck," Mason said.

"Exactly," I said.

John Dickerson of CBS News said, "Did Ms. Soper's politics ever affect your ability to effectively guard her?"

"Absolutely not," I said.

"Not at all," Buddha said.

"No freakin' way," Curtis said.

Patsy looked at the reporter and said, "Tha's wude, thir. The Secwet Sewvice doesn' do powitics. We gawd evwwery puhson th' same—wif' owr wives, thir!"

Before it could get heated I said, "Agent de Vries is right, Mr. Dickerson. I've guarded the president, who I think you will grant is a very conservative man, and I've guarded Ms. Soper, who is decidedly not conservative"—I looked at Soper and she said, "I have 'LIBERAL' tattooed on my butt," which made everybody laugh—"and I didn't see any difference between them. The Secret Service does not acknowledge gender, age, sexual preference, religion, politics or any other identifier concerning its protectees. We treat them all the same: with respect, dignity, honor and our very best efforts. Ms. Soper's politics are irrelevant—and I will guard her until my boss tells me not to."

"My apologies, Agent de Vries," Dickerson said.

"Juth doin' yer job, thir, but it s'ill ma' me angwy," Patsy said.

"You're entitled to some anger, Agent de Vries," Dickerson said. Patsy nodded at him and extended his hand. Dickerson shook it and Gwen Ifill of the PBS NewsHour said, "My last question is just for you, Agent Glickstien. I'm curious why everyone calls you 'Freak.' Isn't that insulting?"

My colleagues all laughed, and I said, "Oh, no, ma'am. I've been called that since my youth. I encourage people to call me that."

"I understand that it came out of your athletic exploits, but what I don't get is why," Ifill said.

"I can show you easier than I can tell you," I said. I stepped over to the cameraman named Jeff and said, "How much do you and your camera weigh, sir?"

"About 350 pounds," he said, "if you include the dolly."

"Can you please hold on to it very tightly and not wiggle around?" I said.

"Sure thing, Agent Glickstien," he said. He gripped up on the dolly and camera and I just bent down and picked him up around the knees. The reporters all gasped, but then I gripped his legs together and hoisted him and the dolly right over my head. I put his feet on my left hand and held him all the way over my head.

The room was completely silent until Jeff said, "Got-damn, girl! You are the strongest mother I've ever seen! You ain't even shakin'!"

I set him down and the reporters just sat there with their mouths open. I looked at Jeff and said, "What rank?"

"Master Sergeant," he said, "First of the Big Red One."

"Sorry about calling you sir, Master Sergeant," I said. "Thanks for the help, and call me Freak."

"Roger that, Freak," he said. He shook my hand as he shook his head, marveling at the fact that without any apparent strain a 167-pound womyn had picked him and his camera up in the air like they were a hank of cotton candy.

The reporters babbled about my strength for a little bit, but eventually they stopped. Dickerson and Mason said goodbye and thanked us for the interview, while Gwen Ifill stayed behind to ask more questions of Old Three Names. She looked at me and said, "Off the record?"

"Sure," I said.

"We got an anonymous tip that the attack was pulled off by the Klan, which is why we pressed you guys so hard about your impressions of the attack. We really weren't questioning your professionalism or your judgment—we were just looking for corroboration of the tip," she said.

"I don't think anybody was upset about it at all. I know that I wasn't," I said.

"You going back on the road with Soper?" Ifill said, trying to confirm that Soper was continuing her campaign without having to look callous by asking Soper directly.

"I don't know if she's going back on the road," I said, lying like a very old Persian rug (it's a saying—I don't know where it came from, but it denotes lying high, wide and hard), "but if—I emphasize that I don't know her intentions, so *if*—she does go out and Director Whitney will let me I'd definitely go."

"You like her?" Ifill said.

"I don't know if I like her or not, but I admire her courage and grit. She'd have made a great Marine, or a special ops operator. If you had seen her charm the crowd at Morehead State you'd know what I mean," I said.

"You think she'd make a good president?" Ifill said.

"We really off the record—like way off the record?" I said.

"I have my own integrity, Agent Glickstien. If I tell you we're off the record and then I repeat any form of what you said all you have to do—especially someone in your position—is tell your boss and poof! my sources dry up. I just wondered if you thought she could handle it," Ifill said.

"I apologize for being patronizing, Ms. Ifill. She's big enough for the job, and she'd be an honorable president. For Secret Service agents those may be the only two criteria necessary for the job," I said.

She shook my hand and said, "Thanks, Freak. I appreciate your honesty."

"What honesty?" I said.

"Who are you again?" Ifill said, getting right away that I was clowning about our off the record conversation.

"I'm just a fat, dumb Secret Service grunt, but I have one question for you, also off the record," I said.

"Ask away. I owe you one anyway," Ifill said.

"Why didn't you ask us more about me taking command of the First of the 101st?" I said.

"Oh, did we really forget to tell you guys? We already had a sit-down with the president—he explained exactly what he did, and what you did once he turned the 101st into Kentucky National Guardsmen and then nationalized them. He had nothing but good things to say about you, your boss and the need to let Soper run. I didn't realize that you even knew him before he told us," Ifill said.

"We met after the New York ambush of our Chicago unit," I said. "He seemed like a genuine guy who really wants the country to be better."

"He is," Ifill said. "In fact, he told me to tell you to treat Soper like she was him."

"If you see him again please tell him I said "You bet your ass I will, sir," willya?" I said

Ifill laughed and said, "You bet your ass I will, Freak." We shook hands and I went out just as Old Three Names was going in. He said, "Well done, Agent Glickstien. Please rejoin your detail—I will be down just as soon as this is over. We have a few things to discuss." He winked at me and I was relieved—apparently we'd been successful in our camouflage efforts.

I went down the hall and found everybody in a much smaller conference room. Soper was talking to Badass and Ed when I walked in, and she came over and gave me a hug. I gave her the hairy eyeball and she said, "Hey, I'm entitled to hug people who save my life, so get used to it. When I'm president I'm calling you back into active service, making you the Commandant of the Marine Corps and seeing to it that you are the first female Chairman of the Joint Chiefs. There'll be a lot more hugging once that happens."

"So you're gonna keep going?" I said.

"After I do two things," she said.

"Like what?" I said.

She told all of us what she wanted to do, and as soon as she was done Badass said, "I'm in, for both." We all made some sound of assent, and I said, "I've got to get something from home before we go." I told them why and Patsy said, "Tha's whi oo're th' bess, Fweak. Wha' a gawwant gess're."

"Did you just try to say 'What a gallant gesture'?" a booming voice said.

Uh-oh. Dr. Hurricane had come ashore.

I spun around to see Dr. Tully Whited, all 4'4½" of her, hands on hips and eyes ablaze as she advanced on Patsy, who was trying to hide behind Bumble, Badass and El Gato.

"Get the fuck out there and confront her, *hermano*," El Gato said. "Show her that you're the boss."

"Oh, like you do with your wife?" Bumble said.

"Is *she* here?" Gato said, his head swinging wildly as he looked for his wife.

"Don't try to hide behind me, Patsy—there is no way I'm fighting with *her*," Badass said.

"ALL OF YOU GUYS CUT THE SHIT!" Hurricane said. They were all instantly silent. She said, "Patsy, front and center now, if you please." She said reasonable words, but her tone said "Do not fuck with me, you assholes."

Patsy came around Badass with his hands up, like he was a bank robber surrendering to the cops. He walked up to Hurricane and she said, "Down on your knees, mister."

"Wight hew in fron' oth God an' evewwybothy?" he said, trying to be funny.

"In your dreams, mister. Down, now!" she said. Patsy dropped like he'd heard sniper fire and Hurricane whipped out a penlight and said, "Stick out your tongue." He did and we all saw the blood in several places on his tongue, which looked like it had been attacked by a crazed badger that thought it was supper. I mean, I'd seen lots of battlefield injuries, but I don't think that any of them were more gross than Patsy's tongue.

Hurricane looked him over thoroughly and then said, "Well, most of 'em held, you ignorant shit-for-brains dumbfuck numbnuts asshole son of a bitch, but there are enough that I'm gonna have to re-stitch some shit after you talk to Director Whitney. Until then DO. NOT. TALK. Are we clear?"

Patsy nodded so vigorously that it looked like he was a bobblehead of himself. We all wanted to laugh, but we were afraid of Hurricane. She turned around, pointed at me and said, "You! You said you'd look out for him, and now he's got stitches loose! Whattya have to say for yourself, Marine?"

"Fuck you, Hurricane," I said. "He's a grown man and we all restrained him as much as we could, but you can't stop a determined U.S. Marine unless you kill him, and you didn't authorize me to do that, now didja, ya damned dwarf tyrant?"

She broke up into laughter and we all joined in, letting loose of the tension we all felt from the whole situation, and probably letting go of the friends we lost, too. When it all wound down Hurricane took Patsy off to get his stitches fixed and I turned to the rest of my detail.

"Ed, who's the most obtuse, obdurate, relentless Secret Service agent you know?" I said.

"Weasel," she said.

"Bumble, same question."

"Jewey," he said.

"El Gato?"

"Joe Cocker," he said, "although I could go with the first two, too."

"Badass, who's the craziest son of a bitch agent you know?" I said.

"Kid Galahad," he said without hesitation.

"He's a Marine, but he is the craziest motherfucker I've ever met, and that's saying something," I said. "Unfortunately we need Secret Service agents."

"Jordan Moerman joined the Secret Service four months ago and is currently assigned to the San Francisco office, but he will be re-assigned soon to the Bismarck, North Dakota office, because he's (a) crazier than a shithouse rat, (b) way smarter than the rest of the San Francisco office combined and (c) so good at his job that everyone up to the assistant director is worried about getting replaced. I could add that he's a royal pain in the ass because he doesn't have a filter, but you already know that," Badass said.

"They actually let Galahad into the Service?" I said, almost stunned.

"Yeah, and gave him a plum post, too," Badass said. "I wonder why that was?"

"SWWFYU," I said, referring to our former commander in Spec Ops, Lieutenant General Natalya Muzhgov-Franklin.

"Oh, yeah, old SWWFYU may have had something to do with that. Remember…" he said.

"…It's who ya know and who ya blow," I said.

Badass shot me with his finger and said, "Four-oh, Freak."

"Who would you pick for the craziest investigator, Freak?" Ed said.

"Mamba," I said.

"Well, I don't know Kid Galahad, but if you put Joe in charge of that detail I'll bet they could get some things done, whatever it is," El Gato said.

"No shit," Bumble said. "How'd you like to have Joe, Jewey, Weasel and Mamba on your tail? All they'd need would be an elephant to knock down doors and they could dig up dirt on the Pope."

Badass and I smiled, because Bumble had just perfectly described Kid Galahad, who I was sure would respond to Joe's leadership the way he'd responded to mine in Spec Ops. I had a sudden thought, just as the rest of my old gang did, too.

"We need…" Bumble said.

"What about…" El Gato said.

"Hey, wouldn't…" Ed said.

"If we added…" I said.

"Jack Soo!" we all said together. "Pepsis all around," I said. "We'll get Old Three Names to pay for 'em."

"What exactly am I paying for?" Edward Otis Whitney said, coming into the room.

So I explained my idea for a flying squad to do our side of the investigation, including who we thought should compose the squad. He listened, and when I was done he said, "Just playing devil's advocate here, but isn't six agents a fairly small group? Also, who would they report to? Agent Cocker is very good, but he's also very junior. Wouldn't we need to have an on-scene supervisor with rank? Say at least an associate director?"

"If you have the right people in place you can operate like a much bigger outfit, just without all the baggage. Remember, we don't want anyone thinking that we take this seriously, or that we have a hope in hell of ever finding anything out—we already know who did it, Eddie, and we're just trying to *look* diligent, not actually investigate. Let's leave the massive, exhaustive, gotta-write-a-comprehensive-report for Congress shit to the FBI, or DHS, or whoever else is in there. Our flying squad will just twinkle-toes around out of the Chicago office, not really going anywhere or doing anything. Have them report to Guru in Chicago, and she can report to Charlie Chan in D.C., but that's where the reporting needs to officially stop, because we already know who did it, right?"

Old Three Names nodded, and Ed said, "And we make sure that the reports Guru gets are informal and don't show very much, except what we already "know""—she made finger quotes—"but we'll have a channel set up to you that tells the real story. And no, before you even ask, Captain Cork and Guru aren't going to get their panties in a bunch about being bypassed—they understand compartmentalization."

"That makes perfect sense," Edward Otis Whitney said. "It will just confirm what we already told the journalists, and should reassure any opposition that we are just confirming what we already know." He made the same finger quotes as Ed.

"And make sure that Charlie Chan selects the agents and assigns them to the detail, and have Joe officially complain about being taken from his new posting to do this useless exercise," El Gato said.

"Good idea, Gato. That'll make it seem even more real that we don't care about the investigation," I said. "How about I call Joe and explain what's going on, so he can really throw himself into the protest?"

"How about you accidentally meet Agent Cocker face-to-face and tell him, and how about we don't talk about this on the telephone, even under secure conditions?" Old Three Names said.

We all let that sink in for a minute before Bumble said, "You think? Really?"

"I really don't know, but I would rather be safe than sorry, and there are a great number of three letter agencies out there who have all sorts of clandestine capabilities," Old Three Names said.

We all nodded, and Badass said, "You are absolutely right, Director. We should make sure that the channel between you and the flying squad are face-to-face meetings, perhaps as part of a tour of all the protective offices? Something that would escape the notice of any particular three letter agency."

"Excellent ideas, all. By the way, the journalists bought it, hook, line and sinker. They are also convinced that it was the Klan and they will be spreading that myth as well. It should start a feeding frenzy, thus making the flying squad's job easier," Old Three Names said.

Soper had been quiet the entire time we were talking, but now she said, "Speaking of feeding frenzies, I could use some food. Director Whitney, can I get Agent Glickstien and Agent Goodenough to take me out for some food? I'm tired of the hospital, and I'm really not all that recognizable with my new nose"—her old one was broken in the crash—"and raccoon mask." Both her eyes were black under the TV makeup. "I'll wear a hat and nondescript clothing, and we won't be long." She looked at Edward Otis Whitney and he said, "Of course you can go to the visitation for the Bliss boy, Ms. Soper. We're not prison guards, but I would like to suggest that you take four agents with you, if you don't mind."

She laughed and said, "Thank you, Director. I'll let Freak choose her detail, and we'll be back tonight."

"Excellent. Freak, please convey the gratitude of the Secret Service to Mr. Bliss's parents, if you would. Director Hessler will also be contacting them, but it would be very nice if agents who knew him, however slightly, could also convey our thanks and sorrow at their loss," Old Three Names said.

"Roger that, Eddie. I really liked that boy and his crowd. They weren't sure how they felt about Soper's lifestyle, but they liked her, and Josie, too—and they were smart enough to listen to her ideas, not just bitch about her being a lesbian. It makes me really want to catch whoever did this, like personally catch them," I said.

Badass knew that look, and he said, "So I'm going to the visitation, and probably Ed and maybe Sparky?"

"We'll take Bumble instead of Ed—she's going to set up our rotation schedules and prepare for a new chief of detail, as well as checking on personal gear and routes after today, especially our route to and from Josie's funeral. We don't know where that is going to be yet, but we're going to plan for both Scotland and Cali, OK?" I said. Ed nodded, and Soper's eyes leaked tears, and all of us felt a heavy weight in our guts, but we had work to do, so we went off to do it, despite our sorrow.

And without knowing that more blood would be spilled because of our actions.

CHAPTER 48

Absolution

We got in a Secret Service car and drove off to Florence, Kentucky, so we could attend the viewing for Elvin Clyde Bliss. Badass drove like he'd stolen the car—we went under 100 a couple of times on curves, I think—but nobody was ever remotely worried, because that son of a bitch could flat *drive*. I'd seen him get up to 140 miles an hour on his custom Victory motorcycle (proudly made in Iowa) without even blinking, and he could make a Humvee act like it was an Indy car, so we rode in relative comfort and got to the viewing just as it was starting.

It was the first of two viewings, held at four in the afternoon so the older crowd could get there before the crush, so it was the perfect time for us to be there. We hadn't let the family know as a security precaution, and I hoped that they were as open-minded as Elvin Clyde had proven to be, because there was a real potential for disaster if the parents reacted badly.

My misgivings increased when I saw two news vans in the parking lot. I looked at Badass and saw that he had the same idea. I cranked around and said, "Soper, you sure you're up for this? The news is here, and if his parents react poorly there's going to be a shitstorm of epic proportions."

She looked out at the news trucks—all local so far—and said, "He deserves it. He tried to save Josie, and he tried to understand me. He was a good young man and I owe him, just like I'd owe someone who died on the battlefield if I were president."

"Yeah, but you don't know how his people are going to react," I said. "If things get hectic the last thing you want to see on the news is us hustling your ass out of there."

Soper looked at me with what I can only describe as her "presidential face" and said, "I'm ordering you not to take me out of there unless my life is in direct physical jeopardy. No matter what is said, no matter how loud it gets, no matter what kind of shit rains down on my head, if it's not guys with guns and knives I'm not leaving until Elvin Clyde's people get their say. Do you understand me, Agent Glickstien?"

I looked right back and said, "Yes, ma'am, we all understand you, but I want to reiterate that this isn't absolutely necessary."

"Too fucking bad," Soper said. "If you want to sit in the big seat you need to be able to take some heat, especially when you are responsible for the shit that happened. That's the problem with the fucking Republicans—they want all of the credit and none of the blame. Hell, that's what's wrong with the whole fucking thing. I caused this man to come into harm's way—and yes, it was his choice, so save the lecture—so I'm taking responsibility for my actions. What the fuck is wrong with that? Isn't that supposed to be the American way? Aren't commanders in chief supposed to take responsibility for everything associated with an operation?"

My respect for her went up from its already high level to something akin to what I felt for my parents. I nodded and said, "Yes, ma'am, that's what is supposed to happen. It's just that it's been so long since I heard anybody say it and mean it that I and my detail are in shocked disbelief. I understand and will comply with your orders, ma'am."

She looked at all of us looking at her and said, "You bet your ass I mean it, and if I ever sit in the big chair I will prove it to you, but right now I'm asking you to trust me."

"We do, ma'am," Badass said.

"Concur," Bumble said.

"Roger, wilco, Boss," Sparky said.

"Good, and thank you," Soper said. "Now let's go get my ass chewed off."

We got out of the car and got in the entrance before anybody knew we were there. The news crews were talking to a guy who looked like a big bowl of blue Jell-o, and who looked so much like Elvin Clyde Bliss that I assumed he was one of Elvin's sibs. There was a lady who was broad shouldered and broad hipped who also looked like Elvin Clyde, but was enough older to make her his mom, and there was a large, round shouldered man in a black suit and white shirt with combed over hair who was the same size and complexion as Elvin Clyde who had to be his dad. We walked down the aisle of the funeral home and stood in line to talk to Elvin Clyde's mother, but the big man noticed us first.

He was on the other side of the room when he saw us, and a TV crew moved to intercept him as he came shambling toward us. He reminded me of a big old bear, except that he might have been bigger than a black bear. Just as he started talking to the TV crew on old lady at the front of the funeral home spotted us, zeroed in on Soper and just bellowed, "ABOMINATION! HARLOT! SINNER!"

Uh-oh. Force five shitstorm bearing down from dead ahead.

The screamer and a whole pack of other old ladies came storming up the aisle, loud as a junior high recess and aiming right for my protectee. Badass moved right in front of Soper, Bumble went forward of him to break the tide, Sparky took up the rear in case of a sneak attack, and I stood right next to Soper on her left. I didn't see any weapons present, but enough people—especially a mob— becomes its own weapon.

But before the little old lady crew could reach us a deep bass voice said, "Myra Montgomery, y'all stop that caterwauling right now, and you leave that womyn alone." The voice was coming from the bear, who was moving to interpose himself between us and the recess mob.

"But Pastor Jim Bob, she's an evil sinner who lays with other wymyn! She's the one who got Elvin Clyde kilt!" the little old lady said.

"Myra, this womyn just lost her wife. Think how y'all would feel if one moment Dale was there at your side and the next the Lord had just taken him off to heaven, never again to be seen in this life," the bear said. "Y'all think that you'd be up to being screeched at by a horde of old busybodies? Or would you rather feel the compassion that the Lord commands us to give even to our enemies?" He never raised his big bass voice, but everybody in the room could hear him just fine. The old lady gang stopped, not sure of how to proceed when their pastor told them exactly the opposite of what they wanted to hear.

"But what about Elvin Clyde?" Myra Montgomery said in a normal tone of voice.

"He's our responsibility, Myra, and the Lord's, now—but not yours," the big shouldered, big hipped womyn said in a lilting alto. "Reverend Jim Bob and I are responsible for all of our children, just like the Bible tells us to be." You could tell the old ladies felt bad now, because it seemed like they were trying to tell the pastor and his wife they didn't care about their children, which just as clearly wasn't true.

The Reverend Pastor Jim Bob Bliss finally got to us. He moved past Bumble and Badass and stopped two feet in front of Soper. He looked even more like a bear up close, with hair on the backs of his big, old hands and the start of a dark beard, even though he'd probably just shaved. His eyes were red, but not cloudy, and he exuded an air of dignity, despite his recent loss. He stopped and stared straight at Soper and said, "As for *you*, well... I only have one thing to say to *you*." His hand moved toward Soper and I prepared to jump his old country ass, preacher or no.

But he only reached out and took Soper's hand to shake it. His face screwed up into a grimace that said "I really don't want to cry" and he said, "Thank you. Thank you, Ms. Soper, for being so good to our son, and for showing him the error of passing judgment on other people for the way that they live their lives. You brought him closer to the Lord than his mother and I ever did, and I know that he died in a state of grace because of you."

You could have knocked all of us down with the proverbial feather. We didn't stop looking out for Soper, but we did all relax. It was as if we'd jumped in the Colosseum with lions and they all said, "Sorry, not eating any people today. How about a nice chardonnay?"

Elvin Clyde's mother said, "And we are sincerely sorry for your loss, Ms. Soper. We didn't know your wife, but we know that she was a Christian womyn and that you loved her. Jim Bob and I are sincerely sorry for what the Klan did to her and everyone else who died." She also shook Soper's hand, and then pulled her into an embrace that lasted for some time. The Reverend Jim Bob Bliss said, "My wife is right. I am very sorry for the loss of the womyn you loved, and for the baby that you never got to know. I assure you that I pray every day that the people who perpetrated this crime against you and everyone else on your bus are caught and put into prison where they belong. Their actions were not Christian, or civilized, regardless of their disagreement with your choice of spouse."

Soper finally recovered from her shock enough to say, "Thank you. I... I, uh, er...didn't expect such a kind reception."

Mrs. Bliss gave a soft laugh and said, "You thought that because we are born again we were going to come at you with fire and brimstone? My husband and I don't believe that we get to judge you or anyone else, Ms. Soper, regardless of who you choose to marry. Only the Lord has that privilege, and I assure you that even though we're good Christian people, we are in no way perfect enough to be Him."

"Furthermore, we believe in your right to choose what to do under the Constitution and in God's eyes. Our son told us that your knowledge of the Bible was as good as his, or maybe even mine, and besides, I never forget Matthew," the Reverend Pastor Bliss said.

"Seven, one through three," Soper said.

"Exactly," Reverend Bliss said. "Besides, Elvin Clyde was a very good judge of character, and he said you were a good person with great intellectual gifts who truly loved her wife and was honest even if it hurt you. He said you kept God's commandments better that anyone he knew except maybe his mother, and that you were making him re-think his position on the LGBTQi community. He liked and admired you, Ms. Soper, and wanted to help with your campaign."

"Reverend, Mrs. Bliss, I want to assure you that the feeling was entirely mutual. Your son and I had several very productive conversations, and I really liked him. You should know that he died trying to protect my wife—he wrapped Josie in his arms in order to shield her from the impact of the truck. In my eyes your son was—is—a hero," Soper said, her eyes dripping tears.

Reverend Bliss put his big old arms around his wife and Soper and they all stood there quietly crying. The local TV crews crowded in with their lights blazing and Reverend Bliss looked up at several other big bowls of Jell-O in primary colors who were standing close. He didn't say anything, but the bowls of Jell-O (all of whom looked a lot like Elvin Clyde (it turned out they were a combination of brothers and cousins—they were kind of like the born-again Mafia), and all of whom clearly did not like the TV people, quickly and efficiently herded the gaggle of reporters away from the Reverend, his wife and Soper, and then maneuvered them right out of the funeral parlor without any words or violence.

I and the rest of the detail moved to screening positions so that Soper, the reverend and Mrs. Bliss had some semblance of privacy, and the big bowls of Jell-O came back and took up screening positions forward of our position, moving the old lady gang further away. A bowl of Jell-O wearing a bright yellow suit with a wide, shiny green tie came over to me and said, "Are you Agent Glickstien?"

I nodded and he said, "I'm Elvin Clyde's brother Virgil Lee. I want to thank you for keeping Miz Soper safe, and for serving your country like you do. My brothers and I appreciate knowing that Elvin Clyde died doing the same, and that you were there for him at the end, and we wanted to know that we'll be praying for you and your team."

I was touched. I'd totally misjudged these people, and now they were thanking me. I nodded again and said, "Your brother was a hero—he tried to save Josephine Boroviak Soper by wrapping her in his arms to shield her from the crash. It was my honor to know him, Mr. Bliss."

The hideously dressed (the suit looked like the sun was visiting for a spell, and the tie hurt my eyes) young man smiled and I knew why he would be successful despite how he dressed—Virgil Lee Bliss was beautiful when he smiled, and you could see the joy just rolling out of him, like heat waves shimmering on a desert highway.

"You served in the military before this? You look like a Marine," Virgil Lee said.

"I was, sir. I served eight years in the Marines and special operations," I said.

A look of the purest admiration and love came across Virgil Lee's face as a giant hand clamped on my shoulder. I spun around and had the hand in a hammerlock before I even thought about it. The Reverend Jim Bob Bliss said, "Stand easy, Marine. I should've told you I was coming, and I shouldn't have touched a special ops operator at all."

I looked in his wise old eyes and said, "Beg your pardon, Reverend, but I really don't like to be touched when I'm on duty." I realized everybody there was staring at me except my detail, and Reverend Bliss said, "Y'all quit staring. Agent Glickstien was in the U.S. Marine Corps, and also U.S. Special Operations Command, and she was trained to do what you just saw so she could defend our country. I'm lucky she didn't over-react and put me on my big dumb butt. Y'all quit staring like she's part of some freak show."

He reached out and took his son's hand, squeezed it and said, "Son, I don't want anybody near your mom and Ms. Soper—they're having a private chat and I want to keep it that way."

Virgil Lee said, "Yes, daddy," but it sounded more like "Sir, yes, sir!" He nodded to me and moved away to inform the rest of the born-again bowls of Jell-O about the plan. I looked at him and then at the Reverend Bliss, who had the same look of love and admiration on his face that Virgil Lee did.

"You've done a magnificent job with your children, sir," I said.

"I've been a Promethean father—all of my boys think that I invented fire and can almost walk on water, which is a good thing when they all have 150 IQs like my wife. She's the real brains of the outfit, and yes, I know how lucky I am. Do you mind if we speak privately for just a moment, Agent Glickstien?" Reverend Bliss said. I nodded at Badass and the reverend and I moved behind where Soper and Mrs. Bliss were sitting. The reverend said, "SOCOM?"

I looked at his genial face and thought about how lucky people were that this big old bear of a man decided to serve the Lord and not some other cause. The look in his eyes would have melted stone, his body was tensed for battle just as surely as if he were holding an assault rifle and the force of his personality was concentrated in that hardass stare of death. It was easy to see him in a suit of chain mail wading through shit to get at the enemy with his battle axe or longsword.

But I was just like him, so I put on my own hard look and said, "Sir, that is classified."

"Bullshit," he said. "I'm a U.S. Marine, too—Second of the Seventh—and I fought in Desert Storm. I need to know that when you find out who did this to my boy you'll give me just an eight-hour head start—and I know that you'll find out, because you're a Marine, and SOCOM operators can find out anything. I pray every day that you discover the cowards who attacked that bus so that I can visit my wrath on them, Agent Glickstien." He hadn't moved, but all of a sudden Reverend Jim Bob Bliss looked like those pictures that you see of John Brown—crazy eyes coupled with absolute belief in his cause. He appeared to be bigger than he was when we started talking, and I was pretty sure that his internal electrical field was crackling on his skin.

I decided that I needed to stop this idea he had of revenge. I'm not saying he didn't have the right to feel the way he did—somebody murders your child you get the right to feel any fucking way you please—but I was worried that this very capable old bear of a man could get the job done, and I wasn't willing to let the motherfuckers who started this get their final revenge by ripping the reverend's family apart and leaving his poor wife alone while he moldered in prison, or in the ground.

So I went all apeshit crazy on him.

I put on my Marine command voice and said, "Bliss, what rank did you achieve in the Corps?" My voice was as harsh as a croaking raven, and my face had that "I'm in-country and not fucking around" look.

He unconsciously straightened up a bit and said, "I was a Master Sergeant, Agent Glickstien."

I pulled back the lapel of my suit jacket to show him my decorations that were always pinned there. His eyes got wide as he saw the Distinguished Service Cross (three times), the Silver Star (four times), the Purple Heart (five times) and the oak leaves of a major in the U.S. Marine Corps. He looked back at me and I said, "I also have decorations that I cannot wear or acknowledge due to how and where they were won, but you will notice my rank insignia."

He nodded and I said, still in my harshest tone, "That won't cut it, Marine. Do you acknowledge that I outrank you?"

"Yes, ma'am," he said. Ain't training a wonderful thing?

"And you acknowledge that "once a Marine, always a Marine" is more than a slogan, and that it applies here?" I said.

"Yes, ma'am," he said.

"Excellent. Then as a superior officer I order you to cease and desist in trying to gain revenge in this matter. Not only is it above your pay grade, it is outside the pale of your area of operation. I further order you to report directly to me any information that you may have received, or may yet receive, regarding this matter, for disposition by the chain of command," I said. I really cranked up my "don't fuck with me" look and said, "Are we clear, Master Sergeant?"

He looked back at me and I saw the agony behind his bravado—he was just mourning his son, and wanting revenge must be the most natural reaction to the senseless loss of a child—but I wasn't willing to let that longing come to fruition, so once I got him to acquiesce to my order I'd need to do one more thing. Finally he said, "We're clear, ma'am."

I said, "I believe you, Master Sergeant, but I want to make sure. Trust but verify, right?"

"Mr. Reagan was so wrong about so much, but he was right about that," Reverend Bliss said.

I picked up an old, well-worn copy of the King James Bible that was laying on the credenza next to us and held it in my hands. I said, "I'm going to swear a holy oath on part of this book, Master Sergeant, and then I'm going to ask you to do the same." I flipped the Bible open to the Old Testament and handed it to him, placing my left hand on the open book and raising my right hand I said, "I swear on the Torah to never rest until I find out who committed these heinous murders and bring them to justice before God and man."

I took the book back and closed it, then held it out to him. Reverend Jim Bob Bliss looked relieved when I said, "Now I'd like you to swear that you will follow my previous orders to the letter and never try to revenge yourself on the dirtbags who murdered your son, Josie Soper and Andria Rogers."

The big old bear drew himself up to attention, placed his left hand on the Bible and raised his right and said, "I swear to follow the orders of my superior officer, Major Glinka Glickstien, USMC, to the letter, and to never try to revenge the death of my son Elvin Clyde Bliss, or the deaths of Josephine Soper or Andria Rogers, so help me God."

Now I was relieved, because the Reverend Jim Bob Bliss might scam me, or even scam himself, but he'd never try to scam God.

Mission accomplished, at least for that part of the operation.

We turned to find Mrs. Bliss and Soper staring at us. Mrs. Bliss got up and hugged her husband, and then folded me in her large embrace. She whispered "Thank you for giving me my husband back" and kissed me on the cheek. I nodded and saw that all of the big bowls of Jell-O were looking at me. Virgil Lee smiled another beatific smile and mouthed "Thank you" at me. I nodded and disengaged myself from his mother.

The reverend looked at me and I said, "Reverend, Mrs. Bliss, with your permission I would like to leave something in the casket with Elvin Clyde. I will completely understand if you do not wish me to do so." I was stiff and formal, because that's the way it was supposed to be when you decorate someone for bravery.

Mrs. Bliss said, "Of course, whatever you'd like, Agent Glickstien, but only if you'll call me Nancy. It's what all of my friends call me—Mrs. Bliss is Jim Bob's mother."

"My friends call me Freak, Nancy," I said. "And I am honored to be your friend."

I looked at the reverend, and he smiled and said, "You're my superior officer, Major. You don't need to ask my permission."

"In this case I do need to ask, Master Sergeant. Do not let my rank influence you, and rest assured that a negative answer will in no way affect our relationship," I said.

"I agree completely with my wife. Please do whatever it is that you feel you need to do, Major," he said.

I nodded and marched up to the casket. I reached up and took the Distinguished Service Cross pin from my lapel and reverently laid it on the pillow next to Elvin Clyde's head. I felt people behind me as I drew myself to rigid attention and saluted the casket, holding the salute as I thanked the young hero for his efforts during the Battle of Morehead. At last I lowered my hand and about-faced to step away from the casket. Badass was behind me, as was the Reverend Jim Bob Bliss. Soper and Mrs. Bliss stood there with their hands over their hearts, as did every other person in the funeral parlor. I looked at all of them and said, "Elvin Clyde Bliss is an example of what is best about this country, and I will never forget his heroism in the defense of an innocent womyn, or his earnest intelligence, or the way that he stood up to an entire arena of people in order to be true to the Constitution that he believed in. He deserves better than he got, but rest assured that we will find out who did this—and they will be delivered to the appropriate authority to face justice."

The little old lady who first started yelling at Soper said, "Well, knock me down and kick me for fallin.' Three cheers for the U.S. Marines, and the Secret Service!"

The cheering was even louder than a junior high recess.

We stayed for three more hours with the family, leaving just before the second visitation began. I exchanged numbers with the Reverend Bliss and Nancy, and Soper promised to keep in touch with them. I got the chance to talk to all of Elvin Clyde's brothers—there were seven of them, all older—and discovered thoughtful, faithful people who were willing to listen, even to a guv'ment employee, or a damned lesbian.

We got in the car to head back to the hospital and my phone rang. It was Old Three Names, calling with orders and information.

"Freak, we've had a small change of plans. Take Ms. Soper to the Cincinnati airport, where the rest of your detail will meet you. Agent Goodenough will take Ms. Soper back to California to stay with her parents, and before you ask, yes, we will be augmenting her detail with other agents. You, Agents Devlin, de Vries, Koenigsblett and Beemond will all be going to DC to be debriefed by Director Hessler, and then you will rejoin Ms. Soper if she should decide to return to the campaign trail. There is a government VC-25 waiting for Ms. Soper. You and your detail are flying commercial to Reagan International, where a car will be waiting for you. Any questions for me?" Edward Otis Whitney sounded tired, but there was something else in his speech.

"One second, sir," I said. I looked at Badass and said, "Cincinnati International Airport, and don't spare the horses." He nodded and we tore out of the parking lot like we just robbed the bank next door.

"About those questions…" I said.

"Pardon me for interrupting, but before I forget, Nurse Mitchell told me to remind you to report any ringing in your ears immediately—it is symptomatic of a delayed onset concussion," Old Three Names said. He was clearly trying to convey some information without articulating it, but what?

Suddenly I thought I got it, so I tried to confirm.

"I'll inform my team, and I'll keep an ear peeled. Speaking of forgetting, Ms. Soper informed me this morning that she still intends to attend the economic conference for the Benelux countries in two months. Will we be on duty for that, or will we be handing her off to the State Department Diplomatic Security Service?" I said.

"Has she given you any kind of itinerary yet?" Old Three Names said.

"She intends to fly into Schiphol—she has friends in Amsterdam," I said. "After Holland she's going to Belgium—the conference is in Bruges, and then she's going to visit some friends in Brussels. She doesn't intend to go to Luxembourg, although that could change," I said. I was asking a question, and I hoped that I was on the same page as Old Three Names, and that he got it.

He did.

"I'll contact the DSS at State, but it sounds like it would be us going along—Ms. Soper won't really be going into dangerous territory—none of those countries care about her being a lesbian, and her trade views are not controversial, especially in those quasi-socialist economies. By the way, you should call it The Netherlands, not Holland—the latter name is considered archaic," Edward Otis Whitney said.

I deliberately didn't answer for a beat too long, and he said, "Agent Glickstien, are you listening?"

Now I got it, completely.

"Sorry, sir. My family is partly from there—they lived in Antwerp, and my grandpa always called the country Holland, not The Netherlands. It always confused me as a kid, because I never understood how you got the term 'Dutch' from either Holland or The Netherlands," I said.

"A question we can debate at a future date when time does not press on us," Old Three Names said.

"Roger that, sir. We are already on the road for Cincinnati—I estimate our ETA as plus or minus thirty-five minutes, depending on traffic," I said, deliberately misstating our estimated time of arrival. With Badass driving we would be there in ten minutes, unless we were there sooner.

"Good, good. You need to deliver Ms. Soper to the private aviation gate, and then go to the gate for D.C. Your tickets are already booked and will have been picked up by the rest of your team. Let me know when you arrive in D.C. and I will give you the schedule for your debriefings. Until then be alert, Agent Glickstien," Old Three Names said.

"Roger that, Eddie. Freak out," I said, ending the call.

"So what is it, Freak?" El Gato said. "Ya got that look on your face."

"Whaddya think of this car?" I said. "Is it nice and quiet?"

"I swept it before we left the funeral home—it's very quiet," Bumble said.

"Excellent work, Agent Beemond," I said.

"So what the fuck is up?" El Gato said.

"Somebody from the FBI is trying to get a line on us, and they may be listening to our comms," I said.

"What the fuck?" Badass said.

"The fuck those assholes think they're doin'?" Bumble said.

"Fart, Barf and Itch is gettin' above their raisin'," El Gato said. "Somebody needs to tell those sons of bitches that we're on the same goddamned side, the fucking maroons."

"Did Director Whitney just tell you that over an open line?" Sparky said. "And is that SOP? The FBI keeping an eye on us?"

"No, that part is a first for me, although I doubt if it's the first time for the Feeble Ones," I said. "And no, Eddie is about one hundred times smarter than whatever asshole is mounting this operation. He fed me the name Mitchell in a perfectly normal line about my health, and I confirmed by using the name Holland in another perfectly normal line, and he confirmed it," I said.

"And that means the FBI is...oh," Sparky 2.0 said as she got it. "Since Mitchell Holland is the Assistant Director of the FBI he was telling you it was them. Wait—he didn't mean that it was the Assistant Director himself, did he?" Sparky said.

The rest of us laughed and El Gato said, "Easy there, rookie. That slicked-back son of a bitch wouldn't know how to do this if a bugging device jumped up and bit him on the ass. He's a pretty boy political appointee who got the job by bundling millions of dollars into donations for his old pal the junior Senator from Michigan and then doing the same thing for the president. He hasn't got the chops for it, and besides, I don't think that he'd have the stomach for it. I mean, what's his motivation?"

"Word on the grapevine is that he's trying to figure out a way to get on the Republican ticket this time. He'd be a perfect fit for some of those dipshits—he's young, good-looking and from Texas," Sparky said.

"All the Republicans need to make sure of Texas, and Holland is so conservative that he makes the NRA seem liberal. If he's really going for the ticket he'd stay as far away from this as humanly possible, so we know it's somebody else," Bumble said.

"Concur," I said. "Besides, it isn't who that concerns me so much as why they are doing it," I said. "I still don't see what attacking me, Soper or anybody else on that bus gained them."

"We may never know either one," Badass said. "Whoever it is will certainly cover their tracks, and we aren't exactly going to be able to just walk up to people and ask them. This is what our British cousins call a sticky fucking wicket, in spades."

We all agreed with him, because none of us knew that we'd find out one day, and all it would cost us was a lot more blood.

Some of it ours.

CHAPTER 49

Badger Squad

So we got to the Cincy airport without incident; and Patsy, Bumble, Ed, Buddha, and I got on a flight to D.C. Everybody else went with Soper, who was going home to Cali to visit her parents and finalize funeral arrangements for Josie.

The D.C. contingent got off the plane and was very happily surprised when we hit the concourse and found Joe, Jewey, Weasel, Jack Soo and Mamba waiting for us. We had a little Chicago reunion there, and then we went out and got in a limo big enough to hold a youth soccer practice in. The faithful James Campbell was still at the wheel, and we all just let our hair down as we headed into town. It was great to have some time to just relax with pals before we had our debriefing, but I never lost sight of what we were really doing here in DC.

Finally Joe said, "OK, Freak, spill it. What the fuck are the Merry Men and I doing here in the Puzzle Palace? You just missed us so much that you took time out from being a badass Army division commander slash superhero agent to slum with the peons?"

A chorus of "Hey, fuck you, Joe," came from Jewey, Weasel, Mamba and Jack Soo. "Pepsis are on Joe," Mamba said.

We all laughed, and then I told James Campbell to please head for Arlington National Cemetery so I could tell Joe what was going on. I told them the whole story, and Ed, Bumble, Buddha and El Gato threw in any details I may have missed, so we were rolling around the Cemetery on Washington Boulevard for the fourth time before I finally said, "So that's why we need you guys."

Joe immediately said, "OK, from what you've told me these assholes are FBI, and they must be at least at the Special Agent in Charge level—no way can something like this get pulled off by even an ASAC. I would also say that this could be someone higher—an associate director, or the director of a big field office."

"But not the Director himself?" I said, wanting to confirm my own opinion.

Joe thought about it for a minute, then said, "I would say no, for two reasons. First, Director Harley doesn't really have time to do it—his days are filled with too much bureaucratic bullshit. Second, he doesn't really have the expertise to pull something like this off. He's not a law enforcement or military person who's done hard core work in the field."

"There's a third reason it's not likely to be him," Mamba said. We all looked at him, but it was Jewey who said, "Motive. Does anyone involved even know him? And if he wants to stay pristine until he retires there can't even be a bit of scandal, so anything like this is kryptonite, to be avoided at all costs."

"That a good point, but what I meant was *cui bono*. I've been trying to figure out who benefits, but it eludes me. Other than something personal I can't think of a single reason anyone would benefit from crashing the bus," Mamba said.

"Is it possible that one of the frontrunners is worried about Soper as a candidate?" Buddha said. "We watched her turn some pretty hostile crowds around before the crash—she's got charisma to burn, and she makes some good points on the campaign trail."

"If there was a snowball's chance in hell of her winning even the nomination I'd say it could be. Political ambition tends to make you crazy, but they can all read the polls—she's at 12 percent nationally, and if she was the nominee she'd only be at 30, 35 percent. The Democrats aren't dumb enough to let that happen," Joe said.

"The world is changing, but not fast enough to elect an openly lesbian womyn," Mamba said sadly.

"Especially when said womyn has written a book called *Men Are the Devil*," Jewey said.

"Even if her wife was killed by the Ku Klux Klan?" Buddha said.

"Unfortunately all that means is that the South would be even more against her because in their opinion the Klan missed," Joe said. "And before you go off on me, Freak, I'm not talking about everyone in the south, just the majority of Southern White men, who last time I looked still keep voting Republican. Remember, all those folks voted for a Mormon before they'd vote for a Democrat. The fact that she can't win in Florida, Georgia and Texas practically eliminate Soper as a viable candidate, so we can cross off any Democrats."

I nodded—he was right—and then said, "OK, so who are we left with? I can't believe that anyone else would be after Soper—I still think it's likely that the unit is the target, or at least I'm the target. Why? What the fuck do I know that would make somebody—especially somebody in the FBI—want to whack me?"

"It's possible that we're dealing with a double agent in the employ of Kim Jong Un," Weasel said. "There's about 900 million reasons for that, not to mention all those guys you whacked and the ones you sent to prison."

"That fat fuck *is* certifiable," Mamba said.

"And he could've bought someone before we broke up the ring, and then had him come after you once it became clear you were the lead dog," Jewey said.

"And if this person was a nice white boy he could get the Klan to do his dirty work, thus insulating himself from any involvement," Ed said.

"He could also be assigned to the investigation right now, and be providing pathways that would lead back to the Klan," Bumble said.

"It also makes sense that he's a nice white boy from Fart, Barf and Itch, because he could get details about your movements without even having to enquire—we don't exactly hide the trails of presidential candidates," Bumble said. "Presidents, yes, but not candidates."

"Which is why you gifted motherfuckers need to get to work on this ASAP," I said.

"But well below the radar, so that we can make it look like we believe the Klan did it," Joe said.

"That's why you're in charge," I said. "We want them to think that so they don't go underground."

"It makes sense—we can find them out and then catch the fuckers before they ever even know that we're there," Jewey said.

"We'll get those racist Klan sons of bitches," Weasel said.

"Those bedsheet bastards don't have a chance against the—what are we calling ourselves?" Jack Soo said.

"Well, since we're digging the dirt why not call ourselves the Badger Squad," Mamba said. "They're fierce creatures who can dig mile-a-minute, and they know how to burrow down without being seen."

"And they don't show up on radar—they're surreptitious as hell," Jack Soo said.

Joe said, "OK, I buy that. We're the Badger Squad. Who do we report to, and how do you want us to play it?"

"Officially you report to Director Hessler—our de-brief is actually briefing her in on the maneuver—but unofficially you report to Edward Otis Whitney, and don't use our regular phones. He'll be sending you some burners for ultra-quiet comms, and you guys will be having some face-to-face meetings through the Chicago office. You are not going to tell anyone else at all, and yes that means Guru and the rest of the Chicago crew," I said.

"You sure that's a good idea? She's pretty sharp," Joe said.

"Irrelevant—you're playing this pissed off at the world. It's the biggest untamed ornithoid (my thanks to the writers of *Star Trek: The Next Generation*) boondoggle ever invented by the brass, and all of you hate it," I said.

"Goddamned motherfucking asshole shithead cocksuckers! I just got promoted to second-in-command of the Chicago Counterfeiting Unit and now I gotta put up with some REMF bullshit about investigating an attack we know was perpetrated by the Ku Klux fucking Klan? Who the hell is running this shithole outfit—Mickey fucking Mouse?" Joe said, his voice tight with anger and shrewish pique.

"How in the hell am I supposed to do real work and catch motherfucking counterfeiters when I gotta move to the seriously fucked up Puzzle Palace just to look at some bullshit domestic terrorism? I'm an expert in anti-counterfeiting, not intrigue, for shit's sake," Weasel said.

"I have a fucking PhD in computer science from fucking MIT, and you want me to investigate a domestic terrorism case. What the fuck! That's a shitload of pavement pounding, which is a damned poor use of my valuable time. What asshole genius cunt thought that shit up? Wile E. Coyote?" Jewey said, his tone implying that someone was about to get torn limb from limb.

"What about my unit in Chicago? You know, that place out there where the piss-assed North Koreans are trying to import more funny money? Instead of catching those assholes there I have to investigate a motherfucking, shit-assed *car accident* that we know was perpetrated by a bunch of defective rednecks in bedsheets. I wish we had a union so that I could file a grievance and stick it up the ass of the moronic fuckface who thought this little fiasco up," Mamba said.

"Exactly like that," I said as we all cracked up. "Drag your feet, ask for clarifications on stuff you already know, stop working early four days out of five, bitch in every bar where you can stand to drink and publicly get as little done as possible. Privately, tear this bitch up and find out who did it. I have a funny feeling about this one—somebody's getting something out of it, and I want to know who."

"Don't worry, Freak—the Badger Squad is on it," Joe said.

"Do we get secret decoder rings and shit?" Weasel said.

"Oohhh, I like secret decoder rings with little secret compartments," Jewey said.

"Especially if we get to wear cool white Bogart suits and slink around in casinos," Bumble said.

"Can my suit be blue or lavender? I don't look good in white, and besides it's *trés gauche* to wear it after Labor Day," Mamba said.

"Hey, you're a member of the Badger Squad—you can wear any motherfucking thing that you want," Joe said.

"Except that gold lamé outfit you wore to the Prince concert," Bumble said. "You looked so good in that one you made my wife jealous."

"Yeah, Bumble's right about that—no skin tight leopard print stuff either," Jewey said. "I can't work when I have an erection, ya little biscuit, you."

"Agreed, but we do have to think about one more thing," Mamba said.

"THE SECRET HANDSHAKE!" everybody said at once. "Pepsi's are on you Freak," Mamba said. "You started this."

"I'll buy the Pepsis just as soon as you wonder workers find something out," I said. "Right now we're going to debrief with the Director and you guys are going to a computer lab and work some magic."

"Badgers, to the dirt!" Joe said.

"To the dirt!" the rest of the Badger Squad said.

"You whack-jobs are going to love Kid Galahad," I said. "James, take us to the Secret Service Field Office at 1100 L Street, will ya?"

We got there in nothing flat—James knew how to handle the big limo and we were just across the river from the FO, so in about eight minutes we were in the lobby and showing our credentials to the duty officer. He looked at mine and said, "Agent Glickstien, you've got someone waiting for you." He pointed across the lobby toward the elevators and I saw Kid Galahad.

He was leaning against the wall talking to a very good-looking blonde womyn in very tight clothing when he saw me, and the smile I got must have made her feel bad, because she said something sharp to him and he said, clear as a bell, "Sorry sweetheart, but there's my girl, there—the redhead with the sweet tits and magnificent guns." He was doing his Bogart imitation, which wasn't bad, and he was wearing a very sharp black suit with Asics sneakers. He was six feet and change, looked to be around 180 pounds, normally built with sandy blonde hair and hazel eyes, and very large wrists and hands. He wore black frame glasses like Charlie Sheen did in *Major League*—ugly, thick, functional glasses—and had a conspicuous ring on his right hand. In all respects he looked like a hipster CEO of a tech startup, and was so ordinary looking that you'd pass him on the street three or five times without noticing.

No one would ever know that he was one of the deadliest special operators in history (and yeah, that's classified).

Kid Galahad was also a walking advertisement for not judging a book by its cover.

He actually weighed 205 sculpted pounds, didn't need the glasses for anything but camouflage, had the brightest blue eyes this side of Paul Newman (colored contacts are a miracle), spoke 11 or 14 languages like a native and had an unmeasurable IQ. He routinely cracked the Pentagon's classified servers for fun and once climbed the Eiffel Tower undetected, just to prove he could do it. He was the fastest underwater swimmer I'd ever seen and the only other person I knew who could hold his breath for over four minutes without straining.

He also knew several styles of hand-to-hand combat and was a master at krav maga, *kendō* and *shotokan* (Okinawan) karate.

I'd only met two people who were his equal in combat, and one of them was dead (do you even need to ask? It's classified).

Did I mention that he was also one smart motherfucker?

We hugged and he said, "Freak."

"Galahad," I said. "Whaddya think?"

"Your tits are still A-One, girlie," he said.

"And you look like you could still be Bond, James Bond," I said.

"Remember that it ain't just the years, it's the mileage. This old carcass doesn't quite function the way it used to," Kid Galahad said.

"Oh, I'll bet it still functions the same way, but I'll bet it doesn't recover as quickly," I said.

He shot me with his thumb and forefinger and said, "Dead on, Freak. My refractory period is just a little bit longer than it used to be."

"As long as you can still get it up when you need to," I said.

"Jesus, you guys just get a room, willya?" Bumble said, his brown face turning slightly red.

"If I knew this was just a booty call I'da turned this goddamned assignment down for real," Joe said.

"What the fuck is a refractory period anyway?" Ed said. "Does it have somethin' to do with drilling?"

Everybody else just cracked up, and once Mamba explained what a refractory period was Ed was laughing as hard (sorry!) as the rest of us.

I introduced Kid Galahad during the laugh fest, and he shook everybody's hand, except Joe, who looked at his hands and wrists and said, "Don't crush my hand, Kid."

"No problem, Boss. I don't trot that out for anybody except assholes, and if Freak thinks you're OK you're aces with me," Galahad said.

The two men shook and Joe said, "Welcome to the Badger Squad, where we dig for shit so you don't have to. Ready to go to work?"

"I was born ready, sir," Kid Galahad said. "But before we go to work you should know that all of that sexual shit earlier was all a farce—Freak and I been through some bad times together and that's the way we dealt with it. I'm actually more interested in men than wymyn, truth be told."

"*Well*, in that case why don't you let *me* give Kid Galahad his *introductory* tour?" Mamba said. He was back in Nathan Lane mode, all tarted up and on the prowl.

Kid Galahad threw back his head and laughed like a demented hyena and said, "Rock on! Another member of the brotherhood in my unit? Too cool! Who knew the Secret Service was so enlightened?"

"We are going to kick some serious Ku Klux Klan ass," Weasel said. "Those rednecks'll never know what hit 'em after the semi-gay Badger Squad gets through diggin' the dirt."

"Don't forget that we're powered by a Jew and two Asians," Jewey said.

"And the boss is a college educated Mick," Jack Soo said.

"Oh fuck yes," Joe said. "We're their worst nightmare—the Rainbow Coalition meets the Yellow Peril meets the Worldwide Zionist Conspiracy meets the IRA meets crazed burrowing mammals—and we have guns! To the Badger Burrow!" They all trooped off toward some workspace, while the rest of us went up to the conference room to meet the Director of the Secret Service.

The first thing that struck everyone about Director Siri Hessler was that she was gorgeous (face and body), the second was that she was short (around five feet, although I never asked her) and the third was she wasn't fucking around (she carried herself like she was an NFL football player, only she was tougher). She was also a very sharp dresser and had the eyes of a killer—she'd shot five men to death when she was a U.S. Marshal, including two who tried to held up a Native American casino in Riverton, Wyoming, while she was trying to celebrate her honeymoon.

The last piece needed to understand the Director was knowing that she was extremely intelligent and understood both strategy and tactics, and the differences between the two.

We all called her Nails, as in "tough as nails." It fit her like a glove.

She was alone when Bumble, Patsy, Buddha, Ed and I entered the conference room, but her personal aide, a guy named Gordie Lidstrom, came in right after us with a laptop under his arm. He set it up in the middle of the table and then sat down beside the Director with a pad of paper.

"OK, Freak, dish," Nails said.

So I did, about everything. It took a while, but she never interrupted, or blinked, or breathed. She was as immobile as the Washington Monument until I was finished. She looked at me and said to Lidstrom, "Is that laptop independent and isolated from the mainframe recording system?"

"Yes, Director, it's completely isolated and independent of the mainframe," Lidstrom said.

Nails rose from her seat, pulled her pistol from its shoulder rig, reversed it, and pounded the laptop into tiny pieces. When she was done the Director said to Lidstrom, "Gordie, please destroy your notes and burn them." Her aide got up and went to a shredder in the corner of the room, shredded the notes and then put them in a locked bag that said, "Top Secret—Burn Contents of Bag Every Day." He locked the bag and came over to sit down again.

Nails said, "Not a word of this to anyone—I mean *no one*. If this is somebody from the FBI we can't even breathe a hint of it or they'll disappear in their bureaucracy so fast it'll make Usain Bolt look like he's using a walker. We need to keep our profile just like you described it to me—a small group of disgruntled agents who eventually discover it was the Ku Klux Klan that was after Soper. As of now none of the rest of you can have any contact with the Badger Squad except as part of normal routine—no special calls, no weekends in Chicago unless you've been routinely doing that and no clandestine meetings of any kind on this subject. You are a part of Soper's protective detail and nothing else. That's the only way this will work. Got it?"

We all nodded, because she was 100% right—the FBI was notorious for covering the tracks of its own, and closing ranks, and basically acting like a fiefdom inside our democracy (it must be said that this was true of virtually every organization within the federal hierarchy), and this case would be no different. We were hunting big game that had already proven it had teeth, and we couldn't afford to spook it back into the impenetrable rain forest of bureaucracy that was the FBI.

It didn't stop anybody from feeling left out, or basically useless in finding out who killed CoD, Josie and Elvin Clyde Bliss, but we all knew that the Badger Squad would leave no stone unturned, and we knew that Nails would also have a big ear to the ground…but you still want to help find the bastards who hurt you, and not passively, either.

It was time to pull up our big girl panties and carry on.

So we finished talking to the Director, established what was acceptable in the way of progress reports, and then asked her a favor.

"We'd all like to be there when we arrest someone," I said.

"All of you?" the Director said. "With weapons?"

We all nodded, and she looked hard at us before she said, "Very well, but if the suspect ends up dead I will prosecute all of you to the fullest extent of the law. *Capische*?"

"Yeah, we got it, Dom Hessler," I said in my best *Godfather* voice.

"Then you can be there," she said, and left.

We went back out to the street, leaving the Badger Squad behind, and got into our government cars. No more limos for us, at least not until the Badgers dug up enough dirt on someone to arrest them and we could socialize with Mamba again. Everybody went home for a while, until it was time to go back out to California and re-join Soper on the campaign trail.

The fallout from the investigation was far in the future, as was the blood price that we paid for finding out the truth.

CHAPTER 50

Zayde's Last Dance

Once Soper finally dropped pout of the race (like we all knew she'd have to—she was way to smart to be president) I surprised my family by flying home unannounced. I called my brother David the Dog-Boy to come and get me from the Kalamazoo-Battle Creek International Airport because I knew that his vet's office was closed on Wednesday afternoons.

As soon as he answered his phone I knew something was wrong.

"Who got ahold of you?" he said.

"What d'you mean, got ahold of me? I flew in to surprise you guys," I said. David was silent, so I said "What the fuck is going on Dog-Boy?"

Before he could answer I saw my brothers Morris (Eggy) and Gabriel (Shyster) walking down the concourse together and I knew something was really wrong. I said, "Doggy, I see Shyster and Eggy—what the fuck is up?"

"Come home with them—they've already got a car," Dog-Boy said before he hung up. I looked at the phone—Glickstien's were not big hangers-up on each other—and looked up to see my brothers steering toward me. Eggy was on the phone, but he hung up when I made eye contact. Both my big brothers reached out and enveloped me in a hug (not a surprise—Glickstiens were and are big huggers), and Eggy said, "Sorry, Freak. We shoulda told you earlier, but *zayde* wouldn't let us. You're the only one in the family who can stand up to him, but he didn't want to distract you from your work."

Before I could answer Shyster said, "Ya gotta be normal for Mumsy and Pops—they're not taking it well, and you know what this is going to do to Mom's practice. No flyin' off the handle, OK?"

I looked at my brothers and said, "What. The. Fuck. Is. Happening."

"Oh, shit," they both said. "You assholes owe me Pepsis," I said. "Now spill it."

Eggy said, "Freak, *zayde* is in the hospital. He's at the end of a long battle with bone cancer. We came home as soon as Mumsy called, but I'm going to guess that you were in transit and nobody got you on the phone before you landed." Her pointed at Shyster and said, "Just for the record, I told you dumbfucks this would happen, did I not?"

My brother Gabriel nodded and said, "That you did, Eggy. You'll recall that Roady and I agreed with you, but we got overruled."

"*Zayde*," I said. "When did you guys find out?" They both looked at me and then at each other, but neither one spoke.

They were afraid of me.

I didn't blame them.

But I wanted to know, so I said, "Just tell me when and no one will get hurt. Don't tell me and neither of you will be out of the hospital for a year. Rehab will be longer." I was kidding, but they didn't know that. I guess I was sort of kidding, because Eggy looked me in the eye and said, "Six months. Mumsy told us the last time we were all home."

"Which is why Pops insisted that he and I have a father-daughter expedition to Kalamazoo to get the barbecue from Barrett's Smokehouse," I said.

"Yeah," Shyster said. "Mumsy and *zayde* swore us to secrecy. *Zayde* insisted that we couldn't distract you from your work, because if you slipped up someone would die."

"Those were his exact words, Freak. He impressed on all of us that working the protective detail required your 100% concentration—you know we weren't going to fight him once he invoked those words," Eggy said.

I looked back over my lifetime and realized that my *zayde* was right, and so were my brothers. When he wanted us to know that the lesson he was teaching us was both serious and lifelong he always said it that way—"this requires your 100% concentration." I decided not to be mad, but rather to be all grown up and just deal with the situation as it was.

I looked at my big brothers, who were now clearly just worried for me, rather than about me, and I said, "It turns out he may have been right. Did you guys get the straight dope on what happened in Kentucky?"

They both shook their heads and Shyster said, "Just what we saw on the news. Did you really take command of the 101st Airborne?"

"First Brigade of the 101st Air Assault Division, United States Army," I said. "And I was given a field rank of lieutenant general under the authority of the president of the United States and the governor of Kentucky."

My brothers exuded nothing but care and interest as they swept me off to their rental car and we headed for Bronson Hospital in Battle Creek (I liked it better when it was Leila Post Hospital, but agglomeration had hit the hospital biz in southwest Michigan) and our appointment with our dying grandfather, the great and powerful Abraham Louis Blumenthal.

My brothers tried to cheer me up by asking about the Battle of Morehead, and I tried to be civil, and I guess we were at least partially successful, because no one died on the way to the hospital. I almost got there clean, but when we turned off Emmet Street onto North Avenue and I saw the hospital on the hill I started crying. Shyster was driving, and Eggy was in the back seat, so I just sat there crying by myself. As soon as we stopped my door jerked open and my dad surged into the car and wrapped me in his arms.

Then the floodgates really opened up.

It took about five minutes, but eventually my eyes stopped gushing tears and snot stopped running out of my nose and the hiccups slash whooping cough stopped and I had to face it for real: my beloved grandfather, my *zayde*, the man who taught me even when I didn't want to be taught, who not only stood by me when I was the ugliest kid on the planet, but also relentlessly stood up for me when it seemed no one else would, the man who told me to follow my dreams and skills wherever I wanted to go, the man who was the only person in my entire family who endorsed my military career, the person who probably saved the rest of the human race by teaching me what the words honor, compassion and humility really meant, and my very best friend *ever* was going to die.

Fuck death, the horse he rode in on, and the family dog, the evil motherfucker.

And then, clear as a bell, I heard my *zayde's* voice in my head saying, '*Wait just a minute, Miss Gigi. Change is the only constant in life, and death is just the ultimate change. No need to call death an evil motherfucker—now Hitler*, that *was an evil motherfucker. Death is just doing his job.*'

I laughed, and then explained why to my assembled family. They all laughed, too, because apparently I sounded just like my *zayde* when I said it. After the laughter died down I looked at my dad and said, "Is everybody here?"

He nodded and said, "Except for Roady—he was stuck in London for his firm. In fact, he may not make it back to sit *shiva*. Your Uncle Mort and Aunt Adele are up there with your mom, and Mrs. Silverman"—*zayde's* girlfriend of many years—"is up there, too. Aaron just went to the funeral home, but he'll be right back. Everybody else is back at the house, just…uh, well…" My dad's face was red and I realized that he was trying not to cry. I reached out and grabbed him back in a hug and said, "They're waiting for *zayde* to depart this plane and experience The Great Unknown Adventure. It's OK, Pops, they're doing it because they love him, just like we do."

We all smiled at that, because it was almost word for word what my *zayde* said the day my *bubbe* died. He was right then and he was right now, so I gave my Pops a squeeze and we went up to say goodbye.

The room was really crowded, but as soon as Mumsy saw my face she rushed out, and so did Uncle Mort and Aunt Adele, and Mrs. Silverman, and Dog-Boy, and Doc (remember my brother Aaron, the doctor?). We looked like a school of herring circling each other in a big ball of hugging and crying, until finally I went in by myself.

Zayde didn't look any different, except for the fact that he was lying in a hospital bed with all sorts of tubes attached to him and several beeping monitors. His eyes were closed, but as soon as I came in the room they flew open and he said, "Gigi, please forgive me for keeping this from you, but I thought it was for the best." His hazel eyes stared right into my green ones, letting me know that his body was breaking down but his mind was still sharp.

The force of his personality was palpable, almost a physical thing itself; but under the usual overwhelming mixture of love, pride, and intelligence I felt his weariness. He'd been a fighter all his life—88 years!—but now the race was over and he knew it. I couldn't feel any sorrow, except for him leaving us, and I didn't feel any regrets, either. What I saw and felt was a man content with the result of his life, secure that he had left a good legacy behind.

He said again, "Gigi, don't be mad at me, or at anyone else in the family—I made them keep it from you. Please forgive me."

I looked at him—the only person besides Square Peg I ever felt understood me and didn't judge me or think me a freak, and I did the only thing I could think of that would show him exactly how much I loved and respected him.

I drew myself up to attention and saluted him.

My *zayde* looked at me and his eyes welled up with tears. I held the salute and stared straight ahead, even when he threw off the covers and struggled to his feet. When he was finally upright he drew himself up to attention and saluted me back. Only when his put his hand down did I drop my salute and really look at him.

Up close and out of bed he looked even less sick, but I realized as I watched that his knees were trembling and that standing was taking all of his concentration, so I went over and helped him back on the bed, but when I tried to cover him back up he said, "Gigi, I want to go home now. I want to die in my own bed, where my Marta died."

I said, "Roger that, *zayde*. Where are your clothes?" He pointed at a cabinet and I said, "I'm going to get Doc to come in and help you get dressed, OK?" He nodded and I went out to where everybody was standing. I grabbed Doc's elbow and said, "Go in and help *zayde* get dressed."

"Say what?" Doc said. I looked at him with my "don't fuck with me" look and he said, "Uh, OK, but Mumsy is gonna come unglued." I just kept looking at him and he said, "Got it. Get *zayde* dressed. Right."

As soon as he went in the room I went over and stood in front of the room door, because I was pretty sure what was going to happen next. Within fifteen seconds, I was proven right. Several bells and whistles went off at the nurses' station and two battleships set sail for *zayde's* room.

They actually looked more like hippos—huge wymyn with giant breasts, more chins than a Chinese phone book and no discernible waistlines. They rolled to a stop in front of me and the one with the wart on her chin and eyes that were looking in different directions at the same time said, "Move out the way, young lady, we need to get in to see our patient."

I said, "Anybody ever tell you that you look like Jack Elam? The old actor who did all those Westerns? Always played the bad guy? Needed eye surgery?"

The shorter battleship said, "Ha, ha, ha. Move yourself and let us in to see our patient, missy."

I reached in my coat pocket, brought out my credentials and held them up in front of her face. I showed the Jack Elam look-alike, too, and then I said, "He isn't going to be your patient for long. He wants to go home, and so he's going home."

"Absolutely not," they both said. "You two owe me Pepsis," I said, "even if your sense of humor sucks."

"Mr. Blumenthal isn't going anywhere," the Jack Elam clone said.

"He's very sick," the smaller battleship said. She bore a striking resemblance to Petunia Pig, only on a much larger scale, so I decided to try out my Porky Pig voice on her.

"B-b-b-b-but Pet-t-t-tunia, what a-b-b-b-out his wi-wi-wi-wishes? Is he a pri-pri-pri-pri-prisoner?"

They really didn't have a sense of humor, because the Jack Elam doppelganger tried to push by me to get in the room. I didn't move at all, so she decided to use sheer bulk to overwhelm me.

It didn't work.

I'd been pushed around by huge college football linemen, and they could in fact move me, but they were trained, and in shape, and even bigger than this battleship-sized nurse…and my *zayde* wanted to go home, so I made like the Black Knight and said, "None shall pass." (If you haven't watched *Monty Python and the Holy Grail* yet you're a loser).

Her fat got all tensed up, her face got red and she began puffing like she'd just run a marathon, but I still didn't move. Her colleague moved in on me from the other side and added her rotundness to the effort to clear the doorway, but I still didn't move. After it got to the point that I was afraid they were going to stroke out I just extended my arms and pushed them away. They both staggered a little bit and then bent over to catch their breath, and Jack Elam's sister said, "You…just…wait… until…doctor…gets…you'll…move…then."

"Doubtful," I said, just as the doctor arrived and said, "What in the hell is going on here? Nurse Carter, why aren't you in the room with Mr. Blumenthal? He could be expiring in there! All of his alarms are going off! What the hell are you doing?"

Both nurses just pointed at me, and the doctor—I noticed right away that he was one good-looking specimen of doctorhood—pointed at me and said, "You. Move." in that imperious, condescending tone that all modern gods of medicine use when addressing we mere mortals.

Before I could respond another voice said, in just as imperious a tone, "Hold that door, Marine!"

I felt relief flood my body, because my reinforcements had arrived, in the form of my brother Marvin Glickstien, Attorney at Law, a.k.a. "Roady."

A word about my brother Roady: he worked for one of the largest law firms in the world as their chief negotiator and litigator, which is an unusual combination, and in a family of very smart people—a veterinarian, a medical doctor, a double PhD physicist, a lawyer with a JD from Yale, and me—he was the smartest. His mental skills were the equivalent of my physical gifts, as evidenced by the fact that he graduated from the University of Chicago in three years, scored so high on the LSATs that they thought he cheated and then demolished Stanford Law as first in his class and editor of their law review. He then clerked for a Supreme Court justice (Sotomayor) and took another degree in international relations from George Washington University.

He was also the person most like *zayde* in our family, and he loved me with a fierceness that bordered on demented parent status. Roady would always back me, even when I was wrong, and it was apparent that I was going to need his help, because by now my whole family was gathered around the door, and they were all yelling, as were the nurses and the good-looking doctor, who'd also called security, since there were five or six rent-a-cops trying to get to me through the crowd.

"SILENCE!" Roady said.

The power of his courtroom voice was so impressive that everybody shut the hell up, and my knight-like brother parted the crowd and came right to my side. He gave me a look that said he was prepared to do battle, and then he kissed my cheek and said, "What the hell is going on here, Freak?"

I said, "*Zayde* wants to go home, to be with us and *bubbe*. Doc's inside getting him dressed, and by now waiting to see what happens at this doorway, and I wouldn't let the battleships in the door, so they tried to push me out of the way."

His eyes widened and he said, "And they're alive?"

"I've learned restraint in my new job," I said.

"Good, because I still don't know how to get blood out of a carpet," Roady said, doing the Blumenthal/Glickstien deflection technique of using humor when one is uncomfortable.

The medical personnel started to yammer about how *zayde* couldn't go home, my family began yammering about 250 things at once and the security guards began moving forward as if they were going to try and remove me from the doorway by force, which made me think about how lucky they were to already be in the hospital, since it wouldn't be far for them to go after we fought.

Roady held up his hand and it got quiet again. He said, "OK, here's the deal. Doctor, nurses, thank you for your concern for and care of my grandfather, but if he wants to go home he's going home. You are his caregivers, not his captors and yes,"—he held up his hand to the doctor—"I know that he will be leaving AMA…but he *will* be leaving. You three are dismissed, and please take your security goons with you before my sister does something stupid and hurts them.

"As for the family—you all please respect the wishes of the best among us and let him go where he wants. None of us want him to die, but he's going to, and he knows it, and despite the decline of his body there isn't anything wrong with his mind, and we all know he's the smartest person we've ever met, and that includes me. Mumsy, Uncle Mort, I know you love your dad, but let him have the end he wants, won't you please?"

His tone was so reasonable that I knew he'd won the family over. My Pops came forward and said, "I'm with you, son." He turned to my mom and said, "You know I love you, and I love Abe, but Roady's right—we've got to let him go home."

Just at that moment the room door opened and my brother Doc said, "Freak, *zayde* wants you." As I went into the room I heard the good-looking doctor say something, and Roady said, "And I'll sue your asses so fast and far that you'll be looking for work in Siberia by next Tuesday. You can't keep patients who want to leave from leaving, unless they're under arrest or committed." The good-looking doc said something else and Roady said, "Try it and I guarantee I'll get an involuntary 72-hour hold put on you and both these bruisers. My *zayde's* as sane as anyone I know, and apparently more sane than some people."

The door closed and I couldn't hear anymore, but there was my *zayde*, looking pale, but much the same as he always did. He was wearing his full coral colored suit, complete with his Phi Beta Kappa key and his old railroad pocket watch with the 22-carat gold fob and chain. He smiled and said, "Roady is tormenting the doctors and nurses, isn't he?"

"He's using the law to beat them like they stole something," I said.

"Good," he said. "Doesn't the biggest nurse look like Jack Elam?"

Doc and I busted up, and so did *zayde*. I said, "Should you be laughing so hard?"

"Why not? What's it going to do, kill me?" he said. We all had another laugh riot before *zayde* said, "Gigi, I can't walk. Can you find me a wheelchair?" I looked at Doc and he said, "He's not kidding, Freak. If he tried to walk he'd have broken bones before we left the hospital. We need a wheelchair."

I went over and said, "No, I think you're both wrong." I smiled at *zayde* and gently put my arm under his legs, bent over so he could put his arms around my neck and then just as gently lifted him off the bed. I said, "Doc, get the door and organize Dog-Boy and Shyster to run interference, willya?"

He nodded and went out of the room. *Zayde* didn't feel frail, but he wasn't all that heavy, either, so I was surprised when he said, "Gigi, I'm too heavy—all of that chemo shit meant that I couldn't exercise, so I got fat. You put me down any time you need to, sweet girl."

I laughed and said, "Did I ever tell you about the time that I carried an unconscious 225-pound Marine ten miles over hill and dale? No? Well, I was serving in…" (Sorry, but the rest is classified. I only told *zayde* because I knew that he wouldn't be around to tell anyone else.)

The door opened after what seemed like a long time and Doc said, "You're not going to believe it… I…you need to come out here, Freak. Now."

493

I walked out of the door with my *zayde* in my arms and almost pissed my pants. The entire corridor was lined by Battle Creek policemen in uniform, led by my old friend Bengt Olafsson. He saw me and said, "Attention!"

All the officers saluted as I walked down the hall to the elevators with *zayde* in my arms. Bengt walked in front of us and my brothers walked behind, and nobody messed with us. As we neared the end of the hall eight officers stepped out from the line and stopped us. *Zayde's* eyes lit up and he said, "Help me stand up, Gigi."

I set him down and he shook the hands of the eight officers. They all said some form of "Thank you, Counselor," or "Thank you, Abe," and they were all very gentle as they took his hand. He called all of them by name, and then everybody cried and gentle hugs were exchanged. I looked at my *zayde* and he said, "These men were wrongly accused, and you know how that offends my sense of order, so I gave them a vigorous defense in court, just like I would anyone else, wrongly accused or not." He looked so vital, so much like the old *zayde*, that it was hard to believe that he was dying.

One of the cops said, "Yeah, right—just like anyone else. You didn't charge me a dime, and you made the city apologize *and* you got me my back pay *and* you unsmirched my good name and gave me my career back. You're like a legal Superman, and I still say ya shoulda let me pay ya."

"Me, too," all the other officers said, but *zayde* held up a hand and said, "That issue is a moot point. We all agreed that public servants get paid like shit, especially police, fire, and teachers, and I'll be damned if I'll contribute to the problem by impoverishing you further. Besides, I had fun making Mr. Garcia and his merry men actually work for a change." Michael Garcia was the Battle Creek prosecutor and a real hardass on police corruption.

"You knocked him ass over applecart in 23 minutes," another policeman said, and they all laughed. "I did knock that one out of the park," my *zayde* said, his face aglow with the good memory. They all had an anecdote to share, but Doc touched my arm and said, in the quietest voice I'd ever heard "Freak, he can't keep this up. It's time to go." I hated to pull him away from it, but my brother was the doctor, so I broke in and said, "Sorry, guys, but we've got to get the hero home for his lunch. Come by the house tomorrow and stay as long as you like, OK."

They were all smart guys who got it, so they gracefully said they'd escort us to the car. I picked *zayde* up and Bengt got an elevator, and we all piled in. Bengt said, "Secure from attention" and all of the officers slowly ended their salute as the doors slowly closed. As we rode down one of the cops touched my arm and said, "Your grandfather saved my life—literally and career wise—so I owe him a debt I can't pay with money. If your family ever needs something just ask, because I pay my debts. So do the rest of these guys." There was a low murmur from the rest of the officers, and Roady said, "Thank you for your kindness. We'll keep that in mind."

The doors opened on the ground floor and there were three TV cameras in our faces—all the local yokels—and Roady said, *sotto voce*, "Officers, time to pay that debt. Clear these assholes out, willya?"

The squad of policemen moved out into the lobby and the TV cameras were jostled back out of the way as I carried *zayde* out through the lobby and to Dog-Boy's waiting car. The thin blue line screened him from view as I loaded him into the front seat and then jumped in back with the rest of my brothers. Eggy went and got their rental car and we prepared to pull out and head for home.

When we got down the hill to Emmett Street there was a cop car waiting to escort us to the big house up on East Roosevelt Avenue that was the ancestral mansion of the Glickstien clan.

We got home, where Mumsy and Pops were already waiting (we'd already argued at the hospital, and as usual *zayde* won, although this time he'd let Roady win the case for him). My Uncle Mort opened the door and I carried *zayde* into the living room and set him down in his wingback chair. He ruffled around and got comfortable, and Mumsy brought him his favorite drink of all time, amaretto and soda. We all gathered around and *zayde* said, "Laissez les bon temps roulez, eh?" as he took a swig of his drink.

It turned into quite a party.

A solid stream of people came by to pay their respects, Speed's Coffee Shop sent us all kinds of food and the Battle Creek Police Department kept the press and other undesirables away.

Zayde was in his glory, holding court like he was Louis XIV at Versailles. He dispensed advice, legal and otherwise, chatted about people alive and dead and generally was the *bon vivant* that he'd always been.

He didn't ignore his family, either. We all got sage advice, compliments on our recent accomplishments, and tips for improving our love lives. He didn't stop for almost eight hours, until Mumsy finally said at midnight, "OK, that's enough old man. We're closing up the Abe Show, at least until tomorrow morning."

We knew how sick *zayde* was when he didn't argue.

All non-family members cleared the door by 12:15, but *zayde* asked us all to stay up with him a while longer, so we all just sat around schmoozing, mostly about all the fun we'd had over the years.

The only truly important piece of information that came out of our gabbing was the fact that Roady no longer worked for the huge firm in New York. When we asked him what happened he said, "Well, they told me I had to pick between staying in London and getting the deal completely done or coming home to my family." He smiled a crocodile smile and said, "I asked my boss if there was any wiggle room involved and he told me to get my Jew ass back in the conference room and finish the deal, so I invited him to kiss my Jewish ass. He objected to my language, so I told him I quit."

"How did he take that?" I asked.

"I don't know, Freak—he was mostly unconscious at that point in time, and I knew that if I wanted to see *zayde* I had to get to Heathrow, so I assume he granted me the release from my contract I asked for as he lay there all in a schlump."

"Unconscious?" Shyster said.

"Well, my resignation letter did come in the form of a really nice left hook and straight right hand," Roady said.

"Oh, shit," Mumsy said. "Do you need legal representation, 'cause I know a good firm." We all got a good laugh out of that, partly because of the way she said it, but mostly because big-time lawyers don't press charges against associates who clock them, especially after making a racial/ethnic/religious epithet the center of their motivational speech.

"So what will you do now?" Pops said.

My tough litigator big brother, the man who once made a prosecutor pee his pants with his cross-examination of a witness, got all teared up and said, "Well, I thought I'd come home and work for the family firm, if they'll have me." We all choked up, because that's what we all wanted.

Mumsy said, "We're not really looking for an associate right now."

Zayde said, "Revenues were down last year, and we've got the note on the building now, and didn't we already promise a job at some point to the neighbor girl who went to Harvard?"

"We may have to let Felicia go, it's so bad," Mumsy said. Felicia Cooper was the firm's paralegal/secretary/bookkeeper/indispensable womyn. Mom and *zayde* were about as likely to let her go as they were to campaign in the nude for the Republican nominee for governor.

Roady'd been in New York for too long, because he didn't get the teasing. He looked genuinely hurt, until *zayde* said, "We could use a part-time person to file papers on divorces and child custody cases."

We all broke up laughing then, because one thing that Blumenthal and Glickstien did not do was divorces and child custody cases—it was one of *zayde's* immutable laws of the universe, like gravity and never getting involved in a land war in Asia (ya really got to read *The Princess Bride*).

Roady shook *zayde's* hand, hugged Mumsy and said, "I'm baaaackkk."

Zayde smiled beneficently and said, "Excellent! I was worried that the practice would falter after its two employees worked themselves into a worn-down frazzle. Remember, all work and no play makes Rachel a dull girl."

We all laughed and *zayde* seemed to relax. Everyone brought up their favorite '*zayde-isms*' and we debated which one was best. Finally Eggy said, "It's even late in Cali guys—and it's really late here. Can we get some sleep and talk more tomorrow over breakfast? *Zayde*? Whattaya think? You had enough?"

Everyone turned to look at him and I knew it was time. I wish I could tell you that my beloved grandfather had some last, great wisdom to impart before he died, or that his last words were so profound that they echoed through the ages, but all he said was, "Goodbye, and remember I love all of you, even you, Phil." He was making a long-standing joke about his relationship with my dad, and everybody else started to laugh except me and Doc, who both moved to his side, realizing what those words meant.

Abraham Louis Blumenthal's eyes closed and he died with grace and dignity at 2:33 a.m. on a beautiful April day, surrounded by his loving family and joking to the end.

We all cried, but not as much as one might think, because we couldn't stop thinking of the grand, beautiful man who had been our father, grandfather, and father-in-law.

Doc checked for a pulse, didn't find one and said, "The royal falcon has flown into the sun." It was a line from Cecil B. de Mille's *The Ten Commandments*—Yul Brynner says it when the old pharaoh dies—and it was what *zayde* had always wanted said when he died. After our brief tearfest we all went out on the porch and waited for the funeral home to come and pick up the body. We didn't touch him—Jews avoid touching dead bodies if at all possible—and we wanted to keep Mumsy and Uncle Mort from looking at him, because it was obvious that they were both near a meltdown. Because of the Holocaust being an orphan has a special significance for Jews, especially for the children of a Holocaust survivor like my *zayde*.

Finally my brother David the Dog-Boy said, "He outlived Hitler by seventy years and left behind a legacy of goodness and love it'll be hard to beat. Not bad for a poor Warsaw Jew, eh?"

"Remember what he always said on his birthday?" Eggy said.

"I'm still alive—and Hitler is still dead!" we all chorused. "I'll get the Pepsis," Mumsy said. She went to the kitchen and came back with a huge cooler of Mexican Pepsis sunk in ice (Mexican Pepsi is made with real sugar and has a touch of vanilla—it's been a family favorite for years). We all pried the cap off our bottles with an old church key that belonged to *zayde* and toasted his life.

My Uncle Mort said, "You know how you idolize your heroes when you're a kid, and then you feel a little bit cheated when you find out they're just people like everybody else? Feet of clay and all that shit?"

We all nodded and he said, "I never had to be disappointed. My hero never put a foot wrong, his feet were made of gold and he was the most steadfast, honorable, and giving person I ever saw. The guy could've went to any white shoe law firm in the world and made a fortune, but instead he picks Battle Creek, because every city should have one big-time defense lawyer. He always thought of everybody else, never himself, and he practiced what he preached. No hypocrisy, no pettiness, no greed…just the burning desire to be the best person he could. Most guys want to distance themselves from their fathers, but I couldn't get enough of him. I still can't believe how lucky I was to grow up with this kind of role model— he was also the best dad I've ever seen."

"And the best teacher," Mumsy said. "He would've made a great rabbi, but remember what he said about the Torah?"

"Yeah, he said it wasn't half as exciting as the Talmud, because thou shalt nots and miracles were like boiled chicken and broccoli—good for you but dry as hell," Uncle Mort said.

"He was a Talmud man," my Aunt Adele said. "Abe loved the law almost as much as he loved Marta and the rest of his family."

Just then the funeral home guys pulled up, and the whirlwind of a Jewish funeral ensued. I'm not going to bore you with the intricacies of Jewish funeral rites, but Jewish funerals are held within forty-eight hours of death whenever possible, and since my *zayde* was among the most organized persons ever born it was a snap—he'd already prearranged all of the details.

His body was going to Hirschfeld's Funeral Home in Springfield (a suburb of Battle Creek) to be washed, dressed, and placed in its plain wood coffin. My brother Doc was going with the body as a *Shomer*, or watchman, as per the Jewish tradition of not leaving the body alone after death (just like the Klingons from *Star Trek*—go figure). My other brothers were prepared to relieve him until the funeral.

We had our only disagreement during the whole process when I suggested that I go as the *Shomer*. My oldest brother told me to butt out, that it was already arranged, and besides I was a girl and traditionally the watchman was a man. I responded by telling him that it should be the person best qualified to guard the body, and give the *neshama*—the soul or essence of *zayde*—the respect and companionship it deserved (Jewish tradition says the soul lingers near the body until the burial), Since I was *zayde's* favorite I argued that was me. When my brothers disagreed the following conversation took place.

> Doc: I'm doing it first, then Roady, then Eggy, then Dog-Boy, then Shyster. We agreed, so let it be written, so let it be done. (If you recognize this, yes, it is from de Mille's *The Ten Commandments*.)

Me: *I* didn't agree to anything.

Eggy: Tough shit. We've already decided. Besides, just because you are some super-agent doesn't mean that you're the only one who can stand guard.

Roady: And just because you're a Secret Service agent don't think that you can take all five of us. We're all grown up and we don't care if you're a girl.

Dog-Boy: Yeah, and we're not afraid of you anymore, either.

Me: You should be.

The brothers: Urk. Waagh. Oofty. Snerk. Zoop. Ferp. Shit. (*Various other sounds that correspond with big bodies hitting various objects while in flight.*)

Me: Who's going to be the first *shomer*?

Shyster: I think it should be you, Freak.

Me: Good answer.

The fact that I had Shyster hauled up off the floor by his belt buckle—and that his pants—and balls—were about a foot north of his belly button because of it—probably had something to do with his answer, which was delivered in a Mickey Mouse soprano. My other brothers wouldn't be speaking for a while, due to serious but non-lethal injuries inflicted by their "little" sister.

Sometimes you just have to put it to people the right way to get them to agree with you.

So I rode with the body to Hirschfeld's. They took it back to be washed and cleaned and dressed in the traditional Jewish manner and I stood guard over the door, just like I was guarding the president. We'd been down there about half an hour when heavy footsteps rumbled down the hall toward me. I wasn't sure who to expect, but it turned out to be my old friend Bengt Olafsson.

He came over and gave me a hug, then said, "I'm very sorry about your grandpa, do'ntcha know. He was the classiest lawyer I ever met., and one of da good guys, even if he was a defense attorney. Battle Creek will miss him, Freak."

"So will everybody else who ever knew him," I said. "He was a *mensch*."

"Dat he was, dat he was. I came down t'day 'cause I've got some other news I wanna tell ya before I forget, so you can let your mind work on it. I been talkin' ta Kristy O'Dowd a little about da whole Tim Miller murder, and I t'ink she's tryin' ta tell me that she and Tim never, ah—did the deed, if y'know what I mean." Bengt's big face was beet red—Norwegians apparently didn't talk about sex much, especially to female friends—and my face must've looked the same as what he said sunk in.

"Did she say they weren't having sex, or did she imply it? Tell me exactly what she said as nearly as you can remember," I said.

"She din't say it exactly, but she did mention dat she had no chance of gettin' pregnant with Tim," Bengt said.

"And the only way to be 100% percent sure of that is to not have sex," I said.

"Dat's what I t'ought," he said.

I thought about it for a minute and said, "Did they love each other? Was their relationship serious?"

"Kristy said they were talkin' about gettin' married when she graduated, but dat Tim wanted to wait for sex 'til then. He said it wasn't fitting—she say's dat's th' word he used—for the niece of a bishop to have sex before she was married. Tim also told her dat he din't want to have sex yet 'cause he wasn't ready for dat kind of responsibility," Bengt said.

"OK, so Tim loved Kristy and wanted to marry her, and he thought sex was irresponsible and premature, but the evidence clearly shows that he had sex the night he died. We know that Tim didn't have sex with Kristy, and we know that he wasn't a typical crazy teenager who'd just throw over his girlfriend for a spur-of-the-moment romp in the hay, especially since it sounds like she was willing…" I said, thinking hard but not coming up with any answers.

Bengt held up two huge fingers and said, "Two more t'ings ta add to dat. One, Kristy showed me a letter from Tim where he called her "the love of my life" and two, his brother Tom was home on leave, and he tol' me dat Tim loved Kristy so much that he was t'inkin' 'bout just going to Kellogg Community College here in Battle Creek, rather den takin' da wrasslin' scholarship to Bloomsburg State."

Suddenly a light bulb went on in my head. Tim staying home…not ready to have sex yet… worried about Kristy's honor…what if…what if it wasn't *just* Kristy that he was worried about?

I looked at my old friend and said, "Bengt, what about Miss Farmer?" I looked at his earnest face, waiting to see if he got to the same place that I did. His eyes narrowed and I could tell he was thinking back to his conversations with Kristy, when suddenly he said, "Ya know, Kristy said dat Tim wasn't ready ta have sex with *her*. I t'ink dat his exact words were "I'm not ready to have sex *with you* because I'm not ready for that kind of responsibility yet." '*Wit' you*' ain't the same as I ain't ready to have sex, which makes perfect sense if you remember Miss Farmer an' da way she was about wrestlers. It could be dat Tim had sex with *Miss Farmer* and some other wrestler had a problem wit' dat."

"Like Ildoberto Cortez, or Bart Stone, or Kurt Featherman, or Simon Harrison?" I said. "Big, tough, strong almost-grown men who could've handled Tim, maybe not easily, but they could've done it," I said.

"What if two or t'ree of dem were t'gether?" Bengt said. "Dey coulda done it, easy. Cortez went 270, and he wadn't fat, either, neither was Bart," Bengt said.

The year after Tim was murdered we had another scandal in Battle Creek, one that involved a pretty young teacher from Florida and five of our wrestlers.

Victoria Farmer came to Harper Creek during our sophomore year right after graduating *summa cum laude* from the University of North Carolina. She was tall, blonde, leggy, so well-built that she made Kate Upton look fat…and she adored high school wrestling. All four of her brothers had been high school wrestlers, and she had been a mat maid (scorekeeper and statistician) in high school and college, so when she volunteered to help the wrestling team no one thought anything about it.

She was also a damned good English teacher—I had her three times and loved it—who threw herself into the school with an unparalleled zeal. Victoria Farmer volunteered for every shit job, any club without a sponsor and every dance, where she chaperoned and was occasionally a DJ. Our principal praised her, the student body loved her and she was considered one of the best teachers in our system for four years.

Until the pictures came out during our senior year.

Then she was considered a criminal, even though it wasn't just her in the pictures.

The four guys we just mentioned as possible candidates who would've objected to Tim fucking Miss Farmer were four of the eight wrestlers she'd been fucking on a regular basis for the four years she was at Harper Creek. One of the other four—Derrick Stratton—was so enamored of Ms. Farmer that he secretly took pictures of them engaging in various activities and sent them to her, apparently trying to get her to agree to an exclusive relationship.

Unfortunately Derrick was as dumb as a box of rocks and sent the pictures to everyone in his smart phone's directory, including his parents, his pastor and Mr. Colley, the wrestling coach. Two things: one, if it's a smart phone how can it not have a blaring alarm that says "Yo! Dipshit! You're sending it to your whole contacts list!" and two, why can't guys be satisfied with taking what they can get? Derrick Stratton was never again going to sleep with someone as good-looking as Ms. Farmer, but he had to have her "all to himself"—why? Guys are stupid, especially when they're having a pissing contest. I mean c'mon, man! Freud was right about penis envy, but it's about guys envying another guy's penis, not that wymyn want one.

Anyway, Mr. Colley promptly showed the pictures to the principal at Harper Creek High School, who showed them to the superintendent, who showed them to the school board, who showed them to the state police…well, suffice to say that the shitstorm it caused was of epic proportions.

Ms. Farmer was arrested on multiple counts of child abuse (if you can call 6'5" 270-pound Ildoberto Cortez a child—in the pictures I saw, he sure didn't look like a child in any respect), and the wrestlers were all suspended because they couldn't resist passing the pictures from phone to phone. After pleading no contest to all the charges Ms. Farmer was fired from her job and went to prison. Once she got out (she only got two years—my *zayde* successfully argued (pre-trial) that most of the wrestlers involved were at least seventeen and appeared to have been enthusiastic participants, not abused sixth graders who were dragged into the relationships) Victoria Farmer disappeared from sight, never to be heard from again.

It was rumored in Battle Creek that she had changed her name and moved to Canada, but I never knew if that was the truth or just more malicious speculation (although I suspect the latter).

"Whatever happened to her, Ms. Farmer fucking Tim Miller on his birthday could certainly have been a reason he was strangled. If a stupid high school senior thought he could blackmail a teacher he was fucking why couldn't another deranged teenage teacher-fucker stalk her and object when she fucked yet another student?" I said.

"Ya read my mind, Freak. He was da right size, da right age and in da right place at the right time. Nobody woulda interviewed Ms. Farmer 'cause no one knew dat she and the wrestlers were gettin' it on then," Bengt said. "It supplies motive, and where he was found woulda meant dat all one a dem had ta be doin' was following her ta have opportunity."

"Yeah, and of course they would've confronted Tim, not Ms. Farmer, 'cause if they confronted her she could've turned off the love tap, as it were," I said.

We both contemplated that idea for a while, and then we both said, "Be nice to talk to Ms. Farmer." We laughed and Bengt said, "I'll bring da Pepsis I owe ya to da *shiva*, Freak, and I'll try ta find Ms. Farmer."

"Deal, Big Man. Thanks for even thinking about it—I know you've got other things to do. And thanks for arranging the police escort for my *zayde*—he got a real kick out of it," I said.

"It was our pleasure. He was a good man for a long time, and he coulda just turned his back on da police, but he din't. Your grampa cared about da law, ya sure he did, but he really cared about justice, and as corny as dat sounds, so does da majority of da force. We was just making sure dat he knew how much we appreciated it," Bengt said.

"You're a good friend, Big Man. Now go home to your wife and kids, and we'll talk tomorrow, OK?" I said, giving him a hug. He hugged me back and said, "Oh, I'll go home in a while. I got da first shift here." He smiled at me, his big blue Norwegian eyes twinkling at the look on my face.

"What the fuck are you talking about, Bengt?" I said, although I thought I knew.

He gave me a big goofy Norwegian grin and said, "Oh, we decided to take turns as *shomer* tonight. Your grampa explained it to us, and me and da chief decided that we needed to help the family, so someone from da force or da sheriff's office will be here until da funeral tomorrow. You can stay, or you can go home and be wit yer family, Freak. We t'ought it might be nice for yer mom and dad if you were all dere at home."

Yes, I'm a Marine, and yes, I was one bad Oscar when I was a special operations operator, and yes, I'm a Secret Service agent who is preternaturally strong and fast, and yes, I can shoot the nuts off a gnat at one hundred feet, but I'm also a human being who'd just lost her favorite person in the world, a human being whose friend was doing the kindest thing she'd ever seen.

I cried like a baby.

I just let it all out while Bengt Olafsson, a Norwegian Lutheran who didn't know diddly-squat about Judaism and wasn't genetically related to us stood with his arm around me as he guarded my *zayde* like Abraham Blumenthal was his own grandfather.

Just when you begin to think that people are shit something happens to prove you wrong. I mean, some people are still shit, but there are still a lot of good folk out there who do their best to be good. If you act right there are times you run into them, often when you most need them.

When I finally finished bawling my eyes out Bengt said, "I called Doc before I got here an' told him what was going on. He's waiting out in da parking lot for ya. Go home an' rest easy—Mr. Abraham's *neshama* won't be lonely, an' I assure ya dat no one will get close to da body who isn't supposed ta, Freak."

I hugged my friend and went out to my waiting brother. We drove home without talking, but when we got there we all talked again, because no one was ready to try and sleep. It was the sweetest time we'd had since we were all still in school, and it comforted Mumsy, Uncle Mort, Aunt Adele and Pops in a way that made them almost happy. Thanks to our friends in the Battle Creek law enforcement community we were able to get it all out before the funeral, so that we were appropriately somber but not devastated the next day (Jews are weird—we're supposed to be sad, but not too sad, and we're expected to mourn, but not excessively. If I ever figure out what the hell we're supposed to actually do I'll let you know, but don't hold your breath).

Of course my *zayde* couldn't just have a regular Jewish funeral…because a Catholic bishop in full regalia delivered the eulogy in the middle of the Harper Creek High School gymnasium, which was full of every kind of person you could possibly imagine, from a group of teenagers with hair colors that definitely weren't a part of any rainbow to eight Sikhs who were in full ceremonial clothes complete with turbans and steel daggers. There weren't any jugglers or circus clowns, or maybe I just missed them in the crowd, which filled the gym to the rafters.

Bishop O'Dowd was in rare form during the eulogy, making my *zayde* sound like a cross between Clarence Darrow and St. Francis of Assisi, with a bit of Moses and Elie Wiesel thrown in for Jewish flavor. I turned to Mumsy and whispered "Was *zayde* able to leap tall buildings in a single bound?"

"No, but he was faster than a speeding bullet if there was Bombay Sapphire or Plymouth gin involved," she whispered back.

"He could hurdle asshole judges, even really fat ones, in the pursuit of justice," Pops whispered from the other side of Mumsy. "I think it was because of his magic green ring."

"Didn't he also have a fiery horse with the speed of light and a hearty hi-ho Silver?" Roady said.

It got out of hand when Dog-Boy started going "Dahdada-dahdada-dahdada-dahdada-dahdada-dahdada" and we all said "Batman!" at the same time, then progressed into "Biffs!" and "Pows!" and "Whams!" which degenerated into the giggles.

We might've been OK at that point—Bishop O'Dowd did have a great sense of humor—but when Eggy said, "Remember when he used his magic shield with the big white star on it to protect Battle Creek from Godzilla's atomic breath?" the entire family appeared to have a collective epileptic seizure.

Bishop O'Dowd stopped his eulogy and said, "I believe that the family has something to say at this time." Mumsy stood up and told the story of *zayde* chasing my *bubbe* around the statue of Sparty at MSU and what was supposed to be a solemn ceremony degenerated into a wild welter of stories about Abraham Blumenthal, *mensch* and all-around good guy.

Which wasn't an altogether bad thing, when you think about it. My *zayde* would've loved all the stories and testimonials and he certainly would've liked to see all the laughter, especially at his expense. The family found out things we didn't know, the community found out stuff they didn't know and everybody had some belly laughs. By the time the bishop told a story about he and *zayde* getting so drunk in a bar in Bellevue that they tried to walk home every single person there had gotten their money's worth, and Battle Creek had sent their favorite son off in high style.

It was exactly the kind of service that my unique grandfather wouldn't have stopped talking about for a hundred years.

After it was all over and all the hands had been shaken and the hugs hugged I found myself standing with Bengt Olafsson and Father Fast Eddie Robinson. Fast Eddie said, "Freak, we got some news for you about Tim Miller."

"I told her about what Kristy told me," Bengt said.

"What about the other thing?" Fast Eddie said. Bengt shook his head and said, "Dat's your news to share." I gave my old friend the priest a quizzical look á la Mr. Spock—eyebrow cocked and head tilted to one side (didn't watch *Star Trek*? Why are you reading this book?)—and he said, "I've got information of a delicate nature, and no, I didn't hear it in the confessional, ya jackass."

I nodded and said, "Oh, I never t'ought you did, Father" in my best Irish accent (which was superb—I really have an ear for accents—not!).

Fast Eddie said, "Fuck you, Freak." We all laughed and he said, "It has come to my attention that Tim Miller may have been—I emphasize *may* have been—a homosexual."

My mouth dropped open and I said, "Whaaaaat?" My brain simply couldn't process that for a few seconds, and then whole new questions opened themselves to me, lines of inquiry that I had never, ever considered before. Several of those lines were both unsavory and explosive. I looked at Bengt and Fast Eddie, both of whom were studiously looking at their fingernails and avoiding eye contact. I looked around and saw that no one was paying us the least attention—we were just three old friends talking at a funeral, so I said, in the most even, innocuous tone that I could muster through my shock, "So Tim was gay? Any idea who he was gay with?"

Fast Eddie still wouldn't look at me, but he said, "Not actually, but there are some reasonable possibilities."

"How about you, Detective Olafsson? You got any ideas?" I said, still using a conversational, even tone.

"Maybe," he said, looking at the state championship football banner from our senior year.

"The bishop?" I said.

Father Robinson zeroed right in on me then and said, "Not a snowball's chance in hell, Freak. The only transgression the old man had he already told you about. He's clear on this one."

I looked at Bengt, and he said, "Fast Eddie's right, Freak. T' bishop was otherwise occupied, an' dere is no hint dat he's ever been gay, even once. I checked everything I could check, too."

I looked back at Fast Eddie and said, "Who was that hippy-dippy parish priest that was here when we were in school? Father Letsrolladoobie?"

Fast Eddie's pleasant brown face got red, and he said, "That would be Father L'Esticaccolli. Ernsesto L'Esticaccoli. Yeah, he's definitely gay—I found him in the Vatican registry, and he left the priesthood to marry a man. They live in Monterrey, California, but Bengt and I haven't been able to really contact him."

"Why the hell not?" I said. My tone of voice was perfectly pleasant, but my eyes were lit up like laser beams trying to destroy an incoming ICBM.

"Because the man he's married to is Ralph Cobb," Fast Eddie said, his eyes blazing back at me.

"Ahh, shit," I said.

"Exactly," Fast Eddie said.

"I tried to get aholt of him, Freak, part of an ongoin' investigation, y'know, but Cobb's people wasn't havin' any of it. Dey stoned me cold as ice and den a nice lawyer from Page, Ellison, Ortega, Slim, and Gates called me ta let me know dat dey din't think dere was any such investigation, an' if I "persisted"—dere word—in spreadin' such "nefarious falsehoods" dey'd be forced ta take action against me and da department an' Battle Creek," Bengt said.

"Well, fuck a duck," I said. "Ralph Cobb is rich enough to buy Battle Creek, and probably the rest of Calhoun County."

"He could probably buy da whole UP, too," Bengt said.

"And his legal firm could squash all of us without really lifting a finger," Fast Eddie said. "You will recall that Mr. Cobb gave a billion dollars to Catholic Charities last year, a fact I was reminded of when Cardinal Pozluszny called Bishop O'Dowd and read him the riot act, complete with the whole "Bishop of East Bumfuck, Bulgaria" reference."

"Da chief let me know dat I was s'posed to butt out, too," Bengt said. "Otherwise I'll be back on patrol in Bellevue."

"OK, you guys are off the investigation, period," I said. "Just absolutely drop it and don't even try to contact me with information if it jumps in your lap and purrs like a kitten."

Both of my old friends looked at me like I was crazy, and finally Fast Eddie said, "Personally I don't give a flying fuck about Father Lestsrolladoobie, but my sense of justice is offended, and I wanna know how likely it is that you think it is that I'll listen to you about dropping it."

"An' I don' care about patrolling in Bellevue, or anywhere else. Poor Missus Miller deserves ta know who killed Tim, and if the chief don' like it, well fuck him, da horse he rode in on, and da family dog," Bengt said. "Ya should remember dat Tim was my friend, too, Freak, an' nobody gets away with murdering one a my friends."

"Ditto what Big Bengt said," Fast Eddie said. "What I do on my free time is my business."

I smiled and said, "Way to live up to my expectations, guys, but I meant it. You are out, and you can't contact me or any other member of my team, because that would fuck everything up." They both drew breath to say something, but I put my hand up and said, "I'm about to break about 17 laws, but I'll tell you why if you'll let me." They both nodded, so I told them about our stealth investigation concerning the possible FBI connection. When I was done they were both nodding, and Bengt said, "OK, so we passively gather information, but no steppin' on any toes ta do it. It's a good plan, Freak, and maybe your Badger Squad can get some info on Father Letsrolladoobie."

Fast Eddie was stroking his chin, clearly trying to come to a decision about telling me who he heard about Tim Miller from. Finally he said, "OK, so do you remember Gary Lyles?"

I said, "Sure—he played basketball at B.C. Central and then—Central Michigan? Or was it Eastern?"

"He played on at CMU, got his degree in finance and was drafted by the Pistons as a courtesy. Six-six power forwards don't go anywhere in the NBA, so once he was cut Gary went to work for a group of players as their investments guy, and then he became the business manager for a bunch of guys, including one NFL star who told him that he'd had a relationship with Tim Miller when they were in high school." Father Fast Eddie paused in his tale to let me catch up, and I did.

"You mean that *Jarius Walker* told you that he had a homosexual relationship with Tim Miller?" I said.

"Lower your voice," Fast Eddie said, "and yes, Jarius Walker told Gary Lyles that he and Tim had a relationship when they were kids, but that Tim broke it off. Jarius apparently thought there was someone else, but he didn't tell Gary who."

I knew it was Jarius Walker because there had only been two NFL players from Battle Creek that I knew of: Jarius Walker and James Sheehan. Sheehan was now Senator James Sheehan of Michigan, who was also running for the Republican nomination for president, while Jarius was an award-winning NFL offensive line coach for the Pittsburgh Steelers, who he'd played thirteen years for after college at Notre Dame.

I also knew it was Jarius Walker who told Gary Lyles, because Jarius told me he was gay after we threw some assholes down some stairs for picking on a gay freshman boy who came out. Jarius and I were forced to step in when our principal, Ms. Walston, refused to stop the bullying, which was pretty typical for Ms. Walston.

It was also pretty typical of Jarius to step in, because he hated bullies almost as much as I did. They'd called us "Law & Order" when we were at good old Harper Creek High School, and nobody ever seriously messed with us, even after Jarius came out his senior year (he was the third gay man ever drafted in the NFL's storied history—I guess being a 6'3", 325-pound All-Pro guard makes people overlook someone's sexuality, much like it made the mackerel-snappers at Notre Dame excuse his liking men, as if it was any of their business anyway). To their credit Pittsburgh and its crazy fans accepted Jarius without any comment other than "Holy fuck can that guy block!" especially when he shitcanned an All-Pro defensive tackle from the Ravens on his first professional snap.

Anyway, if Jarius Walker said he had a relationship with Tim Miller then I believed him, which meant that we really had to look at Father Letsrolladoobie, but we'd need to be very, very, stealthy, or else our possible suspect would simply disappear behind a wall of wealth and privilege.

Which made it Badger Squad work, not out in the open detecting.

So Bengt and Fast Eddie and I agreed to stop talking about it and just shot the shit about my *zayde*. When the whole funeral process was over I went home with Mumsy, Pops and my brothers and we shrouded the mirrors, and did all the other weird Jewish shit so we could sit *shiva* for seven days.

We sat there in the House on East Roosevelt for seven days and received every visitor who wanted to come, with what seemed like people from every city in the northern hemisphere. We never knew how many people *zayde* knew until then—we could've filled Ford Field, Tiger Stadium and the damn Big House at that piss yellow and blue school and still needed more space. People just kept coming and coming, until finally the seven days came to an end and we all prepared to go back to our regular lives.

Except my brother Roady, who announced the last day of *shiva* that he was really staying to partner with mom. We were completely surprised, but Roady said, "Hey, I told those fuckheads in New York to kiss my ass—they told me that I couldn't even come home to sit *shiva* for my grandfather because of some stupid deal, as if their deal was more important than my family. Money isn't everything in the world, ya know. Besides, Mumsy can use the help, especially in litigation, and I miss the old home town."

"How much have you got in the bank?" Doc said.

"More than the president of Kellogg's, but less than Jerry Jones," Eggy said.

"Plus you've got stock options for the last eight years, which I'm going to say you sold at a handsome markup, which means that you've got over ten mil," Dog-Boy said.

"And don't forget that those white-shoe firms all have buyouts built in to their partnership contracts," Shyster said.

"So you have millions in the bank, which means that you can afford to come back and be magnanimous and save the day," I said. Roady gave everybody the superior sneer of a slick New York lawyer and we all said, "Fuck you, Roady" in exactly the same tone of voice.

And then we laughed our asses off before we all went back to the real world. We might not have laughed so hard if we'd known what was going to happen because of that week of mourning, but at the time it was just too far away to see.

Kind of like a freight train that was coming of a tunnel without its headlight on.

CHAPTER 51

Under the Gun

So I went back to D.C. I had three days before Soper was scheduled to be back in New York City, but I got a call at 7:00 a.m. on the second day back from an assistant federal prosecutor for the southern district of New York, a guy named Kevin Wirth, asking me to come to NYC early so that he could ask me about the case against Salvatore Bonnarino and Paul Monteverdi. Their cases were coming up on appeal and Wirth had the reputation of being diligent and dogged, so it wasn't really a surprise that he was lining up all his ducks.

I took the Acela Express train to NYC and Wirth had a car waiting for me. It took me right to the Federal Courthouse at 500 Pearl Street in Manhattan. We bypassed the security stuff and I was whisked up to the 35th floor to talk to Assistant U.S. Attorney Kevin Wirth.

He was a good-looking Black man who said, "Agent Glickstien, I'm sorry, but I have a priority meeting with the District Attorney of New York. I'm going to have to stash you down the hall for a bit—probably not more than 15-20 minutes. I do apologize. I just got the call." He smiled at me and I decided I didn't mind waiting (he was even cuter when he smiled, plus he was built like the proverbial brick shithouse).

Wirth's assistant led me to a nice conference room, got me an ice-cold Pepsi and told me she'd be back when her boss's meeting was over. I'd only had a sip of Pepsi when the door opened and two U.S. Marshals came in. They didn't say a word, just looked to make sure that I was alone, and then two more came in, flanking a guy in a track suit that was too big for him, sun glasses, a Panama hat and handcuffs. They took the cuffs off and left, and the guy took off his hat and glasses and sat down.

It was my "uncle" Paul Monteverdi.

We looked each other up and down for a while, and then he said, "Somebody in the FBI is out ta get ya. That shit storm in Kentucky was a hit, not the Klan tryin' ta kill a rug-muncher."

"Hello to you, too, Mr. Monteverdi. Good to see you looking so good," I said. "What the fuck, ya can't even say hello?"

"Look kid—in about five minutes those marshals are gonna come back and take me away wit'out a word. You wanna waste time on pleasantries, OK by me, but you really don't wanna do that, OK?" he said.

"Roger that," I said. "Now spill—what the fuck do you know and how the fuck do you know it?"

"I ain't gonna tell ya about the how, but the what is pretty fucking weird. Somebody at FBI headquarters is sending a couple a goons around arranging for bad shit ta happen to ya because of something that ain't even connected ta your job guarding Ms. Soper. They're using fake IDs, because their names are different everywhere they go, but they must be connected, because they leaned on that Podunk sheriff to call up his Klan brothers and waste your ass. That's the word—you was the target, not nobody else," my uncle Paul said, his killer's face contorted in obvious disgust.

"But why? Has there been any word about that? What the fuck did I do—is it the Koreans out for revenge?" I said.

"That's what's weird—there don't appear to be no reason at all. It's like ya know something but ya don't know it. I hear that the goons are tellin' people they're trying ta stop ya from fucking shit up, but ain't nobody heard what shit that might be. I tell you, kid, it's a mystery ta me and Mr. Bonnarino, and we been thinking about it," Paul Monteverdi said.

"Any idea how high up this comes from?" I said.

"It has to be at least a SAC from a big office like New York, LA, or Chicago, but Mr. Bonnarino thinks that it's at least an Executive Assistant Director—these goons're connected ta some bigger fish or else they wouldn't get no traction with some a these guys they're leaning on," my uncle Paul said.

"I don't know any of these people—I literally don't know any of them personally, and I really only know a few of the names by reputation," I said.

"That we can help you with," Monteverdi said. "Mr. Bonnarino and me know lots a these guys, and we're pretty sure it ain't the Director or the Deputy Director. Both a them are too straight-up G-Men ta have anything ta do with it, plus they're both incorruptible."

I gave him my best law enforcement "what the fuck are you talking about" look, and he said, "Trust me, kid, we know they ain't going off the rails, no matter what you offer them. We might've tried once or three times, y'know? That Fredds is a good cop and a good person, too, and Harley Henry is retiring in a month, which means whatever bugs he's got up his ass will go away. Mr. Bonnarino thinks it's the Assistant Director, Mitch Holland, but I still think it's either the EAD for Intel, Sam Gwynn, or the EAD for National Security, Malcolm Sorenson. Both a those assholes are mean bastards, and they might do it for somebody else. Mitch Holland is a devious son of a bitch who don't have scruple one, and he wants ta sit in the big chair, which is why I don't think it's him, but Mr. Bonnarino says there's somethin' off about him."

"Which still doesn't answer the question…what the fuck do I know that they want suppressed? I'm not investigating anything, I don't have any power to investigate anything other than counterfeiting, and any operation of any size will be run by someone above me in the food chain. What the fuck is going on here?" I said. I just couldn't get my head around what it was that was driving someone in the FBI to try and basically assassinate me. I wasn't investigating anything, it wasn't the Koreans and Soper wasn't the target… Whiskey Tango Foxtrot? (Military jargon—the international call signs for W-T-F…get it?)

Just then the door opened and two marshals came in. Paul Monteverdi stood up and put his hands behind his back, and said, "Keep that guard up, kid."

I said, "Thanks, Uncle Paul." He nodded, the marshals cuffed him and they all marched out the door. I sat back down, but less than a minute later the door opened and Kevin Wirth's assistant said, "Agent Glickstien? Mr. Wirth can see you now."

We went back to his office, where Wirth thanked me for waiting. He and three assistants then grilled me for three hours about the cases against Bonnarino and Monteverdi. When it was over the assistants left and I said, "OK, what the fuck was this all about, Wirth? You could've done all of this over the phone, and quite frankly you didn't need to do it at all—you've got 'em cold, and the appeal is gonna fail. You're too smart to not know that, so unless you're a real paranoid conspiracy theorist or your sense of duty rivals a character in a Gilbert and Sullivan operetta (sorry—Mumsy and Pops were fans—look it up if the reference doesn't make sense, willya?) I'm at a loss here. Why waste the time?"

Kevin Wirth smiled that dreamy smile and showed me a picture from his desk. It was a beautiful young womyn and three absolutely gorgeous little girls. He said, "These are my girls—my wife Trish and the triplets Charlotte, Emily and Anne. They're my whole life outside this office, and I would do anything to protect them." His smile grew wistful as he set the picture back on the desk, and when he looked up there were tears shining bright in his eyes. "My girls were in a car accident three years ago—they got hit by a drunk driver in a delivery truck. Trish had a broken collarbone and a dislocated elbow and Anne had a concussion, but Emily lost a leg and Charlotte lost an arm and an eye. It turned out that the driver had been drinking in a club all afternoon. His blood alcohol level was .29, so he was what we call super-drunk, what my dad used to call blind drunk. He didn't kill any of my girls, but he really screwed them up for a while. He screwed Emily and Charlotte up for life, and it's taken Trish three years of therapy to just get back to herself."

Wirth paused to collect himself as a single tear crept down his cheek. He smiled another wistful smile and said, "The worst part was that the guy was basically going to get off with a slap on the wrist. He had a perfect driving record and he got an attorney from Patterson, Puskas and Pelfrey—one of the biggest and best white shoe law firms in Manhattan. His company hired them, and his lawyer'd already presented evidence that the truck driver took medication that might have distorted his blood alcohol level. Basically we were looking at a very long, very expensive trial for the City of New York in an accident where no one was killed, which was going to be a non-starter. We were going to accept a plea to impaired driving, which the guy's lawyer said he'd plead *nolo contendere* to—you know what that means? *Nolo contendere?*"

"My mom, uncle, grandpa and a couple of brothers are lawyers, so yeah, I get it—he was going to plead no contest, meaning yeah, I sorta did it, but I'm not admitting any guilt," I said.

"Exactly. So two days before we're going to accept this mutt's plea and he's going to get a sentence of thirty days suspended license I get a visit from a guy who called himself Mr. Green. I'm not on the case—I would've been going for the death penalty—so when this guy starts talking about the case I tell him that he's in the wrong office and try to get rid of him. I was on edge about the whole thing, and I was afraid that I'd lose it on this old guy in the classy blue suit.

"But he told me to relax, that he was an investigator for the truck driver's insurance company and that he just wanted to get a feel for what happened, and that he didn't want to upset Trish any further. He looked at the pictures of my family and he got a little teary-eyed himself, which was weird, because the vibe I was getting from this guy wasn't insurance adjuster, it was more like bar bouncer, or army colonel, or really tough football coach," Wirth said, giving me a look that was anything but confused. I didn't say anything, but I had a pretty good idea where this was going.

"Anyway, Mr. Green and I had a pleasant little meeting—we mostly talked about the girls and the perils facing parents in today's world—and he told me that he'd be in contact about the insurance company paying for the things that were their responsibility. He even left me his card, a very fine embossed card for a national insurance company.

"The very next day I got a call from a friend in the New York District Attorney's office who told me that the truck driver's lawyers had dropped him for non-payment, that the trial judge had recused himself because of some conflict of interest and that the case had been re-assigned to Judge LaSandra Crouch, who had already said that she wouldn't accept a no-contest plea," Wirth said. He paused again as another tear leaked down his cheek, and I was sure where this was going.

"You don't know Judge Crouch, but she's a former school bus driver who put herself through law school, and she is tough as hell—fair, but absolutely hell on drunk drivers. To make a long story short, the prosecutor's office made no plea deals. They went to trial and absolutely destroyed the guy—he got the max for every charge, and Judge Crouch made the sentences consecutive, not concurrent, so the truck driver isn't getting out for at least twenty-five years, which means I should be over the urge to kill the guy.

"The other thing that happened was even better—the truck driver's insurance company paid for everything for the girls. They got Emily and Charlotte state-of-the-art prosthetics, paid for every penny of the rehab and hospital bills and set up irrevocable trusts for the girls' college education. They also gave us a cash indemnity and admitted that their insuree was at fault, which means that anything that happens due to the accident will be paid for by the insurance company in perpetuity. And we didn't even have to have a lawyer involved—they just did it all without being asked," Wirth said.

"Mr. Green must have been a real big shot in the company, huh?" I said.

Wirth smiled a full-wattage smile of joy (it's a good thing that I knew he was married, or I might've made a mess of his desk as I sailed over it to jump his bones) and looked at the picture on his desk. He looked up and said, "Funny thing about that. I called the numbers on the card he left me, but they were all out of service, so I called his company directly and they told me that there wasn't any such person that worked there—never had been, in fact. So I asked around and found out that the insurance company was directed by the company that owned the truck to pay everything that was owed without hassling us, and that they would accept the higher premiums that came with it. In fact, the vice president of the trucking company said that if the insurance company didn't pay they'd be losing a valuable customer, because the trucking company would be taking their business elsewhere."

"What was the company?" I said.

"Sicilio Brothers' Hauling," Wirth said.

"Who was the VP?" I said.

"A guy named Greenmountain," Wirth said.

"Imagine that," I said. "Did you ever dig any deeper, find out who the guy really was?"

Wirth smiled (full wattage again—welcome to squishy panty city) and said, "No, no—I learned a long time ago to not look a gift horse in the mouth, plus every year for Christmas I get a card with a picture of three couples and their kids on it, and it always says the same thing—'A man always pays his debts—I got kids, too. Give those beautiful girls a hug. Mr. Green.' Some of the kids look like the Mr. Green I met."

"And there's no conflict of interest in you prosecuting the Bonnarino and Monteverdi cases?" I said.

"It's an appeal—it's already been prosecuted, I'm just guarding the interests of the state, which I assure you I will do the fullest extent of the law and my abilities, which are considerable," Wirth said.

"You speak Italian?" I said.

"Fuck you, Agent Glickstien," Wirth said with just the right tone and inflection.

I laughed and so did Wirth, and I said, "Can't argue with that. And thanks for arranging the meeting with my uncle. It was helpful."

"I'm sure that I haven't got any idea what you're talking about, Agent Glickstien," Wirth said. "I simply put you in an empty conference room while I met with the District Attorney. Anybody who visited you there did so without my knowledge or permission." He stood up, smiled at me again (nothing I could do about that wet spot on the chair), shook my hand and said, "Thank you for coming. My assistant will show you out."

I went out and got in the waiting car, thinking about what Paul Monteverdi told me and how best to get it to Joe and the Badger Squad. We got to my hotel and I got out to go inside when I heard someone softly whistling "Secret Agent Man," the theme from the TV show *The Man from U.N.C.L.E.* I looked around until I spotted Kid Galahad lounging outside a coffee shop. I also saw Mamba and Jack Soo at a street vendor buying hot dogs. Mamba held one up toward me and I held up three fingers and pointed at the street, meaning I wanted three "street dogs"—New York style boiled hot dogs with sauerkraut and brown mustard. He held up an OK sign and I walked over to Kid Galahad.

He shook my hand and said, rather more loudly than necessary, "Thanks for getting me on this shit detail, Freak. I thought we were friends, but now I'm sure you're just some asshole I used to know." He was stiff and cold, which hurt me even though I knew it was an act.

Mamba was the same way when he brought my dogs. He said, "You owe me $9, Freak. They didn't have any brown mustard, either, so I got yellow."

Jack Soo said, "You owe me for this, Freak. This digging through the Klan bullshit is making me crazier than a shithouse rat. I'm pretty sure that stupidity is catching, y'know?"

"Well, I'm glad to see you, too, fellas—why'n't ya go back and tell Joe I said to fuck off and die. I don't need to be treated like this," I said, throwing a $10 bill at Mamba and generally glaring at the other two like they were meat and I was a hungry wolverine.

"Oh, don't get your panties in a bunch, Freak. We're just bored and tired, plus wading through the Klan cesspool makes us feel like we're always dirty. And before you ask, we're here to interview you and everybody else who was involved, and then we're going to Kentucky—to *Kentucky*—to interview everybody else involved in the attempted assassination of a presidential candidate," Mamba said, clearly outraged that he had to take himself to Kentucky for anything.

We sat down on three benches outside the hotel to eat our dogs, which were delicious, and I said, through a mouthful of dog and kraut, "So what's it looking like?"

"The fucking Klan did it," Jack Soo said. "We're pretty sure their Exalted Cyclops—who is the sheriff—gave the local Klan chapter the idea to strike a blow for men and Christians everywhere by attacking the only lesbian within a hundred miles. We've got a bunch of shit to sift through, but it looks like they had it all set up when Ms. Soper went into the lecture, and then executed it the way it was planned without any help. The only reason they failed is because CoD was right next to the candidate and took the brunt of the force."

"So we aren't getting any picture of some nefarious conspiracy?" I said.

"Joe is calling this "a fucking traffic accident caused by bedsheets," so whatta ya think?" Mamba said. "We've got nothing but the Klan, stupidity and a whole bunch of ignorance, combined with an irresistible opportunity." I looked into his lavender eyes and he blinked at me, using an odd rhythm. I realized it was Morse code—an old trick we'd used in the past—so I watched more closely.

Mamba's eyes sent 'dot-dash-dash-dot...dash-dash-dash...dot-dot-dot...dot-dot...dash...dot-dot...dot-dot-dot-dash...dot...pause...dot-dot-dash-dot...pause...dash-dot-dot-dot...pause...dot-dot' which meant 'positive FBI.'

The Badger Squad had already discovered it was someone in the FBI, which confirmed what Paul Monteverdi had just told me. The Badger Squad needed to know this, so they could concentrate their search, but I wasn't just willing to say it out loud in public, so I decided to take a different tack.

I said, "Well, that's great. How soon can we move against these assholes?"

"Joe's got the warrants in process, but we need to dot the i's and cross the t's—we want it airtight, and we need to coordinate with the U.S. Marshals Service to do the actual takedown. We also want all the interviews in first, in case one of the conspirators wants to unburden themselves, although none of us think that's gonna happen," Jack Soo said.

"Well, hell, that could take two weeks," I said, sounding pissed off again. "What the fuck is taking you guys so long?"

"Understand this clearly, Freak: we got enough on these guys to arrest them right now, but Director Hessler and the Assistant U.S. Attorney we're working with want us to have them completely bundled up into a nice, neat package. They don't know that we're on to them, they're not going to know we're on to them, we're gonna weave a solid web of evidence around them and then, BOOM! We're gonna put 'em away for life," Kid Galahad said. "So you might wanna put that attitude back into the attitude box and play nice with us." He smiled at me and I remembered how good he was on missions, mainly because he could look like he was taking a nap and then be whipping ass in a nanosecond.

I gave a rueful smile and said, "You're right, and yeah, I got that you're stuck on this shit detail, which is almost demeaning for guys with your skill sets, but you can see why I'm impatient."

They all laughed and Mamba said, "You wouldn't be human if you weren't frothing at the mouth, Freak, but surely *you* can see why we're doing it this way."

"Yeah, I do—I just don't like it," I said.

"It's kinda like Christmas isn't it? All the presents waiting under the tree, but you can't open them until Christmas Day. Frustrating," Jack Soo said.

"I'm Jewish, you asshole, and that is a shit analogy," I said. We all laughed, and then I said, "Hey, I'm going up to the room and get changed for a run. Anybody want to come along?" Everybody said they did, especially Kid Galahad, who promised to renew his efforts to kick my ass at distance, since he knew that he couldn't do it sprinting. We all went to our rooms and changed, met back in the lobby, and then took off for an "easy" five miles, which meant we'd start racing at about two miles out.

This was the perfect way to defeat any ongoing surveillance and also to not appear to be conspiring together, because one thing that Secret Service agents did on a regular basis was run—you can't run alongside a car or bus if you don't train. Running for Secret Service agents is the same as it is for cross-country runners, or any other athletes…it's like breathing.

So we ran out from the hotel and set off for a point exactly 2.5 miles from the hotel. I filled everybody in on what Paul Monteverdi had told me, and fielded all of their questions in the first mile and a half, because I knew when we turned for home the race would be on.

"So we know that the FBI is involved from two independent sources," I said.

"Yes," Mamba said. "Weasel and Jewey confirm high level traffic on their phones, and these two mystery inspectors have definitely been playing in the field, but since we've only narrowed them down to a pool of available agents we still don't know who they are."

"So we don't know who sent them, or exactly what they're doing," I said.

"Except that they appear to be intimidating witnesses and setting up alternate versions of events in case their role is discovered," Kid Galahad said.

"The only thing we know for sure is that it isn't Director Harley, because he's been electronically cleared," I said.

"Yeah, and our guts all tell us he's too classy and professional for this. He's been a public servant for over 40 years and he doesn't even have a parking ticket in that time. The guy is clean, which means this operation to get the Freak has been concealed from him, too. If we could just ask questions we'd interview him and probably find out who it was in 10 seconds, but of course we can't," Jack Soo said.

"Life's a bitch and then you die," I said.

"Nobody's bitching about it, it just makes it a bitch to investigate when you have to keep prancing around everyone's toes," Mamba said.

"Prancing?" we all said at once. "I got the Pepsis," Jack Soo said, "since I started the whole thing by sort of semi-bitching."

"Only you would use the word prancing," I said to Mamba.

"Disputatio magnus!" Mamba said, reverting to Latin to show off his language skills. "Lots of people would use the word, because that is precisely what we are doing. We aren't dancing, because that implies having fun and some sense of organization. We aren't stepping in, because that is precisely what we cannot do. We aren't gliding, striding, or slipping—we are strutting around in a highly spirited way, trying not to draw any attention to our true purpose but ostentatiously maintaining our façade without revealing our true purpose—hence we are prancing."

Everybody was talking, agreeing with him, but I knew that we were turning around at the end of the block, so I just went with it until we were 50 meters from the turning point, when I subtly turned up the pace and drew just ahead of the rest of the runners. Mamba was explaining another fine point of prancing when I hit the jets and sped around the sign at the end of the street.

I was 20 meters clear of the rest of the pack when they realized what was going on.

"Shit! Piss! Fuck!" Mamba said.

"Cunt! Cocksucker!" Jack Soo said.

"Motherfucker! Tits!" Kid Galahad said.

I knew what they were doing, so I didn't let their homage to George Carlin (see: *The Seven Words You Can Never Say on Television*) stop me, although I did laugh my ass off for 800 meters. I had to get some kind of lead because I'd run with Mamba and Kid Galahad before, and they would catch me (it turns out that Jack Soo was the guy I had to watch out for—who knew that he ran the 5,000 meters in college? Not me...), but if I had the lead I could simply run them down the last 400 meters or so.

We all ran well and very fast, and all three of them went in front of me, but not by enough. When we were 600 meters from the hotel I just shifted into Freak gear and left them in the dust. At 400 meters I was in front by 20 meters, and by 200 meters I was 60 meters in front of Jack Soo, who was truly fast, but not up to Freak speed.

I was concentrating on finishing when I got a weird feeling and heard a weird sound. The feeling wasn't uncommon—it felt like someone was watching me, but not in a good way. If you've ever read the books by Trevanian—*The Loo Sanction, The Eiger Sanction, Shibumi*—then you know that his hero, Nicholai Hel, has what he calls a proximity sense—he can feel exactly who is near him before they are actually in his presence. I always thought that was a cool skill to have, and I thought that now as I felt someone watching me. Hel could tell who was watching him, but all I knew was that someone had eyes on—and that was usually a bad thing.

The sound confirmed that it was a bad thing, although I don't ever recall thinking about it. When I said the sound I heard was weird I meant "out of context," not odd or strange. My brain registered the weird sound, identified it and a nanosecond later had me stop running.

The sound was a crew-served machine gun bolt being pulled back to charge the weapon.

By the time it was ramming a round forward to be able to started shooting I had flung myself behind a garbage truck while screaming "GUN! GUN! GUN! GUN!" at the top of my voice.

I've asked myself over and over why I even heard it, because my hearing is one of the few things about me that are completely ordinary, but the only answer I ever came up with was that it was so completely out of context that it just registered with my animal brain. Remember, I'd heard machine guns charging hundreds of times in the Marines and special ops, just never in the middle of New York City.

In any case, I was behind the garbage truck when the machine gun opened up on the spot I'd just vacated. It sounded like it always did: a god unzipping to take a .50 caliber piss. Whoever it was had some training and discipline, because they hosed down the sidewalk where I'd been, but then immediately ceased fire to adjust their aim and see if they could hit me, instead of just doing it like they do in the movies and hosing down the garbage truck. That meant two things: they knew the capabilities of their weapon and they knew the specs of a New York City garbage truck. That meant a third thing: this was not random. These assholes knew what they were doing.

Fuck me blind.

Jack Soo and Kid Galahad came creeping along the side of the garbage truck through the screaming people racing away as fast as they could, their backup weapons out and at the ready. I noticed that Jack Soo was a left-handed shooter, which might be an advantage for us, if three people with handguns could have an advantage against what I was sure was a .50 caliber machine gun.

Wait a minute—three people?

"Where's Mamba?" I said.

"He stripped off his clothes and blended into the crowd—he's huddled with the civilians under the front of the building where the shooter is," Jack Soo said.

"Black shorts and a Black Sabbath T-shirt," Kid Galahad said. "Was that a .50?"

"Yeah, and we gotta move now," I said. We were in the front of the truck trying to see the shooters, but in about five seconds they were going to figure that out, and they'd know that they could at least rip up the cab around us, since it wasn't armored. We were going to have to get out of the line of fire and retreat to the rear of the truck, where the bulk and steel of the compactor on the truck might protect us, if they weren't using armor piercing rounds and didn't get lucky by igniting the fuel tank. Luckily this was a new diesel truck, which meant the fuel wasn't as explosive as gas, but that didn't mean that it wouldn't burn if it was ignited by a tracer round.

We all scuttled to the rear of the truck, where there were already two garbage men and several other civilians. "What the fuck is goin' on?" one of the garbage men said. "That was a machine gun—are we under terrorist attack?" His eyes were wild, but his manner was calm and he looked like he was holding it all together. I was trying to decide what to do about the civilians when the machine gun burped again. A burst ripped into the cab of the truck, and then a second one skipped off the pavement under the storage bin in the middle off the truck. The rounds didn't reach us, but they were close and the civilians all screamed, although the two garbage men didn't.

I made up my mind right then. I looked at one of the garbage men and said, "What's your name?"

"Steve Venturi," he said.

"Steve, I'm Agent Glickstien of the U.S. Secret Service. I'm gonna guess that you were in the service, am I right?" His hair was cut in an Army high and tight and he had something else about him—a calmness and detachment that told me he'd heard a machine gun before.

"Yeah, I was four years in the U.S. Army. I made Staff Sergeant," he said.

"Well, Sergeant, I need you to get these civilians out of here so nobody gets killed," I said. "If you take everybody back kitty-corner from the storage tank of this beast to that pizza joint right there it should keep enough steel between them and the shooters to get them out of the line of fire, donchta think?"

He smiled and said, "You were an officer, weren'tcha? Don't worry ma'am, I know how to keep discipline and get shit done." He immediately organized all the civilians into small groups, explained what they were going to do and then sent them off to the pizza joint. When the last civilian was inside the place (and I hoped running like bats out of hell for the rear entrance) Venturi turned back to me and said, "What next, ma'am?" like we were just standing around shooting the shit, instead of having the shit shot out of us.

Before I could answer the machine gun purred again and a hail of slugs pounded against the front of the truck. They let off and we could hear sirens approaching, which wasn't necessarily a good thing, since NYPD cars aren't armored and the officers in them had no way of knowing what they were going up against. If squad cars started arriving they would be sitting ducks.

We had another problem, because one of the bursts had opened the fuel tank. It was literally only a matter of seconds before the shooters figured that out and we were facing a fire. Unless we… hmmm.

I said, "Sergeant, will the fuel tank explode if we set this fuel on fire?"

"No, ma'am—it's diesel, so it burns, but there ain't no vapor, so it really won't explode, even if the fire reaches the tank. It'll smoke like holy hell, but it…oh, I get it. When do you want me to light it?"

"When we get right to the corner of the truck, and then I want you to get the fuck outta here and into that pizza joint. We're going across the street and up under the building. When you get out of the line of fire call the FBI and let them know that we're under fire from a machine gun, OK? And thanks," I said.

He said, "I'd salute ya, ma'am, but it ain't done in-country. Good luck, and get those terrorist bastards, willya?" He grinned and I said, "Bet your ass, Sergeant Venturi. You're one cool customer—I'd have you on my team any time." He nodded and I went to the corner of the truck with Jack Soo and Kid Galahad. Venturi immediately took out a lighter and set the trickle of fuel in the gutter on fire. The fuel caught and began burning toward the fuel tank, aided by some greasy rags Venturi left in its path. Once the fire was going well the former sergeant elbowed us out of the way and grabbed three bags of garbage that were sitting in the back hopper of the truck. He ran to the front of the truck as the .50 cal hammered the truck right in front of us to no effect, thanks to the steel hopper and ten tons of compacted garbage.

The garbage and diesel fuel were really smoking now, and the .50 cal hammered the front of the truck near the fuel tank, but Venturi was hiding behind the engine, big steel bumper and heavy winch on the front of the truck.

As soon as they started up on the front of the truck we were moving toward the front of the building where Mamba and a large group of civilians were huddled. We reached him and Mamba said, "The NYPD knows what's going on—they're sending their SWAT, and the FBI has an HRT inbound, but I don't think we should wait, in case these motherfuckers try to just ease on out of here. I want their asses—they made me break a *nail*." He was bleeding from one of his fingers—the nail was torn completely off.

We all laughed—needed to release some tension—and I said, "Anybody got an idea where they're at? I thought it was the third floor." Just then the .50 cal hammered another long blast at the truck as Venturi ran from the front to the back. He peeked around the corner of the truck and said, "Third time's the charm, Cap'n!"

Whoever was shooting was pretty damned good, because they had a burst inbound a split second after he ducked back behind the steel hopper full of garbage. About five seconds later we saw his feet as he ran back to the front of the truck. This time the .50 cal let fly a fusillade that hammered the front of the truck. The tires went flat, the top of the cab spewed shrapnel everywhere and the passenger door just disintegrated.

As they were shooting we were on the move. Venturi's dash down the truck confirmed that the assholes were on the third floor, in one of the corner windows. We all moved into the building, found the fire door, and moved into the first floor stairs. I said, "Galahad, take point and clear the stairwell. Jack, cover the rear entrance in case they have some way to access it. Mamba, you and I are going up as the assault group. When we get to the third floor we'll case it out, then split and come at them from two directions at once if we can. Galahad, you backstop us unless we can rush them all at once. No quarter on these asshole motherfuckers, OK? We agreed?" Everybody nodded and away we went.

Galahad cleared the stairway and we got to the third-floor fire door, where we got our first piece of good luck.

The door was propped open, and four sets of sanitation worker's coveralls were lying on the floor. We'd found the assholes' escape route.

In case anyone out there is saying to themselves "Hey, this is a stupid move, and your plan sucks, and if they hear you coming no building wall will save you from a .50 caliber machine gun," well… you're right. Our plan was thin, we needed luck to not get killed, but what all of us were thinking about was bad guys with a big gun deciding to shoot their way out of a standoff. We'd still get them, but they'd kill who knows how many before that happened, and besides, we were trained for this shit and we had weapons. As corny as it sounds, we were officers sworn to protect the Constitution, and bad guys with a .50 cal was fucking unconstitutional as all hell.

And yes, we were all too macho to wait for some SWAT or HRT guys, because these shithead motherfuckers were shooting at *us*. In our world you don't get to shoot at Secret Service agents and get away with it, period.

So I poked my head around the door at floor level (less likely to get shot by a lookout there—humans tend to look at things from the height their heads are at, and if they don't they always look high—trust me, I learned that the hard way…and it's still classified), found a nice wide, empty hallway that led to the room they were shooting from, three closed doors and an empty hallway that went the other way with four closed doors.

I ducked back and said, "Mamba, tell Jack to get up here now. This is the only way they can get out unless they take the cross hall, and if they do that it means we're all dead anyway. We'll go as soon as he acknowledges." Mamba got on his phone and as soon as Jack Soo said, "On my way" we were up and ready. I said, "Kid, follow me on my right and two steps back, Mamba, on my left and four steps back. I'm going right down the middle until I get to the door, then I'm going to slam through the door to the right. Mamba, you move up to the left door frame and go low, Kid go the same side and high. I should attract their fire, and you two open up with all you've got, OK?"

"No," they both said. "I'm the smallest and just as quick as you at this—I'll draw fire while you shoot," Mamba said.

"Don't argue, Freak. You're the best pistol shot in the world, and if we get a chance to shoot I want you doing it. Mamba's the logical choice to draw fire, and I'll shoot from low because that gives you the clearest field of fire," Kid Galahad said. Their logic was impeccable, so I just nodded and said, "Let's go."

We crept down the hall in our skewed triangle formation, as quiet as cats after mice. We were about seven steps from the office door when we got our second lucky break. Someone outside the building opened fire with shotguns. We found out later it was three really crazy and courageous NYPD officers who ran out from the pizza joint and opened fire as soon as they were behind the bulk of the truck. Shotguns against a machine gun are no contest, but they figured we needed the distraction after Steve Venturi told them we were in the building trying to take out the terrorists.

Patrol Sergeant Tomasina H. Benton, Patrolman Edwin G. Ross and Patrolman George F. Norris in all likelihood saved our lives, and probably the lives of many civilians, by being incredibly brave in the face of horrendous firepower. The machine gunners decided they were a real threat and opened up on them, hosing the garbage truck in an extended burst and suppressing the shotgun fire, which gave us the chance to finish our move down the hall in a rush.

As soon as we got to the door Mamba threw himself through the right side of the door, firing the whole time. When I hit the doorframe I immediately saw that there were four guys in dark uniforms, three at the machine gun and one dragging something from the back corner of the room.

I was carrying my running gun, a compact Colt Defender with a 3" barrel and eight shot capacity. I had an extra magazine, so I double-tapped the three guys at the gun in the chest. The heavy .45 ACP slugs took them off their feet, and I turned to the fourth guy, but he was already down from Mamba's gun. Kid Galahad put one in the head of each of the guys I'd double-tapped (shot twice in rapid succession—if you did it right it sounded like one report) and Mamba was standing over his guy, so I safed my weapon and whipped out my cell phone.

As I was calling Old Three Names I heard Jack Soo coming down the hall saying "Coming in with coffee, guys! I've even got cream, so don't shoot my sorry Korean ass." That was appropriate, since the guys we'd taken down looked to be Koreans, too.

Edward Otis Whitney answered on the third ring and said, "Agent Glickstien, I'm with the Director. We just got word—"

I cut him off and said, "It's OK, Eddie, we just took the guys with the machine gun down. I think they're all dead"—I looked at Mamba, who said, "Mine's alive"—"and I'm wrong about that. We've got three KIA, one WIA and under control. Tell the SWAT and HRT guys to ease on in here—this may be part of a larger setup, especially since these guys are Asian—they look like they're Korean. I'd say this is an act of terrorism, although it may just be payback for their lost $900 million."

"Are there any casualties?" Old Three Names said.

"Not of ours, but they were hosing the shit out of the street—and I know we had friendlies down there, because they were shooting at the terrorists with shotguns. We're gonna sit on the site until we get HRT or SWAT up here. Tell those eager beavers we're all dressed for running, and that we're still armed, and that we're not giving up our weapons until we're surrounded by a phalanx of friendly faces that are armed, OK? It'd be a real pisser to get shot at by terrorists and have your own guys shoot you instead, y'know?"

Edward Otis Whitney laughed and said, "Good to see you still have your sense of humor, Freak. Sit tight and we'll come and get you."

"Roger that, sir. If you could send a few Pepsis up here it'd be appreciated—we were just finishing a five-mile run when we were attacked, and this was thirsty work," I said.

Old Three Names laughed again and said, "I'll see what I can do." I hung up and turned to my pals. "Pepsis are on the way," I said.

"Thank God—all that running's made me thirsty," Jack Soo said. "I could make some coffee."

"No!" we all said at once. "Pepsis are on me," I said.

"Anybody think there's no one dead out there?" Kid Galahad said.

Nobody said anything, because we all knew that any street that was hosed down by a .50 cal had to have casualties in it, which made us all sad and pissed off, and made me desirous of revenge, because I was sick and tired of shitheads aiming for me and killing innocents instead.

It turned out this wasn't the last time that would happen.

CHAPTER 52

Pissing Contest

Jack Soo was sitting on the floor next to the wounded maybe-Korean, who was trying to sit up. Mamba put his pistol to the guy's head and said, "Lay right the fuck *down*, you motherfucking godless commie, or I'll blow your brains back to Pyongyang. I just had my nails done last week and you *assholes* ruined them. Do you have *any* idea how hard it is to keep good nails?"

The guy didn't get the humor, but he did get the message, because he lay right the fuck down and stopped moving. I looked at Mamba and he said, "They were all wearing vests, Freak. My little .380 didn't get through, but I did break some of his ribs, the *shitheel*." We all laughed, and Jack Soo said, "Maybe I'll talk to the guy. Whattya think? Should we wait for a lawyer?"

"That's like asking if we should wait for a girlfriend who has herpes," I said. "Think he'll answer?"

"Eight to five against," Kid Galahad said. "I'll take some of that action," Jack Soo said. "Hunnert dollars?" Kid Galahad nodded, and I said, "Me, too." Mamba said, "I'll go 200, if that won't break you, Kid."

"I'd just let you take it out in trade if it did," Kid said. We all laughed again and Jack Soo said, "So who sent ya, ya slant-eyed devil?" The guy just looked at him with absolutely zero expression, and Mamba said, "Isn't that just a wee bit racist, Agent Hwang?"

"Only if my name was Murphy, or Tagliano, or Schwartzkopf," Jack Soo said. "If I can't call a slant-eyed devil a slant-eyed devil then what's the fucking point? It's the pot calling the kettle black—it ain't racism if you're calling some asshole something that people routinely call you."

"Well argued, Jack. Now are you gonna ask him some questions in that shit you call a language, or are we gonna sit here until some asshole shows up and says he gets a shyster?" I said.

Jack Soo turned to the guy and asked him a question in Korean. His tone was light and he appeared to be playing the avuncular old uncle role. They guy said something short and defiant, and Jack Soo said something back in as amiable way as you've ever seen. The guy gaped at him and then said something that was considerably less confrontational. Jack Soo said something else and the guy actually smiled a little bit, and then he said something that made Jack smile. Pretty soon they were having a nice little conversation, until finally Jack Soo said, "Kid, can you give me that hunnert dollars in two 50s?"

Kid Galahad looked at him and said, "Sure, Jack, but why it that important?"

"'Cause I promised him 50 dollars if he'd talk," Jack Soo said. The Korean looked at Kid and said, "Fiffy dollah, you give me fiffy dollah." We all laughed, even the Korean guy, and Kid Galahad said, "Guaranteed, sir. In fact, I'll give you $100 dollars if you just tell us who sent you."

The guy acted like he'd just won the lottery, and he said, "Hunner' dollah! Top-dog A-One gennel sen', to kill Seeret Serrice wommin. He say she enemee of DPRK!" He was smiling and laughing and we all joined in, until Jack Soo said, "Yeah, one of the guys was from Hoboken, New Jersey—he was a U.S. national. This guy is from Staten Island. He's a legal immigrant with a green card who works at his uncle's

Korean restaurant. One of the other dead guys is also a legal immigrant, but the guy who was shooting the machine gun was not legal—Staten Island guy says that he was a major in the DPRK army, sent by the Chief of Staff of the DPRK Army on behalf of Kim Jong Un."

"He just spilled all of that, knowing that he's facing jail at least?" I said.

"Welllll, I may have told him that we'd let him go if he cooperated," Jack Soo said.

"Fat fucking chance of that happening," Kid Galahad said. "He just shot up a New York street with a machine gun, probably killed some people and definitely isn't going free—he's gonna have the NYPD on his ass as well as the FBI, Homeland Security and probably NSA, CIA and every other three letter agency that has anything to do with international terrorism."

"Not if he was an FBI informant who was trying to penetrate the North Koreans' intelligence apparatus in the States," I said.

"Oooh, I like it. He was recruited by the FBI because they were watching his uncle's restaurant—the nasty North Koreans were using it as a meeting place for their agents," Mamba said.

"We can't say that because it'd ruin his uncle's business, but we could say they trailed an agent there who was looking for authentic home cooking—and who kept going back because the food was so good," I said.

"There we go. I just have one question, though," Kid Galahad said. We all got it at the same time.

"Ah, shit," I said.

"Fucking-A shit," Jack Soo said.

"I hate people who just *lie*," Mamba said.

"Exactly. If he's a legal immigrant he can't be North Korean, because our fat-assed friend Kim Jong Fuckhead doesn't let anyone just emigrate, and certainly not to the US-of-fucking A," Kid Galahad said.

We all looked at Staten Island guy, who looked down at the floor like he knew the jig was up. Jack Soo said something in Korean, and the guy answered right away, in a tone that just dripped with sadness. Jack said something else to him, and the guy answered in an even sadder tone of voice. Jack Soo said, "Tell them what you just told me."

Staten Island guy said, "I made to come here, or family all die. DPRK man tell me they all die I not do what he tell me, all time. I not wan' to come, I say so, he show me picture of momma an' poppa in Pyongyang. My famiry from North Korean, but I escape to South. He say DPRK keere them I not he'p w' big gun. He know I do big gun in RSK army, I not know how, but he know. I sorry—I not wan' keere you." He never looked at us, but that wasn't unusual—direct eye contact is actively discouraged in some Asian cultures—but I still believed him.

"OK, so our story has to change, but we can still get him off. He was shanghaied here but managed to alert us, which is why we were reconnoitering this street. The DPRK major recognized us as federal agents and they opened fire. This guy was slow to get them more ammo, which helped us take them down. We don't know how they recruited him, but he was blackmailed into this, not a willing participant," I said.

"OK, but do we really believe that the DPRK was behind this?" Mamba said.

"No," the rest of us said. "My Pepsis," I said, "and we need to get everything we can out of this guy before we send him off to some other place, maybe with those guys we sent to Cali. Jack, you gotta volunteer to translate for Staten Island guy. We need it to be an act of DPRK terrorism so that we don't tip our hand about this."

"Why don't you think that this is revenge for the currency bust?" Jack Soo said.

"It's too personal," Mamba said. "If this was revenge for stopping their counterfeiting scam the North Koreans would make it much larger and splashier, or at least guarantee more certain casualties. Killing just one agent who was connected with it—and not even the lead agent? That's just too *parochial*."

"But it would send a definite message," Jack Soo said.

"Then they would've tried to wipe out the whole squad," Kid Galahad said.

"Exactly. They would've come after us when we were in Chicago, or waited until Bumble, El Gato, Ed and I were together, not kill us one at a time. Also, if that was their goal—kill us where they found us—they would've sent snipers. The DPRK military is huge, and we all know they must have a good sniper school, so sending a machine gun and four people to service it is just ridiculous," I said.

"Unless this was another attempt to stop you personally, set up by somebody in the FBI. I'll bet you that there was only supposed to be one survivor from this attack—the DPRK major," Kid Mamba said.

"Leaving us with three dead red-herring bodies, designed to lead us in the direction of the evil empire of North Korea," Jack Soo said.

"Who the *fuck* is that evil *bastard* in the FBI?" Mamba said. "This is getting *irritating*. We need to find his nefarious ass, because it'll take *weeks* for my nails to recover."

"Concur, *mon ami*," I said. "But here comes somebody, so let's shut the fuck up about it and help Staten Island guy here, OK?"

"His name is Pak Bae, by the way, and I concur with Freak," Jack Soo said.

"I don't think anyone is served by sending Mr. Pak to prison, so I'm gonna vote to STFU, too," Kid Galahad said.

"Well, you know I *agree*, and of course I'll *STFU*," Mamba said. "But I am going to have to take a day off to get my nails re-done by Miss Veronica."

"Miss Veronica?" I said, raising an eyebrow.

"His favorite transvestite nail *artiste*, down on Jackson Street," Jack Soo said.

"She's really good?" Kid Galahad said.

"She's simply *fab-u-lous*," Mamba said in his best Nathan-Lane-in-*The-Birdcage* voice.

"She's the biggest nail *artiste* you've ever seen—at least seven feet tall and really built," Jack Soo said.

"As a man or a womyn?" Kid Galahad said.

"Take your pick," Jack Soo said, sounding just like Detective Nick Yamada on *Barney Miller*. We all laughed, until some hardass SWAT guy said, "NYPD! YOU'RE SURROUNDED! THROW OUT YOUR WEAPONS AND COME OUT WITH YOUR HANDS RAISED!

"Didn't we tell them the scene was secure?" I said.

"I knew we forgot *something*," Mamba said.

"Hey, don't look at me—I was busy translating," Jack Soo said.

"You're in charge, Freak, so technically it's your fault," Kid Galahad said.

"The burdens of command," I said. I pushed Pak Bae on the floor and said, "Stay down. Don't move a muscle." Jack Soo translated and when he was done I said, "THIS IS SPECIAL AGENT GLINKA GLICKSTIEN OF THE US SECRET SERVICE! WE HAVE SECURED THE SCENE—ALL SUSPECTS ARE DOWN AND INCAPACITATED! WE ARE ALL STANDING WITH OUR ID CLEARLY DISPLAYED AND OUR RIGHT HANDS BEHIND OUR HEADS!"

"Don't you think that was just a bit *melodramatic*?" Mamba said.

"The pot says as he calls the kettle black," I said.

"I thought it was a bit over the top, too, Freak," Kid Galahad said. "If the HRT is out there I'm not sure the Feebs'll get 'incapacitated,' y'know?"

"And it was so loud—those boys in the HRT don't like loud noises unless they're makin' 'em," Jack Soo said.

"Fuck you fuckers," I said as a flexible camera snaked its way around the corner to look at us. We all had our right hands behind our heads and our IDs held straight out in our left hands, and Mamba started bouncing his hips and singing "Stop! In the name of love, before you break my heart!" and so we all started doing our best imitation of the Supremes, and when the SWAT guys came around the corner we were all dancing and singing and laughing.

The SWAT guys came up to the door and saw us and two of them started singing along until their commander came up and said, "Cut the shit, you assholes." We all stopped, and this fuckhead said, "Give me a sitrep, Glickstien." His tone was nasty, he was trying to act like a macho, macho man (my apologies to The Village People) and we were all just trying to decompress from being shot at with a .50 caliber machine gun, so I said "Fuck off and die, you arrogant prick. You're not in my chain of command and this ain't the Big Green Machine, so find a nice flagpole, sit your ass on it and rotate, willya?"

The SWAT commander's eyes bulged out of his head and his face was as red as a NYFD engine, but before he could say anything Mamba said, "Don't you just *hate* men with small dicks? They're always trying to be so *macho* they forget to be *polite*. It's just *dis-gusting*."

"Yeah, especially since we already did all the hard work. All you guys gotta do is get the body bags and take care of an already secured prisoner," Jack Soo said. "And I could use a cup of coffee."

Kid Galahad didn't say anything at all. He just stared straight into the eyes of the SWAT commander as his hand crept down to where his gun was stuck in his waistband. The Kid's eyes narrowed and his hand flexed like a gunfighter's in an old western. The SWAT guy got a little pale and he started to move his own hand toward his holstered pistol, but the Kid gave a slow, little head shake that said "don't do that, asshole"—and the guy stopped. The tension in the air crept up another notch.

Until one of the SWAT guys said, "Holy fuck! It's the Freak!" He walked into the room and right up to me, his hand out to shake mine. We shook and he said, "You won't remember me, but I was at the Warehouse Massacre." He turned to the rest of the guys and said, "This is the chick that shot the Tromboli Gang to shit in the Bronx—and then she carried four of her guys out at once! It was eight to one and she blew 'em all away—and they had rifles and shotguns!" He shook my hand again and the tension just evaporated.

I looked at the SWAT commander and said, "Sorry about being surly, Captain, but I'm tired of being shot at. We killed three of the guys and took the fourth. He's got broken ribs, but he's definitely coherent, and he's given us some information already. I'd rather not talk about it in the open, and I really don't want to tell the tale more than once, if you know what I mean."

I'd given him a way to save face, and he was smart enough to take it. "I'm sorry I came on so gung-ho—you know how the adrenalin goes up in situations like this, and mine got the best of me. Well done on the takedown," he said. "We'll wait for the brass to show up until we try to debrief, but we'll need to clear this room for the crime scene guys, OK?"

"Thanks, Captain. We'd be glad to clear the room, especially if means we can get some water, although we'd all prefer Pepsi. I will tell you that the machine gun was made by Browning under contract to the U.S. military—I've seen enough to know that it's standard issue to the army and Marines," I said. Then Mamba said, "What about our hero, the brave garbage man?"

I nodded and said, "Is Steve Venturi OK? He's the garbage man who set up our smokescreen so we could stop these shithead terrorists." I used the word deliberately, knowing that it would get around to the media, and that every correspondent in the world would consider a New York SWAT team member a reliable source. Let our FBI mystery man chew on that while the Badger Squad chewed on him.

The SWAT Captain said, "He caught some shrapnel, but he's OK."

Kid Galahad said, "Sir, what about the people who were shooting the shotguns? They drew fire and made it really easy for us to get the drop on these motherfuckers."

The SWAT Captain said, "Two of them are wounded, but Patrolman Ed Ross is dead—a slug got through the truck and hit him in the chest, and you know there's no vest in the world that will stop that."

"God-*DAMMIT*!" Mamba said. He spun around and kicked the dead gunner in the ribs and then stomped out of the room. Jack Soo looked at the floor and quietly said, "Greater love hath no man than this, that he will lay down his life for his brother." Kid Mamba went over to the window and looked out at the shattered garbage truck, his eyes narrowing when he saw something. He pointed out the window and then gave a thumbs-up, so Jack and I went over to look. We saw Steve Venturi being wheeled to an ambulance, and I yelled "Go Army! Beat Navy!" He gave us a thumbs-up and I said, "These asshole shithead terrorists won't ever hurt another person, buddy! You did it—we got 'em!" Venturi yelled back, "Pretty good for Marine pukes! Thanks for saving the city!" before they loaded him in the ambulance.

We turned around and the crime scene guys were at the door, so we went out, went down the fire stairs and out into the street, where Mamba was staring out at the truck, his eyes dry but his face full of anguish. The FBI HRT guys were doing perimeter security, along with the NYPD, and we could see where the dead patrolman was lying behind the truck. We all went over to pay our respects, and the NYPD guy standing over his body said, "Rossie would be proud to know that you got those motherfucking terrorists, agents. He'd a thought it was worth it, y'know?"

We all cried at that, because we didn't think it was worth it to lose even one life, especially when it was one that was brave enough to be part of New York's Finest, and brave enough to take on a fearsome .50 caliber machine gun with a shotgun. I quietly said, "Squad, pre-sent, ARMS!" and we all saluted the body of Patrolman Edwin G. Ross, who we were certain helped save our lives, and probably others, too.

I looked at the guy guarding Ross's body and said, "Anybody else get hit?"

He said, "Three KIA besides Rossie, and about 15 wounded. Most people just ran at the first shots, and it looks like they really didn't like the garbage truck, y'know? Was they shootin' at you guys or what?"

I said, "They were probably shooting at us, although we should let the FBI investigate before we jump to any conclusions."

"Yeah, you're right. Fuckin' North Korean terrorists," he said.

"How'd you know they were North Koreans?" Kid Galahad said.

"The sons of bitches called WFAN and told everybody they were avenging North Korean agents assassinated by the hegemonist, murdering U.S. government," he said. "Anybody know what a fuckin' hegemonist even is?"

I was pretty sure that we all knew, but I was just as sure it didn't matter a tinker's damn, so we just shook our heads and turned away from the NYPD patrolman's body, all of us mad as hell. We were about five steps away when Edward Otis Whitney and Nails rolled up. Old Three Names saw us and they came right over, stopping briefly to show an NYPD officer their IDs. Nails immediately said, "Any of ours hit?"

"No, ma'am," I said. "We're all clean, but they got an NYPD patrolman named Ed Ross and three civilians before we could stop them."

"Our friend again?" Nails said.

"Almost certainly," I said. "You might want to consider sending me to Nome, Alaska, to investigate counterfeit polar bears, because it seems like they're going to keep shooting at me until they get me."

"Nonsense," Nails said. "This is an act of terrorism, retaliation for your part in shutting down the North Korean counterfeiting ring and confiscating $900 million in fake cash. Kim Jong Un is pissed off, and because his dick is the size of a cocktail sausage he's trying to prove he's a man by getting you and your team." Her hazel eyes were boring into my head, daring me to contradict her, which I was never going to do. "Yes, ma'am, I believe that you're right—at least that's what we all thought in the aftermath."

"That's sure how it felt to me, Director," Kid Galahad said.

"The only survivor told us that a top North Korean general sent him as part of a team to stop an enemy of the state," Jack Soo said.

"And it's certain that one of the terrorists was a North Korean officer," Mamba said. "Our survivor claimed he was the ringleader of the op against Freak, again on orders from a top North Korean general."

"So this is another act of terrorism against the people of New York, perpetrated by a known exporter of terrorism and a sworn enemy of the United States," Edward Otis Whitney said.

"And this is exactly what it seems on its face," Nails said, her tone telling us that was the line we'd take in the extensive debriefing we'd all undergo. We all nodded, and Jack Soo said, "Ma'am, I've already got a rapport with the last suspect, so if you could see that I get to interpret for him it may be easier to get the information we need."

"Consider it done," Nails said. Just then the Assistant Director of the FBI, Mitchell Holland, rolled up. His giant black Escalade SUV was followed by several more, plus an FBI armored vehicle and an HRT mobile command post (a giant RV with 'FBI' emblazoned on it in five-foot high letters).

"Shithouse mouse, here comes the circus," Kid Galahad said.

"Son of a bitch! I thought it was Beyoncé," Mamba said.

"Get used to disappointment," Jack Soo said. "This guy is as slimy as a three-day old tuna, and he has the morals of a Borgia."

"I heard he needs at least two Escalades: one for his ride and one for his ego," Edward Otis Whitney said. The look on his face was one of revulsion mixed with fascination, as if he were admiring a king cobra for its grace and cold beauty while recognizing its ability to kill without compunction.

"He's a prick of the first order and will be the Director when Harley retires, and he's got lots of friends in high places, so don't fuck around with him," Nails said. She looked at us and said, "He'll be charming, fawning, and deferential right up until he fucks you over—and you can depend on the fact that he *will* fuck you over if it benefits him. He also likes to preen for the cameras, so don't get in the way of his shot or you may have claw marks on your back."

"So what you're saying is this is the consummate REMF," I said.

"Exactly," Nails said, smiling for our benefit.

Holland swaggered up (and I use that word because that's what he did—swaggered—like he was John Wayne in *True Grit*) and said, "Director Hessler, are all your people safe?" in a deep baritone voice that was charming and smarmy at the same time.

"Yes, Mr. Assistant Director, the Secret Service personnel are all unharmed, although a NYPD patrolman and three civilians were killed by the terrorists," Nails said.

"So our HRT got them? Or was it NYPD SWAT?" he said.

"No, Mr. Assistant Director, it was the team of Secret Service agents who took the terrorists down," Nails said.

"They didn't think to wait for one of the specially trained units? They just charged into the fray without thinking about the consequences?" Assistant Director Holland said, his tone implying that we'd done something wrong.

I shouldn't have done it; but I was tired, hungry, and still pissed off that four people had died because some asshole had it in for me, so I said, "No, it's because of the possible consequences that we went, sir."

"And you are?" he said, his disdain for talking to an underling clear from his tone and demeanor. Holland was a really handsome man—he kind of looked like Channing Tatum, only his face was prettier and his hair was better—and when he sneered it distorted his handsome face into a gargoyle mask. It was odd that someone could go from being good-looking to ugly that quickly, but there it was.

I looked back at him with my best "don't fuck with me" face and said, "U.S. Secret Service Agent Glinka Glickstien, sir."

"And did you take into account that you weren't properly armed for such an effort, or that you might have been killed, or caused more deaths through your actions, Agent Glickstien?" Assistant Director Holland said, sneering again. "Little popguns against a machine gun? Isn't that foolhardy and irresponsible?" He clearly was practicing how he was going to play it with the press, because in his mind we'd gone off half-cocked looking for glory. In reality he was pissed because his Hostage Rescue Team hadn't gotten in on the action, and we had covered ourselves in glory, although we'd trade all the accolades for the lives of Ed Ross and the three civilians who died.

"No sir, what we took into account was that we were under attack, we were armed and the bad guys might've just decided to kill as many civilians as they could before your guys got here. We formed a battle plan and executed it, and yes, we were greatly assisted by the NYPD when three of their officers opened fire with shotguns in defense of the civilians and their city. Patrolman Ross was a tremendous hero who made it possible for us to take down the terrorists, and my squad and I would appreciate it if you did not denigrate his sacrifice by questioning the actions of sworn law officers." Mitchell Holland looked like he'd swallowed habanero peppers, because his face was red and sweaty and his temperature was rising fast. He opened his mouth to say something but I cut him off.

"And Mr. Assistant Director, I'd like to ask you a question. Have you ever faced a combat situation against a machine gun? No? Well, I have, and so has Agent Moerman, and so has Agent Hwang. They are bulky and hard to maneuver when your line of fire isn't clear, so by going in fast and mobile we had the advantage, because they were stuck in a fixed position and we were not. In the urban battlefield mobility gives you the absolute advantage, regardless of the size or capacity of your arms.

"Furthermore, Agent Moerman and I are far more qualified than any FBI HRT team leader to assess such situations and execute counterattack strategies, since we are both veterans of the U.S. Marine Corps and Special Operations Command, as well as veterans of several actions against enemy troops, all of which were harder and more desperate than this situation."

"Well, what would those operations be, Agent Glickstien? Why don't you let us be the judge of your experience in storming buildings defended by machine guns?" Holland said, his face clearly saying that he doubted my story.

Kid Galahad and I both said, "Classified." Kid looked at me and said "Your Pepsis, Freak."

"Roger that, Kid," I said.

"Oh you can tell me about it—I'm the Assistant Director of the FBI, and I have a security clearance," Holland said, his condescension almost a visible thing.

"Sorry, sir, but you're not cleared for this," I said. "The president and I have already discussed this and *he's* not cleared, so I know that you aren't either.

"But that's neither here nor there, sir, because what we did was according to doctrine, and our sidearms are hardly popguns, and further, we are sworn to protect, support and defend the Constitution of the United States, and what those terrorists were doing to this street was certainly against the Constitution, so we did what we swore to do: defend this country and our way of life. We acted according to the highest principles of duty, courage and honor, sir, and if you don't like that I suggest that you go fuck yourself, the horse you rode in on, and the family dog, sir."

"And the fact that you are addressing the best pistol shot in the world when you talk to Agent Glickstien also had an effect on our willingness to take down the terrorists, since we were sure if we could get a clean line of fire she could stop them dead," Mamba said.

"Which she did," Kid Galahad said.

"Then why is one terrorist still *alive*?" Mitchell Holland said, his sneer even more overbearing. His voice also changed, becoming almost catty, like Mamba's when he was trying to be *über* gay.

"Because *I* shot that one," Mamba said.

"Because we needed to capture one so that we could interrogate him," Kid Galahad said.

"Which we did already," Jack Soo said.

The Assistant Director of the FBI said, "And just who are you?" pointing his finger at each of them.

"Secret Service Agent Alec Hwang, anti-counterfeiting office in Chicago," Jack Soo said.

"Secret Service Agent Jordan Moerman, anti-counterfeiting detail, Chicago," Kid Galahad said.

Mamba drew himself up to his full 5'2½" and said "I am Secret Service Agent Almont Phillipe Gilbert de Coucy, Comte de Condé, currently assigned to the anti-counterfeiting office in Chicago. My commanding officer is Special Agent in Charge Narita Singh, and I give you this information as a courtesy, because you, Mr. Assistant Director, are *not* in my chain of command. Good day to you, sir." Mamba turned and walked away from Mitchell Holland and stood watching the crime techs work on the battered garbage truck. Kid Galahad and Jack Soo went and stood with him. I'm sure that Holland had never been talked to before like this, but all I did was fix him with my death stare. The silence built, but I just waited for him to say the first word, knowing that most REMFs had to talk because they couldn't show you how important they were by being quiet.

I was right.

He finally said, "I don't approve of your actions or the way you spoke to me, Agent Glickstien. You and your men were foolhardy in attacking a machine gun with sidearms, you are personally abrasive and all of you are insubordinate. I will be informing the Director that your actions might be criminal, and the FBI will be conducting a full investigation concerning whether or not your egregiously brash and impulsive actions contributed to the death of the NYPD officer and the wounding of the other two." He smiled a cruel smile and said, "I also might be able to make the case that your actions led to the deaths of the civilians, so don't be surprised if that lands on your plate, too."

It was odd, but I was getting some bad vibes from this guy that I didn't know. I understood that he was an REMF, and that as an administrator he was never in the field and probably didn't understand how to take a shit without direction from his superiors (and actual directions on pushing, grunting, and wiping), but his overwhelming hostility and deep animosity didn't reconcile with what I and my team had done. For the life of me I couldn't figure out why he was trying to jam us up when we had solved a huge problem for everybody.

Unless he was the one behind the attempts on our lives.

But that didn't make any sense either, because I'd never really met Assistant Director Holland, and I wasn't involved in any investigations at all, least of all one that involved him. As far as I knew there was no way for me to hurt him even if I wanted to, and why would I want to? We were all on the same team—FBI, CIA, NSA, DIA, Homeland Security—these were all the compatriots of the Secret Service, and I held every institution in high regard, so what the fuck was this asshole's problem?

I was saved from putting my foot in it when a bunch of NYPD command cars rolled up to the barricades and a bunch of guys got out, led by one womyn, who just happened to be the New York City Chief of Police.

Caroline Rose Walton had been an assistant chief in Chicago when Barney Blum, the NYC Police Commissioner, decided it was time for New York City to have an African-America, female chief of police. They made quite a pair: she was a majestic womyn, six feet and change tall, physically beautiful, and impeccably dressed; he was a nebbishy little guy in a rumpled off-the-rack suit who wore thick glasses and whose hair looked like a fright wig, but together they were very effective.

Ms. Walton guilted the city into putting on five hundred new officers in her first year in office, and Mr. Blum insisted that they be as well trained as humanly possible, which meant more and better instructors at the police academy (read as: more real-life cops who could share their experiences and teach the recruits the proper way to police). This novel idea created a more professional police force, which reduced crime, which in turn meant that the police could actually do preventative policing, which led to a downward spiral of crime, which…well, you get the idea. When you combined it with two other ideas Walton and Blum used it meant far less notoriety for the NYPD and far less lawsuits against the department.

First, Chief Walton believed that there should be a rigorous and selective recruitment policy, and she also believed in screening out what she called "the crazed paramilitary idiots" from becoming officers. Her first public statement made it clear that she wouldn't tolerated what she called "stupid machoism." When Blum introduced her Chief Walton said, "The NYPD will no longer tolerate the culture of stupid machoism that has led us to choking suspects to death for committing a misdemeanor. We are here to fully enforce the law using common sense, discipline, and respect for the citizens of New York City, but let me make it clear: we are not the Gestapo, we are not the U.S. Army and we are not demi-gods. The men and wymyn of the NYPD truly are New York's finest, and we are not only going to act like it, but also, from myself to the newest recruit, we are going to live up to that claim, *regardless of the circumstances*."

Her statement, referenced the death of Eric Garner, whose at the hands of a policeman (I'm not making any value judgments here—I wasn't there, so I don't know exactly what went on, although I will say that if someone I'm trying to subdue starts wheezing and says "I can't breathe!" in a voice that finally fades out I'm letting off the hold—and I won't use a choke hold unless I intend to kill someone), raised a shitstorm of protest and controversy. The Chief stuck by her statement, and Commissioner Blum usually mumbled something about common sense and better training, and pretty soon it was a moot point, because the department got better all the way around, and policemen in NYC knew that the chief had their backs, because if you followed SOP she'd stand by you no matter what happened.

The other thing that happened was Commissioner Blum told the city commission that "talent follows money" and got them to grant 15 percent raises to all the people actually in the field. Blum pointed out that the average patrolman did more police work in a day than he and his staff did in a year (absolutely true), and that it didn't make any sense to pay an assistant chief 10 times as much as a patrolman.

In support of that pay raise Blum and all of the other headquarters people started taking regular shifts in the field at the patrolman level, which was a huge hit with the rank and file. Just seeing the brass get back in the blue bag was a hoot, and having them seriously patrol and do the donkey work of policing raised morale and cohesion while alleviating some of the burden on the patrolmen.

As effective as Walton and Blum had been, they were even more effective when you combined them with the current mayor of New York. She was a really smart black liberal who seemed to have the best interests of every person in the city at heart. She didn't ignore anything that had anything to do with the Big Apple, she stood by her people when they were in the right, she took the blame when they (or she) were wrong and she came down on any form of corruption like the righteous Hammer of God.

She also was a calm individual who didn't scream "terrorist" every time something happened in the city, so when I saw her get out of a car right behind the chief and the commissioner I knew we could sell our story, and that these people were here to help us.

The Chief walked right up to the sergeant who was directing the cordon around the crime scene and said, "Where is our officer?" The sergeant pointed to where the medical examiner was finishing up with Patrolman Ross's body and the chief went right over to it. She said something I couldn't hear to the medical examiner and he stood up and said, "It hit him dead center, Chief. He never felt a thing." She said, "I want to see him. Pull that sheet back, willya?"

Before he could do that one of the chief's aides whispered something to her and she said, "No, I told ya—no press at all. Now go keep those dipshits back or I'll break my foot off in somebody's ass."

My estimation of her went up after that.

The press was kept back as the chief, the commissioner, and the mayor all stood over Patrolman Ed Ross's body. Each of them said something and Commissioner Blum bent down and touched his shoulder. I caught a scrap of the *kaddish*, the Hebrew prayer for the dead, and then they all stood up and came over to where Holland, Nails, Old Three Names and I were still standing.

Chief Walton said, "Mr. Assistant Director, good to see you." She shook his hand and then turned her back on him to shake Director Hessler's hand. "Director, I understand that it was your personnel who first responded to the attack. Are they still here?" Hessler pointed at me and I said, "My team and I were first on scene, Chief. We were the ones who went up and got the guys with the machine gun, but we couldn't have done it without your guys. They tried to light up the terrorists with shotguns, and when the terrorists responded we used the noise to catch them with their pants down. Those cops were incredibly brave, ma'am."

She shook my hand and said, "They were, but so were you guys. Thank you for your bravery and initiative." Her eyes were glistening with unshed tears for her patrolman, but they were proud and steady on my face as she continued to pump my hand.

"Now wait a minute," Assistant Director Holland said. "These Secret Service agents were very irresponsible and put a great many lives in jeopardy. They may also have contributed to the death of your patrolman and the civilians. We need to investigate this incident further before we go making any rash claims of bravery."

"That's not the way we heard it," Chief Walton said. "My SWAT commander told me that he and his guys would've walked right into the line of fire without the warning from the Secret Service agents, and he said that the swift action by the agents probably saved the lives off a bunch of your HRT guys, too." She looked at Holland with her deep brown eyes flashing, and I could see why people would follow this womyn. She exuded gallons of the easy confidence that the Corps called "command presence."

"I talked to my terrorism guy and he said that these agents probably saved hundreds of lives by interceding and allowing most of the civilians to escape unharmed. Are you aware that the agents deliberately exposed themselves to draw the fire of the terrorists?" Commissioner Blum said in a rock steady voice, his blue eyes electric behind his thick glasses. "We know for a fact that they saved at least 30 civilians who were sheltering behind the garbage truck, and Patrol Sergeant Tomasina Benton, who was wounded in the attack, tells me that it wasn't five seconds after she and the patrolmen opened fire that she heard the agents shooting the bad guys. She estimates that the bad guys would have killed between 20 and 50 police officers who were responding Code Three to the attack—a New York City patrol car won't stop .50 caliber machine gun rounds. And you think that these agents did something wrong?" The *nebbish* had teeth, and he wasn't afraid to use them.

Holland gave an insincere smile and said, "No doubt that people were possibly saved by the actions of these officers, but of course it was their actions that began the whole thing, wasn't it?" He acted like he'd just scored a point in the debate, but Commissioner Barney Blum locked his blue eyes on the FBI Assistant Director and gave him a smile like a cannibal looking at a fat man. His whole manner appeared apologetic, but then he said, "Listen, asshole, this ain't the fucking movies. When one of my cruisers gets hosed with a .50 caliber machine gun the officer inside dies. They don't get wounded or miraculously escape or outrun the rounds—they fucking *die*. If that was a U.S. issue Browning M2 shooting—well…the armor on our SWAT van wouldn't stop that. So shut your stinking pie-hole about who caused what, you desk jockeying political appointee shithead. I'm the Police Commissioner of New York City and I say these *agents* are heroes. My police chief says they're heroes, and the mayor is about to say they're heroes, so why don't you get the fuck away from this crime scene before I have my grateful officers arrest your lily-white ass for obstruction?"

Commissioner Barney Blum's smile never wavered, but his manner had changed—he was now a bulletproof Godzilla, and the city he was preparing to stomp wasn't named Tokyo, it was named Mitchell Holland. It was clear that Commissioner Barney Blum had a giant pair of brass balls that clanged when he walked, because he wasn't kidding about, or even remotely scared of, arresting the Assistant Director of the FBI, who, even if he was a gigantic dickhead, was still kind of a big deal.

Chief Caroline Rose Walton said, "And I would like to add that you're a giant dickhead who is a disgrace to law enforcement. Just because your fucking suit costs more than my patrolmen make in a year doesn't mean that you get to criticize real live field operators who just saved the city from more horrible terrorism, you *schmuck*."

The mayor came up right then. She immediately felt the tension and said, "Mitch, Carrie, Barney, what the fuck're ya talkin' about? Whatever it is keep it looking civil, because some of those press guys can read lips, and telephoto lenses are a bitch, right?" She laughed and then said, "Mr. Commissioner, what's the situation?"

Barney Blum gave the mayor a very succinct rundown of what happened, finishing with his opinion that we'd saved countless lives in stopping the terrorists the way we did. The mayor looked at Chief Walton, who nodded her agreement. She looked at Nails and said, "Siri, is this an act of terrorism?"

"Mr. Mayor, it's almost certainly terrorism, but for now we should go easy on that word. We have what look like foreign nationals at the gun, but they were using a U.S. Army issue Browning M2, so until we can confirm I'd say suspected terrorists. My investigators will be working with the investigators from DHS and the FBI to try and get you confirmation of that, but it's irresponsible and premature to say that right now," Nails said.

"Any reason for me not saying your agents were heroes here?" the mayor said.

Siri Hessler gave her a tight, satisfied smile and said, "None whatsoever. They put themselves in harm's way for the people of New York just like they were guarding the president, Ms. Mayor, and with the same kind of results we expect of all our agents. It didn't hurt that Agents Glickstien, Moerman and Hwang are all decorated former Marines. Glickstien and Moerman are also veterans of Special Forces."

The mayor looked down at me and I said, "Director Hessler's right about all but one thing, ma'am."

"You're damned right she is—there ain't no such thing as a former Marine," the mayor said. "Once a Marine always a Marine, right?" Her eyes sparkled at me and I said, "Bet your ass, Ms. Mayor." Everybody except Holland laughed a little bit, and the mayor said, "Chief Walton, what do I say about Patrolman Ross?"

The Chief looked at me and said, "Agent Glickstien? You wanna take that?" So I told the mayor what I'd said earlier about us going in under cover of the shotguns and subsequent return fire. She looked at me and said, "I just remembered you—you're the agent they call Freak, right? You saved Aleta Soper's life in Kentucky, right?"

"Yes, ma'am, but I had lots of help there, just like I did here," I said, trying to deflect any praise that might make me appear before the press.

"So if I characterized our three cops as heroes how would you feel about it, Agent Freak?" the mayor said.

"First of all, ma'am, my friends just call me Freak, and second, you would be exactly right. Patrolman Ross, Patrol Sergeant Benton and Patrolman Norris are all huge heroes as far as we're concerned—they really saved our asses by being so brave and bold," I said.

The liberal mayor of New York City said, "Thanks for saving New Yorkers from these terrorists, Freak, and thanks for being so kind about our officers. I'm not going to mention your names because the Secret Service will want to have their own press conference, but I do need to know one thing from you." She gave me a friendly look and said, "How did you guys even get involved? What were you doing here?"

"We were finishing a five-mile run, Ms. Mayor," I said. "Our hotel is right down the street. I'm waiting to rejoin my assignment with Governor Soper and my friends knew I was in town—they were here for training—so they met me and we decided to go for a run."

"Why the hell were you running five miles through the streets of New York?" she said.

"We have to run alongside cars, Ms. Mayor. What better way to train than running the streets of the Big Apple?" I said. We all had a small laugh and the mayor said, "Do you mind if I steal that line about running alongside cars, Freak?"

"No, ma'am," I said, "especially since I stole it from a Clint Eastwood movie." There was more laughter and the mayor shook my hand again. She turned to go down the block to where the press was being held at bay and Assistant Director Holland moved to go with her.

"Where are you going?" the mayor said to Holland.

"To the press conference," Holland said.

"Why?" the mayor said.

"Uh, well…uh, I'm the face of the FBI," Holland said.

"Did the FBI have anything to do with this action?" the mayor said.

"Well…no," Holland said.

"So go get your ass back in your car and stay out of my press conference," the mayor said. "I won't be mentioning the FBI and I sure as hell don't need your help—I have my own professional police officers if I need them." She nodded at Chief Walton and Commissioner Blum, shook my hand and Director Hessler's hand, and then went and had a great press conference.

Mitchell Holland looked as if he'd been slapped. He glared at Nails and I and then stomped off back to his black Escalade. We went over and listened to the mayor.

She started off by saying, "Thank you. I'm pleased to report that today a group of four visiting Secret Service agents and three NYPD officers averted what could have been another senseless act of violence here in New York by stopping a group of bad guys with a .50 caliber machine gun who were attempting to terrorize the city. We will not be releasing the names of the heroic Secret Service agents yet, or the heroic NYPD officers, pending contacting their families, but I think that calling them heroes is not premature. At approximately 2:05 p.m. the persons responsible for this heinous attack opened fire on the street, pinning the Secret Service agents and a group of civilians behind the New York City garbage truck you see down the street…"

The mayor laid out what happened, made everybody involved look good and then took questions. The first question was what you'd expect, and so were the rest of them.

> Reporter: Ms. Mayor, was this an act of terrorism?
>
> Mayor: We don't know enough yet to tell, but I assure you that someone opening fire on a New York City street with an illegal machine gun is pretty terrifying, so in that sense, yes, this was terrorism. The way you mean it, I don't know yet.
>
> Reporter: Were these terrorists Muslim?
>
> Mayor: Again, we don't know if these were foreign terrorists. They were using a machine gun that is also used by the U.S. Army, so we shouldn't jump to any conclusions.
>
> Reporter: Well, what do they look like?
>
> Mayor: They look like three dead guys and a federal prisoner.
>
> Reporter: Were the terrorists wearing suicide vests?
>
> Mayor: Again, we don't know if these guys were terrorists. They were using a machine gun, a Browning M2 like the U.S. Army uses. I have no report of any suicide vests.

Reporter: Why were the Secret Service personnel here? Was this a sting that got out of control? Did the Secret Service bungle an operation that put New Yorkers in danger?

Mayor: The Secret Service agents happened to be in the wrong place at the wrong time. They absolutely *were not* conducting any operation that went bad. These men and wymyn were and are heroes who saved hundreds of lives through their quick, decisive actions that were aided by three heroes in the NYPD.

Reporter: But why were they here? What were they investigating?

Mayor: My understanding was that three of them were here for training, and the fourth was waiting for a new assignment to commence. They were all at the hotel and had previously served together, so they decided to go for a run. They were finishing a five-mile run when the machine gunners opened up on the street and they found themselves trapped behind the garbage truck.

Reporter: But what were they investigating?

Mayor: As I said, they weren't investigating *anything*, they were simply visiting the city on business.

Reporter: Why were they running in the streets of New York? Were they being pursued by the terrorists with the machine gun?

Mayor: Again, we need to be careful about calling the perpetrators terrorists. We don't know who the bad guys were yet. Also, the Browning M2 is a heavy, crew-served machine gun that sits on a tripod. It can't be carried and fired unless it's bolted to a vehicle, so no, they weren't being pursued by the bad guys. What was the other question you asked?

Reporter: Why were they running through the streets?

Mayor: Hey, these agents have to run alongside cars when they're guarding people. What better way to train for that than running in the Big Apple? If you can keep up here a presidential motorcade would be no big deal, right?

(General laughter ensues.)

Reporter: So this was a terrorist attack on the president? Were they secretly guarding the president?

Mayor: Oh, sweet Mother Hubbard. Does anybody have an Excedrin?

When they got to that point Nails looked at all of us and said, "Had enough stupidity for today?" We all nodded, so she said, "C'mon, we need to get you guys food and start the de-brief. I'm not going to ask for your pistols until we get to the field office, and I will send for your on-duty weapons and clean clothes. That OK with you guys?"

"I'd kill a reporter for a Pepsi," I said.

"I'd do it for a lot less than that," Kid Galahad said.

"How does a smart womyn like the mayor manage to keep her cool with that kind of stupidity raging around her every day?" Jack Soo said.

"Not all the press are like that, but because the news is as much about entertainment as about informing the public they have to go for the titillating or salacious as much as they do hard info, or nobody will listen to their version of events," Nails said.

"So you learn to swim in the bullshit?" Kid Galahad said.

"Exactly," Nails said.

We got to her vehicle and she said, "You guys ride with me, OK? Who's the best driver?"

We all pointed at Jack Soo and he said, "Guilty, Director. I've been to the Anti-terrorism Evasive Driving Course at the U.S. Military Police School in Fort Leonard Wood, Missouri, and I drove for two U.S. Ambassadors to the UN, right here in lovely NYC."

"Good. You take the wheel, the rest of you are my security detail until we get home and then we can talk freely." She directed everybody at the car to load up and we shot off like a bat out of hell. Jack Soo was the only person I knew who could drive as well as Badass, but he was basically following a guy, so we didn't really go too fast (compared to zipping along at jet speeds in rural Kentucky).

At least we all lived to do the de-brief, although some barf bags were deployed (I never could ride roller coasters).

CHAPTER 53

Mole Hunt

We debriefed the Director on our suspicions concerning the attack, and how we thought we should deal with it. She had some ideas of her own, and eventually we settled on the best course of action to deal with our mole. Just as we were finishing up her phone rang. She looked at the incoming number and one eyebrow shot up. She said, "Badger Squad, I'm putting you on speaker. You have me, Freak, and the rest of the Badger Squad. Go."

Jewey said, "Do any of you know exactly where Assistant Director Mitchell Holland is right now?" His voice was excited, which meant he was close to something.

I said, "We just left him, Jewey. He can't be more than three miles from us in Manhattan."

"Hot damn!" several voices said at once. "We got the mole," Joe said. "A message was just sent from a burner phone that was purchased in Chevy Chase, Maryland by Malcolm Sorenson, the FBI Executive Assistant Director for National Security. He used a credit card to buy several burners, and we've been sitting on them. The message was between the EAD and the two inspectors who've been running around the country after Freak. The Assistant Director is now excluded since our mole's burner is currently in Santa Fe, New Mexico, which is not three miles from you or your hotel."

"Leaving aside the obvious questions—like how the hell did you do this so fast?—do we have enough evidence to arrest?" Nails said.

"You don't want to know how we did it at all," Weasel said, "or we'll be the ones getting prosecuted."

"We were able to triangulate on these guys because of what we already knew about the previous attempts to get Freak, and because we just assumed guilt and disregarded any evidence that might have proved exculpatory," Joe said.

"We also got lucky because the EAD isn't very smart. If he'd paid cash for the burners, or bought them at different stores we would still be up shit creek," Buzz Lightyear said. "We found the purchase, somebody accidentally came across his financials and we found some anomalies, like payments to two guys named Adam Jones and Tom Smith, which led us to two FBI agents whose work portfolios looked funky and who were connected to just two people: Mitch Holland and Mal Sorenson."

"We have real names on Smith and Jones?" Nails said.

"Turns out to be Smith and Jones," Jewey said. "They were so confident that they could do what they wanted that they didn't hide the payments behind any fronts, they just deposited the money in their accounts like it was a regular paycheck."

"How much?" I said.

"Over a quarter of a million dollars for each asshole," Weasel said. We all just sat there in stunned silence, because in high finance that might not be much money, but to a government field agent who topped out at around $100K it was a whole shitpot of money. For those weak-minded, venal individuals in law enforcement (hey, they're everywhere—we're sworn law officers, not saints. Everybody can't be Melvin Purvis, G-Man) that amount of money would be a powerful inducement.

"And we think that they have more hidden offshore in the Caymans," Jewey said. "Weasel's working on that."

Finally Mamba said, "So we can't arrest yet. How do we get there?"

"We want authorization to pursue the two agents—did we mention that we have witnesses who describe them to a T in New York before the warehouse, and in Kentucky before Morehead?—and to electronically and physically surveil the EAD," Joe said. "And before you give me the money and security speech, Madam Director, the Badger Squad can do it without any help at all."

"Do tell," Nails said. So Joe laid out his plan and it sounded good to all concerned, especially the part about the early warning if another hit was authorized. When Joe was all finished Nails said, "After this is all over we gotta talk about you coming to the Puzzle Palace to work directly for me, but right now I want you to run this operation until we bag this asshole. I also want to make this explicit, although I know that you all get it: on my authority we *are not* involving the FBI or DHS, or any other three letter agency. These are our people being targeted. We are the only agency to lose anyone and we're going to be the one to bring these shits down, even if we get the U.S. Marshals to arrest 'em. Please verbally acknowledge that you understand this order."

Everybody did, and Joe said, "Ma'am, we really will need one more person, and I'd like to make it one of the boys from the Chicago office, LaDavious Bell."

"Great idea, Joe," I said, "Nobody'll ever make Gomer as a Secret Service agent, or any other kind of agent, for that matter. Between Gomer, Mamba, Weasel, Jack and Kid Galahad you'll have five guys for eyes-on surveillance at all times."

"And that means he'll never know, which means we *will* catch this guy," Mamba said. "It also means that Jewey can keep an electronic eye on him, which means we'll know anything that he does within minutes, and we can basically forget about any more surprises."

"We may also be able to turn this to our advantage and trap him, catch him red-handed and tied up with a ribbon on the box," Joe said. "But we need to agree that nobody that Freak and her gang are guarding will feel like a goat tethered in the tyrannosaurus rex paddock at Jurassic Park, least of all Freak. If you want this to be like that, Director, then you need somebody else. I need your permission to act preemptively without any consultation with higher authority."

Siri Hessler said, "Agent Cocker, when I say run something I mean run it—you're in charge of this operation, which means you don't need any consultation. In fact, I'll make it even easier for you. If I try to interfere in this op please tell me to fuck off and die, OK?" Even though she was serious we all laughed. After all, it isn't often that your boss tells you to tell her to fuck off, especially when you work for the government, where everyone forgets the 5th Rule as soon as they're elected or appointed (sorry, Glickstien family shorthand—the 5th Rule explicitly states this: You have taken (or are taking) yourself too seriously. It was my *bubbe's* way to gently tell people they were being a supercilious asshole without having to say the word asshole, which she found repugnant).

After just a bit more palaver the Director said, "Now we have to let our friends from the FBI and DHS in the room for their shot at debriefing you. I'm satisfied we're going down the right road, so I don't see any need to tell them anything more than the truth about the incident. Stick to the story and then go about your business when you're liberated. We'll get this asshole, and then we'll grill him until we find out why he's so hot for your ass, Freak."

Joe said, "Before you go, Director, we do have enough evidence to arrest the sheriff and under-sheriff in Rowan County." Those two shitheads had been released by the U.S. Justice Department because there wasn't sufficient evidence to prove their complicity at the Battle of Morehead. Hearing that they could now be arrested was sweet balm to my ears, because it would scare our FBI mole and also bring some small measure of justice to those who died in the attack on the bus.

"I want to be there if I can, Director. I'd like to take at least Agent Goodenough with me, if that's all right with you," I said.

"That depends," she said. "Agent Cocker, do we know who the Marshals are sending to do the takedown?"

There was a smile in his voice when he said, "Why, yes, yes we do, ma'am." He paused for effect, and then he said, "Honest Tom Vernon and his squad will be arresting the sheriff and under-sheriff."

"You can go," Nails said. "Take anyone you want as long as you remember that Marshal Vernon is in charge."

"I won't be able to forget that, ma'am," I said. "The man isn't given to any ambiguity."

Thomas J. Vernon was a legendary U.S. Marshal who was famous throughout law enforcement circles because of his complete and total honesty, even in the face of the greatest of temptations.

It all began when Tom Vernon was a rookie marshal who went with three other marshals to guard a Mob snitch in Chicago who was going to testify against his former bosses. One of the Chicago crime families offered the four marshals a million dollars each to simply look the other way for 10 minutes while some of their former pals visited the snitch in his hotel. It seemed that the marshals were agreed to do so, until the Mob enforcers showed up, at which point 50 undercover U.S. Marshals surrounded and arrested the mob guys. Tom Vernon himself arrested his three colleagues, explaining to them that he appeared to go along with the scheme because he wanted to catch the Mob guys, not because he thought that he'd have to arrest sworn U.S. Marshals. When one of the guys asked him how much money it would've taken for him to just go along for the ride he said (in the presence of many witnesses) "I'm a sworn U.S. Marshal. Sworn officers don't take bribes, we put the crooks who do away. There isn't enough money in the world to make me violate my oath."

As impressive as that was, it was the next time he was faced with this type of decision that made Tom Vernon a legend.

He and his team were arresting a notorious banker who turned out to be running a Ponzi scheme that made Bernie Madoff look like a petty thief. They got to the guy's apartment and his wife said he was upstairs. Spreading his marshals around downstairs so the guy couldn't escape Tom Vernon and three other marshals went upstairs. They spread out and Honest Tom found the guy standing in his pool room with four large duffel bags full of cash. There was a safe in the pool table that was open and clearly filled with more cash, and the guy had a sealed envelope that he tried to hand to Vernon.

As the other three marshals watched from outside the room they saw the envelope drop on the floor and heard the guy say "There's $10 million here and another 10 in the table safe. The combination to the safe is in the envelope along with the instructions for accessing another $200 million that's in a Cayman Island account. All you have to do is let me go out the back stairs and say that you just missed me. My secretary is prepared to swear that she distracted you just enough to make you miss me."

At that point a beautiful, completely nude womyn came out from a hidden door and moved toward Marshal Vernon. She said (there were three reliable witnesses to this, remember, one of whom was recording the whole thing) "I'll be glad to do whatever you want, Mr. Marshal, if you'll just let poor Jamie here go." She smiled at the poor marshal, who calmly said, "Sir, I'd like your sweater."

The banker smiled and said, "OK. It's cashmere, and we look like the same size." He peeled off the sweater and gave it to Honest Tom, who stepped up to the naked womyn and said, "Miss, please raise your arms over your head." The womyn complied and Marshal Tom Vernon dropped the sweater over her arms, mostly covering her nudity.

The banker said, "See, we aren't that different. I like putting cashmere on her so I can take it off. It spices up the sex afterward, doesn't it?"

Marshal Vernon said, "I wouldn't know sir, and as for us being not that much different, well, I'm not sure that we're from the same species."

With at least $20 million dollars there for the taking, and hundreds of millions more at his fingertips Honest Tom Vernon stepped up to the guy and said, "Please put your hands behind your back, sir. You're under arrest for international money laundering, money laundering, violation of the RICO statute and attempting to bribe a federal officer." The witnesses said the guy's jaw dropped open and he couldn't even talk.

The marshals' jaws dropped open when Vernon turned to the beautiful womyn and said, "Miss, please put your hands behind your back. You're under arrest for obstruction of justice, attempting to bribe a federal officer and attempted money laundering." The womyn looked at him and shot her hip out so that her lower body (and its artfully trimmed pubis) stuck out most provocatively and said, "Are you gay?"

"No, miss, just honest," Tom Vernon said as his fellow marshals fell apart laughing.

The incident might not have been as noteworthy except that when the Ponzi artist was being taken to the car to go to jail the press shouted out questions and he blurted out, "I offered the marshal $250 million and a naked babe to let me go and the dumb son of a bitch arrested me anyway! What's this world coming to?"

"Honesty, I hope," Marshal Vernon said quietly, but people heard him.

A legend was born. Some reporter did a story that called him "Honest" Tom Vernon, and the nickname stuck. Tom Vernon became an unwilling example of the virtuous lawman, kind of like a modern-day Melvin Purvis, or Eliot Ness.

Those sheriffs were in for the surprise of their lives, because U.S. Marshal Thomas J. Vernon was one tough dude, and the most honest man alive.

So we discussed that part of our operation for a few minutes when the intercom chimed and a voice said, "Director, the Department of Homeland Security debriefers are here."

"Very well," Nails said. "Wait three minutes and then send them in." She turned to us and said, "Do not share anything with them about our speculations or Badger Squad. There are a ton of good people at DHS, but they liaise very closely with the FBI, and we're too close to fucking blow it now. The Badger Squad will get that FBI mole and we'll get all the credit, which is a win-win for us. No slipups, OK?"

We all nodded and Nails got up and left. Less than a minute later the door opened and in walked our old friends Miss Bitchy Voice and Dreamboat. Marla Ahumada and Nate Jones didn't look any different than the last time we saw them, although MBV may have been even more beautiful than before.

We all stood up and shook hands, I introduced Kid Galahad, and then we all sat down. Assistant Director of Homeland Security Nathan "Dreamboat" Jones got right to it. He looked at all of us and said, "Officially this is a debriefing about the attack by the North Koreans on America's greatest city that took place today, conducted by myself and my intel chief. It's being conducted by DHS and not the FBI because we have first responsibility for defending the homeland, and because I lied to the Secretary and said that we had some compartmented information that we just couldn't share with the FBI yet. However, that isn't what today is actually about."

He looked at Miss Bitchy Voice and she said (yes, in that same bitchy voice we'd all come to know and love), "I came across something strange when I was looking at some pictures that showed a low-level North Korean agent we were tracking meeting with various people. I would have missed it, but our surveillance team noticed a significant amount of currency being transferred—the North Korean agent took some out to count it—so they took extra pictures, one of which showed the guy passing the cash full face. I recognized him as an FBI agent. I immediately thought that they were running him as a mole, or maybe just for low-level information, and I didn't want to step on anybody's toes, so I called my FBI counterpart to tell him that we had seen the money transfer and offered any assistance that I could.

"He hemmed and hawed for a minute, but finally told me he didn't know anything about it, but that he'd kick it up the chain and let me know. I didn't think anything else about it until the next day, when I got a call on my STE phone." She stopped to let us think about that for a minute. Secure Terminal Units are used with crypto-cards (codes that have to be shared between two STEs) and are completely secure landline communications devices (usually called telephones) that have to be physically invaded in order to hear what is being said—as long as you have the proper crypto-card, of course. Only very serious shit is talked about on STEs, which meant her call had been considered of vital importance to whoever made it.

"So I talked with the Assistant Director of the FBI, who politely told me that I was to butt out and stop the surveillance on the North Korean. He was nice, he took his time, and he never got even remotely worked up, but his intent was clear: what they were doing was above my pay grade, and it wouldn't be good for my career if I pursued this. I acknowledged that I understood and would stop any further inquiries immediately.

"The Deputy Director thanked me for my professionalism and praised me for taking the time to call, which he said saved a vital operation for the FBI and all Americans. He wasn't bombastic, but he made it clear that I'd just helped save the republic and could continue to do so by butting right the hell out. We hung up and I almost forgot about it, until three days later," MBV said.

"Somebody showed up to get the pictures," I said.

"Yes, and they weren't cleared high enough to get them, so I went to my boss," MBV said.

"And he told you to let 'em have the pics, because he'd just gotten a call from Director Harley," I said.

"Yes, which was really weird, since all they would have had to do was seal them in a carry bag and let my office time stamp it, then carry the pics back to the Hoover Building and give them to somebody who had clearance," Nate Jones said. He smiled and said, "Luckily Marla isn't a very good employee, certainly not when it comes to national security affairs."

MBV smiled, batted her lashes, and lowered her eyes in a great facsimile of humility and apology, but it didn't really work, since we all knew she was an egomaniac with serious SGITR (Smartest Guy In The Room, for those of you who aren't) tendencies.

"You kept copies," I said. That was a real no-no in the clandestine intelligence game—only those who needed to see high level pics got to see them, and if copies were made they were numbered and rigidly accounted for, even if they went to the president (probably especially if they went to the president—the White House isn't a great place for keeping secrets).

"I kept copies of three of the hundreds of pictures, because something didn't feel right to me. I shared them with Nate and we both decided that it bore further investigation, so I did some research, especially on the North Korean," MBV said. Her beautiful face lost most of its bitchiness and her voice became almost companionable.

"It didn't take me long to realize that this guy was not ever going to be part of any big-time op. He just didn't have it—he wasn't very smart, he didn't have any big-time contacts and he didn't have the rank for it—he was just a major. Basically he was a guy trying to gather intel on our agricultural capabilities going forward. In no way was he going to go up the food chain for some important job.

"Then I found some phone intercepts that seemed to be about the North Koreans attacking Wall Street. There were 13 calls between this low-level North Korean agent we'd been watching and a number that belonged to the FBI. I tracked the calls back to one office and to one agent in particular," MBV said. She paused and I decided to break the news that we already knew, so I said, "It was either Adam Smith or Tom Jones, probably working out of the office of FBI Executive Assistant Director for National Security Malcolm Sorenson."

Miss Bitchy Voice and Nate Jones both just gawked at me as my fellow agents laughed. Finally they both laughed, too, and MBV said, "Beaten by Jewey and Weasel, again!" Her eyes lit up and her laughter was genuinely happy. "It was Smith, by the way," Dreamboat said.

I said, "Sorry for stealing your thunder, but we just found out. If I promise to shut up while you talk will you share your conclusions with us?"

"Sure," Dreamboat said. "Marla?"

"We think that someone in the FBI, almost certainly EAD Sorenson or his chief of staff, is out to get you, Freak. We can't determine if it's just you, or if it's all of you, but someone wants your ass. Today's op wasn't about hitting Wall Street, although that's the way we want to play it. No, today's op was a straight out hit on you. We've already identified the three guys besides the North Korean agent and they aren't even from North Korean. Two of them were here from South Korea on green cards, and the fourth guy was an American citizen born in Hoboken, New Jersey," MBV said.

"We think that the green card guys were coerced by the North Korean agent, probably by threatening their families, and the American was bought off, probably with some of the FBI money we saw," Nate Jones said. "We have absolutely no motive for why the EAD for the FBI wants you dead, but it's almost certain that he does. We had several other possibilities, but given what we know we're certain it's Mal Sorenson."

So I told them what we were doing with the Badger Squad, and what we knew so far, and how we'd basically eliminated the other suspects. We talked for a bit about motive, but we still didn't come to any conclusions. Finally MBV said, "I'd like to coordinate with the Badger Squad if I could, because then we could do two separate investigations, and mine would be out in the open and clearly focused on *international* terrorism, which might obfuscate anything that the Badger Squad does."

"Having a smoke screen isn't the worst idea I've ever heard," I said.

"It'll let Jewey and Weasel operate completely under the radar, and it'll make it easier for all of us foot soldiers to run shit down, especially if they think we're working for you," Kid Galahad said, looking at MBV with a double twinkle in his eye. He liked the idea of hoodwinking the bad guys, and it was apparent that he liked the idea of Miss Bitchy Voice.

She apparently also liked the idea of the Kid, because she immediately said, "We might lose some IDs with your pictures on them, if we got everything you find out." She looked at me and I said, "Hey, fair's fair—we just need to make sure we're buried completely undercover so that those assholes don't catch a whiff, because I'm tired of being shot at and having people die."

"Well, I get that, and we're officially not talking about this. Marla and I will be the only people who know about it on our end, and I doubt if it'll go much past Nails on your end, right?" Nate Jones said.

"Plus we'll have an advantage in keeping them under surveillance," MBV said. "We can do it passively and they won't know a thing."

"How's that?" Jack Soo said.

"You guys have a secret weapon we don't know about?" Kid Galahad said.

"Is it a new stealth *spy* camera?" Mamba said. "I just love the idea of watching bad guys without them knowing it! It's so *Cold* War!"

I didn't say anything, but after a second I said, "MBV, *how* did you recognize the FBI agent who was delivering the cash to the North Korean agent? Also, do you have pictures of the two guys that Sorenson's been using to run his errands?"

She looked at Dreamboat, who said, "We have pictures of Smith, yes, but you won't need any pictures of Jones, because you'll know who he is as soon as you see him."

"Because he looks like you," I said. "He's your—?"

"Misbegotten little brother, who joined the FBI and fell in with the wrong crowd," Dreamboat said. "He's a good guy and a good agent, but he's easily led and not very smart. Mal Sorenson's a mover and shaker and has charisma, charm, and character to burn. He'd attract Tommie even if he wasn't an EAD, and my brother likes the idea of being the faithful sidekick—we found out when he took the Meyers-Briggs personality test that he's an SJ and really finds comfort in the structure of the FBI's organization."

"And because you're his big brother…" I said.

"He tells me everything, even classified shit that he's not supposed to," Dreamboat said. "I'll prime the pump and if his principal makes another move on you I'll hear about it, and soon thereafter you'll know, and right after that we'll arrest everybody involved, including my brother."

"That works for me. We get an advanced warning apparatus we can trust, as well as a legitimate smokescreen, all without having to expand the circle of who knows, which really enhances our operational security. We'll need to have a means of secure communication that doesn't raise any eyebrows, but I'm sure that we can work that out," I said.

"What if two of us were uh,...*seeing* each other?" MBV said. "That would mean that we could communicate whenever we wanted to without anyone the wiser."

"You mean fake a romantic attachment so that we can communicate? It's a great idea, but it'll be hard to accomplish, since most of us will be on the road, the Badger Squad is based in Chicago and you guys are based in DC," Jack Soo said.

"What if I were moved to Chicago, as part of our effort to decentralize the intel community at DHS?" MBV said.

"There's an effort to decentralize intel gathering in order to have independent sources and evaluation of information to verify its authenticity and accuracy? What a *great* idea!" Mamba said.

"It sure would make it easier to cross-reference shit and cut down on group-think," Jack Soo said. "It'll also keep it completely off the radar of the FBI once they realize the two people are *seeing* each other."

"So who are we going to get to fake a relationship?" I said, although I was pretty sure that I already knew the answer.

"I think we should—" MBV said. "Maybe we could—" Kid Galahad said. They looked at each other and I was sure what the answer would be, but I played along. The Kid said, "Ladies first, please." He smiled and made a royal wave giving MBV the floor, and she nodded at him and said, "Thank you, kind sir" in a plummy little voice that had nothing to do with her normal voice. "I just think that we ought to let that develop organically, once we get a grasp on the dynamics of our group," she said.

"That was almost exactly my point," Kid Galahad said. "We should simply see who's the most comfortable with each other and then let it unspool naturally."

"That way it'll look more plausible and natural to the FBI, if they should ever look," Miss Bitchy Voice said.

Nobody laughed, although by now everybody was aware of the sexual tension between MBV and Kid Galahad. After some strained silence Mamba said, "Well, *I* think it should be The Kid. If the chemistry for a putative romance doesn't work you can always fall back on your semi-gayness as an excuse and the two of you can just become BFFs. In that case you might have to swish it up a bit, Kid."

Kid Galahad smiled and said, "Well, that wouldn't be a problem for me, although I'm fairly sure that two mature adults can find some common ground, don't you Agent Ahumada?"

Miss Bitchy Voice swallowed hard and turned an attractive shade of pink before she said, "I, I, uh, I couldn't agree more, Agent Moerman." Her eyes were like limpid pools of brown toffee (sorry about that—I've always wanted to write a romance novel so I could use that kind of language. It won't happen again) as she stared at Kid Galahad, a slow smile beginning to spread across her beautiful face.

"Call me Kid," The Kid said.

"Only if you'll call me Marla," MBV said.

"Marla is a gorgeous name, filled with mystery and promise," The Kid said. (Hey, he said it, not me. I wasn't trying for romance novel language.)

"I can't wait to find out how you got your nickname," MBV said. "Wasn't there a boxer by that name, back in the 1940s?"

"There was, and the story is long but fascinating," The Kid said.

"Well, I'm sure we'll have plenty of time to discuss it once I'm in Chicago," Miss Bitchy Voice said, in a tone that was more purr than bitchy.

"You do get that we're still here, right?" Jack Soo said.

"You've got some drool on your chin, Kid," I said.

"I sure hope that you don't forget to report in between all of your—ahem—acting," Dreamboat said.

"I think that we could probably get a flight together as soon as tomorrow morning, if we really tried," Kid Galahad said, his eyes never leaving MBV's face.

"Oh, I'm sure we can," Miss Bitchy Voice said. "The only problem is that I won't have any place to stay once I'm there." She put on her best damsel in distress face and Kid Galahad said, "Well…"

"Oh, get a *room*," Mamba said, rolling his eyes along with the rest of US.

"Oh, we intend to," MBV said. "A *private* room."

"At my place," Kid Galahad said.

"Oh, goody," MBV said.

"We've created a *monster*!" Mamba said.

"A *love* monster!" Jack Soo said,

"It's like Romeo and Juliet," I said. "Except from the House of the Secret Service and the House of Homeland Security. Can such a pair of star-cross'd lovers bury their parents' strife with their love?" (My apologies to the Bard. I was just trying to show off in front of Dreamboat.)

"It's more like Godzilla and King Ghidora," Dreamboat said. "Let's just hope that nobody unleashes this force on the human race."

Nobody could really disagree with him. One of them was among the deadliest killers in the world (Kid Galahad) and one of them was an incredibly smart womyn who routinely matched wits with every terror organization on the planet—and won (Miss Bitchy Voice). Put them together and the synergy could be life threatening to anyone or anything that got in their path.

We were all glad they were on our side.

But in the end it turned out to be more like Romeo and Juliet, with blood and sacrifice and hideous loss, although nobody could have known it at the time.

CHAPTER 54

Hoods and Rednecks and Marshals, Oh My!

So Soper came to New York, the detail reacquainted itself, including with our new CoD, a 20-year Secret Service veteran named Henry "Dan'l" Boone, and we went on three trips before I got the call we were waiting for from Director Hessler. I swooped up Badass, Patsy and Buddha and we flew off to the airport in Lexington, Kentucky, where we met Thomas J. Vernon and his team of U.S. Marshals.

Honest Tom Vernon wasn't tall or big—about 5'7", 165—but he was a former collegiate wrestler who moved like a dancer and gave the impression of size because of his no-nonsense demeanor and his ramrod straight posture. The four marshals who worked with him were all cut from the same cloth, if not quite shaped the same. Brady Gates was a former collegiate track athlete, Jason Moyer was a Division II football player, Matt Shimel was a world class pole vaulter who'd just missed the Olympic team and Chris Bingaman was a former national champion wrestler who looked vaguely familiar. They were men whose intentions and attitudes were very much in line with their boss's: honest, morally incorruptible, and fierce, especially when it came to putting bad guys away.

Honest Tom had another squad of guys with him that he didn't introduce, except to say that they were his "Doormen," which we all took to mean that they knocked down doors when he needed them to. Since they were all approximately the size of a full-grown polar bear with shoulders like a water buffalo it wasn't hard to imagine them doing this.

I shook the legend's hand and said, "Marshal, I'm Agent Glinka Glickstien of the U.S. Secret Service. I've been looking forward to meeting you."

"Likewise, Agent Glickstien. May I suggest that you call me Tom for the duration of this op?" he said.

"Only if you'll call me Freak," I said.

"Freak?" Honest Tom said, his face and voice showing his confusion.

"Boss, they call her that because she's a freak of nature—don't get into a handshaking contest with her or you'll regret it," the marshal named Bingaman said. He was about 5'9", maybe 250, none of it fat, with white-blond hair, an easy grin, and a cauliflower ear. I finally realized where I remembered him from.

"Lake Superior State, right?" I said.

"Yeah," Bingaman said. "I saw you at the Midlands that year when our guy slammed you and you got up at the end of injury time to win." If a wrestler gets slammed to the mat without being able to protect themselves, or when they hit the mat before their opponent has a knee back down on the mat it's illegal. If that happens and they get can't continue due to injury the wrestler who did the slamming is disqualified and the slammee is declared the winner. I'd been hurt when the LSSU guy slammed me, but I got up and kept going, eventually pinning him in the third period.

His teammates gave him a raft of shit for slamming a girl, and then for getting pinned by a girl, which made victory even sweeter.

"How is old Samuels?" I said as I shook the marshal's hand.

"Still embarrassed because he got pinned by a girl, although after you took third in the D-I tournament he was a little less embarrassed. He's still an asshole, though." We all laughed and Honest Tom said, "We're going in with just the eight of us, because we're only arresting the sheriff and undersheriff, and we have the full support of the Morehead mayor and the city council. We'll also have an Assistant U.S. Attorney and her guys with us, but like you they're just observers. We don't anticipate any trouble, but if any breaks out you guys are supposed to get the hell out of there."

Honest Tom looked at everybody and then came back to me. I tried to look sincere when I said, "Right, at the first sign of trouble we get the hell out of there." My comrades were nodding when a big, slow smile formed on the U.S. Marshal's face. He gave a slight shake of his head and said, "Seeing as how that won't ever happen I just want to remind you not to shoot any of my guys, OK?"

"What about the U.S. Attorney and her guys?" Badass said.

"I couldn't give two shits about them," Honest Tom said.

"And now you know why they call him Honest Tom," Brady Gates said to general laughter.

"Seriously, we're fairly sure that these clowns are fine as long as they have their sheets and hoods, but are probably cowards when confronted by real authority. However, since nobody can look into the mind of another person, and since even cornered mice will bite, we're going in heavy. We'll send in the Doormen first with the rest of us right behind them. You guys and the AUSA will bring up the rear. Once we serve the warrant the Doormen will get these guys in the car and we'll take their computers and leave," Honest Tom said.

"What about the follow up investigation?" I said.

"Our investigators will be here by the time we take these guys down, assisted by Homeland Security personnel. The FBI wanted in, but apparently that's been nixed above my pay grade," Honest Tom said.

"Tom, I've got an idea about how we can take these guys down really cleanly, without any possibility of resistance or bother, and we can keep it out of the press for a while, too, which means we'll be able to have these *schmucks* in federal custody before anybody even misses them. You mind if I make a phone call?" I said.

"Well, I'd call them more like *schlemiels* than *schmucks*," Badass said.

"Wouldn't *schlub* be even more appropriate?" Buddha said. "I seem to remember that they were fat and exceedingly unattractive."

"Actually, you could also consider them *pishers*, although I suppose that *schlub* actually fits best," Patsy said.

"Fuck all of you *goys* and your Yiddish interpretations," I said. "I'm going to make that call."

Everyone was laughing when I left.

I called Curtis Jeffries. When he answered I said, "Curtis, it's Freak. Who's the one person in Morehead that the sheriff would have to respond to? Who's the one guy that he has to have to get elected?"

"Howdy, Freak. Well, there's two. If Jim Morris called him old DePuis would probably piss himself getting to the phone, because Jim owns about half the businesses in Morehead and gives that fatass more money than everybody else combined. The other person he can't get elected without is Lyle Farnsworth, the editor of the Morehead *News*," Curtis said.

"Which one of those guys would like to do a public service for the U.S. Marshals Service?" I said.

"Either one. Old Man Morris don't like old Ant, but he figures better the devil you know. Farnsworth don't like him, either, but the paper's endorsed him for three elections 'cause the guys they got to run against him was barely alive. Let me ask a question—are ya goin' to take him down?" Curtis said.

"Maybe," I said. "It's theoretically possible that we're taking the undersheriff down, too."

"OK. So there's two things here. First, Farnsworth's office is about a block from the Sheriff's Office, so you'd be too close to the department to really help. Old Man Morris's office is about five miles from the Sheriff's—clear on the other side of town. So if the plan was to get the sher'f and his undersher'f away from all their redneck brethren in order to arrest their sorry asses that'd be the place to do it," Curtis said.

"You said two things," I said.

"Well, the other thing is that the undersher'f, Colt Weaver, is one mean badass. He's a huge MMA fan and has fought in several high amateur contests down there. There's even been some talk of him going pro, so when you go to take him down make sure that y'all keep your guard up. They might also bring a guy named Hunsinger with 'em—you'll recognize him right away because he don't have a neck or a forehead. The sher'f likes to have old Hunsinger drive him around like he's a big-city po-leeceman, but really it's so he's got a bodyguard for his fat ass," Curtis said. "Even though Hunsinger ain't much of a bodyguard he is a big, dumb, mean asshole, so he fits with the sher'f and the undersher'f."

"Roger that, Curtis, and thank you. I can't comment on an ongoing investigation, but it's possible that we might have to get in contact with Mr. Morris and see if we can secure his cooperation. I appreciate your help, but I gotta run and see if I can get this set up, OK? Call ya later after we're done with our hypothetical takedown," I said.

"Well, if you want I can call Farnsworth and have him call Morris—between the three of us I'll bet we can cook up a way to get the Sher'f out to Morris's office by whenever y'all are getting here," Curtis said.

"So you know these guys?" I said.

Curtis laughed and said, "I played ball with Morris's sons, and I'm married to Farnsworth's oldest daughter. They know me, and like I said, they don't like old Ant, they just put up with him."

"OK, but not a word about the arrests until we've cleared town. We're looking at a two p.m. arrival—we'd like to be in and out by three at the latest," I said. "You can't tell anyone what's exactly going on, but you can intimate some of it."

"Oh, don't you worry 'bout that, Freak. Me and my father-in-law get along great, and old man Morris thinks I'm an honorable man. I'll arrange it and get back to ya ASAP," Curtis said.

"Acknowledged. We're leaving the Lexington airport right now, and if I don't hear from you before we're on the outskirts of Morehead I'll call you back," I said.

"Oh, it won't take that long," Curtis said. "I'll call ya within 15 minutes or so with the final details. Jeffries out."

I hung up and went back to the rest of the posse. I told Honest Tom what I was working on and he agreed it sounded like a good modification of the plan. We went out and loaded up in our cars—big Tahoes rented from Hertz—and sped off.

We were just turning into the rendezvous with the Assistant U.S. Attorney when Curtis called and said it was all arranged—everybody would be at Morris's office at two. He sent directions to my phone on the best way to get there and wished us luck.

"Thanks, and Curtis, I owe ya one," I said.

"Oh, hell no," he said. "Y'all got me into the Marshals in the first place, plus I got to have all that fun in Morehead before I left. If anything I still owe you. Call me and let me know how it turns out, willya?"

"Sure thing, but since Marshal Vernon and his squad are doing the takedown I don't think we need all that much luck," I said.

"Shit no—that there is the A-team, Freak. The only trouble you're gonna have is who has to speak to the press," Curtis said.

"Hey, it's his op, so he'll have to do the press," I said, laughing.

"Good one, Freak. Stick to your guns—I hear that he can be pretty persuasive about shit like that," Curtis said, laughing.

"Roger that. Freak out," I said.

I told everybody that it was all arranged, and Honest Tom Vernon said, "Good. If we do this right we'll even be able to avoid the press entirely. We'll also avoid any confrontation with this asshole's department, which is even better. I'll tell the AUSA and we'll go get these dumbass rednecks."

He climbed out of the Tahoe and went over to one of the black Suburbans. A womyn that looked like a rhino stepped out, dwarfing him. They talked for about two minutes, then she nodded and got back in her ride. Honest Tom came back and said, "I like working with smart people."

"The AUSA on board?" I said.

"Her name is Brenda T. Green and she's more than on board—she got it right away, and thinks it's great we got away from any kind of population center, because that way if he resists there will be less chance of hitting any civilians if we have to blow him away. Her people will take perimeter security while we go in—and remember not to shoot any of my guys," Honest Tom said.

"You worked with her before?" I said.

"Don't worry—she's the finest kind. She isn't afraid of anything, has one of the sharpest legal minds I've ever seen and is totally committed to taking down bad guys, especially if they're corrupt asshats like these clowns," Honest Tom said. "And what's the first rule of this op?"

"Don't shoot any of your guys," we all said. "Right—and I'll buy the Pepsis on this one," Honest Tom said. "It should go smooth as silk."

But when we got to the offices of James Morris, Industrialist (hey, that's what his sign said—it's not my fault if some guys have delusions of grandeur) there were five sheriff's cruisers there, plus a big old Mercury Marquis that was clearly the chief's vehicle—it was painted as gold as a Notre Dame football helmet, and had "Sheriff Anthony Livernois DePuis, Sheriff of Rowan County, Kentucky" painted on both sides in bright scarlet paint. It also had "Brilliantly Protecting and Serving the Citizens of Rowan County, Kentucky for 13 Years" painted on the hood and trunk in the same scarlet paint. There were also American flags, side-mounted sirens, four shotguns in a rack in the front seat and the motto "All violators will be prosecuted" stylishly painted across the rear window.

"What the hell kind of sheriff would ride around in that monstrosity?" Brady Gates said.

"An inept asshat one with serious self-esteem issues?" Patsy said.

"More likely one with a teeny-tiny weenie," Buddha said.

"Or one who likes teeny-tiny weenies," Badass said.

"Are you implying that the good sheriff might be a closet homosexual?" Chris Bingaman said.

"That thing would sure attract kids, especially boys," Jason Moyer said.

"Only if they had bad eyesight," I said. "Otherwise it might make you blind."

"There is that," Buddha said.

"It just makes me want to arrest this guy more," Honest Tom said. "A yahoo who's colluding with the Ku Klux Klan *and* drives something like that? 'Brilliantly' protecting his county? I've read this shitkicker's file—and I'll bet you that this is the only time Ant DePuis and brilliant have ever been used together in a sentence."

We all laughed and Honest Tom said, "OK, back to plan A. We're going in really heavy—Doormen with weapons drawn, along with Brady, Jason and all the Secret Service personnel except Freak."

I looked at him and Honest Tom said, "I've read your file, too—I'm well aware of how you shoot, but I also know you're probably better at unarmed takedowns than Chris and I, and we're really, really good. He and I are going to get the sheriff cuffed while you hold off the undersheriff if necessary. As soon as we've got DePuis hooked up you'll take care of the sheriff while Chris and I hook up the undersheriff. Then we bust it out of there so the AUSA can serve the warrants and scare the shit out of his remaining deputies. We'll exfiltrate straight to the county line and then get to the Lexington airport ASAP, where the Justice Department will have a jet waiting for the marshals so we can take these boys to Louisville, where they're going to be arraigned. I don't know where everybody else is going, but I know that you're not going with us—and I'm not trying to be rude about that."

"OK, let's go get these motherfuckers," I said.

"Concur," Honest Tom Vernon said. We got out of the Tahoes, got ourselves arranged and marched right into Jim Morris's office. The Doormen went right through the reception area to the door where four Rowan County deputies stood with shotguns cradled in their arms. With their creds in one hand and their pistols in the other the lead one said, "U.S. Marshals Service. Put down the weapons NOW." His voice was a deep, commanding bass, and the way he emphasized his words made it almost a certainty the deputies would obey him (I was reminded of the Bene Gesserit using the Voice in Frank Herbert's great *Dune* series—if you haven't read the books you should).

Facing armed, imperious federal marshals apparently wasn't the same as facing terrified people with a white hood over your head, because they couldn't put the shotguns down fast enough.

The Doormen kicked the shotguns away, forced the deputies to move aside and swept open the doors to Jim Morris's office. Honest Tom took his squad right into the office, his creds open and his pistol in his hand but held down to his side.

There were six men in uniform in the room, and two more in suits. Four of the men in uniform moved to intercept the squad, but Gates, Bingaman, Shimel and Moyer just zeroed right in on them, putting their pistols right in the faces of the four deputies. The deputies moved away like sheep, huddling in a corner of the office like they were waiting to go to the market. I moved Buddha up to help and Marshal Bingaman detached himself and came back to Honest Tom's side.

"I'm U.S. Marshal Thomas J. Vernon. I'm serving federal arrest warrants for one Anthony "Ant" DePuis and one Colton Weaver," Honest Tom said, staring at the two men left in uniform. He stepped up to the sheriff and said, "Anthony "Ant" DePuis, you are under arrest for the murders of Josephine Boroviak Soper, Elvin Clyde Bliss, Andrea Rogers and Tara Waters." Tara Waters was one of Soper's volunteers who died in intensive care after the crash in Morehead. "You are also under arrest for 35 counts of attempted murder, inciting a riot, assault with intent to commit great bodily harm and conspiracy to commit murder." Honest Tom drew breath to finish his spiel, but before he could finish DePuis said, "Y'all cain't arrest me 'cuz Ah am the law in Rowan County. Ah don't recognize them federal warrants as valid here in mah county." He crossed his fat arms and looked at Honest Tom like a smug toad. The undersheriff just stared off into space, his ugly mug twisted into a disdainful smirk.

The instant was shattered by a bullhorn voice that said, "Nobody gives a shit if you recognize federal warrants or not, Ant. They're legal, and I got the firepower to enforce 'em, so shut the fuck up, you troglodyte."

Everyone stared at the speaker, Assistant U.S. Attorney Brenda T. Green. She was 6'3", 240, a rhino with intelligence. Her voice would have fit a Gunnery Sergeant during Marine Basic Training, as would her belligerence.

Her sparkling eyes bored right into Ant DePuis's, making him squirm, and she said, "Marshal Vernon, arrest that country shitkicker's ass right now, or I'll be forced to walk over and kick his fat ass."

Honest Tom and Chris Bingaman moved in on the sheriff. Honest Tom said, "Sir, please put your hands behind your back" and before DePuis could react Bingaman twisted his right arm up, clapped the iron on that wrist and smoothly completed the process with his left wrist. Once he was cuffed Bingaman nodded at me and I holstered my 1076 as I went to take charge of the sheriff.

Then all hell broke loose.

The ugly undersheriff, Colt Weaver, saw me clearly for the first time and let out an enraged bellow. He was bounding toward me before anyone could react, screaming "I'll punch your tits off!" over and over.

I calmly awaited his rush with my hands spread palm up at shoulder height, like I didn't know what to do. Weaver threw his first punch when he wasn't quite in range, almost jumping off the floor to get at me. It was a wicked punch, with 200 plus pounds of muscle and trained MMA fighter behind it, and it hit me dead center between my tits. I went down like I'd been struck by lightning as everyone started screaming and rushing toward us.

And I came up with Weaver's right hand firmly caught in a claw grip. I rotated his hand counter-clockwise as I popped fully to my feet and placed my left knee right on the point of his elbow. I released my left hand from the claw grip and firmly pushed his arm forward toward his head, gripping his hand in an *aikidō* grip.

I looked down at where his face was mashed into the floor and said, "If you move at all your shoulder and elbow will dislocate. If you understand please tap the floor three times with your left hand." I waited five seconds and he didn't tap, so I moved his arm forward a tad more, at which point he began tapping with great vigor. I eased off on his arm and said, "Colton Weaver, you are under arrest for the murder of Josephine Boroviak Soper, Elvin Clyde Bliss, Andria Rogers and Tara Waters, as well as assorted other counts for attempted murder, conspiracy to commit murder, inciting a riot and any other charges that are extant."

Honest Tom moved in to cuff the undersheriff, but I just held out my hand for the cuffs. He gave them to me and I put one side on, then bent down and grabbed his left wrist. Weaver struggled, not wanting me to get his arm off the floor, but I controlled him like he was a baby. Without any apparent effort or strain I pulled his wrist off the floor and cuffed the still struggling undersheriff's hands behind his back. I stood up and used his cuffed hands to snatch Weaver to his feet. I spun him around and said, "Try to punch my tits off now, ya twerp."

I give him credit. Even with his hands cuffed Colt Weaver was game—he tried to snap kick me in the face. Unfortunately for him I had seen the move before. I stepped on his left foot as I moved inside the kick and lifted his leg so he was doing the horizontal splits. At the same time I let my left fist, which had been cocked at my waist, fly toward his exposed crotch.

It stopped less than an inch from his balls.

Weaver's eyes flew wide open when he realized how close the punch had come to shattering his world forever (unlike in the movies, when someone punches your cookies to mush you stop fighting immediately, often because you need an orchidectomy (orchiectomy)—yeah, that means you need a testicle removed). He looked down at my fist and back up at me and all the fight went out of him. I said, "You're welcome, Mr. Weaver. Now stop behaving like a horse's ass, or next time I won't hold up. Are we clear?"

Colt Weaver swallowed hard and said, "Uh, yes, ma'am, we're clear. Sorry for the trouble."

"No trouble," I said. I let his leg down and turned him over to Marshal Bingaman. "Y'all stop any resistin'," Weaver said to the rest of the deputies in the room.

"We ain't jist gonna give up," Sheriff DePuis said.

"Ant, don't be an idjit. If she hadn't a stopped that punch it woulda went through my nuts and come outta my back. She also picked me up off the floor with one hand—I weigh 209, Ant, and she lifted me up like I was a feather. Ain't no use resistin' when the other side's got a warrior like that— all we gonna do by fighting back is get ourselfs all fucked up." Colt Weaver looked at me and said, "Sorry about being a stupid shit, ma'am, and sorry about the salty language."

"Apology accepted, Undersheriff Weaver. Let's all go to the cars now, OK?" The Doormen came in, took the two soon-to-be former lawmen out and put them in the Tahoes. Everybody holstered their weapons and Honest Tom Vernon said, "Freak, I'd work with you any day. Well done with the prisoner." He shook my hand, as did the AUSA, Brenda T. Green. She said, "I've never seen anything like that, Agent Glickstien. Just how strong are you?" It sounded like a challenge, but before I could answer Badass said, "That's classified ma'am, and you really don't want to find out the hard way."

"I saw her rip the doors off a tour bus without any effort at all," Buddha said.

"I saw her do the same thing to a seat in that bus," Patsy said.

"And I saw her carry three wounded soldiers out of a combat zone while still shooting at the enemy with such devastating effect that they stopped chasing her," Badass said, "and no, I'm not going to be any more specific than that, because the rest of the story is classified."

"I once picked up a mule on a bet," I said.

"What the fuck? A mule? Where was that?" Brenda T. Green said.

"Classified," Badass and I said. "My Pepsis, Freak," Badass said. He said to Green, "Believe me when I tell you that you're punching above your weight on this one. If everybody in this room jumped on her simultaneously there's a chance we could stop her, but God help whoever got there first."

"Well, I'm a large old fellow who was counted as strong in his youth, but even on my best day I couldn't've lifted a struggling 210-pound man straight off the floor with one hand," Jim Morris said. I hadn't noticed his size, but when he stood up from his desk he was 6'7", 285, with big arms and hands and not much fat on him yet, despite his grey hair and lined face. He stepped around the desk and shook my hand, squeezing hard to test me.

I squeezed back at about half pressure and Morris increased his grip, so I just bore down and ground his bones together without doing any permanent damage. The old giant said, "Uncle, Agent, uncle," so I released my grip. Old Man Morris smiled and said, "I never met a person in my whole life who could win a grip contest with me—you're the strongest human being I've ever met, Agent. Well done." He nodded to me and Honest Tom said, "Mr. Morris, thank you for letting us use your office for this arrest. It helped alleviate any possible pressure and made sure that Sheriff DePuis's whole department didn't try to resist us. Thank you." He shook Morris's hand, as did the AUSA.

"No need to thank me, Marshal Vernon. I'm as civic minded as the next guy, and I surely didn't like that the Ku Klux Klan tried to kill a presidential candidate in my town, even if I won't vote for her. Makes the whole town, hell, makes the whole *county* look bad, when in fact Morehead and Rowan County are pretty swell places. I supported old Ant before—lesser of two evils—but I can't look past something like this. I was glad to help."

"And I'm the reason he brought the extra deputies with him, so you can blame me if you want," the other guy in the room said. "Lyle Farnsworth, editor and publisher of the Morehead *News*." We all shook hands and Farnsworth said, "Well, my son-in-law told me I might get a show and I surely did. How much of this can I write about?"

"All of it," Honest Tom said, "as soon as we leave the jurisdiction. We want to be clear of Rowan County before anyone even gets word we've been here."

"Fair enough," Farnsworth said. "About those extra deputies—I told Ant that Jim and I were concerned about the notion that the Klan was active in Rowan County again and he must've figured something was up, which is why he brought all of the deputies he trusted with him." Farnsworth stopped talking and his face screwed up like he was trying to remember something. He turned to Morris and they both said, "Where's Hunsinger?"

We'd forgotten that Curtis told us the sheriff's right-hand man was a brute named Hunsinger, and that the guy was always with him—but he wasn't here now.

Fuck a duck.

I turned and sprinted for the entrance to the office while screaming at the top of my lungs for the marshals who were putting the prisoners in the Tahoes. I hit the door without slowing down, knocking it completely off its hinges and my 1076 leapt into my hand. All the marshals had their guns out, and Honest Tom was yelling at his guys to go as I scanned for targets.

I found one. There was a gun barrel and the front part of a scope on a roof of a three-story building about 50 yards from the office. The shooter was tucked back out of sight behind the wall of the building, so the barrel and scope were the only targets. It must have looked like magic as I processed all of this in under a second and my 1076 barked once, then again.

My first shot hit the scope, shattering it, and my second shot hit the hand holding the stock of the rifle that was exposed when the shooter was rocked forward by the force of the Cor-Bon 165 jacketed hollow point round as it destroyed the scope. The second shot elicited a scream from the roof as the rifle flew end over end and fell down out of the sky.

The marshals had screamed the Tahoes out of the street and toward the highway before I was done shooting, while my fellow Secret Service agents were entering the building where the shooter was and Brenda T. Green was bellowing "Go get that guy!" to her squad. I sprinted over to support the rest of my team, but by the time I got to the building (about 4.5 seconds for the 50-yard dash, according to witnesses) Badass, Buddha and Patsy were already coming down with a prisoner who was cradling a ruined hand.

It was Hunsinger—no forehead, no neck and no brains, since he thought that if he shot the lead marshal his guys would escape and "just melt into the background of Rowan County" (an exact quote from the evil genius himself—I was surprised that he could articulate such a thought, but I'm pretty sure he was just aping the sheriff). Apparently that had been the heroic plan of Ant DePuis and his brilliant deputy Colt Weaver. Somehow they thought that if they killed one federal officer that the rest would just quit, which I guess was about right for three guys with the combined IQ of a rutabaga.

Once the ambulance came and took Hunsinger away to the hospital (AUSA Brenda T. Green sent two guys with him to keep him from escaping, which would have been pretty difficult with his left hand blown to pieces by a nice jacketed bullet) we waited for the Justice Department investigative team. While we sat there at least five Rowan County deputies thanked us for arresting DePuis and Weaver, and they all commented that they had never seen shooting like mine. I thanked them, as well as thanking all of the Justice Department guys who'd also complemented me.

Finally Brenda T. Green couldn't stand it anymore. She snorted and said, "OK, let's get something straight. No way do I believe that you intended to shoot the scope, or that you hit his hand on purpose with the second shot. Admit it—you were lucky. I'm not complaining, I'm just tired of the hero worship and pretending that anyone can do that kind of shooting."

My pals all smiled and Badass said, "You own your own House in D.C.?"

The AUSA looked puzzled. "What the fuck does that have to do with anything?" she said.

"Do you own your own home, or are you a condo girl?" Badass said. He poured on the charm as he looked at her with his cornflower blue eyes.

She said, "I own my House and two others in D.C. My dad was a real estate guy, and when he died I inherited them. What the fuck does that have to do with this?"

Badass said, "I'll bet you my paychecks for the next 20 years that Freak can beat anyone you can find to shoot against her at any distance, using any handgun known to man."

"I'll take some of that action," Patsy said. "The deed for one of your Houses against 20 years of pay?" He smiled sweetly at her as Buddha said, "I'd also like to take that bet, only I'll sweeten the pot. I'll give you my trust fund plus 20 years of pay if Freak misses any shot at anything that is in range of a handgun."

AUSA Brenda T. Green looked at me in amazement, and I smiled like a shark and said, "As long as I can check the rounds before we shoot, I'll take any of those bets. Hell, I'll even do your laundry for 20 years if you want."

The AUSA was a smart womyn, and she knew that she was being hustled, so she said, "You actually hit what you were aiming for?"

I said, "Well, I hit the scope exactly as planned, but you're right, I missed my target on the second shot."

"I knew it—no way you hit his hand like that on purpose," she said.

"I was aiming for his thumb, but he jerked while the bullet was in the air," I said. Her face looked like she'd was having gastric distress and we all laughed, even Brenda T. Green. She looked at me and said, "So you're really that good?"

"I am," I said. "I don't know why, but when I entered the Marine Corps it turned out I had this gift. I trained with some of the best handgun experts in the world, and I was better than every one of them. I know, because they all said 'You're better than me', especially after we'd shot at long range. My *zayde* always used to say "It ain't bragging if you can do it," and believe me, I can. I once shot a guy at 125 yards with a handgun and hit dead on—right in the eye—which was exactly where I was aiming."

"Where were—" Brenda T. Green said, but my whole gang said "Classified," after which we all cracked up again. We told some more stories, the Justice Department investigators arrived, everybody gave statements and we all loaded up to head back to the Lexington airport.

As we were getting in the cars Brenda T. Green said, "You guys ever need anything, you let me know. Without your help we could've had a catastrophe today, so I owe ya."

"Just put those dimwitted shitheads away so that we can get some closure about this whole incident. Soper needs to know that the people who plotted to kill Josie are going away, and so do we. Andria Rogers was the finest kind of boss, and a damned good agent who gave her life to save her principal, and Elvin Clyde Bliss was a keeper, a thoughtful guy who actually thought about stuff, and Tara Waters was working for candy bars and chicken out of a paper bucket for someone she believed in," I said.

"Without being at all rude, what Freak is trying to say is do your job and put these motherfuckers where they belong—in a cage," Badass said.

"Bet your ass I'm going to put them away, and maybe get the sheriff the needle, too," Brenda T. Green said.

"Oh, don't do that," Buddha said.

"We'd much rather see him suffer for years in Marion Federal Prison," Patsy said.

"That way we can send him a picture of all the people he killed every year he's in there, and maybe even visit him from time to time, just to rub it in," I said.

"Consider it done," Brenda T. Green said, her square block of a face lighting up in an evil smile. "See ya when you come to testify." She slammed the doors and we were whisked off to the airport, where we caught a flight back to D.C. to catch up with Soper.

It's a fact that at least one of us visited those country shitkickers in Marion every year until they were all were dead. Usually it was a bunch of us and we always rubbed it in...and that still never stopped the pain we felt from the people we'd lost.

But it did help an awful lot.

CHAPTER 55

Emerald City Calling, Freak

So back we went on the campaign trail. We were there with Soper as she charmed her way across America. We were there when she finished third in Iowa, and second in New Hampshire. We were there when she finished last in South Carolina and Nevada. We were there when she finished third overall on Super Tuesday, but fell further behind in the delegate count. We slogged along through Louisiana, Maine, Michigan, Florida, Illinois, North Carolina, and Washington. Soper never finished higher than second, or lower than fourth, and she won in Wisconsin, but it was apparent that she wasn't going to be able to compete much longer—her delegate count put her in third place behind a sitting U.S. Senator and a 12-term Congressman who was the current governor of Ohio—and her money was drying up.

Oddly enough, the kiss of death came in New York, during a debate about the economy. Under the "debate" (don't get me going about how much these exercises weren't actual debates) format the fourth-place guy, a rich businessman from Florida, got to ask any of the other candidates a question. He chose Soper with this question: Will you absolutely promise to not raise taxes on the middle class?

Remember that this womyn had a PhD in economics and had been a great governor of the largest state by population in the union. She'd asked her legislature to raise taxes twice, in order to rebuild California's infrastructure (the state's economy had boomed) and again to solve the California water problem by building desalinization plants that doubled as wind farms and solar power collectors (the state's economy boomed again). Both of these tax increases were designed to be temporary, but were so successful that California residents voted three times to not cut their taxes when the provisions expired. California was now exporting water to Nevada, Utah, New Mexico, eastern Oregon and North Dakota, and they were supplying electricity to the entire west coast thanks to the new technology the desalinization plants had spurred.

So Soper gave her standard answer. "No president has the power to raise taxes—that's a congressional power, found in Article One, Section Seven, Clause One of the Constitution. Further, good management principles tell us that no chief executive of any entity should ever promise not to do something that may become a necessity. Since no one can see the future, the need to raise taxes for repairing infrastructure, or defense, or education is always a possibility, and a good president will leave her options open on that subject, even though, as I said, that is a congressional power."

If she thought a candidate hadn't answered the question asked the moderator was allowed to press for an answer, and apparently the bubble-headed blonde from Fox News didn't get what Soper had so clearly and succinctly said, so she said, "Ms. Soper, you never actually answered the question. Will you categorically exclude raising taxes on the middle class?"

Soper looked at the moderator, pursed her lips and said, in a voice as patient as someone talking to a three-year old, "As I said, that power is exclusive to Congress, but no, I will not categorically exclude my asking for higher taxes on all classes of Americans, should the need arise due to unforeseen circumstances."

By now even the guy who asked the question was satisfied with Soper's answers, but the clueless moderator wanted to hammer home her point for the intellectually deficient among us, so she said "So you *would* raise taxes on the middle class?"

Soper's face showed iron control as she paused before saying, "As I said, presidents categorically *cannot* raise taxes, since the Constitution grants Congress that right exclusively. Once again I will say this: good management practices require chief executives to keep their options open and not close any doors, so the need to raise taxes on all Americans is theoretically possible, given the uncertainty of the future."

"But you won't make it clear about your position on taxing the middle class, or pledge not to do so?" the moronic moderator said, clearly believing that she was somehow in the middle of a major "gotcha!" moment.

Soper finally lost it. Her face got red, she began to tremble and her eyes glittered like diamonds. She gripped the lectern and said, "Where did you go to college?"

The moderator said, "Why is that important?"

"Because I have nieces and nephews," Soper said, "and I don't want them to waste their money." The moderator didn't get it as fast as the audience did, so she said, "Waste their money on what?"

"A degree from wherever you graduated from." As the moderator got her outrage on Soper pulled out her cell phone and mimed answering a call. She held the phone out and said "It's for you from East BFE University—they want their degree back."

"Well, I never!" the moderator said. "I'm totally insulted!"

"Actually, you're insulting, you idiotic twit. If you didn't understand what I said than you must have the IQ of a kumquat. People in Hunan province in China got it, and most of them don't speak English." Soper said.

It went downhill from there.

Soper never recovered from the debate, even though she was right. Even her opponents came to her defense, with the front-running senator saying her answer couldn't have been more clear, but the Fox News position was that the candidate had been "unclear on her position on taxes, but insulting to the American people with her rhetoric toward the moderator, while the headline in the New York *Post* was "Lesbian Candidate Insults Middle Class; Compares Them to Chinese peasants."

And that was the nice one.

After the dust settled and the primary was over Soper decided to call it quits. She'd finished fourth in New York due to her outburst (another reason that I could never be in politics, because I would've bitch-slapped that pea-brained moderator until her hair went back to its original color) and her funding just dried up. She talked to everybody around her—including all of us, who she'd come to think of as family—and then we flew to Pasadena, California.

She announced that she was withdrawing from the race at Stanford University, giving all of the standard political bullshit reasons every candidate uses, and then she announced that she was taking a position in the economics department at Stanford. Surrounded by her three brothers and four sisters, as well as her nieces and nephews, Soper thanked everybody involved with the campaign, including the United States Secret Service, and then she walked off the stage and back into private life.

We all stood around her for the last time and she shook all of our hands, thanking everybody individually for their hard work and dedication. I was last and she said, "Freak, if you guys ever need anything, anything at all, and I can help you in any way just call me. I owe you my life, and I also owe you for trying to save Josie. I, I don't have many close friends, but I'd be honored if you guys would consider yourselves my friends."

"Well, I don't know," El Gato said. "We Hispanic Catholics aren't supposed to like you non-Catholic lesbians. Aren't you a danger to the social fabric?"

"And doesn't same-sex marriage directly undermine the family?" Buddha said.

"Plus, you lesbians hog all the cute girls," Bumble said. "We straight guys get pretty pissed about that."

"I don't know if I can be friends with a damned tax-raising, socialist-leaning lesbo who picks on poor debate moderators," Badass said. "Plus I agree with Bumble—you get too many of the good-looking wymyn."

"And don't forget that you called middle class Americans dumb as kumquats," Ed said.

"And compared them to Chinese peasants in Hunan province who don't speak English," Flipper said.

"And you're really a bitch in the morning before you have your coffee," Patsy said.

"Fuck you guys," Soper said as we all burst into laughter. There were hugs all around and then we flew home to D.C., while Soper went to be chair of the Stanford economics department.

While we'd been campaigning with Soper the Badger Squad had been digging and digging at the FBI mole. They had enough evidence to at least know who it was, but they had no idea why I was on his shit list, and they couldn't trace the money for the two enforcer agents back to him. In fact, the money was causing all sorts of consternation among the Badgers, because it didn't seem to come from anywhere connected to anybody in this case.

As Joe told me when Soper was campaigning in Chicago, the money "just started appearing in their accounts like it had been transported from the starship *Enterprise*." These were the best minds in the world at tracing the path of money and they kept coming up empty. It wasn't because EAD Malcolm Sorenson didn't have money or multiple accounts—he was from old money and could've dropped multiple millions and probably not noticed—but there was just no connection they could find.

Jewey and Weasel even took the chance of sending Gomer and Mamba into the bad guys' bank to check that the money hadn't been deposited in cash, but of course it wasn't, because then there definitely would've been a paper trail.

No such luck. It turned out that the money had been deposited in $5000 increments over the course of two years, coming from five different offshore banks. There was nothing hinky about the deposits—they were just like thousands of other transactions that went on every day.

After a year and a half of digging Director Hessler ordered the Badger Squad to submit its final report and go dormant. The report inaccurately confirmed that the entire fiasco in Morehead was due to the Ku Klux Klan and its local leaders, Rowan County Sheriff Anthony DePuis and Undersheriff

Colton Weaver. This closed the matter for the public and apparently for the mole, who bought the bogus report and reported to someone at the end of a burner phone line that "everything's copasetic."

It was the only time the two burners were used, and that was literally the only thing said on the line: "Everything's copasetic." No salutations on either side, no chitchat, no goodbye—nothing to identify the other party or EAD Mal Sorenson. The only reason we knew it was Sorenson was because he was still under electronic surveillance by the Badger Squad at the time.

This left all of us wondering who he was calling, and why he had to let them know that our report confirmed what everybody else's said. Director Hessler ordered the Badger Squad to overtly stand down and disband, but to covertly keep tabs on Sorenson, both electronically and eyes-on when possible. The Badger Squad was most disgruntled, but they complied, except for Weasel, who made absolutely no effort to hide the fact that he was tracing the money for the two enforcers back to EAD Sorenson.

Which led to another odd thing: the two agents didn't do anything with the money except let it earn interest in their savings accounts, which made no sense at all. They didn't even put it in CDs or tax-free bonds—they just left it in the bank to do absolutely nothing.

It drove Weasel crazy, and Jewey, too, so they took to having "Badger Weekends," where they ordered takeout, drank gallons of Pepsi and dug like crazy on Sorenson, Smith and Jones. The two best electronic wizards I'd ever seen couldn't find anything at all connecting the money to Sorenson, Smith and Jones, or anything connecting Sorenson to anyone else who was in on the plot.

They didn't find any record of Sorenson sending the two agents to Morehead, just that someone in his office made a call to them three days before the attack.

Like so many other cases we *knew* that EAD Sorenson had a part in the Morehead attack, we *knew* that he'd funneled money to the agents who helped precipitate the attack and we *knew* that Smith and Jones had been sniffing around to find out if we suspected anything except the KKK connection, but we didn't have anything that could be remotely considered evidence in a court of law. In short, we were fucked unless we could come up with something tying one of these disparate parts directly to another, and we were severely hamstrung because we had to try and do it in secret.

We hoped that the interrogation of Ant DePuis and Colt Weaver would give us something more to go on, but that would take time, and life went on…and so did we.

We were all reassigned back to the D.C. field office, and Director Hessler ordered that we all be assigned to the general protection pool. Everybody went off to guard whoever was in town and needed it. Badass, Flipper and I got to guard President Ellen Johnson Sirleaf of Liberia when she came to visit the outgoing president (she was a real hoot—that lady knew how to party without using anything but her charm, intelligence and sense of humor). Patsy, Buddha, Ed and I got to guard President Tsai Ing-wen of Taiwan when she came to New York to meet with U.S. investors (and Sarah was assigned to Adele Winetraub, the U.S. Trade Representative, who wasn't officially at the meeting but may have "dropped by" for a chat—ain't international relations fun?).

All of us were called on when the Pope came to the United Nations to address the General Assembly about worldwide poverty (among other things). We agreed that we'd probably convert to Catholicism if we could guarantee that the Pope would be someone like Pope Francis. He was genuinely good, he had a great sense of humor (you should have seen him when a lady gave him her baby to bless and the kid puked all over him—he laughed and commented in English that "this kind of behavior is how some of the cardinals feel about me being Pope") and his honest love of the people who greeted him might have been the most sincere thing I've ever seen. Oh, and those guys in the funny uniforms who guard the Pope when he's in the Vatican? They're the Swiss Guard, and you should not ever fuck around with them, because those guys are incredibly professional bodyguards who are as good as the Secret Service.

I didn't get to go, but Badass and Flipper were on the detail for the Dali Lama when he came to New York, Philadelphia and Boston, and Ed, Flipper, Buddha, Sarah and I were all assigned to Malala Yousafzai's detail when she came to Detroit for the International Conference on Wymyn's Rights to an Education. It was incredible to think that Malala was only in her twenties and had already won the Nobel Prize and founded a university. She was one of the most polite young wymyn I've ever met, as well as being genuine and true to her cause.

Oh, yeah, we changed presidents during that time, too. Republican Senator James Sheehan of Michigan defeated Democratic Senator Orville Redamacher (not the popcorn guy—that was Orville Redenbacher) of Oregon 278 electoral votes to 260 electoral votes to keep the White House for the Republicans.

The race was tight, mainly because both guys ran a clean campaign and refused to smear each other, but it really turned on Washington State, where Sheehan beat Redamacher by less than 500 votes. There were grumblings of election fraud because the senator from next-door Oregon was ahead by 10 percent in the polls the day before the election, and there were some weird power surges in Seattle and Olympia, which were heavily Democratic, but after a re-count that was mandatory under Washington law Redamacher himself put a stop to the grumbling by conceding, telling the country that "I am satisfied that the voting was done properly and fairly, and that I have lost the great state of Washington to my friend President-elect James Sheehan."

The shifting of Washington's 12 electoral votes from Sheehan to Redamacher would've changed the election—it would've been 272—266 Redamacher, making him president—but everyone from the Federal Election Commission to the losing candidate agreed that the election was fair and legal, so James Sheehan became the first elected president from the great state of Michigan (remember that President Gerald Ford was appointed by President Nixon after Spiro Agnew resigned over a tax scandal).

It wasn't really a surprise that Sheehan won. He was young, good-looking, a Heisman Trophy winner at the University of Michigan, a two-time Super Bowl winning quarterback with the Chicago Bears, a great public speaker and a governor and senator of impeccable reputation and some accomplishment (he finally fixed the Flint water problem caused by former Governor Rick Snyder and his emergency managers, which made him beloved by both Republicans and Democrats in the Wolverine State). President Sheehan was also married to a beautiful (if really bitchy—trust me, you'll find out why later) womyn named Laura Flagler Sheehan; they had two gorgeous daughters named Allison (12 years old) and Brooke (10 years old), little blondes who were clearly going to drive the boys crazy (Allison had bottle green eyes that already knew about the world; Brooke was blue eyed and had one of those precious heart-shaped faces with a pug nose that made her look like a fashion model at age 10).

In short, James Sheehan and his family looked perfect, and they'd been through the most rigorous vetting process in history, so it was a certainty that they were perfect. It was also a certainty that the family had helped the president get elected, especially the cute little girls who made cute little signs for their daddy that said things like "Our hero" and "Our daddy loves puppies" and lots of other stuff that would've made you gag if the girls weren't so goddamned cute. The president's wife was a former college nursing instructor who had a very sharp tongue that she wasn't afraid to use on anyone who tried to denigrate her husband.

The other thing that helped the president win the election was his running mate, former FBI Assistant Director Mitchell Holland, who the president picked to shore up his lack of foreign policy experience, which was his only real weakness.

Former Assistant Director Holland proved to be an engaging public speaker: knowledgeable, glib and drily funny. He was also good-looking, the son of a U.S. Navy admiral and a native of Texas, all of which helped the ticket. He and the president-elect were also close friends, meeting when they both went to that piss yellow and blue school. The first lady and Mrs. Holland were sorority sisters at that school in Ann Arbor, and when the two couples married that cemented the friendship. All in all it was a very attractive ticket, especially when you factored in that Mrs. Holland was Rosanna Mendoza, whose parents were illegal immigrants to the U.S. that turned themselves in, left Rosanna and her siblings with family in Texas and worked their way back into the country.

The only turd in the punchbowl was the fact that the president-elect selected FBI Executive Assistant Director for Homeland Security Malcolm Sorenson to be the new FBI Director, and as soon as the president was sworn in Congress fell all over themselves confirming him.

The mole who tried to kill us was now in the big chair at the Hoover Building as the Director of the FBI.

Well, shit a brick and fuck a duck.

And then nobody had time to worry about it, because things got really busy. Patsy, Bumble and Badass were promoted to the president's detail, Buddha and Flipper were promoted to the first lady's detail and the rest of us were working every day protecting someone, usually in and around DC, although we also got to travel. The apartment house we lived in always had some of us there, but it was rare that we were all there.

It got more interesting a year and a half into President Sheehan's first term. I was off duty, sitting on my little balcony drinking a Pepsi and reading Michael Connelly's latest Harry Bosch novel when there was a thunderous knocking on my door, followed by someone repeatedly pressing the doorbell. I went to the door, taking a 1076 with me just in case (hey, you never know—some assassins like to get the target off balance by doing something disconcerting, perhaps ringing the doorbell like a maniac). I looked at my security camera by the door (never put your eye to a peephole—think about it and you'll see why) and saw nothing, but the bell kept ringing, and then the knocking started up again, so I just whipped the door open and said, "Stop ringing the fucking bell or I'll fucking shoot."

"That's no way to treat a friend," Dr. Tully Whited said. Her hair was just as pink as her eyes, which were twinkling mischievously. She laughed as I stood there gawping at her. "If I had a fucking camera right now I'd win 10 grand from America's Funniest Home Videos, Freak. Close your mouth before a pigeon shits in it, willya?" Hurricane said.

"It was the hair," I said. "I've never seen pink hair that matched someone's eyes like yours does, although I did see a genetically modified rabbit with pink fur and eyes once. You two were about the same size."

"Fuck you, Freak. If you think my hair's bad, you should see my pubes," Hurricane said. "They're going to blow Badass away when he gets home."

"Oh fuck, Hurricane. I can't un-hear that. My ears are bleeding. TMI," I said.

We both laughed our asses off as I put my pistol away and we hugged. "What the fuck are ya doing here?" I said.

"I'm now part of the faculty at the GW Medical School. I decided to leave the country behind me and teach a bunch of smart fuckers how to be brilliant frontier obstetricians. Besides, I like getting laid on a regular basis and I couldn't very well ask Badass to move, now could I?" Hurricane said.

"So are you staying here, or are you living somewhere else?" I said.

"He asked me to stay a couple weeks and see how it goes. If it works—and it will, because with our jobs we won't be together all the time to get on each others' nerves—then I'll move in permanently," she said, her pink eyes twinkling again.

So the apartment house seemed to be full, and the job was going well, and my life was so busy that I didn't mind not having a boyfriend (OK, so that's a lie—I did mind, I just didn't have any time to do anything about it).

Then one day I got a call from Director Hessler that changed everything. After three years of following the Yellow Brick Road, I, too, was moving up to the Emerald City, only mine was white, as in White House. I was going to see the wizard himself, the director told me, because the president wanted to interview me in two days. I was ecstatic, because if you were in the Secret Service on the protection side there was only one goal: the presidential detail (and no, the Vice-Presidential detail wasn't the same thing—John Nance Gardner's comment about the vice presidency—it's not worth a pitcher of warm spit—goes double for Secret Service agents). At the time my meeting with the president at the White House was the biggest thing to ever happen in my life.

I had no idea that it was the beginning of the end of my Secret Service career.

CHAPTER 56

Freak One, Superbitch Zero

I got to the White House 15 minutes early for my meeting, on the theory that I'd rather be early than miss it. Then I waited 10 minutes for the guy at the gate to check my creds and confirm my appointment. Once I got to the lobby I waited another five minutes until Director Hessler swept in and took me in tow. We walked through the West Wing toward the Oval Office (my *zayde* would've been shitting himself about now—he always wanted to visit the Oval) until we got to the outer office, where the president's personal secretary told us that the meeting was moved to the residence.

I kept my disappointment down at not being in the Oval as I followed Director Hessler out of the West Wing and into the residence. We were directed to the president's sitting room (the one with the cool half moon window you saw in the TV program *The West Wing*), where we were once again left waiting.

The president's press secretary came out of the room and said, "Director Hessler, Agent Glickstien, we're just waiting for the first lady to join the president before we begin the meeting. It shouldn't be long."

Thank you, Joanna," Director Hessler said.

Wait a minute. The first lady?

Oh, shithouse mouse. The first lady and I had a history of not getting along that went back to our school days when my brother Aaron beat her out for valedictorian, but that wasn't the real problem.

Shitfuckpisshelldamnsonofabitch!

If we were meeting the president and the first lady I wasn't being seconded to the president's detail, I was being checked out for the *kids* detail, which I wanted about as much as I wanted a root canal, or herpes, or malaria, or…well, you get the idea. It wasn't that I didn't like kids, or that I didn't think that the president's daughters were as cute as little fuzzy ducks, it was the fact that guarding the girls meant that I'd be riding back and forth to school, occasionally escorting them to school functions and chaperoning dates, although that would be rare, since it would take balls the size of Winston Churchill's to ask one of the president's kids out, a trait for which high school (or worse, middle school—yuck!) boys weren't known.

Being assigned to the girls' detail also meant far less travel, since most of the time when they traveled they'd be under the umbrella of the president or first lady.

Fuck me blind.

Just as I had it all worked out the president's body man poked his head out and said, "Director, Agent Glickstien, they're ready for you. Please come in."

Director Hessler took one look at my face and said, "Easy, Freak. This is a singular privilege, to guard the president's children—it's probably second to guarding POTUS himself."

"Great. You do it then, and I'll just go sit in your office. Nobody'll notice, since you REMFs don't really do anything anyway," I said, completely taking a liberty with our relationship that Director Hessler had never given me.

Luckily the Director was a good sport and actually got what Protective Service agents went through when it came to certain assignments. She laughed and said, "You'd last about 35 seconds in a budget meeting, or having to listen to the DHS Secretary bloviate, so just shut the fuck up and give them a good interview. The first lady already doesn't like you, so you probably won't get the assignment anyway." We both laughed and went in to see the most powerful couple in America.

The president stuck his hand out and said, "Freak, how's the best athlete in the history of Battle Creek?"

"I don't know, Mr. President, how are you?" I said. He laughed and I was struck by how handsome, genial, composed and presidential he was. I guess it shouldn't have surprised me—you don't win the national championship and Heisman trophy at that piss yellow and blue school and then win two Super Bowls with the Chicago Bears and not have all the qualities needed to attain public office, especially when you are backed by several conservative gazillionaires who are impressed with your personal charisma, as well as the gaudy jewelry you won on the athletic field.

Did I mention that President James Sheehan was handsome? He was 6'3", 235 pounds now, muscular without being bulky and possessed of that easy, graceful way of moving that all great athletes (and tigers, and jaguars, and leopards, and lions, and cheetahs) possess. He was very handsome in his face, with deep blue eyes, a strong nose, and great teeth, as well as a full head of perfectly cut hair that was just dusted with some gray. His chin could have been chiseled out of granite, with a dimple in just the right place to match the dimples in his cheeks when he smiled or laughed (which was often—he probably laughed more in a day than Calvin Coolidge had in his life). The president also had the strongest looking, most graceful hands you've ever seen, with fingers that tapered to perfectly manicured nails.

James Patrick Liam Sheehan was the whole package, a man's man who was just kind and gentle enough to also be extremely attractive to the female half of the electorate. He was a practicing Catholic who clearly loved his wife and children—not many Presidents went to their kid's junior high choir concerts, but President Sheehan did—and a real patriot who was known to go out to Arlington National Cemetery to watch the changing of the guard at the Tomb of the Unknown Soldier, where he regularly cried as he stood at attention with his hand over his heart as the soldiers of the Old Guard went through their ritual.

I didn't always agree with his politics, but it was impossible not to like him, even when he was trying to pass a law limiting a womyn's reproductive rights, or trying to cut the Wymyn and Infant Children's (WIC) program that provided food to low-income mothers and their children, or trying to cut taxes for millionaires while the middle class floundered, etc. The guy was just attractive in every way it was possible to be attractive, and his political flaws just reinforced everything else about him that was good.

He looked me in the eye and tightened his grip on my hand, challenging me. I squeezed back at about half strength and saw him wince, so I lightened up and said, "How is your shoulder, sir?"

He laughed and said, "Freak, it sucks. Having J. J. Watt and Cornelius Lambert meet at the quarterback wasn't a very good idea then, and it's worse now." The president's playing career had ended during the Super Bowl in Dallas when the two best defensive players on the Houston Texans crushed him to the turf, separating his shoulder and dislocating it and his elbow at the same time. He literally had 11 surgeries and a year of rehab before it became clear that he would never be able to rifle the football with NFL velocity anymore.

Did I mention that the president was personally tough, both mentally and physically? He went through the physical hell of rehab and then went through the mental hell of realizing that even though he was still young he was done with football and ended up making a very mature decision. The president quietly left the game (as quietly as one can in today's world) to go into public service without all the folderol usually associated with star athletes as they retire. He apparently didn't miss the game, although he started a tradition by having a huge Super Bowl blowout wherever he was (House, Senate, governor's mansion, White House).

In short, whether you agreed with his politics or not, it was really hard to not like and/or admire President James Sheehan.

His wife was an entirely different matter.

No one went public with it, but one prominent journalist called her "The Ice Queen," while many on her Secret Service detail called her "The White Witch," after the nasty character in C. S. Lewis's *The Lion, the Witch and the Wardrobe* series (and don't try to tell me you don't know what I'm talking about on that one).

Since our run-in at school I'd always just called her Superbitch.

Regardless of what you called her, Laura Flagler Sheehan was hell on wheels. She was also a shrewd political operator who was her husband's biggest supporter and best adviser, as well as being a great campaigner. Where other presidents sent their vice-presidents to be their hatchet-men, President Sheehan sent his wife. She was a *cum laude* graduate of that piss yellow and blue school in political science and knew how to creatively attack opponents within the boundaries of political decency, and, when necessary, she knew how to be a raging bitch that just tore people apart with her intellect, ingenuity, and acerbity.

I knew that I'd have to physically beat her ass up if I ever wanted to win a fight with her, because nobody beat Laura Flagler Sheehan in a battle of words. Imagine a much better looking and much meaner William F. Buckley, Jr. and you'll have a fair idea of the first lady's capabilities.

The president let go of my hand and the first lady said, "Well, hello, Freak. It's been a long time." She smiled at me and I was taken aback, because it seemed sincere, and her tone was one of conciliation, not condescension. One of the reasons we'd clashed in school was that she acted like her defecation was not odiferous, but that didn't seem to be the case this time.

I said, "Yes, ma'am, it has been a while." I kept my tone and demeanor very carefully neutral so as not to provoke Her Bitchiness (another of my pet names for the first lady in the past) as we shook hands, but she said, "How long have we known each other, Freak? Twenty-five years? I'd think that you could call me Laura."

She stared at me in challenge and I said, "Mrs. Sheehan, if you ask my boss she'll tell you that Secret Service protocol forbids me from using your first name. Even if you were my sister I couldn't do it, ma'am. I'm sorry for that, because I know that "ma'am" makes it seem like I'm calling you old, but I assure you that isn't the case—I'm just trying to be respectful and follow protocol."

Director Hessler said, "She's right, ma'am. We have these protocols to keep people who don't know you from becoming overly familiar. It's difficult for you in the short term because you've known Agent Glickstien for some time, but believe me, these rules work in everybody's favor over the long term. Until your husband leaves office Agent Glickstien won't be able to call you anything but ma'am, madame, First Lady or Mrs. Sheehan—and she'll use those last two as sparingly as possible."

We all just stood there for a moment, until the president said, "Well, now that we've got that settled, let's all sit down and discuss the rest of the situation, shall we?" He was trying to charm all of us, even his wife, and it worked, because she put her hand on his arm and said, "Of course. You know I just hate it when people we've known forever are so formal. I'm sorry if I've been a bi-, uh, pain in the butt." She smiled at Director Hessler and me and I said, "Not at all, ma'am. I have no idea how I'd react in your shoes, but it would probably be the same way."

"Concur," Director Hessler said.

"Well, you know that *I* hate it, so it looks like we're all with you, honey," the president said. He smiled back at her—another thing about the First Couple was that their marriage bond was always on display. A columnist from the Washington *Post* once said that the president would launch a nuclear strike on anybody who tried to get between him and his wife, and said in the same column that the first lady's disposition toward people who went after her husband was roughly the same as that of a University of Michigan Wolverine fan toward anything Ohio State…and like a real wolverine she'd probably kill and eat anyone who tried to pry her away from her husband's side. They were definitely still in love—and it showed.

We settled into seats and the president said, "Freak, you know why we're here, right?"

"Yes, sir. You want me to join the first daughters' detail," I said. I must have sounded like it was a death sentence, because the president laughed and said, "Well, it's not a death sentence. They're not really bad girls, although they are a little bit spoiled."

We all laughed and I said, "Sir, I didn't mean any offense. I'd be honored to protect your daughters."

"Oh, I know that, but there's a specific reason that I—we—are asking you to join the detail. Director Hessler." He looked at my boss, and she nodded and said, "Freak, we've intercepted some low-level chatter that seems to indicate that there is an Islamic terrorist group that would like to kill the president and first lady's daughters."

I sat up even straighter in my seat and said, "Director, is this a credible threat? Have we gotten any intel that confirms the chatter?"

Director Hessler looked at the president, and he said, "Show her. If she's going to be a part of the kids' detail she needs to see it." The director handed me several printed sheets and I started to read.

I'm not going to describe everything in the packet, but somebody had used pictures of the girls and photo-shopped them to show in graphic detail what was going to happen to the first daughters, and anyone else who happened to be in their general vicinity. The pictures were disgusting and not at all crude, which was worrisome—sophisticated terrorists with technical skills meant better bombs, better planning, more funding, etc.—but not as worrisome as the notes that went with them.

"We will slaughter your infidel children as you have slaughtered the children of the Prophet, praised be his name," one message said. "The children of Palestine have paid with their lives for your ignorance and indifference to the words of the Prophet, praised be his name, and now your children will repay the blood debt with their lives," was another. "The Great Satan has murdered our children with his war machine, and now the Faithful will exact vengeance in the Most Holy Name of the Prophet, praised be his name, by taking his children from him," was a third message—and those are just the ones that I'll repeat. The others were too graphic, even for me. Even talking about beheading children is sick business, and again, that was one of the milder threats.

Worse than the threats was the NIE (National Intelligence Estimate) from DHS that called the material a "credible threat." Once something met the credible threat threshold there were primary security measures that were automatically initiated (classified, nimrods—sheesh!) and many secondary measures that the Director and the president could employ, one of which was increasing the size of security details.

That was why I was here. The president wanted me because I was the best pistol shot in the world, stronger than most terrorists and more than willing to shoot dead anyone who was a danger to my protectee (see Morehead, Kentucky, et. al.). The fact the president knew me was also a factor, because he knew that I was honest, trustworthy and willing to take a bullet for the girls if necessary.

It still didn't mean that I wanted to babysit some teenagers, even if they were in danger, but then my common sense brain (thanks mom and dad and *zayde*) kicked in and I realized that I had to protect the girls, whether I wanted to or not, because the person who should be doing a job on any team is the one best suited for it...and I was definitely the best suited for this job.

So I swallowed my pride and said, "Mr. President, I agree that we have a credible threat and that your daughters need an augmented detail, and I'd like to volunteer for the detail. As you know I have a unique skill set, and I believe that it will be well suited to the detail."

"So you don't think that this is a demotion from guarding the Dali Lama, or the president of Paraguay?" the president said, the humor clear in his voice.

I chose to answer in the most professional Secret Service voice you've ever heard. "Sir, guarding any member of the first family is an honor and a privilege. To think that you and the first lady would allow me to guard your children is the highest honor I have ever have received."

"What about what happened during your special ops career? Surely you received higher honors for that?" the First Lady said. Clearly she'd read my service jacket, too, and wanted some details. Anybody would, since for two and a half years I technically didn't exist, but at the risk of pissing Superbitch off I said, still in my serious-as-cancer Secret Service voice, "Sorry, ma'am, but that's classified."

That got her back up. "I'm the First Lady of the United States," she said in full Ice Queen mode.

"Sorry ma'am, but your security classification isn't even high enough for me to tell you where I was stationed during my special operations tour," I said in a voice as cold as space. I knew that it would really wind her up, but hey, why not have a little fun now, since once I was on the detail I wouldn't be having any?

Laura Flagler Sheehan said, "Well, of course you were stationed at Fort MacDill with all of our other Spec Ops soldiers." She smiled a challenge at me, but all I did was give an almost imperceptible "no" shake of my head.

"Well, the president is right here. Perhaps you can tell him the honors you won during your Spec Ops tour?" The White Witch said in her silky-smooth Superbitch voice.

"Sorry, ma'am, but the president's security clearance isn't that high, either," I said. '*That should set her off,*' I thought.

It did.

"Oh you think you're soooo superior! Of course my husband's security clearance is high enough—he's the *Commander in Chief!*—and you're just some low-level Secret Service agent! How dare you try to pull that holier-than-thou shit? Like your security clearance is higher than the *president's*? Bullshit! Now tell him what went on during your special ops career or you're going to be guarding the Undersecretary for Shit-Shoveling from Outer Bumfuckistan!" the Ice Queen said, her face distorted into a nasty sneer.

I stood up and said, "I'm sorry you feel that way, ma'am, but my security clearance is higher than the President's for some things, and this is one of them. I'm sorry I won't be guarding your daughters, ma'am. Mr. President, thank you for thinking of me for this honor. I'm genuinely sorry that I won't be able to serve you in this matter." I didn't move to leave, but I did go stand against the wall of the Oval Office like I was standing post.

Director Hessler stood up and said, "Sir, you've got my list of other potential augmentation agents. Please call me at your convenience and we'll get them in so that you and the first lady can interview them, sir. Ma'am." The Director turned to leave and Superbitch said. "Why don't you just order her to tell us about her career, Director Hessler?"

"Because the part of her service record you want to know about is above my security clearance, ma'am. If you know Freak at all you know that she'll never talk about it, because this is the kind of thing all special operations operators take very seriously," the Director said. "I wouldn't ask her about her honors or anything else connected with her service, because it's against the law and also puts my agent in a position of having to defy me—when I ask I'm making her absolutely insubordinate, which means that she either answers and goes to jail or she doesn't answer and gets fired. Believe me, I'd have to fire her—perhaps my best agent—because Freak will *never* answer questions about her time with SOCOM. Besides," the Director said, "that information is classified above my pay grade."

The first lady looked at the President and said, "Well, why don't *you* order her to tell you? You're the Commander-in-Chief for fuck's sake! Make her tell you!"

President James Patrick Liam Sheehan sighed and said, "Laura, she's right. Her service record *is* classified above my security clearance, and it would be illegal for her to divulge anything from that time."

"WHAT?!?" the first lady said, her face red and contorted into a very ugly expression.

The President said, "Freak, please come back over here and sit down and explain this to the first lady, will you?"

I felt bad for him—I wondered how he was still sane after being married to The White Witch all these years—and I guess I thought that maybe I could alleviate some of that stress, so I went back and sat in the chair indicated. I looked the First Lady/Superbitch/Ice Queen/White Witch right in the eye and said, "Mrs. Sheehan, the only three people who have a security clearance high enough to access my service records are the Chairman of the Joint Chiefs of Staff, the Secretary of Homeland Security and the Director of the CIA. You see, sometimes the Special Operations Command has to send its operators into situations where they need to do things that are necessary but may not reflect well on our country. They also have to send special operators into places where the U.S. is not welcome or even able to enter legally. The only way that we can do this is if we compartmentalize the information about these operations so that word of them never gets out. To not restrict this information jeopardizes the lives of every special operator in the field now or later, and also jeopardizes our relations with specific nations and the rest of the foreign community at large.

"The compartmentalization also protects your husband and every other president, because they need to be able to absolutely deny the actions of our special forces at times. My service record constitutes one of those times. If the president has no access to this information he or she can't be blamed for what the special operations operators have done, and we won't be tipping our hand to the enemy, or giving them ammunition to fuel further animosity towards the United States.

"I'm sorry if it seems like I'm trying to act superior, Ma'am, but I'm not. When I tell you that the information you requested is classified I'm living up to the oath I took when I was commissioned in the U.S. Marine Corps, as well as protecting you, the president, and the country that I love. Sorry if that sounds corny, or melodramatic, or condescending, but I assure you that it is not, Mrs. Sheehan.

"Again, I'm sorry I won't be able to serve on your daughter's detail, ma'am."

"Well, I get the final call on that one, and I'm still asking you to protect our kids," the president said. He looked at his wife, who looked at me with that Ice Queen stare. I stared right back with my "Fuck-you-I'm-a-Marine" death stare. After a few seconds of smoldering silence Superbitch looked at the floor, then looked back up at the president and gave him a short nod.

He smiled and said, "Welcome to the family, Freak. You and the rest of the new squad are going to meet the girls tomorrow, but before you do Laura and I wondered if you had any recommendations for additional personnel. We have a list from Director Hessler, but she tells us that you have a pretty good handle on who might fit in."

I was surprised that the president wanted my input, mainly because it was usually the Chief of Detail that got to set the squads up, not some body agent. I looked at Director Hessler and she said, "Senior Agent Jerilynn Rafferty is the boss of this squad, Freak."

Now it made sense. I laughed and said, "Sir, am I being asked to be second-in-command of this detail?" He nodded and I said, "Good old Major Difficulty! She always said we'd work together again, and so we are. In that case, I would recommend Agents Darah Koenigsblett, Sarah Koenigsblett, Emily Devlin, Alexander de Vries, and Tara Kwyfteralian. Are your daughters interested in sports?"

"Allison is a swimmer, and Brooke likes softball and volleyball, although the president says she's too short for volleyball right now," Superbitch said. She was still pissed at me, but she was very proud of her daughters.

"Well, ma'am, I don't know about her height, but the Koenigsbletts were varsity softball starters at Bowling Green, and Agent Kwyfteralian was a college swimmer and a rescue swimmer for the Coast Guard. That should help establish some bonding with the girls," I said.

"We also have a varsity volleyball player from UCLA, Malik Vaziri, on the detail," the president said. "The rest of the detail is a good mix of youth and experience, according to Chief of Detail Rafferty."

"You called her "Major Difficulty" earlier," Superbitch said. "I take it that the two of you are acquainted?"

"Oh, yes ma'am. We served together in Spec Ops," I said. "Major Difficulty was her nickname then, although I don't know anyone who would have called her that to her face."

"Not even you, Freak?" the president said. "I didn't think that many people intimidated you."

"Oh, it wasn't because she was intimidating, sir, it was out of respect. MD is one of the best, most professional soldiers I've ever met. Everybody in our unit had nothing but the utmost respect for her, although I'm pretty sure that she could be pretty intimidating if she wanted to be," I said.

"What was the basis of the respect? What did she do that made everyone respect her?" Superbitch said.

I thought about it for a minute and decided to tell her as much as I could. "Ma'am, part of it's classified, but Jerilynn Rafferty was the fourth womyn through US Army Ranger School, she led a Ranger company in Desert Storm and she lost her left leg there, ma'am."

"Oh my God," Superbitch said. "And she came back to train people for special operations? That's amazing!"

I laughed and said, "Ma'am, that isn't the half of it. Major Difficulty wasn't a trainer for special ops, she was a field operator. She put herself through the training to prove that she could do it with her prosthesis so that she could remain on active duty. Pardon me for putting it this way, but it was fucking inspirational, ma'am."

Even Superbitch laughed at that. The president said, "So the detail will be filled with extraordinary people, is what you're telling me."

"The finest kind, Mr. President," I said. "I'd go anywhere with the people that I know in the squad, and you can bet that Major Difficulty didn't pick anybody that wasn't the very best at their job. She has a knack for picking people who fit the assignment and then getting them to function like clockwork. Mr. President, Madame First Lady, your daughters will be very safe with this squad, maybe even safer than you will be."

"I just have one more question, Freak," Superbitch said.

"Yes, ma'am?" I said.

"Will you take a bullet for my daughters?" she said, staring at me with real fear on her face.

I looked at her, a womyn that I really didn't like, and I thought about what it must be like to be a mother worried out of your head for the safety of your children. I decided that she deserved a full answer, so I said, "Ma'am, if anybody tries to get at your daughters it'll have to be over my dead body, because I swear to you that I'll guard them like they're my own children. But those are just words. Mr. President, if you would be so kind as to step out of the room for a moment?"

The president looked at me with a curious expression, but he just left the room without arguing. Once the door closed I stood up and took off my jacket, then began unbuttoning my blouse. When it was all undone I said, "Ma'am, are you at all squeamish? If so, I would prepare myself, because what you're about to see isn't for the faint of heart."

The first lady said, "What are you going to show me? I—I've never been squeamish about any-thing, so I can't imagine what it is that—OH MY GOD."

I'd dropped my shirt and turned around so that she could get a look at my ruined back (sorry—classified). It was a gruesome sight that had taken around 440 stitches to close, along with a couple of strips of skin from my butt where a red-hot piece of a Russian tank had burned its way into my body. I've never really looked at it, but I've been told it looks like Frankenstein's monster's face caught fire and the peasants tried to put it out with their pitchforks.

I rarely went out in public without covering up, because the one time I'd gone to the beach after I healed I made a nice lady puke, scared the hell out of a troop of kids and caused two jet skis to crash. Suffice to say my back was as ugly as the rest of me.

I turned around and looked Superbitch right in the eye and said, "Ma'am, I got that defending some guys in a place that I'm not allowed to talk about, and if I'd do that for some guys who weren't even Americans imagine what I'd do for your daughters. In addition to that, ma'am, I promise you that anyone who tries to get near your daughters to harm them will be in a world of shit, because you better believe I'll shoot those motherfuckers dead. Sorry for the language, ma'am."

I give her credit. Even though the first lady was shaken and pale from looking at my back she smiled and said, "Good. That's exactly what I want you to do."

"By your command, ma'am," I said.

Superbitch called out, "Honey, please come back in now." The president came in looking mys-tified, but all he said was, "Satisfied, my love?"

"Bet your ass," the first lady said as we all laughed. Everybody shook hands and we left the sit-ting room. Once we got outside Director Hessler said, "I know you can't tell me, but the guys you were trying to save—did they make it?"

I immediately flashed back to that cold night in the Hindu Kush and the shocked faces of a womyn, a man and their three children as I threw myself on them just before the tank blew up. I remembered how we all stank, and how hard the shrapnel hit me, and the smothered cries of terror that came spilling out from under my body as I surrounded them and squeezed them into a tight ball, but most of all I remembered the looks on those same faces three years ago when I saw them from a distance in their new home.

They were all smiles and happiness, especially the kids, which made it all worth it. I smiled myself and said, "Bet your ass, ma'am."

"Boo-rah," the Director said.

We walked out of the White House and I said, "You realize that this may make the girls more of a target."

"I thought of that, but we're on that asshat now, so we'll get some warning, and besides, we'll arrest his ass if he tries anything at all, regardless of the proof. I'm not worried about it," the Director said.

"Me, either. The Badger Squad is the most capable early warning system in history," I said.

"Concur," she said.

I just wish we'd been right.

CHAPTER 57

The Apples Didn't Fall Far from the Tree

The term "bitch" is probably overused in our society, but in this case, I was sure that it was being kind.

It turns out that the sweet girls we'd seen on TV didn't exist. Instead, the first daughters more closely resembled Audrey II from *Little Shop of Horrors*. In case you haven't seen it, Audrey II was a giant man-eating plant from outer space that devoured people (including Vincent Gardenia and Steve Martin).

Or maybe they were like a pack of ravenous zombie werewolves who turned into vampires.

In any case, these girls were the very definition of the popular epithet "bitches." It was a perfect designation, but of course we couldn't use it, so after the squad met them for the first time Major Difficulty said, "OK, so we can't call them what we want to, so we need a designation that we can all agree on and we need to stick to it, because if we slip and call them bitches we're all gonna get fired."

"How about CIT?" Buddha said.

"CIT?" MD said.

"Cunts in training," Buddha said. We all laughed, but Ed said, "Won't work—sooner or later we'd have to explain it, and then here comes the unemployment line."

"Or Leavenworth," Pedro "Gordo" Velazquez said. He was Mexican-American and one of the thinnest people I'd ever seen, which is why his nickname was 'fat'—we all liked irony.

"How about BLT?" Grant "Sleepy" Rauker said. He was a round-faced young man who had eyes that were perpetually at half-mast, like he was ready to be romantic or he was half asleep.

"Bitchy little twats will get us fired, too," Patsy said.

"How about FIB?" Shemika "Foghorn" Taylor said. She was a muscular Black womyn who could do a dead-on impersonation of the cartoon character Foghorn Leghorn from the old Bugs Bunny program.

"Fired," Flipper said.

"You don't even know what it means," Foghorn said.

"Fucking idiot bitches," Flipper said.

"Definitely fired," I said. "See CIT and BLT."

"What about FBA?" Dung "Hero" Nguyen said. Agent Nguyen was an ordinary looking young man of Vietnamese descent who I knew was one hell of a pistol shot (he was a finalist at the President's Cup the previous year). His nickname was the literal translation of his first name.

"Future Bitches of America means we're fired for sure. I wouldn't even bet a cheesecake on it," Malik "Bookie" Vaziri said. He was a wee lad of 6'6" who'd been a varsity letterman in volleyball at UCLA. He got his nickname because he would bet on anything, anytime—only he preferred to bet baked goods rather than money. He was also one of the best-looking young men I'd ever seen and was trilingual in Portuguese, Arabic and English.

"What about Serbs?" Walter "Count Chocolate" Burgener said. He was a 6'5", broad-shouldered man who got his nickname by telling everyone how awful Hershey's chocolate tasted compared to the chocolate his grandmother from Switzerland always sent him at Christmas. The fact that he was right in his assessment—there certainly is no comparison between Swiss chocolate and any other on earth—didn't stop us from calling him out as a chocolate snob.

"You think the first lady wouldn't fire us for calling her daughters spoiled rotten brats?" Adam "Hot Rod" Seivert said. A former motocross racer, Hot Rod had passed the Academy Defensive Driving course with one of the highest scores in history. He'd also bet "Bookie" two dozen peanut butter cookies that he could drive an armored limo at least 100 miles per hour around a dirt track. He claimed that Bookie was the best cookie baker he'd ever known, and that the 24 cookies only lasted two days.

"I got it," Holly "Gangster" Durante said. She was a short, broad womyn with long brown hair that she always twisted up and stuck a chopstick through. She got her nickname because she had a very thick New Joisey accent (she reminded me of Guru, although you could usually understand Gangster) that made her sound like a Mob guy from a 1950s melodrama. "We'll call them *princesses*. It doesn't stand for anything, but it's perfect because it implies bitchiness, a sense of entitlement, and special privileges, which these two little—*princesses*—both have in spades. The way we use it will all be about tone of voice—when someone is around we use a flat inflection, but when we're trying to blow off steam we'll skew the tone—make it sound like we're saying "bitch" while saying 'princess.' Nobody could object to that."

"And if we're asked we'll just say those little bitches are precious to us, like little princesses," I said. "It's perfect."

"Good. Since they both go to the Friends School we aren't going to have to handle two motorcades, but we are still going to follow standard procedure. We're also going to work in rotating squads, so everyone will get a chance to enjoy the company of the little *princesses*," Major Difficulty said.

"Good plan, ma'am," I said. "That way nobody will have to stay too close to them, which means everybody's shit sandwiches will be smaller." We all laughed and Foghorn said, "They are just young girls—you ever think they'll just grow out of it?"

"Not unless their mother gets hit by a meteor," I said. "I've known her for a long time, and she's always been a superbitch…which means those girls are doomed."

"I'll bet ya three dozen cinnamon rolls that you're wrong," Bookie said. "In three weeks we'll have them eating out of our hands, and they'll consider at least four of us their friends."

"I'll take some a that," Ed said.

"I'll take the bet, but it'll only be two friends," Gordo said.

"I'll take some action, but it's gotta be four dozen cinnamon rolls," Hot Rod said.

"I'll take three dozen at two to one that it's no friends—zero friends," I said. Everybody else chimed in and it took Bookie 15 minutes to get all of the bets down.

We went and got a tour of the Friends School from the principal, Dr. Nancy Puvogel. She was a tall, plain womyn with glorious ash-blonde hair and some really fancy jewelry. She also appeared to have an IQ north of 150 and really understood the Secret Service, since there had already been five First Children through the doors while she was either vice-principal or principal. Having a really smart principal who didn't have to be briefed on Secret Service procedures, as well as having certain other things already in place (c'mon, you know I'm not giving anything away about protective measures) meant that we didn't have as many preliminary things to do, but it also meant that we would have to be more on our toes when the detail commenced tomorrow, because familiarity and routine in security work adds up to disaster—you can't ever let your guard down. Ever. No matter how many times you've done something or how secure you feel, you have to make sure that you are truly alert and paying attention, or else a bad guy or girl can get at your principals—and they only need to be successful one time for all your efforts at protection to be an utter failure.

So we went out and checked the perimeter, considered all the sight lines that might result in a shooter having a chance to hit one of the princesses, and went over ridiculous scenarios, like someone coming in with two helicopters and a company of Russian *spetznaz* (special forces) soldiers. We all agreed we were lucky, because the Friends School had lots of nice grown-up shrubbery that cut down shooting sight lines, and there were enough wires around and overhead that helicopters would have a hard time, and the two drives to the school were well-scouted and easy to secure.

In fact, it all seemed so easy that we needed to be even more on our guard, a fact that Major Difficulty made very apparent when we were all done with our walk through.

We were assembled in the office conference room at the Friends School when MD said, "So we gotta stay sharp the whole time we're here, because this would be a really easy place to screw the pooch. You're gonna wanna relax and coast, and you can't, which is why we'll be doing the rolling squad routine. Believe me, it'll be a royal pain in the ass at the start, but you'll like it, and you'll see why it keeps you on your toes. Any questions?"

"Either of the girls have a boyfriend?" Count Chocolate said.

"Nope, but lots of the boys are gonna wanna hit on Allison—her boobs are growing and she's really cute if you're a 16, 17-year-old boy," MD said. "I also heard from the vice-principal that there are some senior boys who think it's cool to play pinch-the-ass-of-the-freshman-girls game. Obviously we're gonna wanna keep an eye on that and put a stop to it right away."

"You think we're going to have to? Won't these hunyocks know who she is and steer clear?" I said.

"You remember being in high school, Freak?" Sarah said.

"Sort of, but remember that I was already the Freak by then—nobody messed with me," I said.

"But everybody else got some shit from the teenage males there, creatures that had IQs lower than whale shit," Sarah said.

"Abhorrent creatures that were barely human and stank like the grave," Foghorn said.

"Creatures that didn't know what day it was, much less know who the first daughters are," Flipper said.

"These same creatures are in the grip of a terrible flood of hormones that turns their sex drives to the 'hyper-warp' setting," Buddha said.

"You can show these creatures a picture of a crescent wrench and they'll fly into a sexual frenzy," Gangster.

"And since these creatures' brains are naturally set in the "shit for brains" position what you get is a perfect storm of dumbasses who'll try just about anything," Major Difficulty said.

"And since you can't shoot 'em you'll have to try other methods of discouragement," Ed said.

"And no, you can't break their bones, either," MD said.

"Well, shit," I said. "This detail is starting to sound harder than it was originally portrayed."

"You have no idea," Major Difficulty said.

And I didn't.

The next day we had no problem getting loaded up and taking the girls to school, mechanically, that is, but Brooke bitched the whole way about having to get up so early, and Allison bitched about the way her hair looked, and Brooke bitched about not having any cute guys in her classes, and Allison bitched about having two lesbians that lockered next to her and were always kissing each other.

She looked at me with an ugly look on her face and said, "Why do lesbians do that?"

I looked back at her and said, "Miss?" as if I didn't understand what she was asking.

She rolled her eyes and said, "I *said*, why do *lesbians* do that?"

"Do what, miss?" I said, innocent as pie.

"Why do *lesbians* always stand at their lockers and *kiss*?" she said.

"You'll have to ask them, miss," I said.

"Well, I thought that you'd know for sure," Allison said, making eye contact with her sister.

"I wouldn't have any idea about it," I said.

"Well, aren't *you* a *lesbian*?" she said, sneering just like her mother the Superbitch.

"I mean, with that haircut and those clothes you sure look *butchy*," Brooke said. Both the girls were smiling their best *Mean Girls* smiles, and Allison was beaming triumphantly, as if she had just won a debate with William F. Buckley.

I smiled right back, pulled my phone out of my pocket, and called up a picture of Square Peg. I showed it to the *princesses* and said, "You know who that is?" They both looked at the pic and Brooke said, "That's Kel Richardson. He's the captain of the Pistons."

I smiled and scrolled over to a pic with Peg and I holding hands. The caption said, "My Beautiful Girl, Happy Valentine's Day 2016." I showed them the pic and said, "He sent me that—it's from when we were at Disney World. That's my only boyfriend, and I think that we can agree he's a boy, right?" The *princesses* were just goggle-eyed at the pic, but Allison recovered enough to say, "No way you know Kelvin *Richardson*. No way. That picture is photo shopped."

I did my best Mr. Spock eyebrow arch, went into contacts, and pushed a speed dial button. I put the phone on speaker. Peg answered, "Hey, Beautiful Girl, perfect timing. I'm going to shoot a commercial for the Boys and Girls Clubs of America in half an hour, so I just have time talk dirty to you."

I said, "Easy, Peg, I'm here with the first daughters and you're on speaker. They don't believe that I know you."

Square Peg was nothing if not adaptable. He instantly went into schmooze mode and said, "Good morning, Allison, Brooke. When we were in college Freak was my girlfriend, and despite us breaking up she's still one of my best friends."

"You—you really *know* her?" Allison said.

"Like, really *know* her?" Brooke said.

"We've been friends for a really, really long time, and I not only know Freak, I love her like she's my family. I'm friends with all her brothers, I call her parents Mom and Dad and I mourned like my own grandpa died when her *zayde* left us. If you still don't believe me, ask her about the birthmark on her left butt cheek that looks like a duck," Peg said, laughing his deep, rich laugh that always got me. I mean, I know the guy's gay, but he still got me fired up—how could you not be in love with a guy like that?

The *princesses* were speechless.

Finally Allison said, "Uhhh, Mr. Richardson? We, uhhh, well, we, kinda, you know, we sorta thought that Agent Glickstien was, you know, we uhhh, thought she was, well, gay."

Square Peg's laugh boomed over the little speaker and he said, "Oh. My. God. Not that it's any of your business, Allison, but nothing could be further from the truth. Besides, what do you care? She's the best pistol shot in the world, she can run faster than a speeding bullet and she is definitely more powerful than a runaway locomotive. Did I mention that she can probably lift the locomotive off the ground? In case you don't know it, Freak's the best bodyguard in the world, and anybody who messes with you is going to go down for the count. Her sexual orientation is not only none of your business, but also irrelevant. Plus she's got a great sense of humor. Freak's the total package, ladies, and her sexual orientation has absolutely nothing to do with that. Your mom and dad must really love you, if they have Freak on your detail."

"Thanks, Square Peg. Hey, the girls are at school and we gotta go in. Good luck with the Boys and Girls Club spot. Try not to flub it more than three or 12 times, OK?" I said.

"Fu—er, for sure, Beautiful Girl. Call when you can. 'Bye first daughters," he said, hanging up. I shut the phone off and said, "Ready for the day now?"

Both of the girls just stared at me, so I said, "OK, good. You already know the drill, but you *never* open the door or get out before me, and you *always* let me lead, right?" The *princesses* nodded, and Brooke said, "We just talked with Kelvin *Richardson*. Joely and Miranda and Madison are all gonna be *soooo* jealous!" Her comment seemed to break the tension between us, and although neither girl apologized for their intrusion into my personal life I didn't really mind—they were kids, and most kids (including this one during her youth) seldom if ever apologized for being nosy.

We went into school and the daily grind began. It really is boring guarding the kids of famous people, because for the most part they're considered off limits, unlike the other principals I've guarded. Keeping vigilant guarding against crazed lunch ladies or a rogue janitor isn't the same as being on the lookout for the KKK, the Taliban, or some crazed right-winger who wants to take down the Secretary of the Treasury because she's putting tracking chips in the currency.

That was a real threat against SecTreas when I was in the general security pool—the note looked like it had been written by a squirrel with carpal tunnel syndrome, but we had to take it seriously. Good thing we did, too—the guy had two Desert Eagle .50 cal pistols with full mags and an itinerary of SecTreas's movements for the week when we caught him. He also had no regard for his own life—his first words to us were "I'ma kill that bitch fer fuckin' up mah hunnert dollah bills, and ain't no way ta stop me 'cause ah don' care if'n ah lives or dies."

That is the very definition of a nightmare scenario for the Secret Service, because we all know that you can't stop an assassin who is willing to die in the performance of their duty. It's also why anyone guarding anyone important is always on their toes—because those crazies can come from anywhere at any time you have to always be tuned in. It's also why guarding kids at school is so dangerously boring—nothing ever happens at school, so you get lax and lose focus.

Unless your principals are *princesses*, and you're on a rolling schedule, and your boss is like a crazed tweeker whose efforts to obtain Sudafed have all failed, in which case you're bored, but you're not *bored*, mainly because there are unlimited opportunities to keep you focused.

The first week of guarding the *princesses* was filled with drills, endless bitching about everything by our principals and absolutely nothing else. The people at the Friends School were very professional, the teachers appeared to be exceptional and the school itself presented very few problems. We had a great safe room at the opposite end of the school from the main entrance (it was the least likely place for an attack to come from) and we drilled the *princesses* on how to get there in case it was needed (you should have heard them when we got to school at 6:30 am for the practice—it was like an F5 tornado of bitching) and we had no trouble with traffic or anything else.

The second week was much like the first. I liked being in the classroom for Miss Aducci's second hour AP Literature class (Allison) and fourth hour World History with Mr. Messner (Brooke), and I really liked fifth hour economics with Mr. Gunden (Allison), but I couldn't stand third hour algebra with Mr. VonSeggen (Brooke) because Mr. VonSeggen was a sexist asshole. All the other classes were good, especially Ms. Nelson's fiction writing class during first hour (Allison, although most of the rest of the kids weren't awake). The routine wasn't all that routine and everything was proceeding just fine, right up to the Monday morning of the third week.

I was hanging out with Allison and her small herd of friends (a broad spectrum of Hilarys, Ashleys, Ashlees, Ashleighs, Tiffanys, Tiffanis, Samanthas, Rachels, Serenas, Bellas, Heathers, Hollys, Hayleys and Gerta Maartensdottir—her father was the Icelandic ambassador to the U.S.) when I saw a herd of trouble headed down the hall.

It was a gang of senior jocks, led by the son of the Senate Majority Leader, who was also captain of the football team. This was the group we'd been warned about, because apparently they were the ones who tried to pull shit on the underclass girls, like pinching asses, "accidentally" putting their hands on tits and occasionally crowding girls back into their lockers in order to grope everything possible, a process that they called "frisking."

You could smell the hormones from two hallways away, and I could tell from their swagger they'd grown accustomed to us being there, which meant that they might make a run at my principal. I didn't care if she was a *princess*, I wasn't going to let any boy—son of the Majority Leader or not—count coup on my principal by groping her in any way.

Did I mention that I hate sexual harassment, as well as the strong picking on the weak, or high school boys in general (there isn't a segment of the population any dumber, except perhaps

Tea Partiers, the KKK and fundamentalist preachers—and I'm pretty sure that I'm insulting those people).

The Secret Service rule with kids at school was to stay as close as possible to the protectee without being a part of the group, but far enough away that they had some privacy when talking with their friends. That meant that I was close enough to unobtrusively leave my guard position and glide toward my protectee when I saw the herd of trouble deploy in a formation designed to envelop Allison and her friends. That meant that when the football captain reached around behind her to pinch her ass it was my ass that he actually got a grip on. He smiled at the first daughter as he squeezed what he thought was her ass, but the smile dropped off when he realized that he couldn't really pinch her, since the ass he was trying to grip was far too round and muscular to gain any purchase on.

His face really fell when I said, "Sorry, sonny, but you need to buy me dinner for that" as I barged between he and Allison. She said, "Hey, Freak, watch it," but by then Flipper and Patsy were moving in and sweeping her away from the herd of trouble. She looked over her shoulder as her group moved down the hall away from me, a quizzical look on her face.

I turned to the herd of trouble and said, "OK, big boy, let's take a trip to the principal's office." The son of the Senate Majority Leader looked me up and down and tried to brazen his way out of it. "Is there a problem, Officer?" He smirked back at his herd and nearly shit himself when he looked back, because I'd closed the space between us from three feet to three inches and had my creds right in his face.

He tried to step away from me but I wouldn't let him. I flipped my creds to the badge and said, "That's *Agent*, and yeah, you grabbing my buttocks is definitely a problem, laddie."

He recovered nicely and said, "Whaaattt? I most certainly did nothing of the sort, Secret Agent Man." He and the herd smirked at each other until Bookie and Gangster came up on either side of me. Gangster said, "Sonny, we all wear body cams and we got you clean, so just come along to the principal's office so we can get your ass thrown out of school and call the cops to arrest you for assaulting a federal officer and criminal sexual conduct."

"And by the way, that womyn you were addressing is Secret Service Agent Glinka Glickstien, you moron," Bookie said. "You should also know that she's a U.S. Marine and Special Forces operator, so for your own protection I'd watch my mouth and my attitude."

I give him credit—the kid still tried still tried to bull his way through the trouble. He gave us a lazy smile and said, "I imagine that my dad might have something to say about all of this. You do know who he is, don't you?"

I said, "You play poker, laddie?"

He said, "Yeah. So what?" It was the perfect teenage posture: a slope shouldered shrug with no eye contact and the thousand-yard stare of the terminally bored. Like a troop of brain-damaged orangutans (my apologies to orangutans everywhere) his herd of trouble assumed the same posture so perfectly that it almost made me laugh.

"So you're going all in with two pair, but I'm holding a royal flush," I said.

"Oh, yeah?" the kid said, but his apparent boredom was a very effective "fuck you, asshole" face. "I'm sure I have no idea what on earth you're talking about, Agent Cluckstein." His bravado finally got to me. I burst out laughing, unable to take his posturing without just letting go.

He and the herd of trouble stirred restlessly, unsure of how to deal with my dismissive laughter. He started to say something but Gangster said, "The president trumps the majority leader in every way, every day, you supercilious twit. Now stop the crap and let's go to the office so you can get arrested."

The befuddled look that flashed across the kid's face told me something. I realized that his herd may have put him in an awkward position—either he didn't know that he was trying to pinch the first daughter or someone had put a heavy dare on him. That may sound ridiculous to some of you, but to a teenager a challenge of that kind comes fraught with danger: refuse and you may lose your place in the social hierarchy, or worse, be shunned by the group, or worst, be excluded from the herd completely. Since membership and place in the social order were what drove most teens, especially at school, where it mattered most, it was possible that the kid had no alternatives that he could see.

I remembered those days and decided to give him an out.

I snapped my fingers and he looked up at me. I said, "What's your name, laddie?"

"Ryan," he said, "Ryan Horford."

"Mr. Horford, instead of going to the office, I'd like you and four of your friends to accompany my two friends and myself to the gymnasium."

"Why?" he said, not belligerent but curious.

"I'd like to show you something, something that may explain why your conduct isn't the best idea around the first daughters," I said. The entire herd looked apprehensive, so I said, "No one's going to be touched or in any way manhandled. I don't want to haul you somewhere and beat the shit out of you, I just want to show you something, OK?"

"And I won't get in trouble, you know, *arrested* or anything?" young Ryan said.

"If you see what I want to show you and meet one minor condition I won't have you arrested for putting your hand on me," I said.

Ryan stuck out his hand and said, "Your word on it?"

I was touched by his naïveté, but also by his decisiveness, so I stuck out my hand and we shook. He had a politician's handshake—firm but not squeezing. "You have my word," I said.

"Deal," Ryan said. He picked four of his friends and we went down to the gym, and from there into the weight room.

I said, "Can you guys load 225 on a bench press bar, and put the collars on?" Two of the herd moved to put the weights on the bar as I took off my suit coat, folded it up and laid it on a table littered with papers. I unsnapped my shoulder holster rig, took off my 1076s and laid them on top of my coat.

The weights were settled on the bar, so I checked that the safety collars were seated properly and laid down on the bench. I didn't do anything special to get ready, just picked the bar off the rack and started doing reps with 225 pounds. When I got to 10 I said, "You should know that I played football, wrestled and ran track in high school. You should know that I was a varsity wrestler and track athlete at Michigan State University, and that my senior year I played football. You should also know that I am probably pound for pound the strongest human being you will ever meet."

I'd been doing reps with the weight the entire time I was talking. My breathing hadn't changed, I wasn't red in the face (OK, I was, but then again I usually was—you trying being a fair-skinned redhead and see what your face looks like) and I wasn't showing any apparent strain. I did a few more reps and said, "Anybody know how many reps I've done with 225?"

"Thirty-five," Bookie and Gangster said. "You owe me Pepsis, the both of you." I did five more reps for an even 40 and said, "You guys are football players, so you know that the best NFL prospects usually only do 30, maybe 35 of these at the combine, right?" The herd all nodded at me, their eyes wide, so I said, "And those are usually left tackles that weigh 325 pounds plus, right?" Same amazed nods from the kids, same wide eyes, so I said, "And I only weigh 167 pounds, and I'm about to do my 50th rep, right?"

"Holy *fuck*," Ryan Horford said as I did my 50th rep and put the bar back on the rack.

"Exactly," I said. "I didn't tell you that I have black belts in four different martial arts styles, that I still hold the record for running through the Marine Corps obstacle course, or that I can dunk a basketball at 5'7", or that I served several combat tours in places you'd rather not go."

They were all staring at me in complete amazement. I looked at Ryan Horford with my best Special Forces game face and said, "And I didn't tell you that *nobody* is going to touch me *or* one of my girls without their consent, but it's true. Is that *clear*, gentlemen?"

The herd nodded so vigorously that they looked like bobbleheads in the rear window of a low rider. Finally Ryan Horford said, "Ma'am, I apologize for trying to, for actually touching your, ah… for, er—uhhh, you know, I apologize for being a-a, er, dick. It won't happen again, ma'am."

"And you just met my condition to keep our agreement, so what you need to do now is go to class. I'll square the tardy with the principal. Oh, and one other thing."

"Yes, ma'am?" young Ryan said.

"Stop calling me ma'am. You guys can call me Freak, OK?" I said. Once you've broken the enemy you don't beat or berate them, you co-opt them to your side. I was pretty sure that young Ryan and his herd would spread the word about the weight room encounter, and that they would scare off any other idiots who thought that they were going to go after our protectees. I was also pretty sure that that would make our jobs easier, and that it would make the girls' lives easier, too.

It turned out that my ideas were right, right up until they weren't.

Then they were shit.

CHAPTER 58

Princesses Suck

So despite my efforts to make their lives at school better and easier the *princesses* kept being megabitches to everyone, especially me. It wasn't constant, but every time I thought that we were making headway one or the other or both of the *princesses* would jump into the bitchy pool and splash some joy over the rest of us. Rather than bore you with every detail I'll just highlight a few.

The "You're too Ugly for Prom" incident featured Allison getting all tarted up for her prom, greeting her date at the White House and then telling him in full view of the president, first lady and others who'd gathered to see her off that "the Freak and her fat friend from Jersey are too ugly to go to my prom." When her father pointed out that it wasn't our job to be "pretty" but rather to be effective Allison said, "Why can't they be both? Aren't there any good-looking Secret Service agents besides James Bond?"

At that point the president told her that if she didn't stop wailing like a five-year-old she could stay home. The *princess* rolled her eyes and said, "Oh, all right." She turned to me and said, "You just stay out of the pictures. I don't want my prom pictures to have *you* in them—and I don't want the photographer to *break* his camera." That line was delivered so nobody but her date and little cadre of friends could hear, and got quite the laugh.

Once we got into the car it got worse, and the night reached a crescendo when Allison and her date tried to sneak off and ran into Buddha and Foghorn. Once it became clear that she wasn't going to be going to any of the mini-parties associated with the prom, or even be able to sneak off for a snogging session with her date the *princess* went on a tear, calling me a nasty shithead, a fucking bitch and a fun-sucker…even though I wasn't the one who told her no, or stopped her from absconding.

In the car on the way home Allison cried a river of crocodile tears and said, "Thanks a lot, you Freak, for *ruining* my prom with your ugly face and stupid rules! I'm telling my dad I want you *fired*!"

I did not witness the fight she and her parents had about me after we got her back to the White House, but I heard about it from the first lady's Head of Detail, a blonde dreamboat named Gena Boyle, who told me that Superbitch was really fired up about my "unprofessional conduct," although she correctly pointed out that there had been no such thing (to me, not to Superbitch—hey, I didn't blame her—she had mouths to feed and the first lady really was the White Witch). As I told the Director when she questioned us about it I did everything by the book, it was just that Allison didn't like the book.

Major Difficulty put it more succinctly. "She's a little *princess* that's never heard the word no. We're not responsible for bad parenting or bad manners."

Amen, my sister.

The other big blowup was when Brooke went to a birthday party at a roller rink. We had our pre-party briefing and Major Difficulty said, "Any volunteers to skate?" It turned out that Hot Rod,

Hero, Sleepy, Ed and Gangster all had extensive skating experience. In fact, Gangster had been a roller derby babe when she was in college, going by the name Hammerin' Hannah from Hoboken, so she was the leader on the rink, with the others following her lead. The rest of us would secure the perimeter and the two doors in the place.

Brooke immediately objected because she didn't want "some hippo with a New Jersey accent following her around." When Major Difficulty made it clear that Gangster had plenty of experience skating the little *princess* said, "Fine, but tell that whale to stay out of my way. Everyone will want to take pictures of me and she'll definitely get in the way—she's as big as a *house*."

So we got to the rink on that happy note—and the press was there. Some handy-dandy parent squealed so that their little bundle of joy could have their 15 minutes of fame and now we had a problem. Major Difficulty said, "Just hustle her in the building and don't worry about it." So I got out and waited for Brooke, and when she got out I took her arm and prepared to charge in the door behind Bookie and Gordo, with Count Chocolate and Sleepy right behind us. The big Secret Service Suburban was right next to the door, so we had about 10 feet of run-in, which was just about ideal.

Just about.

Both *princesses* constantly bitched about us touching them, and lately Allison had introduced the term "manhandled" to their vocabulary. *Princess* Brooke chose that moment to get her 15-year-old knickers in a knot about being "manhandled." She tried to yank away from me while screaming "Stop *manhandling* me, you *ogre*!"

I let go of her arm and she pitched forward into Gordo's back. He immediately fell over and his legs scythed through the air as he fought for balance, but all he did was take me down. Brooke walked in the door of the rink by walking right over Gordo's face—her foot pushed off his forehead as she regally went out of sight of the press, leaving us to scramble up like a couple of circus clowns.

Count Chocolate and Sleepy helped us get up while the cameras whirred and we went in the rink, where things promptly got worse.

Brooke the *princess* was spouting off to her friends about "putting us in our place" (thanks, Superbitch—I'd heard this tune before from the first lady) when Gordo and I marched up to her. She refused to look at us as she put her skates on, until I finally said, "Brooke, look at me." Her little blonde head came up with such a sneer on it that I almost cracked her across the room (luckily my impulse control was in good shape—thanks, Marine Corps), but all I said was, "You remember that you don't ever pull away from me, right? You remember what your father told you about the Secret Service protection you get, right? The part about you could die if you don't listen to me, right?"

That stopped her in her tracks, and the sneer faded, but she still said, "I just don't know why you have to *manhandle* me. I would've gone in just like you said, but you have to get all *grabby*. I just want you to leave me *alone*."

I squatted down to her eye level. I stared into her brown eyes with my green ones and said, in the quietest voice I owned, "First, I'm sworn to protect you, so I can't just leave you alone. Second, if I really wanted to manhandle you don't you think I could? Third, I took your arm so that I was close enough to stop any bullets aimed at you."

"Yeah, *right*," she sneered.

I lifted the bench she was sitting on up to my eye level. I gave her my best Marine Corps DI look and said, "You better believe it, missy. I'll do anything to keep you safe, and so will anybody else on this detail, including Gordo, whose face you just used as a doormat. You owe him an apology, don't you think?"

Her eyes were about to bug out of her head, but she said, "No. I don't owe anybody an apology for *anything*. I'm certainly not going to apologize to a *Mexican*, even if he is an agent. Why do they let *those* people in the *U.S.* Secret Service anyway?"

Once again my Marine Corps/Secret Service training kicked in and I didn't hurl her and her three little friends who were also sitting on the bench against the wall like I wanted to. Instead I set them down and said, "Very well, Miss Sheehan. Enjoy your skate." I grabbed Gordo by the arm and we marched away to take up positions at the rail to the rink. I was shaking and my face was beet red, Gordo was shaking and muttering in Spanish and all the rest of the agents who'd seen what happened and heard the exchange were seriously contemplating using a certain *princess* like a garden stake.

So the skating began and our *princess* went on the rink. She wasn't a bad skater, but Gangster was clearly the star of the show. She could skate backward faster than any of the kids could skate going forward, and she had some serious horsepower in her thighs, which were just big columns of muscle. In fact, even though Gangster was "built like a refrigerator with a head," (only she wasn't five-foot-six, 215—my apologies to Jim Croce and all the wymyn of roller derby), she could really maneuver on skates.

Not being the center of attention soon annoyed the *princess*. She began bitching about "big fat pigs *hogging* the show" and ended with "I'll show *her*," which is when the real trouble began.

Brooke waited until Gangster was playing crack the whip with some kid, then skated as fast as she could until she was right behind the pair. When Gangster released the kid she spun in a half circle—and there was the *princess*, basically crouched behind her. It was supposed to be like that old playground trick where somebody gets down behind you and then somebody else pushes you over them, but instead it turned into the mother of all goat ropes.

Gangster tried to go right over the *princess* by lifting her front leg straight out in front of her and just spinning in another half circle, but Brooke got scared and stood up right under Gangster's skate, lifting her leg up so she was doing the standing splits. As Gangster tried to keep her balance Brooke panicked and shoved up on her skate, which sent Gangster backwards and down on her ass.

The *princess* thought she was free and tried to just skate away, but as Gangster was falling on her ass her skate kicked Brooke's, which sent the *princess* flying in a flat spin just off the rink's surface.

Brooke looked like a giant weed whacker as she mowed down her friends at the party. There were teenagers falling down everywhere until the only people on their feet were Hot Rod, Hero, Sleepy, Ed and Gangster, who popped up off the surface of the rink like it was electrified. Most of the kids were laughing and whooping it up about falling, and it might have been OK until one of her friends said, "Brooke, you looked so funny flying through the air! How did you do that?" The girl was laughing and clearly kidding, but Brooke reacted like the prize *princess* she was.

She sat up and began screaming and cursing. "It was not my fucking fault it was that fat hippo's fault! I didn't do anything except skate and she deliberately knocked me down and made me look stupid, that *fat fucking bitch whale!*" She then began crying and shrieking a steady stream of curse words that were not in sentence form.

We solved that problem when the mother of the friend whose birthday party it was marched out on the rink, got down next to Brooke and informed her of the facts of life in a firm, furious, but quiet tone.

> Mom of the Birthday Girl: It's time for you to be quiet now, sweetheart.
> Princess: No! That whale embarrassed me on purpose! I—
> MotBG: Now, now, honey, I'm sure that she didn't do that. It's time for you to calm down.
> Princess: You're not my mom, you don't get to tell me what to do! I'll scream if I want to!
> MotBG: Now sweetie, it's Danielle's birthday party, not yours. Please quiet down now.
> Princess: Do you know who my dad is? I can scream whenever I want!
> MotBG: Listen you spoiled little brat, I don't give a damn if your dad is King of the World.
> It's my kid's birthday party and you're ruining it, so shut the fuck up NOW.

I give her a lot of credit, because the MotBG never raised her voice and she kept a smile on her face instead of knocking Brooke ass over tea cart. She also got the *princess* to shut up, and Sleepy (who was the only agent that Brooke liked) helped her up and over to the rail. She kept right on going off the rink and over to the bench to change her shoes. "I want to go home now," the *princess* said.

None of us cheered, but it's a fact that the MotBG got five dozen red roses the next week from an anonymous source known only as A Grateful Badger.

The Great Prom Incident and The Rink Affair were noteworthy bumps in the road of our protection of the *princesses*, but there was one more of even more note.

It was a perfectly ordinary day coming home from school. The girls were their usual snide selves, but we were successfully ignoring them by staying alert for problems on the way to the House. We were approaching a corner when some dumbass cut across six lanes of traffic to turn in front of our motorcade. Hot Rod was driving (like Badass, he was a graduate of the Secret Service driving school) and he stopped on a dime, without really slamming us around too hard, but both the *princesses* shrieked anyway, and Allison was just a bit too vigorous.

She turned toward me and puked her guts out.

It turns out that she'd been feeling a bit queasy since fourth period, when she and her friend Haylee guzzled a pint of vodka in the bathroom, but she was trying to keep it together until she got home. The "car accident" (her words) made the perfect cover for her to let it go and make sure no issue was made of her erratic conduct (several of us had already noticed it and made comments to Major Difficulty).

You already know that I'm tough, that I've been wounded multiple times (sorry, but it's still classified) and that I'm physically gifted, but even Superman has his Kryptonite, and mine is vomit. I can take all sorts of gore and whatnot, but if somebody barfs I'm either going to clear the area immediately or ralph right along with them.

You can't get out of a shower of vomit inside an armored Suburban.

As soon as my olfactory system registered the odor of Allison's vomit I let fly with a gout of my own puke.

Things went to hell in a handbasket after that.

It turned out that Brooke had a bit of an upset tummy too. She barfed all over Flipper, who gagged and then upchucked all over Hot Rod, who couldn't roll down his window before he heaved. The sound and smell of all the puking triggered a sympathetic response from Ed, who spewed all over the front seat, and then sent a small deluge into the next seat, which unfortunately hit Allison as she had her mouth open to once again worship the porcelain goddess.

That set off round two of World War Puke.

By the time we were done everybody was covered in a rainbow confection of vomit, and Allison retched so hard that she shit her pants.

At least we managed to keep the details of World War Puke out of the press, although none of us could keep it out of our olfactory memory.

The president later apologized after Allison told him that she had deliberately held it in so she could barf on me. He was embarrassed by her conduct, but probably not as much as we were about ours as Secret Service agents.

It was a fact that every time we left after that someone would say, "It's time to get mounted up in the Vomit Comet" and we'd all laugh.

I think that we had to burn that Suburban, though.

In any case, it went on like that, although usually at a lower intensity. I wasn't on Allison's first date while a first daughter, which I was told was a shitstorm, but I was present when Brooke went to a Model UN exercise at George Mason University, which was for sure a shitstorm (if your dad is President of the United States you really don't want to have to play Iran at the UN). The entire detail was present at the Kennedy Center Honors when some young pop star who was supposed to be honoring Jon Bon Jovi declared his undying love for Allison and she burst into tears, causing her makeup to run (who doesn't wear waterproof makeup? I don't wear any makeup, but isn't that a thing?), which made her wipe her face off, only she missed getting parts of it, which left her looking like a circus clown on international TV, which of course was our (my) fault.

Welcome to "Let's Eat a Shit Sandwich," the show where highly trained and dedicated and underpaid public servants get abused by teenagers for no reason at all. What do we have for our contestants today, Wayne?

We have SOS, Bill…the Same Old Shit, *ad nauseum.*

If that sounds like bitching, well, it is, sort of, but despite the ongoing battles with the *princesses,* which were certainly fueled by the Superbitch, life was pretty good.

Unfortunately, nothing and nobody lasts forever, except for one simple truth.

Change is the only constant in the universe.

CHAPTER 59

Death Comes for the Bishop (Apologies to Willa Cather)

So life went on as we guarded the princesses. I became really good friends with everybody on the detail, especially Gangster, Flipper and Foghorn, who along with Ed, Hurricane and I formed the so-called Gang of Six.

We went places and did things because we were all relatively young and smart, and five of the six of us were good-looking (age wasn't transforming me into an even average looking broad—dogs still howled when I walked by, and small children still pointed and said, 'Mommy, what is that?' Unfortunately you can't hide the truth).

Everybody seemed to have a love life, even me. Mine was more of the hit and run variety, as in I'd hit it and they'd run. Hurricane said it was because I was too much womyn for any of the callow assholes I dated, Ed said it was because I made love like a Klingon (some of my partners may have required some medical attention after we were done), but I thought it was because of the fright mask that was my face, or the Burning Bush.

The Burning Bush? That's what I call my pubes, because in this era of Brazilians, landing strips, top knots, Chaplins, triangles, reverse triangles, short cuts, French waxes, voids, arrows, bunny ears, princesses and vajazzles I just let my fiery red pubic hair grow uncontrolled, unmanaged, and ungroomed. I'm never going to wear any kind of swimsuit except a full-cut one-piece, so I don't have to worry about anything peeking out of my suit, and since my pubic hair is the approximate density and consistency of a really good Persian rug I don't feel like going through all of the torment to groom it, plus I have to stand for long hours in full view of the public and worldwide television cameras, so I can't be scratching my crotch any time I want to (try the whole shaving routine—it'll itch even if you do everything right). As for waxing, well, the blood loss would probably kill me, or I'd kill whoever was trying to pull the wax off, so that's out. In any case, many modern men are apparently scared off by aggressive natural pubic hair, even if it is clean and beautifully conditioned. I say fuck them, the horse they rode in on, and the family dog if they can't take a forest of fiery red hair in order to make love with me. It's their loss.

In any case, Badass and Hurricane got on so well that they got engaged, and Hurricane asked me to be her maid of honor (I didn't want to think about the dress for that wedding—what does an albino dwarf wear to her wedding? Please don't let it be pink). In Chicago Kid Galahad and Miss Bitchy Face weren't engaged, but they were living together and having a hell of a good time. Mamba found a cool guy named Ben Weigelman, a commodities broker at the Chicago Mercantile Exchange, to hang out with. Everybody seemed happy with their lives, except Weasel and Jewey, who stopped virtually everything except trying to connect now FBI Director Malcolm Sorenson with the two shadowy agents, Smith and Jones, who arranged to have us killed by the Ku Klux Klan in Morehead, Kentucky.

Professionally we were all doing really, really, well. Successfully guarding anyone is usually a thankless job, because your ideal protection involves you not being seen or heard, since that means that nothing happened to your protectee(s), which is what your number one goal was when you started the detail. However, this president was keenly aware of what we did (you wouldn't believe the letters The Man got—there are a lot of stupid, crazy people out there who have too much time on their hands) and always thanked us, looked out for us, and made sure we got our due.

That meant modest pay raises according to the government pay schedule, some public kudos, lots of private thank-yous and no problem staying where we were comfortable. It didn't hurt that the first daughters' detail turned out to be one of the best trained, hardest working and most efficient details in the history of the Secret Service. Like a good professional sports team we became very adept at using our individual strengths to cover any weaknesses we might have. We all probably liked hot dogs too much, and we drank so much Pepsi that we might as well've opened a franchise, but after that…we were damned good at what we did.

So everything was copacetic when I got a call from my brother Doc. He started giving me all the gossip about good old Battle Creek. The best piece was that the captain of the wymyn's volleyball team, who was hugely pregnant, was elected homecoming queen at Harper Creek and proceeded to give birth at the dance after the homecoming game. It was a huge scandal, especially after it was revealed that the principal at the local Catholic high school was the father (it made the national news the day after Doc called me). He talked about Mumsy and Pops, who were really doing well after the death of my *zayde*, and how well my brother Roady was fitting in to the law practice. "He's like a much younger version of *zayde*. He takes on every case like it's going to be in the Supreme Court and everybody loves him for it. He and Mom are both working on a case suing Monsanto for terrorizing local soybean farmers about the seeds they're planting."

"WTF?" I said.

"These three farmers down by Athens decided that seeds were too expensive from Monsanto, so for six years they took turns growing, harvesting, and storing their own seeds. Then they started planting them and crossing their beans with some seeds they bought from Brazil on the internet. After four years they were growing their own hybrid plants and doing pretty well, until one of the farmers mentioned what they'd done to some reporter for WWMT in Kalamazoo, and then Monsanto came down on them like a ton of bricks. The company filed a copyright and patent infringement suit for $850 million dollars against the three guys, and they came to Mumsy and Roady," Doc said. "Guess what Roady said."

"We have to stop these rapacious corporations from crushing the little guys—no, wait, he said "family farmers"—or there won't be anything but corporate agriculture left. Our very way of life is being threatened," I said. "Unless he just said, 'These giant assholes need to fuck off.'"

"It's good! Right down the middle first time, Freak. And who does that sound like?" Doc said.

"*Zayde* always said Roady would follow in his footsteps—sounds like he was right. Cervantes would've loved those two," I said.

"Yeah, he'd've loved you, too, Freak. All three of you—and Mumsy—always tilting at windmills. Just like old Bishop O'Dowd," Doc said.

"What about Bishop O'Dowd?" I said.

"You didn't get a call? Fast Eddie didn't call you?" Doc said.

"No. What the hell's going on?" I said.

"Nothing. The bishop died in his sleep two days ago. I saw Fast Eddie and he said he'd let you know," Doc said.

"I didn't even know he was sick. What the fuck happened?" I said.

"Fast Eddie found him dead in his bed—he was supposed to do a baptism and never showed, so Fast Eddie did it and then rushed over to the bishop's House, but he was already gone. The cops did an autopsy—he had a brain aneurysm that just let go. The coroner said he never felt a thing, just went to sleep and never woke up," Doc said.

"Holy shit," I said. "The town'll never be the same—that old guy *was* Battle Creek."

"No shit," Doc said. "People are already having a fit because it's pretty clear there won't be a replacement bishop toddling down the road to the Cereal City. It looks like Fast Eddie's gonna have to hold the fort by himself, which isn't making the old Catholic ladies happy."

"They still can't get over a black priest? C'mon, man! Fast Eddie's been a priest for what—12 years now? Is it just racial, or is it that he isn't a bishop?" I said.

"Well, Mrs. Miller says it's because Eddie is too young, too modern and too attractive. She told Mumsy and Pops that some of the ladies in her early-bird Mass group think that he tempts the young ladies too much with his—their words—*virility*," Doc said.

"He is a good-looking guy, but I've never seen him even look at a womyn like a womyn, not since he got serious about the church. He wasn't really that much of a hound when we were young. He went with Enir Farouk, and then he was fairly serious with Casey White, but then the Church came into his life and he pretty much packed it up," I said.

"He is black as night—maybe the old ladies are using virility as code for the n-word," Doc said. (In case you think that I edited that word, my brother really used 'n-word.' Nobody in my family would use racial epithets after my *zayde* explained what the word "kike" meant. I can swear like a sailor but it's never going to get racial, because that's just out of bounds. As my Uncle Mort always said, 'A schmuck's a schmuck whatever color they are.')

I agreed that it was possible, and then we went on to other topics until we hung up. I had some time, so I called Fast Eddie.

"Hey, Freak. I been meaning to call you, but I've been kinda busy. The Old Man went and died on me, Freak, and it's hit me pretty hard," Fast Eddie said, his voice quavering with emotion. He grew up without a father, and I know that he treated Bishop O'Dowd like the father he never had, so that wasn't surprising, but what he said next was.

"He lied to you, Freak. The Old Man knew, or he thought he knew, who killed Tim Miller," Fast Eddie said. "I just got through reading his note to me about his files, and the first lines are "I am sorry I lied to your friends about Timothy Miller. I am certain that I know who killed him, and why, but I could not break the sanctity of the confessional. Even now that I am dead I cannot, although I give you permission to let your friends read my notes and diary so that they may solve their case. May God forgive me.'"

I was stunned. Bishop O'Dowd was such an upright, honest, ethical person that I couldn't believe he looked me right in the eye and lied. I also couldn't believe he lied to Fast Eddie, but from the quiet crying that I heard on the phone it was clear that he had. I waited until my old friend took a breath before I said, "Eddie, you can't let one lie demean the memory of a great man. Bishop O'Dowd loved you like you were his son, and sometimes fathers keep secrets from their sons."

"Thanks for that Freak, but I'm not crying about the lie, I'm crying about The Old Man's thoughtfulness in leaving me the note. He was like that, thoughtful, and I'm really crying because he's gone. You remember my so-called dad—the guy with the belt and a taste for other wymyn?— and what he did to me and mt brother and my mom, right? I know it's a cliché, but that asshole with the belt wasn't anything but a sperm donor. The Old Man was my actual father, and I already miss him. I'm never going to be half the man he was—don't bother to try and tell me I will be, because we both know that's a fucking lie—but I'm going to try, because The Old Man wanted me to," Fast Eddie said without drawing a breath.

"Well, I happen to think that you'll be just as good as the Bishop after 40 or so years, but that's just my asshole opinion," I said. "What I really need you to do is shoot me those notes and papers, ya useless fucker." I hoped that my old friend still had his sense of humor, and luckily he did. He laughed and laughed, and I joined him. Finally he said, "Leave it to you, Freak, to still be just like a bull in a China shop. Ain't no delicacy in you, is there?"

"Why change a good thing?" I said. "It's worked this long, and fuck anybody who doesn't like it, y'know?"

Father Fast Eddie Robinson laughed again and said, "The Old Man liked you too, Freak, because he said you lacked the capacity for blarney—it was easy to understand where you stood because you never held back. He commented on what a rare gift that is in today's world, and how much he admired your simplicity—that was a compliment, believe me."

"I always said the bishop was an astute judge of character. I'm sorry for your loss, Eddie, and I'll say the *kaddish* for him," I said. Saying the Jewish Prayers for the Dead was the least I could do if the Bishop's diary was going to give us a clue to solving the murder of Tim Miller.

"It can't hurt, Freak, although if The Old Man isn't going to heaven the rest of us can just give it a rest—he was the best person I ever met, and I've met lots of people, including a Pope. I'll send ya those notes and his diary ASAP," Fast Eddie said.

"Thanks, Eddie. Is it OK if we copy it? It'll save time instead of trying to pass it around, because you know everybody who's met Mrs. Miller is going to want to read it," I said.

"As long as you keep it in the family and don't use it to embarrass the bishop's memory I don't care if you copy it," Fast Eddie said. "I will curse you if it ever causes him any trouble, though." I noted the lack of laughter and decided he probably wasn't kidding about the curse, so I said, "How about this. We'll classify it and only print numbered copies that have to be signed out and then signed back in. After we've all had a chance at one of the numbered copies we'll put all but one in the burn bag. After we're all done I'll keep the copy and send the original to you. Sound OK?"

"Perfect. I'll FedEx 'em to ya, should be there tomorrow. Do me a favor, willya Freak?" Fast Eddie said.

"Absolutely. Who do ya want done and where do ya want the body shipped?" I said. It was an old joke between old friends, designed to alleviate stress and remind the other person how much they meant to whoever told the joke (and it kept things from getting too maudlin—I don't mind genuine emotion, but mushy wasn't my style).

Fast Eddie laughed again and said, "It's not like that, but I do want you to let me know what you find out about Tim's murder. I'd like to think that I did the right thing to rectify the only mistake that I've ever seen the Old Man make. Can you do that, Freak? I don't want you to do it if you'll get in trouble."

"No problem, Father Robinson. Once we catch the motherfucker I'll be able to tell you anything that you want to know. Hell, I'll bring you the case file if you want, because right now everybody is completely in the dark about it—even if the Bishop's notes don't tell us anything at least we'll be re-engaged with the case," I said.

"Roger that. I gotta go, Freak. The parish needs me, and I still got shit to do for the Old Man's funeral mass. The Cardinal is coming from Detroit, but I'm doing most of it, plus I gotta supervise the setup in the church, plus I'm in charge of finding a new principal for St. Phil—you heard about that, right?" Fast Eddie said.

"Yeah, Doc told me. Sounds like a great time for you to be an incisive, forward-thinking church leader," I said.

"Fuck you, Freak. It's a shitstorm of epic proportions," Fast Eddie said. We both laughed and he hung up.

I immediately called Weasel in Chicago. He answered by saying, "No, I haven't found any goddamned connection between those fuckers yet, but I'm fixin' to."

"Ya'll been hanging out with Gomer too, much, Weasel," I said. "And that isn't why I called. I'm gonna send you guys a package of material that I need you to analyze—it's notes and a diary from Bishop O'Dowd of Battle Creek."

"Why'd that jackass give 'em up now? He die or something?" Weasel said, clearly joking.

"Well, yeah, he did. He had an aneurysm and died in his sleep," I said.

"Other than the fact that I'm going to rot in hell, I'm also a fucking dipshit asshole," Weasel said. "I'm sorry, Freak. I'm still pretty strung out looking for the connection between those assholes in Morehead and that fucktard from Fart, Barf and Itch."

"No apology necessary, man. I can't believe your tenacity—don't you know that you're supposed to come in at eight, screw off until lunch and then have the afternoon off? Take a look at the package when you get it, and make enough numbered copies so the squad can look, too. When you guys are done with your analysis send all the copies back to me and I'll take care of them, OK?" I said.

"Roger that, Freak. When will the hard copy be here?" Weasel said.

"I'll get it tomorrow and then send it Fed Ex to you guys, so probably three days all told," I said. I didn't tell him what Fast Eddie said about the bishop lying because I wanted him to approach the documents with an open mind. In fact, I was hoping that the whole Badger Squad would look at the documents independently, because that meant that I'd get independent opinions from eight of the smartest investigators in the world, which increased our chances of catching something. Before I could say anything Weasel said, "Of course we'll all be reading this stuff alone to avoid any group think, which means it'll be a slower process, Freak. It could be 10 days before we get back to you—you know how anal Jewey is about shit."

We both laughed and I said, "Yeah, Weasel, it's all on Jewey. No other anal retentives there. Got it."

"Fuck you, Freak. He's the biggest anal retentive here," Weasel said.

"Because the motherfucker is 6'8", ya maroon," I said. We both laughed and Weasel said, "Hey, I just thought of something. Miss Bitchy Face is in D.C. for meetings today and tomorrow—you could give the package to her to bring back if you get it before she leaves, save some shipping and time."

"Great idea—I'll call her and see if we can get it done. Weasel, thanks again for doing this. You're a good egg," I said.

"Mrs. Miller deserves some answers," Weasel said. "It's a *mitzvah*."

"Roger that. Freak out," I said.

"Badger Squad out," Weasel said.

I called Miss Bitchy Voice, got her voicemail, told her what I wanted and then thought about poor Mrs. Miller for a while. I also thought about how Tom Miller must've felt when his twin was murdered. I knew that I'd probably never get over one of my siblings even dying, much less being murdered, and concluded that if my twin was murdered I'd need serious meds for the duration of my life. I also decided that I'd find out who did it if it killed me, and then I'd kill the guy.

I remembered much later that I also wondered what happened to Tom Miller, and all of Tim's cousins who'd always been at his house when they were kids, but before I did anything to find out about it MBV called me.

"Go for Freak," I said when I saw her number come up. I knew it would piss her off, and I wanted to hear the full Miss Bitchy Voice in irritation mode. I wasn't disappointed.

"Do you *have* to do *that*?" MBV said, clearly irritated with my pretentious, yuppified greeting.

"No, but it makes me giggle when I hear your full treatment, Miss Bitchy Voice," I said, laughing. She laughed and said, "The Kid does the same thing. He says he's just yanking my chain, but I think it turns him on, the dog. I didn't ask for this voice, but I thank my lucky stars I got it, because it helped me meet the love of my life."

"And scares everybody up to Special Assistant to the president," I said. "It'd probably make terrorists piss themselves, too

"There is that," MBV said.

"Cut diamonds and shatter glass," I said.

"Quite possibly," she said.

"Scare small children out of a year's growth," I said.

"Fuck you, Freak," MBV said as we both laughed. We got the business out of the way and then gossiped about the Chicago office for a while, laughing the whole time. Finally she said, "Weasel and Jewey may attack me before I get in the door with this stuff," Miss Bitchy Voice said.

"What's the problem? The Kid would share with them—they're part of his squad, and the squad shares *everything*," I said, knowing what I'd get in response.

"Eeeyyyuuuu! Sick!" MBV said, but she was laughing, too. I laughed along and then said goodbye.

I forgot all about anything else once I'd gotten a half a page into the bishop's diary, and when I finally realized that it was 1:00 a.m. I went to bed shaking my head at all the revelations that I'd read about people back in Battle Creek.

The next day I met MBV and gave her the copies of the diary. We shot the shit for a few minutes and I asked her to read some of it on the plane if she wasn't too busy.

"Sorry, Freak, but no way am I going to have any time to read this. I'm being deliberately vague here, but there appears to be some kind of foreign threat against the first family, especially the first lady," she said.

At least I now knew why she'd been in D.C.—coordinating 17 different intelligence agencies in an effort to define a threat to American personnel or soil wasn't a job for the phone or email, especially when you added in the Secret Service protection component. "What kind of threat?" I said, knowing that she couldn't tell me much.

"Have you ever heard of an organization called Azwaj-i-Tahirat?" Miss Bitchy Voice said.

"No, I'm afraid I'm more interested in homegrown crazies now," I said.

"That's understandable, but this group could become a real pain in the ass if they're real, or if they're serious," MBV said. "Their name means "The Pure Wives," after the wymyn Muhammad married. Sometimes those wives were called "the mothers of the believers," and apparently this group thinks that it's their mission to clean up the first lady's and first daughters' acts, because they're apparently acting like "cheap Western sluts who disgrace the planet with their very presence." That's an exact quote from our latest intercept of their comms. The problem is, we can't tell who they're communicating with—they seem to just broadcast messages hoping that someone will answer."

"That is weird, but you know how some of these splinter groups are—they just want to get their name on the news, or attract the attention of a larger group so that they can be subsumed into the jihad," I said. "Hell, if there were as many groups of jihadists as the media claims there are they'd overwhelm any government they wanted just by sheer numbers. The only problem that I have with this is the specificity—they're just focused on the first lady and first daughters? If that's the case why haven't we heard about it?"

"You will whenever you go in again—the Director was at my briefing yesterday. The truth is, they've only mentioned the first daughters once in passing. Their target really seems to be the first lady. They've talked about her at least nine times that we know of, but the latest stuff is very specific and came right after she got back from her Holland, Belgium and Luxembourg trip," Miss Bitchy Voice said.

"Don't tell me that they had really specific details," I said. MBV nodded and said, "They described her outfits in each place, commented on the fact that one dress was so short that you could almost see her lady parts and also said that in addition to her desecration of wymyn with her dress she also dishonored everyone—we assume that they mean wymyn—by drinking alcohol and fornicating with the Grand Duke of Luxembourg."

"Shithouse mouse," I said. "They had someone watching her like a hawk, because she only accepted a glass of wine at the indoor ceremony, when they toasted the Grand Duke on his ascension to the throne."

"Right. That's also where they took the pictures, and in two of them the first lady has her arm around the Grand Duke. We're pretty sure that's what they mean by fornication, since she and the

Grand Duke were never alone, or even in proximity to each other except for the pictures," MBV said. "No chance that they had sex," MBV said.

"Well, it's no surprise that she put her arm around the guy—what is he, 24, 25 maybe? And I assume that he's as good-looking in person as his press shots," I said.

"Better," MBV said. "I talked to some of the first lady's detail—you know Robin Shaw and Katie Gailhouse?—and they both confirmed that the Grand Duke is one of the best-looking humans they've ever seen," MBV said.

"But…they also confirmed that the flirting was very public, not at all serious and that the first lady did absolutely nothing slutty," I said.

"Exactly. I thought you and the first lady didn't get along?" Miss Bitchy Voice said.

"I don't, but The Ice Queen has class and takes the role of first lady very seriously—she'd never embarrass herself or the president by doing anything even remotely out of line," I said. "She's a stone bitch most of the time, but she's still got standards that she lives up to, y'know?" I said.

"Yeah, I get it. Anyway, this jihadi group has us a little bit worried, mainly because we can't even prove that they exist yet. We'll keep working on it and I'll let you know if anything else comes up," Miss Bitchy Voice said.

"Thanks, MBV. Don't worry too much about Azwaj-i-Tahirat—after all, if we had a beer for every one of these quasi-jihadist groups that threatened somebody the whole world would be drunk," I said. We both laughed our asses off at my *bon mot*, because at the time it seemed like there was a new splinter group of a former splinter group of an offshoot of some fucking organization that was getting a *fatwa* declared against somebody who pissed them off so that they could declare *jihad* against the offending party. It was so common that it became routine, like having cake and ice cream at birthday parties, or weekly mass shootings.

When our laughing seizure wound down I said, "Thanks for the heads-up, MBV, and enjoy Chicago for me. Tell Kid Galahad if he doesn't treat you right I'll come out there and kick his sorry ass," I said.

"Sounds like the right course of action to me," she said in her best bitchy voice. We both laughed again as we hung up.

I always regretted laughing so hard about the whole thing, given subsequent events.

Death will do that to you.

CHAPTER 60

Surprise!

The next day Director Hessler briefed us on Azwaj-i-Tahirat, but with FLOTUS attending the International Wymyn's Conference in Toronto we weren't too worked up about it. The entire atmosphere in D.C. was a bit more relaxed, since POTUS was speaking to the French parliament and then going to London for the G20 summit and Congress was in recess (wow, big surprise there. You ever looked at all of the recesses Congress takes? It's more than your average elementary school—and for longer, too. What a cushy job). The D.C. public school teachers were on strike (nobody blamed them—you try teaching some time, then enjoy your straightjacket in your rubber room), but that didn't really affect us, since we had lots of different routes back to The House (not to mention lights and sirens that sort of cleared the way).

The only real problem was that the princesses' already abominable behavior got worse when their parents were away, which wore everybody out, so by Friday we were really tired and frustrated (we labeled the level of our frustration "The Punch Out Princesses Quotient," or POP-Q. POP-Q One was everyday frustration, POP-Q 10 meant the agent in question needed to be handcuffed or somebody was going to emergency).

It was a POP-Q Nine Friday.

When we left school with the princesses our routine always varied; no one knew when we were leaving, what route we would take or how many vehicles we would be using until we were literally back at the front door of the White House. The Chief of Detail would decide all those things, notify the Director in person or by secure landline and then just grab our assets and go. She notified us by scrambled and coded transmission when we were five minutes from departure and we would assemble the girls to leave.

Also, very few people knew that we had rented three houses that backed onto the drive—one at the top of the drive, one in the middle and one right behind the turnaround drive—or that they were staffed 24-7-365, with two-man teams that were always eyes on the school, which effectively made it impossible for anyone to get near the school without us knowing. Secret Service advance teams also swept the school every morning and searched everyone who came in or out. The princesses were as secure as we could make them, short of imprisoning them in a tower until their hair was long enough for someone to climb up.

That Friday we were in school because the Amicus School was private; its teachers were handsomely compensated, since about two thirds of the kids belonged to VIPs, including some foreign dignitaries whose kids had their own security details. We used a decoy convoy that left the school at 2:35 so it could get caught in the big demonstration the public school teachers had planned for 3 p.m. The actual convoy that carried the princesses wasn't leaving until 3:25, about 15 minutes after school was out. We were also taking the long way home by circling outside the demonstration area and coming up from the south to reach The House.

The decoy worked perfectly—it got caught in the demonstration, just like it was supposed to. Major Difficulty broadcast a sitrep in a simple code that said we were caught in the demonstration but were secure. The U.S. Navy helo that hovered over the convoy only added verisimilitude to the whole charade.

All of these factors made it even more of a surprise when they hit us coming out of the school.

The princesses, Holly Durante and I were just outside the school doors when three things happened at once. First, there was a thunderous volley from several large caliber weapons. Second, there was a volley from smaller caliber arms that brought all four agents who were out in the open down, blood spurting from their lower legs. Third, tires began exploding on the five black Suburbans that ringed the turnaround drive.

Holly and I grabbed our princesses and spun around for the school.

The big guns boomed again and all of the glass on the front of the Amicus School blew out.

I lurched into my princess and brought her and her sister down in a heap.

Holly's right knee exploded from a small-caliber hit, bringing her down on top of us. I grabbed everybody and drug them behind the small wall that projected out from the building at the entrance to the school.

The princesses began screaming like Justin Bieber had just appeared, only their reaction was fueled by terror, so it was louder. Holly also began screaming "Oh fuck! Fucking goddamned shit motherfucker! Son of a bitch cocksucking asshole shitsucking bitch!"

She sounded a lot like a Secret Service agent with Tourette's, although I couldn't blame her—besides the pain, which had to have been considerable, she was also worried about her principal.

The small arms and heavy arms continued their rhythmic firing. I peeked out around the wall and everybody but Flipper, Buddha and Patsy were wounded, including Major Difficulty. She was a trooper, because as she was falling her sidearm was out and firing towards the only place the incoming rounds could be coming from.

The three remaining agents had their FAG (horrible acronym for "Fast-Action Gun") bags out and were firing their HK MP-5 submachine guns at the attackers.

The big guns—I was sure by now that they were Barrett Light .50s, easily acquired on the open market—boomed again and wheels began to fall off the Suburbans. Another volley and the supposedly bullet-proof windows in the vehicles exploded. I realized that they must be using .50 caliber armor-piercing rounds on the vehicles, and smaller arms against the personnel. Several wounded agents had crawled over to the now-useless Suburbans and were attempting to return fire.

Major Difficulty jumped up on one leg and limped towards the nearest car, but another round hit her in the other knee and she went down in a heap.

I suddenly had a thought—the attackers were not shooting to kill. Major Difficulty had been a sitting duck, especially for a .50 cal—but they wounded her instead. "Why?" my shocked brain asked.

As the attack moved into its fifteenth second I realized that the attackers were not trying to just slaughter us—they could have done that in the first volley. Also, they weren't shooting anywhere near the princesses. Most of their fire was directed against our vehicles, which they hammered with another volley.

My blood ran cold as I realized what this was about. In the seventeenth second of the attack I made a command decision. There was a waist-high wall and hedge that ran all the way down the drive to the end of the Amicus School property. It wasn't going to stop a .50 cal slug, but if I was right they weren't going to be shooting at me anyway, because I was taking the prizes with me. If I could get to the end of the hedge intact I could turn the corner and run down the back of the school, aiming for the emergency exit at the rear that would lead me to the safe room inside the school.

It was a crazy idea for a normal agent, but then I wasn't your run-of-the-mill agent, now was I? Of course if I was wrong the princesses and I would be sitting ducks, but fuck it, I wasn't going to just stay where I was until I ran out of ammunition. Nobody was getting my princesses unless I was dead. (I know that sounds corny and melodramatic, but I meant it. Thanks, Mumsy, Pops and U.S. Marine Corps.)

I grabbed Holly's face and said, "I'm going to run with the girls! I need you to give me covering fire from this position—they're probably going to shoot you again when I get clear!" She looked at me and nodded, her face grim and set. She reached under her coat and brought out her MP-5, then turned toward the incoming fire.

I scraped the girls into a princess sandwich on my right side, put a Smith & Wesson 1076 in my left hand and leapt to my feet with the girls clutched to my side like they were a Lycra body suit. I hated to leave Holly and the rest of the detail under fire, but I wasn't going to let anyone get to my principals while I was alive (once again melodramatic, but still true). Holly lunged to her foot and bellowed "DIE YOU MOTHERFUCKERS!" and let fly with the MP-5. I dashed out of the foyer straight to the little alley between the wall with its hedge and turned on the afterburners. Just as I thought, no one fired at us, or even near us, even though we were sitting ducks. I heard small arms fire behind me—Holly's MP-5 stopped right after that.

I saw a security tape of it afterwards, and I am convinced that I was running faster than any human being in history. But that was only the half of it, because the tape didn't have any sound. There I was, running like a crazed female Usain Bolt while the princesses were screaming like a flight of F-18 Super Hornets taking off from the USS *Nimitz* and I was bellowing *"NOT ON MY WATCH YOU MOTHERFUCKERS!"*

Whoever it was shooting at us had never seen me run, because they only got one shot off—a small caliber, not a .50—and that one whinged off the school brick right where my front elbow had been about a second before. We got to the end of the little alley so fast that I wasn't sure I could turn and not expose the princesses, so I slowed down just a bit before turning.

Lucky for all of us that I did, otherwise I wouldn't have seen the sniper prone on the deck of our supposed control station at the head of the school drive. He was perfectly set up to cover the corner, armed with a small caliber rifle and large scope. I didn't even try to ID him or the weapon, I just let off a double tap straight at his chest. I knew I hit him—the muzzle on his weapon immediately went off target—but then I was sprinting for the emergency exit door and screaming into my wrist comm.

"This is Glickstein! We are under attack at the school—most of the detail is down! I am attempting to reach the safe room inside the school!"

I stopped screaming when I realized that something was jamming my supposedly secure comm. There was nothing but static in the earpiece and no response to my emergency call. I turned the little corner into the emergency exit and knew we were sincerely fucked.

There was a bomb attached to the door. It was winking a red light at me and looked to be hooked to several wires running inside the door—contacts which if severed would detonate it? I didn't have time to think about it—it was probably also hooked into a trembler switch or motion sensor. In any case, I instantly realized the safe room was out.

Which is when I saw the bank on the corner. "Bank—vault—safe room" went through my mind so fast that I was already changing direction to get there before the thought was fully conscious. I had cover all the way there, thanks to the privacy fences around the Amicus School playing fields, which meant that I could just run like hell without dodging. I couldn't look around for pursuit, so I screamed, "Allison, is anyone following us?"

The oldest princess just kept screaming, but Brooke stopped screaming long enough to say, "NO! NOBODY'S BACK THERE! I DON'T WANNA DIE!" She then resumed screaming incoherently, but she'd done her job—no pursuit meant that they were scrambling too, probably because no one was supposed to escape the ambush, or get past the end sniper.

I shot the lock off the gate by the road and we blew through it. We got to the bank and I just about ripped the front door off with just my pinky—no way I was letting go of my 1076—and I dashed into the lobby with the princesses in full scream. I saw the open vault door at the back of the bank and ran bellowing "U.S. Secret Service! Open the gate for the vault!" I don't know if it was the gun or the tone of my considerable voice, but one of the clerks opened the gate and I skidded through it. I flung the princesses behind me and into the open vault, turning and pulling my other 1076 in the same motion. Everyone in the bank just stood there, frozen in place by the twin pistols and the murderous look on my face.

"I need the manager, right now!" I said in my command voice. A tall, thin dark-haired guy with glasses and a thick mustache said, "I'm Bob Barth, the manager. Whatcha need?" I gave him credit—my appearance and the pistols didn't appear to faze him. I stuck one of the pistols under my arm, pulled my ID and said, "Special Agent Glinka Glickstien, U.S. Secret Service. I need to know—is your vault vented? Can people survive in there with the door closed?"

Bob Barth said, "Sure. OSHA rules—ya can't have an unvented vault anymore. We have circulation fans in there and the air conditioner needs a vent. Why?"

"I need to borrow your vault—I need you to close it and make sure it's locked, and then I need you to evacuate the bank. There may be very bad people coming here for the girls."

Sometimes people surprise you. Bob Barth surprised me then. He didn't ask any more questions, instead turning to his assistant manager and saying, "Mary Lu, get everybody out as soon as they lock their drawers. Everybody, customers included, goes out the back door and to our emergency assembly point over at the Post Office. Get going, guys." He turned to me and said, "Once I lock it the door won't open for any reason for at least 15 minutes—it has a time lock. I can bump that up to an hour if ya need it."

"Do it," I said. "Anything else I need to know here?" He tossed me a set of keys and said, "These lock the cage at the back where all the cash is. There are two locks and they are a bitch to get open. Might buy ya some time if you need it." He looked at the still screaming princesses and said, "They who I think they are?" I nodded and he said, "Attacked 'em at school?" I nodded again and he said, "Sons of bitches, goin' after kids. If they're pissed off at their old man why not go after him?"

"Because POTUS'd kick their asses back to wherever they came from—the 101st Airborne's a good club to have," I said, liking the guy and wanting him to feel my appreciation for his calm actions.

"Damned straight," Barth said. "Well, I'd offer to stay, but I'd just get in your way. There's a box of Paydays inside the cage door, and a drain in the corner if you need it. Good luck, Special Agent."

He waffled his hand at me to get inside and then swung the door closed. I waited until I saw the big pins clunk home, holstered my 1076s, swept the princesses up off the floor and hustled into the cage area. The vault was in an "L" shape, with the cash in the short leg of the "L" at the back of the vault. I grabbed the Paydays off the shelf and set the princesses down. They were both still trying to scream, so I said, "OK, knock it off! We need to get some stuff done in case they can get at us here."

Oops.

I should have realized that would set off another round of screaming, but I was too buzzed to think about niceties. After about 30 seconds I had enough, so I hauled Allison up to her feet and slapped her, gently, forehand-backhand. She and Brooke both stopped screaming and stared at me.

"Look, I will stipulate that we are all scared shitless and stressed enough to scream our god-damned heads off, but we can't because we have to set up some defenses—just in case. I'll die protecting you, but I'd rather live protecting you, OK? Can you guys help me with some stuff, and then we'll all scream bloody murder?"

People will surprise you, even spoiled rotten brats who are convinced their defecation is not odiferous. Allison nodded, and Brooke said, "You—you'd die for us?"

I wanted to scream, but she was just a 16-year-old kid who didn't know shit about shinola, so I just said, "Yeah, I'd die to protect you, but that ain't gonna happen without a fight, you know? I got my pistols and lots of extra clips, so if we set it up right a Marine division couldn't get at you guys here." Pure hyperbole, that was, because a Marine division can get through anything but a nuke—but it sounded good and I figured their morale needed bucking up.

For once I was right. Both girls stood up, looking a little bit taller. "What do you need us to do, Glinka?" Allison said. I was taken aback—it was the first time she'd ever used my first name, and the first time that there was any trace of respect in her tone.

"Call me Freak," I said, smiling a bit, "and let me tell you what we're gonna do for Operation Fort Apache." Once I explained my plan both girls smiled and said, "Let's dewww it!" like Dr. Phil would.

We all had a good, tension-releasing laugh and then got to work.

CHAPTER 61

Ft. Apache

Once I had everything locked up I actually stopped to check the girls over. I said, "You guys OK? Any bumps or bruises?"

"My, my ribs hurt," Allison said in a very small voice. "Mine, too," Brooke said in the same small, quiet voice. I nodded and said, "I know—that's from me crushing you as we ran. I'm sorry about your ribs—you'll probably bruise up, and I'm sorry about that too—"

Allison—the most arrogant, tightest-assed principal ever who wasn't a POTUS, and a girl that I had come to really despise—shocked the shit out of me when she cut me off and said, "No, Glinka, you don't apologize! You saved our lives—you don't ever apologize again!"

And then she hugged me—really hugged me, like I was her BFF. Brooke also wrapped me in a hug and we all had a good, clean cry.

Which I to this day will deny. Tough, trained Secret Service agents don't cry, even after something as stressful as what we had just gone through. So after we didn't cry for five minutes or so I said, "OK, now I have some stuff to do before that time lock lets the door open again."

Both girls looked like deer in the headlights about to be hit by a semi-truck, and I realized they thought they were off the hook. Brooke's lip trembled and she said, "The bad guys might still be out there? They could try to kill us again?" She looked about to lose it, so I said, "Over my dead body, Brooke, but we have to plan for what the enemy could do, not what we think they will do. So we're going to make some preparations, just in case, OK?" I looked over at Allison, hoping against hope that she would get it. Hey, she'd been a nasty, spoiled rotten, bitch since I'd known her (except for the last five minutes), but she wasn't stupid.

"B, Glinka won't let them through—Dad says she's the best shot in like, the whole world, but we have to think those bad guys could still be around. The assholes were stupid enough to do it once, they could try again, right?"

Hooray, there was a God—Allison had decided to grow up at just the right time.

Her sister nodded, almost reassured, and said, "You're really that good a shot?" I decided to go for funny. "I can shoot the balls off a gnat at 100 yards and hit the balls before they hit the ground," I said in my Al Pacino tough-guy voice. Both girls laughed and when they started to stop I said, "Provided the gnat is at least 6 inches off the ground" which set them off again.

When the laughter wound down I said, "Laughing is good 'cause it keeps us out of shock, but you guys gotta call me Freak. Nobody calls me Glinka, not even my Mumsy."

Finally Allison said, "OK, so what are we going to do, Freak?" I noticed the "we"—a good sign, since I was pretty sure that Allison hadn't ever been part of a cooperative endeavor that she wasn't the leader of before—so I said, "First order of business: does anybody have to do their business?" They looked at me with blank stares, so I elaborated. "Do either of you have to go to the restroom?"

Brooke said, "I really have to ur-i-nate" in a sing-song voice that was clearly an attempt at humor. I said, "Well, good, 'cause I have to piss like a Russian racehorse, and I didn't want to be the only one," which was another very popular joke. I explained that we would take turns over the drain—"Just like when we went to Hong Kong with Mom," Allison said—"a squat toilet." Once that was done I said, "Second order of business: how much water do you guys have?"

God bless their privileged little yuppie hearts, both had full water bottles. I hauled out two Paydays apiece and said, "You guys eat and drink while I get started on my plan."

"No," both girls said at once. "We'll all eat together, then work together on your plan," Allison said. "Yeah," Brooke said. "You have to eat—you just ran like, a mile while carrying us, so you must be hungry."

"And thirsty," Allison said. "I do want some water," I said, once again amazed at how resilient these girls were. Shot at (they thought), carried around like sacks of flour by a screaming maniac with a gun and sequestered in a closed bank vault, and they still wanted to look out for my welfare. Not only was it new behavior for both the princesses, but it severely fucked up my mode of thought concerning them—I wouldn't be calling them princesses after this experience.

But that was for later. We ate and drank, and then I said, "OK, Allison, you and Brooke pull the money bags off the shelves closest to the gates and pull them back here to the forward bunker position. I'm going to take the shelves and turn them into the rear bunker shell, then we'll work together to reinforce them. Got it?"

They looked at me and Allison said, "Freak, shouldn't we stack the bags in a shallow reverse 'U' shape for the forward bunker? So that you can lay down behind it for protection?"

"And shouldn't we put the bags of coins in front of the money, so it can deflect the energy from the bullets and cut down on ricochets?" Brooke said.

I was completely flabbergasted, because that was exactly what I was going to do after I'd built the back bunker frame. I knew that it would be far easier for me to just do it, rather than explain it all to the princesses—I mean the *warrior* princesses—but having them do it would be faster. The fact that they knew what to do astounded me, but I wasn't going to waste time wondering how or why.

"Roger that. The bags of cash first in the reverse 'U,' then the coin in front and on top of the cash. It will take both of you to move the coins and lift them, but by then I'll be able to help. Oh, and leave-"

"A gun slot about 4 inches wide in the center of the bunker, right?" Allison said.

"How the hell do you know that?"

"We played paintball when we were little and dad was in Congress," Brooke said. "All of our friends played and dad said we should learn how to play because it was good for our critical thinking skills. We made bunkers all the time."

"And we were like, really good at it, 'cause dad always talked to us about strategy and tactics—remember he was like, Army ROTC at U of M," Allison said.

I'd forgotten that, but right now I didn't have time to think about it, although it did cause a brief pause in my thought process, something about the attack I couldn't quite put my finger on. In any case, we had work to do—only 22 minutes before the vault door could be opened, and we had no idea what the bad guys were doing.

"Well, like, excellent," I said, imitating their, like, tone and cadence. We all laughed and then got to work. The warrior princesses began stacking bags of cash into the first bunker, while I stomped and bent the metal shelves into flat barriers. I took the flat metal panels back to the rear of the cage and laid them out into a front and two side barriers. The back wall would serve as the rear of the box I was building, until I found an air conditioning vent under the shelving unit in the back right of the cage. I looked at it and thought about tear gas and shifted my box back to take advantage of the vent and the wall—now my bunker would have only two metal sides, with a positive air pressure bunker backed and sided by steel reinforced concrete.

With three of us working it really didn't take too long to get finished. We all looked at each other, sweaty but pleased with our efforts. The front bunker was perfect, bags of cash fronted by bags of coins, with a 4-inch firing slit through the center. Allison had insisted that the slit be protected up top, so we laid a flattened shelf on top and covered it with a layer of coins.

The back bunker was about 48 inches high, with a metal barrier sandwiched between a layer of coins and layer of cash and bearer bonds. There were four shelves left to cover the top, which I would then reinforce from outside with all the stuff we had left. There was enough room inside for the two girls to lay down on their backs with their heads close to the back wall—we all agreed it was better to be hit it the foot by a ricochet or straight shot rather than be hit in the head. The air conditioning vent meant there was plenty of air in the bunker and that it would be harder for tear gas to get inside.

All in all, we had a fairly secure defensive position, considering the limitations of the space and materials.

My watch said that there were seven minutes until the time lock would allow the door to be opened. We hadn't heard any attempts to get in by other means, but that didn't mean anything. The chances were good that the only people coming to the bank were our people, but you have to plan for what the enemy could do, not what they will do, so we weren't going to take any chances.

"OK, it's time for you guys to get situated," I said. Both the girls began to cry, silent tears running down their cheeks, but they went over without protest and stepped over the low wall into the bunker. Before I could tell them to lay down Allison and then Brooke hugged me. I kissed them on the tops of their heads and said, "Remember, the bad guys are a lot bigger than gnats," which made them both laugh through the tears, and then they lay down, each of them clutching a pair of scissors in either hand.

We'd gone over what to do in case I was unsuccessful in keeping the bad guys out.

"First pair of scissors into their foot or ankle, or calf, second pair—"

"Right in their nuts," Brooke said.

"Right in the balls," Allison said. "Nuts sounds juvenile."

"Roger that," Brooke said, sounding enough like me to make us all laugh.

"Remember," I said, "you can't have any mercy. It has to be bang! into a lower limb, preferably the foot and then bang! into their balls. No mercy—make 'em work for it if they want to take you."

"Roger that!" both warrior princesses said, causing more laughter.

I picked up the top shelves and said, "You don't make a sound until you hear me or someone you know tell you to come out—and if it's me I'll say 'Ft. Apache,' right?" They nodded, and I covered them with the metal shelves, and then a layer of coin bags, cash, and other sundry stuff.

I went up and checked the cage door was locked, then went back, stripped off my coat, checked my 1076s, stacked my six spare magazines next to the firing slit and tried my comm one more time.

Nothing but static. I couldn't tell if it was being jammed or just the vault, but we weren't going to get anything until the door opened in two minutes.

"So be it," I said out loud. "Yea, though I walk through the Valley of the Shadow of Death I will fear no evil, for I am the baddest motherfucker in the whole damned valley."

I lay down behind my bunker wall and said, "Come and get me, assholes!"

I can't tell you how satisfied I was to hear the Warrior Princesses giggle from their bunker.

CHAPTER 62

And the Horse You Rode in On

We didn't have to wait long until the door locks were released—we could hear them back in the cage as they clunked open. There was a brief pause and then the door swung open, followed by the sound of shoes in the long part of the 'L' in the vault.

I let them get about four steps in before I put on my Gunnery Sergeant voice and bellowed, "THIS IS SECRET SERVICE AGENT GLINKA GLICKSTIEN! I AM ARMED AND ACTIVELY ENGAGED IN A PROTECTIVE DETAIL! STOP YOUR ADVANCE AND IDENTIFY YOURSELVES OR I WILL FIRE ON YOU!" The Warrior Princesses and I had discussed this tactic—I was hoping to delay them long enough for the girls to hit their panic buttons and give the rest of my service a chance to locate us and send the cavalry. I thought maybe the panic buttons would cut through any jamming better than my comms, which we already knew could be jammed.

What I didn't tell the girls was that I was hoping these sons of bitches would bunch up so I could kill 'em all in one go.

The footsteps stopped and there was some whispering. Finally a voice said, "This is Washington, D.C., Assistant Chief of Police Terrance Carson, Agent Glickstien. I'm the head of the Special Action Section for DC. We were the closest unit to the school and are here to help extract your protectees. I am going to come around the corner with my creds in the air so that you can read them. After that—"

"Your ass will be dead, shithead! I don't know you, and I'll put two in your chest and one in your head before you clear the corner! Send me someone I know—anyone else dies."

"Be reasonable, Agent Glickstien. Of course you know me—I'm on the cleared list for the White House," the voice said, clearly perturbed.

I didn't care how perturbed he was—all I knew about Terrance Carson was his name—so I said, "Go fuck yourself, whoever you are! Unless you want your balls shot off you better stay behind that wall—you are not approaching my principals unless I can positively ID you from a distance."

"I am putting my creds around the corner, Agent Glickstein," the voice said. He was too used to being in charge and his arrogance cost him, because as soon as the creds came around the corner I shot them, right in the center of the picture.

I was very proud of the Warrior Princesses, because they didn't make a sound at the shot. It's more difficult than it sounds to not jump at a loud noise—most people can't control themselves, but my girls did.

The purported Terrance Carson did not control himself.

He screamed like a third grader as his ID got blown away. I thought that was hilarious, because I knew that I hadn't touched his fingers or hand. My little girls were quiet, but this asshole screamed like a third grader, and probably pissed himself, too.

I have always found irony to be my favorite form of humor, and this time was no different.

When he finally got back under control Terrance Carson said, "Goddammit, Glickstien, I'm a fucking D.C. Chief of Police. Stow the weapon immediately and let us do our job!"

"Fuck you, the horse you rode in on, and the family dog, asshole! I've got a shitload of ammo and I'm not afraid to Use it. Send somebody who I know and nobody will get hurt—any other course and you're gonna need body bags."

"Comm your Chief of Detail and have them tell you that I am who I say I am. Will that satisfy you, Glickstien?" He was clearly nonplussed by my behavior, which told me that he wasn't used to field work. I'd heard that Carson had been a political promotion, and besides, the Special Action Section was a bunch of paper pushers who chased dangerous criminals like striking teachers and then had someone else arrest them, which made his behavior more understandable. He thought his badge and badass reputation was all he needed, but I'd believe he was an REMF until I could positively ID him as a real policeman.

Then I'd probably classify him as an REMF, because real policemen don't scream like third graders. Ever.

"My detail chief, if she's alive, is in surgery for two wrecked knees. You need to do better than that, dickhead," I said. "Oh, and it's Agent Glickstien—that's 'Glick—steen,' not 'shtine,' asshole." I wasn't going to let him near my protectees in any case, because I'd decided that I didn't like this guy, even if he was one of the good guys. There was more whispering from the hall, some louder, more heated whispering and then Carson said, "Fuck it! Deploy right and left—fire flash bangs and advance!"

I closed my eyes against the possible blazing light that came from flash-bang grenades when I heard a voice that I hadn't heard in 14 years, but that I could never forget.

"Belay that order! Put the grenades down and let's get our shit together before we do any more shooting. Besides, that's a U.S. Marine in there—your grenades would go off, and then she'd open her eyes and shoot all of you stupid fuckers dead. Ain't that right, reee-cruit?"

"Gunnery Sergeant Thornton?"

She said, "Major Glickstien, I'm going to step around the corner with my hands on top of my head so you don't drill me in the 10-ring, and then we're going to talk." She stepped around the corner and I noticed one big change in 14 years.

It was now Sergeant Major Angela Thornton. She was a little more muscular and thicker in the middle by a smidge, but her face wasn't any different. She was scowling and just as intense as she had been at PI and Basic Training.

She said, "And that's Sergeant *Major*, reee-cruit." Her tone said that she wasn't kidding, and I guess I didn't blame her. Rising to the rank of Sergeant Major in the corps took chutzpah, big balls and the kind of concentration usually associated with great pro athletes. Winning a World Series was just fucking around compared to being a Sergeant Major in the Corps, especially for a womyn. (I wasn't going to mention that to Sergeant Major Thornton, because I was pretty sure that guns or not she'd rip off my head and shit down my neck—she'd say *I was not promoted because of my gender, you little puke cunt!* or some such. I'd pass on that, thank you very much.)

"Sergeant Major Thornton, I apologize about mistaking your rank, and promise to address you properly in the future."

Her scowl relaxed and she almost smiled. She looked at my makeshift bunker and did smile. "Freak, you are wasted on these civilian pukes. Why not come back to the Corps and do some real good?"

"I can't do it, Gun—Sergeant Major. I've got this work in my blood now, and my kids need me, especially now. But you know that you don't really leave the Corps, you're just on temporary detached duty."

"Once a Marine, always a Marine," she said.

"Boo-rah," I said. "But enough of this semper fi shit, Sergeant Major. I need to get these kids out of here and back to the House. How's the weather out there, Sergeant Major?" It was a private code from boot camp. If she said the weather was good or OK someone was compelling her to help them. If the weather was poor, or bad, she was clear.

Sergeant Major Thornton smiled and said, "Freak, it's the biggest shitstorm you've ever seen. Military, locals, Feebs, U.S. Marshals—it's ragin' like a law-enforcement tornado." I nodded and stood up, never taking my guns off her. "You got your own guys out there?"

"A Marine company is right behind me. Just say the word."

I nodded and said, "The word is given. I am requesting relief, Sergeant Major." I didn't let up yet, not until she nodded and said, "Extraction team, get up here" and I heard a gravelly, growly First Sergeant voice say "Ya REMFs get outta our way or I'll shoot ya myself."

A squad of Marines in full battle dress came around the corner and deployed with weapons out. Right after them came a relief squad of Secret Service agents—part of the Vice-President's detail—led by Gabe Berdahl, who was the VP's principal agent. Berdahl came up to me and said, "Got some relief here, Freak. We're bringing up an Army APC for transport, or a helo to The House, if you'd prefer."

Berdahl was a tall, blue-eyed, blonde-haired dreamboat who may have been the best agent in the entire Protective Section of the Secret Service. I appreciated his easy manner, and his giving me a choice of transportation. We both knew what I'd pick, but Berdahl also knew that I was juiced on adrenaline and needed to keep at least a semblance of control so that I didn't just go fucking apeshit crazy. I appreciated the gesture as much as I appreciated his charm and good looks.

I holstered my pistols and said, "Helo straight to The House, as long as there are multiples"—meaning I wanted decoy choppers to fly with us.

Gabe said, "Got eight birds right outside, with a two-mile perimeter manned by Marines from the K Street barracks. We also have over 100 of our agents and 200 Feebs outside. There are four F-16s with white ones on the rails doing CAP and we will be escorted by four AH-64s"—meaning Apache attack helicopters, the deadliest air-to-ground weapons ever known to man.

I smiled and said, "Is that all ya got, Gabe?" He smiled back and said, "Well, Freak, I only had an hour." We kind of giggled, and then I went over to the back bunker and said, "Warrior Princesses, it is I, the mighty Freak. Whattya say we get the fuck outta here?" There wasn't a sound from the bunker.

"Good girls," I said. "Ft. Apache." There was movement beneath the bunker cover as I swept the crap off it and heaved the panels up. Gabe helped me and the warrior princesses jumped out, grabbing me in bearhugs.

"We heard the shot and were so scared!" Brooke said. "Did you have to shoot another bad guy?" Allison said, which caused Gabe to raise an eyebrow. "No, I just had to kill the ID of some asshat who thought he was going to get to you—turns out he's one of our asshats," I said with a smile.

"I'm glad you didn't have to shoot anyone else," Brooke said. She tried to smile, but her tired little 16-year-old-face began to crumble. "C-can we g-go home now, Freak? I'm really tired." She was trying not to cry, so I just hugged her closer and said, "You bet, Warrior Princess Brooke." I stepped back and Gabe and his guys came to stand around the girls, ready to lead them out to the waiting helos.

"No!" they both said at once. "We want Glinka to take us home!" Allison said. Gabe tried to say something, but I raised my hand and said, "OK, my princesses. Let's go have a short helicopter ride and get you home." I knew that they both liked riding in a helo, and I also knew that PTSD was setting in for them. They were teenage girls, not trained, battle-hardened soldiers—you couldn't expect them to get that I needed to be debriefed, or that I wouldn't be seeing them for a while. It was SOP for agents involved in attacks, especially where they discharged their weapons, to undergo batteries of tests and evaluations before being put back on duty—with different protectees. We weren't supposed to become emotionally involved with our protectees because it could lead to impaired judgment, and after this experience I was definitely emotionally involved, and my judgment was certainly impaired.

In fact, right now I felt like I'd kill anyone who tried to even talk to "my" girls.

The Secret Service has a pretty good idea what they're doing.

So I put my arms around the girls, Sergeant Major Thornton and her guys pressed around us and we went off to the helo, escorted the whole way by armed U.S. Marines and Secret Service personnel. The only other way to be safer was if we'd've had an M1A1 main battle tank to ride in, but we were pretty fucking safe as it was.

We got to the helo and I said, "Sergeant Major—" She cut me off and said, "Stow it, Freak. We'll talk later—right now we both got work to do, so get your fucking ass on that bird and let's get the fuck outta here, Marine!" We both knew how brave she'd been to expose herself to my guns, and we also both knew no one would give her any credit, but it was something that I would never forget.

It was a short, impressive ride back to the White House, and then a short, quick run in. There was even more firepower on open display at the House, including a fully armed Marine brigade and at least four APCs. Jets screamed overhead and I could hear the angry buzz of the Apaches somewhere near us.

Once we were inside the V-POTUS guys hustled the warrior princesses off to the residence, where their grandmother was waiting. They both looked at me, and I said, "Go see your grandma—she's probably out of her mind with worry. Your mom will be home soon." I assumed that FLOTUS was already on a plane from Toronto, and that POTUS was also already en route—although he had the Atlantic Ocean to cross. "Go on, Warrior Princesses. Get some sleep—I'll see you later." They nodded, hugged me and were swept away by the best guys I knew to keep them safe.

I turned around to find four agents surrounding me and Secret Service Director Siri Hessler waiting. One of the agents approached me and I handed over my 1076s, and then Director Hessler said, "A goddamned bank vault with a time lock, Freak? What the hell were you thinking?" Her tone and demeanor were harsh, far more so than I had expected. Before I could reply she said, "Why the hell didn't you just get into the safe room at the school? Isn't that SOP in this kind of situation? Or can't you handle following procedure, *Agent* Glickstien?"

I knew that I could be on her and break her neck before anyone on earth could stop me, and I was in the middle of planning just that when my bacon was saved by the nastiest bitch on the face of the planet, the Superbitch White Witch Ice Queen herself, FLOTUS.

Saying that the first lady of the United States and I had never been close was like saying the Palestinians and Israelis were having a spat. My brother had beaten her out for the valedictorian spot in their class at Harper Creek, and apparently she never forgot it, because when I came on the detail she did everything she could to make my life miserable. She also had actively campaigned to have the girls torment me at every opportunity, so what happened next was a total surprise, to everybody.

She took me in her arms and kissed me on the cheek, then hugged me right to her.

I hugged her back, and Laura Flagler Sheehan said, "I owe you, Freak. Thank you for saving my children's lives."

"Ma'am, I was just doing my job. I didn't really do anything extraordinary," I said, completely unsure how to react. I didn't even know how she got home from Toronto so quickly—I'd forgotten that she was flying home at noon.

"Nonsense," FLOTUS said. "You put yourself toward the gunmen, carried the girls away from danger, evaded a bomb at the school, kept them safe—shot a man to save them!—and that isn't extraordinary? Of course it is, and I've known you since school so you don't 'ma'am' me any more—it's Laura, OK?" I nodded, because if I spoke it would be to say that I would never be able to call her Laura, any more than I would ever call the president Jim.

FLOTUS nodded at Director Hessler and swept out of the room. I turned back to the Director and she said, "A bomb? What bomb?"

I said, "Director, can I sit down somewhere? I don't have a lot of gas left in the tank, ma'am."

I stood up straight, but I was about out of it. You can only take so much adrenaline before you burn out...and I had been on the hi-octane juice for about an hour too long.

Director Hessler was a no-shit, for-real tough guy, but she was also a good manager and she heard the tone in my voice. She turned to Gabe and said, "Agent Berdahl, would you please alert the posse that we are going to my office conference room at Treasury?"

I raised a hand to stop her and said, "Sorry, Director, but you don't want to do that. In about 30 minutes the screaming is going to start in the residence, and I am going to have to go up there. My protectees are going to wind it down, get some food in their systems and start to go all PTSD—and they will need me to calm them down before we sedate them, ma'am."

Nails looked at me and said, "I always forget how smart you are, Freak. Gabe, let the posse know that we're in the Roosevelt Room of the White House, would you please?" Berdahl nodded and I followed the director to the Roosevelt Room, which had some people in it. Before the director could even get into it with them the door on the opposite side of the room opened and Charles

Hassenger, the White House Chief of Staff, stepped into the room. He looked at the people around the conference table and said, "Out. Now." They all got up and practically ran for the door, because while Charlie Hassenger was a nice man, he was also an irascible son of a bitch who ran the most disciplined, efficient, and effective White House in recent memory.

The Chief of Staff looked at us and said, "Use our house as long as you need it, Director. I've already had coffee, sandwiches and a dozen cold Pepsis sent here. As for you, Freak,"—Charlie and I were old friends, having gone to the prom together when we were juniors at Harper Creek High—"damned fine job. The president is aware of your actions and is on the way home from France right now. He'll want to talk to you when he gets home in about six hours. Think you can make it that long?"

"Yes, sir," I said. "Anything for the president, sir. And thank you for the Pepsis, sir." Charlie nodded at the Director and winked at me—I'd been a Pepsi freak all my life—and slipped out of the room. I'd be willing to bet that the sandwiches would include kosher pastrami on rye with coleslaw and Russian dressing, which happened to be my all-time favorite sandwich ever.

It never hurt to have friends in high places.

Nails brought me back to reality when she said, "Now what the fuck was this about a bomb?"

…And the de-brief began.

CHAPTER 63

De-Brief Hell

First, I ate like a hog.

Four sandwiches and five Pepsis later, I began talking.

And talking.

And talking.

And talking.

For nearly five hours and eleven more Pepsis I tried to recall everything about the day, the attack, the escape, the warrior princesses—everything that it was humanly possible to report came out of my mouth, because Secret Service agents are trained to observe everything around them at all times, which meant that I had a shitload of information.

I also had a shitload of people listening. The Roosevelt room was full, there was a line open to the Joint Chiefs of Staff and the Chief of Staff was listening from his office.

There was only one interruption, about 45 minutes in, when the Warrior Princesses finally freaked out. I ran to the residence and got there just in time to stop Allison from saying something to her mother that she'd regret later. When I burst into the room the girls turned, threw their hysterical arms around me and burst into tears (not me—I'm a tough guy Secret Service agent, and we don't cry…ah, fuck it—I cried like my dog had just died). The blubbering ran down fairly quickly and Brooke said, "We want you to stay with us, Freak. Only you can protect us from the terrorists."

As she and Allison hung there on my neck I noticed that Brooke had already made the leap to "terrorists" as their assailants, which was the same thing my de-briefers had done, but I also realized that I wasn't so sure about that conclusion. In any case, that could wait for later—for now I had to take care of "my" girls, and I'd already planned for this.

I nodded at the Secret Service agent in the doorway and he stepped aside to admit a tall, handsome Marine major with the shoulders of a water buffalo in standard BDUS. He stopped just inside the door and stiffened to attention. The girls could see him—he was very easy on the eyes—and they both sucked in their breath in that way that wymyn do when they see a hot guy.

I gently disengaged from the warrior princesses and said, "This is Major Morgan Gray, United States Marine Corps. Major Gray won the Medal of Honor in Afghanistan and is currently XO of the K Street Barracks company. Major?"

Morgan Gray was a model of reassurance as he said, "Freak, I'd like to report on the status of White House security." He was still standing at attention, looking great and clearly competent—all you needed to do was look at the pale blue ribbon with the 5 white stars to see that—when FLOTUS looked at me and said, "Freak? Do I?" Laura Flagler Sheehan was a lot of things, but stupid wasn't one of them. She just didn't know what to do, so I said, "Major Gray, please report to the first lady."

"Ma'am, yes ma'am!" he said in his best Marine voice. He looked at FLOTUS and said, "Ma'am, I currently have an 800-man Marine rifle company deployed around the White House, backed up by eight armored personnel carriers manned by Marines and armed with cannons. There are also eight antiaircraft batteries deployed on the ground and four AH-64 Apache attack helicopters in constant patrol of the perimeter. There are Air Force F-16s overhead for a combat air patrol and we also have 200 highly competent Secret Service agents in close protection order. The only way the terrorists could attack the White House would be with a nuke, and they don't have the materials or ball—er, courage to do that, ma'am."

"Can the Marines shoot like Glinka?" Brooke asked.

Morgan Gray smiled and said, "Miss, nobody on earth shoots like the Freak, but we are fair hands with our M4s."

I looked at the girls and said, "He's being modest. It was the Marines who taught me to shoot, and every one of those guys is just as good as me with their long guns."

"Can they shoot the balls off gnats?" Allison said.

"Yes," Major Gray and I said at the same time. "You owe me a Pepsi, Bullhead," I said. That broke the tension. We all laughed and then I said, "Hey, I'm not leaving the building, I'll just be in the Roosevelt Room. If you need me just whistle and I'll come running, but don't doubt that you are safe." We hugged, I kissed them and FLOTUS led them off to sleep.

I went back to de-brief hell.

After repeating everything I'd already said 35,000 more times Nails said, "We need you to go back and describe the terrorists you saw, particularly the one you shot."

"I only saw that one. The shooting came from the houses above the drive, which brings up a question," I said.

"We're asking the questions, Agent Glickstien," Malcolm Sorenson said. "We are trying to determine the reasons for your unorthodox actions during this crisis, and whether or not they were justified." The FBI Director's face was grave, his manner pompous and arrogant, I was tired and I didn't like or trust this motherfucker anyway—a vision of CoD, Josie and Elvin Clyde Bliss swam in front of my exhausted eyes—so rather than completely fucking him up with several karate blows I said, "Fuck you, asshole. Either I get some answers or I'll just put my head down on the table and pass out for the next 14 hours. Besides, I wasn't talking to you, you REMF."

I don't think that Director Sorenson had ever heard that kind of talk, but before he could say anything Nails said, "Everybody calm the fuck down. At the order of the president *I'm* running this meeting and no one else. Are we clear?" Everyone present nodded except Sorenson, who sat back in his chair with a look on his face that was supposed to scare me, but almost made me laugh, since he just looked like he had eaten a lemon, rind and all. It would take more than an outraged bureaucrat to scare me.

Director Hessler then bore in on Sorenson and said, "For the record, we are trying to ascertain exactly what happened during the incident, with the express purpose of assessing the threat against the first lady and first daughters. This group will have absolutely *zero* part in assessing the actions of *my* agents, none of whom have to justify any of their actions to anyone but *me*. Are we clear, Director Sorenson?"

When he didn't answer right away Director Hessler said, "Acknowledge what I just said or get your ass out of *my* meeting, you pompous windbag." Looking like a scared tortoise Sorenson finally gave her a curt nod, but he was smart enough not to say anything. The speakerphone interrupted any further fireworks.

"Agent Glickstien, this is General Terrance X. McAllen, Chairman of the Joint Chiefs. I'd like to hear your question if you and the Director don't mind."

I almost jumped to attention when I heard the voice of my former commanding officer in both basic training and the first part of my Spec Ops career. Despite having a prosthetic leg Mad Dog McAllen had done right well for himself, going from Marine reee-cruit to the highest military rank in the U.S. Armed Forces. He was a truly good man who earned everything that he got and never, ever forgot where he came from—unlike most command officers, Mad Dog McAllen didn't think that he was the Second Coming (of Jesus, or Chesty Puller—take your pick), or that being promoted to Chairman of the Joint Chiefs of Staff made him a demi-god. I respected him as much as I had the Great Pumpkin, or my *zayde*, or my Mumsy or Pops, and I'd've followed that son of a bitch anywhere for any reason.

So it was most welcome when C-JCS supported me against the traitorous asshole director of the FBI.

Director Hessler nodded at me and I said, "Ma'am, what's going on with my squad? I saw most of them get hit and go down. Chief of Detail Rafferty was hit twice. What's the casualty count?"

"I'm sorry to report this, but we have three KIA and 10 wounded, especially CoD Rafferty and Agent Burgener," Hessler said.

"KIA? What the hell—the OpFor (sorry—'Opposition Force'—old Spec Ops jargon) wasn't shooting to kill," I said. "What the fuck?"

"Agent Adam Seivert was hit by small arms fire in the left knee and fell right in front of the front tire of one of the Suburbans as it was being targeted with a larger weapon. He was hit in the head by a heavy caliber round and died instantly. Agent Sarah Koenigsblett was hit by a heavy caliber round that skipped off the pavement and caught her in the femoral artery. Other agents were unable to stop the bleeding before she exsanguinated," Hessler said. Her eyes seemed to soften and she said, "And Agent Alexander de Vries was shot dead at close range when he charged up the slope toward the shooters with an MP-5. He appears to be the only person who was deliberately killed, and we have no idea why."

"I have an idea why," General McAllen said.

"Me, too," I said.

"Well, then I wish you'd enlighten us, because this is the weirdest attack I've ever seen," Nails said.

"Ladies first, Freak," Mad Dog McAllen said.

I looked at Nails and all the other bigwig de-briefers, put my grief at the loss of my friends aside and said, "We're looking at this the wrong way. The shooters could've killed the girls at any time—Agent Durante and I walked out the doors with the girls in plain sight, not two seconds before they opened fire. Think about it. These shooters showed they could hit targets with tremendous precision—they were shooting us in the *knees*, which indicates a desire to incapacitate, not kill—and they were doing it with small caliber weapons, probably .22 magnums. I saw them hit at least 10 knees, and I'll bet that they hit 10 more. They shot the windows of the building out when Agent Durante and I tried to re-enter the school with the girls, but why didn't they just shoot us? They were using .50 cals on the vehicles, and we had no way to stop those—that armor-piercing round would go right through our vests, our chests, the girls' chests and probably anyone standing behind them—but they didn't, because the shooters opted for containment, not death. Why?" I waited just a moment before I said, "Because this was a kidnapping, not an assassination."

All hell broke loose in the silence that followed my statement, until finally Nails bellowed, "EVERYBODY SHUT THE FUCK UP!"

And they did. She glared around the room and said, "That's quite a leap, Freak. We have three agents dead and 10 wounded and absolutely no evidence that there was any attempt to take the first daughters."

"I beg to differ, Director," Mad Dog McAllen said. "Clearly Agent de Vries was killed because he charged the extraction team to prevent them from getting in position to flank the agents who were left alive and then take the girls away. He was a Marine, right? That's standard tactics—disrupt the enemy by presenting yourself as a target so that you can keep the prize away from them. Agent de Vries' actions delayed the extraction team long enough for Freak to escape with the girls, which I'm sure is what he intended when he attacked them."

"That's the way I read it, sir. Patsy knew as soon as he heard the .50 cals and no one was dying that it wasn't an assassination but a kidnap, so he attacked in order to buy time," I said.

"So you're saying that Azwaj-i-Tahirat was trying to kidnap the first daughters? Don't they know that the president would nuke anybody who tried that?" Secretary of Homeland Security Travis Nowicki said.

"Oh, no, sir. This wasn't some terrorist outfit, especially one that is as nebulous as Azwaj-i-Tahirat," I said.

"Well, then what the fuck was it?" Secretary Nowicki said.

"A military op, using very good troops," Mad Dog McAllen said.

"Concur, Mr. Chairman. I'd say these guys were better than a Marine Recon unit, probably as good as a SEAL team," I said.

"How do you figure that?" Arthur Ishikawa, the Deputy Director of Operations for the CIA said.

"Their marksmanship was extraordinary, they were prepared for every contingency except one and they got into position without alerting anyone, even the most paranoid organization in the world. No way a large special ops team all shoot that well without military training," Mad Dog McAllen said.

"Also, there were only two reasons they were unsuccessful," I said. "First, they weren't briefed on my physical gifts, or they didn't believe what they were told, and second, they didn't just slaughter us. If their first volley had been designed to kill us we would've went down without even getting a shot off—they had to have at least 15 shooters to suppress us, with at least five on the strike team," I said.

"Based on what evidence?" Malcolm Sorenson said. "Couldn't it have been a smaller team that just seemed larger in the heat of the moment?"

"No," I said, deliberately omitting the 'sir' that I would've usually added. (Having the Chairman of the Joint Chiefs as your pal can be very useful.) "Nobody shoots that well, not even me. It really felt like we'd run into a SEAL ambush—the shooters' fire discipline was incredible and their accuracy was uncanny. Whoever was in command definitely knew what they were doing, which doesn't fit the profile of a terrorist organization. The bad guys didn't miss and they only killed Patsy because he was close enough to ID some of them. That kind of small unit discipline is only acquired through intense military training—and no fly-by-night terrorist group has that kind of expertise."

"Concur, Freak. Admiral Hannah has a question for you," Mad Dog McAllen said.

Oh, shit. The Admiral's full name was Jordan Wilson Hannah, and she was the first female Chief of Naval Operations in history. Tall, lithe, with the bluest eyes you've ever seen and straight blonde hair, Admiral Wilson was striking looking, but it was what went on in the four pounds of jelly inside her skull that was most impressive. She graduated from the U.S. Naval Academy with four different degrees, spoke at least 15 languages that I knew of and could do mathematical computations in her head that most people couldn't do with a graphing calculator. She also was a decorated combat aviator who was the first female ace in U.S. history, and she'd commanded a carrier and a carrier battle group, which meant she wasn't someone to fuck around with.

She also had the best mind for military strategy and tactics that I'd ever encountered, even better than C-JCS Mad Dog McAllen, which was saying something. (Don't ask how I know all this—it's definitely classified.) You had to be prepared to talk to Admiral Hannah or she'd eviscerate you (possibly literally—she was reputed to be a fantastic knife fighter, although I hadn't seen it myself).

"Freak, what was the range on their firing line?" Admiral Hannah said.

"Between 25 and 50 meters, ma'am. It seemed that their small arms were coming in from closer range, but the heavy guns had elevation and distance, probably since they knew their .50 cals didn't need to be close to be effective," I said.

"And they fired in volleys, not at will?" the Admiral said.

"Yes, ma'am, as near as I could tell. I didn't hear many stragglers until everybody who wasn't hit on the first two volleys started running around. The .50s just methodically shredded the tires on our vehicles while the small arms reached out for knees," I said.

"Tell me again about the man you shot. Are you sure that he wasn't shooting a .50 caliber rifle? And are you sure you hit him?" she said

"Admiral, he was proned out with what looked to be a .22 rifle and a military grade scope that was trained right down the exit road from the school. The scope fucked up his target acquisition at close range, and before he could adjust I shot him twice in the chest and neck—one of those bullets went right down his trachea and into his stomach, ma'am. They had to carry his dead body out," I said.

"Description?" the Admiral said.

"No idea on exact height from direct observation, but extrapolating from what I did see he was about 5'8", 5'9", 175 to 185 pounds, head shaven, muscular but not muscle-bound, definitely a trained marksman, comfortable in the prone position. He was also right-handed, and probably of European extraction," I said. "It seemed like he had a tattoo or some other marking on his left arm, but I couldn't tell what. I was kinda busy at the time, ma'am," I said.

"Yes, you were. Thank you, Freak," Admiral Hannah said.

"You're welcome, ma'am." I looked around the room and said, "I have another question. How did they get by our guys in the houses?"

Nails said, "They gassed everybody on the whole street, civilians and all. They used canisters of some kind of knockout gas, drilled tiny holes in a downstairs window and then waited until they were sure that everybody was out. Once that happened they entered all of the houses, wrapped everybody up in duct tape and then established their firing positions."

"And nobody noticed them doing any of this? Our guys didn't notice and call in?" I said.

"They called *us* purporting to be the gas company and said they had a problem in the area. One of our guys saw an ID that appeared real and then passed out from some kind of aerosol agent. He didn't see a face beyond a bushy red beard and sunglasses—no ID possible. We didn't get suspicious because they did all of this between regular call-in times—and yes, we checked with the gas company beforehand, and they confirmed there were reports of a gas leak in that area," Nails said.

"This was definitely a military operation," three voices said at once. "Great minds think alike, General, Admiral," I said. "Since you guys are in a much better pay grade than me I think that you should buy the Pepsis."

"Gladly, Freak," Mad Dog McAllen said. "The admiral and I were just conferring, and we think that this op was done by mercs being led by a former officer of an elite Special Forces unit. Does this kind of op remind you of anything, Freak?"

"Sir, this sounds like it's right out of the British SAS or SBS playbook," I said. "Tightly run, excellent pre-positioning of assets, minimal loss of life, superb marksmanship and fire discipline—this definitely was not an operation run by terrorists."

"Concur," both members of the Joint Chiefs said.

"Well, I concur with that, too," DHS Secretary Nowicki said. "No way this was done by any jihadi group, not with this kind of planning and organization."

"Plus they planned their escape and cleaned up after themselves, and terrorists just don't do that," CIA DDO Ishikawa said. "They're thinking of paradise and the virgins, not survival."

"Somebody paid a group of mercenaries to pull this off, but we didn't get even a whisper of it on any kind of platform, which seems impossible to me," DHS Secretary Nowicki said.

"Sir, it's really not that surprising," I said. "If one person told another person to assemble a unit for the op they wouldn't do it by normal means—they'd simply go to a few places in the world where mercenaries congregate and dial up whatever unit they wanted. As long as they had the money for it nobody'd ever be the wiser, especially since that kind of money could also get them access to a training facility for their preparations."

"Given everything else we know about this I'd say that Freak's assessment is right on target," Admiral Hannah said. "We should accept this theory for now and try to ascertain who might have a motive for kidnapping the first daughters."

"That list is as long as your arm," DDO Ishikawa said.

"Longer," Nails said. "The president is very unpopular all over the world, especially in what I'd call the crazy places."

"Is that a technical term, Director, or just a lack of geographical expertise on your part?" Secretary Nowicki said.

"It basically means anywhere around the world," Mad Dog McAllen said. "The drone program alone makes him unpopular in more countries than I could name, plus several tribal areas and with organizations like ISIL and Al-Qaeda."

"OK, so let's agree that we need to work on motive and put our ears to the ground to find some clues as to the possible perpetrators of this crime," Nails said. "We've gnawed this bone clean, and I'm sure that Agent Glickstien is tired. We'll resume the de-brief tomorrow with just Secret Service personnel, but I'll send all of you summaries, and I welcome any insights you might have. Thank you for your participation in this exercise."

Everybody said their goodbyes and left, but I noticed that Nails didn't close the phone connection with the Pentagon. Once the room was clear she said, "Mr. Chairman, are you two still there?"

"Yes," Mad Dog Allen said.

"You want to tell her, or should I?" Director Hessler said.

I interrupted her. "Is this a secure line, ma'am?"

"Yes, of course," she said.

"I think that this op was carried out by U.S. personnel, probably Navy SEALs," I said.

"So do we, Freak," Mad Dog McAllen said. The Chairman of the Joint Chiefs sighed and said, "Admiral Hannah advised me that this might be the case as soon as we got the details. What makes you think it was U.S. personnel?"

"Sir, they cared too much about not killing anyone, plus they waited until a day when school was already out, which meant that there were no other civilians around, and it wasn't about having a clear field of fire, because guys who shoot like these guys did don't need clear fields of fire, which means they were worried about casualties again. Having the students at school and milling around actually would've made their jobs easier, although some of them would've for sure died during the op. Mercs would know this and take advantage of it, because civilian casualties wouldn't concern them at all.

"The clincher is that they were so careful about taking down the civilians in the row of Houses at the school—nobody else would give a shit about that. These guys just weren't ruthless enough, which means it's much more likely they were U.S. personnel," I said.

"Concur, Freak," Admiral Hannah said. "A terrorist organization would have killed all the people in the houses above the school to ensure that they weren't ID'd, and also to burden us when it came to the investigation—we'd have to run down every person they killed and at least appear to be concerned about finding out who murdered them. In addition to that would be the jurisdiction issue with the D.C. police and the FBI, and believe me, that asshat tool Sorenson would make that an issue. We all know that suckass has pull with the VP and POTUS."

"I also didn't tell anyone about the Suburbans," Director Hessler said.

I looked at her and said, "We have a witness—or witnesses—who saw our own black Suburbans with lights on pulling out of the neighborhood right after the shooting, don't we."

"Yes," she said. "Three very credible wits all reported six black Suburbans with grill lights and tinted windows hauling ass out of the neighborhood in the direction of the street in front of the Amicus School. They assumed that the vehicles were ours—they were, of course—and that they were going to the rescue, which they were not, since they were being driven by the shooters."

"Shitfuckpisshelldamn!" I said. "These had to be some of our guys—they knew there'd be transport, they knew enough to disable the GPS trackers in the Suburbans and they were going to take the girls out right through the dragnet we'd inevitably set up, which means that they had IDs that would hold up to very close scrutiny. Motherfucking shitheads! Director, they could be Secret Service personnel. What were the descriptions of the people getting into the Suburbans?"

"Two of the wits saw athletic men between 6'2" and 5'8", some white, some black, some brown, jumping into the cars without any wasted motion or hurry. One wit said it looked like a pack of cats jumping onto a sofa," Director Hessler said. "They were all wearing black suits, sunglasses and had short hair and no beards. None of them had guns or gun cases."

"So they'd already loaded the guns in the gas company truck or trucks," I said, "because they couldn't be caught with them in the Suburbans when they were exfiltrating. That means that they purported to be members of one of a dozen agencies, and they had the IDs to back them up."

"We were thinking along the same lines, but due to their extreme expertise in technical matters for covert ops, the fact that the unit was the perfect size for a SEAL team and their extraordinary marksmanship we decided against actual Secret Service personnel," Mad Dog McAllen said.

"It must be rogue SEALs, or a Delta Force unit, or maybe a really, really good Marine Recon unit, but we still don't have any motive for the attack," Admiral Hannah said. "We also don't know how they got the intel about where and when the first daughters were going to be—they hit with perfect timing and placement on a day when a very visible decoy was a semi-stationary target."

"They knew the schedule to the minute and were in position to move in almost immediately, which means they had someone inside," I said. "What about retired SEALs, or Delta, or some other Spec Ops unit? I wonder how many of them are in the Service?"

"Eleven," Admiral Hannah said, "and two of them were with you, which leaves eight, including two who are well-known to you. We've eliminated all of them, which leaves us six people to investigate."

"But that'll have to wait for tomorrow, because right now Freak is about to collapse. I'm going to have her driven home so she can sleep. Good night, Mr. Chairman, Admiral," Nails said. The two Joint Chiefs said their goodbyes and hung up.

Nails looked at me and said, "I know, I know, but it's gonna have to wait. You need to sleep. We'll pick it up tomorrow, but let's not mention anything about it possibly being our own people until it's just our small working group, OK?"

"Yes, ma'am," I said. I was too tired to argue, or grieve for my dead friends, or figure out how I was going to help Buddha function with her twin sister dead, and besides, I was sure we hadn't heard the end of this attack, or the de-brief, by a long shot.

It turned out that I was only too right.

Shit.

CHAPTER 64

Defecation, Meet Air Conditioner

So two agents delivered me home and stayed on to guard my door, just in case the "terrorists" decided to come after me. That's idea's a load of horseshit, by the way. Terrorists don't operate that way, because it isn't personal for them. It's business, which is why they either assassinate big name targets or masses of people—that's the only way to inspire terror. Killing one particular Secret Service agent, or any other single person, just isn't in their repertoire.

Anyway, I got a nice solid six hours of sleep before I woke from a sweet dream where I was shooting FBI Director Malcolm Sorenson in the nuts for killing my friends in Morehead, Kentucky. The only reason(s) I woke up was because (a) my phone was ringing, (b) my emergency pager was going off and (c) someone was pounding on my door and telling me to wake up.

I went to the door in my T-shirt and shorts, flung it open and was greeted by four very serious men. One of them was Badass, all dressed up in his "I'm guarding the president" suit, complete with earpiece. I gave him the hairy eyeball and literally growled at the four guys.

They all backed up a couple of steps, and Badass said, "Before you go ballistic and kill us hear me out." I growled again, and we had a little conversation.

> Me: Wha' fu' yoo wan', yoo fuh'in' assho'?
> Badass: We're under orders here.
> Me: Fu' yoo an' yer or'res, mu'fuh'er.
> Badass: The orders are from The Man.
> Me: I don' gi' a fu'. Tel'ima fuh' off.
> Badass: I don't get to tell the president to do anything.
> Me: Wha' Pres'den'?
> Badass: Of the United States.
> Me: Oh, shit.
> Badass: Exactly. Get dressed.

So I quit growling, silenced all my electronic shit, which all said some version of "come to the White House immediately" (I knew that's what they said as soon as I saw 202-456-1414—the main White House switchboard number), so I didn't answer any of them, I just went with Badass and his guys.

As soon as we got in the limo Badass handed me an ice-cold Pepsi. I drank it down in one go and held out my hand. He slapped another Pepsi in it and I drank that one down, too. After three more Pepsis I let out an enormous burp, apologized to the rest of the car and then burped again for at least 15 seconds.

I looked at Badass and said, "Spill, shithead, like, now, before the sugar high wears off."

He looked back at me and said, "POTUS got in last night just after you left The House. He wanted to talk then, but Nails persuaded him to let you sleep. He functions on five hours a night, so I guess he thought that six hours were plenty. He told me—exact quote—"Go get Freak, now"—end quote, so I did. And no, he's not even remotely pissed at you—he's talking the Presidential Medal of Freedom, and you're a cinch for the DHS Director's Exceptional Service Gold Medal, and the Service's Director's Award of Valor, plus a whole bunch of other shit."

"Then what's the fuckin' rush? If he's not pissed at me…oh, shit, no," I said.

"Oh, shit yeah—The Man is going to sit in on the second de-brief, and he's got a few questions concerning the *how* of what happened," Badass said.

"He's miffed at Major Difficulty and the Director," I said.

"I don't think that 'miffed' is close to the right fucking adjective, Freak. He's so titanically pissed that he can't even see straight—he's talking about replacing the Secretary of DHS, the CIA director and the NSA director, plus Major Difficulty and Nails, as well as a slew of other people," Badass said.

"Because they didn't magically know that some asshats were going to try for his family," I said. "Like anyone ever thought that was a possibility. This isn't the movies, and even the terrorists know that kids are off-limits. Nobody's ever tried it before, and they didn't talk over anything we were monitoring, so how was anybody supposed to anticipate this?"

"I wouldn't use that argument with The Man if I were you," Badass said.

"Fuck a duck," I said.

He didn't say anything except to shoot me with his index finger.

I wished that he'd just shoot me for real; that's how much I was looking forward to this meeting.

We got to the White House, passed through the still increased security and went straight to the Cabinet Room. Every chair was full, except the one right across from the president where the Vice President usually sat. Nails was sitting in the seat to the right of the empty one, and DHS Secretary Nowicki in the seat to the left. The president saw us at the door, jumped up and came right over to me and did something I would've never in a million years expected.

He gave me a hug.

"Thank you for the lives of my children, Freak. Thank you, thank you, thank you," he said, tears streaming down his cheeks.

I was so nonplussed I didn't know what else to do but pat his back and say, "You're welcome, sir. I was just doing my job, sir."

James Patrick Liam Sheehan, POTUS, did something very un-presidential then. "Bullshit! You were so far above doing your job that you should be canonized. Don't give me the fucking self-deprecation, Freak—I've known you too long. Right now you get anything you want from me, you hear? You get the first annual Presidential unconditional favor—name it and it's yours, Freak."

I realized that POTUS was right on the edge of sanity then, so I took advantage of his offer—and him—to help the investigation out. I looked at the Cabinet Room, filled with people who would immediately start leaking about the de-brief (most of that would be inadvertent, but it didn't matter—we needed this to be quiet) and I made a command decision.

"Mr. President, my favor is this: I'd like you to send everybody who is unnecessary to this de-brief out of the room," I said.

"Just tell me who to keep and the rest of them are history," POTUS said.

"Sir, we need the directors of CIA, NSA, the FBI, the Director and Deputy Director of the Secret Service, the Secretary of DHS, the C-JCS and Vice-C-JCS, the commander of Spec Ops, the DDO and DDI of CIA, DHS Assistant Director Nathan Jones and his Intel chief, Marla Ahumada and me. Everybody else goes sir," I said.

President Sheehan turned and addressed the room like he was addressing the huddle of the Bears at the Super Bowl. He called out the names of the people I named and asked everyone else to clear the room. In a surprisingly short time everybody was gone, leaving the smaller group to sit around the nice wooden conference table that Richard Nixon bought with his own money and left for future generations when he left the White House.

The president went over and sat in his usual chair, and the rest of us sat down around him. I sat directly across the table from him, where the VP usually sat, as much because the VP wasn't there—he was probably in another secure location just in case the assholes who went after the girls were actually aiming for the president—and also because I wanted the president to focus on me, not my boss or others.

The Man sat down and immediately looked at DHS Secretary Travis Nowicki. His face got hard and he said, "Mr. Secretary, would you like to give me an explanation as to *how* this happened?"

"No, he wouldn't, Mr. President," I said. Beside me Nails was yanking on my suit coat, but I ignored her and said, "Mr. President, when you were with the Bears did your linebackers try to throw passes? Or did you go out and play defensive end?"

POTUS glared at me and said, "I don't know what relevance that has, and I'm in charge of this meeting, so I'll ask the questions, *Agent* Glickstien. You already used up the presidential favor."

"Mr. President, with all due respect, that would be like Mean Joe Greene telling Terry Bradshaw that he's going to be calling the plays in the Super Bowl against the Cowboys, or you playing defensive end against the Packers. I'm sorry that you're incredibly angry, sir, and that some fucking assholes tried to hurt your daughters, but I also know how good teams work, sir, and this isn't it. If we want to catch these guys we need our team to function at peak efficiency, and having you ask the questions isn't the right way to do it," I said.

"And why is that, Freak? Are you telling me I don't have a right as Commander in Chief to ask my subordinates questions? That I should just shut up and let the professionals do their jobs?" POTUS said. His handsome face was twisted into a very unattractive grimace as he half rose toward me.

I looked right back at him and said, "Jimmy Sheehan, you can coach or you can play, but you can't do both. You're much better as a player, because you don't have the first idea about coaching," I said, trying to duplicate the tone and demeanor of our mutual high school football coach delivering one of his (still applicable) lessons.

Everyone held their breath...until the president sank back in his chair. He put his face in his hands for a moment and then looked up. The ugliness was gone from his face as he looked at me and said, "Coach Horn sure did know his shit, didn't he, Freak?"

"Ya gotta know what ya don't know to be really smart, Jimmy," I said, again echoing our old coach. POTUS and I shared a private smile, thinking of our tough old coach back at Harper Creek, still teaching his tough old lessons. Finally the president said, "OK, Freak, so can I at least run the meeting?" His voice was tired and he looked like hell, which didn't make what I had to do any easier.

"No, sir, you can't. In fact, you shouldn't even be in this meeting. Secretary Nowicki should run this meeting, and then he and Director Sorenson and Director Hessler should brief you, sir, because that's the way the chain of command works. The Secretary is a pro at this, sir, that's why you hired him in the first place, and so are all the other people in this room. You're the only amateur at this, Mr. President, which means you're in the wrong meeting," I said.

"But I've got to do *something*," he said, his frustration showing in both his tome and demeanor. "Someone, some goddamned *terrorists* tried to kill my daughters! It's only by the grace of God and luck that they're alive! *I* need to protect them!" POTUS said.

"No, sir, you don't. That's *my* job. If I haven't proven that the Secret Service will do anything to protect your daughters—I mean *anything*—well, fuck you Mr. President. Ten agents are facing rehabs that will rival your own when you were with the Bears, and three gave their lives for your daughters. One of them charged at least five terrorists *by himself* to give me time to get the girls away from the bad guys. He deliberately sacrificed his life in order to keep your girls safe, just like some of those other agents did. Even though I know you would, you can't do that, Mr. President, which is why we have to do it for you," I said.

"But, my girls...," POTUS said, his voice breaking.

"Need you to go be their dad, and be the president just like before, because if you don't, as trite as it sounds, the terrorists win," I said. "Go be with the girls and your wife—stay in the residence today and watch movies and eat popcorn and let Charlie Hassenger run the country—we all know he does anyway."

"Oh, fuck you, Freak," the president said. He laughed and we all joined in. The tension in the room reduced to DefCon Four from DefCon Oh Fuck as the president stood up and once again came around the table and hugged me. He nodded at everyone else and said, "Travis, I'd like you to chair the meeting so that I don't make a horse's ass of myself."

"No danger of that, Mr. President, and of course I'll chair the meeting. Director Sorenson, Director Hessler and I will brief you as soon as humanly possible, sir." He and the president shook hands, and then the president shook everybody else's hand, and then he left and everybody in the room could breathe again.

Secretary Nowicki looked at me like I'd just sprouted eagle wings from my back and flown around the room. Finally he said, "Freak, you've got the biggest balls I've ever seen, and yes, that's a compliment. What the fuck do you call what you just did?"

"Indomitable *chutzpah*, Mr. Secretary," I said. "It's a Jewish thing, sir—I doubt if a Polish person can understand it." The room roared with laughter as Nowicki shot me the finger while on the way to his chair.

We got down to business, picking up right where we left off the day before after Secretary Nowicki got the secrecy part over.

"Everyone here needs to understand that this is above Top Secret. Nothing we say here can be heard anywhere else. Any tasks you are asked to undertake will be done personally, using the most secure communication possible. We will only use the latest encrypted phones and there are to be no—zero, nada, zilch—emails about the meeting itself or what was discussed. Are we clear?" Secretary Nowicki said. Everyone nodded and Nowicki looked at me, so I said, "And if I find out you did talk about it I will personally fuck your ass up so bad that your mother won't recognize you, and then I'll drag whatever's left to Leavenworth, lock it up and throw away the key. *Capische?*"

Apparently I didn't look like I was joking or indulging in hyperbole, because everyone nodded much more vigorously. That was good, because I meant every word.

I gave them the special ops death stare and recounted the details from the attack on the first daughters so that everyone could get up to speed. There weren't any questions during my recital, but there were plenty when I got done.

"This doesn't sound like a terrorist attack, at least not from Muslim terrorists," Scott Schwartz, Nails' deputy, said.

"I concur. It's too small, too well organized and besides, the jihadis don't specifically target children," the CIA Director said.

"Plus, the jihadis don't have anything like that kind of fire discipline," Miss Bitchy Voice said. "They would've just sprayed everybody with machine guns and then ran."

"And the only chatter we heard was so long ago that it isn't even relevant today. Wasn't the last thing that we heard about the kids back when Freak joined their detail?" the NSA Director said.

"That's right," Nails said. "And that was determined to be two Ukrainian/Russian outfits spit-balling what they'd do if the president followed through with his threat to interdict arms to that area of the world."

"It wasn't an attack, it was a kidnap attempt," Nathan "Dreamboat" Jones said. "These guys wanted to take the first daughters—why? To pressure the president? About what? Their motive is very important—it might lead us to their identities."

"There's a reason I keep him around, and it ain't just for his pretty face," Secretary Nowicki said.

"A kidnap makes much more sense," the CIA Deputy Director (Intelligence) said. "It fits with the fire discipline and methods used, but it can't be from some jihadi group. They couldn't put an op of that size and precision together without some chatter or hum int (human intelligence—i.e., a spy) on it. No way it goes off and we don't get a whiff of it."

"Unless…uh, unless…" Miss Bitchy Voice said, clearly unsure of how far to go with her train of thought.

"Unless they had an inside man and this was an op conducted by our own personnel," Nataliya Muzghov-Franklin, a.k.a. SWWFYU, said.

"The Secret Service has gone rogue?" the DDI said. "That seems pretty unlikely to me, if not downright impossible."

"And besides the DDI's point—which I totally agree with, by the way—except for Freak the Service doesn't have that kind of fire discipline, unless it's a group composed entirely of their sniper section, which again is impossible," the NSA Director said.

"But it's not impossible if it's a coherent U.S. unit, like a Force Recon platoon, or Deltas, or Rangers, or..." Miss Bitchy Voice said, her voice trailing off in disbelief.

"Or Navy SEALs," SWWFYU said.

"Oh, fuck me," the CIA Director said.

We all sat there in silence, contemplating what it meant to have a rogue special ops unit trying to kidnap the first daughters.

What it meant was that we were sincerely fucked every which way, because what we were talking about were Americans born and bred who could be hiding anywhere they wanted. Hell, they wouldn't even need to hide, because they could take their perfectly legitimate U.S. military or diplomatic IDs or plain old driver's licenses and go wherever the fuck they wanted, whenever the fuck they wanted. The fact that these guys (meaning men and wymyn, since there were both varieties in special ops) were experts at hiding in hostile country meant that we'd never find them in their home country without some kind of break, and that wasn't going to happen, since these were probably Navy SEALs we were talking about, all of whom had been voted "Least Likely to Fuck Up" right after they graduated from the SEAL training school in Coronado, California.

Finally Secretary Nowicki said, "We need to check out every goddamned special ops soldier from the last ten years, at least. We have to verify their whereabouts at the time of the attack and we have to check their connections to the Secret Service and we have to do it absolutely without causing a ripple in the Spec Ops pond."

"No shit, Sherlock," General Terrance X. "Mad Dog" McAllen said. "Except that's impossible, because once we make one inquiry the jungle drums will start up and our cover will be busted faster than you can say "Fuck you, Putin." We don't employ any stupid special ops personnel, and they're gonna tumble to us as soon as we even unship an oar, much less start paddling in their pond."

"Unless it was a group of *Russians* who tried to kidnap the first daughters—then they'd *help* us investigate the "terrorist" attack," Admiral Wilson Jordan Hannah said.

"Sweet idea, except make it Russian separatists—dissident Chechens," DDO Arthur Ishikawa said.

"Dissident *expatriate* Chechens, possibly with a cell or three here in the good old USA," Miss Bitchy Voice said.

"Oh, yeah, that works for me," Mad Dog McAllen said. "That'll scare the shit out of the Russians, and probably a bunch of other people, too, which will lead to a bunch of wild goose chases, which'll cover our asses even more."

"It's very elegant and at the same time no one can dispute the contention unless they have access to the actual intel," Admiral Hannah said.

"Which they won't have, especially if we set this up right. We use the CIA, because this is foreign, not domestic. We involve the NSA, but listening to Russian resources...for the most part," the NSA Director said.

"And special ops is involved because neither of those organizations know dick about how someone would set such a thing up, but we have experts on it that we can access," Dreamboat said.

"And we can question them extensively, especially once we mention the word "Russians," because we all know that our special ops are just itching to take on some Russians, right?" Scott Schwartz said.

"The Deputy Director is absolutely correct," said SWWFYU. "We can camouflage the entire op right out in the open and they won't suspect a thing, because it won't involve the FBI, Secret Service or any other domestic entity."

"And meanwhile we can dig in on SigInt (signal intelligence—electronic spying) concerning the attack by piggybacking on our Russian ops," the DDI of the CIA said.

"But we can't do it if there's even a whisper of this outside this room. We have to keep saying "terrorist attack" and implying it was from a foreign source, to everyone outside this room," Nails said.

"Well, for all we *actually* know it was a foreign operation," FBI Director Malcolm Sorenson said. "We don't have any real proof, just surmises and suppositions. And before anyone thinks I'm opposing the surmises and suppositions, I'm not. I totally agree with the assessments the group has made. I'm only saying that when someone asks any of us the inevitable "whodunit" question it won't be hard to prevaricate, since we have no hard evidence." It was a good thing to say and well said, and it gave me an idea about another thing we were going to need to make this work.

I looked at Director Sorenson and said, "Sir, you're absolutely right. What we need to do is start the smokescreen right now. I think that you and the CIA Director need to brief the president immediately. Make sure the Chief of Staff is in there, and preferably the press secretary and anybody else who will start saying the words "foreign terrorist" to the press. If we leave Nails out of the briefing it will look like CIA and FBI are taking over the investigation, which will only reinforce the message that this was foreign assets."

Sorenson looked at the CIA director, who nodded, and Sorenson saw only nodding agreement from everybody else, so he said, "An excellent idea, Agent Glickstien. We'll answer any questions the president has based on the subterfuge that this was a foreign attack—Director MacDonald will float the idea that it may have been expatriate Chechen separatists—and we'll decline to answer just enough questions to confirm the suspicions we plant on them."

I had to admit that the guy was good, dirty or not.

The two directors left to brief the president and DDO Arthur Ishikawa said, "The only problem is that we are going to need some domestic help, because we need to find the mole in the Secret Service."

"We might be able to help with that," Nails said.

"Oh, they're going to love it," I said. Everyone looked at me except Miss Bitchy Voice and Dreamboat Jones, who both looked off into space and imitated whistling, since they already knew what was coming.

So Nails explained about the Badger Squad and their pursuit of another mole, although she didn't specify who or what agency. When she was done Admiral Hannah said, "So what do you suspect the FBI Director did?"

"I never said that it was anyone in the FBI," Nails said, her face as set as Teddy Roosevelt's on Mount Rushmore.

"So why did Freak send the FBI and CIA directors off to prematurely brief the president?" Admiral Hannah said.

"And why did four people in this room heave a sigh of relief?" Mad Dog McAllen said.

I looked at Nails and said, "Contrary to public opinion, we don't have any stupid command officers. Assholes, yes, stupid, no." Everybody laughed and Nails said, "We can't tell you, but we know that it's true. However, the two events don't appear to be connected, and I doubt if it will interfere with this op, but it would be nice if that pompous ass never found out about this."

"About what?" DHS Secretary Nowicki said.

"Weren't we talking about the National's chances this year?" the NSA Director said.

"They'll be right there, but if they face the Tigers in the Series they should just walk Miggy. I've never seen anyone hit like that for as long as he has," Scott Schwartz said.

"Not bad for a 40-year-old, huh?" SWWFYU said. She had a thing for Hispanic men and had always admired Miguel Cabrera's, uh, baseball skills (OK, so she thought he was one hot unit and could benefit from a strong womyn's touch—and no, I'm not going any farther than that, ya pervs).

"How does somebody hit 45 homers and bat .355 at 40 years old?" the CIA DDI said.

"Don't forget he had 152 RBIs and walked ninety times," I said.

"All while playing half his games in Comerica, where homers go to die," DDO Arthur Ishikawa said. We all were still carrying on about baseball when my phone went off. It was the Chicago office, so I answered the call to find Jewey, Weasel, Mamba and what sounded like a whole herd of barking seals at the other end.

"What the fuck is going on, ya fucking nitwits? Are you having another toga party?" I said.

"WE GOT HIM, FREAK!" Weasel said, sounding like he had just won the Power Ball for a billion dollars.

"THAT MOTHERFUCKER'S ASS IS TOAST! WEASEL GOT HIM!" Jewey said. His voice was about three octaves higher than normal.

"Cet imbécile est en baisse pour le comte!" Mamba said, slipping into French to say "That imbecile is going down for the count!"

"Great! What the fuck are you guys talking about? Slow down and tell all of us the story, OK?" I said, trying to warn my fired-up friends that there were other people listening.

They didn't routinely outthink and run down bad guys because they were dumb. Jewey said, "Define everybody."

"You aren't still debriefing, are ya?" Weasel said. I hesitated and he said, "Well, shit, this ain't ready for primetime yet, Freak. Who else is there?"

"Is Nails there?" Mamba said. "Of course she is—no way she leaves you alone after somebody tries to kidnap the president's daughters, so she's sitting on this call, too, which means that…oh, shit. The entire star chamber is still there isn't it?"

"Including several heads or deputy heads of three letter agencies, which means that…oh, shit," Weasel said.

"Then we better let you go, Freak. Call us when you have the chance—we may have something on that big counterfeiting case up in ah, Butte," Jewey said.

"Oh, fuckity-fuck-fuck," Weasel said. "We weren't on speaker, were we?"

"You might as well have been," Nails said from where she'd been listening along with me as my whack-job friends celebrated on the phone. "What the fuck was that infernal racket when Freak answered?"

"Uh, Madame Director, this is Senior Agent William F. Crocker. We, uh, well…that was the rest of our unit giving Agent Wei the uh, er, family seal of approval for his great work on the counterfeiting case in, ah, Butte."

"Joe, you are the worst liar in the entire Secret Service," Nails said. "Don't go anywhere—I'll be right back." She took my phone and put them on hold, then punched another number. It was answered and she said, "Parker, what's the location on POTUS? OK. Who's in with him? The FBI and CIA directors waiting in the outer office? Good. ETA on their getting in the Oval? Good. Call me the instant they step out of the Oval, willya? Thanks, Parker." She hung up and punched back over to the Badger Squad.

"I'm putting you on speaker, Joe." Nails hit the speaker button and Mamba's voice came through loud and clear. "We probably just blew the whole goddamned op because we were acting like fucking children. Shit! All that brilliant work fucking blown because we couldn't keep our fucking shit together for five more fucking minutes!"

"Are you not getting laid enough, Monsieur le Comte? Because your mind seems to be on fucking and not the work," I said.

"Fuck you, Freak. Tell me we're in the clear and I'll stop being fucking pissed off," Mamba said.

"The FBI director is waiting outside the Oval Office to see the president, and he'll be there for at least 20 more minutes, so what the fuck were you fucking going on about, Agent de Coucy?" Nails said.

Mamba said, "Ma'am, I'd like Agents Wei and Silverberg to answer that question, if you don't mind."

"Very well—Agent Wei?" Nails said.

"First of all, ma'am, as for the surveillance expenses, well, I paid for the trip out of my own pocket, ma'am. We've all been paying out of pocket to follow these guys around, although Agent de Coucy has been helping us when we need it," Weasel said.

"Your guys pay for their own expenses during surveillance? How can we get our guys to do that?" DDO Ishikawa said.

"OK, we'll take that up later, Agent Wei. About the why of the surveillance?" Nails said.

"Ma'am, the Badger Squad has never quit digging on who was behind the Morehead State attacks that left three civilians and Secret Service Senior Agent Andria Rogers dead. You authorized us to give it all the attention that we could without compromising our other duties, and so we've been taking turns surveilling the two suspects we had—and we got one bringing $500K back into the U.S. from the Cayman Islands," Weasel said.

"Got how?" Nails said.

"Ma'am, an informant gave him the money at the bank in the Caymans and I kept him and the money in sight all the way to O'Hare International in Chicago. From there we followed him all the way to the World-Famous Billy Goat Tavern, where we arrested him and his partner as they were handing the money over to a representative of the person who ordered the actions against Soper and Glickstien," Weasel said.

"You were on surveillance in the Cayman *Islands*?" Nails said.

"Well, not exactly ma'am. The suspect was in Atlanta, but electronic surveillance indicated that he was going to the Caymans, so I flew there from O'Hare. My informant indicated that he had an appointment at the bank the next day, so I picked him up there the next day, then followed him back to Chicago," Weasel said. "Agents Bell, Greenman, de Coucy and Silverberg joined me at the airport and we followed the suspect to the World-Famous Billy Goat Tavern. Once we saw the money exchange we arrested the three suspects on suspicion of financial crimes against the U.S.," Weasel said.

"I have two questions, Agent Wei. What made you surveil the suspect in the first place? And who was paying for your gallivanting?" Nails said.

"Ma'am, as you know we had these two guys we were trying to link up with the third guy? I noticed in looking at the two guys' bank records that one had booked two tickets to the Caymans in March, and that the other booked two rooms at a luxury hotel for the same time. I checked their personnel records and discovered they were both on vacation during that time.

"I found that odd, so I flew to the Caymans and checked out their hotel. The people there picked them out of photo arrays, and said they remembered the two guys because they appeared to be cheap when they checked in, but later apologized and gave everybody who'd waited on them retroactive tips that were far too large. The help at the resort commented that their generosity seemed to increase after they went to a certain bank there.

"So I went to the bank to see what I could find out about the two guys. We all know that the Caymans are a haven for shady money transfers, primarily due to the bank secrecy laws there, but we should remember that the people who work at the banks are just people. I struck up a conversation with the chief financial secretary at the bank, who happened to be in the market for a new friend. She also happened to be the daughter of a New York City policeman who believed in truth, justice and the American way," Weasel said.

"So how much did it cost to bribe her to get you the info you needed?" I said, only half joking.

"Nothing," Weasel said. "My CI is an American citizen and decided to do her patriotic duty, which is why she provided me with the account info for the two subjects, which is also how I was able to track the first subject and the money—she activated a computer alert on the subject's account."

"So how did you confirm that these two subjects had been paid by someone higher up in the food chain?" Dreamboat Jones said.

"I'd like to let Agent Silverberg answer that, sir," Weasel said.

"We went back and pulled wire transfer records for every transaction on the account and used previously acquired financial records to back trace where the money originated, but that proved to be fruitless...until we discovered that the subjects wire transferred money from a Chicago bank.

"Once we'd established that the account was completely funded from the Chicago wire transfers we went to the bank and asked for their cooperation in an international money-laundering scheme. As you can imagine they were more than happy to help, which is how we discovered that the money was deposited in the account of a Chicago social worker and then transferred to the Cayman Island account which the two subjects co-owned.

"We wondered how a social worker made enough money to send $500K to the Caymans, so we checked and found out that the account holder wasn't just a social worker, she was an ancient, decrepit, retired social worker whose peak salary had been $76K. A check of her financials showed that she had a modest nest egg of around $125K in an investment account, and that she auto deposited monthly retirement checks from both the State of Illinois and Social Security, carrying a balance of around $7K in her checking account. All of her major bills were auto draws and she wrote various small checks each month, including a car payment on a new Cadillac." Jewey paused, so I said, "Not at all unusual, except for the…"

"Two wire transfers of $500K each, two weeks apart, sent from the retired social worker's account to the subjects' Cayman Islands account," Jewey said.

"Wait a minute—are you saying this retired social worker sent a million dollars to our two subjects via wire transfer? How old is this retiree?" Secretary Nowicki said.

"She's 79 years old, and yes, those are the only two times she's ever used a wire transfer in the account's history—and she's had the account for over 25 years," Jewey said.

"Whiskey Tango Foxtrot?" Admiral Hannah said. "Do we know if this old lady even knows how to use wire transfers, and if she does where the hell did she get a million bucks?"

"She didn't, ma'am," Jewey said. "We discovered that there were two $500K deposits made in her account by the same guy, two weeks apart, and then this same guy arranged for the wire transfers to the Cayman account of our subjects."

"How was that done? Wouldn't the old lady have to have sent the cash if it was her account? Did she have a co-signatory on the account?" DDI Silva said.

"I'll bet not, because she's still independent," Miss Bitchy Voice said. "But she's old, so someone's got power of attorney over her accounts just in case she loses it or suffers a stroke or other incapacitating event."

"Bingo! Give the lady a prize—her son has power of attorney over the account and, according to bank access records, routinely checks her accounts for any discrepancies or unusual spending," Jewey said.

"Did you get an ID on the guy?" Mad Dog McAllen said.

"We did, Mr. Chairman. We showed a photo array to the tellers and two of them ID'd the man in question as the guy who made the cash deposits," Weasel said.

"And we also confirmed that he was the guy who called to send the wire transfers," Jewey said.

"What's the old lady's name?" Nails said.

"Her name is Celeste Wilkinson, but that isn't the important name. The name of her son is what's important," Weasel said.

"Well, what the fuck is it?" Secretary Nowicki said. "We need to move fast so that we have this motherfucker under surveillance, unless you've already done that?"

"Oh, we don't have eyes on him, but we don't think that surveillance will be a problem, Mr. Secretary," Weasel said.

"And why the hell not? Who the fuck are we talking about? What's the asshole's name?" Nowicki said.

"Malcolm Francis Sorenson, the Director of the FBI," Jewey said.

Which is when the shit hit the fan, so to speak.

Everybody in the room began cursing, bellowing questions and generally acting as if their hair was on fire. Both the DDO and DDI of the CIA were yelling instructions into their phones about stopping access to certain data for the FBI, the V-JCS was yelling at her phone to make sure that no classified material flowed from the Joint Chiefs to the FBI until further notice, Secretary Nowicki was telling someone to get a guard mounted on the FBI Director's House and Nails was telling the chief of the president's Secret Service detail, Parker Connolly, to personally escort the FBI director back to the Cabinet room as soon as his meeting with the president was over.

When the hullaballoo finally calmed itself Nails said, "Well done, Badger Squad. All of you deserve credit for figuring this out, especially Weasel and Jewey."

"Thank you, but what we told you so far isn't the best part, ma'am," Jewey said.

"The case you've built seems to be very sound—at least we all think that it is," Nails said, getting nods for every head in the room. "What could be better than tha...oh," Nails said. She looked at the cell phone on the table and said, in a soft, reverent voice, "You have one or both of them as cooperating witnesses, don't you?"

"YES!" the entire Chicago contingent said, their voices rising like they were a triumphant chorus of justice.

"It was Kid Galahad—Agent Jordan Moerman—who gave us the clue that broke one of the subjects, whose confession promptly broke the other subject. Both of them independently confirmed that Director Sorenson was the head honcho, which we already knew because we'd seen his mom's bank accounts and had a firm physical ID," Jewey said.

"Exactly how did you turn them, Jewey?" I said. "Please tell me that you gave them an opportunity to have representation present."

"No rubber hoses here, Freak," Weasel said. "We told them we wouldn't proceed until they had lawyers—Joe suggested we not even take a chance on a waiver of their rights, and we all concurred— and we did all the rest by the book. Following the first round of interviews Kid Galahad reminded me of a conversation he'd had with DHS Assistant Director Nathan Jones concerning how to break certain subjects. I proceeded back into the interrogation room where one of the subjects was being interviewed by Agent in Charge Jerry Clune and Agent Alec Hwang and asked him to remember that his grandmother was watching his actions, at which point the subject broke down, confessed to his participation in the enterprises against both Aleta Greenhoe Soper and Agent Glickstien and offered to become a participating witness. The subject's lawyer asked that we draw up a formal agreement concerning the prosecution of the subject before we proceeded, which the U.S. Attorney did and which all parties signed.

"At that time we asked the subject about who ordered the actions against Governor Soper and Agent Glickstien, and he provided us with Director Sorenson's name. We confronted the other subject with his participation in these criminal activities and offered him a deal for his participation, at which point he consulted with his attorney and agreed to our proposal. Subsequent to all parties signing the plea proposal he independently supplied us with Director Sorenson's name as the person who ordered the actions against Soper and Glickstien," Weasel said, his voice as steady as the Rock of Gibraltar despite his evident excitement.

"So there is no question that the subjects' participation in this investigation is voluntary and above board," DHS Secretary Nowicki said.

"None at all, sir. Everything has been signed and notarized and both subjects' attorneys also signed, indicating their agreement with the terms and the fact that the subjects' rights were protected," Weasel said.

"And no warrants were needed for the activities in the Caymans?" Miss Bitchy Voice said.

"No, MBV, because all of my info there came from a CI, plus all we did there was observe what appeared to be suspicious behavior. Once my CI confirmed the money transfer and we watched the suspect transport illegal amounts of cash across international borders we had a financial crime, which is well within the purview of the Secret Service," Weasel said. "We honestly thought that he could be transporting counterfeit cash, although we now know it was just ill-gotten proceeds from the Morehead attempt on the lives of Soper and Freak," Weasel said.

"The big question is why they were bringing the cash back into the U.S. when it was safely offshore," Dreamboat Jones said.

Jewey's big laugh boomed out of the speaker and he said, "You're going to love this one, Dreamboat. The FBI Director demanded a refund of half the cash because the attack failed. The two subjects were ordered to return it to him in cash, so rather than having a wire transfer into the U.S., which we could easily missed, the two geniuses decided to actually hand him the bags full of hundreds."

"What dumb fucks," DDO Ishikawa said. "Why'n the hell would they do that? It's so stupid that it's like they had no knowledge of tradecraft at all."

"They don't," Dreamboat said.

"How do you know?" Secretary Nowicki said. There was silence from everywhere, especially the speaker phone. Finally Dreamboat said, "Jewey, Weasel, it's OK to tell 'em who these dipshits are."

"Roger that. The two subjects are FBI agents Adam Jones and Thomas Smith. They have been stationed at the Baltimore Field Office as investigators, but most of their work has been directly for high-level FBI personnel like Director Sorenson. Also Agent Jones is Assistant Director Jones's brother," Weasel said.

"And he's a real dumbass dipshit who could fuck up tying his shoes. Don't get me wrong, he's a good guy, but he's dumb and easily led. I'm not excusing his actions, but if anybody offered him something shiny he'd take it, because life has always been the path of least resistance for Adam.

"Tom Smith is his best buddy since fifth grade—my family calls them A and A1—and they never do anything apart from each other. If Adam broke Tom would break and vice versa. I'm sorry for all of the shit my brother is responsible for, and I hope everyone involved will accept my apology, especially Freak," Dreamboat Jones said.

"I don't hold anything against anybody, especially your dumbass brother and his asshole friend," I said. "I do reserve the right to hold shit against that motherfucker Sorenson, and no, I'm not begging your pardon for the language. None of the rest of you saw the crushed bodies of the people killed in Morehead, and you didn't see the grief it caused Soper and all the other families that lost people." I turned to Nails and said, "Ma'am, I would suggest that it would be a bad idea for me to arrest that motherfucker Sorenson, although I would like to represent the Service when they clap the iron on him."

She looked at me and said, "I've already arranged to have him arrested right here, in this room, by non-Secret Service personnel, mainly because I don't want there to be any emotions that cause any problems with convicting that son of a bitch, but also so that we can all show him our contempt. Any problems with that, Badger Squad, Freak?"

"No ma'am," said. I could feel my skin reddening and my hair beginning to stand up all over my body as I contemplated the arrest of the motherfucker who ordered the deaths of my pals in Morehead. It really was a good thing I wasn't putting the handcuffs on Sorenson, because it was possible that I would simply wrench his arms off and stick them up his ass.

"No problems with the Badger Squad," Jewey said, "as long as the cuffs are tight and he is prosecuted to the fullest extent of the law."

"And somebody kicks him in the balls for killing CoD," Weasel said.

"And somebody slaps the shit out of him for Josie and the kid," Mamba said.

"And they send him to a prison with a nice general population—you know, like Marion, or better, Ft. Leavenworth," Joe said.

"Lots of rapists and murderers at Leavenworth," Buzz said.

"Maybe we can send a few cards around, let them know about Sorenson," Gomer said.

"What an excellent idea, young Padawan," Joe said.

"Cut the comedy shit, because we're leaving the line open so that you can hear the arrest," Nails said.

"Roger that," Joe said. "Badger Squad, standing by."

"Before he gets here, who's the U.S. Attorney that caught the case?" Dreamboat said.

"Our old friend Brenda T. Green," Joe said. "She's all the way up to speed and she's a killah, if you know what I mean."

"Excellent," I said. "We worked with her in Morehead when we arrested the dumbass sheriff and his dipshit deputy. She won't take shit from anyone and she's as tough as a dollar steak."

"Concur," the entire Badger Squad said.

"I'm glad we're agreed, but he's headed back from the Oval. Be quiet now, because as soon as my arrest team is in place we're taking him down," Nails said.

"Acknowledged. Badger Squad going quiet," Joe said.

"How are we playing this?" DDI Silva of the CIA said.

"Just like we've been discussing the same things we were when he left," Nails said. "I'll get a bump in my ear when the arrest team gets here and then they'll come in and take him down."

So we were all talking about the kidnap attempt when the FBI and CIA directors came back in the room. Sorenson was all smiles when he came in from his meeting with the president. Chairman Mad Dog McAllen was questioning me about the tactics the kidnappers employed, and I was explaining that the shooters killed the vehicles at the same time they began taking the protective agents down, which indicated a large team, especially since someone had wired up the safe room with bombs both inside and out.

Sorenson and CIA Director Joan MacDonald waited until I was done and then MacDonald said, "The smokescreen is successfully started—the president had his inner circle in there with him, and everybody knows that they leak like a sieve, so the word that it's a foreign op won't have any problem getting out, wouldn't you say Mr. Director?"

"I agree, Madam Director. We were just subtle enough to give them the idea, but not explicit enough to actually hand it to them. The media should begin speculating about it today, and the president can be counted on to confirm it by "no commenting on ongoing national security matters." I'd like to give Director MacDonald credit—she was masterful in planting the seeds," Sorenson said.

Everyone nodded their congratulations to the CIA director. She started to speak when there was a loud knock on the door. Without waiting for an answer the door opened and U.S. Marshal Thomas J. Vernon and his four chief deputies entered the Cabinet Room. He looked around the room and then settled on Nails. The marshals marched over to her and she said, "We have the warrant, Marshal Vernon. Please do your duty."

Honest Tom nodded and said, "Yes, ma'am. Will we be notified of the prisoner's destination before we leave the White House?"

"We'll notify you by secure channel once you've cleared the White House," Nails said.

Joan MacDonald didn't become the Director of the CIA because she was weak, shy, or stupid. She stood up and said, "What's the meaning of this, Director Hessler? Who are these men, and why are they here?"

Honest Tom turned toward her and said, "Madame Director, I'm U.S. Marshal Thomas J. Vernon, and I have been instructed to arrest a person wanted by the U.S. Attorney's Office on charges of murder, conspiracy to commit murder, assault with intent to commit murder, assault and battery, bribing a federal officer and multiple other charges. My men and I will be out of your hair in just a moment, ma'am." Honest Tom and his men showed their credentials around the room, and MacDonald said, "Very well, Marshal, do your duty."

He and his men marched over to the FBI Director, who was just sitting in his seat with his mouth hanging wide open. He looked as if he'd just seen Jesus exit the tomb, but like Doubting Thomas he couldn't quite believe it. When Honest Tom looked him in the eye and said, "Mr. Director," Sorenson looked down for a moment, and then he nodded to himself and got out of his chair.

"Malcolm Francis Sorenson, you are under arrest for the murders of Elvin Clyde Bliss, Josephine Boroviak Soper, Andria Rogers and Tara Waters, along with conspiracy to commit murder, assault with intent to commit murder, assault and battery, bribery of a federal officer and many other crimes. You have the right to remain silent, anything you say can and will be used against you in a court of law. You have the right to an attorney. If you cannot afford an attorney one will be provided at no expense to you. Do you understand these rights as I've explained them to you?"

Sorenson nodded, and Honest Tom said, "Sir, I need you to articulate your answer."

"I understand my rights and will remain silent. I also demand that I be allowed to consult my attorney immediately," the (soon to be former) FBI Director said.

"That's fine, sir, as soon as we process you through the system you will get an attorney, and we will not in any way attempt to interrogate or talk to you until your attorney is present," Honest Tom said. "Now if you will please put your hands behind your back for me, sir?"

"Is that really necessary, Marshal?" Joan MacDonald said.

"Yes, ma'am, it really is," several of us said at once. Because of the situation no one mentioned owing anybody any Pepsis, but I planned on claiming some from Nails, Dreamboat, MBV and Mad Dog McAllen.

Sorenson just shrugged and put his hands behind his back. Honest Tom hooked him up and the marshals started for the door. Everyone stood up, and I looked Sorenson right in the eyes. He tried to stare me down, but I'd put on the Spec Ops death stare, combined with my "I'd like to eat you" tiger stare, and he dropped his eyes after just a few moments.

That didn't work for me, so I half-growled and he looked up again. My eyes must have been on the "truth beam" setting, because all of a sudden I was sure he wasn't the final word on the Morehead attack. Sorenson must have felt my doubt, because he said, "I'm sorry for all the lives that were lost. I truly am."

Goddammit, I believed the asshole.

There was someone else out there who was higher on the food chain that had ordered the Morehead attack.

It had to be someone very high up, because there weren't too many people who overtopped the Director of the FBI. The one person who clearly did outrank the FBI director immediately came to mind, but the thought of it being him almost made my heart stop…until I considered the most recent hairy incident in my life…which suddenly made more sense if the two events were connected.

Talk about the shit hitting the fan.

My brain went into overdrive as I considered the fact that maybe the only reason I wasn't dead was because I'd snatched up the first daughters…and the people ordered by their father to make it look like a kidnap attempt while killing me had also ordered that his girls not get hurt during the attack.

Fuck a goddamned duck. It was possible that I was somehow the target of a vendetta being conducted by the president of the United States, which was a fight that I couldn't possibly hope to win.

It turned out I was almost right.

Almost.

CHAPTER 65

Life Goes On, Freak

The arrest of the FBI director on murder charges certainly knocked the attempt on the girls off the airwaves for a while, but it didn't knock it off our radar. Nails and Scott Schwartz didn't know who did it or how they got the intelligence needed for the ambush, and they didn't trust anybody else to investigate, so they brought the Badger Squad to D.C. Everyone was told it was so that they could keep digging into the Sorenson case in preparation for the trial, but in reality, it was to keep working on the ambush case.

Those of us who were ambulatory went to the funerals of Patsy, Sparky 2.0, and Hot Rod, which no one wanted to do, but which were obligatory. At every funeral we were told some version of "get the bastards who did this," and we dutifully promised to do our best, even though none of us knew if it would ever happen. It seemed the least we could do—give the families hope that their loved ones would get justice—but it also left a bad taste in our mouths because of the uncertainty involved. We also missed our comrades, especially because we also had our wounded to think about.

Ed felt particularly morose about the entire deal, since she had been at a dentist appointment the day of the ambush and had missed everything. She really felt bad about Gangster's two ruined knees, since she would've been one of the girls' body agents if she'd been there.

I told her that she needed to get over it, because as the new Chief of Detail for the first daughters I needed her now more than ever. She did get over it, but Ed also went to see Gangster every day she could to assuage her guilt, and to keep Gangster's morale up.

Everybody on the detail the day of the ambush was extensively de-briefed, and then de-briefed again, and again. It was easy to do, since none of them could walk due to their injured kneecaps.

Foghorn and Gangster were injured the worst—both had been hit in both knees, and both had shattered patellas (kneecaps). Foghorn also had both patellar tendons ruptured and surgically repaired, while one of Gangster's patellar tendons was ruptured and required surgical reconstruction. Neither of them would be able to walk for at least nine months, although we all thought that estimate was very optimistic.

Buddha was the least injured. She'd been drilled through her left patella, but the .22-caliber bullet had done just that: it drilled right through the kneecap without any shattering, clipped the ACL (anterior cruciate ligament) and then exited her knee with no other damage. Buddha had actually gotten up after being shot and hauled herself behind one of the Suburbans and used her Heckler & Koch MP-5 to return fire from the attackers. She believed she'd hit one of them, since a position she saw firing immediately ceased after she hit it with three three-round bursts, but we had no confirmation. The docs said that she'd be up and around in four weeks, and probably fully recovered within two months after that.

Everybody else were somewhere between those two extremes on the injured scale, with lots of plates, screws, wire, and mesh in their surgically repaired knees. During personal visits from the president and first lady every one of the injured had vowed that they were coming back to the detail as soon as the docs released them. The president and first lady assured them that their daughters were all in favor of it, and the president said that he'd make it an Executive Order if he had to, which was overkill but still reassuring.

The president and Nails determined that I needed a free hand as the CoD for the Warrior Princesses, so I got to bring in all the old gang that wanted to do protective work, including Coach, Betty Crocker, Mamba (who pulled double duty with the Badger Squad), Badass, El Gato, Bumble and Kid Galahad, along with a whole crew of other agents that were all known to at least one member of the detail.

After a week the Warrior Princesses were cleared to go back to school, although we helicoptered them in and out through the safe room door, which was always covered with a nice Kevlar (semi-bulletproof) arcade canopy. We also saturated the outside of the building with more surveillance gear and kept two agents in the safe room at all times, even overnight (although we managed to keep that from the general public).

The Princesses and I grew very close, to the point where Allison began asking me about colleges (Go Green! Go White!) and Brooke wanted to know if she should let her boyfriend kiss her at the Freshman Dance ("Not unless you want me to pretend he's a gnat"—I got gales of laughter from both princesses over that one).

Once a week the Princesses invited Ed, me and two other agents on their detail up to the residence to watch a movie and eat popcorn and drink Pepsis and burp and giggle, which was fun. More fun was that the president and first lady still liked me enough to not only tolerate this, but actually encouraged it.

I'd also had to come to the residence to help calm the girls after nightmares—three times for Allison and twice for Brooke. I thought that was pretty good—two teens who'd been through the stress of real combat and come through the other side that well are damned strong people in my book.

I also loved the fact that the Warrior Princesses asked me to help them learn to shoot, and that they came with me to the range twice a week. It showed the kind of wymyn they were going to be when we shot, because they always shot at silhouettes, not traditional ring targets.

Brooke always shot the crotch out of the first target, while Allison went for head shots.

Now they really were Warrior Princesses, trained by the Freak who loved them.

The thing that really made it possible to just go on was that it had quickly became clear that the president had not, in fact, been any part of Morehead, New York or the kidnap attempt. After I told the Badger Squad about my suspicions they went into investigative overdrive and found absolutely nothing that would even remotely connect the president to any of the incidents. As Jewey said, "Freak, there's fuck-all that even hints the president was involved. Either he did it by using his telepathic powers or he's as clean as a whistle."

I was absolutely relieved to hear it, especially since POTUS and The First Bitch were still treating me like I was Wonder Woman.

So time rolled on. We got no leads at all on the attempted kidnapping of the first daughters, but the Badger Squad went on looking. We all participated to build an incredibly strong case against the now former FBI Director, who wouldn't talk to us or anyone else, even with his lawyer present. The federal prosecutors used every chance they had to interject the words "seek the death penalty" into their conversations with Malcolm Sorenson, but not only was he not moved, he became more obstinate, finally ceasing all conversation with anyone. I'm not kidding—the guy looked to be trying to break Supreme Court Justice Clarence Thomas's record for longest silence by a federal employee, and he wasn't even an employee anymore.

It looked like the only place the cases were going was to trial, where Brenda T. Green would fricassee the former director of the FBI and at least put him in federal prison for the rest of his life—and maybe get him the death penalty.

So I got to the White House on a perfectly normal Tuesday and we had the usual daily briefing by the chief of POTUS's detail, Parker Connelly. Then it was off to the waiting helicopter and school. I was running on short sleep, but thankfully the Princesses knew me well enough to know it, so it was a relatively quiet ride (or as quiet as it can be inside a tin can with a screaming turbocharged engine right above your head).

When we got to school I got out first, as usual, but as soon as my feet hit the pavement it felt wrong.

I know, I know, the famous gut feeling, right? I wasn't big on following hunches, but this one was a weird feeling, like someone was watching me. I don't have those kind of superpowers—oh to be Nicholai Hel (read Trevanian's *Shibumi*)—but like most people I can tell when someone's watching me. I kept the girls in the helicopter with a hand gesture and spun a slow circle, looking for anything out of the ordinary.

I found nothing unusual.

But the feeling persisted, so I radioed the two agents in the safe room and got an appropriate coded response for all clear, I called the car at the road and got an all clear, and I called the guys in the houses and got appropriate responses from them, too. I decided I was just tired and hurried the girls into the building. Once they were safely in class I went out with Ed and had a look around. We stood at the main entrance and slowly scanned the available scenery.

I went right past a small knot of people who I thought were waiting for the bus, but suddenly realized they were looking at me—not around me, near me or in my direction, but right *at* me. Of course I didn't have any binoculars, but our guys in the last house at the end of the driveway did, and so I called them on the encrypted radio and said, "This is Freak. Get some pics of the group standing by the bus stop sign—one of the guys has on a red shirt, and two of them are wearing blue and yellow jackets."

"Roger that, Freak. We'll get some—what the hell?" the agent said. I was already running for the school, because as soon as my agent started to respond one of the guys dropped something...and there was a huge cloud of dense smoke where the guys had been.

I was screaming "LOCKDOWN! LOCKDOWN! LOCKDOWN! SAFE ROOM NOW!" into my radio as I thundered down the hall toward Allison's classroom. Just as I came around the corner her detail boiled out of the room with her in the middle of them. Their guns were drawn as they flew down the hall. I spun right down the cross corridor toward Brooke's class, but her detail was already racing down the corridor toward me.

"SAFE THE PRINCESSES!" I said. I understand from the people who were there that I sounded like André the Giant in *The Princess Bride* when he yells "Everybody—move!" so it must've been loud. I spun around and pointed my 1076s down the hall toward the entrance, but the only people who appeared were Ed and one of the new agents, Sariya Waite. They had their weapons out and were backing down the hall making sure all the classroom doors were locked and that no students were visible.

But by then I'd already decided to turn this into a drill, because the uniformed Secret Service agents at the new gate to the Amicus School and the agents from the last two houses on the drive had broadcast the all-clear—one of the guys at the bus stop had dropped a new type of firecracker that was supposed to flash and billow smoke. He'd already admitted accidentally dropping it while showing it to the rest of the guys at the bus stop, and he'd been identified by several people as the person responsible. The group of guys had scattered when the smoke went up, but as soon as the wind blew it away they all came back, because they were all really just waiting for the bus. Everybody had lots of ID, nobody tried to run and when the bus came the agents let the guys get on it and leave, since all of them had jobs to get to.

I was OK with the way they handled it, and besides, we'd just done the school a favor by having a very real lockdown drill, which we required periodically in case of some nut-job, lone-wolf shooter who managed to weasel his or her way into the school.

I still couldn't shake the feeling that the whole thing was somehow wrong, but it wasn't. I didn't feel bad about calling for the lockdown, because in the Secret Service biz being paranoid is considered an asset, not a mental defect. Besides, we'd gotten the Warrior Princesses into the safe room and broadcast a sitrep in just 53 seconds, a new record with this crew, which meant that the new agents were almost as good as the old crew had been.

When I gave the code to open the safe room door two agents came out, followed by the Warrior Princesses, who both smiled at me.

"Thank you, Freak," Allison said. "Mrs. Hobart was in the middle of her "writing is the only difference between you and a chimpanzee" lecture and you saved me from falling asleep."

"Hey, Mrs. Hobart is right," I said, smiling back.

"I know she is, but it was still nice to get an unscheduled break," Allison said. She slapped my hand as she went back to class, winking at me, which was our secret code for "I feel safe." Brooke gave me a hug and said, "Thanks for keeping us safe, Freak. Every time we do one of these drills I feel better, especially when I see your 1076s out. Not even gnats can get by you."

Sappy? Yeah. Over the top? Maybe. Made me feel good anyway? Bet your ass, mac.

So we went back to normal for the rest of the day, got the Warrior Princesses back to The House after school and debriefed Nails and Parker Connelly on the incident that prompted the "drill." I was going to call it a day, but the director motioned for me to stay behind after the debrief.

When everybody else was gone she tossed a plane ticket on the table and said, "You're making a flying run to New York to see your uncle, Freak. And before you ask I don't know why, but he was most insistent that he see you ASAP. The message came from the District Attorney of New York herself, so I don't think he's just fucking around. She called me right away because he said if he didn't get to talk to you he might not testify at the death penalty phase of Leona Tromboli's state trial for Mac's murder."

"So I'm going to New York and back tonight?" I said.

"Yeah, and I've got somebody to cover for you tomorrow at school," Nails said. She was smirking, because she knew that after the false alarm that day I was going to protest, which I promptly did.

"C'mon, Director! I'm not going to hand the Warrior Princesses off and you know it, but just out of curiosity who'd you have in mind?" I said.

"Me," Nails said, "so shut the fuck up, Freak."

So I shut the fuck up and took the shuttle to the Big Apple, where we caught the break in the three cases that ignited the biggest shitstorm in the history of the U.S. government.

And all it cost was more lives.

CHAPTER 66

Arrivederci, Paisan

By the time I cleared JFK it was 7 p.m., so I called an Italian place I knew and picked up some food for my uncle. The car the New York DA sent took me to the courthouse, and two nice NYPD detectives led me to a third-floor conference room where they were holding Paul Monteverdi.

He looked like he was going to expire right in front of my eyes. The change was so dramatic that I almost wanted to deny it was him, but then he said, "Did ya bring some cannoli, too, sweetheart? 'Cause I can smell the lasagna and the *spezzatino con cipolline e zucca*, and is dat *pollo con olive e pignoli*?"

"Yeah, it is. I also brought *gnocchi con piselli e gorgonzola*, *capellini alla primavera*, fettucini with red clam sauce and garlic risotto, plus a couple bottles of a nice red from Florence, and of course three kinds of cannoli," I said. The old gangster now looked really old, and I felt inexplicably sad. When I'd encountered him just a few years ago he may have been the most dangerous person I'd ever met (he'd probably done 30 or 50 murders personally, and he'd ordered lots of others), but now he seemed like a really old, tired *paisano* who should be sitting on his sunny porch in Sicily just enjoying what time he had left.

Paul Monteverdi looked at my face and said, "Yeah, OK, I only got a coupla weeks left, maybe t'ree. I got the bone cancer, and it just come on me like a freight train, and den it meta, mesta, uh, y'know, it spread everywhere once it busted out, and yeah, so, I'm gonna die. After all the bad shit I done in my life it's only fair, right?"

I don't know why, but I kind of wished that Paul Monteverdi could go out in a blaze of glory. It didn't seem right that a tough guy like Mr. Green Mountain was going to gasp his life out in a hospital bed, unless he'd taken a dozen slugs in a shootout with other gangsters while defending Don Salvatore Bonnarino.

But that's movie shit, not real life. Most of us die without any theatrics at all, regardless of the cause of death, which is how Paul Monteverdi would go—let's face it, there is just no way to beat the Big D. Sooner or later the Grim Reaper beckons to us all and away we go, off to another plane of existence, or into nothingness, or for a gigantic dirt nap—who really knows, right? And for all of you Bible beaters out there who are going to give me the heaven and hell lecture—well, save it. Ever since I read Mark Twain's *Letters from the Earth* I can't really believe in heaven, and besides, I'm a Jew. Sorry about that.

I gave him a hard look and he said, "Listen, kid, I ain't never been one ta shy away from the facts. The only thing that bugs me is dat Mr. B is gonna be wit'out me to watch over him, but we got a coupla guys wit' us in the joint who're OK. It's just that we been together for a lotta years, and he ain't takin' me dyin' all that well. But I ain't gonna have no pity party or start cryin' or nothin', because I had a good life and did some good shit, even though the bad shit prob'ly weighs more wit' the guy upstairs, y'know?"

"You afraid of going to hell?" I said.

"Nah, I'm goin' in wit' the U.S. Army Rangers' unofficial creed as my shield," he said. "You know it?"

I looked at him and said, "Yea, though I walk through the valley of the shadow of death I will fear no evil, for I am the meanest motherfucker in the whole goddamned valley. Booyah!"

We both laughed and he said, "So yeah, I'm gonna die, but I ain't afraid. I seen too much shit in my day ta be afraid of anything 'cept my wife, God rest her soul, and my old dead pa, who could really swing dat belt. Other'n dat, I ain't really worried."

I looked at him, this tired old guinea gangster, and realized it wasn't bravado talking—he really wasn't afraid to die. It was only then that I understood that when Paul Monteverdi said "death before dishonor" (a Marine aphorism), he really, truly meant it. In contrast to his failing body his bright eyes were locked on me like a hawk on a mouse. My face must've been an open book to him, because when I finally got it he said, "Ah, ya finally got it, din't ya? I ain't afraid ta die, I just don' wanna do it wit'out any dignity. Ain't nobody gonna be changin' my diaper, or wipin' the sweat offa my face, or holdin' my hand an' tellin' me I'm goin' ta a better place. I'm a Army man, an' a man of my word, an' dat's the way I plan on goin' out."

"Fair enough," I said. "I've only got one problem with that."

"Yeah? What's the problem, kid?" he said.

"While you're fucking jawin' the food's getting' cold," I said.

"Well, fuck dat—let's chow down!" he said, a huge smile on his face.

So we did. We ate until we were both stuffed. We called the two nice NYPD cops in and had them eat. There were four U.S. marshals waiting downstairs to escort Monteverdi back to the Marion Federal Penitentiary when he was done testifying and we had them come up and eat, too.

And there was still food left. I may have mentioned who it was for when I called the Italian restaurant, and they may have overdone it just a tad. In any case, there was plenty to go around, and when Monteverdi suggested that we leave the rest for the night janitors to eat I thought it was the perfect way to end the evening.

But Mr. Green Mountain had one more surprise for me

As we sat among the wreckage of the meal we'd just consumed he looked at me and said, "Freak, ya remember dem assholes we was talkin' about last time I seen ya?"

"Yeah, of course. Why?" I said.

"Dere was one in particular dat we put ya on, and it seems like ya took care a dat problem for yourself, din't ya?" Monteverdi said.

"Yeah, we dug in and got his ass," I said.

"Mr. B and me got to talkin' about your story and we t'ought dere might be more to it, so we sorta asked around 'bout it," Monteverdi said. He looked at me with a small smile on his face, like he knew something that I didn't.

"And you found something, didn't you, *zio* Paul," I said.

"Yeah," he said, his smile getting broader.

"Like what? Didn't we get the guy you said was responsible?" I said.

"Yeah, yeah, you did, but Mr. B pointed out dat arresting dat asshole din't satisfy one fundamental question...*cui bono?*" Monteverdi said.

That brought me up short. The Badger Squad and I had sort of glossed over that—*cui bono* was Latin for "who benefits"—but it bothered me, and if it bothered me it definitely bothered the Badgers. The problem was that we'd been so focused on getting our ducks in a row in order to not fuck up the case on a technicality that we hadn't fully explored how or why Malcolm Sorenson would benefit from having me killed. None of us had ever put forward a satisfactory explanation that made any sense, and now Sorenson wasn't talking, at all, to anyone. He'd turned down every deal offered, never said a word to anyone except "No" in response to all offers and wasn't going to testify in his own defense, which meant that he could conceivably be sentenced to death in both state and federal court, which didn't appear to bother him in the least.

There was somebody above him in the food chain that he was protecting.

I looked at Monteverdi and he was smiling like I was Alice and he was the Cheshire Cat (if you don't get that reference it's time to go back and read the classics), his eyes almost twitching with amusement.

Finally I said, "That motherfucker isn't the end of the chain, is he?"

Zio Paul slowly moved his head from side to side.

"Was it the other one, the one Mr. B thought was a possibility?" I said.

Zio Paul slowly moved his head up and down.

Holy fucking shit.

A convicted felon had just told me that while he was the Assistant Director and then Director of the FBI the Vice President of the United States had tried to kill me.

Twice.

Holy. Fucking. Shit.

The Badger Squad was going to go batshit crazy with this, but it still didn't compute—how did Vice President Mitchell Holland benefit from my death? Although there had been several occasions where we were together at the same function I'd only really met the guy twice in my life, including when ai insulted him in New York City. I didn't know anything about him other than he and the president went to Michigan together, were on the football team together, went to law school together and married best friends.

I knew that Vice-President Holland was President Sheehan's best friend and chief political adviser since U of M. He'd also made a pile investing the president's Chicago Bears money while the president was still playing ball, and he'd applied that acumen to do a reasonably good job with the FBI. He was fairly well-liked by most people who met him, he was still handsome and his selection to the ticket was a real boon to President Sheehan, because Mitch Holland was originally from Tyler, Texas, which had helped the president carry the state twice. He was probably going to run for the presidency in the next cycle, and there was every chance he'd win.

And he wanted me dead for no reason that I could fathom.

As Jewey said, fuck me black, blue and blind.

"I don't know why this guy would want me dead, since I don't even know him. This is just baffling, *zio* Paul," I said.

"Yeah, me an' Mr. B are also at a loss wit' this shit. We can't no way connect the two of you, and believe me our sources tried. The only thing we found was a name you can use ta mebbe get Sorenson ta talk," Monteverdi said.

"What name?" I said.

"Shanleigh Cornish. He's a writer or somet'in', here in NYC. Looks like him and Sorenson is tight," Uncle Paul said.

Shanleigh Cornish was an award-winning essayist and columnist for the *New York Times*. He was also one of the leaders of the national gay rights movement.

Say what?

Shanleigh Cornish and the former Director of the FBI were tight, and it never came up through any of the confirmation hearings Malcolm Sorenson went through? Not one rabid Tea Partier raised the question about Sorenson's relationship to one of the most visible gay men in the country? Not once did a smug, self-righteous Mormon member of Congress from Utah make even a passing remark about how Malcolm Sorenson knew Shanleigh Cornish, or the nature of their relationship?

No fucking way.

If the potential Director of the FB-fucking-I knew one of the foremost critics of President Sheehan's "asinine, archaic, almost Neanderthal approach to gay rights" (direct quote from Mr. Cornish) there would have been so many questions about their relationship that even people in East Bumfuck, Antarctica, would've heard them, and yet... Sorenson had been confirmed with just a bare handful of Democratic votes against him, and those weren't because the senators didn't like Sorenson himself, it was because they wanted someone else, like Caroline Fredds, or Nathan "Dreamboat" Jones.

This situation smelled more than a truckload of pig shit left on the Mall in D.C. on a 120-degree day.

There was only one way that the (now former) FBI Director and Shanleigh Cornish had any kind of relationship: if it was the most closely guarded secret since the Manhattan Project, which meant that the relationship was more than just a casual friendship they struck up over a latte at Starbucks. It had to be a sexual relationship, because just being friends with Cornish would be a problem for Sorenson, but not enough to kill his chances at being FBI Director.

Not telling anyone he was gay would cause more than just problems for Sorenson, because he'd lied to Congress, which meant he'd committed fraud, which was a big, fat, motherfucking felony, which meant he could go to federal prison...hence the secret keeping now, as well as keeping it secret before the confirmation hearings.

"And yeah, dat's a real good lever to pull on in order ta get the shithead ta talk, an' dat might shake loose some stones above him in the food chain," Monteverdi said. I gave him another look and he said, "Yeah, I know where this Shanleigh guy is, and yeah, our guys say he'll talk ta ya, as long as it means dat the shithead don't get the death penalty."

"Thanks, *zio* Paul. I owe ya one," I said.

"Yeah, well, make it quick, kid, because I ain't gonna be here long. Besides, I told ya before, Mr. B and I don't like that this thing was done in our names, even though we ain't got shit ta do wit' it, y'know? Just get the assholes who did it an' let everybody know dat it wadn't us and dat'll be enough," Paul Monteverdi said.

"You sure, *zio mio*?" I said.

"Yeah, I'm sure. We neither of us like the fact dat some innocent womyn got killed, and settin' people up to be machine gunned on the streets of our city? Dat ain't kosher, if ya will pardon my bad Jewish," he said.

"All is forgiven, especially if you give me that address," I said.

"He said he'd meet you at the original Nathan's Famous, on the corner of Surf and Stilwell," Monteverdi said. He grinned at me and I said, "He wants me to go to Brooklyn? Seriously? When?"

"Tomorrow at 11:00 a.m. Guy lives out there in Bensonhurst or some place like dat," *zio* Paul said.

Paul Monteverdi and I said our goodbyes and the old gangster said, "Don't forget dat I ain't the good guy here, OK? When you tell people about me remind dem dat I was a real bad guy, not some cartoon who got religion at t'end 'cause he was dyin'. Mr. B and me are doin' ya a good turn, but only because it's to our advantage, y'know?"

"Don't worry, *zio*, I understand that you're a vicious, murdering thug who terrorized old penny candy store owners and killed people if they welshed on their debts," I said.

"Good, 'cause dat's the truth. Now hit the door an' don' make me cry," Paul Monteverdi said.

I left the conference room entirely off balance—the Vice President of the United States had tried to have me killed…twice…and I still didn't know why. A well-known gangster and vicious murderer was helping me find out because he was a patriot with a sense of honor, and his boss, who was an even worse criminal, was also helping me. I was going to meet a gay activist so that I could blackmail the former Director of the FBI into telling me about the Vice-President, which might or might not help me understand why I was his target.

I realized that I had no fucking idea what the fuck was going on, but I had a really bad fucking feeling about it.

Unfortunately it turned out that I was right about the bad feeling.

Dead right.

CHAPTER 67

Freak Finds a Lever to Move the World (Thanks, Archimedes)

I decided to go to bed and get some sleep, since tomorrow promised to be a busy day. I fell asleep within seconds, woke up at 6:00 a.m. and went through my PT, including a quick two-mile stee-plechase through the wilds of NYC, showered and went out to Brooklyn and the original Nathan's Famous Hotdogs stand.

It wasn't Superdawg, but it was pretty fucking close.

I was early, so I ordered three Nathan's with onions, relish and mustard and enjoyed myself until Shanleigh Cornish arrived. He was easily recognizable: around 6'2", with long ash blonde hair in a ponytail, a long, patrician face with a well-shaped and prominent nose, a long neck, large, tapered fingers and smoky grey eyes. He also had a dynamite smile, exuded confidence and capability, and carried himself in a graceful way. His voice was vibrant, smoky and perfectly modulated when he said, "Agent Glickstien? I'm Shanleigh Cornish."

I stood up and we shook hands. He looked at my empty hot dog tray and said, "Need a couple more? Onions, relish and mustard?"

"Well, yeah. Thanks," I said. I reached for my wallet and he said, "Oh, put the money away, Agent Glickstien. I've got more than I know what to do with, and your government salary was prob-ably blown up by the flight of dogs you already ate, am I right? Two or three?"

I held up three fingers and he went off to get us some more hot dogs. When Cornish came back he had my three dogs and five for himself, including two chili-cheese dogs and bacon cheese fries. I looked at the food and then looked again at his lanky frame, and he said, "Yeah, it's genetics. My mom and all of her brothers eat like horses and never gain a pound, and luckily I got the genes from their side. I also run 10 miles a day, but it wouldn't matter if I didn't—I'm always going to be a human clothes rack." I saw why people liked him—he was generous, funny, self-deprecating and his smile was a killer.

I said, "Cholesterol?"

"No thanks, I'm already eating hot dogs and bacon cheese fries," Cornish said. We laughed and I realized that I liked this guy, and that I didn't really want to pump him for information. He seemed to sense it, because he said, "Once the dogs are demolished I'll give you the whole rundown on Mal, but can we just eat right now and have some civil conversation? I'm not trying to duck you, but the food is going to get cold, am I right?"

"One hunnert percent. Let's chow down and then we can have a comfortable inquisition on full bellies," I said.

"Ooooh, an inquisition. Will there be ropes and chains and tongs and stuff?" Cornish said, his smoky eyes twinkling with mischief.

"If that floats your boat we can make it happen, although I don't know how I'll write that shit up in my report," I said. We both whooped with laughter and then proceeded to demolish our food. Shanleigh Cornish polished off the last chili-cheese dog, burped loudly and said, "Excuse me, horrible burp." He looked at me and said, "So Mal and I met in college, but we were both pretty deep in the closet, so we let our mutual love of the Boston Red Sox serve as our beard. We participated in fantasy baseball leagues, which was fun, but really just served as a cover for our love life, which was considerable. When we were seniors I decided to come out, and Mal decided to disavow me so that his career wasn't wrecked—he'd already been recruited by the FBI, which was a good thing."

"Why was that a good thing? Were the two of you done with each other?" I said.

"Not at all, but Mal had the right kind of brain and makeup to be a great FBI agent, and being in the Bureau would help explain the fact that he kept in contact with me—I was his pipeline into certain, ah, shall we say, *subversive* elements in the United States," Cornish said.

"What kind of subversive elements? You're not a communist, or a socialist, or a radical bomb-thrower, so what the hell kind of subversive elements..." My voice trailed off as I thought about it. Shanleigh Cornish just sat there, smiling enigmatically while I worked it out. Finally I said, "He claimed that there were radical gays within the gay rights movement, established that you'd made contact with them and then wrote you up as a confidential informant. The only problem with that is that once you were on record as a CI there'd have to be an ongoing investigation...oh, hell, you're a *writer*. Of course—you started writing the great American novel about some threat to the country from the gay movement, sent the chapters to Sorenson as the gospel truth and kept on seeing him without anyone even batting an eye within the FBI."

"Especially when I met that poor, unhinged boy from Oakland at one of my poetry readings—the one who converted to Islam and then decided he wanted to be a member of ISIS?" Cornish said.

"Fuck yeah—that's the case where Sorenson got himself on the management track at the Bureau," I said. "That was you?"

"Yeah," Cornish said. "The kid was delusional, but he said the magic words on tape, and he started preparations to do the deed, and he had, in fact, made contact with some real ISIS members, even though they basically blew him off as a crazy. Once he went out and surveyed the supports for the Golden Gate and downloaded bomb plans Mal had all he needed, and my *bona fides* were so well established that we could've made love in front of the Hoover Building and no one would have said a thing. We'd stopped a terrorist—I was a gay patriot and Mal was the straight man who befriended me in order to stop terrorism in the gay community, as if there is such a thing."

"So what happened between you two? Why'd you break it off?" I said, since it was clear that Cornish was referring to everything in the past tense.

"I didn't break it off—I still love Mal and wish that we were still together. He broke up with me because once he rose in rank he couldn't handle CIs anymore, so we couldn't very well keep meeting. Once it became clear that he was headed for the top of the FBI he buried anything besides the CI stuff that might connect us and refused to see me, or even talk to me on the phone. I know that it hurt him, because he told me it did, but his career came first," Cornish said.

"And that was OK with you after the initial breakup?" I said.

"Fuck no, it wasn't OK, but I understood it, and I respected Mal's passion for justice, and I loved him, so… I covered up my broken heart by writing three books, threw myself into gay rights causes, took other lovers and generally acted like I didn't care," Shanleigh Cornish said, his eyes bright and clear with unshed tears, "even though I still did."

"So why did you agree to meet with me?" I said. "You must know that I'm trying to understand why Sorenson decided that I needed to die, and how he used his FBI position to make the attempts on mine and Soper's lives. That's what doesn't make sense—if he's gay, why would he want Soper dead? And what the fuck did I do?"

Cornish looked down at the detritus on our table, scooped it all up and went over and threw it away. He came back and said, "Let's go for a walk." We went out into the street and he said, "I never heard him mention you or Soper, ever. He didn't really talk about work, but I can tell you this about Malcolm Sorenson: he doesn't hate anybody, he's very soft-hearted and he is the most loyal man I've ever met. We were together for over 20 years and he never, ever slept with anybody else. Given all that, it's possible that he's protecting someone above him in the food chain."

Cornish stopped talking and I almost said something, but then decided to fall back on the old uncomfortable silence trick. I didn't want to feed Cornish a name—I wanted some kind of independent confirmation about what Paul Monteverde'd told me.

It worked. After about a block Cornish heaved a sigh and said, "OK, the only person Mal ever talked about at work was Mitch Holland. It was always Mitch said this, Mitch did that, Mitch took me into his confidence today, Mitch wants me to head up the task force, Mitch and I had drinks after work…it was all Mitch, all the time. If I had to guess I'd say that Mal had a crush on the guy, especially after he went up to the director's chair. That doesn't prove anything, but knowing Mal like I do I'd say that he's probably protecting the Vice President. No way did Mal do this on his own hook—it just doesn't compute." Cornish hunched his shoulders and seemingly shrank before my eyes. His pain was palpable, rolling off him in waves.

I looked at him and said, "I'm sorry for your pain, but I need to understand your motive in telling me this."

"I'm not letting Mal fry for something I know that he didn't do. Don't get me wrong, he may have ordered something done, but only with great reluctance and in response to orders from higher up the food chain. So my motivation is simple—I don't want him facing the death penalty. When you talk to Mal tell him that I'll take extreme measures to keep him from the death penalty. He'll know what that means and he'll know that I'm serious, too. Push him about the Vice President, but only after you tell him that I'll tell all about Cape Cod. No question that he'll talk after you tell him that, by the way," Cornish said.

I looked a question at him, but he said, "No need for you to know the details, Agent Glickstien, but rest assured that Malcolm will not want that to be public knowledge. Just watch his eyes—they'll start to squinch together as soon as you mention Cape Cod, and right after that he'll talk to you, trust me."

I looked at my phone and saw that I had to hoof it to make my plane. I shook Shanleigh Cornish's hand, thanked him for his time and insights and promised to let him know if the death penalty came off the table for Malcolm Sorenson. He hugged me and said, "If you can let Mal know in private that I still miss him and love him I'd appreciate it."

"Consider it done, Mr. Cornish. I promise you that Sorenson's not going to take the fall for something someone else actually ordered," I said.

"Good. I know that he'll have to take some punishment, but Mal's a fundamentally good person who is just too loyal and duty-driven," Cornish said. "I love him for that, but it seems that this time it may have been misplaced in some nefarious individual or individuals. I don't think he should be put to death for that."

"I concur. I'll keep you posted," I said.

"Thanks, Agent Glickstien. That's all I can ask for," Cornish said. I really liked this guy, so I said, "My friends all call me Freak. I'd be pleased if you'd do the same." He arched an eyebrow at me and said, "Thanks, Freak. My friends call me Lee. And I'm going to want to hear the story about that name next time."

"OK, Lee, but you can't write about it," I said.

"At least not non-fiction, right?" my new friend said, laughing.

"Right," I said, laughing back. We left it like that, laughing, and I grabbed a cab back to JFK and got on the shuttle for D.C. I needed to see the Badger Squad, and interrogate the former Director of the FBI with my newfound leverage. I fell asleep once we were airborne and didn't wake up until we touched down at Reagan International.

I called Joe from the airport and said, "Can you get the Badger Squad together? I've got some new information that might be helpful."

"About which case?" Joe said.

"How about them Nationals," I said.

"I'll have them together at the office ASAP," Joe said, and hung up.

I really like working with smart people.

They were all there when I got there, and they were suitably excited when I told them about what Paul Monteverde said, and my subsequent conversation with Shanleigh Cornish.

"We need to confirm what Cornish said, about his being a CI for the Bureau," Mamba said.

"Not unless we want to alert the Feebs—and we can't do that, because the VP is bound to have people left inside that'll tip him off," Jewey said.

"Oh, fuck, do I need coffee or what?" Mamba said.

"I'll make some," Jack Soo said.

"No!" everybody said at once.

"Lucky I brought Pepsis then," he said, handing everybody an ice cold can from a cooler next to his desk. We all guzzled some sugary caffeine go-juice and finally Joe said, "Well, we need to send an interrogator in with former Director Sorenson, get some shit from him and then launch a blitzkrieg on the confirmation process so that we're done before the VP can even get wind of it."

"Hit it from all points of the compass, get down and dirty corroborating evidence and then present it as a *fait accompli*—I like it," Weasel said.

"I have to admit, I'm still stuck with the *cui bono*/why question?" I said. "None of this makes any sense at all. I barely know that asshole, so why am I the object of his affection?"

"We can't worry about motive right now, Freak, although I agree that this doesn't make sense, unless..." Jewey said. He looked pensive, rubbed his chin and said, "Where is the VP originally from?" at the same time that Joe and Jack Soo did. More Pepsis were tossed from the cooler, and Jack Soo said, "The VP was an Air Force brat—his dad was a bird colonel. He was born in Texas and lived there on and off until Mitchell was 10, when his dad became a command pilot for the C-17 fleet in Charleston, South Carolina. They spent the next eight years there, until Mitch accepted a football scholarship from the University of Michigan and moved to Ann Arbor."

"And our counterfeiters were from where?" I said.

"Near Savannah, Georgia," Weasel said.

"Which is just across the river from South Carolina," Jewey said. "It's also where young Mitchell's mother was from, and where he spent time with his grandparents after his dad was stationed in Charleston."

"Holy shit," I said. "He might be connected to the Korean counterfeit ring."

"Yeah, and everybody knows that you started that shit, and everybody also knows that you won't quit until the job is done, and if the VP found out about the Badger Squad...well, he may have been worried that you'd push us enough that we'd eventually connect him to the case," Jack Soo said.

"And if you died on a protective detail, but especially if Soper died, that's where the story would go—to the first lesbian hopeful for the president, not to her Secret Service detail. The focus and digging would have been on the Klan and all the other crazies that perpetuate the anti-gay agenda, and you guys would've become a footnote. Nobody would've even glanced at the counterfeiting case and tried to make any connections, not with the Klan right in their face," Mamba said, clearly awake after guzzling some Pepsis.

"And if he knew Sorenson at all he'd know that the guy was the perfect cutout—what did Cornish say about him—"he's the most loyal person I know"?" Jewey said. "He could cut all ties with the counterfeiters by killing the person most likely to expose him and could leave behind a monster shitstorm to cover it up, and if anybody did get caught it'd be Sorenson, who would be equally hard to investigate and then prosecute, since he'd know about any normal investigation as soon as it got started."

"There's one other thing that I just looked up," Weasel said. "Kim Yung Sun and Mitchell Holland went to the Wharton School of Business at the University of Pennsylvania at the same time. I don't have a connection yet, but that doesn't mean it isn't there."

"So all of this is about some goddamned funny money? That motherfucking son of a bitch killed all those people because I *might* find out about his connection to the asshole Koreans?" I said, looking like Hurricane Freak about to come ashore.

"It's looking more likely with every passing minute," Joe said. "And yeah, it's senseless and it should piss you off, but we need to focus on making an airtight, iron-clad case, so we need you to hyper down and kick the VP's useless ass at some later date, right Freak?"

Joe was right and we both knew it, so I said, "Bet your, ass, Joe. I'm going to go interrogate that asshole Sorenson and I'd like to take Mamba with me." My anger was dissipated when Joe said, "And I'll come along with the rest of the detail for moral support, and hope that we can stop you when you try to rip off his head and shit down his neck." We all laughed as we headed for our cars, except Joe, who called ahead to get us in to see Sorenson.

We went to the Central Detention Facility (the D.C. Jail) on D Street, where Sorenson was being held under the watchful eyes of the U.S. Marshals Service. We were met at the door to the facility by the team of lawyers who were defending Sorenson, led by V. I. Ingraham, who was semi-famous for arguing civil rights cases before the Supreme Court. No one could seem to find out what his initials stood for, which generated all sorts speculation in the media (most people thought the initials stood for 'Vladimir Ilyich'—you know, like Lenin's) but what the speculation missed was that this was one smart son of a bitch. He was a big, broad-shouldered former basketball player who looked like he might still be able to play, even if his hair was iron grey.

Ingraham looked at us and said, "He's going to be in federal court to plead guilty next week and he's not going to talk to you, regardless of what you have to say, so I'm not sure why we're here in the first place." He didn't seem angry, and he wasn't being a dick, he was just puzzled, so I said, "Mr. Ingraham, I've recently become privy to some new information that I'd like to let Mr. Sorenson hear. If he still wants to remain silent that's his right, but I don't want him to exercise that right until he hears this piece of information. I'm not going to strong-arm him or in any way try to force Mr. Sorenson to tell me anything, unless he wants to after he hears my information. Is that acceptable to you?"

Ingraham looked at me, clearly curious. He looked at the other four lawyers with him and one of them said, "Vee, I'll go tell Mr. Sorenson that someone wants to tell him something, OK?" Ingraham nodded and she went off into the building. Ingraham said, "Agent Glickstien, I'd like to suggest that we leave our respective entourages out here while you and I go in to talk to Malcolm. He certainly won't respond to anything with a crowd around him."

The Badger Squad and I'd discussed this on the ride over, so I said, "Sir, I'd like to bring Agent de Coucy in with me. He has a unique perspective on part of this information that may prove helpful if Mr. Sorenson chooses not to exercise his right to remain silent. Agent de Coucy will not speak unless Mr. Sorenson decides to voluntarily break his silence." Mamba stepped up next to me and nodded at the lawyer, who nodded back and said, "As long as this doesn't turn into some kind of intimidation attempt I'm good with Agent de Coucy, but nobody else."

We nodded and both Mamba and I took off our coats and guns and gave them to the rest of the Badger Squad. Ingraham nodded and led us into the jail, where we went through all of the security procedures necessary to get in to see the most famous prisoner in America. Once we got through all of that Ingraham led us to a conference room, opened the door that was flanked by two U.S. Marshals and ushered us into the presence of the former FBI director.

It didn't look like being in jail had had any effect on old Mal. He was calm, detached, and almost serene as he sat there passively looking at us. He said, "Hello, Vee, hello Agent Glickstien." He looked at Mamba and said, "Do I know you, sir? You look familiar to me."

"I'm Almont Phillipe Gilbert de Coucy, the Comte de Condé, Mr. Sorenson. Perhaps you've seen me before, but I don't recall us ever meeting," Mamba said.

"Well, it's a pleasure to meet you, Monsieur le Comte," Sorenson said.

"Likewise, Mr. Director," Mamba said.

"Not anymore, Monsieur le Comte, not ever again, I'm afraid," Sorenson said. He looked directly at me and said, "I'm invoking my right to remain silent, Agent Glickstien. Sorry you wasted a trip." He wasn't smiling, but he wasn't being a dick either, just stating a fact.

I gave him a slight smile back and said, "I understand, Director Sorenson, but I'm going to ask you a serious question before I tell you something. Is there anything that you don't want your attorney to hear?"

They both looked perplexed and Ingraham said, "I'm his attorney—of course anything he says to me is held in confidence due to the attorney-client privilege, Agent Glickstien."

"Yes, sir, but it's possible there are things that he doesn't want you to hear," I said.

Sorenson's eyes squinched together then, just like Shanleigh Cornish said they would, and he said, "No, there's nothing that Vee can't hear—I've shared everything with him." He was very wary as he really concentrated on me.

"Very well, Mr. Sorenson. I recently returned from New York where I had a conversation with an old friend of yours. This friend wanted me to tell you that they still loved and cared about you and that they wouldn't be able to see you get the death penalty under any circumstances," I said.

Sorenson's eyes squinched together even more visibly, and he said, his voice under tight control, "I'm sure most, if not all, of my old friends feel that way, Agent Glickstien." He tried a smile, but it just caused his lips to turn up at the corners, and it never reached his eyes.

"Yes, I understand that, but this old friend wanted me to tell you that they were going to tell the media about Cape Cod," I said.

Sorenson stood straight up out of his chair, his eyes nearly squinched shut and his face as white as a Minnesota blizzard in January. His mouth opened and closed like the proverbial fish out of water and he was sweating profusely, where just a moment before he'd been as composed as a bishop about to baptize a baby. He looked right at me as if he were trying to communicate telepathically but wasn't able to get through.

I said, "Mr. Sorenson, are you sure you want your lawyer to hear this?"

V. I. Ingraham heaved a huge sigh and said, "Is this friend Shanleigh Cornish?"

Now it was my turn to be astonished. I looked at the lawyer and he said, "Mal told me all about it, and that he didn't think that anybody could even find the connection between them, or that Mr. Cornish wouldn't say or do anything about it anyway. Clearly he was wrong."

Sorenson still stood, only now his face was red and he was trembling. His eyes looked as if he were going to have a stroke, and so I said, "Mr. Sorenson, Shanleigh doesn't think you did it, unless you were under orders, and he really did say that he still loved you, and he wasn't willing to see you get the death penalty for something that you didn't do. This is just my opinion from the outside looking in, but I would say that you are the love of his life, and that he means exactly what he told me."

Sorenson sank into his chair and said, "Did he, did—he tell you...about Cape Cod?" His voice was as harsh as if he'd been screaming for hours.

"No, sir, all he said was I didn't need to know, just that he would tell the media about it in order to save you from the death penalty. I believe that Mr. Cornish will go to any lengths to save your life,

Mr. Sorenson, up to and including exposing things that are sensitive, embarrassing, or hurtful to you or himself. He doesn't want you put to death," I said.

"You have no idea how hard it was—still is—keeping your inner self hidden away just so you can do what you're good at. You have no idea how crushingly idiotic it is to be judged just on your sexuality, as if that actually affected your proferssionalism, or intelligence, or other innate abilities. I've felt like I was tainted somehow since I was eleven years old and realized that I really liked other men, not wymyn," Sorenson said.

"You felt like you were convicted of a crime without being arrested, or allowed to call witnesses on your behalf, or being judged by a jury of your peers at a formal trial," Mamba said. "You were convicted and condemned by the public and the institution of the FBI without being able to defend yourself in any way, which made you bitter and insecure virtually every minute of every day."

Sorenson looked at Mamba like he'd been thrown him a lifeline. He gulped, swallowed hard, nodded and said, "That's exactly it, 100% right, Agent de Coucy."

"Except when you were with Shanleigh, because then you just got to be yourself. You felt like you could fly, and then it was back to the iron maiden that was your real life, back to what the straight world told you was *normal*, even though you knew that was a large, steaming pile of bull-shit," Mamba said, his tone sneering at the straight world.

Malcolm Sorenson was quietly crying his eyes out, shaking gently like an aspen tree quaking in a mountain breeze. He nodded and pointed at Mamba as if to say "You're right," but he couldn't talk. Mamba went over and put his arm around the former director and gave him a hug. Sorenson hugged him back, and the two men just stood there for a bit while Ingraham and I looked at our shoes.

When the tears stopped Mamba said, "Malcolm, you need to let it all out. We know you weren't the top dog on this shit, so you need to unburden yourself, not just because you don't deserve to die, but because it's the right thing to do. I'm not telling you what to do, I'm just telling you what people who've been through what we've been through need to do to heal. You deserve a chance to heal, and to salvage whatever happiness you can with Shanleigh."

My friend came back over next to me and sat down. I put my hand on his shoulder and squeezed, and he put his hand over mine and squeezed back. We both looked at Sorenson, who sat down, shook himself like a dog coming out of a pond and wiped the tears off his face with a Kleenex. He blew his nose with some more Kleenex, threw the tissues into a wastebasket, sat up straight, looked right at Mamba and I and said, "I never meant for any of the people who died to get killed."

V. I. Ingraham said, "Agents, I need a few minutes with my client. We need to—"

"No, Vee, we don't need to talk. I'm going to do this even if it gets me the death penalty," Sorenson said.

"No, you most certainly are not," Ingraham said. He turned to us and said, "If you'll leave now agents?" He went over and opened the door, and we reluctantly started to move toward it, but Sorenson said, "No! Vee, shut that fucking door, sit down and shut the fuck up."

Ingraham said, "Mal, you're upset and you're doing exactly the wrong thing. I've been your lawyer forever and I'm telling you, stop talking *right fucking now*, or you're going to be lined up for the needle, buddy."

"What if we could guarantee that wouldn't happen?" I said.

"No way the U.S. Attorney is going to sign off on that—you're claiming he assassinated a federal agent and a VIP, plus several others. How do you not see the needle in this equation?" Ingraham said.

"If he's got bigger fish to fry I don't see why the U.S. Attorney would even bat an eye," I said.

"How big a fish do you think he's got to fry?" Ingraham said. I didn't say anything, but I knew that meant that old Mal hadn't told his lawyer everything, so I pointed at Sorenson, who looked at Ingraham. Nothing was said, but Ingraham seemed to get it, because he said, "Get the A-USA down here and we might be able to talk."

I whipped out my phone and speed-dialed Brenda T. Green. She answered on the third ring, sounding out of breath.

"Freak, what the hell? Couldn't this have waited? You heard of a personal life?" she said.

"What, you workin' out?" I said.

"Yeah, I'm workin' out. His name's Todd. Now what the fuck ya want?" Brenda T. Green said.

"Malcolm Sorenson wants to deal. He's got something big to tell us, but you gotta get down here right away," I said.

"Look out, Todd, I gotta get dressed!" she said. Her phone sounded like a herd of water buffalo were stampeding down her hallway. When she realized the phone was still on she just yelled, "I'll be there in 20, 25 minutes. And for fuck's sake don't say anything else to him about the case!" She hung up, and I said, "Mamba, we need to scram until Brenda T. gets here."

"I'd like it if Agent de Coucy could stay and talk with me. If you want you can stay too, and I won't talk about the case until the A-USA gets here," Sorenson said. "Vee needs to stay, too, to make sure we don't do anything outside the law or my rights. OK?"

I nodded and went to sit in a chair by the door. Lawyer Ingraham moved a chair over by me and we sat there silently while Mamba and Mal talked.

I could fill the space with the dialogue that went on, but I'm not going to, because I think that some things should be kept private. This is one of those things.

So exactly 23 minutes later there was a knock on the door and Assistant U.S. Attorney Brenda T. Green came through the door like the aforementioned water buffalo. She was in an electric blue suit that might have covered the Roman Colosseum and could've blinded Ray Charles if he weren't already stone blind.

She looked at me, looked at Sorenson, looked at Mamba, looked at Ingraham and finally said, "Somebody wanna tell me what the fuck is going on?"

"I want to talk about a deal for my client that doesn't include the death penalty," Ingraham said.

"I want you to discuss a deal with Mr. Sorenson that doesn't include the death penalty," I said, "because I want the information that he has."

"I want to make a deal so that I don't get the death penalty, even though I probably deserve it," Sorenson said.

Mamba sat there and said nothing, so Brenda T. Green said, "You weren't talking to Mr. Sorenson after I told you not to, were ya?"

"Fuck off, Brenda T.," Mamba said. "I'll talk to whoever I want whenever I want, and besides, it was personal, as in none of your goddamned business."

Before all out war erupted between the large A-USA and the diminutive Secret Service agent V. I. Ingraham said, "I concur with Agent de Coucy about the nature of the conversation he had with my client, and I will attest to the fact that it had nothing to do with the case. It was most definitely a personal conversation. Now, about that deal?"

"What's your client got that I don't already know?" Brenda T. Green said.

"The name of the person who actually ordered the attacks on Agent Glickstien and her comrades," Ingraham said.

Even though Mamba and I were expecting it we were still shaken by the lawyer's matter of fact tone and demeanor. Brenda T. Green wasn't expecting it, so she was considerably more shaken, which she expressed verbally.

"Oh, come on, V.I. This is the oldest trick in the book—give me a deal and I'll give you someone bigger, but this time it won't work, because who's bigger than the damn Director of the FBI? Your client gonna tell me that the Attorney General ordered him to kill a Secret Service agent? Please don't fucking insult my intelligence," the AUSA said.

"I don't know who he's going to tell you about, because he hasn't been specific with me, but he says that the attacks were ordered by someone above him in the food chain. And A-USA Green, this isn't a pig in a poke situation—he says that he has incontrovertible proof of same. Not just idle chatter to save his ass, but actual, stand up in court and convict the perp proof," Ingraham said.

"And you believe that shit? You believe that an asshole criminal who's facing the death penalty won't make fucking shit up out of whole cloth to save his sorry ass? What am I, some night court ADA who just graduated from night school at East Bumfuck U.? I was first in my class at Stanford and I'm not buying this goddamned bullshit," Brenda T. Green said. She glared at me and said, "I can't believe that you're a party to this goat-rope, Freak. Have you lost your fucking mind?"

I stood up and glided over to where the 6'3", 240 pound A-USA stood glowering. I got right up in her face and didn't say a word, but I did give her my "you're about to die" look from my time in Special Forces. I also prepared myself for a lightning martial arts strike that would've basically made Brenda T. Green a large pile of discombobulated protoplasm. I looked in her eyes and mentally said, "My name is Freak. You killed my father. Prepare to die." (My thanks to William Goldman and *The Princess Bride*.)

The A-USA tried to stare me down, but she didn't have a chance. Within 15 seconds, she began to sweat, and 30 seconds in she said, "OK, OK, I'd like to hear a proffer of what Mr. Sorenson is going to say before there's any mention of a deal." She looked away from me and I spun around to point at Mal Sorenson.

"I was ordered to attack the Soper campaign event at Morehead, Kentucky in order to assassinate Agent Glickstien and blame the Ku Klux Klan for it," Sorenson said.

We all just stood there staring at him, but before anyone could say anything he said, "I was also ordered to assassinate Agent Glickstien and any of her comrades in New York City and blame the North Koreans for it," Sorenson said.

"And you have proof of these orders, proof that will hold up in court?" Brenda T. Green said.

"Lots of it," Sorenson said.

The A-USA stood with her chin in her hand, contemplating what came next. Finally she glanced at me and I saw that she'd been mostly acting about not believing Sorenson, probably to get him talking in order to prove her wrong. It's a good tactic, but it'd almost gotten her seriously injured, like, for real. I wasn't angry but there was only so much challenge that I would accept before I responded, and she'd pushed the edge. Now, though, she winked at me and said, "I'm prepared to take the death penalty off the table if—and I emphasize *if*—your information pans out. I can't go any further than that in a case of this magnitude. Your client killed a federal agent and six other people, so you understand my reluctance."

"I do, and I'm going to talk to my client for a moment," Ingraham said. He and Sorenson huddled together and whispered. It only took a few seconds before the lawyer said, "OK, but we want one more thing if this pans out."

"Fuck you," Brenda T. Green said. "You're not really in any position to bargain, since we both know that your client is going to get the needle at Terra Haute Federal Prison in Indiana once I get done with him at trial."

"That's probably true, but all we're asking for is a maximum-security federal prison as near to New York City as possible," Ingraham said, his perfectly calm lawyer's face telling me that his client had not yet shared the name he was about to drop with the unsuspecting attorney.

"Well-l-l-l, if that's it, OK, I'll go for a sentence recommendation that puts Mr. Sorenson away for life at a facility close to New York," Brenda T. Green said. "Now who gave you the orders to assassinate a federal agent?"

"The current Vice-President of the United States, Mitchell Holland," Sorenson said.

Mamba and I knew what was coming and it still surprised US.

Brenda T. Green and V. I. Ingraham were absolutely flabbergasted.

"WHAT!" the lawyer said.

"AREYOUFUCKINGKIDDINGME?" Brenda T. Green said, her voice so loud that the marshals guarding the door came in with their guns half-drawn. I give her credit—the A-USA got herself (almost) under control and said, "It's OK, guys, I was just…just…uh, er, umm, uh…startled. Would one of you please tell your boss that we need a whole squad over here now? Thanks." She turned to Malcolm Sorenson and his still nonplussed attorney and said, "Not another word until my boss gets here and we bring a stenographer in. I want this to be a sworn deposition and I need to talk to my boss. No more talking." She pointed at us and said, "Outside, if you would."

We stepped out in the hall and Brenda T. Green held up a finger while she punched a speed-dial button. Whoever it was finally picked up and she said, "Sir, you need to come down to the Central Detention Facility right now. No sir, I mean ASA-fucking-P, as in wear your pajamas if you have to. Sir, I. Do. Not. Care. She'll get over it once you get down here and see what I'm talking about. Conference Room A. I'm not talking about that over the phone, sir." He was still talking when she hung up and looked at us.

"You guys didn't even flinch when he told me. You expected something like this?" the (soon to be a higher grade) A-USA said.

"No," I said, "we expected exactly this. We recently developed this information on our own, but we wanted to hear it from the horse's mouth. This just corroborates what we've suspected for some time. Sorry to surprise you like that." I stuck out my hand but Brenda T. Green just wrapped her arms around me and whirled me around like I was a little kid. She dropped me and whirled Mamba around, too. She dropped him and did a little dance right there in front of the marshals on duty, then whipped her phone open and called for a bonded stenographer.

We all waited in the hall until the U.S. Attorney for the District of Columbia, Duquanye Quintanilla, came striding down the hall. Quintanilla was a slim, dapper man who'd been an All-American fencer at Notre Dame before he took a Rhodes scholarship and went to Oxford. He came home and went to the Pritzker School of Law at Northwestern in Chicago (yeah, I know that it's in Evanston, but the average person might not, so don't give me shit for using a city people recognize—and that's no offense to Evanston, which is still home to Dave's Italian Kitchen, one of the coolest places to eat in the world). He was fully dressed in an off-the-rack black suit from J.C. Penney, Rockport shoes and a wild Jerry Garcia tie, and he was absolutely, positively focused on Brenda T. Green.

They came face-to-face and the U.S. Attorney for the District of Columbia said, "Ms. Green, I'd like to speak to you about hanging up on me." Brenda T. Green looked down at her clearly enraged boss and said, "No, you really don't. What you want to talk to me about is being appointed Attorney General, and in order for us to do that you're going to have to calm your ass down. I didn't go to Notre Dame, Oxford or Northwestern, but I'm just as smart as you and my JD from Iowa counts just as much as yours, so if you want to be Attorney General—and everybody knows that you want to—then shut the fuck up and listen instead of being stupidly pissed off."

When they handed out big balls Brenda T. Green was right at the front of the line.

It was probable that Duquanye Quintanilla had never been spoken to in that manner in his life, and certainly not since he was appointed U.S Attorney. You have to understand, being a U.S. Attorney is like being a feudal lord. Other than the Attorney General (a duke, perhaps?) and the president (the King) no one *ever* tells a U.S. Attorney what to do, because these people are empowered, powerful and very, very sharp—dummies do not make it to the office of U.S. Attorney.

To challenge one like Brenda T. just did was not only a bad tactical move, it was a very bad long-term strategy, because these men and wymyn all have the ego to go with the talent.

But Duquanye Quintanilla wasn't your average U.S. Attorney. He knew that Brenda T. must have something big to tell him, and he knew she was one smart broad, even if she was built like a rhino and just as ugly, so he visibly curbed himself and said, "Very well, A-USA Green. What is so urgent that you needed to call me away from my daughter's *Quinceañera*?"

"Not in the hall," she said. We went into a small conference room and she said, "Freak, tell the U.S. Attorney what you just told me." So I went through the tale of the discovery that someone above the FBI Director had ordered the attacks on me, leaving out the Vice-President's name (Brenda T. Green deserved to tell him). He listened intently and then said, "OK, given that your information is accurate, does that mean that I'm here because you think you know who actually did it?"

"Oh, we know *exactly* who did it. Malcolm Sorenson just told us who it was, after I offered him a deal," Brenda T. Green said.

"What? What kind of deal? We discussed this—he conspired to kill a federal officer, he has seven murders on his hands and he shows absolutely no remorse. We can't offer him a deal!" Quintanilla said.

"But I did, and I think that you're going to uphold it. The information is worth it, Duquanye," Brenda T. Green said. I think that it was her use of his first name that really caught his attention, because he bit back the reply on his lips, straightened his shoulders and said, "OK, but I hope you made it provisional based on the quality of the information, because if *I* don't agree that it's worth it the offer will be rescinded."

Brenda T. nodded and said, "Of course, Mr. U.S. Attorney."

"So what was the information?" Quintanilla said.

"Well, all Sorenson told us was that the attacks were ordered by the Vice President of the United States, Mitchell Holland," Brenda T. Green said.

"AREYOUFUCKINGKIDDINGME?" the U.S. Attorney for the District of Columbia said. Quintanilla looked at us like pigs smoking little cigars were flying out our asses. I nodded at him and Brenda T. gave him a broad smile.

"What—what did you give him?" Quintanilla said.

"Took the death penalty off the table and told him we'd get him a max security prison close to New York City," Brenda T. said.

"THAT'S IT?" Quintanilla said, totally losing his composure. He danced around, grabbed Brenda T. Green by the hand and danced with her, let her go and grabbed my hand. Apparently he thought that we were going to dance, too, but I gripped his hand tightly and stopped him in mid-dance. He looked at me and I said, "The Vice President killed my boss, two of my friends and four other people. Get your ass under control, get the proof and arrest that motherfucker before you do any more dancing." Quintanilla tried to pull away from me, but I kept a grip on his hand, stared into his eyes and said, "You reading me, counselor?"

He saw the look in my eyes and stopped trying to move at all. He took a deep breath, composed himself and said, "Don't worry, Agent Glickstien, we'll get him."

"You'd better, sir, because if you don't I'm coming for you," I said.

"And I'll be with him," Mamba said.

"Don't worry guys—now that the U.S. Attorney is on board I'm going to nail that bastard's head up on the wall and throw darts at it," Brenda T. Green said.

"And I assure you that I am most definitely on board," Duquanye Quintanilla said. "I shouldn't say this, but I must confess to you that I don't personally like the Vice President. I have no quarrel with the job he's done as VP, and he was actually a fairly good FBI director, but personally he's a nasty, rotten prick who preens like a peacock while kissing up to the president and kicking down on most of his subordinates. I'm as surprised as can be that he did something like this, but I'm not really surprised that he did something like this, if you know what I mean."

We all did, because Mitch Holland seemed to be your typical Washington politician: drunk with power, driven by the conviction that his or her judgment was akin to God's, and certain that his or her defecation wasn't odiferous. The problem was that I still had to answer the question of *cui bono?*, and I had no idea how Mitch Holland benefitted from my death. There was something at the back of my mind bothering me about the whole thing, but I couldn't put my overly muscular finger on it, so I put aside the "who benefits" question when the US Attorney said, "Now let's go get our proof and make history, shall we?"

He was still too smug for me by half, but he had a good reason to be—no U.S. Attorney had ever had the chance to arrest a Vice President for conspiracy to commit murder, especially when he had proof supplied by the former FBI Director. I've never believed the stories that came out of the prosecution claiming that the U.S. Attorney applied particular zeal to the prosecution of the VP because he was a Republican, mainly because I was there and it never happened. I saw everything that went on, and what actually happened was A-USA Brenda T. Green and USA Duquanye Quintanilla tore the former Vice President a new asshole because he was the motherfucker who launched multiple interstate conspiracies to commit murder, which actually resulted in the murders of at least seven people. Nobody on the prosecution team ever mentioned his political proclivities or his position, they just mounted a slam-bang prosecution that landed that murdering son of a bitch on death row at the federal prison in Terre Haute, Indiana.

I do have to admit that the "attagirls" I got from my friends and family were definitely more enthusiastic because Holland was from the "conservative movement," but I truly didn't care about that, because in the end there was as much justice for those he murdered as we could get. And no, I still don't believe in the death penalty, even for that worthless piece of shit.

That's all I truly wanted: justice for Josie, for Elvin Clyde Bliss, for Patsy, for Sparky II, for Hot Rod, for Tara Waters, for the three civilians in New York, and for anybody else the Vice President had harmed. I want to emphasize, I didn't want *revenge*—if I'd wanted that I would've just walked up to the asshole motherfucker and blown his brains out—no, I wanted *justice*, because that was the only way that I wasn't going to stick one of my 1076s up his ass and empty a clip into his worthless body.

So we went in and Mal Sorenson told the U.S. Attorney the whole incredible story. We all listened, but when he said, "And I have proof, too. I have three written notes in the Vice President's handwriting, and I have four burner phones that he left messages on, all of them explicitly telling me what to do in order to assassinate Agent Glickstien," Duquanye Quintanilla said, "Mr. Sorenson, where are these materials? Are they safe?"

Lawyer Ingraham said, "And so you're satisfied that my client's proffer is in good faith? No death penalty? He gets a federal prison near New York City?"

"If the messages and notes are not legitimate then the deal is off, but provisionally we have a deal Mr. Ingraham…but we still need the proof," the United States Attorney said.

Ingraham nodded at Quintanilla and then said, "Go ahead, Mal."

Sorenson gave a small, sad smile and said, "They're in a safe deposit box at a bank on K Street, under my grandmother's name. I have a key and power of attorney so that I can open the box in case something happens to my grandma."

"So we're going to need a court order to open the box," Brenda T. Green said.

"I'm going to give you a waiver and so will my grandma, which should make it easy for a judge to grant the order," Sorenson said "I—it's the least that I can do, given the circumstances." He looked down at the floor and said, in a near whisper, "I don't really deserve a deal, because what I did was wrong on so many levels, and I—uh, well, I-I-I... I knew it was wrong, but I did it anyway. I am so sorry. I have no excuse except my own weakness."

He looked up right at me, and I couldn't help myself. "What the fuck were you thinking, Sorenson? Why the hell didn't you just arrest that asshole and expose him if you had proof? Why the hell go to all the trouble of killing me if all you had to do was just haul out the messages and notes *before* you did all of this shit? Why did anybody have to die?"

The former FBI director looked away from me, cleared his throat and said, "I was afraid that people would find out that I was gay, that I would lose my job over it, and Mitch told me that it was a national security matter, so I did what everybody in the FBI does—I went along to get along. It seemed like a small price to pay at the time, but now it seems like even listening to him made me dirty, and I just don't want to live that way anymore."

I believed him, and I knew why. "You still love Shanleigh Cornish, don't you," I said. It wasn't a question.

"Yes, yes I do, and I knew that Shan would tell me what to do about this, so once our relationship was exposed I decided to do the right thing, so that I could prove to him that I was worthy of his love," Sorenson said. His voice was wistful and forlorn, his face red as he said, "I know that sounds corny, but it's true."

"Did Mr. Cornish know about any of this?" Quintanilla said, his voice rising like a bloodhound that's caught the scent of a rabbit.

"No, no, Shanleigh didn't know anything. We, we broke up, and besides, he's a writer. If I was going to give up my secret it wouldn't be to a writer," Sorenson said.

"For what it's worth, Shanleigh still loves you, without question," I said. "I just saw him and he said so right to my face. I think you're a lucky man, other than the whole going to prison for life thing," I said with my own small smile. It wasn't a great joke, but it seemed like one at the time, so we all sort of giggled and then the real work started.

Everybody had a job to do, and, as U.S. Attorney Duquanye Quintanilla kept reminding us, we were trying to cage a tiger, so the trap had to be perfect. "If we make a mistake we'll get clawed and bitten, maybe even eaten, and we'll certainly never get another chance to catch the tiger," he said.

Nobody argued with him, because we all knew he was right.

So after I informed Nails that the Badger Squad needed to report to USA Quintanilla I went back to my protective detail with the Warrior Princesses. I saw the Vice President three times during the setting of the "tiger trap," and I restrained myself each time, even though when I saw him with the girls I wanted to put his balls into orbit with a nice front kick.

Witnessed and notarized depositions were taken from everyone they needed to be taken from, the proofs from Sorenson's safety deposit box were legally obtained with a court order, the Badger Squad found some nice juicy corroborating evidence once they were able to dig wherever they wanted and everything was proceeding nicely. To all appearances the world was just spinning on its axis on its way around the sun, but in reality there was a giant legal tiger hunt beating its way toward the Vice President, and it was almost ready to flush him into the sights of the U.S. Attorney, who was just waiting to slam the door on the tiger cage shut.

That's when Murphy's Law struck, followed closely by O'Toole's Corollary to Murphy's Law (for those of you who are confused, Murphy's Law says that "anything that can go wrong, will," and O'Toole's Corollary adds "at the worst possible moment, with the worst possible result").

We were literally one day away from moving to arrest the Vice President of the United States when a Murphy/O'Toole wrench got thrown in the works.

It was another (literally) bloody wrench.

CHAPTER 68

Shotgun Symphony

So there we were, a day away from arresting the VP on charges of conspiracy, attempted murder, murder, and lots of other stuff. U.S. Attorney Duquanye Quintanilla had cautioned everybody involved to act as naturally as possible and not to deviate from their routines. He'd promised those of us who'd been on Soper's detail when we were hit in Morehead that we could attend the arrest, even though Honest Tom Vernon and his men would be doing the actual arresting.

We all thought that USA Quintanilla showed remarkable foresight in having the U.S. Marshals do the arresting, because it was possible that the Secret Service personnel might've had a wee bit of a problem maintain objectivity and not punching the Vice President's face into hamburger while clapping the iron on him.

I could guarantee that was the case.

So it was business as usual for everybody. I went with the Warrior Princesses to school, got them back to the House and then took a shower and changed, because we were attending a do at the Kennedy Center that night—the first family was going to see the play *Hamilton*, with Lin-Manuel Miranda in the title role (the Washington <u>Post</u> said he was doing it just for the first daughters, which made them all squishy…me, too—what a biscuit).

We were going in three cars, because POTUS and FLOTUS (you all have this now, right?) were coming from separate venues and didn't want to hold the Warrior Princesses up in case they were late.

It was relatively easy to secure the Kennedy Center, especially when we'd have three details plus the Uniformed Division agents plus the Capital cops for support. The Warrior Princesses were really excited about the play, so we got there a bit early, made our way to the upper boxes where the girls were sitting and then waited, but not for long.

POTUS and FLOTUS arrived within a minute of each other, settled in with the girls and then the play went off for the next three hours or so. From what I saw everybody had a great time, and the girls were burbling about the "utter hotness" of Mr. Miranda while we headed out the side entrance to their car. POTUS and FLOTUS were taking a second car, but were right behind us on the way out.

There was no warning when the shotguns all let loose at once.

There was one huge "BOOM" from the shooters and then things got crazy.

Several agents went down, including two in my detail. The agents with POTUS surrounded him and rushed toward the car that was supposed to carry the Warrior Princesses. They slammed him in the car, two agents piled in on top of him and the car tore out of there like aliens had just landed. They busted up the driveway straight at the crowd of people that were protesting the president's Middle East policies (he was wholly pro-Israel and had just told the BBC in an interview that the Palestinian attitude toward peace made them a "pain in the butt'—there was an outpouring of disgust and anger over that one that made the Vietnam protests seem like Super Bowl parties). The crowd was going to hold its ground until it became apparent that the limo was accelerating toward them with no intention of stopping, and then it looked like the limo was Moses and the crowd was the Red Sea.

The shotguns were still blasting away, but there was something off about the way they sounded. No matter what make or model a combat shotgun is they have a distinct roar (yeah, that's classified), and once you hear that sound it never leaves you. As I was scrambling to cover the Warrior Princesses my ear told me that even though they were loud these shotguns weren't generating enough sound to match what I knew they should sound like.

I had Brooke and Allison down in about one second after the first shotgun volley, with Ed and Coach covering us. I pulled the Princesses back behind a big cement pylon just as another volley from the shotguns whistled in, catching Ed right in the back. She went down hard and Coach fired off three rounds back where the shotguns were shooting from, then fell back to cover the Princesses and I with her body.

I said, "Coach, we got to get the Princesses in the second car. Can we move down the line to get to it?"

Her line of sight was right at the second vehicle, and she said, "No go, Freak. There are four shotgunners flanking it, two on either side. If we move that way we'll be right in the line of fire. There's also five or six bodies in the way of the car—he'd have to drive right over 'em to get up here to us. We need to go back to the building."

I looked to my left and saw the colonnade that led back to the building was littered with bodies. As I was looking I saw the first lady and what was left of her detail crouching behind two decorative flower planters. There was the roar of shotguns and the whine of pellets off the side of the planters. One of them caught the first lady in the cheek and she clapped her hand to face like she'd been stung by a bee, then slowly sat down and collapsed, her eyes rolling up in her head.

There was another volley and Coach said, "Ugh. Hit, Freak. Sorry." Her big body slid down right on top of us, squashing me onto the Princesses. I looked back at the first lady's detail and saw that they were all down now, and surprisingly still. I reached up and grabbed Coach's body, setting her upright. I looked at her back, expecting to see a shitload of blood.

Instead I saw a nice big splatter of what looked like little red paintbrushes, including two that were lodged in her neck.

The motherfuckers were using fléchettes, not shotgun pellets. Fléchettes are little darts, usually little steel darts that help cause maximum damage from a shotgun blast or small artillery shell. They're very effective anti-personnel devices, but these weren't designed to shred flesh—they were designed to incapacitate without causing any lasting injury. I'd bet that they were coated with some kind of knockout agent (yeah, you can do that—darting a person is no different than darting a wild animal). My mind was racing as I realized that this was another kidnap attempt, not an assassination attempt on POTUS.

I pulled Coach back over us and assessed our position. There were still four protective detail agents firing and I knew that the uniformed division guys were gearing up to come out, so the enemy extraction team must be headed inbound, fast—and then I heard the helicopter. I saw movement out of the corner of my eye and saw the shotgunners by the car creeping forward. One of them covered the limo in case the agent inside tried to get out, but the three other guys were advancing on our position. I knew there must be others waiting, but the four guns off to my left were still firing, and I knew the uniformed guys were headed toward us, so I said, "Warrior Princesses, I have an idea." I told them what I wanted to do, and they agreed it seemed like the only way to stop the guys advancing on us.

I scraped together our equipment and we all just lay there, waiting. There was another roar of multiple shotguns on our left, but they were just trying to suppress the four agents still shooting, or maybe they were trying to hold off the uniformed Secret Service agents coming at them. The helicopter clattered closer, cruising up the Potomac behind us. I was sure this was part of the shotgunners' plan, either as a decoy or as the extraction vehicle. The second limo in the driveway was spinning his tires in a giant burnout—it sounded like he was trying to get up the driveway at us but couldn't—and then I saw one of the shotgunners cross my line of vision.

I whispered to the Warrior Princesses to be ready. I counted "one-two-three" in a voice barely above a whisper and then roared "GO!"

All three of US popped up with the shotgunners not twenty feet away. I double-tapped the one in the center and then shot him in the head as he fell.

Brooke shot the one on the left three times in the crotch and then in the head as he fell.

Allison hit the shotgunner on the right six times in the chest, waiting until he hit the ground to put a round in his head.

The Warrior Princesses collapsed back behind the cement pylon and I drilled the fourth shotgunner as he stood by the limo. I spun around the pylon and loosed the rest of my rounds at the shotgunners trying to suppress fire on our right. I re-loaded my 1076s and said, "Saddle up!" The Warrior Princesses stood up facing away from the car and I ran between them, scooping them up into my arms as I raced for the second presidential limo. The Princesses both began shooting behind us just as I got to the car. The driver was out of the car shooting at the shotgunners behind us, but he paused to scream, "They got the car chained to something, Freak! I can't move!"

I ripped the door open, threw the Warrior Princesses inside and said, "Keep those pistols safe, you hear?" They were nodding when I slammed the door on them and said, "Get in, Bobby! I got the chain!"

He jumped in and I threw myself under the car just as the helicopter came screaming down toward the embankment behind the Kennedy Center. I unhooked the chain from around the car's axle, jumped up and hammered the butt of one of my pistols down on the trunk as I got out of the way. Bobby immediately peeled out backwards, spun the wheel to turn the limo 180 degrees and floored it up and out of the driveway and onto New Hampshire Avenue. Within a second or two the car was going eighty miles an hour, speeding off to safety with my Princesses.

I spun around and saw the helo's skids about twenty-five feet from the ground. I immediately classified the helicopter as nonmilitary, a Bell 212, and realized there were men waiting to jump from the open side door. I could also see the back of the pilot's head, so I put three rounds through his helmet and blew his head right off.

The helo dropped like a rock, semi-crashing to earth and throwing all of the guys in the back off their feet. Before I could fire they were all rolling out the open door on the other side, putting the helicopter between themselves and me. The last one out hung up on the door and I hit him twice, although he still managed to get out.

Without the pilot to stabilize it the helo slid down the narrow embankment toward the Potomac. I heard the engine whine as the co-pilot increased power and tried to pull the chopper in the air, but then the rotor struck the Potomac. The big blade broke into pieces and the chopper slowly slid into the river and bobbed there for a minute before it began settling into the cold, dark water. The co-pilot's door banged open and I hit him dead center with a double tap. I didn't bother with a head shot—I was sure he didn't have a heart left—because I was worried about the guys who'd bailed out of the chopper. They weren't shooting, but that didn't mean that they couldn't start right up.

I saw movement to my left and trained on it, but it was four of our guys backed up by a dozen uniforms with long guns. I whistled long and loud, tucked my pistols in my armpits and put two fingers to my eyes. I pointed at the tail of the chopper sticking out of the river, held up ten fingers and pointed at the chopper again. The agents immediately deployed toward the river, guns searching for targets.

I was running toward them at full speed when I heard two more helos coming toward us, only these were cruising down the river. I said into my comms, "Everybody on the net, we've got two helos inbound down the river. It could be more bad guys—be prepared to retreat to the building."

The sweetest sound I'd heard in a long time came back over my earpiece. "Secret Service detail, be advised that two inbound are Marine-1 and Marine-2 out of Fort Meade. ETA one minute. We are armed and hostile, Secret Service—please advise targets."

"Marine-1 and Marine-2, this is Secret Service Agent Glinka Glickstien. Search the banks of the river and the river itself on the backside of the Kennedy Center—advise using FLIR as well as visual, and be advised that targets are armed with unknown long guns."

"Acknowledged, Freak. Marine-1 has activity on the lawn side of the center on FLIR. Say again your position," the pilot said.

"Marine-1, Freak. There are fifteen or sixteen friendlies on the lawn side approaching the backside of the building. All of the targets are on the backside, I say again, backside activity is presumed hostile. If possible pin targets down for possible capture, otherwise weapons free," I said.

Both the Marine choppers blew past us, pivoting in the middle of the river and firing up their "make night like day" spotlights. They began to slowly drift down the river as they looked for the bad guys with their eyes as well as their Forward-Looking Infrared Radar (FLIR). They were menacing, these giant insectile war machines, and I knew they were pissed, because when an AH-64 pilot said they were "armed and hostile" they weren't fucking around.

I came up with the four agents and the uniform guys and we paused to organize ourselves. Badass, Kid Galahad, Greta "Arsenal" Vilmer and Karen "Wopsy" Ianucci were still upright, and they were all staring at me, especially the two newbies. Finally Wopsy said, "I heard the stories, but goddamn, Freak—you looked like a streak of lightning as you ran across the lawn. I ain't never seen anything like it in my whole life."

I said, "Great, thanks, Wopsy, now let's get it together and go get those motherfuckers. We agreed?" Everybody nodded and we started to get organized when we all heard big trucks and sirens. I looked at Badass and he said, "Be my guess that the trucks got a few hopped up Marines in 'em. We might be better off waiting, Freak."

As much as I hated to agree with him I did, so I nodded and we all relaxed a little bit. My comm came up and the helo pilot said, "Freak, Marine-1. Be advised the bad guys may have bugged out. No sign of any activity on the backside of the building, although we have some disturbances on the bank that look like boats may have been pulled up. We also have eight bodies at various places on the terrace and near the building. Marine-1 will continue search while Marine-2 cruises downriver to search for boats."

"Marine-1, Freak. Concur with plan. Please continue to illuminate the area with spotlights and report any contact. We will be sealing the area shortly. Say fuel status," I said.

"Freak, Marine-1. We have six-zero minutes left on station, and we have two backup birds ETA four-zero minutes, as well as mobile re-fueling trucks en route," the pilot said.

"Marine-1, Freak. Thanks for the assist—we owe you one. Freak out," I said.

There was a double click of acknowledgment in my ear as the Marine helicopters continued to search for our attackers, but by now it was fairly certain that they'd escaped, leaving behind only dead bodies. It was possible that they were hiding somewhere close, but given the planning that went into the attack it didn't seem like they'd be that stupid.

Before I could say anything Kid Galahad said, "This was military, Freak. They deliberately fired on POTUS's detail in order to disrupt us, then zeroed in on the kids. If it hadn't been for your quick takedown and our being behind a couple a planters we'd all be dead and they'd have the girls."

"And the timing on the chopper was perfect," Badass said. "They came in just as you were supposed to be overwhelmed by sheer force of numbers with the extraction team, just to make sure that you went down if the shotgunners hadn't already killed ya. It was precision, right down to knowing that most of the agents would be concentrated on POTUS and shooting there first."

"I agree, but there may not be any dead. They were using fléchettes, not shot or slugs," I said. "Coach took some and still had time to tell me she was hit, but then she just passed out like right now—there was some kind of knockout agent on the darts."

Before we could say any more three military 6X6 trucks rumbled right over the curb and onto the Kennedy Center grounds. As soon as they stopped U.S. Marines poured out of them and into neat files, their M4 assault rifles ready and trained toward us. A tall figure jumped out of the first truck and I recognized Major Morgan Gray. Another tall figure jumped out of the second truck and I recognized Sergeant Major Angela Thornton. Both of them recognized me and came running over right behind their troops.

The Marines formed a perimeter around us and Major Gray said, "Sitrep, Freak," so I gave him all the information that I had. "They still out there, Freak?" Sergeant Major Thornton said.

"I don't think so, Sar'nt-Major," I said. "Marine-1 reports that they can see what looks like boat-pullouts—my guess would be that they infiltrated the attack team by boat, and when the helo went down they exfiltrated by boat."

"Sounds plausible—why don't we just go find out, Sar'nt-Major?" Major Gray said.

"Roger that, sir. I'll take first and third squads around the building and Lieutenant Lewis can bring second and fourth squads around this side, leaving you with fifth squad as mobile reserve," Sergeant Major Thornton said.

"Good plan, but let's let Lewis stay with the reserve and I'll bring the two squads from here," Major Gray said. He looked at Sergeant Major Thornton with a silent challenge and she looked right back with the same look.

I was tired of fucking around and pissing contests, so I said, "No go, Major. It's bad doctrine to put the senior officer in the field when we don't know the size and disposition of the enemy, and besides, we need your rank in case we need reinforcements. If you're in the shit and it turns into a firefight we might be overrun because Lieutenant Lewis doesn't have enough shit on his collar to get the same results as you do."

Major Gray and Sergeant Major Thornton both laughed. The Sergeant Major said, "Good lesson in command, Freak."

"Concur," Major Gray said. "I still miss the charge of adrenalin, but you're right on fucking target, Freak. Get started with your guys and apprise me when you're in position, Sar'nt-Major."

"Roger that, sir," Sergeant Major Thornton said. She stood up and bellowed out her orders and the two squads of Marines went off to circle the Kennedy Center. Lieutenant Lewis formed up her guys and they went to the end of the building. Major Gray and his reserve squad stayed put as he spun up the radio to communicate with the attack helos supporting us.

Just then several armored Suburbans pulled up along with about a 100 ambulances (that's not any hyperbole—D.C. ambulance companies were as competitive as the Yankees and Red Sox, and they loved doing business with the government, who always paid promptly and well). Nails jumped out, along with lots of other folks, and the scene went from messy to absolute chaos in 8.9 nanoseconds.

EMTs started running everywhere, checking on our wounded. Secret Service agents began to take control of the scene. Our regular comm channel erupted with so much noise that I just pulled my earpiece out. Nails was barking orders and trying to talk to us at the same time, which finally led to our having a little honest conversation.

Nails: What the hell were you thinking, Freak? Putting your principals in harm's way?
Me: You weren't there, Nails. It was the only realistic alternative to avoid capture.
Nails: You should've retreated or hunkered down and waited for help to arrive.
Me: Fuck you, you REMF. You. Weren't. There.
Nails: That's it, you insubordinate asshole. You're fired, as of now.
Me: Fuck you—I quit.
Nails: No, fuck you. I'll sign your dismissal order before you can write a resignation letter.
Me: It's gonna be hard to sign anything with two broken arms and my foot up your ass.

Luckily the driver of one of the Suburbans came up as Badass and Kid Galahad were separating us and said, "Director Hessler, the president has ordered the remaining agents back to the White House—the first daughters are asking for them."

"The ones who still work for the Service will report in a bit," Nails said.

"No, ma'am, they'll go now. The president said ASAP, ma'am, and beg your pardon, he ranks you, ma'am," the driver, a guy named Eric Stephenson, said. I didn't know him, because he was new on the president's detail and worked the opposite shift as me, but I gave him credit for being both brave and doing his duty in the face of the enraged boss of his division.

Looking like she wanted to gouge my eyes out Nails said, gritting her teeth so hard it seemed as if they might explode, "Very well—all of you go back to the House. We'll debrief later—and some of us will be parting company." Her eyes were blazing at me, so I didn't say anything.

I just stuck my tongue out at her.

It was so incongruous, so child-like, there was only one thing she could do. Nails laughed, as did everybody else. In fact, we were all so stressed that we degenerated into the helpless, doubled-over snorting laughter of those who have just been scared shitless but lived to tell about it.

We finally stopped when snot was coming out of everyone's nose. After we cleaned ourselves up Nails said, "You're not fired, Freak."

"Good, because I'm not quittin'," I said. "Those girls are my responsibility and I'm not leavin' 'em, even if you and I have to have a duel on the South Lawn. No offense, Madam Director."

"None taken, Agent Glickstien," Nails said. "Now get the fuck outta here and back to the House." She turned around and began taking control of the goat-rope that was unfolding across the Kennedy Center lawn.

We all turned around, got in the Suburban and headed for the White House.

When we got there we barely stopped for security. We got out of the car and Charlie Hassenger, the White House Chief of Staff, was waiting for us. He shook all of our hands and said, "You're all employed for life unless you commit murder. The Man is beside himself, but he's convinced that you guys are superheroes, like the Avengers or the Justice League of America."

I looked at him and said, "We've got massive casualties, the bad guys got away, the first lady is down back there and he's *happy*? No offense, Charlie, but is the president off his fucking nut?"

The Chief of Staff gave me a "say what?" look and said, "You don't know?"

"Know what, you obtuse son of a bitch?" I said. Hey, we went to the prom together, so I wasn't about to be intimidated by Charlie's position. Once you've had a guy in a hammerlock so he couldn't put his hand down your pants you sort of lose any fear of them, y'know?

"We don't have any dead back there, just wounded, and most of them aren't really wounded wounded—most of them, including the first lady, are simply recovering from being put to sleep. It turns out that the terrorists were using something called—"

"Fléchettes, yeah we know that much," I said. "No KIA at all?"

"Except for the terrorists, no," Charlie said. "There are seven dead bad guys, but everybody else was asleep, we assume from the darts."

"What about the guys at the back of the Kennedy Center? Were they hit with darts?" Kid Galahad said.

"I don't know that, just that they were somehow knocked out, just like everybody else," Charlie said. "C'mon, The Man is in the Sit Room with the girls and the Joint Chiefs. He wants all of you now." He took off and we followed him through the White House. As we progressed people stood up at their desks and clapped, giving us an ovation as we moved toward the Situation Room. I must admit it was pretty fucking awesome to get a standing O from the whole White House staff, because these were the most composed people I'd ever seen—it was the most respected I've ever felt up to that point.

We arrived outside the Situation Room and Charlie opened the door. We all stopped and he said, "C'mon, the president has personally granted you clearance to come in." When we still hesitated the Chief of Staff said, "Get your asses in here, you hunyocks. The Man wants to give you the keys to the city and he won't take no for an answer." He threw the door open and we walked in.

The Chairman of the Joint Chiefs of Staff saw me and he said, "ATTENTION ON DECK!" All the brass—everybody in the room, in fact—stood to attention, the C-JCS said, "Pree-zent ARMS!" and every single person saluted us.

You have to understand that the only person the Joint Chiefs stand and salute for is the president. There are no other exceptions, but there was all that brass, standing and saluting little old us. It topped the standing O from the White House staff.

Since we were all military trained we all jumped to attention and Badass said, "Pree-zent-ARMS!" and we returned the salute.

Then the Warrior Princesses were slamming into me and we all started crying with relief, and gratitude, and joy. I kept saying "Your mom is OK. They told you, right? Your mom is OK" over and over, and then the Warrior Princesses went and hugged everybody else, and the president wrapped me his large arms and gave me the most sincere hug I'd felt since Square Peg left for Africa. He was weeping, and even most of the crusty old Joint Chiefs had tears in their eyes, even the Commandant of the Marine Corps.

We all hugged ourselves out and then the Vice President was in front of me with his hand out. He had tears on his cheek as he said, "Thank God for you, Agent Glickstien. Thank you for saving the girls again." I felt momentarily squeamish taking his hand, but he seemed totally sincere in his gratitude, and I didn't want to blow the op to arrest him, so I shook his hand and let him pull me in for a faux bro-hug.

Before I could puke he was shoved aside by General Terrance X. McAllen, Chairman of the Joint Chiefs and fellow Marine. "BOOYAH, MARINE!" he bellowed. "I knew you were something special, even way back in Basic. Goddamned well done, you tough leatherneck motherfucker!"

"Amen to that, General," the president said.

"Thank you Chairman, Mr. President, but we were all just doing our jobs. Mr. President, your daughters were incredibly brave under fire and assisted in their own defense," I said.

"What? What do you mean?" the president said. Clearly he didn't know the details about how we escaped the shotgunners. He turned to the girls and said, "What does Freak mean? Brooke? Allison?"

Allison looked her dad right in the eye and said, "We saw Mom get hit and go down, and there was just Freak against four guys with shotguns, and she said she was good but not that good, so we helped her."

"What do you mean you helped her? Helped her how?" the president said.

"I shot my guy in the nuts and the head, Allison shot hers in the chest and the head and Freak shot the other two. Once they were down Freak grabbed us and we guarded her back while we ran to the car. We saw the guys near the entrance turn their shotguns at us, so we let them have it too, although I don't think I hit any of them," Brooke said as if she were reading a grocery list.

"Me, either," Allison said. "But we made 'em duck, and then Freak threw us in the car and the other agents opened up on the guys with shotguns and we were gone."

The president's face was completely chalk white and he was gasping for air. He took a drink of water, loosened his tie and said, "You two each *shot a man?*"

"Yes, dad, we shot them, but it wasn't real hard—they were only about twenty feet away, and they never expected all three of us to stand up at once," Brooke said.

"Besides, dad, they froze when they saw two *little girls* in front of them, just like Freak said they would. They stopped moving and we had easy shots at close range. If we didn't kill them they were going to kill us, so we decided to live." Allison gave her father the perfect parody of the benighted teenager talking to her lame-o parent and said, "I hope you don't *mind.*"

The president of the United States looked at his daughters, looked at me and said, "Well, now I've heard it all. A Secret Service agent used her protectees as a distraction and then has them shoot two of the bad guys because that's the only way to rescue them? What next? We're going to dress them up in tutus and have them dance for the bad guys to distract them?" POTUS's eyes were wild as he looked over at me. It was fairly clear that he was going into shock.

But Brooke walked over, took his hand and said, "Daddy, it *was* the only way. Alli and I had to shoot those guys, 'cause if we didn't they would've put Freak down and taken us, and it wouldn't be like Liam Neeson in the movies, daddy, because once they got Freak down we'd be gone forever. Right now they'd be raping us, or holding us ransom for the nuclear codes, or forcing you to release prisoners, or something else horrible. We had to shoot, daddy, we had to. It was us or them, and we chose us."

"But, but why did you have to do it? There were men with *shotguns* shooting at you," the president said.

"No, dad, they were shooting at Freak and the rest of our Secret Service guys. If they'd been shooting at us we'd've been hit. Brooke and I decided after the last time that no one was going to hurt us or take us without us resisting. We also decided that just because we're *girls* doesn't mean we have to be *helpless*. We didn't ask Freak and Badass and Ed and everybody else to teach us to shoot so we could cower in fear every day," Allison said.

"*But you're my little girls!*" the president said. "Girls don't shoot at the bad guys." His eyes were red and he was sweating—sure signs of shock.

But Allison said, "No, dad, we're your almost adult daughters, and nobody is going to fuck with us without us resisting to the very end. No asshole terrorist is kidnapping me—or my sister!—without me letting them have six in the ten ring and one in the head to make sure they're dead. And before you say I'm a girl one more time, Freak is the best Secret Service agent in history and *she's* a girl and she just shot down a helicopter and hit a bad guy at two hundred feet with a pistol. You don't know anyone else who can do that, but I'm going to train until I can, because I'm never going to be a helpless womyn ever again."

"Me, either, dad," Brooke said. "I'm a goddamned Warrior Princess and you better believe that anyone who tries to do anything to me I don't want done is going to get a real surprise, because nobody gets to fuck with this Warrior Princess without her consent."

"Now snap out of it, dad, and let's find out where Mom is at and go see her, OK?" Allison said.

"Oh, and Dad? You need to give these guys the Presidential Medal of Freedom, or whatever kind of medal you get for being the best, toughest motherfuckers on the planet," Allison said. She and Brooke wrapped their arms around me again, and they both said, "Because they are."

"You guys owe me a Pepsi," I said, hugging them back.

The tension was broken as everybody laughed, even the president, although he still looked like he might start crying uncontrollably at any moment. When the laughter was over POTUS said, "Well, I don't know how we're going to handle this with the media, and your mother will probably have a cow, but we'll work it out. I still want to thank all of the Secret Service agents present for their unparalleled devotion to duty and for helping to save my daughters. I don't know what else to say except that my wife and I thank you, and the country thanks you. I need to attend to other things right now, but there will be time later to personally thank you later."

We took that as our cue to leave and headed for the door. The Warrior Princesses kissed their dad and filed out, too, but Charlie Hassenger caught me at the door and said, "Freak, The Man wants you back for a minute." I raised an eyebrow at him, and he said, "Some intel on the attack just came in and he wants your evaluation."

I went back in the situation room and the president pointed to an open chair two down from him on the right. I sat down and he said, "I want you to know that I'm not mad at you at all for your tactics, which several people have just assured were not only sound but brilliant. I also want to thank you for teaching the girls to shoot, although I'm not sure my wife will be very thrilled. We'll worry about that later, OK? Right now the Chairman has some intel we want you to evaluate. Chairman McAllen?"

The C-JCS looked at everybody in the room and said, "We just intercepted a message intended for a radical Shiite cleric in Qom, Iraq, that purports to be from Ahmed al-Mahsoud." Al-Mahsoud was a leader of the so-called "Foreign Brigade" of ISIS, charged with recruiting disaffected American Muslims to carry out terrorist attacks on American soil, "in order to sow fear among the infidels where they eat, sleep and live." He was at the top of the FBI's Most Wanted list, and hadn't been heard from for at least a month, maybe two.

General McAllen looked grim as he said, "This message said that the packages were missed, but that they were still being tracked and that he was going to contact UPS to find out exactly where they were and when they'd be delivered. He also said that four martyrs had gone to Paradise, but that the infidel lost ten times as many."

"And you think this was about the girls? You think that al-Mahsoud is trying to kidnap them to blackmail the president personally, or just blackmail the country?" I said.

"We want to know what the guys you shot looked like, and if you think this could've been some jihadis hell-bent on revenge for the president's comments the other day," General McAllen said. "So to put it bluntly, were these guys foreign Muslim terrorists? Could you tell?"

I acted like I was pondering the question even though I'd almost said "No" right off the bat. I was stalling because the Vice President was sitting right next to me, and we were going to arrest him the next day, and if I actually said, "No, General, these guys weren't terrorists, they were ordinary looking Americans and their plans were way too sophisticated to be jihadis" then he might find a way to weasel out of everything—the guy had a lot of powerful friends, including the president of the United States, after all.

So I lied.

I looked at General McAllen and said, "Sir, all the men attacking us were dark-complected but not African looking, and shotguns are a good weapon for people who aren't military trained but need firepower. I can't say definitively where the attackers were from, but my first assessment is that they could certainly be from a jihadist group."

"You think they're Muslim terrorists who are angry with me?" the president said. "American Muslims? Because the Chairman didn't tell you this, but we also have some independent confirmation that this was a group of American Muslims who al-Mahsoud recruited for his "American Brigade"—didn't the assessment say they were from local college campuses, Mr. Chairman?"

Mad Dog McAllen nodded as an aide handed him a folded note. He read the note, passed it to Admiral Jordan Wilson Hannah, the Vice-CJS and said, "Yes, sir, it did, and now we actually have a third independent confirmation. The note that is being passed down is the quick transcription of a message on the internet from Ahmed al-Mahsoud himself claiming responsibility for the attack on you, your wife and your children. He claims that it's in retaliation for your repeated attacks on the Palestinian people, and especially for your quote callousness to the plight of Palestinian children end quote. He also claims it will happen again, sir."

"Sir, the implication is that al-Mahsoud will keep recruiting from among Americans, especially Americans that are off our radar, and that he'll be able to keep up this kind of activity because we will be dealing with American citizens," Admiral Hannah said.

"Yes, yes it does, Admiral," the president said. He looked at the Vice President and then me, giving us the same eyebrow lift. The VP said, "Sir, we cannot let this *ever* happen again. We have to know that the girls are safe at all times. I'd recommend a bigger Secret Service detail, and I'd recommend that Agent Glickstien be promoted so she can take care of them full time."

I was stunned. First he wanted to kill me, and then he wanted me promoted? To a bigger, better job, where I could make sure that no one who wasn't family would ever get close to the Warrior Princesses again? Why? How would that serve the asshole's nefarious agenda? (Yeah, I used the word nefarious. Why the fuck not—it fit the situation perfectly and had the added benefit of being cool, and yeah, that's the way I think anyway, so get off my ass about my vocabulary—and no, Shermie, it's not showing off or too trite, either, you language maven. Sorry about the diatribe, but my cousin Shermie is a language professor at Michigan State and always gives me shit about my less than proficient use of the English language. This is for him.)

I was also confused, because the Vice President was really, truly concerned for the Warrior Princesses, and he was absolutely sincere about protecting them and having me in charge of the effort. '*What the fuck is his play on this?*' I thought. I looked up and realized that the president had said something to me while I was grinding my way through the paradoxical positions of the VP.

"Earth to Freak, come in Freak," the president said, making a small joke to ease his own tension. Everyone politely chuckled at the small humor, and I said, "Sir, would you mind repeating yourself? I seem to have concentrated so hard that I effectively blocked any verbal input."

"That's military jargon for 'I wasn't listening to you,' isn't it?" the president said.

"Why yes, yes sir, it is," I said. "How astute of you to notice that, sir."

Everyone laughed at the expression on my face, and the president said, "I just asked you if you were up for expanded duties and a promotion. I know the girls would love it, even though they don't begin to understand what kind of demands the new job would have on your time."

That was when I got it.

The VP wanted to promote me out of the way. If I took the job I would have as much free time as a one-armed paper hanger at Buckingham Palace, which meant that whatever he didn't want me to find out wasn't going to get investigated due to the 100-hour weeks I'd be working. There was something else that was also an obvious conclusion, but it was hovering near the edge of my consciousness and the president was staring at me, so I fell back on my training and said, "I'm yours to command, Mr. President. It would be an honor to lead the first daughters' detail, especially if that's your wish, sir."

"Thank you, Agent Glickstien. It is my wish—I can't think of anyone better to keep my daughters safe, and besides, they actually like you, which is more than I can say," the president said with a rueful smile and harried parent tone of voice.

"If it's any consolation, Mr. President, teenagers hate everyone except their boyfriend or girl friend," Mad Dog McAllen said. "Mine finally grew out of it, sir."

"And how long did that take?" the president said.

"Only twenty years, sir," Mad Dog said, his face completely deadpan.

Everybody laughed at that and I took that as my cue to go. When I got to the door the president said, "Agent Glickstien, thank you again for your exemplary service. It really is extraordinary."

I resisted the urge to salute and said, "Thank you, sir. I wasn't the only one, and it really was the product of the best training on earth." He nodded at me and I nodded back. I also looked at General Mad Dog McAllen and Admiral Jordan Wilson Hannah and gave them nods, too. They both stood up and saluted me (quite improperly, I might add—they weren't wearing their covers, we were indoors, I was a civilian (and I was a junior rank even when I was in uniform), so I (quite improperly) saluted them back. I dropped my salute, executed a perfect parade-ground about face and marched out of the sit room and back to de-brief hell…again.

I had no way of knowing that the military acronym BOHICA (Bend Over, Here It Comes Again—think about it and you'll get it) was about to apply as the situation took another twisty turn into "Are you fucking kidding me?" territory.

And then it got much, much worse.

CHAPTER 69

Justice Is Served

So the de-brief was mercifully brief (sorry about the pun). After all, we already knew who did it, right? Then it was just making the facts fit our premise that it was homegrown Muslim radicals who tried twice to kidnap the first daughters as retaliation for the president's perceived anti-Islam bias (it really wasn't "perceived," it was real—The Man didn't like Muslims in general, and he really didn't like Middle Eastern Muslims).

And before you ask, yeah, the geniuses in Homeland Security determined that it was Ahmed al-Mahsoud and his "American Brigade" who mounted both attacks, even though they didn't have a shred of proof. I felt terrible for lying about the guys who hit us at the Kennedy Center for about thirty seconds, but as far as I knew al-Mahsoud was a real threat to Americans, so having the military and security apparatus of the United States persecute him didn't bother me at all, even if I knew there was no way that the Muslim radical did either attack.

My peeps who were put to sleep during the shotgun attacks all recovered quickly—the fléchette darts that hit them had been coated in Versed, that nice twilight drug that Hurricane had used on Patsy after the Battle of Morehead, so there were no long-term ill effects, just a lot of headaches—and we went back to our routine. The only problem was that something about the attack had been bothering me. After a week I had to talk to somebody about it, so I called Joe. "If the Vice President didn't pull the second attack on the girls, he probably didn't have anything to do with the first one, either," I said. "I've talked about it with the rest of the squad and they agree with you," Joe said. "Let's call DQ and Brenda T. so we can go see our old buddy Mal Sorenson and ask him about it."

That's when we found out the former FBI Dorector hadn't even been questioned about the attacks on the girls.

"I can't believe we never directly asked him about it," Brenda T. Green said. "I feel like a god-damned idiot for just assuming somebody covered it."

"All those hours we questioned him and nobody caught it, Brenda. If you're a goddamned idiot we're all goddamned idiots. I mean, I'm in charge of the prosecution and I never caught it, for fuck's sake," Duquanye Quintanilla said. "Imagine me questioning him about it when he was on the stand—and imagine our case falling into the Grand Canyon, and me crawling off to East Bumfuck, Idaho afterwards." (Don't take offense Idahoans—you have a lovely state, I just picked you because I've already trashed North Dakota).

We got to the jail and went in to the conference room where the former Director of the FBI was waiting. We sat down, everybody smiled and nodded at each other and I said, "So tell us how you and the Vice President planned the kidnapping of the first daughters."

"Pardon me?" Malcolm Sorenson said, looking like a deer in the headlights.

"Did you guys forget that .50-caliber armor-piercing rounds tend to ricochet, or didn't you care?" Joe said.

"Excuse me, but I had *nothing* to do with *that*," Sorenson said. His neck was red and getting redder. A bead of sweat appeared on his forehead and slowly slid down his face, but he made no effort to wipe it off.

"Not only did you kill some of us, you also maimed eleven good people, some of them for life. We want to know why, and how you and the VP did it," Mamba said.

Sorenson was really worked up now. He was shaking, sweat was pouring freely and his eyes were bugging out of his head. He gathered himself and said, "Let me make this perfectly clear. I love those girls and would never, *ever* hurt them. I have no idea what you're talking about." He was really pissed, his hands were shaking, his eyes were red and sweat was just pouring off him, but Malcolm Sorenson mostly looked perplexed.

We'd agreed that we had to be sure, so Kid Galahad said, "Nice words, but they don't wash. You and that asshole Holland tried to kidnap two innocents and got people we knew and loved killed—people who were far more valuable than your sorry ass."

"Now tell us how and why you did it, you worthless motherfucking excuse for a human being," Badass said, his voice like the growl of a grizzly bear.

Malcolm Sorenson stood up and said, "Let me make this perfectly clear. I. HAD. NOTHING. TO. DO. WITH. THESE. ATTACKS! PERIOD." He glared at us and flopped back into his seat, utterly spent.

I believed him.

It was just like the Vice President's reaction to the kidnapping—deep, genuine concern and almost familial love for the girls. Either these two guys were better actors than Robert De Niro and Meryl Streep combined or they were telling the truth.

I looked at everybody in the room and they all had the same stunned look on their faces. They all believed Sorenson, too, and we'd all arrived at the same question at once.

"Then who in the hell did it?" Weasel said.

"Houston, we have a huge fucking problem," Jewey said.

"Ancient Chinese gentleman!" Ed said.

"We have to amend the charges and approach the case entirely differently," US Attorney Duquanye Quintanilla said. "We can't arrest the target tomorrow, or even for the rest of this week." He turned to look at all of us and said, "I would also suggest that you need to figure out who the hell engineered these kidnapping attempts, because I'm certain that Mr. Sorenson is telling the truth, which means that either someone else did the dirty work for the Vice President—" He paused to look at me, and I said, "No fucking way. He was just as surprised as Sorenson and he had much the same reaction, like the girls were his nieces or something. It wasn't them."

"So it was al-Mahsoud and his idiots, although that seems unlikely, or there is another, as yet unknown group that is responsible, which presents even more problems," USA Quintanilla said, succinctly summing up the problem.

"You left out one possibility," Joe said.

"What would that be, Agent Crocker?" Quintanilla said.

"There could be separate groups responsible for the kidnapping attempts," we all said at once.

"I've got the Pepsis, but I'm not sure when we'll have time to drink 'em," Mamba said.

"Ancient Chinese gentleman!" Ed said again.

"You're absolutely right, Ed—this has become a shitstorm of epic proportions—Ah Phuc definitely applies," Jewey said.

Malcolm Sorenson had recovered his composure and he said, "I swear to you, there is no way either I or the Vice President had anything to do with kidnapping those girls. It just isn't possible, especially for Mitch. He talks about them like they're his kids, not the president's."

"We believe you, Mr. Sorenson," I said, "we just can't get our head around the fact that there might be two or three groups trying to kidnap the first daughters."

"And we have absolutely no idea why, do we?" Weasel said. "We have no shred of a motive, unless you believe that fairy tale about al-Mahsoud and the "American Brigade," which we all know is bullshit."

"I'll bite," A-USA Brenda T. Green said. "Why does it have to be bullshit? Isn't it at least possible that the Muslim terrorists did it? Or are we just being politically correct and overly sensitive about our Muslim brothers and sisters?"

"Nobody here is being PC, or sensitive to Muslim sensibilities," Joe said. "There are several reasons why the whole "American Brigade" thing is so much hot air."

"So enlighten me," Brenda T. Green said.

"First of all, their fire discipline was way too good during the school attack. That's Special Forces type shooting, or Marine Corps snipers, or Russian Spetznaz when they were around. There is no way that the guys shooting were jihadis, American or not," Jewey said.

"Second of all, in both attacks the bad guys were shooting to wound, not kill. A Muslim jihadi, American or not, would have no compunction about killing anyone who got in the way of their objective, and they would be especially pleased to be kill any part of the oppressive American security apparatus," Ed said.

"Which brings us to point number three: the word 'jihad' loosely translates to 'holy war,' but in the real sense it means war against the enemies who seek to destroy Islam, and any Muslim who is part of jihad believes that nicely fits America and its decadent people," Weasel said, "which means that the idea of true jihadists leaving anyone but the girls alive is the purest bullshit."

"The fourth point is the easiest to make and understand," Joe said. "These were intricately designed operations that were both complex and simple—and they would've worked if it hadn't been for Freak's unique gifts."

"So what? Are you saying because they're religious zealots the Muslims couldn't design an operation like either of these and then pull them off?" Brenda T. Green said.

"No, not at all," Joe said. "What I am saying is they could never have done it in secret—it would've generated at least some chatter, just because they'd need massive money to make it happen. Also, I'm saying they wouldn't do it, because it just doesn't generate a big enough splash."

"Kidnapping the first daughters isn't *big enough*?" A-USA Green said, her voice rising in disbelief.

"Not if you look at it closely," Mamba said. "Jihadists want to inflict maximum damage in public places, like hospitals, airports, theaters, et cetera, in order to generate maximum terror. They would know that if they kidnapped his daughters President Sheehan would invoke the Twenty-Fifth Amendment to temporarily remove himself from power, at which point the VP, the *former head of the FBI*, would become acting president. The VP is a bigger hawk than the president, and he'd be liable to bomb every Muslim country back to the Stone Age, regardless if they had anything to do with it—and he would for damn sure never negotiate with them, which means the girls would be useless to them, which means these ops would be wasted effort."

"Plus, jihadists don't waste time and resources on ops with no chance of success, which further points to this whole "American Brigade" canard being a sham," Joe said. "Also, the VP would be better equipped to set up and execute the search for the girls, given his background, which would further hamper their efforts to inflict maximum terror on the country. And when the girls were found—dead or alive—the president would give the VP the letter that reinstated him as president and *he* would give the order to obliterate every Muslim he could find. You see? Neither of these ops had a snowball's chance in hell of any kind of success."

"Well, define success," USA Quintanilla said. "They'd have the first daughters, which seems pretty successful to me. These would be fantastic bargaining chips, even if it was just to get the president out of office."

"Have you been listening, counselor?" Jewey said. "First, the jihadis define success as maximum casualties in order to inspire maximum terror. Kidnapping two girls, no matter who their parents are, fails to meet those criteria. Further, I'd rather be facing the president than the VP, who is very hawkish already and might blow his cork if faced with this kind of situation. These jihadis are committed to their cause, but don't mistake them for blind, dumb hicks. They know what's going on here and they'd know they didn't want the former head of America's internal security organ in the big chair."

"So most of us agree that the VP had no knowledge of these attacks, that the jihadis couldn't or wouldn't have pulled them off, and that means an outside third party or parties is still out there contemplating more attacks," Joe said.

Everyone nodded in agreement, even the U.S. Attorney. Duquanye Quintanilla may not have been a strategic genius as he rose to his exalted position, but he wasn't an idiot. He was, however, a straight-line thinker and law and order devotee.

"Well, we can still arrest the Vice-President once we amend the indictment, and we'll have to worry about the other possibilities and consequences later. Even if he didn't know about the attacks on the girls he did know about the murders and attempted murders of Freak and the others—and I won't have a murderer running around so we might tip to some other operation he probably didn't know about. I say we move ahead just as soon as possible," Quintanilla said.

That was definitely straight line thinking, but I couldn't really disagree with him. Josie, Elvin Clyde Bliss, CoD, Patsy and all the rest were still dead, and Vice President Mitch Holland was ultimately responsible for their deaths, so there didn't seem to be anything left but to do except arrest him for what we could prove he was responsible for.

So we all agreed that as soon as the indictments could be amended we'd stand by and watch that asshole get what he deserved. We all left the D.C. Detention Center and went home. The next morning we all went back to do our jobs like we weren't about to arrest the second highest elected official in the United States, but every one of us was thinking about the kidnap attempts on the first daughters. I wasn't as worried about *who* was trying to do it, because I believed that if we could find out *why* they wanted to do it we'd find the who of it. There just didn't seem to be anyone with a motive for taking the president's daughters, at least not one that made any sense, and that's really what we were all worried about, because if there wasn't any real motive it could be some whack job like John Hinckley, a crazy person that was trying to impress someone or make some obscure, obtuse political point.

Then as now, there is no way to stop these kind of crazies unless you put them in the ground, but you can't do that if they don't at least give you a hint.

That's what I was thinking just before my phone rang the night before we were supposed to arrest the Vice President of the United States.

I saw it was Mamba's phone, so I said, "Bon soir, Monsieur le Comte. Comme ca?"

"Bon soir, mademoiselle Freak, je suis très bon, but I have the rest of the Badger Squad here— you're on speaker," Mamba said.

"OK, to what do I owe the pleasure?" I said.

"We've been thinking about the motive for the kidnap attempts and coming up empty, so we decided to ask about the president and first lady before they became famous. Everybody we talked to said that they were perfectly normal people who probably pissed some people off, but not enough for them to carry a grudge all these years," Joe said.

"And you knew 'em before any of us did, so we wanted to ask you what you knew that might help us with a motive," Weasel said.

"Any dirt will do," Jewey said.

"Especially something like a love triangle," Mamba said, "because it seems to us it would have to be extreme unrequited love that led to long-term dissatisfaction or flat-out hatred that has been nurtured long term to give somebody this kind of persistence."

"I've been racking my brain, but believe me nothing has come up," I said, my tone of voice echoing my frustration.

"So good old Pat Sheehan wasn't an asshole in high school?" Jewey said.

"Or the lovely Laura Flagler wasn't a roaring bitch who stole good old Pat from his previous girlfriend?" Weasel said.

"I know that I make jokes about the Super Bitch and the White Ice Queen and all that, but that's mostly personal animus because she and my brother went at it for valedictorian and my brother won. She was understandably upset and said some shit at the time, but the truth is that I don't remember anybody saying anything about her really being bitchy," I said. "Everybody loved the president when he was in school—he might've been the most popular student ever at Harper Creek High School."

"C'mon—there must be something about one of them," Mamba said.

"She wasn't a slut, or he wasn't a real cock-hound?" Jewey said.

"Not at all. They started going together when they were in seventh grade. She volunteered at the local food pantry for the homeless and he worked with handicapped kids for the Special Olympics. When she won the President's Scholarship at Michigan—a four-year full ride—the first lady declined it and made sure someone who couldn't pay for college got it. When the president won the Mr. Football Award he actually ended up giving the trophy to Ernie Springer, a handicapped boy he worked with all through school, because Ernie was his biggest fan and also dying from a dread neuro-muscular disease. When Ernie died Pat Sheehan gave the eulogy, and he put his varsity jacket with all of his medals and awards in the casket with his friend. There wasn't a dry eye in the house," I said.

"Fuck a goddamned fucking duck," Mamba said. "What you're saying is that this guy really is just what his bio says he is—a literal choirboy with tendencies to sainthood."

"Roger that. If either of them has any dirt to dig up I don't know what it is. The only thing either of them has on their record is when the president's frat at Michigan got busted for a party that got out of hand, but even then he came out smelling like a rose, because as the president of the frat he accepted all the responsibility and took all of the punishment on himself, even though he wasn't even on campus when it happened. The guy's for real, and so is his wife," I said.

"Well, sheeeee-it!" the Badger Squad said. They were trying to imitate the way that House used to try and be ghetto, but ended up sounding like the Harlem Wino Choir.

"You guys owe me Pepsis tomorrow after we arrest that son of a bitch Holland. Now go get some sleep so we all look good when the papers take our picture next to that asshole murderer," I said.

They hung up, but the conversation had sparked something in my head. It sort of hung back there, niggling away at my thought process, but I couldn't make it come out, so I just let it go and slept the sleep of the just, knowing that tomorrow I'd get to see a dirty Vice President in handcuffs, which made me very happy.

But that feeling didn't go entirely away. Something was in there, and it would come out when it came out.

The next morning came and we all assembled at the U.S. Attorney's office. Honest Tom Vernon and his guys came in wired and ready to go. Both U.S. Attorney Duquanye Quintanilla and A-USA Brenda T. Green were dressed to the nines, had their arrest warrant in triplicate, and were clearly juiced.

My squad was doing their best Johnny Cash impression—we were all dressed entirely in black. The only break in our monochromatic dress were our creds, which we all wore hanging from our left breast pockets with the badge and photo ID card out. We'd replaced our photos with a photo of Josie, or Elvin Clyde Bishop, or CoD, or Tara Waters. We'd also polished the gold of our shields so that they shone like the crown jewels, because we wanted the VP to know how close to death he was for killing one of our own.

I looked at everybody and said, "OK, we've got the right look, now we've got to get our minds right. We are going to remain absolutely fucking silent, and we're never going to take our eyes off that slimy piece of filth, because that motherfucker murdered some of our own, and we want him to understand that fucking with us is the worst fucking mistake any asshole can make. If anybody says one word I'll send you to emergency and make sure that when you get out of rehab you're transferred to the U.S. Park Service in East Bumfuck, Mississippi (don't get all worked up, Mississippians, it had to be somewhere and I already trashed North Dakota and Idaho). Are we clear?"

The squad all stood at attention and silently raised their right hands in a perfect Marine Corps salute. They all looked at me with the dead fish look every law enforcement officer develops for suspects and then lowered the salute. I nodded back and said, "The Secret Service is ready, U.S. Attorney Quintanilla."

"Let's go arrest the Vice President of the United States," Quintanilla said.

"The U.S. Marshals are ready, sir," Honest Tom Vernon said. The marshals looked ready—they were all just as pissed as we were, but without the personal element attached.

All in all it was one formidable group of federal law enforcement that left the building and headed for the White House.

We pulled up at the North Portico and swept into the White House like Marines taking a beach. My squad was in the lead since we knew where we were going, with the attorneys and the marshals following us in close order.

Every single person in the West Wing who saw us took one look at our faces and moved out of the way without being asked. When we got to the door of the VP's office we went right in to the reception area, where we found three of the VP's aides, an Air Force major, two DHS guys we knew, the VP's personal secretary and the head of his Secret Service detail, Senior Agent Gabriel Berdahl.

Gabe instinctively moved toward the door to the inner office when he saw all of us, his hand coming up so he could get on the radio.

I said, "Senior Agent Berdahl, stay off that radio and move away from the door." My voice was colder than a winter's night in Antarctica as I stared straight into his beautiful blue eyes. His hand paused and he said, "Freak—Agent Glickstien?" He was frozen in place, completely confused but still prepared to do his duty and protect the Vice President if necessary.

I looked at him with my best Special Forces death-stare and said, "Move now, Senior Agent Berdahl, or I'll personally remove you." My voice could've frozen vodka solid as I took a step forward.

He straightened up and said, "What gives you the right to make me move away from my principal?"

U.S. Attorney Duquanye Quintanilla came forward and said, "Senior Agent Berdahl, this gives us the right." He handed Gabe the arrest warrant. His eyes widened when he saw the seal of the U.S. Justice Department on it, and they got wider still when he read the opening of the indictment. Gabe's mouth gaped open and he looked up at all of us with wild eyes.

"That's right, Senior Agent, it's a warrant for the arrest of the Vice President of the United States, Mitchell C. Holland. Is he inside?" Duquanye Quintanilla said.

Gabe nodded dumbly and Quintanilla said, "Marshal Vernon? Let's go." The marshals came up as the VP's secretary reached toward her phone, but Honest Tom Vernon stepped up to the desk and said, "Miss, for his safety and ours please refrain from using any electronic devices until we've secured the Vice President, if you please." The secretary looked sheepish and stopped reaching for the phone. Honest Tom said, "The same goes for the rest of the people in this office. No electronic devices, and no one crosses the threshold of this office once we've secured the Vice President. The FBI will be here to seal the office as a possible crime scene within one minute of our removing the Vice President. Are we clear?"

There were nods all around and Honest Tom nodded to the U.S. Attorney, who opened his phone and hit one button. The phone was immediately answered and Quintanilla said, "Sir, we are affecting the arrest in thirty seconds." Something was said from the other end—it was the Attorney

General, who was waiting to go into the White House Press Room for what the reporters thought was an update on an ongoing investigation into drug charges against a D.C. councilman—and then the U.S. Attorney said, "Yes, sir, right out the North Portico and to our offices." There was some reply and Quintanilla looked up and said, "It's a go. Marshal Vernon?"

Honest Tom Vernon looked at Gabe Berdahl, who stepped aside without speaking. The marshal opened the door to the inner office and the five Marshals went right in, followed by Quintanilla, Brenda T. Green and 11 furiously angry but deadly silent Secret Service agents.

Joe, Mamba, Jewey, Weasel, Ed, Kid Galahad, Badass, El Gato, Bumble, Buddha and I stood in two ranks at the back of the office and twenty-two eyes burning with fury locked on the Vice President. He stood up from his desk and said, "What in the hell is going on here? I'm in a meeting." He was trying for outrage, but I knew he was very conscious of us standing in the back of the room, and his fear sapped his usually rich, deep baritone of any power at all.

He was meeting with the Secretaries of Defense and Homeland Security, and both of them stood up and confronted the U.S. Attorney and the marshals.

"Who the hell are you and what the hell are you doing, barging in like this?" the SecDef said. His name was Lane Zubryd and he was a crusty old coot, a retired four-star Air Force general who was really, truly good at his job. He'd been a servant of both Republican and Democratic administrations and was nobody's fool. He must've seen the U.S. Marshal's badges, because he fell silent after the one outburst, and then looked back at us.

The SecDef and I knew each other slightly (sorry, but…that's classified) and he tried to catch my eye, but I refused to stop staring at the Vice President. My squad just stood there, a monolith of righteous fury that washed over the Vice President like the heat of a thousand suns.

Travis Nowicki, the Secretary of Homeland Security said, "Duquanye, what in the hell are you doing here? This meeting is classified above your pay grade and you need to leave now, or some serious shit is going to pour down on your head, my friend."

U.S. Attorney Duquanye Quintanilla said, "My apologies, Mr. Secretary, but I need you and the Secretary of Defense to stand away from the desk and move to that corner. Now if you would, please sirs."

"Fuck you, asshole," SecDef Zubryd said. "I'm the Secretary of Defense and I've flown over more battlefields than you can imagine, so you don't get to give me orders, sonny." He drew himself up to spew some more invective out, but Duquanye Quintanilla proved why he was going places some day, because he pushed himself right up into the old warrior's face and said, in a dead calm voice, "I'm sorry, Mr. Secretary, but if you don't remove yourself I'm going to arrest you for obstructing a federal investigation, hindering prosecution of a federal felon and interference with federal law enforcement officers in performance of their duty. Your rank means nothing to me and by the way, sir, with the utmost respect, I'm not your son—I'm a U.S. Attorney in pursuit of a man who murdered at least seven people, including two Secret Service agents, so are you going to move, or am I going to arrest your wizened old ass?"

The Secretary of Defense looked at Quintanilla, looked at the Vice President, looked at the 11 Secret Service agents standing silently at the back of the room and said, "Excuse me, Mr. U.S. Attorney, I was not aware that you were just doing your job. Far be it from me to interfere with a federal prosecution, oh, and with respect, I call everyone 'sonny.' It's a privilege you get when you've been around as long as I have." The SecDef smiled and said, "I am impressed that you got the description of my ass exactly right, though," as he stepped away from the desk to the corner of the room. DHS Secretary Nowicki looked thunderstruck, but he didn't say anything further as he joined the SecDef in the corner.

Through it all the Vice President just stood there like he was in a trance. The only thing that showed he understood what was going on was the blush of red slowly rising up his neck to his face. He avoided looking at my squad, but we just bored in on his eyes, unmoving and implacable, the perfect embodiment of the idea of nemesis.

The Vice President finally broke out of his trance when A-USA Brenda T. Green stepped up to him and said, "Mitchell Calvin Holland, you are under arrest for the murder of Josephine Borowiak Soper, Elvin Clyde Bliss, Andria Michelle Rogers, Tara Sue Waters, James Clawson, Dana Louise Gadnicki and Lourdes Maria Serafina Gonzales. You are also charged with conspiracy to commit murder of federal agents, felonious assault of federal agents, conspiracy to commit felonious assault, assault with intent to commit murder, misappropriation of government funds and personnel to commit a felony, to wit: murder, interstate conspiracy to commit multiple felonies and several other lesser charges that will be explained to you once you have retained counsel."

Brenda T. Green stepped back and Honest Tom Vernon stepped up to the Holland and said, "Mr. Vice President, if you would please put your hands behind your back?"

Holland broke his silence and said, "I will not! I'm not being paraded out of here like some common criminal! I'm the Vice President of the United States for Christ's sake! You can't just put me in handcuffs and take me on a perp walk! I'll call the president about this!" He wasn't quite hysterical yet, but it was pretty clear that the soon-to-be-former VP was walking a fine mental line.

Which he got pushed over when Honest Tom Vernon said, "Mr. Vice President, if you don't put your hands behind your back voluntarily I'll have to do it for you, sir, and neither of us want that."

"You keep your hands off me! And you keep me away from those, those, those—" he motioned with his head at my squad because he still couldn't look at us—"those GOONS! I'm the Vice President and the president of the United States is my best friend! He won't let you do this! I have diplomatic immunity, and the *president* is my best friend! You can't even arrest me, much less make me walk out in handcuffs like I'm a crack dealer!"

I think that Holland would've gone on talking like a hysterical third grader for some period of time, except Honest Tom Vernon stepped behind him and smoothly (smooth is fast) clapped the first cuff on and then raked the soon-to-be-former VP's other hand down and into the second cuff before he even had a chance to resist.

"Is that really necessary?" Secretary Nowicki said.

"Yes, sir, it absolutely is," U.S. Attorney Duquanye Quintanilla said. He stood right in front of the soon-to-be-former Vice President and said, "Mitchell Calvin Holland, you have the right to remain silent. Anything you say can and will be used against you in a court of law. You have the right to an attorney, and if you cannot afford one an attorney will be provided at no expense to you. Do you understand these rights as I've explained them to you?"

Mitchell Holland really lost it then. He started crying and babbling about the president being his friend and not being prosecuted and having a bad dream and a bunch of other useless shit, until finally Quintanilla had Brenda T. Green re-read him his rights. She was gentle about it, and that seemed to get through to the soon-to-be-former Vice President, because he nodded and said, "I-I-I, uh, I understand my rights and I would like to speak to my attorney, Shannon Dudek Farrance of Farrance, Hainrihar, Fields, Patten and Seals. I would also like to speak to the president." He still wouldn't look at us, because we were all still giving him our "fuck you, you asshole piece of murderous shit" stares, even though we were ready to cheer at his mini-breakdown.

"I'm sorry, sir, but you'll have to arrange to see anyone else once you see your attorney," Quintanilla said. "Sir, you have invoked your right to an attorney, and my associate will call her right now so that she can meet you at the Washington, D.C. Detention Center. Until that time we will not ask you any questions except those pertaining to your comfort, and I strongly advise you to say absolutely nothing until you have met with your attorney, unless it pertains to your comfort. Please acknowledge that you understand what I've just said, sir." Quintanilla was soft and gentle as he spoke, in complete contrast to the thundercloud of black at the back of the room, which was mentally beating the soon-to-be-former Vice President to his weak knees.

"I understand my rights and that you have just warned me against incriminating myself. I'd like to go now, if we could, and get this over with," Holland said in a very small, broken voice.

Quintanilla looked at Brenda T. Green and she said, "His attorney is on the way, sir." The U.S. Attorney looked at my squad and gave the slightest nod. We all broke ranks, filed out the door and stood shoulder to shoulder in two lines facing each other in the outer office. Badass and I stood at the end of the lines farthest from the outer door.

We were set up for about a minute when the two U.S. Attorneys came out, followed by Marshal Bingaman, the soon-to-be-former Vice President, who was flanked by Marshals Gates and Moyer, who were each holding one of Holland's arms, and finally Marshal Shimel and Honest Tom Vernon.

We all drew ourselves to attention while never taking our eyes off the murderer of our comrades and innocents. He saw us and seemed to shrink into himself, but in the end he couldn't help himself, because he looked at each of us as he moved for the outer door.

El Gato was first in line, his ID picture replaced with a picture of CoD. The soon-to-be-former VP looked at the picture and recoiled, just as he did with all of our IDs. I give him credit, because he moved slowly, really looking at the pictures as his body showed remorse, until he finally got to me.

I'd chosen to put Elvin Clyde Bliss's picture in my creds, because he was truly an innocent who'd only been trying to understand something that was foreign to him. The VP looked at the young man's picture for at least 10 seconds before a single tear slid down his cheek. The soon-to-be-former Vice President finally looked up at me and really recoiled. He opened his mouth to say something, but I gave him a slow, small "no" shake of my head while still looking him right in the eye with my special ops death stare.

I give Mitchell Calvin Holland credit, because he could see in my eyes that if he spoke he would die, so he shut his mouth and moved through the door. We waited until he was out and then formed up and followed him through the West Wing until he was in his car with the five marshals and Brenda T. Green. U.S. Attorney Duquanye Quintanilla stopped and shook all of our hands, thanking us for all we'd done, and when he got to Bumble the big man said, "You fuck this up and I'll fucking kill you and your whole family—you dig, my brother?"

"Indeed I do, Agent Beemond, and I assure you, that motherfucking murdering asshole is going to the federal prison at Marion, Illinois, for the rest of his life or you have my permission to kill me and everybody I know."

Ordinarily we'd've laughed at that, but we settled for grim smiles that day, and then Quintanilla mounted up and it was over.

We all went back to the Secret Service office in the OEOB where we were met by Nails and Gabe Berdahl.

Gabe said, "Freak, what the fuck was that? Why didn't somebody tell me you were coming to arrest *my principal*? You assholes!" He started to move toward me when I fixed him with my death stare and said, "Easy, brother. Your principal murdered people I cared about, that I had to look at after they were dead and explain to their mothers why they died and he was really after me so why don't you eat shit and and die, asshole?" My anger surged up from my belly and I prepared to attack the next thing that moved.

"Thanks for that nice exposition of the English language, Freak, but I'm afraid I'm not going to let you two tear each other apart, even though I must say, Gabe, your judgment has to be called into question, because I'm pretty sure that she'd tear both your arms off and stick 'em up your ass without breaking a sweat, or did you forget that time she put away four of our best agents at once when she was demonstrating unarmed combat techniques? Man, are you barking up the wrong tree," Nails said.

Gabe started to apologize, but Nails rounded on me and said, "And you—do you always threaten people as a way to get them to agree with you? That probably explains why you're single, and maybe why you've got all that anger in the first place. Now apologize, you dipshit."

"Sorry we put you out of a job, Gabe, and sorry for threatening you," I said. "He's a bad guy."

"Sorry I reacted so badly, Freak. Think you could use a former Agent in Charge on your detail with the girls?" Gabe said, those blue eyes sparkling.

"As long as you can stand me giving you shit 23 hours a day," I said.

"We'll see about that later," Nails said. "For right now, I want to congratulate everybody for a job damned well done. Without your persistence and intelligence we'd have never caught that asshole, and there'd still be a threat to the first daughters and the president. I'm proud of each of you personally, and I'm proud to be associated with all of you." She shook all of our hands and I was surprised to see tears in her eyes. While she shook my hand Nails said, "Andria Rogers and I went through training together, and despite working for me she was still one of my best friends, so this is a good day for me, too."

We all cried a little bit then, remembering all the victims, but after a short cry an agent came in and said, "Madame Director? The president would like to see you and Freak in the Oval ASAP. And Director—he, ah, the president said for you to, ah, haul ass ma'am. His exact words, ma'am: tell them to haul ass over here immediately."

"Oh, call POTUS back and tell him not to get his panties in a bunch," Nails said. We all laughed like hell then, until we finally felt cleansed of the deaths associated with the murderous soon-to-be-former Vice President. Finally Nails said, "You ready to go beard the lion in his den, Freak?"

"Bet your ass, ma'am," I said.

We all laughed again before Nails and I left to walk across the alley from the OEOB to the White House and our sure to be sticky meeting with a president who'd just found out his best friend and soon-to-be-former Vice President was a murderer.

I was sure it wouldn't be tougher than facing 1,200 armed Russians with artillery support (sorry, you know the drill—it's classified), but I was also sure it wasn't going to be a cakewalk.

When you're right, you're right—and I was right, in spades.

Unfortunately.

CHAPTER 70

The Lion's Den (Oval Office Edition)

So we got to the Oval Office and the president made us wait for 15 minutes. We knew he was there—we could hear him yelling—but I guess he needed to make a point, so we waited, although it didn't really have the desired effect, since Nails and I could've cared less. We'd seen the evidence and we knew that the case against the soon-to-be-former Vice President was airtight, so we didn't give a flying fuck how long we waited outside the Oval Office.

The yelling finally subsided and Charlie Hassenger came out of the Oval. He looked like he'd aged 10 years in the last 15 minutes. The chief of staff pinched his nose and said, "You two better get in here, and for Christ's sake, keep your mouths shut or I can't guarantee you'll be alive in five minutes."

We went into the Oval Office. The president had his back to us while he looked out at the Rose Garden. The Attorney General and Secretary of Homeland Security were sitting on one of the couches, with the Secretary of Defense and Solicitor General sitting on the other. There didn't seem to be anyplace for us to sit, so we stood at the foot of the couches and waited for the president to begin.

He looked out the window and said, "Tell me why I shouldn't fire your worthless asses right now."

Before I could say anything Nails said, "If you want to fire me that's your prerogative, Mr. President, but you'd better do it to my face, or I'll think that you're a coward, sir." The Director of the Secret Service had balls the size of an elephant and no fear of anything or anyone political.

The president whipped around and said, "What did you say?"

Nails looked back at him and said, "I didn't stutter, Mr. President. Fire me if you want, but do it to my face." She stared at the 6'3" president from her lowly 5'1" and somehow looked bigger than he did.

James Sheehan's face contorted in a way I'd never seen before and he said, "Fine. You want me to fire you to your face? You want to call me a coward? Fine—you're—"

"Resigning," Nails said, interrupting the president. She pulled a letter out of her jacket and handed it to Secretary Nowicki, who was her direct superior. "Mr. Secretary, I hereby resign immediately." She turned and headed for the door to the Oval and the president said, "Where the hell do you think you're going, Hessler? I didn't give you permission to leave yet!"

Nails turned around, her gigantic balls clanking, and said, "Fuck you, *Mr.* President. I don't work for you anymore—I'm worthless, remember?—so that means I'm a private citizen, which means that I can go anywhere I want, any time I want. I don't want to listen to your pissy bitching anymore, so I'm leaving. Just a quick piece of advice—your kids are alive and well because of that agent over there, so I'd treat her with a little more respect than you did me. You owe her. Now if you'll excuse me, I think I'll walk down to Legal Seafood and have some oyster shooters and see if there are some cute Italian diplomats in the bar like there were last time I was there—I could use the distraction. Ciao."

Nails had balls the size of Jupiter and the courage of a wolverine—it was all I could do to keep from laughing, both at her words and the look on the president's face.

SecDef had no such compunction. He burst out laughing, and Secretary Nowicki soon joined him. The Attorney General and the Solicitor General didn't laugh, but they were both tight-assed lawyers, so what do you expect (you'd have an easier time getting an iguana to laugh).

Nails was reaching for the door when the president said, "Director Hessler, I'd consider it a personal favor if you'd wait one second. I—I need a moment to collect myself, if you'd be so kind." His voice was still tense, but Jimmy Sheehan was doing a good job recovering his composure. It was easy to see why people liked him, and why so many of them had voted for him twice.

Nails stopped, and the president went over to Secretary Nowicki and held out his hand. The DHS chief put Nails' resignation letter in his hand and the president tore it to neat shreds and threw them in his wastebasket. He heaved a sigh and said, "Director Hessler, Agent Glickstien, please take a seat." Secretary Nowicki moved over with the AG and SG and we sat on the same couch as SecDef.

The president sat down in his chair and said, "OK, no fucking around—I apologize for being an asshole right then. My only defense is that the Vice President and I have been best friends since our undergrad days at U of M. I was—am—so shocked that I can't tell you, so if you'll accept my apology I'd like you to walk me through this step by step." He looked at both of us and Nails said, "I accept your apology, Mr. President, and I apologize if I was out of line, sir."

"No, no you weren't, Director Hessler, you were just reminding me that I'm the president of the United States and not some whiny shithead. I think I owe you one, Siri," the president said.

"No, sir, it doesn't work that way. Apology accepted and let's move on, sir," Nails said. The president looked at me and said, "Agent Glickstien?"

I looked up like I was startled and said, "Sir?"

James Sheehan looked at me like I was stupid and said, "Do you accept my apology?"

I looked back and said, "Mr. President, you are the commander in chief and my ultimate superior. If it pleases you to yell, scream, have a tantrum, throw things or order me to Afghanistan, well, that's just part of the job. You don't ever owe me an apology, and I don't see any reason to accept something I'm not owed, sir."

SecDef said, "Tell me again how we let you get away?" He looked at the president and said, "Sir, you might want to keep this one for a while. She gets it all, and she knows when to talk and when to shut up, which means she's way smarter than she lets on, and she's the best pistol shot in the world, which can certainly be useful at times."

The wrinkled wing-wiper and I looked at each other and gave a small smile, remembering an old op (sorry, that one is definitely still classified, if not double-secret classified), and then I looked back at the president, who said, "Well, that's enough of an endorsement for me, as if I needed one after what you've already done for my family. I'm afraid Freak'll have to put up with my temper and fits of pique a while longer." The president had apparently gone from being completely discombobulated to at least nominally in control of himself, which I thought was remarkable, considering all of the yelling we heard. It was so remarkable that it was odd, as if the president were schizophrenic and had experienced a dissociative episode, but that wasn't it. Still, there was something off about his whole demeanor, but then there was no more time to think about it, because The Man leaned back in his chair, looked at Nails and I and said, "Now start at the beginning and tell me all about it."

So we did, in every gory detail.

About halfway through U.S. Attorney Duquanye Quintanilla joined us, and right after that Charlie Hassenger came in and said, "Mr. President, the press has been told that you'll be making an announcement shortly and they're gathering in the press room. They assume since we called off the Attorney General earlier that there's been a major development in the D.C. councilman case, and some people are whispering about more arrests, but nobody has the real news—yet."

"We're almost done here, Charlie. Can you give me just a few more minutes?" the president said. "I'd like to tell my wife and kids before I go out there."

"I understand, Mr. President, and I don't mean to pressure you sir, but the clock is ticking. We need to get in front of this as soon as possible, because once the news breaks it will be, ah, very bad, sir," Hassenger said.

"C'mon, Charlie, you can say it's going to be a gigantic shitstorm that dwarfs Hurricane Katrina, or Nixon's resignation, or Clinton's impeachment, or even the OJ trial and verdict. Hell, it'll be bigger than the Super Bowl this year, don't you think?" the president said, looking for some lightness. We all kind of laughed, but it was strained, because we all knew Charlie Hassenger wasn't fucking kidding. When this story broke it was going to be the equivalent of every hurricane that ever made landfall times a hundred. Nixon, Clinton, OJ, the death of Princess Diana—those were all going to look like a Sunday afternoon picnic compared to this.

The president flipped his hand in the universal "continue" gesture and we finished the story. When we were done he looked at the AG and said, "Len, what do you think?"

Henry was a short, muscular man from the South Side of Chicago who'd put himself through law school while working as a mail carrier. He went from there to the public defender's office, the state circuit court and then the Illinois AG under a Democratic governor. He'd been an assistant AG under the previous Democratic president and had been president-elect Sheehan's surprise choice for AG.

The AG was known as a no-bullshit straight shooter who loved putting any sort of criminal in prison. He looked at Duquanye Quintanilla, the president, and finally at me, sighed heavily and said, "Mr. President, the case appears airtight. The Vice President misused his office to try and kill Agent Glickstien and succeeded in killing others. I have a senior U.S. Attorney who has dotted every 'i' and crossed every 't', and I have reams of solid proof of the commission of the crimes. I wish we knew more about the Vice President's motive, but that's irrelevant in the face of all of this proof, especially the money trail. I'd say that Mr. Holland and his attorneys will be pressing for a deal within a week, maybe only three days." The AG looked at the president like he was a pet pug dog who just messed on the floor.

The president looked at Nails and said, "There's no chance these agents who investigated made some kind of mistake?"

"Mr. President, Agents Cocker, Wei and Silverberg literally have 550 IQ points between them, and the other agents helping them investigate are nearly as smart—they didn't make any mistakes, sir," Nails said.

"And you have no idea why Mitch—Vice President Holland—would want you dead?" the president said to me.

"No, sir. I've racked my brain, but he and I never really interacted, and I have absolutely no animosity toward him, sir. I'm absolutely baffled, and so is the rest of the Badger Squad. There doesn't seem to be any connection between us at all," I said.

The president put his hands together and tapped his chin with his forefingers, for a moment, lost in thought. I didn't blame him. If my best friend of over 20 years was suddenly arrested for murder I'd have some contemplating to do, too, especially if he were trying to kill someone who was tasked with protecting me and my family. Finally he looked up and said, "So what we have is the definition of the word conundrum, and what I have to do is perform the most distasteful task of my life by telling the whole world that my best friend is a murderer—or rather that he's accused of murder, even though it is obvious that he's guilty and will be convicted."

The president stood up and we all stood up with him. He had a wan little smile on his face and he said, "Do you know, when I took office I thought that this job was going to be more fun than not. Boy was I wrong."

Before we could say anything the Oval Office door opened and the first lady came in. She saw me and said, "Oh my God! Are the girls—?" I immediately said, "Ma'am, if it were the Warrior Princesses I wouldn't be here, because I'd be dead, ma'am." Melodramatic, I admit, but also truthful, and immediately relaxing to the first lady, who looked at her husband and said, "Jim? Are you all right?" He shook his head and looked like he was going to cry, and Charlie Hassenger said, "Mr. President, we'll be waiting for you outside the Oval Office when you're ready." We all filed out as the president and first lady sat down on one of the couches.

We weren't in the outer office for 30 seconds when two of my newbies on the first daughters' detail, Tomm Dopheide and Lindsay van Order, brought the Warrior Princesses in. Both of them saw me and rushed over to hug me. "What's wrong, Freak? Did something happen to my dad?" Brooke said.

"Is he dead?" Allison said, her face screwing up and preparing to shed tears.

"No, no you guys, your dad and mom are just fine. They've had some bad news, and you need to go in and hear it from your dad, but everything will be OK. I'll wait out here for you with Tomm and Lindsay, OK? Now go in and see your mom and dad."

Like true Warrior Princesses they turned and went in the Oval, and we went back to waiting. The SecDef looked at me and said, "So you're on duty?"

"No, sir," I said, "but they're my principals, and they're going to need me when this is over."

"Won't their mom be with them? Won't that be enough?" SecDef said.

"Not the same thing, sir, and no, I don't think she'll be enough," I said.

"Why not? What can you do that she can't, Marine?" SecDef said.

"Sir, those girls are gonna want to shoot something after they hear that their Uncle Mitch was trying to kill their Secret Service friend, and I'm the person they associate with shooting, therefore I need to be available to them, so that they can blow off steam and get rid of the hatred in their hearts," I said. "Assuming the Attorney General tells me I'm not needed at the press conference." I looked at the AG and he said, "No, we've already decided that Director Hessler will field all Secret Service questions today. In fact, I'm trying to keep all of you guys out of the press spotlight, Freak, because I want you to be able to keep doing your jobs."

"We appreciate that, sir, since we all like our jobs and our principals," I said.

"And it's obvious that they like you," the AG said. "That's what makes all of this so crazy—why the fuck would the VP go after you? Or the girls? I've only seen him with the first daughters a few times, but it's obvious that he's like their favorite uncle, so what's his motive for killing someone who loves them too? You think it's jealousy?" He looked at me and I said, "I don't know how it could be, sir. He's known them since they were born, and I'm positive his relationship with them is much deeper and more intimate—how could I possibly be a threat to the Vice President, especially since he and his wife are their godparents?"

"It's a fair question, and certainly one we haven't answered yet, sir," Nails said. "Motive is usually easy to nail down, but in this case it seems to be the only thing we haven't found out."

"Well, we don't need a motive to convict, and the rest of the case is airtight thanks to great investigative work and excellent prosecutorial skill and diligence," the AG said, giving Nails and Duquanye Quintanilla nods of appreciation.

We didn't get a chance to answer, because the door to the Oval banged open and the Warrior Princesses came out with their mother. They were both crying and the first lady looked like she had been. Their eyes all locked on mine, and then we were all crying and hugging. Finally the first lady said, "Freak, I'm so sorry. I don't know what got into Mitch—he's really not like that."

Both girls tried to apologize, too, but I shushed them and we hugged for a while in silence, until Charlie Hassenger said, "Ma'am, the president is about to go to the press room for the announcement."

Laura Flagler Sheehan disengaged herself from the group hug and said, "I hate to ask, but will you watch over the girls this afternoon, Freak?"

"Of course, ma'am," I said. I mean, what was I gonna say? No, I'm too busy tearing your family apart to be bothered with helping you? Go fuck yourself, I'm not going to look out for a couple of innocent girls because their godfather tried to kill me and mine twice? Satan get thee away from me, when in fact none of the Sheehan family had anything to do with the soon-to-be-former Vice President's actions?

I guess I'm just too soft at heart, because I couldn't do that (it's probably because I'm a namby-pamby liberal from a family of liberal pussies).

So I took the girls away from the White House while their father informed the country that his best friend and Vice President was a murderer who would soon be standing trial for same. We missed the president tearing up, we missed him courageously answering any and all questions that he could (hey, you don't have to like someone to admire his or her courage), and we missed the first lady creeping up beside him to hold his hand as he nearly broke down while answering the "What will you do without your best friend in Washington?" question.

We missed the president's incredible display of grace under pressure because we were busy shredding paper targets at the Secret Service Training Facility at the U.S. Treasury. I methodically cut stars, triangles and other geometric shapes out of my targets, while Brooke just as methodically sawed targets from crotch to the crown of their heads and Allison just obliterated the target's heads, after putting two ceremonial rounds in their chests.

Both the girls were shooting Glock 42s, a nicely balanced, smaller .380 semiauto pistol that fit their smaller hands, but that day they both wanted to move up to a bigger weapon, so I pulled two Glock 19s in 9mil from the armory. The 19 had a customizable grip, carried fifteen rounds in the magazine and was not very heavy, although it was heavier than the Warrior Princesses were used to.

Which turned out to not matter a bit.

The Warrior Princesses had about a five-shot (Brooke, who was a better natural shot) or six-shot (Allison, who actually had smaller hands) adjustment before they settled into their new weapons. I went and watched each of them in turn and offered shooting advice, then drilled them on specific-spot shooting and double-taps. Finally we had a 25-round shoot-off, with my handicap being that I had to loose all my rounds rapid-fire within a five second time frame.

I hit 24 of 25 in the 10-ring and one that was on the line between nine and ten. Brooke hit 19 bull's-eyes, with her other six rounds in the eight or nine ring, and Allison had her best day ever, hitting 21 bull's-eyes and the other four in a close group inside the nine ring.

Afterward we all took our cleaning kits, broke down our weapons, cleaned everything and then reassembled them. The girls carried theirs back to the armory agent and I stowed mine in their shoulder holsters.

We left the range and both girls wrapped me in hugs. We stood like that for a minute until finally Allison said, "Freak, we're sorry. We don't know what Uncle Mitch was doing, but we don't want you to be mad at us. We're truly sorry that he tried to kill you, because you're our friend."

"Probably our best friend," Brooke said.

"At least our best older friend," Allison said.

"I'm not that old," I said in my best mock protest voice.

We all laughed and Allison said, "You know what we mean, right? We love Uncle Mitch, but we love you just as much, and we don't want anyone to try and hurt you."

I looked at the two of them, these Warrior Princesses that I used to absolutely hate but now loved just as much and I said, "I know what you mean, and I also know that you're not responsible for anything that your Uncle Mitch did. I don't hold it against you, and I won't hold it against him, either, because I still don't know why he did it. Maybe he had a good reason, or thought that he had a good reason, because otherwise it just seems random to me. But you guys…you're my Warrior Princesses, and yeah, I love you, and yeah, I really will kill anybody who tries to hurt you, not because I'm supposed to but because, well, you're the little sisters I never had, and sisters take care of each other, period." Trite, maudlin, simpering—use any name you want, but I meant every fucking word, in spades, and fuck you, the horse you rode in on, and the family dog if you don't get it.

We all hugged and cried a little more, and then it was time to head back to the White House. We all went in and found the president and first lady waiting for us. The Man looked like he'd aged 10 years in the three hours since we saw him last, and the Ice Queen looked like somebody'd tried to melt her makeup off her face with a blowtorch. They both looked like they might throw up if they didn't stroke out first.

Both the president and the first lady shook my hand and thanked me for watching over the girls, and I said, "It's my pleasure, sir, ma'am. They're good young wymyn, and they can both shoot, too." My lame-o attempt at humor made them both laugh a little bit, and then the president said,

"Freak, I want to apologize for what Mitch—the Vice President—did to you, and to the people who died. I feel personally responsible even though I didn't know anything about it. I hope you know that I would have stopped Mitch if I'd known. I—I, well, I hope that you'll forgive me."

He looked so forlorn that I just about hugged him, but that was just too far outside the pale, even if I had known him since high school. So instead I looked at the president and his beautiful family (hey, the first lady may have been the Demon Bitch from Hell, but she was still good-looking, and besides, she was kinda growing on me) and I said, "Mr. President, there is nothing to forgive, and I would believe you if you told me that the moon was made of cheese. You are many things, sir, and one of the best is that you are an honest man. I would trust you with my life, Mr. President, and I know that you had nothing to do with anything that the Vice President did. It really is an honor to serve your family, and especially to guard your daughters, sir."

They all looked at me and started crying. After a while the president wiped his eyes and then blew his nose, and then he reached out and gripped my shoulders in a side-by-side "teammate" hug. We stood there for a few seconds and I could feel the president shaking with emotion. I imagined that he felt a lot like I did when I lost the Great Pumpkin, or when my *bubbe* and *zayde* died. I could tell he already felt lonely, which I guess shouldn't have surprised me—when you're President of the United States you can't have that many friends, and losing your best friend because he's a murderer must be a real kick in the balls (although I didn't have any first-hand knowledge of that, obviously).

The president, nodded at me and said, "Freak, I'm giving you a direct order as the Commander-in-Chief: take the next two days off. We're not leaving the House, we've got a massive protective detail and you need some time to yourself, so don't come in, don't think about us, just enjoy yourself. That's an order, Agent Glickstien."

I stood at attention and said, "Sir, yes, sir!" in my best Marine Corps voice. I waved at the Warrior Princesses, nodded to the first lady, turned around and walked right out of the White House to the Metro Center subway station that would take me home to my apartment. I was pretty excited about two straight days off, plus I was happy that we'd caught the son of a bitch that killed my friends, and the first family wasn't pissed about it. I was also happy that there was a nice twelve-ounce ribeye cooling off in my fridge at home, along with a dozen nice cold Pepsis and some really good potato salad that Hurricane had given me.

I should've remembered Wright's Law (that would be Steven Wright, the famous "Dog Named Stay" comedian): If everything seems to be going well, you have obviously overlooked something.

But I didn't, and it turned out that Steven Wright was right.

Dead right, in fact.

CHAPTER 71

The Bishop Lied at Midnight (and every other time)

The first day of my two days off went fabulously. Hurricane and Ed had time off, too, so we went out to Leesburg, Virginia to a joint called Windy City Red Hots to have Chicago style hot dogs and the Italian Combo, which is a nice Italian sausage covered in Italian beef and spiced with hot giardiniera, a mixture of pickled vegetables.

I had four Red Hots (Chicago dogs), two Maxwell Street Polish all the way (with everything) and one Italian combo, plus two fries, all washed down with a gallon of ice-cold Pepsi. It was heavenly, especially since my friends were also pigging out and enjoying it.

We drove back to D.C. by surface roads, went to the Tomb of the Unknown at Arlington National Cemetery to watch them change the guard and then walked the grounds looking for the graves of famous people—it turns out there were a shitload of them. We finally left the sprawling former home of Robert E. Lee at 5:30 p.m. (OK, so they kicked us out) after we found Thurgood Marshall's grave and began chanting "Our hero! Our hero! Our hero!' while bouncing up and down like third graders. Apparently someone thought we were making fun of Mr. Justice Marshall, or maybe they just objected to a black lesbian, an albino dwarf and a really ugly womyn making a spectacle of themselves at a sacred, solemn place. In any case, we never found out because when someone threatened to call security we just booked it out of there as fast as Hurricane's stubby little legs could carry her (OK, so I finally just picked her up and carried her piggy back—ain't nobody got time to wait for some dwarf to run half a mile).

We got back to our apartment building about 6:30 and went our separate ways. I fixed a nice salad for supper and then sat down to do something that I'd been unable to do since the second kidnapping attempt., because I simply hadn't had time to look at them: Bishop O'Dowd's journals that Father Fast Eddie Robinson had sent me from Battle Creek.

I'd only been reading for an hour when I got to the relevant part. I read it the first time and didn't get it, but then a couple of pages later it hit me, so I turned back and there it was, a *bona fide* clue as to the murder of my childhood friend Tim Miller.

The initials MG.

In the bishop's notes he wrote "MG at confession, says he did "terrible thing." Asked for absolution but couldn't grant it w/o knowing the thing in question. Still up in the air if he'll tell me despite sanctity of confessional."

The notes were written on a Monday, 12 May, exactly two days after Tim Miller was murdered.

It was the next set of notes that made it really stand out as a clue. Bishop O'Dowd wrote, "Saw MG at confession again. Told me that the terrible thing he did was unintentional, still no absolution because nature of thing is unknown, but I suspect it had to do with TM. Worried for mental state of MG."

TM.Tim Miller.

That asshole Bishop O'Dowd *knew* who murdered Tim Miller, and he not only didn't tell us, he *lied* about it, right to our faces. He'd also been lying to Mrs. Miller for over 20 years while she slowly deteriorated.

That motherfucking shithead son of a bitch.

I was so angry that I stopped reading, got my pistols and went to the range at headquarters, where I proceeded to shred targets until I'd shot an entire box of shells. I shredded eyes, hearts, balls, foreheads, cut the targets in four pieces, wrote the bishop's name across chests and shot out an outline of a man that looked like it'd been cut out with scissors.

When my anger finally dissipated enough that I could function I called Fast Eddie. He answered on the first ring and said, "I didn't know. They were his private notes—which he shouldn't have kept, by the way—and he never showed them to me when he was alive. I didn't know, Freak, or I swear that I would have told you."

I felt the last of my anger drain away. My old friend wasn't lying—he was the same age as I was, so he wasn't even a priest when Tim died, which meant he hadn't heard the confession that made the bishop nervous—and even if he had known it was up to the bishop to tell us the truth. It was his secret, not Fast Eddie's, which made Fast Eddie an innocent bystander who was trying to do the right thing, so I went easy on him.

"I believe you, Father Robinson. I'm not even mad at that son of a bitch O'Dowd anymore, although I'm not sure how it serves the Lord's higher purpose to lie to a poor womyn who lost her son and just wanted closure. Does that seem right to you?" I said.

"No," Fast Eddie said. "It also doesn't sound anything like the Bishop O'Dowd that I knew. I've racked my brain for some justification for what he did, but if it's out there I can't find it."

"Yeah, that doesn't jibe with the guy who praised Coach Horn for keeping his cool when the refs screwed up the call during the Harrison game and cost us a trip to Ford Field, does it?" I said.

"No, it sure doesn't. He was as sober as a judge and honest as the day is long—and he definitely lied to you, multiple times," Fast Eddie said.

"I haven't read that far. I've only gotten to the first part, about MG telling him about a "terrible thing" he did, and suspecting that it had something to do with TM. That has to be Tim Miller, right? Given the date and all?" I said.

"Yeah, it does—he explicitly writes it later," Fast Eddie said.

"What do you mean? He writes Tim's *name* in his journal?" I said.

"Yeah. The MG person finally tells him that he 'accidentally' caused the death of Tim Miller. The bishop wrote that he believed this MG, that he granted him absolution and that he would now have to wrestle with what to do about it," Fast Eddie said, his voice full of misery.

"What the fuck did that son of a bitch have to wrestle with? This MG admitted he *killed* Tim and the bishop didn't tell the cops? It's not the fucking asshole bishop's job to determine whether or not a crime was committed—that's a secular province, not a spiritual one. Are you telling me the bishop knew for a fact that this MG person *killed Tim* and he didn't tell anyone?" I said as my anger level began to climb again.

"Yeah, he knew and he told nobody corporeal. He did tell God and asked Him for advice, but as far as I can tell he never even told his own confessor. I called Big Bengt about it, and he said that the bishop was only considered tangentially involved. He was never a suspect, so nobody ever interviewed him. Given the way the Old Man felt about the sanctity of the confessional I'm not surprised. Even if he could've proven a crime had been committed I doubt that he would've said anything about it even under direct questioning. The Old Man was old-school about these kinds of things—you knew him a little bit, so you know that," Fast Eddie said.

I heard the pain and distress in his voice and my anger just evaporated. I would probably always be a little bit pissed off at Bishop O'Dowd for what he'd done to Mrs. Miller, but it wouldn't help to give Fast Eddie shit—he was trying to help, after all, and he had nothing to do with the whole thing—so I said, "It's OK, Eddie, I understand. Besides, fear leads to anger, anger leads to hatred and hatred…"

"Leads to the Dark Side," he said. "Yoda was one smart dude, and he was right, then and now. I'm very disappointed in the Old Man, but I can't bring myself to hate him—and I know you won't do that either. Your Mumsy and Pops would kick your ass, and your *zayde* would come back to haunt you, right?"

"'Zxactly," I said, just like I did when we were kids (for some unknown reason I could never say the word 'exactly,' so I said 'Zxactly' instead. Another Freak idiosyncrasy.) We both laughed and I said, "So who the fuck is MG? I don't remember anyone with those initials."

"Me, either," Fast Eddie said. "I've been wracking my brain and coming up empty. I asked Big Bengt to re-examine the file, because he couldn't remember anyone involved with the investigation with the initials MG, either. He said he'd check and probably just get back with you—no sense in playing telephone with the info, right?"

"Right. Keep thinking about it, OK? And if you come up with anything call me any time," I said.

"Roger, wilco, Freak. I'm truly sorry about what the Old Man did," Fast Eddie said.

"Ah, fuck it. You did everything you could to make it right, and he was only doing what he thought was right, the asshole. And notice I didn't say total asshole. I know the bishop was a good guy, and that he was good to you," I said.

"He was an asshole about this. Mrs. Miller looks to be on her last legs, and this is why," Fast Eddie said. "I loved him like a father—no pun intended—but he was a real shithead about this. I guess that just proves that no one is perfect."

"Truer words were never spoken," I said. Just then my call waiting lit up—it was Jewey—so I told Fast Eddie adios and switched over to the other call.

"Hey, Jewey," I said.

"Hey Freak. I've got Joe, Weasel and Mamba on the line, too. We've kinda got some bad news for ya," Jewey said.

"No shit? Let me guess—the motherfucking bishop of Battle Creek fucking lied to us, the asshole shithead son of a bitch. He knew who killed Tim Miller and didn't tell anybody about it, and now we need to find some asshole with the initials MG, only there's shit-all about it in the goddamned file," I said.

There was dead silence on the phone, until Weasel said, "Nobody likes a know-it-all, Freak."

"Sorry, Weasel. I just got off the phone with Fast Eddie, who told me what he knew, which isn't shit, plus I was reading the notes myself," I said.

"OK, so we're all on the same page here, but what I don't get is why the bishop would protect someone in a case like this," Joe said. "I was born and raised Catholic. All the churchmen I ever knew put the secular truth above everything except the redeeming power of Christ, because to them that was the ultimate truth…but even that tenet would seem to require the bishop to tell someone about it—and don't hit me with the "he told God" shit, because that's not what I'm talking about and you smartasses know it."

"That's especially true of Bishop O'Dowd, because he was tied into the power structure of Battle Creek. He played cards with the chief of police, he married the fire chief and his wife, he helped the county sheriff bury his wife after attending to her as she died of cancer—the guy was on a first name basis with everybody who was anybody in town, so it wasn't like he lacked people he trusted to tell," I said.

"And I'm pretty sure that the sanctity of the confessional doesn't include ongoing criminal behavior, or future behavior," Mamba said. "At least that's what I remember from my time as a Catholic."

"Oy, vey!" Jewey said. "I can't even imagine that picture—Monsieur le Comte in the confessional? Wouldn't you need to have a team of cardinals to hear your confession?"

"And about 27 hours?" Weasel said.

"And wouldn't you have to make sure that the cardinals didn't blush?" I said.

"All of the above and more, which is why I now hang out with a bunch of lowlifes who have no reasonable way to get all judgmental on me without indicting themselves," Mamba said.

"Fair point," Jewey said, "but we still need to figure out who this MG is in relation to the bishop. I've read that file over one hundred times—so has Weasel—and we can't find anyone who even remotely fits. The only "G" in the file is some lady named Amy Gleason. She was eighty-four at the time of the murder, is now deceased and was interviewed because she lived at the end of Tim Miller's street and might have seen someone."

"Well, she most certainly didn't see anyone—old Mrs. Gleason was literally stone blind," I said. "I'll bet the state police interviewed her and she gave them nothing."

"Absolutely true," Weasel said. "There were two "M"s in the file: Mike Atherton, wrestling teammate of Tim, and Mickey Trout, ditto. Neither one contributed anything except for the fact that Tim Miller was envied by his teammates because he was sleeping with Kristy O'Dowd. Apparently she was quite the biscuit back in the day."

"Apart from the mixing of decade-speak, that would be accurate. She was beyond beautiful for Battle Creek, and especially for the chicks at Fighting Beaver High," I said. "A couple of semi-pretty boys like Mikey and Mickey would've given 10 years of their lives to be carrying on with Kristy, but they wouldn't've had the balls to do anything about it."

"Because both of them were Catholic boys, and the bishop would've scared the fucking bejeezus out of them," Joe said.

"Spot on, old stick," I said in my horrible English accent.

"So who the fuck was—I guess *is*—the mysterious MG?" Jewey said. "Do you suppose we could get a list of parishioners from back then and look at it?"

"Even if there was such a thing—which is doubtful—Fast Eddie would've already looked at it," Mamba said.

"Yeah, and he would've mentioned it to me when we talked just now," I said.

"Freak, is there anybody you could talk to from back then who might at least remember the Catholic community? Somebody who might recall something about the people who regularly came to confession?" Joe said.

I thought about it and had a "eureka!" moment.

Mr. Munson.

Fred Munson was the lector at St. Philip's church in Battle Creek for at least 187 years, and he had a mind like a steel trap, because he was one of the world's foremost experts on memory. Mr. Munson was actually Dr. Fredrick C. Munson, MD, PhD, a former big-time college professor (at UCLA) who got fed up with the rat-race of academia and moved home to actually teach psychology at Kellogg Community College for 152 years.

Dr. Dr. Munson was also a Catholic man. He'd been a fixture reading the scriptures at St. Phil's for so long that he became like a piece of the building. He also greeted everyone who ever came in the door, every Sunday, and also thanked everybody when they left the church, every Sunday—and I'd bet money that he knew all of their names.

"Tell you what—I might have somebody," I said. "Let me call him and I'll call you right back, OK? Keep thinking about it, because this guy will either know or he won't."

"Roger that. Badger Squad on active standby," Joe said.

"Copy that. Freak out," I said.

"Not until we solve this fucking case," Weasel said.

I was still laughing when I called my Pops to ask about Dr. Dr. Munson. Pops told me that he was still teaching, lecturing and going all over the world to talk about how to build and access memories.

"He's even done one of those TED talks on You Tube," Pops said. "It was very interesting and helpful. Even if I get Alzheimer's I doubt if I'll forget your Mumsy's name."

"Wow, Pops, that's really inspirational. You're not getting Alzheimer's, and we'll just tattoo Mumsy's name on the back of your hand if you do, right before we shuffle you off to the warehouse." Pops always called retirement homes warehouses, claiming that all American children wanted was "out of sight, out of mind" places for their parents to go so they could assuage their guilt. I'm not sure that he wasn't at least partly right.

"In any case, Fred's mind and body are still really sound. He's been helping on political campaigns and writing new books and singing with his rock band, plus he still teaches full time, so I'd say that if anybody could remember somebody with the initials MG it'd be Double Doctor," Pops said.

I got Dr. Dr. Munson's number, thanked Pops and called the old lector.

Who was absolutely no help.

He answered on the first ring. I explained who I was and what I needed and Double Doctor Munson reviewed everything in the memory banks but came up blank.

After twenty minutes of searching Double Doctor said, "Freak, the only M.G. who remotely fits the criteria for killing Tim Miller is his cousin Morgan Gilley, and I don't think that a 12-year-old, 95-pound girl is capable of strangling a 190-pound varsity football player and wrestler, and besides, Lil' Morgy was playing keyboards for us all night when Tim was murdered. No way she slipped away, and again—95 pounds against the physical prowess of Tim? No way I buy it."

I couldn't help but agree with him—Morgan Gilley was still only 5'6", 125 pounds, and she still played with Double Doctor and the Rock Hammers, a pretty good rock band that was locally known from Lansing to Grand Haven and all parts in between. I'd heard them play lots of times and I'd met Lil' Morgy and she just wasn't the type to be able to overpower someone as big and strong as her cousin Tim Miller.

I thanked Double Doctor for his help and was going to hang up when he said, "You know, maybe it's a nickname, or title, instead of a name. I'm not sure of that because Liam—the bishop—wasn't big on that kind of thing, but it could be." I thought about it and realized that it was causing a slow itch in my brain. I could tell that I knew something that related to the nickname thing, but I couldn't retrieve it, which was ironic considering that I was talking to a memory expert.

"I'll keep that in mind, Dr. Munson," I said, "Thanks again for your help."

"Call me anytime, Freak," he said.

I hung up and called the Badger Squad back. I immediately told them Double Doctor's idea about it being a nickname or title, which launched a frenzied round of out-loud conjecturing. We went on brainstorming for at least twenty minutes before Jewey said, "Hey, wait a minute. We're talking about Catholics, right? Tim was a Catholic and obviously so was the bishop."

"It took you this long to figure that out? What are ya, a genius or something?" Weasel said.

"Wait a minute," I said, "I get it, Jewey."

"Me, too," Joe said. "Great catch, Jewey. I'd a never got the connection in a million years."

"OK, slow Asian here. What the fuck are you guys talking about?" Weasel said.

"Aaahhh, yesss," Mamba said. "Weasel, what happens to all Catholics when they get baptized?"

"How the fuck should I know? I'm a fucking Buddhist," Weasel said. "I mean, they get up with their parents and godparents and the priest says some words, and they anoint the baby with holy... Holy fuck! They stand up with their parents and *godparents*."

"Precisely," Jewey said. "And the male godparent of an incipient Catholic boy would call him..."

"MY GODSON!" we all said, sounding like a bad gospel choir.

"Amen," Jewey said, "my godson, a.k.a. MG."

"Joe or Mamba, can a bishop have a godson?" I said. Hey, I'm Jewish—what the fuck did I know about Catholic bishops?

"Anyone who's baptized can be a god parent, including any clergy," Joe said.

"That's true. My grandfather's godfather was the Cardinal Archbishop of Chartres," Mamba said. "My cousin Armand de Coucy's godfather is the Archbishop of Rheims, so it would seem that an American bishop could be one, too."

"Now all we need to do is find out if the bishop had any godsons," Weasel said.

"How the fuck are we going to do that—wander the streets of Battle Creek asking people? Or is there some kind of Catholic list service where they keep track of shit like that?" Jewey said. "Sorry Joe, Mamba, I didn't mean that being baptized and having godparents was shit."

"Got it, Jewey. You mean shit as a substitute for stuff, and yes, there is a listserv for that. It's called the parish records—all churches within the diocese will have a record of who the godparents are of every child ever baptized. The problem is that most of those records will be kept in Bibles or ledgers—we'll have to look at every single one by hand," Joe said.

"Maybe. Fast Eddie was a computer science major in college before he became a priest, and he got his masters in information systems. It's possible that he's computerized the system for the diocese," I said.

"I'd say it was probable," Joe said. The line got real quiet, real quickly, and I realized why just as quickly.

"You don't want to ask Fast Eddie because he's friends with all the players," I said.

"He's at least not an unbiased, trained observer," Joe said.

"And we need somebody who'll know what they're seeing when they look at it, and the father isn't the guy who's been poring over this large raft of shit for a while now," Weasel said.

"So it makes sense that someone who has been poring over this shit does it," Jewey said.

"Like one of us, or better, Detective Lieutenant Bengt Olafsson, BCPD," Mamba said. "He knows all the players, has an investigative mind and can give us a good read on just how many people we'll have to dig in on once we get the names of all the bishop's godsons, assuming there are any."

"I'll call him right now—you guys hang on hold," I said. I dialed Bengt, got his office and then got him.

"Freak, how areya? You in town, or areya still out there in the puzzle palace land?" Bengt said. He sounded positively cheery, so I took a chance that his wife was pregnant again and said, "I'm still here in the land of obfuscation, Big Man. When's Sarah due with number four?"

The big detective lieutenant laughed his huge Norwegian belly laugh and said, "It shows that bad, eh? Well, she's going to bring another boy into this world in just four months. We were both really surprised, because the doc said I was nearly shootin' blanks—but I guess we'll have four-fifths of an offensive line soon. Sarah did tell me that we're both gettin' our tubes tied after this one, just in case one of the procedures doesn't take." We both laughed and I thought of four of Bengt on a high school offensive line—four kids 6'8", 290 with brains—holy shit!

After we were both done laughing I said, "Congratulations, Big Man. I'm glad Sarah's finally putting her foot down about this—you aren't going to be able to retire until you're 75 as it is." There was more laughter and then Bengt said, "So whaddya need, Freak? This can't just be social, right?"

"No, although I don't mind catching up with you. It always reminds me of how great it was, growing up a Fighting Beaver. Anyway, what I need is this: we need to find out if Bishop O'Dowd had any godsons, and if so, who they were," I said, hoping my old friend wouldn't get it, but knowing that he probably would. Bengt was always smart, and he didn't make lieutenant of detectives in a place like Battle Creek by being stupid.

"So you think you found somethin' in the bishop's old files, eh? And you want to keep it from Fast Eddie because you don't know how he'll react if it's a friend?" Bengt said. So much for the generalization about big, dumb football players.

"Yeah, that's it in a nutshell. We need you to find out if there's a database and then search it for anyone who's the bishop's godson. We're not sure, but we think that fits a reference in his notes to a mysterioUS "MG" who did something bad around the time Tim Miller died. The bishop makes a direct reference to it in his notes in several places," I said. My phone beeped—call waiting from Weasel—so I said, "Hold on a sec, Bengt—I'm going to cut Weasel and the guys in on this call."

I made the necessary fiddles with the phone and we were all on a conference call. Weasel didn't even say hello, he just said, "We've confirmed it—the bishop's MG is definitely his godson, and he definitely confessed to being a part of Tim Miller's death, although the bishop claims that his godson told him it was an accident. We need those names ASAP—they'll solve the case, Freak."

Big Bengt said, "Hey, Weasel, guys, it's Bengt. I'm going to look for those records right now. I'll get back to ya as soon as I'm done, OK?"

"Sounds great, Big Man. If you need help cracking into a protected database you got my number," Weasel said. "Not that I would do anything like that, but hypothetically."

We all laughed when Joe said, "Ah, yeah, yeah, that's it—hypothetically," echoing a great Jon Lovitz sketch from Saturday Night Live.

Bengt hung up, but the rest of us all hung out on the phone so I could hear about the new discoveries in the bishop's notes. When Jewey read them to us there was no ambiguity:

> *My godson has done something terrible—he was involved in the death of young Tim Miller, although he claims it was an accident and not murder. He finally told me the truth, without any justification for his actions at all except to say that he did not mean at all to hurt Tim. While I believe him I am still in a quandary—is the crime ongoing since the police have no leads at all, or is it a crime of the past that is protected by the sanctity of the confessional? I must pray over this and let God guide me.*

"We haven't found any place where he acknowledges anything else about it, but I don't think that makes any difference," Jewey said.

"I'm not an attorney, but that seems to be pretty damning evidence," Weasel said. "If we can find which of the bishop's godsons was there at the time of the murder we should be able to at least arrest them and force a DNA sample, which should convict them once we establish motive."

"Well, I am an attorney, and we've got plenty of evidence if we can find a suspect. There could be an elected judge out there in East Bumfuck, Michigan that might not admit the bishop's notes, but if we provide some foundation they'll have a hard time trying to exclude them, as long as Fast Eddie testifies as to chain of custody," Mamba said.

"And with any luck at all we'll find the guy, he'll be alive and we'll arrest his murderous ass and he'll crack once he contemplates life in Jackson State Prison," Weasel said.

"It is the world's largest walled prison," I said, "and it's filled with tough motherfuckers who would like nothing better than making our friend's acquaintance face-to-face."

"Or perhaps front to rear?" Jewey said.

"We can only hope, the motherfucking shithead," Mamba said.

"Such language for an erudite French nobleman," Weasel said.

"This guy has just made me so angry with his treatment of the poor widow Miller that I am really not myself." Mamba said. "Perhaps later we could apply some top-quality alcoholic beverages to alleviate my distress?"

"That's the fucking spirit!" Jewey said.

"Awww, c'mon!" Joe said. "That's a terrible pun, although I have to agree with the spirit of the statement."

"Stop with the fucking puns, willya? I'm trying to think about 17-year-old Scotch, or else really fine, cold beer," Weasel said.

"Does that mean that we're going to try for face plant territory?" Weasel said.

"Only if we find out who this asshole is and solve the case," Joe said. "Otherwise it's just a couple of Laophraig's and home."

"Aw, c'mon, mom. I wanna, like, get shitfaced," Jewey said in his best imitation of a California "Valley Girl" accent (which was both dated and horrible).

We still laughed.

After some more banter we decided that Bengt wasn't calling back right away, so we all rang off after agreeing to meet the next day for lunch.

I went into Virginia to the Steven F. Udvar-Hazy Center—the annex to the Air and Space Museum on the national mall—to see the space shuttle *Discovery* (among many other cool aircraft), and then went to the Mall and visited my old friends the National Portrait Gallery and the Holocaust Museum. I was between boyfriends so I did everything by myself, but the solitude among the throngs of people at the museums and memorials felt kind of good. When everything started closing I went to Legal Seafood and had an excellent dinner and then went home. I read for a couple of hours and then went to bed around eleven.

I got two whole hours of sleep.

My phone went off at exactly 1:07 a.m.

As is usual with phone calls at this hour it wasn't good news. In fact, the news was so bad that it would shake the world to its foundations, and no, that isn't hyperbole or melodrama.

Unfortunately, it was just the fucking truth.

CHAPTER 72

Shit Sandwich, Anyone?

I pawed the phone off the table on the third ring and said, "This better be the goddamned White House switchboard or somebody's goin' to emergency."

It was Bengt. "Come and get me at the airport, agent," he said in a very low voice.

"What the fuck, Be-" I said.

He cut me off and said, "No names, agent. I'm in the Delta terminal at Reagan." Before I could even respond he'd hung up.

What the fuck? It felt like I'd woken up in a spy novel after going to sleep in the real world. I didn't know what the problem was, but I'd be damned if I'd go through it alone, so I called Joe and told him to get the Badger Squad out to the Delta terminal at Reagan. Like the great agent he was Joe never even asked why, he just said "Wilco" and hung up.

I dressed in my agent clothes, put on my shoulder holsters, filled them with my 1076s and headed out to Reagan International Airport. Even at 1:16 a.m. the roads out were crowded, but they actually thinned out when I got closer to the airport. I found the Delta terminal, parked my Secret Service car in the ramp like anybody else and went in.

It was impossible to miss Bengt—6'8" redheads aren't all that common, even in D.C., especially at two o'clock in the morning. I walked toward him and he saw me. Looking completely natural Bengt brushed his nose with his left hand—an old signal from when we were in high school that meant "trouble—avoid me," so I stopped and tied my shoe—"message received and understood"—and then walked right past him to take a seat next to the windows.

We'd only been ignoring each other three or four minutes when I saw the Badger Squad walking toward us in the reflection of the spotless airport glass. I stood up, Bengt stood up and Jewey raised both his hands above his shoulders and said, "So *nu*, Bengt? The airport at two? We couldn't meet at a civilized hour?" (For the goyim among us '*nu*' is Yiddish for "what's up"? In this context it meant "what the fuck?" but that's not something that you just blurt out in a nearly deserted airport, even if you are Secret Service.)

My old friend raised a hand and then put it to his lips like he was thinking, but what he meant was to be quiet. The rest of us shut up and Bengt took out his cell phone and put it in the shoulder bag he was carrying. As he walked past us toward the exits to the terminal he held the bag open and pointed to it. We walked along beside him and all put our phones in the bag, too. We came to a bank of coin lockers and Bengt stuffed the bag in one. He took the key and made a beeline for the nearest men's room.

We all followed him like baby ducks following their mama, even when he went in. A security guard saw me and came right over to stop us, but I held him off with my Secret Service creds. "We're on the job here—sorry about the men's room, but all the conference rooms were full." He smiled and nodded and I followed the guys in.

Bengt didn't even say hello. He just looked at me and said, "Remember dat I have a wife, t'ree children an' another on da way, OK?"

"OK, Bengt. What the fuck is going on?" I said.

He looked at me and I saw that he was afraid, like really, truly, bone-deep afraid. I had a bad feeling about what he was going to say next, but all he said was "What's da president's name, Freak?"

"James Sheehan," I said. "So? Again, what the fuck, Bengt?"

"What's da president's *full* name?" he said.

"James Patrick Liam Sheehan," I said. "What the fu—" I said, my voice involuntarily stopping as an awful thought hit me like a ton of bricks. I looked back at my old friend and knew why he was afraid, because I was just as afraid.

"Oh, fuck me," Joe said as it hit him, too. His voice was shaky and his face was red as the implications of Bengt's question hit him.

"What the hell is wrong with you guys?" Mamba said. "Did you find out who the bishop's godsons are?"

"What was da bishop's *full* name, Freak?" Bengt said.

"Padraig Liam O'Dowd," I said.

"Oh, fuck me," Jewey and Mamba said together. Nobody said anything about Pepsis, mainly because we all felt like we were going to puke.

Weasel still didn't get it, so he said, "OK, what the fuck are you assholes on about? You all look like your dog just died. Give it up to the slow Asian computer genius, willya?"

"Bishop O'Dowd only ha' one godson, a young man named James Patrick Liam Sheehan," Bengt said. "Y'know him better as da President of da United States."

"Oh, fuck the world," Weasel said.

"Fuck me black, blue and blind," Jewey said.

"Fuck me with the Washington Monument," Mamba said.

"Fuck that traitorous bishop with a goddamned duck," Joe said.

"The president killed Tim Miller and the bishop covered it up, and now we're as sincerely fucked as Custer," I said.

"What the fuck was his motive?" Weasel said. "What made a future president of the United States just kill somebody?"

"Kristy O'Dowd," the rest of us said. "Ya owe us a Pepsi, Freak," Bengt said. There was a ghost of a smile on his face, along with the fear we all felt.

"Come on—wasn't he the BMOC at Michigan by the time Tim was killed?" Weasel said. "A guy like that would be hip-deep in pussy before he even played in a game, much less before he beat Ohio State as a freshman."

"Yeah, but what if he *loved* Kristy? It isn't unheard of that a guy loves a girl, thinks the feeling is reciprocated, goes off to college, comes home and finds her fucking some other guy and goes apeshit," Jewey said.

"With the caliber of wymyn he's going to be fucking at *Michigan*? Doesn't that seem just a little bit ridiculous?" Mamba said.

"You underestimate the beauty of Kristy O'Dowd," I said. "She was the best-looking girl in Battle Creek, and maybe the state of Michigan. If she hadn't fallen during her dance routine she would certainly have won the Miss Michigan pageant and been in the Miss America pageant."

"All you've seen is da tired, old Kristy," Bengt said. "Freak's no' kiddin'—grown men made fools a t'emselves when she was around. She caused a riot once when she was swimming against Marshall High because of her bodysuit. T'ink Helen of Troy, guys."

"Bengt's not wrong. She was gorgeous, and if she'd been giving up the biscuit to the pres—er, young Jimmy Sheehan and he found out that she was fucking Tim Miller there's no telling how much rage that might generate," I said.

"And the scenario is easy to see," Joe said. "He goes looking for Kristy, finds her fucking Tim, waits until she leaves and then kills Tim in a fit of jealous rage. He certainly had the strength and size to fit the profile."

"And he's got the biggest hands I've ever seen," I said. "Even compared to Square Peg the president's hands are enormous, and that was one of the definitive things in the coroner's report—somebody with huge, tremendously strong hands killed Tim Miller."

"Oy, vey gevalt!" Jewey said. "This is a giant shit sandwich."

"And us with no mayonnaise," Mamba said.

"We'd need lots and lots of horseradish to cover up the taste of this particular shit sandwich," Weasel said.

"Unfortunately there's plenty to go around," I said.

"I'd rather be in Minnesota," Bengt said. We all agreed with him in one form or another, and then Joe said what we were all thinking.

"Still think that we have more than enough proof to get a conviction?" Joe said to Mamba.

"Hell no!" Mamba said. "Given who it is we don't even have enough evidence to whisper about it outside this john. I'm not even sure that we shouldn't sweep the john for bugs before we say anything else." He was joking, but we all took his point: we were hunting big game, and if we shot at it we couldn't miss, or we'd be trampled into oblivion, or at least clapped into federal prison, or worse, we'd be transferred to West Bumfuck, Utah (sorry, Utah. I could've said North Dakota, but then I thought of all those Mormons…and Utah won—or lost, depending on your perspective) and then clapped into federal prison.

Given what had already happened to us we might even die, which made Bengt's behavior understandable.

I looked at the rest of the group and said, "First thing: Bengt's out, right fucking now. He isn't going to have anything more to do with our investigation and if asked about him our response will be 'Bengt who?'"

"Agreed," Joe said. "We can't put you in the line of fire, big guy, because the guy doing the shooting owns the U.S. military and intelligence apparatus. We're going to discover who the bishop's godson is when we investigate Fast Eddie's database. You never even knew the database existed, right?"

"Well, I 'preciate it, but I don' t'ink we can hide it, since Fast Eddie knows, an' da parish office, an' da lector, and m'wife, and, well, just about anybody who really looks will find me dere. So I'm on da hook, but I'm goin' ta act like a stupid Norwegian an' tell everybody who asks dat I din't find any godsons for da bishop," Bengt said.

"But all anyone has to do is look at the database and they'll know that you're lying," Jewey said.

"Unless my Asian or Jewish computer genius friends erase me an' da entry from da database," Bengt said.

The two computer savants looked at each other and Weasel said, "Goddamn computers are unreliable! Whole pages of databases get misfiled and nobody can find them."

"It's a national fucking tragedy," Jewey said. "To think that so much data is compromised on a daily basis is just sickening."

"If only there was a way that we could help stop that, like if Bengt left his computer in Battle Creek on we could remote in and fix his problem," Weasel said.

"Ah, fuck, I left my computer in BC on, Freak. I'm gonna have ta go home and shut it off," Bengt said.

"And what did you fly all the way out here for?" I said.

"I needed ta give a deposition ta da Secret Service about da counterfeiting operation dat I helped bust, because dey're aboot ta close da appeal of Leona Tromboli, an' some defense lawyer might raise a point aboot my involvement, so rather den make me fly out when it's inconvenient I jus' flew out while my wife an' kids are visitin' her parents in Minnesota so I could get da whole t'ing done. My old friend Freak an' my new friends decided ta take me out for an early breakfast before da deposition," Bengt said.

"Ah, that'll do, Bengt, that'll do," I said, trying to sound like James Cromwell in the movie *Babe*.

"I'm not sure dat I like being complimented like I'm an animatronic pig, but it's better den a sharp stick in da eye," Bengt said.

We all laughed, but then reality came back with a bang.

"Before we say any more let's agree on a code name for the subject of our investigation," Joe said.

"I vote for Little Jimmy, or LJ for short," Mamba said.

"Perfect," Joe said. "Succinct, descriptive, but still kinda cryptic."

"We also need to agree that nothing will be done over email or the phone, no matter the encryption," Weasel said, "'cause we all know that if a human made it a human can break it, and this ain't the kinda thing ya want broken."

"Ya can say dat again," Bengt said.

"We also need to agree that nothing will be done until we strike gold, and gold only," Weasel said.

"Fuck you, Weasel. I agree we need some levity, but are we really saying that we're going to investigate the president of the United States for a 20-year-old murder?" Jewey said. He wasn't incredulous, he just wanted clarity.

"Yes, yes we are, Jewey, and we're doing it in secret, and we're going to find out what the fuck happened and we're going to at least tell Mrs. Miller that we've got a credible lead on her son's murderer, and when this son of a bitch Sheehan leaves office we're going to arrest his fucking narrow white ass and send him to fucking prison for as fucking long as that motherfucker fucking lives," I said. Yes, my "fuck" quotient was up, but I'd had enough of poor Mrs. Miller getting fucked over by some golden boy, even if that asshole was from my high school and hometown. I wanted justice for the poor womyn whose whole life had been one big shit sandwich since her son was murdered.

"I'm wi' ya, Freak. I want justice for Mrs. Miller, an' Timmy. He was a good boy who never hurt no one," Bengt said.

"I also want justice for Mrs. Miller and Tim," Mamba said, "and I swear on my life as Almont Phillipe Gilbert de Coucy, the Comte de Condé that it will be so, even if the president and all his minions stand in the way." Mamba kissed his signet ring and glared at all of us from his full 5',2½", defying any of us to laugh or contradict him.

No one did.

"I'm for justice in every case, not just once in a while or for certain people, so I'm going to agree with all of you and press on for Mrs. Miller and Tim," Jewey said.

"Đừng đứng entre le con rồng và con mồi của mình," Weasel said.

"What the fuck is that, ya Asian asshole?" I said.

"It's Vietnamese for "Do not stand between the dragon and his prey," but it means that I want justice too, for Tim and Mrs. Miller," Weasel said. "I'm willing to sacrifice my life to get justice, if necessary."

"Why?" Mamba said. "You only barely know Tim and you've only met Mrs. Miller once. What's your motivation?"

"Part of it's because where my parents came from there was no justice. My grandfather, three of my uncles and two of my aunties were "disappeared" by the godless commies who ruled Vietnam, just because they weren't important. My father was tortured because he translated for the Americans, and there were lots of other bad things that happened, but I really just agree with Dr. King."

"'Injustice anywhere is a threat to justice everywhere'?" I said.

"Yeah, that's it," Weasel said. "Plus, every time I think of Mrs. Miller I think about my poor grandmother, who sat by the door of their home waiting for my grandfather to come home. When my dad got us out of that hellhole my grandmother wouldn't come at first, because she was sure that my grandfather would come home if she just waited long enough. My dad and I finally just physically hauled her to the boat to leave, and when we got to California she just set her chair up right by the door and watched for him until she died. So I want justice for my grandmother and Mrs. Miller and Tim." We were all crying by that point, and we all hugged Weasel.

Finally I stuck my hand out and said, "Justice for Mrs. Miller and Tim." Everybody else put a hand in and I said, "Mrs. Miller, on three!" and then I counted and we all yelled "Mrs. Miller!" We repeated it for Tim, and for justice, and for Weasel's grandfather, and then we all got the hell outta Dodge. Bengt flew back to Michigan and the rest of us headed back for DC, where we started making a secret case for murder against the president of the United States.

It wasn't the smartest thing we ever did, but it was the absolute right thing to do. The only problem was, we just didn't know how much blood it would take to get the job done.

Unfortunately we found out the hard way.

CHAPTER 73

Revelations from Deep in the Closet

So we all went to bed that night riled up, and the next day we all woke up pissed off, and by noon we'd all decided that we had no idea how to proceed, so I got elected to talk to A-USA Brenda T. Green and feel her out about how one would arrest a sitting president.

I called her and she agreed to meet me for lunch, but I told her it couldn't be anywhere in D.C., so she suggested that we try to catch the Windy City Red Hots truck in Ashburn, Virginia, and I agreed, because hey, you can never have too many Chicago dogs, or Italian beef, or Maxwell Street Polish all the way.

So we arrived separately in Ashburn, met up and went around in her car until we found the food truck. We got our orders (three Chicago dogs, two Maxwell Streets, two Italian combos with giardiniera and five cold Pepsis for me, one Italian beef for her—Brenda T. was a legal heavyweight, but she was a pussy when it came to eating) and went to sit in a nice little park near the truck.

The sky was mostly clear with just a few fluffy clouds, the temperature cool but not cold and there was a fountain burbling gently in the background when I said, "So can the president be arrested for murder?"

Brenda T. Green stopped eating her Italian beef and said, "Hypothetically, of course." I just looked back her like Teddy Roosevelt on Mt. Rushmore. She ate another bite of sandwich and said, "So the quick answer is yes, because of the concept of limited government set forth by John Locke during the Enlightenment and adopted by our Founding Fathers. You understand the concept of limited government?"

"Sure," I said. When your family has as many lawyers as mine you pick up things. "Locke said that all political power is derived from the people, and that since the government is just the people the government has to follow the law like anybody else. That really means that neither the government nor anybody in the government is above the law, with a few exceptions."

"Right. So yes, since there is the no statute limiting judicial actions against the president or anyone else you could *theoretically* arrest a president for a crime," Brenda T. said. She stopped talking and watched me while I annihilated a Maxwell Street Polish and an Italian combo. I finished, drank off most of a Pepsi and then politely belched, but I didn't say anything.

Finally Brenda T. said, "OK, Freak, I'll bite. What the fuck is with this cryptic routine?"

I looked at her and said, "Your mission, Ms. Green, should you choose to accept it, is to prove that the current President of the United States committed murder when he was twenty-one years old and then engaged in a conspiracy to cover up his actions." I was smiling as I said, "This tape will self-destruct in fifteen seconds." (My thanks to the old *Mission: Impossible* TV series.)

The Assistant U.S. Attorney was definitely not smiling as she looked back at me. I could see the wheels turning as she went over things—like how her life would go right down the shitter if she bought whatever I was selling and it turned out to be pure bullshit. Finally she said, "OK. Let's say for one second—just for the sake of argument and purely hypothetically—that I might want to do such a thing. What kind of proof are we talking about?"

So I told her the hypothetical story of a young man who went into a jealous rage when he found what he thought was his exclusive paramour fucking someone else, and how he confronted this usurper of his girlfriend's pulchritude and either (a) on purpose or (b) accidentally killed him. I told her about how we discovered this, about the cover up with the bishop and about how we were even now trying to run down details that might confirm our beliefs. I also told her about how a poor, old widow in Battle Creek, Michigan, was even now winding down her poor, wretched life because she had never gotten justice for her son.

Brenda T. Green looked at me without blinking, but her eyes were full of fire. Finally she said, "Let's say that I buy all of this. What details could you find out that might corroborate the story in the bishop's journals?"

So I told her what was happening with the Badger Squad as we spoke. As I was relating that part my phone rang. The caller ID showed Mamba's number, so I said, "This might be something now" and I took the call and put it on speaker.

"So Ed called me because she had a thought, and I listened to her and then we called some other people we knew and then we decided to call Square Peg, who sort of confirmed our thoughts and we needed to tell you, and we think we need to talk to Duquanye or Brenda T. because we think that we figured something important out about the whole Sorenson slash Holland *mishegoss*," Mamba said without drawing a breath.

"*Oy*, listen to the *goy* with the Yiddish," I said. "And you a baptized person and all."

"Well, I'm a got-damned baptized Baptist, and I also think that *mishegoss* is the correct term for this shit," Ed said. "But what's important is that you remember that Mamba and I are baptized *gay* persons."

"So? What the hell does that have to do with anything? Also, what the hell could Square Peg have to contribute to this case?" I said. I wasn't really as perplexed as I should be, because there had been something hovering at the edge of my consciousness about all of this for some time now.

"In a minute," Mamba said. "How long have the president and Holland been best friends?"

"Since they went to Michigan and joined the same frat," I said.

"And what frat was that?" Ed said.

"How the fuck should I know? I went to Michigan State, and my frat was track and field, and wrestling, and football that one year. What the fuck difference does it make?"

"It was Iota Lambda Omega," Mamba said.

"Hey, Brenda T. Green here. This is fascinating shit, but what the hell does it have to do with the price of tea in China?"

"It turns out that Iota Lambda Omega had some really, really high-powered individuals in it, including two Academy Award winning actors, several captains of industry, lots of elite athletes who went on to professional or Olympic glory, several famous authors, including two Pulitzer Prize winners and one Nobel Laureate, and of, course both a Vice President and President of the United States," Ed said.

Suddenly it hit me. The thought that had been forming in the back of my mind jumped right to the front of the queue. I smiled because I knew what they were going to say next.

"Again, big fucking deal," Brenda T. said. "It surprises you that a bunch of rich, privileged, *male* motherfuckers got together in an exclusive club and *somehow* became richer and more successful? Really?"

"Except for the fact that all of these individuals are either openly or semi-openly gay," Mamba said.

"Except for the athletes, none of whom have come out, even though none of them are married or involved with wymyn except in the most superficial way," Ed said.

"Holy shit!" I said. "We need to meet in person. Don't say another word, but get the rest of the Badgers together and go to the usual place so we can talk. I'll bring Brenda T. and we'll compare notes, OK? Not another word."

"And you better bring your director, too, if what you're saying has any validity at all," Brenda T. green said.

"Acknowledge your last," Ed said, and hung up.

Brenda T. and I looked at each other for a moment and then she said, "Son of a bitch! If they're right the defecation is really going to hit the air conditioner!"

"Especially after we confront the Vice President with it and he confirms that was his motive for the assassination attempts," I said.

We jumped up and ran for her car, our thoughts racing along with us. We jumped in and Brenda T. got on her phone and cancelled the rest of her appointments for the day. She told the person at her office, "Please tell Mr. Quintanilla I have to have an emergency dental procedure, will you? Thanks."

I said, "Code for 'I'm on to something'?"

"Something like that," she said. The A-USA was deep in thought for a moment, and then she said, "Do you suppose the president...?" The thought wasn't finished, but I'd already had much the same thought, so I shrugged and said, "We need more evidence before we go hog wild with the speculations, Brenda T." She nodded and we rode in silence until we got to the Coney & Ivy on 7th Street, the dive bar we used as our local watering hole. This time of day it would be nearly empty, but it wouldn't be odd to see a group of federal law officers just hanging out, and it would be very quiet, which was preferable for what we were about to discuss.

The gang was all there, dressed casually but all carrying their service pistols. We went over to where they were sitting and found drinks already on the table, including a nice cold Oberon for Brenda T., who smiled at Joe and said, "You remembered, Agent Cocker. How nice of you."

Joe grinned at her and said, "Why, you're welcome, A-USA Green. I thought perhaps you might be a bit dry after your drive, and I did remember that you like this excellent beer from Michigan, and, well, I decided that—"

"You should try and seduce A-USA Green while we're about to have the most important meeting of our lives?" Ed said.

"Show yourself to be a Lothario in front of your friends so we can ridicule you when this fine looking and highly intelligent womyn shoots you down in flames?" Mamba said.

"Try to hook up with someone who is clearly out of your league while we have something of the utmost importance in front of us?" I said.

While we all laughed at Joe's beet red face I saw Jewey giving me looks, and Kid Galahad stopped laughing almost right away, a look of curiosity on his handsome face. Nails finally said, "Thanks for the comic relief, but what the fuck is this meeting all about?"

"Madam Director, we believe that we understand the Vice President's motive for his assassination attempts on us," I said.

"And what would that be?" Nails said.

"He was trying to protect his gay lover from being indicted for murder," Ed said.

"And do we know the identity of the former Vice President's gay lover?" Nails said.

"That would be the president of the United States," Mamba said.

There was that eerie silence that always happens right before a battle, and then chaos erupted. Everyone started babbling at once and wouldn't stop. I let it go on for a while and then it got on my nerves, so I used my best Marine Corps officer's voice and said, "NOW HEAR THIS! SHUT THE FUCK UP IMMEDIATELY!"

Everybody shut the fuck up immediately.

After I apologized to the bartender and staff for bellowing an obscenity I said, "Mamba, Ed, will you please give us all you have to support your theory? Nice and easy, if you please." Nails tried to say something and I said, "No questions until they've finished, if you please" in that tone of voice that said "don't fuck with me, you fuckers."

Everybody quelled themselves while Mamba and Ed told their tale. When they were finished everyone looked at each other with wide-eyed incredulity. As crazy as it sounded at first blush the story was simple, powerful, and very, very plausible. In fact, when told dispassionately it not only sounded like the simplest explanation, but also the most plausible one, because the three reasons people commit murder are money, power and love, and love is by far the most common motive.

It was odd, but no one seemed to be too hung up on the fact that the president was gay. I guess I must have realized something was up when he lost it over the VP—his reaction was so vehement that it was bizarre for him.

Lots of things started to make more sense about the attacks, as well as the death of Tim Miller, but we all still had some questions, and only the former VP could answer them, so we decided to call on an old friend to gently interrogate him to see if we could get any answers. Nails opened her phone, hit one number, waited, said, "Come to this address and find me, would you please? Thanks."

Ten minutes later Edward Otis Whitney strolled in the place, saw us and came over after ordering a drink. He smiled at our expressions and said, "Did you just find out something about me that I don't want generally known?"

I smiled back and said, "Would it surprise you to know that the president and vice president are gay and have been lovers since they were together at Michigan?"

"No it would not," Edward Otis Whitney said, "although I am surprised that you found out." He turned to Ed and Mamba and said, "Knowing full well the dangers of doing this, I'm going to assume that it was you two who finally figured it out."

They nodded and Ed said, "It's true, but why would you assume that, sir?"

"It takes one to know one, Agent Devlin," Old Three Names said.

"And how did you find out, Eddie?" I said.

"It takes one to know one, Freak," Edward Otis Whitney said. His drink arrived and he calmly took a sip while we all gawked at him.

Finally Mamba said, "Uhhh, sir—you're *gay*?"

"You didn't think that I became this good a dresser because of my upbringing, did you? Just because I'm the scion of two incredibly wealthy and influential families doesn't mean that I'm going to automatically have a sense of style and know how to color coordinate," Old Three Names said, laughing at himself. "So we already know about the former VP, but what I wonder is why this revelation about the president is so important? It would hurt him politically, of course, but the last time I looked at the Constitution you can't be impeached for being gay, unless you want to look at his remaining closeted as being a fraud perpetrated on the American people, and since he's in his second term he isn't running for president again, so why…" His patrician voice trailed off as his considerable brain worked the problem.

Before his head exploded from concentration Mamba and Ed told him the story and then Nails told him what we wanted him to do. Old Three Names didn't even hesitate. "Of course, I'd be glad to talk to the former VP. Do we have a set of questions?"

We worked everything out as we swigged our drinks, and when we were finished it was decided: Edward Otis Whitney would be the lead interrogator, with Joe, Mamba and I backing him up. We were looking for confirmation that the president either did or didn't know about the attacks on me and the rest of the Secret Service personnel, because if he knew, then president or not, he'd be arrested on the same charges that the former VP was indicted on. If he didn't then we would be pivoting to the old murder case.

We also wanted to know if the president had told the former VP about murdering Tim Miller, or if Holland had found out independently.

Nails assigned everybody else other jobs to do with the investigation, while Old Three Names, Joe, Mamba, and I went off to interrogate the former VP.

We got to the Detention Center and found his attorney, Shannon Dudek Farrance, waiting for US. She was a short, compact blonde womyn with bright blue eyes and beautiful, clear skin. She shook Old Three Names' hand and said, "Assistant Director Whitney, I'm Shannon D. Farrance, the attorney for Vice President Mitchell C. Holland. What exactly are we doing here?"

"Why, we'd like to ask your client a few simple questions to clear up some details of his murderous plot against certain Secret Service agents," Edward Otis Whitney said. He was calm, cool, and very collected in his three-piece bespoke suit from his Savile Row tailor (that means the suit was custom made for him in London—one of the privileges of having two separate trust funds). He smiled gently at Ms. Farrance as he held his hand out toward the interrogation room. She hesitated, then said, "I'm not sure that he'll answer any questions, Assistant Director Whitney, because he's been in a—well, a, a, a bit of a mood lately. I'm telling you this because I don't want to waste anyone's time."

Her statement and body language made it pretty clear that Ms. Farrance had no idea what her client knew, or why he'd done what he did. I looked at Joe, and Joe winked when Mamba whispered,

"Stonewalling his lawyer." I nodded and then we went into a conference room where the former Vice President was being watched by two U.S. marshals.

Old Three Names nodded at him and said, "Mr. Vice President, I am here to ask you some questions concerning the two attempts on the lives of Secret Service Agent Glinka Rose Glickstien and several others. I wish to make it clear that you are under no obligation to answer these questions, neither are you under any legal compulsion to do so, nor will I continue to ask these questions if you do not wish to answer them. I do not wish to be condescending, sir, but I must ask if you understand what I have just old you."

Mitch Holland looked terrible. His face was haggard, he appeared to have lost several pounds since his arrest and his hands were trembling slightly. He looked everywhere but at Joe, Mamba and I, finally looking at Edward Otis Whitney and saying, "I understand you, sir, but I don't know what I could possibly say that would be of any help to you." He looked at his lawyer and she said, "Mr. Assistant Director, the Vice President has plead not guilty to all of the charges and will not answer any questions that I feel might be construed as implicating him in any way. Are we clear on that?"

"Very clear, Ms. Farrance," Old Three Names said. "I am simply trying to verify certain questions that still exist concerning the whereabouts of the Vice President and his agents when he was still the Director of the FBI. I do not believe that any of these questions are incriminating in nature, but leave that to your and the Vice President's discretion. Is this acceptable?"

His courtliness, formal correctness and obvious respect for the former Vice President was disarming the asshole and his lawyer; I think both of them saw a potential ally sitting across the table.

Holland and Farrance exchanged a look and she said, "Yes, but again, I reserve the right to quash any question that I am not comfortable with, Assistant Director."

"Ms. Farrance, if you and the Vice President would like to address me as Edward I would be perfectly comfortable with that," Old Three Names said.

"Thank you, Edward. I'm Shannon, although the Vice President would appreciate you continuing to use his title, or sir, to address him," she said.

"I had no intention of doing otherwise," Old Three Names said. He gave a self-deprecating smile and the former Vice President gave him a slightly condescending one back, while the lawyer nodded.

Old Three Names said, "Mr. Vice President, do you remember when you first met FBI agents Thomas Smith and Adam Jones?"

"I met Agent Smith when he was working on a fraud case for FBI Assistant Director Malcolm Sorenson, who was my subordinate at the time," Holland said. "I met Agent Jones when we worked an arms smuggling case while I was SAC in San Francisco."

"And SAC is Special Agent in Charge, correct? You ran the San Francisco office for the FBI?" Edward Otis Whitney said.

"Yes," Holland said.

That started a very gentle, very respectful round of questions about where and when the former Vice President had been in his career. There were no questions about his relationship with the president, nothing about ordering any murders, or money transfers to pay for the attempted murders, or anything else actually pertaining to the case—just question after question from Edward Otis

Whitney, Jewey and Joe about where and when he had been. I remained silent and appeared to just be taking notes.

After a half hour of gentle probing Old Three Names rubbed his nose with his forefinger—our signal to begin the final phase of questioning—and we sprang our trap. The conversation went like this.

> OTN: Mr. Vice President, do you remember where you were when you got word of the first attack on Agent Glickstien?
>
> The VP: I was in the Situation Room at a briefing with the president, the National Security Council and the Joint Chiefs of Staff.
>
> Joe: And sir, do you remember where you were when you heard about the first attack on the first daughters?
>
> The VP: Certainly. I was in the Roosevelt Room with the Council of Economic Advisors—we were discussing deficit reduction.
>
> OTN: Sir, do you remember where you were when you were told of the second attack on Agent Glickstien?
>
> The VP: I was in New York. The president and I were supposed to attend a Security Council meeting concerning terrorism.
>
> Jewey: I apologize for being picky, Mr. Vice President, but were you at the UN already, or were you at your hotel in New York?
>
> The VP: Neither. We were in transit from the hotel to the UN when the president called and asked me to go check out the incident.
>
> Jewey: Thank you for clearing that up, sir.
>
> The VP: Not at all, Agent Silverberg.
>
> OTN: Mr. Vice President, do you remember where you were when you were notified of the second attack on the first daughters?
>
> The VP: My wife and I were in one of the first cars in line to leave. We were on the road when our car sped up and rapidly returned to the White House.
>
> OTN: Pardon me, Mr. Vice President, but were you at the White House when you were told the first daughters had been attacked again, or did you find out in the car?
>
> The VP: I was told by the Chief of Staff, Charlie Hassenger, once my wife and I were safely inside the White House.
>
> OTN: Thank you for that clarification, Mr. Vice President.
>
> The VP: Not at all, Assistant Director Whitney.
>
> Me: Sir, where were you when you found out that Tim Miller was murdered?
>
> The VP: I was at Fredrick Mei…(silence)
>
> The VP's Attorney: Oh, shit.

There was a silence so absolute in the room that it was like we were in the vacuum of space. The former Vice President dropped his face in his hands, and his attorney had her left hand on her forehead as she shielded her eyes, but the rest of us sat as still as statues, because Jewey'd warned us that Holland would crack or clam up after he slipped, and there really wasn't much we could do about it except fuck it up by talking, so we were all barely breathing during this most delicate time.

After three full minutes of total frozen silence the former VP looked up right at me. I stared back—not with the Death Stare, but with a very neutral look—but I still said nothing. Mitch Holland looked back at me with a blank stare, but after just 30 seconds his face seemed to melt and tears began to drip down his cheeks as he gently shook his head. He looked like he was going to speak, so we followed Jewey's advice and softened our faces, but we still didn't speak, because Jewey said whichever side spoke first would lose the battle.

They did. Shannon D. Farrance, Esquire, said, "Mr. Vice President, I strongly advise you to invoke your Fifth Amendment right to remain silent. Please, sir."

Holland looked at her, looked back at me, looked at Farrance and said, "Please be quiet now, Shannon. She deserves to know why I tried to kill her."

"Mitch, shut the fuck up right now!" Farrance said, but she'd already lost the battle, and now she was about to lose the war.

"No, Shan, I've kept this secret as long as I'm willing to. I'm tired of hiding out and covering and having to listen to people tell sexist jokes about gays. I'm going to prison for a long time, and Jim hasn't got anything to do with this, so why shouldn't I tell her why?" the former VP said, his face coming back to its usual ruddy, good-looking self.

"Mitch, you've *got* to shut up *NOW!*" his lawyer said, but Holland shook his head, patted her hand and said, "No, Shan, it comes out now." He turned and looked at me and I immediately said, "You did it for love, because you love James Patrick Liam Sheehan."

Holland nodded and said, "Since the first time I met him at Michigan. I didn't have any idea I was gay, but once I saw Jim, well, I completely lost interest in the opposite sex, although I was smart enough to not let on. The next day he called me, we went to Zingerman's Deli and got sandwiches and he told me he felt the same way. We were inseparable after that, but we made sure we stayed deep in the closet. We didn't room together the first year at the frat, but after our roommates decided that they wanted to room together it was perfectly natural that we'd room together, and then we just did the best friend thing in public, and because that's the way it goes in college. No one ever suspected a thing, until your Badger Squad guys finally tipped to it."

"Sir, I knew as well—why wasn't I also a target for assassination?" Edward Otis Whitney said.

"Because you weren't getting close to discovering that the president of the United States had murdered Tim Miller, Eddie," I said.

"Right the first time, Freak, although it was an accident that Tim Miller died," Holland said,

"Sir, if we could discuss that later? I would like to know how much the president knew about the plan to assassinate Agent Glickstien and the others, if you wouldn't mind," Old Three Names said, his voice calm and dispassionate even though his face was lit up like a kid at Christmas.

"Before we go any further I'd like a chance to confer with my client," Farrance said.

"No," Holland said. He looked at his poor lawyer and said, "I'm telling you, I'm just going to dump it all now. I don't want a deal, I don't want a trial, and I don't want to drag Jim—the president—into this whole thing, since he didn't know jack shit about it. Sorry, Shan, but if you keep interrupting I'm going to ask you to leave."

I give her credit—she wasn't just going to sit back and draw her fee while her client confessed to trying to kill federal agents. She said, "Fuck you, Mitch, you're paying me to be your lawyer. If you want to confess I can't stop you, but at least get them to take the death penalty off the table."

Holland looked at her again, considered for a moment and then looked at Edward Otis Whitney. Old Three Names made a theatrical presentation out of it, looking at all of us before he nodded and said, "We will not consider this a death penalty case, Mr. Vice President, and we would ask again for your cooperation in ascertaining the other people who conspired with you to carry out the assassinations."

"We'll need that in writing before we continue," Farrance said, but Holland said, "No, we won't." He said, "Your word on that, Assistant Director Whitney?" Old Three Names said, "Yes, Mr. Vice President" and they shook hands on it.

"Sir, who else was involved in the conspiracy to assassinate Agent Glickstien?" Joe said.

"Well, you're not going to believe this, but it was just myself, Malcolm Sorenson and the two agents who did the dirty work, Smith and Jones," Holland said.

"Mr. Vice President, can you explain how that worked?" Jewey said.

So we spent another forty-five minutes as the former vice president laid it all out, from the beginning to the end. When he was done there wasn't a person there who didn't believe him when he said there were no other people involved, because it was all so simple as to be ridiculous. From his time at the FBI Holland had lots of contacts and knew about a wide variety of illicit, immoral, and downright illegal organizations, and he knew that Sorenson would assist and support him, because Sorenson was also a deeply closeted gay man who knew what it was like to be kept from someone you loved by your sense of duty.

The former Vice President knew that he could get Smith and Jones to do almost anything for money, since he had already identified the fact that they had somewhat flexible moral compasses, and also that they were assholes who thought they could prove their manhood by pretending to be tough guys. The idea of siccing the Ku Klux Klukkers on us in Morehead apparently really appealed to the two dimwit shitheads, because, as Holland said, they were "both redneck motherfuckers who hated lesbians."

In any case, once we heard how the former Vice President had set both attempts up it was easy to see why nobody got wind of it. With only four moving parts that actually knew what was going on, and with Smith and Jones believing that Sorenson was the boss, the former Vice President should have completely gotten away with the assassinations.

"Except I forgot about Freak's exceptional abilities, and Murphy's Law, both of which are just as impressive as advertised," Holland said.

"Sir, I want to thank you for your cooperation, but there is something that I need for you to confirm, and one thing I need to follow up on," Edward Otis Whitney said.

"No, I did not have anything to do with trying to kidnap the first daughters," Holland said. "I love those girls like they're my own, and believe me, I tried to move heaven and earth to find out who tried to kidnap them. I still can't understand why the terrorist group responsible hasn't claimed responsibility for the second attack, since it really enhances their credibility."

"Thank you, sir," Old Three Names said. "We didn't believe that you had anything to do with the kidnap attempts, but you understand why we had to ask. I would like to follow up on your contention that Tim Miller's death was an accident."

"Let me just say that I'm not going to go into detail about that, because it's really the president's story to tell, but I am going to tell you as someone who knows the president better than anyone else, I believe him," Holland said.

"Mr. Vice President, I don't mean to be rude in any way, but Tim Miller lived right across the street from me and was my friend. Can I just ask, when the president told you about his death, why did you believe him?" I said, keeping my tone level and respectful even though I was talking to the man who had planned my death. I understood why he'd done it, I maybe even sympathized with him about having to endure the hell of not being able to be with the person you loved, but it didn't mean I had to like it (and I didn't—I really had to suppress my primal feelings, you know, the ones where I wanted to tear his arms off and stick them up his ass?).

Mitchell Holland looked at me and said, "Thank you for being respectful, Agent Glickstien, especially when you must want to kill me, or at least maim me. You all know that the president is a big art lover, right?" We all nodded—the president was always extolling the virtues of art in all aspects of life, and he'd spent more time in the National Galleries than the previous four presidents combined.

"What you don't know is that the president really wanted to be a sculptor, not a football player. He told me about Tim Miller when we were at the Fredrick Meijer Gardens in Grand Rapids, Michigan, which just happens to be the place with the replica of Leonardo da Vinci's giant bronze horse. I know that Jim—the president—was telling the truth because we were standing under that statue when he said, "I accidentally killed the only other man I really loved, Mitch, and then I ran away without taking responsibility. I loved him almost as much as I love you, and I killed him." When I pressed him about it Jim tried to tell me to get away from him so that I didn't get hurt, too, but I wouldn't. In fact I wrapped him up in a 'bro' hug—we've never, ever been affectionate in public—and that's when Jim said, 'I swear on my soul that I didn't mean to hurt him, Mitch.'"

There were tears slowly running down the former Vice President's cheeks when he said, "No way Jim Sheehan killed Tim Miller, except accidentally. He's a real Catholic believer and he never, ever swears on his soul. Also, he's really only loved four people in his life—Tim, his daughters, and me. He'll have to tell you what happened, but I believe him."

Fuck me, so did I.

Imagine living a lie every single minute of your life. Worse, imagine having to live that lie in the glare of the celebrity's life, with eyes, microphones and paparazzi armed with cameras of every variety always aimed at you. Then imagine that you take on the most stressful of careers for someone who's keeping the kind of secret that you are—because believe me, the state of Michigan isn't any place to be a gay politician, not if you want to get elected—and then imagine that you step up to the most stressful and examined position in the world. Imagine that you're living this lie while you're in love with your soul mate—but you can't hold their hand, kiss them goodnight, get a hug when you need one, or in any other way express it. You literally can't make one little slip, because while the Washington press corps catches a ton of shit about being useless, in reality they are very, very good at their jobs, and like great white sharks, they can smell political blood in the water from miles away—and they won't stop until they get fed.

Most of us would crack under that kind of pressure, or we'd go crazier than a shithouse rat, and if someone threatened to take what little happiness you had in your living-a-lie life, and you had the means and opportunity to make the threat go away…well, you look me in the eye and tell me that you wouldn't do what Mitchell Holland did and I'll call you a goddamned liar.

I'm not saying that being under that kind of pressure and not being able to actually love the person you know is your one true love excuses murdering people, but it does make it easier to understand a person's motivation.

I'm a strong person in every way it's possible to be strong, but I know that I'm not that strong. Fuck it, I'd murder anyone who tried to get between me and my soul mate even *without* the pressure cooker of having to live a lie just because society as a whole is filled with a bunch of stupid fucking assholes who think somebody else's sex life is their business.

We all sat there thinking the same thing, and then Edward Otis Whitney said, "Mr. Vice President, I'm not saying that murder is the answer, and I am in no way excusing your conduct, but I think I understand now. Thank you for your honesty, sir, and please know that I, for one, will not be reporting this conversation to my superiors, except as confirmation that you and just three others planned and executed the assassination attempts."

"Sir, I'm satisfied as to your motive in these cases," I said. I gave the former Vice President the hairy eyeball and said, "I don't excuse you, sir, because Josie, Elwin Clyde Bliss, Andria Rogers and Tara Waters were all innocents who died from your machinations, but I hold no personal animosity toward you, and I can see why you thought you had to stop me one way or another. I won't use anything that I heard today against the president, sir."

Joe and Jewey said similar things, and Holland said, "Thank you, and again, please accept my apologies, especially you, Agent Glickstien. I-I, uh, I realize that what I did to you was heinous and I am truly sorry." He looked contrite, sitting there like an old man whose house just burned down, but there's only so much compassion you can give in situations like this, so I stood up and said, "Yes, I believe that you are, Mr. Vice President, but there are some things that you can't apologize for, and you better believe that this is one of them."

I gave him the hairy eyeball again and then spun a perfect about-face and marched out the door. Joe and Jewey followed me, and a moment later so did Old Three Names. Once we were all in the corridor Edward Otis Whitney said, "Not a word to anyone about today, except to confirm that the former VP and his three henchmen were the only ones involved. The rest of it has to kept close until we can hold a council of war with the U.S. Attorney's Office and decide what to do about what that murderer said. Are we agreed?"

We all nodded just as all four of our phones went off with a text alert. All four of the messages were the same: "RTB immediately upon receipt this message. New info essential you see in person. WYA! Weasel."

"WYA!" meant "Watch Your Ass!" and was our code for immediate danger, although if he'd've thought we were in direct danger Weasel would've said "GO!" at the end of the message—"GO!" meant "Guns Out (Now)."

We immediately headed for the car to get back to Secret Service HQ, where the information surrounding the kidnapping attempts would get so deep that we were like the proverbial people buried up to their neck in a vat of shit with people throwing baseballs at our heads.

Put another way, we were caught wading in Shit Creek without our hip waders during a flash flood.

It turned out that drowning was a distinct possibility.

CHAPTER 74

SEAL Trapping

We got back to the Treasury Building and ran up to the bay where the rest of the Badger Squad was working. As soon I saw the looks on Weasel, Mamba, Jack Soo and Kid Galahad's faces I knew that some serious shit was about to hit the fan. Nails was there, too, and she said, "Shut the door and sit down, and don't anybody break anything in the next ten minutes."

We sat down and Weasel said, "OK, so you know how we've been looking back on anything that might be significant about Tim Miller's death, trying to tie the president to it in some physical way, right?" The question was rhetorical, so we all just sat there until Kid Galahad said, "So we found something significant—it doesn't tie the president to Tim's death—but it gives us a possible suspect in the kidnapping attempts."

"Wow! You Badgers are amazing!" I said, really meaning it. The Badger Squad was turning out some of the best investigative work in Secret Service history, and now we might get to use it to stop the guys who were trying to take my Warrior Princesses away from their family.

And just let me stop you before you get all judgy and say, 'But Freak, isn't the murder of Tim Miller more important? Shouldn't you be more worried about poor Mrs. Miller?' The short answer is no, because we knew who killed Tim, we just couldn't prove it. What Mrs. Miller needed to know was that we finally had a suspect, and that we'd pursue that suspect until Tim got justice. The kidnapping attempts were much more immediate and needed our attention far more, since they might be an ongoing threat. So no, I didn't get all het up about Tim Miller's murder.

Instead I got floored by something that I never expected to hear.

Mamba said, "Do you remember what happened to Tom Miller, Freak?"

"Yeah, he served twenty in the Air Force—or maybe Navy?—and then retired to some place in Oregon, or was it Colorado? I don't think that he ever came home after he went in, because his mom never talked about him, and my family never did, either," I said. "So what? That was part of Mrs. Miller's heartache, that she lost two boys on that day."

"Captain Tom Miller served exactly twenty years in the U.S. Navy and then retired to a place called Paisley, Oregon, to live on a four-hundred-acre ranch owned by one of his old Navy friends. He spent a lot of time at a place called the Pioneer Saloon and Restaurant, where everybody said he was very quiet, polite to a fault and in extremely good shape," Weasel said. "A waitress there told me he once stopped a fight just by getting out of his seat and standing near the combatants. She also told me that he had a look on his face that scared everybody in the place, although he never raised his voice or laid a finger on anybody."

Oh shit, oh dear. I think I knew at that point what was coming next, so I said, "What did Tom Miller do for the U.S. Navy for twenty years, Weasel?"

"For the last three years of his career he was the CO of an outfit called SEAL Team Seven out of Coronado, California," Kid Galahad said.

"Oh fuck a duck," Jewey said.

"Goddamn fucking shit," Joe said. "How did we miss that?"

"Sonofagoddamnedbitch," Edward Otis Whitney said, surprising us all with his fluency at cussing.

"Oh fuck me black, blue, and bloody," I said. "We are in some sincerely deep shit if it's him leading the kidnapping attempts."

"Oh, it is," Mamba said. "We also found out that the old Navy buddy of his who bought the ranch near Paisley, Oregon—population 237 or so—also had at least 25 other ranch hands working for him, all of them also Navy veterans. Our wits all said that they deferred to Tom Miller like he was their boss."

"Or their commanding officer," Joe said.

"He assembled an entire SEAL team at a remote location, probably so they could train up in private in order to kidnap the president's daughters," I said.

"Why would he do that? Why not just strike at the president himself?" Old Three Names said. He understood the protection game and was a good boss, but he didn't really know the Spec Ops game, or the warriors that worked in the field.

"Because he knows who killed his twin, and he wants them to suffer just like he and his mother did," I said. "Killing the president would be letting his brother's murderer off way too easy—after 20 years in the SEALs he's bound to be at least somewhat "eye for an eye" in his outlook."

"Even if he wasn't, he'd still want the president to feel some of the agony he felt over the loss of his twin, and his mother felt about the loss of her son. I know that I would," Joe said.

"If that's true—and I don't doubt at all that it is—then we can expect the kidnapping attempts to continue, and possibly succeed," Edward Otis Whitney said.

It was a mark of our professionalism, experience, and pragmatism that no one tried to tell the assistant director that he was wrong. We all knew that the Navy SEALs were more than a match for us. If they went all out and eschewed not killing a bunch of Secret Service agents there was no way that we could stop them.

Kid Galahad said, "This information also explains why the kidnappers were so reluctant to use deadly force—they shot knees and used fléchettes in shotguns because they weren't interested in killing fellow loyal troops, whatever the variety."

"It also explains their fire discipline and the way that they infiltrated and exfiltrated the two sites," Mamba said. "The SEALs are experts at all of those things, plus they know when to cut their losses and just run for it, like they did at the Kennedy Center."

"But their dead at the Kennedy Center weren't SEALs—they were mercenaries, including the two pilots," Old Three Names said.

"Yeah, but that makes sense, because SEALs won't leave their dead behind, and the shotgunners were exposed. Tom Miller is a very experienced officer, so he sent the eight shotgunners in as shock troops, with an infiltration and exfiltration squad, because he was expecting some casualties. He must've known about Freak's abilities before the first attack, and he clearly knew about what she could do after it, so he sent the second string in to do the grunt work—and take the casualties—while the varsity extracted the targets," Kid Galahad said.

"And I'd say that his only real mistake—besides not using deadly force—was that he underestimated how long determined Secret Service agents could hold out against the shotgunners," Joe said. "He thought that his shock troops would take down more of us, and faster, than they actually did. By holding out like we did we threw his timetable off and made his LZ a hot one, with our best marksman there to drop the bird."

"You're all right, but that doesn't change the fact that Captain Miller is still out there, planning his next attack," Edward Otis Whitney said. "Unless you believe that we've successfully scared him off." The Assistant Director of Protective Services looked at all of us with a semi-hopeful smile, which I promptly quashed.

"No way that motherfucker is gonna give up now. Now he's pissed off, mostly at me, but also because some Secret Service rent-a-cops have defeated his elite warriors twice, which means that the asshole and his henchmen are already at work on another way to take the Warrior Princesses, probably by trying to do it when I'm not in the picture," I said.

"'Henchmen'? What the fuck, Freak, you swallow a thesaurus?" Weasel said.

"'Rent-a-cops'? What, just because we never served in some hoo-rah military unit we're all of a sudden pieces of shit?" Jewey said.

"And you're the only one who can stop them, O mighty super-agent?" Joe said.

"I mean, you're the best we got, Freak, but you ain't the only one who can shoot or fight, y'know," Kid Galahad said.

"And while we may be lowly warthog-faced buffoons who can barely find their asses with both hands and directions we did take the same oath as you, O mighty-thewed warrior of the age," Mamba said.

"Fuck you, ya shitheads," I said. "I was talking about what Tom Miller thought of the Secret Service, not what I thought, and you know it."

"We gotta keep your shit quotient up, Freak, or you'll think our bodies have been taken over by aliens," Weasel said.

We all laughed and finally Nails said, "OK, I haven't said anything, but shouldn't we try to locate Captain Miller and his merry men so we can stop them from making another attempt? Would it not behoove us to send some agents out to East Bumfuck, Oregon, and find out if they're back at home planning another, better attack on the first daughters?"

"If we wanted to be straight-up law enforcement that would be the right play," Joe said.

"But that's also what Captain Miller will expect," Kid Galahad said.

"In fact, he's probably counting on us to do that very thing," Mamba said.

"So we should absolutely do exactly that," Weasel said.

I got what they were thinking and said, "What a great idea. We'll paint him a picture by number so that he feels secure—it'll just reinforce his already low opinion of us—and then we can be waiting when he tries to move on us again. It's brilliant, simple and easy to execute."

"Not being a military strategist, I'm gonna require some explanation of this brilliant plan of yours," Nails said.

Jack Soo had been absolutely silent all night long, but it quickly became apparent that he'd just been processing everything that we knew and applying it to our strategy going forward. He said, "Madame Director, the SEALs—in fact, all special ops units—depend on speed and maneuverability to make up for the fact that they're always outmanned and outgunned. They prize speed more than anything because it negates the enemy's size advantage, which means that they want to hit as fast as possible—and you better believe that Captain Miller made contingency plans to hit the first daughters again in case his ops weren't successful, because while he's almost certainly contemptuous of our abilities, he's also a smart, well-trained officer who knows that you have to plan for what the enemy *can* do, not what they *will* do.

"What that means is this: they are already in the vicinity training to hit us. If we go out to their Oregon base of operations they will think that we are going the police route and that we believe we have time to catch them before they hit again. If we give them exactly what they expect they'll wait until we're out of the way and then hit the first daughters—we all know that the only way to truly protect them is to lock them in the Situation Room surrounded by a division of Marines, and we all know that isn't going to happen—and so does Captain Miller.

"You can also bet that he's already sure of his next opportunity, so what we've got to do is fool him into thinking that we're falling for it—that we're thinking like cops, not like special ops operators. So we need to send almost all of the first team out to Paisley, Oregon and show him exactly what he expects to see, so that we can then double back and take his kidnapping ass down."

We all stood up and applauded and Weasel said, "Jack Soo, military genius, ladies and gentlemen."

"Yeah, fuck you assholes. Am I wrong?" Jack Soo said.

We all laughed and I said, "No, no you're not, Jack my boy. In fact, I think that we should leave me and Kid Galahad here and send the rest of you west."

"Do tell," Jewey said.

So I did.

"What if we sent a 767 loaded with every motherfucking Secret Service agent those assholes have ever seen out of Reagan with a flight plan for the airport nearest to Paisley, and had the plane met by some of our guys from a West Coast office?" I said.

"Sounds good, but wouldn't we be kinda far away to help you get Captain Miller and his henchmen?" Weasel said.

"Yeah, if you guys were still on the plane when it got there," I said. "But let's say that our 767 stopped in Pittsburgh, dropped you off while loading up a replacement group that matches all of your descriptions and then proceeded to the Oregon airport?"

"Ah, round eye has formulated exquisite plan for deception of enemy," Jack Soo said in his best Charlie Chan (as portrayed by Warner Oland—I never thought that Sidney Toler really sounded like he was Asian) voice.

"Oh, you are clever, Freak. We'd take choppers back to DC and land at Andrews?" Joe said.

"Yeah, and we'd make sure that we came back in four small groups, wearing high quality disguises," I said.

"And then we'd covertly cover the girls, while you and the Kid kept the second string highly visible—and the investigative group in Oregon would make enough noise to make sure that Captain Miller is convinced we're actually out there, not here," Jewey said.

"Four-oh, Jewey. You need to be the one running the op in Oregon—whoever's supposed to keep tabs on us out there won't be able to miss you, and once they see you they aren't really going to look any further, plus you'll be blundering around enough that you'll really cover up any deficiency in our recon team," I said. "And no, I really don't want you out there, but you gotta admit that it makes sense."

The tallest agent in the Secret Service said, "Well, when ya put it that way…besides, I was going to volunteer anyway, because it really does make sense. I want Weasel to go with me as my XO, because once their watcher sees the two of us together all doubts will be put to rest—and the rest of you will be waiting for that son-of-a-bitch Captain Miller and his merry men."

"Now that's a team player—and I'm with ya, ya big Hebrew," Weasel said. "I figure we can investigate Tim Miller's murder and get confirmation of the president's involvement from anywhere, plus I agree with Jewey—once they see the two of us that's all they'll see, because the watcher ain't gonna be one of the first team, now are they?"

"Nope," Joe said, "they're gonna need all they've got left to deal with the security around the girls, especially if Freak is still here. All we've got do is work out the details and make sure that we don't let them get to the girls."

"Is that all?" Mamba said. "Well, pish, posh, old boy, that shouldn't take more than five minutes, after which I would like to spring for cheeseburgers at the D.C. Grille Express over on DuPont."

"The one where you can get the parmesan Brussels sprouts?" Jack Soo said.

"And a $20 bucket of Corona?" Jewey said.

"And a great grilled fish?" Joe said.

"And the best damned bacon cheeseburgers around?" I said.

"And where the burgers don't cost an arm and a leg?" Badass said.

"That's the place and I'm buying, if we can stop fucking around and work out how we're going to stop a bunch of elite troops from grabbing our principals and hurting more of us," Mamba said.

Everyone agreed that was a damned good idea, and we all turned to look at Edward Otis Whitney. He shrugged his shoulders and did a perfect Alfred E. Newman "What, me worry?" impression (if you don't get that reference you need to go look at some old *Mad* magazines), until Joe said, "OTN, we all know who the expert at planning this kind of shit is—don't be modest—you can probably set up the logistics of this op in your head, right?"

Edward Otis Whitney's eyes were sparking fire as he slowly nodded, a small, tight smile spreading across his patrician face.

"You've already done it, haven't you? You've already worked all of the details out in your head," Weasel said.

"As a matter of fact, I started working on the problem as soon as Agent Glickstien suggested it. The plan made sense and is absolutely feasible, especially if we pre-position some assets in Pittsburgh," Old Three Names said.

"Do tell," Jack Soo said.

So Edward Otis Whitney gave the most concise briefing about a special operation I've ever heard. It lasted exactly 11 minutes and when he was done everyone was shaking their heads in wonder. I mean, I'd been in briefings about going from point A to point B that lasted longer and were less clear—and this plan, while simple at its heart, had more than a few moving parts.

The good news was that while it wasn't a perfect plan, it was virtually guaranteed to draw out our renegade SEALs and give us a chance to take them without any danger to the Warrior Princesses. Of course, that was also the *bad* news, because only a fool underestimated a group of Navy SEALs, or tried to trap them, for that matter—calling these guys tough was like calling Secretariat a good pony.

In fact, you usually only got one chance to fool a SEAL, and if you missed you died. That's no hyperbole—these men are the deadliest soldiers on the planet, bar none (my apologies to the British SAS and SBS, the Israeli commandos and the Gurkhas, as well as all the other men and wymyn who train in the world's special forces, but the U.S. Navy SEALs are the toughest motherfuckers I've ever seen, and I've seen a lot—and yes, that's classified). The SEALs also do not take kindly to being shot at and return fire with incredible speed and accuracy.

We were only going to get one shot at this (no pun intended) and it needed to be our best shot, so we all got our marching orders and went off to set up the subterfuge designed to catch a herd of SEALs.

Jewey and Weasel did all of the overt work, like setting up plane tickets, getting accommodations for the 24 Secret Service agents who were going to be staying in Paisley, Oregon, requisitioning transportation, and all the other mundane details that are required to move a large group of people from one place to another. They did everything right out in the open, and when the Portland police chief wondered what was going on Weasel told him over an unencrypted cell phone that they were coming out to investigate a ranch in Paisley that was owned by a retired Navy SEAL.

We figured that would attract the attention of the watcher(s) in Paisley (it turns out we were right) and that it would also be reported to Captain Tom Miller (we found out later it was), which meant we had to be ready with phase two, which was complicated to set up, but diabolically simple to execute.

First the fake-out group of agents was filtered into Pittsburgh by every transportation device known to man short of oxcarts. Once there they were briefed on their parts, disguised as the people they were going to play and went to the airport in groups of no more than three. They made no contact with each other, but rather just lazed around the airport waiting for the 767 to Oregon to arrive.

The agents who were ostensibly going to Oregon were also briefed and given their disguises, which they would put on once they arrived at the airport in Pittsburgh. They would then proceed to the bus terminal, where they would board a tour bus bound for DC. The tour they were joining was a regularly scheduled senior outing sponsored by a group of retirement communities that were not connected, which made it very convenient for us, since none of the senior tourists would know each other. The agents would then roll into D.C. and take the first tour, but would gradually melt away from the larger group to keep surreptitious surveillance on the first daughters, employing a number of common disguises like being homeless, tourists, military personnel (we thought that was a nice little touch) and business people, among other things.

When the 767 touched down at the Pittsburgh International Airport the surveillance team would move off the plane, go to restrooms around the facility and then wander down to the bus terminal while the replacement team would board the plane and get off *en masse* in Oregon, led by Jewey and Weasel.

While all that other stuff was going on was going on Edward Otis Whitney and a team were going to check out every one of the passengers on the plane to make sure that Tom Miller and his merry men didn't have a sleeper aboard to keep tabs on the unit, even though we didn't think that it was likely

We were having a hard time deciding who to team with Old Three Names when it suddenly hit me. I said, "Hey, what about the Rehab Platoon? They don't need to be ready to fight it out, they've got a vested interest in this shit and we know that we can trust them to just shut the fuck up and get the job done."

"And they'll jump at the chance to do something—anything—to get the guys who fucked them up," Joe said.

"That is a splendid suggestion," Old Three Names said. "I'll brief them in right away and get to work on the passenger manifest. We should know before anyone even arrives at the airport if they are with Captain Miller, and if so, then we'll put the contingency plan to use."

"And just what is our contingency plan if Captain Miller has a sleeper aboard?" Mamba said.

"We take him or her down hard and proceed with the mission," Edward Otis Whitney said.

"What do you mean by hard? Are you talking about local incarceration without Constitutional privileges, like phone calls or access to lawyers, et cetera?" Jack Soo said.

"No, I'm talking about kidnapping their kidnapper asses and holding them for as long as we fucking want at Guantanamo Bay as domestic fucking terrorists," Old Three Names said.

"Rock on, Eddie!" I said.

"Way to have a pair, sir," Kid Galahad said.

"Who'd'a thunk it—an Assistant Director with brains and balls!' Weasel said.

"Why Mr. Assistant Director, wouldn't that be illegal?" Jewey said, teasing Old Three Names.

"Fuck those assholes. I'm tired of them thinking that they can get away with fucking around with the U.S. Secret Service, and besides, only shithead motherfucking asshole *cowards* try to kidnap young wymyn so that they can get back at their daddies, the goddamned dickheads," Edward Otis Whitney said. His face was red, but otherwise he seemed perfectly composed, except for the language, which was completely out of character for him.

"How will we get them to Guantanamo if we do have to haul them away?" Mamba said.

"I'll order up a Gulfstream from DHS and have it standing by at the Pittsburgh private aviation terminal," Old Three Names said.

"Three cheers for the Assistant Director!" Weasel said.

"Hip-hip, hooray!" we all said three times, like we cast members in *Pirates of Penzance*. After that we all laughed and then we turned to our work.

Less than 36 hours later everything was ready and in place. The Rehab Platoon, led by Major Difficulty and ably assisted by Flipper, Buddha, Hero, Sleepy, Gangster, Bookie, Gordo, and Count Chocolate had run roughshod over the lives of the other passengers scheduled on the flight to

Pittsburgh and didn't find a soul that might be remotely connected to Tom Miller, the Navy SEALs or any other agency that might have alerted him to the fact that the Secret Service personnel riding from Pittsburgh to Oregon weren't the same people who rode out from Washington, even though they looked vaguely similar.

Everything was set in place for what we called Operation Pinniped (don't get it? Again, I'm not responsible for your shitty education—look it up). We were set to go in 36 hours when the expanded Badger Squad found out that three Navy SEALs who'd served with Tom Miller in various locations were scheduled to arrive on other flights at the Portland airport shortly before the Secret Service personnel from Washington did. Since none of us believed in such coincidences we decided that these were the lookouts for Tom Miller's operation in Paisley, Oregon, and that we needed to do something about their presence.

That touched off a furious debate about what to do with the three guys, but as Weasel, Joe, Ed, Mamba and Kid Galahad kept pointing out, we wanted to walk them into a trap in Washington, D.C., which meant that we didn't want to spook the bad guys in Oregon so that they alerted the assholes in D.C. to anything unusual. The other group, which included most of the Rehab Platoon, wanted to arrest their asses and then torture the shit out of them (OK, nobody said it, but you could see it in their eyes—you get your knees blown out and spend a year doing rehab and tell me how you'd react), but the other faction had better arguments.

"Our biggest advantage is that they don't have any idea we're on to them—we've got to give them exactly what they expect in order to reinforce the fact that we're clueless," Jewey said.

"It'll also make them think that we haven't even tried to find out about them—we're supposed to be going the police investigation route, right?" Joe said.

"Legerdemain requires holding out the known object and then replacing it with the unknown object," Weasel said. "If we do anything to distract them from looking at the known object they're going to see through the trick—remember that these are not dumb guys."

"We also know that no matter how well we set an op up there is the possibility that these guys—battle hardened special operators—may resist our efforts to subdue them, and that would doom the trap back here," Ed said.

"I think anything on even the local news that includes the phrases Ex-Navy SEALs and/or Secret Service agents might alert even a brain-dead mastermind of a continuing plot to kidnap the president's daughters, and I agree with Weasel—these are not brain-dead guys, especially not Captain Tom Miller," Mamba said.

"You're right, of course, even though I would dearly love to put those three lookouts in jail for life," Edward Otis Whitney said. "However, I concur that that will have to wait until after we have the ringleader and his merry men in hand, so we show them exactly what they expect and wait to spring the trap back here."

We all agreed with that, so we started the clock on the op and Mamba took us to the D.C. Grille Express on DuPont Circle. We took up the entire restaurant, inside and out (it isn't that big anyway), ate like hogs, drank like fish, and generally had an awesome fucking time, especially since everything was paid for by Almont Phillipe Gilbert de Coucy, Monsieur Le Comte de Condé, a.k.a. Mamba. After so much food I thought I'd burst—I had three double bacon cheeseburgers, three fries, two orders of parmesan Brussels sprouts and so much iced tea that I was sloshing as Badass, Jewey, Weasel, Ed and I staggered down 18th Street to the Du Pont Circle Metro station. We were basically staggering from too much food, although Badass and Weasel had certainly held their own in drinking buckets of beer.

We gave each other shit and laughed all the way to the Gallery Place/Chinatown metro station, where we left the Red Line and got on the Green Line for the Anacostia Metro station. As we rode along on the Green Line Badass said, "I don't want to bring up sensitive shit—"

"Then don't!" we all said at once.

"Freak, you owe us Pepsis," Weasel said.

"Why me? I thought that Ed was first," I said.

"Oh, she was, but the rest of us have to travel and you get to stay back here—you don't get the lovely experience of jet-lag, or have to put up with a bunch of dope-smoking Oregon hippies," Weasel said.

"You don't know that they're hippie dopers," I said.

"Oh, come on! They live in *Paisley, Oregon*," Jewey said

I couldn't really argue with that. I mean, I had to admit when I first heard where Tom Miller had his training compound the first thing that popped into my head was a flashback to pictures of Woodstock. Your town's name is Paisley? There must not be a straight guy in the entire town, right?

"As I was saying," Badass said, "I think that Pinniped is one sweet op, and I think we may finally get a chance to ask our friend and his merry men the questions we all want answered."

We couldn't really argue with that, either, since the op appeared to be almost foolproof—none of us were arrogant enough to believe it was perfect (whatever that was), but we were also professional enough to acknowledge that our planning was solid and enhanced our chances of success.

"All we have to do is execute it properly and we'll get those bastards once and for all," Ed said. We all agreed with that, too, so when we got off the Metro to go home we all stopped to get a Pepsi for a "good luck" toast. This was a tradition I'd started to honor my *zayde*, who always said it was "better to be lucky than good" before he went into court (think of it like it's the opening night of a play and people are saying "Break a leg").

We all hoisted our Pepsis and said "Q'APLA!" (it's from *Star Trek*—the Klingon word for success) and then drained the can (well, I drained mine—not everybody was as, ahem, successful as I was).

"We're going to hit it right down the middle and get those motherfucking shithead traitorous asshole kidnappers, and we're going to put them away at Gitmo for the rest of their miserable lives," Badass said. Hurricane was in Boston giving a seminar on how to manage multiple births and Badass wanted to let loose a little bit before the op. OK, so he'd drunk two or five $20 buckets of Corona by himself and was slightly buzzed (drunker than a frat boy on rush night) when he made his melodramatic announcement.

Oddly enough that's almost exactly what the rest of us were thinking, and it's almost what happened.

Almost.

CHAPTER 75

Fried Freak

So the next day we put the op in motion and got ready to take down Tom Miller and his renegade SEALs. We all went off to do our jobs, which meant that Kid Galahad and I went off to cover the Warrior Princesses while everybody else got in position for their flight, which left at two p.m. and got to Pittsburgh about 50 minutes later. The bus trip would take at least four hours (more like six—this tour was senior citizens and they need more pee stops...and before you get all smirky remember: this will be you one day), so the Surreptitious Surveillers (Mamba thought they should have a name) would all be in position by tomorrow morning at six a.m.

The day was uneventful. We went to school and then went to the Treasury Department Shooting Range. We had to shoot quickly because both the girls had a mountain of homework (hey, the Amicus School may have been educating the president's kids, but they also had very high academic requirements—and they didn't give anybody any breaks, privileged or not).

Before we began our practice I took the girls aside and said, "Today I have presents for you both, but you can't tell anyone—especially your parents—about them, and you can't let anyone else see them, either. I mean *nobody* can know about these presents. Am I clear?"

"As crystal, Freak," Allison said.

"Are they pistols of our own?" Brooke said.

"Yes," I said. I pulled out two Smith & Wesson M&P22 Compacts, .22 caliber pistols that held ten in the clip and one in the gun and fired a standard .22 long rifle round. The pistols were only 15 ounces fully loaded and were short enough that you could almost hold them in your hand and no one would notice. They came with small pancake holsters that could be concealed almost anywhere on the body.

We went over the basics of the weapon, the Warrior Princesses loaded up two clips, jacked one in the chamber and then dropped the clips to put one more round in the mag. I always love it in the movies when the hero—always a trained operative of some kind—stands over the bad guy and jacks a round into the chamber to let the bad guy know that he's serious now, boy. What the hell kind of trained operative doesn't always have a round in the chamber? Pistols can't fire without a round up, so anybody who's serious always racks one in. Most of our movie heroes would be dead within seconds if they had to rack one in, the stupid assholes (sorry about the diatribe, but Hollyweird can fuck up a wet dream, especially when it comes to things like taking dramatic license with technical aspects of shooting—it annoys anyone who has ever actually had to do any shooting. Sorry.).

Once we were ready to shoot I said, "Let off the first clip as fast as you can, then take aimed shots with the second one. When you're through with the first 22 rounds see if you can disassemble the weapon, OK? Any questions?"

Both girls shook their heads, so we put on our ear protection and let the rounds fly. I was working on improving my double-tap speed, so I worked very methodically while still trying to operate at combat speed. By the time I'd perforated my last target both Warrior Princesses had their S&Ws apart and were swabbing the barrels down. I felt myself surge with pride, since they were doing what they should be without being told, just like good Marines, and I knew it was as a result of my training.

I don't know what a parent feels like when their child succeeds at something difficult, but what I felt that day must've been damned close.

I went over and we talked about the way the weapons felt, how they were to handle and if they had any tendencies when firing.

"Their recoil makes the weapon shake a bit side to side, rather than going up and off-target," Brooke said.

"It also has a bit of a tendency to miss low and to the left on the last three rounds—oh, because the weight distribution is different and we think that we need to hold it down on target against the recoil," Allison said.

"And we're used to a much more powerful weapon—we're using our 9-millimeter baseline," Brooke said.

I congratulated them on their analysis and then said, "I know these pistols are small, but you remember that they're not toys—they will kill or maim the bad guys just like the 9-millimeter, just with less power. They won't penetrate body armor even at close range, so park every round in their crotch or their head—aim for an eye or ear, if you're at a 90° angle."

They nodded and Brooke said, "Where do we keep them? In our purses?"

"You could, but purses are fickle things that could hang your weapon up," I said.

"What about the small of our backs—under our shirts that are hanging out?" Allison said.

"That's where I'd put it, but if you're in a dress you'll need to find an easily accessible, comfortable spot other than that where you can put it," I said.

"Where would you put it?" Brooke said.

"Well, if the dress or skirt were long enough I'd strap it to the inside of my thigh opposite my dominant hand, so I could just yank the dress up and cross draw it," I said. "You'll have to experiment, and don't be shy about it, either."

"You mean try to put it in, uh, places, where the bad guys won't want to look?" Allison said.

"Like down our bra?" Brooke said. We all kind of giggled and I said, "Sure, although I don't think that'll be an option for you much longer, my Warrior Princess." We giggled again, because Brooke had recently passed her sister in the boob department and looked to be a sure bet for more growth in that area.

After some more girl talk (sorry, some stuff is private) we got ready to leave. Both of the girls had cleaned and reassembled their pistols, filled the clips and racked one in, de-cocked, then fit the pistols in their holsters and stowed them in their bags. When we were ready to leave I said, "Remember, we're not telling anyone yet. Once the time is right I'll ask your parents about it and then we'll take them to the range for a demonstration, but for now…"

"We need to have some personal protection until you catch whoever's trying to take us, but we don't need to worry Mom and Dad," Allison said.

"'Zxactly," I said, making them laugh as we got in the waiting cars and sped off for the White House and three hours of homework.

Once the Warrior Princesses were safely ensconced under the protective umbrella of the president I said good night and went to the Secret Service control center in the White House. I talked to the duty officer, and then to the president's Chief of Detail, Senior Agent Parker H. Connolly. Connolly was a tall guy with a rugged face that clearly showed he'd been an aspiring professional boxer until, as he said, "my face met Earnie Shavers' fist," (Muhammad Ali once said that Earnie Shavers hit him so hard "he rocked my ancestors back in Africa," in case you were wondering who Earnie Shavers was), whereupon he retired after he woke up three days later in the hospital. I don't know if he could've boxed anymore, but he was still in good shape and wasn't someone to fool with. He had a good sense of humor about everything except his middle name, which was Hieronymus, after the great painter Hieronymus Bosch.

I not only liked Connolly, I also respected him for his professionalism and devotion to duty, especially to this Republican president, which must have been a real trial for the son and grandson of Democratic councilmen in Boston.

Anyway, Connolly told me that there had been some chatter (a.k.a. radio intercepts) about some shit concerning the president, and that the White House was on semi-lockdown, and would I like to go inspect the exterior perimeter? It wasn't exactly an order, but Parker Connolly stood about three feet from the president most of the time, and people like that are never bad to have as friends, so I said "Sure" and went off to inspect the exterior perimeter of the White House.

I found everything fairly copacetic, except for the two snipers who were sneaking a cigarette at their post somewhere on the White House grounds (sorry, definitely classified). I chewed their asses out, took their pack of cigarettes, pitched them in the trash and then went to report to Parker H. Connolly that all was well. He told me that Kid Galahad wanted me to know that he was going to the Nationals game with his girlfriend (Miss Bitchy Voice herself, who was now stationed back in D.C.) and that he wouldn't be riding the train home with me.

After talking some more shop I headed out and caught the Metro Blue Line at Farragut West, which took me to the L'Enfant Plaza station and the Green Line for home. It was just getting really dark when I got off at the Anacostia station and began walking the little more than four blocks home, whistling Keb Mo's "Standing at the Station" with a smile on my face as I thought about the Surreptitious Surveillors' bus ride with a bunch of senior citizens.

I was still smiling when two guys whipped out the door of a liquor store and attacked me from the front. They were too close for me to pull a pistol, so I immediately counter-attacked, because I was pretty sure that the two in front of me were the distraction crew, and that I was supposed to back up into the arms of their comrades.

I found out I was right when something clanged off the sidewalk behind me as I attacked the guy on the left side. I put a knife hand in his throat before he could react and then crushed his jaw with an elbow strike while pivoting 90° and kicking the right-hand guy on his left knee cap. The kick was a direct hit that shattered his knee and as he buckled toward me I mashed his nose with a palm strike and hammered his neck with a hammer fist. I felt bones breaking from both strikes as I grabbed his unconscious body and whirled it behind me in a flat spin that knocked down the two guys who were rushing in to attack me from behind.

Both of them had ASP expandable batons, which they lost as they went flying from my impromptu anti-personnel bomb (unlike in the movies, in real life the law of momentum always applies—if you're rushing toward someone and they hit you in the knees with a 200-pound weight your momentum carries you into the weight with more force than your knees can take and you fall down). I scooped up the excellent batons—the Talon Disc Loc 21" models, I noticed—as I whacked both of the attackers in the head to make sure they stayed down. In real life you also can't take a shot to the head with a combat baton (or anything else) employed by a professional and not lose consciousness at least for a little while—these guys weren't getting up any time soon, if ever. Then I faced the three guys armed with batons who were rushing me from three sides.

I instantly attacked the right-hand guy, who was too far in front of his fellow attackers. He realized he was exposed and tried to juke me so that he could get back in position—that was a move that told me these guys were pros—but I did something he never expected when I dove straight under his baton and between his legs. It was a classic John Smith (look him up) inside single leg takedown I'd actually learned from John Smith (look him up) at a wrestling clinic when I was 15 years old, and it left me directly under my attacker's crotch. I popped straight up through said crotch with my shoulder, smashing his balls and throwing him literally 10 feet in the air. I spun in a tight semi-circle with both batons extended and whacked his head, throat, ribs, crotch again and both knees before he hit the ground.

I whipped the two batons over my head as the other two guys smashed theirs down, parrying the strokes that would have knocked me unconscious or killed me. Before the two guys could react I dropped my batons, grabbing theirs and wrenching them free. I smashed the extended forearm of one attacker with both batons, then reversed my stroke and caught the other guy in the ribs and high on the temple, killing him (I knew it when I hit him—crushed temple equals death in the real world—this wasn't the movies, kids).

I turned back to the guy whose arm I had broken and said, "Who the fuck sent you, you weak-assed shithead?"

Which is when I noticed that even though his arm was in a weird Z-shape that must have hurt like hell he was grinning at me.

Which is when I found out that "almost" isn't worth a fucking shit when it comes to disarming a bomb, having a baby, or closing a trap on a herd of Navy SEALs.

Which is also when I felt something smack me in the left ass cheek, kind of like a wasp stinging me.

Which is when my world lit up like the Fourth of July as the eighth attacker triggered the taser whose prongs were stuck in my ass.

As the volts of electricity shot through my body I shook like I was caught in Hurricane Sandy. My head felt like it was going to explode and I was completely paralyzed. I fell to the ground and the guy left off the trigger, stopping the electricity from surging through my body. I wasn't sure I could move, but I tried bucking like a live shrimp on a hot grill and succeeded in dislodging the taser prongs. I rolled over to get to my feet and the ninth attacker shot me with another taser and hit the juice.

I remember bright flashes popping across my eyes, I remember falling again, I remember someone saying "Once more oughta do it, Johnson," and I remember curling into the fetal position and my bladder letting go as the guy squeezed the trigger one more time.

My last conscious thought was 'If I live Tom Miller is going to die,' right before my head blew off my shoulders and everything went black.

CHAPTER 76

Silk Bra Salvation

When I woke up it was black and quiet, and I smelled man-sweat, urine and old, burned coffee. My body felt like I'd been attacked by the Detroit Lions football team and then run over by an 18-wheel tractor-trailer, but it was OK because my mouth felt like the herd of elephants that had been living there had departed, leaving just their enormous piles of shit behind with the slice of the Sahara Desert that used to be my tongue. Jimmy Buffett and the Coral Reefers Band were playing a steel drum concert inside my head as Gregory Hines, Mikhail Baryshnikov, and Bill "Bojangles" Robinson performed tap dancing routines on top of my skull wearing nice steel-toed boots. I was pretty sure there was a writhing ball of mating snakes in my stomach and my eyeballs felt like someone had decided to improve my vision with sandpaper.

The fact was, even if I wasn't tied hand and foot to something that felt like a kitchen chair, I'm not sure that I could've moved. I was sure that I didn't want to move. I was also sure that I wanted about a month's vacation in Harbor Springs, Michigan, accompanied by a thousand Advil tablets, several barrels of Pepsi and a very soft down comforter to cover up with as I lay in my nice, soft bed.

Just then somebody pulled the hood off my head and smacked me across the face.

So much for my fantasies coming true. Where was that fucking fairy godmother when you needed the bitch?

I blinked hard against the harsh light coming from four lamps hanging from the ceiling. I squinted, squinched my eyes in and out of focus a few times and finally got enough vision back in time to see a backhand slap inbound. My head rocked back from the impact, and as I was rolling it forward a fist came into view, inbound for my cheek, so I snapped my head forward and the fist bounced off my forehead. I smiled when I heard a finger break and a knuckle pop, for two reasons. First it meant that one of my captors was hurt, second it meant that these clowns weren't real pros, because unlike the movies, when you punch someone in the head you have as good a chance of hurting yourself as you do inflicting damage on the person that you're hitting, especially if it's someone with a head as hard as mine.

I give the guy credit—he didn't speak, but his breath went in sharply as the pain registered. Someone grabbed my hair and yanked my head back and a different fist popped me on the cheek. Then another fist buried itself in the pit of my stomach, and I let out a huge long burp that rattled the glass in the windows. My stomach immediately felt better, and surprisingly, the punches and slaps seemed to have cleared my fuzzy mental mechanism, because I felt almost like myself, except for a slight shakiness, which I attributed to electricity overdose.

I looked at the three guys who were my captors. They were all around 6', 180, (although the third guy was a bit shorter and thinner), with trim muscled bodies, big hands, and short military-style haircuts. All three were dark haired and dark-eyed, and they sort of looked related, with high foreheads, strong, dimpled chins and noses that looked like they were just off the boat from Palermo.

But I was pretty sure they weren't Navy SEALs, because they just didn't move right, and they seemed to be just knocking me around for the hell of it. SEALs wouldn't waste time doing that. They might waste me, but they'd do it by cutting my throat or shooting me in the head with a silenced 9 mm. Again, unlike the movies, when the bad guys want to get the job done they just do it (my apologies to Nike) like the professionals that they are. No long conversations, no fucking around, just BOOM and you're gone.

After a couple more punches and slaps the shortest one said, "What are your passwords to gain access to the president, bitch?"

Now I knew that they weren't SEALs, and also that they weren't serious about getting any information from me, because anybody with half a brain would know that as soon as it was determined that I'd been taken—and by now somebody definitely knew, because there was almost certainly security footage of my capture and kidnapping—every password I'd ever known for any reason would be changed. Any information I had would be hours too old by now, and besides, we don't do it that way when it came to POTUS and his or her family (sorry, but that's way, way classified).

When I didn't answer him the one with the broken finger and popped knuckle drilled me in the gut with his left hand. It was a good punch, so good that it caused me to explosively break wind. The stench was awful and they all reacted to it, which further proved to me that these guys weren't SEALs, because those guys could care less about smells—they wade through shit every time they go in the field, and it just doesn't affect them (and yes, that is personal, first-hand knowledge talking). That meant that they were the second team, probably the backups from my takedown, and that meant that I had a chance.

While they were gagging and waiting for the air to clear I was subtly checking out the chair I was tied to. The rope was good nylon that was knotted with some skill, so I couldn't worm out that way, but the chair itself...it appeared to be a plain old kitchen chair, and while I couldn't see the whole thing I didn't see any apparent steel reinforcements, or any steel bolts holding a joint together, which meant the chair was vulnerable.

It didn't appear that these guys believed what they'd been told about my abilities, and that really told me that they were at least the second team, because any special operator worth their salt knew better than to try and confine the opposition without accounting for any particular skills or abilities they had, a lesson these guys had clearly never learned.

One of the guys who had a small scar on his face said, "How do we breach the White House communications system, cunt?"

I just smiled at him and he slapped me with his forehand, and then backhanded me in the same stroke. I used the smacking to test the chair again and was really pleased with the results. That's when I decided to let them hit me just three more times. I figured that an even twenty shots to the head and torso were enough, and they were at seventeen, so three it was.

Unless they used an implement. For some reason being hit by their fists didn't bother me, but the thought of being whacked with an implement did. Maybe it was because of my childhood, when my brothers whaled on me with sticks as we played at "sword fighting" (which I am still convinced was brother-speak for "let's beat the crap out of our younger sister and get away with it"), or maybe it was because I really, truly didn't like bullies who whipped up on people weaker than them by using implements of destruction, but probably it was just because I was inherently afraid of penises and/or their symbolic representations (as my good friend Fiona the Freudian psychologist always told me).

Or maybe I was just tired of getting smacked around by three strong motherfuckers.

Especially since they were trying to force information out of me that (a) I was never going to supply and (b) was certainly obsolete, since my supervisor would have changed it the moment he knew that I was taken and (c) the objects they wanted the information for were out of their reach, locked up in the White House behind a Secret Service screen that could be augmented by a Marine regiment in about five minutes (literally).

Or maybe I was just tired of being knocked around by three strong motherfuckers.

In any case, either three more shots with their fists, or one shot with an implement—that was it. I was a stubborn, bullheaded, obtuse bitch with serious anger issues and an iron will, but enough was enough. These clowns were good—clearly well trained and in great physical shape—but they weren't SEALs and had never seen me in action. They were in for a big surprise after just three more punches, or one whack with an implement.

Which is why I was totally unprepared when one of them took out a big Ka-Bar combat knife and sliced my blouse up both sides. He tore the remnants of the blouse off, pulled my bra away from my body and sliced it between the cups, and then threw the whole mess behind him on the floor, leaving my considerable breasts exposed.

It must be said (so I'll say it before anybody else does) that I am not a good-looking womyn, but my boobs are spectacular in their shape, size, and effect on men. Every guy who has ever seen them (even in a business suit) is so awestruck that they pause for a moment in silent reverence for the God of Tits who blessed me with my totally outrageous ta-tas.

Not these guys. They never really looked at them at all, which is when I realized that either (a) I was in the presence of three totally gay guys who could care less about tits (highly unlikely, since these motherfuckers looked and acted mucho hetero) or (b) these were serious professionals bent on truly harming me.

I was betting on (b), especially when the shortest one pulled a circuit board, battery, and some alligator clips on the ends of wires out of a backpack. I realized at that point that it wasn't the information that they wanted—I was going to be a message for POTUS. After they had systematically tortured me they were going to leave my body somewhere it would be readily discovered, and subsequently reported to POTUS, who would undoubtedly get the message that his daughters were next.

All of this flashed through my mind right before the one with the knife yanked my hips away from the chair and slit my pants right down the middle (he cut through my Hermès belt, too, which really pissed me off). One of the other goons stepped up and the two of them yanked my pants down around my ankles, which were still duct-taped to the chair legs. Knife goon sliced through the bunched legs and threw the remnants of my pants into the same pile as my bra and blouse.

I wasn't really bothered about being completely naked in front of the three gomers, until gomer #3 lifted the front of the chair up and set a wide pan down, leaving my feet immersed in water when he gently let the chair back down. I knew what that meant—the next thing out of the backpack would be a probe of some kind that they were going to shove in my vagina or up my ass (if I got to choose I'd have picked vagina, because at least it was used to being probed by my vibrator) right before they used more volts to fry me again.

The three gomers stepped away from me and the one with the scar said, "Not very modern, are we?" They all glanced at my crotch and smirked, I assume because they had never seen a real Burning Bush before (which is what my one college boyfriend had always called my pubes). Having flaming red hair is not a bad thing, unless you have pubic hair that grows like the Brazilian rain forest and covers most of your belly up to your *pipik* (your navel, for the non-Hebrews among us)—then it's a bitch. And no, I never considered having a Brazilian done, since I was sure that even Cedars-Sinai couldn't have stopped the bleeding from that waxing, and no, I wasn't going to shave it, either—you know how bad it is when you have to stand absolutely still and your pubes itch? No? Believe me, it's as bad as having poison ivy in your crotch. And yes, I do know what that feels like.

Besides, my current sex toy liked the Burning Bush (I guess it was inevitable that the nickname would stick) just the way it was, so yeah, I had a mass of curly hairs just sticking up down there. The three gomers did pause just a bit to gaze at the Burning Bush, which is when I decided that having alligator clamps attached to my nipples and a probe shoved up my ass so some gomers could half-electrocute me for information that they clearly didn't give a rat's ass about just wasn't in the cards.

Like I said, the gomers had never seen me in action—clearly they weren't part of the first team, all of whom would have been briefed on my abilities—which is why they were totally unprepared when I ripped the chair apart, fell on my butt and rolled up to my feet before the well-trained gomers could react.

I hit the first one with a knife hand to the solar plexus, caught the second one with a hammer fist to the nose and drove a reverse heel kick into the third one's left knee. I spun and aimed my front elbow at the first gomer's face, but he put his hands up to block, which was OK with me, since it was a feint. My trailing elbow came around in a short, vicious arc and broke four of his ribs, dropping him from the fight. The second gomer was semi-recovered, so I kneed him in the balls and spun an elbow into the mastoid process behind his ear, breaking his jaw in at least three places and also removing him from the fight.

Gomer #3 had recovered enough to pull his Ka-Bar out again, which meant that I was going to get cut. Despite what you see all the time in movies even the best martial artists (of which I was one—black belts in three different styles) cannot casually disarm someone with a knife. The rule was simple: if they get within 10 feet of you with the knife you're going to get cut. No exceptions. Even Bruce Lee or Chuck Norris would have to be just stone lucky to not get cut—and even with luck they'd probably still be bloodied up. Since this gomer was about six feet away I was going to get cut.

So I charged him, hoping he wouldn't hit anything vital until I could subdue him. He stepped back just a tad and then came in low with the knife, aiming right for the Burning Bush (my analytical mind reminded me that this was so I couldn't kick his hand up without taking the thrust somewhere in my body), so I planted my left foot and spun sideways into a desperate wheel kick, which is when my bra intervened.

That's right, my bra.

I know, I know, it's a cliché, right? The heroine is saved by some miraculous occurrence that's totally unbelievable, but this time it was just simple physics. Take 180 pounds of mass and move it along a vector with 850 foot-pounds of thrust at a rate of real quick and the point of the thrusting instrument will arrive at its destination in a certain time with a certain amount of force, provided that the thrust remains constant. This is what should have happened to me, except for the fact that another physical principle—that would be friction—was temporarily suspended at the anchor point of the thrust, changing both the thrusting force and vector of the strike.

The gomer stepped on my 100% silk bra with his back foot as he pushed off. Hand sewn by a little old Chinese-American lady in my neighborhood in D.C., the silk bra did just what it was supposed to do—it slid smoothly across the floor, just like it slid over my boobs when I was wearing my shoulder rig, which was just about all the time. When your boobs are perfectly round, perky 38Cs you need custom bras, because nothing off the rack is ever going to fit right.

So when the gomer slipped on my bra his aim was spoiled, and he didn't have nearly enough force to drive the Ka-Bar through my midriff (or my cooter, for that matter) and gut me.

He did, however, still cut me. The knife slid along my side from my hip up to my armpit, but I just clamped his hand and forearm under my arm and hip-tossed him to the floor. Not letting go of his arm I reversed and spun his shoulder out of socket, broke his arm at the wrist and elbow in a judo hold and kicked him in the trapezius, right where his neck met his shoulder. The gomer's head snapped down and back, then struck the wall at an unnatural angle, breaking his neck. I said a silent thanks to Mrs. Chen for her craftsmanship on the bra—and her insistence that silk was the only proper fabric for a bra—as I stood up from killing the third gomer.

I could feel the wound on my side burning where the knife had cut me as I ripped the tape and chair arm off my left wrist. I then carefully unwound the tape from my right wrist and used it to hold the edges of the wound in my side together. Fortunately the knife had been razor-sharp—further evidence that these gomers were pros—and the wound hadn't yet started to really bleed. I slapped the tape flat over every part of the wound I could see, because I knew when I started to move it would open up. I also carefully unwound the tape from my ankles and used it as cross supports over the wound.

When I was finally tape and chair free I stepped over to the first gomer, the one who had broken ribs and problems breathing from a solar plexus that was certainly bruised all to hell. I knelt down next to him and put my index finger right on the middle one of his broken ribs. He looked like he was thinking of trying to attack me, so I hitched up and put my knee right on his throat. The gomer had a face full of the Burning Bush and 167 rock-solid pounds poised to crush his hyoid bone and slowly suffocate him—and he was a pro who knew that I would do it, too. All the fight went out of his eyes, so I said, "Say, can we talk? I'm just bursting with questions after being assaulted, battered and forced to defend myself against three big, healthy men—the exercise really gets your mind right, y'know?"

He sort of nodded, so I said, "All I want to know is this: where is your boss?"

His eyes got big and he slowly moved his head side to side. I suspected that he was more scared of his boss than he was of me, so I said, "Look, he's a scary guy, but I'm right here, right now, and if you don't tell me I'm gonna have to really, really hurt you." To emphasize my point I gently pushed down on his broken rib with my finger. To his credit the gomer only grunted, so I stiffened my finger into an attack position and really dug in on the rib.

He screamed like a third grader and passed out, which is what I expected to happen. I went over and secured the still unconscious gomer #2 with his own duct tape. Gomer #3 was dead as a doornail, so I didn't duct tape him up. I wrapped gomer #1's feet and hands together with duct tape, so when he woke up I wouldn't have to wrestle with him at all.

He woke up in short order, at which point I again put my finger in an attack position and set it on the rib. I said, "OK, I'm only going to ask you one more time: where is Tom Miller?"

His eyes lit up when I said Tom's name, so I said, "Look, I know what's going on, and I know who's leading the effort, so tell me where Tom is and nobody else has to get hurt. I know that you were just following orders, and I know why Tom wants to do this, but if I can't find him I can't help him. Anybody else is just gonna shoot him on sight, so why not tell me where he is? I'll tell him it was gomer #3—the dead one over there—that told me. He'll never know it was you."

They tell me that I have a sincere and trustworthy face, which really means I can con anybody, but in this case I meant what I said, and the gomer must have seen that. He blew out a breath and said, "We were supposed to meet him at the National Portrait Gallery—just inside the northwest entrance."

"By the Stuart painting of George Washington."

"Yeah. In fact, that bench was the wave-off spot. If we were compromised, or didn't finish the job, one of us was supposed to leave a copy of today's *Post* on the bench, folded open to the second sports page."

I stood up and said, "Thanks, man. I'll call an ambulance for you and gomer #2 as soon as I've seen Tom. Otherwise it could be quite a while before somebody finds you." I stood up and turned to leave the room when I realized that I had a problem.

No fucking clothes.

I was good at what I did—there was no better Secret Service agent alive—but I couldn't go after a bad guy who wanted to harm the first daughters while completely nude. First of all, they'd never let me in the National Gallery, even if I told them I was just a model who was going to a nude sitting. Second, I was pretty sure that Tom Miller would notice a completely nude me trying to stalk him and third, I didn't know where the fuck I was and I didn't have any fucking money for a cab or a fucking car, although I was pretty sure the gomers had some kind of transport—it's hard to take an unconscious Secret Service agent on a bus or the Metro.

There was no question everybody would get a load of the Burning Bush, which would stop traffic just long enough for the cops to arrest my ass and throw me in jail, thus defeating the mission of getting the bad guy.

In other words, I was fucked.

Unless…

I went back to the injured gomer and said, "Dude, I need to borrow your clothes."

"Why'n't you take his clothes," the gomer said, inclining his head toward his dead buddy. "He ain't gonna need 'em no more." I couldn't argue with that logic, especially since the dead gomer was shorter than the other two. I stripped the clothes off his body—outwear only, since I wasn't wearing anybody else's drawers (the only thing more gross than that would be using someone else's tooth-brush—eeeyyeuuu!) and put them on.

The shirt was OK, and the pants were a little long but OK, so I just tightened the belt up, rolled up the shirtsleeves and cut off the pants cuffs with the Ka-Bar. By then the wound scored into my side was burning and trying to leak, but it turned out that the duct tape was just as good as stitches, although nowhere near as good as bourbon for the pain.

I nodded at the conscious gomer and headed out the door.

It opened on a small warehouse, which was nearly empty except for a few boxes near what I guessed was the outside door. I went over and almost just passed by the boxes, but something about the markings made me stop to look at them. I opened one and suddenly knew where Tom Miller and his merry band of rogue SEALs were, and how they were going to get at the first daughters…and I was pretty sure that it was going to work, too.

Shitpisshelldamnfuck!

I grabbed some stuff from the boxes, changed into it and about 3 seconds later I was outside, standing under a faded old sign that said, "Bennie's Tire Repair." There was a really old mercury vapor night-light on a splintered pole that gave just enough light to read "Morgan's Floral" in bright red letters over a blood red rose painted on the side of an old Ford Econoline van. I looked in the window just in case the gomers had left a little present for someone trying to steal their van, but it looked clear—and the keys were in the ignition, so I opened the door and got in, turned the key and started to fasten my seatbelt. As my hand reached down to buckle the belt I felt a piece of smooth leather in the crack between the seat and console.

It was manna from heaven.

Actually, it was my Secret Service creds, which led to my twin S&W 1076s, which led to me being pre-orgasmic. I didn't look the part, but I was almost a fully functional Secret Service agent again. But when I looked for my radio I found it smashed to pieces, along with my cell phone. I pulled back the slide on one 1076 and it just kept sliding—both pistols had parts missing and were non-functional, and I didn't have any rounds for them anyway.

Shit.

I looked at the barren fields around the defunct tire repair shop in the middle of Bumfuck, Egypt, and knew I was severely fucked. With no way to communicate and no way to know even approximately where I was there was no way to get where I thought I needed to be, so I decided to slow down and do a better job of searching the truck.

That's why I found the Maryland road map in the glove box, which confirmed my conclusions from when I found the boxes in the defunct tire repair shop.

Here's how it went in my head.

> Me: (Looking in the boxes) These appear to be Marine BDUS (battle dress uniforms).
> Me: Now why on earth would the bad guys have…hey, wait just a goddamned minute.
> Me: Right—where would the president take his daughters if he thought they were in immediate danger?
> Me: The most secure place he could think of besides the White House.

Me: Right. Someplace surrounded by a regiment of Marines, perhaps?

Me: Shit, yeah.

Me: Someplace like NSF Thurmont, maybe?

Me: Shit, yeah. Camp David'd be perfect—it's remote, inaccessible, and surrounded by a regiment of U.S. Marines.

Me: 'Zxactly.

I had to get to Camp David, convince the gate personnel to let me in and then secure the girls from being kidnapped by a heavily armed SEAL unit led by a fanatic who wanted to punish the president, and I had to do it without weapons, a phone or anything besides myself and some poorly fitting Marine BDUS.

That'd be no problem if I had a big red "S" on my chest, but since I didn't I wasn't sure how to proceed, but I knew one thing.

I wasn't quitting, whatever happened, because I wasn't letting Tom Miller or any other motherfucker kidnap *my* Warrior Princesses as long as I could draw breath. If that sounds melodramatic to you, or if it's too sappy or maudlin, well, then fuck you, the horse you rode in on, and the family dog.

I swore an oath to protect and defend the USA from all threats, foreign and domestic, and by God I meant every fucking word of it.

So I jumped in the flower truck, opened the map, and went off down the deserted road looking for a road sign. I found one, located where I was and discovered that I was only about four miles from the front gate at NSF Thurmont. I popped the truck back in gear and sped off in the right direction.

I was furiously trying to figure out how I was going to get past the gate guards when it hit me. How the fuck was Tom Miller going to get at the girls *at Camp David*, one of the most heavily guarded places in the world? I jammed to a stop at the corner of Cacoctin Hollow Road and Maryland 77 and was about to head for the entrance to the presidential retreat (really? After all we've been through? You think that I'm going to tell you exactly how to get to the presidential retreat? Think again, numbnuts—that's classified) when it hit me like a ton of bricks.

I knew exactly how Tom Miller and his SEALs were going to get to the girls, and I had about a mile and a half to come up with a way to keep from having a firefight near the Princesses (or POTUS) while taking Tom Miller and his guys into custody peacefully, or else people were going to get dead.

Dead was the odds-on favorite.

CHAPTER 77

Turn and Cough

I drove like a crazy person to the gate at Camp David, a.k.a. Naval Support Facility Thurmont, hoping against hope that none of Tom Miller's guys were there ahead of me. When I got to the gate I stopped the flower truck and turned the engine off. Four Marines in full battle dress came out to surround the old van while two Marines with pistols came up on either side of the truck. I was plainly visible, and I kept my hands at ten and two so that none of the Marines thought I was threatening them, because I was fairly sure that they'd shoot first and ask questions later.

The Marine lieutenant who came up to my window was very polite and said, "Ma'am, this is a restricted—" He stopped when he saw my BDUS, and then moved in for a closer look at my name tape. When he saw there wasn't one he very smoothly dropped his clipboard and pulled his M9, as did the Marine at the passenger's window. Both men were scanning everything inside the van, looking for telltale signs of a truck bomb, but they both kept their pistols pointed right at my head.

"Ma'am, please keep your hands where I can see them and exit the vehicle immediately," the Marine lieutenant said. His tone and demeanor were impeccably Marine Corps: calm, cool and polite as hell, with just the right undertone of menace.

I got out of the van with my hands on my head and got down on my knees without being asked. The Marine behind me said, "L-T, she ain't wearin' any shoes, and I don't see any visible wires or weapons."

"Thank you, Gunny. I don't see any weapons, but she's got some sort of case in the front pocket of her BDUS that could be a remote. Henderson, Orozco, check the back of that van," the lieutenant said.

Two of the armed troopers moved to the open door of the van and shined flashlights into the back of the van. "It's completely empty, L-T. There ain't even a candy wrapper we can see," one of the men said.

"Excellent. Now look underneath as well," the lieutenant said.

Within seconds one of the Marines said, "Nothing there, sir, except the exhaust system and axles and shit."

The lieutenant looked at me and said, "Ma'am, what's in the case in your front pocket?"

"My credentials," I said. "I'm Secret Service agent Glinka Glickstien and I need to see the president ASAP."

"Assuming that you check out, ma'am, why the hell is a barefoot Secret Service agent wearing Marine BDUS and driving a flower truck? That's beyond unorthodox, ma'am, it's out there in loony-tunes land," the lieutenant said. He and his men never wavered in keeping their weapons trained on me.

I said, "Lieutenant, I'd like to take my creds out and let you look at them, then I'd like to ask you a question, OK?"

"Ma'am, please take the case out with two fingers and toss it to me. Don't make any other moves, ma'am," he said.

I did what I was told. He scooped up the creds, flopped them open, checked the picture ID against my face, looked at the badge and tapped it with his pistol, then looked back at me and said, "OK, Agent Glickstien, what the fuck is going on?"

"I'd really like to ask you that question now, lieutenant, please," I said.

He nodded and I said, "Has there been anything out of the ordinary about the president's visit this time? Anybody else try to get in without authorization, or any other unusual personnel activity?"

"Who says the president is even here? We do this to anyone who just drives up, whether or not the president is here," the lieutenant said.

"Yeah, I'm sure you do, but let's cut the shit, shall we? He and his family are here, and I need to know if there is anybody else here, and I also need to know if there's anything unusual about this visit," I said.

"Why the hell should I tell you anything, ma'am? You're not in my chain of command, plus you don't need to know anything more about NSF Thurmont than how to get the hell away from here," he said.

"Lieutenant, I've been here twice in a uniform just like yours, and seven times with the first family, and if you don't believe me I'll give you some info that only someone who's been here would know," I said.

"Yeah, like what?" the lieutenant said. So I gave him a whole pile of stuff that only someone who'd been in the presidential retreat would have any hope of knowing (sorry, classified). He finally put his hand up and said, "OK, so I'll buy that you've been here, but you're not on the roster for this trip, and you still haven't told me what the hell is going on, ma'am." He sounded intrigued, so I said, "Look, there is a real threat to the first family and I don't have a lot of time to explain. I need you to call the Pentagon and get the Chairman of the Joint Chiefs on the phone."

They all laughed and the lieutenant said, "Yeah, and right after that I'm gonna grow wings out my ass and fly to Hawai'i."

"OK, lieutenant, who's the senior noncommissioned officer here?" I said.

"Command Sergeant Major Berkey is the senior NCO at NSF Thurmont," the lieutenant said. "I believe she's the second ranking NCO in the corps."

I smiled and said, "Boo-rah, lieutenant. Only Sergeant Major of the Marine Corps Arthur James Williams ranks her. I believe that the Command Sarn't-Major could resolve this right quick. Can you get her to come up to the gate without attracting any attention? Just tell her Freak said she owes me a case of Pepsi."

He looked at me and said, "Well, we call her all the time. She'll probably have a corporal drive her, but—tell her she owes you a case of Pepsi? Freak? You mean *the* Freak?" His eyes got big but he called back to the guardhouse and said, "Martinez, please ask the Command Sarn't-Major to come up to the gate ASAP—tell her Freak said she owes her a case of Pepsi."

"Thank you, lieutenant," I said.

He nodded at me, but he and his men were still locked on with their weapons. We sat there frozen in place, and about three minutes later we heard a vehicle approaching the gate. I looked over and saw my old pistol instructor, Command Sergeant Major Jan Berkey, riding in a jeep. It wasn't even stopped when she jumped out and came striding over to the gate, which slid open enough for her to get through and then was closed again.

She walked right up to me and said, "Freak, get your ass off the ground. Where the fuck are your shoes? Why the fuck are you almost in uniform? And fuck you if you think I still owe you that case—we split our last shoot." She shook my hand and gave me a quick hug, and I said, "Command Sarn't-Major, I shot mine faster than you did—I beat you by almost two seconds."

"Fuck you, Freak. Now what in the hell is goin' on?" Command Sergeant Major Berkey said.

"There's a threat to the first family, and I need to talk to the C-JCS like an hour ago," I said. "I can't talk about it until I get something from him."

Jan Berkey didn't get to be the second highest ranked noncommissioned officer in the United States Marine Corps by being indecisive or weak. She whipped out her cell phone, punched one button, and when the call was picked up after one ring said, "Command Sergeant Major Jan Berkey calling for Sergeant Major of the Marine Corps Arthur J. Williams."

There was a short pause and then she said, "Art? Jan. I need to talk to the Chairman of the Joint Chiefs right now. Can you connect me? Priority One-A, Art, like yesterday. Thanks." There was another short pause and then she said, "Freak for the Chairman." She handed me the phone and Chairman of the Joint Chiefs of Staff Terrence McAllen said, "Freak, where the hell are you? The president went apeshit when you were taken and ran off to NSF Thurmont. I'm sending another brigade up there at his orders, and I've already sent a special comms detail so that he can have full comms without being at the White House, and his chief of staff just called me to say that the president would like an armor contingent up there. Now what the fuck is going on?"

So I told him as concisely as I could, then said, "Sir, I need you to do something for me so that I can take control of this situation. Remember what happened at Morehead? I need the same thing here, sir."

"Put the ranking officer back on," McAllen said. I gave the phone to the lieutenant and saw him straighten to attention. "Lieutenant Sabah Muhammed, sir. Yes, sir. Yes, sir. Right now, sir. Thank you, sir." He handed the phone back to me and I said, "Thank you, Mr. Chairman. Can you please contact my director and my team and get them on helos for this location ASAP? I'm going to go in and try to stop them right now, but in case I fail the team will need to step in." The Chairman interrupted me and I said, "Yes, sir, but they can leave the snipers at home—I have Marines here, sir."

He hung up and I turned to the lieutenant and Command Sergeant Major Jan Berkey, who, along with all the other Marines, were braced to attention. I looked at them and said, "The Chairman of the Joint Chiefs has just reinstated me to the United States Marine Corps with the rank of Major-General. I'm taking temporary command of all forces at NSF Thurmont as of this moment." They all saluted, I saluted back and said, "OK, Marines, I want the gate detail to hold this position against anyone trying to enter or exit, even the president. CSM Berkey and I are going to return to the compound area and see if we can take care of this situation. Before we go, lieutenant, I want to ask you again—any personnel changes for this visit?"

"Ma'am, there was just a special comms detail that flew in right after the president—they were on the list and cleared in from Andrews, ma'am. It was something about the president being able to communicate with several ambassadors across the world at once," Lieutenant Muhammed said.

"How many personnel?' I said.

"Twenty-five men and officers, ma'am," he said.

"OK. Lieutenant, you and your men did exactly right when I pulled up, and you did it well. I'm going to make sure that your CO hears about it. Now hold this position—we'll be sending someone you know to reinforce you." He drew up and saluted and said, "Yes, ma'am. No one in or out without the general's express permission."

I returned the salute and then CSM Berkey and I ran back to the jeep and sped back to the compound. I told her what was going on and how I wanted to play it, and she used her radio to set it up.

We arrived back at the Marine command post for NSF Thurmont to find a Marine colonel in BDUS waiting for us. She started to draw herself up to salute and I said, "Can it, Colonel. I'm just somebody who came down from the gate with Command Sergeant Major Berkey, OK? No salutes, just a couple of fellow officers shooting the shit. Let's go inside so that we can get this set up, preferably out of sight of the special comms unit."

"Yes, ma'am," the Colonel said. "We can go right in here, ma'am." We went into the command post and straight to her office. The plate on the outside of her door had the name "Col. K. J. Brucks, CO" on it, so once we were inside with the door closed I said, "Colonel Brucks, I'm not here to relieve you, but there is a situation within your command that you need to be aware of. Did you meet any of the special comms guys when they came in?"

"Yes, ma'am, I met the CO and the XO," Colonel Brucks said. "The CO is a major named Tom Miller, and the XO is a captain named Hector Vargas. They were very polite and deferential, gave me their orders, promised to stay out of the way and went right down to the comms shack to tie some equipment into the system so that they can be operational soon." She looked at her watch and said, "According to the schedule they gave me they'll be fully operational in just over ten minutes, ma'am."

"Have any of them come up this way yet?" I said.

"Not to my knowledge, ma'am, but we haven't really been keeping track of them," the Colonel said. She had an odd look on her face and I said, "Colonel Brucks, I'm going to literally kick your ass if you're holding out on me. What the fuck is going on? The first family is in danger, probably from the comms unit, so spill it now."

"Goddammit, I *knew* something was wrong with those guys! Excuse me, ma'am, but I need to call someone on the radio. It's important." She held up her radio and said, "Foof, this is Thurmont-Actual. Any movement?"

A very quiet voice said, "Actual, Foof. They're still in the comms shack and there hasn't been anyone in or out."

"Report any movement immediately," Colonel Brucks said. "Roger that," the voice said. I held out my hand and she gave me the radio. I said, "Foof, this is Major General Glinka Glickstien, USMC. Those comm operators are Navy SEALs conducting an op and are extremely dangerous.

Watch your six—be aware that there may be a counter-surveillance unit looking for you. Do not try to interdict—report any movement immediately. Acknowledge."

"Command, Foof. Orders received and understood, ma'am. Foof out."

Colonel Brucks was reaching for her radio, probably to bring up a couple of platoons armed with heavy weapons to surround the comms shack, but I said, "Colonel, they're going to try and kidnap the first daughters. Are the girls in the same cabin as the president and first lady?"

"No, ma'am. They each brought a friend with them—all the girls are in the theater building. The first lady is in the family cabin and the president is talking with the Secretary of State, the Secretary of Defense, the Secretary of Commerce, and several aides in the conference center. Shall I send units to cover them, ma'am?"

"Not yet, Colonel. We need to keep this under control so that there isn't a firefight anywhere around the first family or other civilians. I'm going to try and secure the first daughters with the help of Command Sergeant Major Berkey. Once that happens I'll notify the president's Secret Service detail and you grab the president and first lady and get them the hell out of here by ground transport—we'll have the backup helos on the way and they'll get picked up away from here. Once the first family is clear we'll move in on those traitorous assholes and get them to surrender," I said.

"And if they don't surrender?" the Colonel said.

"Crossing that bridge when we get there, Colonel," I said. "Now, I need a copy of your TO&E (Table of Organization and Equipment), a pair of hair clippers, a steward's uniform that fits and a pistol and two extra clips. Oh, and send a corpsman over here with a full kit, too."

Everything got to the command center and I said, "OK, who's gonna be Sweeney Todd?" They all looked confused, so I said, "I need someone to give me a nice high-and-tight, just like a steward who wants to be a Marine instead of a swabbie." The corpsman who came in with his kit said, "Ma'am, I can do that if you want. I do 'em for people in the field."

"That's exactly what I want, Petty Officer. Cut away," I said. He trimmed all of my flaming red hair off in a nice U.S. Marine regulation cut and I said, "Now I want you to get a nice six-inch Ace bandage and flatten my tits as much as possible."

"Ma'am?" he said, truly confused. "I want to look as much like a guy as possible, Petty Officer Avery, so"—I pulled my BDU blouse over my head and continued—"I want my tits to be as flat as possible. Think you can do that, Avery?"

He looked at my tits and said, "If I had a pneumatic compression machine or a team of good, strong mules I might be able to, ma'am, but with just an Ace bandage?" He shrugged and heaved a big sigh and we all laughed, and I patted Avery on the back and said, "Just do the best you can, corpsman, and don't worry about it."

"Oh, I'm not worried about it, ma'am, I just don't know that I want to cover up such a work of art. I mean, uh, those are some, uh, fine, uh, *ta-tas* you have there, ma'am." The petty officer was grinning and we all laughed again as he began wrapping my tits tight to my body. I told Colonel Brucks there was one more thing that I needed and she called to order it up, and by the time my tits were finished (they weren't all that flat, but they weren't looking like the Grand Tetons, either) and I was properly dressed in the steward's uniform it was there.

I looked at Command Sergeant Major Jan Berkey and said, "Remember, don't shoot anyone if you don't have to, but if you do the only one we want to wound is Tom Miller. Anybody else resists and you have a clear field of fire you dust 'em dead as a door nail, OK?" She nodded and I said, "Colonel Brucks, deploy your APCs on night maneuvers and make sure their magazines are full. Train as many .50 cals as you can on the comms shack and put every Marine you have in the field to back them up. Get your four Apaches in the air and make sure that they know they're facing SEALs—these guys may have shoulder-mounted missiles in their arsenal.

"Last, get your best squad ready and be prepared to attack if you hear gunfire. Either the Command Sergeant Major or I will be yelling 'Geronimo' at the top of our lungs if we need you to enter. Remember, the first family is your first priority—make sure you get them out of here before you worry about anything else. Are we clear?"

"Yes, ma'am," Colonel Brucks said. "We'll put everything in motion as soon as you enter the theater carrying the tray of food, and the special communication unit won't see us coming. Luckily the APC exercise has been on the schedule as pending for about a week, so they won't think a thing about them starting up."

I nodded and said, "Good luck, and make sure if I die that none of these asshole motherfucking kidnappers live to tell about it."

"Bet your ass, General," Colonel Brucks said, her voice growling out like she was Chesty Puller. You gotta love Marines—they really are always faithful.

So I took up my tray of food and let Command Sergeant Major Berkey lead me to the theater. When we got there instead of Secret Service personnel on duty there were Marines, which immediately got my guard up. I was behind the Command Sergeant Major, but I saw her tighten her shoulders up a bit, so I stood ready for anything.

She walked up to the guy on the right and said, "Good evening, Corporal. Where are the Secret Service guys?"

"Chow, Sergeant Major," the guy said, acting natural, but he was acting, and he'd missed the Command Sergeant Major's rank, and…she kneed him in the nuts as she whipped out her M9 and smacked him in the side of the head.

I kept the tray over my right shoulder and hit my guy with a straight left-footed kick to the throat. Before he could fall Command Sergeant Major Berkey smacked him on the side of the head with her M9. He fell down in a heap and didn't move, just like the guy on the other side. I looked at Command Sergeant Major Berkey and she said, "Not my guys, Freak. I think these are our friends in special communications."

Shit.

We were too late—the bad guys were already there ahead of us. There wasn't anything for it—we'd just have to play it as it lay.

So I knocked, said, "Snacks, ladies," opened the door and went in.

Shitfuckpisshelldamn!

The first lady was in the theater, she had a gun in her hand and Tom Miller was standing with a big combat knife at Allison's throat.

Oh shit, oh dear.

I flicked my eyes across the rest of the theater and got the whole picture. There was one other guy in the room, pointing a pistol at the first lady. The first lady's personal agent was flat on the floor, face down and out. Brooke was flat on the floor about ten feet behind Tom Miller and clearly out; the girls' two friends were huddled next to her, whimpering softly. The first lady was holding what I assumed was her agent's pistol in front of her with both hands in a hideous imitation of the Weaver stance, aiming generally at Tom Miller, but also at Allison. The White Witch had sweat pouring down her face and was shaking so much that the pistol she held looked like it was the moon wobbling through an orbit of the earth.

I felt Tom Miller and his other guy flick their eyes over me and got exactly what I hoped for when I walked in.

Dismissal.

Both of them did what I or any other soldier would've done—they instantly classified me as a non-combatant and therefore no threat to their op and turned their attention back to the first lady.

Tom Miller said, "Steward, set the tray down, sit down on your hands and be absolutely silent for me. Do it now, sailor." His voice was calm, level, and full of what the officer's schools call command presence. He wasn't asking me to do something, he was commanding me to do it, and he had every expectation that I would simply comply, more to his tone of voice than his words, and that's exactly what I did.

He and his merry man turned their full attention back on the Superbitch, who'd almost turned the muzzle of the pistol on me, and Tom Miller said, "Once again, Mrs. Sheehan, I don't want to hurt you, but I will if you don't put that pistol down."

The first lady said, "You leave my girls alone, you motherfucker, or I'll shoot both of you. Put that knife down!" She was near hysteria, and Tom Miller said, in a very soothing tone, "Laura, we both know that you don't know how to shoot, and we both know that you're not going to shoot near your daughter, so why don't you put the pistol down before I'm forced to cut poor Allison here?" His hand holding the knife moved the tiniest bit and a very thin trickle of blood appeared at Allison's neck.

The first lady slid forward a step and started to say something, which is when I flung the serving tray full of shit in the face of the second guy in the room, surged to my feet and pulled the pistol from the small of my back. I hit the first lady with the softest hammer fist I could muster right behind her left ear and knocked her cold. As soon as the Superbitch fell Command Sergeant Major Berkey shot the other SEAL in the room from the door that we'd kept partly open when it was supposed to be closed.

I was trained in on Tom Miller, but he wasn't giving me any real shot. He pulled Allison backwards until they were right in front of Brooke, who was still flat on the floor and not moving at all, except to draw shallow, slow breaths. I looked at Allison and was surprised to find that she wasn't even scared. Upset, yes, but I didn't see any sign of fear on her face. She almost smiled at me as she said, "He hit Brookie in the head. I think he killed her." I was right—she'd used the name she called her sister when they were little kids, but she'd done it in a little girl's voice in order to assure Tom Miller that she was completely cowed, despite the look on her face.

I smiled at her and said, "I can see her breathing, Allie, so don't worry about her. You just do exactly what Captain Miller tells you to do, OK? Do everything exactly as he tells you." She smiled back at me and said, "Yes, Agent Glickstien."

Tom Miller said, "Listen to Freak, Allison, she's saving your life. Now take your hands off my arm and put them down at your side." Allison had been gripping the arm Tom Miller had around her neck, but now she instantly did exactly what he told her.

I said, "Tom, I know what happened and we're working on proving it, but this isn't the way to do it. Let the girls go and take me instead. Whattya say?" I wasn't serious, but I needed to distract him, and besides, he was expecting me to negotiate, so I gave him exactly what he expected.

He looked back at me and said, "The motherfucking coward fucked my brother and then killed him. You think I'm ever going to get that out of my head? Would you just let it go, Freak, or would you wreak vengeance on the son of a bitch and his family?"

"I don't know, Tom, I think that I'd probably go for the vengeance, too, but only until I'd had time to think about it, and then I'd realize that vengeance isn't justice. Let the kids go, Tom—they don't have anything to do with it," I said. I was watching his body language and hoping that Allison was noticing, because we were almost there.

"Yeah, well Timmy didn't have anything to do with it either, Freak. Neither did my mom—they were both innocent, and that motherfucker destroyed them both without a thought. Justice is for suckers, Freak." His voice caught and Tom Miller, a man who was raised the right way, turned his head so his mouth wasn't in Allison's ear and gave a soft cough.

Which is when Allison's hand darted under her skirt, grabbed the .22 pistol strapped to her left thigh in its pancake holster and without even drawing it shot Tom Miller in the foot.

He let go of her and she spun away, leaving him without any human shield. I shot the combat knife right out of his hand and charged him, because Mrs. Miller'd already lost one son and she didn't deserve to lose another, especially since he was probably right about what the president had done so long ago.

He dropped into a fighting stance and then I was on him. "Grab Brooke and get the fuck outta here, Allison!" I yelled as I attacked.

Tom Miller was a truly tough son of a bitch, battle hardened and as well trained as any human being can be, a Navy SEAL who was literally a killing machine. If this was the movies we'd've had a big, knockdown, drag-out fight scene that ended with me just barely getting in the last punch to end it. But me, well, I was a Neanderthal throwback who was just as well trained as Tom Miller, and I was stronger, faster and more battle hardened than any human being alive (yes, goddamnit, that's motherfucking classified!), plus I was absolutely furious, because even though I hadn't given birth to them, these were MY GIRLS.

And nobody got to smack my girls around, or cut them, or threaten them with rape and murder without paying a price, no matter what that motherfucker's motivation was.

I turned into Hurricane Freak, Force 35 on the Beaufort scale.

My hands and feet blurred through the air with superhuman speed and power as I broke Tom Miller's right arm in three places, dislocated his left shoulder, broke his left wrist into unidentifiable rubble, broke both his legs and shattered his left kneecap in just three passes. I finished the hurricane attack by picking his sorry ass up and hurling him against the wall. Tom Miller hit flat on and just oozed down the wall like a giant banana slug, slumping over into a senseless pile of flesh. I went over and made sure that he was breathing—he was alive, but there were a couple years of rehab in front of him after the surgeries—and turned to find Allison standing five feet away.

She had her Smith & Wesson M&P22 Compact pointed right at Tom Miller's head, and she said, "He was going to rape Brooke and me, and then kill us, just to hurt our dad? He hit Brooke in the head, like he was swatting a fly. He's, he's evil." I saw the look in her eye and saw her finger tightening, so I stood up and said, "Kill him if you want to, but I think he's already paid for his crimes. He sure as hell won't be threatening you any time soon."

I walked past her, ready to jump her if I needed to, but hoping it wouldn't be necessary. Allison looked at Tom Miller for a long time as he lay in a helpless heap on the floor. Finally she said, "Well, I could kill him, and he certainly deserves it, but I'm a Warrior Princess, and we don't just execute helpless prisoners."

She lowered her pistol, pulled her skirt up, safed the weapon and holstered it. She held out her arms and I wrapped her in a huge hug. We both sank down next to Brooke, who was breathing better but still unconscious. We hugged and hugged each other, and their two friends, until finally other people began streaming into the theater, led by the president of the United States.

He was bellowing "ALLISON! BROOKE! ALLISON! BROOKE!" over and over, until he saw his unconscious wife, at which point James Sheehan burst into tears. "Oh, NOOOOOOO!" he wailed. The president threw himself on the first lady, dislodging the corpsman who was trying to tell him that she was fine, just unconscious. He sat there for a moment, sobbing his eyes out, until Allison said, "Daddy? Brookie's hurt."

The president jumped up and ran to the back of the theatre, looking like he was a hundred years old, and wrapped Allison in a hug. He looked down at Brooke and said, "Is she? Is she? Is she?" until I stood up and smacked him across the face.

Everybody in the room just stopped, and I said, "Mr. President, I think your brain was stuck. Get a grip, willya?" He looked at me, not panicked, but hurt, and I said, "Sir, Brooke's going to be fine. Captain Miller knocked her unconscious, just like I knocked the first lady unconscious. She isn't going to die, Mr. President, but she is going to need a stable parent, and I don't think that's going to be her mother for a while, if you know what I mean."

And then the strangest thing happened, because the president laughed, and then I laughed, and then Allison said, "Well, that's a fucking lock, Dad—Mom's not that stable when she hasn't been knocked unconscious" and we all began laughing. After a bit I said, "I need a medic here, right quick. Petty Officer Avery, is that you?"

"Yes, ma'am," he said.

"Front and center, Avery, and take care of this young womyn. I'm guessing that she attacked Captain Miller, and he knocked her ass over tea cart"—Allison nodded—"and she needs attention. And call your doctor, because I want a neurological workup before we move her."

"Yes, general. The doc is on his way," Avery said.

I turned to Colonel Brucks and said, "Report, Colonel."

"Ma'am, we took the rest of the special communications unit without incident. I persuaded their XO to surrender, probably because I informed him that he was surrounded by enough fire-power to stop a full regiment in its tracks. It also didn't hurt that they had a video feed from the theater in there so they got to see what you did to Captain Miller, ma'am. We have them all under restraints and waiting to be transported to the Navy Yard in D.C. What are your further orders, General Glickstien?"

"Colonel, secure this base and place us under EMCON until the president orders you to call it off. Not a word of this incident gets off this base until the president or his designee authorizes it. Also make sure that none of our comms friends are lurking around somewhere. I'd also like a casualty report at some point," I said.

"That's fairly short, ma'am. We have one KIA—the SEAL with Captain Miller here in the theater. He is—was—Command Master Chief Petty Officer Tory Potts. Otherwise we have several hurt, but no others KIA, unless Captain Miller dies," she said.

"Oh, he'll live," I said. "But he won't be doing any missions for a while, except learning how to piss in a bag."

"Yes, ma'am," Colonel Brucks said. "Ma'am, permission to ask a question?"

"Of course," I said.

"Ma'am, wouldn't one broken arm or leg have been sufficient to incapacitate Captain Miller?" she said.

"Those are my girls, and I'm a motherfucking goddamned leatherneck Marine, and NOBODY gets to fuck with me and mine," I said.

"Oh, yes ma'am," Colonel Brucks said. "Semper fucking fi, ma'am."

"Semper fucking fi, Colonel. Now if you'll excuse me, I'd like to relinquish command of this base to you," I said. "Requesting permission to turn command of NSF Thurmont back to you, Colonel."

"I accept, General. I am assuming command of NSF Thurmont," she said. "Ma'am, it's been a pleasure serving under you, and I would gladly do it again."

"Thank you, Colonel, but let's work to make sure that doesn't happen, OK?" I said.

"Yes, ma'am," Brucks said with a smile.

I needed some air, and the theater was packed with people, so I said, "Permission to disembark this venue, Colonel."

Brucks stood to attention and said, "A-tenn-HUTT! Commanding officer departing!" All of the Marines stood to attention and the Colonel said, "The Old Lady clangs when she walks!"

"The Old Lady clangs when she walks!" everybody said.

"Permission to depart granted, Ma'am," Colonel Brooks said, saluting me. I returned her salute even though I wasn't wearing a cover or outdoors, and then I left the chaos behind and went outside, where I found my unit and my director waiting for me.

"Ya show-off," Badass said.

"Always the glory hound, aren't ya, Freak?" Joe said.

"Couldn't just wait and let us arrest him, could ya? Had to go all kung-fu on his ass," Jack Soo said.

"Trying to make the rest of us look like slackers, weren't ya?" Ed said.

"Ingratiating yourself with the soon to be outgoing President of the United States isn't the best strategy I've ever seen for career advancement, Freak," Mamba said.

"If you think I'm just going to give up my job you're crazy, Freak," Nails said.

"I'd call out the First Armored Division to help you keep it, Nails," Buddha said.

"Yeah, I'm pretty sure that she can't stop a tank with pistols and fists," El Gato said.

"Better get some Air Force support, too, just in case," Bumble said.

"I wouldn't ask any SEALs, though, because their training program has clearly gone for shit," Weasel said.

"Yeah, I've never seen anything like that before, Freak—you turned his ass into a bowl of SEAL jello," Badass said.

"But you still owe us Pepsis, Freak, because I think that you missed with one punch during that barrage," Mamba said.

"I did not," I said.

"Oh, I beg to differ," Jewey said. "Let's go to the videotape, shall we?" He held up an I-Pad and showed me the video from the fight between Tom Miller and me, and sure enough I did miss one punch, right near the end.

"Well, fuck me black, blue and blind," I said. "I did miss once."

"You're slipping, Freak, and paying us off with Pepsis will be entirely appropriate," Ed said.

"Fuckin'-A," Badass said.

"Do you think that Tom Miller will ever walk again?" Buddha said.

"He ought to be just like new in three, four years," I said.

Everybody laughed and gave me big, heavy hugs, which is where we were at when the president came out with the girls. Allison had a small band-aid on her throat where Tom Miller had cut her, and Broke was totally immobilized on a stretcher with a neck brace and all, but the president looked better as he held Allison's hand and walked next to Brooke.

When he saw me the president left Brooke's side and came right over to me. Allison came too, and we all enjoyed a hug. I said, "Allison, I am very proud of you. You kept your cool and did exactly what I told you to, and if you hadn't I don't know what would have happened in there. I owe you one."

"No, no you don't—if it wasn't for you we'd be just like all the other little girls in the world— helpless twits instead of Warrior Princesses. Brooke and I were going to ask you anyway, but you need a couple of sisters? I mean, you have brothers and all, but maybe you want a couple of pain in the ass little sisters? Just for fun?"

It was so unexpected that I almost burst into tears, but instead I just said, "Well, you can never have too much family, and a womyn can't have too many sisters, so yeah, I think that'll work for me." We hugged again and the president said, "This time I'm going to pay up, Freak, whether you want me to or not, so don't argue. We'll talk about it later, but that was damned well done." He shook my hand and then hugged me very tightly, and as we were pulling apart he said, "I only have one complaint."

"I had to knock the first lady out, Mr. President—she was shaking so bad that I was afraid she'd shoot me by accident," I said.

Everyone laughed and the president said, "Well, I'm pretty sure that she'll get over it, and if not, well, we'll just have to live with her disappointment." We laughed again, and then the president and Allison went back over to Brooke's gurney and went toward the infirmary.

I watched them go and then said to Nails, "Madam Director, I'd like to request a vacation day or eight, if that's OK with you. I'm sorta tired, and my ribs hurt, and I haven't had a Pepsi or anything to eat since breakfast yesterday, so is it OK if I just go home for a while?"

"No," Nails said. She turned to Joe and said, "Tell her."

Joe looked at me and said, "We think that Tom Miller had help from within the Cabinet, like at the Secretary level. We managed to intercept and decrypt a communication between Miller and someone with a really high clearance that talked about today and the "fail-safe" option."

My brain was on overload, but it was still working. I grabbed Joe and said, "What did it say exactly?"

Joe said, "'If we fail you're the last line—he'll never suspect it until it's too late. Use the fail-safe option and get the girls.' Now what the fuck is going on?"

I said, "Does anybody know the CV of SecState, SecDef or the Secretary of Commerce? If they served in a particular branch of the service?"

"Sure," Joe said. "SecState was in the Air Force, SecDef was in the Army Reserve and the Secretary of Commerce was in the Navy."

"What did he do in the Navy?" I said.

Joe got pale and said, "Motherfucker! SEALs!"

I turned and burned it for the infirmary, pulling the borrowed pistol from the small of my back while yelling "AVERY! AVERY! AVERY! AVERY! AVERY!" I skidded around a building and saw the corpsman look up from Brooke's gurney. "GET UNDER COVER NOW AVERY! THE SECRETARY OF COMMERCE IS WITH THE SPECIAL COMMS UNIT!" I screamed as loud as I could (I'm told that it was fairly loud).

I give him credit, because the corpsman immediately grabbed the head of the gurney and ran for the nearest building, but too was too late, because the Secretary of Commerce stepped out from behind another building and reached under his coat to pull out a short pistol. He brought the gun up and fired a round that caught Avery and put him down, but he didn't get a chance to fire a second round, because the shot I snapped off right after his blew the gun out of his hand. He screamed and lunged toward the gurney, but was met by a hail of gunfire as several United States Marines, one Secret Service agent and a pissed off sister hit him with everything they had.

I ran up to the gurney just as Allison dropped the empty clip on her .22 and filled it up with a full one she had strapped on her thigh next to her holster. She calmly jacked a round in the pistol and said, "Freak, should I just go shoot the Secretary of State and the Secretary of Defense as a precautionary measure?"

Black humor was a sign of a healthy mind, so I just smiled and ran to Petty Officer Avery. He was in bad shape, with an ugly sucking chest wound, so I knelt down to see if I could stop the bleeding. I yanked a package of four-by-four gauze out of his kit and pressed a handful down on the wound, but they were instantly soaked. I realized that Avery was going to bleed out if we didn't do something right now, and I realized what it needed to be. I grabbed Allison and said, "I need you to do something for me, little sister." I yanked her down by Avery and said, "Put your index finger in that wound and feel your way to the bottom of it."

Allison hesitated and I said, "Alli, he's going to die if you don't," so she slid her long, slender finger into the wound. She'd only gotten about three inches in when she said, "This feels funny, Freak—it's like, fluttering or something."

"Can you push down on it and make it stop fluttering?" I said. She pushed her finger down and said, "It's still kind of doing it, but it's slower."

"Can you get a second finger in there and make it stop?" I said.

She stuck her forefinger and middle finger in the wound, fished around for just a second and then said, "Got it! It's not fluttering at all."

"Good job, sis. Now keep it from fluttering until we can get a doc in there to stop it, OK?" I said.

More Marine medics swarmed over us and I said, "He's got a sucking chest wound, but Allison's got it pinched off."

One of the medics turned out to be the trauma doc assigned to NSF Thurmont, and he took over by telling Allison, "Don't let go, miss. If you do he'll bleed out before we can stop it. We're going to have to have you go into surgery with us so we can fix this young man, OK?" She nodded and then a bunch of Marines grabbed Avery, threw him on a gurney and headed for the infirmary with Allison trotting alongside.

I turned around and Brooke said, "I punched him in the nuts, Freak, but he turned and I missed. He slugged me and it got black all of a sudden." I went over to her and said, "Good job, little sister. If it's any consolation Allison shot him in the foot with her .22, which is how we stopped him."

"Is he dead?" Brooke said.

"No," Buddha said over my shoulder, "but Freak messed him up so bad he'll wish that he was. Howya doin', Brooke?"

"I'm OK, Buddha. How are you?" Brooke said.

"I'm good, and so are the rest of us that're here," Buddha said. "You're safe, so don't worry."

"Oh, I'm not worried. After all, the Freak from Battle Creek is my sister, and she's the baddest motherfucker in the whole damned valley," Brooke said, badly mangling a special ops mantra.

I said, "That's right, little sister. Now do what they tell you and get better, OK?"

"Roger that, big sister," Brooke said as we got to the door of the infirmary. They took her in and the president once again shook my hand and hugged me. When he released me part way I said, so only he could hear, "Mr. President, we need to talk, and soon, sir."

"After the girls are home, at your convenience," he said.

"Thank you, sir," I said. He nodded at me and then there was more commotion at the infirmary as the first lady arrived and my crew surrounded me and took me away.

"For crissakes, Freak, I was fucking kidding about the days off," Nails said.

"I wasn't," I said, just before I fainted.

Talk about embarrassing.

CHAPTER 78

Shit Rolls Uphill

So I woke up in a hospital bed with an IV in my arm, a smell of lemon in the air and two of my squad sitting by my bed.

When she saw I was awake Buddha said, "Oh Freak, please don't die! Come back, Freak, come back!" She sounded like the little kid at the end of the movie *Shane*.

"Don't go, Freak! What would we do without the greatest Secret Service agent of all time?" Jack Soo said.

"I don't know—ask Parker H. Connolly and find out," I said.

"Yeah, there ain't anything wrong with her," Buddha said to Jack Soo.

"Except she's going to have to fight off several very excited lesbian Secret Service agents with that butchy haircut," he said.

"Ain't that the truth," Buddha and I said together.

"My Pepsis, Freak," she said.

"Well, it's about fucking time," I said.

We all laughed and Jack Soo called someone on the phone. "She's awake and with it. Made two jokes in two tries and understood that the sisterhood will probably be right on her ass for a while. OK. See you guys in ten, fifteen minutes? Roger that."

He hung up the phone and said, "Unit incoming, ETA fifteen minutes. Don't know who else is coming."

Right then Hurricane swept in, took one look at me, and said, "I prescribe Chicago dogs and Pepsi at the Coney & Ivy in furthering your recovery from your hideous brush with death" in a tone of voice that was basically the equivalent of "fuck you, Freak." When I didn't say anything the dwarf doctor said, "Did I stutter, you dipshit? Get your ass up and quit wasting my valuable hospital bed."

"Your bed?" I said. "Am I in the fucking maternity ward? What the hell is going on, Hurricane?"

She looked at me with what I recognized was love and said, "Well, I'm your doctor, and I can't be running all over the hospital to see you, and we had an open room, so I had them put you in here, just in case something was really wrong." She crossed her arms and stared at me with those pink eyes and I realized that maybe I had more sisters than I knew.

So I didn't hot-dog it, I just said, "Thanks, Hurricane. I can really leave? 'Cause I really do think I'm just hungry, even though my body feels like I've been run over with a bulldozer."

"It looks like it, too. You've got bruises everywhere, some very deep contusions in your belly and that cut you took was deeper than it looked. We've given you blood and lots of IV fluids, so your electrolytes are good, but your ravenous metabolism probably does need some real food. If you feel like it you can leave, but no real walking and absolutely no fighting, sparring, fooling around or other super-power related shit for at least a week, OK?" Hurricane said.

"Deal, but I still need you to answer a question for me, if you can," I said.

Hurricane was a pretty good doc, because she already knew what I was going to ask. "Petty Officer Avery's in really bad shape. The bullet did a shitload of damage to one of his pulmonary veins and his right lung, and the first mesh graft they put in failed, so he had to go under again. They also discovered that a stray fragment did damage to the hepatic artery, so his surgery was extended. That much time under anesthesia isn't healthy, plus the damage was really extensive. His heart was without fully oxygenated blood for at least twenty minutes—that's the only reason that he's alive, because Allison stopped the bleeding—and we don't know what effect that had on his cognitive functions because he's in a medically induced coma," Hurricane said.

"Prognosis?" I said.

"How the fuck should I know? He's young, strong and seems determined to live, but these kinds of thing are always touch and go. If the mesh grafts in the artery give way he could die before we get him into surgery, or there could be an infection—Allison didn't exactly disinfect before she put her fingers in his chest…" Hurricane said, her voice trailing off.

"OK, I get it. It's a crapshoot for a while whether the kid makes it. Have you seen the reports on Brooke?" I said, trying to put Avery's wounds out of my mind for the time being. I'm not a drunk, but I've always been fond of the Serenity Prayer they use, especially the part about the wisdom to know which things I can change.

Hurricane said, "That little toughie is going places. Perhaps a slight concussion, no lasting head injury and enough attitude to be a Semper Fier like you and Badass. She told me she thought Allison was a pussy for not shooting Captain Miller."

"But how's she doing?" I said.

"Already discharged and home with Mom and Dad. She and Allison wanted to stay with you, but Old Three Names and Nails talked them out of it, citing—ahem—"personal security concerns," which the girls seemed to think was funny," Hurricane said.

"How's Tom Miller? Did I take him down or what? The end of our fight seems kind of fuzzy," I said, my tongue firmly in my cheek.

"Since you ask, you lying sack of shit, he's so thoroughly fucked up that it'll take a year before they can even arraign his kidnapping ass. He's got nothing life threatening, but they already did surgery on his shoulder, which looked like a bunch of kindling wood, and he has at least four more orthopedic procedures scheduled, and that doesn't include his wrist, which they may have to just fuse." Even after that sentence the albino dwarf doctor wasn't out of breath, but she paused as if she was about to give me bad news before she said, "He'd like to see you, by the way. Captain Miller won't talk to anyone else, not even his lawyer, who I must admit is one smart, cute biscuit, even if he is representing that asshole."

"Oh, hell, his attorney isn't going to let me talk to him, regardless of what his client wants," I said. Buddha, Jack Soo, and Hurricane all started laughing and I said, "OK, what the fuck is the joke, you assholes."

"Oh, I don't think the shyster will object, although I think he'll probably want to be there," Buddha said.

"There's sort of like a family bond between him and Tom Miller," Jack Soo said.

"Yeah, the biscuit said he wasn't afraid to let you talk to the asshole, since it was doubtful that you could get anything useful out of him without a rubber hose," Hurricane said, causing them to laugh their asses off again.

They stopped laughing when I got out of bed, pulled the IV out of my arm and started toward them. Buddha said, "OK, OK, that's enough of the Boris Karloff routine—we're laughing because your brother Marvin is representing Tom Miller. He was already in here and told us to tell you that he isn't afraid of you and to stop busting his client's balls."

That stopped me in my tracks. Roady was defending Tom Miller? I guess it made some kind of weird sense—they were high school classmates—but it still seemed strange to think that my brother was defending the guy who tried to kidnap my protectees. Wasn't that some kind of conflict of interest?

Just then I got a chance to find out, because the door to my room opened and the Attorney General of the United States stepped in, followed by U.S. Attorney Duquanye Quintanilla and Assistant U.S. Attorney Brenda T. Green.

There I was in my hospital gown with most of my considerable ass hanging out, and here were some really important people who needed to talk to me about urgent matters of security. It was almost as embarrassing as passing out after saving the girls.

The Attorney General looked at my ass and said, "I'm sorry, Agent Glickstien, but I'm a happily married man, so trying to tempt me with your anatomy isn't going to work." His delivery was so dead-pan perfect that for a second I thought he wasn't kidding, but he had that look in his eye that said he was, so I took a chance and said, "Sorry, sir, but I thought you were here to review me for a promotion."

It turned out that when the AG laughed he brayed like a donkey, and then we all started laughing, and I staggered my considerable ass back into bed while the levity died down.

The AG looked at me and said, "Thanks for that, Freak. I really needed some relief from the last few hours of shit pouring down on my head. You want to tell me exactly what happened, starting with your kidnapping?"

"Sir, my team is about five minutes out—can I just get dressed and we'll go somewhere more comfortable? Maybe get some food? Because I'm just about famished, sir, and I'm going to have to tell them all of this anyway, and it would really save a whole shitpot of time…if that's amenable to you, sir," I said.

"Excellent idea, Freak. We'll clear out and let you get dressed, and then repair to a more comfortable venue," the AG said. Everybody except Hurricane left and I changed into a black Secret Service sweat suit, put on my soft tennis shoes, and walked out of the room and into a whole bunch of hugs and backslaps and kudos from the people I liked and respected most in the world.

After we got all of the "attaboys" out of the way the AG led us out of the hospital and down the street to the George Washington University Inn where we went in to a conference room and found a gigantic Chinese feast laid out for us, courtesy of the wonderful delivery drivers (plural—there was so much food I thought that it was Chinese New Year at my neighbor Mrs. Chen's) from the Peking Garden restaurant just down the street.

There were also five cases of Pepsi cooling off in big tubs of ice and real plates and silverware on the tables.

I thought I'd died and gone to heaven.

It took a while to tell the story, because I was ravenous. I ate so much and with such relish that I finally realized that no one was sitting near me. I looked at Badass, who was two chairs away and said, "Really?"

"Everybody decided to keep their distance—we weren't willing to sacrifice fingers or a hand," my friend said.

I kind of shrugged, nodded and said, "Probably not that bad an idea."

We kind of chuckled, but nobody sat next to me until I got back with my fourth plate of food. Ed was holding a serving tray on its side between our places when I sat down, and she looked at me with a very nervous smile and said "Nice doggy, nice doggy."

We all laughed again and then settled in with some dainties to fill up those little corners of our stomachs that weren't full. While we noshed I told the story, from initial contact of the kidnappers until I was tased, and then what happened after I got to Camp David. I didn't leave anything out, and there were a few questions, so it took almost an hour before Weasel said, "We know how they got into Camp David, Freak."

"Yeah, me too," I said, "They had help manufacturing orders, probably from someone inside the Human Resources command, or possibly in the office of an Assistant Secretary of the Navy or a captain in charge of a combatant command."

"Well done, young Padawan," Joe said. "An Assistant Undersecretary of the Navy was the brother of one of the SEALs and cut them absolutely authentic orders, which they used to impersonate the special comms section that had actually been assigned. He also re-routed the real special comms section to Greenland so that they'd be fully out of touch long enough to complete the kidnapping and escape."

"As much as I hate to admit it, those motherfuckers came up with an absolutely brilliant plan. If the first lady hadn't decided to check in on the girls, or if Allison doesn't shoot Tom Miller in the foot, or, well, if dozens of other things hadn't happened in our favor it would've worked like a charm," Ed said. "You don't know this yet, but Tom Miller's guys had three helos lined up to exfiltrate them, all with authentic orders and more travel on the other end. We think that they were going to take the girls to a place in the Upper Peninsula of Michigan to, uh, well, er—" Ed's face got red as she stammered her way to a stop.

Hurricane said, "What Ed doesn't want to tell you is that it looks like those sick fucks were going to torture the girls on a live internet feed, and then probably send pieces of them to the president." She looked at Ed and said, "Emily, I know it's disgusting, and God bless you for being such a good soul, but you are a Secret Service professional, right? Freak won't like it any more than you do, but she deserves to know it all, right?"

Ed nodded, but it was Buddha who said, "Why don't you look even remotely surprised, Freak?"

"I already realized this was a mission designed to torture the president when the three gomers who had me got out the stuff to fry me. They had no hope of getting anything useful—in fact, they didn't want anything from me at all—so what other reason was there for the shit they pulled? They wanted to send the president a message, and they were going to do me in order to tell him they were serious, and also to terrify him over what they were going to do to the Warrior Princesses," I said.

"It definitely would've been effective," Joe said. "The psychological aspect alone would've torn him apart."

"Especially with the guilt he feels over Tim Miller," Jack Soo said.

"You noticed that, did you?" I said.

"Yeah, he didn't tell the Vice President about Tim's death because he was over it all. You don't tell the person you love most about your deepest, darkest secret because you think it'll deepen your relationship," Jack Soo said. "You do it to jettison the guilt so that you can start over with them."

"So you didn't tell your wife about the time at Mardi Gras when you danced naked on the float full of half-naked sorority girls?" Badass said.

"Oh, no," Jack Soo said. "There has to be some element of intent to do wrong in the deep, dark, secret or it doesn't need to be exposed. Besides, nothing actually happened to feel guilty about in that particular incident."

"That's not how Weasel tells it," Buddha said. "He said something about a dog-pile and a bucket of crème bruleé?"

"Well, Weasel is a notorious liar, a spreader of malicious innuendo and an inventor of fairy tales," Jack Soo said.

"He has eight by ten glossy pictures with circles and arrows on the back explaining what each one is in a court of law," Mamba said (my thanks to Arlo Guthrie and the song *Alice's Restaurant* for that line—we used it all the time, especially Mamba, who I think had quite the crush on old Arlo).

"Oh, fuck Weasel," Jack Soo said. We all laughed, and Badass said, "But there'll be some shit rolling downhill on this one, because too many people know about the president and Tim Miller to ever cover it up."

"Yeah," I said. "All of Tom Miller's guys, all of us, Allison, probably Brooke and maybe even the first lady—I didn't hear what Tom told her before I came in."

"Technically the shit in this case will have to roll *uphill*, since POTUS is considerably above our pay grade," Buddha said. We all laughed, and Ed said, "Well, I'll be damned—I never thought that I'd see the day when shit rolled uphill, but the Wise One is right. We are now officially part of history."

"Yes, you are, because there is no statute of limitations on murder, and as the top law enforcement official in the country I'm duty bound to notify the Michigan Attorney General of the president's crime," the AG said. "You'll be the unit that caused the first arrest of a sitting president, on murder charges no less."

"Somehow that doesn't sound funny at all," Joe said.

"The press'll go fucking apeshit, and the country'll be as crazy as a fucking shithouse rat," Badass said.

"And you'll all get really, really good at saying "No comment" over and over," Hurricane said.

"And that's *all* you're going to say, and you're not going to add anything, uh, colorful when you say it," Duquanye Quintanilla said.

"Wha' you mean coworfoo, roun' eye?" Jack Soo said in a horrible imitation of an Asian accent.

"Wow, was that fucking shitty, Jack. Besides, aren't you from Torrance, California?" Buddha said.

"What the fuck does that have to do with anything?" Jack Soo said. "Everybody knows that the Asian guys are always the comic relief in these kinds of situations. I'm just living up to expectations." He got a mischievous look on his face and said, "Anybody want me to make coffee?"

"NO!" we all said.

"Just to be clear, DQ, we can't say "No magenta comment" to the press once this breaks?" Mamba said.

"Oh, fuck, this is going to be one long headache with you schmucks, isn't it?" the U.S. Attorney said.

"It says "Does not play well with others" in all of our files," Buddha said.

"It's why we like each other so much, I think," Hurricane said.

We were all agreeing with that statement when the doors to the conference room flew open and the first lady came striding in. She wasn't wearing any makeup, her hair was all over the place, she was weaving back and forth a little bit when she walked and either she'd taking up smoking ganja or she hadn't slept in the last two days—her eyes were as red as a robin's breast (which is a weird saying, since robins actually have orange breast feathers—I'm from Michigan, where the robin is the state bird, so I know).

In any case, the White Witch was in quite a state as she came toward me. When she got within five feet she said, "You armed my daughters? You gave them their own GUNS and you didn't tell me?" Her breath was pungent from five feet away and she had the same look on her face as Captain Ahab did when he saw the white whale.

I thought about all the shit the first lady must've been through in the last two days and decided to just take whatever tirade she had for me, so I nodded and said, "Yes, ma'am, I did. I'm sorry I usurped your right to be a parent, but I love your daughters and I never want them hurt, so I gave them personal protection pistols, which I trained them to use. I know I shouldn't have, and you have every right to report me to my director, and even have me fired if you want."

Her wild eyes got wilder and she said, "Fired? Fired? ARE YOU FUCKIN' CRAZY? I wanna adopt your ugly marvelous ass and then staple you to my daughters! Why'n the fuck would I want you fired, you twit?" She threw her arms around me and sobbed so long and loudly that I was afraid she'd have pulled gut muscles. Her tears soaked my shoulder and neck and ran down into my underwear, and she was trembling so hard as she hugged me that I got a bit of motion sickness (not kidding), but I didn't let go of her, because, well, I kind of understood.

I mean, there's having a bad day, and then there's having a bad *year* in a day. Soon the first lady would be the wife of a gay (or bisexual) president who was arrested for murder, which meant impeachment or resignation, prison and leaving Washington in the utmost disgrace. No more privilege, no more respect, no more center of attention, no more perfect family, probably no more marriage, no more money, since the president would lose his retirement and any chance at any other income once he was impeached and then convicted of murder.

If you thought about it, life would probably be harder on her and the girls than it would be on the (soon-to-be-former) president. At least he'd have meals guaranteed, a roof over his head and be out of the limelight, but everywhere she went forevermore the first lady would be "*Laura Flagler Sheehan, former first lady and ex-wife of disgraced president James Sheehan, who is currently serving X years for murder in Jackson Prison*"—and the girls would get the same treatment. Having to live in public would mean that their lives would be destroyed forever, too, even though they hadn't done anything remotely wrong.

So I let the (soon-to-be-former) first lady make a mess of me, until she finally ran out of gas and started hiccupping. I grabbed a handful of napkins off the nearest table and helped her clean up. When we were done she said, "I'm sorry I'm such a mess. It's been a bit trying." Her voice was small and quiet—it reminded me of Allison when she said, "He hit Brookie and she's hurt."

I looked at her and said, "Laura, that's like saying Hurricane Sandy was a spring shower."

Her eyes crinkled like she was going to smile, but then she started to move back into crying mode, until I said, "You've been enveloped in a giant shit-show for the last two days, and you're entitled to scream, cry or break anything you want, girl."

"Ma'am, it's like you stepped into a giant shitstorm inside a tornado," Buddha said.

"I'd call it a shitnado, ma'am, with a giant tsunami of fear to wash you out to sea," Ed said.

"It's a giant shit sandwich with danger dressing, served on a platter of adrenalin," Jack Soo said. "Anybody'd need to let go over that, ma'am."

"You were whirled around by a shitstorm of epic proportions that dropped you into a vat of molten shit while being battered by waves of assholes," Mamba said. "It'd be a miracle if you didn't just explode, ma'am, but all you did was cry, which is what most victims of PTSD do to relieve the pressure."

"Or they just beat the living shit out of somebody," Buddha said.

"And believe me, ma'am, Freak already did that for you, in spades," Hurricane said. "The only thing on Tom Miller that isn't broken are his balls, which I consider to be a grave oversight on Freak's part."

"You didn't pulverize his balls?" the (soon-to-be former) first lady said.

"No, ma'am," I said, "I needed to leave something for you."

"Oh. Thank you for that," she said, and we all burst out laughing. It continued for a while, until the door banged open again and the Warrior Princesses came running in. They wrapped me in a hug, and then they shook everybody else's hands, including the Attorney General, who opened his mouth to say something to them, until he saw all the rest of us looking at him. I gave a very slow, almost imperceptible shake of my head to tell him to shut up, which he thankfully did.

Brooke said, "I really tried to fight that asshole, Freak, but he whacked me away like I was a little kid. I didn't have time to get my pistol out or I would've shot him—it was in the small of my back and he was just right there."

"Don't worry about it—Allison took care of shooting him for you," I said as everyone cheered Allison, who turned beet red.

"She shoulda shot him dead, not just in the foot," Brooke said.

"On the contrary, Allison did exactly what a Warrior Princess should do—she showed mercy to someone who was weaker than she was," I said. "Remember, the strong protect the weak, not hurt them."

"He was way stronger than her—he could've come back to hurt someone," Brooke said.

"Not after Freak got done with him. She tore him up and then splatted him on the wall," Allison said. "She was so fast you couldn't even see her hands or feet—it was like watching a YouTube video on fast forward."

"In any case, you two need to take your Mom and get back to the White House and under cover," I said. The girls started to get clingy and whiny and I said "Don't get your panties in a bunch—I'm coming back to work as soon as Hurricane lets me, which should be fairly soon, and I'll be there almost every day anyway.

"In the meantime you need to get some rest and be prepared to go back to school to resume your schedule. Remember, if you cower in your bubble the bad guys win, right?" I said.

They both nodded and I said, "And take care of your mom, OK? Call her hairdresser up and get her some food and make sure she watches some trash TV and let her take naps in the afternoon for a while. You got it?"

"Yes, Freak," they both said.

"Your Pepsis, Brooke—you didn't get a shot off," Allison said.

"Fair enough," Brooke said.

"Now head for the car—I need to talk to your mom for a second," I said. They hugged me, said their good-byes, and then left. I walked the (soon-to-be-former) first lady to the doors where her security detail was waiting and said, "Ma'am, you need to tell them when the time is right, but soon. Even the Secret Service isn't going to be able to keep this secret for very long, ma'am," I said.

She looked at me with an approximation of her old Super Bitch look and said, "What exactly are we talking about, Agent Glickstien?"

"Laura, drop the act. I know that the president is at least bi-sexual, that he had an affair with Mitch Holland that began at Michigan and I also know that he murdered Tim Miller during his junior year at the university," I said, keeping my voice level and matter-of-fact.

She drooped again and said, "You know? How? Who else knows?"

"Enough people that there're going to be questions from the AG and U.S. Attorney within a couple of weeks. We don't have all the proof to prosecute yet, but you know the AG. He's going to have to follow the evidence to its end, and he's going to have very talented help, and then the Michigan AG will get involved, and then…" I said. I didn't finish my thought, because even though we'd had our differences I didn't want to be cruel to the first lady (OK, I was mainly thinking about my sisters, but I still didn't want to be cruel).

She finished the thought for me, though. "And then Jimmy gets arrested and we all get thrown out in disgrace. The girls and I get hounded for the rest of our lives while Jimmy rots in Jackson Prison, unless he's rotting in some federal prison instead." She rubbed her face like she was trying to take all the skin off it, and then locked her bleary eyes on mine.

"I knew Jimmy was more attracted to men when I met him. When he met Mitch at U of M it was all over—they were in love and have been since the first moment they met. We talked about it and he told me what he wanted to do, and how I was an integral part of all of it, and, well, you know how persuasive he is, and how committed he was to becoming president. I have never felt unloved—he really loves me, even though he's not that physically attracted to me—and the girls…

you already know how fiercely he loves his girls. He's still the best man I've ever known, the most decent, honorable and honest person in every life he touches…and when I think about all the good he's done for the country, how many real people he's helped…"

The (soon-to-be-former) first lady's voice trailed off. Her face got that look everybody calls the "thousand-yard stare" as she contemplated the unbelievable shit-show that was about to be her life. "But what happened all those years ago is just going to blow all of that to a big pile of fucking shit, isn't it, Freak?" she said.

I nodded and she inhaled like she was going to scream, but the (soon-to-be-former) first lady remembered who she was (at least temporarily) and caught herself before breaking down. She reached out, gripped my shoulder, and drew me close to her. "You understand why he did what he did, don't you? Why he never took responsibility for Tim Miller?"

I wasn't sure my voice would work, but I couldn't have her telling me something that would get her put in prison for conspiracy—clearly she knew what had happened, probably because the president had told her—and if she did know and had helped him cover it up the girls were going to be without parents for a while, and that just wasn't going to happen, so I calmly put my hand over her mouth and said, "Ma'am, I don't need or want to know, and I definitely don't want to hear it from you. Don't you think that should be up to the president, to decide if I'm ever told that whole story or not?" I stared at her, willing her to stop talking when I took my hand off her mouth.

The (soon-to-be-former) first lady was a lot of things, but stupid wasn't one of them. Even through the stress and heartache that was enveloping her thought process she realized what I was thinking. Her face lit up like a sunrise over the Himalayas as she realized that I was trying to protect her and the girls. She nodded at me and I took my hand off her mouth. The (soon-to-be-former) first lady reached out and pulled me to her, kissed me on the cheek and said, "Thank you, Glinka. You really are a sister to the girls, and I'm glad I finally realized that. Try not to judge Jimmy too harshly for anything that he might have done, will you?"

"Ma'am, if I were that harsh a judge the president would be in the same condition as Tom Miller," I said in a matter-of-fact tone. Laura Flagler Sheehan looked at my face and realized that I was simply telling the truth. She nodded again and left the room. I turned back to the gathering and said, "Will somebody get me a fucking Pepsi? I'm parched as hell and need some sage counsel. Where are Jewey and Weasel? We need those smart guys if we're going to figure out how to tie this case up, dontcha think?"

Buddha tossed me an ice-cold Pepsi, Mamba led me to a chair and we held a council of war about how to gather enough proof to arrest the president of the United States for murder.

The AG immediately said, "We're agreed that we have enough information to launch an investigation, but not enough proof to indict?" There were several nods of agreement and he said, "So we need to find a way to gather enough proof without alerting the president, correct? Any ideas about how we do that—and I only ask because your unit clearly has experience in this type of operation, given what happened with the Vice President."

"Sir, our two best strategic thinkers are currently in Oregon helping roll up the rest of Tom Miller's rogue SEAL unit. I would suggest that we rest ourselves while we wait for their return and then reconvene to brainstorm. There isn't any statute of limitations for murder, so time isn't an issue," Nails said.

"I'm still not really sure why we can't indict him right now. We've got the former VP's statement and the bishop's notes, plus we've got a time frame that we could flesh out in about two days," El Gato said. He looked at the AG and said, "I'm not questioning your assertion, sir, I'm just wondering about the law."

"We don't have any independent corroboration for the former VP's assertion, plus some judges might consider his statement hearsay, and you better believe the Church will move to quash the bishop's notes as privileged communications from the confessional, and yeah, before you get all militant, lots of judges would buy that, too," I said. Everyone stared at me, and Bumble said, "Freak, you go to night school and become motherfucking F. Lee Bailey without US knowing?"

Through the laughter I said, "Hey, I'm from a family of lawyers. Mumsy or either of my brothers who are in the law would tear what we have right now apart so quickly and with such vigor that the president wouldn't even have to resign, much less get prosecuted."

"Well, there's no question that she's right," Duquanye Quintanilla said. "I doubt if I could get a grand jury to indict with what we have right now, and they're a piece of cake compared to a trial judge. The president's attorneys would tear this apart in pre-trial motions, and probably get all of it expunged, and maybe destroy any chance we have to re-present any further charges."

"And that's assuming that the president doesn't at any point assert executive privilege in his communications with the Vice President, which I'm pretty sure he could and would," Nails said.

"And as a practicing Catholic I can tell you that the Church will march cardinal after cardinal into the prosecutor's office, or the judge's chambers screaming about the sanctity of the confessional, and they'll be followed by about 7,000 church lawyers carrying thousands of boxes of precedents and amicus briefs agreeing with them," El Gato said.

"They'll also fry Fast Eddie for giving up the notes in the first place—he'll be consigned to the East Bumfuck, Mongolia, parish or the Brothers of the Silent Shut the Fuck Up You Asshole monastery for the rest of his life," Joe said.

"True that," Bumble said.

"Plus this will drag the girls and the first lady into the limelight of the loving press, where they'll be crucified," Buddha said.

Once again Jack Soo had been absolutely silent. I looked at him and he said, "There's one thing we're forgetting."

"Do tell," I said.

"Guilt," Jack Soo said.

"We know he's guilty, we just can't prove it," Ed said.

"No, I mean guilt, as in 'that motherfucker feels guilt for what he's done'—like Catholics have guilt for using contraception, or Baptists have guilt for getting drunk, or Mormons have guilt for hiring prostitutes," Jack Soo said.

"You think we can use guilt against the president to get him to confess?" Joe said. "That's a great idea, O Asian Wizard, but Usually you need to have some kind of leverage to make that work. What do you propose to use as…" Joe's voice trailed off as a sudden thought hit him. Several of us got it then, and we all got the same shit-eating grin on or faces at the same time.

"Oh, you wily Oriental sage," Joe said.

"It's very clever, but we'll have to be careful how we play it, on both ends," Mamba said.

"We need to treat it like a Hippocratic Oath situation—first do no harm," I said.

"Absolutely right," Jack Soo said. "But if we're careful and we plan it right, it could work."

The AG looked at us like we'd gone crazy and said, "I have no idea what in the hell you're talking about. Explain, please."

So we did.

After we were done explaining the AG said, "I'm not willing to do any more damage just to get a confession—we'll almost certainly be able to gather enough evidence now that we know where to focus our efforts—but if we can do it, well, it would certainly make it a cleaner, quicker exercise."

"It would also corroborate the former VP's statement, which would then be admissible, and would obviate the need to even use the bishop's notes, which would keep Fast Eddie out of it, too," Brenda T. Green said.

"Thus killing all the proverbial birds with one stone," Ed said.

"But we have to figure out a way to do it that makes sure that nobody else gets hurt any worse," El Gato said.

"I've got an idea," I said.

"Do tell," Joe said.

So I did.

When I was done everybody agreed it was worth a shot, and that if the first part didn't work we wouldn't try the second part, we'd just go to work and dig up evidence the old fashioned way.

That's when it hit me like a ton of bricks that there was another way to help leverage the confession that would ensure that nobody else got hurt.

Joe said, "Freak, that's why everybody loves to play poker with you—your face is transparent as hell. What's up?"

I told them. There was utter silence until Mamba said, "This is how I think we should play it." He laid out his idea and we all were struck by the simplicity and deviousness of it. When Mamba was all done he looked at Jack Soo and said, "How you think it work, Charrie Chan?" in a bad fake Asian accent.

"Roun' eye have good pran, mos' rikery work rike proverbiar crockwork," Jack Soo said in the worst imitation Asian accent we'd ever heard.

We were still laughing when Nails said, "OK, so we're agreed we should try this plan? Mr. Attorney General?"

"Go," the AG said.

"Concur," Duquanye West said.

"Let's take the train to conviction town," Brenda T. Green said.

"I'm sold," Nails said.

"I think we're all for it," Joe said.

"Fuck yeah!" the rest of us said.

"Pepsis all around, and then to work," the AG said. We ate the rest of the Chinese food and then went off to do our assigned tasks so that we could try to get the president of the United States to confess to murder.

Two days later I woke up at 4:45 a.m. and went to my gym to work out. I lifted, ran and jumped, took a shower, and went home to eat breakfast and dress for work. I walked out of my apartment at 6:15 a.m. and met Kid Galahad, El Gato, Bumble, Badass, Ed, Buddha, and Joe. We walked down to the grocery store parking lot where Mamba was waiting with his personal chauffeur and a lovely, huge Lincoln limo.

We all greeted James and then we went to Reagan National Airport, where we picked up Bengt Olafsson, my Mumsy, Kristy O'Dowd and Mrs. Karen Miller.

Greeting hugs were exchanged and then we all piled into the limo and headed for the White House.

"I'm still not sure why I'm here," Mrs. Miller said.

"I'm going to explain that when we get to the White House, ma'am, and then I'm going to give you a tour of the place," I said.

"It's going to be OK for me to tour the White House?" Mrs. Miller said.

"Oh, yes, ma'am, we've already got the president's approval, and my boss, Edward Otis Whitney, has also approved it," I said.

"Well, this is very exciting," Mrs. Miller said. "I've never been to Washington before. I always wanted to take the boys, but we never had the money, and then Timmy passed, and Tommy went away and never came back, and well, there just didn't seem to be any point." She still looked like she was 20 years older than she was, but Mumsy had told her we had a lead on what happened to Tim, so she was trying really hard to be upbeat.

We all hoped she'd be really upbeat in just a little longer.

We got to the White House and were cleared through. We got out at the North Portico and were met by Old Three Names and Nails, who we introduced to everyone that didn't know them. We went into the foyer and I said, "Mrs. Miller, we're going to go on that tour now, but if you don't mind I'm going to send you around with my friends Agent Cocker and Agent Beemond for the first part of it. I've got one thing I have to do, but I'll join you soon, if that's OK?"

"Of course, Freak. Are we going to see the Roosevelt Room? You always hear about it, and I'd like to see if it matches the picture I've painted in my head," Mrs. Miller said.

"You'll absolutely see it, ma'am, and Mumsy will be there so you can compare pictures, because I'm sure she's done the same thing," I said.

"Doesn't it sound exciting Karen? We'll be able to tell everyone back home that we saw the Roosevelt Room, and President Roosevelt's Nobel Peace Prize," Mumsy said. Joe said, "Ladies, if you'll follow me this way?" He and Bumble led them off and the rest of us headed to the Oval Office.

When we got there the AG was waiting with Duquanye Quintanilla. The president's secretaries and his body man, a good-looking kid named Carlos Hill, were all trying to figure out what was going on, but all the AG did was point at the door to the Oval, and we went in. The president was talking to Charlie Hassenger and didn't see us at first. He turned from talking to the chief of staff, saw us and immediately said, "The girls?"

"Are completely safe, sir, no worries at all," I said.

"Well, that's a good thing. What can I do for you, Mr. Attorney General, Agent Glickstien?" the president said.

"Sir, I'm going to request that the chief of staff step out for a moment, unless you want him to hear what I'm about to say," the AG said.

"What is it that you're going to say, Len?" the president said.

"Mr. President, I have some information concerning a murder and the ongoing attempts—a conspiracy, sir—to cover it up," the AG said, his tone flat, his eyes hard as diamonds.

The president paled and said, "Charlie, maybe you should, uh, maybe we should…" He trailed off as his face went from white to red.

"Whatever it is, Mr. President, there's no way I'll leave now. What the hell are you talking about, Len?" Charlie Hassenger said.

But it was me that answered.

"Mr. President, the Secret Service recently became aware that you murdered Tim Miller and then conspired with several individuals to cover it up. When we discovered proof of this we immediately informed the U.S. Attorney, Duquanye Quintanilla, who in turn informed the Attorney General. We have developed enough proof to have you indicted by a federal grand jury, sir."

"That's a bunch of bullshit, and you know it, Len," Charlie Hassenger said. "What, you can't wait to run for president, you've gotta move up early with some bogus charge like this? Have you lost your fucking mind?"

"Charlie, sit down and shut the fuck up, right now," the president said. Hassenger looked thunderstruck, but he sat down and shut the fuck up.

The president looked at me and said, "I never murdered anybody, Freak, least of all Tim Miller. I was at college when he died. What the hell is this really all about, Freak?"

"Sir, you definitely murdered Tim Miller, and we absolutely have proof. The AG thought that due to your position you deserved the chance to hear the proofs before we got down to brass tacks," I said.

"I thank you for that, Len, but I'm still mystified about my motive for killing Tim Miller. And I really was at U of M when he died," the president said. His face was recovering, and he settled comfortably into the chair behind his desk. He was starting to look a bit more confident, too, so I said, "Sir, we know what your motive was." I got up, went over to the door, and said, "Send her in."

Kristy O'Dowd came in and said, "Hello, Jim, I mean, Mr. President. Sorry about that."

The president stood up, then abruptly flopped back in his chair like he was having a stroke. He clearly couldn't speak, so Charlie Hassenger said, "That's it! This interview is over right now. You people get the fuck out of the Oval Office. Mr. President, I'm calling the White House Counsel and getting her in here." He was reaching for the phone when the president said, "No, no Charlie. Sit down and just listen, OK. Trust me, we need to listen right now."

"Ms. O'Dowd, why did the president leave Ann Arbor and come home to see Tim Miller?" I said.

"Tim told me that he and Jimmy—the president—loved each other, and that's why we never had sex, because he had sex with Jimmy—the president," Kristy said. "He told me that Jimmy was coming home from U of M to see him that weekend, but that they had to keep it a secret." She lied so sweetly that I almost believed her, even though I knew it was a crock of shit.

"You were afraid that he'd betray your secret just like this, Mr. President, so you killed him to keep him from squealing," I said.

"That's utterly ridiculous, and besides, that's just some hearsay between two people who had reason to be jealous of the president," Charlie Hassenger said, but he was clearly starting to doubt what he was saying. I'd known the guy a long time and I could tell that doubt was creeping in.

When the president didn't reply to Kristy's accusation it was clearly time for phase two. I went to the door and said, "Send him in."

Bengt Olafsson came in and said, "Mr. President, I wish we were seeing each other under better circumstances." The president stood up and shakily offered his hand to the big detective, who shook it and said, "Sir, you should sit down before you fall down." The president fell into the chair like he was a marionette whose strings had been cut, and Bengt stepped back from the desk to stand by one of the couches in the office. He looked at me and I nodded, so he said, "Mr. President, do you remember that you led the blood drive at Harper Creek High School when you were a senior there?"

The president nodded, and Bengt said, "Sir, do you remember that you and the other officers of your high school class volunteered to take part in a Kellogg Community College study about the ancestry of people in the Battle Creek area?"

The president nodded and Bengt said, "Sir, do you remember that one of the parts of the project was an early DNA analysis, and that you signed a release that allowed the school to use your results in the study?"

The president nodded, and Bengt said, "Sir, using the Freedom of Information Act I acquired those results in order to compare them to the DNA found at the Tim Miller murder, which the Attorney General has assured me was perfectly legal, since the study was in the public domain." My old friend was also lying beautifully. Once again I believed the big detective, even though I knew it was just sunshine he was pulling out of his ass.

"Sir, I had the Michigan State Police crime lab compare those two samples, and I had the FBI Crime Lab at Quantico and the University of Michigan biology lab confirm the findings." Bengt looked at the president, who stared back with a horrified expression on his face.

"Sir, those samples were confirmed to be an exact match, with a one in twenty-six trillion chance of error. You were there, sir, at the site of Tim Miller's murder, and I can prove that you had sexual relations with him," Bengt said, his big voice remarkably gentle in the complete silence of the Oval Office.

The silence stretched on until the president finally said, "Everybody except Freak out of the office." When nobody moved he said, "I said everybody get the fuck out of this office except Freak, *right now!*"

Charlie Hassenger said, "Mr. President, you need to stop talking and let me get the White House counsel in here, sir."

The president went to his discombobulated chief of staff, patted his back and said, "Thanks, Charlie, but I want to talk to Freak before we do anything else. Trust me, we'll talk off the record, but Freak and I *are* going to talk. Now everybody leave."

And they did.

James Patrick Liam Sheehan sat down in one arm chair and motioned me into the other, and we sat there for a moment before he said, "I guess now it doesn't matter if this is off the record or not, but I'd like to tell you what actually happened that night, Freak."

"I'd like to hear it, Mr. President, and believe me, with the evidence that we have it won't matter," I said, lying my ass off just like Kristy and Bengt.

"I believe you," the president said. "Now let me tell you exactly what happened."

And he did.

CHAPTER 79

A Mother's Voice

The president looked at the eagle in the carpet of the Oval Office for a few seconds before he said, "Tim and I loved each other and had been having sex for over a year before that day. I want you to know that I didn't murder him. It was consensual sex that got rough, and the backseat of the car was small and awkward for two guys our size, and Tim kind of liked being choked and, well, I lost control of myself and it just happened. I didn't even realize that Tim was dead until I was done and he didn't react at all." The president stared back down at the eagle on the carpet and said, "I panicked and ran, but came back after I realized that I might be able to revive him, but when I got back there it was obvious that I wouldn't be able to do CPR. He was dead."

"His hyoid bone was fractured, sir. Once it was broken the only thing that would've saved him was a tracheotomy," I said. Joe and the AG had counseled me to say nothing and let him get it all out, but I felt like I needed to push the conversation along, using a little bit of reality to imply sympathy, even though I didn't feel any such thing.

It worked. The president spewed out the whole sordid story in great detail, and I listened and nodded for the next ten minutes until he wound down. I let the silence build until the president said, "So what do I do, Freak? I didn't mean to hurt Tim, and I certainly didn't murder him, although I suppose that you could consider it manslaughter. What do I do now?" It was apparent that the president was trying to defend himself and work his way to some kind of absolution, so before he got there and decided to ask all of us to join a giant criminal conspiracy I said, "Mr. President, were you serious about owing me for saving your family the last time?"

"Absolutely," the president said. "Whatever you want, Freak." He looked at me with some of the old James Sheehan, Master of the Universe confidence and I said, "OK, I want you to take a meeting with myself and one other person, sir."

"Whenever you want, Freak," the president said.

"In just about five minutes, Mr. President," I said. "Please excuse me one moment, sir." I went out into the Oval Office, where Mumsy and Mrs. Miller arrived right on schedule. I took Mrs. Miller's arm and said, "Ma'am, you need to sit down for a moment."

She sat down and I said, "Agent Goodenough, clear this room." Badass shoved everybody out of the office and I told Mrs. Miller what we knew about Tim's death. I was gentle, but firm about the proofs and what we absolutely knew, including what the president had just told me.

She cried at first, but as I moved further into my narrative her face changed. She started to look younger, and her chin firmed up, and her eyes began flashing with anger, and she lost all of the doddering characteristics she'd had for so long, until finally she was giving off waves of righteous indignation. I don't know how else to put it, but Mrs. Miller was transformed right in front of my eyes into a womyn who was ready to rain down some serious guilt on the person who killed her son, to the point where she said, "I'd like to talk to the president now, Glinka."

"Are you sure you're ready, Mrs. Miller?" I said, even though I was sure that she was more than ready.

She looked at me with the eyes of a warrior princess and said, "Take me to him now, Glinka." So I did.

She walked in the office and the president's face drained of all color. He staggered back and tried to get back behind the desk, but Mrs. Miller went right up to him and slapped his face. The president staggered back but didn't fall down, catching himself on the edge of the desk. Mrs. Miller looked him right in the eye and said, "Good people don't kill those they love, Jimmy Sheehan, and good people surely don't put the family of their victim through the hell of not knowing what happened for 25 years. You're a bad person, Jimmy Sheehan, and you should be ashamed of yourself." Tears streamed down her cheeks, but at that moment Mrs. Miller looked like an Old Testament warrior princess, full of the wrath of God and willing to rain it down on the unrighteous.

The president clung to the corner of his desk like a man adrift in a sea of sharks would hold on to his life raft, but Mrs. Miller refused to back down. She grabbed the president by the ear, dragged him over to one of the armchairs and shoved him into the seat. She dragged the other chair over so the two were facing each other from about six inches away and sat down. Her eyes were like twin lasers as they bored into the president's eyes.

"Now tell me everything, Jimmy Sheehan, and don't you dare leave anything out," Mrs. Miller said.

"But, but, er, uh—Mrs. Miller, I, I, I, uh, there are some things that…uh, well, Tim and I, we, uh—"

Mrs. Miller cut him off by reaching out and grabbing his face. She pulled the president over to her and said, "Jimmy Sheehan, if you think that I didn't know that my boy liked boys better than girls, or that he had sex with other boys, well, you've got another think coming. I'm perfectly aware that my Tim was a gay man and I don't care, but you *will* tell me everything. You owe me that much, Jimmy Sheehan." Her voice was steady, firm, and irresistible, a mother's voice commanding a child to tell her the truth.

The president heaved a huge sigh, looked away from Mrs. Miller and then looked back at the floor. He began to say something while looking at the floor, but Mrs. Miller said, "Look me in the eye, Jimmy Sheehan. I've been waiting for 25 years, and I don't want to miss anything about my Tim's last moments, regardless of how gruesome they may have been."

I give him credit, because the president looked at Mrs. Miller and spewed it all out. I'm not going to detail their whole conversation, because some things should be private, and this is one of those things. They both cried multiple times, there were Kleenexes passed back and forth, and after 45 minutes of conversation, they both were wrung out, and that's all you need to know.

The president looked at Mrs. Miller and said, "You know my parents are both gone, and I really don't have anyone else to ask, so can I ask you what to do, Mrs. Miller? What should I do?" In that moment James Sheehan's voice was that of a son asking his mom what to do about his pregnant girlfriend, or about whether or not to come out of the closet.

Mrs. Miller gently took his hand between hers and held it in her lap. "I knew your parents and your grandparents, Jimmy, and they were all good, honorable people. I watched you grow up and learn to be a man from Marv Horn, and Bishop O'Dowd, and your mom and dad, so I know that you were raised properly," she said in the kindest voice that I've ever heard.

"But, what—I still don't know what to do, ma'am. I still don't know what to do. Help me, please," the president said, his voice soft and wavering just a tiny bit.

"Jimmy, do you remember what Coach Horn used to say about making choices?" Mrs. Miller said. "Do you remember what he said about cancelling the game after my Tim died?"

The president was lost in thought for a moment, and then he gave a small nod. He looked at Mrs. Miller and she gave him a Mona Lisa smile, and he nodded again, and said, "I remember. Coach Horn said that when you're faced with two choices, a hard one and an easy one, that the hard one was usually the right choice. That's why the Beavers played the week after Tim died, because that was the hard choice."

"Never take the path of least resistance, the man said to me, and I agreed with him," Mrs. Miller said.

"Because men take the hard road in order to avoid becoming weak," the president said.

"So I think you just answered your own question, Jimmy," Mrs. Miller said.

"But, I… I have to…what can I do to make it up to you, Mrs. Miller? I've treated you horribly, and I… I did kill Tim, even though I didn't mean to, I really didn't mean to, Mrs. Miller," the president said as his voice broke and he began to cry again.

Through her own tears Mrs. Miller said, "Some things can't be made right, Jimmy Sheehan, and some things you can't apologize for, but I'm a good Catholic womyn and I believe that the Lord forgives all who ask for it. Ask for forgiveness and the Lord will grant it, Jimmy.

"As for me, well, I forgave you as soon as you told me what happened, because you may have killed my Timmy, but he was a willing participant, and it was an accident of love. I'm not excusing your conduct since, which was absolutely shitty, but I do understand, and I forgive you for Tim's death. I'm afraid that I can't do more than that, except to remind you that you're a good Catholic boy who knows where to turn for absolution."

They looked at each other for a long time, until finally the president said, "You're right, Mrs. Miller, I do know what to do, and I'm going to do it, for you, for myself and especially for Tim. Tim was an innocent who deserves better than he got, and I'm the only one who can provide him with justice. You have my word that I'll do that, ma'am."

"Your word is good enough for me, Mr. President," Mrs. Miller said. She and the president stood up and embraced each other. Mrs. Miller patted him on the back and said, "Under it all you're a good man, Jimmy, you just need to remember your raising all the time, like this one does," jerking a thumb over her shoulder at me.

I'd been standing post the whole time they talked, listening while not listening, and now I said, "Mr. President, may I make one suggestion? Take your time and think about any course of action you might take, because right now you're suffering from PTSD, sleep deprivation and probably dehydration. All of those things combine to skew your thought processes, and you need to be very clear headed about this, sir."

"Thanks, Freak, and you're right about all of that. Any suggestions on how to deal with a problem like that?" the president said.

"Sir, you look ill to me—I'd say that you have a high fever and are probably contagious with oh, I'd say the flu," I said.

"No, he's got strep throat, with a case of pink eye thrown in. Both are really contagious and are best served by staying in bed and near isolation," Mrs. Miller said.

"Well, I'm certainly not going to be out in public with such contagious diseases, so I guess it's going to be three days or so in the residence, without any real work," the president said.

"And you won't be able to talk very much, either, Mr. President, because strep throat really hurts," Mrs. Miller said. "You need to rest your voice and remember to eat well, because that fever is trying to lower your blood sugar and make you feel worse."

The president nodded and said, "So it is, Mrs. Miller." He hugged her again. She patted his cheek and said, "Remember your raising, Jimmy Sheehan, and put your trust in the Lord." She turned to me and said, "I'd like to go, now, Freak. Can you take me back to your mother?"

I opened the door and said, "Kid, Badass, will you please escort Mrs. Miller back to my mother so they can finish their tour? And let everybody back in their office, please. I'll meet everybody back at the bullpen in five minutes."

I went back in the office and said, "Mr. President, may I make one more suggestion?"

James Patrick Liam Sheehan looked up from his desk—the *Resolute* desk that so many presidents had used—and said, "Absolutely, Freak. Having that meeting with Mrs. Miller doesn't settle my obligation to you, by the way, so suggest away."

I told him my suggestion and he agreed that it was the best idea possible, given the situation, and then I went out and sent the president's body man in to see him. I heard him say, "Carlos, I need the chief of staff, my personal physician and the first lady, in that order. I also need you to call..."

I went out of the Oval Office anteroom and straight to the Secret Service bullpen. Within five minutes all of my squad was there, as well as the AG, Nails and Old Three Names. Once we were all assembled Jack Soo said, "He's going to go for it, isn't he? Good plan, Freak, and it worked like a charm."

"How the fuck do you know that, you overconfident asshole?" Buddha said.

"I've played poker with Freak, and I'll bet you that Joe, Kid Galahad and Badass all knew, too," Jack Soo said.

"Of course we knew," Mamba said. "Freak's face might as well be a billboard with lights flashing 'Mission Accomplished'."

"Oh, fuck you assholes," I said. "I can keep secrets, and I'm a *great* poker player." That was such obvious bullshit that even Old Three Names joined in the laughter.

"So our testimony worked," Bengt said.

"Yes, you guys helped persuade the president to do the right thing," I said.

"Even though we were lying like rugs," Kristy O'Dowd said.

"Yeah, it put him over the edge. He didn't know that Tim kept his sexuality a secret from you, and he didn't know that the study at KCC was a double-blind, anonymous project," I said.

"Which means that there is no way of knowing which DNA sample is the president's, just that he actually gave one," Bengt said. "I checked—there's no way to identify a single sample, and besides, those samples were destroyed long ago, after the study was over."

"So when's it going to happen?" Nails said.

"Probably four days. I advised him to treat his PTSD slash exhaustion, et cetera by resting, so he's going to get strep throat and pink eye for the next three days. During that time he'll consult with his attorney, spend time with his family and get the rest of his house in order," I said.

"We should be ready to adjust our coverage once he does whatever it is he's going to do," Edward Otis Whitney said. "We'll need to continue with the first family, but once the president is in custody by law we'll be absolved of any duty on him. The law also says that we won't have any responsibility for the first lady or the first daughters after three months, although we could extend that."

Nails said, "We'll work on that. We'll need everybody else to act normally, and we'll need to talk to Tom Miller, and we need to contact the FBI about the rest of the investigation, because they're the logical agency for it, once the president does whatever he's going to do."

Every eye in the place swung toward me and I said, "Look all you want, but don't expect any prognostication. Remember that the president is a tough, capable man with enormous resources available to him. He may decide to admit that something happened and then spin it. All he promised Mrs. Miller was to do the right thing—he didn't specify what that was, and I can't predict what it'll be."

The AG said, "In that case, I'm going to arrange for the president to be taken into custody at the close of business in four days, just in case he does nothing. We are going to continue with this as an exclusive Secret Service investigation until we see what happens, and we are not going to inform any other agencies until I give the go-ahead. Director Hessler, who are you going to assign to talk to Tom Miller?"

"Freak, Joe and Ed will go in first, with Jewey, Weasel and Jack Soo on the second interview. After that we'll see who's made the best connection and send them in for the third interview. That should get us what we need, and if it doesn't we'll have teams from other agencies interview him," Nails said.

"Good. If we need to do anything else we'll coordinate through USA Quintanilla's office, since he and A-USA Green will be doing the ground work on this case. I can do it, but I was appointed by the president and I don't want any seeming conflicts of interest," the AG said.

"That's a good move, sir, especially if we get a quick conviction for less than the top count," Quintanilla said.

"Yes, God forbid we seem to be lenient on someone who had to stay in the closet nearly his whole life because some in our society still can't accept that what someone does in their own bedroom is a private affair," the AG said.

"That's not what I meant, sir. What I meant is that *you* can't be lenient if necessary, but I can—this president didn't appoint me, and after I prosecute him I'm going home to Nevada to run for the House, which means that you can still run for president without any blemish on your record, sir," Duquanye Quintanilla said.

The AG was clearly touched by the loyalty, but he said, "Remember, the murder is a Michigan matter, not federal. Only the conspiracy to cover up is federal, and the conviction for that won't matter so much after the murder conviction. Now let's get to work."

So Joe, Ed and I went to see Tom Miller.

We set the time up with his lawyer (my brother! Sheesh!) and then went to the hospital armed with warrants in case Roady got frisky. In fact, we took A-USA Brenda T. Green with us as our legal adviser, even though she wasn't going to go into the interview, since we were afraid that'd get Tom and Roady's backs up.

We arrived at Tom Miller's hospital room and identified ourselves to the two U.S. Marshals guarding the door and went in, where we found two more U.S. Marshals, a Secret Service guy, Alvin Firkkensen, my brother and Tom Miller.

All the law enforcement personnel shot the shit for a minute, before my brother said, "Hello? Fascist pigs? My client has lots of wounds that could become infected, what with all the defecation flying around in here, so could we get on with this before you either kill him with germs or he dies from boredom?"

"Sure thing, Counselor," I said, looking Roady straight in the eye. I didn't intimidate him—the guy went through Stanford Law without breaking a sweat and then clerked for Justice Sotomayor on the Supreme Court before becoming a great defense lawyer in a firm in Boston—but I had most of the cards, and he knew it, so the bravado was a delaying tactic…but why? I needed to know what Roady was up to before I talked to Tom Miller, but the only way I was going to get the chance to sound out Roady's strategy was by talking to his client. Goddamned Joseph Heller would've loved the situation (yes, that's another literary reference—look it up), but we were all kind of pissed off about it.

Until Roady said, "My client waives his right to remain silent and is prepared to answer any questions you might have. You can even bring the A-USA you have waiting outside in if you'd like."

Our collective jaws hit the floor, because we'd figured that there were about 22 avenues for Tom Miller to take in order to not get sent to prison for 350 years, but this wasn't one of them.

"Will you put that in writing?" Joe said.

Roady pulled out a sheaf of papers, pulled the top one off and said, "Already signed and notarized, and before you question the signature, my client's signing hand is so fucked up that he'll be lucky if he can ever use it again, so we had the notary add a note explaining that she witnessed the physical distress my client was under when he was signing." Roady was glaring at me when he said it, which didn't sit very well with me.

In fact, it pissed me off royally, so I decided to strike back at my big brother's anger with a demonstration. I didn't say a thing, but I did take off my jacket, unsnap and remove my shoulder holster rig, unbutton my shirt and pull it off, and unsnap my bra and remove it.

Everyone was staring at me as I did a slow pirouette, showing off my bruises and the knife scar that ran from my armpit until it disappeared into my pants just above my hip. There was dead silence as everyone took in the full extent of the beating the three gomers sent by Tom Miller had given me, but that wasn't enough for me, so I reached in my pocket and brought my creds case out.

I snapped it open and got three pictures out of the pocket behind the badge. I fanned them out and walked right up to shove them in Roady's face. I let him look at them for a few seconds before I said, "Agent Adam Seivert, Agent Sarah Koenigsblett, Agent Alexander de Vries, all killed by .50-caliber fire initiated by your client at the Amicus School. They were shot down like dogs while doing their sworn duty, protecting two teenage girls who never hurt anybody in their lives." My voice was steady, and as cold as Antarctica during a winter blizzard.

I stood there half-naked and looked Roady right in the eyes before I said, "So cry me a fucking river about his damned hand, counselor. Your client is nothing more than an asshole murderer, and I could give a shit about him getting his ass kicked in a fair fight that was only fair after he lost the combat knife he was holding at the throat of one of those teenage girls."

Bravery ran in our family, because Roady said, "It seems that the fair "fight" may have turned into a beating, not just a subduing of my client." He actually used finger quotes when he said fair fight, which torked me off even more.

"It's not my fault if that fucking piece of shit can't defend himself. I only made three passes at him, and I'm a sworn federal law officer who was subduing a highly dangerous Navy SEAL, and did I mention that he's a murderous piece of shit who goes around trying to kidnap innocent teenage *girls*? You go for a "poor old Tom Miller" defense because he got his ass kicked and I'll get on the stand and turn you into dog food, you lame-ass piece-of-shit shyster," I said.

Roady smiled and said, "First of all, that's lame-ass piece-of-shit shyster *brother*, and second, I'd like to see you try it, you misshapen lump of murderous protoplasm."

"Stop that shit, you two. Roady, you lost this pissing contest, because hers really is bigger than yours, and actually, she's right," Tom Miller said, interrupting what could have been a very ugly family feud.

"Eh?" Roady said. "Tom, I need to mount a vigorous defense or—"

"No way they go for the death penalty, and besides, what I did was wrong," Tom Miller said. "Look at your sister's body—I told those guys to torture her and send the pieces to the president as another way to torture him. I could've just killed the son of a bitch who killed my brother, but I had to go and get all Greek tragedy on his ass and look what happened. Lots of innocent people died and here I lay, busted up beyond all recognition. My guys were all a part of the conspiracy, so those good and honorable men, who only did what they did because they loved and trusted me, are also going to jail for a very long time."

Tom Miller looked at me and said, "I'm sorry, Freak. Something popped in my head and I lost sight of myself, and no, that isn't an excuse, it's just a fact. I'm truly sorry about what happened."

I believed him, so all I did was put my clothes back on and walk up to his bed to shake his hand, which I found he really couldn't do, since they had him shackled to the bed.

That really pissed me off, and I stomped over, opened the door and said, "Who the hell's cuffs are on the prisoner?"

One of the marshals said, "They're mine. We're under orders to make sure he can't escape."

"Have you noticed the shape he's in? Come in and take them off," I said.

"No way that's going to happen. My boss said shackle him, so he stays shackled, whether you like it or not," the marshal said. Alvin Firkkensen took one look at my face and began to back away from me, but I just said, "Oh, OK" and went back in the room, where I promptly grabbed the shackles and tore them to pieces.

I picked up the now useless shackles and went out the door. I said, "A-USA Green, would you please come in and take a statement from Captain Tom Miller?"

"Of course," she said.

"Oh, and here're your piece-of-shit shackles," I said to the marshals as I tossed the scrap metal at their feet. The look on their faces was worth a thousand words—and it was clear that they now understood how the prisoner got the way he was.

I went back in and shook Tom Miller's hand. "I accept your apology, but there is still a price to be paid, and I'm afraid you'll have to pay most of it, although I'd make sure I was watching TV in three days."

Tom Miller's eyes were filled with hope and he said, "Yeah? Why is that, Freak?"

"I can't tell ya, but it might be worth it," I said. "I do have one good piece of news for you."

"I'll still get my pension when I'm in Leavenworth?" he said.

"Are you kidding me? The cheap-ass bastards who let contracts to the lowest bidder? Let you keep your pension? The sun'll rotate backward before that happens," I said, eliciting laughter from everybody. "No, your mother is in town and she'd like to see you, even in this condition. Can I bring her by?"

"Yes," Roady and Tom Miller said together.

"I'll get the Pepsis, Roady, since I can't really pay ya," Tom Miller said.

My brother said, "Fair enough, Captain Miller. I see the A-USA…shall we get the statement done?"

"Yes," Tom Miller said as Brenda T. Green came over to the bed. They got all of the paperwork out of the way—actually, Roady'd already done all of it—and then we all stood there and listened to Tom Miller tell his story.

He'd always suspected that Tim was killed by a gay lover—twins really have no secrets from each other—but he could never figure out who it was, even though it seemed to be all he thought about in his free time.

At first that wasn't a problem, because his life was so busy. He finished high school, enlisted in the navy, went to OCS and then was selected for the SEALs. "I was so tired all of the time that I kind of forgot about Timmy, and then I was on assignment to several interesting places (all classified) and I needed to think about my men and myself first, and, well, I really put Timmy out of my mind," Tom Miller said.

"What happened that triggered your obsession?" I said.

"I got wounded in a far away, fairy tale place and spent six months in bed, first in a field hospital and then Walter Reed. There's lots of time to think when you're just lying there, and so naturally I started thinking about Tim.

"At first it was just the usual speculation about who did it and how they got away with it, but then I started to think about why they did it, and specifically, how did someone subdue my very physically gifted brother, who was a wrestler and could really, truly take care of himself, and not get all busted up? That led me to start thinking about other athletes, and that led me to think about other athletes who might have been able to strangle Timmy without him ripping them up," Tom Miller said.

"Which meant it had to be someone bigger and stronger than him," Joe said.

"Exactly. It wasn't until later that I realized that it could also be someone who had another attribute," Tom said.

"An *older* athlete who was also bigger and stronger," Ed said. "Someone who was training at a much higher level than your brother."

"Maybe a collegiate athlete in a highly physical sport, like, say, football?" I said.

"Yeah, I got on to Jimmy Sheehan pretty quickly. I knew that Timmy liked him, and I kinda had a feeling that Jimmy was gay, although I didn't have any proof. I also had another suspect that I knew was gay and had the opportunity to do it, and I knew he had a motive for keeping Timmy quiet about their relations," Tom Miller said. He looked at me and raised one eyebrow and I said, "Oh, shit. Are you telling me that—"

"Yep, I am. Jarius Walker told me that he was gay, and that he and Tim had been a couple for a while but decided to break up when Jarius went to Notre Dame. I was sure that it was Jarius for a long time, because you remember that he was at the party, and, well, he was the logical suspect. Jimmy was off at U of M and it was in-season, so he was kinda out as a suspect," Tom Miller said.

"Wait a minute," Ed said. "Are we talking about Jarius Walker, the former All-Pro right guard for the New Orleans Saints? That Jarius Walker?"

"Yeah," Tom Miller and I said.

"My Pepsis," I said.

"Shit, yeah. You'll even have to hold it for me, at least for a year or three," Tom Miller said. "By the way, the fucking Taliban didn't kick my ass as bad as you did. I'm an expert at martial arts and as good a hand-to-hand fighter as there's ever been in the SEALs…but what you did defies logic, and in a couple of places the laws of physics. I'm lucky to be alive, although I don't think luck had much to do with it, did it?"

I slowly shook my head and said, "You're alive because of your mother, and the fact that what the president did was shitty, and because if it'd been one of my brothers I can't say it wouldn't have been me doing something like what you did, although I wouldn't have been willing to pay the cost in innocent blood you did."

"You'd've been a bit more direct, I'm thinking," Tom Miller said.

"Bet your ass," I said. We all laughed and then Joe said, "OK, so you had another suspect that you pursued and discarded. What finally tipped you to the president?"

"I confronted Jarius after the NFC championship game that they lost to the Lions—he was low, and really beaten up, and he wouldn't have lied to me anyway, because we were pals, and he told me that he had nothing to do with it, and he gave me an iron-clad alibi, so I went back to thinking about it, and then I got deployed again.

"I was sitting in a USO tent in Afghanistan and looking at an ancient *Sports Illustrated*—the one with Jimmy Sheehan on the cover, you know, after he won the Heisman and the Wolverines won the national championship?" Tom Miller said.

"Sure," I said, "it was the one Coach Horn put in the window of his office. It might still be there, for all I know."

"That's the one. Anyway, I read the whole article, and it remarked on the fact that Jimmy'd had one bad game in four years, the game against Purdue during his junior season. He had three interceptions in the first half, and two of them were returned for touchdowns, and U of M almost lost, until Jimmy came back and threw three TD passes in seven minutes to pull the game out. The article also mentioned that Jimmy'd taken a hell of a beating during the previous week, when the Wolverines beat Wisconsin, and that maybe all the time he spent in the training room that week had affected his play."

Tom Miller paused and looked at me, and I felt the hair stand up on the back of my neck, because I was back at home, watching the U of M—Wisconsin game with my family as Michigan's ground game wore the Badgers down and hometown hero Jimmy Sheehan threw a pair of play-action touchdown passes in the fourth quarter to help U of M beat the #2 ranked Badgers.

And later that day we went across the street to the birthday party for Tom and Tim Miller.

"Oh, shit," I said.

"Yeah, I finally figured it out when I tracked down the Michigan trainer from that year, and he told me it was the weirdest thing, because Jimmy hadn't mentioned anything about being hurt right after the game, but by Sunday at noon he was in the training room with multiple injuries, including a huge bruise on his left buttock, a deep scratch on his neck and three bruised ribs. The trainer figured that the adrenalin from the win covered up the pain, and when he wound down it all started to affect him," Tom Miller said.

"But you figured that he didn't get the injuries until *after* the game, when he and your brother hooked up," Ed said.

"Right down the middle, first time," Tom said. "It made more sense—he and Timmy made Klingon love (see *Star Trek: Deep Space 9*, reference Mr. Worf and Jadzia Dax), and in the process Timmy marked him up. He went to the trainer to register the injuries as football ones, just in case he was somehow implicated. It was brilliant, and the beginning of the cover-up."

"And nobody would even question him, because playing quarterback in the Big Ten is physically demanding in just the right way to cover injuries incurred during rough sex," Joe said.

"Yeah," Tom Miller said. "It was brilliant on his part because it covered him for the murder as well as padding his reputation as a football tough guy."

"Which kept him off everybody else's radar, but once you thought he was your guy you ran down enough information to convince you that he *was* your guy, and then..." I said.

"I lost my fucking mind, especially after I went home my one and only time and saw what had happened to my mother. I was teetering on the edge of obsession then, and when I went to the old bishop to confess my sins he was very solicitous about his sorrow at Timmy's death. It'd been a while, so I kind of wondered what was still bothering him, and he slipped up and said he'd just talked about it with his godson, Jimmy Sheehan, and they agreed what a tragedy it was," Tom Miller said.

"Ancient Chinese gentleman!" Joe said. "If the president was already on your radar that was a red flag before a bull, wasn't it?"

"Yeah, it set me off. I pressed the old bishop until he finally confessed that he was worried that his godson was involved in Timmy's death. I just lost it then. I went into revenge mode and I've been there ever since. It never got in the way of me doing my duty, or kept me from being myself, but I was planning every minute of every day how to make Jimmy Sheehan suffer as much as Kristy, my mom and I had suffered over the years. I wrote shit down, made maps, checked travel itineraries, and told every one of my close personal friends what that son of a bitch had done to my twin brother, until I was consumed by the hate. My teammates hated him, too, so it was really easy to recruit people to my "get that motherfucking murderer" squad," Tom Miller said.

"So you retired in order to have time to set your plans in motion, and then your guys did the same thing," I said.

"And you had multiple plans—why?" Joe said. "It seems odd that you didn't think that your first plan would work."

Tom Miller looked at me and I said, "In special ops you always plan for the first plan to fail, and the second, and probably the third, so you always make at least five plans based on what the enemy *can* do, not what he *will* do. I'm betting that once the team and I showed just how good we were the plans got updated, which is why the second team took me down with tasers—that was a good stroke, by the way."

"It was brilliant," Ed said. "You took out our best agent and guaranteed that the president would retreat to the exact place that you wanted him to be."

"I figured that even if you took all those poor, mercenary schmucks down you'd have to de-brief, and the president would still head for the safest place on earth short of a nuclear bunker. It would've worked, too, except for the fact that you're a freak of nature," Tom Miller said, pointing at me. "And I guess I'm glad it didn't, because getting the shit completely beat out of me has made me realize what an asshole I was for attacking the president's daughters."

"You can say that again," Joe said. "If your beef was with the president why not just bring the evidence forward and let somebody like us bring him to justice? Why the psychological and physical torture of innocents? I know that you wanted to torture the president, but you ended up torturing the girls—and even though the president killed your brother, he definitely didn't torture him—and the girls didn't ask for their father to be an asshole."

"Or why not just cripple the president, or the first lady? You had plenty of chances to make a statement and make him suffer without involving the girls," Ed said.

I looked hard at Tom Miller and said, "He was in the field too long. Seven tours to Afghanistan and two more to Iraq left you empty didn't it? In the tribal areas it's SOP to threaten the family because the fanatics don't really care about themselves—but their children…well, that's a different story." I looked at my brother and said "I wouldn't try to use that in your defense, Counselor—it would take a jury of Spec Ops warriors to understand what the fuck we were just talking about. The average citizen has no idea about what happens out there, or why it happens. If you try to sell the PTSD defense, or the 'violence leads to more violence' argument it could backfire, especially since your client seems to be completely sane."

"Thanks for the advice, Freak, but there isn't going to be a defense, at least not in that sense," Roady said.

"Whaddaya mean there isn't going to be a defense? There has to be a defense or the death penalty will become a very real possibility," Joe said.

Tom Miller said, "Let's get one thing straight—Roady'd fight until hell froze over for me, and he gave me great legal advice, but I'm going to plead guilty to every single charge, and then I'm going to tell my story in court, and then I'm going to take whatever I get, because (a) I did everything they're charging me with, and (b) I was sane, then and now, and (c) when you play you've got to pay, and I deserve to pay."

"That doesn't mean that there weren't extenuating circumstances," I said. "What you did was totally wrong, but you *were* provoked, and when you factor in what Tim's murder did to your mother…well, I'm not the lawyer in my family…" I said, looking at Roady.

"And I'll argue that during the penalty phase, which is how we're going to try and keep the death penalty out of the equation," my brother said, looking hard at A-USA Brenda T. Green.

She looked back and started to say something, but then she stopped. She looked at me and Roady, and then just turned around and went out the door.

"Well, she didn't say they had the needle ready," Tom Miller said, kind of half laughing.

"Wouldn't it be a firing squad?" Ed said.

"That would seem to be poetic justice," Joe said.

"I'd go for drawing and quartering," I said.

"With a dull jackknife," Ed said.

"Because of your agent who charged us at the school," Tom Miller said. "The other two were accidents, but he came up the hill at one of our firing positions and the security guys had to put him away. That's the one I feel the worst about, because that was just one brave motherfucker doing his job, and doing it well, and getting killed because of my Captain Ahab complex." His eyes were watery and he almost let out a sob, but swallowed it back and said, "I'm truly sorry about all of them, but that guy—what was his name? De Vries? He was a man and a half, and I want to honor his memory. Did any of you serve with him before that detail? Was he as brave as he looked?"

So Ed and I told Tom Miller the tale of the Battle of Morehead, and how Patsy wouldn't leave us even though he was really fucked up. When I got to Patsy saying "I'm a dod-damned U Eth Mawine! We don' weave any'n behin'!" I thought Tom Miller was going to pop a gasket. Just then the door opened and A-USA Brenda T. Green came back in.

"If you'll allocute to all of your activities and outline all the parts played by everyone who helped you the death penalty won't be an issue," she said.

"As long as we're clear that my client won't be the star witness in any other prosecutions," Roady said. "Most of what they did was simply following his orders, even those men who fired rounds that killed someone."

"We understand your position, and we're working on it vis-à-vis charges against the other men involved," Brenda T. Green said. "I can tell you that we're seeking manslaughter charges against everybody who fired fatal rounds except the man or men who killed Agent Alexander de Vries and, of course, your client, as the mastermind of the operations."

Roady looked at Tom Miller, who said, "I'm OK with that, but you'll have all manslaughter charges except for me. Whoever shot my sidekick at Camp David did the taxpayers a favor, because

Command Master Chief Petty Officer Tory Potts was the one who killed Agent de Vries. His two gunners will verify that, and yeah, I'm still responsible for all of it, including any murder charges. As long as my guys are treated fairly I'll do whatever you need me to, Miss A-USA."

She nodded and said, "That's what I told my boss you'd say, so while your lawyer and I go work out the details I think you have another visitor." She looked at me and I said, "OK, we'll clear out so you can have some privacy, but we'll probably be back with more questions."

"Fair enough, Freak," Tom Miller said. "Leave Agent de Vries's full CV with Roady, will ya? I wanna do something nice for his family before I head to Leavenworth."

"Roger that," I said. We went out the door and Mrs. Miller was waiting with my Mumsy, who smiled when she saw Roady and I.

"I told you she wouldn't hurt you," Mumsy said.

"It was a near thing," Roady said.

"I never said it wouldn't be nerve-wracking," my mom said.

As I came out the door the four U.S. Marshals tried to go in. I stopped in the doorway and said, "The prisoner's gonna have some private time with his mom. You fellas mount guard out here until they're done, OK?"

"We don't answer to you, and our boss said at least two of us in the room at all times in order to make sure he doesn't try and escape," the young, cocky one who'd given me shit about the shackles said. I noticed that he had some new shackles with him and an attitude like a small dog at a big dog convention. He tried to muscle by me and I casually blocked him. He looked at me and said, "You need get out of the way, or we'll have to escort you away from here and call your supervisor, sweetheart."

We already know how I react to being called some form of endearment, but I managed to quell my desire to smash his face in and say, "Uh, Joe, is the room next door open?"

Joe and Ed readied themselves to try and peel me off the marshal after I put him down, but Joe was smart and realized I was going to try and let the guy off the hook first, so he said, "Why yes, Freak, it is. Why on earth do you ask?" His tone was all sarcastic and ironic and smarmy, and I didn't say anything; I just looked back at Tom Miller in his bed and then back at the young U.S. Marshal a couple of times.

He got the implication, because he backed off and handed the shackles to one of his pals and said, "I said you need to move, Agent, or I'll move you, regardless of your reputation, which I doubt, by the way." He smiled at me, but before I could say anything Alvin Firkkensen said, "Dude, have you lost your fucking mind?" They had an interesting conversation after that.

> Young Marshal: Orders are orders, and she's not my boss.
> Alvin Firkkenen: But she is your superior in every way.
> YM: I can take care of myself.
> AF: Not against the Freak, you can't. She's badder than Leroy Brown.
> YM: So everybody says, but I'm from Missouri. She'll have to show me. (Smirks)
> AF: Dude, the schmo layin' in that bed is a motherfucking Navy SEAL. What more proof do you need?

YM: I heard she shot him first, and then she had help.

AF: Man, are you fucking stupid. If everybody here jumped her at once she'd beat the shit out of us without breaking a sweat.

YM: So you're afraid of her?

AF: You bet your ass, dipshit.

YM: Why? Is this bitch really that bad?

AF: Let him live, Freak—he's just young, dumb, and full of come.

YM: Who're you callin' dumb?

Alvin Firkkensen just shook his head and stepped away from the young marshal, who smirked again and turned around to find me within an inch of him. He tried to jump back, but I grabbed his belt buckle and kept him close, took my left index finger and placed it on his right subclavian nerve cluster (just under his right collarbone) and crushed it, paralyzing his right arm.

Then I lifted him straight off the floor with one arm, using his belt buckle as my lifting point. I held him over my head and inclined his body until I was looking up directly into his face, which was parallel to the floor.

"Tom Miller is going to have as much private time with his mother as he wants," I said. "Is that clear?"

The young marshal nodded, but I said, "Articulate my last" and he said "Uh, Tom Miller and his mom aren't to be disturbed."

"Very good, young woodchuck," I said, setting him back on his feet. I thought that would be it, but this kid had moxie. He stepped back and went for his pistol, and things were about to go sideways when Honest Tom Vernon and his guys came around the corner.

"Salisbury, what the hell are you doing?" Honest Tom said.

"Sir, she won't let us in to guard the prisoner, and Marshal Ollbee gave us explicit orders," the young marshal said. "I was going to arrest her for obstruction of justice."

"Don't you have to be alive to arrest someone?" Marshal Gates said.

"Why yes, indeedy-do, you must be breathing to actually arrest a perpetrator," Marshal Bingaman said.

"Which young Salisbury is about to not be, if his hand comes out from under that coat with anything but air," Marshal Moyer said.

"Sir?" young Salisbury said, to Honest Tom Vernon. "What do they mean, sir?"

"They're trying to tell you that a man's got to know his limitations, and Agent Glickstien is well beyond your capabilities to restrain, son. Pull that hand out slowly and step away from the nice lady. Save us all from having to watch the surgery to get your gun out of your ass."

"Well, with you here, sir—" Salisbury started to say, but Honest Tom cut him off and said "Easy, junior! I only brought my flying squad, not the entire U.S. Marshals Service. You need to stand down, now."

"You don't think that we could take her, the nine of us?" the young marshal said. Everybody started laughing and Honest Tom Vernon said, "I'm not sure that every U.S. Marshal to ever carry the badge could stop the Freak from Battle Creek, but I for damn sure know that those of us here can't, so let's stop talking about it and let Mrs. Miller in to see her son, shall we?"

I said, "Marshal Salisbury, I understand following orders, but sometimes they don't make any sense, and sometimes they violate good taste, and sometimes they're just plain stupid. When all three of those things occur simultaneously I would suggest that you use good sense in order to determine a course of action in situations like this, rather than just slavishly 'following orders.' God gave you a brain to use, not to do what Adolf Eichmann did when he ran the Nazi death camps."

"Discipline is the basis of our organization, just like yours," Salisbury said. "If everybody just went around making up their own orders where would we be?"

"That's not what I'm talking about and you know it, dumbass. If you can look at someone and see that they're completely disabled—can't walk, can't run, hell, can't even stand upright without assistance—you oughta be able to have enough human compassion to take their shackles off and let them have a talk with their mother. If you can't see why that's the thing to do here then maybe you should go into carpentry, kid," I said.

Salisbury bristled, but then he realized that everyone was looking at him and making a value judgment about his innermost workings—really, his fitness for the Marshals Service was being assessed, and by some pretty senior and serious U.S. Marshals, too, along with other highly trained personnel whose resumés were above reproach. How he went about his business right here was probably going to determine how far he went in the U.S. Marshals Service.

It turned out that young Salisbury was pretty smart. He felt the vibe and understood what it meant, because he stopped bristling and said, "Yes, ma'am, I see what you're getting at. I apologize if I was too much of an ass to you."

"Marshal Salisbury, you don't need to apologize for trying to do your job," I said. "Just remember that you're a human being first and U.S. Marshal second, willya?"

"What?" all the other marshals said.

"That damned manual lied!" Marshal Bingaman said. "Imagine an official U.S. government publication not telling the truth."

"I'm a human being? I'm not a wooden caricature who only simulates human activities?" Marshal Gates said.

"I told ya that your ex-wife was just being a bitch," Marshal Shimel said. "You're a real little boy, just like Pinocchio."

"If I'm human first why haven't I gotten a vacation in four years?" Marshal Moyer said. "I thought that I was just an android, like Commander Data from *Star Trek*."

"Fuck you, you assholes," I said. We all laughed, even Salisbury, and I held the door open for Mrs. Miller, who went in the door and stopped, shocked by the condition of her only remaining son.

But he was her son, so after a moment Mrs. Miller moved forward and said, "Tommy?"

"Mom?" Tom Miller said, sounding like he was 10 years old. "Mom, I'm so sorry for…" was the last thing I heard before I closed the door so they could have some privacy.

Honest Tom Vernon said, "Thanks for educating our young'uns, Freak. Sometimes we hurry them into the field and they don't get the full training time needed."

"Ah, he's a good one, just too fucking zealous about the whole orders thing. Why do bosses who aren't in the field always think they know best? Why do they teach us about small-unit leadership and command presence and situational and operational awareness and then tie our hands with stupid REMF orders? Can you explain that, Marshal Vernon, sir?"

"Fuck no," Honest Tom Vernon said. "I can't even tell you how to turn a computer on, which is why I'm permanently barred from advancement in my service."

"Which is why you're the best U.S. Marshal since Matt Dillon," Chris Bingaman said.

"It's also why I named my oldest son after you," Jason Moyer said.

"And why I've listed you as my next of kin on my emergency card," Matt Shimel said.

"And why we'd follow you to hell and back," Brady Gates said. "You're a real U.S. Marshal, boss, not a paper tiger or self-promoting REMF who wants to move up the ladder any way they can."

"It's because you can't have the line animals actually making the rules or everything we do might start to make perfect sense, which means we wouldn't need all of that flabby administrative tail, which means many of the REMFs would get shitcanned, and since they can't have that they issue their standard orders, knowing that most of these orders will run afoul of actual operational reality," Joe said.

"Which means the REMFs will have to clarify the orders, and rules and regs, which means that..." Ed said.

"They'll all stay employed, and we'll be plagued by REMFs who think you can run an op from a Washington office with a view of the Mall," Honest Tom Vernon said.

"So young, so cynical," I said.

"Truthful," everybody said.

"We'll take care of Mrs. Miller, Freak, and when we're done you guys can stand us Pepsis," Honest Tom Vernon said.

"It'll be a pleasure, Marshal Vernon," I said. I looked at young Salisbury, who looked right back, fearless, and I said, "I work out at the Treasury Department gym at 1500 Pennsylvania, and I shoot at their range. Call me, Missouri, and I'll show you whatever you want to see—well, almost everything you might want to see—any time at all."

"I'll look forward to it," young Salisbury said.

"Hey, Missouri, just remember two things when you go work out with her," Joe said.

"What's that?" young Salisbury said.

"Make sure your insurance is paid up, and bring money for the shooting part," Ed said.

"Best advice I've heard in a long time, Salisbury," Honest Tom Vernon said.

"How much money?" young Salisbury said.

"How much ya got?" everyone said at once.

"Secret Service is owed some Pepsis," I said. "Concur," Honest Tom said.

"She can't be that good," young Salisbury said, disbelief showing on his face.

"Don't bet your ass on it, Missouri," Ed said.

"Ya think?" young Salisbury said.

"No, I *know*," Joe said.

Everybody laughed at the poor young marshal, and then we left to go back and report that there wouldn't be a trial of the century because an essentially good man decided to do the right thing, and Mrs. Miller got reacquainted with her only remaining son.

It was a good day to be a Secret Service agent.

CHAPTER 80

Almost Full Circle

So we went about our business as usual, but two days later, we heard that the president was having a press conference. We also heard that he'd requested a meeting with Nails and several Cabinet members, and that she'd gone to it, but not what was discussed. Then we heard that Nails went to another meeting with several congressional leaders, but we got no report on what came of that meeting either.

The Washington press speculated that the high-level meetings were the result of the assaults on the first family, and were being held in order to discuss the expansion of the Secret Service, and/or to request extra money for training and newer, better equipment.

The *Washington Post* had an editorial that said it was about time that the Secret Service was fully staffed and funded, and that the appropriation of money for such a cause should be easy, since Congress was protected on a bipartisan basis, and so was every first family, regardless of their political persuasion. Most of the other papers agreed, and several members of Congress who weren't privy to the meetings said that they would be glad to get on board and co-sponsor an appropriations bill for such a cause.

Only one paper, the *Washington Times*, reported that Nails was about to get the boot for the supposed "failures of the Secret Service," but since they were a rag who always "reported" that the sky was falling nobody really paid attention, especially after the White House press secretary adamantly denied the report and gave the Secret Service glowing reviews from the president.

There was also some chatter about who the president was going to nominate for the open vice-presidency, and that Nails might make an attractive choice, but the White House quickly denied it, and that talk blew away.

The Warrior Princesses seemed normal, the detail was functioning perfectly, and everybody was relieved to have Tom Miller and his merry men behind bars, although we were advised by Dreamboat and Miss Bitchy Voice to keep our guard up, since copycat crimes weren't uncommon. MBV also pointed out that there was an awful lot of international chatter about the first family, and that terrorists were not above attacking when one least expected it.

So the fourth day came after the president had vowed to "do the right thing" and we hadn't heard a word about anything going on, until we got the Warrior Princesses home from school. Once the girls were safe upstairs in the residence we all went back to the Secret Service bullpen to de-brief—that was SOP—and Nails was waiting for us.

She said, "Anybody who needs to perform any ablutions should do it now, because there isn't going to be time later. The whole protective detail for the first daughters needs to present itself in the Oval Office in exactly 30 minutes, and before you ask I don't know, and if I did I wouldn't say. Take a piss, wash your face, drink a Pepsi, but be ready to move in 29 minutes."

We all looked at each other and then we went off to get cleaned up. I hit the locker room, stripped everything off and jumped in the shower. So did Coach, Ed, Flipper (who was back from rehab and completely recovered), Foghorn (ditto) and Buddha. We talked about Major Difficulty and Gangster's rehabs, how long before they got back, how we'd change the detail once they were back, the beauty of Flipper's body—swimmers have got the most beautiful bodies you've ever seen, especially once they stop training and let their boobs grow back—in short, we talked about everything except what was about to happen, because we just didn't know enough to even speculate, and because to do so would seem like we were on the "Real Secret Service Agents of Washington" (man did we hate those stupid "Real Housewives" shows. I thought Flipper and Buddha would stroke out every time someone mentioned them).

As we were adjusting our guns on the way out of the locker room Ed said, "So why all of us? I get having one or two in the office, but all of us? Seems like overkill."

"Who knows? Maybe we're getting gold plated pistols for valor, maybe we're all getting drummed out of the Service as a unit, maybe we're going to be inducted into the Secret Service Hall of Fame," I said.

"You're awfully insouciant on such a momentous occasion," Buddha said.

"I woulda used 'flippant' instead of 'insouciant'," Foghorn said.

"Why not just use nonchalant?" Flipper said. "It's direct, on point and has a nice sophisticated feel to it when it rolls out of your mouth."

"And insouciant doesn't?" Buddha said. "The blithe spirit there just seemed to be blowing it off, and insouciant has just the right ring of flippancy to be effective."

"Oooh, I like that, folding the two words into a single meaningful phrase," Foghorn said.

"It's funny what kind of conversations occur when everybody's as nervous as we are," I said.

"Ain't it, though?" Ed said.

We all walked out of the locker room, joined up with the male contingent and went off to the office outside the Oval. We waited about two minutes and then Charlie Hassenger opened the door to the Oval Office and said, "Come in, Director Hessler, and bring the squad with you, please." The chief of staff looked tired but not haggard, and he also had an air of pride about him.

The president and first lady were standing in front of the desk, and the girls were with them, looking edgy but almost relieved. The president stepped out and shook all of our hands, saying something to everybody when he did. The first lady did the same thing, as did the Warrior Princesses. When all the handshaking was done the president said, "We wanted you to know exactly how much we appreciated your excellent work and your utter dedication to protecting us. It's damned impressive, what you did, and how you did it even if it cost you. None of it would've happened if it wasn't for my selfishness and stupidity, but even though I put my daughters in jeopardy they were saved because of your professionalism, toughness and incredible dedication. What we say here this afternoon won't ever be repeated, so I'd like to give you all a chance to say anything you'd like, and please forget that I'm the president when you do."

None of us said anything, and the president said, "You have my permission to speak freely. If you need to bitch me out, please feel free to do it—nobody's going to stop you, and trust me, it won't have any effect on your careers."

Finally Badass said, "Sir, we're sworn officers of the United States Secret Service, and that means that we don't bitch you out, regardless of what you've done. We were assigned to protect your daughters and that's what we did, but nobody here is going to judge you, sir. You did what you did, we did what we did, and that's that. For me personally, well, I resent the deaths of my fellow agents, but I still don't hold that to be your fault directly, and even if I did, well, I'm a Secret Service agent, Mr. President, and I will never comment on the first family for any reason, not to the press, not to you, not now, not ever. I swore an oath, sir, ma'am, young ladies, and I meant it."

Buddha said, "What Agent Goodenough said, sir. I would like to tell you that my twin sister felt it was an enormous privilege to guard your daughters, and that she liked them. We both agreed that dying in the line of duty was the ultimate honor. She wouldn't be angry with you, sir, and I know that I'm not."

"Mr. President, whatever you did in the past—and I'm not excusing it, sir, it was wrong, especially what you did to Mrs. Miller—but whatever you did, it was Tom Miller, the Vice President and the FBI Director who were the assholes, sir, not you, and certainly not your family. If I were angry with anyone it would be them, but I'm not angry," Weasel said.

"But it was my actions that precipitated everything that happened," the president said.

"No, sir, it was the warped actions of three defectives that caused what happened," Jewey said. "Sorry to butt in, Weasel, but Mr. President, all of those *schmucks* had a choice, and they chose to do wrong, sir, and everybody knows that two wrongs don't make a right. Yeah, you were a *putz* for about 10 minutes when you were 19 years old—everybody knows that teenagers don't have normal thought processes, begging your pardon ladies—and there's no way to hold that against you. You did wrong, sir, but you didn't pull any triggers, and besides, Badass is right—we're Secret Service agents, and we don't squeal about our principals, period. It's just not done, sir, and I don't intend to start a new tradition of non-excellence."

We all nodded, and I said, "Mr. President, none of us are happy about whatever's about to happen here, but we'd still respect your office even if we didn't respect you personally, and without putting words in anyone's mouth, I think we all do, sir." There was a general murmuring of consensus and lots of head nodding, and I said, "None of us can imagine what it must've been like to have to hide who you were every minute of every day, sir, and we can't begin to imagine how you became the good father and president that we all know under those circumstances. I know that I couldn't have done anything like that, and my parents have always said that only God gets to judge, so if you'll excuse my bluntness, sir, you're not going to get absolution from any of us, because we aren't carrying any grudges." I held up my badge and said, "This means that I swore to give my life for my country, my principal and even assholes I don't like, like the First Secretary of the Chinese Communist Party or the president of Venezuela, who's not fit to carry your shoes, sir."

I looked at James Patrick Liam Sheehan and said, "I'm a sworn Secret Service agent, Mr. President, and I'd like to echo my colleagues. We. Don't. Comment. On. The. First. Family. EVER."

Everybody had tears in their eyes or on their cheeks, and my Warrior Princesses rushed me, crushing me in a huge hug, which set off a whole bunch of hugging, until the door to the Oval Office opened and Charlie Hassenger said, "Mr. President, ma'am, it's time."

The first lady and the Warrior Princesses hugged the president and walked out the door without saying anything more, leaving us alone with the president. He said, "Please sit down, because I have something that I'd like to tell you."

We all sat down and the president said, "My wife and children are being taken to Air Force One and Andrews to wait for me." He paused and I said, "You're going to resign, sir?"

"I'm going to resign, yes, but I'm going to do a lot more than that," the president said. He paused, as sad as I've ever seen a human being look, wiped his face with his hand and said, "In about eight minutes I'm going to walk into the press room and tell the country that I'm resigning, effective at 6:00 p.m., and at 6:01 p.m. the Speaker of the House is going to walk in that door with the Chief Justice, the Secretary of State and some other guests and get sworn in—and your squad is going to witness it.

"At 6:02 p.m. I'm going to surrender myself to five U.S. Marshals, who are going to take me out to Marine One and on to Andrews, where we will board Air Force One and fly to the Kalamazoo/ Battle Creek International Airport. From there I'll be arrested for the murder of Tim Miller and transported to the Calhoun County jail in Battle Creek, where I'm going to sit until such time as I can be put on trial. Once on trial I'm going to plead no contest to all the charges and then I'm going to let a jury of my peers decide what happens.

"And after that I don't know what happens, but I do know that my conscience will be as clear as it can be," the (soon-to-be-former) President said.

"Sir, you'd probably do better to fight the charges, since you can't depend on what a jury'll do," Joe said.

"You need to make sure that your side is heard, sir, especially the extenuating circumstances, or Roady'll open a can of whup-ass on the Appeals Court, whether you want him to or not," I said. "He'll almost have to, or he could face disciplinary action from the American Bar Association."

"Thank you for your advice, and be assured that my side will be heard. But somebody has to pay for what happened to Tim, and his mother, and I am the person responsible, and I will be paying the price, regardless of what it is."

The (soon-to-be-former) President stood up and gave all of us a look of gratitude as we rose around him. He shook all of our hands and said, "I said I was going to do the right thing and I am, no matter what it costs me. I'm doing that because you promised an old womyn that you'd find out what happened to her son, and in the process showed me what the right thing to do was. It probably sounds strange, but I'm grateful to you for doing what you did, and for finally giving me a chance to step out of the closet, and for making me a hero in the eyes of my children."

From the door Charlie Hassenger said, "Mr. President, it's time."

The (soon-to-be-former) President of the United States smiled and said, "Wish me luck, you guys. Here goes nothing."

"Break a leg, Mr. President," El Gato said.

"He's not doin' a play, ya dipshit," Bumble said.

"But he is going on a stage, so it isn't that inappropriate," Mamba said,

"There's only one thing to say at a time like this," I said, looking at Jewey.

"Correct," the big Jewish agent said. "Everybody, Jewish wedding cry on four…one, two… four!" he said.

"Mazel tov!" we all said.

"I've already got those Pepsis cooling for you in the East Room, where the new President is going to give their first address to the nation, surrounded by the best protective detail on the world," Jimmy Sheehan, the soon-to-be-former President of the United States said, smiling at us as he left the Oval Office for the last time.

We all watched on the TVs in the outer office as he gave a little speech announcing his resignation, and kept watching as he explained why he was resigning, and then kept watching when he surrendered to Honest Tom Vernon and his flying squad of U.S. Marshals and was escorted from the White House briefing room and onto Air Force One.

We went back into the Oval Office and at 6:02 p.m. the Speaker of the House, the Chief Justice of the Supreme Court, the Secretary of State, and lots of other people crowded into the office to witness the peaceful transfer of the most powerful position in the world from one person and one party to another.

The Speaker stood tall and looked at the bible the Secretary of State held out, kept the left hand that was supposed to go there where it was alongside a thigh and raised a right hand as the Chief Justice said, "Please repeat after me. I do solemnly swear that I will faithfully execute the Office of the President of the United States, and will to the best of my ability, preserve, protect and defend the Constitution of the United States."

Aleta Greenhoe Soper, Representative from the great state of California and Speaker of the House of Representatives, smiled and said, "I do solemnly affirm that I will faithfully execute the Office of the President of the United States, and will to the best of my ability, preserve, protect and defend the Constitution of the United States."

The Chief Justice said, "Madame President, I apologize for forgetting to say 'affirm' instead of 'swear.' It's a habit, ma'am."

"Well, if I'd've sworn in five presidents saying 'swear' I'm sure the same thing would've happened. I don't expect it makes any difference, does it?" President Soper said.

"No Madame President, it does not," the Chief Justice said. "Congratulations." They shook hands, and then Soper—shit! *President* Soper—shook everybody else's hands. She hugged Josie's parents, who'd flown over from Scotland for the announcement, although they didn't know what was happening until five minutes before, and she also hugged Nails.

"Thank you for having my squad assembled for the ceremony, Director Hessler," President Soper said.

"I serve at the pleasure of the president, so your wish is my command, Madame President," Nails said.

"I appreciate it anyway," President Soper said. Charlie Hassenger said, "Madame President, they're ready in the East Room, and the networks would like it if they could get going before their regularly scheduled broadcast of the evening news."

"Oh, fuck the networks. I'll get there when I get there, and if they don't like it they can get in line," President Soper said. She looked at the Secret Service contingent and said, "Did I say it right, Freak? Jewey? Ed? Weasel? Joe?"

"Almost, Madame President," I said.

"You'll need to work on your inflection on the 'fuck,' ma'am," Joe said.

"Yeah, it was a little bit too hard, like you might've actually meant it to be insulting, ma'am," Jewey said.

"Z'xctly," Weasel said. "You need a bit more insouciance when you say it."

"It's kind of like a verbal flip of your hair, Madame President," Ed said. "That takes the sting out of it and lets the listener know that you're joking." We all started laughing, and Soper—damn it! *President* Soper!—said, "I've missed you guys."

"Your fuckin' telephone broken?" I said. "Nobody's changed their numbers. Ma'am."

"Ya got me on that one, Freak. My bad," the president of the United States said.

Everybody else in the room was just staring at us with their mouths open, because this wasn't how they were used to presidents addressing their Secret Service details. Finally the Secretary of State said, "Madame President, is this really what you want to do right now? Banter with your protective detail while we're facing this national crisis?"

SecState was a crusty old rich white Republican who thought that the U.S. should continue to just bomb the shit out of anybody who disagreed with us, bully everyone else with our economic power and close our borders to anyone who wasn't a rich, white, English-speaking person. He was the past, and President Soper was the future, and I suspected that the old coot wouldn't last more than 10 days with her, which suspicion she confirmed when she said, "What the hell are you talking about, Ellis? You sound like a Fox News headline waiting to happen."

"Madame President, we have a crisis of confidence in this country that needs to be addressed by a president that takes it seriously," SecState said. "This may be the most dangerous situation our country has ever faced."

"What the fuck are you talking about?" President Soper said. "We've got a president, soon we'll have a vice president in case something happens to me, our economy is booming and is going to go even higher, Congress and the president are going to be able to get a shitload of work done now that we're all going to be on almost the same page"—the Senate was still Republican controlled, but the margin was 51–49 and President Soper was very persuasive when she wanted to be—"and the only confidence that is shaking is yours, because you and your Neanderthal colleagues are deathly afraid of someone like me in this office. Isn't that about right?" She looked at everybody assembled and several of them nodded, so Soper said, "OK, if you don't have any confidence in me please let me have your resignations by seven a.m. tomorrow so I can fill your positions. Except for you, Mr. Secretary of State. I want you to walk over to the desk and write yours right now, effective immediately."

The crusty old coot looked at her, smiled a very confident smile and said, "And if I don't? You need me to keep the international community calm, and you also—"

President Soper cut him off and said, "I was hoping that you'd take that approach, Mr. Secretary. You're fired, effective immediately. And before you try to say anything else, this isn't Andrew Johnson's administration, and there isn't any Tenure of Office Act, so you serve at my pleasure, and you don't please me. Get out of this office, get in the car, and go home. I'll have the FBI clean out your office at State and deliver it to your home. You can deliver all of your credentials to the agents who take you home, and no, I'm not going to shake your hand and thank you for your service, you horrid excuse for a diplomat."

The former SecState's face turned purple and he said, "You-you-you…you can't…fire me, you damned dyke! I'm the Secretary of State!"

"Were," President Soper. "And fuck you." She pointed at the door and the crusty old bastard staggered out of the Oval Office on the arm of an aide.

"You said it right that time," Weasel said.

"Absolutely nailed it," Jewey said.

"Perfect rhythm, pitch and diction," Ed said.

"Well done, ma'am," Joe said.

"Thanks, guys," President Soper said. "Anybody else?"

The NSA Director, Don Crais, a good spook who had a sense of humor (sorry, still classified) said, "Madame President, have you given any thought to a vice president? I'm not trying to be morbid or forward, but Senator Grimes is ninety-three and in the hospital, and he's next in line, ma'am."

"Thanks for reminding me, Director Crais. As it happens I have given some thought to that, and I'd like to introduce you to my nominee for vice president. She looked at Charlie Hassenger, who opened the door to the Oval and said, "Sir? The president would like to see you now."

Chairman of the Joint Chiefs of Staff Terrance X. McAllen walked into the office and said, "Madame President, it's good to see you. We have a lot to talk about, ma'am, but I could've sent someone else to brief you, and I don't have the nuclear codes with me, ma'am." Everybody laughed and President Soper said, "Mr. Chairman, I need you to do something for me, if you could."

"Of course, ma'am. You're my commander in chief, so you can order me to do anything you need as long as it's legal, ma'am." There was more laughter and the president said, "No orders, Mr. Chairman, just a request."

"Ma'am?" he said.

"I need you to resign your position and commission, Mr. Chairman…" the president said.

"Ma'am?" C-JCS said.

"…so you can be confirmed as my vice president," President Soper said.

Terry McAllen didn't get to be the Chairman of the Joint Chiefs because he was stupid or indecisive. He looked at the president and said, "Why me, ma'am?"

President Soper looked at him and said, "Because if something happens to me I want to be sure that there's a person of intelligence, character, compassion, strength and great fortitude to take my place, and Mr. Chairman, when I think of those things, I think of you. Isn't the motto of the Marine Corps 'semper fidelis'—always faithful?"

"Oh, yes, ma'am, it is," the C-JCS said.

"And you've proven yourself to be an excellent example of that motto, General McAllen. So whattya say? Ya wanna jump into the fire with me?" the president said.

General Terrance X. McAllen stood at attention and said, in his best Marine Corps voice, "Ma'am, I request permission to resign temporarily from the Marine Corps and my position as Chairman of the Joint Chiefs of Staff so that I might further serve my country, ma'am." He saluted perfectly and held it at rigid attention.

Soper drew herself up like we'd taught her and snapped off a return salute with some panache and said, "Permission granted, General. Welcome aboard the USS "What The Fuck Do We Do Now.""

"We fix shit, Madame President," McAllen said, smiling at her.

"Amen to that," President Soper said, shaking his hand.

"Semper fucking fi!" I said.

"Semper fucking fi!" the rest of the Secret Service detail and some of the spectators said.

"OK, everybody head for the East Room. I want a word with my Secret Service detail, and then I'll be right along," President Soper said.

When we were alone she shook all of our hands and made us sit down. She sat with us and said, "First rule, no formality when it's just us, even in this office. I'm still just Soper, OK?" We all sort of nodded, and she said, "You guys ever think that we'd be sitting here like this?"

"Oh, fuck yeah, Madame President," I said.

"You've got the second biggest balls I've ever seen, and I work five feet from the womyn with the biggest balls, so fuck yeah I thought you'd be president," Badass said.

"I thought it would take longer, but yeah, I was pretty sure that you're too smart to be kept down, ma'am," Ed said.

Weasel looked at the president and then at Jewey and said, "Tell her, big man."

"Ma'am, we were flying back from rounding up the last of Tom Miller's guys in East Bumfuck, Oregon, and we got stuck on a layover at McCarron International in Lost Wages, and Weasel and I went into town because it was going to be four hours and we went to Harrah's and well, we each placed a $100 bet on you becoming president within 10 years."

"What kind of odds did you get?" President Soper said.

"That's it, ma'am—you were at one hundred thousand to one," Weasel said.

"Holy fuck-fuck, you assholes are stinking rich!" Bumble said.

"Nah, Mamba's stinking rich, but we're doin' pretty fucking well right now," Jewey said.

"Could this day get any better?" Buddha said.

"You mean that we'll never have to buy a Pepsi again, as long as we keep one of these assholes with us?" El Gato said.

"You mean that we're going to have front row seats to every sporting event we ever go to?" Coach said.

"You mean that we'll be eating real barbeque at Jewey's every Saturday, imported from Memphis every Friday night?" Foghorn said.

"You mean that Jewey and Weasel can buy the apartment house next to us and completely renovate it so that they have two floors apiece?" Kid Galahad said.

"Or do you mean that our country just got its smartest president since Jed Bartlet?" Flipper said.

"Oh, yeah, there is that," I said. Once again we all laughed, and slapped hands, and bumped fists and generally made horse's asses of ourselves in the Oval Office, until Charlie Hassenger stuck his head in the door and said, "President Soper, the fucking circus can wait—you need to get to the East Room before the press eats the podium. Wear old shoes, ma'am—they've been foaming at the mouth."

"Those fuckers!" President Soper said.

"Nailed it again, ma'am," Ed said.

"Sure did," Joe said. "I think you're getting the hang of it, Madame President."

"Will you guys just call me Soper when we're alone?" the president said.

"No way, ma'am!" we all said.

"I got the Pepsis," Weasel said.

"And I'm next," Jewey said.

We finally stopped with the levity and President Soper put on her dealing with the press face. Everybody except Badass, Ed and I preceded her out the door, and when she got there President Soper stopped and said to us, "Well, here we go. For the next year and a half it'll be a real pain in your ass every time I decide to even walk around the house. You guys ready for this?"

"Bet your ass, ma'am," I said.

"Just remember that you're the president, ma'am, and it'll be all right," Ed said.

"Yeah, I was only in the House for four years, I was only Speaker for six months, I'm the first openly gay, openly atheist president ever, I'm unelected, I just fired the Secretary of State, the most recognizable face from the previous administration, and oh, yeah, I'm also the most liberal president to occupy the office since FDR. What could possibly go wrong?" the president said as she left the Oval Office.

It turns out that a shitload of things could go wrong…

…but that's another story for another time.

ACKNOWLEDGMENTS

Why do authors always wait to thank their families until after everybody else has been featured? I don't know, but I want to thank my family first, especially my wife, Katie. She deserves a medal and a cookie for suffering through my natterings and babblings and thinking-out-loud fits over this novel for over seven years, virtually without complaint. I couldn't have written the novel without her love, support, and fierce editing. I should also mention that she is living proof that you can be the nicest person who ever lived and still not be a pushover. Thank you, my sweet. I owe you some beach time.

I would also like to thank my parents, Sharon and Gene, who showed me at an early age that reading and writing were acceptable forms of entertainment preferable to most others. I never had to worry about not having television or other forms of distraction because I had books and the worlds they opened up to me. My mom and dad taught me a ton of things, and they are most certainly (at least indirectly) responsible for this work. I was a terrible kid, which makes what they did for me even more amazing. I can't repay that debt except to go forward and be as good a man as they taught me to be (I'm still trying).

I won't name all the people in my home group who encouraged me to step up and write this novel, but I owe you everything, even more than I owe my wife. I want to give a special thanks to my friend Norm (not his or her real name), whose encouragement of "Stop being a pussy and write the goddamned book, you asshole" was truly good motivation.

I owe all my students who gave me ideas for use in this and further books. I can't name you all, but you know who you are.

My friends Joe Dorwin and Barry Shanley Jr. took the time to read parts of this novel when it was just a pile of disconnected thoughts and then gave me sage advice on how to make it sound like an actual book. There aren't enough hot dogs or Mexican dinners to pay you guys back, but I hope we can keep trying. If you'll keep reading, I'll keep buying. My friend Corey Aukerman didn't read the novel, but he has been the best of friends about everything else, so I owe him, too.

I can't give the proper due to everyone who ever taught me, but I would like to say that not only did all of you have the patience of saints, but you also inspired me to write this novel, and probably others. Sorry it took me so long to do it, but here it is, the culmination of your efforts at educating that horrible little boy and horrible fat man. Sorry about the language, Mennonite doctorii, but that's the way these people talk. I especially owe Ms. Jerilyn Adducci, Mrs. Nancy Rafferty, Ms. Pat Brundige, Mr. Don Fry, and Ms. Karin Nelson, all of whom labored long and hard to give me the skills necessary to be a thinking, writing human being. I'm still amazed you guys didn't have me assassinated, or at least exiled. Sorry about all the awful shit I put you through.

My third-grade teacher, Mrs. Tracy, and my fifth-grade teacher, Miss Joslin (a.k.a. the Great Pumpkin), were/are real people who saved my life.

That isn't hyperbole; it's reality.

I'm not sure what I would've done if I didn't have Mrs. Tracy in third grade, but I'm sure it wouldn't have been pleasant. Up to that point, school had been the Chinese water torture for me, but that old lady made education fun, and learning became my shibboleth because she figured out that I was bored and challenged me to pass through the boredom into the realm of questing minds. Mrs. Tracy has passed away, but she still lives in me every time I'm challenged.

I lost track of Miss Joslin, but the real Great Pumpkin probably had more of an effect on me than any other person in the world except my family. Her grace, strength, implacable attention to every student ever placed in her room and her incredible sense of joy permeate my thinking even today. I can't say enough about her, so I'll just say this one last thing: I know that I would've literally burned the school down without her gentle but firm treatment of me as a person, not a data point or problem child. I can never repay my debt to you, wherever you are, O Great Pumpkin, but I'm going to keep trying. Again, sorry for the language in this book, but it was necessary.

There is also a long list of authors who helped me write this book. Ellery Queen, Rex Stout, Sir Arthur Conan Doyle, Edgar Allan Poe, Daniel Silva, Robert Crais, Stephen Hunter, Don Winslow, Harlan Coben, Mickey Spillane, Jeffery Deaver, Randy Wayne White, William Goldman, Aaron Sorkin, Larry Bond, Tom Clancy, Stephen King, Mary Stewart, Isaac Asimov, Arthur C. Clarke, Edgar Rice Burroughs, P. T. Deutermann, Loren D. Estleman, Paul Levine, Jonathan Kellerman, Harry Kemelman, Dashiell Hammett, Ross Macdonald, Christopher Moore, G. M. Ford, Bill Pronzini, Ed McBain, Donald Westlake, Robert A. Heinlein, Douglas Adams, Poul Anderson, Margaret Atwood, Lisa Lutz, Carl Hiaasen, Jimmy Buffett, and L. Frank Baum all had a hand in this novel, whether they knew it or not.

But the people who really drove me to write are the eight Knights of the Golden Pen and Silver Parchment: J. R. R. Tolkien, John D. MacDonald, Lee Child, John Sandford (Camp), Elmore Leonard, Michael Connolly, Tony Hillerman, and Robert B. Parker. These authors are so good to me that I've read everything they ever wrote multiple times, not only because the stories were so good, but also because their writing was/is so crisp, clean, and clear. I never got to meet Robert B. Parker, but his style certainly influenced my writing a great deal, and Elmore Leonard gave great writing advice, and Tony Hillerman's physical descriptions defy belief. And I could go on, but you get the picture. No author writes in a vacuum, and I certainly did not. I owe everybody on this list a great debt, and I hope this book meets with your approval (those of you who are still with us).

I also had tremendous college professors, including but not limited to Theron Schlabach, James Hertzler, Randy Gunden, John D. Roth, Lucy Morgan, Elizabeth Attaway Hayes, and the Three Kings of Knowledge at Glen Oaks: Dave Greenhoe, Tom Soper, and Leland W. Thornton. Those three men were transformative for me, driving me to do more than my best and making me conscious of the fact that the written word should be explicit, not full of "implicities," since your reader is probably ignorant of your topic and needs the full exposition. You were right then, and you're right now, O Three Kings, and I, your humble subject, beg forgiveness if this tome in any way violates that stricture.

The final blame for this book falls squarely on the shoulders of my freshman English prof, Herr Toby Fulwiler, then of Michigan Technological University. Toby was a stranger in a strange land way up in frozen Houghton, an English prof in the land of engineers, but he still gave it his all and was one of the most consistently interesting teachers I ever had. It was Herr Fulwiler who told us in class that there was no tale so fantastic that it shouldn't be told, and he also told us that "reality was overrated" when it came to writing. He pointed me toward a raft of books that helped convince me that one could tell a "real" story without having to make every detail "accurate," and he also told me privately that my writing could use an injection of creativity, even when writing history. He was absolutely right about that, and this book is proof of what can happen when one gets just a bit creative.

So I don't know if Herr Fulwiler will even remember me—I was his student, briefly, forty-three years ago, after all—but if you want someone to blame, blame him, because I never forgot his advice or his efforts to make me be creative. This story (and hopefully the others to follow) is the result of a lifelong search for the right characters and story line to make people laugh, cry, and throw things—and it's all your fault, Herr Fulwiler. Thank you. (Remember, if you don't like the story, throw things at Herr Fulwiler, not me. I just wrote what he told me to.)

I would also like to particularly thank Dave, Justin, Ginny Lu, Charmaine, Anna, Doug, Rick, Ron, Mary, Bob Hall, Jeff and all the other fine folks at LaRue's Family Restaurant in Kalamazoo. The Pepsi is always cold, the food is always excellent and the service is truly magnificent. Thanks for taking care of me in my little corner while this book took shape and flew away.

If I forgot anybody I was supposed to thank, I'm profoundly sorry. Maybe I'll remember you for the second book, but if you know me, you know that I'll probably forget, so email me and make it bitchy so I have to write your name down or risk your continued bitchy emails. You might want to bitch me out in person too, since I often forget and hit "Delete all" when it comes to emails. Remember, I'm captain of the Luddite team.

Until we meet again, I remain, as always, your faithful servant.

AJ Hartman
from the Highgate House
8 March 2021

ABOUT THE AUTHOR

AJ Hartman is a retired teacher and coach living in Kalamazoo, Michigan, with his wife, Katie. He enjoys cooking, gardening, sports, reading, and writing. He also enjoys eating, especially hot dogs washed down with ice-cold Pepsi (yes, he's a big, old, fat man). This is his first novel.

CPSIA information can be obtained
at www.ICGtesting.com
Printed in the USA
LVHW061936060822
725291LV00009B/215

9 781662 450938